# THE
# ELENIUM

By David and Leigh Eddings

## THE BELGARIAD

Book One: *Pawn of Prophecy*
Book Two: *Queen of Sorcery*
Book Three: *Magician's Gambit*
Book Four: *Castle of Wizardry*
Book Five: *Enchanters' End Game*
Book Six: *Belgarath the Sorcerer*

## THE MALLOREON

Book One: *Guardians of the West*
Book Two: *King of the Murgos*
Book Three: *Demon Lord of Karanda*
Book Four: *Sorceress of Darshiva*
Book Five: *The Seeress of Kell*

## THE ELENIUM

Book One: *The Diamond Throne*
Book Two: *The Ruby Knight*
Book Three: *The Sapphire Rose*

## THE TAMULI

Book One: *Domes of Fire*
Book Two: *The Shining Ones*
Book Three: *The Hidden City*

## POLGARA THE SORCERESS

## THE REDEMPTION OF ALTHALUS

## THE RIVAN CODEX

## REGINA'S SONG

# THE ELENIUM

.

# DAVID EDDINGS

BALLANTINE BOOKS

NEW YORK

2007 Del Rey Books Trade Paperback Edition

Copyright © 1989, 1990, 1991
Front matter map and maps for *The Diamond Throne* by Shelly Shapiro
Part opener maps © 1990, 1991 by Claudia Carlson

Published in the United States by Del Rey Books, an imprint of The Random House Publishing Group, a division of Random House, Inc., New York.

DEL REY is a registered trademark and the Del Rey colophon is a trademark of Random House, Inc.

Originally published in three separate volumes in the United States by Del Rey Books, an imprint of The Random House Publishing Group, a division of Random House, Inc., as *The Diamond Throne* in 1989, *The Ruby Knight* in 1990, and *The Sapphire Rose* in 1991.

ISBN 978-0-345-50093-9

Printed in the United States of America

www.delreybooks.com

9  8  7  6  5

# CONTENTS

SEA OF

R. Horset
Horset
Heid
Ksema
R. Ksema
Husdal
R. Emsat
Yosut
Ksema
Emsat
Straits of Thalesia
Chael
R. Matern
PELOS
Asabel
R. Asabel
Amir.
Endahl
DEIRA
Acie
Gatas
Alaris
Kaneas
Gulf of Acie
Acie
Fenvl
Adera
Endde
Endde
Styric R.
DEIRAN
SEA
Cardos
ELENIA
Zenda
Arruka
R. Arruk
Cimmura R.
Cimmura
Demos
Chyrellos
Vardenais
Ucera R.
Ucera
Dieros
Darra
ARCIUM
Ucera
R. Symm R.
Coombe R.
Larium
Zand
Arcian Strait
Coombe
Tiroch
Gule R.
Kodhl
RENDOR
Umanthum
THE
Dabour
INM

Miles    100    200    300
Leagues  25  50  75  100

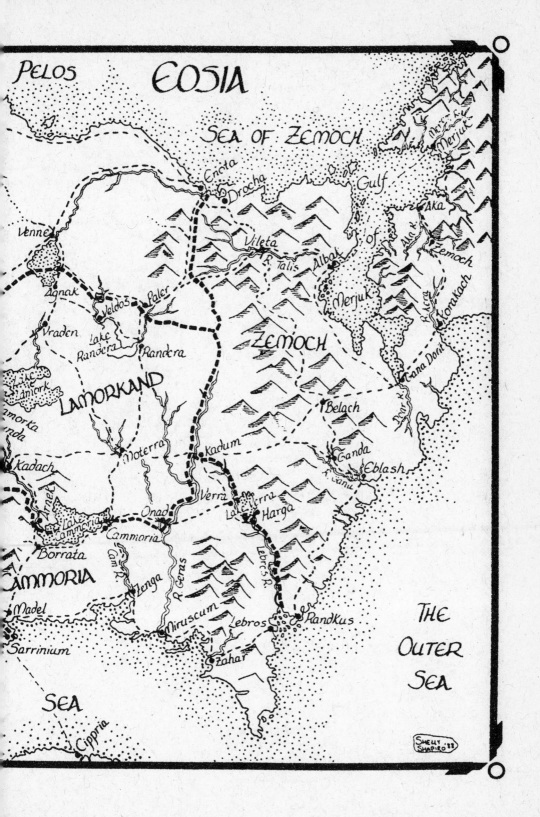

# THE DIAMOND
# THRONE

*For Eleanor and for Ralph,*
*for courage and faith.*
*Trust me.*

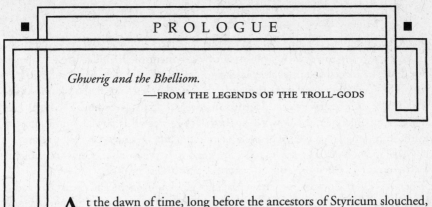

# PROLOGUE

*Ghwerig and the Bhelliom.*
—FROM THE LEGENDS OF THE TROLL-GODS

At the dawn of time, long before the ancestors of Styricum slouched, fur-clad and club-wielding, out of the mountains and forests of Zemoch onto the plains of central Eosia, there dwelt in a deep cavern lying beneath the perpetual snows of northern Thalesia a dwarfed and misshapen Troll named Ghwerig. Now, Ghwerig was an outcast by reason of his ugliness and his overwhelming greed, and he labored alone in the depths of the earth, seeking gold and precious gems that he might add to the treasure-hoard which he jealously guarded. Finally there came a day when he broke into a deep gallery far beneath the frozen surface of the earth and beheld by the light of his flickering torch a deep blue gemstone, larger than his fist, embedded in the wall. Trembling with excitement in all his gnarled and twisted limbs, he squatted on the floor of that passage and gazed with longing at the huge jewel, knowing that its value exceeded that of the entire hoard which he had labored for centuries to acquire. Then he began with great care to cut away the surrounding stone, chip by chip, so that he might lift the precious gem from the spot where it had rested since the world began. And as more and more of it emerged from the rock, he perceived that it had a peculiar shape, and an idea came to him. Could he but remove it intact, he might by careful carving and polishing enhance that shape and thus increase the value of the gem a thousandfold.

When at last he gently took the jewel from its rocky bed, he carried it straightway to the cave wherein lay his workshop and his treasure hoard. Indifferently, he shattered a diamond of incalculable worth and fashioned from its fragments tools with which he might carve and shape the gem which he had found.

For decades, by the light of smoky torches, Ghwerig patiently carved and polished, muttering all the while the spells and incantations which would infuse this priceless gem with all the power for good or ill of the Troll-Gods. When at last the carving was done, the gem was in the shape of a rose of deepest sapphire blue. And he named it Bhelliom, the flower-gem, and he believed that by its might all things might be possible for him.

But though Bhelliom was filled with all the power of the Troll-Gods, it would not yield up that power unto its misshapen and ugly owner, and Ghwerig pounded his fists in rage upon the stone floor of his cavern. He consulted with his Gods and made offerings to them of heavy gold and bright silver, and his Gods revealed to him that there must be a key to unlock the power of Bhelliom, lest its might be unleashed by the whim of any who came upon it. Then the Troll-Gods told Ghwerig what he must do to gain mastery over the gem which he had wrought. Taking the shards which had fallen unnoticed in the dust about his feet as he had labored to shape the sapphire rose, he fashioned a pair of rings. Of finest gold were the rings, and each was mounted with a polished oval fragment of Bhelliom itself. When it was done, he placed the rings one on each of his hands and then lifted the sapphire rose. The deep, glowing blue of the stones mounted in his rings fled back into Bhelliom itself, and the jewels that adorned his twisted hands were now as pale as diamond. And as he held the flower-gem, he felt the surge of its power and he rejoiced in the knowledge that the jewel he had wrought had consented to yield to him.

As the uncounted centuries rolled by, great were the wonders Ghwerig wrought by the power of Bhelliom. But the Styrics came at last into the land of the Trolls. When the Elder Gods of Styricum learned of Bhelliom, each in his heart coveted it by reason of its power. But Ghwerig was cunning and he sealed up the entrances to his cavern with enchantments to repel their efforts to wrest Bhelliom from him.

Now at a certain time, the Younger Gods of Styricum took counsel with each other, for they were disquieted about the power which Bhelliom would confer upon whichever God came to possess it, and they concluded that such might should not be unloosed in the earth. They resolved then to render the stone powerless. Of their number they selected the nimble Goddess Aphrael for the task. Then Aphrael journeyed to the north, and, by reason of her slight form, she was able to wriggle her way through a crevice so small that Ghwerig had neglected to seal it. Once she was within the cavern, Aphrael lifted her voice in song. So sweetly she sang that Ghwerig was all bemused by her melody and he felt no alarm at her presence. So it was that Aphrael lulled him. When, with dreamy smile, the Troll-Dwarf closed his eyes, she tugged the ring from off his right hand and replaced it with a ring set with a common diamond. Ghwerig started up when he felt the tug; but when he looked at his hand, a ring still encircled his finger, and he sat him down again and took his ease, delighting in the song of the Goddess. When once again, in sweet reverie, his eyes drooped shut, the nimble Aphrael tugged the ring from off his left hand, replacing it with yet another ring mounted with yet another diamond. Again Ghwerig started to his feet and looked with alarm at his left hand, but he was reassured by the presence there of a ring which looked for all the world like one of the pair which he had fashioned from the shards of the flower-gem. Aphrael continued to sing for him until at last he lapsed into deep slumber. Then the Goddess stole away on silent feet, bearing with her the rings which were the keys to the power of Bhelliom.

Now, upon a later day, Ghwerig lifted Bhelliom from the crystal case wherein it lay that he might perform a task by its power, but Bhelliom would not yield to him, for he no longer possessed the rings which were the keys to its power. The rage of Ghwerig was beyond measure, and he went up and down in the land seeking the Goddess Aphrael that he might wrest his rings from her, but he found her not, though for centuries he searched.

Thus it was for as long as Styricum held sway over the mountains and plains of Eosia. But there came a time when the Elenes rode out of the east and intruded themselves into this place. After centuries of random wandering to and fro in the land, some of their number came at last into far northern Thalesia and dispossessed the Styrics and their Gods. And when the Elenes heard of Ghwerig and his Bhelliom, they sought the entrances to the Troll-Dwarf's cavern throughout the hills

and valleys of Thalesia, all hot with their lust to find and own the fabled gem by reason of its incalculable worth, for they knew not of the power locked in its azure
petals.

It fell at last to Adian of Thalesia, mightiest and most crafty of the heroes of antiquity, to solve the riddle. At peril of his soul, he took counsel with the Troll-Gods
and made offering to them, and they relented and told him that Ghwerig went
abroad in the land at certain times in search of the Goddess Aphrael of Styricum
that he might reclaim a pair of rings which she had stolen from him, but of the true
meaning of those rings they told him not. And Adian journeyed to the far north
and there he awaited each twilight for a half-dozen years the appearance of
Ghwerig.

When at last the Troll-Dwarf appeared, Adian went up to him in a dissembling
guise and told him that he knew where Aphrael might be found and that he would
reveal her location for a helmet full of fine yellow gold. Ghwerig was deceived and
straightaway led Adian to the hidden mouth of his cavern and he took the hero's
helm and went into his treasure chamber and filled it to overflowing with fine gold.
Then he emerged again, sealing the entrance to his cavern behind him. And he gave
Adian the gold, and Adian deceived him again, saying that Aphrael might be found
in the district of Horset on the western coast of Thalesia. Ghwerig hastened to
Horset to seek out the Goddess. And once again Adian imperiled his soul and implored the Troll-Gods to break Ghwerig's enchantments that he might gain entrance to the cavern. The capricious Troll-Gods consented and the enchantments
were broken.

As rosy dawn touched the ice fields of the north into flame, Adian emerged
from Ghwerig's cavern with Bhelliom in his grasp. He journeyed straightway to his
capital at Emsat and there he fashioned a crown for himself and surmounted it with
Bhelliom.

The chagrin of Ghwerig knew no bounds when he returned empty-handed to
his cavern to find that not only had he lost the keys to the power of Bhelliom, but
that the flower-gem itself was no longer in his possession. Thereafter he usually
lurked by night in the fields and forests about the city of Emsat, seeking to reclaim
his treasure, but the descendants of Adian protected it closely and prevented him
from approaching it.

Now as it happened, Azash, an Elder God of Styricum, had long yearned in his
heart for possession of Bhelliom and of the rings which unlocked its power and he
sent forth his hordes out of Zemoch to seize the gems by force of arms. The kings
of the west took up arms to join with the knights of the Church to face the armies
of Otha of Zemoch and of his dark Styric God, Azash. And King Sarak of Thalesia
took ship with some few of his vassals and sailed south from Emsat, leaving behind
the royal command that his earls were to follow when the mobilization of all Thalesia was complete. As it happened, however, King Sarak never reached the great battlefield on the plains of Lamorkand, but fell instead to a Zemoch spear in an
unrecorded skirmish near the shores of Lake Venne in Pelosia. A faithful vassal,
though mortally wounded, took up his fallen lord's crown and struggled his way to
the marshy eastern shore of the lake. There, hard-pressed and dying, he cast the
Thalesian crown into the murky, peat-clouded waters of the lake, even as Ghwerig,

who had followed his lost treasure, watched in horror from his place of concealment in a nearby peat bog.

The Zemochs who had slain King Sarak immediately began to probe the brown-stained depths, that they might find the crown and carry it in triumph to Azash, but they were interrupted in their search by a column of Alcione Knights sweeping down out of Deira to join the battle in Lamorkand. The Alciones fell upon the Zemochs and slew them to the last man. The faithful vassal of the Thalesian king was given an honorable burial, and the Alciones rode on, all unaware that the fabled crown of Thalesia lay beneath the turbid waters of Lake Venne.

It is sometimes rumored in Pelosia, however, that on moonless nights the shadowy form of the immortal Troll-Dwarf haunts the marshy shore. Since, by reason of his malformed limbs, Ghwerig dares not enter the dark waters of the lake to probe its depths, he must creep along the marge, alternately crying out his longing to Bhelliom and dancing in howling frustration that it will not respond to him.

PART ONE

# CIMMURA

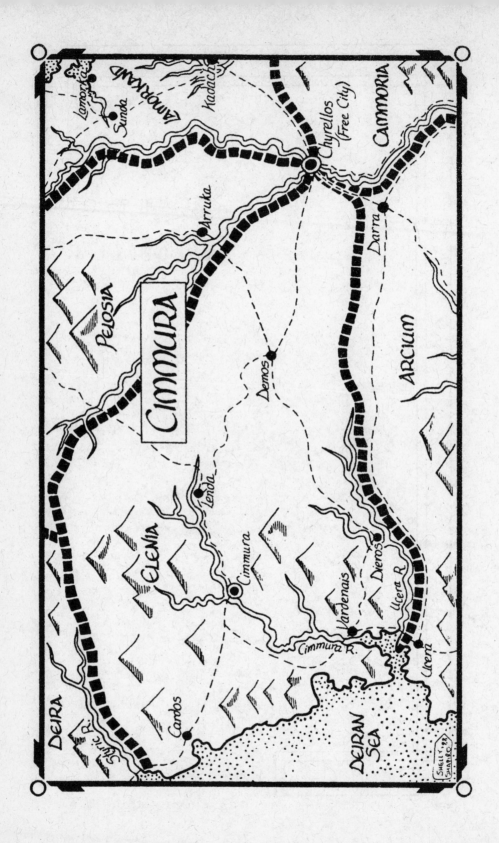

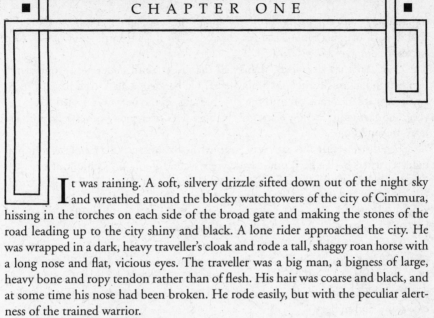

# CHAPTER ONE

It was raining. A soft, silvery drizzle sifted down out of the night sky and wreathed around the blocky watchtowers of the city of Cimmura, hissing in the torches on each side of the broad gate and making the stones of the road leading up to the city shiny and black. A lone rider approached the city. He was wrapped in a dark, heavy traveller's cloak and rode a tall, shaggy roan horse with a long nose and flat, vicious eyes. The traveller was a big man, a bigness of large, heavy bone and ropy tendon rather than of flesh. His hair was coarse and black, and at some time his nose had been broken. He rode easily, but with the peculiar alertness of the trained warrior.

His name was Sparhawk, a man at least ten years older than he looked, who carried the erosion of his years not so much on his battered face as in a half-dozen or so minor infirmities and discomforts and in the several wide purple scars upon his body which always ached in damp weather. Tonight, however, he felt his age and he wished only for a warm bed in the obscure inn which was his goal. Sparhawk was coming home at last after a decade of being someone else with a different name in a country where it almost never rained—where the sun was a hammer pounding down on a bleached white anvil of sand and rock and hard-baked clay, where the walls of the buildings were thick and white to ward off the blows of the sun, and where graceful women went to the wells in the silvery light of early morning with large clay vessels balanced on their shoulders and black veils across their faces.

The big roan horse shuddered absently, shaking the rain out of his shaggy coat, and approached the city gate, stopping in the ruddy circle of torchlight before the gatehouse.

An unshaven gate guard in a rust-splotched breastplate and helmet, and with a patched green cloak negligently hanging from one shoulder, came unsteadily out of the gatehouse and stood swaying in Sparhawk's path. "I'll need your name," he said in a voice thick with drink.

Sparhawk gave him a long stare, then opened his cloak to show the heavy silver amulet hanging on a chain about his neck.

The half-drunk gate guard's eyes widened slightly, and he stepped back a pace. "Oh," he said, "sorry, my Lord. Go ahead."

Another guard poked his head out of the gatehouse. "Who is he, Raf?" he demanded.

"A Pandion Knight," the first guard replied nervously.

"What's his business in Cimmura?"

"I don't question the Pandions, Bral," the man named Raf answered. He smiled ingratiatingly up at Sparhawk. "New man," he said apologetically, jerking his thumb back over his shoulder at his comrade. "He'll learn in time, my Lord. Can we serve you in any way?"

"No," Sparhawk replied, "thanks all the same. You'd better get in out of the rain, neighbor. You'll catch cold out here." He handed a small coin to the green-cloaked guard and rode on into the city, passing up the narrow, cobbled street beyond the gate with the slow clatter of the big roan's steel-shod hooves echoing back from the buildings.

The district near the gate was poor, with shabby, run-down houses standing tightly packed beside each other with their second floors projecting out over the wet, littered street. Crude signs swung creaking on rusty hooks in the night wind, identifying this or that tightly shuttered shop on the street-level floors. A wet, miserable-looking cur slunk across the street with his ratlike tail between his legs. Otherwise, the street was dark and empty.

A torch burned fitfully at an intersection where another street crossed the one upon which Sparhawk rode. A sick young whore, thin and wrapped in a shabby blue cloak, stood hopefully under the torch like a pale, frightened ghost. "Would you like a nice time, sir?" she whined at him. Her eyes were wide and timid, and her face gaunt and hungry.

He stopped, bent in his saddle, and poured a few small coins into her grimy hand. "Go home, little sister," he told her in a gentle voice. "It's late and wet, and there'll be no customers tonight." Then he straightened and rode on, leaving her to stare in grateful astonishment after him. He turned down a narrow side street clotted with shadow and heard the scurry of feet somewhere in the rainy dark ahead of him. His ears caught a quick, whispered conversation in the deep shadows somewhere to his left.

The roan snorted and laid his ears back.

"It's nothing to get excited about," Sparhawk told him. The big man's voice was very soft, almost a husky whisper. It was the kind of voice people turned to hear. Then he spoke more loudly, addressing the pair of footpads lurking in the shadows. "I'd like to accommodate you, neighbors," he said, "but it's late, and I'm not in the mood for casual entertainment. Why don't you go rob some drunk young nobleman instead, and live to steal another day?" To emphasize his words, he threw back his damp cloak to reveal the leather-bound hilt of the plain broadsword belted at his side.

There was a quick, startled silence in the dark street, followed by the rapid patter of fleeing feet.

The big roan snorted derisively.

"My sentiments exactly," Sparhawk agreed, pulling his cloak back around him. "Shall we proceed?"

They entered a large square surrounded by hissing torches where most of the brightly colored canvas booths had their fronts rolled down. A few forlornly hopeful enthusiasts remained open for business, stridently bawling their wares to indifferent passersby hurrying home on a late, rainy evening. Sparhawk reined in his horse as a group of rowdy young nobles lurched unsteadily from the door of a seedy tavern, shouting drunkenly to each other as they crossed the square. He waited calmly until they vanished into a side street and then looked around, not so much wary as alert.

Had there been but a few more people in the nearly empty square, even Sparhawk's trained eye might not have noticed Krager. The man was of medium height and he was rumpled and unkempt. His boots were muddy, and his maroon cape carelessly caught at the throat. He slouched across the square, his wet, colorless hair plastered down on his narrow skull and his watery eyes blinking nearsightedly as he peered about in the rain. Sparhawk drew in his breath sharply. He hadn't seen Krager since that night in Cippria, almost ten years ago, and the man had aged considerably. His face was grayer and more pouchy-looking, but there could be no question that it was Krager.

Since quick movements attracted the eye, Sparhawk's reaction was studied. He dismounted slowly and led his big horse to a green canvas food vendor's stall, keeping the animal between himself and the nearsighted man in the maroon cape. "Good evening, neighbor," he said to the brown-clad food vendor in his deadly quiet voice. "I have some business to attend to. I'll pay you if you'll watch my horse."

The unshaven vendor's eyes came quickly alight.

"Don't even think it," Sparhawk warned. "The horse won't follow you, no matter what you do—but I *will,* and you wouldn't like that at all. Just take the pay and forget about trying to steal the horse."

The vendor looked at the big man's bleak face, swallowed hard, and made a jerky attempt at a bow. "Whatever you say, my Lord," he agreed quickly, his words tumbling over each other. "I vow to you that your noble mount will be safe with me."

"Noble what?"

"Noble mount—your horse."

"Oh, I see. I'd appreciate that."

"Can I do anything else for you, my Lord?"

Sparhawk looked across the square at Krager's back. "Do you by chance happen to have a bit of wire handy—about so long?" He measured out perhaps three feet with his hands.

"I may have, my Lord. The herring kegs are bound with wire. Let me look."

Sparhawk crossed his arms and leaned them on his saddle, watching Krager across the horse's back. The past years, the blasting sun, and the women going to the wells in the steely light of early morning fell away, and quite suddenly he was back in the stockyards outside Cippria with the stink of dung and blood on him, the taste of fear and hatred in his mouth, and the pain of his wounds making him weak as his pursuers searched for him with their swords in their hands.

He pulled his mind away from that, deliberately concentrating on this moment rather than the past. He hoped that the vendor could find some wire. Wire was good. No noise, no mess, and with a little time it could be made to look exotic— the kind of thing one might expect from a Styric or perhaps a Pelosian. It wasn't so much Krager, he thought as the tense excitement built in him. Krager had never been more than a dim, feeble adjunct to Martel—an extension, another set of hands, just as the other man, Adus, had never been more than a weapon. It was what Krager's death would do to Martel—that was what mattered.

"This is the best I could find, my Lord," the greasy-aproned food vendor said respectfully, coming out of the back of his canvas booth and holding out a length of rusty, soft-iron wire. "I'm sorry. It isn't much."

"It's just fine," Sparhawk replied, taking the wire. He snapped the rusty strand taut between his hands. "It's perfect, in fact." Then he turned to his horse. "Stay here, Faran," he said.

The horse bared his teeth at him. Sparhawk laughed softly and moved out into the square, some distance behind Krager. If the nearsighted man were found in some shadowy doorway, bowed tautly backward with the wire knotted about his neck and ankles and with his eyes popping out of a blackened face, or facedown in the trough of some back-alley public urinal, that would unnerve Martel, hurt him, perhaps even frighten him. It might be enough to bring him out into the open, and Sparhawk had been waiting for years for a chance to catch Martel out in the open. Carefully, his hands concealed beneath his cloak, he began to work the kinks out of his length of wire, even as he stalked his quarry.

His senses had become preternaturally alert. He could clearly hear the guttering of the torches along the sides of the square and see their orange flicker reflected in the puddles of water lying among the cobblestones. That reflected glow seemed for some reason very beautiful. Sparhawk felt good—better perhaps than he had for ten years.

"Sir Knight? Sir Sparhawk? Can that be you?"

Startled, Sparhawk turned quickly, swearing under his breath. The man who had accosted him had long, elegantly curled blond hair. He wore a saffron-colored doublet, lavender hose, and an apple-green cloak. His wet maroon shoes were long and pointed, and his cheeks were rouged. The small, useless sword at his side and his broadbrimmed hat with its dripping plume marked him as a courtier, one of the petty functionaries and parasitic hangers-on who infested the palace like vermin.

"What are you doing back here in Cimmura?" the fop demanded, his high-pitched, effeminate voice startled. "You were banished."

Sparhawk looked quickly at the man he had been following. Krager was nearing the entrance to a street that opened into the square, and in a moment he would be out of sight. It was still possible, however. One quick, hard blow would put this overdressed butterfly before him to sleep, and Krager would still be within reach. Then a hot disappointment filled Sparhawk's mouth as a detachment of the watch marched into the square with lumbering tread. There was no way now to dispose of this interfering popinjay without attracting their attention. The look he directed at the perfumed man barring his path was flat with anger.

The courtier stepped back nervously, glancing quickly at the soldiers who were moving along in front of the booths, checking the fastenings on the rolled-down canvas fronts. "I insist that you tell me what you're doing back here," he said, trying to sound authoritative.

"Insist? You?" Sparhawk's voice was full of contempt.

The other man looked quickly at the soldiers again, seeking reassurance, then he straightened boldly. "I'm taking you in charge, Sparhawk. I demand that you give an account of yourself." He reached out and grasped Sparhawk's arm.

"Don't touch me." Sparhawk spat out the words, striking the hand away.

"You hit me!" the courtier gasped, clutching at his hand in pain.

Sparhawk took the man's shoulder in one hand and pulled him close. "If you ever put your hands on me again, I'll rip out your guts. Now get out of my way."

"I'll call the watch," the fop threatened.

"And how long do you think you'll continue to live after you do that?"

"You can't threaten me. I have powerful friends."

"But they're not here, are they? I *am,* however." Sparhawk pushed him away in disgust and turned to walk on across the square.

"You Pandions can't get away with this highhanded behavior anymore. There are laws in Elenia now," the overdressed man called after him shrilly. "I'm going straight to Baron Harparin. I'm going to tell him that you've come back to Cimmura and about how you hit me and threatened me."

"Good," Sparhawk replied without turning. "Do that." He continued to walk away, his irritation and disappointment rising to the point where he had to clench his teeth tightly to keep himself under control. Then an idea came to him. It was petty—even childish—but for some reason it seemed quite appropriate. He stopped and straightened his shoulders, muttering under his breath in the Styric tongue, even as his fingers wove intricate designs in the air in front of him. He hesitated slightly, groping for the word for carbuncle. He finally settled for boils instead and completed the incantation. He turned slightly, looked at his tormentor, and released the spell. Then he turned back and continued on across the square, smiling slightly to himself. It was, to be sure, quite petty, but Sparhawk was like that sometimes.

He handed the food vendor a coin for minding Faran, swung up into his saddle, and rode across the square in the misty drizzle, a big man shrouded in a rough wool cloak, astride an ugly-faced roan horse.

Once he was past the square, the streets were dark and empty again, with guttering torches hissing in the rain at intersections and casting their dim, sooty orange glow. The sound of Faran's hooves was loud in the empty street. Sparhawk shifted slightly in his saddle. The sensation he felt was very faint, a kind of prickling of the skin across his shoulders and up the back of his neck, but he recognized it immediately. Someone was watching him, and the watcher was not friendly. Sparhawk shifted again, carefully trying to make the movement appear to be no more than the uncomfortable fidgeting of a saddle-weary traveller. His right hand, however, was concealed beneath his cloak and it sought the hilt of his sword. The oppressive sense of malevolence increased, and then, in the shadows beyond the flickering torch at the next intersection, he saw a figure robed and hooded in a dark gray garment that blended so well into the shadows and wreathing drizzle that the watcher was almost invisible.

The roan tensed his muscles, and his ears flicked.

"I see him, Faran," Sparhawk replied very quietly.

They continued on along the cobblestone street, passing through the pool of orange torchlight and on into the shadowy street beyond. Sparhawk's eyes readjusted to the dark, but the hooded figure had already vanished up some alleyway or through one of the narrow doors along the street. The sense of being watched was gone, and the street was no longer a place of danger. Faran moved on, his hooves clattering on the wet stones.

The inn which was Sparhawk's destination was on an unobtrusive back street. It was gated at the front of its central courtyard with stout oaken planks. Its walls were peculiarly high and thick, and a single, dim lantern glowed beside a much-weathered wooden sign that creaked mournfully as it swung back and forth in the rain-filled night breeze. Sparhawk pulled Faran close to the gate, leaned back in his saddle, and kicked the rain-blackened planks solidly with one spurred foot. There was a peculiar rhythm to the kicks.

He waited.

Then the gate creaked inward and the shadowy form of a porter, hooded in black, looked out. He nodded briefly, then pulled the gate wider to admit Sparhawk. The big knight rode into the rain-wet courtyard and slowly dismounted. The porter swung the gate shut and barred it, then he pushed his hood back from his steel helm, turned, and bowed. "My Lord," he greeted Sparhawk respectfully.

"It's too late at night for formalities, Sir Knight," Sparhawk responded, also with a brief bow.

"Formality is the very soul of gentility, Sir Sparhawk," the porter replied ironically. "I try to practice it whenever I can."

"As you wish." Sparhawk shrugged. "Will you see to my horse?"

"Of course. Your man, Kurik, is here."

Sparhawk nodded, untying the two heavy leather bags from the skirt of his saddle.

"I'll take those up for you, my Lord," the porter offered.

"There's no need. Where's Kurik?"

"First door at the top of the stairs. Will you want supper?"

Sparhawk shook his head. "Just a bath and a warm bed." He turned to his horse, who stood dozing with one hind leg cocked slightly so that his hoof rested on its tip. "Wake up, Faran," he told the animal.

Faran opened his eyes and gave him a flat, unfriendly stare.

"Go with this knight," Sparhawk instructed firmly. "Don't try to bite him, or kick him, or pin him against the side of the stall with your rump—and don't step on his feet, either."

The big roan briefly laid back his ears and then sighed.

Sparhawk laughed. "Give him a few carrots," he instructed the porter.

"How can you tolerate this foul-tempered brute, Sir Sparhawk?"

"We're perfectly matched," Sparhawk replied. "It was a good ride, Faran," he said then to the horse. "Thank you, and sleep warm."

The horse turned his back on him.

"Keep your eyes open, Sir Knight," Sparhawk cautioned the porter. "Someone was watching me as I rode here, and I got the feeling that it was a little more than idle curiosity."

The knight porter's face hardened. "I'll tend to it, my Lord," he said.

"Good." Sparhawk turned and crossed the wet, glistening stones of the courtyard and mounted the steps leading to the roofed gallery on the second floor of the inn.

The inn was a well-kept secret that few in Cimmura knew about. Though ostensibly no different from any of dozens of others, this particular establishment was owned and operated by the Pandion Knights and it provided a safe haven for any of their number who, for one reason or another, were reluctant to avail themselves of the facilities of their chapterhouse on the eastern outskirts of the city.

At the top of the stairs, Sparhawk stopped and tapped his fingertips lightly on the first door. After a moment, the door opened. The man inside was burly and he had iron-gray hair and a coarse, short-trimmed beard. His hose and boots were of black leather, and his long vest was of the same material. A heavy dagger hung from his belt, steel cuffs encircled his wrists, and his heavily muscled arms and shoulders were bare. He was not a handsome man, and his eyes were as hard as agates. "You're late," he said flatly.

"A few interruptions along the way," Sparhawk replied laconically, stepping into the warm, candlelit room. The bare-shouldered man closed the door behind him and slid the bolt with a solid clank. Sparhawk looked at him. "I trust you've been well, Kurik?" he said to the man he had not seen for ten years.

"Passable. Get out of that wet cloak."

Sparhawk grinned, dropped his saddlebags to the floor, and undid the clasp of his dripping wool cloak. "How are Aslade and the boys?"

"Growing," Kurik grunted, taking the cloak. "My sons are getting taller and Aslade's getting fatter. Farm life agrees with her."

"You like plump women, Kurik," Sparhawk reminded his squire. "That's why you married her."

Kurik grunted again, looking critically at his lord's lean frame. "You haven't been eating, Sparhawk," he accused.

"Don't mother me, Kurik." Sparhawk sprawled in a heavy oak chair. He looked around. The room had a stone floor and stone walls. The ceiling was low, with heavy black beams supporting it. A fire crackled in an arched fireplace, filling the room with dancing light and shadows. Two candles burned on the table, and two narrow cots stood, one against either wall. It was to the heavy rack beside the single blue-draped window that Sparhawk's eyes went first, however. Hanging on that rack was a full suit of armor, enameled shiny black. Leaning against the wall beside it was a large black shield with the emblem of his family, a hawk with flared wings and with a spear in its talons, worked in silver upon its face. Beside the shield stood a massive, sheathed broadsword with a silver-bound hilt.

"You forgot to oil it when you left," Kurik accused. "It took me a week to get the rust off. Give me your foot." He bent and worked off one of Sparhawk's riding boots and then the other. "Why do you always have to walk in the mud?" he growled, tossing the boots over beside the fireplace. "I've got a bath ready for you in the next room," he said then. "Strip. I want to see those wounds of yours anyway."

Sparhawk sighed wearily and stood up. With his gruff squire's peculiarly gentle help, he undressed.

"You're wet clear through," Kurik noted, touching his lord's clammy back with one rough, callused hand.

"Rain does that to people sometimes."

"Did you ever see a surgeon about these?" the squire demanded, lightly touching the wide purple scars on Sparhawk's shoulders and left side.

"A physician looked at them. There wasn't a surgeon handy, so I left them to heal by themselves."

Kurik nodded. "It shows," he said. "Go get in the tub. I'll fetch something for you to eat."

"I'm not hungry."

"That's too bad. You look like a skeleton. Now that you're back, I'm not going to let you walk around in that condition."

"Why are you bullying me, Kurik?"

"Because I'm angry. You frightened me half to death. You've been gone for ten years, and there's been little news—and all of it bad." The gruff man's eyes grew momentarily soft, and he roughly grasped Sparhawk's shoulders in a grip that might have brought a lesser man to his knees. "Welcome home, my Lord," he said in a thick voice.

Sparhawk roughly embraced his friend. "Thank you, Kurik," he said, his voice also thick. "It's good to be back."

"All right," Kurik said, his face hard again. "Now go bathe. You stink." And he turned on his heel and went to the door.

Sparhawk smiled and walked into the next room. He stepped into the wooden tub and sank gratefully down into the steaming water. He had been another man with another name—a man called Mahkra—for so long now that he knew that no simple bath would wash that other identity away, but it was good to relax and let the hot water and coarse soap rinse the dust of that dry, sunblasted coast from his skin. In a kind of detached reverie as he washed his lean, scarred limbs, he remembered the life he had led as Mahkra in the city of Jiroch in Rendor. He remembered the small, cool shop where, as an untitled commoner, Mahkra had sold brass ewers, candied sweetmeats, and exotic perfumes while the bright sunlight reflected blindingly from the thick, white walls across the street. He remembered the hours of endless talk in the little wine shop on the corner, where Mahkra had sipped sour, resinous Rendorish wine by the hour and had delicately, subtly, probed for the information which was then passed on to his friend and fellow Pandion, Sir Voren—information concerning the reawakening of Eshandist sentiment in Rendor, of secret caches of arms hidden in the desert and of the activities of the agents of Emperor Otha of Zemoch. He remembered the soft, dark nights filled with the clinging perfume of Lillias, Mahkra's sulking mistress, and of the beginning of each day when he had arisen and gone to the window to watch the women going to the wells in the steel-gray light of sunless dawn. He sighed. "And who are you now, Sparhawk?" he asked himself softly. "No longer a merchant in brass and candied dates and perfumes, certainly, but once again a Pandion Knight? A magician? The Queen's Champion? Perhaps not. Perhaps no more than a battered and tired man with a few too many years and scars and far too many skirmishes behind him."

"Didn't it occur to you to cover your head while you were in Rendor?" Kurik asked sourly from the doorway. The burly squire held a robe and a rough towel.

"When a man starts talking to himself, it's a sure sign that he's been out in the sun too long."

"Just musing, Kurik. I've been a long time away from home, and it's going to take a while to get used to it again."

"You may not have a while. Did anyone recognize you when you rode in?"

Sparhawk remembered the fop in the square and nodded. "One of Harparin's toadies saw me in the square near the west gate."

"That's it, then. You're going to have to present yourself at the palace tomorrow, or Lycheas will have Cimmura taken apart stone by stone searching for you."

"Lycheas?"

"The prince regent—bastard son to Princess Arissa and whatever drunken sailor or unhanged pickpocket got him on her."

Sparhawk sat up quickly, his eyes hardening. "I think you'd better explain a few things, Kurik," he said. "Ehlana's the queen. Why does her kingdom need a prince regent?"

"Where have you been, Sparhawk? On the moon? Ehlana fell ill a month ago."

"Not dead?" Sparhawk demanded with a sudden sinking in his stomach and a wrench of unbearable loss at the memory of the pale, beautiful girl-child with the grave, serious gray eyes whom he had watched throughout her childhood and whom, in a peculiar way, he had come to love, though she had been but eight years old when King Aldreas had sent him into his exile in Rendor.

"No," Kurik replied, "not dead, though she might as well be." He picked up the large, rough towel. "Come out of the tub," he ordered. "I'll tell you about it while you eat."

Sparhawk nodded and stood up. Kurik roughly toweled him off and then draped the soft robe about him. The table in the other room was laid with a platter of steaming slices of meat swimming in gravy, a half loaf of rough, dark peasant bread, a wedge of cheese, and a pitcher of chilled milk. "Eat," Kurik said.

"What's been going on here?" Sparhawk demanded as he seated himself at the table and started to eat. He was surprised to find that he was suddenly ravenous. "Start at the beginning."

"All right," Kurik agreed, drawing his dagger and starting to carve thick slices of bread from the loaf. "You knew that the Pandions were confined to the motherhouse at Demos after you left, didn't you?"

Sparhawk nodded. "I heard about it. King Aldreas was never really very fond of us."

"That was your father's fault, Sparhawk. Aldreas was *very* fond of his sister, and then your father forced him to marry someone else. That sort of soured his attitude toward the Pandion Order."

"Kurik," Sparhawk said, "it's not proper to talk about the king that way."

Kurik shrugged. "He's dead now, so it doesn't hurt him, and the way he felt about his sister was common knowledge anyway. The palace pages used to take money from anyone who wanted to watch Arissa walk mother-naked through the upper halls to her brother's bedchamber. Aldreas was a weak king, Sparhawk. He was totally under the control of Arissa and the Primate Annias. With the Pandions confined at Demos, Annias and his underlings had things pretty much the way they wanted them. You were lucky not to have been here during those years."

"Perhaps," Sparhawk murmured. "What did Aldreas die from?"

"They say that it was the falling-sickness. My guess would be that the whores Annias used to slip into the palace for him after his wife died finally wore him out."

"Kurik, you gossip worse than an old woman."

"I know," Kurik admitted blandly. "It's a vice I have."

"And then Ehlana was crowned queen?"

"Right. And then things started to change. Annias was certain that he'd be able to control her the same way that he'd been able to control Aldreas, but she brought him up short. She summoned Preceptor Vanion from the motherhouse at Demos and made him her personal advisor. Then she told Annias to make preparations to retire to a monastery to meditate on the virtues proper to a churchman. Annias was livid, of course, and he started to scheme immediately. The messengers were as thick as flies on the road between here and the cloister where the Princess Arissa has been confined. They're old friends, and they had certain common interests. At any rate, Annias suggested that Ehlana should marry her bastard cousin, Lycheas, but she laughed in his face."

"That sounds fairly characteristic," Sparhawk smiled. "I raised her myself and I taught her what was appropriate. What is this illness of hers?"

"It appears to be the same one that killed her father. She had a seizure and never regained consciousness. The court physicians all maintained that she wouldn't live out the week, but then Vanion took steps. He appeared at court with Sephrenia and eleven other Pandions—all in full armor and with their visors down. They dismissed the queen's attendants, took her from her bed, clothed her in her state robes, and put the crown on her head. Then they carried her to the great hall and set her on the throne and locked the door. Nobody knows what they did in there, but when they opened the door again, Ehlana sat on her throne encased in crystal."

"What?" Sparhawk exclaimed.

"It's as clear as glass. You can see every freckle on the queen's nose, but you can't get near her. The crystal's harder than diamond. Annias had workmen hammering on it for five days, and they couldn't even chip it." Kurik looked at Sparhawk. "Could you do something like that?" he asked curiously.

"Me? Kurik, I wouldn't even know where to start. Sephrenia taught us the basics, but we're like babies compared to her."

"Well, whatever it was that she did, it's keeping the queen alive. You can hear her heart beating. It echoes through the throne room like a drum. For the first week or so, people were flocking in there just to listen to it. There was even talk that it was some kind of miracle and that the throne room ought to be made a shrine. But Annias locked the door and summoned Lycheas the bastard to Cimmura and set him up as prince regent. That was about two weeks ago. Since then Annias has had the church soldiers rounding up all his enemies. The dungeons under the cathedral are bulging with them. That's where things stand right now. You picked a good time to come back." He paused, looking directly into his lord's face. "What happened in Cippria, Sparhawk?" he asked. "The news we got here was pretty sketchy."

Sparhawk shrugged. "It wasn't much. Do you remember Martel?"

"The renegade Vanion stripped of his knighthood? The one with white hair?"

Sparhawk nodded. "He came to Cippria with a couple of underlings, and they hired fifteen or twenty cutthroats to help them. They waylaid me in a dark street."

"Is that where you got the scars?"

"Yes."

"But you got away."

"Obviously. Rendorish murderers are a trifle squeamish when the blood on the cobblestones and splashed all over the walls happens to be theirs. After I cut down a dozen or so of them, the rest sort of lost heart. I got clear of them and made my way to the edge of town. I hid in a monastery until the wounds healed, then I took Faran and joined a caravan for Jiroch."

Kurik's eyes were shrewd. "Do you think there's any possibility that Annias might have been involved in it?" he asked. "He hates your family, you know, and it's fairly certain that he was the one who persuaded Aldreas to exile you."

"I've had the same thought from time to time. Annias and Martel have had dealings before. At any rate, I think the good primate and I have several things to discuss."

Kurik looked at him, recognizing the tone in his voice. "You're going to get in trouble," he warned.

"Not as much as Annias will if I find out that he had a hand in that attack." Sparhawk straightened. "I'm going to need to talk with Vanion. Is he still here in Cimmura?"

Kurik nodded. "He's at the chapterhouse on the east edge of town, but you can't get there right now. They lock the east gate at sundown. I think you'd better present yourself at the palace right after the sun comes up, though. It won't take Annias long to come up with the idea of declaring you outlaw for breaking your exile, and it's better to appear on your own, rather than be dragged in like a common criminal. You're still going to have to do some fast talking to stay out of the dungeon."

"I don't think so," Sparhawk disagreed. "I've got a document with the queen's seal on it authorizing my return." He pushed back his plate. "The handwriting's a little childish, and there are tearstains on it, but I think it's still valid."

"She cried? I didn't think she knew how."

"She was only eight at the time, Kurik, and quite fond of me, for some reason."

"You have that effect on a few people." Kurik looked at Sparhawk's plate. "Have you had all of that you want?"

Sparhawk nodded.

"Then get you to bed. You've got a busy day ahead of you tomorrow."


It was much later. The room was faintly lit with the orange coals of the banked fire, and Kurik's regular breathing came from the cot on the other side of the room. The insistent, nagging bang of an unlatched shutter swinging freely in the wind several streets over had set some brainless dog to barking, and Sparhawk lay, still half-bemused by sleep, patiently waiting for the dog to grow wet enough or weary enough of his entertainment to seek his kennel again.

Since it had been Krager he had seen in the square, there was no absolute certainty that Martel was in Cimmura. Krager was an errand boy and was frequently half a continent away from Martel. Had it been the brutal Adus who had crossed that rainy square, there would be no question of Martel's presence in the city. Of necessity, Adus had to be kept on a short leash.

Krager would not be hard to find. He was a weak man with the usual vices and the usual predictability of weak men. Sparhawk smiled bleakly into the darkness. Krager would be easy to find and Krager would know where Martel could be found. It would be a simple matter to drag that information out of him.

Moving quietly to avoid waking his sleeping squire, Sparhawk swung his legs out of the bed and crossed silently to the window to watch the rain slant past into the deserted, lantern-lit courtyard below. Absently he wrapped his hand about the silver-bound hilt of the broadsword standing beside his formal armor. It felt good—like taking the hand of an old friend.

Dimly, as always, there was the remembered sound of the bells. It had been the bells he had followed that night in Cippria. Sick and hurt and alone, stumbling through the dung-reeking night in the stockyards, he had half crawled toward the sound of the bells. He had come at last to the wall and had followed it, his good hand on the ancient stones, until he had come finally to the gate, and there he had fallen.

Sparhawk shook his head. That had been a long time ago. It was strange that he could still remember the bells so clearly. He stood with his hand on his sword, looking out at the tag end of night, watching it rain and remembering the sound of the bells.

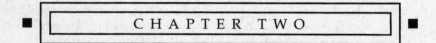

## CHAPTER TWO

Sparhawk was dressed in his formal armor and he strode clanking back and forth in the candlelit room to settle it into place. "I'd forgotten how heavy this is," he said.

"You're getting soft," Kurik told him. "You need a month or two on the practice field to toughen you up. Are you sure you want to wear it?"

"It's a formal occasion, Kurik, and formal occasions demand formal dress. Besides, I don't want any confusion in anybody's mind when I get there. I'm the Queen's Champion, and I'm supposed to wear armor when I present myself to her."

"They won't let you in to see her," Kurik predicted, picking up his lord's helmet.

"Won't let?"

"Don't do anything foolish, Sparhawk. You're going to be all alone."

"Is the Earl of Lenda still on the council?"

Kurik nodded. "He's old, and he doesn't have much authority, but he's too much respected for Annias to dismiss him."

"I'll have one friend there anyway." Sparhawk took his helmet from his squire and settled it in place. He pushed up his visor.

Kurik went to the window to pick up Sparhawk's sword and shield. "The rain's letting up," he noted, "and it's starting to get light." He came back, laid the sword and shield on the table, and picked up the silver-colored surcoat. "Hold out your arms," he instructed.

Sparhawk spread his arms wide, and Kurik draped the surcoat over his shoulders, then he laced up the sides. He then took up the long sword belt and wrapped it twice about his lord's waist. Sparhawk picked up his sheathed sword. "Did you sharpen this?" he asked.

Kurik gave him a flat stare.

"Sorry." Sparhawk locked the scabbard onto the heavy steel studs on the belt and shifted it around into place on his left side.

Kurik fastened the long black cape to the shoulder plates of the armor, then stepped back and looked Sparhawk up and down appraisingly. "Good enough," he said. "I'll bring your shield. You'd better hurry. They rise early at the palace. It gives them more time for mischief."

They went out of the room and on down the stairs to the innyard. The rain for the most part had passed, with only a few last intermittent sprinkles slanting into the yard in the gusty morning wind. The dawn sky, however, was still covered with tattered cloud, although there was a broad band of pale yellow off to the east.

The knight porter led Faran out of the stable, and he and Kurik boosted Sparhawk up into his saddle.

"Be careful when you get inside the palace, my Lord," Kurik warned in the formal tone he used when they were not alone. "The regular palace guards are probably neutral, but Annias has a troop of church soldiers there as well. Anybody in red livery is likely to be your enemy." He handed up the embossed black shield.

Sparhawk buckled the shield into place. "You're going to the chapterhouse to see Vanion?" he asked his squire.

Kurik nodded. "Just as soon as they open the east gates of the city."

"I'll probably go there when I'm through at the palace, but you come back here and wait for me." He grinned. "We may have to leave town in a hurry."

"Don't go out of your way to force the issue, my Lord."

Sparhawk took Faran's reins from the porter. "All right then, Sir Knight," he said. "Open the gate and I'll go present my respects to the bastard Lycheas."

The porter laughed and swung open the gate.

Faran moved out at a proud, rolling trot, lifting his steel-shod hooves exaggeratedly and bringing them down in a ringing staccato on the wet cobblestones. The big horse had a peculiar flair for the dramatic and he always pranced outrageously when Sparhawk was mounted on his back in full armor.

"Aren't we both getting a little old for exhibitionism?" Sparhawk asked drily.

Faran ignored that and continued his prancing.

There were few people abroad in the city of Cimmura at that hour—rumpled artisans and sleepy shopkeepers for the most part. The streets were wet, and the gusty wind set the brightly painted wooden signs over the shops to swinging and creaking. Most of the windows were still shuttered and dark, although here and there golden candlelight marked the room of some early riser.

Sparhawk noted that his armor had already begun to smell—that familiar compound of steel, oil, and the leather harness that had soaked up his sweat for years. He had nearly forgotten that smell in the sun-blasted streets and spice-fragrant shops of Jiroch; almost more than the familiar sights of Cimmura, it finally convinced him that he was home.

An occasional dog came out into the street to bark at them as they passed, but Faran disdainfully ignored them as he trotted through the cobblestone streets.

The palace lay in the center of town. It was a very grandiose sort of building, much taller than those around it, with high, pointed towers surmounted by damply flapping colored pennons. It was walled off from the rest of the city, and the walls were surmounted by battlements. At some time in the past, one of the kings of Elenia had ordered the exterior of those walls sheathed in white limestone. The climate and the pervasive pall of smoke that lay heavy over the city in certain seasons, however, had turned the sheathing a dirty, streaked gray.

The palace gates were broad and patrolled by a half-dozen guards wearing the dark blue livery that marked them as members of the regular palace garrison.

"Halt!" one of them barked as Sparhawk approached. He stepped into the center of the gateway, holding his pike slightly advanced. Sparhawk gave no indication that he had heard, and Faran bore down on the man. "I said to halt, Sir Knight!" the guard commanded again. Then one of his fellows jumped forward, seized his arm, and pulled him out of the roan's path. "It's the Queen's Champion," the second guard exclaimed. "Don't *ever* stand in his way."

Sparhawk reached the central courtyard and dismounted, moving a bit awkwardly because of the weight of his armor and the encumbrance of his shield. A guard came forward, his pike at the ready.

"Good morning, neighbor," Sparhawk said to him in his quiet voice.

The guard hesitated.

"Watch my horse," the knight told him then. "I shouldn't be too long." He handed the guard Faran's reins and started up the broad staircase toward the heavy double doors that opened into the palace.

"Sir Knight," the guard called after him.

Sparhawk did not turn, but continued on up the stairs. There were two blue-liveried guards at the top, older men, he noted, men he thought he recognized. One of the guard's eyes widened, then he suddenly grinned. "Welcome back, Sir Sparhawk," he said, pulling the door open for the black-armored knight.

Sparhawk gave him a slow wink and went on inside, his mail-shod feet and his spurs clinking on the polished flagstones. Just beyond the door, he encountered a palace functionary with curled and pomaded hair and wearing a maroon-colored doublet. "I will speak with Lycheas," Sparhawk announced in a flat tone. "Take me to him."

"But—" The man's face had gone slightly pale. He drew himself up, his expression growing lofty. "How did you—"

"Didn't you hear me, neighbor?" Sparhawk asked him.

The man in the maroon doublet shrank back. "A-at once, Sir Sparhawk," he stammered. He turned then and led the way down the broad central corridor. His shoulders were visibly trembling. Sparhawk noted that the functionary was not leading him toward the throne room, but rather toward the council chamber where King Aldreas had customarily met with his advisors. A faint smile touched the big man's lips as he surmised that the presence of the young queen sitting encased in crystal on the throne might have had a dampening effect on her cousin's attempts to usurp her crown.

They reached the door to the council chamber and found it guarded by two men wearing the red livery of the church—the soldiers of the Primate Annias. The two automatically crossed their pikes to bar entry to the chamber.

"The Queen's Champion to see the prince regent," the functionary said to them, his voice shrill.

"We have had no orders to admit the Queen's Champion," one of them declared.

"You have now," Sparhawk told him. "Open the door."

The man in the maroon doublet made a move as if to scurry away, but Sparhawk caught his arm. "I haven't dismissed you yet, neighbor," he said. Then he looked at the guards. "Open the door," he repeated.

It hung there for a long moment, while the guards looked first at Sparhawk and then nervously at each other. Then one of them swallowed hard and, fumbling with his pike, he reached for the door handle.

"You'll need to announce me," Sparhawk told the man whose arm he still held firmly in his gauntleted fist. "We wouldn't want to surprise anyone, would we?"

The man's eyes were a little wild. He stepped into the open doorway and cleared his throat. "The Queen's Champion," he blurted with his words tumbling out over each other. "The Pandion Knight, Sir Sparhawk."

"Thank you, neighbor," Sparhawk said. "You can go now."

The functionary bolted.

The council chamber was very large and was carpeted and draped in blue. Large candelabra lined the walls, and there were more candles on the long, polished table in the center of the room. Three men sat at the table with documents before them, but the fourth had half risen from his chair.

The man on his feet was the Primate Annias. The churchman had grown leaner in the ten years since Sparhawk had last seen him, and his face looked gray and emaciated. His hair was tied back from his face and was now shot with silver. He wore a long black cassock, and the bejeweled pendant of his office as primate of Cimmura hung from a thick gold chain about his neck. His eyes were wide with surprised alarm as Sparhawk entered the room.

The Earl of Lenda, a white-haired man in his seventies, was dressed in a soft gray doublet and he was grinning openly, his bright blue eyes sparkling in his lined face. The Baron Harparin, a notorious pederast, sat with an astonished expression on his face. His clothing was a riot of conflicting colors. Seated next to him was a grossly fat man in red, whom Sparhawk did not recognize.

"Sparhawk!" Annias said sharply, recovering from his surprise. "What are you doing here?"

"I understand that you've been looking for me, your Grace," Sparhawk replied. "I thought I'd save you some trouble."

"You've broken your exile, Sparhawk," Annias accused angrily.

"That's one of the things we need to talk about. I'm told that Lycheas the bastard is functioning as prince regent until the queen regains her health. Why don't you send for him so we won't have to go through all this twice?"

Annias's eyes widened in shock and outrage.

"That's what he is, isn't it?" Sparhawk said. "His origins are hardly a secret, so why tiptoe around them? The bell pull, as I recall, is right over there. Give it a yank, Annias, and send some toady to fetch the prince regent."

The Earl of Lenda chuckled openly.

Annias gave the old man a furious look and went to the pair of bell pulls hanging down the far wall. His hand hesitated between the two.

"Don't make any mistakes, your Grace," Sparhawk warned him. "All sorts of things could go terribly wrong if a dozen soldiers come through that door instead of a servant."

"Go ahead, Annias," the Earl of Lenda urged. "My life is almost over anyway, and I wouldn't mind going out with a bit of excitement."

Annias clenched his teeth and yanked the blue bell pull instead of the red one. After a moment the door opened, and a liveried young man entered. "Yes, your Grace?" he said, bowing to the primate.

"Go tell the prince regent that we require his presence here at once."

"But—"

"*At once!*"

"Yes, your Grace." The servant scurried out.

"There, you see how easy that was?" Sparhawk said to Annias. Then he went over to the white-haired Earl of Lenda, removed his gauntlet, and took the old man's hand. "You're looking well, my Lord," he said.

"Still alive, you mean?" Lenda laughed. "How was Rendor, Sparhawk?"

"Hot, dry, and very dusty."

"Always has been, my boy. Always has been."

"Are you going to answer my question?" Annias demanded.

"Please, your Grace," Sparhawk responded piously, holding up one hand, "not until the bastard regent arrives. We must mind our manners, mustn't we?" He lifted one eyebrow. "Tell me," he added, almost as an afterthought, "how's his mother—her health, I mean? I wouldn't expect a churchman to be able to testify to the carnal talents of the Princess Arissa—although just about everybody else in Cimmura could."

"You go too far, Sparhawk."

"You mean you didn't know? My goodness, old boy, you really should try to stay abreast of things."

"How *rude*!" Baron Harparin exclaimed to the fat man in red.

"It's not the sort of thing you'd understand, Harparin," Sparhawk told him. "I hear that your inclinations lie in other directions."

The door opened and a pimpled young man with muddy blond hair and a slack-lipped mouth entered. He wore a green, ermine-trimmed robe and a small gold coronet. "You wanted to see me, Annias?" His voice had a nasal, almost whining quality to it.

"A state matter, your Highness," Annias replied. "We need to have you pass judgment in a case involving high treason."

The young man blinked stupidly at him.

"This is Sir Sparhawk, who has deliberately violated the command of your late uncle, King Aldreas. Sparhawk here was ordered to Rendor, not to return unless summoned back by royal command. His very presence in Elenia convicts him."

Lycheas recoiled visibly from the bleak-faced knight in black armor, his eyes going wide and his loose mouth gaping. "Sparhawk?" he quailed.

"The very same," Sparhawk told him. "The good primate, however, has slightly overstated the case, I'm afraid. When I assumed my position as hereditary champion of the crown, I took an oath to defend the king—or the queen—whenever the royal life was endangered. That oath takes precedence over any command—royal or otherwise—and the queen's life is clearly in danger."

"That's merely a technicality, Sparhawk," Annias snapped.

"I know," Sparhawk replied blandly, "but technicalities are the soul of the law."

The Earl of Lenda cleared his throat. "I have made a study of such matters," he said, "and Sir Sparhawk has correctly cited the law. His oath to defend the crown does in fact take precedence."

Prince Lycheas had gone around to the other side of the table, giving Sparhawk a wide berth. "That's absurd," he declared. "Ehlana's sick. She's not in any physical danger." He sat down in the chair next to the primate.

"The queen," Sparhawk corrected him.

"What?"

"Her proper title is 'her Majesty'—or at the least, 'Queen Ehlana.' It's extremely discourteous simply to call her by name. Technically, I suppose, I'm obliged to protect her from discourtesy as well as physical danger. I'm a little vague on that point of law, so I'll defer to the judgment of my old friend, the Earl of Lenda, on the matter before I have my seconds deliver my challenge to your Highness."

Lycheas went pasty white. "Challenge?"

"This is sheer idiocy," Annias declared. "There will be no challenges delivered or accepted." His eyes narrowed then. "The prince regent's point is well taken, however," he said. "Sparhawk has simply seized this flimsy excuse to violate his banishment. Unless he can present some documentary evidence of having been summoned, he stands convicted of high treason." The primate's smile was thin.

"I thought you'd never ask, Annias," Sparhawk said. He reached under his sword belt and drew out a tightly folded parchment tied with a blue ribbon. He untied the ribbon and opened the parchment, the blood-red stone on his ring flashing in the candlelight. "This all seems to be in order," he said, perusing the document.

"It has the queen's signature on it and her personal seal. Her instructions to me are quite explicit." He stretched out his arm, offering the parchment to the Earl of Lenda. "What's your opinion, my Lord?"

The old man took the parchment and examined it. "The seal is the queen's," he confirmed, "and the handwriting is hers. She commands Sir Sparhawk to present himself to her immediately upon her ascension to the throne. It's a valid royal command, my Lords."

"Let me see that," Annias snapped.

Lenda passed it on down the table to him.

The primate read the document quickly, his teeth tightly clenched. "It's not even dated," he accused.

"Excuse me, your Grace," Lenda pointed out, "but there is no legal requirement that a royal decree or command be dated. Dating is merely a convention."

"Where did you get this?" the primate asked Sparhawk, his eyes narrowing.

"I've had it for quite some time."

"It was obviously written before the queen ascended the throne."

"It does appear that way, doesn't it?"

"It has no validity." The primate took the parchment in both hands as if he would tear it in two.

"What's the penalty for destroying a royal decree, my Lord of Lenda?" Sparhawk asked mildly.

"Death."

"I rather thought it might be. Go ahead and rip it up, Annias. I'll be more than happy to carry out the sentence myself—just to save time and the expense of all the tiresome legal proceedings." His eyes locked with those of Annias. After a moment, the primate threw the parchment on the table in disgust.

Lycheas had watched all of this with a look of growing chagrin. Then he seemed to notice something for the first time. "Your ring, Sir Sparhawk," he said in his whining voice. "That is your badge of office, is it not?"

"In a manner of speaking, yes. Actually the ring—and the queen's ring—are symbolic of the link between my family and hers."

"Give it to me."

"No."

Lycheas's eyes bulged. "I just gave you a royal command!" he shouted.

"No. It was a personal request, Lycheas. You can't give royal commands, because you're not the king."

Lycheas looked uncertainly at the primate, but Annias shook his head slightly. The pimpled young man flushed.

"The prince regent merely wished to examine the ring, Sir Sparhawk," the churchman said smoothly. "We have sought its mate, the ring of King Aldreas, but it seems to be missing. Would you have any idea where we might find it?"

Sparhawk spread his hands. "Aldreas had it on his finger when I left for Cippria," he replied. "The rings are not customarily taken off, so I assume he was still wearing it when he died."

"No. He was not."

"Perhaps the queen has it, then."

"Not so far as we're able to determine."

"I want that other ring," Lycheas insisted, "as a symbol of my authority."

Sparhawk looked at him, his face amused. "What authority?" he asked bluntly. "The ring belongs to Queen Ehlana, and if someone tries to take it from her, I imagine that I'll have to take steps." He suddenly felt a faint prickling of his skin. It seemed that the candles in their gold candelabra lowered slightly and the blue-draped council chamber grew perceptibly dimmer. Instantly, he began to mutter under his breath in the Styric tongue, carefully weaving the counter-spell even as he searched the faces of the men sitting around the council table for the source of the rather crude attempt at magic. When he released the counterspell, he saw Annias flinch and he smiled bleakly. Then he drew himself up. "Now," he said, his voice crisp, "let's get down to business. Exactly what happened to King Aldreas?"

The Earl of Lenda sighed. "It was the falling-sickness, Sir Sparhawk," he replied sadly. "The seizures began several months ago, and they grew more and more frequent. The king grew weaker and weaker, and finally—" He shrugged.

"He didn't have the falling-sickness when I left Cimmura," Sparhawk said.

"The onset was sudden," Annias said coldly.

"So it seems. It's rumored that the queen fell ill with the same affliction."

Annias nodded.

"Didn't that strike any of you as odd? There's never been a history of the disease in the royal family, and isn't it peculiar that Aldreas didn't develop symptoms until he was in his forties, and his daughter fell ill when she was little more than eighteen?"

"I have no medical background, Sparhawk," Annias told him. "You may question the court physicians if you wish, but I doubt that you're going to unearth anything that we haven't already discovered."

Sparhawk grunted. He looked around the council chamber. "I think that covers everything we need to discuss here," he said. "I'll see the queen now."

"Absolutely not!" Lycheas said.

"I'm not *asking* you, Lycheas," the big knight said firmly. "May I have that?" He pointed at the parchment still lying on the table in front of the primate.

They passed it down to him, and he ran through it quickly. "Here it is," he said, picking out the sentence he wanted. " 'You are commanded to present yourself to me immediately upon your return to Cimmura.' That doesn't leave any room for argument, does it?"

"What are you up to, Sparhawk?" the primate asked suspiciously.

"I'm just obeying orders, your Grace. I'm commanded by the queen to present myself to her and I'm going to do precisely that."

"The door to the throne room is locked," Lycheas snapped.

The smile Sparhawk gave him was almost benign. "That's all right, Lycheas," he said. "I've got a key." He put his hand suggestively on the silver-bound hilt of his sword.

"You wouldn't!"

"Try me."

Annias cleared his throat. "If I may speak, your Highness?" he said.

"Of course, your Grace," Lycheas replied quickly. "The crown is always open to the advice and counsel of the church."

"Crown?" Sparhawk asked.

"A formula, Sir Sparhawk," Annias told him. "Prince Lycheas speaks for the crown for so long as the queen is incapacitated."

"Not to me, he doesn't."

Annias turned back toward Lycheas. "It is the advice of the church that we accede to the somewhat churlish request of the Queen's Champion," he said. "Let no one accuse *us* of incivility. Moreover, the church advises that the prince regent and all of the council accompany Sir Sparhawk to the throne room. He is reputed to be adept at certain forms of magic, and—to protect the queen's life—we must not permit him to employ precipitously those arts without full consultation with the court physicians."

Lycheas made some pretense of thinking it over. Then he rose to his feet. "It shall be as you advise, then, your Grace," he declared. "You are directed to accompany us, Sir Sparhawk."

"Directed?"

Lycheas ignored that and swept regally toward the door.

Sparhawk let Baron Harparin and the fat man in red pass, then fell in beside Primate Annias. He was smiling in a relaxed fashion, but there was little in the way of good humor in the low voice that came from between his teeth. "Don't ever try that again, Annias," he said.

"What?" The primate sounded startled.

"Your magic. You're not very good at it in the first place, and it irritates me to have to waste the effort of countering the work of amateurs. Besides, churchmen are forbidden to dabble in magic, as I recall."

"You have no proof, Sparhawk."

"I don't need proof, Annias. My oath as a Pandion Knight would be sufficient in any civil or ecclesiastical court. Why don't we just leave it there? But don't mutter any more incantations in my direction."

With Lycheas in the lead, the council and Sparhawk went down a candlelit corridor to the broad double doors of the throne room. When they reached the doors, Lycheas took a key from inside his doublet and unlocked them. "All right," he said to Sparhawk. "It's open. Go present yourself to your queen—for all the good it's going to do you."

Sparhawk reached up and took a burning candle from a silver sconce jutting from the wall of the corridor and went into the dark room beyond the doors.

It was cool, almost clammy inside the throne room, and the air smelled musty and stale. Methodically, Sparhawk went along the walls, lighting candles. Then he went to the throne and lighted the ones standing in the candelabra flanking it.

"You don't need *that* much light, Sparhawk," Lycheas said irritably from the doorway.

Sparhawk ignored him. He put out his hand, tentatively touched the crystal which encased the throne, and felt Sephrenia's familiar aura permeating the crystal. Then slowly he raised his eyes to look into Ehlana's pale young face. The promise that had been there when she had been a child had been fulfilled. She was not simply pretty as so many young girls are pretty; she was beautiful. There was an almost luminous perfection about her countenance. Her pale blond hair was long and loosely framed her face. She wore her state robes, and the heavy gold crown of Elenia encircled her head. Her slender hands lay upon the arms of her throne, and her eyes were closed.

He remembered that at first he had bitterly resented the command of King Aldreas that had made him the young girl's caretaker. He had quickly found, however, that she was no giddy child, but rather was a serious young lady with a quick, retentive mind and an overwhelming curiosity about the world. After her initial shyness had passed, she had begun to question him closely about palace affairs and thus, almost by accident, had begun her education in statecraft and the intricacies of palace politics. After a few months they had grown very close, and he had found himself looking forward to their daily private conversations during which he had gently molded her character and had prepared her for her ultimate destiny as queen of Elenia.

To see her as she was now, locked in the semblance of death, wrenched at his heart, and he swore to himself that he would take the world apart if need be to restore her to health and to her throne. For some reason it made him angry to look at her, and he felt an irrational desire to lash out at things, as if by sheer physical force he could return her to consciousness.

And then he heard and felt it. The sound appeared to grow more pronounced, and it grew louder moment by moment. It was a regular, steady thudding sound, not quite like the beating of a drum, and it did not change nor falter, but echoed through the room, its volume steadily increasing as it announced to any who might enter that Ehlana's heart was still beating.

Sparhawk drew his sword and saluted his queen with it. Then he sank to one knee in a move of profoundest respect and a peculiar form of love. He leaned forward and gently kissed the unyielding crystal, his eyes suddenly filling with tears. "I am here now, Ehlana," he murmured, "and I'll make everything all right again."

The heartbeat grew louder, almost as if in some peculiar way she had heard him.

From the doorway he heard Lycheas snicker derisively and he promised himself that should the opportunity arise, he would do a number of unpleasant things to the queen's bastard cousin. Then he rose and went toward the door again.

Lycheas stood smirking at him, still holding the key to the throne room in his hand. As Sparhawk passed the prince, he reached out and took the key. "You won't need this any more," he said. "I'm here now, so I'll take care of it."

"Annias," Lycheas said in a voice shrill with protest.

Annias, however, took one look at the bleak face of the Queen's Champion and decided not to press the issue. "Let him keep it," he said shortly.

"But—"

"I said to let him keep it," the primate snapped. "We don't need it anyway. Let the Queen's Champion hold the key to the room in which she sleeps." There was a vile innuendo in the churchman's voice, and Sparhawk clenched his still-gauntleted left fist.

"Will you walk with me as we return to the council chamber, Sir Sparhawk?"

the Earl of Lenda said, placing a lightly restraining hand on Sparhawk's armored forearm. "My steps sometimes falter, and it's comforting to have a strong young person at my side."

"Certainly, my Lord," Sparhawk replied, unclenching his fist. When Lycheas had led the members of the council back down the corridor toward their meeting room, Sparhawk closed the door and locked it. Then he handed the key to his old friend. "Will you keep this for me, my Lord?" he asked.

"Gladly, Sir Sparhawk."

"And if you can, keep the candles burning in the throne room. Don't leave her sitting there in the dark."

"Of course."

They started down the corridor.

"Do you know something, Sparhawk?" the old man said, "they left a great deal of bark on you when they were giving you the last polishing touches."

Sparhawk grinned at him.

"You can be *truly* offensive when you set your mind to it." Lenda chuckled.

"I can but try, my Lord."

"Be very careful here in Cimmura, Sparhawk," the old man cautioned seriously in a low voice. "Annias has a spy on every street corner. Lycheas won't even sneeze without his permission, so the primate is the real ruler here in Elenia and he hates you."

"I'm not overly fond of him, either." Sparhawk thought of something. "You've been a good friend here today, my Lord. Is that going to put you in danger?"

The Earl of Lenda smiled. "I doubt it. I'm too old and powerless to be any kind of threat to Annias. I'm hardly more than an irritation, and he's far too calculating to take action against me for that."

The primate awaited them at the door to the council chamber. "The council has discussed the situation here, Sir Sparhawk," he said coldly. "The queen is quite obviously in no danger. Her heartbeat is strong, and the crystal which encloses her is quite impregnable. She has no real need of a protector at this particular time. It is the command of the council, therefore, that you return to the chapterhouse of your order here in Cimmura and remain there until you receive further instructions." A chill smile touched his lips. "Or until the queen herself summons you, of course."

"Of course," Sparhawk replied distantly. "I was about to suggest that myself, your Grace. I'm just a simple knight and I'll be far more at ease in the chapterhouse with my brothers than here in the palace." He smiled. "I'm really quite out of place at court."

"I noticed that."

"I thought you might have." Sparhawk briefly clasped the hand of the Earl of Lenda by way of farewell. Then he looked directly at Annias. "Until we meet again, then, your Grace."

"*If* we meet again."

"Oh, we will, Annias. Indeed we will." Then Sparhawk turned on his heel and walked on down the corridor.

The chapterhouse of the Pandion Knights in Cimmura lay just beyond the eastern gate of the city. It was, in every sense of the word, a castle, with high walls surmounted by battlements and with bleak towers at each corner. It was approached by way of a drawbridge which spanned a deep fosse bristling with sharpened stakes. The drawbridge had been lowered, but it was guarded by four black-armored Pandions mounted on war horses.

Sparhawk reined Faran in at the outer end of the bridge and waited. There were certain formalities involved in gaining entry into a Pandion chapterhouse. Oddly, he found that he did not chafe at those formalities. They had been a part of his life for all the years of his novitiate, and the observance of these age-old ceremonies seemed somehow to mark a renewal and a reaffirmation of his very identity. Even as he awaited the ritual challenge, the sun-baked city of Jiroch and the women going to the wells in the steel-gray light of morning faded back in his memory, becoming more remote and taking their proper place among all his other memories.

Two of the armored knights rode forward at a stately pace, the hooves of their chargers booming hollowly on the foot-thick planks of the drawbridge. They halted just in front of Sparhawk. "Who art thou who entreateth entry into the house of the Soldiers of God?" one of them intoned.

Sparhawk raised his visor in the symbolic gesture of peaceable intent. "I am Sparhawk," he replied, "a Soldier of God and a member of this order."

"How may we know thee?" the second knight inquired.

"By this token may you know me." Sparhawk reached his hand into the neck of his surcoat and drew out the heavy silver amulet suspended on the chain about his neck. Every Pandion wore such an amulet.

The pair made some pretence of looking carefully at it.

"This is indeed Sir Sparhawk of our order," the first knight declared.

"Truly," the second agreed, "and shall we then—uh—" He faltered, frowning.

"'Grant him entry into the house of the Soldiers of God,'" Sparhawk prompted.

The second knight made a face. "I can never remember that part," he muttered. "Thanks, Sparhawk." He cleared his throat and began again. "Truly," he said, "and shall we then grant him entry into the house of the Soldiers of God?"

The first knight was grinning openly. "It is his right freely to enter this house," he said, "for he is one of us. Hail, Sir Sparhawk. Prithee, come within the walls of this house, and may peace abide with thee beneath its roof."

"And with thee and thy companion as well, wheresoever you may fare," Sparhawk replied, concluding the ceremony.

"Welcome home, Sparhawk," the first knight said warmly then. "You've been a long time away."

"You noticed," Sparhawk answered. "Did Kurik get here?"

The second knight nodded. "An hour or so ago. He talked with Vanion and then left again."

"Let's go inside," Sparhawk suggested. "I need a large dose of that peace you mentioned earlier, and I've got to see Vanion."

The two knights turned their horses, and the three rode together back across the drawbridge.

"Is Sephrenia still here?" Sparhawk asked.

"Yes," the second knight replied. "She and Vanion came from Demos shortly after the Queen fell ill, and she hasn't gone back to the motherhouse yet."

"Good. I need to talk with her as well."

The three of them halted at the castle gate. "This is Sir Sparhawk, a member of our order," the first knight declared to the two who had remained at the gate. "We have confirmed his identity and vouch for his right to enter the house of the Knights Pandion."

"Pass then, Sir Sparhawk, and may peace abide with thee whilst thou remain within this house."

"I thank thee, Sir Knight, and may peace also be thine."

The knights drew their mounts aside, and Faran moved forward without any urging.

"You know the ritual as well as I do, don't you?" Sparhawk murmured.

Faran flicked his ears.

In the central courtyard, an apprentice knight who had not yet been vested with his ceremonial armor or spurs hurried forward and took Faran's reins. "Welcome, Sir Knight," he said.

Sparhawk hooked his shield to his saddlebow and swung down from Faran's back with his armor clinking. "Thank you," he replied. "Do you have any idea of where I might find Lord Vanion?"

"I believe he's in the south tower, my Lord."

"Thanks again." Sparhawk started across the courtyard, then stopped. "Oh, be careful of the horse," he warned. "He bites."

The novice looked startled and then cautiously stepped away from the big, ugly roan, though still firmly holding the reins.

The horse gave Sparhawk a flat, unfriendly stare.

"It's more sporting this way, Faran," Sparhawk explained. He started up the worn steps that led into the centuries-old castle.

The inside of the chapterhouse was cool and dim, and the few members of the order Sparhawk met in those halls wore cowled monk's robes, as was customary inside a secure house, although an occasional steely clink betrayed the fact that, beneath their humble garb, the members of this order wore chain mail and were inevitably armed. There were no greetings exchanged, and the cowled brothers of Pandion went resolutely about their duties with bowed heads and shadowed faces.

Sparhawk put the flat of his hand out in front of one of the cowled men. Pandions seldom touched each other. "Excuse me, brother," he said. "Do you know if Vanion is still in the south tower?"

"He is," the other knight replied.

"Thank you, brother. Peace be with you."

"And with you, Sir Knight."

Sparhawk went on along the torchlit corridor until he came to a narrow stairway which wound up into the south tower between walls of massive, unmortared stones. At the top of the stairs there was a heavy door guarded by two young Pandions. Sparhawk did not recognize either of them. "I need to talk with Vanion," he told them. "The name is Sparhawk."

"Can you identify yourself?" one of them asked, trying to make his youthful voice sound gruff.

"I just did."

It hung there while the two young knights struggled to find a graceful way out of the situation. "Why not just open the door and tell Vanion that I'm here?" Sparhawk suggested. "If he recognizes me, fine. If he doesn't, the two of you can try to throw me back down the stairs." He laid no particular emphasis on the word *try*.

The two looked at each other, then one of them opened the door and looked inside. "A thousand pardons, my Lord Vanion," he apologized, "but there's a Pandion here who calls himself Sparhawk. He says that he wants to talk with you."

"Good," a familiar voice replied from inside the room. "I've been expecting him. Send him in."

The two knights looked abashed and stepped out of Sparhawk's way.

"Thank you, my brothers," Sparhawk murmured to them. "Peace be with you." And then he went on through the door. The room was large, with stone walls, dark green drapes at the narrow windows, and a carpet of muted brown. A fire crackled in the arched fireplace at one end, and there was a candlelit table surrounded by heavy chairs in the center. Two people, a man and a woman, sat at the table.

Vanion, the Preceptor of the Pandion Knights, had aged somewhat in the past ten years. His hair and beard were iron gray now. There were a few more lines in his face, but there were no signs of feebleness there. He wore a mail shirt and a silver surcoat. As Sparhawk entered the room, he rose and came around the table. "I was about to send a rescue party to the palace for you," he said, grasping Sparhawk's armored shoulders. "You shouldn't have gone there alone, you know."

"Maybe not, but things worked out all right." Sparhawk removed his gauntlets and helmet, laying them on the table. Then he unfastened his sword from its studs and laid it beside them. "It's good to see you again, Vanion," he said, taking the older man's hand in his. Vanion had always been a stern teacher, tolerating no shortcomings in the young knights he had trained to take their places in Pandion ranks. Although Sparhawk had come close to hating the man during his novitiate, he now regarded the blunt-spoken preceptor as one of his closest friends, and their handclasp was warm, even affectionate.

Then the big knight turned to the woman. She was small and had that peculiar neat perfection one sometimes sees in small people. Her hair was as black as night, though her eyes were a deep blue. Her features were obviously not Elene, but had that strangely foreign cast that marked her as a Styric. She wore a soft, white robe, and there was a large book on the table in front of her. "Sephrenia," he greeted her warmly, "you're looking well." He took both of her hands in his and kissed her palms in the ritual Styric gesture of greeting.

"You have been long away, Sir Sparhawk," she replied. Her voice was soft and musical and had an odd, lilting quality to it.

"And will you bless me, little mother?" he asked, a smile touching his battered face. He knelt before her. The form of address was Styric, reflecting that intimate personal connection between teacher and pupil which has existed since the dawn of time.

"Gladly." She lightly touched her hands to his face and spoke a ritual benediction in the Styric tongue.

"Thank you," he said simply.

Then she did something she rarely did. With her hands still holding his face, she leaned forward and lightly kissed him. "Welcome home, dear one," she murmured.

"It's good to be back," he replied. "I've missed you."

"Even though I scolded you when you were a boy?" she asked with a gentle smile.

"Scoldings don't hurt that much." He laughed. "I even missed those, for some reason."

"I think that perhaps we did well with this one, Vanion," she said to the preceptor. "Between us, we've made a good Pandion."

"One of the best," Vanion agreed. "I think Sparhawk's what they had in mind when they formed the order."

Sephrenia's position among the Pandion Knights was a peculiar one. She had appeared at the gates of the order's motherhouse at Demos upon the death of the Styric tutor who had been instructing the novices in what the Styrics referred to as the secrets. She had neither been selected nor summoned, but had simply appeared and taken up her predecessor's duties. Generally, Elenes despised and feared Styrics. They were a strange, alien people who lived in small, rude clusters of houses deep in the forests and mountains. They worshipped strange Gods and practiced magic. Wild stories about hideous rites involving the use of Elene blood and flesh had circulated among the more gullible in Elene society for centuries, and periodically mobs of drunken peasants would descend on unsuspecting Styric villages, bent on massacre. The Church vigorously denounced such atrocities. The Church Knights, who had come to know and respect their alien tutors, went perhaps a step further than the Church, letting it be generally known that unprovoked attacks on Styric settlements would result in swift and savage retaliation. Despite such organized protection, however, any Styric who entered an Elene village or town could expect taunts and abuse and, not infrequently, showers of stones and offal. Thus, Sephrenia's appearance at Demos had not been without personal risk. Her motives for coming had been unclear, but over the years she had served faithfully; to a man the Pandions had come to love and respect her. Even Vanion, the preceptor of the order, frequently sought her counsel.

Sparhawk looked at the volume lying on the table before her. "A book, Sephrenia?" he said in mock amazement. "Has Vanion finally persuaded you to learn how to read?"

"You know my beliefs about that practice, Sparhawk," she replied. "I was merely looking at the pictures." She pointed at the brilliant illuminations on the page. "I was ever fond of bright colors."

Sparhawk drew up a chair and sat, his armor creaking.

"You saw Ehlana?" Vanion asked, resuming his seat across the table.

"Yes." Sparhawk looked at Sephrenia. "How did you do that?" he asked her. "Seal her up like that, I mean?"

"It's a bit complex." Then she stopped and gave him a penetrating look. "Perhaps you're ready, at that," she murmured. She rose to her feet. "Come over here, Sparhawk," she said, moving toward the fireplace.

Puzzled, he rose and followed her.

"Look into the flames, dear one," she said softly, using that odd Styric form of address she had used when he was her pupil.

Compelled by her voice, he stared at the fire. Faintly, he heard her whispering in Styric, and then she passed her hand slowly across the flames. Unthinking, he sank to his knees and stared into the fireplace.

Something was moving in the fire. Sparhawk leaned forward and stared hard at the little bluish curls of flame dancing along the edge of a charred oak log. The blue color expanded, growing larger and larger, and within that nimbus of coruscating blue, he seemed to see a group of figures that wavered as the flame flickered. The image grew stronger, and he realized that he was looking at the semblance of the throne room in the palace, many miles away. Twelve armored Pandions were crossing the flagstone floor bearing the slight figure of a young girl. She was borne, not upon a litter, but upon the flat sides of a dozen gleaming sword blades held rock-steady by the twelve black-armored and visored men. They stopped before the throne, and Sephrenia's white-robed figure stepped out of the shadows. She raised one hand, seeming to say something, though all Sparhawk could hear was the crackling flames. With a dreadful jerking motion, the young girl sat up. It was Ehlana. Her face was distorted and her eyes wide and vacant.

Without thinking, Sparhawk reached toward her, thrusting his hand directly into the flames.

"No," Sephrenia said sharply, pulling his hand back. "You may watch only."

The image of Ehlana, trembling uncontrollably, jerked to its feet, following, it seemed, the unspoken commands of the small woman in the white robe. Imperiously, Sephrenia pointed at the throne, and Ehlana stumbled, even staggered, up the steps of the dais to assume her rightful place.

Sparhawk wept. He tried once again to reach out to his queen, but Sephrenia held him back with a gentle touch that was strangely like an iron chain. "Continue to watch, dear one," she told him.

The twelve knights then formed a circle around the enthroned queen and the white-robed woman standing at her side. Reverently, they extended their swords so that the two women on the dais were ringed in steel. Sephrenia raised her arms and spoke. Sparhawk could clearly see the strain on her face as she uttered the words of an incantation he could not even begin to imagine.

The point of each of the twelve swords began to glow and grew brighter and brighter, bathing the dais in intense silvery-white light. The light from those sword tips seemed to coalesce around Ehlana and her throne. Then Sephrenia spoke a single word, bringing her arm down as she did so in a peculiar cutting motion. In an instant the light around Ehlana solidified, and she became as she had been when Sparhawk had seen her in the throne room that morning. The image of Sephrenia, however, wilted and collapsed on the dais beside the crystal-encased throne.

The tears were streaming openly down Sparhawk's face, and Sephrenia gently enfolded his head in her arms, holding him to her. "It is not easy, Sparhawk," she comforted him. "To look thus into the fire opens the heart and allows what we really are to emerge. You are gentler far more than you would have us believe."

He wiped at his eyes with the back of his hand. "How long will the crystal sustain her?" he asked.

"For so long as the thirteen of us who were there continue to live," Sephrenia replied. "A year at most, as you Elenes measure time."

He stared at her.

"It is our life force that keeps her heart alive. As the seasons turn, we will one by one drop away, and one of us who was there will then have to assume the burden of the fallen. Eventually—when we have each and every one given all we can—your queen will die."

"No!" he said fiercely. He looked at Vanion. "Were you there, too?"

Vanion nodded.

"Who else?"

"It wouldn't serve any purpose for you to know that, Sparhawk. We all went willingly and we knew what was involved."

"Who's going to take up the burden you mentioned?" Sparhawk asked Sephrenia.

"I will."

"We're still arguing that point," Vanion disagreed. "Any one of us who was there can do it, actually."

"Not unless we modify the spell, Vanion," she told him just a bit smugly.

"We'll see," he said.

"But what good does it do?" Sparhawk demanded. "All you've done is to give her a year more of life at a dreadful cost—and she doesn't even know."

"If we can isolate the cause of her illness and find a cure, the spell can be reversed," Sephrenia replied. "We have suspended her life to give us time."

"Are we making any progress?"

"I've got every physician in Elenia working on it," Vanion said, "and I've summoned others from various parts of Eosia. Sephrenia's looking into the possibility that the illness may not be of natural origin. We're encountering some resistance, though. The court physicians refuse to cooperate."

"I'll go back to the palace then," Sparhawk said bleakly. "Perhaps I can persuade them to be more helpful."

"We thought of that already, but Annias has them all closely guarded."

"What *is* Annias up to?" Sparhawk burst out angrily. "All we want to do is to restore Ehlana. Why is he putting all these stumbling blocks in our path? Does he want the throne for himself?"

"I think he has his eyes on a bigger throne," Vanion said. "The Archprelate Cluvonus is old and in poor health. I wouldn't be at all surprised if Annias believes that the miter of the archprelacy might fit him."

"Annias? Archprelate? Vanion, that's an absurdity."

"Life is filled with absurdities, Sparhawk. The militant orders are all opposed to him, of course, and our opinion carries a great deal of weight with the Church Hierocracy, but Annias has his hands in the treasury of Elenia up to the elbows and he's very free with his bribes. Ehlana would have been able to cut off his access to that money, but she fell ill. That may have something to do with his lack of enthusiasm about her recovery."

"And he wants to put Arissa's bastard on the throne to replace her?" Sparhawk was growing angrier by the minute. "Vanion, I've just seen Lycheas. He's weaker— and stupider—than King Aldreas was. Besides, he's illegitimate."

Vanion spread his hands. "A vote of the royal council could legitimize him, and Annias controls the council."

"Not all of it, he doesn't," Sparhawk grated. "Technically, I'm *also* a member of the council, and I think I might just want to sway a few votes if that ever came up. A public duel or two might change the minds of the council."

"You're rash, Sparhawk," Sephrenia told him.

"No, I'm angry. I feel a powerful urge to hurt some people."

Vanion sighed. "We can't make any decisions just yet," he said. Then he shook his head and turned to another matter. "What's *really* going on in Rendor?" he asked. "Voren's reports were all rather carefully worded in the event they fell into unfriendly hands."

Sparhawk rose and went to one of the embrasured windows with his black cape swirling about his ankles. The sky was still covered with dirty-looking cloud, and the city of Cimmura seemed to crouch beneath that scud as if clenched to endure yet another winter. "It's hot there," he mused, almost as if to himself, "and dry and dusty. The sun reflects back from the walls and pierces the eye. At first light, before the sun rises and the sky is like molten silver, veiled women in black robes with clay vessels on their shoulders pass in silence through the streets on their way to the wells."

"I've misjudged you, Sparhawk," Sephrenia said in her melodic voice. "You have the soul of a poet."

"Not really, Sephrenia. It's just that you need to get the feel of Rendor to understand what's happening there. The sun is like the blows of a hammer on the top of your head, and the air is so hot and dry that it leaves no time for thought. Rendors seek simplistic answers. The sun doesn't give them time for pondering. That might explain what happened to Eshand in the first place. A simple shepherd with his brains half baked out isn't the logical receptacle for any kind of profound epiphany. It's the aggravation of the sun, I think, that gave the Eshandist Heresy its impetus in the first place. Those poor fools would have accepted *any* idea, no matter how absurd, just for the chance to move around—and perhaps find some shade."

"That's a novel explanation for a movement that plunged all of Eosia into three centuries of warfare," Vanion observed.

"You have to experience it," Sparhawk told him, returning to his seat. "Anyway, one of those sun-baked enthusiasts arose at Dabour about twenty years ago."

"Arasham?" Vanion surmised. "We've heard of him."

"That's what he calls himself," Sparhawk replied. "He was probably born with a different name, though. Religious leaders tend to change their names fairly often to fit the prejudices of their followers. From what I understand, Arasham is an unlettered, unwashed fanatic with only a tenuous grip on reality. He's about eighty or so and he sees things and hears voices. His followers have less intelligence than their sheep. They'd gladly attack the kingdoms of the north—if they could only figure out which way north is. That's a matter of serious debate in Rendor. I've seen a few of them. These heretics that send the members of the Hierocracy in Chyrellos trembling to their beds every night are little more than howling desert dervishes, poorly armed and with no military training. Frankly, Vanion, I'd worry more about the next winter storm than any kind of resurgence of the Eshandist Heresy in Rendor."

"That's blunt enough."

"I've just wasted ten years of my life on a nonexistent danger. I'm sure you'll forgive a certain amount of discontent about the whole thing."

"Patience will come to you, Sparhawk." Sephrenia smiled. "Once you have reached maturity."

"I thought that I already had."

"Not by half."

He grinned at her then. "Just how old are you, Sephrenia?" he asked.

Her look was filled with resignation. "What is it about you Pandions that makes you all ask that same question? You *know* I'm not going to answer you. Can't you just accept the fact that I'm older than you are and let it go at that?"

"You're also older than I am," Vanion added. "You were my teacher when I was no older than those boys who guard my door."

"And do I look so very, very old?"

"My dear Sephrenia, you're as young as spring and as wise as winter. You've ruined us all, you know. After we've known you, the fairest of maidens have no charm for us."

"Isn't he nice?" She smiled at Sparhawk. "Surely no other man alive has so beguiling a tongue."

"Try him sometime when you've just missed a pass with the lance," Sparhawk replied sourly. He shifted his shoulders under the weight of his armor. "What else is afoot? I've been gone a long time and I'm hungry for news."

"Otha's mobilizing," Vanion told him. "The word that's coming out of Zemoch is that he's looking eastward toward Daresia and the Tamul Empire, but I've got a few doubts about that."

"And I have more than a few," Sephrenia agreed. "The kingdoms of the west are suddenly awash with Styric vagabonds. They camp at crossroads and hawk the rude goods of Styricum, but no local Styric band acknowledges them as members. For some reason the Emperor Otha and his cruel master have innundated us with watchers. Azash has driven the Zemochs to attack the west before. Something lies hidden here that he desperately wants, and he's not going to find it in Daresia."

"There have been Zemoch mobilizations before," Sparhawk said, leaning back. "Nothing ever came of it."

"I think that this time might be a bit more serious," Vanion disagreed. "When he gathered his forces before, it was always on the border; as soon as the four militant orders moved into Lamorkand to face him, he disbanded his armies. He was testing us, nothing more. This time, though, he's massing his troops back behind the mountains—out of sight, so to speak."

"Let him come," Sparhawk said bleakly. "We stopped him five hundred years ago and we can do it again if we have to."

Vanion shook his head. "We don't want a repetition of what happened after the battle at Lake Randera—a century of famine, pestilence, and complete social collapse. No, my friend, *that* we don't want."

"*If* we can avoid it," Sephrenia added. "I am Styric, and I know even better than you Elenes just how totally evil the Elder God Azash is. If he comes west again, he *must* be stopped—no matter what the cost."

"That's what the Church Knights are here for," Vanion said. "Right now, about all we can do is keep our eyes on Otha."

"I just remembered something," Sparhawk said. "When I was riding into town last night, I saw Krager."

"Here in Cimmura?" Vanion asked, sounding surprised. "Do you think Martel could be with him?"

"Probably not. Krager's usually Martel's errand boy. Adus is the one who has to be kept on a short chain." He squinted his eyes. "How much did you hear about the incident in Cippria?" he asked them.

"We heard that Martel attacked you," Vanion replied. "That's about all."

"There was a bit more to it than that," Sparhawk told him. "When Aldreas sent me to Cippria, I was supposed to report to the Elenian consul there—a diplomat who just *happens* to be the cousin of the Primate Annias. Late one night, he summoned me. I was on my way to his house when Martel, Adus, and Krager—along with a fair number of local cutthroats—came charging out of a side street. There's no way that they could have known that I'd be passing that way unless someone had told them. Put that together with the fact that Krager's back in Cimmura, where there's a price on his head, and you start to come up with some interesting conclusions."

"You think that Martel is working for Annias?"

"It's a possibility, wouldn't you say? Annias wasn't very happy about the way my father forced Aldreas to give up the notion of marrying his own sister, and it's entirely possible that he felt that he'd have a freer hand here in Elenia if the family of Sparhawk became extinct in a back alley in Cippria. Of course, Martel has his *own* reasons for disliking me. I really think you made a mistake, Vanion. You could have saved us all a lot of trouble if you hadn't ordered me to withdraw my challenge."

Vanion shook his head. "No, Sparhawk," he said. "Martel had been a brother in our order, and I didn't want you two trying to kill each other. Besides, I couldn't be entirely sure who'd win. Martel is very dangerous."

"So am I."

"I'm not taking any unnecessary chances with you, Sparhawk. You're too valuable."

"Well, it's too late to worry about it now."

"What are your plans?"

"I'm *supposed* to stay here in the chapterhouse, but I think I'll drift around the
city a bit and see if I can run across Krager again. If I can connect him with anybody
who's working for Annias, I'll be able to answer a few burning questions."

"Perhaps you should wait a bit," Sephrenia advised. "Kalten's on his way back
from Lamorkand."

"Kalten? I haven't seen him in years."

"She's right, Sparhawk," Vanion agreed. "Kalten's a good man in tight quarters,
and the streets of Cimmura can be just as dangerous as the alleys of Cippria."

"When's he likely to arrive?"

Vanion shrugged. "Soon, I think. It could even be today."

"I'll wait until he gets here." An idea came to Sparhawk then. He smiled at his
teacher and rose to his feet.

"What are you doing, Sparhawk?" she asked him suspiciously.

"Oh, nothing," he replied. He began to speak in Styric, weaving his fingers in
the air in front of him as he did so. When he had built the spell, he released it and
held out his hand. There came a humming vibration, followed by a dimming of the
candles and a lowering of the flames in the fireplace. When the light came up again,
he was holding a bouquet of violets. "For you, little mother," he said, bowing
slightly and offering the flowers to her, "because I love you."

"Why, thank you, Sparhawk." She smiled, taking them. "You were always the
most thoughtful of my pupils. You mispronounced *staratha,* though," she added
critically. "You came very close to filling your hand with snakes."

"I'll practice," he promised.

"Do."

There was a respectful knock at the door.

"Yes?" Vanion called.

The door opened and one of the young knights stepped inside. "There's a messenger from the palace outside, Lord Vanion. He says that he has been commanded
to speak with Sir Sparhawk."

"*Now* what do they want?" Sparhawk muttered.

"You'd better send him in," Vanion told the young knight.

"At once, my Lord." The knight bowed slightly and went out again.

The messenger had a familiar face. His blond hair was still elegantly curled. His
saffron-colored doublet, lavender hose, maroon shoes, and apple-green cloak still
clashed horribly. The young fop's face, however, sported an entirely new embellish-
ment. The very tip of his pointed nose was adorned with a large and extremely
painful-looking boil. He was trying without much success to conceal the excres-
cence with a lace-trimmed handkerchief. He bowed elegantly to Vanion. "My Lord
Preceptor," he said, "the prince regent sends his compliments."

"And please, convey mine back to him," Vanion replied.

"Be assured that I shall, my Lord." The elegant fellow then turned to Sparhawk. "My message is for you, Sir Knight," he declared.

"Say on then," Sparhawk answered with exaggerated formality. "My ears hunger for your message."

The fop ignored that. He removed a sheet of parchment from inside his doublet and read grandly from it. " 'By royal decree, you are commanded by his Highness to journey straightway to the motherhouse of the Pandion Knights at Demos, there to devote yourself to your religious duties until such time as he sees fit to summon you once again to the palace.' "

"I see," Sparhawk replied.

"Do you understand the message, Sir Sparhawk?" the fop asked, handing over the parchment.

Sparhawk did not bother to read the document. "It was quite clear. You have completed your mission in a fashion which does you credit." Sparhawk peered at the perfumed young fellow. "If you don't mind some advice, neighbor, you ought to have that boil looked at by a surgeon. If it isn't lanced soon, it's going to keep growing to the point where you won't be able to see around it."

The fop winced at the word *lanced.* "Do you really think so, Sir Sparhawk?" he asked plaintively, lowering his handkerchief. "Wouldn't a poultice, perhaps—"

Sparhawk shook his head. "No, neighbor," he said with false sympathy. "I can almost guarantee you that a poultice won't work. Be brave, my man. Lancing is the only solution."

The courtier's face grew melancholy. He bowed and left the room.

"Did *you* do that to him, Sparhawk?" Sephrenia asked suspiciously.

"Me?" He gave her a look of wide-eyed innocence.

"*Somebody* did. That eruption is not natural."

"My, my," he said. "Imagine that."

"Well?" Vanion said. "Are you going to obey the bastard's orders?"

"Of course not," Sparhawk snorted. "I've got too many things to do here in Cimmura."

"You'll make him very angry."

"So?"

## CHAPTER FOUR

The sky had turned threatening again when Sparhawk emerged from the chapterhouse and clanked down the stairs into the courtyard. The novice came from the stable door leading Faran, and Sparhawk looked thoughtfully at him. He was perhaps eighteen and quite tall. He had knobby wrists that stuck out of an earth-colored tunic that was too small for him. "What's your name, young man?" Sparhawk asked him.

"Berit, my Lord."

"What are your duties here?"

"I haven't been assigned anything specific as yet, my Lord. I just try to make myself useful."

"Good. Turn around."

"My Lord?"

"I want to measure you."

Berit looked puzzled, but he did as he was told. Sparhawk measured him across the shoulders with his hands. Although he looked bony, Berit was actually a husky youth. "You'll do fine," Sparhawk told him.

Berit turned, his face baffled.

"You're going to be making a trip," Sparhawk told him. "Gather up what you'll need while I go get the man who's going to go with you."

"Yes, my Lord," Berit replied, bowing respectfully.

Sparhawk took hold of the saddlebow and hauled himself up onto Faran's back. Berit handed him the reins, and Sparhawk nudged the big roan into a walk. They crossed the courtyard, and Sparhawk responded to the salutes of the knights at the gate. Then he rode on across the drawbridge and through the east gate of the city.

The streets of Cimmura were busy now. Workmen carrying large bundles wrapped in muddy-colored burlap grunted their way through the narrow lanes, and merchants dressed in conventional blue stood in the doorways of their shops with their brightly colored wares piled around them. An occasional wagon clattered along the cobblestones. Near the intersection of two narrow streets, a squad of church soldiers in their scarlet livery marched with a certain arrogant precision. Sparhawk did not give way to them, but instead bore down on them at a steady trot. Grudgingly, they separated and stood aside as he passed. "Thank you, neighbors," Sparhawk said pleasantly.

They did not answer him.

He reined Faran in. "I said, thank you, neighbors."

"You're welcome," one of them replied sullenly.

Sparhawk waited.

". . . my Lord," the soldier added grudgingly.

"Much better, friend." Sparhawk rode on.

The gate to the inn was closed, and Sparhawk leaned over and banged on its timbers with his gauntleted fist. The porter who swung it open for him was not the same knight who had admitted him the evening before. Sparhawk swung down from Faran's back and handed him the reins.

"Will you be needing him again, my Lord?" the knight asked.

"Yes. I'll be going right back out. Would you saddle my squire's horse, Sir Knight?"

"Of course, my Lord."

"I appreciate that." Sparhawk laid one hand on Faran's neck. "Behave yourself," he said.

Faran looked away, his expression lofty.

Sparhawk clinked up the stairs and rapped on the door of the room at the top.

Kurik opened the door for him. "Well? How did it go?"

"Not bad."

"You came out alive, anyway. Did you see the queen?"

"Yes."

"That's surprising."

"I sort of insisted. Do you want to get your things together? You're going back to Demos."

"You didn't say 'we,' Sparhawk."

"I'm staying here."

"I suppose there are good reasons."

"Lycheas has ordered me back to the motherhouse. I more or less plan to ignore him, but I want to be able to move around Cimmura without being followed. There's a young novice at the chapterhouse who's about my size. We'll put him in my armor and mount him on Faran. Then the two of you can ride to Demos with a grand show of obedience. As long as he keeps his visor down, the primate's spies will think I'm obeying orders."

"It's workable, I suppose. I don't like the idea of leaving you here alone, though."

"I won't be alone. Kalten's coming in either today or tomorrow."

"That's a little better. Kalten's steady." Kurik frowned. "I thought that he'd been exiled to Lamorkand. Who ordered him back?"

"Vanion didn't say, but you know Kalten. Maybe he just got bored with Lamorkand and took independent action."

"How long do you want me to stay at Demos?" Kurik asked as he began to gather up his things.

"A month or so at least. The road's likely to be watched. I'll get word to you. Do you need any money?"

"I always need money, Sparhawk."

"There's some in the pocket of that tunic." Sparhawk pointed at his travel clothes draped across the back of a chair. "Take what you need."

Kurik grinned at him.

"Leave me a *little*, though."

"Of course, my Lord," Kurik said with a mocking bow. "Do you want me to pack up your things?"

"No. I'll be coming back here when Kalten arrives. It's a little hard to get in and out of the chapterhouse without being seen. Is the back door to that tavern still open?"

"It was yesterday. I drop in there from time to time."

"I thought you might."

"A man needs a few vices, Sparhawk. It gives him something to repent when he goes to chapel."

"If Aslade hears that you've been drinking, she'll set fire to your beard."

"Then we'll just have to make sure that she doesn't hear about it, won't we, my Lord?"

"Why do I always get mixed up in your domestic affairs?"

"It keeps your feet planted in reality. Get your own wife, Sparhawk. Then other women won't feel obliged to take special note of you. A married man is safe. A bachelor is a constant challenge to any woman alive."

About half an hour later, Sparhawk and his squire went down the stairs into the courtyard, mounted their horses, and rode out through the gate. They clattered along the cobblestone streets toward the east gate of the city.

"We're being watched, you know," Kurik said quietly.

"I certainly *hope* so," Sparhawk replied. "I'd hate to have to ride around in circles until we attract somebody's attention."

They went through the ritual again at the drawbridge of the chapterhouse and then rode on into the courtyard. Berit was waiting for them.

"This is Kurik," Sparhawk told him as he dismounted. "The two of you will be going to Demos. Kurik, the young man's name is Berit."

The squire looked the acolyte up and down. "He's the right size," he noted. "I might have to shorten a few straps, but your armor should come close to fitting him."

"I thought so myself."

Another novice came out and took their reins.

"Come along then, you two," Sparhawk said. "Let's go tell Vanion what we're going to do, and then we'll put my armor on our masquerader here."

Berit looked startled.

"You're being promoted, Berit," Kurik told him. "You see how quickly one can move up in the Pandions? Yesterday a novice; today Queen's Champion."

"I'll explain it to you when we see Vanion," Sparhawk told Berit. "It's not so interesting a story that I want to go over it more than once."

It was midafternoon when the three of them emerged from the chapterhouse door again. Berit walked awkwardly in the unaccustomed armor, and Sparhawk was dressed in a plain tunic and hose.

"I think it's going to rain," Kurik said, squinting at the sky.

"You won't melt," Sparhawk told him.

"I'm not worried about that," the squire replied. "It's just that I'll have to scour the rust off your armor again."

"Life is hard."

Kurik grunted, and then the two of them boosted Berit up into Faran's saddle. "You're going to take this young man to Demos," Sparhawk told his horse. "Try to behave as if it were me on your back."

Faran gave him an inquiring look.

"It would take much too long to explain. It's entirely up to you, Faran, but he's wearing my armor, so if you try to bite him, you'll probably break your teeth." Sparhawk turned to his squire. "Say hello to Aslade and the boys for me," he said.

"Right," Kurik nodded. Then he swung up into his saddle.

"Don't make *too* big a show when you leave," Sparhawk added, "but make sure that you're seen—and make sure that Berit keeps his visor down."

"I know what I'm doing, Sparhawk. Come along then, my Lord," Kurik said to Berit.

"My Lord?"

"You might as well get used to it, Berit." Kurik pulled his horse around. "I'll see you, Sparhawk." Then the two of them rode out of the courtyard toward the drawbridge.

The rest of the day passed quietly. Sparhawk sat in the cell which Vanion had assigned to him, reading a musty old book. At sundown he joined the other brothers in the refectory for the simple evening meal, then marched in quiet procession with them to chapel. Sparhawk's religious convictions were not profound, but there was again that sense of renewal involved in the return to the practices of his novitiate. Vanion conducted the services that evening and spoke at some length on the virtue of humility. In keeping with his long-standing practice, Sparhawk fell into a doze about halfway through the sermon.

He was awakened at the end of the sermon by the voice of an angel. A young knight with hair the color of butter and a neck like a marble column lifted his clear tenor voice in a hymn of praise. His face shone, and his eyes were filled with adoration.

"Was I really all that boring?" Vanion murmured, falling in beside Sparhawk as they left the chapel.

"Probably not," Sparhawk replied, "but I'm not really in any position to judge. Did you do the one about the simple daisy being as beautiful in the eyes of God as the rose?"

"You've heard it before?"

"Frequently."

"The old ones are the best."

"Who's your tenor?"

"Sir Parasim. He just won his spurs."

"I don't want to alarm you, Vanion, but he's too good for this world."

"I know."

"God will probably call him home very soon."

"That's God's business, isn't it, Sparhawk?"

"Do me a favor, Vanion. Don't put me in a situation where I'm the one who lets him get killed."

"That's also God's business. Sleep well, Sparhawk."

"You, too, Vanion."

It was probably about midnight when the door to Sparhawk's cell banged open. He rolled quickly out of his narrow cot and came to his feet with his sword in his hand.

"*Don't* do that," the big blond-haired man in the doorway said in disgust. He was holding a candle in one hand and a wineskin in the other.

"Hello, Kalten," Sparhawk greeted his boyhood friend. "When did you get in?"

"About a half hour ago. I thought I was going to have to scale the walls there for a while." He looked disgusted. "It's peacetime. Why do they raise the drawbridge every night?"

"Probably out of habit."

"Are you going to put that down?" Kalten asked, pointing at the sword in Sparhawk's hand, "or am I going to have to drink this whole thing by myself?"

"Sorry," Sparhawk said. He leaned his plain sword against the wall.

Kalten set his candle on the small table in the corner, tossed the wineskin onto Sparhawk's bed, and then caught his friend in a huge bear hug. "It's good to see you," he declared.

"And you, too," Sparhawk replied. "Have a seat." He pointed at the stool by the table and sat down on the edge of his cot. "How was Lamorkand?"

Kalten made an indelicate sound. "Cold, damp, and nervous," he replied. "Lamorks are not my favorite people in the world. How was Rendor?"

Sparhawk shrugged. "Hot, dry, and probably just as nervous as Lamorkand."

"I heard a rumor that you ran into Martel down there. Did you give him a nice funeral?"

"He got away."

"You're slipping, Sparhawk." Kalten unfastened the collar of his cloak. A great mat of curly blond hair protruded out of the neck of his mail coat. "Are you going to sit on that wineskin all night?" he asked pointedly.

Sparhawk grunted, unstopped the skin, and lifted it to his lips. "Not bad," he said. "Where did you get it?" He handed the skin to his friend.

"I picked it up in a wayside tavern about sundown," he replied. "I remembered that all there is to drink in Pandion chapterhouses is water—or tea, if Sephrenia happens to be around. Stupid custom."

"We *are* a religious order, Kalten."

"There are a half dozen patriarchs in Chyrellos who get drunk as lords every night." Kalten lifted the wineskin and took a long drink. Then he shook the skin. "I should have picked up two," he observed. "Oh, by the way, Kurik was in the tavern with some young puppy wearing your armor."

"I should have guessed that," Sparhawk said wryly.

"Anyway, Kurik told me that you were here. I was going to spend the night there, but when I heard that you'd come back from Rendor, I rode on the rest of the way."

"I'm touched."

Kalten laughed and handed back the wineskin.

"Were Kurik and the novice staying out of sight?" Sparhawk asked.

Kalten nodded. "They were in one of the back rooms, and the young fellow was keeping his visor down. Have you ever seen anybody try to drink through his visor? Funniest thing I ever saw. There were a couple of local whores there, too. Your young Pandion might be getting an education along about now."

"He's due," Sparhawk observed.

"I wonder if he'll try to do that with his visor down as well."

"Those girls are usually adaptable."

Kalten laughed. "Anyhow, Kurik told me about the situation here. Do you really believe you can sneak around Cimmura without being recognized?"

"I was thinking along the lines of a disguise of some sort."

"Better come up with a false nose," Kalten advised. "That broken beak of yours makes you fairly easy to pick out of a crowd."

"You should know," Sparhawk said. "You're the one who broke it."

"We were only playing," Kalten said, sounding a bit defensive.

"I've gotten used to it. We'll talk with Sephrenia in the morning. She should be able to come up with something in the way of disguises."

"I'd heard that she was here. How is she?"

"The same. Sephrenia never changes."

"Truly." Kalten took another drink from the wineskin and wiped his mouth with the back of his hand. "You know, I think I was always a big disappointment to her. No matter how hard she tried to teach me the secrets, I just couldn't master the Styric language. Every time I tried to say *'ogeragekgasek,'* I almost dislocated my jaw."

*"Okeragukasek,"* Sparhawk corrected him.

"However you say it. I'll just stick to my sword and let others play with magic." He leaned forward on his stool. "They say that the Eshandists are on the rise again in Rendor. Is there any truth to that?"

"It's no particular danger." Sparhawk shrugged, lounging back on his cot. "They howl and spin around in circles out in the desert and recite slogans to each other. That's about as far as it goes. Is anything very interesting going on in Lamorkand?"

Kalten snorted. "All the barons there are involved in private wars with each other," he reported. "The whole kingdom reeks with the lust for revenge. Would you believe that there's actually a war going on over a bee sting? An earl got stung and declared war on the baron whose peasants owned the hive. They've been fighting each other for ten years now."

"That's Lamorkand for you. Anything else happening?"

"The whole countryside east of Motera is crawling with Zemochs."

Sparhawk sat up quickly. "Vanion did say that Otha was mobilizing."

"Otha mobilizes every ten years." Kalten handed his friend the wineskin. "I think he does it just to keep his people from getting restless."

"Are the Zemochs doing anything significant in Lamorkand?"

"Not that I was able to tell. They're asking a lot of questions—mostly about old folklore. You can find two or three of them in almost every village. They question old women and buy drinks for the loafers in the village taverns."

"Peculiar," Sparhawk murmured.

"That's a fairly accurate description of just about anybody from Zemoch," Kalten said. "Sanity has never been particularly prized there." He stood up. "I'll go find a cot someplace," he said. "I can drag it in here and we can talk old times until we both fall asleep."

"All right."

Kalten grinned. "Like the time your father caught us in that plum tree."

Sparhawk winced. "I've been trying to forget about that for almost thirty years now."

"Your father *did* have a very firm hand, as I recall. I lost track of most of the rest of that day—and the plums gave me a bellyache besides. I'll be right back." He turned and went out the door of Sparhawk's cell.

It was good to have Kalten back. The two of them had grown up together in the house of Sparhawk's parents at Demos after Kalten's family had been killed and before the pair of boys had entered their novitiate training at the Pandion motherhouse. In many ways, they were closer than brothers. To be sure, Kalten had some rough edges to him, but their close friendship was one of the things Sparhawk valued more than anything else.

After a short time, the big blond man returned, dragging a cot behind him, and then the two of them lay in the dim candlelight reminiscing until quite late. All in all, it was a very good night.

Early the following morning, they rose and dressed themselves, covering their mail coats with the hooded robes Pandions wore when they were inside their chapterhouses. They rather carefully avoided the morning procession to chapel and went in search of the woman who had trained whole generations of Pandion Knights in the intricacies of what were called the secrets.

They found her seated with her morning tea before the fire high up in the south tower.

"Good morning, little mother," Sparhawk greeted her from the doorway. "Do you mind if we join you?"

"Not at all, Sir Knights."

Kalten went to her, knelt, and kissed both her palms. "Will you bless me, little mother?" he asked her.

She smiled and put one hand on each side of his face. Then she spoke her benediction in Styric.

"That always makes me feel better for some reason," he said, rising to his feet again. "Even though I don't understand all the words."

She looked at them critically. "I see that you chose not to attend chapel this morning."

"God won't miss us all that much." Kalten shrugged. "Besides, I could recite all of Vanion's sermons from memory."

"What other mischief are you two planning for today?" she asked.

"Mischief, Sephrenia?" Kalten asked innocently.

Sparhawk laughed. "Actually, we weren't even contemplating any mischief. We just have a fairly simple errand in mind."

"Out in the city?"

He nodded. "The only problem is that we're both fairly well known here in Cimmura. We thought you might be able to help us with some disguises."

She looked at them, her expression cool. "I'm getting a strong sense of subterfuge in all this. Just exactly what is this errand of yours?"

"We thought we'd look up an old friend," Sparhawk replied. "A fellow named Krager. He has some information he might want to share with us."

"Information?"

"He knows where Martel is."

"Krager won't tell you that."

Kalten cracked his big knuckles, the sound unpleasantly calling to mind the sharp noise of breaking bones. "Would you care to phrase that in the form of a wager, Sephrenia?" he asked.

"Won't you two ever grow up? You're a pair of eternal children."

"That's why you love us so much, isn't it, little mother?" Kalten grinned.

"What sort of disguise would you recommend?" Sparhawk asked her.

She pursed her lips and looked at them. "A courtier and his squire, I think."

"No one could ever mistake me for a courtier," he objected.

"I was thinking of it the other way around. I can make you look *almost* like a good honest squire, and once we dress Kalten in a satin doublet and curl that long blond hair of his, he can pass for a courtier."

"I *do* look good in satin," Kalten murmured modestly.

"Why not just a couple of common workmen?" Sparhawk asked.

She shook her head. "Common workmen cringe and fawn when they encounter a nobleman. Could either of you manage a cringe?"

"She's got a point," Kalten said.

"Besides, workmen don't carry swords, and I don't imagine that either of you would care to go into Cimmura unarmed."

"She thinks of everything, doesn't she?" Sparhawk observed.

"All right," she said. "Let's see what we can do."

Several acolytes were sent scurrying to various places in the chapterhouse for a number of articles. Sephrenia considered each one of them, selecting some and discarding others. What emerged after about an hour were two men who only faintly resembled the pair of Pandions who had first entered the room. Sparhawk now wore a plain livery not unlike Kurik's, and he carried a short sword. A fierce black beard was glued to his face, and a purple scar ran across his broken nose and up under a black patch that covered his left eye.

"This thing itches," he complained, reaching up to scratch at the false beard.

"Keep your fingers off of it until the glue dries," she told him, lightly slapping his knuckles. "And put on a glove to cover that ring."

"Do you actually expect me to carry this toy?" Kalten demanded, flourishing a light rapier. "I want a sword, not a knitting needle."

"Courtiers don't carry broadswords, Kalten," she reminded him. She looked at him critically. His doublet was bright blue, gored and inset with red satin. His hose matched the goring, and he wore soft half boots, since no pair of the pointed shoes currently in fashion could be found to fit his huge feet. His cape was of pale pink, and his freshly curled blond hair spilled down over the collar. He also wore a broadbrimmed hat adorned with a white plume. "You look beautiful, Kalten," she complimented him. "I think you might pass—once I rouge your cheeks."

"Absolutely not!" He backed away from her.

"Kalten," she said quite firmly, "sit down." She pointed at a chair and reached for a rouge pot.

"Do I have to?"

"Yes. Now sit."

Kalten looked at Sparhawk. "If you laugh, we're going to fight, so don't even think about it."

"Me?"

Since the chapterhouse was watched at all times by the agents of the Primate Annias, Vanion came up with a suggestion that was part subterfuge and part utilitarian. "I need to transfer some things to the inn anyway," he explained. "Annias knows that the inn belongs to us, so we're not giving anything away. We'll hide Kalten in the wagon bed and turn this good, honest fellow into a teamster." He looked pointedly at the patch-eyed, bearded Sparhawk. "Where on earth did you find so close a match to his real hair?" he asked Sephrenia curiously.

She smiled. "The next time you go into the stables, don't look too closely at your horse's tail."

"*My* horse?"

"He was the only black horse in the stable, Vanion, and I didn't take all that much, really."

"*My* horse?" he repeated, looking injured.

"We must all make sacrifices now and then," she told him. "It's a part of the Pandion oath, remember?"

## CHAPTER FIVE

The wagon was rickety, and the horse was spavined. Sparhawk slouched on the wagon seat with the reins held negligently in one hand and apparently paying very little attention to the people in the street around him.

The wheels wobbled and creaked as the wagon jolted over a rutted place in the stone-paved street. "Sparhawk, do you have to hit every single bump?" Kalten's muffled voice came from under the boxes and bales loosely piled around him in the back of the wagon.

"Keep quiet," Sparhawk muttered. "Two church soldiers are coming this way."

Kalten grumbled a few choice oaths, then fell silent.

The church soldiers wore red livery and disdainful expressions. As they walked through the crowded streets, the workmen and blue-clad merchants stepped aside for them. Sparhawk reined in his nag, stopping the wagon in the exact center of the street so that the soldiers would be forced to go around him. " 'Morning, neighbors," he greeted them.

They glared at him, then walked on around the wagon.

"Have a pleasant day," he called after them.

They ignored him.

"What was that all about?" Kalten demanded in a low voice from the wagon bed.

"Just checking my disguise," Sparhawk replied, shaking the reins.

"Well?"

"Well what?"

"Does it work?"

"They didn't give me a second glance."

"How much farther to the inn? I'm suffocating under all this."

"Not too much farther."

"Give me a big surprise, Sparhawk. Miss a bump or two—just for the sake of variety."

The wagon creaked on.

At the barred gate of the inn, Sparhawk climbed down from the wagon and pounded the rhythmic signal on its stout timbers. After a moment the knight porter opened the gate. He looked at Sparhawk carefully. "Sorry, friend," he said. "The inn's all full."

"We won't be staying, Sir Knight," Sparhawk told him. "We just brought a load of supplies from the chapterhouse."

The porter's eyes widened and he peered more closely at the big man. "Is that you, Sir Sparhawk?" he asked incredulously. "I didn't even recognize you."

"That was sort of the idea. You aren't supposed to."

The knight pushed the gate open, and Sparhawk led the weary horse into the courtyard. "You can get out now," he said to Kalten as the porter closed the gate.

"Help get all this off me."

Sparhawk moved a few of the boxes, and Kalten came squirming out.

The knight porter gave the big blond man an amused look.

"Go ahead and say it," Kalten said in a belligerent tone.

"I wouldn't dream of it, Sir Knight."

Sparhawk took a long, rectangular box out of the wagon bed and hoisted it up onto his shoulder. "Get somebody to help you with these supplies," he told the porter. "Preceptor Vanion sent them. And take care of the horse. He's tired."

"Tired? Dead would be closer." The porter eyed the disconsolate-looking nag.

"He's old, that's all. It happens to all of us sooner or later. Is the back door to the tavern open?" He looked across the courtyard at a deeply inset doorway.

"It's always open, Sir Sparhawk."

Sparhawk nodded and he and Kalten crossed the courtyard.

"What have you got in the box?" Kalten asked.

"Our swords."

"That's clever, but won't they be a little hard to draw?"

"Not after I throw the box down on the cobblestones, they won't." He opened the inset door. "After you, my Lord," he said, bowing.

They passed through a cluttered storeroom and came out into a shabby-looking tavern. A century or so of dust clouded the single window, and the straw on the floor was moldy. The room smelled of stale beer and spilled wine and vomit. The low ceiling was draped with cobwebs, and the rough tables and benches were battered and tired-looking. There were only three people in the place, a sour-looking tavern keeper, a drunken man with his head cradled in his arms on a table by the door, and a blowsy-looking whore in a red dress dozing in the corner.

Kalten went to the door and looked out into the street. "It's still a little under-populated out there," he grunted. "Let's have a tankard or two while we wait for the neighborhood to wake up."

"Why not have some breakfast instead?"

"That's what I just said."

They sat at one of the tables, and the tavern keeper came over, giving no hint that he recognized them as Pandions. He made an ineffective swipe at a puddle of spilled beer on the table with a filthy rag. "What would you like?" His voice had a sullen, unfriendly tone.

"Beer," Kalten replied.

"Bring us a little bread and cheese, too," Sparhawk added.

The tavern keeper grunted and left them.

"Where was Krager when you saw him?" Kalten asked quietly.

"In that square near the west gate."

"That's a shabby part of town."

"Krager's a shabby sort of person."

"We could start there, I suppose, but this might take a while. Krager could be down just about any rat hole in Cimmura."

"Did you have anything else more pressing to do?"

The whore in the red dress hauled herself wearily to her feet and shuffled across the straw-covered floor to their table. "I don't suppose either of you fine gentlemen would care for a bit of a frolic?" she asked in a bored-sounding voice. One of her front teeth was missing, and her red dress was cut very low in front. Perfunctorily she leaned forward to offer them a view of her flabby-looking breasts.

"It's a bit early, little sister," Sparhawk said. "Thanks all the same."

"How's business?" Kalten asked her.

"Slow. It's always slow in the morning." She sighed. "I don't suppose you could see your way clear to offer a girl something to drink?" she asked hopefully.

"Why not?" Kalten replied. "Tavern keeper," he called, "bring the lady one, too."

"Thanks, my Lord," the whore said. She looked around the tavern. "This is a sorry place," she said with a certain amount of resignation in her voice. "I wouldn't even come in here—except that I don't like to work the streets." She sighed. "Do you know something?" she said. "My feet hurt. Isn't that a strange thing to happen to someone in my profession? You'd think it would be my back. Thanks again, my Lord." She turned and shuffled back to the table where she had been sitting.

"I like talking with whores," Kalten said. "They've got a nice, uncomplicated view of life."

"That's a strange hobby for a Church Knight."

"God hired me as a fighting man, Sparhawk, not as a monk. I fight whenever He tells me to, but the rest of my time is my own."

The tavern keeper brought them tankards of beer and a plate with bread and cheese on it. They sat eating and talking quietly.

After about an hour the tavern had attracted several more customers—sweat-smelling workmen who had slipped away from their chores and a few of the keepers of nearby shops. Sparhawk rose, went to the door, and looked out. Although the narrow back street was not exactly teeming with traffic, there were enough people moving back and forth to provide some measure of concealment. Sparhawk returned to the table. "I think it's time to be on our way, my Lord," he said to Kalten. He picked up his box.

"Right," Kalten replied. He drained his tankard and rose to his feet, swaying slightly and with his hat on the back of his head. He stumbled a few times on the way to the door and he was reeling just a bit as he led the way out into the street. Sparhawk followed him with the box once again on his shoulder. "Aren't you overdoing that just a little?" he muttered to his friend when they turned the corner.

"I'm just a typical drunken courtier, Sparhawk. We just came out of a tavern."

"We're well past it now. If you act too drunk, you'll attract attention. I think it's time for a miraculous recovery."

"You're taking all the fun out of this, Sparhawk," Kalten complained. He stopped staggering and straightened his white-plumed hat.

They moved on through the busy streets with Sparhawk trailing respectfully behind his friend as a good squire would.

When they reached another intersection, Sparhawk felt a familiar prickling of his skin. He set down his wooden box and wiped at his brow with the sleeve of his smock.

"What's the matter?" Kalten asked, also stopping.

"The case is heavy, my Lord," Sparhawk explained in a voice loud enough to be heard by passersby. Then he spoke in a half whisper. "We're being watched," he said as his eyes swept the sides of the street.

The robed and hooded figure was in a second-floor window, partially concealed behind a thick green drape. It looked very much like the one that had watched him in the rain-wet streets the night he had first arrived back in Cimmura.

"Have you located him?" Kalten asked quietly, making some show of adjusting the collar of his pink cloak.

Sparhawk grunted, raising the box to his shoulder again. "Second floor window—over the chandler's shop."

"Let's be off then, my man," Kalten said in a louder voice. "The day's wearing on." As he started on up the street, he cast a quick, furtive glance at the green-draped window.

They rounded another corner. "Odd-looking sort, wasn't he?" Kalten noted. "Most people don't wear hoods when they're indoors."

"Maybe he's got something to hide."

"Do you think he recognized us?"

"It's hard to say. I'm not positive, but I think he was the same one who was watching me the night I came into town. I didn't get a good look at him, but I could feel him, and this one feels just about the same."

"Would magic penetrate these disguises?"

"Easily. Magic sees the man, not the clothes. Let's go down a few alleys and see if we can shake him off in case he decides to follow us."

"Right."

It was nearly noon when they reached the square near the west gate where Sparhawk had seen Krager. They split up there. Sparhawk went in one direction and Kalten the other. They questioned the keepers of the brightly colored booths and the more sedate shops closely, describing Krager in some detail. On the far side of the square, Sparhawk rejoined his friend. "Any luck?" he asked.

Kalten nodded. "There's a wine merchant over there who says that a man who looks like Krager comes in three or four times a day to buy a flagon of Arcian red."

"That's Krager's drink, all right." Sparhawk grinned. "If Martel finds out that he's drinking again, he'll reach down his throat and pull his heart out."

"Can you actually do that to a man?"

"You can if your arm's long enough, and if you know what you're looking for.

Did your wine merchant give you any sort of hint about which way Krager usually comes from?"

Kalten nodded. "That street there." He pointed.

Sparhawk scratched at his horse-tail beard, thinking.

"If you pull that loose, Sephrenia's going to turn you over her knee and paddle you."

Sparhawk took his hand away from his face. "Has Krager picked up his first flagon of wine this morning?" he asked.

Kalten nodded. "About two hours ago."

"He's likely to finish that first one fairly fast. If he's drinking the way he used to, he'll wake up in the mornings feeling a bit unwell." Sparhawk looked around the busy square. "Let's go on up that street a ways where there aren't quite so many people and wait for him. As soon as he runs out of wine, he'll come out for more."

"Won't he see us? He knows us both, you know."

Sparhawk shook his head. "He's so shortsighted that he can barely see past the end of his nose. Add a flagon of wine to that, and he wouldn't be able to recognize his own mother."

"Krager's got a mother?" Kalten asked in mock amazement. "I thought he just crawled out from under a rotten log."

Sparhawk laughed. "Let's go find someplace where we can wait for him."

"Can we skulk?" Kalten asked eagerly. "I haven't skulked in years."

"Skulk away, my friend," Sparhawk said.

They walked up the street the wine merchant had indicated. After a few hundred paces, Sparhawk pointed toward the narrow opening of an alley. "That ought to do it," he said. "Let's go do our skulking in there. When Krager goes by, we can drag him into the alley and have our little chat in private."

"Right," Kalten agreed with an evil grin.

They crossed the street and entered the alley. Rotting garbage lay heaped along the sides, and some way farther on was a reeking public urinal. Kalten waved one hand in front of his face. "Sometimes your decisions leave a lot to be desired, Sparhawk," he said. "Couldn't you have picked someplace a little less fragrant?"

"You know," Sparhawk said, "that's what I've missed about not having you around, Kalten—that steady stream of complaints."

Kalten shrugged. "A man needs something to talk about." He reached under his azure doublet, took out a small, curved knife, and began to strop it on the sole of his boot. "I get him first," he said.

"What?"

"Krager. I get to start on him first."

"What gave you that idea?"

"You're my friend, Sparhawk. Friends always let their friends go first."

"Doesn't that work the other way around, too?"

Kalten shook his head. "You like me better than I like you. It's only natural, of course. I'm a lot more likable than you are."

Sparhawk gave him a long look.

"That's what friends are for, Sparhawk," Kalten said ingratiatingly, "to point out our little shortcomings to us."

They waited, watching the street from the mouth of the alley. It was not a particularly busy street, for there were but few shops along its sides. It seemed rather to be given over largely to storehouses and private dwellings.

An hour dragged by, and then another.

"Maybe he drank himself to sleep," Kalten said.

"Not Krager. He can hold more than a regiment. He'll be along."

Kalten thrust his head out of the opening of the alleyway and squinted at the sky. "It's going to rain," he predicted.

"We've both been rained on before."

Kalten plucked at the front of his gaudy doublet and rolled his eyes. "But *Thpar*hawk," he lisped outrageously. "You *know* how thatin thpotth when it getth wet."

Sparhawk doubled over with laughter, trying to muffle the sound.

They waited once more, and another hour dragged by.

"The sun's going to go down before long," Kalten said. "Maybe he found another wine shop."

"Let's wait a little longer," Sparhawk replied.

The rush came without warning. Eight or ten burly fellows in rough clothing came charging down the alley with swords in their hands. Kalten's rapier came whistling out of its sheath even as Sparhawk's hand flashed to the hilt of his short sword. The man leading the charge doubled over and gasped as Kalten smoothly ran him through. Sparhawk stepped past his friend as the blond man recovered from his lunge. He parried the sword stroke of one of the attackers and then buried his sword in the man's belly. He wrenched the blade as he jerked it out to make the wound as big as possible. "Get that box open!" he shouted at Kalten as he parried another stroke.

The alleyway was too narrow for more than two of them to come at him at once; even though his sword was not as long as theirs, he was able to hold them at bay. Behind him he heard the splintering of wood as Kalten kicked the rectangular box apart. Then his friend was at his shoulder with his broadsword in his hand. "I've got it now," Kalten said. "Get your sword."

Sparhawk spun and ran back to the mouth of the alley. He discarded the short sword, jerked his own weapon out of the wreckage of the box, and whirled back again. Kalten had cut down two of the attackers, and he was beating the others back step by step. He did, however, have his left hand pressed tightly to his side, and there was blood coming out from between his fingers. Sparhawk rushed past him, swinging his heavy sword with both hands. He split one fellow's head open and cut the sword arm off another. Then he drove the point of his sword deep into the body of yet a third, sending him reeling against the wall with a fountain of blood gushing from his mouth.

The rest of the attackers fled.

Sparhawk turned and saw Kalten coolly pulling his sword out of the chest of the man with the missing arm. "Don't leave them behind you like that, Sparhawk," the blond man said. "Even a one-armed man can stab you in the back. Besides, it isn't tidy. Always finish one job before you go on to the next." He still had his left hand tightly pressed to his side.

"Are you all right?" Sparhawk asked him.

"It's only a scratch."

"Scratches don't bleed like that. Let me have a look."

The gash in Kalten's side was sizable, but it did not appear to be too deep. Sparhawk ripped the sleeve off the smock of one of the casualties, wadded it up, and placed it over the cut in Kalten's side. "Hold that in place," he said. "Push in on it to slow the bleeding."

"I've been cut before, Sparhawk. I know what to do."

Sparhawk looked around at the crumpled bodies littering the alley. "I think we ought to leave," he said. "Somebody in the neighborhood might get curious about all the noise." Then he frowned. "Did you notice anything peculiar about these men?" he asked.

Kalten shrugged. "They were fairly inept."

"That's not what I mean. Men who make a living by waylaying people in alleys aren't usually very interested in their personal appearance, and these fellows are all clean-shaven." He rolled one of the bodies over and ripped open the front of his canvas smock. "Isn't *that* interesting?" he observed. Beneath the smock the dead man wore a red tunic with an embroidered emblem over the left breast.

"Church soldier," Kalten grunted. "Do you think that Annias might possibly dislike us?"

"It's not unlikely. Let's get out of here. The survivors might have gone for help."

"The chapterhouse then—or the inn?"

Sparhawk shook his head. "Somebody's seen through our disguises, and Annias would expect us to go to one of those places."

"You could be right about that. Any ideas?"

"I know of a place. It's not too far. Are you all right to walk?"

"I can go as far as you can. I'm younger, remember?"

"Only by six weeks."

"Younger is younger, Sparhawk. Let's not quibble about numbers."

They tucked their broadswords under their belts and walked out of the mouth of the alley. Sparhawk supported his wounded friend as they moved out into the open.

The street along which they walked grew progressively shabbier, and they soon entered a maze of interconnecting lanes and unpaved alleys. The buildings were large and run-down, and they teemed with roughly dressed people who seemed indifferent to the squalor around them.

"It's a rabbit warren, isn't it?" Kalten said. "Is this place much farther? I'm getting a little tired."

"It's just on the other side of that next intersection."

Kalten grunted and pressed his hand more tightly to his side.

They moved on. The looks directed at them by the inhabitants of this slum were unfriendly, even hostile. Kalten's clothing marked him as a member of the ruling class, and these people at the very bottom of society had little use for courtiers and their servants.

When they reached the intersection, Sparhawk led his friend up a muddy alley. They had gone about halfway when a thick-bodied man with a rusty pike in his hands stepped out of a doorway to bar their path. "Where do you think you're going?" he demanded.

"I need to talk to Platime," Sparhawk replied.

"I don't think he wants to hear anything you have to say. If you're smart, you'll get out of this part of town before nightfall. Accidents happen here after dark."

"And sometimes even before dark," Sparhawk said, drawing his sword.

"I can have a dozen men here in two winks."

"And my broken-nosed friend here can have your head off in one," Kalten told him.

The man stepped back, his face apprehensive.

"What's it to be, neighbor?" Sparhawk asked. "Do you take us to Platime, or do you and I play for a bit?"

"You've got no right to threaten me."

Sparhawk raised his sword so that the fellow could get a good look at it. "This gives me all sorts of rights, neighbor. Lean your pike against that wall and take us to Platime—now!"

The thick-bodied man flinched and then carefully set his pike against the wall, turned, and led them on up the alley. It came to a dead end a hundred paces farther on, and a stone stairway ran down to what appeared to be a cellar door.

"Down there," the man said, pointing.

"Lead the way," Sparhawk told him. "I don't want you behind me, friend. You look like the sort who might make errors in judgment."

Sullenly, the fellow went down the mud-coated stairs and rapped twice on the door. "It's me," he called. "Sef. There are a couple of nobles here who want to talk to Platime."

There was a pause followed by the rattling of a chain. The door opened and a bearded man thrust his head out. "Platime doesn't like noblemen," he declared.

"I'll change his mind for him," Sparhawk said. "Step back out of the way, neighbor."

The bearded man looked at the sword in Sparhawk's hand, swallowed hard, and opened the door wider.

"Press right along, Sef," Kalten said to their guide.

Sef went through the door.

"Join us, friend," Sparhawk told the bearded man when he and Kalten were inside. "We like lots of company."

The stairs continued down between moldy stone walls that wept moisture. At the bottom, the stair opened out into a very large cellar with a vaulted stone ceiling. There was a fire burning in a pit in the center of the room, filling the air with smoke, and the walls were lined with roughly constructed cots and straw-filled pallets. Two dozen or so men and women in a wide variety of garments sat on those cots and pallets drinking and playing at dice. Just beyond the firepit a huge man with a fierce black beard and a vast paunch sprawled in a large chair with his feet thrust out toward the flames. He wore a satin doublet of a faded orange color, spotted and stained down the front, and he held a silver tankard in one beefy hand.

"That's Platime," Sef said nervously. "He's a little drunk, so you should be careful, my Lords."

"We can deal with it," Sparhawk told him. "Thanks for your help, Sef. I don't know how we'd have managed without you." Then he led Kalten on around the firepit.

"Who are all these people?" Kalten asked in a low voice, looking around at the men and women lining the walls.

"Thieves, beggars, a few murderers probably—that sort of thing."

"You've got some very nice friends, Sparhawk."

Platime was carefully examining a necklace with a ruby pendant attached to it. When Sparhawk and Kalten stopped in front of him, he raised his bleary eyes and looked them over, paying particular attention to Kalten's finery. "Who let these two in here?" he roared.

"We sort of let ourselves in, Platime," Sparhawk told him, thrusting his sword back under his belt and turning up his eye patch so that it no longer impaired his vision.

"Well, you can sort of let yourselves back out again."

"That wouldn't be convenient right now, I'm afraid," Sparhawk told him.

The gross man in the orange doublet snapped his fingers, and the people lining the walls stood up. "You're badly outnumbered, my friend." Platime looked around suggestively at his cohorts.

"That's been happening fairly often lately," Kalten said with his hand on the hilt of his broadsword.

Platime's eyes narrowed. "Your clothes and that sword don't exactly match," he said.

"And I try so hard to coordinate my attire." Kalten sighed.

"Just who are you two?" Platime asked suspiciously. "This one is dressed like a courtier, but I don't think he's really one of those walking butterflies from the palace."

"He sees right to the core of things, doesn't he?" Kalten said to Sparhawk. He looked at Platime. "Actually, we're Pandions," he said.

"Church Knights? I thought it might be something like that. Why the fancy clothes, then?"

"We're both fairly well known," Sparhawk told him. "We wanted to be able to move around without being recognized."

Platime looked meaningfully at Kalten's bloodstained doublet. "It looks to me as if *somebody* saw through your disguises," he said, "or maybe you just frequent the wrong taverns. Who stabbed you?"

"A church soldier." Kalten shrugged. "He got in a lucky thrust. Do you mind if I sit down? I'm feeling a little shaky for some reason."

"Somebody bring him a stool," Platime shouted. Then he looked back at the two of them. "Why would Church Knights and church soldiers be fighting?" he asked.

"Palace politics." Sparhawk shrugged. "They get a little murky sometimes."

"That's God's own truth. What's your business here?"

"We need a place to stay for a while," Sparhawk told him. He looked around. "This cellar of yours ought to work out fairly well."

"Sorry, friend. I can sympathize with a man who's just had a run-in with the church soldiers, but I'm conducting a business here, and there's no room for outsiders." Platime looked at Kalten, who had just sunk down on a stool that a ragged beggar had brought him. "Did you kill the man who stabbed you?"

"He did." Kalten pointed at Sparhawk. "I killed a few others, but my friend here did most of the fighting."

"Why don't we get down to business?" Sparhawk said. "I think you owe my family a debt, Platime."

"I don't have any dealings with nobles," Platime replied, "except to cut a few of their throats from time to time—so it's unlikely that I owe your family a thing."

"This debt has nothing to do with money. A long time ago, some church soldiers were hanging you. My father stopped them."

Platime blinked. "You're Sparhawk?" he said in surprise. "You don't look that much like your father."

"It's his nose," Kalten said. "When you break a man's nose, you change his whole appearance. Why were the soldiers hanging you?"

"It was all a misunderstanding. I knifed a fellow. He wasn't wearing his uniform, so I didn't know he was an officer in the primate's guard." He looked disgusted. "And all he had in his purse were two silver coins and a handful of copper."

"Do you acknowledge the debt?" Sparhawk pressed.

Platime pulled at his coarse black beard. "I guess I do," he admitted.

"We'll stay here, then."

"That's all you want?"

"Not quite. We're looking for a man—a fellow named Krager. Your beggars are all over town, and I want them to look for him."

"Fair enough. Can you describe him?"

"I can do better than that. I can show him to you."

"That doesn't exactly make sense, friend."

"It will in a minute. Have you got a basin of some kind—and some clean water?"

"I think I can manage that. What have you got in mind?"

"He's going to make an image of Krager's face in the water," Kalten said. "It's an old trick."

Platime looked impressed. "I've heard that you Pandions are all wizards, but I've never seen anything like that before."

"Sparhawk's better at it than I am," Kalten admitted.

One of the beggars furnished a chipped basin filled with slightly cloudy water. Sparhawk set the basin on the floor and concentrated for a moment, muttering the Styric words of the spell under his breath. Then he passed his hand slowly over the basin, and Krager's puffy-looking face appeared.

"Now *that* is really something to see," Platime marveled.

"It's not too difficult," Sparhawk said modestly. "Have your people here look at it. I can't keep it there forever."

"How long can you hold it?"

"Ten minutes or so. It starts to break up after that."

"Talen!" the fat man shouted. "Come here."

A grubby-looking boy of about ten slouched across the room. His tunic was ragged and dirty, but he wore a long, red satin vest that had been fashioned by cutting the sleeves off a doublet. There were several knife-holes in the vest. "What do you want?" he asked insolently.

"Can you copy that?" Platime asked, pointing at the basin.

"Of course I can, but why should I?"

"Because I'll box your ears if you don't."

Talen grinned at him. "You'd have to catch me first, fat man, and I can run faster than you can."

Sparhawk dug a finger into a pocket of his leather jerkin and took out a small silver coin. "Would this make it worth your while?" he asked, holding up the coin.

Talen's eyes brightened. "For that, I'll give you a masterpiece," he promised.

"All we want is accuracy."

"Whatever you say, my patron." Talen bowed mockingly. "I'll go get my things."

"Is he really any good?" Kalten asked Platime after the boy had scurried over to one of the cots lining the wall.

Platime shrugged. "I'm not an art critic," he said. "He spends all his time drawing pictures, though—when he isn't begging or stealing."

"Isn't he a little young for your line of work?"

Platime laughed. "He's got the nimblest fingers in Cimmura," he said. "He could steal your eyes right out of their sockets, and you wouldn't even miss them until you went to look closely at something."

"I'll keep that in mind," Kalten said.

"It could be too late, my friend. Weren't you wearing a ring when you came in?"

Kalten blinked, then raised his bloodstained left hand and stared at it. There was no ring on the hand.

## CHAPTER SIX

Kalten winced. "Easy, Sparhawk," he said. "That *really* hurts."

"It has to be cleaned before I can bandage it," Sparhawk replied, continuing to wipe the cut on his friend's side with a wine-soaked cloth.

"But do you have to do it so hard?"

Platime waddled around the smoky firepit and stood over the cot where Kalten lay. "Is he going to be all right?" he asked.

"Probably," Sparhawk replied. "He's had the blood let out of him a few times before, and he usually recovers." He laid aside the cloth and picked up a long strip of linen. "Sit up," he told his friend.

Kalten grunted and pushed himself into a sitting position. Sparhawk began to wind the strip about his waist.

"Not so tight," Kalten said. "I have to be able to breathe."

"Quit complaining."

"Were those church soldiers after you for any particular reason?" Platime asked, "or were they just amusing themselves?"

"They had reasons," Sparhawk told him as he knotted Kalten's bandage. "We've managed to be fairly offensive to Primate Annias lately."

"Good for you. I don't know how you noblemen feel about him, but the common people all hate him."

"We moderately despise him."

"That's one thing we all have in common then. Is there any chance that Queen Ehlana might recover?"

"We're working on that."

Platime sighed. "I think she's our only hope, Sparhawk. Otherwise Annias is going to run Elenia to suit himself, and that would really be too bad."

"Patriotism, Platime?" Kalten asked.

"Just because I'm a thief and a murderer doesn't mean that I'm disloyal. I respect the crown as much as any man in the kingdom. I even respected Aldreas, weak as he was." Platime's eyes grew sly. "Did his sister ever really seduce him?" he asked. "There were all kinds of rumors."

Sparhawk shrugged. "That's sort of hard to say."

"She went absolutely wild after your father forced Aldreas to marry Queen Ehlana's mother, you know." Platime sniggered. "She was totally convinced that she was going to marry her brother and get control of the throne."

"Isn't that sort of illegal?" Kalten asked.

"Annias said that he'd found a way around the law. Anyway, after Aldreas got married, Arissa ran away from the palace. They found her a few weeks later in that cheap brothel over by the river. Just about everybody in Cimmura had tried her before they dragged her out of the place." He squinted at them. "What did they finally do with her anyway? Chop off her head?"

"No," Sparhawk told him. "She's cloistered in the nunnery at Demos. They're very strict there."

"At least she's getting some rest. From what I hear, the Princess Arissa was a very busy young woman." He straightened and pointed at a nearby cot. "You can use that one," he told Sparhawk. "I've got every thief and beggar in Cimmura out looking for this Krager fellow of yours. If he sets foot in the streets, we'll know about it within an hour. In the meantime, you might as well get some sleep."

Sparhawk nodded and rose to his feet. "Are you all right?" he asked Kalten.

"I'm fine."

"Do you need anything?"

"How about some beer—just to restore all the blood I lost, of course."

"Of course."

It was impossible to tell what time it was since the cellar had no windows. Sparhawk felt a light touch and came awake immediately, catching the hand that had touched him.

The grubby-looking boy, Talen, made a sour face. "Never try to pick a pocket when you're shivering," he said. He mopped the rain out of his face. "It's really a miserable morning out there," he added.

"Were you looking for anything in particular in my pockets?"

"No, not really—just anything that might turn up."

"Would you like to give me back my friend's ring?"

"Oh, I suppose so. I only took it to keep in practice anyway." Talen reached inside his wet tunic and drew out Kalten's ring. "I cleaned the blood off it for him," he said, admiring it.

"He'll appreciate that."

"Oh, by the way, I found that fellow you were looking for."

"Krager? Where?"

"He's staying in a brothel in Lion Street."

"A brothel?"

"Maybe he needs affection." ·

Sparhawk sat up. He touched his horsehair beard to make sure it was still in place. "Let's go talk to Platime."

"Do you want me to wake your friend?"

"Let him sleep. I'm not going to take him out in the rain in his condition anyway."

Platime was snoring in his chair, but his eyes opened instantly when Talen touched his shoulder.

"The boy found Krager," Sparhawk told him.

"You're going after him, I suppose?"

Sparhawk nodded.

"Do you think the primate's soldiers are still looking for you?"

"Probably."

"And they know what you look like?"

"Yes."

"You won't get very far then."

"I'll have to chance it."

"Platime," Talen said.

"What?"

"Do you remember that time when we had to get Weasel out of town in a hurry?"

Platime grunted, scratching at his paunch and looking speculatively at Sparhawk. "How much are you attached to that beard?" he asked.

"Not too much. Why?"

"If you'd be willing to shave it off, I know a way you might be able to move around Cimmura without being recognized."

Sparhawk began pulling off chunks of the false beard.

Platime laughed. "You really *aren't* attached to it, are you?" He looked at Talen. "Go get what he'll need out of the bin."

Talen went to a large wooden box in the corner of the cellar and started rummaging around inside as Sparhawk finished removing the beard. When the boy came back, he was carrying a ragged-looking cloak and a pair of shoes that were little more than rotting leather bags.

"How much of the rest of your face will come off?" Platime asked.

Sparhawk took the ragged cloak from Talen and poured some of Platime's wine on one corner. Then he vigorously scrubbed his face, removing the remnants of Sephrenia's glue and the purple scar.

"The nose?" Platime asked.

"No. That's real."

"How did it get broken?"

"It's a long story."

Platime shrugged. "Take off your boots and those leather breeches. You'll wear the cloak and those shoes."

Sparhawk pulled off his boots and peeled off the leather hose. Talen draped the cloak around him, then pulled one corner across the front and fastened it to the opposite shoulder so that it covered Sparhawk's body and reached about halfway to his knees.

Platime squinted at him. "Put on the shoes and rub some dirt on your legs. You look a bit too clean." Talen went back to the bin and returned with a scuffed leather cap, a long, slender stick, and a length of dirty sackcloth.

"Put on the cap and tie the rag across your eyes," Platime instructed.

Sparhawk did that.

"Can you see well enough through the bandage?"

"I can make things out, but that's about all."

"I don't want you to see too well. You're supposed to be blind. Get him a begging bowl, Talen." Platime turned back to Sparhawk. "Practice walking around a bit. Swing the stick in front of you, but bump into things from time to time and don't forget to stumble."

"It's an interesting idea, Platime, but I know exactly where I'm going. Won't that make people suspicious?"

"Talen will lead you. You'll just be a pair of ordinary beggars."

Sparhawk hitched up his belt and shifted his broadsword around.

"You're going to have to leave that here," Platime told him. "You can hide a dagger under the cloak, but a broadsword's a little too obvious."

"I suppose you're right." Sparhawk pulled out his sword and handed it to the fat man in the orange doublet. "Don't lose it," he said. Then he began to practice the blind man's groping walk, tapping the long, slender stick Talen had given him on the floor as he went.

"Not too bad," Platime said after several minutes. "You pick things up fast, Sparhawk. It ought to be good enough to get you by. Talen can teach you how to beg as you go along."

Talen came back from the large wooden storage box. His left leg looked grotesquely twisted, and he limped along with the aid of a crutch. He had removed his gaudy vest, and he was now dressed in rags.

"Doesn't that hurt?" Sparhawk asked, pointing at the boy's leg with his stick.

"Not much. All you have to do is walk on the side of your foot and turn your knee in."

"It looks very convincing."

"Naturally. I've had a lot of practice."

"Are you both ready then?" Platime asked.

"Probably as ready as we'll ever be," Sparhawk replied. "I don't think I'll be very good at begging, though."

"Talen can teach you the basics. It's not too hard. Good luck, Sparhawk."

"Thanks. I might need it."

It was the middle of a gray rainy morning when Sparhawk and his young guide emerged from the cellar and started back down the muddy alleyway. Sef was once again standing watch in a recessed doorway. He did not speak to them as they passed.

When they reached the street, Talen took hold of the corner of Sparhawk's cloak and led him along by it. Sparhawk groped his way behind him, his stick tapping the cobblestones.

"There are several ways to beg," the boy said after they had gone a short distance. "Some prefer just to sit and hold out the begging bowl. That doesn't bring in too many coins, though—unless you do it outside a church on a day when the sermon's been about charity. Some people like to shove the bowl into the face of everybody who walks by. You get more coins that way, but sometimes it irritates people, and every so often you'll get punched in the face. You're supposed to be blind, so we'll have to work out something a little different."

"Do I have to say anything?"

Talen nodded. "You've got to get their attention. 'Charity' is usually good enough. You don't have time for long speeches, and people don't like to talk with beggars anyway. If somebody decides to give you something, he wants to get it over with as quickly as possible. Make your voice sound hopeless. Whining isn't all that good, but try to put a little catch in your voice—as if you were just about to cry."

"Begging's quite an art, isn't it?"

Talen shrugged. "It's just selling something, that's all. But you've got to do all the selling with just one or two words, so put your heart in it. Do you have any coppers with you?"

"Unless you've stolen them already. Why?"

"When we get to the brothel, you'll need to bait the bowl. Drop in a couple of coppers to make it look as if you've already gotten something."

"I don't quite follow what you've got in mind."

"You want to wait for this Krager to come out, don't you? If you go in after him, you're likely to run into the bruisers who keep order in the place." He looked Sparhawk up and down. "You might be able to deal with them at that, but that sort of thing gets noisy, and the madame would probably send for the watch. It's usually better just to wait outside."

"All right. I suppose we'll wait then."

"We'll station ourselves outside the door and beg until he shows up." The boy paused. "Are you going to kill him?" he asked. "And if you are, can I watch?"

"No. I just want to ask him a few questions."

"Oh." Talen's voice sounded a little disappointed.

It was raining harder now, and Sparhawk's cloak had begun to drip down the backs of his bare legs.

They reached Lion Street and turned left. "The brothel's just up ahead," Talen said, tugging Sparhawk along by the corner of his dripping cloak. Then he stopped suddenly.

"What's the matter?" Sparhawk asked him.

"Competition," Talen replied. "There's a one-legged man leaning against the wall beside the door."

"Begging?"

"What else?"

"Now what?"

"It's no particular problem. I'll just tell him to move on."

"Will he do it?"

Talen nodded. "He will when I tell him that we've rented the spot from Platime. Wait here. I'll be right back."

The boy crutched his way up the rainy street to the red-painted brothel door and spoke briefly with the one-legged beggar stationed there. The man glared at him for a moment, then his leg miraculously unfolded out from under his rough smock and he stalked off, carrying his crutch and muttering to himself. Talen came back down the street and led Sparhawk to the door of the brothel. "Just lean against the wall and hold the bowl out when anybody comes by. Don't hold it right in front of them, though. You're not supposed to be able to see them, so sort of stick it off to one side."

A prosperous-looking merchant came by with his head down and his dark cloak wrapped tightly about him. Sparhawk thrust out his bowl. "Charity," he said in a pleading tone of voice.

The merchant ignored him.

"Not too bad," Talen said. "Try to put that little catch I mentioned in your voice, though."

"Is that why he didn't put anything in the bowl?"

"No. Merchants never do."

"Oh."

Several workmen dressed in leather smocks came along the street. They were talking loudly and were a bit unsteady on their feet.

"Charity," Sparhawk said to them.

Talen sniffled, wiping his nose on his sleeve. "Please, good masters," he said in a choked voice. "Can you help my poor blind father and me?"

"Why not?" one of the workmen said good-humoredly. He fished around in one of his pockets, drew out a few coins, and looked at them. Then he selected one small copper and dropped it into Sparhawk's bowl.

One of the others sniggered. "He's trying to get enough together to go in and visit the girls," he said.

"That's his business, isn't it?" the generous one replied as they went on down the street.

"First blood," Talen said. "Put the copper in your pocket. We don't want the bowl to have *too* many coins in it."

In the next hour, Sparhawk and his youthful instructor picked up about a dozen more coins. It became challenging after the first few times, and Sparhawk felt a small surge of triumph each time he managed to wheedle a coin out of a passerby.

Then an ornate carriage drawn by a matched pair of black horses came up the street and stopped in front of the red door. A liveried young footman jumped down from the back, lowered a step from the side of the vehicle, and opened the door. A nobleman dressed all in green velvet stepped out. Sparhawk knew him.

"I may be a while, love," the nobleman said, fondly touching the footman's boyish face. "Take the carriage up the street and watch for me." He giggled girlishly. "Someone might recognize it, and I certainly wouldn't want people to think I was frequenting a place like *this*." He rolled his eyes and then minced toward the red door.

"Charity for the blind," Sparhawk begged, thrusting out his bowl.

"Out of my way, knave," the nobleman said, fluttering one hand as if shooing away a bothersome fly. He opened the door and went inside as the carriage moved off.

"Peculiar," Sparhawk murmured.

"Wasn't he, though?" Talen grinned.

"Now that's a sight I thought I'd never see—the Baron Harparin going into a brothel."

"Noblemen get urges, too, don't they?"

"Harparin gets urges, all right, but I don't think the girls inside would satisfy them. He might find *you* interesting, though."

Talen flushed. "Never mind *that*," he said.

Sparhawk frowned. "Why would Harparin go into the same brothel where Krager's staying?" he mused.

"Do they know each other?"

"I wouldn't think so. Harparin's a member of the council and a close friend of the Primate Annias. Krager's a third-rate toad. If they're meeting in there, I'd give a great deal to hear what they're saying."

"Go on in, then."

"What?"

"It's a public place, and blind men need affection, too. Just don't start any fights." Talen looked around cautiously. "Once you get inside, ask for Naween. She works for Platime on the side. Tell her that he sent you. She'll get you to someplace where you can eavesdrop."

"Does Platime control the whole city?"

"Only the underside of it. Annias runs the top half."

"Are you going in with me?"

Talen shook his head. "Shanda's got a twisted sense of morality. She doesn't allow children inside—not male ones, anyway."

"Shanda?"

"The madame of this place."

"I probably should have guessed. Krager's mistress is named Shanda—Thin woman?"

Talen nodded. "With a very sour mouth?"

"That's her."

"Does she know you?"

"We met once about twelve years ago."

"The bandage hides most of your face, and the light inside isn't too good. You should be able to get by if you change your voice a bit. Go on in. I'll stay out here and keep watch. I know every policeman and spy in Cimmura by sight."

"All right."

"Have you got the price for a girl? I can lend you some if you need it. Shanda won't let you see any of her whores unless you pay her first."

"I can manage it—unless you've picked my pocket again."

"Would I do that, my Lord?"

"Probably, yes. I might be in there for a while."

"Enjoy yourself. Naween's very frisky—or so I've been told."

Sparhawk ignored that. He opened the red-painted door and went inside.

The hallway he entered was dim and filled with the cloyingly sweet scent of cheap perfume. Maintaining his pose as a blind man, Sparhawk swung his stick from side to side, tapping the walls. "Hello," he called in a squeaky voice. "Is anybody here?"

The door at the far end of the hall opened, and a thin woman in a yellow velvet dress emerged. She had limp, dirty-blonde hair, a disapproving expression, and eyes as hard as agates. "What do you want?" she demanded. "You can't beg in here."

"I'm not here to beg," Sparhawk replied. "I'm here to buy—or at least rent."

"Have you got money?"

"Yes."

"Let's see it."

Sparhawk reached inside his ragged cloak and took several coins out of a pocket. He held them out on the palm of his hand.

The thin woman's eyes narrowed shrewdly.

"Don't even think about it," he told her.

"You're not blind," she accused him.

"You noticed."

"What's your pleasure, then?" she asked.

"A friend told me to ask for Naween."

"Ah, Naween. She's been very popular lately. I'll send for her—just as soon as you pay."

"How much?"

"Ten coppers—or a silver half crown."

Sparhawk gave her a small silver coin, and she went back through the door. She came back a moment later with a buxom brunette girl of about twenty. "This is Naween," Shanda said. "I hope you enjoy yourselves." She simpered briefly at Sparhawk, then the smile seemed to drain off her face. She turned and went back into the room at the end of the hall.

"You're not really blind, are you?" Naween asked coquettishly. She was wrapped in a sleazy-looking dressing gown of bright red, and her cheeks were dimpled.

"No," Sparhawk admitted, "not really."

"Good. I've never done a blind man before, so I wouldn't know what to expect. Let's go upstairs, shall we?" She led him to a stairway that climbed into the upper parts of the house. "Anything in particular that you'd like?" she asked, smiling back over her shoulder at him.

"At the moment, I'd like to listen," he told her.

"Listen? To what?"

"Platime sent me. Shanda's got a friend staying here—a fellow named Krager."

"Mousy-looking little man with bad eyes?"

"That's him. A nobleman dressed in green velvet just came in here, and I think that he and Krager might be talking. I'd like to hear what they're saying. Can you arrange it?" He reached up and took the bandage off his eyes.

"Then you don't really want to. . . ?" She left it hanging, and her generous lower lip took on a slight pout.

"Not today, little sister," he told her. "I've got other things on my mind."

She sighed. "I like your looks, friend," she said. "We could have had a very nice time."

"Some other day, maybe. Can you take me someplace where I can hear what Krager and his friend are saying?"

She sighed again. "I suppose so," she said. "It's on up the stairs. We can use Feather's room. She's visiting her mother."

"Her mother?"

"Whores have mothers, too, you know. Feather's room is right next to the one where Shanda's friend is staying. If you put your ear to the wall, you should be able to hear what's going on."

"Good. Let's go. I don't want to miss anything."

The room near the far end of the upper hallway was small, and its furnishings were sparse. A single candle burned on the table. Naween closed the door, then she removed the dressing gown and lay down on the bed. "Just for the sake of appearances," she whispered archly, "in case someone looks in on us. *Or* in case you change your mind later." She gave him a suggestive little leer.

"Which wall is it?" he asked in a low voice.

"That one." She pointed.

He crossed the room and put the side of his head to the wall's grimy surface.

". . . to my Lord Martel," a familiar voice was saying. "I need something that proves that you're really from Annias and that what you tell me comes from him."

It was Krager. Sparhawk grinned exultantly and continued to listen.

## CHAPTER SEVEN

"The primate said that you might be a little suspicious," Harparin said in his effeminate voice.

"There's a price on my head here in Cimmura, Baron," Krager told him. "Under those circumstances, a certain amount of caution seems to be in order."

"Would you recognize the primate's signature—and his seal—if you saw them?"

"I would," Krager replied.

"Good. Here's a note from him that will identify me. Destroy it after you've read it."

"I don't think so. Martel might want to see the proof with his own eyes." Krager paused. "Why didn't Annias just write down his instructions?"

"Be sensible, Krager," Harparin said. "A message can fall into unfriendly hands."

"So can a messenger. Have you ever seen what the Pandions do to people who have information they want?"

"We would assume that you'd take steps to keep yourself from being questioned."

Krager laughed derisively. "Not a chance, Harparin," he said in a slightly slurred voice. "My life isn't all that much, but it's all I've got."

"You're a coward."

"And you're—whatever it is that you are. Let me see that note."

Sparhawk heard paper rustling. "All right," Krager's mushy-sounding voice said. "This is the primate's seal, I'll agree."

"Have you been drinking?"

"Naturally. What else is there to do in Cimmura? Unless you have other entertainments—like some I could name."

"I don't like you very much, Krager."

"I'm not fond of you either, Harparin, but we can both live with that, can't we? Just give me the message and go away. That perfume you're wearing is beginning to turn my stomach."

There was a stiff silence, and then the baron spoke very precisely, as if to a child or a simpleton. "This is what the Primate Annias wants you to say to Martel: Tell him to gather up as many men as he'll need and to dress them all in black armor. They are to carry the banners of the Pandion Knights—any seamstress can counterfeit them for you, and Martel knows what they look like. They are then to ride with great show to the castle of Count Radun, uncle of King Dregos of Arcium. Do you know the place?"

"It's on the road between Darra and Sarrinium, isn't it?"

"Precisely. Count Radun is a pious man and he'll admit the Church Knights without question. Once Martel is inside the walls, his men are to kill the inhabitants. There shouldn't be much resistance, because Radun doesn't maintain a large garrison. He has a wife and a number of unmarried daughters. Annias wants them all repeatedly raped."

Krager laughed. "Adus would do that anyway."

"Good, but tell him not to be self-conscious about it. Radun has several churchmen in his castle. We want them to witness it all. After Adus and the others finish with the women, cut their throats. Radun is to be tortured and then beheaded. Take his head with you when you leave, but leave enough personal jewelry and clothing on the body so that it can be identified. Butcher everybody else in the castle, *except* for the churchmen. After they've witnessed everything, let them go."

"Why?"

"To report the outrage to King Dregos at Larium."

"The idea then is that Dregos will declare war on the Pandions?"

"Not quite, no—although that's possible, too. As soon as the business is finished, dispatch a man on a fast horse to me here in Cimmura to tell me that it's been done."

Krager laughed again. "Only an idiot would carry that kind of message. He'd have a dozen knives in him as soon as he finished talking."

"You *are* suspicious, aren't you, Krager?"

"Better suspicious than dead, and the people Martel will hire are likely all to feel pretty much the same way. You'd better tell me a little more about this scheme, Harparin."

"You don't need to know any more."

"Martel will. He won't be a cat's-paw for anybody."

Harparin muttered an oath. "All right then. The Pandions have been interfering with the primate's activities. This atrocity will give him an excuse to confine them in their motherhouse at Demos again. Then he will personally carry a report of the affair to Chyrellos to lay before the Church Hierocracy and the archprelate himself. They will have no choice but to disband the Pandion Order. The leaders—Vanion, Sparhawk, and the others—will be imprisoned in the dungeons beneath the Basilica of Chyrellos. No man has ever come out of those dungeons alive."

"Martel will like that idea."

"Annias thought that he might. The Styric woman, Sephrenia, will be burned as a witch, of course."

"We'll be well rid of her." There was another pause. "There's more, isn't there?" Krager added.

Harparin did not answer.

"Don't be coy, Harparin," Krager told him. "If *I* can see through all this, you can be sure that Martel will, too. Let's have the rest of it."

"All right." Harparin's voice was sullen. "The Pandions are likely to resist confinement and they'll certainly try to protect their leaders. At that point, the army will move against them. That will give Annias and the royal council an excuse to declare a state of emergency and to suspend certain laws."

"Which laws are those?"

"The ones having to do with the succession to the throne. Elenia will technically be in a state of war, and Ehlana is obviously in no condition to deal with that. She'll abdicate in favor of her cousin, the Prince Regent Lycheas."

"Arissa's bastard—the sniveler?"

"Legitimacy can be bestowed by a decree of the council, and I'd really watch what I say about Lycheas, Krager. Disrespect for the king is high treason and it *can* be made retroactive, you know."

There was an apprehensive silence. "Wait a minute," Krager said then. "I've heard that Ehlana's unconscious—and sealed in some kind of crystal."

"That's no particular problem."

"How can she sign the instrument of abdication?"

Harparin laughed. "There's a monk at the monastery near Lenda. He's been practicing the queen's signature for a month now. He's very good."

"Clever. What happens to her after she abdicates?"

"As soon as Lycheas is crowned king, we'll give her a splendid funeral."

"But she's still alive, isn't she?"

"So? If need be, we'll entomb her throne and all."

"There's only one problem then, isn't there?"

"I don't see any problem."

"That's because you're not looking, Harparin. The primate is going to have to move very fast. If the Pandions find out about this before he can get to the Hierocracy in Chyrellos, they'll take steps to counter his accusations."

"We're aware of that. That's why you have to send the message to me as soon as the count and his people are dead."

"The message would never reach you. Any man we send will realize that he'll be killed as soon as he delivers it—and he'll find an excuse to go to Lamorkand or Pelosia instead." Krager paused. "Let me see that ring of yours," he said.

"My ring? Why?"

"It's a signet, isn't it?"

"Yes—with the coat of arms of my family."

"All noblemen have rings like that, don't they?"

"Of course."

"Good. Tell Annias to pay close attention to the collection plate in the cathedral of Cimmura here. One of these days a ring will show up among the pennies. The ring will bear the coat of arms of Count Radun's family. He'll understand the message, and the messenger can slip away unharmed."

"I don't think Annias will like that."

"He doesn't have to like it. All right, how much?"

"How much what?"

"Money. What is Annias willing to pay Martel for his assistance? He's getting the crown for Lycheas and absolute control of Elenia for himself. What's it worth to him?"

"He told me to mention the sum of ten thousand gold crowns."

Krager laughed. "I think Martel might want to negotiate that point just a bit."

"Time is important here, Krager."

"Then Annias probably won't be too stubborn about the price, will he? Why don't you go back to the palace and suggest to him that a bit more generosity might be in order? I could wind up spending the whole winter riding back and forth between Annias and Martel carrying proposals and counterproposals."

"There's only so much money in the treasury, Krager."

"Simplicity in itself, my dear Baron. Just increase taxes—or have Annias dip into church funds."

"Where is Martel now?"

"I'm not at liberty to say."

Sparhawk swore under his breath and took his ear away from the wall.

"Was it interesting?" Naween asked. She still lounged on the bed.

"Very."

She stretched voluptuously. "Are you sure that you won't change your mind?" she asked. "Now that you've taken care of your business?"

"Sorry, little sister," Sparhawk declined. "I've got a great deal left to do today. Besides, I've already paid Shanda your price. Why work if you don't have to?"

"Professional ethics, I suppose. Besides, I sort of like you, my big broken-nosed friend."

"I'm flattered." He reached into his pocket, took out a gold coin, and gave it to her. She stared at him in amazed gratitude. "I'll slip out the front door before Krager's friend gets ready to leave," he told her. He went to the door.

"Come back sometime when your mind's not so occupied," she whispered.

"I'll think about it," he promised. He tied the bandage over his eyes again, opened the door, and stepped quietly into the hall. Then he went on down into the dimly lit lower hall and back out to the street.

Talen was leaning against the wall beside the door, trying to stay out of the rain. "Did you have fun?" he asked.

"I found out what I needed to know."

"That's not what I meant. Naween's supposed to be the best in Cimmura."

"I really wouldn't know about that. I was there on business."

"I'm disappointed in you, Sparhawk." Talen grinned impudently, "But probably not nearly so much as Naween was. They say that she's a girl who likes her work."

"You've got a nasty mind, Talen."

"I know, and you've got no idea how much I enjoy it." His young face grew serious, and he looked around cautiously. "Sparhawk," he said, "is somebody following you?"

"It's possible, I suppose."

"I'm not talking about a church soldier. There was a man at the far end of the street—at least I think it was a man. He was wearing a monk's habit, and the hood covered his face, so I couldn't be sure."

"There are a lot of monks in Cimmura."

"Not like this one. It made me cold all over just to look at him."

Sparhawk looked at him sharply. "Have you ever had this kind of feeling before, Talen?"

"Once. Platime had sent me to the west gate to meet somebody. Some Styrics were coming into the city, and after they passed, I couldn't even keep my mind on what I was supposed to be doing. It was two days before I could shake off the feeling."

There was not really any point in telling the boy the truth about the matter. Many people were sensitives, and it seldom went any further. "I wouldn't worry about it," Sparhawk advised. "We all get these peculiar feelings now and then."

"Maybe," Talen said dubiously.

"We're finished here," Sparhawk said. "Let's go back to Platime's place."

The rainy streets of Cimmura were a bit more crowded now, filled with nobles wearing brightly colored cloaks and with workmen dressed in plain brown or gray. Sparhawk was obliged to grope his way along, swinging his blindman's stick in front of him to avoid suspicion. It was noon by the time he and Talen descended the steps into the cellar again.

"Why didn't you wake me up?" Kalten demanded crossly. He was sitting on the edge of his cot holding a bowl of thick stew.

"You needed your rest." Sparhawk untied the bandage from his eyes. "Besides, it's raining out there."

"Did you see Krager?"

"No, but I heard him, which is just as good." Sparhawk went on around the firepit to where Platime sat. "Can you get me a wagon and a driver?" he asked.

"If you need one." Platime lifted his silver tankard and drank noisily, spilling beer on the front of his spotted orange doublet.

"I do," Sparhawk said. "Kalten and I have to get back to the chapterhouse. The primate's soldiers are probably still looking for us, so I thought that we could hide in the back of a wagon to stay out of sight."

"Wagons don't move very fast. Wouldn't a carriage with the curtains drawn be faster?"

"Do you have a carriage?"

"Several, actually. God's been good to me lately."

"I'm delighted to hear it." Sparhawk turned. "Talen," he called.

The boy came over to where he was standing.

"How much money did you steal from me this morning?"

Talen's face grew cautious. "Not too much. Why?"

"Be more specific."

"Seven coppers and one silver piece. You're a friend, so I put the gold coins back in your pocket."

"I'm touched."

"You want the money back, I suppose."

"Keep it—as payment for your services."

"You're generous, my Lord."

"I'm not finished yet. I want you to keep an eye on Krager for me. I think I'm going to be out of town for a while and I want to keep track of him. If he leaves Cimmura, go to the inn on Rose Street. Do you know it?"

"The one that's run by the Pandions?"

"How did you find out about that?"

"Everybody knows about it."

Sparhawk let that pass. "Knock on the gate three times, then pause. Then knock twice more. A porter will open the gate. Be polite to him because he's a knight. Tell him that the man Sparhawk was interested in has left town. Try to give him the direction Krager took. Can you remember all that?"

"Do you want me to recite it back to you?"

"That won't be necessary. The knight porter at the inn will give you half a crown for the information."

Talen's eyes brightened.

Sparhawk turned back to Platime. "Thank you, my friend," he said. "Consider your debt to my father paid."

"I've already forgotten it." The fat man grinned.

"Platime's very good at forgetting debts," Talen said. "The ones he owes, anyway."

"Someday your mouth is going to get you in serious trouble, boy."

"Nothing that my feet can't carry me away from."

"Go tell Sef to hitch the gray team to the carriage with the blue wheels and to bring it to the alley door."

"What's in it for me?"

"I'll postpone the thrashing I'm just about to give you."

"That sounds fair." The boy grinned and scampered away.

"That's a very clever young man," Sparhawk said.

"He's the best," Platime agreed. "It's my guess that he'll replace me when I retire."

"He's the crown prince, then."

Platime laughed uproariously. "The crown prince of thieves. It has a nice ring to it, doesn't it? You know, I like you, Sparhawk." Still laughing, the fat man clapped the big knight on the shoulder. "If there's ever anything else I can do for you, let me know."

"I will, Platime."

"I'll even give you a special rate."

"Thanks," Sparhawk said drily. He picked up his sword from beside Platime's chair and went back to his cot to change back into his own clothes. "How are you feeling?" he asked Kalten.

"I'm fine."

"Good. You'd better get ready to leave."

"Where are we going?"

"Back to the chapterhouse. I found out something that Vanion needs to know."

The carriage was not new, but it was soundly constructed and well maintained. The windows were draped with heavy curtains which effectively hid the passengers from prying eyes. The team which drew the carriage was a pair of matched grays, and they moved out at a brisk trot.

Kalten leaned back against the leather cushion. "Is it my imagination, or does thieving pay better than knighting?"

"We didn't go into the business for the money, Kalten," Sparhawk reminded him.

"That's painfully obvious, my friend." Kalten stretched out his legs and crossed his arms contentedly. "You know," he said, "I could get to like this sort of thing."

"Try not to," Sparhawk advised him.

"You have to admit that it's a great deal more comfortable than pounding your backside on a hard saddle."

"Discomfort's good for the soul."

"My soul's just fine, Sparhawk. It's my behind that's starting to wear out."

The carriage moved rapidly through the streets, and they soon passed through the east gate of the city and pulled up at the drawbridge of the chapterhouse. Sparhawk and Kalten stepped out into the drizzly afternoon, and Sef immediately turned the carriage around and clattered back toward the city.

Following the ritual which gained them entrance into the fortified house, Sparhawk and Kalten went immediately to the preceptor's study in the south tower.

Vanion was seated at the large table in the center of the room with a stack of documents in front of him, and Sephrenia sat by the crackling fire with her ever-present teacup in her hand. She was looking into the dancing flames, her eyes a mystery.

Vanion looked up and saw the bloodstains on Kalten's doublet. "What happened?" he asked.

"Our disguises didn't work." Kalten shrugged. "A group of church soldiers waylaid us in an alley. It's not serious."

Sephrenia rose from her chair and came over to them. "Did you have it tended?" she asked.

"Sparhawk put a bandage on it."

"Why don't you let me look at it? Sometimes Sparhawk's bandages are a little rudimentary. Sit down and open your doublet."

Kalten grumbled a bit, but did as he was told.

She untied the bandage and looked at the cut in his side with pursed lips. "Did you clean it at all?" she asked Sparhawk.

"I wiped it down with some wine."

She sighed. "Oh, Sparhawk." She rose, went to the door, and sent one of the young knights outside for the things she would need.

"Sparhawk picked up some information," Kalten told the preceptor.

"What kind of information?" Vanion asked.

"I found Krager," Sparhawk told him, drawing up a chair. "He's staying in a brothel near the west gate."

One of Sephrenia's eyebrows shot up. "What were you doing in a brothel, Sparhawk?"

"It's a long story," he replied, flushing slightly. "Someday I'll tell you all about it. Anyway," he continued, "the Baron Harparin came to the brothel, and—"

"Harparin?" Vanion looked startled. "In a brothel? He had less business there than you did."

"He was there to meet with Krager. I managed to get inside and into the room next to the one where they were meeting." He quickly sketched out the details of the involuted scheme of the Primate Annias.

Vanion's eyes were narrow as Sparhawk finished his report. "Annias is even more ruthless than I'd imagined," he said. "I never thought that he'd stoop to mass murder."

"We're going to stop them, aren't we?" Kalten asked as Sephrenia began to cleanse his wound.

"Of course we are," Vanion replied absently. He stared up at the ceiling, his eyes lost in thought. "I think I see a way to turn this around." He looked at Kalten. "Are you fit to ride?" he asked.

"This is hardly more than a scratch," Kalten assured him as Sephrenia laid a compress over the cut.

"Good. I want you to go to the motherhouse at Demos. Take every man you can get your hands on and start out for Count Radun's castle in Arcium. Stay off the main roads. We don't want Martel to know you're coming. Sparhawk, I want you to lead the knights from here in Cimmura. Join Kalten down there in Arcium someplace."

Sparhawk shook his head. "If we ride out in a body, Annias will know that we're up to something. If he gets suspicious, he could postpone the whole thing and then attack the count's castle some other time when we aren't around."

Vanion frowned. "That's true, isn't it? Maybe you could sneak your men out of Cimmura a few at a time."

"It would take too long that way," Sephrenia told him, winding a clean bandage around Kalten's waist, "and sneaking attracts more attention than riding out openly." She pursed her lips in thought. "Does the order still own that cloister on the road to Cardos?" she asked.

Vanion nodded. "It's in total disrepair, though."

"Wouldn't this be an excellent time to restore it?"

"I don't quite follow you, Sephrenia."

"We need to find some excuse for most of the Pandions here in Cimmura to ride out of town together. If you were to go to the palace and tell the council that you're going to take all your knights and go repair that cloister, Annias would think you're playing right into his hands. Then you could take wagonloads of tools and building materials to make it look genuine and leave town with them. Once you're out of Cimmura, you can change direction with no one the wiser."

"It sounds workable, Vanion," Sparhawk said. "Will you be coming with us?"

"No," Vanion replied. "I'm going to have to ride to Chyrellos and alert a few friendly members of the Church Hierocracy to what Annias has planned."

Sparhawk nodded; then he remembered something. "I'm not entirely positive about this," he said, "but I think there's someone here in Cimmura who's been watching me, and I don't think he's an Elene." He smiled at Sephrenia. "I've been trained to recognize the subtle touch of a Styric mind. Anyway, this watcher seems to be able to pick me out no matter what kind of disguise I wear. I'm almost certain that he's the one who set the church soldiers on Kalten and me, and that means that he has ties to Annias."

"What does he look like?" Sephrenia asked him.

"I can't really say. He wears a hooded robe and keeps his face hidden."

"He can't report to Annias if he's dead," Kalten shrugged. "Lay an ambush for him somewhere on the road to Cardos."

"Isn't that a little direct?" Sephrenia asked disapprovingly, tying the bandage firmly in place.

"I'm a simple man, Sephrenia. Complications confuse me."

"I want to work out a few more details," Vanion said. He looked at Sephrenia. "Kalten and I will be riding together as far as Demos. Do you want to return to the motherhouse?"

"No," she replied. "I'll go with Sparhawk just in case this Styric who's been watching him tries to follow us. I should be able to deal with that without resorting to murder."

"All right, then," Vanion said, rising to his feet. "Sparhawk, you and Kalten go see to the wagons and the building materials. I'll go to the palace and lie a little bit. As soon as I get back, we'll all leave."

"And what would you like to have me do, Vanion?" Sephrenia asked him.

He smiled. "Why don't you have another cup of tea, Sephrenia?"

"Thank you, Vanion. I believe I will."

# CHAPTER EIGHT

The weather had turned cold, and the sullen afternoon sky was spitting pellets of hard-frozen snow. A hundred cloaked and black-armored Pandion Knights rode at a jingling trot through the heavily forested region near the Arcian border with Sparhawk and Sephrenia in the lead. They had been travelling for five days.

Sparhawk glanced up at the sky and reined in the black horse he was riding. The horse reared, pawing at the air with his front hooves. "Oh, stop that," Sparhawk told him irritably.

"He's very enthusiastic, isn't he?" Sephrenia said.

"He's also not very bright. I'll be glad when we catch up with Kalten and I can get Faran back."

"Why are we stopping?"

"It's close to evening, and that grove over there seems to be fairly clear of undergrowth. We may as well set up our night's encampment here." He raised his voice then, calling back over his shoulder. "Sir Parasim," he shouted.

The young knight with the butter-colored hair rode forward. "Yes, my Lord Sparhawk?" he said in his light tenor voice.

"We'll stop for the night here," Sparhawk told him. "As soon as the wagons get here, set up Sephrenia's tent for her and see to it that she has everything she needs."

"Of course, my Lord."

The sky had turned a chill purple by the time Sparhawk had overseen the setting up of their encampment and had posted sentries. He walked past the tents and the flickering cook fires to join Sephrenia at the small fire before her tent, which was set slightly apart from the rest of the camp. He smiled when he saw her ever-present teakettle hanging from a metal tripod which she had set over the flames.

"Something amusing, Sparhawk?" she asked.

"No," he said. "Not really." He looked back toward the youthful knights moving around their cook fires. "They all seem so young," he said almost as if to himself, "hardly more than boys."

"That's the nature of things, Sparhawk. The old make the decisions, and the young carry them out."

"Was I ever that young?"

She laughed. "Oh yes, dear Sparhawk," she told him. "You couldn't begin to believe how young you and Kalten were when you came to me for your first lessons. I felt as if a pair of babies had been placed in my care."

He made a rueful face. "I guess that answers that question, doesn't it?" He held out his hands to the warmth of her fire. "It's a cold night. I think my blood thinned out while I was in Jiroch. I haven't been really warm since I came back to Elenia. Did Parasim bring you your supper?"

"Yes. He's a very nice boy, isn't he?"

Sparhawk laughed. "He'd probably be offended if he heard you say that."

"It's the truth, isn't it?"

"Of course, but he'd be offended all the same. Young knights are always sensitive."

"Have you ever heard him sing?"

"Once. In chapel."

"He has a glorious voice, doesn't he?"

Sparhawk nodded. "I don't think he really belongs in a militant order. A regular monastery would probably suit his temperament a little better." He looked around, then stepped outside the circle of firelight, dragged a log to the side of the fire, and covered it with his cloak. "It's not exactly an easy chair," he apologized, "but it's better than sitting on the ground."

"Thank you, Sparhawk." She smiled. "That was very thoughtful of you."

"I do have a few manners, I suppose." He looked at her gravely. "This is going to be a hard journey for you, I'm afraid."

"I can endure it, my dear."

"Perhaps, but don't go out of your way to be unnecessarily brave. If you get tired or cold, don't hesitate to say something to me."

"I'll be just fine, Sparhawk. Styrics are a hardy people."

"Sephrenia," he said then, "how long will it be until the twelve knights who were in the throne room with you begin to die?"

"That's really impossible to say, Sparhawk."

"Will you know—each time it happens, I mean?"

"Yes. At the moment, I'm the one to whom their swords will be delivered."

"Their swords?"

"The swords were the instruments of the spell, and they symbolize the burden that must be passed on."

"Wouldn't it have been wiser to have distributed that responsibility?"

"I chose not to."

"That might have been a mistake."

"Perhaps, but it was mine to make."

He began to pace angrily. "We should be working on a cure instead of riding halfway across Arcium," he burst out.

"This is important, too, Sparhawk."

"I couldn't bear to lose you and Ehlana," he said, "and Vanion, too."

"There's still time, dear one."

He sighed. "Are you all settled in, then?" he asked her.

"Yes. I have everything I need."

"Try to get a good night's sleep. We'll be starting early. Good night, Sephrenia."

"Sleep well, Sparhawk."

He awoke as daybreak had begun to spread its light through the wood. He strapped on his armor, shivering at the touch of the cold plate. He emerged from the tent he shared with five other knights and looked around the sleeping camp. Sephrenia's fire was flickering in front of her tent again, and her white robe gleamed in the steely light of dawn and the glow of her fire.

"You're up early," he said as he approached her.

"So are you. How far is it to the border?"

"We should cross into Arcium today."

And then from somewhere out in the forest they heard a strange, flutelike sound. The melody was in a minor key, but it was not sad; rather it seemed filled with an ageless joy.

Sephrenia's eyes grew wide, and she made a peculiar gesture with her right hand.

"A shepherd maybe?" Sparhawk said.

"No," she replied. "Not a shepherd." She stood up. "Come with me, Sparhawk," she said, and then she led him away from the fire.

The sky was growing lighter as they moved out into the meadow lying just to the south of their encampment, following the flutelike sound. They approached the sentry Sparhawk had stationed there.

"You heard it, too, my Lord Sparhawk?" the black-armored knight asked.

"Yes. Can you see who it is or where it's coming from?"

"I can't make out who it is yet, but it seems to be coming from that tree out in the center of the meadow. Do you want me to come along with you?"

"No. Stay here. We'll investigate."

Sephrenia had already gone on ahead, moving directly toward the tree that seemed to be the source of the strange melody.

"You'd better let me go first," Sparhawk said when he caught up with her.

"There's no danger, Sparhawk."

When they reached the tree, Sparhawk peered up through the shadowy limbs and saw the mysterious musician. It was a little girl of six or so. Her long hair was black and glossy, and her large eyes were as deep as night. A headband of plaited grass encircled her brow, holding her hair back. She was sitting on a limb breathing sound into a simple, many-chambered set of pipes such as a goatherd might play.

Although it was quite cold, she wore only a short, belted linen smock that left her arms and legs bare. Her grass-stained, unshod feet were crossed, and she perched on the limb with a sedate sureness.

"What's she doing here?" Sparhawk asked, puzzled. "There aren't any houses or villages around."

"I think she's been waiting for us," Sephrenia replied.

"That doesn't make any sense." He looked up at the child. "What's your name, little girl?" he asked.

"Let me question her, Sparhawk," Sephrenia said. "She's a Styric child, and they tend to be shy." She pushed back her hood and spoke to the little girl in a dialect Sparhawk did not understand.

The child lowered her rude pipe and smiled. Her lips were like a small, pink bow.

Sephrenia asked her another question in a strange, gentle tone.

The little girl shook her head.

"Does she live in some house back in the forest?" Sparhawk asked.

"She has no home nearby," Sephrenia said.

"Doesn't she talk?"

"She chooses not to."

Sparhawk looked around. "Well, we can't leave her here." He reached up his arms to the child. "Come down, little girl," he said.

She smiled at him and slipped off the limb into his hands. Her weight was very slight, and her hair smelled of grass and trees. She confidently put her arms about his neck and then wrinkled her nose at the smell of his armor.

He set her down on her feet, and she immediately went to Sephrenia, took the small woman's hands in hers, and kissed them. Something peculiarly Styric seemed to pass between the woman and the little girl, something that Sparhawk could not understand. Sephrenia lifted the child into her arms and held her close. "What will we do with her, Sparhawk?" she asked in a strangely intent tone. For some reason it seemed very important to her.

"We'll have to take her with us, I guess—at least until we find some people to leave her with. Let's go back to camp and see if we can find something for her to wear."

"And some breakfast, I think."

"Would you like that, Flute?" Sparhawk asked the child.

The little girl smiled and nodded.

"Why did you call her that?" Sephrenia asked him.

"We have to call her something, at least until we find out her real name—if she has one. Let's go back to the fire where it's warm." He turned and led the way back across the meadow toward the camp.

They crossed the border into Arcium near the city of Dieros, once again avoiding contact with the local inhabitants. They paralleled the road leading eastward, staying well back from that heavily travelled highway. The countryside of the kingdom of Arcium was noticeably different from that of Elenia. Unlike its northern neighbor, Arcium seemed to be a kingdom of walls. They stretched along the roads or cut across open pastureland, often for no apparent reason. The walls were thick and high, and Sparhawk was frequently obliged to lead his knights on long detours to go around them. Wryly he remembered the words of a twenty-fourth century patriarch of the Church who, after travelling from Chyrellos to Larium, had referred to Arcium as "God's rock garden."

The following day they entered a large forest of winter-bare birch trees. As they rode deeper into the chill wood, Sparhawk began to smell smoke and he soon saw a dark pall lying low among the stark white tree trunks. He halted the column and rode on ahead to investigate.

He had gone perhaps a mile when he came to a cluster of rudely built Styric houses. They were all on fire, and bodies littered the open area around the houses. Sparhawk began to swear. He wheeled the young black horse and galloped back to where he had left his troops.

"What is it?" Sephrenia asked him, looking at his bleak expression. "Where's the smoke coming from?"

"There was a Styric village up ahead," he replied darkly. "We both know what the smoke means."

"Ah." She sighed.

"You'd better keep the little girl back here until I can get a burial detail up there."

"No, Sparhawk. This sort of thing is a part of her heritage, too. All Styrics know that it happens. Besides, I might be able to help the survivors—if there are any."

"Have it your own way," he said shortly. A huge rage had descended upon him, and he curtly motioned the column forward.

There was some evidence that the hapless Styrics had made an attempt to defend themselves, but that they had been swarmed under by people carrying only the crudest of weapons. Sparhawk put his men to work—some of them digging graves and others extinguishing the fires.

Sephrenia came across the littered field, her face deathly pale. "There are only a few women among the dead," she reported. "I'd guess that the rest fled back into the woods."

"See if you can persuade them to come back," he said. He looked over at Sir Parasim, who was weeping openly as he spaded dirt out of a grave. The young knight was obviously not emotionally suited for this kind of work. "Parasim," Sparhawk ordered, "go with Sephrenia."

"Yes, my Lord," Parasim sobbed, dropping his spade.

The dead were finally all committed to the earth, and Sparhawk briefly murmured an Elene prayer over the graves. It was probably not appropriate for Styrics, but he didn't really know what else to do.

After about an hour, Sephrenia and Parasim returned. "Any luck?" Sparhawk asked her.

"We found them," she replied, "but they won't come out of the woods."

"I can't really blame them very much," he said. "We'll see if we can fix up at least a few of these houses for them to keep them out of the weather."

"Don't waste your time, Sparhawk. They won't come back to this place. That's a part of the Styric religion."

"Did they give you some idea of which way the Elenes who did this went?"

"What are you planning, Sparhawk?"

"Chastisement. That's a part of the Elene religion."

"No. I won't tell you which way they went, if that's what you've got in mind."

"I'm not going to let this pass, Sephrenia. You can tell me or not, whichever you choose. I can find their trail by myself if I need to."

She looked at him helplessly. Then her eyes became shrewd. "A bargain, Sparhawk?" she suggested.

"I'll listen."

"I'll tell you where to find them if you promise not to kill anybody."

"All right," he agreed grudgingly, his face still black with anger. "Which way did they go?"

"I'm not done yet," she said. "You'll stay here with me. I know you, and you sometimes go to extremes. Send someone else to do it."

He glared at her, then turned. "Lakus!" he bellowed.

"No," she said, "not Lakus. He's as bad as you are."

"Who, then?"

"Parasim, I think."

"Parasim?"

"He's a gentler person. If we tell him not to kill anybody, he won't make any mistakes."

"All right, then," he said from between clenched teeth. "Parasim," he said to the young knight standing sorrowfully nearby, "take a dozen men and run down the animals who did this. Don't kill anybody, but make them all very, very sorry that they ever came up with the idea."

"Yes, my Lord," Parasim said, his eyes suddenly glinting like steel. Sephrenia gave him directions, and he started back to where the other knights were gathered. On his way, he stopped and uprooted a thorn bush. He seized it in one gauntleted fist and swung it very hard at an unoffending birch tree, ripping off a fair-sized chunk of white bark.

"Oh, dear," Sephrenia murmured.

"He'll do just fine." Sparhawk laughed mirthlessly. "I have great hopes for that young man and great faith in his sense of the appropriate."

Some distance away, Flute was standing over the scattered graves. She was playing her pipes softly, and her melody seemed to convey eons of sorrow.

The weather continued cold and unpleasant, though no significant amounts of snow fell. After a week of steady travel, they reached a ruined castle some six or eight leagues west of the city of Darra. Kalten and the main body of the Pandion Knights awaited them there.

"I thought you'd got lost," the blond man said as he reined up in front of Sparhawk. He looked curiously at Flute, who sat in front of Sparhawk's saddle, her bare feet both on one side of the black horse's neck and with Sparhawk's cloak wrapped around her. "Isn't it a little late for you to be starting a family?"

"We found her along the way," Sparhawk replied. He took the little girl and handed her across to Sephrenia.

"Why didn't you put some shoes on her?"

"We did. She keeps losing them. There's a nunnery on the other side of Darra. We'll drop her off there." Sparhawk looked at the ruin crouched on the hill above them. "Is there any kind of shelter in there?"

"Some. It breaks the wind, at least."

"Let's get inside, then. Did Kurik bring Faran and my armor?"

Kalten nodded.

"Good. This horse is a little unruly, and Vanion's old armor has rubbed me raw in more places than I care to count."

They rode up into the ruin and found Kurik and the young novice, Berit, waiting for them. "What took you so long?" Kurik asked bluntly.

"It's a long way, Kurik," Sparhawk replied a bit defensively, "and the wagons can only move so fast."

"You should have left them behind."

"They were carrying the food and extra equipment."

Kurik grunted. "Let's get in out of the weather. I've got a fire going in what's left of that watchtower over there." He looked rather peculiarly at Sephrenia, who carried Flute in her arms. "Lady," he greeted her respectfully.

"Dear Kurik," she said warmly. "How are Aslade and the boys?"

"They're well, Sephrenia," he replied. "Very well indeed."

"I'm so glad to hear it."

"Kalten said you'd be coming along," he said to her. "I have water boiling for your tea." He looked at Flute, who had her face nestled against Sephrenia's. "Have you been keeping secrets from us?"

She laughed, a rippling cascade of a laugh. "That's what Styrics do best, Kurik."

"Let's get you all inside where it's warm." He turned and led the way across the rubble-strewn courtyard of the ruin, leaving Berit to care for the horses.

"Was it a good idea to bring him along?" Sparhawk asked, jerking his thumb back over his shoulder in the direction of the novice. "He's a little young for an all-out battle."

"He'll be all right, Sparhawk," Kurik said. "I took him to the practice field at Demos a few times and gave him some instruction. He handles himself well and he learns fast."

"All right, Kurik," Sparhawk said, "but when the fighting starts, stay close to him. I don't want him getting hurt."

"I never let *you* get hurt, did I?"

Sparhawk grinned at his friend. "No. As I recall, you didn't."

They stayed the night in the ruin and rode out early the following morning. Their combined forces numbered just over five hundred men, and they rode south under a still-threatening sky. Just beyond Darra stood a nunnery with yellow sandstone walls and a red tile roof. Sparhawk and Sephrenia turned aside from the road and crossed a winter-browned meadow toward the building.

"And what is the child's name?" the black-robed mother superior asked when they were admitted into her presence in a severely simple room with only a small brazier to warm it.

"She doesn't talk, Mother," Sparhawk replied. "She plays those pipes all the time, so we call her Flute."

"That is an unseemly name, my son."

"The child doesn't mind, Mother Superior," Sephrenia told her.

"Did you make some effort to find her parents?"

"There was no one in the vicinity when we found her," Sparhawk explained.

The mother superior looked gravely at Sephrenia. "The child is Styric," she pointed out. "Would it not perhaps be better to put her with a family of her own race and her own faith?"

"We have pressing business," Sephrenia said, "and Styrics can be very difficult to find when they choose to be."

"You know, of course, that if she stays with us, we will raise her in the Elene faith."

Sephrenia smiled. "You will *try*, Mother Superior. I think you will find that she's not amenable to conversion, however. Coming, Sparhawk?"

They rejoined the column and rode south under clearing skies, moving first at a rolling trot and then at a thunderous gallop. They crossed a knoll, and Sparhawk reined Faran in sharply, staring in astonishment at Flute, who sat cross-legged on a large white rock playing her pipes. "How did you—" he began, then broke off. "Sephrenia," he called, but the white-robed woman had already dismounted. She approached the child, speaking gently to her in that strange Styric dialect.

Flute lowered her pipes and gave Sparhawk an impish little grin. Sephrenia laughed and took the child in her arms.

"How did she get ahead of us?" Kalten asked, his face baffled.

"Who knows?" Sparhawk replied. "I guess I'd better take her back."

"No, Sparhawk," Sephrenia said firmly. "She wants to go with us."

"That's too bad," he said bluntly. "I'm not going to take a little girl into battle."

"Don't concern yourself with her, Sparhawk. I'll care for her." She smiled at the child nestled in her arms. "I'll care for her as if she were my own." She laid her cheek against Flute's glossy black hair. "In a way, she is."

He gave up. "Have it your own way," he said. Just as he began to wheel Faran around, he felt a sudden chill accompanied by the sense of an implacable hatred. "Sephrenia!" he said sharply.

"I felt it, too!" she cried, drawing the little girl closer to her. "It's directed at the child!"

Flute struggled briefly, and Sephrenia, looking surprised, set her down. The little girl's face was set, looking more annoyed than angered or frightened. She set her pipes to her lips and began to play. The melody this time was not that light air in a minor key which she had played before. It was sterner and peculiarly ominous.

Then from some distance away they heard a sudden howl of pain and surprise. The howl immediately began to fade, as if whoever or whatever had made it were fleeing at an unimaginable rate.

"What was that?" Kalten exclaimed.

"An unfriendly spirit," Sephrenia replied calmly.

"What drove it away?"

"The child's song. It seems that she has learned to protect herself."

"Do you understand any of what's going on here?" Kalten asked Sparhawk.

"No more than you do. Let's keep moving. We've still got a couple of days hard riding ahead of us."

The castle of Count Radun, the uncle of King Dregos, was perched atop a high, rocky promontory. Like so many of the castles in this southern kingdom, it was surrounded by massive walls. The weather had cleared off, and the noonday sun was very bright as Sparhawk, Kalten, and Sephrenia, who still carried Flute in front of her saddle, rode across a broad meadow of yellow grass toward the fortress.

They were admitted without question; in the courtyard they were met by the count, a blocky man with heavy shoulders and silver-shot hair. He wore a dark green doublet trimmed in black and surmounted by a heavily starched white ruff of a collar. It was a style which had gone out of fashion in Elenia decades ago. "My house is honored to welcome the Knights of the Church," he declared formally after they had introduced themselves.

Sparhawk swung down off Faran's back. "Your hospitality is legendary, my Lord," he said, "but our visit is not entirely social. Is there someplace private where we can talk? We have a matter of some urgency to discuss with you."

"Of course," the count replied. "If you will all be so good as to come with me." They followed him through the broad doors of his castle and along a candlelit corridor strewn with rushes. At the end of the corridor, the count produced a brass key and unlocked a door. "My private study," he said modestly. "I'm rather proud of my collection of books. I have almost two dozen."

"Formidable," Sephrenia murmured.

"Perhaps you might care to read some of them, madame?"

"The lady doesn't read," Sparhawk told him. "She's a Styric and an initiate in the secrets. She feels that reading might somehow interfere with her abilities."

"A witch?" the count said, looking at the small woman. "Truly?"

"We prefer to use other terms, my Lord," she replied mildly.

"Please, sit down," the count said, pointing at a large table standing in a chill patch of wintery sunlight coming through a heavily barred window. "I'm curious to hear about this urgent matter."

Sparhawk removed his helmet and gauntlets and laid them on the table. "Are you familiar with the name of Annias, primate of Cimmura, my Lord?"

The count's face hardened. "I've heard of him," he said shortly.

"You know his reputation then?"

"I do."

"Good. Quite by accident, Sir Kalten and I unearthed a plot hatched by the primate. Fortunately, he isn't aware of the fact that we know about it. Is it your common practice so freely to admit Church Knights?"

"Of course. I revere the Church and honor her knights."

"Within a few days—a week at most—a sizable group of men in black armor and bearing the standards of Pandion Knights will ride up to your gates. I strongly advise you not to admit them."

"But—"

Sparhawk held up one hand. "They will *not* be Pandions, my Lord. They're mercenaries under the command of a renegade named Martel. If you let them in, they will kill everyone within your walls—excepting only a churchman or two who will spread word of the outrage."

"Monstrous!" the count gasped. "What reason could the primate of Cimmura have to bear me such hatred?"

"The plot isn't directed at you, Count Radun," Kalten told him. "Your murder is designed to discredit the Pandion Knights. Annias hopes that the Hierocracy of the Church will be so infuriated that they'll disband the order."

"I must send word to Larium at once," the count declared, coming to his feet. "My nephew can have an army here in a few days."

"That won't be necessary, my Lord," Sparhawk said. "I have five hundred fully armed Pandions—real ones—concealed in the woods just to the north of your castle. With your permission, I'll bring a hundred of them inside your walls to reinforce your garrison. When the mercenaries arrive, find some excuse not to admit them."

"Won't that seem strange?" Radun asked. "I have a reputation for hospitality—for the Knights of the Church in particular."

"The drawbridge," Kalten said.

"I beg your pardon?"

"Tell them that the windlass that operates your drawbridge is broken. Then tell them that you have men working on it and ask them to be patient."

"I will not lie," the count said stiffly.

"That's all right, my Lord," Kalten assured him. "I'll break the windlass for you myself, so you won't really be lying."

The count stared at him for a moment, then burst out laughing.

"The mercenaries will be outside the castle," Sparhawk went on, "and your walls will give them very little room for maneuvering. That's when we'll attack them from behind."

Kalten grinned broadly. "It should be almost like a cheese grater when we start to grind them up against your walls."

"And I can drop some interesting things on them from my battlements as well," the count added, also grinning. "Arrows, large rocks, burning pitch—that sort of thing."

"We're going to get on splendidly, my Lord," Kalten told him.

"I will, of course, make arrangements to lodge this lady and the little girl here in safety," the count said.

"No, my Lord," Sephrenia disagreed. "I will accompany Sir Sparhawk and Sir Kalten back to our hiding place. This Martel Sparhawk mentioned is a former Pandion and he has delved deeply into secret knowledge that is forbidden to honest men. It may be necessary to counter him, and I'm best equipped to do that."

"But surely the child—"

"The child must stay with me," Sephrenia said firmly. She looked over at Flute, who was in the act of curiously opening a book. "No!" she said, probably more sharply than she had intended. She rose and took the book away from the little girl.

Flute sighed, and Sephrenia spoke briefly to her in that dialect Sparhawk did not understand.

Since there was no way to know when Martel's mercenaries might arrive, the Pandions built no fires that night, and when the next morning dawned clear and cold, Sparhawk unrolled himself from his blankets and looked with some distaste at his armor, knowing that it would take at least an hour for the heat of his body to take the clammy chill out of it. He decided that he was not ready to face that just yet, so he belted on his sword, pulled his stout cloak around his shoulders, and walked down through the sleeping camp toward a small brook that trickled through the woods where he and his knights lay hidden.

He knelt beside the brook and drank from his cupped hands, then braced himself and splashed icy water on his face. Then he rose, dried his face with the hem of his cloak, and stepped across the brook. The just-risen sun streamed golden into the leafless wood, slanting between the dark trunks and touching fire into the dewdrops collected like strings of beads along the stems of the grass about his feet. Sparhawk walked on through the woods.

He had gone perhaps half a mile when he saw a grassy meadow through the trees. As he approached the meadow, he heard the thudding of hooves. Somewhere ahead, a single horse was loping across the turf at a canter. And then he heard the sound of Flute's pipes rising in the morning air.

He pushed his way to the edge of the meadow, parted the bushes, and peered out.

Faran, his roan coat glistening in the morning sun, cantered easily in a wide circular course around the meadow. He wore no saddle nor bridle, and there was something almost joyful about his stride. Flute lay faceup on his back with her pipes at her lips. Her head was nestled comfortably on his surging front shoulders, her knees were crossed, and she was beating time on Faran's rump with one little foot.

Sparhawk gaped at them, then stepped out into the meadow to stand directly in the big roan's path. He spread his arms wide, and Faran slowed to a walk and then stopped in front of his master.

"What do you think you're doing?" Sparhawk barked at him.

Faran's expression grew lofty and he looked away.

"Have you completely taken leave of your senses?"

Faran snorted and flicked his tail even as Flute continued to play her song. Then the little girl slapped her grass-stained foot imperiously on his rump several times, and he neatly sidestepped the fuming Sparhawk and cantered on with Flute's song soaring above him.

Sparhawk swore and ran after them. After a few yards, he knew it was hopeless and he stopped, breathing hard.

"Interesting, wouldn't you say?" Sephrenia said. She had come out from among the trees and stood at the edge of the meadow with her white robe gleaming in the morning sun.

"Can you make them stop?" Sparhawk asked her. "She's going to fall off and get hurt."

"No, Sparhawk," Sephrenia disagreed, "she will not fall." She said it in that strange manner into which she sometimes lapsed. Despite the decades she had spent in Elene society, Sephrenia remained a Styric to her fingertips, and Styrics had always been an enigma to Elenes. The centuries of close association between the militant orders of the Elene Church and their Styric tutors, however, had taught the Church Knights to accept the words of their instructors without question.

"If you're sure," Sparhawk said a bit dubiously as he looked across the turf at Faran, who seemed somehow to have lost his normally vicious temperament.

"Yes, dear one," she said, laying an affectionate hand on his arm in reassurance. "I'm absolutely sure." She looked out at the great horse and his tiny passenger joyously circling the dew-drenched meadow in the golden morning sunlight. "Let them play a while longer," she advised.

About midmorning Kalten returned from the vantage point to the south of the castle where he and Kurik had been keeping watch over the road coming up from Sarrinium. "Nothing yet," he reported as he dismounted, his armor clinking. "Do you think Martel might just try to come across country and avoid the roads?"

"It's not very likely," Sparhawk replied. "He *wants* to be seen, remember? He needs lots of witnesses."

"I suppose I hadn't thought of that," Kalten admitted. "Have you got the road coming down from Darra covered?"

Sparhawk nodded. "Lakus and Berit are watching it."

"Berit?" Kalten sounded surprised. "The apprentice? Isn't he a little young?"

"He'll get over it. He's steady and he's got good sense. Besides, Lakus can keep him out of trouble."

"You're probably right. Is there any of that roast ox the count sent us left?"

"Help yourself. It isn't hot, though."

Kalten shrugged. "Better cold meat than no meat."

The day dragged on, as days spent only in waiting will do; by evening, Sparhawk was pacing the camp with his impatience gnawing at him. Finally Sephrenia emerged from the rough little tent she shared with Flute. She placed herself directly in front of the big knight in black armor with her hands on her hips. "*Will* you stop that?" she demanded crossly.

"Stop what?"

"Pacing. You jingle at every step, and the noise is very distracting."

"I'm sorry. I'll go jingle on the other side of camp."

"Why not just go sit down?"

"Nerves, I guess."

"Nerves? You?"

"I get twinges now and then."

"Well, go twinge someplace else."

"Yes, little mother," he replied obediently.

It was cold again the following morning. Kurik rode quietly into camp just before sunrise. He carefully picked his way past the sleeping knights wrapped in their black cloaks to the place where Sparhawk had spread his blankets. "You'd better get up," he said, lightly touching Sparhawk's shoulder. "They're coming."

Sparhawk sat up quickly. "How many?" he asked, throwing off his blankets.

"I make it about two hundred and fifty."

Sparhawk stood up. "Where's Kalten?" he asked as Kurik began to buckle the black armor over his lord's padded tunic.

"He wanted to make sure that there wouldn't be any surprises, so he joined the end of their column."

"He did *what?*"

"Don't worry, Sparhawk. They're all wearing black armor, so he blends right in."

"Do you want to tie this on?" Sparhawk handed his squire the length of bright ribbon that each knight was to wear as a means of identification during a battle in which both sides would be dressed in black.

Kurik took the red ribbon. "Kalten's wearing a blue one," he noted. "It matches his eyes." He tied the ribbon around Sparhawk's upper arm, then stepped back and looked at his lord appraisingly. "Adorable," he said, rolling his eyes.

Sparhawk laughed and clapped his friend on the shoulder. "Let's go wake the children," he said, looking across the encampment of generally youthful knights.

"I've got some bad news for you, Sparhawk," Kurik said as the two of them moved out through the camp, shaking the sleeping Pandions awake.

"What's that?"

"The man leading the column isn't Martel."

Sparhawk felt a hot surge of disappointment. "Who is it?" he asked.

"Adus. He had blood all over his chin. I think he's been eating raw meat again." Sparhawk swore.

"Look at it this way. At least the world's going to be a cleaner place without Adus, and I'd imagine that God would like to have a long talk with him anyway."

"We'll have to see what we can do to arrange that."

Sparhawk's knights were assisting each other into their armor when Kalten rode into camp. "They've pulled up just beyond that hill to the south of the castle," he reported, not bothering to dismount.

"Is Martel possibly lurking around somewhere among them?" Sparhawk asked hopefully.

Kalten shook his head. "I'm afraid not." He stood up in his stirrups, shifting his sword around. "Why don't we just go ahead and attack them?" he suggested. "I'm getting cold."

"I think Count Radun would be disappointed if we didn't let him take part in the fight."

"That's true, I suppose."

"Is there anything unusual about the mercenaries?"

"Run of the mill—except that about half of them are Rendors."

"Rendors?"

"They don't smell very good, do they?"

Sephrenia, accompanied by Parasim and Flute, came up to join them.

"Good morning, Sephrenia," Sparhawk greeted her.

"Why all the bustle?" she asked.

"We have company coming. We thought we'd ride out to greet them."

"Martel?"

"No. I'm afraid it's only Adus—and a few friends." He shifted the helmet he was holding under his left arm. "Since Martel isn't leading them, and since Adus can barely speak Elenic, much less Styric, there isn't anybody out there who could stir up enough magic to knock a fly off the wall. I'm afraid that means that you've made the trip for nothing. I want you to stay back here in the woods, well hidden and out of danger. Sir Parasim will stay with you."

The young knight's face filled with disappointment.

"No, Sparhawk," Sephrenia replied. "I need no guard, and this is Parasim's first battle. We won't deprive him of it."

Parasim's face shone with gratitude.

Kurik came back through the woods from the place where he had been keeping watch. "The sun's coming up," he reported, "and Adus is leading his men over the top of that hill."

"We'd better mount up, then," Sparhawk said.

The Pandions swung up into their saddles and moved cautiously through the wood until they reached the edge of the broad meadow that surrounded the count's castle. Then they waited, watching the black-armored mercenaries riding down the hill in the golden dawn sunlight.

Adus, who normally spoke in grunts and belches, rode up to the gate of Count Radun's castle and read haltingly from a piece of paper which he held in front of him at arm's length.

"Can't he extemporize?" Kalten asked quietly. "He's only asking for permission to enter the castle."

"Martel doesn't take chances," Sparhawk replied, "and Adus usually has trouble remembering his own name."

Adus continued to read his request. He had some trouble with the word *admission,* since it had more than one syllable.

Then Count Radun appeared on the battlements to announce regretfully that the windlass which raised and lowered the drawbridge was broken and to beg them to be patient until it was repaired.

Adus mulled that over. It took him quite a while. The mercenaries dismounted and lounged about on the grass at the foot of the castle wall.

"This is going to be almost too easy," Kalten muttered.

"Let's just make sure that none of them get away," Sparhawk told him. "I don't want anybody riding to Annias with word of what *really* happens today."

"I still think Vanion's trying to be too clever about this."

"Maybe that's why he's the preceptor and we're only knights."

A red banner appeared atop the count's walls.

"There's the signal," Sparhawk said. "Radun's forces are ready." He put on his helmet, gathered his reins, and rose in his stirrups, firmly holding Faran in. Then he raised his voice. "Charge!" he roared.

# CHAPTER NINE

"Any chance at all?" Kalten asked.

"No," Sparhawk replied with deep regret as he lowered Sir Parasim to the ground. "He's gone." He smoothed the young knight's hair with his hand, then gently closed the vacant eyes.

"He wasn't ready to come up against Adus," Kalten said.

"Did that animal get completely away?"

"I'm afraid so. After he cut down Parasim, he rode off to the south with about a dozen other survivors."

"Send some people after him," Sparhawk said bleakly as he straightened the fallen Sir Parasim's limbs. "Tell them to run him into the sea if necessary."

"Do you want me to do it?"

"No. You and I have to go to Chyrellos." He raised his voice then. "Berit," he shouted.

The novice approached at a half run. He was wearing an old mail shirt splashed with blood and a dented foot soldier's helmet with no visor. He carried a grim, long-handled battle-axe.

Sparhawk looked closely at the blood on the rangy youth's mail shirt. "Is any of that yours?" he asked.

"No, my Lord," Berit answered. "All theirs." He looked pointedly at the mercenary dead littering the field.

"Good. What's your feeling about a long ride?"

"As my Lord commands."

"He's got good manners, at least," Kalten observed. "Berit," he said then, "ask 'Where?' before you agree so quickly."

"I'll remember that, my Lord Kalten."

"I want you to come with me," Sparhawk said to the novice. "We need to talk with Count Radun before you leave." He turned to Kalten. "Get a group of men to chase Adus," he said. "Push him hard. I don't want him to have time to send one of his people to Cimmura to report all of this to Annias. Tell the rest of the men to bury our dead and care for the wounded."

"What about these?" Kalten pointed at the dead bodies of the mercenaries heaped in front of the castle walls.

"Burn them."

Count Radun met Sparhawk and Berit in the courtyard of his castle. He was wearing full armor and held his sword in his hand. "I see that the reputation of the Pandions is well deserved," he said.

"Thank you, my Lord," Sparhawk replied. "I have a favor—no, two favors—to ask of you."

"Anything, Sir Sparhawk."

"Are you known to any members of the Hierocracy in Chyrellos?"

"Several, actually, and the patriarch of Larium is a distant cousin of mine."

"Very good. I know it's a bad season for travel, but I'd like for you to join me in a little ride."

"Of course. Where are we going?"

"To Chyrellos. The next favor is a bit more personal. I'll need your signet ring."

"My ring?" The count lifted his hand and looked at the heavy gold ring bearing his coat of arms.

Sparhawk nodded. "And worse yet, I can't guarantee that I'll be able to return it."

"I'm not sure that I understand."

"Berit here is going to take the ring to Cimmura and drop it in the collection plate during services in the cathedral there. The Primate Annias will take that to mean that his scheme has succeeded and that you and your family have all been murdered. He will then rush to Chyrellos to lay charges against the Pandions before the Hierocracy."

Count Radun grinned broadly. "But then you and I will step forward and refute those charges, right?"

Sparhawk grinned back. "Exactly," he said.

"That might cause the primate a certain amount of embarrassment," the count said as he tugged the ring off his finger.

"That was sort of what we had in mind, my Lord."

"The ring is well lost, then," Radun said, handing his signet to Berit.

"All right," Sparhawk said to the young novice. "Don't kill any horses on your way to Cimmura. Give us time to get to Chyrellos before Annias does." He squinted thoughtfully. "Morning service, I think."

"My Lord?"

"Drop the count's ring in the collection plate during morning services. Let's give Annias a whole day to gloat before he starts out for Chyrellos. Wear ordinary clothes when you go into the cathedral and pray a bit—just to make it look convincing. Don't go near the chapterhouse or the inn on Rose Street." He looked at the young novice, feeling a renewed pang at the loss of Sir Parasim. "I can't assure you that your life won't be in danger, Berit," he said soberly, "so I can't order you to do this."

"There's no need to order me to do it, my Lord Sparhawk," Berit replied.

"Good man," Sparhawk said. "Now go get your horse. You've got a long ride ahead of you."

It was nearly noon when Sparhawk and Count Radun emerged from the castle. "How long do you think it's going to take for Primate Annias to reach Chyrellos?" the count asked.

"Two weeks at least. Berit has to get to Cimmura before Annias can even start for Chyrellos."

Kurik came riding up to them. "Everything's ready," he told Sparhawk.

Sparhawk nodded. "You'd better go get Sephrenia," he said.

"Is that really a good idea, Sparhawk? Things might get a little chancy when we get to Chyrellos."

"Do *you* want to be the one to tell her that she has to stay behind?"

Kurik winced. "I see what you mean," he said.

"Where's Kalten?"

"Over there at the edge of the woods. He's building a bonfire for some reason."

"Maybe he's cold."

The winter sun was very bright in the cold blue sky as Sparhawk and his party set out. "Surely, madame," Count Radun objected to Sephrenia, "the child would have been quite safe within the walls of my castle."

"She would not have stayed there, my Lord," Sephrenia replied in a small voice. She laid her cheek against Flute's hair. "Besides," she added, "I take great comfort in having her with me." Her voice sounded weak somehow, and she looked very pale and tired. In one hand she carried Sir Parasim's sword.

Sparhawk pulled Faran in beside her white palfrey. "Are you all right?" he asked her quietly.

"Not really," she answered.

"What's the matter?" He felt a sudden alarm.

"Parasim was one of the twelve knights in the throne room in Cimmura." She sighed. "I've just been obliged to shoulder his burden as well as my own." She gestured slightly with the sword.

"You're not ill, are you?"

"Not in the way that you mean, no. It's just that it's going to take a little while to adjust to the additional weight."

"Is there any way that I could carry it for you?"

"No, dear one."

He drew in a deep breath. "Sephrenia," he said, "is what happened to Parasim today a part of what you told me was going to happen to the twelve knights?"

"There's no way to know, Sparhawk. The compact we made with the Younger Gods was not that specific." She smiled wanly. "If another of the knights dies this moon, though, we'll know that it was merely an accident and had nothing to do with the compact."

"We're going to lose them one every month?"

"Moon," she corrected. "Twenty-eight days. Most probably yes. The Younger Gods tend to be methodical about such things. Don't concern yourself about me, Sparhawk. I'll be all right in a little while."

It was some sixty leagues from the count's castle to the city of Darra, and on the morning of the fourth day of their journey, they crested a hill and looked down upon the red tile roofs and the hundreds of chimneys sending pale blue columns of smoke straight up into the windless air. A black-armored Pandion Knight awaited them on the hilltop. "Sir Sparhawk," the knight said, raising his visor.

"Sir Olven," Sparhawk replied, recognizing the knight's scarred face.

"I have a message for you from Preceptor Vanion. He instructs you to proceed directly to Cimmura with all possible speed."

"Cimmura? Why the change in plans?"

"King Dregos is there, and he's invited Wargun of Thalesia and Obler of Deira to join him. He wants to investigate the illness of Queen Ehlana—and the justification for the appointment of the bastard Lycheas as prince regent. Vanion believes that Annias will level his charges against our order at that council in order to deflect an inquiry that might be embarrassing."

Sparhawk swore. "Berit's a good way ahead of us by now," he said. "Have all the kings gathered in Cimmura yet?"

Olven shook his head. "King Obler is too old to travel very fast, and it's likely to take a week to sober King Wargun up before he can make the voyage from Emsat."

"Let's not gamble on that," Sparhawk said. "We'll cut across country to Demos and then ride directly to Cimmura. Is Vanion still at Chyrellos?"

"No. He came through Demos on his way to Cimmura. The Patriarch Dolmant was with him."

"Dolmant?" Kalten said. "That's a surprise. Who's running the Church?"

"Sir Kalten," Count Radun said stiffly. "The guidance of the Church is in the hands of the archprelate."

"Sorry, my Lord," Kalten apologized. "I know how much Arcians revere the Church, but let's be honest. Archprelate Cluvonus is eighty-five years old and he sleeps a great deal. Dolmant doesn't make an issue of it, but most of the decisions that come out of Chyrellos are his."

"Let's ride," Sparhawk said.

It took them four days of hard travelling to reach Demos, where Sir Olven left them to return to the Pandion motherhouse, and it was three more days before they arrived at the gates of the chapterhouse in Cimmura.

"Do you know where we can find Lord Vanion?" Sparhawk asked the novice who came out into the courtyard to take their horses.

"He's in his study in the south tower, my Lord—with the Patriarch Dolmant."

Sparhawk nodded and led the way inside and up the narrow stairs.

"Thank God you arrived in time," Vanion greeted them.

"Did Berit deliver the count's ring yet?" Sparhawk asked him.

Vanion nodded. "Two days ago. I had men inside the cathedral watching." He frowned slightly. "Was it altogether wise to entrust that kind of mission to a novice, Sparhawk?"

"Berit's a solid young man," Sparhawk explained, "and he isn't widely known here in Cimmura. Most of the full-fledged knights are."

"I see. It was your command, Sparhawk. The decision was yours. How did things go in Arcium?"

"Adus led the mercenaries," Kalten replied. "We didn't see a sign of Martel. Otherwise, things went more or less as planned. Adus got away, though."

Sparhawk drew in a deep breath. "We lost Parasim," he said sadly. "I'm sorry, Vanion. I tried to keep him out of the fight."

Vanion's eyes clouded with sudden grief.

"I know," Sparhawk said, touching the older man's shoulder. "I loved him, too." He saw the quick look that passed between Vanion and Sephrenia. She nodded slightly as if to advise the preceptor that Sparhawk knew that Parasim had been one of the twelve. Then Sparhawk straightened and introduced Count Radun and Vanion to each other.

"I owe you my life, Lord Vanion," Radun said as they shook hands. "Please tell me how I can repay you."

"Your presence here in Cimmura is ample repayment, my Lord."

"Have the other kings joined my nephew as yet?" the count asked.

"Obler has," Vanion replied. "King Wargun is still at sea, though."

A thin man dressed in a severe black cassock sat near the window. He appeared to be in his late fifties and had silvery hair. His face was ascetic and his eyes were very keen. Sparhawk crossed the room and knelt respectfully before him. "Your Grace," he greeted the patriarch of Demos.

"You're looking well, Sir Sparhawk," the churchman told him. "It's good to see you again." Then he looked over Sparhawk's shoulder. "Have you been going to chapel, Kurik?" he asked the squire.

"Uh—whenever there's opportunity, your Grace," Kurik answered, flushing slightly.

"Excellent, my son," Dolmant said. "I'm sure that God is always glad to see you. How are Aslade and the boys?"

"Well, your Grace. Thank you for asking."

Sephrenia had been looking critically at the patriarch. "You haven't been eating properly, Dolmant," she told him.

"Sometimes I forget," he said. Then he smiled slyly at her. "My overwhelming concern with the conversion of the heathens fills all my waking thoughts. Tell me, Sephrenia, are *you* ready at last to put aside your pagan ways and embrace the true faith?"

"Not yet, Dolmant," she replied, also smiling. "It was nice of you to ask, though."

He laughed. "I thought I'd get the question out of the way early so we can converse without having it hanging over our heads." He looked curiously at Flute, who was walking about the room examining the furnishings. "And who is this beautiful child?" he asked.

"She's a foundling, your Grace," Sparhawk replied. "We came across her near the Arcian border. She doesn't talk, so we call her Flute."

Dolmant looked at the little girl's grass-stained feet. "And was there no time to bathe her?" he asked.

"That would not be appropriate, your Grace," Sephrenia replied.

The patriarch looked puzzled at that. Then he looked again at Flute. "Come over here, child," he said.

Flute approached him warily.

"And will you not speak—even to me?"

She raised her pipes and blew a questioning little note.

"I see," Dolmant said. "Well, then, Flute, will you accept my blessing?"

She looked at him gravely, then shook her head.

"She is a Styric child, Dolmant," Sephrenia explained. "An Elene blessing would have no meaning for her."

Flute then reached out and took the patriarch's thin hand and placed it over her heart. Dolmant's eyes grew suddenly very wide and his expression troubled.

"She will give you *her* blessing, however," Sephrenia told him. "And will *you* accept it?"

Dolmant's eyes were still wide. "I think perhaps that I should not," he said, "but God help me, I will—and gladly."

Flute smiled at him and then kissed both of his palms. Then she pirouetted away, her black hair flying and her pipes sounding joyously. The patriarch's face was filled with wonder.

"I expect that I'll be summoned to the palace as soon as King Wargun arrives," Vanion said. "Annias wouldn't want to miss the chance to confront me personally." He looked at Count Radun. "Did anyone see you arrive, my Lord?" he asked.

Radun shook his head. "I had my visor down, my Lord Vanion, and at Sparhawk's suggestion, I had covered the crest on my shield. I'm positive that no one knows that I'm in Cimmura."

"Good." Vanion grinned suddenly. "We wouldn't want to spoil the surprise for Annias, would we?"

The expected summons from the palace arrived two days later. Vanion, Sparhawk, and Kalten put on the simple robes Pandions customarily wore inside the chapterhouse, though beneath them they wore mail coats and their swords. Dolmant and Radun wore the cowled black robes of monks. Sephrenia wore her usual white. She had spoken at some length with Flute, and it appeared that the little girl had agreed to remain behind. Kurik belted on a sword. "Just in case there's trouble," he grunted to Sparhawk before the party left the chapterhouse.

The day was cold and raw. The sky was leaden, and a chill wind whistled through the streets of Cimmura as Vanion led them toward the palace. There were few people abroad in the streets. Sparhawk could not be sure if the citizens were staying inside because of the weather or because some rumors had leaked out about the possibility of trouble.

Not too far from the palace gate, Sparhawk saw a familiar figure. A lame beggar boy wrapped in a ragged cloak crutched his way out from the corner where he had been sheltering himself. "Charity, my Lords, charity," he begged in a broken-hearted voice.

Sparhawk reined Faran in and reached inside his robe for a few coins.

"I need to talk with you, Sparhawk," the boy said quietly after the others had ridden out of earshot.

"Later," Sparhawk replied, bending to his saddle to place the coins in the boy's begging bowl.

"Not too much later, I hope," Talen said, shivering. "I'm freezing out here."

There was a brief delay at the palace gate where the guards tried to deny entrance to Vanion's escort. Kalten resolved the problem by pulling open his robe and putting his hand meaningfully on his sword hilt. The discussion ended abruptly at that point, and the party rode on into the palace courtyard and dismounted.

"I *love* doing that," Kalten said blithely.

"It doesn't take very much to make you happy, does it?" Sparhawk said.

"I'm a simple man, my friend—with simple pleasures."

They proceeded directly to the blue-draped council chamber where the kings of Arcium, Deira, and Thalesia sat on thronelike chairs, flanking the slack-lipped Lycheas. Behind each king stood a man in formal armor. The crests of the three other militant orders were emblazoned on their surcoats. Abriel, preceptor of the Cyrinic Knights in Arcium, stood sternly behind King Dregos; Darellon, preceptor of the Alcione Knights of Deira, had taken up a similar position behind the aged King Obler; and the big-boned Komier, leader of the Genidian Knights, stood behind King Wargun of Thalesia. Although it was early in the day, Wargun was already bleary-eyed. He held a large silver cup in a hand that was visibly shaking.

The Royal Council of Advisors sat to one side of the room. The face of the Earl of Lenda was troubled, while that of the Baron Harparin was smug.

The Primate Annias wore a purple satin cassock, and the expression on his emaciated face was coldly triumphant as Vanion entered. When he saw the rest of them accompanying the Pandion preceptor, however, his eyes flashed angrily. "Who authorized this entourage of yours, Lord Vanion?" he demanded. "The summons did not mention an escort."

"I require no authorization, your Grace," Vanion answered coldly. "My rank is all the authority I need."

"That's true," the Earl of Lenda said. "Law and custom support the preceptor's position."

Annias gave the old man a look filled with hate. "What a comfort it is to have the advice of one so versed in the law," he said in a sarcastic voice. Then his eyes fell on Sephrenia. "Remove that Styric witch from my presence," he demanded.

"No," Vanion said. "She stays."

Their eyes locked for a long moment, and Annias finally looked away. "Very well, then, Vanion," he said. "Because of the seriousness of the matter I am about to present to their majesties, I will control my natural revulsion at the presence of a heathen sorceress."

"You're too kind," Sephrenia murmured.

"Just get on with it, Annias," King Dregos said irritably. "We're gathered here to examine certain irregularities involving the throne of Elenia. What is this burning matter that is important enough to delay our inquiry?"

Annias straightened. "The matter concerns you directly, your Majesty. Last week a body of armed men attacked a castle in the eastern part of your kingdom."

King Dregos's eyes blazed. "Why was I not informed?" he demanded.

"Forgive me, your Majesty," Annias apologized. "I myself learned of the incident only recently and I felt it wiser to present the matter to this council rather than to advise you in advance. Although this outrage occurred within the boundaries of your kingdom, the implications of it spread beyond your borders to all four western kingdoms."

"Get on with it, Annias," King Wargun growled. "Save the flowery language for your sermons."

"As your Majesty wishes," Annias said, bowing. "There are witnesses to this criminal act, and I think perhaps it were best that your Majesties hear their accounts directly rather than at secondhand from me." He turned and gestured to one of the red-liveried church soliders who lined both walls of the council chamber. The soldier stepped to a side door and admitted a nervous-looking man whose face went visibly pale when he saw Vanion.

"Don't be afraid, Tessera," Annias told him. "So long as you tell the truth, no harm will come to you."

"Yes, your Grace," the nervous man mumbled.

"This is Tessera," Annias introduced him, "a merchant of this city who has recently returned from Arcium. Tell us what you saw there, Tessera."

"Well, your Grace, it was as I told you before. I was in Sarrinium on business. I was returning from there when I was overtaken by a storm and I took shelter in the castle of Count Radun, who was kind enough to take me in." Tessera's voice had the singsong quality some people assume when they are reciting something previously committed to memory. "Anyway," he went on, "after the weather cleared, I was preparing to leave and I was in the count's stables seeing to my horse. I heard the sounds of many men in the courtyard, so I peered out the stable door to see what was happening. It was a sizable body of Pandion Knights."

"Are you certain that they were Pandions?" Annias prompted him.

"Yes, your Grace. They were wearing black armor and carrying Pandion banners. The count is well known to be most respectful of the Church and her knights, so he had admitted them without challenge. As soon as they were inside the walls, however, they all drew their swords and began to kill everyone in sight."

"My uncle!" King Dregos exclaimed.

"The count tried to fight them, of course, but they quickly disarmed him and tied him to a stake in the center of the courtyard. They killed all the men inside the castle, and then—"

"*All* the men?" Annias interrupted him, his face suddenly stern.

"They killed all the men inside the castle, and then—" Tessera faltered. "Oh, I almost forgot that part. They killed all the men inside the castle—*except* for the churchmen—and then they brought out the count's wife and daughters. They were all stripped naked and then violated before the count's eyes."

A sob escaped the king of Arcium. "My aunt and my cousins," he cried.

"Steady, Dregos," King Wargun said, putting his hand on the other king's shoulder.

"Then," Tessera continued, "after the count's womenfolk had all been repeatedly raped, they were dragged one by one to a spot directly before where the count was tied and their throats were cut. The count wept and tried to tear his hands free, but his bonds were too tight. He pleaded with the Pandions to stop, but they only laughed and continued their butchery. Finally, when his wife and daughters were all dead and lying in their own blood, he asked them why they were doing this. One of them, the leader, I think, replied that it was on the orders of Lord Vanion, the preceptor of the Pandions."

King Dregos leaped to his feet. He was weeping openly and clawing at his sword hilt. Annias stepped in front of him. "I share your outrage, your Majesty, but a quick death for this monstrous Vanion would be far too merciful. Let us hear this good, honest man out. Go on with your account, Tessera."

"There isn't much more to tell, your Grace," Tessera replied. "Once the Pandions had killed all the women, they tortured the count to the point of death and then they beheaded him. After that, they drove the churchmen out of the castle and looted the place."

"Thank you, Tessera," Annias said. He motioned to another of his soldiers, and the guard went to the same side door to admit a man dressed in a peasant smock. The peasant had a slightly furtive look and he was trembling noticeably.

"Say your name, fellow," Annias ordered.

"I am Verl, your Grace, an honest serf from the estate of Count Radun."

"And why are you in Cimmura? A serf may not leave the estate of his lord without permission."

"I fled, your Grace, after the murder of the count and all his family."

"Can you tell us what happened? Did you witness this atrocity?"

"Not directly, your Grace. I was working in a field near the count's castle when I saw a large group of men dressed in black armor and carrying the banners of the Pandion Knights ride out of the castle. One of them had the count's head on the point of his spear. I hid myself and I could hear them talking and laughing as they rode by."

"What were they saying?"

"The one who was carrying the count's head said, 'We must carry this trophy to Demos to prove to Lord Vanion that we have carried out his orders.' After they had gone past, I ran to the castle and found everyone inside dead. I was afraid that the Pandions might come back, so I ran away."

"Why did you come to Cimmura?"

"To report the crime to you, your Grace, and to place myself under your protection. I was afraid that if I stayed in Arcium, the Pandions would hunt me down and kill me."

"Why did you do this?" Dregos demanded of Vanion. "My uncle has never given any offense to your order."

The other kings were also glaring at the Pandion preceptor accusingly.

Dregos wheeled to glare at Prince Lycheas. "I insist that this murderer be placed in chains!"

Lycheas tried without much success to look like a king. "Your demand is reasonable, your Majesty," he said in his nasal voice. He cast a quick look at Annias, seeking reassurance. "We therefore command that this miscreant Vanion be placed—"

"Um, excuse me, your Majesties," the Earl of Lenda interposed, "but by law, Lord Vanion is entitled to present his defense."

"What defense can there possibly be?" Dregos asked in a sick voice.

Sparhawk and the others had remained at the back of the council chamber. Sephrenia made a small gesture, and Sparhawk leaned toward her. "Someone here is using magic," she whispered. "That's why the kings are so willing to accept the infantile charges against Vanion. The spell induces belief."

"Can you counter it?" he whispered back.

"Only if I know who's doing it."

"It's Annias. He tried a spell on me when I first came back to Cimmura."

"A churchman?" she looked surprised. "All right. I'll take care of it." Her lips began to move, and she concealed her hands in her sleeves to hide their gesturing.

"Well, Vanion," Annias sneered, "what have you to say for yourself?"

"These men are obviously lying," Vanion replied scornfully.

"Why would they lie?" Annias turned to the kings seated at the front of the room. "As soon as I received the reports of these witnesses, I dispatched a troop of church soldiers to the count's castle to verify the details of this crime. I expect their report within the next week. In the meantime, it is my recommendation that the Pandion Knights all be disarmed and confined within their chapterhouses to prevent any further atrocities."

King Obler stroked his long gray beard. "Under the circumstances, that would be the prudent course," he said sagely. He turned to Darellon of the Alcione Knights. "My Lord Darellon," he said. "Dispatch a rider to Deira. Tell him to bring your knights to Elenia. They are to assist the civil authorities here in disarming and confining the Pandions."

"It shall be as your Majesty commands," Darellon replied, glaring at Vanion.

The aged king of Deira looked at King Wargun and King Dregos. "I would strongly advise that the Cyrinics and Genidians also send forces," he said. "Let us seal up these Pandions until we can separate the innocent from the guilty."

"See to it, Komier," King Wargun said.

"Send your knights as well, Abriel," King Dregos commanded the preceptor of the Cyrinics. He glared at Vanion with hate-filled eyes. "I pray that your underlings attempt to resist," he said fiercely.

"A splendid idea, your Majesties," Annias said, bowing. "I would further suggest that as soon as we receive confirmation of the murders, your Majesties travel with me and these two honest witnesses to Chyrellos. There we can lay the entire affair before the Hierocracy of the Church and the archprelate himself with our strong recommendation that the Pandion Order be disbanded. Strictly speaking, that order is under Church authority, and only the Church can make the final decision."

"Truly," Dregos grated. "Let us rid ourselves of this Pandion infection once and for all."

A thin smile touched the primate's lips. Then he flinched, and his face went deathly pale as Sephrenia released her counterspell.

It was at that point that Dolmant stepped forward, pushing back the hood of his monk's robe to reveal his face. "May I speak, your Majesties?" he asked.

"Y—your Grace," Annias stammered in surprise, "I didn't know that you were in Cimmura."

"I didn't think you did, Annias. As you've so correctly pointed out, the Pandions are under Church authority. As the ranking churchman present, I think it's proper for me to take charge of this inquiry. You are to be commended for the way in which you have conducted things thus far, however."

"But—"

"That will be all, Annias," Dolmant dismissed him. He turned then to the kings and to Lycheas, who was staring openmouthed at him.

"Your Majesties," the patriarch began, pacing back and forth with his hands clasped behind him as if deep in thought. "This is indeed a serious accusation. Let us, however, consider the character of the accusers. On the one hand, we have an untitled merchant, and on the other, a runaway serf. The accused is the preceptor of an order of Church Knights, a man whose honor has always been above question. Why would a man of Lord Vanion's stature commit such a crime? Indeed, we have as yet received no substantiation that the crime *did* in fact take place. Let us not move in haste."

"As I mentioned, your Grace," Annias injected, "I have dispatched church soldiers to Arcium to view the scene of the crime with their own eyes. I have also ordered them to seek out the churchmen who were in the castle of Count Radun and witnessed this horror and to return with them to Cimmura. Their reports should leave no doubts whatsoever."

"Ah, yes," Dolmant agreed. "None whatsoever. I think, however, that I might be able to save us a bit of time. As it happens, I myself have with me a man who witnessed what happened at the castle of Count Radun and I don't think his testimony can be questioned by any man here." He looked at the robed and cowled Count Radun, who had remained unobtrusively at the rear of the chamber. "Would you be so good as to step forward, brother?" he said.

Annias was gnawing on a fingernail. His expression clearly showed his chagrin at having the proceedings taken out of his grasp and at the appearance of Dolmant's unexpected witness.

"Would you reveal your identity to us, brother?" Dolmant asked mildly as the count joined him before the kings.

There was a tight grin on Radun's face as he pushed back his hood.

"Uncle!" King Dregos gasped in astonishment.

"Uncle?" King Wargun exclaimed, coming to his feet and spilling his wine.

"This is Count Radun—my uncle," Dregos told him, his eyes still wide with amazement.

"You seem to have made an astonishing recovery, Radun," Wargun laughed. "My congratulations. Tell me, how did you stick your head back on?"

Annias had gone very pale. He stared in stunned disbelief at Count Radun. "How did you—" he blurted. Then he recovered. He looked around wildly for an instant as if seeking a way to escape. Then he seemed to get hold of himself. "Your Majesties," he stammered, "I have been misled by false witnesses. Please forgive me." He was visibly sweating now. Then he spun about. "Seize those two liars!" He pointed at Tessera and Verl, who were both cringing in terror. Several red-liveried guards quickly rushed the pair from the room.

"Annias thinks very fast on his feet, doesn't he?" Kalten murmured to Sparhawk. "How much would you care to wager that those two will manage somehow to hang themselves before the sun goes down—with a certain amount of help, of course?"

"I'm not a betting man, Kalten," Sparhawk replied. "Not on a proposition like that, anyway."

"Why don't you tell us what *really* happened at your castle, Count Radun?" Dolmant suggested.

"It was really fairly simple, your Grace," Radun replied. "Sir Sparhawk and Sir Kalten arrived at my gates some time ago and warned me that a group of men dressed in the armor of Pandion Knights were planning to gain entry by subterfuge and murder me and my family. They had a number of *real* Pandions with them. When the imposters arrived, Sir Sparhawk led his knights against them and drove them off."

"Fortuitous," King Obler observed. "Which of these stalwarts is Sir Sparhawk?"

Sparhawk stepped forward. "I am, your Majesty."

"How did you become aware of this plot?"

"It was quite by accident, your Majesty. I happened to overhear a conversation concerning it. I immediately informed Lord Vanion, and he ordered Kalten and me to take preventive steps."

King Dregos rose to his feet and came down from the dais. "I have wronged you, Lord Vanion," he said in a thick voice. "Your motives were the very best, and I accused you. Can you forgive me?"

"There is nothing to forgive, your Majesty," Vanion replied. "Under the circumstances, I'd have done exactly the same."

The Arcian king took the preceptor's hand and clasped it warmly.

"Tell me, Sir Sparhawk," King Obler asked, "could you by chance identify the plotters?"

"I couldn't see their faces, your Majesty."

"A shame, really," the old king sighed. "It would appear that the plot was fairly widespread. The two who came before us to testify would also seem to have been a part of it, and at some prearranged signal were to have stepped forward with their obviously well-coached lies."

"That same thought had occurred to me, your Majesty," Sparhawk agreed.

"But who was behind it? And against whom was it really directed? Count Radun, perhaps? Or King Dregos? Or even Lord Vanion?"

"That might be impossible to determine—unless the so-called witnesses can be persuaded to identify their fellow plotters."

"Excellent point, Sir Sparhawk." King Obler looked sternly at the Primate Annias. "It lies upon you, your Grace, to ensure that the merchant Tessera and the serf Verl are available for questioning. We would all be most distressed should anything of a permanent nature happen to either of them."

Annias's face grew stiff. "I shall have them both closely guarded, your Majesty," he assured the king of Deira. He gestured to one of his soldiers and muttered some instructions to the man, who blanched slightly, then hurried from the room.

"Sir Sparhawk," Lycheas blustered, "you were ordered to Demos and told to remain there until you received permission to leave. Why is it that you—"

"Be still, Lycheas," Annias snapped at him.

A slow flush crept up the pimpled young man's face.

"I would say that you owe Lord Vanion an apology, Annias," Dolmant said pointedly.

Annias paled and then turned stiffly to the Pandion chief. "Please accept my apologies, Lord Vanion," he said shortly. "I was misled by liars."

"Of course, my dear Primate," Vanion replied. "We all blunder from time to time, don't we?"

"I believe that more or less concludes this matter then," Dolmant said. He cast a sidelong glance at Annias, who was obviously making a great effort to control his emotions. "Be assured, Annias," the patriarch of Demos said to him, "I will cast this entire matter in as charitable a light as I can when I make my report to the Hierocracy in Chyrellos. I'll try my very best not to make you look like a *complete* idiot."

Annias bit his lip.

"Tell us, Sir Sparhawk," King Obler said, "could you in any way identify the people who approached the count's castle?"

"The man who was leading them is named Adus, your Majesty," Sparhawk told him. "He's a thick-witted savage who does the bidding of a renegade Pandion named Martel. Many of his men were just ordinary mercenaries. The rest were Rendors."

"Rendors?" King Dregos said, his eyes narrowing. "There *have* been tensions of late between my kingdom and Rendor, but this plot seems a bit involuted for the Rendorish mind."

"We could spend hours in speculation, Dregos," King Wargun said, holding his empty wine cup out for a serving man to refill. "An hour or so on the rack should persuade the merchant and the serf down in the dungeon to tell us what they know about their fellow plotters."

"The Church does not approve of such methods, your Majesty," Dolmant said.

Wargun snorted derisively. "The dungeons beneath the Basilica of Chyrellos are reputed to employ the most expert interrogators in the world," he said.

"That practice is being discontinued."

"Perhaps," Wargun said, "but this is a civil matter. We're not constrained by churchly delicacy, and I for one don't propose to wait while you pray an answer out of those two."

Lycheas, who had been smarting from the almost absentminded rebuke Annias had delivered to him, straightened on his thronelike chair. "We are delighted that this matter has been resolved so amicably," he announced, "and we rejoice that the reports concerning the death of Count Radun have proved to be unfounded. I agree with the patriarch of Demos that we can consider this inquiry concluded—unless Lord Vanion's excellent witnesses can shed further light on just who might have been behind this monstrous conspiracy."

"No, your Highness," Vanion told him. "We are not prepared at this time to do so."

Lycheas turned to the kings of Thalesia, Deira, and Arcium, trying with scant success to look regal. "Our time, your Majesties, is short," he said. "We each have kingdoms to rule, and there are other matters requiring our attention. I suggest that we tender Lord Vanion our appreciation for his aid in clarifying this situation and give him permission to withdraw so that we may turn to state matters."

The kings nodded their agreement.

"You and your friends may leave now, Lord Vanion," Lycheas said grandly.

"Thank you, your Highness," Vanion replied with a stiff bow. "We are all happy to have been of service to you." He turned and started toward the door.

"A moment, Lord Vanion," Darellon, the slightly built preceptor of the Alcione Knights said. Then he stepped forward. "Since your Majesties' conversations will now turn on state matters, I think that I, Lord Komier, and Lord Abriel will also withdraw. We are little versed in statecraft and could contribute nothing of value to your discussions. The matter that has come to light this morning, however, requires some consultation among the militant orders. Should conspiracies of this nature recur, we must make preparations to meet them."

"Well said," Komier agreed.

"A splendid idea, Darellon," King Obler assented. "Let's not be caught asleep again. Keep me advised of the thrust of your discussions."

"You may rely upon me, your Majesty."

The preceptors of the other three orders marched down from the dais and joined Vanion, who led the way from the ornate audience chamber. Once they were out in the corridor, Komier, the hulking preceptor of the Genidian Knights, grinned openly. "Very neat, Vanion," he said.

"I'm glad you liked it." Vanion grinned back.

"My head must have been packed in wool this morning," Komier confessed. "Would you believe I almost accepted all that tripe?"

"It was not entirely your fault, Lord Komier," Sephrenia told him.

He gave her a questioning look.

"Let me think my way through it a bit more," she said, frowning.

The big Thalesian looked at Vanion. "It was Annias, wasn't it?" he guessed shrewdly as they progressed down the hall. "The scheme was his, I take it?"

Vanion nodded. "The Pandion presence in Elenia is hindering his operations. He saw this as a way to remove us."

"Elenian politics get a bit dense sometimes. We're much more direct in Thalesia. Just how powerful is the primate of Cimmura?"

Vanion shrugged. "He controls the royal council. That makes him more or less the ruler of the kingdom."

"Does he want the throne for himself?"

"No, I don't think so. He prefers to manipulate things from behind the scenes. He's trying to groom Lycheas for the throne."

"Lycheas is a bastard, isn't he?"

Vanion nodded again.

"How can a bastard be king? Nobody knows who his father is."

"Annias probably believes he can get around that problem. Until Sparhawk's father intervened, our good primate had very nearly convinced King Aldreas that it was perfectly legitimate for him to marry his own sister."

"That's disgusting," Komier shuddered.

"I've heard that Annias has certain ambitions involving the archprelate's throne in Chyrellos," Abriel, the gray-haired preceptor of the Cyrinic Knights, said to Patriarch Dolmant.

"I've heard some of the same rumors myself," Dolmant replied blandly.

"This humiliation is going to be quite a setback for him, isn't it? The Hierocracy's likely to look with some disfavor on a man who makes a total ass of himself in public."

"That thought had crossed my mind as well."

"And your report will be quite detailed, I expect?"

"That is my obligation, Lord Abriel," Dolmant said piously. "As a member of the Hierocracy myself, I could hardly conceal any of the facts, could I? I will have to present the *whole* truth to the high councils of the Church."

"We wouldn't have it any other way, your Grace."

"We're going to need to talk, Vanion," Darellon, the preceptor of the Alcione Knights, said seriously. "This scheme was directed at you and your order this time, but it concerns us all. It could be any one of us the next time. Is there someplace secure where we can discuss this matter?"

"Our chapterhouse is on the eastern edge of the city," Vanion replied. "I can guarantee that none of the primate's spies are inside its walls."

As they rode out through the palace gates, Sparhawk remembered something and slowed to ride with Kurik at the rear of the column.

"What's the matter?" Kurik asked.

"Let's drop behind a little bit. I want to talk with that beggar boy."

"That's hardly good manners, Sparhawk," Kurik said. "A meeting of the preceptors of all four orders happens about once in a lifetime, and they're going to have some questions for you."

"We can catch up with them before they get to the chapterhouse."

"What do you want to talk to a beggar for?" Kurik sounded more than a little irritated.

"He's working for me." Sparhawk gave his friend an appraising look. "What's bothering you, Kurik?" he asked. "Your face looks like a rain cloud."

"Never mind," Kurik replied shortly.

Talen was still huddled in the angle between two intersecting walls. He had his ragged cloak wrapped about him and he was shivering.

Sparhawk dismounted a few feet from the boy and made some pretense of checking his saddle girth. "What did you want to tell me?" he said quietly.

"That man you had me watching," Talen began. "Krager, wasn't that his name? He left Cimmura about the same time you did, but he came back a week or so later. There was another man with him—a fellow with white hair. It sort of stands out because he's not really that old. Anyway, they went to the house of that baron who's so fond of little boys. They stayed there for several hours, then they rode out of town again. I got close enough to them at the east gate to hear them talking with the gate guards. When the guard asked their destination, they said they were going to Cammoria."

"Good lad," Sparhawk congratulated him, dropping a gold crown into the begging bowl.

"Child's play." Talen shrugged. He bit the coin and then tucked it inside his tunic. "Thanks, Sparhawk."

"Why didn't you tell the porter at the inn on Rose Street?"

"The place is being watched. I decided to play it safe." Then Talen looked over the big knight's shoulder. "Hello, Kurik," he said. "I haven't seen you for a long time."

"You two know each other?" Sparhawk was a bit surprised.

Kurik flushed, looking embarrassed.

"You wouldn't believe how far back our friendship goes, Sparhawk," Talen said with a sly little smile at Kurik.

"That's enough, Talen," Kurik said sharply. Then his expression softened slightly. "How's your mother?" he asked. There was a strange, wistful note in his voice.

"She's doing quite well, actually. When you add what I make to what you give her from time to time, she's comfortably off."

"Am I missing something here?" Sparhawk asked mildly.

"It's a personal matter, Sparhawk," Kurik told him. Then he turned to the boy. "What are you doing out here in the streets, Talen?" he demanded.

"I'm begging, Kurik. You see?" Talen held out his bowl. "That's what this is for. Would you like to drop something in for old times' sake?"

"I put you in a very good school, boy."

"Oh, it was very good indeed. The headmaster used to tell us how good it was three times a day—at mealtimes. He and the other teachers ate roast beef. The students got porridge. I don't like porridge all that much, so I enrolled in a different school." He gestured extravagantly at the street. "This is my classroom now. Do you like it? The lessons I learn here are much more useful than rhetoric or philosophy or all that tiresome theology. If I pay attention, I can earn enough to buy my own roast beef—or anything else, for that matter."

"I ought to thrash you, Talen," Kurik threatened.

"Why, Father," the boy replied, wide-eyed, "what a thing to suggest!" He laughed. "Besides, you'd have to catch me first. That's the first lesson I learned in my new school. Would you like to see how well I learned it?" He took up his crutch and begging bowl and ran off down the street. He was, Sparhawk noted, very fast on his feet.

Kurik started to swear.

"Father?" Sparhawk asked.

"I told you that this is none of your business, Sparhawk."

"We don't keep any secrets from each other, Kurik."

"You're going to push this, aren't you?"

"Me? I'm just curious, that's all. This is a side of you I've never seen before."

"I was indiscreet some years ago."

"That's a delicate way to put it."

"I can do without the clever remarks, Sparhawk."

"Does Aslade know about this?"

"Of course not. It would only make her unhappy if I told her. I kept quiet about it to spare her feelings. A man owes that to his wife, doesn't he?"

"I understand perfectly, Kurik," Sparhawk assured him. "And was Talen's mother so very beautiful?"

Kurik sighed, and his face grew oddly soft. "She was eighteen and like a spring morning. I couldn't help myself, Sparhawk. I love Aslade, but . . ."

Sparhawk put his arm about his friend's shoulder. "It happens sometimes, Kurik," he said. "Don't beat yourself over the head about it." Then he straightened. "Why don't we see if we can catch up with the others?" he suggested, as he swung back up into his saddle.

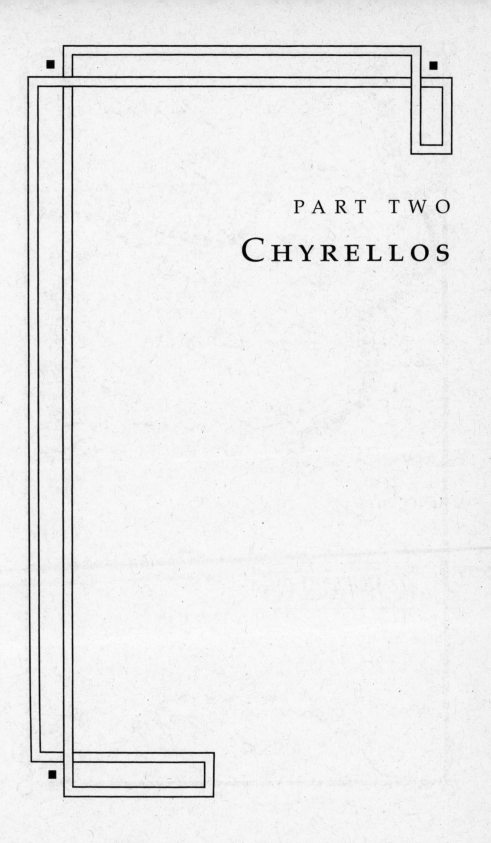

PART TWO

# CHYRELLOS

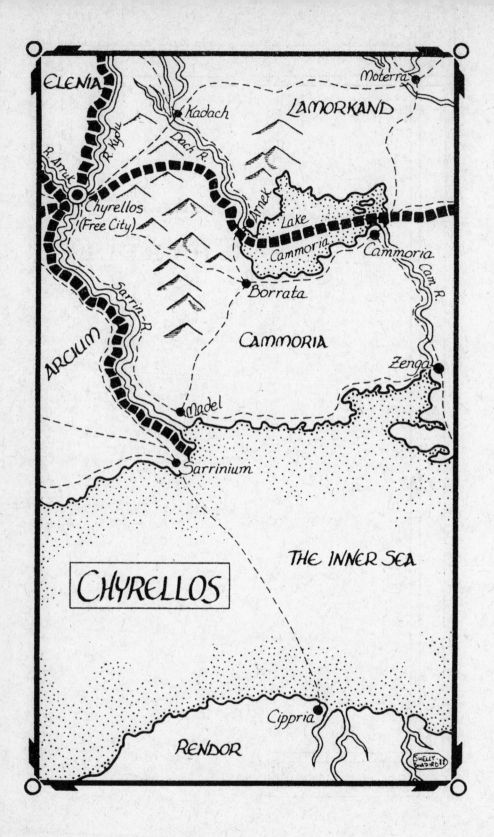

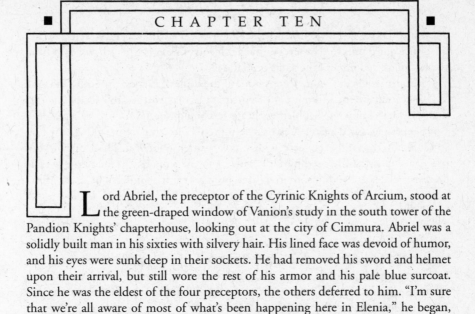

Lord Abriel, the preceptor of the Cyrinic Knights of Arcium, stood at the green-draped window of Vanion's study in the south tower of the Pandion Knights' chapterhouse, looking out at the city of Cimmura. Abriel was a solidly built man in his sixties with silvery hair. His lined face was devoid of humor, and his eyes were sunk deep in their sockets. He had removed his sword and helmet upon their arrival, but still wore the rest of his armor and his pale blue surcoat. Since he was the eldest of the four preceptors, the others deferred to him. "I'm sure that we're all aware of most of what's been happening here in Elenia," he began, "but there are a few things that need a little clarification, I think. Would you mind if we asked you some questions, Vanion?"

"Not at all," Vanion replied. "We'll all try our best to answer any that you might have."

"Good. We've had our differences in the past, my Lord, but in this situation we'll want to set those aside." Abriel, like all the Cyrinics, spoke in a considered, even formal, fashion. "I think we need to know more about this Martel person."

Vanion leaned back in his chair. "He was a Pandion," he replied with a trace of sadness in his voice. "I was forced to expel him from the order."

"That's a little terse, Vanion," Komier said. Unlike the others, Komier wore a mail shirt rather than formal armor. He was a heavy-boned man with thick shoulders and large hands. Like most Thalesians, the preceptor of the Genidian Knights was blond, and his shaggy eyebrows gave his face an almost brutish look. As he spoke, he continually toyed with the hilt of his broadsword, which lay on the table before him. "If this Martel's going to be a problem, we all ought to know as much about him as we can."

"Martel was one of the best," Sephrenia said quietly. She sat in her hooded white robe before the fire, holding her teacup. "He was extremely proficient in the secrets. That, I think, is what led to his disgrace."

"He was good with a lance, too," Kalten admitted ruefully. "He used to unhorse me on a regular basis on the practice field. Sparhawk was probably the only one who was a match for him."

"Exactly what was this disgrace you mentioned, Sephrenia?" Lord Darellon asked. The preceptor of the Alcione Knights of Deira was a slender man in his late forties. His massive Deiran armor looked almost too heavy for his slight frame.

Sephrenia sighed. "The secrets of Styricum are myriad," she replied. "Some are fairly simple—common spells and incantations. Martel mastered those very quickly. Beyond commonplace magic, however, lies a deeper and far more dangerous realm. Those of us who instruct the Knights of the Church in the secrets do not introduce our pupils to that level of magic. It serves no practical purpose and it involves things that imperil the souls of Elenes."

Komier laughed. "Many things imperil the souls of Elenes, my Lady," he said. "I felt a certain wrench in mine the first time I contacted the Troll-Gods. I gather that this Martel of yours dabbled in things he should not have?"

Sephrenia sighed again. "Yes," she admitted. "He came to me asking that I instruct him in the forbidden secrets. He was very intense about it. That's one of Martel's characteristics. I refused him, of course, but there are renegade Styrics, even as there are renegade Pandions. Martel came from a wealthy family, so he could afford to pay for the instruction he wanted."

"Who found him out?" Darellon asked.

"I did," Sparhawk said. "I was riding from Cimmura to Demos. That was shortly before King Aldreas sent me into exile. There's a patch of woods three leagues this side of Demos. It was just about dusk when I passed those woods, and I saw a strange light back among the trees. I went to investigate and saw Martel. He'd raised some kind of glowing creature. Its light was very bright—so bright that I couldn't make out its face."

"I don't think you'd have wanted to see its face, Sparhawk," Sephrenia told him.

"Perhaps not," he agreed. "Anyway, Martel was speaking to the creature in Styric, commanding it to do his bidding."

"That doesn't seem like anything out of the ordinary," Komier said. "We've all raised spirits or ghosts of one kind or another from time to time."

"This was not precisely a spirit, Lord Komier," Sephrenia told him. "It was a Damork. The Elder Gods of Styricum created them to serve as slaves to their will. The Damorks have extraordinary powers, but they are soulless. A God can summon them from that unimaginable place where they dwell and control them. For a mortal to attempt that, however, is sheer folly. No mortal can control a Damork. What Martel had done is absolutely forbidden by all of the Younger Gods."

"And the Elder Gods?" Darellon asked.

"The Elder Gods have no rules, my Lord—only whims and desires."

"Sephrenia," Dolmant pointed out, "Martel is an Elene. Perhaps he felt no obligation to observe the prohibitions of the Gods of Styricum."

"So long as one is practicing the arts of Styricum, one is subject to the Styric Gods, Dolmant," she replied.

"I wonder if perhaps it might have been a mistake to arm the Church Knights with Styric magic as well as conventional weapons," Dolmant mused. "We seem to be dabbling in an area best left untapped."

"That decision was made over nine hundred years ago, your Grace," Abriel reminded him, coming back to the table, "and if the Knights of the Church had not been proficient in magic, the Zemochs would have won that battle on the plains of Lamorkand."

"Perhaps," Dolmant said.

"Go on with your story, Sparhawk," Komier suggested.

"There's not too much more, my Lord. I didn't know what the Damork was until Sephrenia told me about it later, but I knew that it was something we were forbidden to contact. After a while, the thing vanished, and I rode in to talk with Martel. We were friends, and I wanted to warn him that what he was doing was prohibited, but he seemed almost mad somehow. He shrieked at me and told me to mind my own business. That didn't leave me any choice. I rode on to our mother-house at Demos and reported what I'd seen to Vanion and Sephrenia. She told us what the creature was and how dangerous it was to have it loose in the world. Vanion ordered me to take a number of men and to apprehend Martel and to bring him to the motherhouse for questioning. He went completely wild when we approached him and he went to his sword. Martel's very good to begin with, and his madness made him all the more savage. I lost a couple of very close friends that day. We finally managed to overpower him and we dragged him back to the motherhouse in chains."

"By the ankles, as I recall," Kalten added. "Sparhawk can be very direct when he's irritated." He smiled at his friend. "You didn't endear yourself to him by doing it that way, Sparhawk," he said.

"I wasn't trying to. He'd just killed two of my friends, and I wanted to give him plenty of reasons to accept my challenge when Vanion was finished with him."

"Anyway," Vanion took up the story, "when they brought Martel back to Demos, I confronted him. He didn't even try to deny what he'd been doing. I ordered him to stop practicing the forbidden secrets, and he defied me. I had no choice but to expel him from the order at that point. I stripped him of his knighthood and his armor and turned him out the front gate."

"That could have been a mistake," Komier grunted. "I'd have had him killed. Did he raise that thing again?"

Vanion nodded. "Yes, but Sephrenia appealed to the Younger Gods of Styricum, and they exorcized it. Then they stripped Martel of the most significant of his powers. He went away weeping and swearing revenge upon us all. He's still dangerous, but at least he can't summon up horrors anymore. He left Elenia and he's been hiring his sword out to the highest bidder in other parts of the world for the past ten or twelve years."

"He's just a common mercenary then?" Darellon asked. The slender Alcione preceptor had an intent look on his narrow face.

"Not quite common, my Lord," Sparhawk disagreed. "He's had Pandion training. He could have been the very best of us and he's very clever. He has wide contacts with mercenaries all over Eosia. He can raise an army at a moment's notice and he's totally ruthless. I don't believe that Martel believes in anything anymore."

"What does he look like?" Darellon asked.

"A little bigger than medium size," Kalten replied. "He's about the same age as Sparhawk and me, but he's got white hair—he has had it since he was in his twenties."

"I think we might all want to keep an eye out for him," Abriel suggested. "Who's the other one—Adus?"

"Adus is an animal," Kalten told him. "After Martel was expelled from the Pandions, he recruited Adus and a man named Krager to help him in his activities.

Adus is a Pelosian, I think—or maybe a Lamork. He can barely talk, so his accent is a little hard to identify. He's a total savage, devoid of human feelings. He enjoys killing people—slowly—and he's very good at it."

"And the other one?" Komier asked. "Krager?"

"Krager's fairly intelligent," Sparhawk replied. "Basically, he's a criminal—false coins, extortion, fraud, that sort of thing—but he's weak. Martel trusts him to perform tasks that Adus wouldn't be able to understand."

"What's the link between Annias and Martel?" Count Radun asked.

"Probably nothing more than money, my Lord." Sparhawk shrugged. "Martel is for hire and he has no strong convictions about anything. There are rumors that he has about half a ton of gold hidden somewhere."

"I was right," Komier said bluntly. "You should have killed him, Vanion."

"I made the offer," Sparhawk said, "but Vanion said no."

"I had reasons," Vanion said.

"Was there anything significant about the fact that there were Rendors in the party that attacked Count Radun's house?" Abriel asked then.

"Probably not," Sparhawk replied. "I've just come back from Rendor. There's a pool of mercenaries there in the same way that there is in Pelosia, Lamorkand, and Cammoria. Martel draws on those people whenever he needs men. Rendorish mercenaries have no particular religious convictions, Eshandist or otherwise."

"Do we have enough evidence against Annias to take before the Hierocracy in Chyrellos?" Darellon asked.

"I don't think so," Patriarch Dolmant said. "Annias has bought many voices in the higher councils of the Church. Any charges we might bring against him would have to be supported by overwhelming proof. All we have now is an overheard conversation between Krager and Baron Harparin. Annias could wriggle out of that rather easily—or simply buy his way out of it."

Komier leaned back in his chair, tapping at his chin with one finger. "I think the patriarch has just put his finger on the key to the whole affair. As long as Annias has his hands on the Elenian treasury, he can finance these schemes of his and continue to buy support in the Hierocracy. If we aren't careful, he'll bribe his way to the archprelacy. We've all stood in his path from time to time, and I'd guess that his first act as archprelate would be to disband all four militant orders. Is there any way we can cut off his access to those funds?"

Vanion shook his head. "He controls the Royal Council—except for the Earl of Lenda. They vote him all the money he needs."

"What about your queen?" Darellon asked. "Did he control her, too—before she fell ill, I mean?"

"Not even a little," Vanion replied. "Aldreas was a weak king who did anything Annias told him to do. Ehlana's an altogether different matter and she despises Annias." He shrugged. "But she's ill, and Annias will have a free hand until she recovers."

Abriel began to pace up and down, his lined face deep in thought. "That would seem to be our logical course then, gentlemen. We must bend all of our efforts to finding a cure for Queen Ehlana's illness."

Darellon leaned back, his fingers tapping on the polished table. "Annias is very cunning," he observed. "He will easily guess what our course is likely to be and he's certain to try to block us. Even if we succeed in finding a cure, won't that immediately put the queen's life in danger?"

"Sparhawk is her champion, my Lord," Kalten told him. "He can cope—particularly if I'm there to back him up."

"Are you making any progress on a cure, Vanion?" Komier asked.

"The local physicians are all baffled," Vanion replied. "I've sent out requests for others, though, but most of them haven't arrived as yet."

"Physicians don't always respond to requests," Abriel noted. "This might be particularly true in a situation where the head of the royal council has a certain interest in *not* seeing the queen recover." He considered the problem. "The Cyrinics have many contacts in Cammoria," he said. "Have you considered taking your queen to the medical faculty at the University of Borrata in that kingdom? They're reputed to be experts in obscure ailments."

"I don't think we dare dissolve the encasement that surrounds her," Sephrenia said. "At the moment it's all that sustains her life. She could not survive a trip to Borrata."

The preceptor of the Cyrinic Knights nodded thoughtfully. "Perhaps you're right, madame," he said.

"Not only that," Vanion added. "Annias would never let us take her out of the palace."

Abriel nodded bleakly. He considered it for a moment. "There's an alternative. It's not as good as having the physician actually look at the patient, but sometimes it works—or so I've been told. A skilled physician can learn a great deal from a detailed description of symptoms. That would be my suggestion, Vanion. Write down everything you know about Queen Ehlana's illness and send someone to Borrata with the documents."

"I'll take it," Sparhawk said quietly. "I have certain personal reasons for wanting the queen restored to health. Besides, Martel's in Cammoria—or at least he's reputed to be—and he and I have a few things to discuss."

"That raises another point," Abriel said. "There's a great deal of turmoil in Cammoria right now. Someone's been stirring up civil unrest there. It's not the safest place in the world."

Komier leaned back again. "What would you gentlemen say to a little show of unity?" he said to the other preceptors.

"What did you have in mind?" Darellon asked.

"I'd say that we all have a stake in this," Komier replied. "Our common goal is to keep Annias off the archprelate's throne. We all have champions who stand above their comrades in skill and bravery. I think it might be a good idea for us each to select one of those champions and send him to join Sparhawk in Cammoria. The assistance couldn't hurt, and the sending of men from all four orders would convince the world that the Church Knights stand as one in this matter."

"Very good, Komier," Darellon agreed. "The militant orders have had their differences in the past few centuries, and too many people still think that we're divided." He turned to Abriel. "Have you any idea who's behind the trouble in Cammoria?" he asked.

"Many believe that it's Otha," the Cyrinic replied. "He's been infiltrating the central kingdoms for the past six months or so."

"You know," Komier said, "I've got a strong feeling that someday we're going to have to do something about Otha—something fairly permanent."

"That would involve coming up against Azash," Sephrenia said, "and I'm not sure we want to do that."

"Can't the Younger Gods of Styricum do something about him?" Komier asked her.

"They choose not to," she replied. "The wars of men are bad enough, but a war between the Gods would be dreadful beyond imagining." She looked at Dolmant. "The God of the Elenes is reputed to be all-powerful," she said. "Couldn't the Church appeal to Him to confront Azash?"

"It's possible, I suppose," the patriarch said. "The only problem is that the Church does not admit the existence of Azash—or any other Styric God. It's a matter of theology."

"How very shortsighted."

Dolmant laughed. "My dear Sephrenia," he said. "I thought you knew that was the nature of the ecclesiastical mind. We're all like that. We find one truth and embrace it. Then we close our eyes to everything else. It avoids confusion." He looked at her curiously. "Tell me, Sephrenia, which heathen God do *you* worship?"

"I'm not permitted to say," she answered gravely. "I *can* tell you that it's not a God, though. I serve a Goddess."

"A female deity? What an absurd idea."

"Only to a man, Dolmant. Women find it very natural."

"Is there anything else you think we ought to know, Vanion?" Komier asked.

"I think we've just about covered everything, Komier." Vanion looked at Sparhawk. "Anything you want to add?" he asked.

Sparhawk shook his head. "No," he said. "I don't think so."

"What about that Styric who set the church soldiers on us?" Kalten asked.

Sparhawk grunted. "I'd almost forgotten that," he admitted. "It was at about the time that I heard Krager and Harparin talking. Kalten and I were wearing disguises, but there was a Styric who saw through them. Not long after that, we were attacked by some of Annias's people."

"You think there's a connection?" Komier asked.

Sparhawk nodded. "The Styric had been following me around for several days, and I'm fairly sure he was the one who pointed Kalten and me out to the soldiers. That would connect him to Annias."

"It's pretty thin, Sparhawk. Annias has some fairly well known prejudices where Styrics are concerned."

"Not so many that he wouldn't seek out their help if he thought he needed it. On two occasions I've caught him using magic."

"A churchman?" Dolmant's expression was startled. "That's strictly forbidden."

"So was plotting the murder of Count Radun, your Grace. I don't think Annias pays too much attention to the rules. He's not much of a magician, but the fact that he knows how it's done indicates that he's had instruction, and that means a Styric."

Darellon interlaced his slender fingers on the table in front of him. "There are

Styrics and then there are Styrics," he noted. "As Abriel pointed out, there's been a great deal of Styric activity in the central kingdoms of late—much of it coming out of Zemoch. If Annias sought out a Styric to instruct him in the secrets, he might possibly have contacted the wrong one."

"I think you're overcomplicating things, Darellon," Dolmant said. "Not even Annias would have dealings with Otha."

"That's presuming that he *knows* he's dealing with Otha."

"My Lords," Sephrenia said very quietly, "consider what happened this morning." Her eyes were very intent. "Would any of you—or the kings you serve—have been deceived by the transparent accusations of the Primate Annias? They were crude, obvious, even childish. You Elenes are a subtle, sophisticated people. If your minds had been alert, you'd have laughed at Annias's clumsy attempts to discredit the Pandions. But you didn't. Neither did your kings. And Annias, who's as subtle as a serpent, presented his case as if he believed it was a stroke of genius."

"Exactly what are you getting at, Sephrenia?" Vanion asked.

"I think we should give some consideration to Lord Darellon's line of thought. The presentation this morning would have overwhelmed a Styric. We are a simple people, and our magicians do not have to work very hard to persuade us to their way of thinking. You Elenes are more skeptical, more logical. You are not so easily deceived—unless you've been tampered with."

Dolmant leaned forward, his eyes betraying his eagerness for a contest at logic. "But Annias is also an Elene, with a mind trained in theological disputation. Why would he have been so clumsy?"

"You're assuming that Annias was speaking in his own voice this morning, Dolmant. A Styric sorcerer—or some creature subject to one—would present his case in terms that would be understood by a simple Styric and then rely upon magic to induce belief."

"Was someone using that kind of magic in that room this morning?" Darellon asked, his face troubled.

"Yes," she replied simply.

"I think we're getting a bit far afield," Komier said. "What we need to do right now is get Sparhawk on his way to Borrata. The quicker we find a cure for Queen Ehlana's illness, the quicker we can eliminate the threat of Annias altogether. Once we cut off his supply of ready cash, he can consort with anybody—or anything—he wants to, for all I care."

"You'd better get ready to ride, Sparhawk," Vanion said. "I'll write down the queen's symptoms for you."

"I don't think that's necessary, Vanion," Sephrenia told him. "I know her condition in much greater detail than you do."

"But you can't write, Sephrenia," he reminded her.

"I won't have to, Vanion," she said sweetly. "I'll tell the physicians in Borrata about the symptoms personally."

"You're going with Sparhawk?" Vanion looked surprised.

"Of course. There are things afoot that seem to be focusing on him. He might need my help when he gets to Cammoria."

"I'll go along, too," Kalten said. "If Sparhawk catches up with Martel in Cammoria, I want to be there to see what happens." He grinned at his friend. "I'll let you have Martel," he offered, "if you'll give me Adus."

"Sounds fair," Sparhawk agreed.

"You'll be passing through Chyrellos on your way to Borrata," Dolmant said. "I'll ride along with you as far as that."

"We'll be honored to have you, your Grace." Sparhawk looked at Count Radun. "Might you want to join us as well, my Lord?" he asked.

"No. Thanks all the same, Sir Sparhawk," the count replied. "I'll return to Arcium with my nephew and Lord Abriel."

Komier was frowning slightly. "I don't want to delay you, Sparhawk," he said, "but Darellon is right. Annias is sure to guess what our next step is likely to be. There are only so many centers of medical learning in Eosia; if this Martel fellow is already in Cammoria and still taking orders from Annias, he's almost certain to try to keep you from reaching Borrata. I think it might be best if you waited in Chyrellos until the knights from our other orders catch up with you. A show of force can sometimes avoid difficulties."

"That's a good idea," Vanion agreed. "The others can join him at the Pandion chapterhouse in Chyrellos and ride out together from there."

Sparhawk rose to his feet. "That's it, then," he said. He glanced at Sephrenia. "Are you going to leave Flute here?"

"No. She goes with me."

"It's going to be dangerous," he warned.

"I can protect her if she needs protection. Besides, the decision is not mine to make."

"Don't you love talking with her?" Kalten said. "All the mental stimulation of trying to puzzle out the meaning of what she's saying."

Sparhawk ignored that.


Later in the courtyard where Sparhawk and the others were preparing to mount for the ride to Chyrellos, the novice, Berit, approached. "There's a lame beggar boy at the gate, my Lord," he said to Sparhawk. "He says he has something urgent to tell you."

"Let him through the gates," Sparhawk said.

Berit looked a bit shocked.

"I know the boy," Sparhawk said. "He works for me."

"As you wish, my Lord," Berit said, bowing. He turned back toward the gate.

"Oh, by the way, Berit," Sparhawk said.

"My Lord?"

"Don't walk too close to the boy. He's a thief and he can steal everything you own before you go ten paces." ·

"I'll keep that in mind, my Lord."

A few minutes later, Berit came back escorting Talen.

"I've got a problem, Sparhawk," the boy said.

"Oh?"

"Some of the primate's men found out that I've been helping you. They're looking for me all over Cimmura."

"I told you that you were going to get in trouble," Kurik growled at him. Then the squire looked at Sparhawk. "What do we do now?" he asked. "I don't want him locked up in the cathedral dungeon."

Sparhawk scratched his chin. "I guess he'll have to go with us," he said, "at least as far as Demos." He grinned suddenly. "We can leave him with Aslade and the boys."

"Are you insane, Sparhawk?"

"I thought you'd be delighted at the notion, Kurik."

"That's the most ridiculous thing I've ever heard in my life."

"Don't you want him to get to know his brothers?" Sparhawk looked at the boy. "How much did you steal from Berit here?" he bluntly asked the young thief.

"Not very much, really."

"Give it all back."

"I'm very disappointed in you, Sparhawk."

"Life is filled with disappointments. Now give it back."

## CHAPTER ELEVEN

It was midafternoon when they rode across the drawbridge and onto the road leading to Demos and beyond. The wind still blew, but the sky was clearing. The long road stretching toward Demos was teeming with traffic. Carts and wagons rattled by, and drably dressed peasants with heavy bundles on their shoulders plodded slowly toward the market places of Cimmura. The raw winter wind bent the yellow grass at the sides of the road. Sparhawk rode a few paces in advance of the others, and the travellers on their way to Cimmura gave way to him. Faran was prancing again as they rode along at a steady trot.

"Your horse seems restive, Sparhawk," the Patriarch Dolmant, wrapped in a heavy black ecclesiastical cloak over his cassock, observed.

"He's just showing off," Sparhawk replied back over his shoulder. "He has some notion that it impresses me."

"It gives him something to do while he's waiting for the chance to bite somebody." Kalten laughed.

"Is he vicious?"

"It's the nature of the war horse, your Grace," Sparhawk explained. "They're bred for aggressiveness. In Faran's case they just went too far."

"Has he ever bitten you?"

"Once. Then I explained to him that I'd rather he didn't do it anymore."

"Explained?"

"I used a stout stick. He got the idea almost immediately."

"We're not going to get too far this afternoon, Sparhawk," Kurik called from his position at the rear of the party where he rode with their pair of pack horses. "We started late. There's an inn I know of about a league ahead. What do you think of the idea of stopping there, getting a good night's sleep, and starting out early in the morning?"

"It makes sense, Sparhawk," Kalten agreed. "I don't enjoy sleeping on the ground that much anymore."

"All right," Sparhawk said. He glanced at Talen, who was riding a tired-looking bay horse beside Sephrenia's white palfrey. The boy kept looking back over his shoulder apprehensively. "You're being awfully quiet," he said.

"Young people aren't supposed to talk in the presence of their elders, Sparhawk," Talen replied glibly. "That's one of the things they taught me in that school Kurik sent me to. I try to obey the rules—when it doesn't inconvenience me too much."

"The young man is pert," Dolmant observed.

"He's also a thief, your Grace," Kalten warned. "Don't get too close to him if you have any valuables about you."

Dolmant looked sternly at the boy. "Aren't you aware of the fact that thievery is frowned upon by the Church?"

"Yes," Talen sighed, "I know. The Church is very straitlaced about things like that."

"Watch your mouth, Talen," Kurik snapped.

"I can't, Kurik. My nose gets in the way."

"The lad's depravity is perhaps understandable," Dolmant said tolerantly. "I doubt that he's received much instruction in doctrine or morality." He sighed. "In many ways, the poor children of the streets are as pagan as the Styrics." He smiled slyly at Sephrenia, who rode with Flute bundled up in an old cloak in front of her saddle.

"Actually, your Grace," Talen disagreed, "I attend Church services regularly and I always pay close attention to the sermons."

"That's surprising," the patriarch said.

"Not really, your Grace," Talen said. "Most thieves go to church. The offertory provides all sorts of splendid opportunities."

Dolmant looked suddenly aghast.

"Look at it this way, your Grace," Talen explained with mock seriousness. "The Church distributes money to the poor, doesn't she?"

"Of course."

"Well, I'm one of the poor, so I take my share when the plate goes by. It saves the Church all the time and trouble of looking me up to give me the money. I like to be helpful when I can."

Dolmant stared at him, then suddenly burst out laughing.

Some few miles farther along, they encountered a small band of people dressed in the crude, homespun tunics that identified them as Styric. They were on foot and, as soon as they saw Sparhawk and the others, they ran fearfully out into a nearby field.

"Why are they so frightened?" Talen asked, puzzled.

"News travels very rapidly in Styricum," Sephrenia replied, "and there have been incidents lately."

"Incidents?"

Briefly, Sparhawk told him what had happened in the Styric village in Arcium. Talen's face went very pale. "That's awful!" he exclaimed.

"The Church has tried for hundreds of years to stamp out that sort of thing," Dolmant said sadly.

"I think we stamped it out fairly completely in that part of Arcium," Sparhawk assured him. "I sent some men out to deal with the peasants who were responsible."

"Did you hang them?" Talen asked fiercely.

"Sephrenia wouldn't let us, so my men gave them a switching instead."

"That's all?"

"They used thorn bushes for switches. Thorns grow very long down in Arcium, and I instructed my men to be thorough about it."

"A bit extreme, perhaps," Dolmant said.

"It seemed fitting at the time, your Grace. The Church Knights have close ties with the Styrics and we don't like people who mistreat our friends."

The pale winter sun was sliding into a bank of chill purple cloud behind them when they arrived at a run-down wayside inn. They ate a barely adequate meal of thin soup and greasy mutton and retired early.

It was clear and cold the following morning. The road was frozen iron-hard, and the bracken lining its sides was white with frost. The sun was very bright, but there was little warmth to it. They rode briskly, wrapped tightly in their cloaks to ward off the biting chill.

The road undulated across the hills and valleys of central Elenia, passing through fields lying fallow under the winter sky. Sparhawk looked about as he rode. This was the region where he and Kalten had grown up, and he felt that peculiar sense of homecoming all men feel when returning after many years to the scenes of their childhood. The self-discipline which was so much a part of Pandion training usually made Sparhawk suppress any form of emotionalism, but, despite his best efforts, certain things sometimes touched him deeply.

About midmorning, Kurik called ahead. "There's a rider coming up behind us," he reported. "He's pushing his horse hard."

Sparhawk reined in and wheeled Faran around. "Kalten," he said sharply.

"Right," the big blond man replied, thrusting his cloak aside so that his sword hilt was clear.

Sparhawk also cleared his sword, and the two of them rode several hundred yards back along the road to intercept the oncoming horseman.

Their precautions, however, proved unnecessary. The rider was the young novice, Berit. He was wrapped in a plain cloak, and his hands and wrists were chapped by the morning chill. His horse, however, was lathered and steaming. He reined in and approached them at a walk. "I have a message for you from Lord Vanion, Sir Sparhawk," he said.

"What is it?" Sparhawk asked him.

"The Royal Council has legitimized Prince Lycheas."

"They did *what?*"

"When the kings of Thalesia, Deira, and Arcium insisted that a bastard could not serve as prince regent, the Primate Annias called the council into session, and they declared the prince to be legitimate. The primate produced a document that stated that Princess Arissa had been married to Duke Osten of Vardenais."

"That's absurd," Sparhawk fumed.

"That's what Lord Vanion thought. The document appeared to be quite genuine, though, and Duke Osten died years ago, so there wasn't any way to refute the claim. The Earl of Lenda examined the parchment very closely and finally even he had to vote to legitimize Lycheas."

Sparhawk swore.

"I knew Duke Osten," Kalten said. "He was a confirmed bachelor. There's no way he'd have married. He despised women."

"Is there some problem?" Patriarch Dolmant asked, riding back down the road to join them with Sephrenia, Kurik, and Talen close behind him.

"The royal council has voted to legitimize Lycheas," Kalten told him. "Annias produced a paper that says that Princess Arissa was married."

"How strange," Dolmant said.

"And how convenient," Sephrenia added.

"Could the document have been falsified?" Dolmant asked.

"Easily, your Grace," Talen told him. "I know a man in Cimmura who could provide irrefutable proof that Archprelate Cluvonus has nine wives—including a lady Troll and an Ogress."

"Well, it's done now," Sparhawk said. "It puts Lycheas one step closer to the throne, I'm afraid."

"When did this happen, Berit?" Kurik asked the novice.

"Late last night."

Kurik scratched at his beard. "Princess Arissa's cloistered at Demos," he said. "If Annias came up with this scheme just recently, she may not know she's a wife."

"Widow," Berit corrected.

"All right—widow, then. Arissa's always been rather proud of the fact that she lay down with just about every man in Cimmura—begging your pardon, your Grace—and that she did it on her own terms without ever having been to the altar. If someone approached her right, it shouldn't be too hard to get her to sign a statement that she's never been married. Wouldn't that sort of muddy up the waters a little?"

"Where did you find this man, Sparhawk?" Kalten asked admiringly. "He's a treasure."

Sparhawk was thinking very fast now. "Legitimacy—or illegitimacy—is a civil matter," he noted, "since it has to do with inheritance rights and things such as that, but the wedding ceremony is always a religious one, isn't it, your Grace?"

"Yes," Dolmant agreed.

"If you and I were to get the kind of statement from Arissa that Kurik just mentioned, could the Church issue a declaration of her spinsterhood?"

Dolmant considered it. "It's highly irregular," he said dubiously.

"But it *is* possible?"

"I suppose so, yes."

"Then Annias could be ordered by the Church to withdraw his spurious document, couldn't he?"

"Of course."

Sparhawk turned to Kalten. "Who inherited Duke Osten's lands and titles?" he asked.

"His nephew—a complete ass. He's very impressed with his dukedom and he spends money faster than he earns it."

"How would he react if he were suddenly disinherited and the lands and title were passed to Lycheas instead?"

"You'd be able to hear the screams in Thalesia."

A slow smile crossed Sparhawk's face. "I know an honest magistrate in Vardenais, and the affair would be in his jurisdiction. If the current duke were to take the matter into litigation, and if he presented the Church declaration to support his position, the magistrate would rule in his favor, wouldn't he?"

Kalten grinned broadly. "He wouldn't have any choice."

"Wouldn't that sort of de-legitimize Lycheas again?"

Dolmant was smiling. Then he assumed a pious expression. "Let us press on to Demos, dear friends," he suggested. "I feel a sudden yearning to hear the confession of a certain sinner."

"Do you know something?" Talen said. "I always thought that thieves were the most devious people in the world, but nobles and churchmen make us look like amateurs."

"How would Platime handle the situation?" Kalten asked as they set off again.

"He'd stick a knife in Lycheas." Talen shrugged. "Dead bastards can't inherit thrones, can they?"

Kalten laughed. "It has a certain direct charm, I'll admit."

"You cannot solve the world's problems by murder, Kalten," Dolmant said disapprovingly.

"Why, your Grace, I wasn't talking about murder. The Church Knights are the Soldiers of God. If God tells us to kill somebody, it's an act of faith, not murder. Do you suppose the Church could see its way clear to instruct Sparhawk and me to dispatch Lycheas—and Annias—and Otha too, as long as we're at it?"

"Absolutely not!"

Kalten sighed. "It was only a thought."

"Who's Otha?" Talen asked curiously.

"Where did you grow up, boy?" Berit asked him.

"In the streets."

"Even in the streets you must have heard of the emperor of Zemoch."

"Where's Zemoch?"

"If you'd stayed in that school I put you in, you'd know," Kurik growled.

"Schools bore me, Kurik," the boy responded. "They spent months trying to teach me my letters. Once I learned how to write my own name, I didn't think I needed any of the rest of it."

"That's why you don't know where Zemoch is—or why Otha may be the one who kills you."

"Why would somebody I don't even know want to kill me?"

"Because you're an Elene."

"Everybody's an Elene—except for the Styrics, of course."

"This boy has a long way to go," Kalten observed. "Somebody ought to take him in hand."

"If it please you, my Lords," Berit said, choosing his words carefully, largely, Sparhawk guessed, because of the presence of the revered patriarch of Demos. "I know that you have pressing matters on your minds. I was never more than a passing fair scholar of history, but I will undertake the instruction of this urchin in the rudiments of the subject."

"I love to listen to this young man talk," Kalten said. "The formality almost makes me swoon with delight."

"Urchin?" Talen objected loudly.

Berit's expression did not change. With an almost casual backhanded swipe he knocked Talen out of his saddle. "Your first lesson, young man, is respect for your teacher," he said. "Never question his words."

Talen came up sputtering and with a small dagger in his fist. Berit leaned back in his saddle and kicked him solidly in the chest, knocking the wind out of him.

"Don't you just adore the learning process?" Kalten asked Sparhawk.

"Now, get back on your horse," Berit said firmly, "and pay attention. I will test you from time to time, and your answers had better be correct."

"Are you going to let him do this?" Talen appealed to his father.

Kurik grinned at him.

"This isn't fair," Talen complained, climbing back into his saddle. He wiped at his bleeding nose. "You see what you did?" he accused Berit.

"Press your finger against your upper lip," Berit suggested, "and don't speak without permission."

"What was that?" Talen demanded incredulously.

Berit raised his fist.

"All right. All right," Talen said, cringing away from the offered blow. "Go ahead. I'll listen."

"I always enjoy seeing a hunger for knowledge in the young," Dolmant observed blandly.

And so Talen's education began as they rode on to Demos. At first he was quite sullen about it, but after a few hours of listening to Berit, he began to be caught up in the story. "Can I ask questions?" he said finally.

"Of course," Berit replied.

"You said that there weren't any kingdoms in those days—just a lot of duchies and the like?"

Berit nodded.

"Then how did this Abrech of Deira gain control of the whole country in the fifteenth century? Didn't the other nobles fight him?"

"Abrech had control of the iron mines in central Deira. His warriors had steel weapons and armor. The people facing him were armed with bronze—or even flint."

"That would make a difference, I guess."

"After he had consolidated his hold on Deira, he turned south into what's now Elenia. It didn't take him very long to conquer the entire region. Then he moved down into Arcium and repeated the process there. After that, he turned toward central Eosia, Cammoria, Lamorkand, and Pelosia."

"Did he conquer all of Eosia?"

"No. It was about that time that the Eshandist Heresy arose in Rendor, and Abrech was persuaded by the Church to give himself over to its suppression."

"I've heard about the Eshandists," Talen said, "but I could never get the straight of what they really believe."

"Eshand was antihierarchical."

"What does that mean?"

"The Hierarchy is composed of higher church officials—primates, patriarchs, and the archprelate. Eshand believed that individual priests should decide matters of theology for their congregations and that the Hierocracy of the Church should be disbanded."

"I can see why high churchmen disliked him then."

"At any rate, Abrech gathered a huge army from western and central Eosia to move against Rendor. His eyes were fixed on heaven and so when the earls and dukes of the lands he had conquered asked for steel weapons—the better to fight the heretics, they said—he gave his consent without considering the implications. There were a few battles, but then Abrech's empire suddenly disintegrated. Now that they had the advanced technology that the Deirans had kept secret before, the nobles of west and central Eosia no longer felt obliged to pay homage to Abrech. Elenia and Arcium declared their independence, and Cammoria, Lamorkand, and Pelosia all coalesced into strong kingdoms. Abrech himself was killed in a battle with the Eshandists in southern Cammoria."

"What's all this got to do with Zemoch?"

"I'll get to that in due time."

Talen looked over at Kurik. "You know," he said, "this is a good story. Why didn't they tell it in that school you put me in?"

"Probably because you didn't stay long enough to give them the chance."

"That's possible, I suppose."

"How much farther is it to Demos?" Kalten asked, squinting at the late afternoon sun to gauge the time.

"About twelve leagues," Kurik replied.

"We'll never make that before nightfall. Is there an inn or a tavern hereabouts?"

"There's a village a ways up ahead. They have an inn."

"What do you think, Sparhawk?" Kalten asked.

"I suppose we might as well," the big man agreed. "We wouldn't do the horses any good by riding them all night in the cold."

The sun was going down as they rode up a long hill toward the village. Since it was behind them, it projected their shadows far out to the front. The village was small, with thatched-roofed stone houses clustered together on either side of the road. The inn at the far end was hardly more than a taproom with a sleeping loft on the second floor. The supper they were provided, however, was far better than the poor fare they had been offered the previous night.

"Are we going to the motherhouse when we get to Demos?" Kalten asked Sparhawk after they had eaten in the low, torchlit common room.

Sparhawk considered it. "It's probably being watched," he said. "Escorting the patriarch back to Chyrellos gives us an excuse to be passing through Demos, but I'd rather not have anyone see his Grace and me go into the cloister to talk with Arissa. If Annias gets any clues about what we've got planned, he'll try to counter us. Kurik, have you got any spare room at your house?"

"There's an attic—and a hayloft."

"Good. We'll be visiting you."

"Aslade will be delighted." Kurik's eyes grew troubled. "Can I talk with you for a moment, Sparhawk?"

Sparhawk pushed back his stool and followed his squire to the far side of the flagstone-floored room.

"You weren't really serious about leaving Talen with Aslade, were you?" Kurik asked quietly.

"No," Sparhawk replied, "probably not. You were right when you said that she might be very unhappy if she finds out about your indiscretion, and Talen has a busy mouth. He could let things slip."

"What are we going to do with him, then?"

"I haven't decided yet. Berit's looking after him and keeping him out of trouble."

Kurik smiled. "I expect it's the first time in his life that Talen's come up against somebody who won't tolerate his clever mouth. That lesson may be more important than all the history he's picking up."

"The same thought had occurred to me." Sparhawk glanced over at the novice, who was talking respectfully with Sephrenia. "I've got a feeling that Berit's going to make a very good Pandion," he said. "He's got character and intelligence, and he was very good in that fight down in Arcium."

"He was fighting on foot," Kurik said. "We'll know better when we see how he handles a lance."

"Kurik, you've got the soul of a drill sergeant."

"Somebody's got to do it, Sparhawk."

It was cold again the following morning, and the horses' breath steamed in the frosty air as they set out. After they had gone about a mile, Berit resumed his instruction. "All right," he said to Talen, "tell me what you learned yesterday."

Talen was tightly wrapped in a patched old gray cloak that had once belonged to Kurik and he was shivering, but he glibly recited back what Berit had told him the day before. So far as Sparhawk could tell, the boy repeated Berit's words verbatim.

"You have a very good memory, Talen," Berit congratulated him.

"It's a trick," Talen replied with uncharacteristic modesty. "Sometimes I carry messages for Platime, so I've learned how to memorize things."

"Who's Platime?"

"The best thief in Cimmura—at least he was before he got so fat."

"Do you consort with thieves?"

"I'm a thief myself, Berit. It's an ancient and honorable profession."

"Hardly honorable."

"That depends on your point of view. All right, what happened after King Abrech got killed?"

"The war with the Eshandists settled down into a stalemate," Berit took up the account. "There were raids back and forth across the Inner Sea and the Arcian Straits, but the nobles on both sides had other things on their minds. Eshand had died, and his successors were not nearly as zealous as he'd been. The Hierocracy of the Church in Chyrellos kept trying to prod the nobility into pressing the war, but the nobles were far more interested in politics than in theology."

"How long did it go on like that?"

"For nearly three centuries."

"They took their wars seriously in those days, didn't they? Wait a minute. Where were the Church Knights during all of this?"

"I'm just coming to that. When it became obvious that the nobility had lost its enthusiasm for the war, the Hierocracy gathered in Chyrellos to consider alternatives. What finally emerged was the idea of founding the militant orders to continue the struggle. The knights of the four orders all received training far beyond that given ordinary warriors; in addition, they were given instruction in the secrets of Styricum."

"What are those?"

"Magic."

"Oh. Why didn't you say so?"

"I did. Pay attention, Talen."

"Did the Church Knights win the war then?"

"They conquered all of Rendor, and the Eshandists finally capitulated. During their early years the militant orders were ambitious, and they began to carve Rendor up into four huge duchies. But then a far worse danger came out of the east."

"Zemoch?" Talen guessed.

"Exactly. The invasion of Lamorkand came without any—"

"Sparhawk!" Kalten said sharply. "Up there!" He pointed at a nearby hilltop. A dozen armed men had suddenly come riding over the crest and were crashing down through the bracken at a gallop.

Sparhawk and Kalten drew their swords and spurred forward to meet the charge. Kurik ranged out to one side shaking a spiked chain mace free from his saddle. Berit took the other side wielding his heavy-bladed battle-axe.

The two armored knights crashed into the center of the charge. Sparhawk felled two of the attackers in quick succession as Kalten chopped another out of his saddle with a rapid series of savage sword strokes. One man tried to flank them, but fell twitching as Kurik's mace crushed in the side of his head. Sparhawk and Kalten were in the very center of the attackers now, swinging their heavy broadswords in vast overhand strokes. Then Berit charged in from the flank, his axe crunching into the bodies of the riders on that side. After a few moments of concerted violence, the survivors broke and fled.

"What was that all about?" Kalten demanded. The blond man was red-faced and panting from his exertions.

"I'll chase one of them down and ask him, my Lord," Berit offered eagerly.

"No," Sparhawk told him.

Berit's face fell.

"A novice must not volunteer, Berit," Kurik told the young man sternly, "at least, not until he's proficient with his weapons."

"I did all right, Kurik," Berit protested.

"Only because these people weren't very good," Kurik said. "Your swings are too wide, Berit. You leave yourself open for counterstrokes. When we get to my farm in Demos, I'll give you some more instruction."

"Sparhawk!" Sephrenia cried from the bottom of the hill.

Sparhawk spun Faran quickly around and saw five men on foot wearing the rough smocks of Styrics running out of the bushes beside the road toward Sephrenia, Dolmant, and Talen. He swore and drove his spurs into Faran's flanks.

It quickly became obvious that the Styrics were trying to reach Sephrenia and Flute. Sephrenia, however, was not utterly defenseless. One of the Styrics fell squealing to the ground, clutching at his belly. Another dropped to his knees, clawing at his eyes. The other three faltered, fatally as it turned out, because by then Sparhawk was there. He sent one man's head flying with a single swipe of his sword, then drove his blade into the chest of another. The last Styric tried to flee, but Faran took the bit between his teeth and ran him down with three quick bounds and trampled him into the earth with his steel-shod forehooves.

"There!" Sephrenia said sharply, pointing at the hilltop. A robed and hooded figure sat astride a pale horse, watching. Even as the small Styric woman began her incantation, the figure turned and rode back over the hill and out of sight.

"Who were they?" Kalten asked as he joined them on the road.

"Mercenaries," Sparhawk replied. "You could tell by their armor."

"Was that one up on the hill the leader?" Dolmant asked.

Sephrenia nodded.

"He was a Styric, wasn't he?"

"Perhaps, but perhaps something else. I sensed something familiar about him. Once before something tried to attack the little girl. Whatever it was, it was driven off. This time it tried more direct means." Her face grew dreadfully serious. "Sparhawk," she said, "I think we should ride on to Demos as quickly as we can. It's very dangerous out here in the open."

"We could question the wounded," he suggested. "Maybe they could tell us something about this mysterious Styric who seems so interested in you and Flute."

"They won't be able to tell you anything, Sparhawk," she disagreed. "If what was up there on that hill was what I think it was, they won't even have any memory of it."

"All right," he decided, "let's ride then."

It was midafternoon when they reached Kurik's substantial farmstead just outside Demos. The farm showed Kurik's careful attention to detail. The logs forming the walls of his large house had been adze squared and they fit tightly together with no need for chinking. The roof was constructed of overlapping split shakes. There were several outbuildings and storage sheds all built back into the side of the hill just behind the house, and the two-story barn was of substantial size. The carefully tended kitchen garden was surrounded by a sturdy rail fence. A single brown and white calf stood at the fence looking wistfully at the wilted carrot tops and frost-browned cabbages inside the garden.

Two tall young men about the same age as Berit were splitting firewood in the yard, and two others, slightly older, were repairing the barn roof. They all wore rough canvas smocks.

Kurik swung down from his saddle and approached the two in the yard. "How long has it been since you sharpened those axes?" he demanded gruffly.

"Father!" one of the young men exclaimed. He dropped his axe and roughly embraced Kurik. He was, Sparhawk noticed, at least a head taller than his sire.

The other lad shouted to his brothers on the roof of the barn, and they came sliding down to leap from the edge with no apparent concern for life or limb.

Then Aslade came bustling out of the house. She was a plump woman wearing a gray homespun dress and a white apron. Her hair was touched at the temples with silver, but the dimples in her cheeks made her look girlish. She caught Kurik in a warm embrace, and for several moments Sparhawk's squire was surrounded by his family. Sparhawk watched almost wistfully.

"Regrets, Sparhawk?" Sephrenia asked him gently.

"A few, I suppose," he admitted.

"You should have listened to me when you were younger, dear one. That could be you, you know."

"My profession's a little too dangerous for me to include a wife and children in my life, Sephrenia." He sighed.

"When the time comes, dear Sparhawk, you won't even consider that."

"The time, I think, has long since passed."

"We'll see," she replied mysteriously.

"We have guests, Aslade," Kurik told his wife.

Aslade dabbed at her misty eyes with one corner of her apron and crossed to where Sparhawk and the others sat, still mounted. "Welcome to our home," she greeted them simply. She curtsied to Sparhawk and Kalten, both of whom she had known since they were boys. "My Lords," she said formally. Then she laughed. "Come down here, you two," she said, "and give me a kiss."

Like two clumsy boys, they slid from their saddles and embraced her. "You're looking well, Aslade," Sparhawk said, trying to recover some degree of dignity in the presence of Patriarch Dolmant.

"Thank you, my Lord," she said with a mocking little curtsey. Aslade had known them far too long to pay much attention to customary usages. Then she smiled broadly. She patted her ample hips. "I'm getting stouter, Sparhawk," she said. "It comes from all the tasting when I cook, I think." She shrugged good-humoredly. "But you can't tell if it's right unless you taste it." Then she turned to Sephrenia. "Dear, dear Sephrenia," she said, "it's been so long."

"Too long, Aslade," Sephrenia replied, sliding down from the back of her white palfry and taking Aslade in her arms. Then she said something in Styric to Flute, and the little girl came shyly forward and kissed Aslade's palms.

"What a beautiful child," Aslade said. She looked a bit slyly at Sephrenia. "You should have told me, my dear," she said. "I'm a very good midwife, you know, and I'm just a little hurt that you didn't invite me to officiate."

Sephrenia looked startled at that, then suddenly burst out laughing. "It's not like that at all, Aslade," she said. "There's a kinship between the child and me, but not the one you suggested."

Aslade smiled at Dolmant. "Come down from your horse, your Grace," she invited the patriarch. "Would the Church permit us an embrace—a chaste one, of course? Then you'll get your reward. I've just taken five loaves from the oven, and they're still nice and hot."

Dolmant's eyes brightened, and he quickly dismounted. Aslade threw her arms about his neck and kissed him noisily on the cheek. "He married Kurik and me, you know," she said to Sephrenia.

"Yes, dear. I was there, remember?"

Aslade blushed. "I remember very little about the ceremony," she confessed. "I had my mind on other things that day." She gave Kurik a wicked little smile.

Sparhawk carefully concealed a grin when he saw his squire's face redden noticeably.

Aslade looked inquiringly at Berit and Talen.

"The husky lad is Berit," Kurik introduced them. "He's a Pandion novice."

"You're welcome here, Berit," she told him.

"And the boy is my—uh—apprentice," Kurik fumbled. "I'm training him up to be a squire."

Aslade looked appraisingly at the young thief. "His clothes are a disgrace, Kurik," she said critically. "Couldn't you have found him something better to wear?"

"He's only recently joined us, Aslade," Kurik explained a little too quickly.

She looked even more sharply at Talen. "Do you know something, Kurik?" she said. "He looks almost exactly the way you looked when you were his age."

Kurik coughed nervously. "Coincidence," he muttered.

Aslade smiled at Sephrenia. "Would you believe that I was after Kurik from the time I was six years old? It took me ten years, but I got him in the end. Come down from your horse, Talen. I have a trunk full of clothes my sons have outgrown. We'll find something suitable for you to wear."

Talen's face had a strange, almost wistful expression as he dismounted, and Sparhawk felt a sharp pang of sympathy as he realized what the usually impudent boy must be feeling. He sighed and turned to Dolmant. "Do you want to go to the cloister now, your Grace?" he asked.

"And leave Aslade's freshly baked bread to get cold?" Dolmant protested. "Be reasonable, Sparhawk."

Sparhawk laughed as Dolmant turned to Kurik's wife. "You have fresh butter, I hope?" he asked.

"Churned yesterday morning, your Grace," she replied, "and I just opened a pot of that plum jam you're so fond of. Shall we step into the kitchen?"

"Why don't we?"

Almost absently, Aslade picked up Flute in one arm and wrapped the other about Talen's shoulders. And then, with the children close to her, she led the way into the house.

• • •

The walled cloister in which Princess Arissa was confined stood in a wooded glen on the far side of the city. Men were seldom admitted into this strict community of women, but Dolmant's rank and authority in the Church gained them immediate entry. A submissive little sister with doelike eyes and a bad complexion led them to a small garden near the south wall where they found the princess, sister of the late King Aldreas, sitting on a stone bench in the wan winter sunlight with a large book in her lap.

The years had touched Arissa only lightly. Her long, dark blonde hair was lustrous, and her eyes a pale blue, so pale as to closely resemble the gray eyes of her niece, Queen Ehlana, although the dark circles beneath them spoke of long, sleepless nights filled with bitterness and a towering resentment. Her mouth was thin-lipped rather than sensual, and there were two hard lines of discontent at its corners. Although Sparhawk knew that she was approaching forty, her features were those of a much younger woman. She did not wear the habit of the sisters of the nunnery, but was wrapped instead in a soft red woolen robe open at the throat, and her head was crowned with an intricately folded wimple. "I'm honored by your visit, gentlemen," she said in a husky voice, not bothering to rise. "I have so few visitors."

"Your Highness," Sparhawk greeted her formally. "I trust you've been well?"

"Well, but bored, Sparhawk." Then she looked at Dolmant. "You've aged, your Grace," she observed spitefully, closing her book.

"But you have not," he replied. "Will you accept my blessing, Princess?"

"I think not, your Grace. The Church has done quite enough for me already." She looked meaningfully around at the walls enclosing the garden, and her refusal of the customary blessing seemed to give her some pleasure.

He sighed. "I see," he said. "What is the book you read?" he asked her.

She held it up for him to see.

*"The Sermons of the Primate Subata,"* he noted, "a most instructional work."

She smiled maliciously. "This particular edition is even more so," she told him. "I had it made especially for me, your Grace. Within this innocent-looking cover, which deceives the mother superior who is my jailer, there lurks a volume of salacious erotic poetry from Cammoria. Would you care to have me read you a few verses?"

His eyes hardened. "No, thank you, Princess," he replied coldly. "You have not changed, I see."

She laughed mockingly. "I see no reason to change, Dolmant. I have merely altered my circumstances."

"Our visit here is not social, Princess," he said. "A rumor has surfaced in Cimmura that prior to your being cloistered here, you were secretly married to Duke Osten of Vardenais. Would you care to confirm—or deny—that rumor?"

"Osten?" She laughed. "That dried-up old stick? Who in her right mind would marry a man like that? I like my men younger, more ardent."

"You deny the rumor, then?"

"Of course I deny it. I'm like the Church, Dolmant. I offer my bounty to *all* men—as everyone in Cimmura knows."

"Would you sign a document declaring the rumor to be false?"

"I'll think about it." She looked at Sparhawk. "What are you doing back in Elenia, Sir Knight? I thought my brother exiled you."

"I was summoned back, Arissa."

"How very interesting."

Sparhawk thought of something. "Did you receive a dispensation to attend your brother's funeral, Princess?" he asked her.

"Why, yes, Sparhawk. The Church generously granted me three whole days of mourning. My poor, stupid brother looked very regal as he lay on his bier in his state robes." She critically examined her long, pointed fingernails. "Death improves some people," she added.

"You hated him, didn't you?"

"I held him in contempt, Sparhawk. There's a difference. I always used to bathe whenever I left him."

Sparhawk held out his hand, showing her the bloodred ring on his finger. "Did you happen to notice if he had the mate to this on his finger?" he asked her.

She frowned slightly. "No," she said. "As a matter of fact, he didn't. Perhaps the brat stole it after he died."

Sparhawk clenched his teeth.

"Poor, poor Sparhawk," she said mockingly. "You cannot bear to hear the truth about your precious Ehlana, can you? We used to laugh about your attachment to her when she was a child. Did you have hopes, great champion? I saw her at my brother's funeral. She's not a child anymore, Sparhawk. She has the hips and breasts of a woman now. But she's sealed up in a diamond, isn't she, so you can't even touch her? All that soft, warm skin, and you can't even put so much as a finger on it."

"I don't think we need to pursue this, Arissa." He narrowed his eyes. "Who is your son's father?" he asked her suddenly, hoping to startle the truth out of her.

She laughed. "How could I possibly know that?" she asked. "After my brother's wedding, I amused myself in a certain establishment in Cimmura." She rolled her eyes. "It was both enjoyable and profitable. I made a very great deal of money. Most of the girls there overpriced themselves, but I learned as a child that the secret of great wealth is to sell cheaply to many." She looked maliciously at Dolmant. "Besides," she added, "it's a renewable resource."

Dolmant's face grew stiff, and Arissa laughed coarsely.

"That's enough, Princess," Sparhawk told her. "You would not care then to hazard a guess as to the identity of your bastard's father?" He said it quite deliberately, hoping to sting her into some inadvertent revelation.

Her eyes flashed with momentary anger, then she leaned back on the stone bench with a heavy-lidded look of voluptuous amusement. She put her hands to the front of her scarlet robe. "I'm a bit out of practice, but I suppose I could improvise. Would you like to try me, Sparhawk?"

"I don't think so, Arissa." Sparhawk's voice was flat.

"Ah, the well-known prudery of your family. What a shame, Sparhawk. You interested me when you were a young knight. Now you've lost your queen, and there's not even that pair of rings to prove the connection between the two of you. Wouldn't that mean that you're no longer her champion? Perhaps—if she recovers—you might be able to establish a closer bond with her. She shares my blood, you know, and it might flow as hotly through her veins as it does through mine. If you were to try me, you could compare and find out."

He turned away in disgust, and she laughed again.

"Shall I send for parchment and ink, Princess?" Dolmant asked, "so that we may compose your denial of the rumor concerning your marriage?"

"No, Dolmant," she replied, "I don't think so. This request of yours hints at the interest of the Church in this matter. The Church has done me few favors of late, so why should I exert myself in her behalf? If the people in Cimmura want to amuse themselves with rumors about me, let them. They licked their lips over the truth, now let them enjoy a lie."

"That's your final word then?"

"I might change my mind. Sparhawk's a Church Knight, your Grace, and you're a patriarch. Why don't you order him to see if he can persuade me? Sometimes I persuade easily—sometimes not. It all depends on the persuader."

"I think we've concluded our business here," Dolmant said. "Good day, Princess." He turned on his heel and started across the winter-brown lawn of the garden.

"Come back some time when you can leave your stuffy friend behind, Sparhawk," Arissa said. "We could amuse ourselves."

He turned without answering and followed the patriarch out of the garden. "I think we've wasted our time," he muttered, his face dark and angry.

"Ah, no, my boy," Dolmant said serenely. "In her haste to be offensive, the princess overlooked an important point in canon law. She has just made a free admission in the presence of two ecclesiastical witnesses—you and me. That has all the validity of a signed statement. All it takes is our oaths as to what she said."

Sparhawk blinked. "Dolmant," he said, "you're the most devious man I've ever known."

"I'm glad you approve, my son." The patriarch smiled.

---

# CHAPTER TWELVE

They left Kurik's farmstead early the following morning. Aslade and her four sons stood in the dooryard waving as they rode out. Kurik remained behind for a few personal farewells, promising to catch up with them a bit later.

"Are we going through the city?" Kalten asked Sparhawk.

"I don't think so," Sparhawk replied. "We can take the road that goes around the north side. I'm fairly sure that we'll be seen, but let's not make it easy for them."

"Would you mind a personal observation?"

"Probably not."

"You really ought to give some thought to letting Kurik retire, you know. He's getting older and he should be spending more time with his family instead of trailing along behind you all over the world. Besides, so far as I know, you're the only Church Knight who still has a squire. The rest of us have learned to get along without them. Give him a good pension and let him stay home."

Sparhawk squinted at the sun which was just rising above the wooded hilltop lying to the east of Demos. "You're probably right," he agreed, "but how would I go about telling him? My father placed Kurik in my service before I completed my novitiate. It has to do with being hereditary champion of the royal house of Elenia." He smiled wryly. "It's an archaic position that requires archaic usages. Kurik's a friend more than a squire, and I'm not going to hurt him by telling him that he's too old to serve anymore."

"It's a problem, isn't it?"

"Yes," Sparhawk said, "it is."

Kurik came riding up behind them as they were passing the cloister where Princess Arissa was confined. His bearded face was a bit glum, but then he straightened his shoulders and assumed a businesslike expression.

Sparhawk looked gravely at his friend, trying to imagine life without him. Then he shook his head. It was totally impossible.

The road leading toward Chyrellos passed through an evergreen forest where the morning sun streamed down through the boughs to spatter the forest floor with gold. The air was crisp and bright, although there was no frost. After they had gone about a mile farther, Berit resumed his narrative. "The Knights of the Church were consolidating their position in Rendor," he told Talen, "when word reached Chyrellos that Emperor Otha of Zemoch had massed a huge army and was marching into Lamorkand."

"Wait a minute," Talen interrupted him. "When did all this happen?"

"About five hundred years ago."

"It wasn't the same Otha Kalten was talking about the other day then, was it?"

"So far as we know, it was."

"That's impossible, Berit."

"Otha is perhaps nineteen hundred years old," Sephrenia told the boy.

"I thought this was a history," Talen accused, "not a fairy tale."

"When Otha was a boy, he encountered the Elder God Azash," she explained. "The Elder Gods of Styricum have great powers and are not controlled by any form of morality. One of the gifts they can bestow upon their followers is the gift of a greatly expanded lifetime. That is why some men are willing to follow them."

"Immortality?" he asked her skeptically.

"No," she corrected, "not that. No God can bestow that."

"The Elene God can," Dolmant said, "in a spiritual sense, anyway."

"That's an interesting theological point, your Grace." She smiled. "Someday we'll have to discuss it. Anyway," she continued, "when Otha agreed to worship Azash, the God granted him enormous power, and Otha eventually became emperor of Zemoch. The Styrics and the Elenes in Zemoch have intermarried, and so a Zemoch is not truly a member of either race."

"An abomination in the eyes of God," Dolmant added.

"The Styric Gods feel much the same way," Sephrenia agreed. She looked at Talen again. "To understand Otha—and Zemoch—one needs to understand Azash. He is the most totally evil force on earth. The rites of the worship of him are obscene. He delights in perversion and in blood and in the agonies of sacrificial victims. In their worship of him, the Zemochs have become much less than human and their incursion into Lamorkand was accompanied by unspeakable horrors. Had the invading armies been only Zemochs, however, they might have been met and turned back by conventional forces. But Azash had reinforced them with creatures from the underworld."

"Goblins?" Talen asked disbelievingly.

"Not exactly; but the word will serve, I suppose. It would take most of the morning for me to describe the twenty or so varieties of inhuman creatures Azash has at his command, and you wouldn't like the descriptions."

"This story is getting less believable by the minute," Talen noted. "I like the battles and all, but when you start telling me about goblins and fairies, I begin to lose interest. I'm not a child anymore, after all."

"In time you may come to understand—and to believe," she said. "Go on with the story, Berit."

"Yes, ma'am," he said. "When the Church realized the nature of the forces that were invading Lamorkand, they summoned the Church Knights back from Rendor. They reinforced the ranks of the four orders with other knights and with common soldiers until the forces of the west were nearly as numerous as those of the Zemoch horde of Otha."

"Was there a battle then?" Talen asked eagerly.

"The greatest battle in the history of mankind," Berit replied. "The two armies met on the plains of Lamorkand near Lake Randera. The physical battle was gigantic, but the supernatural battle on that plain was even more stupendous. Waves of darkness and sheets of flame swept the field. Fire and lightning rained from the sky. Whole battalions were swallowed up by the earth or burned to ashes in sudden flame. The crash of thunder rolled perpetually from horizon to horizon, and the ground itself was torn by earthquakes and the eruption of searing liquid rock. The magic of the Zemoch priests was countered each time by the concerted magic of the Knights of the Church. For three days, the armies were locked in battle before the Zemochs were pushed back. Their retreat became more rapid, eventually turning into a rout. Otha's horde finally broke and ran toward the safety of the border."

"Terrific!" Talen exclaimed excitedly. "And then did our army invade Zemoch?"

"They were too exhausted," Berit told him. "They had won the battle, but not without great cost. Fully half of the Church Knights lay slain upon the battlefield, and the armies of the Elene kings numbered their dead by the scores of thousands."

"They could have done *something*, couldn't they?"

Berit nodded sadly. "They cared for their wounded and buried their dead. Then they went home."

"That's all?" Talen asked incredulously. "This isn't much of a story if that's all they did, Berit."

"They had no choice. They'd stripped the western kingdoms of every able-bodied man to fight the war and had left the crops untended. Winter was coming, and there was no food. They managed to eke their way through that winter, but so many men had been killed or maimed in the battle that when spring came, there weren't enough people—in the west or in Zemoch—to plant new crops. The result was famine. For a century, the only concern in all of Eosia was food. The swords and lances were put aside, and the war horses were hitched to plows."

"They never talk about that sort of thing in other stories I've heard." Talen sniffed.

"That's because those are only stories," Berit told him. "This really happened. Anyway," he went on, "the war and the famine which followed caused great changes. The militant orders were forced to labor in the fields beside the common people and they gradually began to distance themselves from the Church. Pardon me, your Grace," he said to Dolmant, "but at that time, the Hierocracy was too far removed from the concerns of the commons fully to understand their suffering."

"There's no need to apologize, Berit," Dolmant replied sadly. "The Church has freely admitted her blunders during that era."

Berit nodded. "The Church Knights became increasingly secularized. The original intent of the Hierocracy had been that the knights should be armed monks who would live in their chapterhouses when they weren't fighting. That concept began to fade. The dreadful casualties in their ranks made it necessary for them to seek a source for new recruits. The preceptors of the orders journeyed to Chyrellos and laid the problem before the Hierocracy in the strongest of terms. The main stumbling block to recruitment had always been the vow of celibacy. At the insistence of the preceptors, the Hierocracy relaxed that rule, and Church Knights were permitted to take wives and father children."

"Are you married, Sparhawk?" Talen suddenly asked.

"No," the knight replied.

"Why not?"

"He hasn't found any woman silly enough to have him." Kalten laughed. "He's not very pretty to begin with and he's got a foul temper."

Talen looked at Berit. "That's the end of the story, then?" he asked critically. "A good story needs an end, you know—something like, 'and they all lived happily ever after.' Yours just sort of dribbles off without going any place."

"History just keeps going, Talen. There aren't any ends. The militant orders are now as much involved in political affairs as they are in the affairs of the Church, and no one can say what lies in store for them in the future."

Dolmant sighed. "All too true," he agreed. "I wish it might have been otherwise, but perhaps God had His reasons for ordaining things this way."

"Wait a minute," Talen objected. "This all started when you were going to tell me about Otha and Zemoch. He sort of fell out of the story a ways back. Why are we so worried about him now?"

"Otha is mobilizing his armies again," Sparhawk told him.

"Are we doing anything about it?"

"We're watching him. If he comes again, we'll meet him the same way we did last time." Sparhawk looked around at the yellow grass gleaming in the bright morning sunlight. "If we want to get to Chyrellos before the month's out, we're going to have to move a little faster," he said, touching his spurs to Faran's flanks.

They rode east for three days, stopping each night in wayside inns. Sparhawk concealed a certain tolerant amusement as Talen, inspired by Berit's recounting of the age-old story, fiercely beheaded thistles with a stick as they rode along. It was midafternoon of the third day when they crested a long hill to look down upon the vast sprawl of Chyrellos, the seat of the Elene Church. The city lay within no specific kingdom, but sat instead at the place where Elenia, Arcium, Cammoria, Lamorkand, and Pelosia touched. It was by far the largest city in all of Eosia. Since it was a Church city, it was dotted with spires and domes; at certain times of the day, the air above it shimmered with the sound of bells, calling the faithful to prayer. No city so large, however, could be given over entirely to churches. Commerce, almost as much as religion, dominated the society of the holy city, and the palaces of wealthy merchants vied with those of the patriarchs of the Church for splendor and opulence. The center and focus of the city, however, was the Basilica of Chyrellos, a vast, domed cathedral of gleaming marble erected to the glory of God. The power emanating from the Basilica was enormous, and it touched the lives of all Elenes from the snowy wastes of northern Thalesia to the deserts of Rendor.

Talen, who until now had never been out of Cimmura, gaped in astonishment at the enormous city spread before them, gleaming in the winter sunlight. "Good God!" he breathed almost reverently.

"Yes," Dolmant agreed. "He is good, and this is one of His most splendid works."

Flute, however, seemed unimpressed. She drew out her pipes and played a mocking little melody on them as if to dismiss all the splendors of Chyrellos as unimportant.

"Will you go directly to the Basilica, your Grace?" Sparhawk asked.

"No," Dolmant replied. "It's been a tiring journey, and I'll need my wits about me when I present this matter to the Hierocracy. Annias has many friends in the highest councils of the Church, and they won't like what I'm going to say to them."

"They can't possibly doubt your words, your Grace."

"Perhaps not, but they can try to twist them around." Dolmant tugged thoughtfully at one earlobe. "I think my report might have more impact if I have corroboration. Are you any good at public appearances?"

"Only if he can use his sword," Kalten said.

Dolmant smiled faintly. "Come to my house tomorrow, Sparhawk. We'll go over your testimony together."

"Is that altogether legal, your Grace?" Sparhawk asked.

"I won't ask you to lie under oath, Sparhawk. All I want to do is suggest to you how you should phrase your answers to certain questions." He smiled again. "I don't want you to surprise me when we're before the Hierocracy. I hate surprises."

"All right then, your Grace," Sparhawk agreed.

They rode on down the hill to the great bronze gates of the holy city. The guards there saluted Dolmant and let them all pass without question. Beyond the gate lay a broad street that could only be called a boulevard. Huge houses stood on either side, seeming almost to shoulder at each other in their eagerness to command the undivided attention of passersby. The street teemed with people. Although many of them wore the drab smocks of workmen, the vast majority were garbed in somber, ecclesiastical black.

"Is everybody here a churchman?" Talen asked. The boy's eyes were wide as the sights of Chyrellos overwhelmed him. The cynical young thief from the back alleys of Cimmura had finally seen something he could not shrug off.

"Hardly," Kalten replied, "but in Chyrellos, one commands a bit more respect if he's thought to be affiliated with the Church, so everybody wears black."

"Frankly, I wouldn't mind seeing a bit more color in the streets of Chyrellos," Dolmant said. "All this unrelieved black depresses me."

"Why not start a new trend then, your Grace?" Kalten suggested. "The next time you present yourself at the Basilica, wear a pink cassock—or maybe emerald green. You'd look very nice in green."

"The dome would collapse if I did," Dolmant said wryly.

The patriarch's house, unlike the palaces of most other high churchmen, was simple and unadorned. It was set slightly back from the street and was surrounded by well-trimmed shrubs and an iron fence.

"We'll go on to the chapterhouse then, your Grace," Sparhawk said as they stopped at Dolmant's gate.

The patriarch nodded. "And I'll see you tomorrow."

Sparhawk saluted and then led the others on down the street.

"He's a good man, isn't he?" Kalten said.

"One of the best," Sparhawk replied. "The church is lucky to have him."

The chapterhouse of the Pandion Knights in Chyrellos was a bleak-looking stone building on a little-travelled side street. Although it was not moated as was the one in Cimmura, it was nonetheless surrounded by a high wall and blocked off from the street by a formidable gate. Sparhawk went through the ritual which gained them entry, and they dismounted in the courtyard. The governor of the chapterhouse, a stout man named Nashan, came bustling down the stairs to greet them. "Our house is honored, Sir Sparhawk," he said, clasping the big knight's hand. "How did things turn out in Cimmura?"

"We managed to pull Annias's teeth," Sparhawk replied.

"How did he take it?"

"He looked a little sick."

"Good." Nashan turned to Sephrenia. "Welcome, little mother," he greeted her, kissing both her palms.

"Nashan," she replied gravely. "I see that you're not missing too many meals."

He laughed and slapped at his paunch. "Every man needs a vice or two," he said. "Come inside, all of you. I've smuggled a skin of Arcian red into the house— for my stomach's sake, of course—and we can all have a goblet or two."

"You see how it works, Sparhawk?" Kalten said. "Rules can be bent if you know the right people."

Nashan's study was draped and carpeted in red, and the ornate table which served as his desk was inlaid with gold and mother-of-pearl. "A gesture," he said apologetically as he led them into the room and looked about. "In Chyrellos, we must make these little genuflections in the direction of opulence if we are to be taken seriously."

"It's all right, Nashan," Sephrenia told him. "You weren't selected as governor of this chapterhouse because of your humility."

"One must keep up appearances, Sephrenia," he said. He sighed. "I was never that good a knight," he admitted. "I'm at best only mediocre with the lance, and most of my spells tend to crumble on me about halfway through." He drew in a deep breath and looked around. "I'm a good administrator, though. I know the Church and her politics and I can serve the order and Lord Vanion in that arena probably far better than I could on the field."

"We all do what we can," Sparhawk told him. "I'm told that God appreciates our best efforts."

"Sometimes I feel that I've disappointed Him," Nashan said. "Somewhere deep inside me I think I might have done better."

"Don't flagellate yourself, Nashan," Sephrenia advised. "The Elene God is reputed to be most forgiving. You've done what you could."

They took seats around Nashan's ornate table, and the governor summoned an acolyte who brought goblets and the skin of the deep red Arcian wine. At Sephrenia's request, he also sent for tea for her and milk for Flute and Talen.

"We don't necessarily need to mention this to Lord Vanion, do we?" Nashan said to Sparhawk as he lifted the wineskin.

"Wild horses couldn't drag it out of me, my Lord," Sparhawk told him, holding out his goblet.

"So," Kalten said, "what's happening here in Chyrellos?"

"Troubled times, Kalten," Nashan replied. "Troubled times. The archprelate ages, and the entire city is holding its breath in anticipation of his death."

"Who will be the new archprelate?" Sparhawk asked.

"At the moment there's no way to know. Cluvonus is in no condition to name a successor, and Annias of Cimmura is spending money like water to gain the throne."

"What about Dolmant?" Kalten asked.

"He's too self-effacing, I'm afraid," Nashan replied. "He's so dedicated to the Church that he doesn't have the sense of self that one needs to have to aspire to the golden throne in the Basilica. Not only that, he's made enemies."

"I like enemies." Kalten grinned. "They give you a reason to keep your sword sharp."

Nashan looked at Sephrenia. "Is there something afoot in Styricum?" he asked her.

"What exactly do you mean?"

"The city is suddenly awash with Styrics," he replied. "They say that they're here to seek instruction in the Elene faith."

"That's absurd."

"I thought so myself. The Church has been trying to convert the Styrics for three thousand years without much success, and now they come flocking to Chyrellos on their own accord, begging to be converted."

"No sane Styric would do that," she insisted. "Our Gods are jealous, and they punish apostasy severely." Her eyes narrowed. "Have any of these pilgrims identified their place of origin?" she asked.

"Not that I've heard. They all look like common rural Styrics."

"Perhaps they've made a longer journey than they're willing to reveal."

"You think they might be Zemochs?" Sparhawk asked her.

"Otha's already infested eastern Lamorkand with his agents," she replied. "Chyrellos is the center of the Elene world. It's a logical place for espionage and disruption." She considered it. "We're likely to be here for a while," she observed. "We have to wait for the arrival of the knights from the other orders. I think that perhaps we might spend the time investigating these unusual postulants."

"I can't really get too much involved in that," Sparhawk disagreed. "I have things far more important on my mind just now. We'll deal with Otha and his Zemochs when the time comes. Right now I have to concentrate on restoring Ehlana to her throne and preventing the deaths of certain friends." He spoke obliquely, since he had kept to himself the details of what she had told him had taken place in the throne room in Cimmura.

"It's all right, Sparhawk," she assured him. "I understand your concern. I'll take Kalten with me, and we'll see what we can turn up."

They spent the remainder of the day in quiet conversation in Nashan's ornate study, and the following morning Sparhawk dressed in a mail coat and a simple hooded robe and rode across town to Dolmant's house, where the two of them carefully went over what had happened in Cimmura and Arcium. "It would be futile to level any direct charges at Annias," Dolmant said, "so it's probably best to omit any references to him—or to Harparin. Let's just present the affair as a plot to discredit the Pandion Order and leave it at that. The Hierocracy will draw its own conclusions." He smiled faintly. "The least damaging of those conclusions will be that Annias made a fool of himself in public. If nothing else, that might help to stiffen the resolve of the neutral patriarchs when the time comes to select a new archprelate."

"That's something, anyway," Sparhawk said. "Are we going to present the matter of Arissa's so-called marriage at the same time?"

"I don't think so," Dolmant replied. "It's really not a significant enough thing to require the consideration of the entire Hierocracy. The declarations of Arissa's spinsterhood can come from the patriarch of Vardenais. The alleged wedding took place in his district, and he would be the logical one to draw up the denial that it took place." A smile touched his ascetic face. "Besides," he added, "he's a friend of mine."

"Clever," Sparhawk said admiringly.

"I rather liked it," Dolmant said modestly.

"When are we going before the Hierocracy?"

"Tomorrow morning. There's no point in waiting. All that would do is give Annias time to alert his friends in the Basilica."

"Do you want me to come by here and ride to the Basilica with you?"

"No. Let's go in separately. Let's not give them the slightest hint of what we're up to."

"You're very good at political chicanery, your Grace." Sparhawk grinned.

"Of course I am. How do you think I got to be a patriarch? Come to the Basilica during the third hour after sunrise. That should give me time to present my report first—and to answer all the questions and objections that Annias's supporters are likely to raise."

"Very well, your Grace," Sparhawk said, rising to his feet.

"Be careful tomorrow, Sparhawk. They'll try to trip you up. And for God's sake, don't lose your temper."

"I'll try to remember that."

The following morning Sparhawk dressed carefully. His black armor gleamed, and his cape and silver surcoat had been freshly pressed. Faran had been groomed until his roan coat shone, and his hooves had been oiled to make them glossy.

"Don't let them back you into a corner, Sparhawk," Kalten warned as he and Kurik boosted the big man into his saddle. "Churchmen can be very devious."

"I'll watch myself." Sparhawk gathered his reins and nudged Faran with his heels. The big roan pranced out through the chapterhouse gate and into the teeming streets of the holy city.

The domed Basilica of Chyrellos dominated the entire city. It was built on a low hill, and it soared toward heaven, gleaming in the wintery sun. The guards at the bronze portal admitted Sparhawk respectfully, and he dismounted before the marble stairs that led up to the great doors. He handed Faran's reins to a monk, adjusted the strap on his shield, and then mounted the steps, his spurs ringing on the marble. At the top of the stairs, an officious young churchman in a black cassock blocked his path. "Sir Knight," the young man protested, "you may not enter while under arms."

"You're wrong, your Reverence," Sparhawk told him. "Those rules don't apply to the militant orders."

"I've never heard of any such exception."

"You have now. I don't want any trouble with you, friend, but I've been summoned by Patriarch Dolmant and I'm going inside."

"But—"

"There's an extensive library here, neighbor. Why don't you go look up the rules again? I'm sure you'll find that you've missed a few. Now stand aside." He brushed past the man in the black cassock and went on into the cool incense-smelling cathedral. He made the customary bow toward the jewel-encrusted altar and moved on down the broad central aisle in the multicolored light streaming through tall, stained-glass windows. A sacristan stood by the altar vigorously polishing a silver chalice.

"Good morning, friend," Sparhawk said to him in his quiet voice.

The sacristan almost dropped the chalice. "You startled me, Sir Knight," he said, laughing nervously. "I didn't hear you come up behind me."

"It's the carpeting," Sparhawk said. "It muffles the sound of footsteps. I understand that the members of the Hierocracy are in session."

The sacristan nodded.

"Patriarch Dolmant summoned me to testify in a matter he's presenting this morning. Could you tell me where they're meeting?"

"In the archprelate's audience chamber, I believe. Do you want me to show you the way, Sir Knight?"

"I know where it is. Thanks, neighbor." Sparhawk went across the front of the nave and out through a side door into an echoing marble corridor. He removed his helmet and tucked it under his arm and proceeded along the corridor until he reached a large room where a dozen churchmen sat at tables sorting through stacks of documents. One of the black-robed men looked up, saw Sparhawk in the doorway, and rose. "May I help you, Sir Knight?" he asked. The top of his head was bald, and wispy tufts of gray hair stuck out over his ears like wings.

"The name is Sparhawk, your Reverence. The Patriarch Dolmant summoned me."

"Ah, yes," the bald churchman said. "The patriarch advised me that he was expecting you. I'll go tell him that you've arrived. Would you care to sit down while you're waiting?"

"No thanks, your Reverence. I'll stand. It's a little awkward to sit down when you're wearing a sword."

The churchman smiled a bit wistfully. "I wouldn't know about that," he said. "What's it like?"

"It's overrated," Sparhawk told him. "Would you tell the patriarch that I'm here?"

"At once, Sir Sparhawk." The churchman turned and crossed the room to the far door with his sandals slapping on the marble floor. After a few moments he came back. "Dolmant says that you're to go right on in. The archprelate's with them."

"That's a surprise. I've heard that he's been ill."

"This is one of his better days, I think." The churchman led the way across the room and opened the door for Sparhawk.

The audience chamber was flanked on either side by tier upon tier of high-backed benches. The benches were filled with elderly churchmen in sober black, the Hierocracy of the Elene Church. At the front of the room on a raised dais sat a large golden throne, and seated upon that throne in a white satin robe and golden miter was the Archprelate Cluvonus. The old man was dozing. In the center of the room stood an ornate lectern. Dolmant was there with a sheaf of parchment on the slanted shelf before him. "Ah," he said, "Sir Sparhawk. So good of you to come."

"My pleasure, your Grace," Sparhawk replied.

"Brothers," Dolmant said to the other members of the Hierocracy, "I have the honor to present the Pandion Knight, Sir Sparhawk."

"We have heard of Sir Sparhawk," a lean-faced patriarch seated in the front tier on the left said coldly. "Why is he here, Dolmant?"

"To present evidence in the matter we were just discussing, Makova," Dolmant replied distantly.

"I have heard quite enough already."

"Speak for yourself, Makova," a jovial-looking fat man said from the right tier. "The militant orders are the arm of the Church, and their members are always welcome at our deliberations."

The two men glared at each other.

"Since Sir Sparhawk was instrumental in uncovering and thwarting this plot," Dolmant said smoothly, "I thought that his testimony might prove enlightening."

"Oh, get on with it, Dolmant," the lean-faced patriarch on the left said irritably. "We have matters of much greater importance to take up this morning."

"It shall be as the esteemed patriarch of Coombe wishes." Dolmant bowed. "Sir Sparhawk," he said then, "do you give your oath as a Knight of the Church that your testimony shall be the truth?"

"I do, your Grace," Sparhawk affirmed.

"Please tell the assembly how you uncovered this plot."

"Of course, your Grace." Sparhawk then recounted most of the conversation between Harparin and Krager, omitting their names, the name of the Primate Annias, and all references to Ehlana.

"Is it your custom to eavesdrop on private conversations, Sir Sparhawk?" Makova asked a bit spitefully.

"When it involves the security of the Church or the State, yes, your Grace. I'm sworn to defend both."

"Ah, yes. I'd forgotten that you are also the champion of the queen of Elenia. Does that sometimes not divide your loyalties, Sir Sparhawk?"

"It hasn't so far, your Grace. The interests of the Church and the State are seldom in conflict with each other in Elenia."

"Well said, Sir Sparhawk," the fat churchman on the right approved.

The patriarch of Coombe leaned over and whispered something to the sallow man sitting beside him.

"What did you do after you learned of this conspiracy, Sir Sparhawk?" Dolmant asked then.

"We gathered our forces and rode down into Arcium to intercept the men who were to carry out the attack."

"And why did you not advise the primate of Cimmura of this so-called conspiracy?" Makova asked.

"The scheme involved an attack on a house in Arcium, your Grace," Sparhawk replied. "The primate of Cimmura has no authority there, so the matter didn't concern him."

"Nor the Pandions either, I should say. Why did you not just alert the Cyrinic Knights and let them deal with things?" Makova looked around smugly at those seated near him as if he had just made a killing point.

"The plot was designed to discredit *our* order, your Grace. We felt that gave us sufficient reason to attend to the matter ourselves. Besides, the Cyrinics have their own concerns, and we didn't want to trouble them with so minor an affair."

Makova grunted sourly.

"What happened then, Sir Sparhawk?" Dolmant asked.

"Things went more or less as expected, your Grace. We alerted Count Radun; then, when the mercenaries arrived, we fell on them from behind. Not very many of them escaped."

"You attacked them from behind without warning?" Patriarch Makova looked outraged. "Is this the vaunted heroism of the Pandion Knights?"

"You're nitpicking, Makova," the jovial-looking man on the other side of the aisle snorted. "Your precious Primate Annias made a fool of himself. Quit trying to smooth it over by attacking this knight or trying to impugn his testimony." He looked shrewdly at Sparhawk. "Would you care to hazard a guess as to the source of this conspiracy, Sir Sparhawk?" he asked.

"We are not here to listen to speculation, Emban," Makova snapped quickly. "The witness can testify only to what he knows, not what he guesses."

"The patriarch of Coombe is right, your Grace," Sparhawk said to Patriarch Emban. "I swore to speak only the truth, and guesses usually fly wide of that mark. The Pandion Order has offended many people in the past century or so. We are sometimes an acerbic group of men, stiff-necked and unforgiving. Many find that quality in us unpleasant, and old hatreds die hard."

"True," Emban conceded. "If it came to the defense of the faith, however, I would prefer to place my trust in you stiff-necked and unforgiving Pandions rather than some others I could name. Old hatreds, as you say, die hard, but so do new ones. I've heard about what's going on in Elenia, and it's not too hard to pick out somebody who might profit from the Pandions' disgrace."

"Do you dare to accuse the Primate Annias?" Makova cried, jumping to his feet with his eyes bulging.

"Oh, sit down, Makova," Emban said in disgust. "You contaminate us by your very presence. Everybody in this chamber knows who owns you."

"You accuse *me*?"

"Who paid for that new palace of yours, Makova? Six months ago you tried to borrow money from me, but now you seem to have all you need. Isn't that curious? Who's subsidizing you, Makova?"

"What's all the shouting about?" a feeble voice asked.

Sparhawk looked sharply at the golden throne at the front of the chamber. The Archprelate Cluvonus had come awake and was blinking in confusion as he looked around. The old man's head was wobbling on his stringy neck, and his eyes were bleary.

"A spirited discussion, Most Holy," Dolmant said mildly.

"Now you went and woke me up," the archprelate said petulantly, "and I was having such a nice dream." He reached up, pulled off his miter, and threw it on the floor. Then he sank back on his throne, pouting.

"Would the Archprelate care to hear of the matter under discussion?" Dolmant asked.

"No, I wouldn't," Cluvonus snapped. "So there." Then he cackled as if his infantile outburst had been some enormous joke. The laughter trailed off and he scowled at them. "I want to go back to my room," he declared. "Get out of here, all of you."

The Hierocracy rose to its feet and began to file out.

"You, too, Dolmant," the archprelate insisted in a shrill voice. "And send Sister Clentis to me. She's the only one who really cares about me."

"As you wish, Most Holy," Dolmant said, bowing.

When they were outside, Sparhawk walked beside the patriarch of Demos. "How long has he been like this?" he asked.

Dolmant sighed. "For a year now at least," he replied. "His mind has been failing for quite some time, but it's only in the past year that his senility has reached this level."

"Who is Sister Clentis?"

"His keeper—his nursemaid, actually."

"Is his condition widely known?"

"There are rumors, of course, but we've managed to keep his true state a secret." Dolmant sighed again. "Don't judge him by the way he is now, Sparhawk. When he was younger, he honored the throne of the archprelacy."

Sparhawk nodded. "I know," he agreed. "How is his health otherwise?"

"Not good. He's very frail. It cannot be much longer."

"Perhaps that's why Annias is beginning to move so quickly." Sparhawk shifted his silver-embossed shield. "Time's on his side, you know."

Dolmant made a sour face. "Yes," he agreed. "That's what makes your mission so vital."

Another churchman came up to join them. "Well, Dolmant," he said, "a very interesting morning. Just how deeply was Annias involved in the scheme?"

"I didn't say anything about the primate of Cimmura, Yarris," Dolmant protested with mock innocence.

"You didn't have to. It all fits together a bit too neatly. I don't think anybody on the council missed your point."

"Do you know the patriarch of Vardenais, Sparhawk?" Dolmant asked.

"We've met a few times." Sparhawk bowed slightly to the other churchman, his armor creaking. "Your Grace," he said.

"It's good to see you again, Sir Sparhawk," Yarris replied. "How are things in Cimmura?"

"Tense," Sparhawk said.

Patriarch Yarris looked at Dolmant. "You know that Makova's going to report everything that happened this morning to Annias, don't you?"

"I wasn't trying to keep it a secret. Annias made an ass of himself. Considering his aspirations, that element of his personality is highly relevant."

"It is indeed, Dolmant. You've made another enemy this morning."

"Makova's never been that fond of me anyway. Incidentally, Yarris, Sparhawk, and I would like to present a certain matter to you for your consideration."

"Oh?"

"It involves another ploy by the primate of Cimmura."

"Then let's thwart him, by all means."

"I was hoping you might feel that way about it."

"What's he up to this time?"

"He presented a spurious marriage certificate to the Royal Council in Cimmura."

"Who got married?"

"Princess Arissa and Duke Osten."

"That's ridiculous."

"Princess Arissa said almost the same thing."

"You'll swear to that?"

Dolmant nodded. "So will Sparhawk," he added.

"I assume that the point of the whole thing was to legitimize Lycheas?"

Dolmant nodded again.

"Well, then. Why don't we see if we can disrupt that? Let's go speak with my secretary. He can draw up the necessary document." The patriarch of Vardenais chuckled. "Annias is having a bad month, I'd say. This will make two plots in a row that have failed—and Sparhawk's been involved both times." He looked at the big Pandion. "Keep your armor on, my boy," he suggested. "Annias might decide to have the area between your shoulder blades decorated with a dagger hilt."

After Dolmant and Sparhawk had given their depositions concerning the statements of Princess Arissa, they left the patriarch of Vardenais and continued along the corridor to the nave of the Basilica.

"Dolmant," Sparhawk said, "do you have any idea about why so many Styrics are here in Chyrellos?"

"I've heard about it. The story is that they're seeking instruction in our faith."

"Sephrenia says that's an absurdity."

Dolmant made a wry face. "She's probably right. I've labored for a lifetime and I haven't as yet managed to convert a single Styric."

"They're very attached to their Gods," Sparhawk said. "I'm not trying to be offensive, Dolmant, but there seems to be a very close personal relationship between the Styrics and their Gods. Our God is perhaps a bit remote."

"I'll mention that the next time I talk to Him." Dolmant smiled. "I'm sure He values your opinion."

Sparhawk laughed. "It *was* a bit presumptuous, wasn't it?"

"Yes, as a matter of fact, it was. How long do you think it's going to be until you can leave for Borrata?"

"Several days, anyway. I hate to lose the time, but the knights from the other orders have long journeys to make to reach Chyrellos, and I'm more or less obliged to wait for them. All this waiting is making me very impatient, but there's no help for it, I'm afraid." He pursed his lips. "I think I'll spend the time nosing around a bit. It'll give me something to do, and all these Styrics are making me curious."

"Be careful in the streets of Chyrellos, Sparhawk," Dolmant advised seriously. "They can be very dangerous."

"The whole world is dangerous lately, Dolmant. I'll keep you posted on what I find out." Then Sparhawk turned and went down the corridor with his spurs clinking on the marble floor.

I t was nearly noon when Sparhawk returned to the chapterhouse. He had ridden slowly through the busy streets of the holy city, paying scant attention to the crowds around him. The deterioration of the Archprelate Cluvonus had saddened him. Despite the rumors that had been circulating of late, actually to see the revered old man's condition had come as a profound personal shock.

He stopped at the heavy gate and perfunctorily went through the ritual that admitted him. Kalten was waiting in the courtyard. "Well?" the blond man asked. "How did it go?"

Sparhawk dismounted heavily and pulled off his helmet. "I don't know if we changed any minds," he replied. "The patriarchs who support Annias still support him; the ones who oppose him are still on our side; and those who are neutral are still sitting on the fence."

"It was a waste of time, then?"

"Not entirely, I guess. After this, it might be a little harder for Annias to win over any more uncommitted votes."

"I wish you'd make up your mind, Sparhawk." Kalten looked closely at his friend. "You're in a sour mood. What really happened?"

"Cluvonus was there."

"That's a surprise. How did he look?"

"Awful."

"He *is* eighty-five, Sparhawk. You couldn't expect him to look very impressive. People wear out, you know."

"His mind has gone, Kalten," Sparhawk said sadly. "He's childish now. Dolmant doesn't think he's going to last much longer."

"That bad?"

Sparhawk nodded.

"That makes it fairly important for us to get to Borrata and back in a hurry then, doesn't it?"

"Urgent," Sparhawk agreed.

"Do you think we should ride on ahead and let the knights from the other orders catch up with us later?"

"I wish we could. I hate the idea of Ehlana sitting alone in that throne room, but I don't think we dare. Komier was right about a show of unity, and the other orders are sometimes a little touchy. Let's not start off by offending them."

"Did you and Dolmant talk to somebody about Arissa?"

Sparhawk nodded. "The patriarch of Vardenais is handling it."

"The day wasn't an absolute waste, then."

Sparhawk grunted. "I want to change out of this." He rapped on the breastplate of his armor with his knuckles.

"You want me to unsaddle Faran for you?"

"No, I'll be going back out. Where's Sephrenia?"

"In her room, I think."

"Have somebody saddle her horse."

"Is she going somewhere?"

"Probably." Sparhawk went on up the stairs and entered the chapterhouse.

It was about a quarter hour later when he tapped on Sephrenia's door. He had removed his armor and now wore a mail coat beneath a nondescript gray cloak that bore no insignia of his rank or his order. "It's me, Sephrenia," he said through the panels of the door.

"Come in, Sparhawk," she said.

He opened the door and stepped in quietly.

She was sitting in a large chair with Flute in her lap. The child was sleeping with a contented little smile on her face. "Did things go well at the Basilica?" Sephrenia asked.

"It's a little hard to say," he replied. "Churchmen are very good at hiding their emotions. Did you and Kalten find out anything yesterday about all the Styrics here in Chyrellos?"

She nodded. "They're concentrated in the quarter near the east gate. They have a house there somewhere that seems to be a headquarters of some sort. We weren't able to locate it exactly, though."

"Why don't we go see if we can find it?" he suggested. "I need something to do. I'm feeling a bit restless."

"Restless? You, Sparhawk? The man of stone?"

"Impatience, I suppose. I want to get started for Borrata."

She nodded. Then she rose, lifting Flute easily, and laid the child on the bed. Gently she covered the little girl with a gray wool blanket. Flute briefly opened her dark eyes, then smiled and went back to sleep. Sephrenia kissed the small face, then turned to Sparhawk. "Shall we go then?" she said.

"You're very fond of her, aren't you?" Sparhawk asked as the two of them walked along the corridor leading toward the courtyard.

"It goes a bit deeper than that. Someday perhaps you'll understand."

"Have you any idea where this Styric house might be?"

"There's a shopkeeper in the market near the east gate. He sold some Styrics a number of sides of meat. The porter who delivered them knows where the house is."

"Why didn't you question the porter?"

"He wasn't there yesterday."

"Maybe he'll make it to work today."

"It's worth a try."

He stopped and gave her a direct look. "I'm not trying to pry into the secrets you've chosen not to reveal, Sephrenia, but could you distinguish between ordinary rural Styrics and Zemochs?"

"It's possible," she admitted, "unless they're taking steps to conceal their true identity."

They went down into the courtyard where Kalten waited with Faran and

Sephrenia's white palfrey. The blond knight had an angry expression on his face. "Your horse bit me, Sparhawk," he said accusingly.

"You know him well enough not to turn your back on him. Did he draw blood?"

"No," Kalten admitted.

"Then he was only being playful. It shows that he likes you."

"Thanks," Kalten said flatly. "Do you want me to come along?"

"No. I think we want to be more or less inconspicuous, and on occasion you have trouble managing that."

"Sometimes your charm overwhelms me, Sparhawk."

"We're sworn to speak the truth." Sparhawk helped Sephrenia into her saddle, then mounted Faran. "We should be back before dark," he told his friend.

"Don't hurry on my account."

Sparhawk led the small Styric woman out through the gate and into the side street beyond.

"He turns everything into a joke, doesn't he?" Sephrenia observed.

"Most things, yes. He's been laughing at the world since he was a boy. I think that's why I like him so much. My view of things tends to be a little more bleak, and he helps me keep my perspective."

They rode on through the now-teeming streets of Chyrellos. Although many local merchants affected the somber black of churchmen, visitors usually did not, and their bright clothing stood out by contrast. Travellers from Cammoria in particular were highly colorful, since their customary silk garments did not fade with the passage of time and remained brightly red or green or blue.

The marketplace to which Sephrenia led him was some distance from the chapterhouse, and it was perhaps three-quarters of an hour before they reached it.

"How did you find this shopkeeper?" Sparhawk asked.

"There are certain staples in the Styric diet," she replied. "Elenes don't eat those things very often."

"I thought you said that this porter delivered some sides of meat."

"Goat, Sparhawk. Elenes don't care much for goat."

He shuddered.

"How provincial you are," she said lightly. "If it doesn't come from a cow, you won't eat it."

"I suppose it's what you're used to."

"I'd better go to the shop alone," she said. "Sometimes you're a bit intimidating, dear one. We want answers from the porter, and we might not get them if you frighten him. Watch my horse." She handed him her reins and then moved off through the market. Sparhawk watched as she went across the bustling square to speak with a shabby-looking fellow in a blood-smeared canvas smock. After a short time she returned. He got down and helped her back onto her horse.

"Did he tell you where the house is?" he asked.

She nodded. "It's not far—near the east gate."

"Let's go have a look."

As they started out, Sparhawk did something uncharacteristically impulsive.

He reached out and took the small woman's hand. "I love you, little mother," he told her.

"Yes," she said calmly, "I know. It's nice of you to say it, though." Then she smiled. It was an impish little smile that somehow reminded him of Flute. "Another lesson for you, Sparhawk," she said. "When you're having dealings with a woman, you cannot say *I love you* too often."

"I'll remember that. Does the same thing apply to Elene women?"

"It applies to all women, Sparhawk. Gender is a far more important distinction than race."

"I shall be guided by you, Sephrenia."

"Have you been reading medieval poetry again?"

"Me?"

They rode through the marketplace and on into the run-down quarter near the east gate of Chyrellos. While not perhaps the same as the slums of Cimmura, this part of the holy city was far less opulent than the area around the Basilica. There was less color here, for one thing. The tunics of the men in the street were uniformly drab, and the few merchants there were in the crowd wore garments which were faded and threadbare. They did, however, have the self-important expressions which all merchants, successful or not, automatically assume. Then, at the far end of the street, Sparhawk saw a short man in a lumpy, unbleached smock of home-spun wool. "Styric," he said shortly.

Sephrenia nodded and drew up the hood of her white robe so that it covered her face. Sparhawk straightened in his saddle and carefully assumed an arrogant, condescending expression such as the servant of some important personage might wear. They passed the Styric, who stepped cautiously aside without paying them any particular heed. Like all members of his race, the Styric had dark, almost black, hair and pale skin. He was shorter than the Elenes who passed him in this narrow street, and the bones in his face were prominent, as if he had somehow not quite been completed.

"Zemoch?" Sparhawk asked after they had passed the man.

"It's impossible to say," Sephrenia replied.

"Is he concealing his identity with a spell?"

She spread her hands helplessly. "There's no way to tell, Sparhawk. Either he's just an ordinary backwoods Styric with nothing on his mind but his next meal, or he's a very subtle magician who's playing the bumpkin to block out attempts to probe him."

Sparhawk swore under his breath. "This might not be as easy as I thought," he said. "Let's go on then and see what we can find out."

The house to which Sephrenia had been directed sat at the end of a cul-de-sac, a short street that went nowhere.

"That's going to be difficult to watch without being obvious," Sparhawk said as they rode slowly past the mouth of the narrow street.

"Not really," Sephrenia disagreed. She reined in her palfrey. "We need to talk with the shopkeeper there on the corner."

"Did you want to buy something?"

"Not exactly buy, Sparhawk. Come along. You'll see." She slid down out of her saddle and tied the reins of her delicate white horse to a post outside the shop she had indicated. She looked around briefly. "Will your great war horse discourage anyone who might want to steal my gentle little Ch'iel?" she asked. She laid her hand affectionately on the white horse's neck.

"I'll talk to him about it."

"Would you?"

"Faran," Sparhawk said to the ugly roan, "stay here and protect Sephrenia's mare."

Faran nickered, his ears pricked eagerly forward.

"You big old fool." Sparhawk laughed.

Faran snapped at him, his teeth clacking together at the empty air inches from Sparhawk's ear.

"Be nice," Sparhawk murmured.

Inside the shop, a room devoted to the display of cheap furniture, Sephrenia's attitude became ingratiating, even oddly submissive. "Good master merchant," she said with an uncharacteristic tone in her voice, "we serve a great Pelosian noble who has come to Chyrellos to seek solace for his soul in the holy city."

"I don't deal with Styrics," the merchant said rudely, glowering at Sephrenia. "There are too many of you filthy heathens in Chyrellos already." He assumed an expression of extreme distaste, all the while making what Sparhawk knew to be totally ineffective gestures to ward off magic.

"Look, huckster," the big knight said, affecting an insulting Pelosian-accented manner, "do not rise above yourself. My master's chatelaine and I will be treated with respect, regardless of your feeble-minded bigotry."

The shopkeeper bristled at that. "Why—" he began to bluster.

Sparhawk smashed the top of a cheap table into splinters with a single blow of his fist. Then he seized the shopman's collar and pulled him forward so that they were eye to eye. "Do we understand each other?" he said in a dreadful voice that hovered just this side of a whisper.

"What we require, good master merchant," Sephrenia said smoothly, "is a goodly set of chambers facing the street. Our master has been ever fond of watching the ebb and flow of humanity." She lowered her eyelashes modestly. "Have you such a place above-stairs?"

The shopkeeper's face was a study in conflicting emotions as he turned to mount the stairs toward the upper floor.

The chambers above were shabby—one might even go so far as to say ratty. They had at some time in the past been painted, but the pea-soup-green paint had peeled and now hung in long strips from the walls. Sparhawk and Sephrenia were not interested in paint, however. It was to the dirty window at the front of the main chamber that their eyes went.

"There's more, little lady," the shopkeeper said, more respectfully than before.

"We can conduct our own inspection, good master merchant." She cocked her head slightly. "Was that the step of a customer I heard from below?"

The shopkeeper blinked and then he bolted downstairs.

"Can you see the house up the street from the window?" Sephrenia asked.

"The panes are dirty." Sparhawk lifted the hem of his gray cloak to wipe away the dust and grime.

"Don't," she said sharply. "Styric eyes are very sharp."

"All right," he said. "I'll look through the dust. Elene eyes are just as sharp." He looked at her. "Does that happen every time you go out?" he asked.

"Yes. Common Elenes are not much smarter than common Styrics. Frankly I'd rather have a conversation with a toad than with either breed."

"Toads can talk?" He was a little surprised at that.

"If you know what you're listening for, yes. They're not very stimulating conversationalists, though."

The house at the end of the street was not impressive. The lower floor was constructed of fieldstone, crudely mortared together, and the second story was of roughly squared-off timbers. It seemed somehow set off from the houses around it, as if drawing in a kind of isolated separateness. As they watched, a Styric wearing the poorly woven wool smock which was the characteristic garb of his race moved up the street toward the house. He looked around furtively before he entered.

"Well?" Sparhawk asked.

"It's hard to say," Sephrenia replied. "It's the same as with that one we saw in the street. He's either simple or very skilled."

"This could take a while."

"Only until dark, if I'm right," she said as she drew a chair up to the window.

In the next several hours, a fair number of Styrics entered the house, and, as the sun sank into a dense, dirty-looking cloud bank on the western horizon, others began to arrive. A Cammorian in a bright yellow silk robe went furtively up the cul-de-sac and was immediately admitted. A booted Lamork in a polished steel cuirass and accompanied by two crossbow-bearing men-at-arms marched arrogantly up to the doors of the house and gained entry just as quickly. Then, as the chill winter twilight began to settle over Chyrellos, a lady in a deep purple robe and attended by a huge manservant in bullhide armor such as that commonly worn by Pelosians went up the center of the short street, moving with a stiff-legged, abstracted pace. Her eyes seemed vacant and her movements jerky. Her face, however, bore an expression of ineffable ecstasy.

"Strange visitors to a Styric house," Sephrenia commented.

Sparhawk nodded and looked around the darkening room. "Do you want some light?" he asked her.

"No. Let's not be seen to be here. I'm certain that the street is being watched from the upper floor of the house." Then she leaned against him, filling his nostrils with the woody fragrance of her hair. "You can hold my hand, though," she offered. "For some reason, I've always been a little afraid of the dark."

"Of course," he said, taking her small hand in his big one. They sat together for perhaps another quarter hour as the street outside grew darker.

Suddenly Sephrenia gave an agonized little gasp.

"What's the matter?" he asked in alarm.

She did not immediately reply but rose to her feet instead, raising her hands, palms up, above her. A dim figure seemed to stand before her, a figure that was more shadow than substance, and a faint glow seemed to stretch between its widespread, gauntleted hands. Slowly it held forth that silvery nimbus. The glow grew momentarily brighter, then coalesced into solidity as the shadow before her vanished. She sank back into her chair, holding the long, slender object with a curious kind of sorrowful reverence.

"What was that, Sephrenia?" Sparhawk demanded.

"Another of the twelve knights has fallen," she said in a voice that was almost a moan. "This is his sword, a part of my burden."

"Vanion?" he asked, almost choking with a dreadful sense of fear.

Her fingers sought the crest on the pommel of the sword she held, feeling the design in the darkness. "No," she said. "It was Lakus."

Sparhawk felt a wrench of grief. Lakus was an elderly Pandion, a man with snowy hair and a grim visage whom all the knights of Sparhawk's generation had revered as a teacher and a friend.

Sephrenia buried her face in Sparhawk's armored shoulder and began to weep. "I knew him as a boy, Sparhawk," she lamented.

"Let's go back to the chapterhouse," he suggested gently. "We can do this another day."

She lifted her head and wiped at her eyes with her hand. "No, Sparhawk," she said firmly. "Something's happening in that house tonight—something that may not happen again for a while."

He started to say something, but then he felt an oppressive weight that seemed to be located just behind his ears. It was as if someone had just placed the heels of his hands at the back of his skull and pushed inward. Sephrenia leaned intently forward. "Azash!" she hissed.

"What?"

"They're summoning the spirit of Azash," she said with a terrible note of urgency in her voice.

"That nails it down, then, doesn't it?" he said, rising to his feet.

"Sit down, Sparhawk. This isn't played out yet."

"There can't be that many."

"And what will you learn if you go up the street and chop the house and everyone in it to pieces? Sit down. Watch and learn."

"I'm obliged, Sephrenia. It's part of the oath. It has been for five centuries."

"Bother the oath," she snapped. "This is more important."

He sank back into his chair, troubled and uncertain. "What are they doing?" he asked.

"I told you. They're raising the spirit of Azash. That can only mean that they're Zemochs."

"What are the Elenes doing in there, then? The Cammorian, the Lamork, and that Pelosian woman?"

"Receiving instruction, I think. The Zemochs didn't come here to learn, but to teach. This is serious, Sparhawk—more deadly serious than you could ever imagine."

"What do we do?"

"For the moment, nothing. We sit here and watch."

Again Sparhawk felt that oppressive weight at the base of his skull, and then a fiery tingling that seemed to run through all his veins.

"Azash has answered the summons," Sephrenia said quietly. "It's very important to sit quietly now and for both of us to keep our thoughts neutral. Azash can sense hostility directed at him."

"Why would Elenes participate in the rites of Azash?"

"Probably for the rewards he will give them for worshipping him. The Elder Gods have always been most lavish with their rewards—when it suits them to be."

"What kind of reward could possibly pay for the loss of one's soul?"

She shrugged, a barely perceptible motion in the growing darkness. "Longevity, perhaps. Wealth, power—and in the case of the woman, beauty. It could even be other things—things I don't care to think about. Azash is twisted and he soon twists those who worship him."

In the street below, a workman with a handcart and a torch clattered along over the cobblestones. He took an unlighted torch from the cart, set it in an iron ring protruding from the shop front below, and ignited it. Then he rattled on.

"Good," Sephrenia murmured. "Now we'll be able to see them when they come out."

"We've already seen them."

"They'll be different, I'm afraid."

The door to the Styric house opened, and the silk-robed Cammorian emerged. As he passed through the circle of torchlight below, Sparhawk saw that his face was very pale, and his eyes were wide with horror.

"That one will not return," Sephrenia said quietly. "Most likely he'll spend the rest of his life trying to atone for his venture into the darkness."

A few minutes later, the booted Lamork came out into the street. His eyes burned, and his face was twisted into an expression of savage cruelty. His impassive crossbowmen marched along behind him.

"Lost," Sephrenia sighed.

"What?"

"The Lamork is lost. Azash has him."

Then the Pelosian lady emerged from the house. Her purple robe was carelessly open at the front, and beneath it she was naked. As she came into the torchlight, Sparhawk could see that her eyes were glazed and that her nude body was splattered with blood. Her hulking attendant made some effort to close the front of her robe, but she hissed at him, thrusting his hand away, and went off down the street shamelessly flaunting her body.

"And that one is more than lost," Sephrenia said. "She will be dangerous now. Azash rewarded her with powers." She frowned. "I'm tempted to suggest that we follow her and kill her."

"I'm not sure that I could kill a woman, Sephrenia."

"She's not even a woman anymore, but we'd have to behead her, and that could cause some outrage in Chyrellos."

"Do *what*?"

"Behead her. It's the only way to be certain that she's really dead. I think we've seen enough here, Sparhawk. Let's go back to the chapterhouse and talk with

Nashan. Tomorrow I think we should report this to Dolmant. The Church has ways to deal with this sort of thing." She rose to her feet.

"Let me carry the sword for you."

"No, Sparhawk. It's *my* burden. I must carry it." She tucked Lakus's sword inside her robe and led the way toward the door.

They went downstairs again, and the shopkeeper came out of the back of his establishment rubbing his hands together. "Well?" he said eagerly, "will you be taking the rooms?"

"Totally unsuitable," Sephrenia sniffed. "I wouldn't keep my master's dog in a place like that." Her face was very pale, and she was visibly trembling.

"But—"

"Just unlock the door, neighbor," Sparhawk said, "and we'll be on our way."

"What took you so long, then?"

Sparhawk gave him a flat, cold stare, and the shopkeeper swallowed hard and went to the door, fishing in his tunic pocket for the key.

Outside, Faran was standing protectively beside Sephrenia's palfrey. There was a torn scrap of rough cloth on the cobblestones under his hooves.

"Trouble?" Sparhawk asked him.

Faran snorted derisively.

"I see," Sparhawk said.

"What was that about?" Sephrenia asked wearily as Sparhawk helped her to mount.

"Someone tried to steal your horse," he shrugged. "Faran persuaded him not to."

"Can you really communicate with him?"

"I more or less know what he's thinking. We've been together for a long time." He hauled himself up into his saddle, and the two of them rode off down the street in the direction of the Pandion chapterhouse.

They had gone perhaps a half mile when Sparhawk had a momentary premonition. He reacted instantly, driving Faran's shoulder against the white palfrey. The smaller horse lurched to one side, even as a crossbow bolt buzzed spitefully through the space where Sephrenia had been an instant before. "Ride, Sephrenia!" he barked as the bolt clashed against the stones of a house fronting the street. He looked back, drawing his sword. But Sephrenia had already thumped her heels to the white horse's flanks and plunged off down the street at a clattering gallop with Sparhawk closely behind her, shielding her body with his own.

After they had crossed several streets, Sephrenia slowed her pace. "Did you see him?" she asked. She had Lakus's sword in her hand now.

"I didn't have to see him. A crossbow means a Lamork. Nobody else uses them."

"The one who was in the house with the Styrics?"

"Probably—unless you've gone out of your way to offend other Lamorks of late. Could Azash or one of his Zemochs have sensed your presence back there?"

"It's possible," she conceded. "No one can be absolutely certain just how far the power of the Elder Gods goes. How did you know that we were about to be attacked?"

"Training, I suppose. I've learned to know when someone's pointing a weapon at me."

"I thought it was pointed at me."

"It amounts to the same thing, Sephrenia."

"Well, he missed."

"*This* time. I think I'll talk to Nashan about getting you a mail shirt."

"Are you mad, Sparhawk?" she protested. "The weight alone would put me on my knees—not to mention the awful smell."

"Better the weight and the smell than an arrow between the shoulder blades."

"Totally out of the question."

"We'll see. Put the sword away and let's move on. You need rest, and I want to get you inside the chapterhouse where it's safe before someone else takes a shot at you."

---

## CHAPTER FOURTEEN

The following day, about midmorning, Sir Bevier arrived at the gates of the Pandion chapterhouse in Chyrellos. Sir Bevier was a Cyrinic Knight from Arcium. His formal armor was burnished to a silvery sheen, and his surcoat was white. His helmet had no visor, but rather bore heavy cheekpieces and a formidable nose guard. He dismounted in the courtyard, hung his shield and his Lochaber axe on his saddlebow, and removed his helmet. Bevier was young and somewhat slender. His complexion was olive and his hair curly and blue-black.

With some show of ceremony, Nashan descended the steps of the chapterhouse with Sparhawk and Kalten to greet him. "Our house is honored, Sir Bevier," he said.

Bevier inclined his head stiffly. "My Lord," he responded, "I am commanded by the preceptor of my order to convey to you his greetings."

"Thank you, Sir Bevier," Nashan said, somewhat taken aback by the young knight's stiff formality.

"Sir Sparhawk," Bevier said then, again inclining his head.

"Do we know each other, Bevier?"

"Our preceptor described you to me, my Lord Sparhawk—you and your companion, Sir Kalten. Have the others arrived yet?"

Sparhawk shook his head. "No. You're the first."

"Come inside, Sir Bevier," Nashan said then. "We'll assign you a cell so that you can get out of your armor, and I'll speak to the kitchen about a hot meal."

"And if it please you, my Lord, might I first visit your chapel? I have been some days on the road and I feel sorely the need for prayer in a consecrated place."

"Of course," Nashan said to him.

"We'll see to your horse," Sparhawk told the young man.

"Thank you, Lord Sparhawk." Bevier bent his head again and followed Nashan up the steps.

"Oh, he's going to be a jolly travelling companion," Kalten said ironically.

"He'll loosen up once he gets to know us," Sparhawk said.

"I hope you're right. I'd heard that the Cyrinics are a shade formal, but I think our young friend there might be carrying it to extremes." Curiously, he unhooked the Lochaber from the saddlebow. "Can you imagine using this thing on somebody?" He shuddered. The Lochaber axe had a heavy, two-foot blade surmounted at its forward end with a razor-sharp, hawklike bill. Its heavy handle was about four feet long. "You could shuck a man out of his armor like an oyster out of its shell with this."

"I think that's the idea. It *is* sort of intimidating, isn't it? Put it away, Kalten. Don't play with another man's toys."

After Sir Bevier had completed his prayers and changed out of his armor, he joined them in Nashan's ornate study.

"Did they give you something to eat?" Nashan asked.

"It isn't necessary, my Lord," Bevier replied. "If I may be permitted, I'll join you and your knights in refectory for the noon meal."

"Of course," Nashan replied. "You're more than welcome to join us, Bevier."

Sparhawk then introduced Bevier to Sephrenia. The young man bowed deeply to her. "I have heard much of you, Lady," he said. "Our instructors in the Styric secrets hold you in great esteem."

"You're kind to say so, Sir Knight. My skills are the result of age and practice, however, and do not result from any particular virtue."

"Age, Lady? Surely not. You can scarce be much older than I, and I will not see my thirtieth year for some months yet. The bloom of youth has not yet left your cheeks, and your eyes quite overwhelm me."

Sephrenia smiled warmly at him, then looked critically at Kalten and Sparhawk. "I hope you two are paying attention," she said. "A little polish wouldn't hurt either of you."

"I was never much good at formality, little mother," Kalten confessed.

"I've noticed," she said. "Flute," she said a bit wearily then, "please put the book down. I've asked you again and again not to touch one."

Several days later, Sir Tynian and Sir Ulath arrived, riding together. Tynian was a good-humored Alcione Knight from Deira, the kingdom lying to the north of Elenia. His broad, round face was open and friendly. His shoulders and chest were powerfully muscled as the result of years of bearing Deiran armor, the heaviest in the world. Over his massive armor he wore a sky-blue surcoat. Ulath was a hulking Genidian Knight, fully a head taller than Sparhawk. He did not wear armor, but rather a plain mail shirt and a simple conical helmet. Covering his shirt, he wore a green surcoat. He carried a large round shield and a heavy war axe. Ulath was a silent, withdrawn man who seldom spoke. His blond hair hung in two braids down his back.

"Good morning, gentlemen," Tynian said to Sparhawk and Kalten as he dismounted in the courtyard of the chapterhouse. He looked at them closely. "You would be Sir Sparhawk," he said. "Our preceptor said that you'd broken your nose sometime." He grinned then. "It's all right, Sparhawk. It doesn't interfere with your kind of beauty."

"I'm going to like this man," Kalten said.

"And you must be Kalten," Tynian said. He thrust out his hand, and Kalten took it before he realized that the Alcione was holding a dead mouse concealed in his palm. With a startled oath, he jerked his hand back. Tynian howled with laughter.

"I think I could get to like him as well," Sparhawk noted.

"My name is Tynian," the Alcione Knight introduced himself. "My silent friend there is Ulath from Thalesia. He caught up with me a few days ago. Hasn't spoken ten words since then."

"You talk enough for both of us," Ulath grunted, sliding out of his saddle.

"That's God's own truth," Tynian admitted. "I have this overwhelming fondness for the sound of my own voice."

Ulath thrust out his huge hand. "Sparhawk," he said.

"No mice?" Sparhawk asked.

A faint smile touched Ulath's face as they clasped hands. Then he shook hands with Kalten, and the four of them went up the steps into the chapterhouse.

"Has Bevier arrived yet?" Tynian asked Kalten.

"A few days back. Have you ever met him?"

"Once. Our preceptor and I made a formal visit to Larium, and we were introduced to the Cyrinics in their motherhouse there. I found him to be a bit stiff-necked and formal."

"That hasn't changed much."

"Didn't think it had. Exactly what are we going to do down in Cammoria? Preceptor Darellon can be infuriatingly closemouthed on occasion."

"Let's wait until Bevier joins us," Sparhawk suggested. "I get the feeling that he might be a little touchy, so let's not offend him by talking business out of his presence."

"Good thinking, Sparhawk. This show of unity could fall apart on us if Bevier starts sulking. I'll have to admit that he can be a good man in a fight, though. Is he still carrying that Lochaber?"

"Oh, yes," Kalten said.

"Gruesome thing, isn't it? I saw him practicing with it at Larium. He cut the top off a post as thick as my leg with one swipe at a full gallop. I get the feeling that he could ride through a platoon of foot troops and leave a trail of loose heads behind him ten yards wide."

"Let's hope it doesn't come to that," Sparhawk said.

"If that's your attitude, Sparhawk, you're going to take all the fun out of this excursion."

"I *am* going to like him," Kalten said.

Sir Bevier joined them in Nashan's study after the completion of noon services in the chapel. As closely as Sparhawk could determine, Bevier had not missed services once since his arrival.

"All right then," Sparhawk said, rising to his feet when they were all assembled, "this is sort of where we stand. Annias, the primate of Cimmura, has his eyes on the archprelate's throne here in Chyrellos. He controls the Elenian royal council, and they're giving him money out of the royal treasury. He's trying to use that money to buy enough votes in the Hierocracy to win election after Cluvonus dies. The preceptors of the four orders want to block him."

"No decent churchman would accept money for his vote," Bevier said, his voice verging on outrage.

"I'll grant that," Sparhawk agreed. "Unfortunately, many churchmen are far from decent. Let's be honest about it, gentlemen. There's a wide streak of corruption in the Elene Church. We might wish it were different, but we have to face the facts. Many of those votes *are* for sale. Now—and this is important—Queen Ehlana is unwell; otherwise, she wouldn't allow Annias to have access to the treasury. The preceptors agree that the best way to stop Annias is to find some way to cure the queen and put her back in power. That's why we're going to Borrata. There are physicians at the university there who might be able to determine the nature of her illness and find a cure for it."

"Are we taking your queen with us?" Tynian asked.

"No. That's quite impossible."

"It's going to be a little hard for the physicians to find out much then, isn't it?"

Sparhawk shook his head. "Sephrenia, the Pandion instructor in the secrets, will be going with us. She can describe Queen Ehlana's symptoms in great detail and she can raise an image of the queen if the physicians need a closer look."

"Seems a bit roundabout," Tynian noted, "but if that's the way we have to do it, then that's the way we'll do it."

"There's a great deal of unrest in Cammoria right now," Sparhawk went on. "The central kingdoms are all infested with Zemoch agents, and they're trying to stir up as much trouble as they can. Not only that, Annias is fairly certain to guess at what we're trying to do, so he'll try to interfere."

"Borrata's a long way from Cimmura, isn't it?" Tynian asked. "Does Primate Annias have so long an arm?"

"Yes," Sparhawk said, "he does. There's a renegade Pandion in Cammoria who sometimes works for Annias. His name is Martel, and he's likely to try to stop us."

"Only once," Ulath grunted.

"Let's not go out of our way looking for a fight, though," Sparhawk cautioned. "Our main task is to get Sephrenia safely to Borrata and back. There's been at least one attempt on her life already."

"We'll want to discourage that," Tynian said. "Are we taking anybody else with us?"

"My squire, Kurik," Sparhawk replied, "and probably a young Pandion novice named Berit. He shows some promise, and Kurik's going to need somebody along to help him care for the horses." He thought a moment. "I think we'll take a boy along as well," he said.

"Talen?" Kalten sounded surprised at that. "Is that really a good idea, Sparhawk?"

"Chyrellos is corrupt enough already. I don't think it's a good idea to turn that little thief loose in the streets. Besides, I think we may find uses for his specialized talents. The only other person going with us will be a little girl named Flute."

Kalten stared at him in astonishment.

"Sephrenia won't leave her behind," Sparhawk explained, "and I'm not sure she *can* be left behind. You remember how easily she got out of that nunnery in Arcium?"

"You've got a point there, I guess," Kalten conceded.

"A very straightforward presentation, Sir Sparhawk," Bevier said approvingly. "When will we leave?"

"First thing in the morning," Sparhawk replied. "It's a long way to Borrata, and the archprelate isn't getting younger. Patriarch Dolmant says that he could die at any time, and that's when Annias will start to move."

"We must make our preparations then," Bevier said, rising to his feet. "Will you gentlemen be joining me in the chapel for evening services?" he asked.

Kalten sighed. "I suppose we should," he said. "We *are* Church Knights, after all."

"And a bit of God's help wouldn't hurt, would it?" Tynian added.

Late that afternoon, however, a company of church soldiers arrived at the gates of the chapterhouse. "I have a summons from the Patriarch Makova for you and your companions, Sir Sparhawk," the captain in charge of the soldiers said when Sparhawk and the others came down into the courtyard. "He would speak with you in the Basilica at once."

"We'll get our horses," Sparhawk said. He led the rest of the knights into the stables. Once inside, he swore irritably.

"Trouble?" Tynian asked him.

"Makova's a supporter of Primate Annias," Sparhawk replied, leading Faran out of his stall. "I've got a strong suspicion that he's going to try to hinder us."

"We must respond to his summons, however," Bevier said, swinging his saddle up onto his horse's back. "We are Church Knights and must obey the commands of a member of the Hierocracy, no matter what his affiliation."

"And there's that company of soldiers out there, too," Kalten added. "I'd say that Makova doesn't take too many chances."

"Surely he doesn't think we'd refuse?" Bevier said.

"You don't know Sparhawk that well yet," Kalten told him. "He can be contrary at times."

"Well, we don't have any choice in the matter," Sparhawk said. "Let's go to the Basilica and see what the patriarch has to say to us."

They led their horses out into the courtyard and mounted. At a crisp command from the captain, the soldiers formed up around them.

The square in front of the Basilica was strangely deserted as Sparhawk and his friends dismounted.

"Looks to me as if they're expecting trouble," Kalten noted as they started up the broad marble stairs.

When they entered the vast nave of the church, Bevier went down on his knees and clasped his hands in front of him.

The captain and a squad of his soldiers entered behind them. "We must not keep the patriarch waiting," he said. There was a certain arrogant tone in his voice that irritated Sparhawk for some reason. He muffled that feeling, however, and piously dropped to his knees beside Bevier. Kalten grinned and also knelt. Tynian nudged Ulath, and they, too, went down on their knees.

"I said—" the captain began, his voice rising slightly.

"We heard you, neighbor," Sparhawk said to him. "We'll be with you presently."

"But—"

"You can wait over there. We won't be too long."

The captain turned and stalked off.

"Nice touch, Sparhawk," Tynian murmured.

"We *are* Church Knights, after all," Sparhawk replied. "It won't hurt Makova to wait awhile. I'm sure he'll enjoy the anticipation."

"I'm sure," Tynian agreed.

The five knights remained kneeling for perhaps ten minutes while the captain stalked about impatiently.

"Have you finished, Bevier?" Sparhawk asked politely when the Cyrinic unclasped his hands.

"Yes," Bevier answered, his face alight with devotion. "I feel cleansed now and at peace with the world."

"Try to hang on to that feeling. The patriarch of Coombe is likely to irritate us all." Sparhawk rose to his feet. "Shall we go, then?"

"Well, *finally*," the captain snapped as they joined him and his men.

Bevier looked at him coldly. "Have you any rank, Captain?" he asked, "aside from your military one, I mean?"

"I am a marquis, Sir Bevier."

"Excellent. If our devotions offend you, I will be more than happy to give you satisfaction. You may have your seconds call upon me at any time. I will be at your complete disposal."

The captain paled visibly and shrank back. "I am merely following my orders, my Lord. I would not dream of giving offense to a Knight of the Church."

"Ah," Bevier said distantly. "Let us proceed, then. As you stated so excellently earlier, we must not keep the patriarch of Coombe waiting."

The captain led them to a hallway branching out from the nave.

"Nicely done, Bevier," Tynian whispered.

The Cyrinic smiled briefly.

"There's nothing like the offer of a yard or so of steel in his belly to remind a man of his manners," Kalten added.

The chamber to which the captain led them was grandiose with deep maroon carpeting and drapes and polished marble walls. The lean-faced patriarch of Coombe sat at a long table reading a parchment. He looked up as they were admitted, his face angry. "What took so long?" he snapped at the captain.

"The Knights of the Church felt obliged to spend a few moments in devotions before the main altar, your Grace."

"Oh. Of course."

"May I withdraw, your Grace?"

"No. Stay. It shall fall to you to enforce the dictates I will issue here."

"As it please your Grace."

Makova then looked sternly at the knights. "I am told that you gentlemen are planning a foray into Cammoria," he said.

"We haven't made any secret of it, your Grace," Sparhawk replied.

"I forbid it."

"Might one ask why, your Grace?" Tynian asked mildly.

"No. One may not. The Church Knights are subject to the authority of the Hierocracy. Explanations are not required. You are all to return to the Pandion chapterhouse and you will remain there until it pleases me to send you further instructions." He smiled a chill smile. "I believe you will all be returning home very shortly." Then he drew himself up. "That will be all. You have my permission to withdraw. Captain, you will see to it that these knights do not leave the Pandion chapterhouse."

"Yes, your Grace."

They all bowed and silently filed out the door.

"That was short, wasn't it?" Kalten said as they went back down the corridor with the captain some distance in the lead.

"There wasn't much point in fogging the issue with lame excuses," Sparhawk replied.

Kalten leaned toward his friend. "Are we going to obey his orders?" he whispered.

"No."

"Sir Sparhawk," Bevier gasped, "surely you would not disregard the commands of a patriarch of the Church?"

"No, not really. All I need is a different set of orders."

"Dolmant?" Kalten guessed.

"His name does sort of leap to mind, doesn't it?"

They had, however, no opportunity for side trips. The officious captain insisted upon escorting them directly back to the chapterhouse. "Sir Sparhawk," he said as they reached the narrow street where the house stood, "you will be so good as to advise the governor of your establishment that this gate is to remain closed. No one is to enter or leave."

"I'll tell him," Sparhawk replied. Then he nudged Faran and rode on into the courtyard.

"I didn't think he'd actually seal the gate," Kalten muttered. "How are we going to get word to Dolmant?"

"I'll think of something," Sparhawk said.

Later, as twilight crept in over the city, Sparhawk paced along the parapet surmounting the wall of the chapterhouse, glancing from time to time down into the street outside.

"Sparhawk," Kurik's gruff voice came from the yard below, "are you up there?"

"Yes. Come on up."

There was the sound of footsteps on the stone stairs leading up to the parapet. "You wanted to see us?" Kurik asked as he, Berit, and Talen came up out of the shadows clotting the stairway.

"Yes. There's a company of church soldiers outside. They're blocking the gate, and I need to get a message to Dolmant. Any ideas?"

Kurik scratched his head as he mulled it over.

"Give me a fast horse and I can ride through them," Berit offered.

"He'll make a good knight," Talen said. "Knights love to charge, I'm told."

Berit looked sharply at the boy.

"No hitting," Talen said, shrinking back. "We agreed that there wasn't going to be any more hitting. I pay attention to the lessons, and you don't hit me anymore."

"Have you got a better idea?" Berit asked.

"Several." Talen looked over the wall. "Are the soldiers patrolling the streets outside the walls?" he asked.

"Yes," Sparhawk said.

"That's not really a problem, but it might have been easier if they weren't." Talen pursed his lips as he thought it over. "Berit," he said, "are you any good with a bow?"

"I've been trained," the novice said a bit stiffly.

"That's not what I asked. I said are you any good?"

"I can hit a mark at a hundred paces."

Talen looked at Sparhawk. "Don't you people have anything better to do?" he asked. Then he looked at Berit again. "You see that stable over there?" he asked, pointing across the street, "the one with the thatched roof?"

"Yes."

"Could you get an arrow into the thatch?"

"Easily."

"Maybe training pays off after all."

"How many months did you practice cutting purses?" Kurik asked pointedly.

"That's different, Father. There's a profit involved in that."

"Father?" Berit sounded astonished.

"It's a long story," Kurik told him.

"Any man in the world listens to a bell that rings for any reason whatsoever," Talen said, affecting a schoolteacherish tone, "and no man can possibly avoid gawking at a fire. Can you lay your hands on a length of rope, Sparhawk?"

"How long a length?"

"Long enough to reach the street. Here's how it goes. Berit wraps his arrow with tinder and sets fire to it. Then he takes a shot at that thatched roof. The soldiers will all run to this street to watch the fun. That's when I go down the rope on the far side of the building. I can be out on the street in less than a minute with no one the wiser."

"You can't set fire to a man's stable," Kurik objected, sounding horrified.

"They'll put it out, Kurik," Talen said in a patient tone. "They'll have lots of warning, because we'll all stand up here shouting 'Fire!' at the top of our lungs. Then I'll skin down the rope on the far wall and be five streets away before the excitement dies down. I know where Dolmant's house is and I can tell him whatever you want him to know."

"All right," Sparhawk approved.

"Sparhawk!" Kurik exclaimed. "You're not going to let him do this, are you?"

"It's tactically sound, Kurik. Diversion and subterfuge are part of any good plan."

"Do you have any idea of how much thatch—and wood—there is in this part of town?"

"It might give the church soldiers something useful to do," Sparhawk shrugged.

"That's hard, Sparhawk."

"Not nearly as hard as the notion of Annias sitting on the archprelate's throne. Let's get what we need. I want to be out of Chyrellos before the sun comes up tomorrow and I can't do that with all those soldiers camped outside the gate."

They went down the stairs to fetch rope, a bow, and a quiver of arrows.

"What's afoot?" Tynian asked as he, Kalten, Bevier, and Ulath met them in the courtyard.

"We're going to get word to Dolmant," Sparhawk told him.

Tynian looked at the bow Berit was carrying. "With that?" he asked. "Isn't that rather a long shot?"

"There's a little more to it than that," Sparhawk told him. He quickly sketched in the plan. Then, as they started up the steps, he put his hand on Talen's shoulder. "This isn't going to be the safest thing in the world," he told the boy. "I want you to be careful out there."

"You worry too much, Sparhawk," Talen replied. "I could do this in my sleep."

"You might need some kind of note to give to Dolmant," Sparhawk said.

"You're not serious? If I get stopped, I can lie my way out of trouble, but not if I've got a note in my pocket. Dolmant knows me, and he'll know that the message is from you. Just leave everything to me, Sparhawk."

"Don't stop to pick any pockets along the way."

"Of course not," Talen replied, just a little too glibly.

Sparhawk sighed. Then he quickly told the boy what to say to the patriarch of Demos.

The plan went more or less as Talen had outlined it. As soon as the patrol had passed in the narrow street, Berit's arrow arched out like a falling star and sank into the thatched stable roof. It sputtered there for a moment or two, and then a bluish-colored flame ran quickly up to the ridgepole, turning sooty orange first, then bright yellow as the flames began to spread.

"Fire!" Talen yelled.

"Fire!" the rest echoed.

In the street below, the church soldiers came pounding around the corner to be met by the nearly hysterical owner of the stables. "Good masters!" the poor man cried, wringing his hands. "My stable! My horses! My house! My God!"

The officious captain hesitated, looking first at the fire then back at the looming wall of the chapterhouse in an agony of indecision.

"We'll help you, Captain," Tynian called down from the wall. "Open the gate!"

"No!" the captain shouted back. "Stay inside."

"You could lose half of the holy city, you blockhead!" Kalten roared at him. "That fire will spread if you don't do something immediately."

"You!" the captain snapped at the commoner who owned the stable. "Fetch buckets and show me the nearest well." He turned quickly to his men. "Form up a line," he commanded. "Go to the front gate of the Pandion house and bring back every man we can spare." He sounded decisive now. Then he squinted up at the knights on the parapet. "But leave a detachment on guard there," he ordered.

"We can still help, Captain," Tynian offered. "There's a deep well here. We can turn out our men and pass buckets to your men outside the gate. Our major concern here must be the saving of Chyrellos. Everything else must be secondary to that."

The captain hesitated.

"Please, Captain!" Tynian's voice throbbed with sincerity. "I beg of you. Let us help."

"Very well," the captain snapped. "Open your gate. But no one is to leave the chapterhouse grounds."

"Of course not," Tynian replied.

"Nicely done," Ulath grunted, tapping Tynian on the shoulder with his fist.

Tynian grinned at him. "Talking *does* pay off now and then, my silent friend. You should try it sometime."

"I'd rather use an axe."

"Well, I guess I'll be leaving now, my lords," Talen said. "Was there anything you'd like to have me pick up for you—since I'll be out and about anyway?"

"Keep your mind on what you're supposed to do," Sparhawk told him. "Just go talk to Dolmant."

"And be careful," Kurik growled. "You're a disappointing son sometimes, but I don't want to lose you."

"Sentimentality, Father?" Talen said, affecting surprise.

"Not really," Kurik replied. "Just a certain sense of responsibility to your mother."

"I'll go with him," Berit said.

Talen looked critically at the rangy novice. "Forget it," he said shortly. "You'd just be in my way. Forgive me, revered teacher, but your feet are too big and your elbows stick out too far to move around quietly, and I don't have time to teach you how to sneak right now." The boy disappeared into the shadows along the parapet.

"Where did you find that rare youth?" Bevier asked.

"You wouldn't believe it, Bevier," Kalten replied. "You absolutely wouldn't believe it."

"Our Pandion brothers are perhaps a bit more worldly than the rest of us, Bevier," Tynian said sententiously. "We who fix our eyes firmly on heaven are not so versed in the seamier side of life as they are." He looked piously at Kalten. "We all serve, however, and I'm sure that God appreciates your efforts, no matter how dishonest or depraved."

"Well put," Ulath said with an absolutely straight face.

The fire in the thatched roof continued to smoke and steam as the church soldiers threw bucket after bucket of water onto it during the next quarter hour. Gradually, by sheer dint of numbers and the volume of water poured on it, the fire was quenched, leaving the owner of the stable bemoaning the saturation of his store of fodder, but preventing any spread of the flames.

"Bravo, Captain, bravo!" Tynian cheered from atop the wall.

"Don't overdo it," Ulath muttered to him.

"It's the first time I've ever seen any of those fellows do anything useful," Tynian protested. "That sort of thing ought to be encouraged."

"We could set some more fires, if you'd like," the huge Genidian offered. "We could keep them hauling water all week."

Tynian tugged at one earlobe. "No," he said after a moment's thought. "They might get bored with the novelty and decide to let the city burn." He glanced at Kurik. "Did the boy get away?" he asked.

"As slick as a snake going down a rat hole," Sparhawk's squire replied, trying to conceal the note of pride in his voice.

"Someday you'll have to tell us about why the lad keeps calling you father."

"We might get to that one day, my Lord Tynian," Kurik muttered.

As the first light of dawn crept up the eastern sky, there came the measured tread of hundreds of feet some distance up the narrow street outside the front gate of the chapterhouse. Then the Patriarch Dolmant, astride a white mule, came into view at the head of a battalion or more of red-liveried soldiers.

"Your Grace," the soot-smeared captain who had been blocking the gate of the chapterhouse exclaimed, rushing forward with a salute.

"You are relieved, Captain," Dolmant told him. "You may return with your men to your barracks." He sniffed a bit disapprovingly. "Tell them to clean up," he suggested. "They look like chimney sweeps."

"Your Grace," the captain faltered, "I was commanded by the patriarch of Coombe to secure this house. May I send to him for confirmation of your Grace's counterorder?"

Dolmant considered it. "No, Captain," he said. "I don't think so. Retire at once."

"But, your Grace!"

Dolmant slapped his hands sharply together, and the troops massed at his back moved into position, their pikes advanced. "Colonel," Dolmant said in the mildest of tones to the commander of his troops, "would you be so good as to escort the captain and his men back to their barracks?"

"At once, your Grace," the officer replied with a sharp salute.

"And I think they should be confined there until they are presentable."

"Of course, your Grace," the colonel said soberly. "I myself shall conduct the inspection."

"Meticulously, Colonel—most meticulously. The honor of the Church is reflected in the appearance of her soldiers."

"Your Grace may rely upon my attention to the most minute detail," the colonel assured him. "The honor of our service is also reflected by the appearance of our lowliest soldier."

"God appreciates your devotion, Colonel."

"I live but to serve Him, your Grace," the colonel bowed deeply.

Neither man smiled, nor winked.

"Oh," Dolmant said then, "before you leave, Colonel, bring me that ragged little beggar boy. I think I'll leave him with the good brothers of this order—as an act of charity, of course."

"Of course, your Grace." The colonel snapped his fingers, and a burly sergeant dragged Talen by the scruff of the neck to the patriarch. Then Dolmant's battalion advanced on the captain and his men, effectively pinning them against the high wall of the chapterhouse with their pikes. The sooty soldiers of the patriarch of Coombe were quickly disarmed and then marched off under close guard.

Dolmant affectionately reached down and patted the slender neck of his white mule; then he looked critically up at the parapet. "Haven't you left yet, Sparhawk?" he asked.

"We were just making our preparations, your Grace."

"The day wears on, my son," Dolmant told him. "God's work cannot be accomplished by sloth."

"I'll keep that in mind, your Grace," Sparhawk said. Then his eyes narrowed, and he stared hard down at Talen. "Give it back," he commanded.

"What?" Talen answered with a note of anguish in his voice.

"All of it. Every last bit."

"But, Sparhawk—"

"*Now,* Talen."

Grumbling, the boy began to remove all manner of small, valuable objects from inside his clothes, depositing them in the hands of the startled patriarch of Demos. "Are you satisfied now, Sparhawk?" he demanded a bit sullenly, glaring up at the parapet.

"Not entirely, but it's a start. I'll know better after I search you once you're inside the gate."

Talen sighed and dug into several more hidden pockets, adding more items to Dolmant's already overflowing hands.

"I assume you're taking this boy with you, Sparhawk?" Dolmant asked, tucking his valuables inside his cassock.

"Yes, your Grace," Sparhawk replied.

"Good. I'll sleep better knowing that he's not roaming the streets. Make haste, my son, and Godspeed." Then the patriarch turned his mule and rode on back up the street.

## CHAPTER FIFTEEN

"At any rate," Sir Tynian continued his obviously embellished account of certain adventures of his youth, "the local Lamork barons grew tired of these brigands and came to our chapterhouse to enlist our aid in exterminating them. We had all grown rather bored with patrolling the Zemoch border, so we agreed. To be honest about the whole thing, we looked upon the affair as something in the nature of a sporting event—a few days of hard riding and a nice brisk fight at the end."

Sparhawk let his attention wander. Tynian's compulsive talking had been virtually uninterrupted since they had left Chyrellos and crossed the border into the southern kingdom of Cammoria. Although the stories were at first amusing, they eventually grew repetitious. To hear Tynian tell it, he had figured prominently in every major battle and minor skirmish on the Eosian continent in the past ten years. Sparhawk concluded that the Alcione Knight was not so much an unabashed brag- gart as he was an ingenious storyteller who put himself in the center of the action of each story to give it a certain immediacy. It was a harmless pastime, really, and it helped to make the miles go faster as they rode down into Cammoria on the road to Borrata.

The sun was warmer here than it had been in Elenia, and the breeze that skipped puffball clouds across the intensely blue sky smelled almost springlike. The fields around them, untouched by frost, were still green, and the road unwound like a white ribbon, dipping into valleys and snaking up verdant hillsides. It was a good day for a ride, and Faran was obviously enjoying himself.

Sparhawk had already begun to make an assessment of his companions. Tynian was very nearly as happy-go-lucky as Kalten. The sheer bulk of his upper torso, however, and the professional way he handled his weapons indicated that he would be a solid man in a fight, should it come to that. Bevier was perhaps a bit more high- strung. The Cyrinic Knights were known for their formality and their piety. They were also touchy. Bevier would need to be handled carefully. Sparhawk decided to have a word in private with Kalten. His friend's fondness for casual jesting might need to be curbed where Bevier was concerned. The young Cyrinic, though, would obviously also be an asset in the event of trouble.

Ulath was an enigma. He had a towering reputation, but Sparhawk had not had many dealings with the Genidian Knights of far northern Thalesia. They were reputed to be fearsome warriors, but the fact that they wore chain mail instead of steel-plate armor concerned him a bit. He decided to feel out the huge Thalesian on that score. He reined Faran in slightly to allow Ulath to catch up with him.

"Nice morning," he said pleasantly.

Ulath grunted. Getting him to talk might prove difficult. Then, surprisingly, he actually volunteered something. "In Thalesia, there's still two feet of snow on the ground," he said.

"That must be miserable."

Ulath shrugged. "You get used to it, and snow makes for good hunting—boars, stags, Trolls, that sort of thing."

"Do you actually hunt Trolls?"

"Sometimes. Every so often a Troll goes crazy. If he comes down into the val- leys where Elenes live and starts killing cows—or people—we have to hunt him down."

"I've heard that they're fairly large."

"Yes. Fairly."

"Isn't it a bit dangerous to fight one with only chain-mail armor?"

"It's not too bad, really. They only use clubs. A man might get his ribs broken sometimes, but that's about all."

"Wouldn't full armor be an advantage?"

"Not if you have to cross any rivers—and we have a lot of rivers in Thalesia. A man can peel off a mail shirt even if he's sitting on the bottom of a river. It might be a little hard to hold your breath long enough to get rid of a full suit of armor, though."

"That makes sense."

"We thought so ourselves. We had a preceptor a while back who thought that we should wear full armor like the other orders—for the sake of appearances. We threw one of our brothers dressed in a mail shirt into the harbor at Emsat. He got out of his shirt and came to the surface in about a minute. The preceptor was wearing full armor. When we threw him in, he didn't come back up. Maybe he found something more interesting to do down there."

"You drowned your preceptor?" Sparhawk asked in astonishment.

"No," Ulath corrected. "His armor drowned him. Then we elected Komier as preceptor. He's got better sense than to make foolish suggestions like that."

"You Genidians appear to be an independent sort of order. You actually elect your own preceptors?"

"Don't you?"

"Not really, no. We send a panel of names to the Hierocracy and let them do the choosing."

"We make it easier for them. We only send them one name."

Kalten came back down the road at a canter. The big blond man had been riding about a quarter of a mile in the lead to scout out possible danger. "There's something strange up ahead, Sparhawk," he said tensely.

"How do you mean strange?"

"There's a pair of Pandions at the top of the next hill." There was a slightly strained note in Kalten's voice, and he was visibly sweating.

"Who are they?"

"I didn't go up there to ask."

Sparhawk looked sharply at his friend. "What's the matter?" he asked.

"I'm not sure," Kalten replied. "I just had a strong feeling that I shouldn't go near them, for some reason. I think they want to talk with you. Don't ask me where I got that idea either."

"All right," Sparhawk said. "I'll go see what they want." He spurred Faran into a gallop and thudded up the long slope of the road toward the hilltop. The two mounted men wore black Pandion armor, but they gave none of the customary signs of greeting as Sparhawk approached, and neither of them raised his visor. Their horses were peculiarly gaunt, almost skeletal.

"What is it, brothers?" Sparhawk asked, reining Faran in a few yards from the pair. He caught a momentary whiff of an unpleasant smell, and a chill ran through him.

One of the armored figures turned slightly and pointed a steel-clad arm down into the next valley. He did not speak, but appeared to be pointing at a winter-denuded elm grove at one side of the road about a half mile farther on.

"I don't quite—" Sparhawk started; then he caught the sudden glint of sunlight on polished steel among the spidery branches of the grove. He shaded his eyes with one hand and peered intently at the cluster of trees. He saw a hint of movement and another flash of reflected light. "I see," he said gravely. "Thank you, my brothers. Would you care to join us in routing the ambushers waiting below?"

For a long moment, neither black-armored figure responded, then one of them inclined his head in assent. They both moved then, one to either side of the road, and sat their horses, waiting.

Puzzled by their strange behavior, Sparhawk rode back down the road to rejoin the others. "We've got some trouble up ahead," he reported. "There's a group of armed men hiding in a grove of trees in the next valley."

"An ambush?" Tynian asked.

"People don't usually hide unless they've got some mischief in mind."

"Could you tell how many there are?" Bevier asked, loosening his Lochaber from its sling on his saddlebow.

"Not really."

"One way to find out," Ulath said, reaching for his axe.

"Who are the two Pandions?" Kalten asked nervously.

"They didn't say."

"Did they give you the same kind of feeling they gave me?"

"What kind of feeling?"

"As if my blood had just frozen."

Sparhawk nodded. "Something like that," he admitted. "Kurik," he said then, "you and Berit take Sephrenia, Flute, and Talen to some place out of sight."

The squire nodded curtly.

"All right then, gentlemen," Sparhawk said to the other knights, "let's go have a look."

They started out at a rolling trot, five armored knights mounted on war horses and wielding a variety of unpleasant-looking weapons. At the top of the hill they were joined by the two silent men in black armor. Once again Sparhawk caught that unpleasant smell, and once again his blood ran strangely cold.

"Has anybody got a horn?" Tynian asked. "We should let them know we're coming."

Ulath unbuckled one of his saddlebags and took out the curled and twisted horn of some animal. It was quite large and had a brass mouthpiece at its tip.

"What kind of an animal has horns like that?" Kalten asked him.

"Ogre," Ulath replied. Then he set the mouthpiece to his lips and blew a shattering blast.

"For the glory of God and the honor of the Church!" Bevier exclaimed, rising in his stirrups and flourishing his Lochaber.

Sparhawk drew his sword and drove his spurs into Faran's flanks. The big horse plunged eagerly ahead, his ears laid back and his teeth bared.

There were shouts of chagrin from the elm grove as the Church Knights plunged down the hill at a gallop with the grass whipping at the legs of their chargers. Then perhaps eighteen armored men on horseback broke out of their concealment and rode out into the open to meet the charge.

"They want a fight!" Tynian shouted jubilantly.

"Watch yourselves when we mix with them!" Sparhawk warned. "There may be more hiding in the grove!"

Ulath continued to sound his horn until the last moment. Then he quickly stuffed it back into his saddlebag and began to whirl his great war axe about his head.

Three of the ambushers had held back; just before the two parties crashed together, they turned tail and rode off at a dead run, flogging their horses in sheer panic.

The initial impact might easily have been heard a mile away. Sparhawk and Faran were slightly in the lead, with the others fanned out and back in a kind of wedge formation. Sparhawk stood up in his stirrups to deliver broad overhand strokes to the right and the left as he crashed into the strangers. He split open a helmet and saw blood and brains come gushing out as the man fell stiffly out of his saddle. On his next stroke his sword sheared through an upraised shield, and he heard a scream as his blade bit into the arm to which the shield was strapped. Behind him he could hear the sounds of other blows and shrieks as his friends followed him through the mêlée.

Their rush through the center of the ambushers left ten down, killed or maimed, but, as they whirled to attack again, a half-dozen more came crashing out of the grove to attack them from the rear.

"Go ahead!" Bevier shouted as he wheeled his horse. "I'll hold these off while you finish the rest!" He raised his Lochaber and charged.

"Help him, Kalten!" Sparhawk called to his friend, then led Tynian, Ulath, and the two strangers against the dazed survivors of their first attack. Tynian's broadsword had a much wider blade than those of the Pandions and thus a great deal more weight. That weight made the weapon savagely efficient, and Tynian cut through flesh or armor with equal ease. Ulath's axe, of course, had no finesse or subtlety. He hewed at men as a woodsman might hew at trees.

Sparhawk briefly saw one of the two strange Pandions rise in his stirrups to deliver a vast overhand blow. What the knight held in its gauntleted fist, however, was not a sword, but rather that same kind of glowing nimbus that had been given to Sephrenia in the shabby upstairs apartment in Chyrellos by the insubstantial ghost of Sir Lakus. The nimbus appeared to pass completely through the body of the awkward mercenary the Pandion faced. The man's face went absolutely white, and he stared down at his chest in horror, but there was no blood, and his rust-splotched armor remained intact. With a shriek of terror, he threw his sword away and fled. Then Sparhawk's attention was diverted by another enemy.

When the last of the ambushers had fallen, Sparhawk wheeled Faran to go to the aid of Bevier and Kalten, but saw that it was largely unnecessary. Three of the men who had come charging out of the elm grove were already down. Another was doubled over in his saddle with both hands pressed to his belly. The other two were trying desperately to parry the blows of Kalten's sword and Bevier's Lochaber axe. Kalten feinted with his sword, then smoothly slapped his opponent's weapon out of his hand, even as Bevier lopped the head off his man with an almost casual backhand swipe.

"Don't kill him!" Sparhawk shouted to Kalten as the blond man raised his sword.

"But—" Kalten protested.

"I want to question him."

Kalten's face grew bleak with disappointment as Sparhawk rode back across the littered turf toward him and Bevier.

Sparhawk reined Faran in. "Get off your horse," he told the frightened and exhausted captive.

The man slid down. Like that worn by his fallen companions, his armor was a mishmash of unmatched pieces. It was rusty and dented in places, but the sword Kalten had knocked from his hand was polished and sharp.

"You're a mercenary, I take it," Sparhawk said to him.

"Yes, my Lord," the fellow faltered in a Pelosian accent.

"This didn't turn out too well, did it?" Sparhawk asked in an almost comradely fashion.

The fellow laughed nervously, looking at the carnage around him. "No, my Lord, not at all the way we expected."

"You did your best," Sparhawk said to him. "Now, we'll need the name of the man who hired you."

"I didn't ask his name, my Lord."

"Describe him then."

"I—I cannot, my Lord."

"This interview is going to get a lot less pleasant, I think," Kalten said.

"Stand him in a fire," Ulath suggested.

"I've always liked pouring boiling pitch inside their armor—slowly," Tynian said.

"Thumbscrews," Bevier said firmly.

"You see how it is, neighbor," Sparhawk said to the now ashen-faced prisoner. "You *are* going to talk. We're here, and the man who hired you isn't. He might have threatened you with unpleasant things, but we're going to do them to you. Save yourself a great deal of discomfort and answer my questions."

"My Lord," the man blubbered, "I *can't*—even if you torture me to death."

Ulath slid down from his saddle and approached the cringing captive. "Oh, stop that," the Genidian said. He raised a hand, palm outstretched, over the prisoner's head and spoke in a harsh, grating language Sparhawk did not understand but uneasily suspected was not a human tongue. The captured mercenary's eyes went blank, and he fell to his knees. Falteringly and with absolutely no expression in his voice, he began to speak in the same language as Ulath had.

"He's been bound in a spell," the Genidian Knight reported. "Nothing we could have done to him would have made him talk."

The mercenary went on in that dreadful language, speaking more rapidly now.

"There were two who hired him," Ulath translated, "a hooded Styric and a man with white hair."

"Martel!" Kalten exclaimed.

"Very likely," Sparhawk agreed.

The prisoner spoke again.

"It was the Styric who put the spell on him," Ulath said. "It's one I'm not familiar with."

"I don't think I am either," Sparhawk admitted. "We'll see if Sephrenia knows it."

"Oh," Ulath added, "that's one other thing. This attack was directed at her."

*"What?"*

"The orders these men had were to kill the Styric woman."

"Kalten!" Sparhawk barked, but the blond man was already spurring his horse.

"What about him?" Tynian pointed at the prisoner.

"Let him go," Sparhawk shouted as he galloped off after Kalten. "Come on!"

As they rode over the hilltop, Sparhawk looked back. The two strange Pandions were nowhere in sight. Then, up ahead, he saw them. A group of men had surrounded the rocky knoll where Kurik had hidden Sephrenia and the others. The two black-armored knights were sitting their horses coolly between the attackers and the knoll. They were making no effort to fight, but merely stood their ground. As Sparhawk watched, one of the attackers launched a javelin which appeared to pass directly through the body of one of the black-armored Pandions with no visible effect.

"Faran!" Sparhawk barked, "run!" It was something he seldom did. He called upon Faran's loyalty instead of his training. The big horse shuddered slightly, then stretched himself out in a run that quickly outdistanced the others.

The attackers numbered perhaps ten men. They were recoiling visibly from the two shadowy Pandions blocking their path. Then one of them looked around and saw Sparhawk descending upon them with the others rushing along behind him, and he shouted a warning. After a moment of stunned paralysis, the shabby attackers bolted, fleeing across the meadow, fleeing in a kind of panic Sparhawk had seldom seen in professionals. He charged up the side of the outcrop with Faran's steel-shod hooves striking sparks from the stones. Just below the crest, he reined in. "Is everybody all right?" he called to Kurik.

"We're fine," Kurik replied, looking over the hasty breastwork of stone he and Berit had erected. "It was touch and go until those two knights got here, though." Kurik's eyes looked a bit wild as he stared at the pair who had warded off the assailants. Sephrenia came up to the breastwork beside him, and her face was deathly pale.

Sparhawk turned to the two strange Pandions. "I think it's time for introductions, brothers," he said, "and some explanations."

The two made no reply. He looked at them a bit more closely. The horses upon which they sat now appeared even more skeletal, and Sparhawk shuddered as he saw that the animals had no eyes, but only vacant eye sockets, and that their bones protruded through their tattered coats. Then the two knights removed their helmets. Their faces seemed somehow filmy and indistinct, almost transparent, and they, too, were eyeless. One of them appeared very young and he had butter-colored hair. The other was old, and his hair was white. Sparhawk recoiled slightly. He knew both of them; he knew that they both were dead.

"Sir Sparhawk," the ghost of Parasim said, his voice hollow and emotionless, "pursue thy quest with diligence. Time will not stay for thee."

"Why have you returned from the house of the dead?" Sephrenia asked the two in a profoundly formal tone. Her voice was trembling.

"Our oath hath the power to bring us out of the shadows if need be, little mother," the form of Lakus replied, his voice also hollow and void of all emotion. "Others will also fall, and our company will increase ere the queen returns to health." The hollow-eyed shade turned then to Sparhawk. "Guard well our beloved mother, Sparhawk, for she is in grave peril. Should she fall, our deaths are without purpose, and the queen will die."

"I will, Lakus," Sparhawk promised.

"Know also one last thing. In Ehlana's death, thou shalt lose more than a queen. The darkness hovers at the gate, and Ehlana is our only hope of light." Then the two of them shimmered and vanished.

The four other knights came charging up the rocky slope and reined in. Kalten's face was pallid and he was visibly trembling. "Who were they?" he asked.

"Parasim and Lakus," Sparhawk replied quietly.

"Parasim? He's dead."

"So's Lakus."

"Ghosts?"

"So it would seem."

Tynian dismounted and pulled off his massive helmet. He was also pale and sweating. "I've dabbled at times in necromancy," he said, "though not usually by choice. Usually a spirit has to be summoned, but sometimes they'll appear on their own—particularly if they left something important unfinished."

"This was important," Sparhawk said bleakly.

"Was there something else you wanted to tell us, Sparhawk?" Ulath asked then. "You seem to have left a few things out."

Sparhawk looked at Sephrenia. Her face was still deathly pale, but she straightened and nodded to him.

Sparhawk took a deep breath. "Ehlana would be dead, but is being preserved by a spell that keeps her sealed within a crystal. The spell was the result of the combined efforts of Sephrenia and twelve Pandions," he explained.

"I'd been sort of wondering about that," Tynian said.

"There's only one problem with it," Sparhawk continued. "The knights will die one by one until only Sephrenia is left."

"And then?" Bevier asked, his voice shaking.

"Then I will also depart," Sephrenia replied simply.

A stifled sob escaped the young Cyrinic. "Not while I have breath," he said in a choked voice.

"Someone, however, is trying to speed things up," Sparhawk went on. "This is the third attempt on Sephrenia's life since we left Cimmura."

"But I have survived them," she said as if they were of no moment. "Were you able in any way to identify the people behind this attack?"

"Martel and some Styric," Kalten told her. "The Styric had put a spell on the mercenaries to keep them from talking, but Ulath broke it somehow. He spoke with a prisoner in a language I didn't understand. The man answered in the same tongue."

She looked inquiringly at the Thalesian knight.

"We spoke in the language of the Trolls," Ulath shrugged. "It's a nonhuman tongue, so it circumvented the spell."

She stared at him in horror. "You called upon the Troll-Gods?" she gasped.

"Sometimes it's necessary, Lady," he replied. "It's not too dangerous if you're careful."

Bevier's face was tear-streaked. "And it please you, my Lord Sparhawk," he said, "I shall personally undertake the protection of the Lady Sephrenia. I shall remain constantly at this valiant lady's side, and should there be further encounters, I pledge you my life that she shall not be harmed."

A brief expression of consternation crossed Sephrenia's face, and she looked appealingly at Sparhawk.

"Probably not a bad idea," he said, ignoring her unspoken objection. "All right then, Bevier. Stay with her."

Sephrenia gave him a withering look.

"Are we going to get the dead under the ground?" Tynian asked.

Sparhawk shook his head. "We don't have time to be gravediggers. My brothers are dying one by one, and Sephrenia's at the end of the list. If we see some peasants, we'll tell them where the bodies are. The loot they'll get will more than pay for the digging. Let's move along."


Borrata was a university town that had grown up around the stately buildings of the oldest center of higher learning in Eosia. On occasion in the past, the Church had strongly urged that the institution be moved to Chyrellos, but the faculty had always resisted that notion, obviously desiring to maintain their independence and the absence of Church supervision.

Sparhawk and his companions took rooms in one of the local inns late in the afternoon on the day they arrived. The inn was more comfortable and certainly cleaner than the roadside ones in which they had stayed in Elenia and here in Cammoria.

The following morning, Sparhawk put on his mail coat and his heavy wool cloak.

"Do you want us to go with you?" Kalten asked as his friend came down into the common room on the main floor of the inn.

"No," Sparhawk replied. "Let's not turn it into a parade. The university isn't very far from here, and I can protect Sephrenia along the way."

Sir Bevier looked as if he were about to protest. He had taken his self-appointed role as Sephrenia's protector very seriously, seldom moving more than a few feet from her side during the journey to Borrata. Sparhawk looked at the earnest young Cyrinic. "I know you've been keeping watch outside her door every night, Bevier," he said. "Why don't you get some sleep? You won't be much good to her—or the rest of us—if you fall out of your saddle."

Bevier's face stiffened.

"He didn't mean it personally, Bevier," Kalten said. "Sparhawk just hasn't quite figured out the meaning of the word *diplomatic* yet. We're all hoping that someday it might come to him."

Bevier smiled faintly, then he laughed. "I think it might take me some time to adjust to you Pandions," he said.

"Look upon it as educational," Kalten suggested.

"You know that if you and the lady are successful in finding that cure, we're likely to encounter all kinds of trouble on the way back to Cimmura," Tynian said to Sparhawk. "We'll probably run into whole armies trying to stop us."

"Madel," Ulath suggested cryptically, "or Sarrinium."

"I don't quite follow," Tynian admitted.

"Those armies you mentioned will try to block the road to Chyrellos to keep us from getting there—and then on into Elenia. If we ride south to either of those seaports, we can hire a ship and sail around to Vardenais on the west coast of Elenia. It's faster to travel by sea anyway."

"Let's decide that after we find the cure," Sparhawk said.

Sephrenia came down the stairs with Flute. "Are we ready then?" she asked.

Sparhawk nodded.

She spoke briefly to Flute. The little girl nodded and crossed the room to where Talen sat. "You've been selected, Talen," Sephrenia told the boy. "Watch over her while I'm gone."

"But—" he started to object.

"Just do as she says, Talen," Kurik told him wearily.

"I was going to go out and have a look around."

"No," his father said, "as a matter of fact, you weren't."

Talen's expression grew sulky. "All right," he said as Flute climbed up into his lap.

Since the university grounds were so close, Sparhawk decided against taking their horses, and he and Sephrenia walked through the narrow streets of Borrata. The small woman looked around. "I haven't been here in a long time," she murmured.

"I can't imagine what interest a university could hold for you," Sparhawk smiled, "considering your views on reading."

"I wasn't studying, Sparhawk. I was teaching."

"I should have guessed, I suppose. How are you getting on with Bevier?"

"Fine, except that he won't let me do anything for myself—and that he keeps trying to convert me to the Elene faith." Her tone was slightly tart.

"He's just trying to protect you—your soul as well as your person."

"Are you trying to be funny?"

He decided not to answer that.

The grounds of the University of Borrata were parklike, and students and members of the faculty strolled contemplatively across the well-kept lawns.

Sparhawk stopped a young man in a lime-green doublet. "Excuse me, neighbor," he said, "but could you direct me to the medical college?"

"Are you ill?"

"No. A friend of mine is, though."

"Ah. The physicians occupy that building over there." The student pointed at a squat-looking structure made of gray stone.

"Thank you, neighbor."

"I hope your friend gets better soon."

"So do we."

When they entered the building, they encountered a rotund man in a black robe.

"Excuse me, sir," Sephrenia said to him. "Are you a physician?"

"I am."

"Splendid. Have you a few moments?"

The rotund man had been looking closely at Sparhawk. "Sorry," he said curtly. "I'm busy."

"Could you direct us to one of your colleagues, then?"

"Try any door," he said, waving his hand and walking quickly away from them.

"That's an odd attitude for a healer," Sparhawk said.

"Every profession attracts its share of louts," she replied.

They crossed the antechamber and Sparhawk rapped on a dark-painted door.

"What is it?" a weary voice said.

"We need to consult a physician."

There was a long pause. "Oh, all right," the weary voice replied, "come in."

Sparhawk opened the door and held it for Sephrenia.

The man seated behind the cluttered desk in the cubicle had deep circles beneath his eyes, and it appeared that he had foregone shaving some weeks ago. "What is the nature of your illness?" he asked Sephrenia in a voice hovering on exhaustion.

"I'm not the one who's ill," she replied.

"Him, then?" the doctor pointed at Sparhawk. "He looks robust enough to me."

"No," she said. "He's not ill either. We're here on behalf of a friend."

"I don't go to people's houses."

"We weren't asking you to do that," Sparhawk said.

"Our friend lives some distance away," Sephrenia said. "We thought that if we described her symptoms to you, you might be able to hazard a guess as to the cause of her malady."

"I don't make guesses," he told her shortly. "What are the symptoms?"

"Much like those of the falling-sickness," Sephrenia told him.

"That's it, then. You've already made the diagnosis yourself."

"There are certain differences, however."

"All right. Describe the differences."

"There's a fever involved—quite a high one—and profuse sweating."

"The two don't match, little lady. With a fever, the skin is dry."

"Yes, I know."

"Have you a medical background?"

"I'm familiar with certain folk remedies."

He snorted. "My experience tells me that folk remedies kill more than they cure. What other symptoms did you notice?"

Sephrenia meticulously described the illness that had rendered Ehlana comatose.

The physician, however, seemed not to be listening, but was staring instead at Sparhawk. His face became suddenly alert, his eyes narrowed and his expression sly. "I'm sorry," he said when Sephrenia had finished. "I think you'd better go back and take another look at your friend. What you just described matches no known illness." His tone was abrupt, even curt.

Sparhawk straightened, clenching his fist, but Sephrenia laid her hand on his arm. "Thank you for your time, learned sir," she said smoothly. "Come along then," she told Sparhawk.

The two of them went back out into the corridor.

"Two in a row," Sparhawk muttered.

"Two what?"

"People with bad manners."

"It stands to reason, perhaps."

"I don't follow you."

"There's a certain natural arrogance in those who teach."

"*You've* never displayed it."

"I keep it under control. Try another door, Sparhawk."

In the next two hours, they spoke with seven physicians. Each of them, after a searching look at Sparhawk's face, pretended ignorance.

"I'm starting to get a peculiar feeling about this," he growled as they emerged from yet another office. "They take one look at me, and they suddenly become stupid—or is that just my imagination?"

"I've noticed that, too," she replied thoughtfully.

"My face isn't that exciting, I know, but it's never struck anyone dumb before."

"It's a perfectly good face, Sparhawk."

"It covers the front of my head. What else can you expect from a face?"

"The physicians of Borrata seem less skilled than we'd been led to believe."

"We've wasted more time, then?"

"We haven't finished yet. Don't give up hope."

They came finally to a small, unpainted door set back in a shabby alcove. Sparhawk rapped, and a slurred voice responded, "Go away."

"We need your help, learned sir," Sephrenia said.

"Go bother somebody else. I'm busy getting drunk right now."

"That does it!" Sparhawk snapped. He grasped the door handle and pushed, but the door was locked from the inside. Irritably, he kicked it open, splintering the frame.

The man inside the tiny cubicle blinked. He was a shabby little man with a crooked back and bleary eyes. "You knock very loudly, friend," he observed. Then he belched. "Well, don't just stand there. Come in." His head weaved back and forth. He was shabbily dressed, and his wispy gray hair stuck out in all directions.

"Is there something in the water around here that makes everybody so churlish?" Sparhawk asked acidly.

"I wouldn't know," the shabby man replied. "I never drink water." He drank noisily from a battered tankard.

"Obviously."

"Shall we spend the rest of the day exchanging insults, or would you rather tell me about your problem?" The physician squinted myopically at Sparhawk's face. "So you're the one," he said.

"The one what?"

"The one we aren't supposed to talk to."

"Would you like to explain that?"

"A man came here a few days ago. He said that it would be worth a hundred gold pieces to every physician in the building if you left empty-handed."

"What did he look like?"

"He had a military bearing and white hair."

"Martel," Sparhawk said to Sephrenia.

"We should have guessed almost immediately," she replied.

"Take heart, friends," the messy little man told them expansively. "You've found your way to the finest physician in Borrata." He grinned then. "My colleagues all fly south with the ducks in the fall going, 'Quack, quack, quack.' You couldn't get a sound medical opinion out of any one of them. The white-haired man said that you'd describe some symptoms. Some lady someplace is very ill, I understand, and your friend—this Martel you mentioned—would prefer that she didn't recover. Why don't we disappoint him?" He drank deeply from his tankard.

"You're a credit to your profession, good doctor," Sephrenia said.

"No. I'm a vicious-minded old drunkard. Do you really want to know why I'm willing to help you? It's because I'll enjoy the screams of anguish from my colleagues when all that money slips through their fingers."

"That's as good a reason as any, I suppose," Sparhawk said.

"Exactly." The slightly tipsy physician peered at Sparhawk's nose. "Why didn't you have that set when it got broken?" he asked.

Sparhawk touched his nose. "I was busy with other things."

"I can fix it for you if you'd like. All I have to do is take a hammer and break it again. Then I can set it for you."

"Thanks all the same, but I'm used to it now."

"Suit yourself. All right, what are these symptoms you came here to describe?"

Once again Sephrenia ran down the list for him.

He sat scratching at his ear with his eyes narrowed. Then he rummaged through the litter piled high on his desk and pulled out a thick book with a torn leather cover. He leafed through it for several moments, then slammed it shut. "Just as I thought," he said triumphantly. He belched again.

"Well?" Sparhawk said.

"Your friend was poisoned. Has she died yet?"

A chill caught at Sparhawk's stomach. "No," he replied.

"It's only a matter of time." The physician shrugged. "It's a rare poison from Rendor. It's invariably fatal."

Sparhawk clenched his teeth. "I'm going to go back to Cimmura and disembowel Annias," he grated, "with a dull knife."

The disreputable little physician suddenly looked interested. "You do it this way," he suggested. "Make a lateral incision just below the navel. Then kick him over backward. Everything ought to fall out at that point."

"Thank you."

"No charge. If you're going to do something, do it right. I take it that this Annias person is the one you think was responsible?"

"Undoubtedly."

"Go ahead and kill him then. I despise a poisoner."

"Is there an antidote for this poison?" Sephrenia asked.

"None that I know of. I'd suggest talking with several physicians I know in Cippria, but your friend will be dead before you could get back."

"No," Sephrenia disagreed. "She's being sustained."

"I'd like to know how you managed that."

"The lady is Styric," Sparhawk told him. "She has access to certain unusual things."

"Magic? Does that really work?"

"At times, yes."

"All right, then. Maybe you do have time." The seedy-looking doctor ripped a corner off one of the papers on his desk and dipped a quill into a nearly dry inkpot. "The first two names here are those of a couple of fairly adept physicians in Cippria," he said as he scrawled on the paper. "This last one is the name of the poison." He handed the paper to Sparhawk. "Good luck," he said. "Now get out of here so I can continue what I was doing before you kicked in my door."

## CHAPTER SIXTEEN

"Because you don't look like Rendors," Sparhawk told them. "Foreigners attract a great deal of attention there—usually unfriendly. I can pass for a native in Cippria. So can Kurik. Rendorish women wear veils, so Sephrenia's appearance won't be a problem. The rest of you are going to have to stay behind."

They were gathered in a large room on the upper floor of the inn near the university. The room was bare with only a few benches along the walls and no curtains at the narrow window. Sparhawk had reported what the tipsy physician had said and the fact that Martel had attempted subterfuge this time rather than a physical confrontation.

"We could put something on our hair to change the color," Kalten protested. "Wouldn't that get us by?"

"It's the manner, Kalten," Sparhawk explained. "I could dye you green, and people would still know that you're an Elenian. The same's more or less true of the rest of you. You all have the bearing of knights. It takes years to erase that."

"You want us to stay here, then?" Ulath asked.

"No. Let's all go down to Madel," Sparhawk decided. "If something unexpected comes up in Cippria, I can get word to you there faster."

"I think you're overlooking something, Sparhawk," Kalten said. "We know that Martel's moving around down here, and he's probably got eyes everywhere. If we all ride out of Borrata in full armor, he'll know about it before we cover half a league."

"Pilgrims," Ulath grunted cryptically.

"I don't quite follow you," Kalten said, frowning.

"If we pack our armor in a cart and dress in sober clothes, we can join a group of pilgrims, and nobody's going to give us a second glance." He looked at Bevier. "Do you know very much about Madel?" he asked.

"We have a chapterhouse there," Bevier replied. "I visit it from time to time."

"Are there any shrines or holy places there?"

"Several. But pilgrims seldom travel in winter."

"They do if they get paid. We'll hire some—and a clergyman to sing hymns as we go along."

"It's got possibilities, Sparhawk," Kalten said. "Martel doesn't really know *which* way we're going when we leave here, so his spies are going to be spread fairly thin."

"How will we know this Martel person?" Bevier asked. "Should we encounter him while you're in Cippria, I mean?"

"Kalten knows him," Sparhawk replied, "and Talen has seen him once." Then he remembered something. He looked over at the boy, who was making a cat's cradle to entertain Flute. "Talen," he said, "could you draw pictures of Martel and Krager?"

"Of course."

"And we can conjure up the image of Adus as well," Sephrenia added.

"Adus is easy," Kalten said. "Just put armor on a gorilla and you've got him."

"All right, we'll do it that way, then," Sparhawk said. "Berit."

"Yes, Lord Sparhawk?"

"Go find a church somewhere—a poor one. Talk with the vicar. Tell him that we'll finance a pilgrimage to the shrines in Madel. Ask him to pick a dozen or so of his neediest parishioners and to bring them here tomorrow morning. We'll want him to come with us as well—to be the caretaker of our souls. And tell him that we'll make a sizable contribution to his church if he agrees."

"Won't he ask about our motives, my Lord?"

"Tell him that we've committed a dreadful sin and want to atone for it," Kalten shrugged. "Just don't be too specific about the sin."

"Sir Kalten!" Bevier gasped. "You would lie to a churchman?"

"It's not exactly a lie, Bevier. We've all committed sins. I've sinned at least a half-dozen times this week already. Besides, the vicar of a poor church isn't going to ask too many questions when there's a contribution involved."

Sparhawk took a leather pouch from inside his tunic. He shook it a few times, and a distinctive jingling sound came from it. "All right, gentlemen," he said, untying the top of the pouch, "we've reached the part of this service you all enjoy the most—the offertory. God appreciates a generous giver, so don't be shy. The vicar will need cash to hire pilgrims." He passed the pouch around.

"Do you think God might accept a promissory note?" Kalten asked.

"God might. I won't. Put something in the pouch, Kalten."

The group that gathered in the innyard the following morning was uniformly shabby—widows in patched mourning, out-of-work artisans and several hungry beggars. They were all mounted on weary nags or sleepy-looking mules. Sparhawk looked at them from the window. "Tell the innkeeper to feed them," he said to Kalten.

"There's quite a number of them, Sparhawk."

"I don't want them fainting from hunger a mile out of town. You take care of that while I go talk with the vicar."

"Anything you say." Kalten shrugged. "Should I bathe them, too? Some of them look a bit unwashed."

"That won't be necessary. Feed their horses and mules as well."

"Aren't we being a little overgenerous?"

"You get to carry any horse that collapses."

"Oh. I'll see to it right away, then."

The vicar of the poor church was a thin, anxious-looking man in his sixties. His silvery hair was curly, and his face was drawn and deeply lined with care. "My Lord," he said, bowing deeply to Sparhawk.

"Please, good vicar," Sparhawk said to him, "just 'pilgrim' is adequate. We are all equal in the service of God. My companions and I wish simply to join with your good, pious folk and to journey to Madel that we may worship at the holy shrines there for the solace of our souls and in the certain knowledge of the infinite mercy of God."

"Well said—uh—pilgrim."

"Would you join us at table, good vicar?" Sparhawk asked him. "We will go many miles before we sleep tonight."

The vicar's eyes grew suddenly bright. "I would be delighted, my Lord—uh, pilgrim, that is."

The feeding of the Cammorian pilgrims and their mounts took quite some time and stretched the capacity of the kitchen and the stable grain bins to a considerable degree.

"I've never seen people eat so much," Kalten grumbled. Clad in a sturdy, unmarked cloak, he swung up into his saddle just outside the inn.

"They were hungry," Sparhawk told him. "At least we can see to it that they get a few good meals before they have to return to Borrata."

"Charity, Sir Sparhawk?" Bevier asked. "Isn't that a bit out of character? The grim-faced Pandions are not noted for their tender sensibilities."

"How little you know them, Sir Bevier," Sephrenia murmured. She mounted her white palfrey, then held down her hands to Flute, but the little girl shook her head, walked over to Faran, and reached out her tiny hand. The big roan lowered his head, and she caressed his velvety nose. Sparhawk felt an odd quiver run through his mount's body. Then Flute insistently raised her hands to the big Pandion. Gravely, Sparhawk leaned over and lifted her into her accustomed place in front of the saddle and enfolded her in his cloak. She nestled against him, took out her pipes, and began to play that same minor melody she had been playing when they had first found her.

The vicar at the head of their column intoned a brief prayer, invoking the protection of the God of the Elenes during their journey, an invocation punctuated by questioning—even skeptical—trills from Flute's pipes.

"Behave yourself," Sparhawk whispered to her. "He's a good man and he's doing what he thinks is right."

She rolled her eyes roguishly. Then she yawned, snuggled closer to him, and promptly went to sleep.

They rode south out of Borrata under a clear morning sky with Kurik and the two-wheeled cart containing their armor and equipment clattering along behind them. The breeze was gusty and it tugged at the ragged clothing of the pilgrims patiently plodding along behind their vicar. A line of low mountains lay to the west, touched with snow on their peaks, and the sunlight glistened on those white fields. Their pace as they rode seemed to Sparhawk leisurely—even lackadaisical—though the panting and wheezing of the poor mounts of the pilgrims was a fair indication that the beasts were being pressed as hard as was possible.

It was about noon when Kalten rode forward from his station at the rear of the column. "There are riders coming up behind us," he reported quietly to avoid alarming nearby pilgrims. "They're pushing hard."

"Any idea of who they are?"

"They're wearing red."

"Church soldiers, then."

"Notice how quick he is?" Kalten observed to the others.

"How many?" Tynian asked.

"It looks to be a reinforced platoon."

Bevier loosened his Lochaber axe in its sling.

"Keep that under cover," Sparhawk told him. "The rest of you hide your weapons as well." Then he raised his voice. "Good vicar," he called ahead. "How about a hymn? The miles go easier with sacred music for company."

The vicar cleared his throat and began to sing in a rusty, off-key voice. Wearily, but responding automatically to their pastor's lead, the other pilgrims joined in.

"Sing!" Sparhawk commanded his companions, and they all raised their voices in the familiar hymn. As they bawled their song, Flute lifted her pipes and played a mocking little counterpoint.

"Stop that," Sparhawk murmured to her. "And if there's trouble, slide down and run out into that field."

She rolled her eyes at him.

"Do as you're told, young lady. I don't want you getting trampled if there's a fight."

The church soldiers, however, pounded past the column of hymn-singing pilgrims with hardly a glance and were soon lost in the distance ahead.

"Tense," Ulath commented.

"Truly," Tynian agreed. "Trying to fight in the middle of a crowd of terrified pilgrims might have been interesting."

"Do you think they were searching for us?" Berit asked.

"It's hard to say," Sparhawk replied. "I wasn't going to stop them to ask, though."

They moved southward toward Madel in easy stages to conserve the sorry mounts of the vicar's parishioners, and they arrived on the outskirts of the port city about noon on the fourth day out of Borrata. When the town came into view, Sparhawk rode forward to join the vicar at the head of the column. He handed the good man a pouch full of coins. "We'll be leaving you here," he said. "A matter has come up that needs our attention."

The vicar gave him a speculative look. "This was all subterfuge, wasn't it, my Lord?" he asked gravely. "I may be only the poor pastor of a poverty-stricken chapel, but I recognize the manner and bearing of Church Knights when I see them."

"Forgive us, good vicar," Sparhawk replied. "Take your people to the holy places here in Madel. Lead them in prayer and then see to it that they're well-fed. Then return to Borrata and use whatever money is left as you see fit."

"And may I do this with a clear conscience, my son?"

"The clearest, good pastor. My friends and I serve the Church in a matter of gravest urgency, and your aid will be appreciated by the members of the Hierocracy in Chyrellos—most of them, at any rate." Then Sparhawk turned Faran around and rode back to his companions. "All right, Bevier," he said. "Take us to your chapterhouse."

"I have been considering that, Sir Sparhawk," Bevier replied. "Our chapterhouse here is closely watched by local authorities and all manner of other folk. Even garbed as we are, we would surely be recognized."

Sparhawk grunted. "You're probably right. Can you think of any alternatives?"

"Perhaps so. As it happens, I have a kinsman—a marquis from eastern Arcium—who has a villa on the outskirts of the city. I have not seen him for some years—our family disapproves of him because he's in trade—but perhaps he will remember me. He's a good-natured fellow, and if I approach him right, he might extend his hospitality."

"It's worth a try, I guess. All right. Lead the way."

They rode around the western outskirts of Madel to an opulent house surrounded by a low wall built of the local sandstone. The house was set back some distance from the road and was surrounded by tall evergreens and well-groomed lawns. There was a graveled court directly in front of the house, and they dismounted there. A servant in sober livery emerged from the house and approached inquiringly.

"Would you be so good as to advise the marquis that his second cousin, Sir Bevier, and several friends would like to have a word with him?" the Cyrinic inquired politely.

"At once, my Lord." The servant turned and reentered the house.

The man who emerged from the house a few moments later was stout and had a florid face. He wore one of the colorful silk robes common in southern Cammoria rather than Arcian doublet and hose, and his welcoming grin was broad. "Bevier," he greeted his distant cousin with a warm handclasp. "What are you doing in Cammoria?"

"Seeking refuge, Lycien," Bevier replied. His open young face clouded momentarily. "The family has not treated you well, Lycien," he admitted. "I could not blame you if you turned me and my friends away."

"Nonsense, Bevier. The decision to take up trading was mine. I knew how the rest of the family would feel about it. I'm delighted to see you. You mentioned refuge?"

Bevier nodded. "We're here on Church business of some delicacy," he said, "and there are a few too many eyes watching the Cyrinic chapterhouse in the city. I know it's a great deal to ask, but might we impose on your hospitality?"

"By all means, my boy, by all means." Marquis Lycien clapped his hands sharply, and several grooms came out of the stables. "See to the mounts of these visitors and their cart," the marquis ordered. Then he laid his hand on Bevier's shoulder. "Come in," he invited them all. "My house is yours." He turned and led the way through the low, arched doorway and on into the house. Once they were inside, they followed him to a pleasant room with low, cushioned furniture and a fireplace where several logs crackled and snapped. "Please, friends, sit," Lycien said. Then he looked speculatively at them. "This Church business of yours must be very important, Bevier," he guessed. "Gathering from their features, I'd say that your friends represent all four of the militant orders."

"Your eyes are sharp, Marquis," Sparhawk told him.

"Am I going to get in trouble over this?" Lycien asked. Then he grinned. "Not that I care, mind you. It's just that I like to be prepared."

"It's not too likely," Sparhawk assured him. "Particularly if we're successful in our mission. Tell me, my Lord, do you have contacts in the harbor?"

"Extensive ones, Sir . . ."

"Sparhawk," the Pandion supplied.

"Champion of the queen of Elenia?" Lycien looked surprised. "I heard that you'd returned from your exile in Rendor; but aren't you a bit far afield? Shouldn't you be in Cimmura trying to circumvent the attempts of the Primate Annias to depose your lady?"

"You're well-informed, my Lord," Sparhawk said.

"I have widespread commercial contacts." Lycien shrugged. He winked at Bevier. "That's what disgraced me in the eyes of the family. My agents and the masters of my ships gather much information in the course of their dealings."

"I gather, my Lord, that you're not overly fond of the primate of Cimmura?"

"The man's a scoundrel."

"Our sentiments exactly," Kalten agreed.

"Very well, then, my Lord," Sparhawk said. "What we're involved with is an attempt to counter the growing power of the primate. If we're successful, we can stop him in his tracks. I'd tell you more, but it might be dangerous for you if you knew too many of the details."

"I can appreciate that, Sir Sparhawk," Lycien said. "Tell me, in what way can I help?"

"Three of us need to go to Cippria," Sparhawk replied. "For the sake of your own safety, it might be better if we were to take the ship of an independent sea captain rather than one of your own vessels. If you could direct us to such a captain and perhaps give us a discreetly worded letter of introduction to him, we can take care of the rest."

"Sparhawk," Kurik said sharply, looking around the room, "what happened to Talen?"

Sparhawk turned quickly. "I thought he was bringing up the rear when we came in."

"So did I."

"Berit," Sparhawk said, "go find him."

"At once, my Lord." The novice hurried from the room.

"Some problem?" Lycien asked.

"A wayward boy, cousin," Bevier told him. "From what I gather, he needs to be watched rather closely."

"Berit will find him." Kalten laughed. "I have a great deal of confidence in that young man. Talen may come back with a few bumps and contusions, but I'm sure they'll be very educational for him."

"Well, if it's all under control, then," Lycien said, "why don't I send word to the kitchen? I'm sure you're all hungry. And in the meantime, perhaps some wine?" He assumed a pious expression that was obviously feigned. "I know that the Knights of the Church are abstemious, but a touch or so of wine is good for the digestion, or so I've heard."

"I've heard that, too," Kalten agreed.

"Could I prevail upon you for a cup of tea, my Lord?" Sephrenia asked, "and some milk for the little girl? I'm not sure that wine would be good for either of us."

"Of course, madame," Lycien replied jovially. "I should have thought of that myself."

It was midafternoon when Berit returned with Talen in tow. "He was down near the harbor," the novice reported, still firmly holding the boy by the neck of his tunic. "I searched him thoroughly. He hadn't had time to steal anything yet."

"I just wanted to look at the sea," the boy protested. "I've never seen the sea before."

Kurik was grimly removing his wide leather belt.

"Now, wait a minute, Kurik," Talen said, struggling to free himself from Berit's grasp. "You wouldn't really do that, would you?"

"Watch me."

"I picked up some information," Talen said quickly. "If you thrash me, I'll keep it to myself." He looked appealingly at Sparhawk. "It's important," he said. "Tell him to put his belt back on, and I'll let you know what I found out."

"All right, Kurik," Sparhawk said. "Let it pass—for the moment anyway." Then he looked sternly at the boy. "This had better be good, Talen," he threatened.

"It is, Sparhawk. Believe me."

"Let's have it."

"Well, I was going down this street. As I said, I wanted to see the harbor and all the ships and things. Anyway, I was passing a wine shop and I saw a man coming out."

"Amazing," Kalten said. "Do people in Madel actually frequent wine shops?"

"You both know this man. It was Krager, the one you had me watching in Cimmura. I followed him. He went into a shabby-looking inn down by the waterfront. I can take you there if you want."

"Put your belt back on, Kurik," Sparhawk said.

"Do we have time for this?" Kalten asked.

"I think we should take time. Martel's already tried to interfere with us a couple times. If it *was* Annias who poisoned Ehlana, he'll definitely want to keep us from finding any kind of antidote. That means that Martel will try to get to Cippria before I do. We can wring that information out of Krager if we can catch him."

"We'll go with you," Tynian said eagerly. "This whole thing will be easier if we can cut Annias's hands off here in Madel."

Sparhawk considered it, then shook his head. "I don't think so," he said. "Martel and his hirelings know Kalten and me. He doesn't know the rest of you. If the two of us can't catch up with Krager, you'll all be looking around Madel for him. That's going to be easier if he doesn't know what you look like."

"Makes sense," Ulath agreed.

Tynian looked profoundly disappointed. "Sometimes you think too much, Sparhawk," he said.

"It's a trait of his," Kalten told him.

"Will these cloaks of ours attract any attention in the streets of Madel, my Lord?" Sparhawk asked the marquis.

Lycien shook his head. "It's a port city," he said. "There are people here from all over the world, so two more strangers won't attract that much notice."

"Good," Sparhawk said. He started toward the door with Kalten and Talen at his heels. "We should be back before long," he said.

They left their horses behind and went into the city on foot. Madel was situated on an estuary, and the smell of the sea was very strong, carried inland by a stiff onshore breeze. The streets were narrow and crooked and grew increasingly rundown as the two knights and the boy approached the harbor.

"How far is this inn?" Kalten asked.

"Not too much farther," Talen assured him.

Sparhawk stopped. "Did you get the chance to look around a bit after Krager went inside?" he asked the boy.

"No. I was going to, but Berit caught me before I had time."

"Why don't you do it now? If Kalten and I go marching up to the front door and Krager happens to be watching, he'll be out the back door before we get inside. See if you can find that back door for us."

"Right," Talen said, his eyes sparkling with excitement. He scurried off down the street.

"Good lad there," Kalten said, "in spite of his bad habits." He frowned. "How do you know this inn has a back door?" he asked.

"Every inn has a back door, Kalten—in case of fire, if nothing else."

"I guess I hadn't thought of that."

When Talen returned, he was running as hard as he could. There were about ten men chasing him; in the lead, roaring unintelligibly, was Adus.

"Look out!" Talen shouted as he ran past.

Sparhawk and Kalten whipped their swords out from under their cloaks and stepped slightly apart to meet the charge. The men following Adus were shabbily dressed and carried a variety of weapons, rusty swords, axes, and spiked maces. "Kill them!" Adus bellowed, slowing slightly and waving his men on.

The fight was short. The men rushing up the narrow street appeared to be common waterfront roughnecks, and they were no match for the two trained knights. Four of them were down before the others realized that they had made a tactical blunder. Two more collapsed onto the bloody stones before the rest could turn to flee. Then Sparhawk leaped over the sprawled bodies and rushed at Adus. The brute parried the knight's first stroke, then seized his sword hilt in both hands and flailed at Sparhawk with it. Sparhawk easily deflected those blows and countered deftly, inflicting painful cuts and bruises on his opponent's mailed ribs and shoulders. After a moment, Adus fled, running hard and clutching at his side with a bloody hand.

"Why didn't you chase him?" Kalten demanded, coming up puffing and with his blood-smeared sword still in his hand.

"Because Adus can run faster than I can," Sparhawk shrugged. "I've known that for years."

Talen came back down the street, breathing hard. He looked admiringly at the hacked and bleeding bodies sprawled on the cobblestones. "Well done, my Lords," he congratulated them.

"What happened?" Sparhawk asked.

"I went on past the inn." Talen shrugged. "Then I went around back. That big one who just got away was hiding in the alley with these others. He made a grab for me, but I dodged. Then I ran."

"Good thinking," Kalten said.

Sparhawk sheathed his sword. "Let's get away from here," he said.

"Why not follow Adus?" Kalten asked.

"Because they're setting traps for us. Martel's using Krager as bait to lead us around by the nose. That's probably why we keep finding him so easily."

"Would that mean that they can recognize me as well?" Talen sounded shocked.

"Probably," Sparhawk said. "They found out that you were working for me in Cimmura, remember? Krager probably knew that you were following him around and gave your description to Adus. Adus may not have a brain, but his eyes are sharp." He muttered an oath. "Martel's even more clever than I thought, and he's starting to irritate me."

"It's about time," Kalten murmured as they started back up the crooked street.

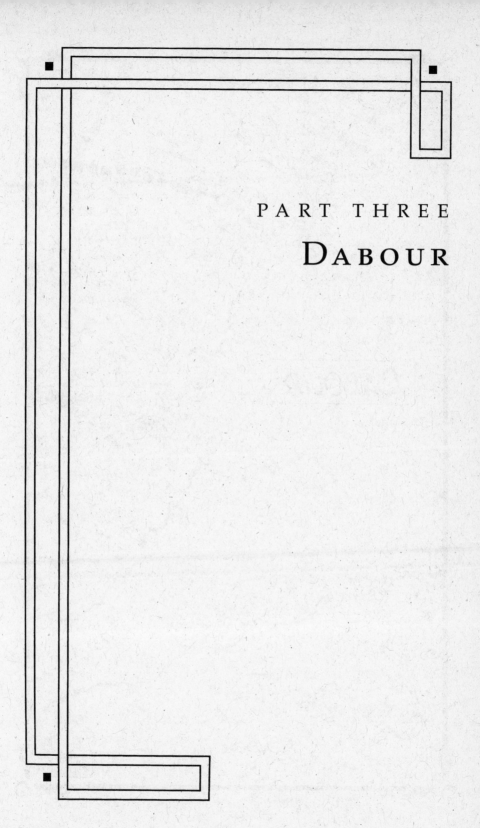

PART THREE

# DABOUR

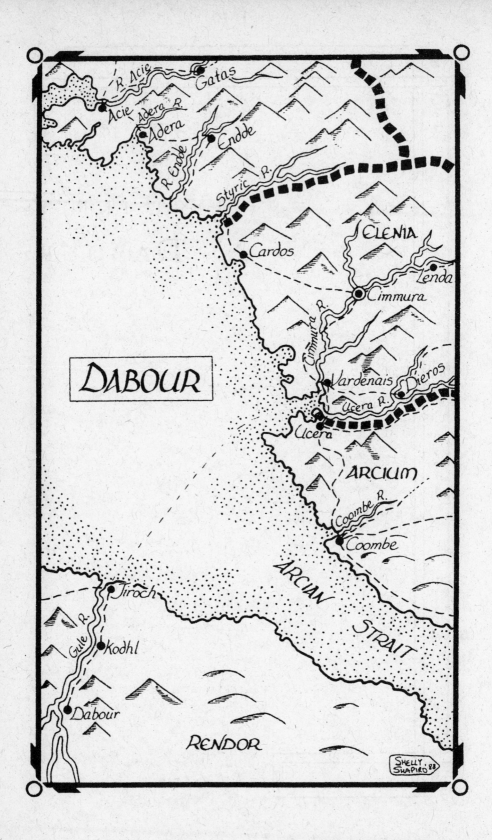

A purple twilight was settling in the narrow streets of Madel, and the stars were coming out. Sparhawk, Kalten, and Talen moved through the narrow, crooked streets, frequently turning corners and occasionally even doubling back to throw off anyone who might possibly be following them.

"Aren't we being just a little overcautious?" Kalten said after about a half hour.

"Let's not take any chances with Martel," Sparhawk replied. "He's entirely capable of throwing a few people away just for the chance to hunt us down. I'd rather not wake up in the middle of the night to find Lycien's house surrounded by mercenaries."

"You've got a point there, I suppose."

They slipped out through the west gate of Madel as the light faded even more. "In here," Sparhawk said as they passed a thicket some distance up the road. "Let's wait for a while and make sure that no one's trying to follow us."

They crouched down among the rustling saplings and peered back along the road leading down to the city. A sleepy bird somewhere in the thicket muttered complainingly, and then an ox cart with creaking wheels passed, rumbling slowly down the road toward Madel.

"It's not too likely that anybody's going to leave town this close to nightfall, is it?" Kalten asked quietly.

"That's what I'm counting on," Sparhawk told him. "Anybody who comes out now probably has serious business."

"And the business could be us, right?"

"It's altogether possible."

A creaking sound came from the city, followed by a dull boom and the rattling of a heavy chain.

"They just closed the gate," Talen whispered.

"That was what I was waiting for," Sparhawk said, rising to his feet. "Let's go."

They emerged from the thicket and continued along the road. Stands of trees loomed up out of the darkness on either side, and clumps of shadowy bushes lined the edges of the fields stretching off into the night. Talen nervously stayed close to the two knights, his eyes darting this way and that.

"What's the matter, boy?" Kalten asked him.

"I've never been out in the countryside after dark before," Talen explained. "Is it always this black?"

The blond man shrugged. "That's why they call it night."

"Why doesn't somebody put up some torches?" Talen complained.

"What for? So the rabbits can see where they're going?"

Lycien's house stood in the deep shadows of the surrounding evergreens with only a single torch at the gate. Talen was visibly relieved when they walked into the graveled yard in front of the entrance.

"Any luck?" Tynian asked, emerging from the main entrance.

"We ran into some trouble," Sparhawk replied. "Let's go inside."

"I told you that you should have let the rest of us come along," the bulky-shouldered Alcione said accusingly as they entered the building.

"It wasn't *that* much trouble," Kalten assured him.

The others were waiting in the large room to which Lycien had first led them. Sephrenia rose to her feet, looking closely at the blood spatters on the two Pandions' cloaks. "Are you all right?" she asked, her voice mirroring her concern.

"We ran into a group of sportive fellows," Kalten replied lightly. He looked down at his cloak. "The blood is all theirs."

"What happened?" she asked Sparhawk.

"Adus tried to ambush us when we got to the inn," he told her. "He had a group of waterfront toughs with him." He paused reflectively. "You know, we've been running across Krager just about every time we turn around. Once—or even twice—might have been sheer coincidence, but it's starting to happen just a little too frequently, and every time we try to follow him, there's some kind of ambush."

"You think it's deliberate?" Tynian asked.

"It's beginning to look that way, isn't it?"

"Would this Martel put a friend in such danger?" Bevier sounded surprised.

"Martel doesn't have any friends," Sparhawk told him. "Adus and Krager are hirelings, nothing more. They're useful, but he feels no particular attachment for them. I don't think he'd shed many tears if something happened to Krager." He began to pace up and down, staring thoughtfully at the floor. "Maybe we can turn the tables on him." He looked at Kalten. "Why don't you let yourself be seen in the streets of Madel?" he suggested. "Don't take too many chances, but let people know you're in town."

"Why not?" Kalten shrugged.

Tynian grinned. "Martel and his hirelings don't know the rest of us, so we can sort of loiter along behind Kalten without attracting attention. Is that the idea?"

Sparhawk nodded. "If they think Kalten's alone, it might bring them out into the open. I'm getting a little tired of Martel's games, so maybe it's time for us to play a few of our own." He looked at Bevier's cousin. "How excited do the local authorities get about street brawls, my Lord?" he asked.

Lycien laughed. "Madel is a seaport, Sir Sparhawk. Brawling is second nature to sailors. The authorities don't pay much attention to their little scuffles—except to remove the bodies, of course. Public sanitation, you understand."

"Good." Sparhawk looked at his friends. "You may not get a chance at Krager or Adus, but you might be able to divide Martel's attention. That could be what it takes to get Kurik and Sephrenia and me aboard a ship unnoticed. I'd rather not have to keep looking over my shoulder when we get to Cippria."

"About the only tricky part is going to be getting you to the harbor without being seen," Kalten said.

"It won't be necessary to go to the harbor," Lycien said. "I have some ware-houses on the river about five miles from here. A fair number of independent sea captains deliver cargoes to me there, and I'm sure arrangements for your passage can be made without any need for going into the city."

"Thank you, my Lord," Sparhawk said. "That solves a problem."

"When do you plan to leave?" Tynian asked.

"I don't see much point in delaying."

"Tomorrow, then?"

Sparhawk nodded.

"I need to talk with you, Sparhawk," Sephrenia said. "Would you mind com-ing to my room?"

He followed her out the door, slightly puzzled. "Is it something we can't discuss in front of the others?" he asked her.

"It might be better if they don't hear us arguing."

"Are we going to argue?"

"Probably." She opened the door to her room and led him inside. Flute sat cross-legged on the bed, her dark eyebrows knit in concentration as she wove the in-tricate mesh of a cat's cradle out of a strand of wool yarn. It was far more complex than the one Talen had made when he had demonstrated it to her. She looked up, smiled at them, and proudly extended her little hands to show them her handiwork.

"She'll be going with us," Sephrenia said.

"Absolutely not!" Sparhawk said sharply.

"I told you we'd argue about this."

"It's an absurd idea, Sephrenia."

"We all do many absurd things, dear one." She smiled affectionately at him.

"Don't do that," he said. "You're not going to win me over that way."

"Don't be tiresome, Sparhawk. You've been around her long enough to know that she always does what she decides to do, and she's decided that she's going with us to Rendor."

"She won't if I have anything to say about it."

"That's the whole point, Sparhawk. You don't. You're dealing with something you can't understand. She's going to come with us in the end anyway, so why not just give in gracefully?"

"Gracefulness is not one of my strong points."

"I've noticed."

"All right, Sephrenia," he said flatly, "just who is she, anyway? You recognized her the first moment we saw her, didn't you?"

"Of course."

"Why of course? She's only about six years old, and you haven't left the Pan-dions for generations. How could you possibly know her?"

She sighed. "Elene logic always clouds an issue with facts. The child and I are kindred in a rather peculiar sense of the word. We know each other in a way you couldn't begin to comprehend."

"Thanks," he said drily.

"I'm not belittling your intelligence, dear one," she told him, "but there's a part of Styric life you're not prepared to accept—either intellectually or philosophically."

He frowned slightly, his eyes narrowed in thought. "All right, Sephrenia," he said, "let me have a try at the Elene logic you're so fond of dismissing. Flute is a child, hardly more than a baby."

The little girl made a face at him.

He ignored that and went on. "She suddenly appeared in an uninhabited region near the Arcian border far from any kind of human habitation. We tried to leave her at that nunnery south of Darra, and she not only managed to escape but also got a goodly distance ahead of us even though we were travelling at a gallop. Then she somehow managed to persuade Faran to let her on his back, and Faran won't let anybody near him except me unless I tell him to. When she met Dolmant, you could tell by his face that he sensed something very unusual about her. Not only that, you bully full-grown knights like a drill sergeant, but anytime Flute decides to do something or go someplace, you give in without a fight. Wouldn't you say that all of that suggests that she's not an ordinary child?"

"You're the one who's exercising his logic. I wouldn't dream of interfering."

"All right then. Let's see where logic takes us. I've seen a fair number of Styrics. With the exception of you and the other magicians, they're all fairly primitive and not very bright—no offense intended, of course."

"Of course." Her expression was amused.

"Since we've already established the fact that Flute is not an ordinary child, what does that leave us?"

"What would be your guess, Sparhawk?"

"Since she's not ordinary, she must be special. In Styricum, that can only mean one thing. She's a magician. Nothing else could explain her."

She applauded ironically. "Excellent, Sparhawk," she congratulated him.

"But that's impossible, Sephrenia. She's only a child. She hasn't had time to learn the secrets."

"Some few are born with that knowledge. Besides, she's older than she looks."

"How old?"

"You know that I won't tell you that. The knowledge of the exact moment of one's birth can be a powerful weapon in the hands of an enemy."

A disturbing thought came to him. "You're preparing for your own death, aren't you, Sephrenia? If we fail, the twelve Pandions who were in the throne room with you will die one by one, and then you'll die, too. You're preparing Flute to be your successor."

She laughed. "Now *that*, dear Sparhawk, is a very interesting idea. I'm surprised you came up with it, considering the fact that you're an Elene."

"That's a very irritating habit you've picked up lately, you know? Don't try to be mysterious with me, Sephrenia, and don't treat me like a child just because I'm an Elene."

"I'll try to remember that. You'll agree to let her come with us, then?"

"Do I have any choice?"

"No. As a matter of fact, you don't."

·    ·    ·

They rose early the next morning and gathered in the dew-drenched yard in front of Marquis Lycien's house. The newly risen sun was very bright and it slanted down through the trees, casting the peculiarly bluish-colored shadows of early morning.

"I'll get word to you from time to time," Sparhawk told those who were remaining behind.

"Be careful down there, Sparhawk," Kalten said.

"I'm always careful." Sparhawk swung himself up onto Faran's back.

"Godspeed, Sir Sparhawk," Bevier said.

"Thank you, Bevier." Sparhawk looked around at the other knights. "Don't be so glum, gentlemen," he told them. "If we're lucky, this won't take very long." He looked at Kalten again. "If you run into Martel, give him my regards."

Kalten nodded. "With an axe in the face, I think."

Marquis Lycien mounted a fat bay horse and led the way out onto the road which passed his house. The morning was crisp, though not actually cold. Spring, Sparhawk decided, was not very far off. He shifted his shoulders slightly. The sober businessman's doublet Lycien had lent him did not really fit very well. It bound in some places and was uncomfortably loose in others.

"We'll turn off just up ahead," Lycien told them. "There's a track through the woods that leads down to my wharves and the little settlement that's grown up around them. Will you want me to bring your horses back after you go on board ship?"

"No, my Lord," Sparhawk replied. "I think we'll take them with us. We don't know exactly what's going to happen in Rendor. We might need dependable mounts, and I've seen what passes for a horse in Cippria."

What Lycien had modestly called a "little settlement" turned out to be a fair-sized village complete with shipyards, houses, inns, and taverns. A dozen vessels were moored at the wharves with longshoremen swarming over them.

"Quite an operation, my Lord," Sparhawk said as they rode down the muddy street toward the river.

"One has had a certain success," Lycien said self-deprecatingly. He smiled. "Besides, I save enough in moorage fees to offset more than the cost of keeping the place up." He looked around. "Why don't you and I step into that tavern over there, Sir Sparhawk?" he suggested. "The independent sea captains favor that one."

"All right," Sparhawk agreed.

"I'll introduce you as Master Cluff," Lycien said as he swung down from his bay. "It's not much of a name, I'll admit, but it's fairly nondescript, and I've discovered that seafaring men love to talk, but they're not always very selective in their choice of listeners. I've gathered that you might prefer to keep this business of yours more or less confidential."

"You're perceptive, my Lord," Sparhawk replied, also dismounting. "This shouldn't take too long," he said to Kurik and Sephrenia.

"Isn't that what you said the last time you went to Rendor?" Kurik asked him.

"We can all hope that this time might be different."

Lycien led the way into a rather sedate wharfside tavern. The ceiling was low, with dark, heavy beams decorated here and there with ships' lanterns. There was a broad window near the front, and golden morning sunlight streamed in through it, setting the fresh straw on the floor to gleaming. Several substantial-looking men of middle years sat at a table by the window, talking over brimming tankards. They looked up as the marquis led Sparhawk to their table. "My Lord," one of them respectfully greeted Lycien.

"Gentlemen," Lycien said, "this is Master Cluff, an acquaintance of mine. He's asked me to introduce him."

They all looked at Sparhawk inquiringly.

"I have a bit of a problem, gentlemen," Sparhawk told them. "May I join you?"

"Have a seat," one of the sea captains, a solid-looking man with silver-shot curly hair, invited.

"I'll leave you gentlemen, then," Lycien said. "There's something that needs my attention." He inclined his head slightly, turned, and went back out of the tavern.

"He probably wants to see if there's some way he can raise the mooring fees," one of the captains said wryly.

"My name's Sorgi," the captain with the curly hair introduced himself to Sparhawk. "What's this problem you mentioned, Master Cluff?"

Sparhawk coughed slightly as if a little embarrassed. "Well," he said, "it all started a few months ago. I happened to hear about a lady who lives not far from here," he began, embellishing as he went along. "Her father is old and very wealthy, so the lady stands to inherit a sizable estate. One of my problems has always been the fact that I have some expensive tastes and very little in my purse to support them. It occurred to me that a rich wife might solve that problem."

"That makes sense," Captain Sorgi said. "That's about the only reason I can think of for getting married at all."

"I couldn't agree more," Sparhawk replied. "Anyway, I wrote her a letter pretending that we had some mutual friends and I was a little surprised when she answered my letter with a great deal of warmth. Our letters grew more and more friendly, and she finally invited me to call on her. I went even deeper in debt to my tailor and set out for her father's house in high spirits and splendid new clothes."

"Sounds to me as if everything was going according to your plan, Master Cluff," Sorgi said. "What's this problem of yours?"

"I'm just getting to that, Captain. The lady is of middle years and very wealthy. If she were even remotely presentable, someone would have snapped her up years ago, so I didn't have my hopes too high on that score. I assumed that she was plain—perhaps even homely. I had not, however, expected a horror." He feigned a shudder. "Gentlemen, I cannot even describe her to you. No matter how rich she was, it wouldn't have been worth waking up to *that* every morning. We spoke together briefly—about the weather, I think—and then I made my apologies and left. She has no brothers, so I wasn't worried about the possibility of someone looking me up to object to my bad manners. What I didn't count on, though, was all her cousins. She's got a whole platoon of them, and they've been following me for weeks now."

"They don't want to kill you, do they?" Sorgi asked.

"No," Sparhawk replied in an anguished tone. "They want to drag me back and force me to marry her."

The captains all roared with laughter, pounding on the table in glee. "I think you've outsmarted yourself, Master Cluff," one of them said, wiping the tears of mirth from his eyes.

Sparhawk nodded glumly. "You're probably right," he admitted.

"You should have found some way to get a look at her before you sent the first letter," Sorgi grinned.

"I know that now," Sparhawk agreed. "Anyhow, I think it's time I left the country for a while until the cousins stop looking for me. I've got a nephew living in Cippria in Rendor who's been doing fairly well of late. I'm sure I can impose on him until I can get my feet on the ground again. Is it possible that one of you gentlemen might be sailing there soon? I'd like to book passage for myself and a couple of family retainers. I'd go to the main docks in Madel, but I've got a strong feeling that the cousins are watching them."

"What say you, gentlemen?" Captain Sorgi said expansively. "Shall we help this good fellow out of his predicament?"

"I'm going to Rendor, right enough," one of the others replied, "but I'm committed to Jiroch."

Sorgi thought about it. "I was going to Jiroch myself," he mused, "and then on to Cippria, but I might be able to rearrange my schedule just a bit."

"I won't be able to help," a rough-voiced sea captain growled. "My ship's having her bottom scraped. I can give you some advice, though. If these cousins are watching the main wharves in Madel, they're probably watching these as well. Everybody in town knows about Lycien's docks here." He tugged at one earlobe. "I've smuggled a few people out of a few places in my time—when the price was right." He looked at the captain who was bound for Jiroch. "When do you sail, Captain Mabin?"

"With the noon tide."

"And you?" the helpful captain asked Sorgi.

"The same."

"Good. If the cousins are watching the docks here, they may try to hire a ship and follow our bachelor friend. Have him openly board Mabin's ship. Then, when you're downriver a ways and out of sight, transfer him to Sorgi's ship. If the cousins decide to follow, Mabin can lead them off toward Jiroch, and Master Cluff will be safe on his way to Cippria. That's the way I'd do it."

"You've got a very ingenious mind, my friend." Sorgi laughed. "Are you sure that people are the only things you've smuggled in the past?"

"We've all avoided customs officers from time to time, haven't we, Sorgi?" the rough-voiced captain said. "We live at sea. Why should we pay taxes to support the kingdoms of the landsmen? I'd gladly pay taxes to the King of the Ocean, but I can't seem to find his palace."

"Well said, my friend." Sorgi applauded.

"Gentlemen," Sparhawk said. "I'm eternally in your debt."

"Not exactly eternally, Master Cluff," Sorgi said. "A man who admits to having financial difficulties pays for his passage *before* he boards. He does on my ship, at least."

"Would you accept half here and half when we reach Cippria?" Sparhawk countered.

"I'm afraid not, my friend. I like you well enough, but I'm sure you can see my position in the matter."

Sparhawk sighed. "We have horses," he added. "I suppose you'll charge extra to carry them as well?"

"Naturally."

"I was afraid of that."

The loading of Faran, Sephrenia's palfrey, and Kurik's stout gelding took place behind a screen of sailcloth Sorgi's sailors were ostensibly mending. Shortly before noon, Sparhawk and Kurik boarded the ship bound for Jiroch. They moved openly up the gangway, followed by Sephrenia, who carried Flute in her arms.

Captain Mabin greeted them on the quarterdeck. "Ah," he grinned, "here's our reluctant bridegroom. Why don't you and your friends walk around the deck until we sail? Give all the cousins plenty of chances to see you."

"I've had a few second thoughts about this, Captain Mabin," Sparhawk said. "If the cousins hire a ship and follow you—and if they catch up with you—it's going to be fairly obvious that I'm not on board."

"Nobody's going to catch up with me, Master Cluff." The captain laughed. "I've got the fastest ship on the Inner Sea. Besides, it's obvious that you don't know very much about seafaring etiquette. Nobody boards another man's ship at sea unless he's prepared for a fight. It's just not done."

"Oh," Sparhawk said. "I didn't know that. We'll stroll around the deck, then."

"Bridegroom?" Sephrenia murmured as they moved away from the captain.

"It's a long story," Sparhawk told her.

"There seem to be a fair number of these long stories cropping up lately. Someday we'll have to sit down so that you can tell them to me."

"Someday perhaps."

"Flute," Sephrenia said quite firmly, "come down from there."

Sparhawk looked up. The little girl was halfway up a rope ladder stretching from the rail to the yardarm. She pouted just a bit, then did as she was told. "You always know exactly where she is, don't you?" he asked Sephrenia.

"Always," she replied.

The transfer from one ship to the other took place in midriver some distance downstream from Lycien's wharves and was concealed by a great deal of activity on both ships. Captain Sorgi quickly bustled his passengers belowdecks to get them out of sight, and then the two ships proceeded sedately downriver, bobbing side by side like two matrons returning home from church.

"We're passing the wharves of Madel," Sorgi called down the companionway to them some short time later. "Keep your face out of sight, Master Cluff, or I may have a deck full of your betrothed's cousins on my hands."

"This is *really* making me curious, Sparhawk," Sephrenia said. "Couldn't you give me just the tiniest clue?"

"I made up a story." He shrugged. "It was lurid enough to seize the attention of a group of sailors."

"Sparhawk's always been very good at making up stories," Kurik observed. "He used to lie himself in and out of trouble regularly when he was a novice." The grizzled squire was seated on a bunk with the drowsing Flute nestled in his lap. "You know," he said quietly, "I never had a daughter. They smell better than little boys, don't they?"

Sephrenia burst out laughing. "Don't tell Aslade," she cautioned. "She may decide to try for one."

Kurik rolled his eyes upward in dismay. "Not again," he said. "I don't mind babies around the house, but I couldn't bear the morning sickness again."

About an hour later, Sorgi came down the companionway. "We're clearing the mouth of the estuary now," he reported, "and there's not a single vessel to the rear. I'd say that you've made good your escape, Master Cluff."

"Thank God," Sparhawk replied fervently.

"Tell me, my friend," Sorgi said thoughtfully, "is the lady really as ugly as you say?"

"Captain Sorgi, you wouldn't believe how ugly."

"Maybe you're a bit too delicate, Master Cluff. The sea's getting colder, my ship's getting old and tired, and the winter storms are making my bones ache. I could stand a fair amount of ugliness if the lady's estate happened to be as large as you say. I might even consider returning some of your passage money in exchange for a letter of introduction. Maybe you overlooked some of her good qualities."

"We could talk about that, I suppose," Sparhawk conceded.

"I need to go topside," Sorgi said. "We're far enough past the city that it's safe for you and your friends to come on deck now." He turned and went back up the companionway.

"I think I can save you all the trouble of telling me that long story you mentioned earlier," Sephrenia told Sparhawk. "You didn't actually use that tired old fable about the ugly heiress, did you?"

He shrugged. "As Vanion says, the old ones are the best."

"Oh, Sparhawk, I'm disappointed in you. How are you going to avoid giving that poor captain the imaginary lady's name?"

"I'll think of something. Why don't we go up on deck before the sun sets?"

Kurik spoke in a whisper. "I think the child's asleep," he said. "I don't want to wake her. You two go on ahead."

Sparhawk nodded and led Sephrenia out of the cramped cabin.

"I always forget how gentle he is," Sephrenia said softly.

Sparhawk nodded. "He's the best and kindest man I know," he said simply. "If it weren't for class distinctions, he'd have made an almost perfect knight."

"Is class really all that important?"

"Not to me, it isn't, but I didn't make the rules."

They emerged on deck in the slanting, late-afternoon sunlight. The breeze blowing offshore was brisk, catching the tops of the waves and turning them into sun-splashed froth. Captain Mabin's vessel, bound for Jiroch, was heeling over in that breeze on a course almost due west through the broad channel of the Arcian Strait. Her sails bellied out, snowy white in the afternoon sun, and she ran before the wind like a skimming sea bird.

"How far do you make it to Cippria, Captain Sorgi?" Sparhawk asked as he and Sephrenia stepped up onto the quarterdeck.

"A hundred and fifty leagues, Master Cluff," Sorgi replied. "Three days, if this wind holds."

"That's good time, isn't it?"

Sorgi grunted. "We could make better if this poor old tub didn't leak so much."

"Sparhawk!" Sephrenia gasped, taking him urgently by the arm.

"What is it?" He looked at her in concern. Her face had gone deathly pale.

"Look!" She pointed.

Some distance from where Captain Mabin's graceful ship was running through the Arcian Strait, a single, densely black cloud had appeared in an otherwise unblemished sky. It seemed somehow to be moving against the wind, growing larger and more ominously black by the moment. Then it began to swirl, ponderously at first, but then faster and faster. As it spun, a long, dark finger twitched and jerked down from its center, reaching down and down until its inky tip touched the roiling surface of the strait. Tons of water were suddenly drawn up into the swirling maw as the vast funnel moved erratically across the heaving sea.

"Waterspout!" the lookout shouted down from the mast. The sailors rushed to the rail to gape in horror at the swirling spout.

Inexorably the vast thing bore down on Mabin's helpless ship, and then the vessel, which suddenly appeared very tiny, vanished in the seething funnel. Chunks and pieces of her timbers spun out of the great waterspout hundreds of feet in the air to settle with agonizing slowness to the surface again. A single piece of sail fluttered down like a stricken white bird.

Then, as suddenly as they had come, the black cloud and its deadly waterspout were gone.

So was Mabin's ship.

The surface of the sea was littered with debris, and a vast cloud of white gulls appeared, swooping and diving over the wreckage as if to mark the vessel's passing.

## CHAPTER EIGHTEEN

Captain Sorgi combed the wreckage-strewn water where Mabin's ship had gone down until after dark, but he found no survivors. Then, sadly, he turned his ship southeasterly again, setting his course toward Cippria.

Sephrenia sighed and turned from the rail. "Let's go below, Sparhawk."

He nodded and followed her down the companionway.

Kurik had lighted a single oil lamp, and it swung from a low overhead beam, filling the small, dark-paneled compartment with swaying shadows. Flute had awakened and she sat at the bolted-down table in the center of the cabin, looking suspiciously at the bowl sitting in front of her.

"It's just stew, little girl," Kurik was saying to her. "It won't hurt you."

She delicately dipped her fingers into the thick gravy and lifted out a dripping chunk of meat. She sniffed at it, then looked questioningly at the squire.

"Salt pork," he told her.

She shuddered and dropped the chunk back into the gravy. Then she firmly pushed the bowl away.

"Styrics don't eat pork, Kurik," Sephrenia told him.

"The ship's cook said that this is what the sailors eat," he said defensively. He looked at Sparhawk. "Was the captain able to find any survivors from the other ship?"

Sparhawk shook his head. "That waterspout tore it all to pieces. The same thing probably happened to the crew."

"It's lucky we weren't on board that one."

"Very lucky," Sephrenia agreed. "Waterspouts are like tornadoes. They don't appear out of completely clear skies and they don't move against the wind or change direction the way that one did. It was being consciously directed."

"Magic?" Kurik said. "Is that really possible—to call up weather like that, I mean?"

"I don't think *I* could do it."

"Who did then?"

"I don't know for certain." Her eyes, however, showed a certain suspicion.

"Let's get it out into the open, Sephrenia," Sparhawk said. "You've guessed something, haven't you?"

Her expression grew a bit more certain. "In the past few months we've had several encounters with a hooded figure in a Styric robe. You saw it several times in Cimmura, and it tried to have us ambushed on our way to Borrata. Styrics seldom cover their faces. Have you ever noticed that?"

"Yes, but I don't quite make the connection."

"This thing had to cover its face, Sparhawk. It's not human."

He stared at her. "Are you sure?"

"I can't be absolutely positive until I see its face, but the evidence is beginning to pile up, wouldn't you say?"

"Could Annias actually do something like that?"

"It's not Annias. He might know a little rudimentary magic, but he couldn't begin to raise a thing like that. Only Azash could have done it. He's the only one who dares to summon such beings. The Younger Gods will not, and even the other Elder Gods have forsworn the practice."

"Why would Azash want to kill Captain Mabin and his crew?"

"The ship was destroyed because the creature thought that we were on board."

"That goes a little far, Sephrenia," Kurik objected skeptically. "If it's so powerful, why did it sink the wrong boat?"

"The creatures of the underworld are not very sophisticated, Kurik," she replied. "Our simple ruse may have deceived it. Power and wisdom don't always go hand in hand. Many of the greatest magicians of Styricum were as stupid as stumps."

"I don't quite follow this," Sparhawk admitted with a puzzled frown. "What we're doing has nothing to do with Zemoch. Why would Azash go out of his way to help Annias?"

"It may be that there isn't any connection. Azash always has his own motives. It's quite possible that what he's doing has nothing to do with Annias at all."

"It doesn't wash, Sephrenia. If you're right about this thing, it's been working for Martel, and Martel works for Annias."

"Are you so sure that the creature is working for Martel and not the other way around? Azash can see the shadows of the future. One of us might be a danger to him. The seeming alliance between Martel and the creature may be no more than a matter of convenience."

He began to gnaw worriedly at a fingernail. "That's all I need," he said, "something else to worry about." Then a thought struck him. "Wait a minute. Do you remember what the ghost of Lakus said—that darkness was at the gate and that Ehlana was our only hope of light? Could Azash be that darkness?"

She nodded. "It's possible."

"If that's the case, then wouldn't it be Ehlana he's trying to destroy? She's totally protected by that crystal that encases her, but if something happens to us before we can find a way to heal her, she'll die, too. Maybe that's why Azash has joined forces with the primate."

"Aren't you both stretching things a bit?" Kurik asked. "You're basing a great deal of speculation on a single incident."

"It doesn't hurt to be ready for eventualities, Kurik," Sparhawk replied. "I hate surprises."

The squire grunted and rose to his feet. "You two must be hungry," he said. "I'll go down to the galley and get you some supper. We can talk some more while you're eating."

"No pork," Sephrenia told him firmly.

"Bread and cheese, then?" he suggested. "And maybe some fruit?"

"That would be fine, Kurik. You'd probably better bring enough for Flute as well. I know she's not going to eat that stew."

"That's all right," he said. "I'll eat it for her. I don't have the same kind of prejudices that you Styrics do."


It was overcast when they reached the port city of Cippria three days later. The cloud cover was high and thin, and there was no trace of moisture in it. The city was low, with squat white buildings thickly walled to ward off the heat of the southern sun. The wharves jutting out into the harbor were constructed of stone, since Rendor was a kingdom largely devoid of trees.

Sparhawk and the others came up on deck, wearing hooded black robes, just as the sailors were mooring Captain Sorgi's ship to one of the wharves. They went up the three steps to the quarterdeck to join the curly-haired seaman.

"Get some fenders between our side and that wharf!" Sorgi roared at the seamen who were snubbing off the mooring lines. He shook his head in disgust. "I have to tell them that every single time we dock," he muttered. "All they can think about when we make port is the nearest alehouse." He looked at Sparhawk. "Well, Master Cluff," he said. "Have you changed your mind?"

"I'm afraid not, Captain," Sparhawk replied, setting down the bundle containing his spare clothing. "I'd like to oblige you, but the lady I mentioned seems to have all her hopes pinned on me. It's for your own good, actually. If you show up at her house with an introduction from me, her cousins might decide to wring my location out of you—and being wrung is not anybody's idea of a good time. Besides, I don't want to take any chances."

Sorgi grunted. Then he looked at them all curiously. "Where did you come by the Rendorish clothing?"

"I did some bargaining in your forecastle yesterday." Sparhawk shrugged, plucking at the front of the hooded black robe he wore. "Some of your sailors like to be unobtrusive when they make port here in Rendor."

"How well I know," Sorgi said wryly. "I spent three days looking for the ship's cook the last time I was in Jiroch." He looked at Sephrenia, who was also robed in black and wore a heavy veil across her face. "Where did you find anything to fit her?" he asked. "None of my sailors are that small."

"She's very adept with her needle." Sparhawk did not think it necessary to explain exactly how Sephrenia had changed the color of her white robe.

Sorgi scratched at his curly hair. "I can't for the life of me understand why most Rendors wear black," he said. "Don't they know that it's twice as hot?"

"Maybe they haven't realized that yet," Sparhawk replied. "Rendors are none too bright in the first place, and they've only been here for five thousand years."

Sorgi laughed. "Maybe that's it," he said. "Good fortune here in Cippria, Master Cluff," he said. "If I happen to run across any cousins, I'll tell them that I've never heard of you."

"Thank you, Captain," Sparhawk said, clasping Sorgi's hand. "You have no idea how much I appreciate that."

They led their horses down the slanting gangway to the wharf. At Kurik's suggestion, they covered their saddles with blankets to conceal the fact that they were not of Rendorish construction. Then they all tied their bundles to their saddles, mounted, and moved away from the harbor at an unobtrusive walk. The streets were teeming with Rendors. The city dwellers sometimes wore lighter-colored clothing, but the desert people were all dressed in unrelieved black and had their hoods up. There were few women in the street, and they were all veiled. Sephrenia rode subserviently behind Sparhawk and Kurik with her hood pulled far forward and her veil drawn tightly across her nose and mouth.

"You know the customs here, I see," Sparhawk said back over his shoulder.

"I was here many years ago," she replied, drawing her robe around Flute's knees.

"How many years?"

"Would you like to have me tell you that Cippria was only a fishing village then?" she asked archly. "Twenty or so mud huts?"

He looked back at her sharply. "Sephrenia, Cippria's been a major seaport for fifteen hundred years."

"My," she said, "has it really been that long? It seems like only yesterday. Where *does* the time go?"

"That's impossible!"

She laughed gaily. "How gullible you can be sometimes, Sparhawk," she said. "You know I'm not going to answer that kind of question, so why keep trying?"

He suddenly felt more than a little sheepish. "I suppose I asked for that, didn't I?" he admitted.

"Yes, you did."

Kurik was grinning broadly.

"Go ahead and say it," Sparhawk told him sourly.

"Say what, my Lord?" Kurik's eyes were wide and innocent.

They rode up from the harbor, mingling with robed Rendors in the narrow, twisting streets. Although the overcast veiled the sun, Sparhawk could still feel the heat radiating out from the white-plastered walls of the houses and shops. He could also catch the familiar scents of Rendor. The air was close and dusty, and there was the pervading odor of mutton simmering in olive oil and pungent spices. There was the cloying fragrance of heavy perfumes, and overlaying it all was the persistent reek of the stockyards.

Near the center of town, they passed the mouth of a narrow alley. A chill touched Sparhawk, and suddenly, as clearly as if they were actually ringing out their call, he seemed once again to hear the sound of the bells.

"Something wrong?" Kurik asked as he saw his lord shudder.

"That's the alley where I saw Martel last time."

Kurik peered up the alley. "Tight quarters in there," he noted.

"That's all that kept me alive," Sparhawk replied. "They couldn't come at me all at once."

"Where are we going, Sparhawk?" Sephrenia asked from the rear.

"To the monastery where I stayed after I was wounded," he replied. "I don't think we want to be seen in the streets. The abbot and most of the monks out there are Arcian and they know how to keep secrets."

"Will I be welcome there?" she asked dubiously. "Arcian monks are conservative and they have certain prejudices where Styrics are concerned."

"This particular abbot is a bit more cosmopolitan," Sparhawk assured her, "and I have a few suspicions about his monastery, anyway."

"Oh?"

"I don't think these monks are entirely what they seem and I wouldn't be at all surprised to find a secret armory inside the monastery, complete with burnished armor, blue surcoats, and a variety of weapons."

"Cyrinics?" she asked, a bit surprised.

"The Pandions aren't the only ones who want to keep an eye on Rendor," he replied.

"What's that smell?" Kurik asked as they approached the western outskirts of town.

"The stockyards," Sparhawk told him. "A great deal of beef is shipped out of Cippria."

"Do we have to go through any kind of a gate to get out?"

Sparhawk shook his head. "The city walls were pulled down during the suppression of the Eshandist Heresy. The local people didn't bother to rebuild them."

They emerged from the narrow street they were following into acre upon acre of stock pens filled with bawling, scrubby-looking cows. It was late afternoon by now, and the overcast had begun to take on a silvery sheen.

"How much farther to the monastery?" Kurik asked.

"A mile or so."

"It's quite a distance from that alley back there, isn't it?"

"I noticed that myself about ten years ago."

"Why didn't you take shelter someplace closer?"

"There wasn't anyplace safe. I could hear the bells from the monastery, so I just kept following the sound. It gave me something to think about."

"You could have bled to death."

"That same thought crossed my mind a few times that night."

"Gentlemen," Sephrenia said, "do you suppose we could move along? The night comes on very quickly here in Rendor, and it gets cold in the desert after the sun goes down."

The monastery lay beyond the stockyards on a high, rocky hill. It was surrounded by a thick wall, and the gate was closed. Sparhawk dismounted before the gate and tugged on a stout cord hanging beside it. A small bell tinkled inside. After a moment, the shutter of a narrow, barred window cut into the stones beside the gate opened. The brown-bearded face of a monk peered out warily.

"Good evening, brother," Sparhawk said. "Do you suppose I might have a word with your abbot?"

"Can I give him your name?"

"Sparhawk. He might remember me. I stayed here for a time a few years back."

"Wait," the monk said brusquely, closing the shutter again.

"Not very cordial, is he?" Kurik said.

"Churchmen aren't really welcome in Rendor," Sparhawk replied. "A bit of caution is probably only natural."

They waited as the twilight faded.

Then the shutter opened again. "Sir Sparhawk!" a voice more suited to a parade ground than a religious community boomed.

"My Lord Abbot," Sparhawk replied.

"Wait there a moment. We'll open the gate."

There was a rattling of chains and the grating sound of a heavy bar sliding through thick iron rings. Then the gate ponderously swung open, and the abbot came out to greet them. He was a bluff, hearty-looking man with a ruddy face and an imposing black beard. He was quite tall, and his shoulders were massive. "It's good to see you again, my friend," he said, clasping Sparhawk's hand in a crushing grip. "You're looking well. You seemed a bit pale and wan when you left the last time you were here."

"It's been ten years, my Lord," Sparhawk pointed out. "In that length of time a man either heals or dies."

"So he does, Sir Sparhawk. So he does. Come inside and bring your friends."

Sparhawk led Faran through the gate with Sephrenia and Kurik close behind. There was a court inside, and the walls surrounding it were as bleak as those surrounding the monastery. They were unadorned by the white mortar customary on the walls of Rendorish buildings, and the windows which pierced them were perhaps a trifle narrower than monastic architecture would have dictated. They would, Sparhawk noted professionally, make excellent vantage points for archers.

"How can I help you, Sparhawk?" the abbot asked.

"I need refuge again, my Lord Abbot," Sparhawk replied. "That's getting to be sort of a habit, isn't it?"

The abbot grinned at him. "Who's after you this time?" he asked.

"No one that I know of, my Lord, and I think I'd like to keep it that way. Is there someplace we can talk privately?"

"Of course." The abbot turned to the brown-bearded monk who had first opened the shutter. "See to their horses, brother." It was not a request, but had all the crispness of a military command. The monk straightened noticeably, though he did not quite salute.

"Come along then, Sparhawk," the abbot boomed, clapping the big knight on the shoulder with one meaty hand.

Kurik dismounted and went to help Sephrenia. She handed Flute down to him and slipped from her saddle.

The abbot led them through the main door and into a vaulted stone corridor dimly lighted at intervals by small oil lamps. Perhaps it was the scent of the oil, but the place had a peculiar odor of sanctity—and of safety—about it. That smell sharply reminded Sparhawk of the night ten years before. "The place hasn't changed much," he noted, looking around.

"The Church is timeless, Sir Sparhawk," the abbot replied sententiously, "and her institutions try to match that quality."

At the far end of the corridor, the abbot opened a severely simple door, and they followed him into a book-lined room with a high ceiling and an unlighted charcoal brazier in the corner. The room was quite comfortable-looking—far more so than the studies of abbots in the monasteries of the north. The windows were made of thick triangular pieces of glass joined with strips of lead and they were draped in pale blue. The floor was strewn with white sheepskin rugs, and the unmade bed in the far corner was quite a bit wider than the standard monastic cot. The jammed bookcases reached from floor to ceiling.

"Please, sit down," the abbot said, pointing at several chairs standing in front of a table piled high with documents.

"Still trying to catch up, my Lord?" Sparhawk smiled, pointing at the documents and taking one of the chairs.

The abbot made a wry face. "I give it a try every month or so," he replied. "Some men just aren't made for paperwork." He looked sourly at the litter on his table. "Sometimes I think a fire in here might solve the problem. I'm sure the clerks in Chyrellos wouldn't even miss all my reports." He looked curiously at Sparhawk's companions.

"My man Kurik," Sparhawk introduced his squire.

"Kurik." The abbot nodded.

"And the lady is Sephrenia, the Pandion instructor in the secrets."

"Sephrenia herself?" The abbot's eyes widened and he rose to his feet respectfully. "I've been hearing stories about you for years, madame. Your reputation is quite exalted." He smiled broadly at her in welcome.

She removed her veil and returned his smile. "You're very kind to say so, my Lord." She sat and gathered Flute up into her lap. The little girl nestled down and regarded the abbot with her large dark eyes.

"A beautiful child, Lady Sephrenia," the abbot said. "Your daughter by any chance?"

She laughed. "Oh, no, my Lord Abbot," she said. "The child's a Styric found-ling. We call her Flute."

"What an odd name," he murmured. Then he returned his gaze to Sparhawk. "You hinted at a matter you wanted to keep private," he said curiously. "Why don't you tell me about it."

"Do you get much news about what's happening on the continent, my Lord?"

"I'm kept informed, yes." The bearded abbot said it rather cautiously as he sat down again.

"Then you know about the situation in Elenia?"

"The queen's illness, you mean? And the ambitions of Primate Annias?"

"Right. Anyway, a while back, Annias came up with a very complicated scheme to discredit the Pandion Order. We were able to thwart it. After the general meeting in the palace, the preceptors of the four orders gathered in a private session. Annias hungers for the archprelate's throne and he knows that the militant orders will oppose him."

"With swords if necessary," the abbot agreed fervently. "I'd like to cut him down myself," he added. Then he realized that he had perhaps gone too far. "If I weren't a member of a cloistered order, of course," he concluded lamely.

"I understand perfectly, my Lord," Sparhawk assured him. "The preceptors discussed the matter and they concluded that all of the primate's power—and any hope he has of extending it to Chyrellos—is based on his position in Elenia, and he'll keep that authority only for so long as Queen Ehlana's indisposed." He grimaced. "That's a silly word, isn't it? She's barely clinging to her life, and I called it *indisposed*. Oh, well, you know what I'm talking about."

"We all flounder from time to time, Sparhawk," the abbot forgave him. "I know most of the details already. Last week I got word from Patriarch Dolmant about what was afoot. What did you find out in Borrata?"

"We talked with a physician there, and he told us that Queen Ehlana has been poisoned."

The abbot came to his feet swearing like a pirate. "You're her champion, Sparhawk! Why didn't you go back to Cimmura and run your sword through Annias?"

"I was tempted," Sparhawk admitted, "but I decided that it's more important right now to see if we can find an antidote. There'll be plenty of time later to deal with Annias, and I'd rather not be rushed when it gets down to that. Anyway, the physician in Borrata told us that he thinks the poison is of Rendorish origin and he directed us to a couple of his colleagues here in Cippria."

The abbot began to pace up and down, his face still dark with rage. When he began to speak, all traces of monkly humility were gone from his voice. "If I know Annias, he's probably been trying to stop you every step of the way. Am I right?"

"Fairly close, yes."

"And the streets of Cippria aren't the safest places in the world—as you found out that night ten years ago. All right, then," he said decisively, "this is the way we're going to do it. Annias knows that you're looking for medical advice, right?"

"If he doesn't, then he's been asleep."

"Exactly. If you go near a physician, you'll probably need him for yourself, so I won't let you do that."

"Won't let, my Lord?" Sephrenia asked mildly.

"Sorry," the abbot mumbled. "Maybe I got a little carried away there. What I meant to say is that I advise against it in the strongest possible terms. What I'll do instead is send some monks out to bring the physicians here. That way you'll be able to talk with them without chancing the streets of Cippria. We'll work out a way afterward to slip you out of town."

"Would an Elenian physician actually agree to call on a patient at home?" Sephrenia asked him.

"He will if his own health is of any concern to him," the abbot replied darkly. He suddenly looked a bit sheepish. "That didn't sound very monkly, did it?" he apologized.

"Oh, I don't know," Sparhawk said blandly. "There are monks, and then there are monks."

"I'll send some of the brothers into the city to fetch them right now. What are the names of these physicians?"

Sparhawk fished the scrap of parchment the tipsy doctor in Borrata had given him out of an inside pocket and handed it to the abbot.

The bluff man glanced at it. "You know this first one already, Sparhawk," he said. "He's the one who treated you the last time you were here."

"Oh? I didn't really catch his name."

"I'm not surprised. You were delirious most of the time." The abbot squinted at the parchment. "This other one died about a month ago," he said, "but Doctor Voldi here can probably answer just about any question you might have. He's a little impressed with himself, but he's the best physician in Cippria." He rose, went to the door, and opened it. A pair of youthful monks stood outside. They were, Sparhawk noted, quite similar to the two young Pandions who normally stood guard outside Vanion's door in the chapterhouse in Cimmura. "You," the abbot sharply ordered one of them, "go into the city and bring Doctor Voldi to me. Don't take no for an answer."

"At once, my Lord," the young monk replied. With a certain amusement, Sparhawk noted that the monk's feet twitched slightly as if he were about to snap his heels together.

The abbot closed the door and returned to his seat. "It should be about an hour, I expect." He looked at Sparhawk's grin. "Something funny, my friend?" he asked.

"Not at all, my Lord. It's just that your young monks have a very crisp manner about them."

"Does it really show that much?" the abbot asked, looking a little abashed.

"Yes, my Lord. If you know what you're looking for, it does."

The abbot made a wry face. "Fortunately, the local people aren't very familiar with that sort of thing. You'll be discreet about this discovery, won't you, Sparhawk?"

"Of course, my Lord. I was fairly sure about the nature of your order when I left here ten years ago and I haven't told anyone yet."

"I should have guessed, I suppose. You Pandions tend to have very sharp eyes." He rose to his feet. "I'll have some supper sent up. There's a fairly large partridge that grows hereabouts, and I have an absolutely splendid falcon." He laughed. "That's what I do instead of making out the reports I'm supposed to send to Chyrellos. What do you say to a bit of roast fowl?"

"I think we could manage that," Sparhawk replied.

"And in the meantime, could I offer you and your friends some wine? It's not Arcian red, but it's not too bad. We make it here on the grounds. The soil hereabouts isn't much good for anything but raising grapes."

"Thank you, my Lord Abbot," Sephrenia replied, "but might the child and I have milk instead?"

"I'm afraid that all we have is goat's milk, Lady Sephrenia," he apologized.

Her eyes brightened. "Goat's milk would be just fine, my Lord. Cow's milk is so bland, and we Styrics prefer something a bit more robust."

Sparhawk shuddered.

The abbot sent the other young monk to the kitchen for milk and supper, then poured red wine for Sparhawk, Kurik, and himself. He leaned back in his chair then, idly toying with the stem of his goblet. "Can we be frank with each other, Sparhawk?" he asked.

"Of course."

"Did any word get to you in Jiroch about what happened here in Cippria after you left?"

"Not really," Sparhawk replied. "I was a bit submerged at that time."

"You know how Rendors feel about the use of magic?"

Sparhawk nodded. "They call it witchcraft, as I recall."

"They do indeed, and they look on it as a worse crime than murder. Anyway, just after you left, we had an outbreak of that sort of thing. I got involved in the investigation since I'm the ranking churchman in the area." He smiled ironically. "Most of the time Rendors spit as I go by, but the minute somebody whispers 'witchcraft,' they come running to me with their faces white and their eyes bulging out. Usually the accusations are completely false. The average Rendor couldn't remember the Styric words of the simplest spell if his life depended on it, but charges crop up from time to time—usually based on spite, jealousy, and petty hatreds. This time, though, the affair was quite different. There was actual evidence that somebody in Cippria was using magic of a fair degree of sophistication." He looked at Sparhawk. "Were any of the men who attacked you that night at all adept in the secrets?"

"One of them is, yes."

"Perhaps that answers the question then. The magic seems to have been a part of an attempt to locate something—or someone. Maybe you were the object of that search."

"You mentioned sophistication, my Lord Abbot," Sephrenia said intently. "Could you be a bit more specific?"

"There was a glowing apparition stalking the streets of Cippria," he replied. "It seemed to be sheathed in lightning of some kind."

She drew in her breath sharply. "And what exactly did this apparition do?"

"It questioned people. None of them could remember the questions afterward, but the questioning appears to have been quite severe. I saw a number of the burns with my own eyes."

"Burns?"

"The apparition would seize whomever it wanted to question. Wherever it touched them, it left a burned place. One poor woman had a burn that encircled her entire forearm. I'd almost say that it was in the shape of a hand—except that it had far too many fingers."

"How many fingers?"

"Nine, and two thumbs."

She hissed. "A Damork," she said.

"I thought you said that the Younger Gods had stripped Martel of the power to summon those things," Sparhawk said to her.

"Martel didn't summon it," she replied. "It was sent to do his bidding by someone else."

"It amounts to almost the same thing, then, doesn't it?"

"Not exactly. The Damork is only marginally under Martel's control."

"But all this happened ten years ago," Kurik shrugged. "What difference does it make now?"

"You're missing the point, Kurik," she replied gravely. "We thought that the Damork had appeared only recently, but it was here in Cippria ten years ago, before anything we're involved with now even began."

"I don't quite follow you," he admitted.

Sephrenia looked at Sparhawk. "It's you, dear one," she said in a deadly quiet voice. "It's not me or Kurik or Ehlana or even Flute. The Damork's attacks have all been directed at you. Be very, very careful, Sparhawk. Azash is trying to kill you."

## CHAPTER NINETEEN

Doctor Voldi was a fussy little man in his sixties. His hair was thinning on top, and he had carefully combed it forward to conceal the fact. It was also quite obvious that he dyed it to hide the encroaching gray. He removed his dark cloak, and Sparhawk saw that he wore a white linen smock. He smelled of chemicals and he had an enormous opinion of himself.

It was quite late when the little physician was ushered into the abbot's littered study, and he was struggling without much success to cover his irritation at having been called out at that hour. "My Lord Abbot," he stiffly greeted the black-bearded churchman with a jerky little bow.

"Ah, Voldi," the abbot said, rising to his feet, "so good of you to come."

"Your monk said that the matter was urgent, my Lord. May I see the patient?"

"Not unless you're prepared to make a very long journey, Doctor Voldi," Sephrenia murmured.

Voldi gave her a long, appraising look. "You appear not to be a Rendor, madame," he noted. "Styric, I should say, judging from your features."

"Your eyes are keen, Doctor."

"I'm sure you remember this fellow," the abbot said, pointing at Sparhawk.

The doctor looked blankly at the big Pandion. "No," he said, "I can't say that—" Then he frowned. "Don't tell me," he added, absently brushing his hair forward with the palm of his hand. "It was about ten years ago, wasn't it? Weren't you the one who'd been knifed?"

"You have a good memory, Doctor Voldi," Sparhawk said. "We don't want to keep you out too late, so why don't we get down to cases? We were referred to you by a physician in Borrata. He greatly respects your opinion in certain areas." Sparhawk quickly appraised the little fellow and decided to apply a bit of judicious flattery. "Of course, we'd have probably come to you anyway," he added. "Your reputation has spread far beyond the borders of Rendor."

"Well," Voldi said, preening himself slightly. Then he assumed a piously modest expression. "It's gratifying to know that my efforts on behalf of the sick have received some small recognition."

"What we need, good Doctor," Sephrenia injected, "is your advice in treating a friend of ours who has recently been poisoned."

"Poisoned?" Voldi said sharply. "Are you sure?"

"The physician in Borrata was quite certain," she replied. "We described our friend's symptoms in great detail, and he diagnosed the condition as being the effects of a rather rare Rendorish poison called—"

"Please, madame," he said, holding up one hand. "I prefer to make my own diagnoses. Describe the symptoms for me."

"Of course." Patiently she repeated what she had told the physicians at the University of Borrata.

The little doctor paced up and down as she talked, his hands clasped behind him and his eyes on the floor. "I think we can rule out the falling-sickness right at the outset," he mused when she had finished. "Some other diseases, however, do result in convulsions." He affected a wise expression. "It's the combination of the fever and sweating that's the crucial clue," he lectured. "Your friend's illness is not a natural disease. My colleague in Borrata was quite correct in his diagnosis. Your friend has indeed been poisoned, and I would surmise that the poison involved was darestim. The desert nomads here in Rendor call it deathweed. It kills sheep in the same way that it kills people. The poison is very rare, since the nomads uproot every bush they come across. Does my diagnosis agree with that of my Cammorian colleague?"

"Exactly, Doctor Voldi," she said admiringly.

"Well, that's it, then." He reached for his cloak. "I'm glad to have been of help."

"All right," Sparhawk said. "Now what do we do?"

"Make arrangements for a funeral," Voldi shrugged.

"What about an antidote?"

"There isn't any. I'm afraid your friend is doomed." There was an irritating smugness about the way he said it. "Unlike most poisons, darestim attacks the brain instead of the blood. Once it's ingested—poof." He snapped his fingers. "Tell me, does your friend have rich and powerful enemies? Darestim is fearfully expensive."

"The poisoning was politically motivated," Sparhawk said bleakly.

"Ah, politics." Voldi laughed. "Those fellows have all the money, don't they?" He frowned then. "It does seem to me—" He broke off, palming at his hair again. "Where *did* I hear that?" He scratched at his head, disturbing the carefully slicked-down hair. Then he snapped his fingers again. "Ah yes," he said triumphantly, "I have it now. I've heard some rumors—only rumors, mind you—that a physician in Dabour has effected a few cures among members of the king's family in Zand. Normally that information would have been immediately disseminated to all other physicians, but I have some suspicions about the matter. I know the fellow, and there have been some ugly stories about him circulating in medical circles for years now. There are some who maintain that his miraculous-appearing cures are the result of certain forbidden practices."

"Which practices?" Sephrenia asked intently.

"Magic, madame. What else? My friend in Dabour would immediately lose his head if word got out that he was practicing witchcraft."

"I see," she said. "Did this rumor about a cure come to you from one single source?"

"Oh, no," he replied. "Any number of people have told me about it. The king's brother and several nephews fell ill. The physician from Dabour—Tanjin his name is—was summoned to the palace. He confirmed that they had all been poisoned with darestim, then he cured them. Out of gratitude, the king suppressed the information of exactly how the cures were effected, and he issued Tanjin a full pardon just to make sure." He smirked. "Not that the pardon is much good, mind you, since the king's authority doesn't go much beyond the walls of his own palace in Zand. Anyway, anyone with the slightest bit of medical knowledge knows how it was done." He assumed a lofty expression. "I wouldn't stoop to that myself," he declared, "but Doctor Tanjin is notoriously greedy, and I imagine that the king paid him handsomely."

"Thank you for your assistance, Doctor Voldi," Sparhawk said then.

"I'm sorry about your friend," Voldi said. "By the time you get to Dabour and back, he'll be long since dead, I'm afraid. Darestim works rather slowly, but it's always fatal."

"So's a sword through the belly," Sparhawk said grimly. "At the very least, we'll be able to avenge our friend."

"What a dreadful thought," Voldi shuddered. "Are you at all acquainted with the kind of damage a sword does to someone?"

"Intimately," Sparhawk replied.

"Oh, that's right. You would be, wouldn't you? Would you like to have me take a look at those old wounds of yours?"

"Thanks all the same, Doctor. They're quite healed now."

"Splendid. I'm rather proud of the way I cured those, you know. A lesser physician would have lost you. Well, I must be off now. I have a full day ahead of me tomorrow." He wrapped his cloak about him.

"Thank you, Doctor Voldi," the abbot said. "The brother at the door will escort you home again."

"My pleasure, my Lord Abbot. It's been a stimulating discussion." Voldi bowed and left the room.

"Pompous little ass, isn't he?" Kurik muttered.

"Yes, he is," the abbot agreed. "He's very good, though."

"It's thin, Sparhawk," Sephrenia sighed, "very, very thin. All we have are rumors, and we don't have time for wild-goose chases."

"I don't see that we have any choice, do you? We have to go to Dabour. We can't ignore the slightest chance."

"It may not be quite as thin as you think, Lady Sephrenia," the abbot said. "I know Voldi very well. He wouldn't confirm anything he hasn't seen with his own eyes, but I've heard a few rumors myself to the effect that some members of the family of the king of Rendor fell ill and then recovered."

"It's all we've got," Sparhawk said. "We've got to follow through on it."

"The fastest way to Dabour is by sea along the coast and then up the Gule River," the abbot suggested.

"No," Sephrenia said firmly. "The creature that's been trying to kill Sparhawk has probably realized by now that it failed last time. I don't think we want to be looking over our shoulders for waterspouts every foot of the way."

"You'll have to go to Dabour by way of Jiroch anyway," the abbot told them. "You can't go overland. No one crosses the desert between here and Dabour, even at this time of year. It's totally impassable."

"If that's the way we have to do it, then that's the way we'll do it," Sparhawk said.

"Be careful out there," the abbot cautioned seriously. "The Rendors are in a state of turmoil right now."

"They're always in a state of turmoil, my Lord."

"This is a bit different. Arasham's at Dabour preaching up a new holy war."

"He's been doing that for over twenty years now, hasn't he? He stirs up the desert people all winter, and then in the summer they go back to their flocks."

"That's what's different about this time, Sparhawk. Nobody pays much attention to the nomads, but somehow the old lunatic's beginning to sway the people who live in the cities, and that makes it a little more serious. Arasham's elated, of course, and he's holding his desert nomads firmly at Dabour. He's got quite an army."

"The city people in Rendor aren't all *that* stupid. What's impressing them so much?"

"I've heard that there are some people spreading rumors. They're telling the townsfolk that there's a great deal of sympathy for the resurgence of the Eshandist movement in the northern kingdoms."

"That's absurd," Sparhawk scoffed.

"Of course it is, but they've managed to persuade a fair number of people here in Cippria that for the first time in centuries a rebellion against the Church might have some chance of success. Not only that, there have been fairly large shipments of arms filtering into the country."

A suspicion began to grow in Sparhawk's mind. "Have you any idea who's been circulating these rumors?" he asked.

The abbot shrugged. "Merchants, travellers from the north, and the like. They're all foreigners. They usually stay in that quarter near the Elenian consulate."

"Isn't *that* curious?" Sparhawk mused. "I'd been summoned to the Elenian consulate that night when I was attacked in the street. Is Elius still the consul?"

"Why, yes, as a matter of fact, he is. What are you getting at, Sparhawk?"

"One more question, my Lord. Have your people by any chance seen a white-haired man going in and out of the consulate?"

"I couldn't really say. I didn't tell them to look for that sort of thing. You have someone particular in mind, I gather?"

"Oh, I do indeed, my Lord Abbot." Sparhawk rose and began to pace up and down. "Why don't I have another try at Elene logic, Sephrenia," he said. He began to tick items off on his fingers. "One: The Primate Annias aspires to the archprelate's throne. Two: All four militant orders oppose him, and their opposition could block his ambitions. Three: In order to get that throne, he must discredit or divert the Church Knights. Four: The Elenian consul here in Cippria is his cousin. Five: The consul and Martel have had dealings with each other before. I got some personal evidence of that ten years ago."

"I didn't know that Elius was related to the primate," the abbot said, looking a bit surprised.

"They don't make an issue of it," Sparhawk told him. "Now then," he continued, "Annias wants the Church Knights out of Chyrellos when the time comes to elect a new archprelate. What would the Church Knights do if there were an uprising here in Rendor?"

"We'd descend on the kingdom in full battle array," the abbot declared, forgetting that his choice of words clearly confirmed Sparhawk's suspicions about the nature of his order.

"And that would effectively remove the militant orders from the debate over the election in Chyrellos, wouldn't it?"

Sephrenia looked at Sparhawk speculatively. "What kind of man is this Elius?"

"He's a petty time server with little intelligence and less imagination."

"He doesn't sound very impressive."

"He isn't."

"Then someone else would have to be giving him instructions, wouldn't they?"

"Precisely." Sparhawk turned once more to the abbot. "My Lord," he said, "do you have any way to get messages to Preceptor Abriel at your motherhouse in Larium? Messages that can't be intercepted?"

The abbot gave him a frosty stare.

"We agreed to be frank with each other, my Lord," Sparhawk reminded him. "I'm not trying to embarrass you, but this is a matter of the greatest urgency."

"All right, Sparhawk," the abbot replied a bit stiffly. "Yes, I can get a message to Lord Abriel."

"Good. Sephrenia knows all the details and she can fill you in. Kurik and I have something to attend to."

"Just what are you planning?" the abbot demanded.

"I'm going to pay a call on Elius. He knows what's been going on, and I think I can persuade him to share the information. We need confirmation of all this before you send the message to Larium."

"It's too dangerous."

"Not as dangerous as having Annias in the archprelacy, is it?" Sparhawk considered it. "Do you happen to have a secure cell someplace?" he asked.

"We have a penitent's cell down in the cellar. The door can be locked, I suppose."

"Good. I think we'll bring Elius back here to question him. Then you can lock him up. I can't let him go, once he knows I'm here, and Sephrenia disapproves of random murders. If he just disappears, there'll be some uncertainty about what happened to him."

"Won't he make an outcry when you take him captive?"

"Not very likely, my Lord," Kurik assured him, drawing his heavy dagger. He slapped the hilt solidly against his palm. "I can practically guarantee that he'll be asleep."

The streets were quiet. The overcast which had obscured the sky that afternoon had cleared, and the stars were very bright overhead.

"No moon," Kurik said quietly as he and Sparhawk crept through the deserted streets. "That's a help."

"It's been rising late the past three nights," Sparhawk said.

"How late?"

"We've got a couple more hours."

"Can we make it back to the monastery by then?"

"We have to." Sparhawk stopped just before they reached an intersection and peered around the corner of a house. A man wearing a short cape and carrying a spear and a small lantern was shuffling sleepily along the street.

"Watchman," Sparhawk breathed, and he and Kurik stepped into the shadows of a deeply recessed doorway.

The watchman plodded on past, the lantern swinging from his hand casting looming shadows against the walls of the buildings.

"He should be more alert," Kurik growled disapprovingly.

"Under the circumstances your sense of what's proper might be a little misplaced."

"Right is right, Sparhawk," Kurik replied stubbornly.

After the watchman was out of sight, they crept on up the street.

"Are we just going to walk up to the gate of the consulate?" Kurik asked.

"No. When we get close to it, we'll go in over the rooftops."

"I'm not a cat, Sparhawk. Leaping from roof to roof isn't my idea of entertainment."

"The houses are all built up against each other in that part of town. The rooftops are just like a highway."

"Oh," Kurik grunted. "That's different, then."

The consulate of the kingdom of Elenia was a fairly large building surrounded by a high, white-mortared wall. There were torches set on long poles at each corner, and a narrow lane running alongside the wall.

"Does that lane run all the way around it?" Kurik asked.

"It did the last time I was here."

"There's a significant hole in your plan then, Sparhawk. I can't jump all the way from one of these rooftops to the top of that wall."

"I don't think I could either." Sparhawk frowned. "Let's go around and look at the other side."

They crept through a series of narrow streets and alleys that wound along the back sides of the houses facing the consulate wall. A dog came out and barked at them until Kurik shied a rock at him. The dog yelped and ran off on three legs.

"Now I know how a burglar feels," Kurik muttered.

"There," Sparhawk said.

"There where?"

"Right over there. Some helpful fellow is doing some repairs on his roof. See that pile of beams stacked up against the side of that wall? Let's go see how long they are."

They crossed the alley to the stack of building material. Kurik studiously measured the beams off with his feet. "Marginal," he observed.

"We'll never know until we try," Sparhawk told him.

"All right. How do we get up on the roof?"

"We'll lean the beams against the wall. If we slant them up right, we should be able to scramble up and then pull them up after us."

"I'm glad you don't have to construct your own siege engines, Sparhawk," Kurik observed sourly. "All right. Let's try it."

They leaned several beams against the wall, and Kurik, grunting and sweating, hauled himself up to the roof. "All right," he whispered down over the edge, "come on up."

Sparhawk climbed up the beam, picking up a large splinter in his hand in the process. Then he and Kurik laboriously hauled the beams up after them and carried them one by one across the roof to the side facing the consulate wall. The flickering torches atop the wall cast a faint glow across the rooftops. As they were carrying the last beam, Kurik stopped suddenly. "Sparhawk," he called softly.

"What?"

"Two roofs over. There's a woman lying there."

"How do you know it's a woman?"

"Because she's stark naked, that's how."

"Oh," Sparhawk said, "that. It's a Rendorish custom. She's waiting for the moon to rise. They have a superstition here that the first rays of the moon on a woman's belly increases her fertility."

"Won't she see us?"

"She won't say anything if she does. She's too busy waiting for the moon. Press on, Kurik. Don't stand there gawking at her."

They struggled manfully to push a beam out over the narrow lane, a task made more difficult by the fact that their leverage diminished as they shoved the beam out farther and farther. Finally the stubborn beam clunked down on top of the consulate wall. They slid several more beams across along its top, then rolled them to one side to form a narrow bridge. As they were shoving the last one across, Kurik suddenly stopped with a muttered oath.

"What's wrong?" Sparhawk asked him.

"How did we get up on this roof, Sparhawk?" Kurik asked acidly.

"We climbed up a slanted beam."

"Where did we want to go?"

"To the top of the wall of the consulate over there."

"Then why are we building bridges?"

"Because—" Sparhawk stopped, feeling suddenly very foolish. "We could have just leaned a beam against the wall of the consulate, couldn't we?"

"Congratulations, my Lord," Kurik said sarcastically.

"The bridge was such a perfect solution to the problem," Sparhawk said defensively.

"But totally unnecessary."

"That doesn't really invalidate the solution, does it?"

"Of course not."

"Why don't we just go on across?"

"You go ahead. I think I'll go talk with the naked lady for a while."

"Never mind, Kurik. She has her mind on other things."

"I'm sort of an expert on fertility, if that's what's really bothering her."

"Let's go, Kurik."

They crossed their makeshift bridge to the top of the consulate wall and then crept along it until they reached a place where the branches of a well-watered fig tree reached up out of the shadows below. They climbed down the tree and stood for a moment or two beside it while Sparhawk got his bearings.

"You wouldn't happen to know where the consul's bedchamber is, would you?" Kurik whispered.

"No," Sparhawk replied softly, "but I can guess. It's the Elenian consulate, and all official Elenian buildings are more or less the same. The private quarters will be upstairs in the back."

"Very good, Sparhawk," Kurik said drily. "That narrows things down considerably. Now we only have to search about a quarter of the building."

They crept through a shadowy garden and entered by way of an unlocked back door. They passed through a darkened kitchen and into the dimly lit central hall. Kurik suddenly jerked Sparhawk back into the kitchen.

"What—" Sparhawk started to object in a hoarse whisper.

"Shhh!"

Out in the hall there was the bobbing glow of a candle. A matronly woman, a housekeeper or perhaps a cook, walked toward the kitchen door. Sparhawk shrank back as she stood framed in the doorway. Then she took hold of the handle and firmly closed the door.

"How did you know she was coming?" Sparhawk whispered.

"I don't know," Kurik whispered back. "I just did." He put his ear to the door. "She's moving on," he reported softly.

"What's she doing up at this time of the night?"

"Who knows? Maybe she's just making sure all the doors are locked. Aslade does that every night." He listened again. "There," he said, "she just closed another door, and I can't hear her out there anymore. I think she went to bed."

"The staircase should be just opposite the main entryway," Sparhawk whispered. "Let's get up on the second floor before somebody else comes wandering by."

They darted out into the hallway and up a broad flight of stairs to the upper floor.

"Look for an ornate door," Sparhawk whispered. "The consul's the master of the house, so he's likely to have the most luxurious room. You go that way, and I'll go this."

They separated and went in opposite directions on tiptoe. At the end of the hallway, Sparhawk found an elaborately carved door decorated with gilt paint. He opened it carefully and looked inside. By the light of a single dimly glowing oil lamp he saw a stout, florid-faced man of fifty or so lying on his back in the bed. The man was snoring loudly. Sparhawk recognized him. He softly closed the door and went looking for Kurik. His squire met him at the head of the stairs.

"How old a man is the consul?" Kurik whispered.

"About fifty."

"The one I saw wasn't him, then. There's a carved door at the far end. There's a young fellow about twenty in bed with an older woman."

"Did they see you?"

"No. They were busy."

"Oh. The consul's sleeping alone. He's down at this end of the hall."

"Do you suppose the woman at the other end could be his wife?"

"That's their business, isn't it?"

Together they tiptoed back down to the gilt-painted door. Sparhawk eased it open, and they went inside and crossed the floor to the bed. Sparhawk reached out and took the consul's shoulder. "Your Excellency," he said quietly, shaking the man.

The consul's eyes flew open, then glazed and went blank as Kurik rapped him sharply behind the ear with the hilt of his dagger. They trussed the unconscious man up in a dark blanket, and Kurik unceremoniously slung the limp form over his shoulder. "Is that everything we need here?" he asked.

"That's it," Sparhawk said. "Let's go."

They crept back down the stairs and into the kitchen again. Sparhawk carefully, closed the door leading into the main part of the house. "Wait here," he breathed to Kurik. "Let me check the garden. I'll whistle if it's clear." He slipped out into the shadowed garden and carefully moved from tree to tree, his eyes alert. He suddenly realized that he was enjoying himself immensely. He hadn't had so much pure fun since he and Kalten had been boys and had regularly slipped out of his father's house in the middle of the night bent on mischief.

He whistled a very poor imitation of a nightingale.

After a moment, he heard Kurik's hoarse whisper coming from the kitchen door. "Is that you?"

For an instant, he was tempted to whisper back, "No," but then he got himself under control again.

They had some difficulty getting the inert body of the consul up the fig tree, but finally managed by main strength. Then they crossed their makeshift bridge and pulled the beams back onto the roof.

"She's still there," Kurik whispered.

"Who is?"

"The naked lady."

"It's her roof."

They dragged the beams back to the far side of the roof and lowered them again. Then Sparhawk climbed down and caught the consul's body when Kurik lowered it to him. Kurik joined him a moment later, and they restacked the beams against the wall.

"All nice and neat," Sparhawk said with satisfaction, brushing his hands together.

Kurik hefted the body up onto his shoulder again. "Won't his wife miss him?" he asked.

"Not very much, I wouldn't think—if that was her in the bedroom at the other end of the hall. Why don't we go back to the monastery?"

They traded off carrying the body and reached the outskirts of town in about half an hour, dodging several watchmen along the way. The consul, draped over Sparhawk's shoulder, groaned and stirred weakly.

Kurik rapped him on the head again.

When they entered the abbot's study, Kurik unceremoniously dumped the unconscious man on the floor. He and Sparhawk looked at each other for a moment, then they both burst into uncontrollable laughter.

"What's so funny?" the abbot demanded.

"You should have come along, my Lord," Kurik gasped. "I haven't had so much fun in years." He began laughing again. "The bridge was the best, I think."

"I sort of liked the naked lady," Sparhawk disagreed.

"Have you two been drinking?" the abbot asked suspiciously.

"Not a drop, my Lord," Sparhawk replied. "It's a thought, though, if you've got anything handy. Where's Sephrenia?"

"I persuaded her that she and the child should get some sleep." The abbot paused. "*What* naked lady?" he demanded, his eyes afire with curiosity.

"There was a woman up on a roof going through that fertility ritual," Sparhawk told him, still laughing. "She sort of distracted Kurik for a moment or two."

"Was she pretty?" The abbot grinned at Kurik.

"I couldn't really say, my Lord. I wasn't looking at her face."

"My Lord Abbot," Sparhawk said then, a bit more seriously, though he still felt enormously exuberant, "we're going to question Elius as soon as he wakes up. Please don't be alarmed by some of the things we say to him."

"I quite understand, Sparhawk," the abbot replied.

"Good. All right, Kurik, let's wake up his Excellency here and see what he has to say for himself."

Kurik stripped the blanket off the consul's limp body and began pinching the unconscious man's ears and nose. After a moment, the consul's eyelids fluttered. Then he groaned and opened his eyes. He stared blankly at them for a moment, then sat up quickly. "Who are you? What's the meaning of this?" he demanded.

Kurik smacked him firmly across the back of the head.

"You see how it is, Elius," Sparhawk said blandly. "You don't mind if I call you Elius, do you? Possibly you may remember me. The name's Sparhawk."

"Sparhawk?" the consul gasped. "I thought you were dead."

"That's a highly exaggerated rumor, Elius. Now, the fact of the matter is that you've been abducted. We have a number of questions for you. Things will go much more pleasantly for you if you answer them freely. Otherwise, you're in for a very bad night."

"You wouldn't dare!"

Kurik hit him again.

"I'm the consul of the kingdom of Elenia," Elius blustered, trying to cover the back of his head with both hands, "and the cousin of the primate of Cimmura. You can't do this to me."

Sparhawk sighed. "Break a few of his fingers, Kurik," he suggested, "just to show him that we *can* do this to him."

Kurik set his foot against the consul's chest, pushed him back onto the floor, and seized the weakly struggling captive's right wrist.

"No!" Elius squealed. "Don't! I'll tell you anything you want."

"I told you he'd cooperate, my Lord," Sparhawk said conversationally to the abbot, pulling off his Rendorish robe to stand revealed in his mailcoat and sword belt, "just as soon as he understood the seriousness of the situation."

"Your methods are direct, Sir Sparhawk," the abbot noted.

"I'm a plain man, my Lord," Sparhawk replied, scratching at one mailed armpit. "Subtlety isn't one of my strong points." He nudged the captive with one foot. "All right, then, Elius, I'll make things simple for you. All you have to do at first is confirm a number of statements." He drew up a chair and sat down, crossing his legs. "First of all, your cousin, the primate of Cimmura, has his eyes on the throne of the archprelacy, right?"

"You have no proof of that."

"Break his thumb, Kurik."

Still holding the consul's wrist in his grip, Kurik pried open the man's clenched fist and grasped his thumb. "In how many places, my Lord?" he asked politely.

"Do as many as you can, Kurik. Give him something to think about."

"No! No! It's true!" Elius gasped, his eyes wide with terror.

"We're making real progress here," Sparhawk observed with a relaxed smile. "Now. You've had dealings in the past with a white-haired man named Martel. He works for your cousin from time to time. Am I right?"

"Y—yes," Elius faltered.

"Notice how it gets easier as you go along? In fact it was you who set Martel and his hirelings on me that night about ten years ago, wasn't it?"

"It was his idea," Elius blurted quickly. "I'd received orders from my cousin to cooperate with him. He suggested that I summon you that night. I had no idea that he intended to kill you."

"You're very naïve then, Elius. Lately, a fair number of travellers from the northern kingdoms have been circulating rumors here in Cippria that there's a ground swell of sympathy for Rendorish aims in those kingdoms. Is Martel in any way connected with that campaign?"

Elius started at him, his lips pressed fearfully shut.

Slowly, Kurik began to bend his thumb back.

"Yes! Yes!" Elius squeaked, arching back in pain.

"You were almost backsliding there, Elius," Sparhawk chided. "I'd watch that if I were you. The whole purpose of Martel's campaign here is to persuade the city dwellers of Rendor to join with the desert nomads in an Eshandist uprising against the Church. Am I right?"

"Martel doesn't confide in me all that much, but I suppose that's his ultimate goal, yes."

"And he's supplying weapons, right?"

"I've heard that he is."

"This next one is tricky, Elius, so listen carefully. The real point here is to stir things up so that the Church Knights will have to come here and quiet them down again. Isn't that so?"

Elius nodded sullenly. "Martel himself hasn't said so, but my cousin intimated as much to me in his last letter."

"And the uprising is to be timed to coincide with the election of the new archprelate in the Basilica of Chyrellos?"

"I really don't know that, Sir Sparhawk. Please believe me. You're probably right, but I can't really say for certain."

"We'll let that one pass for the moment. Now, I have a burning curiosity. Just where is Martel right now?"

"He's gone to Dabour to talk with Arasham. The old man's trying to whip his followers into a frenzy so that they'll start burning churches and expropriating Church lands. Martel was very upset when he heard about it and he hurried to Dabour to try to head it off."

"Probably because it was premature?"

"I'd imagine as much, yes."

"I guess that's about all then, Elius," Sparhawk said benignly. "I certainly want to thank you for your cooperation tonight."

"You're letting me go?" the consul asked incredulously.

"No, I'm afraid not. Martel's an old friend of mine. I want to surprise him when I get to Dabour, so I can't risk having you get word to him that I'm coming. There's a penitent's cell down in the cellar of this monastery. I'm sure you feel very penitent just now and I want to give you some time to reflect on your sins. The cell is quite comfortable, I'm told. It has a door, four walls, a ceiling, and even a floor." He looked at the abbot. "It *does* have a floor, doesn't it, my Lord?"

"Oh, yes," the abbot confirmed, "a nice cold stone one."

"You can't do that!" Elius protested shrilly.

"Sparhawk," Kurik agreed, "you really can't confine a man in a penitent's cell against his will. It's a violation of Church law."

"Oh," Sparhawk said peckishly, "I suppose you're right. I did want to avoid all the mess. Go ahead and do it the other way, then."

"Yes, my Lord," Kurik said respectfully. He drew his dagger. "Tell me, my Lord Abbot," he said, "does your monastery have a graveyard?"

"Yes, rather a nice one, actually."

"Oh, good. I hate just to drag them out into the open countryside and leave them for the jackals." He took hold of the consul's hair and tipped his head back. Then he set the edge of his dagger against the cringing man's throat. "This won't take a moment, your Excellency," he said professionally.

"My Lord Abbot," Elius squealed.

"I'm afraid it's altogether out of my hands, your Excellency," the abbot said with mock piety. "The Church Knights have their own laws. I wouldn't dream of interfering."

"Please, my Lord Abbot," Elius pleaded. "Confine me to the penitent's cell."

"Do you sincerely repent your sins?" the abbot asked.

"Yes! Yes! I am heartily ashamed!"

"I am afraid, Sir Sparhawk, that I must intercede on this penitent's behalf," the abbot said. "I cannot permit you to kill him until he has made his peace with God."

"That's your final decision, my Lord Abbot?" Sparhawk asked.

"I'm afraid it is, Sir Sparhawk."

"Oh, all right. Let us know as soon as he's completed his penance. Then we'll kill him."

"Of course, Sir Sparhawk."

After the violently trembling Elius had been taken away by a pair of burly monks, the three men in the room began to laugh.

"That was rare, my Lord," Sparhawk congratulated the abbot. "It was exactly the right tone."

"I'm not a complete novice at this sort of thing, Sparhawk," the abbot said. He looked at the big Pandion shrewdly. "You Pandions have a reputation for brutality— particularly where questioning captives is concerned."

"It seems to me I've heard some rumors to that effect, yes," Sparhawk admitted.

"But you don't really do anything to people, do you?"

"Not usually, no. It's the reputation that persuades people to cooperate. Do you have any idea how hard—and messy—it is actually to torture people? We planted those rumors about our order ourselves. After all, why work if you don't have to?"

"My feelings exactly, Sparhawk. Now," the abbot said eagerly, "why don't you tell me about the naked lady and the bridge—and anything else you might have run across? Don't leave anything out. I'm only a poor cloistered monk and I don't really get much fun out of life."

## ■ CHAPTER TWENTY ■

Sparhawk winced and drew his breath in sharply. "Sephrenia, do you have to dig straight in?" he complained.

"Don't be such a baby," she told him, continuing to pick at the sliver in his hand with her needle. "If I don't get it all out, it's going to fester."

He sighed and gritted his teeth together as she continued to probe. He looked at Flute, who had both hands across her mouth as if to stifle a giggle.

"You think it's funny?" he asked her crossly.

She lifted her pipes and blew a derisive little trill.

"I've been thinking, Sparhawk," the abbot said. "If Annias has people in Jiroch the same as he has here in Cippria, wouldn't it be safer just to go around it and avoid the possibility of being recognized?"

"I think we'll have to chance it, my Lord," Sparhawk said. "I've got a friend in Jiroch I need to talk with before we go upriver." He looked down at his black robe. "These ought to get us past a casual glance."

"I think it's dangerous, Sparhawk."

"Not if we're careful, I hope."

Kurik, who had been saddling their horses and loading the pack mule the abbot had given them, came into the room. He was carrying a long, narrow wooden case. "Do you really have to take this?" he asked Sephrenia.

"Yes, Kurik," she replied in a sad voice. "I do."

"What's in it?"

"A pair of swords. They're a part of the burden I bear."

"It's a pretty large box for only two swords."

"There'll be others, I'm afraid," she sighed, then began to wrap Sparhawk's hand with a strip of linen cloth.

"It doesn't need a bandage, Sephrenia," he objected. "It was only a splinter."

She gave him a long, steady stare.

He gave up. "All right," he said. "Do whatever you think is best."

"Thank you." She tied off the end of the bandage.

"You'll send word to Larium, my Lord?" Sparhawk asked the abbot.

"On the next ship that leaves the harbor, Sir Sparhawk."

Sparhawk thought a moment. "I don't think we'll be going back to Madel," he said. "We have some companions staying at the house of the Marquis Lycien there."

The abbot nodded. "I know him," he said.

"Could you get word to them as well? Tell them that if everything works out at Dabour, we'll be going home from there. I think they might as well go on back to Cimmura."

"I'll see to it, Sparhawk."

Sparhawk tugged thoughtfully at the knot on his bandage.

"Leave it alone," Sephrenia told him.

He took his hand away. "I'm not trying to tell the preceptors what to do," he said to the abbot, "but you might suggest in your message that a few small contingents of Church Knights in the streets of Rendorish cities right now might remind the local population of just how unpleasant things can get if they pay too much attention to all these rumors."

"And head off the need for whole armies later on," the abbot agreed. "I'll definitely mention it in my report."

Sparhawk rose to his feet. "I'm in your debt again, my Lord Abbot," he said. "You always seem to be here when I need you."

"We serve the same master, Sparhawk," the abbot replied. He grinned then. "Besides," he added, "I sort of like you. You Pandions don't always do things the way we would, but you get results, and that's what counts, isn't it?"

"We can hope."

"Be careful in the desert, my friend, and good luck."

"Thank you, my Lord."

They went down to the central court of the monastery as the bells began to chime their call to morning prayers. Kurik tied Sephrenia's sword case to the pack mule's saddle, and they all mounted. Then they rode out through the front gate with the sound of the bells hovering in the air above them.

Sparhawk's mood was pensive as they reached the dusty coast road and turned west toward Jiroch.

"What is it, Sparhawk?" Sephrenia asked him.

"Those bells have been calling me for ten years now," he replied. "Somehow I've always known that someday I'd come back to this monastery." He straightened in his saddle. "It's a good place," he said. "I'm a little sorry to leave it, but . . ." He shrugged and rode on.

The morning sun was very bright and it reflected back blindingly from the wasteland of rock, sand, and gravel lying on the left side of the road. On the right side was a steep bank leading down to a gleaming white beach, and beyond that lay the deep blue waters of the Inner Sea. Within an hour it was quite warm. A half hour later it was hot.

"Don't they ever get a winter down here?" Kurik asked, mopping at his stream-ing face.

"This *is* winter, Kurik," Sparhawk told him.

"What's it like in the summer?"

"Unpleasant. In the summer you have to travel at night."

"How far is it to Jiroch?"

"About five hundred leagues."

"Three weeks at least."

"I'm afraid so."

"We should have gone by ship—waterspouts or no."

"No, Kurik," Sephrenia disagreed. "None of us could be of any help to Ehlana if we're all lying on the bottom of the sea."

"Won't that thing that's after us just use magic to locate us anyway?"

"It seems that it can't do that," she replied. "When it was looking for Sparhawk ten years ago, it had to question people. It couldn't just sniff him out."

"I'd forgotten that," he admitted.

They rose early each day, even before the stars faded, and pushed their horses hard during the early morning hours before the sun became a bludgeon at midday. Then they rested in the scant shade of the tent the abbot had pressed on them, while their mounts grazed listlessly on scrubby forage in the blistering sun. As the sun lowered toward the west, they rode on, usually until well after dark. Occasionally, they reached some desert spring, inevitably surrounded by lush vegetation and shade. At times, they lingered for a day to rest their horses and to gather the strength to face the savage sun again.

It was at such a spring, where crystal water came purling out of a rocky slope to gather in an azure pool surrounded by palm trees, that the shade of a black-armored Pandion Knight visited them. Sparhawk, clad in only a loincloth, had just emerged dripping from the pool when he saw the mounted figure approaching from the west. Although the sun stood at the figure's back, it cast no shadow, and he could clearly see the sun-blasted hillsides through both horse and man. Once again he caught that charnelhouse reek; as the figure approached, he saw that its horse was little more than a vacant-eyed skeleton. He made no attempt to reach a weapon, but stood shivering despite the furnacelike heat as the mounted specter bore down on them. Some few yards away, the shade reined in its skeletal mount and, with a deadly slow motion, drew its sword. "Little mother," it intoned hol-lowly to Sephrenia, "I have done all that I could." It raised the hilt of its weapon to its visor in a salute, then reversed the blade and offered the hilt across its insubstan-tial forearm.

Sephrenia, pale and faltering, crossed the hot gravel to the specter and took the sword hilt in both hands. "Thy sacrifice shall be remembered, Sir Knight," she said in a trembling voice.

"What is remembrance in the House of the Dead, Sephrenia? I did what duty commanded of me. That alone is my solace in the eternal silence." Then it turned its visored countenance toward Sparhawk. "Hail, brother," it said in that same empty voice. "Know that thy course is aright. At Dabour shalt thou find that answer which we have sought. Shouldst thou succeed in thy quest, we shall salute thee with our hollow cheers in the House of the Dead."

"Hail, brother," Sparhawk replied in a choked voice, "and farewell."

Then the specter vanished.

With a long, shuddering moan, Sephrenia collapsed. It was as if the weight of the suddenly materialized sword had crushed her to earth.

Kurik rushed forward, scooped her slight form up in his arms, and carried her back into the shade beside the pool.

Sparhawk, however, moved at a resolute pace toward the spot where she had fallen, heedless of the blistering gravel under his naked feet, and retrieved his fallen brother's sword.

Behind him, he heard the sound of Flute's pipes. The melody was one that he had not heard before. It was questioning and filled with a deep sadness and an aching kind of longing. He turned around with the sword in his hand. Sephrenia lay on a blanket in the shade of the palms. Her face seemed drawn, and quite suddenly dark circles had appeared beneath her now-closed eyes. Kurik knelt anxiously beside her, and Flute sat cross-legged not far away with her pipes to her lips, sending her strange, hymnlike song soaring into the air.

Sparhawk crossed the gravel and stopped in the shade. Kurik rose and joined him. "She won't be able to go on today," the squire said quietly, "perhaps not even tomorrow."

Sparhawk nodded.

"This is weakening her terribly, Sparhawk," Kurik continued gravely. "Each time one of those twelve knights dies, she seems to wilt a little more. Wouldn't it be better to send her back to Cimmura when we get to Jiroch?"

"Perhaps so, but she wouldn't go."

"You're probably right," Kurik agreed glumly. "You *do* know that you and I could move faster if we didn't have her and the little girl along, though, don't you?"

"Yes, but what would we do without her when we got to where we're going?"

"You've got a point there, I guess. Did you happen to recognize that ghost?"

Sparhawk nodded. "Sir Kerris," he said shortly.

"I never got to know him very well," Kurik admitted. "He always seemed a little stiff and formal."

"He was a good man, though."

"What did he say to you? I was too far away to hear him."

"He said that we're on the right course and that we'll find the answer we need at Dabour."

"Well, now," Kurik said. "That helps, doesn't it? I was about half-afraid that we were chasing shadows."

"So was I," Sparhawk admitted.

Flute had laid aside her pipes and now sat beside Sephrenia. She reached out and took the stricken woman's hand and held it. Her small face was grave, but betrayed no other emotion.

An idea came to Sparhawk. He went to where Sephrenia lay. "Flute," he said quietly.

The little girl looked up at him.

"Can you do something to help Sephrenia?"

Flute shook her head a bit sadly.

"It is forbidden." Sephrenia's voice was hardly more than a whisper, and her eyes were still closed. "Only those of us who were present can bear this burden." She drew in a deep breath. "Go put some clothes on, Sparhawk," she said then. "Don't walk around like that in front of the child."

They remained in the shade beside the pool for the remainder of that day and all of the next. On the morning of the third day, Sephrenia rose and resolutely began to gather up her things. "Time is moving along, gentlemen," she said crisply, "and we still have a long way to go."

Sparhawk looked closely at her. Her face was still haggard, and the deep circles beneath her eyes had not lessened. As she bent to pick up her veil, he saw several silvery strands in her glistening black hair. "Wouldn't you be stronger if we stayed here another day?" he asked her.

"Not appreciably, Sparhawk," she replied in a weary voice. "My condition can't be improved by resting. Let's move on. It's a long way to Jiroch."

They rode at an easy pace at first, but after a few miles, Sephrenia spoke rather sharply. "Sparhawk," she said, "it's going to take all winter if we keep sauntering along like this."

"All right, Sephrenia, whatever you say."

It was perhaps ten days later when they arrived in Jiroch. Like Cippria, the port city in western Rendor was a low, flat town with thick-walled, flat-roofed houses thickly plastered with white mortar. Sparhawk led them through a series of twisting alleys to a section of town not far from the river. It was a quarter where foreigners were, if not actually encouraged, at least tolerated. While most of the people in the streets were still Rendors, there was a fair spattering of brightly robed Cammorians, a number of Lamorks, and even a few Elenians in the crowd. Sparhawk and the others kept their hoods up and rode slowly to avoid attracting attention.

It was late morning when they reached a modest house set some distance back from the street. The man who owned the house was Sir Voren, a Pandion Knight, although few in Jiroch were aware of that fact. Most people in the port city thought of him as a moderately prosperous Elenian merchant. He did, in fact, engage in trade. Some years, he even made a profit. Sir Voren's real purpose for being in Jiroch was not commercial, however. There were a goodly number of Pandion Knights submerged in the general population of Rendor, and Voren was their only contact with the motherhouse at Demos. All their communications and dispatches passed through his hands to be concealed in the boxes and bales of goods he shipped from the harbor.

A slack-lipped servant with dull, uncurious eyes led Sparhawk and the others through the house and on into a walled garden filled with the shade of fig trees and the musical trickle of a marble fountain in the center. Neatly tended flowerbeds lined the walls, and the nodding blossoms were a riot of colors. Voren was seated on a bench beside the fountain. He was a tall, thin man with a sardonic sense of humor. His years in this southern kingdom had browned his skin until it was the color of an old saddle. Though he was of late middle age, his hair was untouched by gray, but his tanned face was a tracery of wrinkles. He wore no doublet, but rather a plain linen shirt open at the neck. He rose as they entered the garden.

"Ah, Mahkra," he greeted Sparhawk with a brief, sidelong glance at the servant, "so good to see you again, old boy."

"Voren," Sparhawk responded with a Rendorish bow, a sinuous movement that was half genuflection.

"Jintal," Voren said to the servant then, "be a good fellow and take this to my factor down at the docks." He folded a sheet of parchment in half and handed it to the swarthy-faced Rendor.

"As you command, Master," the servant replied, bowing.

They waited until the sound of the front door of the house closing announced that the servant had departed.

"Nice enough fellow there," Voren observed. "Of course he's fearfully stupid. I'm always careful to hire servants who aren't too bright. An intelligent servant is usually a spy." Then his eyes narrowed. "Wait here a moment," he said. "I want to be sure he really left the house." He crossed the garden and went back inside.

"I don't remember his being that nervous," Kurik said.

"This is a nervous part of the world," Sparhawk replied.

After a few moments, Voren returned. "Little mother," he greeted Sephrenia warmly, kissing her palms. "Will you give me your blessing?"

She smiled, touched his forehead, and spoke in Styric.

"I've missed that," he confessed, "even though I haven't done much lately that deserves blessing." Then he looked at her more closely. "Aren't you well, Sephrenia?" he asked her. "Your face seems very drawn."

"The heat, perhaps," she said, passing a slow hand across her eyes.

"Sit here," he said, pointing at his marble bench. "It's the coolest place in all of Jiroch." He smiled sardonically. "Which isn't saying all that much, I'll grant you."

She sat on the bench, and Flute clambered up beside her.

"Well, Sparhawk," Voren said, clasping his friend's hand, "what brings you back to Jiroch so soon? Did you leave something behind, perhaps?"

"Nothing I can't live without," Sparhawk replied drily.

Voren laughed. "Just to show you how good a friend I am, I won't tell Lillias that you said that. Hello, Kurik. How's Aslade?"

"She's well, my Lord Voren."

"And your sons? You have three, don't you?"

"Four, my Lord. The last one was born after you left Demos."

"Congratulations," Voren said, "a little late, maybe, but congratulations all the same."

"Thank you, my Lord."

"I need to talk with you, Voren," Sparhawk said, cutting across the pleasantries, "and we don't have much time."

"And here I thought this was a social visit." Voren sighed.

Sparhawk let that pass. "Has Vanion managed to get word to you about what's been going on in Cimmura?"

The lightly ironic smile faded from Voren's face, and he nodded seriously. "That's one of the reasons I was surprised to see you," he said. "I thought you were going to Borrata. Did you have any luck there?"

"I don't know how lucky it was, but we found out something we're trying to track down." He clenched his teeth together. "Voren," he said darkly, "Ehlana was poisoned."

Voren stared at him for a moment, then swore. "I wonder how long it'd take me to get back to Cimmura," he said in an icy voice. "I think I'd like to rearrange Annias just a bit. He'd look much better without his head, don't you think?"

"You'd have to stand in line, my Lord Voren," Kurik assured him. "I know at least a dozen other people with the same idea."

"Anyway," Sparhawk went on, "we found out that it was a Rendorish poison and we've heard of a physician in Dabour who might know of an antidote. That's where we're going now."

"Where are Kalten and the others?" Voren asked. "Vanion wrote that you had him and some knights from the other orders with you."

"We left them in Madel," Sparhawk replied. "They didn't look—or act—very Rendorish. Have you heard of a Doctor Tanjin in Dabour?"

"The one who's reputed to have cured the king's brother of some mysterious ailment? Of course. He might not want to talk about it, though. There are some shrewd guesses going around about how he managed those cures, and you know how Rendors feel about magic."

"I'll persuade him to talk about it," Sparhawk told him.

"You might wish that you hadn't left Kalten and the others behind," Voren told him. "Dabour's a very unfriendly place right now."

"I'll have to manage alone. I sent word to them from Cippria to go back home and wait for me there."

"Whom did you find in Cippria that you could really trust enough to carry messages for you?"

"I went to the abbot of that Arcian monastery on the east side of town. I've known him for a long time."

Voren laughed. "Is he still trying to conceal the fact that he's a Cyrinic?"

"Do you know *everything*, Voren?"

"That's what I'm here for. He's a good man, though. His methods are a little pedestrian, but he gets things done."

"What's happening in Dabour right now?" Sparhawk asked. "I don't want to walk in there with my eyes closed."

Voren sprawled on the grass near Sephrenia's feet and hooked his hands about one knee. "Dabour's always been a strange place," he replied. "It was Eshand's home, and the desert nomads think of it as a holy city. At any given time there are usually a dozen or so religious factions all fighting with each other for control of the holy places there." He smiled wryly. "Would you believe that there are twenty-three tombs there, all purporting to be the final resting place of Eshand? I strongly suspect that at least some of them are spurious—unless they dismembered the holy man after his death and buried him piecemeal."

Sparhawk sank to the grass beside his friend. "This is just a thought," he said, "but could we throw some clandestine support to one of the other factions and undermine Arasham's position?"

"It's a nice idea, Sparhawk, but at the moment there *aren't* any other factions. After Arasham received his epiphany, he spent forty years exterminating all possible rivals. There was a bloodbath in central Rendor of colossal proportions. Pyramids of skulls dot the desert out there. Finally, he gained control of Dabour and he rules there with an authority so total that he makes Otha of Zemoch look like a liberal. He has thousands of rabid followers who blindly follow his every lunatic whim. They roam the streets with sun-baked brains and burning eyes, searching for any infraction of obscure religious laws. Hordes of the unwashed and lice-ridden and only marginally human rage through the streets in search of the opportunity to burn their neighbors at the stake."

"That's direct enough," Sparhawk said. He glanced at Sephrenia. Flute had dipped a handkerchief into the fountain and was gently bathing the small woman's face with it. Peculiarly, Sephrenia had her head laid against the little girl's shoulder as if *she* were the child. "Arasham has gathered an army, then?" he asked Voren.

Voren snorted. "Only an idiot would call it an army. They can't march anywhere because they have to pray every half hour, and they blindly obey even the obvious misstatements of that senile old man." He laughed harshly. "Arasham sometimes stumbles over the language—which isn't surprising, since he's probably at least half baboon—and once, during his campaigns back in the hinterlands, he gave an order. He meant to say, 'Fall upon your foes,' but it came out wrong. Instead, he said, 'Fall upon your swords,' and three whole regiments did exactly that. Arasham rode home alone that day, trying to figure out what had gone wrong."

"You've been here too long, Voren." Sparhawk laughed. "Rendor's starting to sour your disposition."

"I can't abide stupidity and filth, Sparhawk, and Arasham's followers believe devoutly in the sanctity of ignorance and dirt."

"You're starting to develop a fine flair for rhetoric, though."

"Contempt is a powerful seasoning for one's words," Voren admitted. "I can't say what I think openly here in Rendor, so I have plenty of time to polish my phrases in private." His face grew serious. "Be very careful in Dabour, Sparhawk," he advised. "Arasham has a couple dozen disciples—some of whom he even knows. They're the ones who really control the city and they're all as crazy as he is."

"That bad?"

"Worse, probably."

"You've always been such a cheerful fellow, Voren," Sparhawk said drily.

"It's a failing of mine. I try to look on the bright side of things. Is anything happening in Cippria I ought to know about?"

"You might want to look into this," Sparhawk said, plucking at the grass beside him. "There are some foreigners going about there trying to encourage the belief that the peasantry in the Elene kingdoms in the north is on the verge of open rebellion against the Church because they support the goals of the Eshandist movement."

"I've heard some rumors about that," Voren said. "It hasn't gone very far here in Jiroch yet."

"It's just a question of time until it does, I think. It's fairly well organized."

"Any idea of who's behind it?"

"Martel, and we all know for whom he works. The whole idea is to stir up the city dwellers to join with Arasham in an uprising against the Church here in Rendor at the same time that the Hierocracy is gathering in Chyrellos to elect a new archprelate. The Church Knights would have to come here to put the fire out, and that would give Annias and his supporters a free hand in the election. We've passed the word to the militant orders, so they should be able to take steps." Sparhawk rose from the grass. "How long is your servant likely to take to run his errand?" he asked. "It might be better if we were gone when he came back. He may not be too bright, but I know Rendors, and they like to gossip."

"I think you've got a little time left. Jintal's fastest pace is a leisurely saunter. You'll have time to eat something, and I'll give you some fresh supplies."

"Is there any safe place to stay in Dabour?" Sephrenia asked the sardonic man.

"No place in Dabour is really safe, Sephrenia," Voren replied. He looked at Sparhawk. "Do you remember Perraine?" he asked.

"Lean fellow? Almost never talks?"

"That's him. He's in Dabour posing as a cattle buyer. He goes by the name Mirrelek, and he's got a place near the stockyards. The desert people need him—unless they want to eat all their own cows—so he has more or less the free run of the city. He'll put you up and keep you out of trouble." Voren grinned a bit slyly. "Speaking of trouble, Sparhawk," he said, "I'd strongly advise you to get out of Jiroch before Lillias finds out that you're back."

"Is she still unhappy?" Sparhawk said. "I thought that she'd have found someone to comfort her by now."

"I'm sure she has—several, probably—but you know Lillias. She holds grudges."

"I left her full title to the shop," Sparhawk said a bit defensively. "She should be doing very well by now if she pays attention to business."

"The last I heard, she was, but that's not the point. The whole thing is that you said your farewells—and left your bequest—in a note. You didn't give her the chance to scream, weep, and threaten to kill herself."

"That was sort of the idea."

"You were terribly unkind to her, my friend. Lillias thrives on high drama; when you slipped out in the middle of the night the way you did, you robbed her of a wonderful opportunity for histrionics." Voren was grinning openly.

"Do you really have to pursue this?"

"I'm just trying to give you a friendly warning, Sparhawk. All you'll have to face at Dabour are several thousand howling fanatics. Here in Jiroch, you'll have to face Lillias, and she's much, much more dangerous."

## CHAPTER TWENTY-ONE

They left Voren's house quietly about a half hour later. Sparhawk looked closely at Sephrenia as they mounted their horses. Although it was scarcely past noon, she already looked weary. "Could this thing that's after us stir up a waterspout on the river?" he asked her.

She frowned. "It's hard to say," she replied. "Normally, I'd say no, there's not enough open water. But the creatures of the underworld can overcome some natural laws if they choose." She thought a moment. "How wide is the river here?" she asked.

"Not very," he replied. "There's not enough water in the whole of Rendor to make a wide river."

"The riverbanks would make it very hard to direct a spout," she said thoughtfully. "You saw how erratically the one that destroyed Mabin's ship was moving."

"We'll have to chance it, then," he said. "You're too exhausted to ride all the way to Dabour, and it's going to get hotter as we ride south."

"Don't take unnecessary chances just for my sake, Sparhawk."

"It's not entirely for your sake," he told her. "We've lost a lot of time already, and going by boat is faster than riding. We'll stay close to the riverbank in case we need to get off the boat in a hurry."

"Whatever you think best," she said, slumping slightly in her saddle.

They rode out into the teeming street where black-robed nomads from the desert mingled with the more brightly garbed city dwellers and the merchants from the northern kingdoms. The street was filled with noise and with those peculiarly Rendorish scents—spices, perfumes, and the pervading odor of smoking olive oil.

"Who's this Lillias?" Kurik asked curiously as they rode down along the street toward the river.

"It's not important," Sparhawk replied shortly.

"If this person is dangerous, I'd say that it's fairly important for me to know about it."

"Lillias isn't dangerous in that particular way."

"We're talking about a woman, I gather."

It was obvious that Kurik did not intend to be put off. Sparhawk made a sour face. "All right," he said. "I was here in Jiroch for ten years. Voren set me up in a little shop where I went by the name Mahkra. The idea was that I could drop out of sight so that Martel's hirelings couldn't find me. In order to keep busy, I gathered information for Voren. To do that, I needed to look like all the other merchants on that street. They all had mistresses, so I needed one, too. Her name was Lillias. Satisfied?"

"That was quick. The lady has a short temper, I take it?"

"No, Kurik. She has a very long one. Lillias is the kind of woman who nurses grudges."

"Oh, that kind. I'd like to meet her."

"No, you wouldn't. I don't think you'd care for all the screaming and dramatics."

"That bad?"

"Why do you think I slipped out of town in the middle of the night? Do you suppose we could drop this?"

Kurik started to chuckle. "Excuse me for laughing, my Lord," he said, "but as I recall, you weren't exactly brimming with sympathy when I told you about *my* indiscretion with Talen's mother."

"All right. We're even, then." Sparhawk clamped his lips shut and rode on, ignoring Kurik's laughter.

The docks that jutted out into the muddy flow of the Gule River were rickety affairs and they were draped with smelly fishnets. Dozens of the wide-beamed river boats that plied the stream between Jiroch and Dabour were moored to them. Dark-skinned sailors clad in loincloths and with cloths wound about their heads lounged on their decks. Sparhawk dismounted and approached an evil-looking one-eyed man in a loose-fitting striped robe. The one-eyed man stood on the dock bawling orders at a lazy-looking trio of sailors aboard a mud-smeared scow.

"Your boat?" the knight asked.

"What of it?"

"Is it for hire?"

"That depends on the price."

"We can work that out. How many days to Dabour?"

"Three, maybe four days, depending on the wind." The captain was assessing Sparhawk and the others with his good eye. His surly expression changed, and he smiled an oily smile. "Why don't we talk about the price, noble sir?" he suggested.

Sparhawk made some pretense at haggling, then dipped into the pouch of coins Voren had given him and counted silver into the riverman's grimy hand. The man's single eye came alight when he saw the pouch.

They boarded the boat and tethered their horses amidships as the three sailors slipped the hawsers, pushed the boat out into the current, and raised the single, slanted sail. The river was sluggish, and the stiff onshore breeze blowing in off the Arcian Strait pushed them upstream against the current at a goodly speed.

"Watch yourselves," Sparhawk muttered to his companions as they unsaddled their mounts. "Our captain appears to be an independent businessman with his eye open for opportunities." He walked aft to where the one-eyed man stood at the tiller. "I want you to keep as close to shore as you can," he said.

"What for?" The captain's lone eye became suddenly wary.

"My sister's afraid of water," Sparhawk improvised. "If I give you the word, put your boat up against the bank so that she can get off."

"You're paying." The captain shrugged. "We'll do it any way you like."

"Do you run at night?" Sparhawk asked him.

The captain shook his head. "Some do, but I don't. There are too many snags and hidden rocks for my taste. We moor up against the bank when it gets dark."

"Good. I like prudence in a sailor. It makes for safer journeys—which brings up a point." He opened the front of his robe to reveal his mail coat and the heavy broadsword belted at his side. "Do you get my meaning?" he asked.

The captain's face clouded with chagrin. "You have no right to threaten me on my own boat," he blustered.

"As you said before, I'm paying. Your crew looks a little undependable to me, Captain, and your own face isn't one to inspire trust."

The captain's face grew sullen. "You don't have to be insulting," he said.

"If I've misjudged you, I'll apologize later. We have certain valuables with us and we'd prefer to keep them. My friends and I will sleep on the foredeck. You and your men can sleep aft. I trust that won't inconvenience you too much?"

"Aren't you being a little overcautious?"

"Nervous times, neighbor. Nervous times. Remember, when we tie up to the bank for the night, keep your men on the aft deck—and warn them against sleep-walking. A boat can be a very dangerous place for that sort of thing, and I'm a light sleeper." He turned and walked back forward.

The riverbanks on either side were covered with thick, rank vegetation, though the hills rising behind those narrow strips of green were barren and rock-strewn. Sparhawk and his friends sat on the foredeck, keeping a careful eye on the captain and his sailors and watching for any signs of unusual-looking weather. Flute sat astride the bowsprit playing her pipes while Sparhawk spoke quietly with Sephrenia and Kurik. Sephrenia already knew the customs of the country, so Sparhawk's instruction was directed primarily at his squire. He cautioned him about the many minor things that could be taken as personal insults, and about other things that were considered sacrilegious.

"Who made up all these stupid rules?" Kurik demanded.

"Eshand," Sparhawk replied. "He was crazy, and crazy people take great comfort in rituals."

"Anything else?"

"One other thing. If you should happen to encounter any sheep, you have to step aside for them."

"Say that again?" Kurik's tone was incredulous.

"It's very important, Kurik."

"You're not serious!"

"Deadly serious. Eshand was a shepherd when he was a boy and he used to go absolutely wild when someone rode through his flock. When he came to power, he announced that God had revealed to him that sheep were holy animals and that everyone had to give way to them."

"That's crazy, Sparhawk," Kurik protested.

"Of course it is. It's the law here, though."

"Isn't it strange how the Elene God's revelations always seem to coincide exactly with the prejudices of His prophets?" Sephrenia murmured.

"Do they do anything at all like normal people?" Kurik asked.

"Not many things, no."

As the sun went down, the captain moored his boat against the riverbank, and he and his sailors spread pallets on the aft deck. Sparhawk rose and went amidships. He laid his hand on Faran's neck. "Stay awake," he told the big roan. "If someone starts creeping around in the middle of the night, let me know about it."

Faran bared his teeth and shifted around until he was resolutely facing aft. Sparhawk patted his rump familiarly and went back forward.

They took a cold supper of bread and cheese, then spread their blankets on the deck.

"Sparhawk," Kurik said after they had settled down for the night.

"Yes, Kurik?"

"I just had a thought. Are there many people riding in and out of Dabour?"

"Usually, yes. Arasham's presence there tends to attract large crowds."

"I sort of thought so. Wouldn't we be a little less conspicuous if we got off this boat a league or so this side of Dabour and joined one of the groups of pilgrims riding into the city?"

"You think of everything, don't you, Kurik?"

"That's what you pay me for, Sparhawk. Sometimes you knights aren't too practical. It's a squire's job to keep you out of trouble."

"I appreciate that, Kurik."

"No extra charge," Kurik said.

The night passed uneventfully, and at dawn the sailors cast off their moorings and raised the sail again. They passed the town of Kodhl about midmorning of the following day and sailed on up river toward the holy city of Dabour. The river between the two towns was heavily travelled. There seemed to be no organized pattern to the traffic, and the boats occasionally bumped into each other. Such incidents were usually accompanied by an exchange of curses and insults.

It was about noon on the fourth day when Sparhawk went aft to have a word with the one-eyed captain. "We're getting fairly close, aren't we?" he asked.

"About five more leagues," the captain replied, moving his tiller slightly to avoid an oncoming boat. "Mangy son of a three-legged donkey!" he bellowed at the steersman of the other vessel.

"May your mother break out in warts!" the steersman replied pleasantly.

"I think my friends and I might want to go ashore before we actually reach the city," Sparhawk said to the captain. "We want to look around a bit before we meet any of Arasham's followers, and the docks are likely to be watched rather closely."

"That might be a wise move," the captain agreed. "Besides, I get a feeling that you might be up to no good and I'd rather not get involved."

"It works out for both of us, then, doesn't it?"

It was early afternoon when the captain put his tiller over and drove the prow of his boat up onto a narrow strip of sandy beach. "This is about as close as I can get you," he told Sparhawk. "The bank gets marshy just up ahead."

"How far is Dabour from here?" Sparhawk asked him.

"Four, maybe five miles."

"Close enough, then."

The sailors ran the gangway out to the sand from amidships, and Sparhawk and his friends led their horses and their pack mule down to the beach. They had no sooner disembarked than the sailors pulled in the gangway and pushed the boat out into the river with long poles. Then the captain maneuvered his craft out into the current and moved back down river. There was no exchange of farewells.

"Are you going to be all right?" Sparhawk asked Sephrenia. Her face was still drawn, although the dark circles under her eyes had begun to fade.

"I'll be fine, Sparhawk," she assured him.

"If we lose too many more of those knights, though, you won't be, will you?"

"I don't really know," she replied. "I've never been in this exact position before. Let's go on to Dabour and talk with Doctor Tanjin."

They rode up off the beach through the scrubby bushes that bordered it and soon reached the dusty road that led to Dabour. There were other travellers on that road, black-robed nomads for the most part, with their dark eyes afire with religious fervor. Once they were forced to the side of the road by a herd of sheep. The herders, mounted on mules, rode arrogantly and deliberately blocked the road as much as possible with their animals. Their expressions clearly dared anyone to object.

"I never liked sheep very much," Kurik muttered, "and I like sheepherders even less."

"Don't let it show," Sparhawk advised him.

"They eat a lot of mutton down here, don't they?"

Sparhawk nodded.

"Isn't it sort of inconsistent to butcher and eat a sacred animal?"

"Consistency is not one of the more notable characteristics of the Rendorish mind."

As the sheep passed, Flute raised her pipes and played a peculiarly discordant little melody. The sheep suddenly grew wild-eyed, milled for a moment, then stampeded across the desert with the sheepherders in frantic pursuit. Flute covered her mouth with a soundless giggle.

"Stop that," Sephrenia chided.

"Did what I think happened just happen?" Kurik said in amazement.

"I wouldn't be at all surprised," Sparhawk said.

"I really like that little girl, you know?" Kurik was grinning broadly.

They rode on at the tail end of a crowd of pilgrims. After a time they crested a low hill and saw the city of Dabour spread out below them. There were the usual white-plastered houses clustered near the river, but beyond them, stretching in all directions, were hundreds of large black tents. Sparhawk shaded his eyes with one hand and scanned the city. "The cattle pens are over there," he said, pointing to the eastern edge of town. "We should be able to find Perraine there somewhere."

They angled down the hill, avoiding the buildings and tents in the southern section of Dabour. As they began to ride through a cluster of tents pitched between them and the pens, a bearded nomad with a brass pendant set with a bit of glass hanging on a chain about his neck stepped out from behind a tent to bar their path. "Where do you think you're going?" he demanded. He made a quick, imperious gesture with one hand, and a dozen other black-robed men came out into the open with long pikes in their hands.

"We have business at the cattle pens, noble sir," Sparhawk replied mildly.

"Oh, really?" the bearded man sneered. "I see no cows." He looked around at his followers with a self-congratulatory smirk as if terribly pleased with his own cleverness.

"The cows are coming, noble sir," Sparhawk told him. "We were sent on ahead to make arrangements."

The man with the pendant knit his brows, trying hard to find something wrong with that. "Do you know who I am?" he demanded finally in a pugnacious tone of voice.

"I'm afraid not, noble sir," Sparhawk apologized. "I haven't had the pleasure of making your acquaintance."

"You think you're very clever, don't you?" the officious fellow demanded. "All these soft answers don't deceive me in the least."

"I wasn't trying to be deceptive, neighbor," Sparhawk said with a slight edge coming into his voice, "merely polite."

"I am Ulesim, favored disciple of holy Arasham," the bearded man said, striking his chest with his fist.

"I'm overwhelmed by the honor of meeting you," Sparhawk said, bowing in his saddle.

"That's all you have to say?" Ulesim exclaimed, his eyes bulging at the imagined insult.

"As I said, Lord Ulesim, I'm overwhelmed. I hadn't expected to be greeted by so illustrious a man."

"I'm not here to greet you, cowherd. I'm here to take you into custody. Get down off your horses."

Sparhawk gave him a long look, assessing the situation. Then he swung down from Faran's back and helped Sephrenia to dismount.

"What's this all about, Sparhawk?" she whispered as she lifted Flute down.

"I'd guess that he's a minor bootlicker trying to assert his own importance," Sparhawk whispered back. "We don't want to stir anything up, so let's do as he says."

"Take the prisoners to my tent," Ulesim commanded grandly after a moment's hesitation. The favored disciple didn't seem to know exactly what to do.

The pikemen stepped forward threateningly, and one of them led the way toward a tent surmounted by a dropping pennon made of dirty green cloth.

They were roughly shoved into the tent, and the flap was tied down.

Kurik's expression was filled with contempt. "Amateurs," he muttered. "They hold those pikes like shepherd's crooks and they didn't even search us for weapons."

"They may be amateurs, Kurik," Sephrenia said softly, "but they've managed to take us prisoner."

"Not for long," Kurik growled, reaching under his robe for his dagger. "I'll cut a hole in the back of the tent, and we can be on our way."

"No," Sparhawk said quietly. "We'd have a horde of howling fanatics on our heels in about two minutes if we did that."

"We're not just going to sit here?" Kurik asked incredulously.

"Let me handle it, Kurik."

They sat waiting in the stifling tent as the minutes dragged by.

After a bit, the tent flap opened and Ulesim entered with two of his men close behind him. "I will have your name from you, cowherd," he said arrogantly.

"I am called Mahkra, Lord Ulesim," Sparhawk replied meekly, "and this is my sister, her daughter, and my servant. May I ask why we have been detained?"

Ulesim's eyes narrowed. "There are those who refuse to accept holy Arasham's authority," he declared. "I, Ulesim, his most favored disciple, have taken it upon myself to root out these false prophets and send them to the stake. Holy Arasham relies upon me completely."

"Is that still going on?" Sparhawk asked in mild surprise. "I thought that all op-position to Arasham had been stamped out decades ago."

"Not so! Not so!" Ulesim half shrieked. "There are still plotters and conspira-tors hiding in the desert and lurking in the cities. I will not rest until I have un-earthed every one of these criminals and consigned them to the flames."

"You have nothing to fear from me or my band, Lord Ulesim," Sparhawk as-sured him. "We revere the holy prophet of God and pay him homage in our prayers."

"So you say, Mahkra, but can you prove your identity and satisfy me that you have legitimate business in the holy city?" The fanatic smirked at his two cohorts as if he had just scored a tremendous point.

"Why yes, Lord Ulesim," Sparhawk replied calmly, "I believe I can. We are here to speak with a cattle buyer named Mirrelek. Do you perhaps know him?"

Ulesim puffed himself up. "What would I, the favored disciple of holy Arasham, have to do with some common cattle buyer?"

One of the disciple's toadies leaned forward and whispered at some length in Ulesim's ear. The disciple's expression grew less and less certain and finally even a bit frightened. "I will send for this cattle buyer you mentioned," he declared grudg-ingly. "If he confirms your story, well and good; but if not, I will take you to holy Arasham himself for judgment."

"As the Lord Ulesim wishes," Sparhawk bowed. "If you would have your mes-senger tell Mirrelek that Mahkra is here with greetings from his little mother, I'm sure he'll come here immediately and clear up this whole matter."

"You'd better hope so, Mahkra," the bearded disciple said threateningly. He turned to the toady who had whispered in his ear. "Go fetch this Mirrelek. Repeat the message of this cowherd to him and tell him that I, Ulesim, favored disciple of holy Arasham, command his presence immediately."

"At once, favored one," the fellow replied and scurried from the tent. Ulesim glowered at Sparhawk for a moment, then he and his other sycophant left the tent.

"You've still got your sword, Sparhawk," Kurik said. "Why didn't you just let the air out of that windbag? I could have dealt with the other two."

"It wasn't necessary." Sparhawk shrugged. "I know Perraine well enough to know that by now he's managed to make himself indispensable to Arasham. He'll be here shortly and put Ulesim-favored-disciple-of-holy-Arasham in his place."

"Aren't you gambling, Sparhawk?" Sephrenia asked. "What if Perraine doesn't recognize the name Mahkra? As I recall, you were in Jiroch, and he's been here in Dabour for years."

"He may not recognize the name I go by here in Rendor," Sparhawk replied, "but he can't fail to recognize yours, little mother. It's a very old password. The Pandions have been using it for years."

She blinked. "I'm very flattered," she said, "but why didn't someone tell me?"

Sparhawk turned to her in some surprise. "We all thought you knew."

It was perhaps a quarter of an hour later when Ulesim escorted a lean, saturnine man in a striped robe into the tent. Ulesim's manner was obsequious and his expression worried. "This is the fellow I was telling you about, honored Mirrelek," he fawned.

"Ah, Mahkra," the lean man said, coming forward to take Sparhawk's hand warmly in his own. "So good to see you again. What seems to be the trouble here?"

"A slight misunderstanding is all, Mirrelek," Sparhawk replied, bowing slightly to his fellow Pandion.

"Well, that's all straightened out now." Sir Perraine turned to the favored disciple. "Isn't it, Ulesim?"

"O—of course, honored Mirrelek," Ulesim faltered, his face visibly pale now.

"Whatever possessed you to detain my friends?" Perraine's tone was mild, but there was a slight edge to it.

"I—I'm only trying to protect holy Arasham."

"Oh? And did he ask for your protection?"

"Well—not in so many words."

"I see. That was very brave of you, Ulesim. Surely you know how holy Arasham feels about those who act independently of his instructions? Many have lost their heads for taking too much upon themselves."

Ulesim began to tremble violently.

"I'm sure he'll forgive you when I tell him of the incident, however. A lesser man would be sent to the block immediately, but after all, you're his favorite disciple, aren't you? Was there anything else, Ulesim?"

Mutely, his face pasty white, Ulesim shook his head.

"My friends and I will be going, then. Coming, Mahkra?" Sir Perraine led them from the tent.

As they rode through the city of tents that had grown up on the outskirts of Dabour, Perraine talked at length about how depressed the cattle market currently was. The tents they passed had apparently been pitched at random, and there was nothing resembling a street. Hordes of dirty children ran and played in the sand, and dispirited-looking dogs rose from the shady side of each tent they passed to bark indifferently a few times before returning to flop down out of the sun again.

Perraine's house was a square, blocklike structure that stood in the center of a patch of weedy ground just beyond the tents. "Come inside," the knight told them loudly as they reached the door. "I want to hear more about this cattle herd of yours."

They went in, and he closed the door. It was dim and cool inside. The house had but a single room. There were rudimentary cooking facilities on one side and an unmade bed on the other. A number of large, porous jugs hung from the rafters, each seeping moisture which dripped into puddles on the floor. A table and two benches sat in the middle of the room. "It's none too ornate," Perraine apologized.

Sparhawk looked meaningfully at the lone window at the back of the house, a window that seemed only loosely shuttered. "Is it safe to talk?" he asked in a low voice.

Perraine laughed. "Oh, yes, Sparhawk," he replied. "In my spare time I've been nurturing a thorn bush outside that window. You'd be amazed at how much it's grown and how long the thorns are. You're looking well, my friend. I haven't seen you since we were novices." Perraine spoke with the faintest trace of an accent. Unlike most Pandions, he was not an Elenian, but came instead from somewhere in the vast reaches of central Eosia. Sparhawk had always liked him.

"You seem to have learned how to talk, Perraine," Sephrenia said. "You were always so silent before."

He smiled. "It was my accent, little mother," he said. "I didn't want people making fun of me." He took her wrists and kissed her palms in greeting and asked her blessing.

"You remember Kurik?" Sparhawk said.

"Of course," Perraine replied. "He trained me with the lance. Hello, Kurik. How's Aslade?"

"Very well, Sir Perraine," Kurik said. "I'll tell her you asked. What was that business back there all about—with Ulesim, I mean?"

"He's one of the officious toads who've attached themselves to Arasham."

"Is he really a disciple?"

Perraine snorted. "I doubt that Arasham even knows his name," he said. "Of course there are days when Arasham doesn't even know his own. There are dozens like Ulesim—self-appointed disciples who go around bothering honest people. He's probably five miles out into the desert by now and riding very hard to get away. Arasham is very firm with people who overstep what little authority he gives them. Why don't we all sit down?"

"How did you manage to accumulate so much power, Perraine?" Sephrenia asked him. "Ulesim behaved as if you were some kind of king."

"It wasn't really too hard," he replied. "Arasham has only two teeth in his head—and they don't meet. I give him a tender, milk-fed veal every other week as a token of my unspeakable regard for him. Old men are very interested in their bellies, so Arasham is profuse in his thanks. The disciples aren't blind, so they defer to me because of Arasham's supposed favor. Now, what brings you to Dabour?"

"Voren suggested that we look you up," Sparhawk said. "We need to talk with someone here and we didn't want to attract too much attention."

"My house is yours," Perraine said ironically, "such as it is. Who is it you need to talk with?"

"A physician named Tanjin," Sephrenia told him, removing her veil.

Perraine looked at her rather closely. "You *are* looking a bit unwell, Sephrenia," he said, "but couldn't you find a physician in Jiroch?"

She smiled briefly. "It's not for me, Perraine," she told him. "It has to do with someone else. Do you know this Tanjin?"

"Everybody in Dabour knows him. He keeps quarters in the back of an apothecary shop in the central square. His house is being watched, though. There are rumors going about that he dabbles in magic sometimes, and the zealots have been trying to catch him at it."

"It might be better to walk to the square, wouldn't you say?" Sparhawk asked. Perraine nodded.

"And I think we'll wait until just before the sun goes down. That way we'll have some darkness when we come out—just in case we need it."

"You want me to go with you?"

"It might be better if Sephrenia and I went alone," Sparhawk replied. "You have to stay here, and we don't. If Tanjin's under suspicion, visiting him could jeopardize your position here in Dabour."

"Stay out of alleys, Sparhawk," Kurik growled.

Sparhawk motioned to Flute, and she came to him obediently. He put his hands on her shoulders and looked directly into her face. "I want you to stay here with Kurik," he told her.

She looked at him gravely, then impudently crossed her eyes at him.

"Stop that," he said. "Listen to me, young lady, I'm serious."

"Just ask her, Sparhawk," Sephrenia advised. "Don't try to order her around."

"Please, Flute," he implored. "Will you *please* stay here?"

She smiled sweetly, put her hands together in front of her, and curtsied.

"You see how easy it is?" Sephrenia said.

"Since we've got some time, I'll fix you all something to eat," Perraine said, rising to his feet.

"Did you know that all your bottles are leaking, Sir Perraine?" Kurik said, pointing at the dripping vessels hanging from the rafters.

"Yes," Perraine replied. "They make a mess on the floor, but they help to keep it cool in here." He went to the hearth and fumbled for a few moments with flint, steel, and tinder. He built up a very small fire of twigs and twisted chunks of the branches of desert shrubs. Then he set a kettle on the fire, took a large pan, and poured oil in it. He set the pan on the coals and took several chunks of meat out of a covered bowl. As the oil began to smoke, he dropped the meat into the pan. "I'm afraid it's only mutton," he apologized. "I wasn't expecting company." He spiced the sizzling meat liberally to disguise its flavor, then brought heavy plates to the table. He went back to the fire and opened an earthenware jar. He took a pinch of tea from the jar, dropped it into a mug, and poured hot water from the kettle into the mug. "For you, little mother," he said, delivering the mug to her with a flourish.

"How very nice," she said. "You're such a dear, Perraine."

"I live but to serve," he said a bit grandiosely. He brought fresh figs and a slab of cheese to the table, then set the smoking pan in the center of it.

"You've missed your calling, my friend," Sparhawk said.

"I learned to cook for myself a long time ago. I could afford a servant, but I don't trust strangers." He sat down. "Be careful out there, Sparhawk," he cautioned as they began to eat. "Arasham's followers are a bit limp between the ears and they're all obsessed with the idea of catching some neighbor committing a minor transgression. Arasham preaches every evening, after the sun goes down, and he manages to come up with some new prohibition every night."

"What's the latest one?" Sparhawk asked.

"Killing flies. He says that they're the messengers of God."

"You're not serious."

Perraine shrugged. "I think he's running out of things to forbid, and his imagination is severely limited. You want some more of this mutton?"

"Thanks all the same, Perraine," Sparhawk said, taking a fig instead, "but one chunk of mutton is my limit."

"One chunk a day?"

"No. One a year."

■ | CHAPTER TWENTY-TWO | ■

The sun was turning the western sky a rusty color when Sparhawk and Sephrenia entered the square near the center of Dabour, and the light reflecting from the late-afternoon sky bathed the walls of the buildings and the faces of the people in the square with a ruddy glow. Sephrenia had her left arm bound up in a makeshift sling, and Sparhawk held her other elbow solicitously as they walked.

"It's right over there," he said quietly, nodding his head toward the far side.

Sephrenia drew her veil a bit tighter across her nose and mouth, and they moved through the crowd milling around in the middle of the square.

Here and there along the walls of the buildings leaned hooded nomads in black robes, their eyes alert and filled with suspicion as they peered at every face that passed.

"True believers," Sparhawk muttered sardonically, "ever alert for the sins of their neighbors."

"It's always been that way, Sparhawk," she replied. "Self-righteousness is one of the most common—and least attractive—characteristics of man." They passed one of the watchers and entered the smelly shop.

The apothecary was a chubby little man with an apprehensive expression on his face. "I don't know if he'll consent to see you," he said when they asked to speak with Doctor Tanjin. "He's being watched, you know."

"Yes," Sparhawk said. "We saw several of the watchers outside. Please advise him that we're here. My sister's arm needs attention."

The nervous apothecary scurried through a curtained doorway at the back of the shop. A moment later, he came back. "I'm sorry," he apologized. "He said he's not taking any new patients."

Sparhawk raised his voice. "How can a healer refuse to see an injured person? Does the oath they take mean so little to them here in Dabour? In Cippria, the physicians are more honorable. My good friend, Doctor Voldi, would never refuse his aid to the sick or hurt."

It hung there for a moment, and then the curtains parted. The man who thrust his head out between them had a very large nose, a pendulous lower lip, jutting ears, and weak, watery eyes. He wore the white smock of a physician. "Did you say Voldi?" he asked in a high-pitched, nasal voice. "Do you know him?"

"Of course," Sparhawk replied. "He's a small man who's going bald, and he dyes his hair. He has a very large opinion of himself."

"That's Voldi, all right. Bring your sister back here—and be quick. Don't let anybody outside the shop see you."

Sparhawk took Sephrenia's elbow and escorted her back through the curtains.

"Did anyone see you come in?" the big-nosed man asked nervously.

"Any number of them, I'd imagine." Sparhawk shrugged. "They line the walls of the square like a flock of vultures, trying to sniff out sin."

"It's not safe to talk that way in Dabour, my friend," Tanjin warned.

"Perhaps." Sparhawk looked around. The room was shabby and was piled high in the corners with open wooden boxes and stacks of books. A persistent bumble-bee batted its head against the single dirty window, trying to get out. There was a low couch against one wall and several straight-backed wooden chairs and a table in the center. "Shall we get down to business, Doctor Tanjin?" he suggested.

"All right," the physician said to Sephrenia, "sit here, and I'll have a look at that arm."

"You may if it's going to make you happy, Doctor," she replied, taking the chair and removing her arm from the sling. She pulled back the sleeve of her robe to reveal a surprisingly girlish arm.

The doctor looked a bit hesitantly at Sparhawk. "You understand, of course, that I'm not being forward with your sister's person, but I must examine her."

"I understand the procedure, Doctor."

Tanjin took a deep breath and then bent Sephrenia's wrist back and forth several times. Then he gently ran his fingers up her forearm and bent her elbow. He swallowed hard and probed at her upper arm. Then he moved her arm up and down with his fingers lightly touching her shoulder. His close-set eyes narrowed. "There's nothing wrong with this arm," he accused.

"How kind you are to say so," she murmured, removing her veil.

"Madame!" he said in a shocked voice. "Cover yourself!"

"Oh, do be serious, Doctor," she told him. "We're not here to talk about arms and legs."

"You're spies!" he gasped.

"In a manner of speaking, yes," she replied calmly. "But even spies have reason to consult with physicians once in a while."

"Leave at once," he ordered.

"We just got here," Sparhawk said, pushing back his hood. "Go ahead, sister dear," he said to Sephrenia. "Tell him why we're here."

"Tell me, Tanjin," she said, "does the word 'darestim' mean anything to you?"

He started guiltily and looked at the curtained doorway, backing away from her.

"Don't be modest, Doctor," Sparhawk told him. "Word's been going about that you cured the king's brother and several of his nephews after they'd been poisoned with darestim."

"There's no proof of that."

"I don't need proof. I need a cure. A friend of ours has the same condition."

"There's no antidote or cure for darestim."

"Then how is it that the king's brother still lives?"

"You're working with them," the doctor accused, pointing vaguely out toward the square. "You're trying to trick me into a confession."

"Them who?" Sparhawk asked.

"The fanatics who follow Arasham. They're trying to prove that I use witchcraft in my practice."

"Do you?"

The doctor shrank back. "Please leave," he begged. "You're putting my life in terrible danger."

"As you've probably noticed, Doctor," Sephrenia said, "we are not Rendorish. We do not share the prejudices of your countrymen, so magic does not offend us. It's quite routine in the place we come from."

He blinked at her uncertainly.

"This friend of ours—the one I mentioned before—is very dear to us," Sparhawk told him, "and we'll go to any lengths to find a cure for this poison." To emphasize his point, he opened his robe. "Any lengths at all."

The doctor gaped at his mail coat and sheathed sword.

"There's no need to threaten the doctor, brother dear," Sephrenia said. "I'm sure he'll be more than happy to describe the cure he's found. He *is* a healer, after all."

"Madame, I don't know what you're talking about," Tanjin said desperately. "There is no cure for darestim. I don't know where you heard all these rumors, but I can assure you that they're absolutely false. I do *not* use witchcraft in my practice." He threw another quick, nervous glance at the curtained doorway.

"But Doctor Voldi in Cippria told us that you *did,* in fact, cure members of the king's family."

"Well—yes, I suppose I did, but the poison wasn't darestim."

"What was it, then?"

"Un—porgutta—I think." He was obviously lying.

"Then why was it that the king sent for you, Doctor?" she pressed. "A simple purge will cleanse the body of porgutta. Any apprentice physician knows that. Surely it couldn't have been so mild a poison."

"Un—well, maybe it was something else. I forget, exactly."

"I think, dear brother," Sephrenia said then to Sparhawk, "that the good doctor needs some reassurance—some positive proof that he can trust us and that we are what we say we are." She looked at the irritating bumblebee still stubbornly trying to break its way out through the window. "Have you ever wondered why you never see a bumblebee at night, Doctor?" she asked the frightened physician.

"I've never given it any thought."

"Perhaps you should." She began to murmur in Styric as her fingers wove the designs of the spell.

"What are you doing?" Tanjin exclaimed. "Stop that!" He started to move toward her with one hand outstretched, but Sparhawk stopped him.

"Don't interfere," the big knight said.

Then Sephrenia pointed her finger and released the spell.

The buzzing sound of insect wings was suddenly joined by a tiny, piping voice that sang joyously in a tongue unknown to man. Sparhawk looked quickly at the dust-clouded window. The bumblebee was gone, and in its place there hovered a tiny female figure directly out of folklore. Her pale hair cascaded down her back between her rapidly beating gossamer wings. Her little nude body was perfectly formed, and her minuscule face was so lovely as to stop the breath.

"That is how bumblebees think of themselves," Sephrenia said quite calmly, "and perhaps that is what they truly are—by day a common insect, but by night a creature of wonder."

Tanjin had fallen back on his shabby couch with his eyes wide and his mouth agape.

"Come here, little sister," Sephrenia crooned to the fairy, extending one hand.

The fairy swooped about the room, her transparent wings buzzing and her tiny voice soaring. Then she delicately settled on Sephrenia's outstretched palm with her wings still fanning at the air. Sephrenia turned and stretched her hand out to the shaking physician. "Isn't she beautiful?" she asked. "You may hold her if you like— but be wary of her sting." She pointed at the tiny rapier in the fairy's hand.

Tanjin shrank away with his hands behind his back. "How did you do that?" he asked in a trembling voice.

"Do you mean that you can't? The charges against you *must* be false, then. This is a very simple spell—quite rudimentary, actually."

"As you can see, Doctor," Sparhawk said, "we have no qualms about magic. You can speak freely to us with no fear of being denounced to Arasham or his fanatic followers."

Tanjin tightly clamped his lips shut, continuing to stare at the fairy seated sedately on Sephrenia's palm with fluttering wings.

"Don't be tiresome, Doctor," Sephrenia said. "Just tell us how you cured the king's brother, and we'll be on our way."

Tanjin began to edge away from her.

"I think, dear brother, that we're wasting our time here," she said to Sparhawk. "The good doctor refuses to cooperate." She raised her hand. "Fly, little sister," she told the fairy, and the tiny creature soared once again into the air. "We'll be going now, Tanjin," she said.

Sparhawk started to object, but she laid one restraining hand on his arm and started toward the door.

"What are you going to do about that?" Tanjin cried, pointing at the circling fairy.

"Do?" Sephrenia said. "Why nothing, Doctor. She's quite happy here. Feed her sugar from time to time, and put out a small dish of water for her. In return, she'll sing for you. Don't try to catch her, though. That would make her very angry."

"You can't leave her here!" he exclaimed in anguish. "If anyone sees her here, I'll be burned at the stake for witchcraft."

"He sees directly to the central point, doesn't he?" Sephrenia said to Sparhawk.

"The scientific mind is noted for that." Sparhawk grinned. "Shall we go, then?"

"Wait!" Tanjin cried.

"Was there something you wanted to tell us, Doctor?" Sephrenia asked mildly.

"All right. All right. But you must swear to keep it a secret that I told you this."

"Of course. Our lips are sealed."

Tanjin drew in a deep breath and scurried to the curtained doorway to make certain that no one was listening outside. Then he turned and motioned them into a far corner where he spoke in a hoarse whisper. "Darestim is so virulent that there's no natural remedy or antidote," he began.

"That's what Voldi told us," Sparhawk said.

"You'll note that I said no *natural* remedy or antidote," Tanjin continued. "Some years ago in the course of my studies, I came across a very old and curious book. It predated Eshand's time and it had been written before his prohibitions came into effect. It seems that the primitive healers here in Rendor routinely utilized magic in treating their patients. Sometimes it worked, sometimes it didn't— but they effected some astonishing cures. The practice had one common element. There are a number of objects in the world which have enormous power. The physicians of antiquity used that sort of thing to cure their patients."

"I see," Sephrenia said. "Styric healers sometimes resort to the same desperate measure."

"The practice is quite common in the Tamul Empire on the Daresian continent," Tanjin went on, "but it's fallen into disfavor here in Eosia. Eosian physicians prefer scientific techniques. They're more reliable, for one thing, and Elenes have always been suspicious of magic. But darestim is so potent that none of the customary antidotes have any effect. Magical objects are the only possible cure."

"And what did you use to cure the king's brother and nephews?" Sephrenia asked.

"It was an uncut gem of a peculiar color. I think it originally came from Daresia, though I can't really be sure. It's my belief that the Tamul Gods infused it with their power."

"And where is that gem now?" Sparhawk asked intently.

"Gone, I'm afraid. I had to grind it to a powder and mix it with wine to cure the king's relatives."

"You idiot!" Sephrenia exploded. "That is *not* the way to use such an object. You need only touch it to the patient's body and call forth its power."

"I'm a trained physician, madame," he replied stiffly. "I cannot turn insects into fairies, nor levitate myself, nor cast spells upon my enemies. I can only follow the normal practices of my profession, and that means that the patient must ingest the medication."

"You destroyed a stone that might have healed thousands for the sake of just a few!" With some effort she controlled her anger. "Do you know of any other such objects?" she asked him.

"A few." He shrugged. "There's a great spear in the imperial palace in Tamul, several rings in Zemoch, though I doubt that they'd be much good in healing people. It's rumored that there's a jeweled bracelet in Pelosia somewhere, but that might be only a myth. The sword of the king of the island of Mithrium was reputed to have great power, but Mithrium sank into the sea eons ago. I've also heard that the Styrics have quite a few magic wands."

"That's also a myth," she told him. "Wood is too fragile for that kind of power. Any others?"

"The only one I know of is the jewel on the royal crown of Thalesia, but that's been lost since the time of the Zemoch invasion." He frowned. "I don't think this will help very much," he added, "but Arasham has a talisman that he claims is the most holy and powerful thing in all the world. I've never seen it myself, so I can't say for sure, and Arasham's wits aren't so firmly set in his head that he'd be any kind of an authority. You'd never be able to get it away from him in any case."

Sephrenia reattached her veil across the lower part of her face. "Thank you for your candor, Doctor Tanjin," she said. "Be assured that no one will learn of your secret from us." She thought a moment. "I think you should splint this," she said, holding out her arm. "That should prove to the curious that we had a legitimate reason for this visit, and it should protect you as well as us."

"That's a very good idea, madame." Tanjin fetched a couple of slats and a long strip of white cloth.

"Would you take a bit of friendly advice, Tanjin?" Sparhawk asked him as he began to splint Sephrenia's arm.

"I'll listen."

"Do that. If it were me, I'd gather up a few things and go to Zand. The king can protect you there. Get out of Dabour while you still can. Fanatics make the jump from suspicion to certainty very easily, and it won't do you much good if you're proved innocent *after* you've been burned at the stake."

"But everything I own is here."

"I'm sure that'll be a great comfort to you when your toes are on fire."

"Do you really think I'm in that much danger?" Tanjin asked in a weak voice, looking up from his task.

Sparhawk nodded. "That much and more. I'd estimate that you'll be lucky to live out the week if you stay here in Dabour."

The doctor began to tremble violently as Sephrenia slipped her splinted arm back into the sling. "Wait a minute," he said as they started toward the door. "What about that?" He pointed at the fairy swooping through the air near the window.

"Oh," Sephrenia said. "Sorry. I almost forgot about her." She mumbled a few words and made a vague gesture.

The bumblebee went back to batting its head against the window.

It was dark when they emerged from the apothecary's shop into the nearly deserted square.

"It's not very much," Sparhawk said dubiously.

"It's more than we had before. At least we know how to cure Ehlana. All we need to do now is to find one of these objects."

"Would you be able to tell if Arasham's talisman has any real power?"

"I think so."

"Good. Perraine says that Arasham preaches every night. Let's go find him. I'll listen to a dozen sermons if it puts me close to a cure."

"How do you propose to get it away from him?"

"I'll think of something."

A black-robed man suddenly blocked their path. "Stop right there," he commanded.

"What's your problem, neighbor?" Sparhawk asked him.

"Why are you not at the feet of holy Arasham?" the robed man asked accusingly.

"We were just on our way," Sparhawk replied.

"All Dabour knows that holy Arasham speaks to the multitudes at sundown. Why are you deliberately absenting yourselves?"

"We arrived only today," Sparhawk explained, "and I had to seek medical attention for my sister's injured arm."

The fanatic scowled suspiciously at Sephrenia's sling. "Surely you did not consult with the wizard Tanjin?" he said in an outraged tone.

"When one is in pain, one does not ask to see the healer's credentials," Sephrenia told him. "I can assure you, however, that the doctor used no witchcraft. He set the broken bone and splinted it for me in the same way any other physician would have."

"The righteous do not consort with wizards," the zealot declared stubbornly.

"I'll tell you what, neighbor," Sparhawk said pleasantly. "Why don't I break *your* arm? Then you can visit the doctor yourself. If you watch him very closely, you should be able to tell if he's using witchcraft or not."

The fanatic stepped back apprehensively.

"Come now, friend," Sparhawk told him enthusiastically, "be brave. It won't hurt all that much, and think of how much holy Arasham will appreciate your zeal in rooting out the abomination of witchcraft."

"Could you tell us where we might find the place where holy Arasham speaks to the multitudes?" Sephrenia interposed. "Our souls hunger and thirst for his words."

"Over that way," the nervous man said, pointing. "You can see the light from the torches."

"Thanks, friend," Sparhawk said, bowing slightly. He frowned. "How is it that you yourself are not at the services this evening?"

"I—uh—I have a sterner duty," the fellow declared. "I must seek out those who are absent without cause and deliver them up for judgment."

"Ah," Sparhawk said, "I see." He turned away, then turned back. "Are you sure you wouldn't like to have me break your arm for you? It won't take but a minute."

The fanatic hurried away from them.

"Must you threaten everyone you meet, Sparhawk?" Sephrenia asked.

"He irritated me."

"You irritate very easily, don't you?"

He considered it. "Yes," he admitted, "I suppose I do. Shall we go?"

They went through the dark streets of Dabour until they reached the tents pitched on the outskirts. Some distance toward the south a ruddy glow pulsed up toward the glittering stars. They moved quietly past the tents toward the light.

The flickering torches were set on tall poles surrounding a kind of natural amphitheater on the southern edge of town, a sort of depression between two hills. The hollow was filled with Arasham's followers, and the deranged holy man himself stood atop a large boulder halfway up the side of one of the hills. He was tall and gaunt with a long gray beard and bushy black eyebrows. His voice was strident as he harangued his followers, but his words were difficult to understand because of his lack of teeth. When Sparhawk and Sephrenia joined the crowd, the old man was in the middle of an extended and highly involuted proof of God's special favor—which had, he declared, been bestowed upon him in a dream. There were huge logical gaps in his argument and great leaps of what passed for faith here in Rendor.

"Is he making any sense at all?" Sephrenia whispered to Sparhawk in a puzzled tone as she removed the splints and the sling.

"Not that I can detect," he whispered back.

"I didn't think so. Does the Elene God actually encourage that sort of hysterical gibberish?"

"He never has to me."

"Can we get any closer?"

"I don't think so. The crowd's pretty thick in front of where he's standing."

Arasham then turned to one of his favorite topics, a denunciation of the Church. The organized Elene religion, he maintained, was cursed by God for its failure to recognize his exalted status as the chosen and beloved spokesman of the Most High.

"But the wicked shall be punished!" he lisped in a toothless shriek with spittle flying from his lips. "My followers are invincible! Be patient for but a little more time, and I will raise my holy talisman and lead you into war against them! They will send their accursed Church Knights to do war upon us, but fear them not! The power of this holy relic will sweep them before us like chaff before the wind!" He held something high over his head in his tightly clenched fist. "The spirit of the blessed Eshand himself has confirmed this to me!"

"Well?" Sparhawk whispered to Sephrenia.

"He's too far away," she murmured. "I can't feel anything one way or the other. We're going to have to get closer. I can't even tell what he's holding."

Arasham's voice sank into a harshly conspiratorial tone. "I tell you this, O ye faithful, and my words are true. The voice of God has revealed to me that even now our movement is spreading through the fields and forests of the kingdoms of the north. The ordinary people there—our brothers and sisters—grow weary of the yoke of the Church and they will join our holy cause."

"It was Martel who told him that," Sparhawk muttered, "and if he thinks that Martel is the voice of God, then he's even crazier than I thought." He rose up on his tiptoes and looked over the heads of the crowd. A large pavilion stood some distance down the hill from where Arasham was preaching. It was surrounded by a palisade of stout poles. "Let's work our way around this crowd," he suggested. "I think I've located the old man's tent."

Slowly they moved back until they were at the edge of the crowd. Arasham continued his rambling harangue, but his slurred words were lost in the distance and the murmuring of his followers. Sparhawk and Sephrenia slipped around the crowd toward the palisade and the dark pavilion inside it. When they were perhaps twenty paces away, Sparhawk touched Sephrenia's arm, and they stopped. A number of armed men stood before the opening at the front of the palisade. "We'll have to wait until he finishes preaching," Sparhawk murmured.

"Would you like to tell me what you have in mind?" she said. "I hate surprises."

"I'm going to see if I can get us into his tent. If that talisman of his really has any power, it might be difficult to get it away from him in the middle of this crowd."

"How do you propose to manage that, Sparhawk?"

"I thought I'd try flattery."

"Isn't that a bit dangerous—and very obvious?"

"Of course it's obvious, but you have to be obvious when you're dealing with deranged people. They don't have the concentration to grasp subtlety."

Arasham's voice was rising to a shrill climax, and his followers cheered at the end of each of his mumbled pronouncements. Then he delivered his benediction, and the crowd began to break up. Surrounded by a knot of jealous disciples, the holy man began to walk slowly through the milling throng toward his tent. Sparhawk and Sephrenia moved to place themselves in his path.

"Stand aside!" one of the disciples commanded harshly.

"Forgive me, exalted disciple," Sparhawk said loudly enough for his words to carry to the tottering old man, "but I bear a message from the king of Deira for holy Arasham. His majesty sends greetings to the true head of the Elene Church."

Sephrenia made a slightly strangled noise.

"Holy Arasham takes no note of kings," the disciple sneered arrogantly. "Now stand aside."

"A moment there, Ikkad," Arasham mumbled in a surprisingly weak voice. "We would hear more of this message from our brother of Deira. It may well be that this is the communication mentioned by God when last He spoke with us."

"Most holy Arasham," Sparhawk said with a deep bow, "His majesty, King Obler of Deira, greets you as his brother. Our king is very old, and age always brings wisdom."

"Truly," Arasham agreed, stroking his own long, gray beard.

"His majesty has long contemplated the teachings of the blessed Eshand," Sparhawk continued, "and he has also eagerly followed your own career here in Rendor. He has regarded the activities of the Church with increasing disfavor. He has found churchmen to be hypocritical and self-serving."

"My very words," Arasham said ecstatically. "I have said so myself a hundred times and more."

"His majesty acknowledges that you are the source and wellspring of his thought, holy Arasham."

"Well," Arasham replied, preening himself slightly.

"His majesty believes that the time has come for a purification of the Elene Church and he further believes that you are the one who has been chosen by God to purge the Church of her sins."

"Did you hear my sermon tonight?" the old man asked eagerly. "I preached to that self-same topic."

"Truly," Sparhawk said. "I was amazed at how closely your words coincided with those of his majesty when he charged me with his message to you. Know, however, holy Arasham, that his majesty intends to provide more aid to you than the mere comfort of his greetings and his respectful affection. The details of his further intentions, though, must be for your ears alone." He looked around suspiciously at the crowd pressing in upon them. "In a gathering so large as this, there may be several who are not what they seem, and if what I have to tell you should reach Chyrellos, the Church would bend all her efforts to hinder his majesty's design."

Arasham tried without much success to look shrewd. "Your prudence becomes you, young man," he agreed. "Let us go into my pavilion so that you may more fully disclose the mind of my dear brother Obler to me."

Pushing aside the officious disciples, Sparhawk thrust his way through their ranks to offer the support of his arm and shoulder to the elderly zealot. "Holy one," he said in a fawning tone, "fear not to lean upon me, for as the blessed Eshand has commanded, it is the duty of the young and strong to serve the aged and wise."

"How truly you speak, my son."

They passed thus through the gate of the palisade and across a stretch of sand dotted with sheep droppings.

The interior of Arasham's pavilion was far more luxurious than might have been expected from its severe exterior. A single lamp burned expensive oil in the center, and priceless carpets covered the rude sand floor. Silken fabric curtained off the rearward portions of the pavilion, and from behind those curtains came the giggling of adolescent boys.

"Please sit and take your ease," Arasham invited expansively, sinking down upon a cluster of silken cushions. "Let us take some refreshment, and then you may tell me of the intent of my dear brother Obler of Deira." He clapped his hands sharply together, and a doe-eyed boy emerged from behind one of the silken panels.

"Bring us some of the fresh melon, Saboud," Arasham told him.

"As you command, Most Holy." The boy bowed and retired behind the silken screen.

Arasham leaned back on his cushions. "I am not at all surprised at the communication you have brought me concerning the growing sentiment for our cause in Deira," he lisped to Sparhawk. "Word has reached me that such feelings are not uncommon in the kingdoms of the north. Indeed, another such message has but recently arrived." He paused thoughtfully. "It occurs to me—perhaps at the prompting of God Himself, who ever joins His thought with mine—that you and the other messenger may know each other." He turned toward a silken panel that concealed a dimly lighted part of the tent. "Come forth, my friend and advisor. Look upon the face of our noble visitor from Deira and tell me if you know him."

A shadow moved behind the panel. It seemed to hesitate for a moment, and then a robed and hooded figure emerged into the lamplight. The hooded man was only slightly shorter than Sparhawk and he had the heavy shoulders of a warrior. He reached up and pushed back his hood to reveal his piercing black eyes and his thick mane of snowy white hair.

In a kind of curious detachment, Sparhawk wondered what it was exactly that kept him from instantly drawing his sword.

"Indeed, most holy Arasham," Martel said in his deep, resonant voice, "Sparhawk and I have known each other for a long time."

## CHAPTER TWENTY-THREE

"It's been a long time, hasn't it, Sparhawk?" Martel said in a neutral tone. His eyes, however, were watchful.

With some effort Sparhawk relaxed his tightly clenched muscles. "Yes, it has," he replied. "It must be ten years now at least. We should try to get together more often."

"We'll have to make a point of that."

It hung there. The two continued to look directly into each other's faces. The air seemed to crackle with tension as each waited for the other to make the first move.

"Sparhawk," Arasham mused, "a most unusual name. It seems to me that I've heard it somewhere before."

"It's a very old name," Sparhawk told him. "It's been passed down through my family for generations. Some of my ancestors were men of note."

"Perhaps that's where I heard it, then," Arasham mumbled complacently. "I'm delighted to have been able to reunite two old and dear friends."

"We are forever in your debt, Most Holy," Martel replied. "You cannot imagine how I've hungered for the sight of Sparhawk's face."

"No more than I hungered for the sight of yours," Sparhawk said. He turned to the ancient lunatic. "At one time Martel and I were almost as close as brothers, Most Holy. It's a shame that the years have kept us apart."

"I've tried to find you, Sparhawk," Martel said coolly, "several times."

"Yes, I heard about that. I always hurried back to the place where you'd been seen, but by the time I got there, you'd already left."

"Pressing business," Martel murmured.

"It is ever thus," Arasham lisped sententiously, his ruined mouth collapsing over the words. "The friends of our youth slip away from us, and we are left alone in our old age." His eyes dropped shut in melancholy reverie. He did not reopen them; after a moment he began to snore.

"He tires easily," Martel said quietly. He turned to Sephrenia, although still keeping a wary eye on Sparhawk. "Little mother," he greeted her in a tone between irony and regret.

"Martel." She inclined her head in the briefest of nods.

"Ah," he said. "It seems that I've disappointed you."

"Not so much as you've disappointed yourself, I think."

"Punishment, Sephrenia?" he asked sardonically. "Don't you think I've been punished enough already?"

"It's not in my nature to punish people, Martel. Nature gives neither rewards nor punishment—only consequences."

"All right, then. I accept the consequences. Will you at least permit me to greet you—and to seek your blessing?" He took her wrists and turned her palms up.

"No, Martel," she replied, closing her hands, "I don't think so. You're no longer my pupil. You've found another to follow."

"That wasn't entirely my idea, Sephrenia. You rejected me, you remember." He sighed and released her wrists. Then he looked back at Sparhawk. "I'm really rather surprised to see you, brother mine," he said, "considering all the times I've sent Adus to deal with you. I'll have to speak sharply with him about that—provided you haven't killed him, of course."

"He was bleeding a little the last time I saw him," Sparhawk said, "but not very seriously."

"Adus doesn't pay much attention to blood—not even his own."

"Would you like to step out of the way, Sephrenia?" Sparhawk said, opening the front of his robe and shifting his sword hilt around slightly. "Martel and I were having a little discussion the last time we saw each other. I think it's time we continued it."

Martel's eyes narrowed, and he opened his own robe. Like Sparhawk, he also wore mail and a broadsword. "Excellent notion, Sparhawk," he said, his deep voice dropping to little more than a whisper.

Sephrenia stepped between them. "Stop that, both of you," she commanded. "This isn't the time or the place. We're right in the middle of an army. If you play this game of yours here in Arasham's tent, you'll have half of Rendor in here with you before it's over."

Sparhawk felt a hot surge of disappointment, but he knew that she was right. Regretfully, he took his hand away from his sword hilt. "Sometime soon, however, Martel," he said in a dreadfully quiet voice.

"I'll be happy to oblige you, dear brother," Martel replied with an ironic bow. His eyes narrowed speculatively. "What are you two doing here in Rendor?" he asked. "I thought you were still in Cammoria."

"It's a business trip."

"Ah, you've found out about the darestim, I see. I hate to tell you this, but you're wasting your time. There's no antidote. I checked that very carefully before I recommended it to a certain friend in Cimmura."

"You're pressing your luck, Martel," Sparhawk told him ominously.

"I always have, brother mine. As they say, no risk, no profit. Ehlana will die, I'm afraid. Lycheas will succeed her, and Annias will become archprelate. I expect to reap quite a handsome profit from that."

"Is that all you ever think about?"

"What else is there?" Martel shrugged. "Everything else is only an illusion. How's Vanion been lately?"

"He's well," Sparhawk replied. "I'll tell him you asked."

"That's assuming that you live long enough to see him again. Your situation here is precarious, my old friend."

"So's yours, Martel."

"I know, but I'm used to it. You're weighted down with scruples and the like. I left all that behind a long time ago."

"Where's your tame Damork, Martel?" Sephrenia asked suddenly.

He looked only slightly surprised and he recovered instantly. "I really haven't the slightest idea, little mother," he replied. "It comes to me without being summoned, so I never know when it's going to turn up. Perhaps it returned to the place it came from. It has to do that every so often, you know."

"I've never been that curious about the creatures of the underworld."

"That could be a serious oversight."

"Perhaps."

Arasham stirred on his cushions and opened his eyes. "Did I doze off?" he asked.

"Only briefly, Most Holy," Martel said. "It gave Sparhawk and me time to renew our friendship. We had much to discuss."

"Very much," Sparhawk agreed. He hesitated slightly, but then decided that Martel was so sure of himself that he'd probably miss the significance of the question. "You mentioned a talisman during your sermon, holy one," he said to Arasham. "Might we be permitted to see it?"

"The holy relic? Of course." The old man fumbled inside his robe and drew out something that appeared to be a twisted lump of bone. He held it out proudly. "Do you know what this is, Sparhawk?" he asked.

"No, Most Holy. I'm afraid not."

"The blessed Eshand began life as a shepherd, you know."

"Yes, I'd heard so."

"One day when he was quite young, a ewe in his flock gave birth to a pure white lamb that was like none other he had ever seen. Unlike all other sheep of that breed, this infant ram bore horns upon its head. It was, of course, a sign from God. The pure lamb, obviously, symbolized the blessed Eshand himself, and the fact that the lamb was horned could only mean one thing—that Eshand had been chosen to chastise the Church for her iniquity."

"How mysterious are the ways of God," Sparhawk marveled.

"Truly, my son. Truly. Eshand cared for the ram most tenderly, and in time it began to speak to him, and its voice was the voice of God himself. And thus God instructed Eshand in that which he must do. This holy relic is a piece of the horn of that very ram. Now you can see why it has such enormous power."

"Clearly, Most Holy," Sparhawk said in a reverent tone of voice. "Come closer, little sister," he said to Sephrenia. "View this miraculous relic."

She stepped forward and looked intently at the twisted bit of horn in Arasham's hand. "Remarkable," she murmured. She glanced at Sparhawk, shaking her head almost imperceptibly.

The bitter taste of disappointment filled his mouth.

"The power of this talisman will overcome all the concerted might of the accursed Church Knights and their foul witchcraft," Arasham declared. "God Himself has told me so." He smiled almost shyly. "I have discovered a truly remarkable thing," he told them confidentially. "When I am alone, I can lift the holy relic to my ear and hear the voice of God. Thus He instructs me even as He instructed the blessed Eshand."

"A miracle!" Martel said in mock amazement.

"Is it not?" Arasham beamed.

"We are quite overcome with gratitude that you have consented to let us view the talisman, Most Holy," Sparhawk said, "and we will spread word of it throughout the kingdoms of the north, won't we, Martel?"

"Oh, of course, of course." Martel's face was slightly puzzled, and he was looking suspiciously at Sparhawk.

"I perceive now that our coming here is a part of God's design," Sparhawk continued. "It is our mission to tell all the kingdoms of the north of this miracle—through every village and at every crossroads. Even now I feel the spirit of God infusing my tongue with eloquence so that I might better describe what I have seen." He reached out and clapped Martel on the left shoulder—quite firmly. "Don't you feel it as well, dear brother?" he asked enthusiastically.

Martel winced slightly, and Sparhawk could feel the shoulder shrinking from under his hand. "Why, yes," Martel admitted in a slightly pained voice, "as a matter of fact, I believe I do."

"Wondrous is the might of God!" Arasham exulted.

"Yes," Martel said, rubbing at his shoulder, "wondrous."

The idea had been slow in coming, in part perhaps because of the surprise of once again seeing Martel, but now it all began to fall into place. Sparhawk was suddenly glad that Martel was here. "And now, Most Holy," he said, "let me give you the remainder of his majesty's message to you."

"Of course. My ears are open to you."

"His majesty commands me to implore you to give him time to marshal his forces before you move against the venal Church here in Rendor. He must move with caution in his mobilization because the Hierocracy in Chyrellos has spies everywhere. He wishes devoutly to aid you, but the Church is powerful, and he must mass sufficient force to overcome her might in Deira at one stroke, lest she recover and crush him. It is his thought that should you mount your campaign here in the south at the same time he mounts his in the north, the Church will be confounded, not knowing which way to turn, and by moving swiftly you may take advantage of her confusion and win victory after victory. The impact of these victories will dishearten and demoralize the forces of the Church, and you may both march triumphant upon Chyrellos."

"Praise God!" Arasham exclaimed, starting to his feet and brandishing his sheep's horn like a weapon.

Sparhawk raised one hand. "*But,*" he cautioned, "this grand design, which can only have come from God Himself, has no chance of success unless you and his majesty attack simultaneously."

"I can see that, of course. God's own voice has instructed me in just such strategy."

"I was sure that he had." Sparhawk let his face assume an expression of extreme cunning. "Now," he went on, "the Church is as sly as a serpent, and she has ears everywhere. Despite our best efforts to maintain secrecy, she may uncover our plan. Her first recourse has always been deceit."

"I have seen that in her," Arasham admitted.

"It may well be that once she has uncovered our plan, she will attempt deception, and what better way to deceive you than to send false messengers to you to declare that his majesty is in readiness when indeed he is not? Thus the Church could defeat you and your disciples one by one."

Arasham frowned. "That's true, isn't it?" he said. "But how may we avoid being deceived?"

Sparhawk pretended to think about it. Then he suddenly snapped his fingers. "I have it!" he exclaimed. "What better way to confound the deceitfulness of the Church than by the word—a word known only to you and to me and to King Obler of Deira? Thus may you know that a message is genuine. Should any come to you with the message that the time has come, but who cannot repeat the word to you, that man will be most surely a serpent of the Church sent to deceive you, and you should deal with him accordingly."

Arasham thought about it. "Why, yes," he mumbled finally. "I believe that might indeed confound the Church. But what word can be so locked in our hearts that none may seek it out?"

Sparhawk threw a covert glance at Martel, whose face was suddenly filled with chagrin. "It must be a word of power," he said, squinting at the roof of the tent as if deep in thought. The whole ploy was obvious—even childish—but it was the kind of thing that would appeal to the senile old Arasham, and it provided a marvelous opportunity to settle a few scores with Martel, just for old times' sake.

Sephrenia sighed and lifted her eyes in resignation. Sparhawk felt a little ashamed of himself at that point. He looked at Arasham, who was leaning forward in anticipation, chewing upon emptiness with his toothless mouth and setting his long beard to waggling.

"I will, of course, accept your pledge of secrecy without question, Most Holy," Sparhawk said in feigned humility. "I, however, swear by my life that the word I am about to give you in profoundest secrecy shall never again pass my lips until I divulge it to King Obler in Acie, the capital of his kingdom."

"And I also pledge my oath to you, noble friend Sparhawk," the old man cried in an excess of enthusiasm. "Torture will not drag the word from my lips." He made some attempt to draw himself up regally.

"Your pledge honors me, Most Holy," Sparhawk replied with a deep Rendorish bow. He approached the old man, bent, and whispered, "Ramshorn." Arasham, he noted, didn't smell very good.

"The perfect word!" Arasham cried. He seized Sparhawk's head in a pair of wiry arms and kissed him soundly full on the mouth.

Martel, his face pale with anger, had tried to draw near enough to hear, but Sephrenia stepped in front of him. His eyes flashed angrily, and with obvious effort he restrained his first impulse to thrust her out of his way.

She raised her chin and looked him full in the face. "Well?" she said.

He muttered something, turned, and stalked to the far side of the tent where he stood gnawing at a knuckle in frustration.

Arasham still clung to Sparhawk's neck. "My beloved son and deliverer," he cried with his rheumy eyes filled with tears. "Surely you have been sent to me by God Himself. We cannot fail now. God is on our side. Let the wicked tremble before us."

"Truly," Sparhawk agreed, gently disengaging the old man's arms from about his neck.

"A thought, holy one," Martel said shrewdly, though his face was still white with fury. "Sparhawk is only human and, therefore, mortal. The world is full of mischance. Might it not be wiser to—"

"Mischance?" Sparhawk cut him off quickly. "Where is your faith, Martel? This is God's design, not mine. God will not permit me to die until I have performed this service for Him. Have faith, dear brother. God will sustain and keep me against all perils. It is my destiny to fulfill this task, and God will see to it that I do not fail."

"Praise God!" Arasham exclaimed ecstatically, ending the discussion.

The doe-eyed boy brought in the melons at that point, and the conversation shifted to more general matters. Arasham delivered another rambling diatribe against the Church while Martel sat scowling at Sparhawk. Sparhawk kept his eyes on his melon, which was surprisingly good. It had all been too easy, somehow, and that worried him just a little. Martel was too clever, too devious, to have been so easily circumvented. He looked appraisingly across the tent at the white-haired man he had hated for so long. Martel's expression was baffled, frustrated—and that was also not like him. The Martel he had known as a youth would never have revealed such emotions. Sparhawk began to feel a little less sure of himself.

"A thought has just occurred to me, Most Holy," he said. "Time is crucial in this affair, and it is essential that my sister and I return to Deira at once to advise his majesty that all here in Rendor is ready, and to convey to his ears alone that word which is locked in both our hearts. We have good horses, of course, but a fast boat could take us downriver and deliver us to the seaport at Jiroch days earlier. Perhaps you—or one of your disciples—might know of some dependable boat-owner here in Dabour whom I could hire."

Arasham blinked at him vaguely. "A boat?" he mumbled.

A faint movement caught Sparhawk's eye, and he saw Sephrenia move her arm as if only shaking back her sleeve. Instantly he knew what she had been doing all along.

"Hire, my son?" Arasham beamed at him. "Let there be no talk of hiring. I have a splendid boat at my disposal. You will take it, and with my blessing. I will send armed men with you and a regiment—no, a legion—to patrol the banks of the river to make sure you reach Jiroch safely."

"It shall be as you command, Most Holy," Sparhawk said. He looked across the tent at Martel with a beatific smile. "Is it not amazing, dear brother," he said. "Truly such wisdom and generosity can only come from God."

"Yes," Martel replied darkly, "I'm sure of it."

"I must make haste, holy Arasham," Sparhawk rushed on, rising to his feet. "We left our horses and belongings in the care of a servant in a house on the outskirts of town. My sister and I will retrieve them at once and return within the hour."

"As you see fit, my son," Arasham said eagerly, "and I will instruct my disciples to have the boat and the soldiers made ready for your journey downriver."

"Let me show you the way out of the compound, dear brother," Martel said from between clenched teeth.

"Gladly, dear brother," Sparhawk said. "Your company, as always, fills my heart with joy."

"Return directly, Martel," Arasham instructed. "We must discuss this wondrous turn of fortune and offer thanks to God for His grace in providing it."

"Yes, Most Holy," Martel said, bowing. "I shall come back immediately."

"Within the hour, Sparhawk," Arasham said.

"Within the hour, Most Holy," Sparhawk agreed with a deep bow. "Come along then, Martel," he said, once again smacking his hand down on the renegade's shoulder.

"Of course." Martel winced, once again shrinking from Sparhawk's comradely blow.

Once they were outside the pavilion, Martel turned on Sparhawk, his face white with fury. "Just what do you think you're doing?" he demanded.

"Testy today, aren't we, old boy?" Sparhawk said mildly.

"What are you up to, Sparhawk?" Martel snarled, looking around to be sure that no one in the crowd of hovering disciples could hear him.

"I just spiked your wheel, Martel," Sparhawk replied. "Arasham will sit here until he petrifies unless someone brings him that secret word. I can almost guarantee you that the Church Knights will be in Chyrellos when the time comes to elect the new archprelate, because there won't be anything going on in Rendor to drag them away."

"Very clever, Sparhawk."

"I'm glad you liked it."

"This is one more debt you owe me," Martel grated.

"Feel free to call them in at any time, dear brother," Sparhawk said. "I'll be more than happy to accommodate you." He took Sephrenia by the elbow and led her away.

"Are you completely out of your senses, Sparhawk?" she demanded once they were out of earshot of the fuming Martel.

"I don't think so," he replied. "Of course crazy people never really know, do they?"

"What were you *doing* in there? Do you realize how many times I had to step in to keep you out of trouble?"

"I noticed that. I couldn't have pulled it off without you."

"Will you stop smirking and tell me what was behind all that?"

"Martel was getting too close to our real reason for being here," he explained. "I had to throw something else in his path to keep him from realizing that we'd unearthed a possible antidote for the poison. It all worked out rather well, even if I do say so myself."

"If you knew you were going to do that before you went into the tent, why didn't you tell me?"

"How could I have known, Sephrenia? I didn't even know Martel was there until I saw him."

"You mean . . ." Her eyes went suddenly very wide.

He nodded. "I sort of made it up as I went along," he confessed.

"Oh, Sparhawk," she said disgustedly, "you know better than that."

He shrugged. "It was about the best I could do on short notice."

"Why did you keep hitting Martel on the shoulder like that?"

"He broke that shoulder when he was about fifteen. It's always been very sensitive."

"That was cruel," she accused.

"So was what happened in that alley back in Cippria ten years ago. Let's go get Kurik and Flute. I think we've done about all we can here in Dabour."


Arasham's boat was more like a barge than the scow which had carried them upriver and it was perhaps four times as large. Banks of oarsmen lined each side, and black-robed zealots with swords and javelins clustered in the torchlit bow and stern. Martel had preceded them to the rickety dock and he stood alone there, some distance from the hot-eyed disciples on shore, as Sparhawk, Sephrenia, Kurik, and Flute embarked. The renegade's white hair gleamed in the starlight, and his face was very nearly as pale.

"You're not going to get away with this, Sparhawk," he said in a low voice.

"Oh?" Sparhawk said. "I think you'd better look again, Martel. It seems to me that I already did. You can try to follow me, of course, but all those troops patrolling the river banks are probably going to get in your way. Besides, I think that once you get over your pique, you'll realize that about the only thing you can do is stay here and try to wheedle that magic word out of Arasham. Everything you've set up here in Rendor will be at a standstill until you do."

"You'll pay for this, Sparhawk," Martel promised darkly.

"I thought I already had, old boy," Sparhawk replied, "in Cippria, I believe it was." He reached out, and Martel jerked his shoulder out of range. Instead, however, Sparhawk patted him on the cheek insultingly. "Take care of yourself, Martel," he said. "I want to see you again—soon—and I want you to be well and in full possession of your faculties. Believe me, you're going to need them." Then he turned and went up the gangway to the waiting barge.

The sailors cast off all lines and pushed the barge out into the slowly moving current. Then they ran out their oars and began to row slowly downriver. The dock behind them and the solitary man standing on the end of it shrank out of sight.

"Oh, God!" Sparhawk cried exultantly, "I loved that!"

The run downriver took them a day and a half, and they disembarked a league or so upstream from Jiroch to avoid any watchers Martel might have managed to get to the docks ahead of them. The precaution was probably unnecessary, Sparhawk admitted, but there was no point in taking chances. They entered the city through the west gate and mingled with the crowds as they made their way to Voren's house again. It was late afternoon when they entered.

Voren was a trifle surprised at their reappearance. "That was quick," he said as they entered his garden.

"We were lucky," Sparhawk shrugged.

"More than lucky," Sephrenia said darkly. The small woman's temper had not noticeably improved since they had left Dabour, and she still refused even to talk to Sparhawk.

"Did something go wrong?" Voren asked mildly.

"Not that *I* noticed," Sparhawk replied blithely.

"Stop congratulating yourself, Sparhawk," she snapped. "I'm vexed with you, very vexed."

"I'm sorry about that, Sephrenia, but I did the best I could." He turned to Voren. "We ran into Martel," he explained, "and I managed to stop him in his tracks. His whole scheme just collapsed around his ears."

Voren whistled. "I don't see anything wrong with that, Sephrenia."

"It's not what he did, Voren. It was the way he did it."

"Oh?"

"I don't want to talk about it." She gathered Flute up in her arms, went to the bench by the fountain, and sat muttering darkly to the little girl in Styric.

"We need a way to get aboard a fast ship bound for Vardenais without being seen," Sparhawk told Voren. "Can you come up with something?"

"Quite easily," Voren replied. "Every so often the true identity of one of our brothers is exposed. We've devised a way to get them out of Rendor safely." He smiled ironically. "It was the first thing I did when I got to Jiroch, actually. I was fairly sure I was going to need it for myself almost immediately. I have a wharf down in the harbor. There's a waterfront inn not far away. It's run by one of our brothers, and it has all the things an inn usually has—taproom, stables, sleeping rooms upstairs, and the like. It's also got a cellar, and there's a passageway running from that one to the cellar of my main warehouse. At low tide you can board a ship directly from that cellar without being seen by anyone on shore."

"Would that fool the Damork, Sephrenia?" Sparhawk asked her.

She glared at him for a moment, then relented. She touched the fingertips of one hand lightly to her temple. Sparhawk noted that there was more silver there now. "I think it would," she replied. "We don't even know that the Damork is here. Martel could actually have been telling us the truth."

"I wouldn't count on it," Kurik grunted.

"Even so," she continued, "the Damork probably couldn't begin to grasp the concept of a cellar—much less underground passageways."

"What's a Damork?" Voren asked.

Sparhawk told him and described what had happened to Captain Mabin's ship in the Arcian Straits just out from Madel.

Voren rose and began to pace up and down. "That's not the sort of thing our escape route was designed to cope with," he admitted. "I think I'd better take some additional precautions. I've got six ships in port just now. Why don't I just send them all out at the same time? If you sail out in the middle of a flotilla, it might add a bit more confusion."

"Isn't that a bit elaborate?" Sparhawk asked him.

"Sparhawk, I know how modest you are, but you're probably the most important man in the world just now—at least you are until you get to Cimmura and make your report to Vanion. I'm not going to take any chances with you if I can help it." He went to the garden wall and squinted at the setting sun. "We're going to have to hurry," he told them. "Low tide this evening comes just after dusk, and I'll want you in the cellar when the ship's rail drops below the edge of the wharf. I'll go with you to make sure you get on board safely."

They all rode out together toward the waterfront. Their route took them through the familiar quarter where Sparhawk had maintained his shop during the years he had been hidden here. The buildings on either side of the streets were almost like old friends, and he thought he recognized a few of the people hurrying home through the narrow streets as the sun sank toward the western horizon.

"Brute!" The voice from behind them probably carried halfway across the Arcian Straits, and it was painfully familiar. "Assassin!"

"Oh, no!" Sparhawk groaned, reining Faran in. "And we were so close." He looked longingly at the waterfront inn to which Voren was leading them and which was but one street away.

"Monster!" the voice went on in a strident tone.

"Uh—Sparhawk," Kurik said mildly, "is it my imagination, or is that lady trying to get your attention?"

"Just let it lie, Kurik."

"Anything you say, my Lord."

"Assassin! Brute! Monster! Deserter!"

There was a brief pause. "Murderer!" the woman added.

"I never did that," Sparhawk murmured. He sighed and turned Faran around. "Hello, Lillias," he said to the robed and veiled woman who had been shouting at him. He spoke in as mild and inoffensive a tone as he could manage.

"Hello, Lillias?" she shrieked. "*Hello, Lillias!* Is that all you have to say for yourself, brigand?"

Sparhawk tried very hard not to smile. In a peculiar way, he loved Lillias and he was pleased to see her enjoying herself so much. "You're looking well, Lillias," he said conversationally, knowing that a comment like that would spur her to new heights.

"Well? *Well?* When you have murdered me? When you have cut my heart out? When you have sunk me in the mire of deepest despair?" She leaned back in a tragic posture, head up and arms thrown wide. "Hardly a morsel of food has passed my lips since that hateful day when you abandoned me penniless in the gutter."

"I left you the shop, Lillias," he protested. "It fed us both before I left. Surely it still feeds you."

"Shop! What do I care about the shop? It is my heart that you have broken, Mahkra!" She thrust back her hood and ripped off her veil. "Assassin!" she cried. "Look at your handiwork!" She began to tear at her long, glossy black hair and to gouge at her dark, full-lipped face with her fingernails.

"Lillias!" Sparhawk barked in the tone he had only had to use a few times during their years together. "Stop that! You'll hurt yourself."

But Lillias was in full voice now, and there was no stopping her. "Hurt?" she cried tragically. "What do I care about hurt? How can you hurt a dead woman? You want to see hurt, Mahkra? Look at my heart!" She ripped open the front of her robe. It was not her heart, however, that she revealed.

"Oh, my goodness," Kurik said in an awed voice, staring at the woman's suddenly revealed attributes. Voren turned his head aside, concealing a smile. Sephrenia, however, looked at Sparhawk with a slightly different expression.

"Oh, God," Sparhawk groaned. He swung down from his saddle. "Lillias!" he muttered sharply to her, "cover yourself! Think of the neighbors—and all the children watching."

"What do I care about the neighbors? Let them look!" She thrust out her full breasts. "What does shame mean to a woman whose heart is dead?"

Grimly, Sparhawk advanced on her. When he got close enough, he spoke quietly to her from between clenched teeth. "They're very nice, Lillias," he said, "but I don't really think they're much of a surprise to any man within six streets in any direction. Do you really want to go on with this?"

She suddenly looked a little less certain, but she did not close the front of her robe.

"Have it your way," he shrugged. Then he, too, raised his voice. "Your heart is not dead, Lillias," he declared to the audience breathlessly clustered on the second-floor balconies. "Far from it, I think. What of Georgias the baker? And Nendan the sausage maker?" He was selecting names at random.

Her face blanched, and she shrank back, covering her generous bosom with her robe. "You know?" she faltered.

That hurt him just a little, but he covered it. "Of course," he declared, still playing to the balconies, "but I forgive you. You are much woman, Lillias, and not meant to be alone." He reached out and gently covered her hair with her hood again. "Have you been well?" he asked her very softly.

"I get by," she whispered.

"Good. Are we almost done?"

"I think we need something to round it out, don't you?" Her face looked hopeful.

He tried very hard to keep from laughing.

"This is serious, Mahkra," she hissed. "My position in the community depends on it."

"Trust me," he murmured. "You have betrayed me, Lillias," he said to the balconies, "but I forgive you, for I have not been here to keep you from straying."

She considered that for a moment, then sobbed, fell into his arms, and buried her face in his chest. "It's just that I missed you so much, my Mahkra. I weakened. I am but a poor, ignorant woman—a slave to my passions. Can you ever truly forgive me?"

"What is there to forgive, my Lillias?" he said grandly. "You are like the earth, like the sea. To give is a part of your nature."

She thrust herself back from him. "Beat me!" she demanded. "I deserve to be beaten!" Huge tears, genuine for all he knew, stood in her glowing black eyes.

"Oh, no," he refused, knowing exactly where *that* would lead. "No beatings, Lillias," he said. "Only this," and he gave her a single chaste kiss full on the lips. "Be well, Lillias," he murmured softly. Then he stepped back quickly before she could wrap her arms about his neck. He knew just how strong her arms were. "And now, though it rends my soul, I must leave you again," he declaimed. He reached out and drew her veil once again across her face. "Think of me from time to time whilst I seek out the fate that destiny has in store for me." He did manage to resist the impulse to lay his hand on his heart.

"I knew it!" she cried, more to the onlookers than to him. "I knew that you were a man of affairs! I shall carry our love in my heart for all eternity, my Mahkra, and I shall remain faithful to you to the grave. And if you live, come back to me." She had both arms spread wide again. "And if you do not, send your ghost to me in my dreams, and I will comfort your pale shade as best I can."

He backed away from her outstretched arms. Then he spun so that his robe would swirl dramatically—he owed her that much—and vaulted into Faran's saddle. "Farewell, my Lillias," he said melodramatically, jerking the reins to make Faran rear and paw the air with his front hooves. "And if we do not meet again in this world, may God grant that we meet once more in the next." And he drove his heels into Faran's flanks and charged past her at a gallop.

"Did you do all that on purpose?" Sephrenia asked as they dismounted in the courtyard of the waterfront inn.

"I might have gotten a little carried away," Sparhawk admitted. "Lillias does that to a man from time to time." He smiled a bit ruefully. "She gets her heart broken on an average of three times a week," he noted clinically. "She was always militantly unfaithful and just a little dishonest where the cashbox was concerned. She's vain and vulgar and self-indulgent. She's deceptive and greedy and grossly overdramatic." He paused then, thinking back over the years. "I liked her, though. She's a good girl, despite her faults, and living with her was never dull. I owed her that performance. She'll be able to walk through the quarter like a queen now, and it didn't really cost me all that much, did it?"

"Sparhawk," she said gravely, "I will never understand you."

"That's what makes it all so much fun, isn't it, little mother?" He grinned at her.

Flute, still sitting on Sephrenia's white horse, blew a mocking little trill on her pipes.

"Talk with her," Sparhawk suggested to Sephrenia. "She understands."

Flute rolled her eyes at him, then generously held out her hands to permit him to help her down.

■ CHAPTER TWENTY-FOUR ■

The voyage across the mouth of the Arcian Strait passed without incident. They ran northeasterly under clear skies with a fair following breeze and with the other ships of Voren's flotilla clustered about them protectively.

About noon on the third day out, Sparhawk came up on deck to join Sephrenia in the bow where she and Flute stood looking out over the sparkling waves. "Are you still cross with me?" he asked her.

She sighed. "No. I suppose not."

Sparhawk was not entirely certain how to put his vague sense of unease into words, so he approached it obliquely. "Sephrenia," he said, "did it seem to you that everything in Dabour went just a little too smoothly? I somehow get the feeling that I'm being led around by the nose again."

"How do you mean, exactly?"

"I know you tampered with Arasham a few times that night, but did you do anything to Martel?"

"No. He'd have felt it if I'd tried and he'd have countered me."

"That's what I thought. What was wrong with him, then?"

"I'm not sure I follow you."

"He acted almost like a schoolboy. We both know Martel. He's intelligent and he thinks very fast on his feet. What I did was so obvious that he should have seen through it almost immediately, but he didn't do a thing. He just stood there like an idiot and let me pull his whole scheme down around his ears. It was just too easy, and that worries me."

"He didn't really expect to see us in Arasham's tent, Sparhawk. Maybe the surprise threw him off balance."

"Martel doesn't surprise all that easily."

She frowned. "No," she admitted, "he doesn't, does he?" She thought about it. "Do you remember what Lord Darellon was saying before we left Cimmura?"

"Not exactly, no."

"He said that Annias behaved like a simpleton when he presented his case to the Elene kings. He announced the death of Count Radun without even verifying the fact that the count had really died."

"Oh, yes, now I remember. And you said that the whole scheme—the attempt to murder the count and to lay the blame on the Pandions—might have originated with a Styric magician."

"Perhaps it goes a little further than that. We know that Martel has had contacts with a Damork, and that means that Azash is involved somehow. Azash has always dealt with Styrics, so he's had very little experience with the subleties of the Elene mind. The Gods of Styricum are very direct and they seldom prepare for contingencies—probably because of the Styric lack of sophistication. Now, the whole purpose of the plot in Arcium and the one in Rendor has been to keep the Church Knights out of Chyrellos during the election. Annias behaved the way a Styric would have in the palace at Cimmura, and Martel behaved the same way in Arasham's tent."

"You're a little inconsistent, Sephrenia," he objected. "First you try to tell me that Styrics are unsophisticated, then you come up with an explanation so complicated that I can't even follow it. Why don't you just say what you mean?"

"Azash has always dominated the minds of his followers," she replied, "and for the most part, they've been Styrics. If Annias and Martel both start behaving like Styrics, it raises some very interesting possibilities, wouldn't you say?"

"I'm sorry, Sephrenia, but I can't accept that. Whatever other faults he may have, Martel's still an Elene; and Annias is a churchman. Neither one of them would give his soul to Azash."

"Not consciously, perhaps, but Azash has ways to subvert the minds of people he finds useful."

"Where does all this lead?"

"I'm not entirely sure, but it seems that Azash has some reason to want Annias to be the new archprelate. It's something we might want to keep in mind. If Azash is controlling Annias and Martel, they're both going to be thinking like Styrics, and Styrics don't react very fast when they're surprised. It's a racial trait. Surprise could be our best weapon."

"Was that why you were so angry with me—because I surprised you?"

"Of course. I thought you knew that."

"Next time, I'll try to warn you."

"I'd appreciate that."

Two days later their ship entered the estuary of the River Ucera and sailed up toward the Elenian port city of Vardenais. As they approached the wharves, however, Sparhawk saw trouble. Men in red tunics were patrolling the waterfront.

"Now what?" Kurik asked as the two of them crouched behind a low deck-house to keep out of sight.

Sparhawk frowned. "I suppose we could sail across the bay and go inland on the Arcian side."

"If they're watching the seaports, they're bound to be patrolling the border as well. Use your head, Sparhawk."

"Maybe we could slip across at night."

"Isn't what we're doing a little too important to hang it all on a *maybe*?" Kurik asked pointedly.

Sparhawk started to swear. "We've *got* to get to Cimmura," he said. "It's getting close to the time when another of the twelve knights is going to die, and I don't know how much more of the weight Sephrenia can carry. Think, Kurik. You're always better at tactics than I am."

"That's because I don't wear armor. The sense of invincibility does funny things to a man's brains."

"Thanks," Sparhawk said drily.

Kurik knit his brows in thought.

"Well?" Sparhawk said impatiently.

"I'm working on it. Don't rush me."

"We're getting closer to that wharf, Kurik."

"I can see that. Can you tell if they're searching any of the ships?"

Sparhawk raised his head and peered over the top of the deckhouse. "They don't seem to be."

"Good. That means we won't have to make any spur-of-the-moment decisions. We can go below and work this out."

"Any ideas at all?"

"You're pushing, Sparhawk," Kurik said disapprovingly. "That's one of your failings, you know. You always want to dash into the middle of things before you've thought your way completely through what you're going to do."

Their ship hove to beside a tar-smeared wharf, and the sailors cast lines to the longshoremen clustered there. Then they ran out the gangway and began to carry boxes and bales down to the wharf.

There was a clattering sound from the hold, and Faran trotted up on deck. Sparhawk stared at his war horse in amazement. Flute sat cross-legged on the big roan's broad back playing her pipes. The melody she played was a peculiarly drowsy one, almost like a lullaby. Before Sparhawk and Kurik could run to intercept her, she tapped Faran's back with the side of her foot, and he placidly walked down the gangway to the wharf.

"What is she *doing*?" Kurik exclaimed.

"I can't even begin to guess. Go get Sephrenia—fast!"

On the wharf, Flute rode directly toward the squad of church soldiers stationed at the far end. The soldiers had been closely examining every disembarking passenger and sailor, but they paid no attention to Flute and the roan horse. She impudently rode back and forth in front of them several times, then turned. She seemed to be looking directly at Sparhawk and, still playing her pipes, she raised one little hand and motioned to him.

He stared at her.

She made a little face and then quite deliberately rode directly through the soldiers' ranks. They absently stepped aside for her, but not one of them so much as looked at her.

"What's going on down there?" he demanded as Sephrenia and Kurik joined him behind the deckhouse.

"I'm not altogether sure," Sephrenia replied, frowning.

"Why aren't the soldiers paying any attention to her?" Kurik asked as Flute rode through the ranks of red tunics once again.

"I don't think they can see her."

"But she's right there in front of them."

"That doesn't seem to matter." Her face slowly took on an expression of wonder. "I'd heard about this," she murmured. "I thought it was just an old folktale, but perhaps I was wrong." She turned to Sparhawk. "Has she looked back at the ship at all since she rode down onto that wharf?"

"She sort of motioned to me to follow her," he said.

"You're sure?"

"That's the way it looked to me."

She drew in a deep breath. "Well," she said, "there's one way to find out, I suppose." Before Sparhawk could stop her, she rose and walked out from behind the deckhouse.

"Sephrenia!" he called after her, but she continued on across the deck as if she had not heard him. She reached the rail and stood there.

"She's right out in plain sight," Kurik said in a strangled tone.

"I can see that."

"The soldiers are certain to have a description of her. Has she gone out of her mind?"

"I doubt it. Look." Sparhawk pointed toward the soldiers on the wharf. Although Sephrenia was standing in plain view, they did not even appear to look at her.

Flute, however, saw her and made another of those imperious little gestures.

Sephenia sighed and looked at Sparhawk. "Wait here," she said.

"Wait where?"

"Here—on board ship." She turned, walked to the gangway, and went on down to the wharf.

"That rips it," Sparhawk said bleakly, rising to his feet and drawing his sword. Quickly he counted the soldiers on the wharf. "There aren't that many of them," he said to Kurik. "If we can take them by surprise, there might be a chance."

"Not a very good one, Sparhawk. Let's wait a moment and see what happens."

Sephrenia walked up the wharf and stopped directly in front of the soldiers.

They ignored her.

She spoke to them.

They paid no attention.

Then she turned back toward the ship. "It's all right, Sparhawk," she called. "They can't see us—or hear us. Bring the other horses and our things."

"Magic?" Kurik asked in a stunned voice.

"Not any kind that *I* ever heard about," Sparhawk replied.

"I guess we'd better do what she says, then," Kurik advised, "and sort of immediately. I'd hate to be right in the middle of those soldiers when the spell wears off."

It was eerie to walk down the gangway in plain view of the church soldiers and to saunter casually up the wharf until they were face-to-face with them. The soldiers' expressions were bored, and they gave no indication that anything at all was amiss. They routinely stopped every sailor and passenger leaving the wharf, but paid no attention whatsoever to Sparhawk, Kurik, and the horses. The soldiers stepped out of the way with no command from their corporal and immediately closed ranks again once Sparhawk and Kurik had led the horses off the wharf and onto the cobblestones of the street.

Without a word, Sparhawk lifted Flute down from Faran's back and saddled the big roan. "All right," he said to Sephrenia when he had finished, "how did she do it?"

"The usual way."

"But she can't talk—or at least she doesn't. How did she cast the spell?"

"With her pipes, Sparhawk. I thought you knew that. She doesn't speak the spell, she plays it on her pipes."

"Is that possible?" His tone was incredulous.

"You just saw her do it."

"Could you do it that way?"

She shook her head. "I'm just a bit tone deaf, Sparhawk," she confessed. "I can't really tell one note from another, except in a general sort of way, and the melody has to be very precise. Shall we go, then?"

They rode up through the streets of Vardenais from the harbor.

"Are we still invisible?" Kurik asked.

"We're not actually invisible, Kurik," Sephrenia replied, wrapping her cloak about Flute, who still played the drowsy tune on her pipes. "If we were, we would-n't be able to see each other."

"I don't understand at all."

"The soldiers knew we were there, Kurik. They stepped out of the way for us, remember? They just chose not to pay any attention to us."

"Chose?"

"Perhaps that was the wrong word. Let's say they were encouraged not to."

They rode out through the north gate of Vardenais without being stopped by the guards posted there and were soon on the high road to Cimmura. The weather had changed since they had left Elenia many weeks before. The chill of winter had gone now, and the first budding leaves of spring tipped the branches of the trees at the sides of the road. Peasants plodded across their fields behind their plows, turning over the rich black loam. The rains had passed, and the sky was bright blue, dotted here and there with puffy white clouds. The breeze was fresh and warm, and the earth smelled of growth and renewal. They had discarded their Rendorish robes before leaving the ship, but Sparhawk still found his mail coat and padded tunic uncomfortably warm.

Kurik was looking out at the freshly plowed fields they passed with an appraising eye. "I hope the boys have finished with the plowing at home," he said. "I'd hate to have that chore in front of me when I get back."

"Aslade will see to it that they get it done," Sparhawk assured him.

"You're probably right." Kurik made a wry face. "When you get right down to it, she's a better farmer than I am."

"Women always are," Sephrenia told him. "They're more in tune with the moon and the seasons. In Styricum, women always manage the fields."

"What do the men do?"

"As little as possible."

It took them nearly five days to reach Cimmura, and they arrived on an early spring afternoon. Sparhawk reined in atop a hill a mile or so west of town. "Can she do it again?" he asked Sephrenia.

"Can who do what again?"

"Flute. Can she make people ignore us again?"

"I don't know. Why don't you ask her?"

"Why don't *you* ask her? I don't think she likes me."

"Whatever gave you that idea? She adores you." Sephrenia leaned forward slightly and spoke in Styric to the little girl who rested against her.

Flute nodded and made an obscure kind of circling gesture with one hand.

"What did she say?" Sparhawk asked.

"Approximately that the chapterhouse is on the other side of Cimmura. She suggests that we circle the city rather than ride through the streets."

"Approximately?"

"It loses a great deal in translation."

"All right. We'll do it her way, then. I definitely don't want Annias to find out that we're back in Cimmura."

They rode on around the city, passing through open fields and sparse woodlands and keeping about a mile back from the city wall. Cimmura was not an attractive city, Sparhawk decided. The peculiar combination of its location and the prevailing weather seemed to capture the smoke from its thousands of chimneys and to hold it in a continual pall just above the rooftops. That lowering cloud of smoke made the place look perpetually grimy.

They finally reached a thicket about a half mile from the walls of the chapterhouse. Once again the land was dotted with peasants at work, and the road leading out from the east gate was alive with brightly dressed travellers.

"Tell her it's time," Sparhawk said to Sephrenia. "I'd imagine that a fair number of those people out there are working for Annias."

"She knows, Sparhawk. She's not stupid."

"No. Only a little flighty."

Flute made a face at him and began to play her pipes. It was that same lethargic, almost drowsy tune she had played in Vardenais.

They started across the field toward the few houses clustered outside the chapterhouse. Though he was certain that the people they passed would pay no attention to them, Sparhawk instinctively tensed at each encounter.

"Relax, Sparhawk," Sephrenia ordered him crisply. "You're making it harder for her."

"Sorry," he mumbled. "Habit, I guess." With some effort he pulled a kind of calm about himself.

A number of workmen were repairing the road that led up to the gates of the fortress.

"Spies," Kurik grunted.

"How do you know that?" Sparhawk asked.

"Look at the way they're laying the cobblestones, Sparhawk. They haven't got the faintest idea of what they're doing."

"It does look a bit slipshod, doesn't it?" Sparhawk agreed, looking critically at the section of newly laid stone as they rode past the unseeing road gang.

"Annias must be getting old," Kurik said. "He never used to be this obvious."

"He's got a lot on his mind, I guess."

They clattered up the road to the drawbridge and then on across it and into the courtyard, passing the indifferent quartet of armored knights on guard at the gate.

A young novice was drawing water from the well in the center of the courtyard, laboriously winding the creaking windlass mounted at the well mouth. With a final little flourish, Flute took her pipes from her lips.

The novice choked out a startled oath and reached for his sword. The windlass squealed as the bucket plummeted down again.

"Easy, brother," Sparhawk told him, dismounting.

"How did you get past the gate?" the novice exclaimed.

"You wouldn't believe it," Kurik told him, swinging down from his gelding's back.

"Forgive me, Sir Sparhawk," the novice stammered. "You startled me."

"It's all right," Sparhawk assured him. "Did Kalten get back yet?"

"Yes, my Lord. He and the knights from the other orders arrived some time back."

"Good. Do you know where I might find them?"

"I believe they're with Lord Vanion in his study."

"Thank you. Would you see to our horses?"

"Of course, Sir Sparhawk."

They entered the chapterhouse and went down the central corridor toward the south end of the building. Then they climbed the narrow flight of stairs to the tower.

"Sir Sparhawk," one of the young knights on guard at the top said respectfully, "I'll advise Lord Vanion that you've arrived."

"Thank you, brother," Sparhawk said.

The knight tapped on the door, then opened it. "Sir Sparhawk is here, my Lord," he reported to Vanion.

"It's about time." Sparhawk heard Kalten's voice inside the room.

"Please go in, Sir Sparhawk," the young knight said, stepping aside and bowing.

Vanion sat at the table. Kalten, Bevier, Ulath, and Tynian had risen from their seats and come forward to greet Sparhawk and the others. Berit and Talen sat on a bench in the corner.

"When did you get in?" Sparhawk asked as Kalten roughly clasped his hand.

"Early last week," the blond man replied. "What kept you?"

"We had a long way to go, Kalten," Sparhawk protested. Wordlessly he gripped the hands of Tynian, Ulath, and Bevier. Then he bowed to Vanion. "My Lord," he said.

"Sparhawk," Vanion nodded.

"Did you get my messages?"

"If there were only two, I did."

"Good. Then you're fairly well up-to-date on what's going on down there."

Vanion, however, was looking closely at Sephrenia. "You're not looking too well, little mother," he said.

"I'll be all right," she said, passing one hand wearily across her eyes.

"Sit down," Kalten said, holding a chair for her.

"Thank you."

"What happened in Dabour, Sparhawk?" Vanion asked, his eyes intent.

"We found that physician," Sparhawk reported. "As it turns out, he *did* in fact cure some people who'd been poisoned with the same thing Annias gave the queen."

"Thank God!" Vanion said, letting his breath out explosively.

"Don't be too quick about that, Vanion," Sephrenia told him. "We know what the cure is, but we've got to find it before we can use it."

"I don't quite follow you."

"The poison is extremely potent. The only way to counteract it is through the use of magic."

"Did the physician give you the spell he used?"

"Apparently there's no spell involved. There are a number of objects in the world that have enormous power. We have to find one of them."

He frowned. "That could take time," he said. "People usually hide those things to keep them from being stolen."

"I know."

"Are you absolutely certain you've identified the right poison?" Kalten asked Sparhawk.

Sparhawk nodded. "I got confirmation from Martel," he said.

"Martel? You actually gave him time to talk before you killed him?"

"I didn't kill him. The time wasn't right."

"Any time is right for that, Sparhawk."

"I felt that way myself when I first saw him, but Sephrenia persuaded the two of us to put away our swords."

"I'm terribly disappointed in you, Sephrenia," Kalten said.

"You almost had to have been there to understand," she replied.

"Why didn't you just get whatever it was the physician used to cure those other people?" Tynian asked Sparhawk.

"Because he ground it to a powder, mixed it with wine, and had them drink it."

"Is that the way it's supposed to be done?"

"No, as a matter of fact, it's not. Sephrenia spoke to him rather sharply about that."

"I think you'd better start at the beginning," Vanion said.

"Right," Sparhawk agreed, taking a chair. Briefly he told them about Arasham's "holy talisman" and about the ploy that had gotten them into the old man's tent.

"You were being awfully free with the name of my king, Sparhawk," Tynian objected.

"We don't necessarily need to tell him about it, do we?" Sparhawk replied. "I needed to use the name of a kingdom a long way from Rendor. Arasham probably has only the vaguest idea of where Deira is."

"Why didn't you say you were from Thalesia, then?"

"I doubt if Arasham's ever heard of Thalesia. Anyway, the 'holy talisman' turned out to be a fake. Martel was there and he was trying to persuade the old lunatic to postpone his uprising until the time of the election of the new archprelate." He went on to describe the means by which he had overturned the white-haired man's scheme.

"My friend," Kalten said admiringly, "I'm proud of you."

"Thank you, Kalten," Sparhawk said modestly. "It did turn out rather well, I thought."

"He's been patting himself on the back ever since we came out of Arasham's tent," Sephrenia said. She looked at Vanion. "Kerris died," she told him sadly.

Vanion nodded, his face somber. "I know," he said. "How did you find out?"

"His ghost came to us to deliver his sword to Sephrenia," Sparhawk told him. "Vanion, we're going to have to do something about that. She can't go on carrying all those swords and everything they symbolize. She gets weaker every time somebody gives her another one."

"I'm all right, Sparhawk," she insisted.

"I hate to contradict you, little mother, but you're definitely *not* all right. It's all you can do right now to hold up your head. About two more of those swords is all it's going to take to put you on your knees."

"Where are the swords now?" Vanion asked.

"We brought a mule with us," Kurik replied. "They're in a box in his pack."

"Would you get them for me, please?"

"Right away," Kurik said, going to the door.

"What have you got in mind, Vanion?" Sephrenia asked suspiciously.

"I'm going to take the swords." He shrugged. "And everything that goes with them."

"You can't."

"Oh, yes, I can, Sephrenia. I was in the throne room, too, and I know which spell to use. You don't have to be the one who has to carry them. Any one of us who was there can do it."

"You're not strong enough, Vanion."

"When you get down to it, I could carry you and everything you've got in your arms, my teacher, and right now you're more important than I am."

"But—" she started.

He held up his hand. "The discussion is ended, Sephrenia. I am the preceptor. With or without your permission, I'm taking those swords away from you."

"You don't know what it means, my dearest one. I won't let you." Her face was suddenly wet with tears, and she wrung her hands in an uncharacteristic display of human emotion. "I won't let you."

"You can't stop me," he said in a gentle voice. "I can cast the spell without your help, if I have to. If you want to keep your spells a secret, little mother, you should-n't chant them out loud, you know. You should know by now that I've got a very re-tentive memory."

She stared at him. "I'm shocked at you, Vanion," she declared. "You were not so unkind when you were young."

"Life is filled with these little disappointments, isn't it?" he said urbanely.

"I can stop you," she cried, still wringing her hands. "You forget just how much stronger I am than you are." There was a shrill triumph in her voice.

"Of course you are. That's why I'd have to call in help. Could you deal with ten knights all chanting in unison? Or fifty? Or half a thousand?"

"That's unfair!" she exclaimed. "I did not know that you would go this far, Vanion—and I trusted you."

"And well you should, dear one," he said, assuming suddenly the superior role, "for I will not permit you to make this sacrifice. I'll force you to submit to me, be-cause you know I'm right. You'll release the burden to me, because you know that what you have to do is more important than anything else right now, and you'll sac-rifice anything to do what we both know must be done."

"Dear one," she began in an agonized voice. "My dearest one—"

"As I said," he cut her off, "the discussion is ended."

There was a long and awkward silence as Sephrenia and Vanion stood with their eyes locked on each other's faces.

"Did the physician in Dabour give you any hints about which objects might cure the queen?" Bevier asked Sparhawk a bit uneasily.

"He mentioned a spear in Daresia, several rings in Zemoch, a bracelet some-where in Pelosia, and a jewel on the royal crown of Thalesia."

Ulath grunted. "The Bhelliom."

"That solves it, then," Kalten said. "We go to Thalesia, borrow Wargun's crown, and come back here with it."

"Wargun doesn't have it," Ulath told him.

"What do you mean, Wargun doesn't have it? He's the king of Thalesia, isn't he?"

"That crown was lost five hundred years ago."

"Could we possibly find it?"

"Almost anything is possible, I suppose," the big Thalesian replied, "but people have been looking for it for five hundred years without much success. Do we have that kind of time?"

"What is this Bhelliom?" Tynian asked him.

"The legends say that it's a very large sapphire carved in the shape of a rose. It's supposed to have the power of the Troll-Gods in it."

"Does it?"

"I wouldn't know. I've never seen it. It's lost, remember?"

"There are bound to be other objects," Sephrenia declared. "We live in a world with magic all around us. In all of the eons since the beginning of time, I'd imagine that the Gods have seen fit to create any number of things with the kind of power we're looking for."

"Why not just make one?" Kalten asked. "Get a group of people together and have them cast a spell on something—some jewel or stone or ring or whatever?"

"Now I can see why you never became proficient in the secrets, Kalten." Sephrenia sighed. "You don't even understand the basic principles. All magic comes from the Gods, not from us. They allow us to borrow—if we ask them in the proper fashion—but they *won't* let us make the kind of thing we're looking for in this case. The power that's instilled in those objects is a part of the power of the Gods themselves, and they don't sacrifice that sort of thing lightly."

"Oh," the blond man said. "I didn't know that."

"You should have. I told you about it when you were fifteen."

"I must have forgotten."

"About all we can do is start looking," Vanion said. "I'll send word to the other preceptors. We'll have every Church Knight in all four orders working on it."

"And I'll get word to the Styrics in the mountains," Sephrenia added. "There are many such things known only to Styricum."

"Did anything interesting happen in Madel?" Sparhawk asked Kalten.

"Not really," Kalten replied. "We caught a few glimpses of Krager, but always from a distance. By the time we got close to where he'd been, he'd given us the slip. He's a tricky little weasel, isn't he?"

Sparhawk nodded. "That's what made me finally realize that he was being used as bait. Could you get any idea of what he was doing?"

"No. We could never get close enough. He was up to something, though. He was scurrying around Madel like a mouse in a cheese factory."

"Did Adus drop out of sight?"

"More or less. Talen and Berit saw him once—when he and Krager rode out of town."

"Which way were they going?" Sparhawk asked the boy.

Talen shrugged. "They were headed back toward Borrata the last time we saw them," he said. "They might have changed direction once they got out of sight, though."

"The big one had some bandages on his head, Sir Sparhawk," Berit reported, "and his arm was in a sling."

Kalten laughed. "It seems that you got a bigger piece of him than either one of us realized, Sparhawk," he said.

"I was trying," Sparhawk said grimly. "Getting rid of Adus is one of my main goals in life."

The door opened, and Kurik came back in carrying the wooden case containing the swords of the fallen knights.

"You insist on doing this, Vanion?" Sephrenia asked.

"I don't see that there's any choice," he replied. "You have to be fit to move around. I can do my job sitting down—or lying in bed—or dead, probably, if it comes to that."

The movement was but a faint one of Sephrenia's eyes. She looked for the briefest instant at Flute, and the little girl gravely nodded her head. Sparhawk was positive that only he had witnessed the exchange; for some reason it troubled him profoundly.

"Only take the swords one at a time," Sephrenia instructed Vanion. "The weight is considerable, and you'll need to give yourself time to get used to it."

"I've held swords before, Sephrenia."

"Not like these, and it's not the weight of the swords I'm talking about. It's the weight of all that goes with them." She opened the case and took out the sword of Sir Parasim, the young knight whom Adus had killed in Arcium. She took the blade and gravely extended the hilt across her forearm to Vanion.

He rose and took it from her. "Correct me if I make any mistakes," he said and started to chant in Styric. Sephrenia raised her voice with his, though her tone was softer, less certain, and her eyes were filled with doubt. The spell rose to a climax, and Vanion suddenly sagged, his face turning gray. "God!" he gasped, almost dropping the sword.

"Are you all right, dear one?" Sephrenia asked sharply, reaching out and touching him.

"Let me get my breath for a minute," Vanion said. "How can you stand this, Sephrenia?"

"We do what we must," she replied. "I feel better already, Vanion. There's no need for you to take the other two."

"Yes, there is. We're going to lose another of the twelve of us any day now, and his ghost will deliver another sword to you. I'm going to see to it that your hands are free when it comes." He straightened. "All right," he said grimly. "Give me the next one."

Sparhawk found that he was unusually tired that evening. The rigors of what had taken place in Rendor seemed to catch up with him all at once, but despite his weariness, he tossed and turned fitfully on the narrow cot in his cell-like room. The moon was full and it cast its pale light through the narrow window directly into Sparhawk's face. He muttered a sour oath and covered his head with his blanket to hide his eyes from the light.

Perhaps he dozed, or perhaps not. He hovered on the verge of sleep for what seemed hours; but, try though he might to slip through that soft door, he could not. He threw off his blanket and sat up.

It was spring, or very nearly. It seemed that the winter had been interminable, but what had he really accomplished? The months had slipped away, and with them Ehlana's life. Was he really any closer to freeing her from her crystal entombment? In the cold light of the midnight moon, he suddenly came face-to-face with a chilling thought. Might it not be entirely possible that all of the scheming and the complicated plots of Annias and Martel had been with but a single aim—to delay him, to fill the time Ehlana had left with senseless activity? He had been dashing from crisis to crisis since he had returned to Cimmura. Perhaps the plots of his enemies had not been intended to succeed. Perhaps their only purpose had been delay. He felt somehow that he was being manipulated and that whoever or whatever was behind it was taking pleasure in his anger and frustration, toying with him with cruel amusement. He lay back again to consider that.

It was a sudden chill that awoke him, a cold that seemed to penetrate to his bones, and he knew even before he opened his eyes that he was not alone.

An armored figure stood at the foot of his cot, with the moonlight gleaming on the enameled black steel. The familiar charnelhouse reek filled the room. "Awaken, Sir Sparhawk," the figure commanded in a chillingly hollow tone. "I would have words with thee."

Sparhawk sat up. "I'm awake, brother," he replied. The specter raised its visor, and Sparhawk saw a familiar face. "I'm sorry, Sir Tanis," he said.

"All men die," the ghost intoned, "and my death was not without purpose. That thought alone doth comfort me in the House of the Dead. Attend to me, Sparhawk, for my time with thee must be short. I bring thee instruction. This is the purpose for which I died."

"I will hear thee, Tanis," Sparhawk promised.

"Go thou then this very night to the crypt which doth lie beneath the cathedral of Cimmura. There shalt thou meet another restless shade which will instruct thee further in the course which thou must follow."

"Whose shade?"

"Thou shalt know him, Sparhawk."

"I will do as you command, my brother."

The specter at the foot of the cot drew its sword. "And now I must leave thee, Sparhawk," it said. "I must deliver up my sword ere I return to the endless silence."

Sparhawk sighed. "I know," he said.

"Hail then, brother, and farewell," the ghost concluded. "Remember me in thy prayers." Then the armored figure turned and walked silently from the room.

The towers of the cathedral of Cimmura blotted out the stars, and the pale moon lay low on the western horizon, filling the streets with silvery light and inky black shadows. Sparhawk moved silently down a narrow alleyway and stopped in the dense shadow at its mouth. He was directly across the street from the main doors of the cathedral. Beneath his traveller's cloak he wore mail, and his plain sword was belted at his waist.

He felt a peculiar detachment as he stared across the street at the pair of church soldiers standing guard at the cathedral door. Their red tunics were leached of all color by the pale moon, and they leaned inattentively against the stones of the cathedral wall.

Sparhawk considered the situation. The guarded door was the only way into the cathedral. All others would be locked. By tradition, however, if not by Church law, the locking of the main doors of any church was forbidden.

The guards would be sleepy and far from alert. The street was not wide. One quick rush would eliminate the problem. Sparhawk straightened and reached for his sword. Then he stopped. Something seemed wrong with the notion. He was not squeamish, but it seemed somehow that he should not go to this meeting with blood on his hands. Then, too, he decided, two bodies lying on the cathedral steps would announce louder than words that someone had gone to a great deal of trouble to get inside.

All he really needed was about a minute to cross the street and slip through the doors. He thought about it. What would be most likely to pull the soldiers from their posts? He came up with a half-dozen possibilities before he finally settled on one. He smiled when the notion came to him. He ran over the spell in his mind, making sure that he had all the words right, and then he began to mutter under his breath in Styric.

The spell was fairly long. There were a number of details he wanted to get exactly right. When it was done, he raised his hand and released it.

The figure that appeared at the end of the street was that of a woman. She wore a velvet cloak with its hood thrown back, and her long blonde hair tumbled down her back. Her face was lovely beyond belief. She walked toward the doors of the cathedral with a seductive grace and, when she reached the steps, she stopped, looking up at the now fully awake pair of guards. She did not speak. Speech would have unnecessarily complicated the spell, and she did not need to say anything. Slowly, she unfastened the neck of her cloak and then opened it. Beneath the cloak, she was naked.

Sparhawk could clearly hear the suddenly hoarse breathing of the two soldiers.

Then, with inviting glances over her shoulder, she walked back up the street. The two guards looked after her, then at each other, then up and down the street to be sure that no one was watching. They leaned their pikes against the stone walls beside them and ran down the steps.

The figure of the woman had stopped beneath the torch flaring at the corner. She beckoned again, then stepped out of the light and disappeared up the side street.

The guards ran after her.

Sparhawk was out of the shadows at the mouth of the alley before the pair had rounded the corner. He was across the street in seconds and he bounded up the steps two at a time, seized the heavy handle of one of the great arched doors, and pulled. Then he was inside. He smiled faintly to himself, wondering how long the soldiers would search for the now-vanished apparition he had created.

The inside of the cathedral was dim and cool, smelling of incense and candle wax. Two lone tapers, one on either side of the altar, burned fitfully, stuttering in the faint breath of night air that had followed Sparhawk into the nave. Their light was little more than two flickering pinpoints that were reflected only faintly in the gems and gold decorating the altar.

Sparhawk moved silently down the central aisle, his shoulders tense and his senses alert. Although it was late at night, there was always the possibility that one of the many churchmen who lived within the confines of the cathedral might be up and about, and Sparhawk preferred to keep his visit a secret and to avoid noisy confrontations.

He knelt perfunctorily before the altar, rose, and moved out of the nave into the dim, latticed corridor leading toward the chancel.

There was light ahead, dim but steady. Sparhawk moved quietly, keeping close to the wall. A curtained archway stood before him, and he carefully parted the thick purple drapes a finger's width and peered in.

The Primate Annias, garbed not in satin but in harsh monk's cloth, knelt before a small stone altar inside the sanctuary. His emaciated features were twisted in an agony of self-loathing, and he wrung his hands together as if he would tear his fingers from their sockets. Tears streamed openly down his face, and his breath rasped hoarsely in his throat.

Sparhawk's face went bleak, and his hand went to his sword hilt. The soldiers at the cathedral door had been one thing. Killing them would have served no real purpose. Annias, however, was an entirely different matter. The primate was alone. A quick rush and a single thrust would remove this filthy infection from Elenia once and for all.

For a moment the life of the primate of Cimmura hung in the balance as Sparhawk, for the first time in his life, contemplated the deliberate murder of an unarmed man. But then he seemed to hear a light, girlish voice and saw before him a wealth of pale blonde hair and a pair of unwavering gray eyes. Regretfully, he let the velvet drapes close again and went to serve his queen, who, even in her slumber, had reached out with her gentle hand to save his soul.

"Another time, Annias," he whispered under his breath. Then he went down the corridor past the chancel toward the entrance to the crypt.

The crypt lay beneath the cathedral, and entry was gained by walking down a flight of stone stairs. A single tallow candle guttered at the top of the stairs, set in a grease-encrusted sconce. Careful to make no noise, Sparhawk snapped the candle in two, relit the fragment remaining in the sconce, and went on down, holding his half candle aloft.

The door at the bottom of the stairs was of heavy bronze. Sparhawk closed his fist about the latch and twisted very slowly until he felt the bolt grate open. Then, a fraction of an inch at a time, he opened the thick door. The faint creaking of the hinges seemed very loud in the silence, but Sparhawk knew that the sound would not carry up to the main floor of the church, and Annias was too caught up in his personal agonizing to hear anyway.

The inside of the crypt was a vast, low place, cold and musty-smelling. The circle of yellow light from Sparhawk's bit of candle did not reach far, and beyond that circle, huge expanses lay lost in darkness. The arched buttresses which supported the roof were draped with cobwebs, and dense shadows clotted the irregular corners. Sparhawk placed his back against the bronze door and very slowly closed it again. The sound of its closing echoed through the crypt like the hollow crack of doom.

The shadowed crypt extended back in unrelieved darkness far under the nave of the cathedral. Beneath the vaulted ceiling and the web-draped buttresses lay the former rulers of Elenia, rank upon silent rank of them, each enclosed in a leprous marble tomb with a dusty leaden effigy reposing on its top. Two thousand years of Elenian history lay moldering slowly into dust in this dank cellar. The wicked lay beside the virtuous. The stupid bedded down with the wise. The universal leveler had brought them all to this same place. The customary funerary sculpture decorated the stone walls and the corners of many of the sarcophagi, adding an even more mournful air to the silent tomb.

Sparhawk shuddered. The hot meeting of blood, bone, flesh, and bright, sharp steel were familiar to him, but not this cold, dusty silence. He was not sure of exactly how to proceed, since the specter of Sir Tanis had provided him with few details. He stood uncertainly near the bronze door, waiting. Although he knew it was foolish, he wrapped his hand about his sword hilt, more for comfort than out of any belief that the weapon at his side would be of any use in this dreadful place.

At first the sound seemed no more than a breath, a vagrant movement of the stale air inside the crypt. Then it came again, slightly louder this time. "Sparhawk," it sighed in a hollow whisper.

Sparhawk lifted his guttering candle, peering into the shadows.

"Sparhawk," the whisper came again.

"I'm here."

"Come closer."

The whisper seemed to be coming from somewhere among the more recent burials. Sparhawk moved toward them, growing more certain as he did so. Finally, he stopped before the last sarcophagus, the one bearing the name of King Aldreas, father of Queen Ehlana. He stood before the lead effigy of the late king, a man he was sworn to serve but for whom he had held but little respect. The sculptor who had created the effigy had made some effort to make Aldreas's features look regal, but the weakness was still there in the slightly harried expression and the uncertain chin.

"Hail, Sparhawk." The whisper came not from the sculptured form atop the marble lid, but from within the tomb itself.

"Hail, Aldreas," Sparhawk replied.

"And dost thou still bear me enmity and hold me in contempt, my champion?"

A hundred slights and insults leaped into Sparhawk's mind, a half-score years of humiliation and denigration by the man whose sorrowing shade now spoke from the hollow confines of his marble sepulcher. But what would it prove to twist a knife in the heart of one already dead? Quietly, Sparhawk forgave his king. "I never did, Aldreas," he lied. "You were my king. That's all I needed to know."

"Thou art kind, Sparhawk," the hollow voice sighed, "and thy kindness rends mine insubstantial heart far more than any rebuke."

"I'm sorry, Aldreas."

"I was not suited to wear the crown," the sepulchral voice admitted with a melancholy regret. "There were so many things happening that I didn't understand, and people around me I thought were my friends, but were not."

"We knew, Aldreas, but there was no way we could protect you."

"I could not have known of the plots which surrounded me, could I, Sparhawk?" The ghost seemed to have a desperate need to explain and justify the things Aldreas had done in life. "I was raised to revere the Church, and I trusted the primate of Cimmura above all others. How could I have known that his intent was to deceive me?"

"You could not have, Aldreas." It was not difficult to say it. Aldreas was no longer an enemy, and if a few words would comfort his guilt-ridden ghost, they cost no more than the breath it took to express them.

"But I should not have turned my back on my only child," Aldreas said in a voice filled with pain. "It is that which I repent most sorely. The primate turned me against her, but I should not have listened to his false counsel."

"Ehlana knew that, Aldreas," Sparhawk said. "She knew that it was Annias who was her enemy, not you."

There was a long pause. "And what has become of my dear, dear sister?" The late king's words came out as from between teeth tightly clenched with hate.

"She's still in the cloister at Demos, your Majesty," Sparhawk reported in as neutral a tone as he could manage. "She will die there."

"Then entomb her there, my champion," Aldreas commanded. "Do not defile my slumber by placing my murderess at my side in this place."

"Murderess?" Sparhawk was stunned.

"My life had become a burden to her. Her sycophant and paramour, Primate Annias, arranged to have her conveyed in secret here to me. She beguiled me with wildest abandon, wilder than I had ever known from her. In exhaustion, I took a cup from her hands and drank, and the drink was death. She taunted me with that, standing over my nerveless body with her flagrant nudity and her face contorted with hatred and contempt as she reviled me. Avenge me, my champion. Take vengeance upon my foul sister and her twisted consort, for they have brought me low and dispossessed my true heir, the daughter I ignored and despised throughout her childhood."

"As God gives me breath, it shall be as you say, Aldreas," Sparhawk swore.

"And when my pale little daughter ascends to her rightful place upon my throne, tell her, I pray thee, that I did truly love her."

"If that, please God, should come to pass, Aldreas, I will."

"It must, Sparhawk. It must—else all that Elenia hath ever been shall be as naught. Only Ehlana is the true heir to the throne of Elenia. I charge thee, do not let my throne be usurped by the fruit of the unclean coupling of my sister and the primate of Cimmura."

"My sword shall prevent it, my king," Sparhawk pledged fervently. "All three will lie dead in their own blood before this week sees its end."

"And thy life as well shall be lost in thy rush to vengeance, Sparhawk, and how will thy sacrifice restore my daughter to her rightful place?"

Aldreas, Sparhawk concluded, was far wiser in death than he had been in life.

"The time for vengeance will come in its own proper order, my champion," the ghost told him. "First, however, I charge thee to restore my daughter Ehlana. And to that end I am permitted to reveal certain truths to thee. No nostrum nor talisman of lesser worth may heal my child, for only Bhelliom can make her whole again."

Sparhawk's heart sank.

"Be not dismayed, Sparhawk, for the time hath come for Bhelliom to emerge from the place where it hath lain hidden and once again to stir the earth with its power. It moves in its own time and with its own purpose, and this is that time, for events have moved mankind to the place where its purpose may now be accomplished. No force in all the world can prevent Bhelliom from coming forth into the sunlight again, and whole nations await its coming. Be *thou* the one who finds it, however, for only in *thy* hand can its full power be released to roll back the darkness which even now stalks the earth. Thou art no longer my champion, Sparhawk, but the champion of all this world. Shouldst thou fail, all will fail."

"And where should I seek, my king?"

"That I am forbidden to reveal. I can, however, tell thee how to unleash its power once it lies in thy grasp. The blood-red ring which adorns thy hand and that which in life adorned mine are older far than we had imagined. He who fashioned Bhelliom fashioned the rings, also, and they are the keys which will unlock the power of the jewel."

"But your ring is lost, Aldreas. The primate of Cimmura tore the palace apart again and again searching for it."

A ghostly chuckle came from the sarcophagus. "I still have it, Sparhawk," Aldreas said. "After my dear sister had given me her last fatal kiss and departed, I had moments of lucidity. I concealed the ring to deny possession of it to my enemies. Despite all the desperate efforts of the primate of Cimmura, it was buried with me. Think back, Sparhawk. Remember the old legends. At the time my family and thine were bonded together by these rings, thy ancestor gave to mine his own war spear in token of his allegiance. Thus I return it."

A ghostly hand rose from the sarcophagus holding a short-handled, broad-bladed spear in its grasp. The weapon was very old, and its symbolic importance had been forgotten over the centuries. Sparhawk reached out his hand and took it from the ghostly hand of Aldreas. "I will carry it with pride, my king," he said.

"Pride is a hollow thing, Sparhawk. The significance of the spear goes far beyond that. Detach the blade from the shaft and look within the socket."

Sparhawk set down his candle, put his hand to the blade, and twisted the tough wood of the shaft. With a dry squeak, the two separated. He looked into the ancient steel socket of the blade. The blood-red glitter of a ruby winked back at him.

"I have but one more instruction for thee, my champion," the ghost continued. "Should it come to pass that thy quest reaches its conclusion only after my daughter joins me in the House of the Dead, it lies upon thee to destroy Bhelliom, though this shall surely cost thee thy life."

"But how may I destroy a thing of such power?" Sparhawk protested.

"Keep thou my ring in the place where I have concealed it. Should all go well, return it to my daughter when she sits again in splendor upon her throne; but should she die, continue thy quest for Bhelliom, though the search takes thee all the days of thy life. And when it comes to pass that thou findest it, seize the spear in the hand which bears thy ring and drive it into the heart of Bhelliom with all thy might. The jewel will be destoyed, as will the rings—and in that act shalt thou lose thy life. Fail not in this, Sparhawk, for a dark power doth bestride the earth, and Bhelliom must never fall into its hands."

Sparhawk bowed. "It shall be as you command, my king," he swore.

A sigh came from the sarcophagus. "It is done, then," Aldreas whispered. "I have done what I could to aid thee, and this completes the task which I left unfinished. Do not fail me. Hail then, Sparhawk, and farewell."

"Hail and farewell, Aldreas."

The crypt was still chill and empty, save for the ranks of the royal dead. The hollow whisper had fallen silent now. Sparhawk rejoined the parts of the spear, then reached out his hand and laid it over the heart of the leaden effigy. "Sleep well, Aldreas," he said softly. Then with the ancient spear in his grasp, he turned and quietly left the tomb.

# THE RUBY
# KNIGHT

*For young Mike*
*"Put it in the car"*
*And for Peggy*
*"What happened to my balloons?"*

*A History of the House of Sparhawk*

—FROM THE CHRONICLES OF
THE PANDION BROTHERHOOD

It was in the twenty-fifth century when the hordes of Otha of Zemoch invaded the Elene kingdoms of western Eosia and swept all before them with fire and sword in their march to the west. Otha appeared invincible until his forces were met on the great, smoke-shrouded battlefield at Lake Randera by the combined armies of the western kingdoms and the concerted might of the Knights of the Church. The battle there in central Lamorkand is said to have raged for weeks before the invading Zemochs were finally pushed back and turned to flee for their own borders.

The victory of the Elenes was thus complete, but fully half of the Church Knights lay slain upon the battlefield, and the armies of the Elene kings numbered their dead by the scores of thousands. When the victorious but exhausted survivors returned to their homes, they faced an even grimmer foe—the famine that is one of the common results of war.

The famine in Eosia endured for generations, threatening at times to depopulate the continent. Inevitably, social organization began to break down, and political chaos reigned in the Elene kingdoms. Rogue barons paid only lip service to their oaths of fealty to their kings. Private disputes often resulted in ugly little wars, and open banditry was common. These conditions generally prevailed until well into the early years of the twenty-seventh century.

It was in this time of turmoil that an accolyte appeared at the gates of our motherhouse at Demos, expressing an earnest desire to become a member of our order. As his training began, our preceptor soon realized this young postulant, Sparhawk by name, was no ordinary man. He quickly outstripped his fellow novices and even mastered seasoned Pandions on the practice field. It was not merely his physical prowess, however, that so distinguished him, since his intellectual gifts were also towering. His aptitude for the secrets of Styricum was the delight of his tutor in those arts, and the aged Styric instructor guided his pupil into areas of magic far beyond those customarily taught the Pandion Knights. The Patriarch of Demos was no less enthusiastic about the intellect of this novice, and by the time Sir Sparhawk had won his spurs, he was also skilled in the intricacies of philosophy and theological disputation.

It was at about the time that Sir Sparhawk was knighted that the youthful King Antor ascended the Elenian throne in Cimmura, and the lives of the two young men soon became intricately intertwined. King Antor was a rash, even foolhardy youth, and an outbreak of banditry along his northern border enraged him to the point where he threw caution to the winds and mounted a punitive expedition into that portion of his kingdom with a woefully inadequate force. When word of this reached Demos, the Preceptor of the Pandion Knights dispatched a relief column to rush north to the king's aid, and among the knights in that column was Sir Sparhawk.

King Antor was soon far out of his depth. Although no one could dispute his personal bravery, his lack of experience often led him into serious tactical and strategic blunders. Since he was oblivious to the alliances between the various bandit barons of the northern marches, he ofttimes led his men against one of them without giving thought to the fact that another was very likely to come to the aid of his ally. Thus, King Antor's already seriously outnumbered force was steadily whittled down by surprise attacks directed at the rear of his army. The barons of the north gleefully outflanked him again and again as he charged blindly forward, and they steadily decimated his reserves.

And so it stood when Sparhawk and the other Pandion Knights arrived in the war zone. The armies that had been so sorely pressing the young king were largely untrained, a rabble recruited from local robber bands. The barons who led them fell back to take stock of the situation. Although their numbers were still overwhelming, the reputed skill of the Pandions on the battlefield was something to be taken into account. A few of their number, made rash by their previous successes, urged their allies to press the attack, but older and wiser men advised caution. It seems relatively certain that a fair number of the barons, young and old alike, saw the way to the throne of Elenia opening before them. Should King Antor fall in battle, his crown might easily become the property of any man strong enough to wrest it from his companions.

The barons' first attacks on the combined forces of the Pandions and King Antor's troops were tentative, more in the nature of tests of the strength and resolve of the Church Knights and their allies. When it became evident that the response was in large measure defensive, these assaults grew more serious, and ultimately there was a pitched battle not far from the Pelosian border. As soon as it became evident that the barons were committing their full forces to the struggle, the Pandions reacted with their customary savagery. The defensive posture they had adopted during the first probing attacks had been clearly a ruse designed to lure the barons into an all-out confrontation.

The battle raged for the better part of a spring day. Late in the afternoon, when bright sunlight flooded the field, King Antor became separated from the troops of his household guard. He found himself horseless and hard-pressed and he resolved to sell his life as dearly as possible. It was at this point that Sir Sparhawk entered the fray. He quickly cut his way through to the king's side, and, in the fashion as old as the history of warfare, the two stood back to back, holding off their foes. The combination of Antor's headstrong bravery and Sparhawk's skill was convincing enough to hold their enemies at bay until by mischance, Sparhawk's sword was broken. With triumphant shouts the force encircling the two rushed in for the kill. This proved to be a fatal error.

Snatching a short, broad-bladed battle spear from one of the fallen, Sparhawk decimated the ranks of the charging troops. The culmination of the struggle came when the swarthy-faced baron who had been leading the attack rushed in to slay the sorely wounded Antor and died with Sparhawk's spear in his vitals. The baron's fall demoralized his men. They fell back and ultimately fled the scene.

Antor's wounds were grave, and Sparhawk's only slightly less so. Exhausted, the two sank side by side to the ground as evening settled over the field. It is impossible to reconstruct the conversation of the two wounded men there on that bloody field during the early hours of the night, since in later years neither would reveal what had passed between them. What is known, however, is that at some point during their discussions, they traded weapons. Antor bestowed the royal sword of Elenia upon Sir Sparhawk and took in exchange the battle spear with which Sir Sparhawk had saved his life. The king was to cherish that rude weapon to the end of his days.

It was nearly midnight when the two injured men saw a torch approaching through the darkness, and, not knowing if the torchbearer was friend or foe, they struggled to their feet and wearily prepared to defend themselves. The one who approached, however, was not an Elene, but was rather a white-robed and hooded Styric woman. Wordlessly, she tended their wounds. Then she spoke to them briefly in a lilting voice and gave them the pair of rings that came to symbolize their lifelong friendship. Tradition has it that the oval stones set in the rings were as pale as diamond when the two received them, but that their mingled blood permanently stained the stones, and they appear to this day to be deep red rubies. Once she had done this, the mysterious Styric woman turned without a further word and walked off into the night, her white robe glowing in the moonlight.

As misty dawn lightened the field, the troops of Antor's household guard and a number of Sparhawk's fellow Pandions found the two wounded men at last, and they were borne on litters to our motherhouse here at Demos. Their recovery consumed months; by the time they were well enough to travel, they were fast friends. They went by easy stages to Antor's capital at Cimmura, and there the king made a startling announcement. He declared that henceforth the Pandion Sparhawk would be his champion and that, so long as both their families survived, the descendants of Sparhawk would serve the rulers of Elenia in that capacity.

As inevitably happens, the king's court at Cimmura was filled with intrigues. The various factions, however, were taken aback somewhat by the appearance at court of the grim-faced Sir Sparhawk. After a few tentative attempts to enlist his support for this or that faction had been sternly rebuffed, the courtiers uncomfortably concluded that the King's Champion was incorruptible. Moreover, the friendship between the king and Sparhawk made the Pandion Knight the king's confidant and closest adviser. Since Sparhawk, as has been pointed out, had a towering intellect, he easily saw through the ofttimes petty scheming of the various officials at court and brought them to the attention of his less-gifted friend. Within a year, the court of King Antor had become remarkably free of corruption as Sparhawk imposed his own rigid morality upon those around him.

Of even greater concern to the various political factions in Elenia was the growing influence of the Pandion order in the kingdom. King Antor was profoundly grateful, not only to Sir Sparhawk, but also to his champion's brother knights. The king and his friend journeyed often to Demos to confer with the preceptor of our order, and major policy decisions were more often made in the motherhouse than in the chambers of the royal council where courtiers had customarily dictated royal policy with an eye more to their own advantage than to the good of the kingdom.

Sir Sparhawk married in middle life, and his wife soon bore him a son. At Antor's request, the child was also named Sparhawk, a tradition which, once established, has continued unbroken in the family to this very day. When he had reached a suitable age, the younger Sparhawk entered the Pandion motherhouse to begin the training for the position he would one day fill. To their fathers' delight, young Sparhawk and Antor's son, the crown prince, had become close friends during their boyhood, and the relationship between king and champion was thus ensured to continue unbroken.

When Antor, filled with years and honors, lay on his deathbed, his last act was to bestow his ruby ring and the short, broad-bladed spear upon his son; at the same time, the elder Sparhawk passed his ring and the royal sword on to *his* son. This tradition has also persisted down to this very day.

It is widely believed among the common people of Elenia that for so long as the friendship between the royal family and the house of Sparhawk shall persist, the kingdom will prosper and that no evil can befall it. Like many superstitions, this one is to some degree based in fact. The descendants of Sparhawk have always been gifted men and, in addition to their Pandion training, they have also received special instruction in statecraft and diplomacy, the better to prepare them for their hereditary task.

Of late, however, there has been a rift between the royal family and the house of Sparhawk. The weak King Aldreas, dominated by his ambitious sister and the Primate of Cimmura, rather coldly relegated the current Sparhawk to the lesser, even demeaning position as caretaker of the person of Princess Ehlana—possibly in the hope that the champion would be so offended that he would renounce his hereditary position. Sir Sparhawk, however, took his duties seriously and educated the child who would one day be Queen of Elenia in those areas that would prepare her to rule.

When it became obvious that Sparhawk would not willingly give up his post, Aldreas, at the instigation of his sister and Primate Annias, sent the Knight Sparhawk into exile in the Kingdom of Rendor.

Upon the death of King Aldreas, his daughter Ehlana ascended the throne as Queen. Hearing this news, Sparhawk returned to Cimmura only to find that his young Queen was gravely ill and that her life was being sustained only by a spell cast by the Styric sorceress Sephrenia—a spell, however, which could keep Ehlana alive for no more than a year.

In consultation, the preceptors of the four militant orders of Church Knights decided that the four orders must work in concert to discover a cure for the Queen's illness and to restore her to health and power, lest the corrupt Primate Annias achieve his goal, the throne of the Archprelacy in the basilica of Chyrellos. To that end, the preceptors of the Cyrinics, the Alciones, and the Genidians dispatched their own champions to join with the Pandion Sparhawk and his boyhood friend Kalten to seek out the cure that would not only restore Queen Ehlana, but also her kingdom, which suffered in her absence from a grave malaise.

Thus it stands. The restoration of the Queen's health is vital not only to the Kingdom of Elenia, but to the other Elene kingdoms as well, for should the venal Primate Annias gain the Archprelate's throne, we may be sure that the Elene kingdoms will be wracked by turmoil, and our ancient foe, Otha of Zemoch, stands poised on our eastern frontier, ready to exploit any division or chaos. The cure of the Queen who is so near to death, however, may daunt even her champion and his stalwart companions. Pray for their success, my brothers, for should they fail, the whole of the Eosian continent will inevitably fall into general warfare, and civilization as we know it will cease to exist.

PART ONE

# LAKE RANDERA

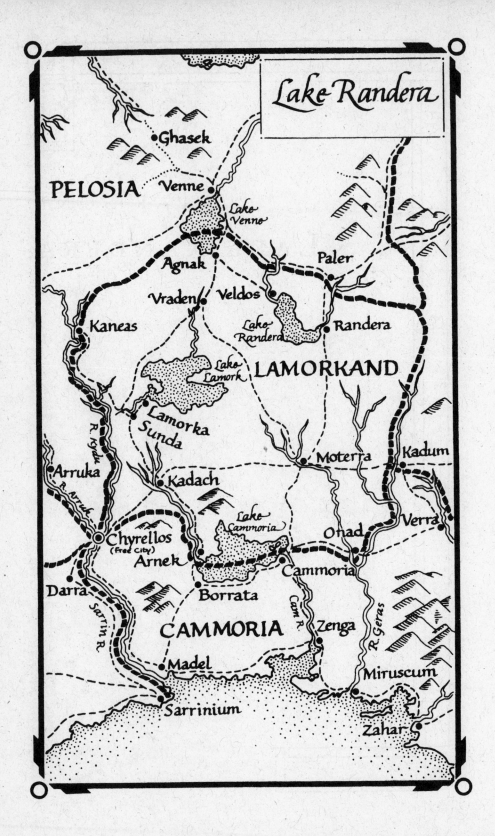

Lake Randera

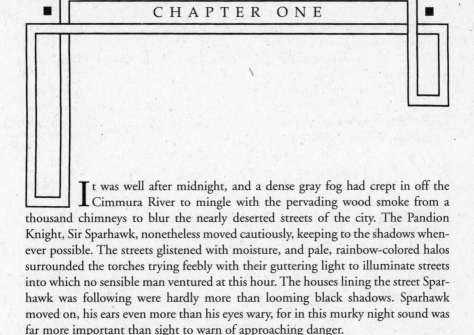

# CHAPTER ONE

It was well after midnight, and a dense gray fog had crept in off the Cimmura River to mingle with the pervading wood smoke from a thousand chimneys to blur the nearly deserted streets of the city. The Pandion Knight, Sir Sparhawk, nonetheless moved cautiously, keeping to the shadows whenever possible. The streets glistened with moisture, and pale, rainbow-colored halos surrounded the torches trying feebly with their guttering light to illuminate streets into which no sensible man ventured at this hour. The houses lining the street Sparhawk was following were hardly more than looming black shadows. Sparhawk moved on, his ears even more than his eyes wary, for in this murky night sound was far more important than sight to warn of approaching danger.

This was a bad time to be out. By day, Cimmura was no more dangerous than any other city. By night, it was a jungle where the strong fed upon the weak and unwary. Sparhawk, however, was neither of those. Beneath his plain traveller's cloak he wore chain mail, and a heavy sword hung at his side. In addition, he carried a short, broad-bladed battle spear loosely in one hand. He was trained, moreover, in levels of violence no footpad could match, and a seething anger inflamed him at this point. Bleakly, the broken-nosed man almost hoped that some fool might try an attack. When provoked, Sparhawk was not the most reasonable of men and he had been provoked of late.

He was also, however, aware of the urgency of what he was about. Much as he might have taken some satisfaction in the rush and cut and slash of a meeting with unknown and unimportant assailants, he had responsibilities. His pale young Queen hovered near death, and she silently demanded absolute fidelity from her champion. He would not betray her, and to die in some muddy gutter as a result of a meaningless encounter would not serve the Queen he was oath-bound to protect. And so it was that he moved cautiously, his feet more silent than those of any paid assassin.

Somewhere ahead he saw the bobbing of hazy-looking torches and heard the measured tread of several men marching in unison. He muttered an oath and ducked up a smelly alley.

A half-dozen men marched by, their red tunics bedewed by the fog and with long pikes leaning slantwise over their shoulders. "It's that place in Rose Street," their officer was saying arrogantly, "where the Pandions try to hide their ungodly subterfuge. They know we're watching, of course, but our presence restricts their movements and leaves his Grace, the primate, free from their interference."

"We know the reasons, Lieutenant," a bored-sounding corporal said. "We've been doing this for over a year now."

"Oh." The self-important young lieutenant sounded a bit crestfallen. "I just want to be sure that we all understood, is all."

"Yes, sir," the corporal said tonelessly.

"Wait here, men," the lieutenant said, trying to make his boyish voice sound gruff. "I'll look on ahead." He marched on up the street, his heels smashing noisily on the fog-wet cobblestones.

"What a jackass," the corporal muttered to his companions.

"Grow up, Corporal," an old, gray-haired veteran said. "We take the pay, so we obey their orders and keep our opinions to ourselves. Just do your job and leave opinions to the officers."

The corporal grunted sourly. "I was at court yesterday," he said. "Primate Annias had summoned that young puppy up there, and the fool absolutely *had* to have an escort. Would you believe the lieutenant was actually fawning all over the bastard Lycheas?"

"That's what lieutenants do best." The veteran shrugged. "They're born boot-lickers, and the bastard *is* the Prince Regent, after all. I'm not sure if that makes his boots taste any better, but the lieutenant's probably got calluses on his tongue by now."

The corporal laughed. "That's God's truth, but wouldn't he be surprised if the Queen recovered and he found out that he'd eaten all that boot polish for nothing?"

"You'd better hope she doesn't, Corporal," one of the other men said. "If she wakes up and takes control of her own treasury again, Annias won't have the money to pay us next month."

"He can always dip into the church coffers."

"Not without giving an accounting, he can't. The Hierocracy in Chyrellos squeezes every penny of church money until it squeaks."

"All right, you men," the young officer called out of the fog, "the Pandion inn is just up ahead. I've relieved the soldiers who were on watch, so we'd better go there and take up our positions."

"You heard him," the corporal said. "Move out." The church soldiers marched off into the fog.

Sparhawk smiled briefly in the darkness. It was seldom that he had the opportunity to hear the casual conversations of the enemy. He had long suspected that the soldiers of the Primate of Cimmura were motivated more by greed than from any sense of loyalty or piety. He stepped out of the alley and then jumped soundlessly back as he heard other footsteps coming up the street. For some reason the usually empty nighttime streets of Cimmura were awash with people. The footsteps were loud, so whoever it was out there was not trying to sneak up on anybody. Sparhawk shifted the short-handled spear in his hands. Then he saw the fellow looming out of the fog. The man wore a dark-colored smock, and he had a large basket balanced on one shoulder. He appeared to be a workman of some kind, but there was no way to be sure of that. Sparhawk remained silent and let him pass. He waited until the sound of the footsteps was gone, then he stepped into the street again. He walked carefully, his soft boots making little sound on the wet cobblestones, and he kept his gray cloak wrapped tightly about him to muffle any clinking of his chain mail.

He crossed an empty street to avoid the flickering yellow lamplight coming through the open door of a tavern where voices were raised in bawdy song. He shifted the spear to his left hand and pulled the hood of his cloak even farther forward to shadow his face as he passed through the mist-shrouded light.

He stopped, his eyes and ears carefully searching the foggy street ahead of him. His general direction was toward the east gate, but he had no particular fanaticism about that. People who walk in straight lines are predictable, and predictable people get caught. It was absolutely vital that he leave the city unrecognized and unseen by any of Annias' men, even if it took him all night. When he was satisfied that the street was empty, he moved on, keeping to the deepest shadows. At a corner beneath a misty orange torch, a ragged beggar sat against a wall. He had a bandage across his eyes and a number of authentic-looking sores on his arms and legs. Sparhawk knew that this was not a profitable time for begging, so the fellow was probably up to something else. Then a slate from a rooftop crashed into the street not far from where Sparhawk stood.

"Charity!" the beggar called in a despairing voice, although Sparhawk's soft-shod feet had made no sound.

"Good evening, neighbor," the big knight said softly, crossing the street. He dropped a couple of coins into the begging bowl.

"Thank you, my Lord. God bless you."

"You're not supposed to be able to see me, neighbor," Sparhawk reminded him. "You don't know if I'm a lord or a commoner."

"It's late," the beggar apologized, "and I'm a little sleepy. Sometimes I forget."

"Very sloppy," Sparhawk chided. "Pay attention to business. Oh, by the way, give my best to Platime." Platime was an enormously fat man who ruled the underside of Cimmura with an iron fist.

The beggar lifted the bandage from his eyes and stared at Sparhawk, his eyes widening in recognition.

"And tell your friend up on that roof not to get excited," Sparhawk added. "You might tell him, though, to watch where he puts his feet. That last slate he kicked loose almost brained me."

"He's a new man." The beggar sniffed. "He still has a lot to learn about burglary."

"That he does," Sparhawk agreed. "Maybe you can help me, neighbor. Talen was telling me about a tavern up against the east wall of the city. It's supposed to have a garret that the tavern keeper rents out from time to time. Do you happen to know where it's located?"

"It's in Goat Lane, Sir Sparhawk. It's got a sign that's supposed to look like a bunch of grapes. You can't miss it." The beggar squinted. "Where's Talen been lately? I haven't seen him for quite a while."

"His father's sort of taken him in hand."

"I didn't know Talen even *had* a father. That boy will go far if he doesn't get himself hanged. He's just about the best thief in Cimmura."

"I know," Sparhawk said. "He's picked my pocket a few times." He dropped a couple more coins in the begging bowl. "I'd appreciate it if you'd keep the fact that you saw me tonight more or less to yourself, neighbor."

"I never saw you, Sir Sparhawk." The beggar grinned.

"And I never saw you and your friend on the roof, either."

"Something for everybody then."

"My feelings exactly. Good luck in your enterprise."

"And the same to you in yours."

Sparhawk smiled and moved off down the street. His brief exposure to the seamier side of Cimmuran society had paid off again. Though not exactly a friend, Platime and the shadowy world he controlled could be very helpful. Sparhawk cut over one street to make sure that should the clumsy burglar on the roof be surprised in the course of his activities, the inevitable hue and cry would not bring the watch running down the same street he was traversing.

As they always did when he was alone, Sparhawk's thoughts reverted to his Queen. He had known Ehlana since she had been a little girl, though he had not seen her during the ten years he had been in exile in Rendor. The memory of her seated on her throne, encased in diamond-hard crystal, wrenched at his heart. He began to regret the fact that he had not taken advantage of the opportunity to kill the Primate Annias earlier tonight. A poisoner is always contemptible, but the man who had poisoned Sparhawk's Queen had placed himself in mortal danger, since Sparhawk was not one to let old scores simmer too long.

Then he heard furtive footsteps behind him in the fog, and he stepped into a recessed doorway and stood very still.

There were two of them, and they wore nondescript clothing. "Can you still see him?" one of them whispered to the other.

"No. This fog's getting thicker. He's just ahead of us, though."

"Are you sure he's a Pandion?"

"When you've been in this business as long as I have, you'll learn to recognize them. It's the way they walk and the way they hold their shoulders. He's a Pandion all right."

"What's he doing out in the street at this time of night?"

"That's what we're here to find out. The primate wants reports on all their movements."

"The notion of trying to sneak up behind a Pandion on a foggy night makes me just a little nervous. They all use magic, and they can feel you coming. I'd rather not get his sword in my guts. Did you ever see his face?"

"No. He had his hood up, so his face was in shadow."

The two of them crept on up the street, unaware of the fact that their lives had hung in the balance for a moment. Had either of them seen Sparhawk's face, they would have died on the spot. Sparhawk was a very pragmatic man about things like that. He waited until he could no longer hear their footfalls. Then he retraced his steps to an intersection and went up a side street.

The tavern was empty except for the owner, who dozed with his feet up on a table and with his hands clasped over his paunch. He was a stout, unshaven man wearing a dirty smock.

"Good evening, neighbor," Sparhawk said quietly as he entered.

The tavern keeper opened one eye. "Morning is more like it," he grunted.

Sparhawk looked around. The tavern was a fairly typical workingman's place with a low, beamed ceiling smudged with smoke and with a utilitarian counter across the back. The chairs and benches were scarred, and the sawdust on the floor had not been swept up and replaced for months. "It seems to be a slow night," he noted in his quiet voice.

"It's always slow this late, friend. What's your pleasure?"

"Arcian red—if you've got any."

"Arcium's hip deep in red grapes. Nobody ever runs out of Arcian red." With a weary sigh the tavern keeper heaved himself to his feet and poured Sparhawk a goblet of red wine. The goblet, Sparhawk saw, was none too clean. "You're out late, friend," the fellow observed, handing the big knight the sticky goblet.

"Business." Sparhawk shrugged. "A friend of mine said you have a garret on the top floor of the house."

The tavern keeper's eyes narrowed suspiciously. "You don't look like the sort of fellow who'd have a burning interest in garrets," he said. "Does this friend of yours have a name?"

"Not one he cares to have generally known," Sparhawk replied, taking a sip of his wine. It was a distinctly inferior vintage.

"Friend, I don't know you, and you have a sort of official look about you. Why don't you just finish your wine and leave? That's unless you can come up with a name I can recognize."

"This friend of mine works for a man named Platime. You may have heard the name."

The tavern keeper's eyes widened slightly. "Platime must be branching out. I didn't know that he had anything to do with the gentry—except to steal from them."

Sparhawk shrugged. "He owed me a favor."

The unshaven man still looked dubious. "Anybody could throw Platime's name around," he said.

"Neighbor," Sparhawk said flatly, setting his wineglass down, "this is starting to get tedious. Either we go up to your garret or I go out looking for the watch. I'm sure they'll be very interested in your little enterprise."

The tavern keeper's face grew sullen. "It'll cost you a silver half crown."

"All right."

"You're not even going to argue?"

"I'm in a bit of a hurry. We can haggle about the price next time."

"You seem to be in quite a rush to get out of town, friend. You haven't killed anybody with that spear tonight, have you?"

"Not yet." Sparhawk's voice was flat.

The tavern keeper swallowed hard. "Let me see your money."

"Of course, neighbor. And then let's go upstairs and have a look at this garret."

"We'll have to be careful. With this fog, you won't be able to see the guards coming along the parapet."

"I can take care of that."

"No killing. I've got a nice little sideline here. If somebody kills one of the guards, I'll have to close it down."

"Don't worry, neighbor. I don't think I'll have to kill anybody tonight."

The garret was dusty and appeared unused. The tavern keeper carefully opened the gabled window and peered out into the fog. Behind him, Sparhawk whispered in Styric and released the spell. He could feel the fellow out there. "Careful," he said quietly. "There's a guard coming along the parapet."

"I don't see anybody."

"I heard him," Sparhawk replied. There was no point in going into extended explanations.

"You've got sharp ears, friend."

The two of them waited in the darkness as the sleepy guard strolled along the parapet and disappeared in the fog.

"Give me a hand with this," the tavern keeper said, stooping to lift one end of a heavy timber up onto the windowsill. "We slide it across to the parapet, and then you go on over. When you get there, I'll throw you the end of this rope. It's anchored here, so you'll be able to slide down the outside of the wall."

"Right," Sparhawk said. They slid the timber across the intervening space. "Thanks, neighbor," Sparhawk said. He straddled the timber and inched his way across to the parapet. He stood up and caught the coil of rope that came out of the misty darkness. He dropped it over the wall and swung out on it. A few moments later, he was on the ground. The rope slithered up into the fog, and then he heard the sound of the timber sliding back into the garret. "Very neat," Sparhawk muttered, walking carefully away from the city wall. "I'll have to remember that place."

The fog made it a bit difficult to get his bearings, but, by keeping the looming shadow of the city wall to his left, he could more or less determine his location. He set his feet down carefully. The night was quiet, and the sound of a stick breaking would be very loud.

Then he stopped. Sparhawk's instincts were very good, and he knew that he was being watched. He drew his sword slowly to avoid the telltale sound it made as it slid out of its sheath. With the sword in one hand and the battle spear in the other, he stood peering out into the fog.

And then he saw it. It was only a faint glow in the darkness, so faint that most people would not have noticed it. The glow drew closer, and he saw that it had a slight greenish cast to it. Sparhawk stood perfectly still and waited.

There was a figure out there in the fog, indistinct perhaps, but a figure nonetheless. It appeared to be robed and hooded in black, and that faint glow seemed to be coming out from under the hood. The figure was quite tall and appeared to be impossibly thin, almost skeletal. For some reason it chilled Sparhawk. He muttered in Styric, moving his fingers on the hilt of the sword and the shaft of the spear. Then he raised the spear and released the spell with its point. The spell was a relatively simple one, its purpose being only to identify the emaciated figure out in the fog. Sparhawk almost gasped when he felt the waves of pure evil emanating from the shadowy form. Whatever it was, it was certainly not human.

After a moment, a ghostly metallic chuckle came out of the night. The figure turned and moved away. Its walk was jerky as if its knees were put together backward. Sparhawk stayed where he was until that sense of evil faded away. Whatever the thing was, it was gone now. "I wonder if that was another of Martel's little surprises," Sparhawk muttered under his breath. Martel was a renegade Pandion Knight who had been expelled from the order. He and Sparhawk had once been friends, but no more. Martel now worked for Primate Annias, and it had been he who had provided the poison with which Annias had very nearly killed the Queen.

Sparhawk continued slowly and silently now, his sword and the spear still in his hands. Finally he saw the torches that marked the closed east gate of the city, and he took his bearings from them.

Then he heard a faint snuffling sound behind him, much like the sound a tracking dog would make. He turned, his weapons ready. Again he heard that metallic chuckle. He amended that in his mind. It was not so much a chuckle as it was a sort of stridulation, a chittering sound. Again he felt that sense of overpowering evil, which once again faded away.

Sparhawk angled slightly out from the city wall and the filmy light of those two torches at the gate. After about a quarter of an hour, he saw the square, looming shape of the Pandion chapterhouse just ahead.

He dropped into a prone position on the fog-wet turf and cast the searching spell again. He released it and waited.

Nothing.

He rose, sheathed his sword, and moved cautiously across the intervening field. The castlelike chapterhouse was, as always, being watched. Church soldiers, dressed as workmen, were encamped not far from the front gate with piles of the cobblestones they were ostensibly laying heaped around their tents. Sparhawk, however, went around to the back wall and carefully picked his way through the deep, stake-studded fosse surrounding the structure.

The rope down which he had clambered when he had left the house was still dangling behind a concealing bush. He shook it a few times to be certain the grappling hook at its upper end was still firmly attached. Then he tucked the war spear under his sword belt. He grasped the rope and pulled down hard.

Above him, he could hear the points of the hook grating into the stones of the battlement. He started to climb up, hand over hand.

"Who's there?" The voice came sharply out of the fog overhead. It was a youthful voice and familiar.

Sparhawk swore under his breath. Then he felt a tugging on the rope he was climbing. "Leave it alone, Berit," he grated, straining to pull himself up.

"Sir Sparhawk?" the novice said in a startled voice.

"Don't jerk on the rope," Sparhawk ordered. "Those stakes in the ditch are very sharp."

"Let me help you up."

"I can manage. Just don't displace that hook." He grunted as he heaved himself up over the battlement, and Berit caught his arm to help him. Sparhawk was sweating from his exertions. Climbing a rope when one is wearing chain mail can be very strenuous.

Berit was a novice Pandion who showed much promise. He was a tall, rawboned young man who was wearing a mail shirt and a plain, utilitarian cloak. He carried a heavy-bladed battle-ax in one hand. He was a polite young fellow, so he did not ask any questions, although his face was filled with curiosity. Sparhawk looked down into the courtyard of the chapterhouse. By the light of a flickering torch, he saw Kurik and Kalten. Both of them were armed, and sounds from the stable indicated that someone was saddling horses for them. "Don't go away," he called down to them.

"What are you doing up there, Sparhawk?" Kalten sounded surprised.

"I thought I'd take up burglary as a sideline," Sparhawk replied dryly. "Stay there. I'll be right down. Come along, Berit."

"I'm supposed to be on watch, Sir Sparhawk."

"We'll send somebody up to replace you. This is important." Sparhawk led the way along the parapet to the steep stone stairs that led down into the courtyard.

"Where have you been, Sparhawk?" Kurik demanded angrily when the two had descended. Sparhawk's squire wore his usual black leather vest, and his heavily muscled arms and shoulders gleamed in the orange torchlight that illuminated the courtyard. He spoke in the hushed voice men use when talking at night.

"I had to go to the cathedral," Sparhawk replied quietly.

"Are you having religious experiences?" Kalten asked, sounding amused. The big blond knight, Sparhawk's boyhood friend, was dressed in chain and had a heavy broadsword belted at his waist.

"Not exactly," Sparhawk told him. "Tanis is dead. His ghost came to me about midnight."

"Tanis?" Kalten's voice was shocked.

"He was one of the twelve knights who were with Sephrenia when she encased Ehlana in crystal. His ghost told me to go to the crypt under the cathedral before it went to give up its sword to Sephrenia."

"And you went? At night?"

"The matter was of a certain urgency."

"What did you do there? Violate a few tombs? Is that how you got the spear?"

"Hardly," Sparhawk replied. "King Aldreas gave it to me."

*"Aldreas!"*

"His ghost anyway. His missing ring is hidden in the socket." Sparhawk looked curiously at his two friends. "Where were you going just now?"

"Out to look for you." Kurik shrugged.

"How did you know I'd left the chapterhouse?"

"I checked in on you a few times," Kurik said. "I thought you knew I usually did that."

"Every night?"

"Three times at least," Kurik confirmed. "I've been doing that every night since you were a boy—except for the year you were in Rendor. The first time tonight, you were talking in your sleep. The second time—just after midnight—you were gone. I looked around, and when I couldn't find you, I woke up Kalten."

"I think we'd better go wake the others," Sparhawk said bleakly. "Aldreas told me some things, and we've got some decisions to make."

"Bad news?" Kalten asked.

"It's hard to say. Berit, tell those novices in the stable to go replace you on the parapet. This might take awhile."

They gathered in Preceptor Vanion's brown-carpeted study in the south tower. Sparhawk, Berit, Kalten, and Kurik were there, of course. Sir Bevier, a Cyrinic Knight, was there as well, as were Sir Tynian, an Alcione Knight, and Sir Ulath, a huge Genidian Knight. The three were the champions of their orders, and they had joined with Sparhawk and Kalten when the preceptors of the four orders had decided that the restoration of Queen Ehlana was a matter that concerned them all. Sephrenia, the small, dark-haired Styric woman who instructed the Pandions in the secrets of Styricum, sat by the fire with the little girl they called Flute at her side. The boy, Talen, sat by the window, rubbing at his eyes with his fists. Talen was a sound sleeper, and he did not like being awakened. Vanion, the preceptor of the Pandion Knights, sat at the table he used for a writing desk. His study was a pleasant room, low, dark beamed, and with a deep fireplace that Sparhawk had never seen unlighted. As always, Sephrenia's simmering teakettle stood on the hob.

Vanion did not look well. Roused from his bed in the middle of the night, the Preceptor of the Pandion Order, a grim, careworn knight who was probably even older than he looked, wore an uncharacteristic Styric robe of plain white homespun cloth. Sparhawk had watched this peculiar change in Vanion over the years. Caught at times unawares, the preceptor, one of the stalwarts of the Church, sometimes seemed almost half Styric. As an Elene and a Knight of the Church, it was Sparhawk's duty to reveal his observations to the Church authorities. He chose, however, not to. His loyalty to the Church was one thing—a commandment from God. His loyalty to Vanion, however, was deeper, more personal.

The preceptor was gray faced, and his hands trembled slightly. The burden of the swords of the three dead knights he had compelled Sephrenia to relinquish to him was obviously weighing him down more than he would have admitted. The spell Sephrenia had cast in the throne room and which sustained the Queen had involved the concerted assistance of twelve Pandion Knights. One by one those knights would die, and their ghosts would deliver their swords to Sephrenia. When the last had died, she would follow them into the House of the Dead. Earlier that evening, Vanion had compelled her to give those swords to him. It was not the weight of the swords alone that made them such a burden. There were other things that went with them, things about which Sparhawk could not even begin to guess. Vanion had been adamant about taking the swords. He had given a few vague reasons for his action, but Sparhawk privately suspected that the preceptor's main reason had been to spare Sephrenia as much as possible. Despite all the strictures forbidding such things, Sparhawk believed that Vanion loved the dear, small woman who had instructed all Pandions for generations in the secrets of Styricum. All Pandion Knights loved and revered Sephrenia. In Vanion's case, however, Sparhawk surmised that love and reverence went perhaps a step further. Sephrenia also, he had noticed, seemed to have a special affection for the preceptor that went somehow beyond the love of a teacher for her pupil. This was also something that a Church Knight should reveal to the Hierocracy in Chyrellos. Again, Sparhawk chose not to.

"Why are we gathering at this unseemly hour?" Vanion asked wearily.

"Do you want to tell him?" Sparhawk asked Sephrenia.

The white-robed woman sighed and unwrapped the long, cloth-bound object she held to reveal another ceremonial Pandion sword. "Sir Tanis has gone into the House of the Dead," she told Vanion sadly.

"Tanis?" Vanion's voice was stricken. "When did this happen?"

"Just recently, I gather," she replied.

"Is that why we're here tonight?" Vanion asked Sparhawk.

"Not entirely. Before he went to deliver his sword to Sephrenia, Tanis visited me—or at least his ghost did. He told me that someone in the royal crypt wanted to see me. I went to the cathedral and I was confronted by the ghost of Aldreas. He told me a number of things and then gave me this." He twisted the shaft of the spear out of its socket and shook the ruby ring from its place of concealment.

"So *that's* where Aldreas hid it," Vanion said. "Maybe he was wiser than we thought. You said he told you some things. Such as what?"

"That he had been poisoned," Sparhawk replied. "Probably the same poison they gave Ehlana."

"Was it Annias?" Kalten asked grimly.

Sparhawk shook his head. "No. It was Princess Arissa."

"His own *sister*?" Bevier exclaimed. "That's monstrous!" Bevier was an Arcian, and he had deep moral convictions.

"Arissa's fairly monstrous," Kalten agreed. "She's not the sort to let little things stand in her way. How did she get out of the cloister in Demos to dispose of Aldreas, though?"

"Annias arranged it," Sparhawk told him. "She entertained Aldreas in her usual fashion, and when he was exhausted, she gave him the poisoned wine."

"I don't quite understand." Bevier frowned.

"The relationship between Arissa and Aldreas went somewhat beyond what is customary for a brother and sister," Vanion told him delicately.

Bevier's eyes widened and the blood drained from his olive-skinned face as he slowly gathered Vanion's meaning.

"Why did she kill him?" Kalten asked. "Revenge for locking her up in that cloister?"

"No, I don't think so," Sparhawk told him. "I think it was a part of the overall scheme she and Annias had hatched. First they poisoned Aldreas and then Ehlana."

"So the way to the throne would be clear for Arissa's bastard son?" Kalten surmised.

"It's sort of logical," Sparhawk agreed. "It fits together even tighter when you know that Lycheas the bastard is Annias' son, too."

"A Primate of the Church?" Tynian said, looking a bit startled. "Do you people here in Elenia have different rules from the rest of us?"

"Not really, no," Vanion replied. "Annias seems to feel that he's above the rules, and Arissa goes out of her way to break them."

"Arissa's always been just a little indiscriminate," Kalten added. "Rumor has it that she was on very friendly terms with just about every man in Cimmura."

"That might be a slight exaggeration," Vanion said. He stood up and went to the window. "I'll pass this information on to Patriarch Dolmant," he said, looking out at the foggy night. "He may be able to make some use of it when the time comes to elect a new Archprelate."

"And perhaps the Earl of Lenda might be able to use it as well," Sephrenia suggested. "The royal council is corrupt, but even they might balk if they find that Annias is trying to put his own bastard son on the throne." She looked at Sparhawk. "What else did Aldreas tell you?" she asked.

"Just one other thing. We know we need some magic object to cure Ehlana. He told me what it is. It's Bhelliom. It's the only thing in the world with enough power."

Sephrenia's face blanched. "No!" she gasped. "Not Bhelliom!"

"That's what he told me."

"It presents a big problem," Ulath declared. "Bhelliom's been lost since the Zemoch war, and even if we're lucky enough to find it, it won't respond unless we have the rings."

"Rings?" Kalten asked.

"The Troll-Dwarf Ghwerig made Bhelliom," Ulath explained. "Then he made a pair of rings to unlock its power. Without the rings, Bhelliom's useless."

"We already have the rings," Sephrenia told him absently, her face still troubled.

"We do?" Sparhawk was startled.

"You're wearing one of them," she told him, "and Aldreas gave you the other this very night."

Sparhawk stared at the ruby ring on his left hand, then back at his teacher. "How's that possible?" he demanded. "How did my ancestor and King Antor come by these particular rings?"

"I gave them to them," she replied.

He blinked. "Sephrenia, that was three hundred years ago."

"Yes," she agreed, "approximately."

Sparhawk stared at her, then swallowed hard. *"Three hundred years?"* he demanded incredulously. "Sephrenia, just how old *are* you?"

"You know I'm not going to answer that question, Sparhawk. I've told you that before."

"How did *you* get the rings?"

"My Goddess Aphrael gave them to me—along with certain instructions. She told me where I'd find your ancestor and King Antor, and she told me to deliver the rings to them."

"Little mother," Sparhawk began, and then broke off as he saw her bleak expression.

"Hush, dear one," she commanded. "I will say this only once, Sir Knights," she told them all. "What we do puts us in conflict with the Elder Gods, and that is not lightly undertaken. Your Elene God forgives; the Younger Gods of Styricum can be persuaded to relent. The Elder Gods, however, demand absolute compliance with their whims. To counter the commands of an Elder God is to court worse than death. They obliterate those who defy them—in ways you cannot imagine. Do we *really* want to bring Bhelliom back into the light again?"

"Sephrenia! We have to!" Sparhawk exclaimed. "It's the only way we can save Ehlana—and you and Vanion for that matter."

"Annias will not live forever, Sparhawk, and Lycheas is hardly more than an inconvenience. Vanion and I are temporary, and so, for that matter—regardless of how you feel personally—is Ehlana. The world won't miss any of us all that much." Sephrenia's tone was almost clinical. "Bhelliom, however, is another matter—and so is Azash. If we fail and put the stone into that foul God's hands, we will doom the world forever. Is it worth the risk?"

"I'm the Queen's Champion," Sparhawk reminded her. "I have to do whatever I possibly can to save her life." He rose and strode across the room to her. "So help me God, Sephrenia," he declared, "I'll break open Hell itself to save that girl."

Sephrenia sighed. "He's such a child sometimes," she said to Vanion. "Can't you think of some way to make him grow up?"

"I was sort of considering going along," the preceptor replied, smiling. "Sparhawk might let me hold his cloak while he kicks in the gate. I don't think anybody's assaulted Hell lately."

"You too?" She covered her face with her hands. "Oh, dear. All right then, gentlemen," she said, giving up, "if you're all so bent on this, we'll try it—but only on one condition. If we do find Bhelliom, and it restores Ehlana, we must destroy it immediately after the task is done."

"*Destroy it?*" Ulath exploded. "Sephrenia, it's the most precious thing in the world."

"And also the most dangerous. If Azash ever comes to possess it, the world will be lost, and all mankind will be plunged into the most hideous slavery imaginable. I must insist on this, gentlemen. Otherwise, I'll do everything in my power to prevent your finding that accursed stone."

"I don't see that we've got much choice here," Ulath said gravely to the others. "Without her help, we don't have much hope of unearthing Bhelliom."

"Oh, somebody's going to find it all right," Sparhawk told him firmly. "One of the things Aldreas told me was that the time has come for Bhelliom to see the light of day again, and no force on earth can prevent it. The only thing that concerns me right now is whether it's going to be one of us who finds it or some Zemoch, who'll carry it back to Otha."

"Or if it rises from the earth all on its own," Tynian added moodily. "Could it do that, Sephrenia?"

"Probably, yes."

"How did you get out of the chapterhouse without being seen by the primate's spies?" Kalten asked Sparhawk curiously.

"I threw a rope over the back wall and climbed down."

"How about getting in and out of the city after the gates were all closed?"

"By pure luck, the gate was still open when I was on my way to the cathedral. I used another way to get out."

"That garret I told you about?" Talen asked.

Sparhawk nodded.

"How much did he charge you?"

"A silver half crown."

Talen looked shocked at that. "And they call *me* a thief. He gulled you, Sparhawk."

Sparhawk shrugged. "I needed to get out of the city."

"I'll tell Platime about it," the boy said. "He'll get your money back. A half crown? That's outrageous." The boy was actually spluttering.

Sparhawk remembered something. "Sephrenia, when I was on my way back here, something was out in the fog watching me. I don't think it was human."

"The Damork?"

"I couldn't say for sure, but it didn't feel the same. The Damork's not the only creature subject to Azash, is it?"

"No. The Damork is the most powerful, but it's stupid. The other creatures don't have its power, but they're more clever. In many ways, they can be even more dangerous."

"All right, Sephrenia," Vanion said then. "I think you'd better give me Tanis' sword now."

"My dear one—" she began to protest, her face anguished.

"We've had this argument once already tonight," he told her. "Let's not go through it again."

She sighed. Then the two of them began to chant in unison in the Styric tongue. Vanion's face turned a little grayer at the end when Sephrenia handed him the sword and their hands touched.

"All right," Sparhawk said to Ulath after the transfer had been completed. "Where do we start? Where was King Sarak when his crown was lost?"

"No one really knows," the big Genidian Knight replied. "He left Emsat when Otha invaded Lamorkand. He took a few retainers and left orders for the rest of his army to follow him to the battlefield at Lake Randera."

"Did anyone report having seen him there?" Kalten asked.

"Not that I've ever heard. The Thalesian army was seriously decimated, though. It's possible that Sarak did get there before the battle started, but that none of the few survivors ever saw him."

"I expect that's the place to start then," Sparhawk said.

"Sparhawk," Ulath objected, "that battlefield is immense. All the Knights of the Church could spend the rest of their lives digging there and still not find the crown."

"There's an alternative," Tynian said, scratching his chin.

"And what is that, friend Tynian?" Bevier asked him.

"I have some skill at necromancy," Tynian told him. "I don't like it much, but I know how it's done. If we can find out where the Thalesians are buried, I can ask them if any of them saw King Sarak on the field and if any know where he might be buried. It's exhausting, but the cause is worth it."

"I'll be able to aid you, Tynian," Sephrenia told him. "I don't practice necromancy myself, but I know the proper spells."

Kurik rose to his feet. "I'd better get the things we'll need together," he said. "Come along, Berit. You too, Talen."

"There'll be ten of us," Sephrenia told him.

"Ten?"

"We'll be taking Talen and Flute along with us."

"Is that really necessary?" Sparhawk objected, "or even wise?"

"Yes, it is. We'll be seeking the aid of some of the Younger Gods of Styricum, and they like symmetry. We were ten when we began this search, so now we have to be the same ten every step of the way. Sudden changes disturb the Younger Gods."

"Anything you say." He shrugged.

Vanion rose and began to pace up and down. "We'd better get started with this," he said. "It might be safer if you left the chapterhouse before daylight and before this fog lifts. Let's not make it too easy for the spies who watch the house."

"I'll agree with that," Kalten approved. "I'd rather not have to race Annias' soldiers all the way to Lake Randera."

"All right, then," Sparhawk said, "Let's get at it. Time's running a little short on us."

"Stay a moment, Sparhawk," Vanion said as they began to file out.

Sparhawk waited until the others had left, and then he closed the door.

"I received a communication from the Earl of Lenda this evening," the preceptor told his friend.

"Oh?"

"He asked me to reassure you. Annias and Lycheas are taking no further action against the Queen. Apparently the failure of their plot down in Arcium embarrassed Annias a great deal. He's not going to take the chance of making a fool of himself again."

"That's a relief."

"Lenda added something I don't quite understand, though. He asked me to tell you that the candles are still burning. Do you have any idea what he meant by that?"

"Good old Lenda," Sparhawk said warmly. "I asked him not to leave Ehlana sitting in the throne room in the dark."

"I don't think it makes much difference to her, Sparhawk."

"It does to me," Sparhawk replied.

## ■ CHAPTER TWO ■

The fog was even thicker when they gathered in the courtyard a quarter of an hour later. The novices were busy in the stables saddling horses.

Vanion came out through the main door, his Styric robe gleaming in the mist-filled darkness. "I'm sending twenty knights with you," he quietly told Sparhawk. "You might be followed, and they'll offer some measure of protection."

"We sort of need to hurry, Vanion," Sparhawk objected. "If we take others with us, we won't be able to move any faster than the pace of the slowest horse."

"I know that, Sparhawk," Vanion replied patiently. "You won't need to stay with them for very long. Wait until you're out in open country and the sun comes up. Make sure nobody's too close behind you and then slip away from the column. The knights will ride on to Demos. If anybody's following, they won't know you aren't still in the middle of the column."

Sparhawk grinned. "Now I know how you got to be preceptor, my friend. Who's leading the column?"

"Olven."

"Good. Olven's dependable."

"Go with God, Sparhawk," Vanion said, clasping the big knight's hand, "and be careful."

"I'm certainly going to try."

Sir Olven was a bulky Pandion Knight with a number of angry red scars on his face. He came out of the chapterhouse wearing full armor enamelled black. His men trailed out behind him. "Good to see you again, Sparhawk," he said as Vanion went back inside. Olven spoke very quietly to avoid alerting the church soldiers camped outside the front gate. "All right," he went on, "you and the others ride in the middle of us. With this fog, those soldiers probably won't see you. We'll drop the drawbridge and go out fast. We don't want to be in sight for more than a minute or two."

"That's more words than I've heard you use at one time in the last twenty years," Sparhawk said to his normally silent friend.

"I know," Olven agreed. "I'll have to see if I can't cut back a little."

Sparhawk and his friends wore mail shirts and traveller's cloaks, since formal armor would attract attention out in the countryside. Their armor, however, was carefully stowed in packs on the string of a half-dozen horses Kurik would lead. They mounted, and the armored men formed up around them. Olven made a signal to the men at the windlass that raised and lowered the drawbridge, and the men slipped the rachets, allowing the windlass to run freely. There was a noisy rattle of chain, and the drawbridge dropped with a huge boom. Olven was galloping across it almost before it hit the far side of the fosse.

The dense fog helped enormously. As soon as he had galloped across the bridge, Olven cut sharply to the left, leading the column across the open field toward the Demos road. Behind them, Sparhawk could hear startled shouts as the church soldiers ran out of their tents to stare after the column in chagrin.

"Slick," Kalten said gaily. "Across the drawbridge and into the fog in under a minute."

"Olven knows what he's doing," Sparhawk said, "and what's even better is that it's going to be at least an hour before the soldiers can mount any kind of pursuit."

"Give me an hour's head start, and they'll never catch me." Kalten laughed delightedly. "This is starting out very well, Sparhawk."

"Enjoy it while you can. Things will probably start to go wrong later on."

"You're a pessimist, do you know that?"

"No. I'm just used to little disappointments."

They slowed to a canter when they reached the Demos road. Olven was a veteran, and he always tried to conserve his horses. Speed might be necessary later, and Sir Olven took very few chances.

A full moon hung above the fog, and it made the thick mist deceptively luminous. The glowing white fog around them confused the eye and concealed far more than it illuminated. There was a chill dampness in the fog, and Sparhawk pulled his cloak about him as he rode.

The Demos road swung north toward the city of Lenda before turning south-easterly again to Demos, where the Pandion motherhouse was located. Although he could not see it, Sparhawk knew that the countryside along the road was gently rolling and that there were large patches of trees out there. He was counting on those trees for concealment once he and his friends left the column.

They rode on. The fog had dampened the dirt surface of the road, and the sound of their horses' hooves was muffled.

Every now and then the black shadows of trees loomed suddenly out of the fog at the sides of the road as they rode by. Talen shied nervously each time it happened.

"What's the problem?" Kurik asked him.

"I hate this," the boy replied. "I absolutely hate it. Anything could be hiding beside the road—wolves, bears—or even worse."

"You're in the middle of a party of armed men, Talen."

"That's easy for you to say, but I'm the smallest one here—except for Flute, maybe. I've heard that wolves and things like that always drag down the smallest when they attack. I really don't want to be eaten, Father."

"That keeps cropping up," Tynian noted curiously to Sparhawk. "You never did explain why the boy keeps calling your squire by that term."

"Kurik was indiscreet when he was younger."

"Doesn't anybody in Elenia sleep in his own bed?"

"It's a cultural peculiarity. It's not really as widespread as it might seem, though."

Tynian rose slightly in his stirrups and looked ahead to where Bevier and Kalten rode side by side deep in conversation. "A word of advice, Sparhawk," he said confidentially. "You're an Elenian, so you don't seem to have any problem with this sort of thing, and in Deira we're fairly broad-minded about such things, but I don't know that I'd let Bevier in on this. The Cyrinic Knights are a pious lot—just like all Arcians—and they disapprove of these little irregularities very strongly. Bevier's a good man in a fight, but he's a little narrow-minded. If he gets offended, it might cause problems later on."

"You're probably right," Sparhawk agreed. "I'll talk with Talen and ask him to keep his relationship with Kurik to himself."

"Do you think he'll listen?" the broad-faced Deiran asked skeptically.

"It's worth a try."

They occasionally passed a farmhouse standing beside the foggy road with hazy golden lamplight streaming from its windows, a sure sign that, even though the sky had not yet started to lighten, day had already begun for the country folk.

"How long are we going to stay with this column?" Tynian asked. "Going to Lake Randera by way of Demos is a very long way around."

"We can probably slip away later this morning," Sparhawk replied, "once we're sure that nobody's following us. That's what Vanion suggested."

"Have you got somebody watching to the rear?"

Sparhawk nodded. "Berit's riding about a half mile back."

"Do you think any of the primate's spies saw us leave your chapterhouse?"

"They didn't really have very much time for it," Sparhawk said. "We'd already gone past them before they came out of their tents."

Tynian grunted. "Which road do you plan to take when we leave this one?"

"I think we'll go across country. Roads tend to be watched. I'm sure that Annias has guessed that we're up to something by now."

They rode on through the tag end of a foggy night. Sparhawk was pensive. He privately admitted to himself that their hastily conceived plan had little chance of success. Even if Tynian could raise the ghosts of the Thalesian dead, there was no guarantee that any of the spirits would know the location of King Sarak's final resting place. This entire journey could well be futile and serve only to use up what time Ehlana had left. Then a thought came to him. He rode on forward to speak with Sephrenia. "Something just occurred to me," he said to her.

"Oh?"

"How well known is the spell you used to encase Ehlana?"

"It's almost never practiced because it's so very dangerous," she replied. "A few Styrics might know of it, but I doubt that any would dare to perform it. Why do you ask?"

"I think I'm right on the edge of an idea. If no one but you is really willing to use the spell, then it's rather unlikely that anybody else would know about the time limitation."

"That's true. They wouldn't."

"Then nobody could tell Annias about it."

"Obviously."

"So Annias doesn't know that we only have so much time left. For all he knows, the crystal could keep Ehlana alive indefinitely."

"I'm not certain that gives us any particular advantage, Sparhawk."

"I'm not either, but it's something to keep in mind. We might be able to use it someday."

The eastern sky was growing gradually lighter as they rode, and the fog was swirling and thinning. It was about a half hour before sunrise when Berit came galloping up from the rear. He was wearing his mail shirt and plain blue cloak, and his war ax was in a sling at the side of his saddle. The young novice, Sparhawk decided almost idly, was going to need some instruction in swordsmanship soon, before he grew too attached to that ax.

"Sir Sparhawk," he said, reining in, "there's a column of church soldiers coming up behind us." His hard-run horse was steaming in the chill fog.

"How many?" Sparhawk asked him.

"Fifty or so, and they're galloping hard. There was a break in the fog, and I saw them coming."

"How far back?"

"A mile or so. They're in that valley we just came through."

Sparhawk considered it. "I think a little change of plans might be in order," he said. He looked around and saw a dark blur back in the swirling fog off to the left. "Tynian," he said, "I think that's a grove of trees over there. Why don't you take the others and ride across this field and get into the grove before the soldiers catch up?

I'll be right along." He shook Faran's reins. "I want to talk with Sir Olven," he told the big roan.

Faran flicked his ears irritably, then moved alongside the column at a gallop.

"We'll be leaving you here, Olven," Sparhawk told the scar-faced knight. "There's a half-hundred church soldiers coming up from the rear. I want to be out of sight before they come by."

"Good idea," Olven approved. Olven was not one to waste words.

"Why don't you give them a bit of a run?" Sparhawk suggested. "They won't be able to tell that we're not still in the column until they catch up with you."

Olven grinned crookedly. "Even so far as Demos?" he asked.

"That would be helpful. Cut across country before you reach Lenda and pick up the road again south of town. I'm sure Annias has spies in Lenda too."

"Good luck, Sparhawk," Olven said.

"Thanks," Sparhawk said, shaking the scar-faced knight's hand. "We might need it." He backed Faran off the road, and the column thundered past him at a gallop.

"Let's see how fast you can get to that grove of trees over there," Sparhawk said to his bad-tempered mount.

Faran snorted derisively, then leaped forward at a dead run.

Kalten waited at the edge of the trees, his gray cloak blending into the shadows and fog. "The others are back in the woods a ways," he reported, "Why's Olven galloping like that?"

"I asked him to," Sparhawk replied, swinging down from his saddle. "The soldiers won't know that we've left the column if Olven stays a mile or two ahead of them."

"You're smarter than you look, Sparhawk," Kalten said, also dismounting. "I'll get the horses back out of sight. The steam coming off them might be visible." He squinted at Faran. "Tell this ugly brute of yours not to bite me."

"You heard him, Faran," Sparhawk told his war-horse.

Faran laid his ears back.

As Kalten led their horses back among the trees, Sparhawk sank down onto his stomach behind a low bush. The grove of trees lay no more than fifty yards from the road; as the fog began to dissipate with the onset of morning, he could clearly see that the whole stretch of road they had just left was empty. Then a single red-tunicked soldier galloped along, coming from the south. The man rode stiffly, and his face seemed strangely wooden.

"A scout?" Kalten whispered, crawling up beside Sparhawk.

"More than likely," Sparhawk whispered back.

"Why are we whispering?" Kalten asked. "He can't hear us over the noise of his horse's hooves."

"You started it."

"Force of habit, I guess. I always whisper when I'm skulking."

The scout reined in his mount at the top of the hill, then wheeled and rode back along the road at a dead run. His face was still blank.

"He's going to wear out that horse if he keeps doing that," Kalten said.

"It's his horse."

"That's true, and he's the one who gets to walk when the horse plays out on him."

"Walking is good for church soldiers. It teaches them humility."

About five minutes later, the church soldiers galloped by, their red tunics dark in the dawn light. Accompanying the leader of the column was a tall, emaciated figure in a black robe and hood. It might have been a trick of the misty morning light, but a faint greenish glow seemed to emanate from under the hood, and the figure's back appeared to be grossly deformed.

"They're definitely trying to keep an eye on that column," Kalten said.

"I hope they enjoy Demos," Sparhawk replied. "Olven's going to stay ahead of them every step of the way. I need to talk with Sephrenia. Let's go back to the others. We'll sit tight for an hour or so until we're sure the soldiers are out of the area and then move on."

"Good idea. I'm about ready for some breakfast anyway."

They led their horses back through the damp woods to a small basin surrounding a trickling spring that emerged from a fern-covered bank.

"Did they go by?" Tynian asked.

"At a gallop." Kalten grinned. "And they didn't look around very much. Does anybody have anything to eat? I'm starving."

"I've got a slab of cold bacon," Kurik offered.

"Cold?"

"Fire makes smoke, Kalten. Do you really want these woods full of soldiers?"

Kalten sighed.

Sparhawk looked at Sephrenia. "There's somebody—or something—riding with those soldiers," he said. "It gave me a very uneasy feeling, and I think it was the same thing I caught a glimpse of last night."

"Can you describe it?"

"It's quite tall and very very thin. Its back seems to be deformed, and it's wearing a black hooded robe, so I couldn't see any details." He frowned. "Those church soldiers in the column seemed to be half-asleep. They usually pay closer attention to what they're doing."

"This thing you saw," she said seriously. "Was there anything else unusual about it?"

"I can't say for sure, but it seemed to have a sort of greenish light coming from its face. I noticed the same thing last night."

Her face grew bleak. "I think we'd better leave immediately, Sparhawk."

"The soldiers don't know we're here," he objected.

"They will before long. You've just described a Seeker. In Zemoch they're used to hunt down runaway slaves. The lump on its back is caused by its wings."

"Wings?" Kalten said skeptically. "Sephrenia, no animal has wings—except maybe a bat."

"This isn't a mammal, Kalten," she replied. "It more closely resembles an insect—although neither term is very exact when you're talking about the creatures Azash summons."

"I hardly think we need to worry about a bug," he said.

"We do with this particular creature. It has very little in the way of a brain, but that doesn't matter, because the spirit of Azash infuses it and provides its thoughts for it. It can see a long ways in the dark or fog. Its ears are very sharp, and it has a very keen sense of smell. As soon as those soldiers come in sight of Olven's column, it's going to know that we're not riding with the knights. The soldiers will come back at that point."

"Are you saying that church soldiers will take orders from an insect?" Bevier asked incredulously.

"They have no choice. They have no will of their own anymore. The Seeker controls them utterly."

"How long does that last?" he asked her.

"For as long as they live—which usually isn't very long. As soon as it has no further need of them, it consumes them. Sparhawk, we're in very great danger. Let's leave here at once."

"You heard her," Sparhawk said grimly. "Let's get out of here."

They rode out of the grove of trees at a canter and crossed a wide green meadow where brown and white spotted cows grazed in knee-deep grass. Sir Ulath pulled in beside Sparhawk. "It's really none of my business," the shaggy-browed Genidian Knight said, "but you had twenty Pandions with you back there. Why didn't you just turn around and eliminate those soldiers and their bug?"

"Fifty dead soldiers scattered along a road would attract attention," Sparhawk explained, "and new graves are almost as obvious."

"Makes sense, I guess." Ulath grunted. "Living in an overpopulated kingdom has its own special problems, doesn't it? Up in Thalesia, the Trolls and Ogres usually clean up that sort of thing before anybody chances by."

Sparhawk shuddered. "Will they really eat carrion?" he asked, looking back over his shoulder for any sign of pursuit.

"Trolls and Ogres? Oh, yes—as long as the carrion's not too ripe. A nice fat church soldier will feed a family of Trolls for a week or so. That's one of the reasons there aren't very many church soldiers or their graveyards in Thalesia. The point, though, is that I don't like leaving live enemies behind me. Those church soldiers might come back to haunt us, and, if that thing they've got with them is as dangerous as Sephrenia says, we probably should have gotten it out of the way while we had the chance."

"Maybe you're right," Sparhawk admitted, "but it's too late now, I'm afraid. Olven's far out of reach. About all we can do is make a run for it and hope the soldiers' horses play out before ours do. When we get a chance, I'll want to talk with Sephrenia some more about that Seeker. I've got a feeling there were some things about it she wasn't telling me."

They rode hard for the rest of the day and saw no signs that the soldiers were anywhere behind them.

"There's a roadside inn just ahead," Kalten said as evening settled over the rolling countryside. "Do you want to chance it?"

Sparhawk looked at Sephrenia. "What do you think?"

"Only for a few hours," she said, "just long enough to feed the horses and give them some rest. The Seeker knows that we're not with that column by now, and it's certain to be following our trail. We have to move on."

"We could at least get some supper," Kalten added, "and maybe a couple hours of sleep. I've been up for a long time. Besides, we might be able to pick up some information if we ask the right questions."

The inn was run by a thin, good-humored fellow and his plump, jolly wife. It was a comfortable place and meticulously clean. The broad fireplace at one end of the common room did not smoke, and there were fresh rushes on the floor.

"We don't see many city folk this far out in the country," the innkeeper noted as he brought a platter of roast beef to the table, "and very seldom any knights—at least I judge from your garb that you're knights. What brings you this way, my Lords?"

"We're on our way to Pelosia," Kalten lied easily. "Church business. We're in a hurry, so we decided to cut across country."

"There's a road that runs on up into Pelosia about three leagues to the south," the innkeeper advised helpfully.

"Roads wander around a lot," Kalten said, "and, as I told you, we're in a hurry."

"Anything interesting happening hereabouts?" Tynian asked as if only mildly curious.

The innkeeper laughed wryly. "What can possibly happen in a place like this? The local farmers spend all their time talking about a cow that died six months ago." He drew up a chair and sat down uninvited. He sighed. "I used to live in Cimmura when I was younger. Now, there's a place where things really happen. I miss all the excitement."

"What made you decide to move out here?" Kalten asked, spearing another slice of beef with his dagger.

"My father left me this place when he died. Nobody wanted to buy it, so I didn't have any choice." He frowned slightly. "Now that you mention it, though," he said, returning to the previous topic, "there has been something a little unusual happening around here for the last few months."

"Oh?" Tynian said carefully.

"We've been seeing bands of roving Styrics. The countryside's crawling with them. They don't usually move around that much, do they?"

"Not really," Sephrenia replied. "We're not a nomadic people."

"I thought you might be Styric, lady—judging from your looks and your clothes. We've got a Styric village not far from here. They're nice enough people, I suppose, but they keep pretty much to themselves." He leaned back in his chair. "I do think you Styrics could avoid a lot of the trouble that breaks out from time to time if you'd just mingle with your neighbors a little more."

"It's not our way," Sephrenia murmured. "I don't believe Elenes and Styrics are supposed to mingle."

"There could be something to what you say," he agreed.

"Are these Styrics doing anything in particular?" Sparhawk asked, keeping his voice neutral.

"Asking questions is about all. They seem to be very curious about the Zemoch war for some reason." He rose to his feet. "Enjoy your supper," he said and went back to the kitchen.

"We have a problem," Sephrenia said gravely. "Western Styrics do not wander about the countryside. Our Gods prefer to have us stay close to their altars."

"Zemochs then?" Bevier surmised.

"Almost certainly."

"When I was in Lamorkand, there were reports of Zemochs infiltrating the country east of Motera," Kalten remembered. "They were doing the same thing— wandering about the country asking questions, mostly having to do with folklore."

"Azash seems to have a plan that closely resembles ours," Sephrenia said. "He's trying to gather information that will lead him to Bhelliom."

"It's a race then," Kalten said.

"I'm afraid so, and he's got Zemochs out there ahead of us."

"And church soldiers behind," Ulath added. "You've gone and got us surrounded, Sparhawk. Could that Seeker be controlling those wandering Zemochs the same way it's controlling the soldiers?" the big Thalesian asked Sephrenia. "We could be riding into an ambush if it is, you know."

"I'm not entirely certain," she replied. "I've heard a great deal about Otha's Seekers, but I've never actually seen one in action."

"You didn't have time to be very specific this morning," Sparhawk said. "Exactly how is that thing controlling Annias' soldiers?"

"It's venomous," she said. "Its bite paralyzes the will of its victims—or of those it wants to dominate."

"I'll make a point of not letting it bite me then," Kalten said.

"You may not be able to stop it," she told him. "That green glow is hypnotic. That makes it easier for it to get close enough to inject the venom."

"How fast can it fly?" Tynian asked.

"It doesn't fly at this stage of its development," she replied. "Its wings don't mature until it becomes an adult. Besides, it has to be on the ground to follow the scent of the one it's trying to catch. Normally, it travels on horseback, and since the horse is controlled in the same way people are, the Seeker simply rides the horse to death and then finds another. It can cover a great deal of ground that way."

"What does it eat?" Kurik asked. "Maybe we can set a trap for it."

"It feeds primarily on humans," she told him.

"That would make baiting a trap a little difficult," he admitted.

They all went to bed directly after supper, but it seemed to Sparhawk that his head had no sooner touched the pillow when Kurik shook him awake.

"It's about midnight," the squire said.

"All right," Sparhawk said wearily, sitting up in bed.

"I'll wake the others," Kurik said, "and then Berit and I'll go saddle the horses."

After he had dressed, Sparhawk went downstairs to have a word with the sleepy innkeeper. "Tell me, neighbor," he said, "is there by any chance a monastery hereabouts?"

The innkeeper scratched his head. "I think there's one near the village of Verine," he replied. "That's about five leagues east of here."

"Thanks, neighbor," Sparhawk said. He looked around. "You've got a nice, comfortable inn here," he said, "and your wife keeps clean beds and sets a very fine table. I'll mention your place to my friends."

"Why, that's very kind of you, Sir Knight."

Sparhawk nodded to him and went outside to join the others.

"What's the plan?" Kalten asked.

"The innkeeper thinks there's a monastery near a village about five leagues away. We should reach it by morning. I want to get word of all this to Dolmant in Chyrellos."

"I could take the message to him for you, Sir Sparhawk," Berit offered eagerly.

Sparhawk shook his head. "The Seeker probably has your scent by now, Berit. I don't want you getting ambushed on the road to Chyrellos. Let's send some anonymous monk instead. That monastery's on our way anyhow, so we won't be losing any time. Let's mount up."

The moon was full and the night sky was clear as they rode away from the inn. "That way," Kurik said, pointing.

"How do you know that?" Talen asked him.

"The stars," Kurik replied.

"Do you mean you can actually tell direction by the stars?" Talen sounded impressed.

"Of course you can. Sailors have been doing that for thousands of years."

"I didn't know that."

"You should have stayed in school."

"I don't plan to be a sailor, Kurik. Stealing fish sounds a little too much like work to me."

They rode on through the moon-drenched night, moving almost due east. By morning they had come perhaps five leagues, and Sparhawk rode to a hilltop to look around. "There's a village just ahead," he told the others when he returned. "Let's hope it's the one we're looking for."

The village lay in a shallow valley. It was a small place, perhaps a dozen stone houses with a church at one end of its single cobbled street and a tavern at the other. A large, walled building stood atop a hill just outside of town. "Excuse me, neighbor," Sparhawk asked a passerby as they clattered into town. "Is this Verine?"

"It is."

"And is that the monastery up on that hill there?"

"It is," the man replied again, his voice a bit sullen.

"Is there some problem?"

"The monks up there own all the land hereabouts," the fellow replied. "Their rents are cruel."

"Isn't that always the way? All landlords are greedy."

"The monks insist on tithes as well as the rent. That's going a bit far, wouldn't you say?"

"You've got a point there."

"Why do you call everybody 'neighbor'?" Tynian asked as they rode on.

"Habit, I suppose." Sparhawk shrugged. "I got it from my father, and it sort of puts people at their ease."

"Why not call them 'friend'?"

"Because I never know that for sure. Let's go talk to the abbot of that monastery."

The monastery was a severe-looking building surrounded by a wall made of yellow sandstone. The fields around it were well tended, and monks wearing conical hats woven from local straw worked patiently under the morning sun in long, straight rows of vegetables. The gates of the monastery stood open, and Sparhawk and the others rode into the central courtyard. A thin, haggard-looking brother came out to meet them, his face a bit fearful looking.

"Good day, brother," Sparhawk said to him. He opened his cloak to reveal the heavy silver amulet hanging on a chain about his neck that identified him as a Pandion Knight. "If it's not too much trouble, we'd like to have a word with your abbot."

"I'll bring him immediately, my Lord." The brother scurried back inside the building.

The abbot was a jolly little fat man with a well-shaved tonsure and a bright red, sweaty face. His was a small, remote monastery and had little contact with Chyrellos. He was almost embarrassingly obsequious at the sudden unexpected appearance of Church Knights on his doorstep. "My Lords." He almost grovelled. "How may I serve you?"

"It's a small thing, my Lord Abbot," Sparhawk told him gently. "Are you acquainted with the Patriarch of Demos?"

The abbot swallowed hard. "Patriarch Dolmant?" he said in an awed voice.

"Tall fellow," Sparhawk agreed. "Sort of lean and underfed-looking. Anyway, we need to get a message to him. Have you a young monk who's got some stamina and a good horse who could carry a message to the Patriarch for us? It's in the service of the Church."

"O-of course, Sir Knight."

"I'd hoped you'd feel that way about it. Do you have a quill pen and ink handy, my Lord Abbot? I'll compose the message, and then we won't bother you anymore."

"One other thing, my Lord Abbot," Kalten added. "Might we trouble you for a bit of food? We've been some time on the road, and our supplies are getting low. Nothing too exotic, mind—a few roast chickens, perhaps, maybe a ham or two, a side of bacon, a hindquarter of beef, maybe?"

"Of course, Sir Knight," the abbot agreed quickly.

Sparhawk composed the note to Dolmant while Kurik and Kalten loaded the supplies on a pack horse.

"Did you have to do that?" Sparhawk asked Kalten as they rode away.

"Charity is a cardinal virtue, Sparhawk," Kalten replied loftily. "I like to encourage it whenever I can."

The countryside through which they galloped grew increasingly desolate. The soil was thin and poor, fit only for thornbushes and weeds. Here and there were pools of stagnant water, and the few trees standing near them were stunted and sick-looking. The weather had turned cloudy, and they rode through the tag end of a dreary afternoon.

Kurik pulled his gelding in beside Sparhawk. "Doesn't look too promising, does it?" he noted.

"Dismal," Sparhawk agreed.

"I think we're going to have to make camp somewhere tonight. The horses are almost played out."

"I'm not feeling too spry myself," Sparhawk admitted. His eyes felt gritty, and he had a dull headache.

"The only trouble is that I haven't seen any clean water for the last league or so. Why don't I take Berit and see if we can find a spring or stream?"

"Keep your eyes open," Sparhawk cautioned.

Kurik turned in his saddle. "Berit," he called, "I need you."

Sparhawk and the others rode on at a trot while the squire and the novice ranged out in search of clean water.

"We could just ride on, you know," Kalten said.

"Not unless you feel like walking before morning," Sparhawk replied. "Kurik's right. The horses don't have very much left in them."

"That's true, I suppose."

Then Kurik and Berit came pounding down a nearby hill at a gallop. "Get ready!" Kurik shouted, shaking loose his chain mace. "We've got company!"

"Sephrenia!" Sparhawk barked, "take Flute and get back behind those rocks. Talen, get the pack horses." He drew his sword and moved to the front, even as the others armed themselves.

There were fifteen or so of them, and they drove their horses over the hilltop at a run. It was an oddly assorted group, church soldiers in their red tunics, Styrics in homespun smocks, and a few peasants. Their faces were all blank, and their eyes dull. They charged on mindlessly, even though the heavily armed Church Knights were rushing to meet them.

Sparhawk and the others spread out, preparing to meet the charge. "For God and the Church!" Bevier shouted, brandishing his Lochaber ax. Then he spurred his horse forward, crashing into the middle of the oncoming attackers. Sparhawk was taken off guard by the young Cyrinic's rash move, but he quickly recovered and charged in to his companion's aid. Bevier, however, appeared to need little in the way of help. He warded off the clumsy-appearing sword strokes of the mindlessly charging ambushers with his shield, and his long-handled Lochaber whistled through the air to sink deep into the bodies of his enemies. Though the wounds he inflicted were hideous, the men he struck down made no outcry as they fell from their saddles. They fought and died in an eerie silence. Sparhawk rode behind Bevier, cutting down any of the numb-faced men who tried to attack the Cyrinic from behind. His sword sheared a church soldier almost in half, but the man in the red tunic did not even flinch. He raised his sword to strike at Bevier's back, but Sparhawk split his head open with a vast overhand stroke. The soldier toppled out of his saddle and lay twitching on the bloodstained grass.

Kalten and Tynian had flanked the attackers on either side and were chopping their way into the mêlée, while Ulath, Kurik, and Berit intercepted the few survivors who managed to make their way through the concerted counterattack.

The ground was soon littered with bodies in red tunics and bloody white Styric smocks. Riderless horses plunged away from the fight, squealing in panic. In normal circumstances, Sparhawk knew the attackers bringing up the rear would falter and then flee when they saw what had befallen their comrades. These expressionless men, however, continued their attack, and it was necessary to kill them to the last man.

"Sparhawk!" Sephrenia shouted. "Up there!" She was pointing toward the hilltop over which the attack had come. It was the tall, skeletal figure in the black hooded robe that Sparhawk had seen twice before. It sat its horse atop the hill with that faint green glow emanating from its concealed face.

"That thing's starting to bore me," Kalten said. "The best way to get rid of a bug is to step on it." He raised his shield and thumped his heels to his horse's flanks. He started to gallop up the hill, his blade held menacingly aloft.

"Kalten! No!" Sephrenia's shout was shrill with fright. But Kalten paid no attention to her warning. Sparhawk swore and started after his friend.

But then Kalten was suddenly hurled from his saddle by some unseen force as the figure atop the hill gestured almost contemptuously. With revulsion Sparhawk saw that what emerged from the sleeve of the black robe was not a hand, but more closely resembled the front claw of a scorpion.

And then, even as he swung down from Faran's back to run to Kalten's aid, Sparhawk gaped in astonishment. Somehow Flute had escaped from Sephrenia's watchful eye and had advanced to the foot of the hill. She stamped one grass-stained little foot imperiously and lifted her rude pipes to her lips. Her melody was stern, even slightly discordant; for some peculiar reason, it seemed to be accompanied by a vast, unseen choir of human voices. The hooded figure on the hilltop reeled back in its saddle as if it had been struck a massive blow. Flute's song rose, and that unseen choir swelled its song in a mighty crescendo. The sound was so overpowering that Sparhawk was forced to cover his ears. The song had reached the level of physical pain.

The figure shrieked, a dreadfully inhuman sound, and it also clapped its claws to the sides of its hooded head. Then it wheeled its horse and fled down the far side of the hill.

There was no time to pursue the monstrosity. Kalten lay gasping on the ground, his face pale and his hands clutching at his stomach.

"Are you all right?" Sparhawk demanded, kneeling beside his friend.

"Leave me alone," Kalten wheezed.

"Don't be stupid. Are you hurt?"

"No. I'm lying here for fun." The blond man drew in a shuddering breath. "What did it hit me with? I've never been hit that hard before."

"You'd better let me have a look at you."

"I'm all right, Sparhawk. It just knocked the breath out of me, that's all."

"You idiot. You know what that thing is. What were you thinking of?" Sparhawk was suddenly, irrationally angry.

"It seemed like a good idea at the time." Kalten grinned weakly. "Maybe I should have thought my way through it a little more."

"Is he hurt?" Bevier asked, dismounting and coming toward them, his face showing his concern.

"I think he'll be all right." Then Sparhawk rose, controlling his temper with some effort. "Sir Bevier," he said rather formally, "you've had training in this sort of thing. You know what you're supposed to do when you're under attack. What possessed you to dash into the middle of them like that?"

"I didn't think there were all that many of them, Sparhawk," Bevier replied defensively.

"There were enough. It only takes one to kill you."

"You're vexed with me, aren't you, Sparhawk?" Bevier's voice was mournful.

Sparhawk looked at the young knight's earnest face for a moment. Then he sighed. "No, Bevier, I guess not. You just startled me, that's all. Please, for the sake of my nerves, don't do unexpected things any more. I'm not getting any younger, and surprises age me."

"Perhaps I didn't consider the feelings of my comrades," Bevier admitted contritely. "I promise it will not happen again."

"I appreciate that, Bevier. Let's help Kalten back down the hill. I want Sephrenia to take a look at him, and I'm sure she'll want to have a talk with him—a nice long one."

Kalten winced. "I don't suppose I could talk you into leaving me here? This is nice soft dirt."

"Not a chance, Kalten," Sparhawk replied ruthlessly. "Don't worry, though. She likes you, so she probably won't do anything to you—nothing permanent, anyway."

## CHAPTER THREE

Sephrenia was tending a large, ugly-looking bruise on Berit's upper arm when Sparhawk and Bevier helped the weakly protesting Kalten down the hill to her.

"Is it bad?" Sparhawk asked the young novice.

"It's nothing, my Lord," Berit said bravely, although his face was pale.

"Is that the very first thing they teach you Pandions?" Sephrenia asked acidly. "To make light of your injuries? Berit's mail shirt stopped most of the blow, but in about an hour his arm's going to be purple from elbow to shoulder. He'll barely be able to use it."

"You're in a cheerful humor this afternoon, little mother," Kalten said to her.

She pointed a threatening finger at him. "Kalten," she said, "sit. I'll deal with you after I've tended Berit's arm."

Kalten sighed and slumped down onto the ground.

Sparhawk looked around. "Where are Ulath, Tynian, and Kurik?" he asked.

"They're scouting around to make sure there aren't any more ambushes laid for us, Sir Sparhawk," Berit replied.

"Good idea."

"That creature didn't look so very dangerous to me," Bevier said. "A little mysterious perhaps, but not all that dangerous."

"It didn't hit *you*," Kalten told him. "It's dangerous, all right. Take my word for it."

"It's more dangerous than you could possibly imagine," Sephrenia said. "It can send whole armies after us."

"If it's got the kind of power that knocked me off my horse, it doesn't *need* armies."

"You keep forgetting, Kalten. Its mind is the mind of Azash. The Gods prefer to have humans do their work for them."

"The men who came down that hill were like sleepwalkers," Bevier said, shuddering. "We cut them to pieces, and they didn't make a sound." He paused, frowning. "I didn't think Styrics were so aggressive," he added. "I've never seen one with a sword in his hand before."

"Those weren't western Styrics," Sephrenia said, tying off the padded bandage around Berit's upper arm. "Try not to use that too much," she instructed. "Give it time to heal."

"Yes, ma'am," Berit replied. "Now that you mention it, though, it *is* getting a little sore."

She smiled and put an affectionate hand on his shoulder. "This one may be all right, Sparhawk. His head isn't *quite* solid bone—like some I could name." She glanced meaningfully at Kalten.

"Sephrenia," the blond knight protested.

"Get out of the mail shirt," she told him crisply. "I want to see if you've broken anything."

"You said the Styrics in that group weren't western Styrics," Bevier said to her.

"No. They were Zemochs. It's more or less what we guessed at back at that inn. The Seeker will use anybody, but a western Styric is incapable of using weapons made of steel. If they'd been local people, their swords would have been bronze or copper." She looked critically at Kalten, who had just removed his mail shirt. She shuddered. "You look like a blond rug," she told him.

"It's not my fault, little mother," he said, suddenly blushing. "All the men in my family have been hairy."

Bevier looked puzzled. "What finally drove that creature off?" he asked.

"Flute," Sparhawk replied. "She's done it before. She even ran off the Damork once with her pipes."

"This tiny child?" Bevier's tone was incredulous.

"There's more to Flute than meets the eye," Sparhawk told him. He looked out across the slope of the hill. "Talen," he shouted, "stop that."

Talen, who had been busily pillaging the dead, looked up with some consternation. "But Sparhawk—" he began.

"Just come away from there. That's disgusting."

"But—"

"Do as he says!" Berit roared.

Talen sighed and came back down the hill.

"Let's go round up the horses, Bevier," Sparhawk said. "As soon as Kurik and the others get back, I think we'll want to move on. That Seeker is still out there, and it can come at us with a whole new group of people at any time."

"It can do that at night as well as in the daylight, Sparhawk," Bevier said dubiously, "and it can follow our scent."

"I know. At this point I think speed is our only defense. We're going to have to try to outrun that thing again."

Kurik, Ulath, and Tynian returned as dusk was settling over the desolate landscape. "There doesn't seem to be anybody else out there," the squire reported, swinging down from his gelding.

"We're going to have to keep going," Sparhawk told him.

"The horses are right on the verge of exhaustion, Sparhawk," the squire protested. He looked at the others. "And the people aren't in much better shape. None of us has had very much sleep in the past two days."

"I'll take care of it," Sephrenia said calmly, looking up from her examination of Kalten's hairy torso.

"How?" Kalten sounded just a bit grumpy.

She smiled at him and wiggled her fingers under his nose. "How else?"

"If there's a spell that counteracts the way we're all feeling right now, why didn't you teach it to us before?" Sparhawk was also feeling somewhat surly, since his headache had returned.

"Because it's dangerous, Sparhawk," she replied. "I know you Pandions. Given certain circumstances, you'd try to go on for weeks."

"So? If the spell really works, what difference does it make?"

"The spell only makes you *feel* as if you've rested, but you have not, in fact. If you push it too far, you'll die."

"Oh. That stands to reason, I guess."

"I'm glad you understand."

"How's Berit?" Tynian asked.

"He'll be sore for a while, but he's all right," she replied.

"The young fellow shows some promise," Ulath said. "When his arm heals, I'll give him some instruction with that ax of his. He's got the right spirit, but his technique's a little shaky."

"Bring the horses over here," Sephrenia told them. She began to speak in Styric, uttering some of the words under her breath and concealing her moving fingers from them. Try though he might, Sparhawk could not catch all of the incantation nor even guess at the gestures that enhanced the spell. Then he suddenly felt enormously refreshed. The dull headache was gone, and his mind was clear. One of the pack horses, whose head had been drooping and whose legs had been trembling violently, actually began to prance around like a colt.

"Good spell," Ulath said laconically. "Shall we get started?"

They helped Berit into his saddle and rode out in the luminous twilight. The full moon rose an hour or so later, and it gave them sufficient light to risk a canter.

"There's a road just over that hill up ahead," Kurik told Sparhawk. "We saw it when we were looking around. It goes more or less in the right direction, and we could make better time if we follow it instead of stumbling over broken ground in the dark."

"I expect you're right," Sparhawk agreed, "and we want to get out of this area as quickly as possible."

When they reached the road, they pushed on to the east at a gallop. It was well past midnight when clouds moved in from the west, obscuring the night sky. Sparhawk muttered an oath and slowed their pace.

Just before dawn they came to a river, and the road turned north. They followed it, searching for a bridge or a ford. The dawn was gloomy under the heavy cloud cover. They rode upriver a few more miles, and then the road bent east again and ran down into the river to emerge on the far side.

Beside the ford stood a small hut. The man who owned the hut was a sharp-eyed fellow in a green tunic who demanded a toll to cross. Rather than argue with him, Sparhawk paid what he asked. "Tell me, neighbor," he said when the transaction was completed, "how far is the Pelosian border?"

"About five leagues," the sharp-eyed fellow replied. "If you move along, you should reach it by afternoon."

"Thanks, neighbor. You've been most helpful."

They splashed on across the ford. When they reached the other side, Talen rode up beside Sparhawk. "Here's your money back," the young thief said, handing over several coins.

Sparhawk gave him a startled look.

"I don't object to paying a toll to cross a bridge," Talen sniffed. "After all, somebody had to go to the expense of building it. That fellow was just taking advantage of a natural shallow place in the river, though. It didn't cost him anything, so why should he make a profit from it?"

"You cut his purse, then?"

"Naturally."

"And there was more in it than just my coins?"

"A bit. Let's call it my fee for recovering your money. After all, I deserve a profit too, don't I?"

"You're incorrigible."

"I needed the practice."

From the other side of the river there came a howl of anguish.

"I'd say he just discovered his loss," Sparhawk observed.

"It does sort of sound that way, doesn't it?"

The soil on the far side of the river was not a great deal better than the scrubby wasteland through which they had just passed. Occasionally they saw poor farmsteads where shabby-looking peasants in muddy brown smocks labored long and hard to wrest scanty crops from the unyielding earth. Kurik sniffed disdainfully. "Amateurs," he grunted. Kurik took farming very seriously.

About midmorning, the narrow track they were following joined a well-travelled road that ran due east. "A suggestion, Sparhawk," Tynian said, shifting his blue-blazoned shield.

"Suggest away."

"It might be better if we took this road to the border rather than cutting across country again. Pelosians tend to be sensitive about people who avoid the manned border crossings. They're obsessively concerned about smugglers. I don't think we'd accomplish very much in a skirmish with one of their patrols."

"All right," Sparhawk agreed. "Let's stay out of trouble if we can."

Not very long after a dreary, sunless noon, they reached the border and passed without incident into the southern end of Pelosia. The farmsteads here were even more run-down than they had been in northeastern Elenia. The houses and out-buildings were universally roofed with sod, and agile goats grazed on the roofs. Kurik looked about disapprovingly, but said nothing.

As evening settled over the landscape, they crested a hill and saw the twinkling lights of a village in the valley below. "An inn perhaps?" Kalten suggested. "I think Sephrenia's spell is starting to wear off. My horse is staggering, and I'm not in much better shape."

"You won't sleep alone in a Pelosian inn," Tynian warned. "Their beds are usu-ally occupied by all sorts of unpleasant little creatures."

"Fleas?" Kalten asked.

"And lice and bedbugs the size of mice."

"I guess we'll have to risk it," Sparhawk decided. "The horses won't be able to go much farther, and I don't think the Seeker would attack us inside a building. It seems to prefer open country." He led the way down the hill to the village.

The streets of the town were unpaved, and they were ankle-deep in mud. They reached the town's only inn, and Sparhawk carried Sephrenia to the porch while Kurik followed with Flute. The steps leading up to the door were caked with mud, and the boot scraper beside the door showed little signs of use. Pelosians, it ap-peared, were indifferent to mud. The interior of the inn was dim and smoky, and it smelled strongly of stale sweat and spoiled food. The floor had at one time been covered with rushes, but, except in the corners, the rushes were buried in dried mud.

"Are you sure you don't want to reconsider this?" Tynian asked Kalten as they entered.

"My stomach's fairly strong," Kalten replied, "and I caught a whiff of beer when we came in."

The supper the innkeeper provided was at least marginally edible, although a bit overgarnished with boiled cabbage, and the beds, mere straw pallets, were not nearly so bug-infested as Tynian had predicted.

They rose early the next morning and rode out of the muddy village in a murky dawn.

"Doesn't the sun ever shine in this part of the world?" Talen asked sourly.

"It's spring," Kurik told him. "It's always cloudy and rainy in the spring. It's good for the crops."

"I'm not a radish, Kurik," the boy replied. "I don't need to be watered."

"Talk to God about it." Kurik shrugged. "I don't make the weather."

"God and I aren't on the best of terms," Talen said glibly. "He's busy, and so am I. We try not to interfere with each other."

"The boy is pert," Bevier observed disapprovingly. "Young man," he said, "it is not proper to speak so of the Lord of the Universe."

"You are an honored Knight of the Church, Sir Bevier," Talen pointed out. "I am but a thief of the street. Different rules apply to us. God's great flower garden needs a few weeds to offset the splendor of the roses. I'm a weed. I'm sure God forgives me for that, since I'm a part of his grand design."

Bevier looked at him helplessly, and then began to laugh.

They rode warily across southeastern Pelosia for the next several days, taking turns scouting on ahead and riding to hilltops to survey the surrounding countryside. The sky remained dreary as they pushed on to the east. They saw peasants—serfs actually—laboring in the fields with the crudest of implements. There were birds nesting in the hedges, and occasionally they saw deer grazing among herds of scrubby cattle.

While there were people about, Sparhawk and his friends saw no more church soldiers or Zemochs. They remained cautious, however, avoiding people when possible, and continuing their scouting, since they all knew the black-robed Seeker could enlist even normally timid serfs to do its bidding.

As they came closer to the border of Lamorkand, they received increasingly disturbing reports concerning turmoil in that kingdom. Lamorks were not the most stable people in the world. The King of Lamorkand ruled only at the sufferance of the largely independent barons, who retreated in times of trouble to positions behind the walls of massive castles. Blood feuds dating back a hundred years or more were common, and rogue barons looted and pillaged at will. For the most part, Lamorkand existed in a state of perpetual civil war.

They made camp one night perhaps three leagues from the border of that most troubled of western kingdoms, and Sparhawk stood up directly after a supper of the last of Kalten's hindquarter of beef. "All right," he said, "what are we walking into? What's stirring things up in Lamorkand? Any ideas?"

"I spent the last eight or nine years in Lamorkand," Kalten said seriously. "They're strange people. A Lamork will sacrifice anything he owns for the sake of revenge—and the women are even worse than the men. A good Lamork girl will spend her whole life—and all her father's wealth—for the chance to sink a spear into somebody who refused her invitation to dance at some midwinter party. I spent all those years there, and in all that time, I never heard anyone laugh or saw anyone smile. It's the bleakest place on earth. The sun is forbidden to shine in Lamorkand."

"Is this universal warfare we've been hearing about from the Pelosians a common thing?" Sparhawk asked.

"Pelosians are not the best judges of Lamork peculiarities," Tynian replied thoughtfully. "It's only the influence of the Church—and the presence of the Church Knights—that's kept Pelosia and Lamorkand from blithely embarking on a war of mutual extinction. They despise each other with a passion that's almost holy in its mindless ferocity."

Sephrenia sighed. "Elenes," she said.

"We have our faults, little mother," Sparhawk conceded. "We're going to run into trouble when we cross the border then, aren't we?"

"Not entirely," Tynian said, rubbing his chin. "Are you open to another sugges-tion, maybe?"

"I'm always open to suggestions."

"Why don't we put on our formal armor? Not even the most wild-eyed Lam-ork baron will willingly cross the Church, and the Church Knights could grind western Lamorkand into powder if they felt like it."

"What if somebody calls our bluff?" Kalten asked. "There are only five of us, after all."

"I don't think they'd have any reason to," Tynian said. "The neutrality of the Church Knights in these local disputes is legendary. Formal armor might be just the thing to avoid misunderstandings. Our purpose is to get to Lake Randera, not to engage in random disputes with hotheads."

"It might work, Sparhawk," Ulath said. "It's worth a try, anyway."

"All right, let's do it then," Sparhawk decided.

When they arose the following morning, the five knights unpacked their for-mal armor and began to put it on with the help of Kurik and Berit. Sparhawk and Kalten wore Pandion black with silver surcoats and formal black capes. Bevier's armor was burnished to a silvery sheen, and his surcoat and cape were pristine white. Tynian's armor was simply massive steel, but his surcoat and cape were a bril-liant sky blue. Ulath put aside the utilitarian mail shirt he had worn on the trail and replaced it with chain-mail trousers and a mail coat that reached to midthigh. He stowed away his simple conical helmet and green traveller's cloak and put on instead a green surcoat and a very impressive-looking helmet surmounted by a pair of the curled and twisted horns he had identified as having come from an Ogre.

"Well?" Sparhawk said to Sephrenia when they had finished putting on their finery, "how do we look?"

"Very impressive," she complimented them.

Talen, however, eyed them critically. "They look sort of like an ironworks that sprouted legs, don't they?" he observed to Berit.

"Be polite," Berit said, concealing a smile behind one hand.

"That's depressing," Kalten said to Sparhawk. "Do you think we really look that ridiculous to the common people?"

"Probably."

Kurik and Berit cut lances from a nearby yew grove and affixed steel points to them.

"Pennons?" Kurik asked.

"What do you think?" Sparhawk asked Tynian.

"It couldn't hurt. Let's try to look as impressive as we can, I suppose."

They mounted with some difficulty, adjusted their shields and moved their pennon-flagged lances into positions where they were prominently displayed, and rode out. Faran immediately began to prance. "Oh, stop that," Sparhawk told him disgustedly.

They crossed into Lamorkand not much past noon. The border guards looked suspicious, but automatically gave way to the Knights of the Church dressed in their formal armor and wearing expressions of inexorable resolve.

The Lamork city of Kadach stood on the far side of a river. There was a bridge, but Sparhawk decided against going through that bleak, ugly place. Instead, he checked his map and turned north. "The river branches upstream," he told the others. "We'll be able to ford it up there. We're going more or less in that direction anyway, and towns are filled with people who just might want to talk to alien strangers asking questions about us."

They rode on north to the series of small streams that fed into the main channel. It was when they were crossing one of those shallow streams that afternoon that they saw a large body of Lamork warriors on the far bank.

"Spread out," Sparhawk commanded tersely. "Sephrenia, take Talen and Flute to the rear."

"You think they might belong to the Seeker?" Kalten asked, moving his hand up the shaft of his lance.

"We'll find out in a minute. Don't do anything rash, but be ready for trouble."

The leader of the group of warriors was a burly fellow wearing a chain coat, a steel helmet with a protruding, pig-faced visor, and stout leather boots. He advanced into the stream alone and raised his visor to show that he had no hostile intentions.

"I think he's all right, Sparhawk," Bevier said quietly. "He doesn't have that blank look on his face that the men we killed back in Elenia had."

"Well met, Sir Knights," the Lamork said.

Sparhawk nudged Faran forward a bit through the swirling current. "Well met indeed, my Lord," he replied.

"This is a fortunate encounter," the Lamork continued. "It seemed me that we might have ridden even so far as Elenia ere we had encountered Church Knights."

"And what is your business with the Knights of the Church, my Lord?" Sparhawk asked politely.

"We require a service of you, Sir Knight—a service that bears directly on the well-being of the Church."

"We live but to serve her," Sparhawk said, struggling to conceal his irritation. "Speak further concerning this necessary service."

"As all the world knows, the Patriarch of Kadash is the paramount choice for the Archprelate's throne in Chyrellos," the helmeted Lamork stated.

"I hadn't heard that," Kalten said quietly from behind.

"Hush," Sparhawk muttered over his shoulder. "Say on, my Lord," he said to the Lamork.

"Misfortunately, civil turmoil mars western Lamorkand presently," the Lamork continued.

"I like 'misfortunately,'" Tynian murmured to Kalten. "It's got a nice ring to it."

"*Will* you two be quiet?" Sparhawk snapped. Then he looked back at the man in the chain coat. "Rumor has advised us of this discord, my Lord," he replied. "But surely this is a local matter, and does not involve the Church."

"I will speak to the point, Sir Knight. The Patriarch Ortzel of Kadach has been forced by the turmoil I but recently mentioned to seek shelter in the stronghold of his brother, the Baron Alstrom, whom I have the honor to serve. Rude civil discord rears its head here in Lamorkand, and we anticipate with some certainty that the foes of my Lord Alstrom will shortly besiege his fortress."

"We are but five, my Lord," Sparhawk pointed out. "Surely our aid would be of little use in a protracted siege."

"Ah, no, Sir Knight," the Lamork said with a disdainful smile. "We can sustain ourselves and my Lord Alstrom's castle without the aid of the invincible Knights of the Church. My Lord Alstrom's castle is impregnable, and his foes may freely dash themselves to bits against its walls for a generation or more without causing us alarm. As I have said, however, the Patriarch Ortzel is the paramount choice for the Archprelacy—in the event of the demise of the revered Cluvonus, which, please God, may be delayed for a time. Thus I charge you and your noble companions, Sir Knight, to convey his Grace safe and whole to the sacred city of Chyrellos so that he may stand for election, should that mournful necessity come to pass. With that end in view, I will forthwith convey you and your knightly companions to the stronghold of my Lord of Alstrom so that you may undertake this noble task. Let us then proceed."

## CHAPTER FOUR

The castle of Baron Alstrom was situated on a rocky promontory on the east bank of the river. The promontory jutted out into the main channel a few leagues above the town of Kadach. It was a bleak, ugly fortress, squatting toad-like under a cheerless sky. Its walls were thick and high, seeming to reflect the stiff, unyielding arrogance of its owner.

"Impregnable?" Bevier murmured derisively to Sparhawk as the knight in the chain coat preceded them along the short causeway that led out to the castle gate. "I could reduce these walls within the space of two years. No Arcian noble would feel secure within such flimsy fortifications."

"Arcians have more time to build their castles," Sparhawk pointed out to the white-caped knight. "It takes longer to start a war in Arcium than it does here in Lamorkand. You can start a war here in about five minutes, and it's likely to go on for generations."

"Truly," Bevier agreed. He smiled faintly. "In my youth I gave some time to the study of military history. When I turned to the volumes dealing with Lamorkand, I threw up my hands in despair. No rational man could sort out all the alliances, betrayals, and blood feuds that seethe just below the surface of this unhappy kingdom."

The drawbridge boomed down, and they clattered on across it into the castle's main court. "And it please you, Sir Knights," the Lamork knight said, dismounting, "I will convey you directly into the presence of the Baron Alstrom and his Grace, the Patriarch Ortzel. Time is pressing, and we must see his Grace safely out of the castle ere the forces of Count Gerrich mount their siege."

"Lead on, Sir Knight," Sparhawk said, clanking down from Faran's back. He leaned his lance against the wall of the stable, hung his silver-embossed black shield on his saddle, and handed his reins to a waiting groom.

They went up a broad stone staircase and through the pair of massive doors at its top. The hallway beyond was torchlit, and the stones of its walls were massive. "Did you warn that groom?" Kalten asked, falling in beside Sparhawk, his long black cape swirling about his ankles.

"About what?"

"Your horse's disposition."

"I forgot," Sparhawk confessed. "He'll find out on his own, I imagine."

"He probably already has."

The room to which the Lamork knight led them was bleak. In many respects it was more like an armory than living quarters. Swords and axes hung on the walls, and pikes in clusters of a dozen or so leaned in the corners. A fire burned in a huge, vaulted fireplace, and the few chairs were heavy and unpadded. There was no carpeting on the floor, and a number of huge wolfhounds dozed here and there.

Baron Alstrom was a grim-faced, melancholy-looking man. His black hair and beard were shot with gray. He wore a mail coat and had a broadsword at his waist. His surcoat was black and elaborately embroidered in red, and like the knight in the pig-faced helmet, he wore boots.

Their escort bowed stiffly. "By good fortune, my Lord, I encountered these Knights of the Church no more than a league from your walls. They were gracious enough to accompany me here."

"Did we have any choice?" Kalten muttered.

The Baron rose from his chair with a movement made clumsy by the encumbrance of armor and sword. "Greetings, Sir Knights," he said in a voice without much warmth. "It was indeed fortuitous that Sir Enmann encountered you so near this stronghold. The forces of mine enemy will presently besiege me here, and my brother must be safely away before they come."

"Yes, my Lord," Sparhawk replied, removing his black helmet and looking after the departing Lamork in the chain coat. "Sir Enmann advised us of the circumstances. Might it not have been more prudent, however, to have sent your brother on his way with an escort of your own troops? It was only a chance meeting that brought us to your gate before your enemies come."

Alstrom shook his head. "The warriors of County Gerrich would certainly attack my men on sight. Only under escort of the Knights of the Church will my brother be safe, Sir—?"

"Sparhawk."

Alstrom looked briefly surprised. "The name is not unknown to us," he said. He looked inquiringly at the others, and Sparhawk made the introductions.

"An oddly assorted party, Sir Sparhawk," Alstrom observed after he had bowed perfunctorily to Sephrenia. "But is it wise to take the lady and the two children on a journey that might involve danger?"

"The lady is essential to our purpose," Sparhawk replied. "The little girl is under her care, and the boy is her page. She would not leave them behind."

"Page?" he heard Talen whisper to Berit. "I've been called a lot of things, but that's a new one."

"Hush," Berit whispered back.

"What astonishes me even more, however," Alstrom continued, "is the fact that all four of the militant orders are represented here. Relations between the orders have not been cordial of late, I've been told."

"We are embarked upon a quest which directly involves the Church," Sparhawk explained, taking off his gauntlets. "It is of such pressing urgency that our preceptors brought us together that we might by our unity prevail."

"The unity of the Church Knights, like that of the Church herself, is long overdue," a harsh voice said from the far side of the room. A churchman stepped out of the shadows. His black cassock was plain, even severe, and his hollow-cheeked face was bleakly ascetic. His hair was pale blond, streaked with gray, and it fell straight to his shoulders, appearing to have been hacked off at that point with the blade of a knife.

"My brother," Alstrom introduced him, "the Patriarch Ortzel of Kadach."

Sparhawk bowed, his armor creaking slightly. "Your Grace," he said.

"This Church matter you mentioned interests me," Ortzel said, coming forward into the light. "What can it be that is of such urgency that it impels the preceptors of the four orders to set aside old enmities and to send their champions forth as one?"

Sparhawk thought only a moment, then gambled. "Is your Grace perhaps acquainted with Annias, Primate of Cimmura?" he asked, depositing his gauntlets in his helmet.

Ortzel's face hardened. "We've met," he said flatly.

"We've also had that pleasure," Kalten said dryly, "often enough more than to satisfy me, at least."

Ortzel smiled briefly. "I gather that our opinions of the good primate more or less coincide," he suggested.

"Your Grace is perceptive," Sparhawk noted smoothly. "The Primate of Cimmura aspires to a position in the Church for which our preceptors feel he is unqualified."

"I have heard of his aspirations in that direction."

"This is the main thrust of our quest, your Grace," Sparhawk explained. "The Primate of Cimmura is deeply involved in the politics of Elenia. The lawful Queen of that realm is Ehlana, daughter to the late King Aldreas. She is, however, gravely ill, and Primate Annias controls the royal council—which means, of course, that he also controls the royal treasury. It is his access to that treasury that fuels his hopes to ascend the throne of the Archprelacy. He has more or less unlimited funds at his disposal, and certain members of the Hierocracy have proved to be susceptible to his blandishments. It is our mission to restore the Queen to health so that she might once again take the rulership of her kingdom into her own hands."

"An unseemly state of affairs," Baron Alstrom observed disapprovingly. "No kingdom should be ruled by a woman."

"I have the honor to be the Queen's Champion, my Lord," Sparhawk declared, "and, I hope, her friend as well. I have known her since she was a child and I assure you that Ehlana is no ordinary woman. She has more steel in her than almost any other monarch in all of Eosia. Once she is restored to health, she will be more than a match for the Primate of Cimmura. She will cut off his access to the treasury as easily as she would snip off a stray lock of hair, and without that money, the Primate's hopes die."

"Then your quest is a noble one, Sir Sparhawk," Patriarch Ortzel approved, "but why has it brought you to Lamorkand?"

"May I speak frankly, your Grace?"

"Of course."

"We have recently discovered that Queen Ehlana's illness is not of natural origin, and to cure her we must resort to extreme measures."

"You're speaking too delicately, Sparhawk," Ulath growled, removing his Ogre-horned helmet. "What my Pandion brother is trying to say, your Grace, is that Queen Ehlana has been poisoned, and that we'll have to use magic to bring her back to health."

"Poisoned?" Ortzel paled. "Surely you do not suspect Primate Annias?"

"Everything points that way, your Grace," Tynian said, pushing back his blue cape. "The details are tedious, but we have strong evidence that Annias was behind it all."

"You must bring these charges before the Hierocracy!" Ortzel exclaimed. "If they are true, this is monstrous."

"The matter is already in the hands of the Patriarch of Demos, your Grace," Sparhawk assured him. "I think we can trust him to lay it before the Hierocracy at the proper time."

"Dolmant is a good man," Ortzel agreed. "I'll abide by his decision in the matter—for the time being, at least."

"Please be seated, Sir Knights," the baron said. "The urgency of this present situation has made me remiss in matters of courtesy. Might I offer you some refreshment?"

Kalten's eyes brightened.

"Never mind," Sparhawk muttered to him, holding a chair for Sephrenia. She sat, and Flute came over and climbed up into her lap.

"Your daughter, Madame?" Ortzel surmised.

"No, your Grace. She's a foundling—of sorts. I'm fond of her, however."

"Berit," Kurik said, "we're just in the way here. Let's go to the stables. I want to check over the horses." And the two of them left the room.

"Tell me, my Lord," Bevier said to Baron Alstrom, "what is it that has brought you to the brink of war? Some ancient dispute, perhaps?"

"No, Sir Bevier," the baron replied, his face hardening, "this is an affair of more recent origin. Perhaps a year ago my only son became friendly with a knight who said he was from Cammoria. I have since discovered that the man is a villain. He encouraged my young and foolish son in a vain hope of obtaining the hand of the daughter of my neighbor, Count Gerrich. The girl seemed amenable, though her father and I have never been friends. Not long after, however, Gerrich announced that he had promised his daughter's hand to another. My son was enraged. His so-called friend goaded him on in this and proposed a desperate plan. They could abduct the girl, find a priest willing to marry her to my son, and present Gerrich with a number of grandchildren to still his wrath. They scaled the walls of the count's castle and crept into the girl's bedchamber. I have since discovered that my son's supposed friend had alerted the count, and Gerrich and his sister's seven sons sprang from hiding as the two entered. My son, believing that it had been the count's daughter who had betrayed him, plunged his dagger into her breast before the count's nephews fell upon him with their swords." Alstrom paused, his teeth clenched and his eyes brimming.

"My son was obviously in the wrong," he admitted, continuing his story, "and I would not have pursued the matter, grieved though I was. It was what happened after my son's death that has set eternal enmity between Gerrich and myself. Not content with merely killing my son, the count and his sister's savage brood mutilated his body and contemptuously deposited it at my castle gate. I was outraged, but the Cammorian knight, whom I still trusted, advised guile. He pled matters of pressing urgency in Cammorian, but promised me the aid of two of his trusted retainers. It was but last week when the two arrived at my door to tell me that the time for my revenge had come. They led my soldiers to the house of the count's sister, and there they slaughtered the count's seven nephews. I have since discovered that these two underlings inflamed my soldiers, and they took certain liberties with the person of Gerrich's sister."

"That's a delicate way to put it," Kalten whispered to Sparhawk.

"Be still," Sparhawk whispered back.

"The lady was dispatched—naked, I'm afraid—to her brother's castle. Reconciliation is now quite impossible. Gerrich has many allies, as do I, and western Lamorkand now hovers on the brink of general war."

"A melancholy tale, my Lord," Sparhawk said sadly.

"The impending war is *my* concern. What is important now is to remove my brother from this house and to convey him safely to Chyrellos. Should he also fall during Gerrich's attack, the Church will have no choice but to send in her Knights. The murder of a patriarch—particularly one who is a strong candidate for elevation to the Archprelacy—would be a crime she could not ignore. Thus it is that I implore you to safeguard him on his way to the Holy City."

"One question, my Lord," Sparhawk said. "The activities of this Cammorian knight have a familiar ring to them. Can you describe him and his underlings to us?"

"The knight himself is a tall man with an arrogant bearing. One of his companions is a huge brute, scarcely human. The other is a rabbity fellow with an excessive fondness for strong drink."

"Sounds a bit like some old friends, doesn't it?" Kalten said to Sparhawk. "Was there anything unusual about this knight?"

"His hair was absolutely white," Alstrom replied, "and he was not that old."

"Martel certainly moves around, doesn't he?" Kalten observed.

"You know this man, Sir Kalten?" the baron asked.

"The white-haired man is named Martel," Sparhawk explained. "His two hirelings are Adus and Krager. Martel's a renegade Pandion Knight who hires out his services in various parts of the world. Most recently, he's been working for the Primate of Cimmura."

"But what would be the primate's purpose in fomenting discord between Gerrich and me?"

"You've already touched on that, my Lord," Sparhawk replied. "The preceptors of the four militant orders are firmly opposed to the notion of Annias sitting on the Archprelate's throne. They will be present—and voting—during the election in the Basilica of Chyrellos, and their opinion carries great weight with the Hierocracy. Moreover, the Knights of the Church would respond immediately to the first hint of any irregularities in the election. If Annias is to succeed, he must get the Church Knights out of Chyrellos before the election. We were recently able to thwart a plot that Martel was hatching in Rendor that would have pulled the Knights out of the Holy City. It's my guess that this unhappy affair you told us about is yet another. Martel, acting on orders from Annias, is roaming the world building bonfires in the hope that sooner or later the Knights of the Church will be forced to move out of Chyrellos to extinguish them."

"Is Annias truly so depraved?" Ortzel asked.

"Your Grace, Annias will do *anything* to ascend that throne. I'm positive that he'd order the massacre of half of Eosia to get what he wants."

"How is it possible for a churchman to stoop so low?"

"Ambition, your Grace," Bevier said sadly. "Once it sinks its claws into a man's heart, the man becomes blind to all else."

"This is all the more reason to get my brother safely to Chyrellos," Alstrom said gravely. "He is much respected by the other members of the Hierocracy, and his voice will carry great weight in their deliberations."

"I must advise you and your brother, my Lord Alstrom, that there is a certain risk involved in your plan," Sparhawk warned them. "We are being pursued. There are those bent on thwarting us in our quest. Since your brother's safety is your first concern, I should tell you that I cannot guarantee it. The ones who are pursuing us are determined and very dangerous." He spoke obliquely, since neither Alstrom nor Ortzel would give him much credence if he told them the bald truth about the nature of the Seeker.

"I'm afraid I have no real choice in the matter, Sir Sparhawk. With this anticipated siege hanging over my head, I have to get my brother out of the castle, no matter what the risk."

"As long as you understand, my Lord." Sparhawk sighed. "Our mission is of the gravest urgency, but this matter overshadows even that."

"Sparhawk!" Sephrenia gasped.

"We have no choice, little mother," he told her. "We absolutely *must* get his Grace safely out of Lamorkand and to Chyrellos. The baron is right. If anything happens to his brother, the Church Knights will ride out of Chyrellos to retaliate. Nothing could prevent it. We'll have to take his Grace to the Holy City and then try to make up for lost time."

"What precisely is the object of your search, Sir Sparhawk?" the Patriarch of Kadach asked.

"As Sir Ulath explained, we are forced to resort to magic to restore the Queen of Elenia to health, and there's only one thing in the world with that much power. We're on our way to the great battlefield at Lake Randera to seek out the jewel, which once surmounted the royal crown of Thalesia."

"The Bhelliom?" Ortzel was shocked. "Surely you would not bring that accursed thing to light again?"

"We have no choice, your Grace. Only Bhelliom can restore my Queen."

"But Bhelliom is tainted. All the wickedness of the Troll-Gods infects it."

"The Troll-Gods aren't all that bad, your Grace," Ulath said. "They're capricious, I'll grant you, but they're not truly evil."

"The Elene God forbids consorting with them."

"The Elene God is wise, your Grace," Sephrenia told him. "He has also forbidden contact with the Gods of Styricum. He made an exception to his prohibition, however, when the time came to form the militant orders. The Younger Gods of Styricum agreed to assist Him in His design. One wonders if He might not also be able to enlist the aid of the Troll-Gods. He is, I understand, most persuasive."

"Blasphemy!" Ortzel gasped.

"No, your Grace, not really. I am Styric and therefore not subject to Elene theology."

"Hadn't we better get going?" Ulath suggested. "It's a long ride to Chyrellos, and we need to get his Grace out of this castle before the fighting starts."

"Well put, my laconic friend," Tynian approved.

"I shall make ready at once," Ortzel said, going to the door. "We will be able to depart within the hour." And he went out.

"How long do you think it's likely to be before the count's forces reach here, my Lord?" Tynian asked the baron.

"No more than a day, Sir Tynian. I have friends who are impeding his march northward from his keep, but he has a sizeable army, and I'm certain he will soon break his way through."

"Talen," Sparhawk said sharply, "put it back."

The boy made a wry face and laid a small dagger with a jeweled hilt back on the table from which he had taken it. "I didn't think you were watching," he said.

"Don't ever make that mistake," Sparhawk said. "I always watch you."

The baron looked puzzled.

"The boy has not yet learned to grasp some of the finer points of property ownership, my Lord," Kalten said lightly. "We've been trying to teach him, but he's a slow learner."

Talen sighed and took up his sketch pad and pencil. Then he sat at a table on the far side of the room and began to draw. He was, Sparhawk remembered, very talented.

"I am most grateful to you all, gentlemen," the baron was saying. "The safety of my brother has been my only concern. Now I shall be able to concentrate on the business at hand." He looked at Sparhawk. "Do you think you might possibly encounter this Martel person during the course of your quest?"

"I most certainly *hope* so," Sparhawk said fervently.

"And is it your intention to kill him?"

"That's been Sparhawk's intention for the last dozen years or so," Kalten said. "Martel sleeps very lightly when Sparhawk's in the same kingdom with him."

"May God aid your arm then, Sir Sparhawk," the baron said. "My son will rest more peacefully once his betrayer joins him in the House of the Dead."

The door burst open, and Sir Enmann hurried into the room. "My Lord!" he said to Alstrom in urgent tones, "come quickly!"

Alstrom came to his feet. "What is it, Sir Enmann?"

"Count Gerrich has deceived us. He has a fleet of ships on the river, and even now his forces are landing on both sides of this promontory."

"Sound the alarm!" the baron commanded, "and raise the drawbridge!"

"At once, my Lord." Enmann hurried from the room.

Alstrom sighed bleakly. "I'm afraid it's too late, Sir Sparhawk," he said. "Both your quest and the task I set you are doomed now. We are under siege, and we will all be trapped within these walls for a number of years, I fear."

# CHAPTER FIVE

The booming crash of boulders slamming against the walls of Alstrom's castle came with monotonous regularity as the siege engines of Count Gerrich moved into place and began pounding the fortress.

Sparhawk and the others had remained in the cheerless, weapons-cluttered room at Alstrom's request, and they sat awaiting his return.

"I've never been under siege before," Talen said, looking up from his drawings. "How long do they usually last?"

"If we can't come up with a way to get out of here, you'll be shaving by the time it's over," Kurik told him.

"Do something, Sparhawk," the boy said urgently.

"I'm open to suggestions."

Talen looked at him helplessly.

Baron Alstrom came back into the room. His face was bleak. "I'm afraid we're completely encircled," he said.

"A truce, perhaps?" Bevier suggested. "It's customary in Arcium to grant safe passage to women and churchmen before pressing a siege."

"Unfortunately, Sir Bevier," Alstrom replied, "this is not Arcium. This is Lamorkand, and there's no such thing as a truce here."

"Any ideas?" Sparhawk asked Sephrenia.

"A few, perhaps," she said. "Let me have a try at your excellent Elene logic. First, the use of main force to break out of the castle is quite out of the question, wouldn't you say?"

"Absolutely."

"And, as you pointed out, a truce would probably not be honored?"

"I certainly wouldn't want to gamble his Grace's life or yours on a truce."

"Then there's the possibility of stealth. I don't think that would work either, do you?"

"Too risky," Kalten agreed. "The castle is surrounded, and the soldiers will be on the alert for people trying to sneak out."

"Subterfuge of some kind?" she asked.

"Not under these circumstances," Ulath said. "The troops surrounding the castle are armed with crossbows. We'd never get close enough to tell them stories."

"That leaves only the arts of Styricum, doesn't it?"

Ortzel's face stiffened. "I will not be a party to the use of heathen sorcery," he declared.

"I was afraid he might look at it that way," Kalten murmured to Sparhawk.

"I'll try to reason with him in the morning," Sparhawk replied under his breath. He looked at Baron Alstrom. "It's late, my Lord," he said, "and we're all tired. Some sleep might clear our heads and hint at other solutions."

"Well said, Sir Sparhawk," Alstrom agreed. "My servants will convey you and your companions to safe quarters, and we shall consider this matter further on the morrow."

They were led through the bleak halls of Alstrom's castle to a wing that, while comfortable, showed little signs of use. Supper was brought to them in their rooms, and Sparhawk and Kalten removed their armor. After they had eaten they sat talking quietly in the chamber they shared.

"I could have told you that Ortzel would feel the way he does about magic. The churchmen here in Lamorkand feel almost as strongly about it as Rendors."

"If it'd been Dolmant, we might have talked our way around him," Sparhawk agreed glumly.

"Dolmant's more cosmopolitan," Kalten said. "He grew up next door to the Pandion motherhouse, and he knows a great deal more about the secrets than he lets on."

There was a light rap on the door. Sparhawk rose and answered it. It was Talen. "Sephrenia wants to see you," he told the big knight.

"All right. Go to bed, Kalten. You're still looking a bit worse for wear. Lead the way, Talen."

The boy took Sparhawk to the end of the corridor and tapped on the door.

"Come in, Talen," Sephrenia replied.

"How did you know it was me?" Talen asked curiously as he opened the door.

"There are ways," she said mysteriously. The small Styric woman was gently brushing Flute's long black hair. The child had a dreamy look on her small face, and she was humming to herself contentedly. Sparhawk was startled. It was the first vocal sound he had ever heard her utter. "If she can hum, why is it she can't talk?" he asked.

"Whatever gave you the idea she can't talk?" Sephrenia continued her brushing.

"She never has done so."

"What does that have to do with it?"

"What did you want to see me about?"

"It's going to take something rather spectacular to get us out of here," she replied, "and I may need your help and that of the others to manage it."

"All you have to do is ask. Have you got any ideas at all?"

"A few. Our first problem is Ortzel, though. If he bows his neck on this, we'll never get him out of the castle."

"Suppose I just hit him on the head before we leave and tie him across his saddle until we're safely away?"

"Sparhawk," she chided him.

"It was a thought." He shrugged. "What about Flute here?"

"What about her?"

"She made those soldiers on the docks at Vardenais and the spies outside the chapterhouse ignore us. Couldn't she do that here too?"

"Do you realize how large that army outside the gate is, Sparhawk? She's just a little girl, after all."

"Oh. I didn't know that would make a difference."

"Of course it does."

"Couldn't you put Ortzel to sleep?" Talen asked her. "You know, sort of wiggle your fingers at him until he drops off?"

"It's possible, I suppose."

"Then he won't know you used magic to get us out of here until he wakes up."

"Interesting notion," she conceded. "How did you come up with it?"

"I'm a thief, Sephrenia." He grinned impudently. "I wouldn't be very good at it if I couldn't think faster than the other fellow."

"However we manage Ortzel is beside the point," Sparhawk said. "Our main concern is getting Alstrom's cooperation. He might be a little reluctant to risk his brother's life on something he doesn't understand. I'll talk with him in the morning."

"Be *very* persuasive, Sparhawk," Sephrenia said.

"I'll try. Come along, Talen. Let the ladies get some sleep. Kalten and I have a spare bed in our room. You can sleep there. Sephrenia, don't be afraid to call on me and the others if you need help with any spells."

"I'm never afraid, Sparhawk—not when I have you to protect me."

"Stop that," he told her. Then he smiled. "Sleep well, Sephrenia."

"You too, dear one."

"Good night, Flute," he added.

She blew him a little trill on her pipes.

The following morning, Sparhawk rose early and went back into the main part of the castle. As chance had it, he encountered Sir Enmann in the long, torchlit corridor. "How do things stand?" he asked the Lamork knight.

Enmann's face was gray with fatigue. He had obviously been up all night. "We've had some success, Sir Sparhawk," he replied. "We repelled a fairly serious assault on the castle's main gate about midnight, and we're moving our own engines into place. We should be able to begin destroying Gerrich's siege machines—and his ships—before noon."

"Will he pull back at that point?"

Enmann shook his head. "More likely, he'll begin digging earthwork fortifications. It's probable that the siege will be protracted."

Sparhawk nodded. "I thought that might be the case," he agreed. "Have you any idea where I might find Baron Alstrom? I need to talk with him—out of the hearing of his brother."

"My Lord Alstrom is atop the battlements at the front of the castle, Sir Sparhawk. He wants Gerrich to be able to see him. That may goad the count into some rash move. He's alone there. His brother is customarily in chapel at this hour."

"Good. I'll go talk with the baron then."

It was windy atop the battlements. Sparhawk had drawn his cloak about his armor to conceal it, and the wind whipped it around his legs.

"Ah, good morning, Sir Sparhawk," Baron Alstrom said. His voice was weary. He wore a full suit of armor, and the visor of his helmet had that peculiar pointed construction common in Lamorkand.

"Good morning, my Lord," Sparhawk replied, staying back from the battlements. "Is there someplace back out of sight where we can talk? I'm not sure it's a good idea to let Gerrich know that there are Church Knights inside your walls just yet, and I'm sure he has a number of sharp-eyed men watching you."

"The tower there above the gate," Alstrom suggested. "Come along, Sir Sparhawk." He led the way along the parapet.

The room inside the tower was grimly functional. A dozen crossbowmen stood at the narrow embrasures along its front unloosing their bolts at the troops below.

"You men," Alstrom commanded, "I have need of this room. Go shoot from the battlements for a while."

The soldiers filed out, their metal-shod feet clinking on the stone floor.

"We have a problem, my Lord," Sparhawk said when the two of them were alone.

"I noticed that," Alstrom said dryly, glancing out one of the embrasures at the troops massed before his walls.

Sparhawk grinned at this rare flash of humor in a usually dour race. "That particular problem is yours, my Lord," he said. "Our mutual one is what we're going to do about your brother. Sephrenia got directly to the point last night. No purely natural effort is going to effect his escape from the siege. We have no choice. We have to use magic—and his Grace appears to be unalterably opposed."

"I would not presume to instruct Ortzel in theology," Alstrom said.

"Nor would I, my Lord. Might I point out, however, that should his Grace ascend to the Archprelacy, he's going to have to modify his position—or at least learn to look the other way when this sort of thing happens. The four orders are the military arm of the Church, and we routinely utilize the secrets of Styricum in completing our tasks."

"I'm aware of that, Sir Sparhawk. My brother, however, is a rigid man and unlikely to change his views."

Sparhawk began to pace up and down, thinking fast. "Very well, then," he said carefully. "What we'll have to do to get your brother out of the castle will seem unnatural to you, but I assure you that it will be very effective. Sephrenia is highly skilled in the secrets. I've seen her do things that verge on the miraculous. You have my guarantee that she will in no way endanger your brother."

"I understand, Sir Sparhawk."

"Good. I was afraid that you might object. Most people are reluctant to rely on things they don't understand. Now, then, his Grace will in no way participate in what we may have to do. To put it bluntly, he'd just be in the way. All he's going to do is take advantage of it. He will in no way be personally involved in what he considers a sin."

"Understand me, Sir Sparhawk, I am not opposed to you in this. I will try reason with my brother. Sometimes he listens to me."

"Let's hope this is one of those times." Sparhawk glanced out the window and swore.

"What is it, Sir Sparhawk?"

"Is that Gerrich standing on top of that knoll at the rear of his troops?"

The baron looked out the embrasure. "It is."

"You might recognize the man standing beside him. That's Adus, Martel's underling. It seems that Martel's been playing both sides in this affair. The one that concerns me, though, is that figure standing off to one side—the tall one in the black robe."

"I don't think it poses much of a threat, Sir Sparhawk. It seems to be hardly more than a skeleton."

"You notice how its face seems to glow?"

"Now that you mention it, yes, I do. Isn't that odd?"

"It's more than odd, Baron Alstrom. I think I'd better go talk with Sephrenia. She needs to know about this immediately."

Sephrenia sat beside the fire in her room with her ever-present teacup in her hands. Flute sat cross-legged on the bed, weaving a cat's cradle of such complexity that Sparhawk pulled his eyes away from it, lest his entire mind become lost in trying to trace out the individual strands. "We've got trouble," he told his tutor.

"I noticed that," she replied.

"It's a little more serious than we'd thought. Adus is out there with Count Gerrich, and Krager's probably lurking around somewhere in the background."

"Martel's beginning to make me very tired."

"Adus and Krager don't add much to the problems we've already got, but that thing, the Seeker, is out there too."

"Are you sure?" She came quickly to her feet.

"It's the right size and shape, and that same glow is coming out from under its hood. How many humans can it take over at any one time?"

"I don't think there are any limits, Sparhawk, not when Azash is controlling it."

"Do you remember those ambushers back near the Pelosian border? How they just kept coming even though we were cutting them to pieces?"

"Yes."

"If the Seeker can gain control of Gerrich's whole army, they'll mount an assault that Baron Alstrom's forces won't be able to withstand. We'd better get out of here in a hurry, Sephrenia. Have you come up with anything yet?"

"There are a few possibilities," she replied. "The presence of the Seeker complicates things a bit, but I think I know a way to get around it."

"I hope so. Let's go talk with the others."

It was perhaps a half hour later when they all gathered again in the room where they had first met the previous day. "Very well, gentlemen," Sephrenia said to them. "We are in great danger."

"The castle is quite secure, Madame," Alstrom assured her. "In five hundred years it has never once fallen to besiegers."

"I'm afraid things are different this time. A besieging army usually assaults the walls, doesn't it?"

"It's the common practice, once the siege engines have weakened the fortifications."

"After the assaulting force has taken heavy casualties, they normally fall back, don't they?"

"That's been my experience."

"Gerrich's men will *not* fall back. They will continue their attack until they overwhelm the castle."

"How can you be so sure?"

"You remember the figure in the black robe I pointed out to you, my Lord?" Sparhawk said.

"Yes. It seemed to cause you some concern."

"With good reason, my Lord. That's the creature that's been pursuing us. It's called a Seeker. It's not human, and it's subject to Azash."

"Beware of what you say, Sir Sparhawk," Patriarch Ortzel said ominously. "The Church does not recognize the existence of the Styric Gods. You are treading very close to the brink of heresy."

"Just for the purposes of this discussion, let's assume that I know what I'm talking about," Sparhawk replied. "Putting Azash aside for the moment, it's important for you and your brother to understand just how dangerous that thing out there really is. It will be able to control Gerrich's troops completely, and it will hurl them against this castle until they succeed in taking it."

"Not only that," Bevier added bleakly, "they will pay no attention to wounds that would incapacitate a normal man. The only way to stop them is to kill them. We've met men under the Seeker's control before and we had to kill every last one of them."

"Sir Sparhawk," Alstrom said, "Count Gerrich is my mortal enemy, but he's still an honorable man and a faithful son of the Church. He would not consort with a creature of darkness."

"It's entirely possible that the count doesn't even know it's there," Sephrenia said. "The whole point here, however, is that we're all in deadly peril."

"Why would that creature join forces with Gerrich?" Alstrom asked.

"As Sparhawk said, it's been pursuing us. For some reason, Azash looks upon Sparhawk as a threat. The Elder Gods have some ability to see into the future, and it's possible that Azash has caught a glimpse of something He wants to prevent. He's already made several attempts on Sparhawk's life. It's my belief that the Seeker is here for the express purpose of killing Sparhawk—or at the very least preventing his recovering Bhelliom. We must leave, my Lord, and quickly." She turned to Ortzel. "I'm afraid, your Grace, that we have no choice. We're compelled to resort to the arts of Styricum."

"I will not be a party to that," he said stiffly. "I know that you are Styric, Madame, and therefore ignorant of the dictates of the true faith, but how dare you propose to practice your black arts in my presence? I am a churchman, after all."

"I think that in time you may be obliged to modify your views, your Grace," Ulath said calmly. "The militant orders are the arms of the Church. We receive instruction in the secrets so that we may better serve her. This practice has been approved by every Archprelate for nine hundred years."

"Indeed," Sephrenia added, "no Styric will consent to teach the Knights until approval is given by each new Archprelate."

"Should it come to pass that I ascend the throne in Chyrellos, that practice shall cease."

"Then the West will surely be doomed," she predicted, "for without these arts, the Church Knights will be helpless against Azash, and without the Knights, the West will fall before the hordes of Otha."

"We have no evidence that Otha is coming."

"We have no evidence that summer is coming either," she said dryly. She looked at Alstrom. "I believe I have a plan that may effect our escape, my Lord, but first I'll need to go to your kitchen and talk with your cook."

He looked puzzled.

"The plan involves certain ingredients normally found in kitchens. I need to be certain they're available."

"There's a guard at the door, Madame," he said. "He will escort you to the kitchen."

"Thank you my Lord. Come along, Flute." And she went out.

"What's she up to?" Tynian asked.

"Sephrenia almost never explains things in advance," Kalten told him.

"Or afterward either, I've noticed," Talen added, looking up from his drawing.

"Speak when you're spoken to," Berit told him.

"If I did that, I'd forget how to talk."

"Surely you're not going to permit this, Alstrom," Ortzel said angrily.

"I don't have much choice," Alstrom replied. "We absolutely must get you to safety, and this seems to be the only way."

"Did you see Krager out there too?" Kalten asked Sparhawk.

"No, but I imagine he's around somewhere. Somebody's got to keep an eye on Adus."

"Is this Adus so very dangerous?" Alstrom asked.

"He's an animal, my Lord," Kalten replied, "and a very stupid one. Sparhawk's promised that I get to kill Adus if I don't interfere when he goes after Martel. Adus can barely talk, and he kills for the sheer pleasure of it."

"He's dirty and he smells bad too," Talen added. "He chased me down a street once in Cammoria, and the odor almost knocked me off my feet."

"You think Martel might be with them?" Tynian asked hopefully.

"I doubt it," Sparhawk said. "I think I nailed his foot to the floor down in Rendor. It's my guess that he set things up here in Lamorkand and then went to Rendor to hatch things there. Then he sent Krager and Adus back here to set things in motion."

"I think the world would be better off without this Martel of yours," Alstrom said.

"We're going to do what we can to arrange that, my Lord," Ulath rumbled.

A few moments later, Sephrenia and Flute returned.

"Did you find the things you need?" Sparhawk asked.

"Most of them," she replied. "I can make the others." She looked at Ortzel. "You might wish to retire, your Grace," she suggested. "I don't want to offend your sensibilities."

"I will remain, Madame," he said coldly. "Perhaps my presence will prevent this abomination from coming to pass."

"Perhaps, but I rather doubt it." She pursed her lips and looked critically at the small earthen jar she had carried from the kitchen. "Sparhawk," she said, "I'm going to need an empty barrel."

He went to the door and spoke with the guard.

Sephrenia walked to the table and picked up a crystal goblet. She spoke at some length in Styric, and with a soft rustling sound, the goblet was suddenly filled with a powder that looked much like lavender sand.

"Outrageous," Ortzel muttered.

Sephrenia ignored him. "Tell me, my Lord," she said to Alstrom, "you have pitch and naphtha, I assume."

"Of course. They're a part of the castle's defenses."

"Good. If this is to work, we're going to need them."

The soldier entered, rolling a barrel.

"Right here, please," she instructed, pointing to a spot away from the fire.

He set the barrel upright, saluted the baron, and left.

Sephrenia spoke briefly to Flute. The little girl nodded and lifted her pipes. Her melody was strange, hypnotic, and almost languorous.

The Styric woman stood over the barrel, speaking in Styric and holding the jar in one hand and the goblet in the other. Then she began to pour their contents into the barrel. The pungent spices in the jar and the lavender sand in the goblet came spilling out, but neither vessel emptied. The two streams, mixing as they fell, began to glow, and the room was suddenly filled with starlike glitterings that soared, fireflylike, and sparkled on the walls and ceiling. Sephrenia poured on and on. Minute after minute the small woman continued to pour from the two seemingly inexhaustible containers.

It took nearly half an hour to fill the barrel. "There," Sephrenia said at last, "that should be enough." She looked down into the glowing barrel.

Ortzel was making strangling sounds.

She put the two containers far apart on the table. "I wouldn't let these two get mixed together, my Lord," she cautioned Alstrom, "and keep them away from any kind of fire."

"What are we doing here?" Tynian asked her.

"We must drive the Seeker away, Tynian. We'll mix what's in this barrel with naphtha and pitch and load the baron's siege engines with the mixture. Then we'll ignite it and throw it in among Count Gerrich's troops. The fumes will force them to withdraw, temporarily at least. That's not the main reason we're doing it, however. The Seeker has a much different breathing apparatus than humans do. The fumes are noxious to humans. To the seeker, they're lethal. It will either flee or die."

"That sounds encouraging," he said.

"Was it really all so very terrible, your Grace?" she asked Ortzel. "It's going to save your life, you know."

His face was troubled. "I had always thought that Styric sorcery was mere trickery, but there was no way you could have done what I just saw by charlatanism. I will pray on this matter. I will seek guidance from God."

"I wouldn't take too long, your Grace," Kalten advised. "If you do, it could be that you'll arrive in Chyrellos just in time to kiss the ring of the Archprelate Annias."

"That must never happen," Alstrom declared sternly. "The siege at the gates is *my* concern, Ortzel, not yours. Therefore I must regretfully withdraw my hospitality. You will leave my castle just as soon as it's convenient."

"Alstrom!" Ortzel gasped. "This is my home. I was born here."

"But our father left it to *me. Your* proper home is in the Basilica of Chyrellos. I advise you to go there at once."

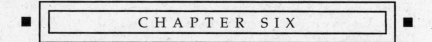

## CHAPTER SIX

"We'll need to go to the highest point in your castle, my Lord," Sephrenia said after the Patriarch of Kadach had angrily stormed from the room.

"That would be the north tower," he replied.

"And can one see the besieging army from there?"

"Yes."

"Good. First, however, we must give your soldiers instructions on how to proceed with this." She pointed at the barrel. "All right, gentlemen," she said crisply, "don't just stand there. Pick the barrel up and bring it along, and whatever you do, don't drop it or get it near any fire."

Her instructions to the soldiers manning the catapults were fairly simple, explaining the proper mixture of the powder, naphtha, and pitch. "Now," she went on, "listen very carefully. Your own safety depends on this. Do not set fire to the naptha until the last possible instant, and if any of the smoke blows in your direction, hold your breath and run. Under no circumstances breathe any of those fumes."

"Will they kill us?" one soldier asked in a frightened voice.

"No, but they'll make you ill and confuse your minds. Cover your noses and mouths with damp cloths. That may protect you a bit. Wait for the baron's signal from the north tower." She tested the wind direction. "Hurl the burning material to the north of those troops on the causeway," she told them, "and don't forget to throw some at those ships in the river as well. Very well then, Baron Alstrom. Let's go to the tower."

As it had been for the last several days, the sky was cloudy, and a brisk wind whistled through the unpaned embrasures of the north tower. Like all such purely defensive constructions, the tower was severely utilitarian. The besieging army of Count Gerrich looked oddly antlike, a mass of tiny men with armor glinting the color of pewter in the pale light. Despite the height of the tower, an occasional crossbow bolt chinked against its weathered stones.

"Be careful," Sparhawk murmured to Sephrenia as she thrust her head out of one of the embrasures to peer at the troops massed before the gate.

"There's no danger," she assured him as the wind whipped at her hooded white robe. "My Goddess protects me."

"You can believe in your Goddess all you want," he replied, "but your safety is *my* responsibility. Have you any idea of what Vanion would do to me if I let you get hurt?"

"And that's only after *I* got through with him," Kalten growled.

She stepped back from the embrasure and stood tapping one finger thoughtfully against her pursed lips.

"Forgive me, Madame," Alstrom said. "I recognize the necessity of chasing off that creature out there, but a purely temporary withdrawal of Gerrich's troops won't really do us all that much good. They'll return as soon as the smoke dissipates, and we still won't be any closer to getting my brother safely away from here."

"If we do this right, they won't return for several days, my Lord."

"Are the fumes that powerful?"

"No. They'll clear off in an hour or so."

"That's hardly time enough for you to make good your escape," he pointed out. "What's to prevent Gerrich from coming back and continuing the siege?"

"He's going to be very busy."

"Busy? With what?"

"He's going to be chasing some people."

"And who is that?"

"You, me, Sparhawk, and the others, your brother, and a fair number of men from your garrison."

"I don't think that's wise, Madame," Alstrom said critically. "We have secure fortifications here. I don't propose to abandon them and risk all our lives in flight."

"We're not going anywhere just yet."

"But you just said—"

"Gerrich and his men will think they're pursuing us. What they'll actually be chasing, however, will be an illusion." She smiled briefly. "Some of the best magic is illusion," she said. "You trick the mind and the eye into believing wholly in something that's not really there. Gerrich will be absolutely convinced that we're trying to take advantage of the confusion to bolt. He'll follow with his army, and that should give us plenty of time to slip your brother away to safety. Is that forest on the horizon fairly extensive?"

"It goes on for several leagues."

"Very good. We'll lead Gerrich in there with our illusion and let him wander around among the trees for the next few days."

"I think there's a flaw here, Sephrenia," Sparhawk said. "Won't the Seeker come back just as soon as the smoke clears? I don't think an illusion would deceive it, would it?"

"The Seeker won't come back for at least a week," she assured him. "It will be very, very ill."

"Should I signal the troops manning the catapults?" Alstrom asked.

"Not yet, my Lord. We have other things to do first. Timing is very important in this. Berit, I'll need a basin of water."

"Yes, ma'am." The novice went toward the stairs.

"Very well, then," she continued. "Let's get started." She began patiently to instruct the Church Knights in the spell. There were Styric words Sparhawk had not learned before, and Sephrenia adamantly insisted that each of them repeat them over and over until pronunciation and intonation were absolutely perfect. "Stop that!" she commanded at one point when Kalten tried to join in.

"I thought I could help," he protested.

"I know just how inept you are at this, Kalten. Just stay out of it. All right, gentlemen, let's try it again."

Once she was satisfied with their pronunciation, she instructed Sparhawk to weave the spell. He began to repeat the Styric words and to gesture with his fingers. The figure that appeared in the center of the room was vaguely amorphous, but it did appear to be wearing Pandion black armor.

"You didn't put a face on it, Sparhawk," Kalten pointed out.

"I'll take care of that," Sephrenia said. She spoke two words and gestured sharply.

Sparhawk stared at the shape before him. It was much like looking into a mirror.

Sephrenia was frowning.

"Something wrong?" Kalten asked her.

"It's not too hard to duplicate familiar faces," she replied, "or those of people who are actually present, but if I have to go look at the face of everybody in the castle, this could take days."

"Would these help?" Talen asked, handing her his sketch pad.

She leafed through the pages, her eyes widening as she turned each page. "The boy's a genius!" she exclaimed. "Kurik, when we get back to Cimmura, apprentice him to an artist. That might keep him out of trouble."

"It's only a hobby, Sephrenia," Talen said, blushing modestly.

"You do know that you could make far more as a painter than as a thief, don't you?" she said pointedly.

He blinked, and then his eyes narrowed speculatively.

"All right. Now it's your turn, Tynian," Sephrenia told the Dieran.

After each had created a mirror image of himself, she led them to an embrasure overlooking the courtyard. "We'll build the large illusion down there," she told them. "It might get a little crowded if we tried to do it up here."

It took them an hour to complete the illusion of a mass of armed and mounted men down in the courtyard. Then Sephrenia went through Talen's sketch pad again and put a face on each figure. Then she made a broad sweep of her arm, and the images of the Church Knights joined the illusion below.

"They aren't moving," Kurik said.

"Flute and I will take care of that," Sephrenia told him. "The rest of you will need to concentrate to keep the images from breaking up. You'll have to hold them together until they reach that forest over there."

Sparhawk was already sweating. Building a spell and then releasing it was one thing. Holding one in place was quite something else. He suddenly realized how much strain Sephrenia was bearing.

It was early afternoon by now. Sephrenia looked out the embrasure at Count Gerrich's troops. "All right," she said. "I guess we're ready. Signal the catapults, my Lord," she said to Alstrom.

The baron took a piece of red cloth out from under his sword belt and waved it out of the embrasure. Below, the catapults began to thud, hurling their burning missiles over the wall and into the midst of the besieging army while other engines showered the ships in the river. Even from this distance, Sparhawk could hear the soldiers coughing and choking on the dense cloud of lavender smoke coming from the burning balls of pitch, naphtha, and Sephrenia's powder. The smoke rolled across the field in front of the castle, sparkling with that firefly glitter. Then it engulfed the knoll where Gerrich, Adus, and the Seeker were standing. Sparhawk heard an animal-like screech, and then the black-robed Seeker burst from the smoke, flogging its horse mercilessly. It seemed unsteady in its saddle, and it was holding the edge of its hood tightly across its face with one pale claw. The soldiers who had been blocking the road leading from the castle gate came reeling out of the smoke, coughing and retching.

"All right, my Lord," Sephrenia said to Alstrom, "lower the drawbridge."

Alstrom signalled again, this time with a green cloth. A moment later, the drawbridge boomed down.

"Now, Flute," Sephrenia said, and began to speak rapidly in Styric even as the little girl raised her pipes.

The mass of illusory men in the courtyard, who had until now been rigidly immobile, seemed to come to life all at once. They rode out through the gate at a gallop and plunged directly into the smoke. Sephrenia passed her hand over the basin of water Berit had brought to the tower and peered intently into it. "Hold them, gentlemen," she said. "Keep them intact."

A half-dozen of Gerrich's soldiers who had escaped from the smoke stood coughing, retching, and digging at their eyes on the causeway leading away from the castle. The illusory army rode directly through them. The soldiers fled screaming.

"Now we wait," Sephrenia said. "It's going to take a few minutes for Gerrich to get his wits together and realize what seems to be happening down there."

Sparhawk heard startled shouts coming from below and then bellowed commands.

"A little faster, Flute," Sephrenia said quite calmly. "We don't want Gerrich to catch up with the illusion. He might begin to grow suspicious if his sword goes through the baron here without any effect."

Alstrom was staring at Sephrenia in awe. "I would not have believed this possible, my Lady," he said in a shaking voice.

"It did turn out rather well, didn't it?" she said. "I wasn't entirely positive I could pull it off."

"You mean—"

"I've never done it before, but we can't learn without experimentation, can we?"

On the field below, Gerrich's troops were scrambling into their saddles. Their pursuit was disorganized, a chaos of galloping horses and brandished weapons.

"They didn't even think to charge that open drawbridge," Ulath noted critically. "Very unprofessional."

"They aren't thinking very clearly just now," Sephrenia told him. "The smoke does that to people. Are they all clear of the area yet?"

"There are a few still floundering around down there," Kalten advised. "They seem to be trying to catch their horses."

"Let's give them time to get out of our way. Continue to hold the illusion, gentlemen," she said, looking into her basin of water. "It's still a couple of miles to those woods."

Sparhawk clenched his teeth. "Can't you speed things up a bit?" he asked her. "This isn't easy, you know."

"Nothing worthwhile is ever easy, Sparhawk," she told him. "If the images of those horses start to fly, Gerrich is going to get very, very suspicious—even in his present condition."

"Berit," Kurik said, "you and Talen come with me. Let's go down and get the horses ready. I think we all might want to leave in a hurry."

"I'll go with you," Alstrom said. "I want to talk with my brother before he leaves. I'm sure I've offended him, and I'd rather have us part friends."

The four of them went on down the stairs.

"Just a few minutes longer now," Sephrenia said. "We're almost to the edge of the woods."

"You look as if you just fell into a river," Kalten said, glancing at Sparhawk's sweaty face.

"Oh, shut up," Sparhawk said irritably.

"There," Sephrenia said finally. "Let it go now."

Sparhawk let out an explosive breath of relief and released the spell. Flute lowered her pipes and winked at him.

Sephrenia continued to look into her basin. "Gerrich's about a mile from the edge of the trees," she reported. "I think we should let him get well into the woods before we leave."

"Whatever you say," Sparhawk replied, leaning wearily against a wall.

It was about fifteen minutes later when Sephrenia set her basin on the floor and straightened. "I think we can go down now," she said.

They descended to the courtyard where Kurik, Talen, and Berit had the horses. The Patriarch Ortzel, stiff-lipped and pale with anger, was with them, and his brother was at his elbow. "I shall not forget this, Alstrom," he said, pulling his black ecclesiastical robe tighter about him.

"You may feel differently after you've had time to think about it. Go with God, Ortzel."

"Stay with God, Alstrom," Ortzel replied, more out of habit, Sparhawk thought, than from any real sense of emotion.

They mounted and rode out through the gate and on across the drawbridge. "Which way?" Kalten asked Sparhawk.

"North," Sparhawk replied. "Let's get clear of this place before Gerrich comes back."

"That's supposed to be a number of days."

"Let's not take any chances."

They rode north at a gallop. It was late afternoon by the time they reached the shallow ford where they had first encountered Sir Enmann. Sparhawk reined in and dismounted. "Let's consider our options," he said.

"What precisely did you do back there, Madame?" Ortzel was saying to Sephrenia. "I was in the chapel, and so I did not see what happened."

"A bit of deception is all, your Grace," she replied. "Count Gerrich thought he saw your brother and the rest of us escaping. He gave chase."

"That's all?" He looked surprised. "You didn't—" He left it hanging.

"Kill anybody? No. I strongly disapprove of killing."

"That's one thing we agree about, anyway. You're a very strange woman, Madame. Your morality seems to coincide rather closely with that laid down by the true faith. I would not have expected that from a heathen. Have you ever given any thought to conversion?"

She laughed. "You too, your Grace? Dolmant's been trying to convert me for years now. No, Ortzel. I'll remain faithful to my Goddess. I'm far too old to change religions at this stage in my life."

"Old, Madame? You?"

"You wouldn't believe it, your Grace," Sparhawk told him.

"You have all given me much to consider," Ortzel said. "I have followed what I perceived to be the letter of Church doctrine. Perhaps I should look beyond that perception and seek guidance from God." He walked a ways upstream, his face lost in thought.

"It's a step," Kalten muttered to Sparhawk.

"A fairly big one, I'd say."

Tynian had been standing at the edge of the shallow ford looking thoughtfully toward the west. "I have a sort of an idea, Sparhawk," he said.

"I'm willing to listen."

"Gerrich and his soldiers are all searching that forest, and, if Sephrenia's right,

the Seeker will be unable to give chase for at least a week. There won't be any enemies on the other side of this river."

"That's true, I suppose. We should probably have a look around on the other
side before we get overconfident, though."

"All right. That's the safest way, I suppose. What I'm getting at is that, if there
aren't any troops over there, it wouldn't take more than a couple of us to escort his
Grace safely to Chyrellos while the rest of us go on to Lake Randera. If things are
quiet, we don't all have to ride to the Holy City."

"He's got a good point, Sparhawk," Kalten agreed.

"I'll think about it," Sparhawk said. "Let's go on across and have a look around
before we make any decisions."

They remounted and splashed on across the shallow ford. There was a thicket
on the far side. "It's going to get dark soon, Sparhawk," Kurik said, "and we're going
to have to make camp. Why don't we hole up in that thicket for the night? Once it
gets completely dark, we can come out and look for campfires. No group of soldiers
is going to set up for the night without building fires, and we'll be able to see them.
That would be a lot easier and faster than riding up and down the river all day tomorrow trying to flush them out."

"Good idea. Let's do it that way then."

They made camp for the night in the center of the thicket and built only a
small cook-fire. By the time they had finished eating, night had fallen over Lamorkand. Sparhawk rose to his feet. "All right," he said, "let's go have a look. Sephrenia, you and the children and his Grace stay here out of sight." He led the way out
of the thicket. Once they were clear of the trees, he and his companions fanned out,
all of them peering intently into the night. The clouds obscured the moon and stars
and made the darkness almost total.

Sparhawk moved around the thicket. On the far side he bumped into Kalten.

"It's darker than the inside of your boots out here," Kalten said.

"Did you see anything?"

"Not a glimmer. There's a hill on the back side of these trees, though. Kurik's
going up to the top to look around."

"Good. I'll trust Kurik's eyes any time."

"Me too. Why don't you get him knighted, Sparhawk? When you get right
down to it, he's better than any of us."

"Aslade would kill me. She's not set up to be the wife of a knight."

Kalten laughed as they moved on, straining their eyes into the blackness.

"Sparhawk." Kurik's voice came from not far away.

"Over here."

The squire joined them. "That's a fairly high hill," he puffed. "The only light
I saw was coming from a village a mile or so to the south."

"You're sure it wasn't a campfire?" Kalten asked him.

"Campfires make a different kind of light from lamps shining through a dozen
windows, Kalten."

"That's true, I suppose."

"I guess that's it, then," Sparhawk said. He raised his fingers to his lips and
whistled, a signal for the others to return to the camp.

"What do you think?" Kalten asked as they pushed their way through the stiffly rustling brush toward the center of the thicket where the dim light of their banked cook-fire was scarcely more than a faint red glow in the darkness.

"Let's ask his Grace," Sparhawk replied. "It's his neck we'll be risking." They entered the brush-clogged encampment and Sparhawk pushed back the hood of his cloak. "We have a decision to make, your Grace," he told the patriarch. "The area appears to be deserted. Sir Tynian has suggested that two of us could escort you to Chyrellos in as much safety as the whole group. Our search for Bhelliom must not be delayed, if we're to keep Annias off the Archprelate's throne. The choice is up to you, though."

"I can go on to Chyrellos alone, Sir Sparhawk. My brother is overly concerned about my well-being. My cassock alone will protect me."

"I'd rather not gamble on that, your Grace. You'll recall that I mentioned that something was pursuing us?"

"Yes. I believe you called it a Seeker."

"Exactly. The creature is ill now because of the fumes Sephrenia created, but there's no way to be positive of how long its illness will last. It wouldn't look upon you as an enemy, though. If it should attack, run away. It's unlikely that it would follow you. I think that under the circumstances, though, Tynian's right. Two of us will be enough to ensure your safety."

"As you see fit, my son."

The others had entered the camp during the conversation, and Tynian volunteered immediately.

"No," Sephrenia rejected that idea. "You're the one most skilled at necromancy. We're going to need you as soon as we reach Lake Randera."

"I'll go," Bevier said. "I have a fast horse and can catch up with you at the lake."

"I'll go with him," Kurik offered. "If you run into more trouble, Sparhawk, you'll need knights with you."

"There's not that much difference between you and a knight, Kurik."

"I don't wear armor, Sparhawk," the squire pointed out. "The spectacle of Church Knights charging with lances makes people start thinking about their own mortality. It's a good way to avoid serious fighting."

"He's right, Sparhawk," Kalten said, "and if we run into more Zemochs and Church soldiers, you're going to need men wearing steel around you."

"All right," Sparhawk agreed. He turned to Ortzel. "I want to apologize for having offended your Grace," he said. "I don't really see that we had much choice, though. If we'd all been forced to stay penned up in your brother's castle, both of our missions would have failed, and the Church could not afford that."

"I still do not entirely approve, Sir Sparhawk, but your argument is most cogent. No apology is necessary."

"Thank you, your Grace," Sparhawk said. "Try to get some sleep. You'll be a long time in the saddle tomorrow, I think." He stepped away from the fire and rummaged through one of the packs until he found his map. Then he motioned to Bevier and Kurik. "Ride due west tomorrow," he told them. "Try to get back across the border into Pelosia before dark. Then go south to Chyrellos on that side of the line. I don't think even the most rabid Lamork soldier will violate that boundary and risk a confrontation with Pelosian border patrols."

"Sound reasoning," Bevier approved.

"When you get to Chyrellos, drop Ortzel off at the Basilica, then go see Dolmant. Tell him what's been going on here and ask him to pass the word on to Vanion and the other preceptors. Urge them very strongly to resist the idea of sending the Church Knights out here into the hinterlands to put out the brush fires Martel's been starting. We're going to need the four orders in Chyrellos if Archprelate Cluvonus dies, and luring them out of the Holy City's what's been behind all of Martel's scheming."

"We will, Sparhawk," Bevier promised.

"Make the trip as quickly as you can. His Grace appears to be fairly robust, so a little hard riding won't hurt him. The quicker you get across the border into Pelosia, the better. Don't waste any time, but be careful."

"You can count on that, Sparhawk," Kurik assured him.

"We'll rejoin you at Lake Randera as soon as we can," Bevier declared.

"Have you got enough money?" Sparhawk asked his squire.

"I can get by." Then Kurik grinned, his teeth flashing white in the dim light. "Besides, Dolmant and I are old friends. He's always good for a loan."

Sparhawk laughed. "Get to bed, you two," he said. "I want you and Ortzel on your way to Pelosia at first light in the morning."

They arose before dawn and sent Bevier and Kurik off to the west with the Patriarch of Kadach riding between them. Sparhawk consulted his map again by the light of their cook-fire. "We'll go back across this ford again," he told the others. "There's a larger channel east of here, so we'll probably need to find a bridge. Let's go north. I'd rather not run across any of Count Gerrich's patrols."

They splashed across the ford after breakfast and angled away from it as a ruddy light to the east indicated that somewhere behind the dreary cloud cover the sun had risen.

Tynian fell in beside Sparhawk. "I don't want to sound disrespectful," he said, "but I rather hope that the election doesn't fall to Ortzel. I think the Church—and the four orders—would be in for a bad time if he ascends the throne."

"He's a good man."

"Granted, but he's very rigid. An Archprelate needs to be flexible. Times are changing, Sparhawk, and the Church needs to change with them. I don't think the notion of change would appeal to Ortzel very much."

"That's in the hands of the Hierocracy, though, and I'd definitely prefer Ortzel to Annias."

"That's God's own truth."

About midmorning, they overtook the clattering wagon of a shabby-looking itinerant tinker who was also travelling northward. "What cheer, neighbor?" Sparhawk asked him.

"Scant cheer, Sir Knight," the tinker replied glumly. "These wars are bad for business. Nobody worries about a leaky pot when his house is under siege."

"That's probably very true. Tell me, do you know of a bridge or a ford hereabouts where we can get across that river ahead?"

"There's a toll bridge a couple of leagues north," the tinker advised. "Where are you bound, Sir Knight?"

"Lake Randera."

The tinker's eyes brightened. "To search for the treasure?" he asked.

"What treasure?"

"Everybody in Lamorkand knows that there's a vast treasure buried somewhere on the old battlefield at the lake. People have been digging there for five hundred years. About all they turn up is rusty swords and skeletons, though."

"How did people find out about it?" Sparhawk asked him, sounding casual.

"It was the oddest thing. The way I understand it, not too long after the battle, people started seeing Styrics digging there. Now, that doesn't really make any sense, does it? What I mean is that everybody knows that Styrics don't pay very much attention to money, and Styric menfolk are very reluctant to pick up shovels. That sort of tool doesn't seem to fit their hands, for some reason. At any rate, or so the story goes, people began to wonder just exactly what it was the Styrics were looking for. That's when the rumors started about the treasure. That ground's been plowed and sifted over a hundred times or more. Nobody's sure what they're looking for, but everybody in Lamorkand goes there once or twice in his lifetime."

"Maybe the Styrics know what's buried there."

"Maybe so, but no one can talk to them. They run away any time somebody gets near them."

"Peculiar. Well, thank you for the information, neighbor. Have a nice day."

They rode on, leaving the tinker's clanking wagon behind. "That's gloomy," Kalten said. "Somebody got there with a shovel before we did."

"A lot of shovels," Tynian amended.

"He's right about one thing, though," Sparhawk said. "I've never known a Styric to be interested enough in money to go out of his way for it. I think we'd better find a Styric village and ask a few questions. Something's going on at Lake Randera that we don't know about, and I don't like surprises."

# CHAPTER SEVEN

The toll bridge was narrow and in some disrepair. A shabby hut stood at its near end with several dirty, hungry-looking children sitting listlessly in front of it. The bridge tender wore a ragged smock, and his unshaven face was gaunt and hopeless. His eyes clouded with disappointment when he saw the armor of the knights. "No charge," he sighed.

"You'll never make a living that way, friend," Kalten told him.

"It's a local regulation, my Lord," the bridge tender said unhappily. "No charge is made to Church people."

"Do very many people cross here?" Tynian asked him.

"No more than a few a week," the fellow replied. "Hardly enough to make it possible for me to pay my taxes. My children haven't had a decent meal in months."

"Are there any Styric villages hereabouts?" Sparhawk asked him.

"I believe there's one on the other side of the river, Sir Knight—in that cedar forest over there."

"Thank you, neighbor," Sparhawk said, pouring some coins into the startled fellow's hand.

"I can't charge you to cross, my Lord," the man objected.

"The money's not for crossing, neighbor. It's for the information." Sparhawk nudged Faran and started across the bridge.

As Talen passed the bridge tender, he leaned over and handed him something. "Get your children something to eat," he said.

"Thank you, young master," the man said, tears of gratitude standing in his eyes.

"What did you give him?" Sparhawk asked.

"The money I stole from that sharp-eyed fellow back at the ford," Talen replied.

"That was very generous of you."

The boy shrugged. "I can always steal more. Besides, he and his children need it more than I do. I've been hungry a few times myself, and I know how it feels."

Kalten leaned forward in his saddle. "You know, there might be some hope for this boy after all, Sparhawk," he said quietly.

"It could be a little early to say for sure."

"At least it's a start."

The damp forest on the far side of the river was composed of mossy old cedars with low-swooping green boughs, and the trail leading into it was poorly marked. "Well?" Sparhawk said to Sephrenia.

"They're here," she told him. "They're watching us."

"They'll hide when we approach their village, won't they?"

"Probably. Styrics have little reason to trust armed Elenes. I should be able to persuade at least some of them to come out, though."

Like all Styric villages, the place was rude. The thatch-roofed huts were scattered haphazardly in a clearing, and there was no street of any kind. As Sephrenia had predicted, there was no one about. The small woman leaned over and spoke briefly to Flute in that Styric dialect Sparhawk did not understand. The little girl nodded, lifted her pipes, and began to play.

At first nothing happened.

"I think I just saw one of them back in the trees," Kalten said after a few moments.

"Timid, aren't they?" Talen said.

"They have reason to be," Sparhawk told him. "Elenes don't treat Styrics very well."

Flute continued to play. After a time, a white-bearded man in a smock made of unbleached homespun emerged hesitantly from the forest. He put his hands together in front of his chest and bowed respectfully to Sephrenia, speaking to her in Styric. Then he looked at Flute, and his eyes widened. He bowed again, and she gave him an impish little smile.

"Aged one," Sephrenia said to him, "do you perchance speak the language of the Elenes?"

"I have a passing familiarity with it, my sister," he replied.

"Good. These knights have a few questions, and then we'll leave your village and trouble you no more."

"I will answer as best I can."

"Some time back," Sparhawk began, "we chanced upon a tinker who told us something a bit disquieting. He said that Styrics have been digging in the battlefield at Lake Randera for centuries, searching for a treasure. That doesn't seem like the sort of thing Styrics would do."

"It is not, my Lord," the old man said flatly. "We have no need of treasure, and we would most certainly not violate the graves of those who sleep there."

"I thought that might be the case. Have you any idea of who those Styrics might be?"

"They are not of our kindred, Sir Knight, and they serve a God whom we despise."

"Azash?" Sparhawk guessed.

The old man blanched slightly. "I will not speak his name aloud, Sir Knight, but you have hit upon my meaning."

"Then the men digging at the lake are Zemochs?"

The old man nodded. "We have known of their presence there for centuries. We do not go near them, for they are unclean."

"I think we'd all agree to that," Tynian said. "Have you got any idea of what they're looking for?"

"Some ancient talisman that Otha craves for his God."

"The tinker we spoke with said that most people around here believe there's a vast treasure there somewhere."

The old man smiled. "Elenes tend to exaggerate things," he said. "They cannot believe that the Zemochs would devote so much effort to the finding of one single thing—although the thing they seek is of greater worth than all the treasure in the world."

"That answers that question, doesn't it?" Kalten noted.

"Elenes have an indiscriminate lust for gold and precious gems," the old Styric went on, "and so it's entirely possible that they don't even know what they're looking for. They expect huge chests of treasure, but there are no such chests to be found on that field. It's not impossible that some one of them might already have found the object and cast it aside, not knowing its worth."

"No, aged master," Sephrenia disagreed. "The talisman of which you speak has not yet been found. Its uncovering would ring like a giant bell through all the world."

"It may be as you say, my sister. Do you and your companions also journey to the lake in search of the talisman?"

"Such is our intent," she replied, "and our quest is of some urgency. If nothing else, we must deny possession of the talisman to Otha's God."

"I shall pray to *my* God for your success then." The old Styric looked back at Sparhawk. "How fares it with the head of the Elene Church?" he asked carefully.

"The Archprelate is very old," Sparhawk told him truthfully, "and his health is failing."

The old man sighed. "It is as I feared," he said. "Although I am sure he would not accept the good wishes of a Styric, I nonetheless also pray to my God that he will live for many more years."

"Amen to that," Ulath said.

The white-bearded Styric hesitated. "Rumor states that the primate of a place called Cimmura is most likely to become the head of your Church," he said cautiously.

"That could be a bit exaggerated," Sparhawk told him. "There are many in the Church who oppose the ambitions of Primate Annias. A part of *our* purpose is to thwart him as well."

"Then I shall pray for you doubly, Sir Knight. Should Annias reach the throne in Chyrellos, it will be a disaster for Styricum."

"And for just about everybody else as well," Ulath grunted.

"It will be far more deadly for Styrics, Sir Knight. The feelings of Annias of Cimmura about our race are widely known. The authority of the Elene Church has kept the hatred of the Elene commons in check, but should Annias succeed, he will probably remove that restraint, and I fear Styricum will be doomed."

"We will do all we can to prevent his reaching the throne," Sparhawk promised.

The old Styric bowed. "May the hands of the Younger Gods of Styricum protect you, my friends." He bowed again to Sephrenia and then to Flute.

"Let's move on," Sephrenia said. "We're keeping the other villagers away from their homes."

They rode out of the village and back into the forest.

"So the people digging up the battlefield are Zemochs," Tynian mused. "They're creeping all over western Eosia, aren't they?"

"We have known that it's all part of Otha's plan for generations," Sephrenia said. "Most Elenes cannot tell the difference between western Styrics and Zemochs. Otha does not want any kind of alliance or reconciliation between western Styrics and Elenes. A few well-placed atrocities have kept the prejudices of the Elene common people inflamed, and the stories of such incidents grow with every telling. This has been the source of centuries of general oppression and random massacres."

"Why does the possibility of an alliance worry Otha so much?" Kalten sounded puzzled. "There aren't enough Styrics in the west to pose that much of a threat, and since they won't touch steel weapons, they wouldn't be of much use if war breaks out again, would they?"

"The Styrics would fight with magic, not steel, Kalten," Sparhawk told him, "and Styric magicians know a lot more about it than the Church Knights."

"The fact that the Zemochs are at Lake Randera is promising, though," Tynian said.

"How so?" Kalten asked.

"If they're still digging, it means they haven't found Bhelliom yet. It also sort of hints at the fact that we're going to the right place."

"I'm not so sure," Ulath disagreed. "If they've been looking for Bhelliom for the last five hundred years and still haven't found it, maybe Lake Randera's *not* the right place."

"Why haven't the Zemochs tried necromancy the way we're going to?" Kalten asked.

"Thalesian spirits would not respond to a Zemoch necromancer," Ulath replied. "They'll probably talk to me, but not to anybody else."

"It's a good thing you're along then, Ulath," Tynian said. "I'd hate to go to all the trouble of raising ghosts and then find out that they won't talk to me."

"If you raise them, I'll talk with them."

"You didn't ask him about the Seeker," Sparhawk said to Sephrenia.

"There was no need. It would only have frightened him. Besides, if those villagers had known the Seeker was in this part of the world, the village would have been abandoned."

"Maybe we should have warned him."

"No, Sparhawk. Life is hard enough for those people without turning them into vagabonds. The Seeker is looking for *us*. The villagers are in no danger."

It was late afternoon by the time they reached the edge of the woods. They halted there and peered out over seemingly deserted fields. "Let's camp back here among the trees," Sparhawk said. "That's awfully open ground out there. I'd rather not have anyone see our fires if I can avoid it."

They rode back among the trees a ways and set up camp for the night. Kalten walked out to the edge of the wood to keep watch. Shortly after dark, he returned. "You'd better hide that fire a little better," he told Berit. "You can see it from the edge of the trees."

"Right away, Sir Kalten," the young novice replied. He took a spade and banked more earth around their small cook-fire.

"We're not the only ones around here, Sparhawk," the big blond Pandion said seriously. "There are a couple of fires about a mile out there in those fields."

"Let's go have a look," Sparhawk said to Tynian and Ulath. "We'll need to pinpoint the locations so we can slip around them in the morning. Even if the Seeker won't be a problem for several more days, there are still other people trying to keep us away from the lake. Coming, Kalten?"

"Go ahead," his friend said. "I haven't eaten yet."

"We might need you to point the fires out to us."

"You can't miss them," Kalten said, filling his wooden bowl. "Whoever built them wants lots of light."

"He's very attached to his stomach, isn't he?" Tynian said as the three knights walked toward the edge of the wood.

"He eats a great deal," Sparhawk admitted, "but he's a big man, so it takes a lot of food to keep him going."

The fires far out in the open fields were clearly visible. Sparhawk carefully noted the locations. "We'll swing north, I think," he said quietly to the others.

"Probably we'll want to stay in the woods until we get well past those camps out there."

"Peculiar," Ulath said.

"What is?" Tynian asked.

"Those camps aren't very far apart. If the men out there know each other, why didn't they make just one camp?"

"Maybe they don't like each other."

"Why did they camp so close together then?"

Tynian shrugged. "Who knows why Lamorks do anything?"

"There's nothing we can do about them tonight," Sparhawk said. "Let's go back."

Sparhawk awoke just before dawn. When he went to rouse the others, he found that Tynian, Berit, and Talen were missing. Tynian's absence was easily explained. He was on watch at the edge of the woods. The novice and the boy, however, had no business being out of their beds. Sparhawk swore and went to wake Sephrenia. "Berit and Talen have gone off somewhere," he told her.

She looked around at the darkness pressing in on their well-hidden camp. "We'll have to wait until it gets light," she said. "If they're not back by then, we'll have to go look for them. Stir up the fire, Sparhawk, and put my teakettle near the flame."

The sky to the east was growing lighter when Berit and Talen returned to camp. They both looked excited, and their eyes were very bright.

"Just where have you two been?" Sparhawk demanded angrily.

"Satisfying a curiosity," Talen replied. "We went to pay a visit on our neighbors."

"Can you translate that for me, Berit?"

"We crept across the fields to have a look at the people around those campfires out there, Sir Sparhawk."

"Without asking me first?"

"You were asleep," Talen explained quickly. "We didn't want to wake you."

"They're Styrics, Sir Sparhawk," Berit said seriously, "at least some of them are. There's a fair scattering of Lamork peasants among them, though. The men around the other fire are all Church soldiers."

"Could you tell if the ones you saw were western Styrics or Zemochs?"

"I can't tell one kind of Styric from another, but the ones out there have swords and spears." Berit frowned. "This might have been my imagination, but all the men out there are sort of numb-looking. Do you remember how blank the faces of that group of ambushers back in Elenia were?"

"Yes."

"The people out there look more or less the same, and they're not talking to each other or even sleeping, and they haven't posted any sentries."

"Well, Sephrenia?" Sparhawk said. "Could the Seeker have recovered more quickly than you thought it would?"

"No," she replied, frowning. "It could have set those men in our path before it went on to Cimmura, however. They'd follow any instructions it might have given them, but they wouldn't be able to respond to any new situations without its presence."

"They'd recognize us though, wouldn't they?"

"Yes. The Seeker would have implanted that in their minds."

"And they'd attack us if they saw us?"

"Inevitably."

"Then I think we'd better move on," he said. "Those people out there are just a little too close to make me feel entirely comfortable. I don't like riding through strange country before it's fully light, but under the circumstances—" Then he turned sternly to Berit. "I appreciate the information you've brought us, Berit, but you shouldn't have gone off without telling me first, and you most definitely should not have taken Talen along. You and I are paid to take certain risks, but you had absolutely no right to endanger him."

"He didn't know I was tagging along behind him, Sparhawk," Talen said glibly. "I saw him get up, and I was curious about what he was doing, so I sneaked after him. He didn't even know I was there until we were almost to those campfires."

"That's not precisely true, Sir Sparhawk," Berit disagreed with a pained look. "Talen woke me and suggested that the two of us should go have a look at those men out there. It seemed like a very good idea at the time. I'm sorry. I didn't even think of the fact that I was putting him in danger."

Talen looked at the novice with some disgust. "Now why did you do that?" he asked. "I was telling him a perfectly good lie. I could have kept you out of trouble."

"I've taken an oath to tell the truth, Talen."

"Well, I haven't. All you had to do was keep your mouth shut. Sparhawk won't hit *me* because I'm too little. He might decide to thrash you, though."

"I love these little arguments about comparative morality before breakfast," Kalten said. "Speaking of which—" He looked meaningfully toward the fire.

"It's your turn," Ulath told him.

"What?"

"It's your turn to do the cooking."

"It surely can't be my turn again already."

Ulath nodded. "I've been keeping track."

Kalten put on a pious expression. "Sparhawk's probably right, though. We really should move on. We can have something to eat later."

They broke camp quietly and saddled their horses. Tynian came back from the edge of the woods where he had been keeping watch. "They're breaking up into small parties," he reported. "I think they're going to scour the countryside."

"We'll want to keep to the woods then," Sparhawk said. "Let's ride."

They moved cautiously, staying well back from the edge of the trees. Tynian rode out to the fringe of the forest from time to time to scout out the movements of the numb-faced men out in the open fields. "They seem to be ignoring these woods entirely," he said after one such foray.

"They're unable to think independently," Sephrenia explained.

"No matter," Kalten said. "They're between us and the lake. As long as they're patrolling those fields out there, we can't get through. We're going to run out of woods eventually, and then we'll be at a standstill."

"Just exactly which ones are patrolling this section?" Sparhawk asked Tynian.

"Church soldiers. They're riding in groups."

"How many in each group?"

"About a dozen."

"Are the groups staying in sight of each other?"

"They're spreading out more and more."

"Good." Sparhawk's face was bleak. "Go keep an eye on them and let me know when they're far enough apart so they can't see each other."

"All right."

Sparhawk dismounted and tied Faran's reins to a sapling.

"What have you got in your mind, Sparhawk?" Sephrenia asked suspiciously as Berit helped her and Flute down from her white palfrey.

"We know that the Seeker was probably sent by Otha—which means Azash."

"Yes."

"Azash knows that Bhelliom's about to emerge again, right?"

"Yes."

"The Seeker's primary task is to kill us, but if it fails to do that, wouldn't it settle for keeping us away from Lake Randera?"

"Elene logic again," she said disgustedly. "You're transparent, Sparhawk. I can see where you're leading with this."

"Even though their minds are blank, the church soldiers would still be able to pass information to each other, wouldn't they?"

"Yes." She said it grudgingly.

"Then we don't have any choice in the matter. If any of them see us, we'll have them all right behind us within an hour."

"I don't quite follow," Talen said, looking puzzled.

"He's going to kill all the men in one of those patrols," Sephrenia said.

"To the last man," Sparhawk said grimly, "and just as soon as the others are all out of sight."

"They can't even run away, you know."

"Good. Then I won't have to chase them."

"You're plotting deliberate murder, Sparhawk."

"That's not precisely accurate, Sephrenia. They'll attack as soon as they see us. What we'll be doing is defending ourselves."

"Sophistry," she snapped, and stalked away, muttering to herself.

"I didn't think she even knew what that word means," Kalten said.

"Do you know how to use a lance?" Sparhawk asked Ulath.

"I've been trained with it," the Thalesian replied. "I much prefer my ax, though."

"With a lance you don't have to get in quite so close. Let's not take too many chances. We should be able to put a fair number of them down with our lances, and then we can finish up with our swords and axes."

"There are only five of us, you know," Kalten said, "counting Berit."

"So?"

"I just thought I'd mention it."

Sephrenia came back, her face pale. "Then you're absolutely set on this?" she demanded of Sparhawk.

"We have to get to the lake. Can you think of any alternatives?"

"No, as a matter of fact, I can't." Her tone was sarcastic. "Your impeccable Elene logic has completely disarmed me."

"I've been meaning to ask you something, little mother," Kalten said, obviously trying to head off an argument by changing the subject. "Exactly what does this Seeker thing look like? It seems to go to a great deal of trouble to keep itself hidden."

"It's hideous." She shuddered. "I've never seen one, but the Styric magician who taught me how to counter it described it to me. Its body is segmented, very pale and very thin. At this stage, its outer skin has not yet completely hardened, and it oozes out a kind of ichor from between its segments to protect the skin from contact with the air. It has crablike claws, and its face is horrible beyond belief."

"Ichor? What's that?"

"Slime," she replied shortly. "It's in its larval stage—sort of like a caterpillar or a worm, although not quite. When it reaches adulthood, its body hardens and darkens and its wings emerge. Not even Azash can control an adult. All they're concerned with at that stage is reproducing. Set a pair of adults loose, and they'd turn the entire world into a hive and feed every living creature on earth to their young. Azash keeps a pair for breeding purposes in a place from which they can't escape. When one of the larvae he uses as Seekers approaches adulthood, he has it killed."

"Working for Azash has its risks, doesn't it? But I've never seen any kind of insect that looks like that."

"Normal rules don't apply to the creatures who serve Azash." She looked at Sparhawk, her expression agonized. "Do we really have to do this?" she asked him.

"I'm afraid we do," he replied. "There's no other way."

They sat on the damp forest loam, waiting for Tynian to return. Kalten went to one of the pack saddles and cut large slabs from a cheese and a loaf of bread with his dagger. "This takes care of my turn at cooking, right?" he said to Ulath.

Ulath grunted. "I'll think about that."

The sky overhead was still cloudy, and birds drowsed among the dark green cedar boughs that filled the wood with their fragrance. Once, a deer approached them, stepping delicately along a forest trail. One of the horses snorted, and the deer bounded away, his white tail flashing and his velvet-covered antlers flaring above his head. It was peaceful here, but Sparhawk pushed that peace from his mind, steeling himself for the task ahead.

Tynian returned. "There's one group of soldiers sort of stationed a few hundred yards north of us," he reported quietly. "All the others are out of sight."

"Good," Sparhawk said, rising to his feet. "We might as well get started. Sephrenia, you stay here with Talen and Flute."

"What's the plan?" Tynian asked.

"No plan," Sparhawk replied. "We're just going to ride out there and eliminate that patrol. Then we'll ride on to Lake Randera."

"It has a certain direct charm," Tynian agreed.

"Remember, all of you," Sparhawk went on, "they won't react to wounds the way normal people would. Make sure of them so they won't come at you from behind when you move on to the next one. Let's go."

The fight was short and brutal. As soon as Sparhawk and the others burst from the wood in a thundering charge, the blank-faced Church soldiers drove their horses across the grassy field toward them, their swords aloft. When the two parties were perhaps fifty paces apart, Sparhawk, Kalten, Tynian, and Ulath lowered their lances and set themselves. The shock of the impact was terrific. The soldier Sparhawk struck was picked out of his saddle by the lance that drove through his chest and emerged from his back. Sparhawk reined Faran in sharply to avoid breaking his lance. He pulled it free of the body and then charged on. His lance broke off in the body of another soldier. He discarded it and drew his sword. He lopped an arm off a third soldier then drove the point of his sword through the man's throat. Ulath had broken his lance on the first soldier he attacked but then had driven the broken end into the body of another. Then the big Genidian had reverted to his ax. He smoothly brained yet another soldier. Tynian had driven his lance through another soldier's belly and had finished him with his sword and moved on to another. Kalten's lance had shattered against a soldier's shield, and he was being hard-pressed by two others until Berit rode in and chopped the top off one of their heads with his ax. Kalten finished the other with a broad stroke. The remaining soldiers were milling around in confusion, their venom-numbed minds unable to react quickly enough to the assault by the Knights of the Church. Sparhawk and his companions crushed them together in a tangle and methodically butchered them.

Kalten swung down from his saddle and walked among the fallen soldiers lying in huddled heaps on the bloody grass. Sparhawk turned his head away as his friend systematically ran his sword into each body. "Just wanted to be sure," Kalten said, sheathing his sword and remounting. "None of them are going to do any talking now."

"Berit," Sparhawk said, "go get Sephrenia and the children. We'll keep watch here. Oh, one other thing. You'd better cut us some new lances as well. The ones we had seem to be all used up."

"Yes, Sir Sparhawk," the novice said, and rode back toward the woods.

Sparhawk looked around and saw a brush-choked draw not far away. "Let's hide these," he said, looking at the bodies. "We don't want to make it obvious that we've come this way."

"Did their horses all run off?" Kalten asked, looking around.

"Yes," Ulath replied. "Horses do that when there's fighting."

They dragged the mutilated corpses to the draw and dumped them into the brush. By the time they had finished, Berit was returning with Sephrenia, Talen, and Flute. He carried the new lances across his saddle. Sephrenia kept her eyes averted from the bloodstained grass where the fight had taken place.

It took but a few minutes to affix the steel points to the lances, and then they all remounted.

"Now I'm *really* hungry," Kalten said as they set out at a gallop.

"How *can* you?" Sephrenia demanded in a tone of revulsion.

"What did I say?" Kalten asked Sparhawk.

"Never mind."

The next several days passed without incident, although Sparhawk and the others kept wary eyes to the rear as they galloped on. They took shelter each night in places of concealment and built small, well-shielded fires. And then the cloudy skies finally fulfilled their promise. A steady drizzle began to fall as they pushed on toward the northeast.

"Wonderful," Kalten said sardonically, looking up at the soggy sky.

"Just pray that it rains harder," Sephrenia told him. "The Seeker should be moving about again by now, but it won't be able to follow our scent if it's been washed out by rain."

"I suppose I hadn't thought of that," he admitted.

Sparhawk periodically dismounted to cut a stick from a particular kind of low-lying bush and to lay it carefully on the ground pointing in the direction they were going.

"Why do you keep doing that?" Tynian asked him finally, pulling his dripping blue cloak tighter about him.

"To let Kurik know which way we've gone," Sparhawk replied, remounting.

"Very clever, but how will he know which bush to look behind?"

"It's always the same kind of bush. Kurik and I worked that out a long time ago."

The sky continued to weep. It was a depressing kind of rain that soaked into everything. Campfires were difficult to get started and tended to go out without much advance notice. Occasionally they passed Lamork villages and now and then an isolated farmstead. The people for the most part were staying in out of the rain, and the cattle grazing in the fields were wet and dispirited-looking.

They were not too far from the lake when Bevier and Kurik finally caught up with them on a blustery afternoon when the steady rain was blowing almost horizontally to the ground.

"We delivered Ortzel to the Basilica," Bevier reported, wiping his dripping face. "Then we went to Dolmant's house and told him about what was happening here in Lamorkand. He agrees that the upheaval is probably designed to pull the Church Knights out of Chyrellos. He'll do what he can to block that."

"Good," Sparhawk said. "I like the notion of all Martel's efforts being wasted. Did you have any problems along the way?"

"Nothing serious," Bevier said. "The roads are all being patrolled, though, and Chyrellos is crawling with soldiers."

"And all the soldiers are loyal to Annias, I suppose?" Kalten said sourly.

"There are other candidates for the Archprelacy, Kalten," Tynian pointed out. "If Annias is bringing his troops into Chyrellos, it stands to reason that the others would bring in theirs as well."

"We certainly don't want open fighting in the streets of the Holy City," Sparhawk said. "How's Archprelate Cluvonus?" he asked Bevier.

"He's fading fast, I'm afraid. The Hierocracy can't even hide his condition from the common people any more."

"That makes what we're doing all the more urgent," Kalten said. "If Cluvonus dies, Annias will start to move, and at that point, he won't *need* the Elenian treasury any more."

"Let's press on, then," Sparhawk said. "It's still a day or so to the lake."

"Sparhawk," Kurik said critically, "you've let your armor get rusty."

"Really?" Sparhawk pulled back his sodden black cloak and looked at his red-tinged shoulder plates with some surprise.

"Couldn't you find the oil bottle, my Lord?"

"I had my mind on other things."

"Obviously."

"I'm sorry. I'll deal with it."

"You wouldn't know how. Don't fool with the armor, Sparhawk. I'll tend to it."

Sparhawk looked around at his companions. "If anybody makes an issue of this, there's going to be a fight," he said ominously.

"We would sooner die than offend you, my Lord Sparhawk," Bevier promised with an absolutely straight face.

"I appreciate that," Sparhawk told him, and then rode resolutely off into the driving rain, his rusty armor creaking.

## CHAPTER EIGHT

The ancient battlefield at Lake Randera in north central Lamorkand was even more desolate than they had been led to believe. It was a vast waste-land of turned-over earth with mounds of dirt heaped up everywhere. There were huge holes and trenches in the ground filled with muddy water, and the steady rain had turned the vast field into a quagmire.

Kalten sat his horse beside Sparhawk, looking helplessly out at the muddy field that seemed to stretch off to the horizon. "Where do we start?" he asked, sounding baffled at the enormity of the task before them.

Sparhawk remembered something. "Bevier," he called.

The Arcian rode forward. "Yes, Sparhawk?"

"You said that you'd made a study of military history."

"Yes."

"Since this was the biggest battle that's ever been fought, you probably devoted some time to it, didn't you?"

"Of course."

"Do you think you might be able to locate the general area where the Thalesians were fighting?"

"Give me a few moments to orient myself." Bevier rode slowly out into the soggy field, looking around intently for some landmark. "There," he said finally, pointing toward a nearby hill that was half obscured in the misty drizzle. "That's where the troops of the King of Arcium made their stand against the hordes of Otha and their supernatural allies. They were hard-pressed, but they held on until the Knights of the Church reached this field." He squinted thoughtfully into the rain. "If my memory serves me correctly, the army of King Sarak of Thalesia swept down around the east side of the lake in a flanking maneuver. They would have fought much farther to the east."

"At least that narrows things down a little bit," Kalten said. "Would the Genidian Knights have been with Sarak's army?"

Bevier shook his head. "All the Church Knights had been engaged in the campaign in Rendor. When word reached them of Otha's invasion, they sailed across the inner sea to Cammoria and then made a forced march to get here. They arrived on the field from the south."

"Sparhawk," Talen said quietly, "over there. Some people are trying to hide behind that big mound of dirt—the one with that tree stump halfway up the side."

Sparhawk carefully avoided turning. "Could you get any kind of a look at them?"

"I couldn't tell what kind of people they are," the boy replied. "They're all covered with mud."

"Did they have any kind of weapons?"

"Shovels, mostly. I think a couple of them had crossbows."

"Lamorks, then," Kalten said. "Nobody else uses that weapon."

"Kurik," Sparhawk said to his squire, "what's the effective range of a crossbow?"

"Two hundred paces with any kind of accuracy. After that, you sort of have to rely on luck."

Sparhawk looked around, trying to appear casual. The heaped-up mound of dirt was perhaps fifty yards away. "We'll want to go on that way," he said in a voice loud enough to be heard by the lurking treasure seekers. He raised one steel-gauntleted hand and pointed east. "How many are there, Talen?" he asked quietly.

"I saw eight or ten. There could be more."

"Keep your eyes on them, but don't be too obvious about it. If any of them starts to raise his crossbow, warn us."

"Right."

Sparhawk started out at a steady trot. Faran's hooves splashed up the semi-liquid mud. "Don't look back," he warned the others.

"Wouldn't a gallop be more appropriate about now?" Kalten asked in a strained voice.

"Let's not let them know that we've seen them."

"This is very hard on my nerves, Sparhawk," Kalten muttered, shifting his shield. "I've got this very uneasy feeling right between my shoulder blades."

"So do I," Sparhawk admitted. "Talen, are they doing anything?"

"Just watching us," the boy replied. "I can see a head pop up every so often."

They trotted on, splashing through the mud.

"We're almost clear," Tynian said tensely.

"The rain's settling down around that hill," Talen reported. "I don't think they can see us now."

"Good," Sparhawk said, letting out an explosive breath of relief. "Let's slow down. It's obvious that we're not alone out here, and we don't want to blunder into anything."

"Nervous," Ulath commented.

"Wasn't it, though?" Tynian agreed.

"I don't know why *you* were worried," Ulath said, eyeing Tynian's massive Deiran armor, "considering all the steel you've got wrapped around you."

"At close range, a crossbow bolt will penetrate even this." Tynian rapped his fist on the front of his armor. It made a ringing sound, almost like a bell. "Sparhawk, the next time you talk to the Hierocracy, why don't you suggest that they outlaw crossbows? I felt positively naked out there."

"How do you carry all that armor?" Kalten asked him.

"Painfully, my friend, very painfully. The first time they strapped it on me, I collapsed. It took me an hour to get back on my feet."

"Keep your eyes open," Sparhawk cautioned. "A few Lamork treasure hunters are one thing, but men controlled by the Seeker are something else; if it had those men back there near the woods, it's certain to have some here as well."

They splashed on through the mud, looking about cautiously. Sparhawk consulted his map again, shielding it from the rain with his cloak. "The city of Randera's up on the east shore of the lake," he said. "Bevier, did any of your books say anything about whether the Thalesians occupied it?"

"That portion of the battle is a bit obscure in the chronicles I've read," the white-cloaked knight replied. "About the only accounts of that part of the battle just say that the Zemochs occupied Randera fairly early in their campaign. Whether or not the Thalesians did anything about that, I simply don't know."

"They wouldn't have," Ulath declared. "Thalesians have never been very good at sieges. We don't have that kind of patience. King Sarak's army probably bypassed it."

"This might be easier than I thought," Kalten said. "The only area we have to search is what lies between Randera and the south end of the lake."

"Don't get your hopes up too much, Kalten," Sparhawk told him. "It's still a lot of ground." He looked off into the drizzle toward the lake. "The lake shore seems to be sand, and wet sand is better to ride on than mud." He turned Faran and led the others toward the lake.

The sandy beach that stretched off into the distance along the south shore of the lake did not seem to have been excavated in the same way the rest of the field had. Kalten looked around as they rode out onto the expanse of damp sand. "I wonder why they haven't been digging here," he said.

"High water," Ulath replied cryptically.

"I beg your pardon?"

"The water level rises in the winter, and it washes the sand back into any holes they might have dug."

"Oh. That makes sense, I suppose."

They rode cautiously along the edge of the water for the next half hour.

"How far do we have to go?" Kalten asked Sparhawk. "You're the one with the map."

"Ten leagues, anyway," Sparhawk replied. "This beach seems to be open enough to make a gallop safe." He nudged Faran with his heels and led the way.

The rain continued unabated, and the dimpled surface of the lake was the color of lead. They had ridden some miles along the water's edge when they saw another group of men digging somewhat furtively out in the sodden field.

"Pelosians," Ulath disdainfully identified them.

"How can you tell?" Kalten asked him.

"Those silly pointed hats."

"Oh."

"I think they fit the shape of their heads. They probably heard rumors about the treasure and came down from the north. Do you want us to run them off, Sparhawk?"

"Let them dig. They're not bothering us—at least not as long as they stay where they are. Men who belong to the Seeker wouldn't be interested in treasure."

They rode on along the beach until late afternoon. "What do you say to making camp up there?" Kurik suggested, pointing to a large pile of driftwood just ahead. "I've got some dry wood in one of the packs, and we ought to be able to find more near the bottom of that pile."

Sparhawk looked up at the dripping clouds, gauging the time of day. "It's time to stop anyway," he agreed.

They reined in beside the driftwood, and Kurik built his fire. Berit and Talen began pulling relatively dry sticks out from under the pile, but after a little while, Berit went back to his horse for his battle-ax.

"What are you going to do with that?" Ulath asked him.

"I'm going to chop up some of those larger pieces with it, Sir Ulath."

"No, you're not."

Berit looked a bit startled.

"That's not what it was made for. You'll dull the edge, and you might need that edge before long."

"My ax is in that pack over there, Berit," Kurik told the shamefaced novice. "Use that. I don't plan to hit anybody with it."

"Kurik," Sephrenia said from inside the tent Sparhawk and Kalten had just erected for her and Flute, "put up a cover near the fire, and string a rope under it." She emerged from the tent wearing a Styric smock and carrying her dripping white robe in one hand and Flute's garment in the other. "It's time to dry out some clothes."

After the sun went down, a night breeze began to blow in off the lake, making the tents flap and tossing the flames of their fire. They ate a meager supper and then sought their beds.

About midnight, Kalten came back from where he had been standing watch. He shook Sparhawk awake. "It's your turn," he said quietly to avoid waking the others.

"All right." Sparhawk sat up, yawning. "Did you find a good place?"

"That hill just behind the beach. Watch your step climbing it, though. They've been digging in the sides of it."

Sparhawk began to put on his armor.

"We're not alone here, Sparhawk," Kalten said, removing his helmet and his dripping black cloak. "I saw a half-dozen fires a good ways out in that field."

"More Pelosians and Lamorks?"

"It's a little hard to say. A fire doesn't usually have any kind of identifying marks on it."

"Don't tell Talen and Berit. I don't want them creeping around in the dark any more. Get some sleep, Kalten. Tomorrow might be a long day."

Sparhawk carefully climbed the pitted side of the hill and took up a position on top. He immediately saw the fires Kalten had mentioned, but saw also that they were a long way off and posed little threat.

They had been long on the road now, and a growing sense of impatient urgency gnawed at Sparhawk. Ehlana sat alone in the silent throne room back in Cimmura with her life ticking away. A few more months and her heartbeat would falter and then stop. Sparhawk pulled his mind away from that thought. As he usually did when that apprehension came over him, he deliberately set his mind on other matters and other memories.

The rain was chill and damp and unpleasant, so he turned his thoughts to Rendor, where the blistering sun burned all trace of moisture from the air. He remembered the lines of black-veiled women gracefully going to the well at dawn before the sun made the streets of Jiroch unbearable. He remembered Lillias with a wry smile, and he wondered if the melodramatic scene in the street near the docks had earned her the kind of respect she so desperately needed.

And then he remembered Martel. That night in Arasham's tent in Dabour had been a good one. To see his hated enemy filled with chagrin and frustration had been almost as satisfying as killing him might have been. "Someday, though, Martel," he muttered. "You have a lot to pay for, and I think it's almost time for me to collect." It was a good thought, and Sparhawk dwelt on it as he stood in the rain. He thought about it in some detail until it was time to rouse Ulath for his turn on watch.

They broke camp at daybreak and rode on down the rain-swept beach.

About midmorning, Sephrenia reined in her white palfrey with a warning hiss. "Zemochs," she said sharply.

"Where?" Sparhawk asked.

"I can't be sure. They're close, though, and their intentions are unfriendly."

"How many?"

"It's very hard to tell, Sparhawk. At least a dozen, but probably fewer than a score."

"Take the children and ride back to the edge of the water." He looked at his companions. "Let's see if we can flush them out," he said. "I don't want them following us."

The knights advanced across the muddy field at a walk, their lances lowered. Berit and Kurik flanked them on either side.

The Zemochs were hiding in a shallow trench less than a hundred yards from the beach. When they saw the seven Elenes resolutely bearing down on them, they rose with their weapons in their hands. There were perhaps fifteen of them, but the fact that they were on foot put them at a distinct disadvantage. They made no sound, uttered no war cries, and their eyes were empty.

"The Seeker sent them," Sparhawk barked. "Be careful."

As the knights approached, the Zemochs shambled forward, and several even blindly hurled themselves on the lance points. "Drop the lances!" Sparhawk commanded. "They're too close!" He cast aside his lance and drew his sword. Again the men controlled by the Seeker charged in eerie silence, and paid no attention to their fallen comrades. Although they had the advantage of numbers, they were really no match for the mounted knights, and their doom was sealed when Kurik and Berit outflanked them and came at them from the rear.

The fight lasted for perhaps ten minutes, and then it was over.

"Is anybody hurt?" Sparhawk asked, looking around quickly.

"Several, I'd say," Kalten replied, looking at the bodies lying in the mud. "This is getting to be a little too easy, Sparhawk. They charge in, almost asking to be killed."

"I'm always glad to oblige," Tynian said, wiping his sword with a Zemoch smock.

"Let's drag them back to that trench they were hiding in," Sparhawk said. "Kurik, go back and get your spade. We'll cover them over."

"Hide the evidence, eh?" Kalten said gaily.

"There may be others around," Sparhawk said. "Let's not announce that we've been here."

"Right, but I want to make sure of them before we start dragging. I'd rather not have one wake up when my hands are occupied with his ankles."

Kalten dismounted and went through the grim business of making sure of them. Then they all fell to work. The slippery mud made dragging the inert bodies easier. Kurik stood at the edge of the trench scooping mud over the corpses with his spade.

"Bevier," Tynian said, "are you really so attached to that Lochaber?"

"It's my weapon of choice," Bevier replied. "Why do you ask?"

"It's a little inconvenient when the time comes to tidy up. When you lop off their heads like that, it means we have to make two trips with each one." Tynian bent over and picked up two severed heads by the hair as if to emphasize his point.

"How droll," Bevier said dryly.

After they had dropped all the bits and pieces of the Zemoch bodies and their weapons in the trench and Kurik had covered them with mud, they rode back to the beach, where Sephrenia sat on her horse, carefully keeping Flute's face covered with the hem of her cloak and trying to keep her own eyes turned away. "Have you finished?" she asked as Sparhawk and the others approached.

"It's all over," he assured her. "You can look now." He frowned. "Kalten just raised a point. He said that this was getting to be almost too easy. These people just charge in without thinking. It's as if they want to be killed."

"That's not really it, Sparhawk," she replied. "The Seeker has men to spare. It will throw away hundreds just to kill one of us—and hundreds more to kill the next one."

"That's depressing. If it has so many, why is it sending them out in such small groups?"

"They're scouting parties. Ants and bees do exactly the same thing. They send out small groups to find what the colony is looking for. The Seeker is still an insect, after all, and, in spite of Azash, it still thinks like one."

"At least they're not reporting back," Kalten said. "None of the ones we've met so far, anyway."

"They already have," she disagreed. "The Seeker knows when its forces have been diminished. It may not know precisely where we are, but it knows that we've been killing its soldiers. I think we'd better leave here. If there was one group out there, there are probably others as well. We don't want them converging on us."

Ulath was talking seriously to Berit as they rode out at a trot. "Keep your ax under control at all times," he advised. "Don't ever make a swing so wide that you can't recover instantly."

"I think I see," Berit replied seriously.

"An ax can be just as delicate a weapon as a sword—if you know what you're doing," Ulath said. "Pay attention, boy. Your life might depend on this."

"I thought the whole idea was to hit somebody with it as hard as you can."

"There's no real need of that," Ulath replied. "Not if you keep it sharp. When you're cracking a walnut with a hammer, you hit it just hard enough to break the shell. You don't want to smash it into little bits. It's the same with an ax. If you hit somebody too hard with one, there's a fair chance that the blade's going to hang up in the body somewhere, and that leaves you at a definite disadvantage when you have to face your next opponent."

"I didn't know an ax was that complicated a weapon," Kalten said quietly to Sparhawk.

"I think it's a part of the Thalesian religion," Sparhawk replied. He looked at Berit, whose face was rapt as he listened to Ulath's instruction. "I hate to say this, but we've probably lost a good swordsman there. Berit's very fond of that ax, and Ulath's encouraging him."

Late in the day the lake shore began to curve toward the northeast. Bevier looked around, getting his bearings. "I think we'd better stop here, Sparhawk," he advised. "As closely as I can tell, this is approximately where the Thalesians came up against the Zemochs."

"All right," Sparhawk agreed. "I guess the rest is up to you, Tynian."

"First thing in the morning," the Alcione Knight replied.

"Why not now?" Kalten asked him.

"It's going to start getting dark soon," Tynian said, his face bleak. "I don't raise ghosts at night."

"Oh?"

"Just because I know how to do it doesn't mean that I like it. I want lots of daylight around me when they start to appear. These men were killed in battle, so they won't be very pretty to look at. I'd rather not have any of them coming up to me in the dark."

Sparhawk and the other knights scouted the general area while Kurik, Berit, and Talen set up camp. The rain was slacking slightly as they returned.

"Anything?" Kurik asked, looking out from under the sheets of canvas he had erected at an angle over the fire.

"There's some smoke a few miles off to the south," Kalten replied, swinging down from his horse. "We didn't see anybody, though."

"We'll still have to post a watch," Sparhawk said. "If Bevier knows that this is the general area where the Thalesians were fighting, we can be fairly sure the Zemochs will too, and the Seeker probably knows what we're looking for, so it's certain to have people in this area."

They were all unusually quiet that evening as they sat under Kurik's makeshift canvas cover that kept the rain from quenching their fire. This place had been their goal in the weeks since they had left Cimmura, and very soon they would find out if the trip had served any real purpose. Sparhawk in particular was anxious and worried. He definitely wanted to get on with it, but he respected Tynian's feeling in the matter. "Is the process very complicated?" he asked the broad-shouldered Deiran. "Necromancy, I mean?"

"It's not your average spell, if that's what you mean," Tynian replied. "The incantation's fairly long, and you have to draw diagrams on the ground to protect yourself. Sometimes the dead don't want to be awakened, and they can do some fairly nasty things to you if they're really upset."

"How many of them do you plan to raise at a time?" Kalten asked him.

"One," Tynian said very firmly. "I don't want a whole brigade of them coming at me all at once. It might take a little longer, but it's a great deal safer."

"You're the expert, I guess."

The morning dawned wet and dreary. The rain had returned during the night. The sodden earth had already received more water than it could hold, and rain-dimpled puddles stood everywhere.

"A perfect day for raising the dead," Kalten observed sourly. "It just wouldn't seem right if we did it in the sunshine."

"Well," Tynian said, rising to his feet, "I suppose we might as well get started."

"Aren't we going to eat breakfast first?" Kalten objected.

"You really don't want anything in your stomach, Kalten," Tynian replied. "Believe me, you don't."

They walked out into the field.

"They don't seem to have been doing as much digging here," Berit said, looking around. "Maybe the Zemochs don't know where the Thalesians are buried after all."

"We can hope," Tynian said. "I guess this is as good a place to start as any." He picked up a dead stick and prepared to draw a diagram on the sodden ground.

"Use this instead," Sephrenia advised, handing him a coil of rope. "A diagram drawn on dry ground is all right, but there are puddles here, and the ghosts might not see the whole thing."

"We really wouldn't want that to happen," Tynian agreed. He began to lay out the rope on the ground. The design was a strangely compelling one with obscure curves and circles and irregularly shaped stars. "Is that about right?" he asked Sephrenia.

"Move that one slightly to the left," she said, pointing.

He did that.

"Much better," she said. "Repeat the spell out loud. I'll correct you if you do anything wrong."

"Just out of curiosity, why don't *you* do this, Sephrenia?" Kalten asked her. "You seem to know more about it than anybody."

"I'm not strong enough," she admitted. "What you're really doing in this ritual is wrestling with the dead to compel them to rise. I'm a little small for that sort of thing."

Tynian began to speak in Styric, intoning the words sonorously. There was a peculiar cadence to his speech, and the gestures he made had a slow stateliness to them. His voice grew louder and more commanding. Then he raised both his hands and brought them together sharply.

At first nothing seemed to happen. Then the ground inside his diagram seemed to ripple and shudder. Slowly, almost painfully, something rose from the earth.

"God!" Kalten gasped in horror as he stared at the grotesquely mutilated thing.

"Talk to it, Ulath," Tynian said from between clenched teeth. "I can't hold it here very long."

Ulath stepped forward and began to speak in a harshly guttural language.

"Old Thalesian," Sephrenia identified the dialect. "Common soldiers at the time of King Sarak would have spoken it."

The ghastly apparition replied haltingly in a dreadful voice. Then it made a jerky pointing motion with one bony hand.

"Let it go back, Tynian," Ulath said. "I've got what we need."

Tynian's face was gray and his hands were shaking. He spoke two words in Styric, and the apparition sank back into the earth.

"That one didn't really know anything," Ulath told them, "but it pointed out the spot where an earl is buried. The earl was in the household of King Sarak, and if anyone around here knows where the king's buried, he would. It's right over there."

"Let me get my breath first," Tynian said.

"Is it really that difficult?"

"You have no idea, my friend."

They waited while Tynian stood gasping painfully. After a few moments he coiled up his rope and straightened. "All right. Let's go wake up the earl."

Ulath led them to a small knoll that stood nearby. "Burial mound," he said. "It's customary to raise one when you bury a man of importance."

Tynian laid out his design atop the mound, then stepped back and began the ritual again. He finished it and clapped his hands once more.

The apparition that rose from the mound was not as hideously mutilated as the first had been. It was dressed in traditional Thalesian chain mail and had a horned helmet on its head. "Who art thou who hast disturbed my sleep?" it demanded of Tynian in the archaic speech of five centuries past.

"He hath brought thee once again into the light of day at my urging, my Lord," Ulath replied. "I am of thy race and would speak with thee."

"Speak quickly then. I am discontent that thou hast done this thing."

"We seek the resting place of his Majesty King Sarak," Ulath said. "Knowest thou, my Lord, where we might search?"

"His Majesty doth not lie on this battlefield," the ghost responded.

Sparhawk's heart sank.

"Knowest thou what befell him?" Ulath pressed.

"His Majesty departed from his capital at Emsat when word reached him of the invasion of Otha's hordes," the ghost declared. "He took with him a small party of his household retainers. The rest of us remained behind to marshal the main force. We were to follow when the army was gathered. When we arrived here, his Majesty was nowhere to be found. None here knoweth what befell him. Seek ye, therefore, elsewhere."

"One last question, my Lord," Ulath said. "Knowest thou perchance which route it was his Majesty's intention to follow to reach this field?"

"He sailed to the north coast, Sir Knight. No man—alive or dead—knoweth where he made landfall and disembarked. Seek ye therefore in Pelosia or Deira, and return me to my rest."

"Our thanks, my Lord," Ulath said with a formal bow.

"Thy thanks have no meaning for me," the ghost said indifferently.

"Let him go back, Tynian," Ulath said sadly.

Once again, Tynian released the spirit as Sparhawk and the others stood looking at each other, their faces filled with chagrin.

## CHAPTER NINE

Ulath walked over to where Tynian sat on the wet ground with his head between his hands. "Are you all right?" he asked. Sparhawk had noticed that the huge, savage Thalesian was strangely gentle and solicitous with his companions.

"I just feel a little tired, that's all," Tynian replied weakly.

"You can't keep doing this, you know," Ulath told him.

"I can hold out for a little longer."

"Teach me the spell," Ulath urged. "I can wrestle with the best—alive or dead."

Tynian smiled wanly. "I'll wager that you could, my friend. Have you ever been bested?"

"Not since I was about seven," Ulath said modestly. "That was when I crammed my older brother's head into the wooden well-bucket. It took our father two hours to get him out of it. My brother's ears got caught. He always had those big ears. I sort of miss him. He came out second best in a fight with an Ogre." The big man looked at Sparhawk. "All right," he said, "now what?"

"We certainly can't search all of northern Pelosia or Deira," Kalten said.

"That's fairly obvious," Sparhawk replied. "We don't have time. We've got to get more precise information somehow. Bevier, can you think of anything that might give us a clue of where to look?"

"The accounts of this part of the battle are very sketchy, Sparhawk," the white-cloaked knight replied dubiously. He smiled at Ulath. "Our Genidian brothers are a bit lax in keeping records."

"Writing in runes is tedious," Ulath confessed. "Particularly on stone. Sometimes we let those things slide for a generation or so."

"I think we need to find a village or a town of some sort, Sparhawk," Kurik said. "Oh?"

"We've got a lot of questions, and we aren't going to get the answers unless we ask somebody."

"Kurik, the battle was five hundred years ago," Sparhawk reminded him. "We're not going to find anybody alive who saw what happened."

"Of course not, but sometimes local people—particularly commoners—keep track of an area's traditions, and landmarks have names. The name of a mountain or a stream could be just the clue we need."

"It's worth a try, Sparhawk," Sephrenia said seriously. "We're not getting anywhere here."

"It's very slim, Sephrenia."

"What other options do we have?"

"We'll keep going north then, I suppose."

"And probably past all the excavations," she added. "If the ground's been ploughed over, it's a fairly sure sign that Bhelliom's not there."

"That's true, I suppose. All right, we'll go on north, and if something promising turns up, Tynian can raise another ghost."

Ulath looked dubious at that. "I think we'll have to be careful there," he said. "Just the effort of raising these two almost put him on his back."

"I'll be all right," Tynian protested weakly.

"Of course you will—at least you would be if we had time to let you rest in bed for several days."

They helped Tynian into his saddle, pulled his blue cape around him, and rode north in the continuing drizzle.

The city of Randera stood on the east shore of the lake. It was surrounded by high walls, and there were grim watchtowers at each corner.

"Well?" Kalten said, looking speculatively at the bleak Lamork city.

"Waste of time," Kurik grunted. He pointed at a large mound of dirt slowly melting down in the rain. "We're still coming across diggings. We need to go farther north."

Sparhawk looked critically at Tynian. Some of the color had returned to the Alcione Knight's face, and he seemed to be slowly recovering. Sparhawk nudged Faran into a canter and led his friends through the dreary landscape.

It was midafternoon by the time they passed the last signs of excavations. "There's some kind of a village down there by the lake, Sir Sparhawk," Berit said, pointing.

"It's probably not a bad place to start," Sparhawk agreed. "Let's see if we can find an inn down there. I think it's time for us to have a hot meal, get in out of the rain, and dry out a bit anyway."

"And a tavern, perhaps," Kalten added. "People in taverns usually like to talk, and there are always a few old men around who pride themselves on how well they know local history."

They rode on down to the shore of the lake and into the village. The houses were uniformly run-down, and the cobbled streets were in disrepair. At the lower end of town, a series of docks protruded out into the lake, and there were nets hanging on poles along the shore. The smell of long-dead fish permeated the air in the narrow streets. A suspicious-eyed villager directed them to the only inn the village had, a very old, sprawling stone building with a slate roof.

Sparhawk dismounted in the innyard and went inside. A fat man with a bright red face and raggedly cut hair was rolling a beer barrel across the floor toward a wide door near the back. "Have you any empty rooms, neighbor?" Sparhawk asked him.

"The whole loft is empty, my Lord," the fat man replied respectfully, "but are you sure you want to stop here? My accommodations are good enough for ordinary travellers, but they're hardly suitable for the gentry."

"I'm sure they'd be better than sleeping under a hedge on a rainy night."

"That's surely true, my Lord, and I'll be happy to have guests. I don't get many visitors at this time of year. That taproom back there is about the only thing that keeps me in business."

"Are there any people in there at the moment?"

"A half dozen or so, my Lord. Business picks up when the fishermen come in off the lake."

"There are ten of us," Sparhawk told him, "so we'll need quite a few rooms. Do you have someone who can see to our horses?"

"My son takes care of the stables, Sir Knight."

"Warn him to be careful of the big roan. The horse is playful, and he's very free with his teeth."

"I'll mention it to my son."

"I'll get my friends then, and we'll go upstairs and have a look at your loft. Oh, incidentally, do you happen to have a bathtub? My friends and I have been out in the weather, and we're a little rusty-smelling."

"There's a bathhouse out back, my Lord. Nobody uses it very often, though."

"All right. Have some of your people start heating water, and I'll be right back." He turned and went back outside into the rain.

The rooms, though a bit dusty from lack of use, were surprisingly comfortable-looking. The beds were clean and seemed bug-free, and there was a large common room at one end of the loft.

"Very nice, actually," Sephrenia said, looking around.

"There's a bathhouse as well," Sparhawk told her.

"Oh, that's just lovely." She sighed happily.

"We'll let you use it first."

"No, dear one. I don't like to be rushed when I bathe. You gentlemen go ahead." She sniffed at them critically. "Don't be afraid to use soap," she added. "Lots and lots of soap—and wash your hair as well."

"After we bathe, I think we'll want to change into plain tunics," Sparhawk advised the others. "We want to ask these people questions, and armor's just a bit intimidating."

The five knights pulled off their armor, took up their tunics, and trooped with Kurik, Berit, and Talen down the back stairs in the padded and rust-splotched undergarments they wore beneath their steel. They bathed in large, barrellike tubs, and emerged feeling refreshed and cleansed.

"This is the first time I've been warm for a week," Kalten said. "I think I'm ready to visit that taproom now."

Talen was pressed into service to carry their padded undergarments back upstairs, and he was a little sullen about it.

"Don't make faces," Kurik told him. "I wasn't going to let you go into the taproom, anyway. I owe that much to your mother. Tell Sephrenia that she and Flute can have the bathhouse now. Come back down with her and guard the door to make sure they're not interrupted."

"But I'm hungry."

Kurik put his hand threateningly on his belt.

"All right, all right, don't get excited." The boy hurried on up the stairs.

The taproom was a bit smoky, and the floor was covered with sawdust and silvery fish scales. The five plain-clad knights, along with Kurik and Berit, entered unobtrusively and seated themselves at a vacant corner table.

"We'll have beer," Kalten called to the serving wench, "lots of beer."

"Don't overdo it," Sparhawk muttered. "You're heavy, and we don't want to have to carry you back upstairs."

"Never fear, my friend," Kalten replied expansively. "I spent a full ten years here in Lamorkand and never once got fuddled. The beer here is weak and watery stuff."

The serving girl was a typical Lamork woman—large-hipped, blond, busty, and none too bright. She wore a peasant blouse, cut very low, and a heavy red skirt. Her wooden shoes clattered across the floor, and she had an inane giggle. She brought them large, copper-bound wooden tankards of foamy beer. "Don't go just yet, lass," Kalten said to her. He lifted his tankard and drained it without once taking it from his lips. "This one seems to have gone empty on me. Be a good girl and fill it again." He patted her familiarly on the bottom. She giggled and scurried away with his tankard.

"Is he always like this?" Tynian asked Sparhawk.

"Every chance he gets."

"As I was saying before we came in," Kalten said loudly enough to be heard in most parts of the room, "I'll wager a silver half crown that the battle never got this far north."

"And I'll wager two that it did," Tynian replied, picking up the ruse immediately.

Bevier looked puzzled for an instant, and then his eyes showed that he understood. "It shouldn't be too hard to find out," he said, looking around. "I'm sure that someone here would know."

Ulath pushed back his bench and stood up. He thumped his huge fist on the table for attention. "Gentlemen," he said loudly to the other men in the taproom. "My two friends here have been arguing for the last four hours, and they've finally got to the point of putting money down on the issue. Frankly, I'm getting a little tired of listening to them. Maybe some of you can settle the matter and give my ears a rest. There was a battle here five hundred years ago or so," He pointed at Kalten. "This one with the beer foam on his chin says that the fighting didn't get this far north. The other one with the round face says that it did. Which one is right?"

There was a long silence, and then an old man with pink cheeks and wispy white hair shambled across the room to their table. He was shabbily dressed, and his head wobbled on his neck. "I b'leeve I kin settle yer dispute, good masters," he said in a squeaky voice. "My old gaffer, he used to tell me stories about that there battle ye was talkin' about."

"Bring this good fellow a tankard, dearie," Kalten said familiarly to the serving girl.

"Kalten," Kurik said disgustedly, "keep your hand off her bottom."

"Just being friendly is all."

"Is that what you call it?"

The serving girl blushed rosily and went back for more beer, rolling her eyes invitingly at Kalten.

"I think you've just made a friend," Ulath said dryly to the blond Pandion, "but try not to take advantage of it here in public." He looked at the old man with the wobbly neck. "Sit down, old fellow," he invited.

"Why, thankee, good master. I read by the look of 'ee that ye be from far north Thalesia." He sat down shakily on the bench.

"You read well, old man," Ulath said. "What did your gaffer tell you about that ancient battle?"

"Well," the wobbly fellow said, scratching at his stubbled cheek, "as I recall it, he says to me, he says—" He paused as the busty serving girl slid a tankard of beer to him. "Why, thankee, Nima," he said.

The girl smiled, sidling up to Kalten. "How's yours?" she asked, leaning against him.

Kalten flushed slightly. "Ah—just fine, dearie," he faltered. Oddly, her directness seemed to take him off guard.

"You *will* let me know if you want anything, won't you?" she encouraged. "*Anything* at all. I'm here to please, you know."

"At the moment—no," Kalten told her. "Maybe later."

Tynian and Ulath exchanged a long look, and then they both grinned.

"You northern knights look at the world differently than we do," Bevier said, looking slightly embarrassed.

"You want some lessons?" Ulath asked him.

Bevier suddenly blushed.

"He's a good boy." Ulath smiled broadly to the others and patted Bevier on the shoulder. "We just have to keep him out of Arcium for a while until we have time to corrupt him. Bevier, you're my dear brother, but you're awfully stiff and formal. Try to relax a bit."

"Am I so very rigid?" Bevier asked, looking a bit shamefaced.

"We'll fix it for you," Ulath assured him.

Sparhawk looked across the table at the toothlessly grinning old Lamork. "Can you settle this stupid argument for us, grandfather? Did the battle really come this far north?"

"Why, yes indeed it did, young master," the old man mumbled, "and even further, if the truth be known. My old gaffer, he tole me as there was fightin' an' killin' as far north as up into Pelosia. Y'see, the hull army of the Thalesians, they come slippin' around the upper end of the lake an' fell on them Zemochs from behind. Only thing is, was that there was a hull lot more of them there Zemochs than there was Thalesians. Well, sir, the way I understand it was that the Zemochs got over their surprise an' come roarin' back up this way, killin' most ever'thin' in sight. Folks hereabouts hid in their cellars while they was goin' on, let me tell you." He paused to take a long drink from his tankard. "Well, sir," he continued, "the battle *seemed* t' be more or less over, the Zemochs havin' won an' all, but then a hull bunch of them Thalesian lads, what had probably had to wait around for boats up there in the north country, come chargin' in an' done some real awful things to them there Zemochs." He glanced at Ulath. "Yer people are a real bad-tempered sort, if y' don't mind my sayin' so, friend."

"I think it has to do with the climate," Ulath agreed.

The old man looked mournfully into his tankard. "Could ye maybe see yer way clear to do this again?" he asked hopefully.

"Of course, grandfather," Sparhawk said. "See to it, Kalten."

"Why me?"

"Because you're on better speaking terms with the barmaid than I am. Go on with your story, grandfather."

"Well, sir, I been told there was this awful battle that went on about a couple leagues or so north of here. Them Thalesian fellers was *real* unhappy about what had happened to their friends an' kinfolk down to the south end of the lake, an' they went at the Zemochs with axes an' such. They's graves up there as has got a thousand or more in 'em—an' they hain't all human, I'm told. The Zemochs wasn't none too particular about who they took up with, or so the story goes. Ye kin see the graves up there in the fields—big heaps of dirt all growed over with grass an' bushes an' such like. Local farmers been turnin' up bones an' old swords an' spears an' axheads with their plows fer nigh onto five hunnerd years now."

"Did your gaffer by any chance tell you who led the Thalesians?" Ulath asked carefully. "I had some kin in that battle, and we could never find out what happened to them. Do you think the leader might possibly have been the King of Thalesia?"

"Never heard one way or t'other," the old Lamork admitted. "Course, the folks hereabouts wasn't none too anxious to get right down there in the middle of the killin' an' all. Common folks don't have no business gettin' mixed up in that sort of thing."

"He wouldn't have been too hard to recognize," Ulath said. "The old legends in Thalesia say that he was near to seven feet tall, and that his crown had a big blue jewel on top of it."

"Never heard of nobody matchin' that description—but like I said, the common folk was stayin' *real* far back from the fightin'."

"Do you think there might be somebody else around here who's perhaps heard other stories about the battle?" Bevier asked in a neutral tone.

"It's possible, I s'pose," the old fellow said dubiously, "but my old gaffer, he was one of the best storytellers in these here parts. He got hisself runned over by a wagon when he was fifty or so, an' it broke up his back real cruel. He used to set hisself on a bench out there on the porch of this very inn, him an' his cronies. They'd swap the old stories by the hour, an' he took real pleasure in it—not havin' nothin' else to do, him bein' so crippled up an' all, don't y' know. An' he passed all the old tales down t' me—me bein' his favorite an' all, on accounta I used t' bring him his bucket of beer from this very taproom." He looked at Ulath. "No, sir," he said. "None of the old stories I ever heard say nothin' about no king such as you described, but like I say, it was a awful big battle, an' the local folk stayed a long way back from it. It could be that this here king of yers was there, but nobody I ever knew mentioned it."

"And this battle took place a couple or so leagues north of here, you say?" Sparhawk prompted.

"Maybe as much as seven mile," the old fellow replied, taking a long drink from the fresh tankard the broad-hipped serving wench had brought him. "T' be downright honest with'ee, young master, I been a bit stove up of late, an' I don't walk out so far no more." He squinted at them appraisingly. "If y' don't mind me sayin' it, young masters, y' seem t' have a powerful curiosity about that there long ago King of Thalesia an' what not."

"It's fairly simple, grandfather," Ulath said easily. "King Sarak of Thalesia was one of our national heroes. If I can track down what really happened to him, I'll get a great deal of credit out of it. King Wargun might even reward me with an earldom—that's if he ever gets sober enough."

The old man cackled. "I heered of him," he said. "Does he really drink as much as they say?"

"More, probably."

"Well, now—an earldom, y' say? Now, that's a goal that's worth goin' after. What y' might want to do, yer earlship, is go on up t' that there battlefield an' poke around a bit. Might could be that ye kin turn up somethin' as'll give 'ee a clue. A man seven feet tall—an' a king to boot—well, sir, he'd have some mighty impressive armor an' such. I know a farmer up there—name of Wat. He's fond of the old tales same as me, an' that there battleground is in his back yard, so t' speak. If anybody's turned up anythin' that might lead ye t' what yer lookin' fer, he'd know it."

"The man's name is Wat, you say?" Sparhawk asked, trying to sound casual.

"Can't miss him, young master. Walleyed feller. Scratches hisself a lot. He's had the seven-year itch fer about thirty year now." He shook his tankard hopefully.

"Ho there, my girl," Ulath called, fishing several coins out of the pouch at his belt. "Why don't you keep your old friend here drinking until he falls under the table?"

"Why, thankee, yer earlship." The old man grinned.

"After all, grandfather," Ulath laughed, "an earldom ought to be spread around, shouldn't it?"

"I couldn't of put it better meself, me Lord."

They left the taproom and started up the stairs. "That worked out rather well, didn't it?" Kurik said.

"We were lucky," Kalten said. "What if that old fellow hadn't been in the taproom tonight?"

"Then someone would have directed us to him. Common people like to be helpful to the ones buying the beer."

"I think we'll want to remember the story Ulath told the old fellow," Tynian said. "If we tell people that we want the king's bones to take back to Thalesia, they won't start speculating about our real reason for being so curious about where he's buried."

"Isn't that the same as lying?" Berit said.

"Not really," Ulath told him. "We *do* plan to rebury him after we get his crown, don't we?"

"Of course."

"Well, there you are, then."

Berit looked a little dubious about that. "I'll go see about supper," he said, "but I think there's a hole in your logic, Sir Ulath."

"Really?" Ulath said, looking surprised.

It was still raining the following morning. At some time during the night, Kalten had slipped from the room he shared with Sparhawk. Sparhawk had certain suspicions about his friend's absence in which the broad-hipped and very friendly barmaid Nima figured rather prominently. He did not press the issue, however. Sparhawk was, after all, a knight and a gentleman.

They rode north for the better part of two hours until they came to a broad meadow dotted with grass-covered burial mounds. "I wonder which one I should try first," Tynian said as they all dismounted.

"Take your pick," Sparhawk replied. "This Wat we heard about might be able to give you more precise information, but let's try it this way first. It might save some time, and we're starting to get short on that."

"You worry about your Queen all the time, don't you, Sparhawk?" Bevier asked shrewdly.

"Of course. It's what I'm supposed to do."

"I think, my friend, that it might go a bit deeper than that. Your affection for your Queen is more than a duty."

"You're being absurdly romantic, Bevier. She's only a child." Sparhawk felt suddenly offended, and at the same time defensive. "Before we get started, gentlemen," he said brusquely, "let's have a look around. I don't want any stray Zemochs watching us, and I definitely don't want any of the Seeker's empty-headed soldiers creeping up behind us while we're busy."

"We can deal with them," Kalten said confidently.

"Probably, yes, but you're missing the point. Every time we kill one of them, we announce our general location to the Seeker."

"Otha's bug is beginning to irritate me," Kalten said. "All this sneaking and skulking is unnatural."

"Maybe so, but I think you'd better get used to it for a while."

They left Sephrenia and the children in the shelter of a propped-up sheet of canvas and scoured the general vicinity. They found no sign of anyone. Then they rode back to the burial mound.

"How about that one?" Ulath suggested to Tynian, pointing at a low earthen mound. "It looks sort of Thalesian."

Tynian shrugged. "It looks as good as any of the others."

They dismounted again. "Don't overdo this," Sparhawk told Tynian. "If you start to get too tired, back away from it."

"We need information, Sparhawk. I'll be all right." Tynian removed his heavy helmet, dismounted, took his coil of rope, and began to lay it out on the top of the mound in the same design as he had the previous day. Then he straightened with a slight grimace. "Well," he said, "here goes." He threw back his blue cloak and began to speak sonorously in Styric, weaving the intricate gestures of the spell with his hands as he did. Finally, he clapped his hands sharply together.

The mound shook violently as if it had been seized by an earthquake, and what came up from the ground this time did not rise slowly. It burst from the ground roaring—and it was not human.

"Tynian!" Sephrenia shouted. "Send it back!"

Tynian, however, stood transfixed, his eyes starting from his head in horror.

The hideous creature rushed at them, bowling over the thunderstruck Tynian and falling on Bevier, clawing and biting at his armor.

"Sparhawk!" Sephrenia cried as the big Pandion drew his sword. "Not that! It won't do any good! Use Aldreas' spear instead!"

Sparhawk spun and wrenched the short-handled spear from his saddle skirt.

The monstrous thing that was attacking Bevier lifted the white-cloaked knight's armored body as easily as a man might lift a child and smashed it to the ground with terrible force. Then it leaped at Kalten and began wrenching at his helmet. Ulath, Kurik, and Berit dashed to their friend's aid, hacking at the monster with their weapons. Astonishingly, their heavy axes and Kurik's mace did not sink into the thing's body, but bounced off in great showers of glowing sparks. Sparhawk dashed in, holding the spear low. Kalten was being shaken like a rag doll, and his black helmet was dented and scarred.

Deliberately, Sparhawk drove the spear into the monster's side with all his strength. The thing shrieked and turned on him. Again and again Sparhawk struck, and with each blow he felt a tremendous surge of power flowing through the spear. At last he saw an opening, feinted once, and then sank the spear directly into the monster's chest. The hideous mouth gaped open, but what gushed forth was not blood, but a kind of black slime. Grimly, Sparhawk twisted the spear inside the creature's body, making the wound bigger. It shrieked again and fell back. Sparhawk jerked his spear out of the beast's body, and the creature fled, howling and clutching at the gaping hole in its chest. It staggered up the side of the burial mound to the place whence it had emerged from the earth and plunged back into the depths.

Tynian was on his knees in the mud, clutching at his head and sobbing. Bevier lay motionless on the ground, and Kalten sat moaning.

Sephrenia moved quickly to Tynian and, after a quick glance at his face, began to speak rapidly in Styric, weaving the spell with her fingers. Tynian's sobbing lessened, and after a moment, he toppled over on his side. "I'll have to keep him asleep until he recovers," she said. "*If* he recovers. Sparhawk, you help Kalten. I'll see to Bevier."

Sparhawk went to Kalten. "Where are you hurt?" he asked.

"I think it cracked some of my ribs," Kalten gasped. "What was that thing? My sword just bounced off it."

"We can worry about what it was later," Sparhawk said. "Let's get you out of that armor and wrap those ribs. We don't want one of them jabbing into your lungs."

"I'd agree to that." Kalten winced. "I'm sore all over. I don't need any other problems. How's Bevier?"

"We don't know yet. Sephrenia's looking after him."

Bevier's injuries appeared to be more serious than Kalten's. After Sparhawk had bound a wide linen cloth tightly around his friend's chest and checked him over for any other injuries, he wrapped his cloak about him and then went to check on the Arcian. "How is he?" he asked Sephrenia.

"It's fairly serious, Sparhawk," she replied. "There aren't any cuts or gashes, but I think he may be bleeding inside."

"Kurik, Berit," Sparhawk called. "Set up the tents. We've got to get them in out of the rain." He looked around and saw Talen riding away at a gallop. "Now where's *he* going?" he demanded in exasperation.

"I sent him off to see if he can find a wagon," Kurik told him. "These men need to get to a physician fast, and they're in no condition to sit a saddle."

Ulath was frowning. "How did you manage to get your spear into that thing, Sparhawk?" he asked. "My ax just bounced off."

"I'm not sure," Sparhawk admitted.

"It was the rings," Sephrenia said, not looking up from Bevier's unconscious form.

"I *thought* I felt something happening while I was stabbing at that monster," Sparhawk said. "How is it that they've never seemed to have that sort of power before?"

"Because they were separated," she replied. "But you've got one on your hand and the other is in the socket of the spear. When you put them together like that, they have great power. They're a part of Bhelliom itself."

"All right," Ulath said. "What went wrong? Tynian was trying to raise Thalesian ghosts. How did he wake up that monstrosity?"

"Apparently he opened the wrong grave by mistake," she said. "Necromancy's not the most precise of the arts, I'm afraid. When the Zemochs invaded, Azash sent certain of his creatures with them. Tynian accidentally raised one of them."

"What's the matter with him?"

"The contact with that being has almost destroyed his mind."

"Is he going to be all right?"

"I don't know, Ulath, I really don't."

Berit and Kurik finished erecting the tents, and Sparhawk and Ulath moved their injured friends inside one of them. "We're going to need a fire," Kurik said, "and that's not going to be easy today, I'm afraid. I've got a little dry wood left, but not enough to last for very long. Those men are wet and cold, and we absolutely have to get them dried out and warm."

"Any suggestions?" Sparhawk asked him.

"I'll work on it."

It was sometime after noon when Talen returned, driving a rickety wagon that was hardly more than a cart. "This was the best I could find," he apologized.

"Did you have to steal it?" Kurik asked him.

"No. I didn't want the farmer chasing me. I bought it."

"With what?"

Talen looked slyly at the leather purse hanging from his father's belt. "Don't you feel just a little light on that side, Kurik?"

Kurik swore and looked closely at the purse. The bottom had been neatly slit open.

"Here's what I didn't need, though," Talen said, handing over a small handful of coins.

"You actually stole from *me*?"

"Be reasonable, Kurik. Sparhawk and the others are all wearing armor, and their purses are on the inside. Yours was the only one I could get to."

"What's under that canvas?" Sparhawk asked, looking into the wagon bed.

"Dry firewood," the boy replied. "The farmer had stacks of it in his barn. I picked up a few chickens, too. I didn't steal the wagon," he noted clinically, "but I *did* steal the firewood and the chickens—just to keep in practice. Oh, incidentally, the farmer's name is Wat. He's a walleyed fellow who scratches a lot. It seems to me that when I was outside the taproom door last night somebody was saying that he might be sort of significant for some reason."

PART TWO

# GHASEK

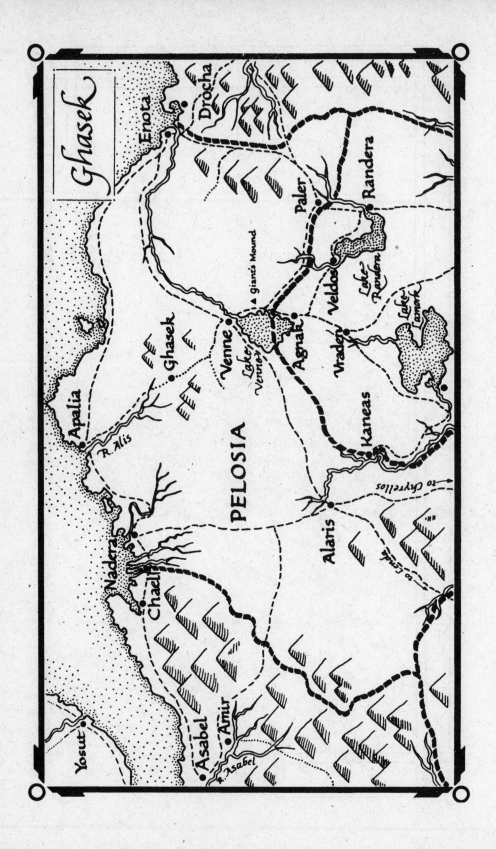

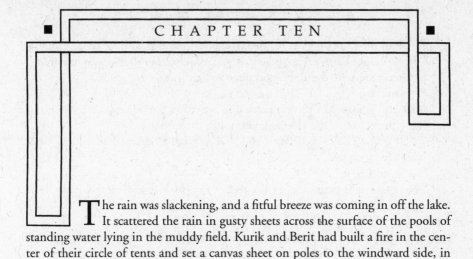

The rain was slackening, and a fitful breeze was coming in off the lake. It scattered the rain in gusty sheets across the surface of the pools of standing water lying in the muddy field. Kurik and Berit had built a fire in the center of their circle of tents and set a canvas sheet on poles to the windward side, in part to protect the blaze from being quenched, but also in part to deflect its heat into the tent where the injured knights lay.

Ulath came out of one of the other tents, wrapping a dry cloak about his huge mailed shoulders. He raised his shaggy-browed face toward the sky. "It seems to be letting up," he said to Sparhawk.

"We can hope," Sparhawk said. "I don't think putting Tynian and the others in that wagon in a rainstorm would do them much good."

Ulath grunted his agreement. "This really didn't turn out very well, did it, Sparhawk?" he said morosely. "We've got three men down, and we're still not any closer to finding Bhelliom."

There was not much Sparhawk could say to that. "Let's go see how Sephrenia's doing," he suggested.

They went around the fire and entered the tent where the small Styric woman hovered over the injured. "How are they coming along?" Sparhawk asked her.

"Kalten's going to be all right," she replied, pulling a red wool blanket up under the blond Pandion's chin. "He's had bones broken before, and he mends fast. I gave Bevier something that may stop the bleeding. It's Tynian who worries me the most, though. If we can't do something—and fairly soon—his mind will slip away."

Sparhawk shuddered at that. "Can't you do anything at all?"

She pursed her lips. "I've been thinking it over. The mind is a much more difficult thing to work with than the body. You have to be very careful."

"What actually happened to him?" Ulath asked her. "I didn't quite follow what you said before."

"At the end of his incantation, he was totally open to that creature from the mound. The dead usually wake slowly, so you've got time to put up your defenses. That beast isn't really dead, so it came at him before he had time to protect himself." She looked down at Tynian's ashen face. "There's one thing that might work," she mused doubtfully. "It's worth a try, I suppose. I don't think anything else will save his sanity. Flute, come here."

The little girl rose from where she had been sitting cross-legged on the canvas ground sheet of the tent. Her bare feet were grass-stained, Sparhawk noted absently.

In spite of all the mud and wet, Flute's feet always seemed to have those greenish stains on them. She softly crossed the tent to Sephrenia, her dark eyes questioning.

Sephrenia spoke to her in that peculiar Styric dialect.

Flute nodded.

"All right, gentlemen," Sephrenia said to Sparhawk and Ulath, "there's nothing you can do here, and at the moment, you're just underfoot."

"We'll wait outside," Sparhawk said, feeling slightly abashed at the crisp way they had been dismissed.

"I'd appreciate it."

The two knights went out of the tent. "She can be very abrupt, can't she?" Ulath noted.

"When she has something serious on her mind."

"Has she always treated you Pandions this way?"

"Yes."

Then they heard the sound of Flute's pipes coming from inside the tent. The melody was much like the peculiarly drowsy one she had played to lull the attention of the spies outside the chapterhouse and the soldiers on the dock at Vardenais. There were slight differences, however, and Sephrenia was speaking sonorously in Styric as a sort of counterpoint. Suddenly, the tent began to glow with a peculiar golden light.

"I don't believe I've ever heard that spell before," Ulath admitted.

"Our instruction only covers the things we're likely to need to know," Sparhawk replied. "There are whole realms of Styric magic we don't even know exist. Some are too difficult, and some are too dangerous." Then he raised his voice. "Talen," he called.

The young thief poked his head out of one of the other tents. "What?" he said flatly.

"Come here. I want to talk to you."

"Can't you do it inside? It's wet out there."

Sparhawk sighed. "Just come here, Talen," he said. "Please don't argue with me every time I ask you to do something."

Grumbling, the boy came out of the tent. He approached Sparhawk warily. "Well, am I in trouble again?"

"Not that I know of. You said that farmer you bought the wagon from is named Wat?"

"Yes."

"How far is his farm from here?"

"A couple of miles."

"What does he look like?"

"His eyes look off in two different directions, and he scratches a lot. Isn't he the fellow that old man in the taproom was telling you about?"

"How did you know about that?"

Talen shrugged. "I was listening outside the door."

"Eavesdropping?"

"I don't know if I'd really put it that way. I'm a child, Sparhawk—or at least people think I am. Grownups don't think they have to tell things to children. I've found that if I really need to know anything, I'm going to have to find it out for myself."

"He's probably got a point, Sparhawk," Ulath said.

"You'd better get your cloak," Sparhawk told the boy. "In just a little bit, you and I are going to pay a visit to this itchy farmer."

Talen looked out over the rainy field and sighed.

From inside the tent, Flute's pipesong broke off, and Sephrenia ceased her incantation.

"I wonder if that's a good sign or a bad one," Ulath said.

They waited tensely. Then, after a few moments, Sephrenia looked out. "I think he'll be all right now. Come in and talk to him. I'll know better once I hear how he answers."

Tynian was propped up on a pillow, although his face was still ashy gray and his hands were trembling. His eyes, however, though still haunted, appeared rational.

"How are you feeling?" Sparhawk asked him, trying to sound casual.

Tynian laughed weakly. "If you really want to know the truth, I feel as if I'd been turned inside out and then put together again backward. Did you manage to kill that monstrosity?"

"Sparhawk drove it off with that spear of his," Ulath told him.

A haunted fear came into Tynian's eyes. "It might come back then?" he asked.

"Not very likely," Ulath replied. "It jumped back into the burial mound and pulled the ground in after it."

"Thank God," Tynian said with relief.

"I think you'd better sleep now," Sephrenia told him. "We can all talk more later."

Tynian nodded and lay back again.

Sephrenia covered him with a blanket, motioned to Sparhawk and Ulath, and led them outside. "I think he's going to be all right," she said. "I felt much better when I heard him laugh. It's going to take some time, but at least he's on the mend."

"I'm going to take Talen and go talk to that farmer," Sparhawk told them. "He seems to be the one the old man at the inn told us about. He might be able to give us some idea of where to go next."

"It's worth a try, I suppose," Ulath said a bit doubtfully. "Kurik and I'll keep an eye on things here."

Sparhawk nodded and went into the tent he normally shared with Kalten. He removed his armor and put on his plain mail shirt and stout woolen leggings instead. He belted on his sword and then pulled his gray, hooded traveller's cloak about his shoulders. He went back out to the fire. "Come along, Talen," he called.

The boy came out of the tent with a look of resignation on his face. His still-damp cloak was wrapped tightly about him. "I don't suppose I could talk you out of this," he said.

"No."

"I hope that farmer hasn't looked into his barn yet, then. He might be a little touchy about the missing firewood."

"I'll pay for it if I have to."

Talen winced. "After I went to all the trouble of stealing it? Sparhawk, that's degrading. It might even be immoral."

Sparhawk looked at him quizzically. "Someday you're going to have to explain the morality of a thief to me."

"It's really very simple, Sparhawk. The first rule is not to pay for anything."

"I thought it might be something like that. Let's go."

The sky to the west was definitely growing lighter as Sparhawk and Talen rode toward the lake, and the rain had become no more than sporadic showers. That in itself lightened Sparhawk's mood. It had been a bleak time. The uncertainty that had dogged his steps from the moment they had left Cimmura had proved to be fully justified, but even now the certainty that they had taken a wrong course provided him with firm ground for a new beginning. Sparhawk accepted his losses stoically and went on toward the lightening sky.

The house and outbuildings of the farmer Wat lay in a little dell. It was a slovenly-looking sort of place, surrounded by a log palisade that leaned dispiritedly away from the prevailing wind. The house, half log and half stone, had a poorly thatched roof and looked definitely run-down. The barn was even worse, appearing to continue to stand more out of habit than from any structural integrity. A broken-down cart sat in the muddy yard, and rusting tools lay wherever their owner had discarded them. Wet, dishevelled chickens scratched in the mud without much hope, and a scrawny black and white pig rooted near the doorstep of the house.

"Not very neat, is he?" Talen observed as he and Sparhawk rode in.

"I saw the cellar you were living in back in Cimmura," Sparhawk replied. "It wasn't exactly what you'd call tidy."

"But at least it was out of sight. This fellow's messy in public."

A man with eyes that did not track together and unkempt, dirty hair shambled out of the house. His clothing appeared to be tied together with bits of twine, and he was absently scratching at his stomach. "What's yer business here?" he asked in an unfriendly tone. He levelled a kick at the pig. "Get outta there, Sophie," he said.

"We were talking with an old man back there in the village," Sparhawk replied, pointing with his thumb back over his shoulder. "He was a white-haired fellow with a wobbly neck who seemed to know a lot of old stories."

"You must mean old Farsh," the farmer said.

"Never did catch his name," Sparhawk said easily. "We met him in the taproom at the inn."

"That's Farsh, all right. He likes to stay close to the beer. What's this got to do with me?"

"He said you were fond of the old stories, too—the ones that have to do with the battle that went on here some five hundred or so years ago."

The walleyed man's face brightened. "Oh, so that's it," he said. "Me'n Farsh always used to swap those old tales. Why don't you an' yer boy come inside, yer worship? I ha'nt had a chance t' talk about the good ol' days fer a long time now."

"Why, that's mighty obliging of you, neighbor," Sparhawk said, swinging down from Faran's back. "Come along, Talen."

"Lemme put yer mounts in the barn," the itchy fellow offered.

Faran looked at the rickety structure and shuddered.

"Thanks all the same, neighbor," Sparhawk said, "but the rain's letting up, and the breeze ought to dry their coats. We'll just put them out in your meadow, if that's all right."

"Somebody might come along an' try to steal 'em."

"Not this horse," Sparhawk told him. "This is not the sort of horse people want to steal."

"Yer the one as gets to walk if yer wrong." The walleyed man shrugged, turning to open the door to his house.

The interior of the house was if anything more untidy than the yard had been. The remains of several meals sat on the table, and dirty clothes lay in heaps in the corners. "The name's Wat," the walleyed man identified himself. He flopped down in a chair. "Sit yerselves," he invited. Then he squinted at Talen. "Say, you was the young fella as bought my ol' wagon."

"Yes," Talen replied a bit nervously.

"She run all right fer you? I mean, none of the wheels fell off or nothin'?"

"It worked just fine," Talen said with some relief.

"Glad t' hear it. Now, which particular stories was you interested in?"

"What we're really looking for, Wat," Sparhawk began, "is any information you might be able to give us about what happened to the old King of Thalesia during the battle. A friend of ours is distantly related to him, and the family wants his bones brought back to Thalesia for proper burial."

"Never heard nothin' about no Thalesian king," Wat admitted, "but that don't mean all that much. This was a big battle, and there was Thalesians fightin' with the Zemochs from the south end of the lake all the way up into Pelosia. Y'see now, what happened was that when the Thalesians started to land on the north coast up there, Zemoch patrols they seen 'em, an' Otha, he started to send some good-sized forces up there to try to keep 'em from gettin' to the main battlefield. At first, the Thalesians come down in small groups, an' the Zemochs, they had things pretty much their own way. There was a pretty fair number of runnin' fights up there when this group or that of the Thalesians got theirselves waylaid. But then the main body of the Thalesian army landed, an' they turned things around. Say, I got some home-brewed beer back there. Could I interest you in some?"

"I wouldn't mind," Sparhawk said, "but the boy's a bit young."

"Got some milk, if that'd suit you, young feller," Wat offered.

Talen sighed. "Why not?" he said.

Sparhawk thought things over. "The Thalesian King would have been one of the first to land," he said. "He left his capital before his army did, but he never got as far as the battlefield."

"Then most likely he's layin' somewhere up there in Pelosia or maybe someplace in Deira," Wat replied. He rose to fetch beer and milk.

"It's a big stretch of country." Sparhawk winced.

"That it is, friend, that it is, but yer followin' the right trail. There's them in Pelosia an' Deira as takes the same pleasure in the old tales as me 'n' old Farsh does, an' the closer y' get to wherever it is this king yer lookin' fer is buried, the better yer chances are gonna be of findin' somebody as kin tell y' what y' want to know."

"That's true, I suppose." Sparhawk took a sip of beer. It was cloudy, but it was about the best he had ever tasted.

Wat leaned back in his chair, scratching at his chest. "Fact of the matter is, friend, that the battle was just too big fer any one man t' see it all. I pretty much know what went on around here, an' Farsh, he knows what went on down around the village an' on south. We all know in a general sorta way what happened overall, but when y' want to get down to specifics, y' gotta talk with somebody as lives fairly close to where it actual happened."

Sparhawk sighed. "It's just a matter of pure luck, then," he said glumly. "We could ride right past the man who knows the story and never even think to ask him."

"Now, that's not entirely true, friend," Wat disagreed. "Us fellers as like to swap stories, we knows one another. Old Farsh, he sent y' t' me, an' I kin send y' on to another feller I know in Paler up there in Pelosia. He's gonna know a lot more about what went on up there than I do, an' he'll know others as knows even more about what went on close t' where *they* live. That's what I meant when I said y' was followin' the right trail. All y' need t' do is go from feller t' feller until y' git the story y' want. It's a lot faster'n diggin' up all of northern Pelosia or Deira."

"You might be right at that."

The walleyed man grinned crookedly. "Not meanin' no offense, yer worship, but you gentlefolk think that us commoners don't know nothin', but when y' stack us all together, there's not very much in this world we *don't* know."

"I'll remember that," Sparhawk said. "Who's this man in Paler?"

"He's a tanner, name of Berd—silly name, but Pelosians is like that. His tanyard's just outside the north gate of the city. They wouldn't let him set up inside the walls on accounta the smell, y' know. You go see Berd, an' if he don't know the story y' want to hear, he'll probably know somebody as does—or at least somebody as kin tell y' who y' oughta talk to."

Sparhawk rose to his feet. "Wat," he said, "you've been a real help." He handed the fellow a few coins. "The next time you go to the village, have yourself a few tankards of beer, and if you run into Farsh, buy him one too."

"Why, thankee, yer worship," Wat said. "I most surely will. An' good luck in yer search."

"Thank you." Then Sparhawk remembered something. "I'd like to buy some firewood from you, if you can spare any." He handed Wat a few more coins.

"Why, certainly, yer worship. Come along to the barn, an' I'll show you where it's stacked."

"That's all right, Wat," Sparhawk smiled. "We've already got it. Come along, Talen."

The rain had stopped entirely when Sparhawk and Talen came out of the house, and they could see blue sky out over the lake to the west.

"You had to go and do that, didn't you?" Talen said in a disgusted tone of voice.

"He *was* very helpful, Talen," Sparhawk said defensively.

"That has nothing to do with it. Did we really get very far with this?"

"It was a start," Sparhawk replied. "Wat may not look very bright, but he's really very shrewd. The plan of going from storyteller to storyteller is about the best we've come up with so far."

"It's going to take awhile, you know."

"Not as long a while as some of the other notions we've had."

"The trip wasn't wasted then."

"We'll know better after we talk with that tanner in Paler."

Ulath and Berit had strung a rope near the fire and were hanging wet clothes over it when Sparhawk and the boy returned to camp. "Any luck?" Ulath asked.

"Some, I hope," Sparhawk replied. "It's fairly certain that King Sarak didn't get this far south. It seems that there was a lot more fighting up in Pelosia and Deira than Bevier read about."

"What next, then?"

"We go to the town of Paler up in Pelosia and talk to a tanner named Berd. If he hasn't heard about Sarak, he can probably send us on to someone who has. How's Tynian?"

"He's still asleep. Bevier's awake, though, and Sephrenia got him to drink some soup."

"That's a good sign. Let's go inside and talk with her. Now that the weather's clearing, I think it's safe to move on."

They trooped into the tent, and Sparhawk repeated the gist of what Wat had said.

"The plan has merit, Sparhawk," Sephrenia approved. "How far is it to Paler?"

"Talen, go get my map, would you?"

"Why me?"

"Because I asked you to."

"Oh. All right."

"Just the map, Talen," Sparhawk added. "Don't take anything else out of the pack."

The boy returned after a few moments, and Sparhawk unfolded the map. "All right," he said. "Paler's up here at the north end of the lake—just across the Pelosian border. I make it about ten leagues."

"That wagon won't move very fast," Kurik told him, "and we don't want to jolt these men around. It's probably going to take at least two days."

"At least once we get them to Paler we should be able to find a physician for them," Sephrenia said.

"We really don't have to use the wagon," Bevier objected. His face was pale, and he was sweating profusely. "Tynian is much better, and Kalten and I aren't hurt that badly. We can ride."

"Not while I'm giving the orders, you can't," Sparhawk told him. "I'm not going to gamble your lives just to save a few hours." He went to the door of the tent and looked out. "It's coming on to evening," he noted. "We'll all get a good night's sleep and start out first thing in the morning."

Kalten grunted and sat up painfully. "Good," he said. "Now that that's settled, what's for supper?"

After they had eaten, Sparhawk went out and sat by the fire. He was staring morosely into the flames when Sephrenia joined him. "What is it, dear one?" she asked him.

"Now that I've had time to think about it, this is really a farfetched notion, isn't it? We could wander around Pelosia and Deira for the next twenty years listening to old men tell stories."

"I don't really think so, Sparhawk," she disagreed. "Sometimes I get hunches— little flashes of the future. Somehow I feel that we're on the right course."

"Hunches, Sephrenia," he said with some amusement.

"Maybe a little stronger than that, but it's a word that Elenes wouldn't understand."

"Are you trying to say you can actually see into the future?"

She laughed. "Oh, no," she replied. "Only the Gods can do that, and even they're imperfect at it. About all I can really perceive is when something's right and when it isn't. This somehow *feels* right. There's one other thing, too," she added. "The ghost of Aldreas told you that the time has come for Bhelliom to emerge again. I know what Bhelliom is capable of. It can control things in ways we can't even imagine. If it wants *us* to be the ones who find it, nothing on earth will be able to stop us. I think you might find that the storytellers up there in Pelosia and Deira will tell us things they've thought they've forgotten, and even things they never knew."

"Isn't that just a little mystic?"

"Styrics *are* mystics, Sparhawk. I thought you knew that."

## CHAPTER ELEVEN

They slept late the following morning. Sparhawk awoke before daybreak, but decided to let his companions rest. They had been long on the road, and the horror of the previous day had taken its toll. He went out some way from the tents to watch the sunrise. The sky overhead was clear, and the stars were still out. Despite Sephrenia's assurances the previous evening, Sparhawk's mood was somber. When they had begun, the sense that their cause was just and noble had led him to believe that somehow they would prevail against almost anything. The events of the previous day, however, had proved to him just how wrong he had been about that. He would venture anything to bring his pale young Queen back to health, even to the point of throwing his own life into the crucible, but did he have the right to risk his friends'?

"What's the problem?" He recognized Kurik's voice without looking around.

"I don't know, Kurik," he admitted. "It all feels as if I'm trying to hold sand in my fist, and this plan of ours doesn't really make much sense, does it? Trying to track down five-hundred-year-old stories is really kind of absurd, don't you think?"

"No, Sparhawk," Kurik said, "not really. You could run around northern Pelosia or Deira with a spade for the next two hundred years and not even come close to Bhelliom. That farmer was right, you know. Trust the people, my Lord. In many ways, the people are wiser than the nobility—or even the Church, for that matter." Kurik coughed uncomfortably. "You don't necessarily have to tell Patriarch Dolmant I said that," he amended.

"Your secret is safe, my friend." Sparhawk smiled. "There's something we're going to have to talk about."

"Oh?"

"Kalten, Bevier, and Tynian are more or less out of action."

"You know, I believe you're right."

"That's a bad habit, Kurik."

"Aslade says the same thing."

"Your wife's a wise woman. All right. Part of our success in getting around difficulties has been the presence of men in armor. Most people don't interfere with the Knights of the Church. The trouble is that now there's only going to be Ulath and me."

"I can count, Sparhawk. What's your point?"

"Could you fit into Bevier's armor?"

"Probably. It might not be very comfortable, but I could adjust the straps a bit. The point, though, is that I won't do it."

"What's the problem? You've worn armor on the practice field."

"That was on the field. Everybody knew who I was, and they knew why I was doing it. This is out in the world, and that's altogether different."

"I really don't see the distinction, Kurik."

"There are laws about that sort of thing, Sparhawk. Only knights are permitted to wear armor, and I'm not a knight."

"The difference is very slight."

"But it's still a difference."

"You're going to make me order you to do this, aren't you?"

"I wish you wouldn't."

"I wish I didn't have to. I'm not trying to offend your sensibilities, Kurik, but this is an unusual situation. It involves our safety. You'll wear Bevier's armor, and I think we can stuff Berit into Kalten's. He's worn mine before, and Kalten and I are about the same size."

"You're going to insist, then?"

"I don't really have any choice. We've got to get through to Paler without any incidents along the way. I've got some injured men, and I don't want to risk them."

"I understand the reasons, Sparhawk. I'm not stupid, after all. I don't like it, but you're probably right."

"I'm glad we agree."

"Don't get too ecstatic about it. I want it clearly understood that I'm doing this under protest."

"If there's ever any trouble about it, I'll swear to that."

"That's assuming you're still alive," Kurik replied sourly. "You want me to wake the others?"

"No. Let them sleep. You were right last night. It's going to take two days to get to Paler. That gives us a little time to play with."

"You're very worried about time, aren't you, Sparhawk?"

"We've only got so much of it left," Sparhawk replied somberly. "This business of running around listening to old men tell stories is likely to chew up a great deal of it. It's coming up to the point where another one of the twelve knights is going to die, and he'll give his sword to Sephrenia. You know how that weakens her."

"She's a lot stronger than she looks. She could probably carry as much as you and I put together." Kurik glanced back toward the tents. "I'll go build up the fire and put her teakettle on to boil. She usually wakes up early." And he went back toward the camp.

Ulath, who had been standing watch nearby, loomed out of the shadows. "That was a very interesting conversation," he rumbled.

"You were listening."

"Obviously. Voices carry a long way at night for some reason."

"You don't approve—about the armor, I mean?"

"It doesn't bother me, Sparhawk. We're a lot less formal in Thalesia than you are down here. A fair number of Genidian Knights are not, strictly speaking, of noble birth." He grinned, his teeth flashing. "We usually wait until King Wargun is roaring drunk and then file them in so he can bestow titles on them. Several of my friends are barons of places that don't even exist." He rubbed at the back of his neck. "Sometimes I think this whole nobility business is a farce, anyway. Men are men— titled or not. I don't think God cares, so why should we?"

"You're going to stir up a revolution talking like that, Ulath."

"Maybe it's time for one. It's starting to get light over there." Ulath pointed toward the eastern horizon.

"Right. It looks as if we might have good weather today."

"Check with me this evening, and I'll let you know."

"Don't people in Thalesia try to predict the weather?"

"Why? You can't do anything about it. Why don't we go have a look at your map? I know a bit about ships and currents and prevailing winds and the like. It could just be that I can make some guesses about where King Sarak made his landfall. We might be able to figure out which route he took. That could narrow things down just a bit."

"Not a bad idea," Sparhawk agreed. "If we can work that out, at least we'll have some idea of where to start asking questions." Sparhawk hesitated. "Ulath," he said seriously, "is Bhelliom really as dangerous as they say it is?"

"Probably even more so. Ghwerig made it, and he's not really very pleasant— even for a Troll."

"You said 'is.' Don't you mean 'was'? He's dead by now, isn't he?"

"Not that I've heard, and I sort of doubt it. There's something you ought to know about Trolls, Sparhawk. They don't die of old age like other creatures. You have to kill them. If somebody had managed to kill Ghwerig, he'd have boasted about it, and I'd have heard the story. There's not much to do in Thalesia in the wintertime except listen to stories. The snow piles up by the foot there, so we usually stay inside. Let's go have a look at that map."

As they walked back toward the tents, Sparhawk decided that he liked Ulath.

The huge Genidian Knight was normally very silent, but once you managed to unlock his friendship, he spoke with a kind of droll understatement that was often even more amusing than Kalten's exaggerated humor. Sparhawk's companions were good men—the best, actually. They were all different, of course, but that was only to be expected. Whatever the outcome of their search might be, he was glad that he had had the opportunity to know them.

Sephrenia stood by the fire drinking tea. "You're up early," she noted as the two knights came into the circle of light. "Have the plans changed? Are we in some hurry to leave?"

"Not really," Sparhawk told her, kissing her palm in greeting.

"Please don't spill my tea," she cautioned.

"No, ma'am," he agreed. "We're not going to be able to cover much more than five leagues today, so let the others sleep awhile longer. That wagon's not going to move very fast, and besides, after what's been happening, I don't think wandering around in the dark would be such a good idea. Is Berit awake yet?"

"I think I heard him stirring around."

"I'm going to put him in Kalten's armor and have Kurik wear Bevier's. Maybe we can intimidate anybody who might be feeling unfriendly."

"Is that all you Elenes ever think about?"

"A good bluff is sometimes better than a good fight," Ulath growled. "I like deceiving people."

"You're as bad as Talen is."

"No, not really. My fingers aren't nimble enough for cutting purses. If I decide I want what's in a man's purse, I'll hit him on the head and take it."

She laughed. "I'm surrounded by scoundrels."

The day dawned bright and sunny. The sky was very blue, and the wet grass that covered the surrounding hills was shiny green.

"Whose turn is it to cook breakfast?" Sparhawk asked Ulath.

"Yours."

"Are you sure?"

"Yes."

They roused the others, and Sparhawk got the cooking utensils out of one of the packs.

After they had eaten, Kurik and Berit cut spare lances from a nearby thicket while Sparhawk and Ulath helped their injured friends into Talen's rickety wagon.

"What's wrong with the ones we've got?" Ulath asked when Kurik returned with the lances.

"They tend to break," Kurik said, tying the poles to the side of the wagon, "particularly in view of the way you gentlemen use them. It never hurts to have extra ones along."

"Sparhawk," Talen said quietly, "there are some more of those people in white smocks out there. They're hiding in that brush along the edge of the field."

"Could you tell what kind they were?"

"They had swords," the boy replied.

"Zemochs then. How many of them are there?"

"I saw four."

Sparhawk went over to Sephrenia. "There's a small group of Zemochs hiding at the edge of the field. Would the Seeker's people try to hide?"

"No. They'd attack immediately."

"That's what I thought."

"What are you going to do?" Kalten asked.

"Run them off. I don't want any of Otha's men trailing along behind us. Ulath, let's mount up and chase those people for a while."

Ulath grinned and hauled himself into his saddle.

"You want your lances?" Kurik asked.

Ulath grunted, drawing his ax. "Not for a job this small."

Sparhawk climbed up onto Faran's back, strapped on his shield, and drew his sword. He and Ulath set out at a menacing walk. After a few moments, the hidden Zemochs broke from their cover and fled, crying out in alarm. "Let's run them for a bit," Sparhawk suggested. "I want them to be too winded to turn around and come back."

"Right," Ulath agreed, pushing his horse into a canter.

The two mounted knights crashed through the bushes at the edge of the field and pursued the fleeing Zemochs across a broad stretch of ploughed ground.

"Why not just kill them?" Ulath shouted to Sparhawk.

"It's probably not really necessary," Sparhawk shouted back. "There are only four of them, and they don't pose much of a threat."

"You're getting soft, Sparhawk."

"Not really."

They pursued the Zemochs for perhaps twenty minutes, then reined in.

"They run very well, don't they?" Ulath chuckled. "Why don't we go on back now? I'm getting tired of looking at this place."

They rejoined the others, and they all set out, going north along the lake. They saw peasants in the fields, but no signs of any other Zemochs. They rode at a walk with Ulath and Kurik in the lead.

"Any guesses about what those people were up to?" Kalten asked Sparhawk. The blond knight was driving the wagon, the reins held negligently in one hand and the other pressed against his injured ribs.

"I'd imagine that Otha's having his men keep an eye on anybody poking around the battlefield," Sparhawk replied. "If somebody happens to stumble across Bhelliom, he'd definitely want to know about it."

"There may be more, then. It might not hurt to keep our eyes open."

The sun grew warmer as the day progressed, and Sparhawk began almost to wish for a return of the clouds and rain of the past week or more. Grimly he rode on, sweltering in his black-enamelled armor.

They camped that night in a grove of stately oaks not far from the Pelosian border and rose early the following morning. The guards posted at the boundary stood aside for them respectfully, and by midafternoon they crested a hill and looked down on the Pelosian city of Paler.

"We made better time than I thought we would," Kurik noted as they rode down the long slope toward the city. "Are you sure that map of yours is accurate, Sparhawk?"

"No map is entirely accurate. About the best you can hope for is an approximation."

"Knew a map maker in Thalesia once," Ulath said. "He set out to map the country between Emsat and Husdal. At first he paced everything off very carefully, but after a day or so he bought himself a good horse and started guessing. His map doesn't even come close, but everybody uses it because nobody wants to take the trouble of drawing a new one."

The guards at the south gate of the city passed them after only the briefest of questions, and Sparhawk obtained the name and location of a respectable inn from one of them. "Talen," he said, "do you think you'll be able to find your way to that inn by yourself?"

"Of course. I can find any place in any town."

"Good. Stay here then, and keep your eyes on that road coming up from the south. Let's see if those Zemochs are still curious about us."

"No problem, Sparhawk." Talen dismounted and tied his horse at the side of the gate. Then he strolled back out and sat in the grass at the side of the road.

Sparhawk and the others rode on into the city with the wagon clattering along behind them. The cobbled streets of Paler were crowded, but people gave way to the Knights of the Church, and they reached the inn within perhaps half an hour. Sparhawk dismounted and went inside.

The innkeeper wore one of the tall, pointed hats common in Pelosia and had a slightly haughty expression.

"You have rooms?" Sparhawk asked him.

"Of course. This is an inn."

Sparhawk waited, his expression cold.

"What's your trouble?" the innkeeper asked.

"I was just waiting for you to finish your sentence. I think you left something out."

The innkeeper flushed. "Sorry, my Lord," he mumbled.

"Much better," Sparhawk congratulated him. "Now then, I have three injured friends. Does there happen to be a physician nearby?"

"Down at the end of this street, my Lord. He has a sign out."

"Is he any good?"

"I really couldn't say. I haven't been sick lately."

"We'll chance him, I guess. I'll bring my friends inside and go get him."

"I don't think he'll come, my Lord. He has a very high opinion of himself. He thinks it's beneath his dignity to leave his quarters. He makes the sick and injured come to him."

"I'll persuade him," Sparhawk said bleakly.

The innkeeper laughed a bit nervously at that. "How many in your party, my Lord?"

"Ten of us. We'll help the injured inside, and then I'll go have a chat with this self-important physician."

They aided Kalten, Tynian, and Bevier into the inn and up the stairs to their rooms. Then Sparhawk came back down and walked resolutely toward the end of the street, his black cape billowing out behind him.

The physician maintained his quarters on the second floor over a greengrocer's shop, and entry was gained by way of an outside stairway. Sparhawk clanked up the stairs and entered without knocking. The physician was a weaselly little fellow dressed in a flowing blue robe. His eyes bulged slightly when he looked up from his book to see a grim-faced man in black armor enter uninvited. "I *beg* your pardon," he objected.

Sparhawk ignored that. He had decided that the best course was to cut through any possible arguments. "You are the physician?" he asked in a flat voice.

"I am," the man replied.

"You will come with me." It was not a request.

"But—"

"No buts. I have three injured friends who require your attention."

"Can't you bring them here? I do not customarily leave my quarters."

"Customs change. Get what you'll need and come along. They're at the inn just up the street."

"This is outrageous, Sir Knight."

"We're not going to argue about this, are we, neighbor?" Sparhawk's voice was deadly quiet.

The physician flinched back. "Ah—no. I don't believe so. I'll make an exception in this case."

"I was hoping you'd feel that way."

The physician rose quickly. "I'll get my instruments and some medicines. What sort of injuries are we talking about?"

"One of them has some broken ribs. Another seems to be bleeding inside somewhere. The third suffers mostly from exhaustion."

"Exhaustion is easily cured. Just have your friend spend several days in bed."

"He doesn't have time. Just give him something that'll get him back on his feet."

"How did they receive these injuries?"

"Church business," Sparhawk said shortly.

"I'm always eager to serve the Church."

"You've got no idea of how happy that makes me."

Sparhawk led the reluctant physician back up the street to the inn and on up to the second floor. He drew Sephrenia aside as the healer began his examinations. "It's a little late," he said to her. "Why don't we hold off on visiting the tanner until morning? I don't think we want him to be rushed. He might forget things we need to know."

"Truly," she agreed. "Besides, I want to be sure this physician knows what he's doing. He looks a little unreliable to me."

"He'd better be reliable. He's already got a fair idea of what's going to happen to him if he isn't."

"Oh, Sparhawk," she said reprovingly.

"It's really a very simple arrangement, little mother. He fully understands that either they get healthy or he gets sick. That sort of encourages him to do his best."

Pelosian cooking, Sparhawk had noticed, leaned heavily in the direction of boiled cabbage, beets, and turnips, only lightly garnished with salt pork. The latter, of course was totally unacceptable to Sephrenia and Flute, and so the two made a meal of raw vegetables and boiled eggs. Kalten, however, ate everything in sight.

It was after dark when Talen arrived at the inn. "They're still following us, Sparhawk," he reported, "only there are a lot more of them now. I saw maybe forty of them on top of that hill just south of town, and they're on horses now. They stopped at the hilltop and looked things over. Then they pulled back into the woods."

"That's a little more serious than just four, isn't it?" Kalten said.

"It is indeed," Sparhawk agreed. "Any ideas, Sephrenia?"

She frowned. "We haven't really been moving all that fast," she said. "If they're on horseback, they could have caught up with us without much trouble. I'd guess that they're just following us. Azash seems to know something that we don't. He's been trying to kill you for months, but now he sends his people out with orders just to follow us at a distance."

"Can you think of any reason for the change in tactics?"

"Several, but they're all pure speculation."

"We'll have to be alert when we leave town," Kalten said.

"Maybe doubly alert," Tynian added. "They might be just biding their time until we come to a deserted stretch of road where they can ambush us."

"That's a cheerful thought," Kalten said wryly. "Well, I don't know about the rest of you, but I'm going to bed."

The sun was very bright again the following morning, and a freshening breeze blew in off the lake. Sparhawk dressed in his mail shirt, a plain tunic, and woolen leggings. Then he and Sephrenia rode out from the inn toward the north gate of Paler and the tanyard of the man named Berd. The people in the street appeared for the most part to be common workmen carrying a variety of tools. They wore sober blue smocks and the tall, pointed hats.

"I wonder if they realize just how silly those things look," Sparhawk murmured.

"Which things were those?" Sephrenia asked him.

"Those hats. They look like dunce caps."

"They're no more ridiculous than those plumed hats the courtiers in Cimmura wear."

"I suppose you're right."

The tanyard was some distance beyond the north gate, and it smelled vile. Sephrenia wrinkled her nose as they approached. "This is not going to be a pleasant morning," she predicted.

"I'll cut it as short as I can," Sparhawk promised.

The tanner was a heavy-set, bald man wearing a canvas apron stained with dark brown splotches. He was stirring at a large vat with a long paddle as Sparhawk and Sephrenia rode into his yard. "I'll be right with you," he said. His voice sounded like gravel being poured across a slate. He stirred for a moment or two longer, looking critically into the vat. Then he laid aside his paddle and came toward them, wiping his hands on his apron. "How can I help you?" he asked.

Sparhawk dismounted and helped Sephrenia down from her white palfrey. "We were talking with a farmer named Wat down in Lamorkand," he told the tanner. "He said you might be able to help us."

"Old Wat?" The tanner laughed. "Is he still alive?"

"He was three days ago. You're Berd, aren't you?"

"That's me, my Lord. What's this help you need?"

"We've been going around talking to people who know stories about that big battle they had around here some years back. There are some people up in Thalesia who are distantly related to the man who was their king during that battle. They want to find out where he's buried so they can take his bones back home."

"Never heard of no kings involved in the fights around here," Berd admitted. "Course that don't mean there wasn't a few. I don't imagine kings go around introducin' theirselves to common folks."

"Then there *were* battles up here?" Sparhawk asked him.

"I don't know as I'd call 'em battles exactly—more what you might call skirmishes an' the like. Y' see, my Lord, the main battle was down at the south end of the lake. That's where the armies drew up their lines of regiments an' battalions an' such. What was goin' through up here was small groups of men—Pelosians mostly at first, an' then later the Thalesians started to filter on down. Otha's Zemochs, they had out their patrols, an' there was a bunch of nasty little fights, but nothin' as you could really call a battle. They was a couple not far from here, but I don't know as any Thalesians was involved. Most of *their* fights went on up around Lake Venne, an' even as far north as Ghasek." He suddenly snapped his fingers. "Now *that's* the one you really ought to talk to," he said. "Can't think why I didn't remember that right off."

"Oh?"

"Of course. Can't imagine where my brain had went. That Count of Ghasek, he went to some university down in Cammoria, an' he got to studyin' up on history an' the like. Anyhow, all the books he read on that there battle, they sorta concentrated on what went on down to the south end of the lake. They didn't say hardly nothin' about what happened up here. Anyhow, when he finished up his studyin', he come back home, an' he started goin' around collectin' all the old stories he could come across. Wrote 'em all down, too. He's been at it for years now. I expect he's gathered up just about every story in northern Pelosia by now. He even come an' talked to me, an' it's some fair distance from Ghasek to here. He tole me that what he's tryin' to do is to fill in some mighty big gaps in what they teach at that there university. Yes, sir, you go talk to Count Ghasek. If anybody in all Pelosia knows anythin' about this king you're lookin' for, the count woulda found out about it an' wrote it down in that there book he's puttin' together."

"My friend," Sparhawk said warmly, "I think you've just solved our problem for us. How do we find the count?"

"Best way is to take the road to Lake Venne. The city of Venne itself is up at the north end of the lake. Then you go north from there. It's a real bad road, but it's passable—particularly at this time of year. Ghasek ain't no real town. Actual, it's just the count's estate. There's a few villages around it—mostly belongin' to the count hisself—but anybody up there can direct you to the main house—more like a palace, really, or maybe a castle. I've been past it a few times. Bleak-lookin' place it is, but I never went inside, though." He laughed a rusty-sounding laugh. "Me an' the count, we don't exactly move in the same circles, if you take my meanin'."

"I understand perfectly," Sparhawk said. He took out several coins. "Your work here looks hot, Berd."

"It surely is, my Lord."

"When you finish up for the day, why don't you get yourself something cool to drink?" He gave the tanner the coins.

"Why, thankee, my Lord. That's uncommon generous of you."

"I'm the one who should be thanking you, Berd. I think you've just saved me months of travel." Sparhawk helped Sephrenia back onto her horse and then re-mounted himself. "I'm more grateful to you than you can possibly imagine, Berd," he said to the tanner by way of farewell.

"Now that turned out extremely well, didn't it?" Sparhawk exulted as he and Sephrenia rode back into the city.

"I told you it would," she reminded him.

"Yes, as a matter of fact, you did. I shouldn't have doubted you for a moment, little mother."

"It's natural to have doubts, Sparhawk. We'll go on to Ghasek, then?"

"Of course."

"I think we'd better wait until tomorrow, though. That physician said that none of our friends is in any danger, but another day's rest won't hurt them."

"Will they be able to ride?"

"Slowly at first, I'm afraid, but they'll grow stronger as we go along."

"All right. We'll leave first thing tomorrow morning then."

The mood of the others brightened considerably when Sparhawk repeated what Berd had told him.

"Somehow this is beginning to seem too easy," Ulath muttered, "and easy things make me nervous."

"Don't be so pessimistic," Tynian told him. "Try to look on the bright side of things."

"I'd rather expect the worst. That way, if things turn out all right, I'm pleasantly surprised."

"I suppose you'll want me to get rid of the wagon then?" Talen said to Spar-hawk.

"No. Let's take it along just to be on the safe side. If any one of these three takes a turn for the worse, we can always put him back in it."

"I'm going to check the supplies, Sparhawk," Kurik said. "It could be quite some time before we come to another town with a market place. I'll need some money."

Even that could not dampen Sparhawk's elation.

They spent the rest of the day quietly and retired early that evening.

Sparhawk lay in his bed staring up into the darkness. It was going to be all right; he was sure of that now. Ghasek was a long distance away, but if Berd had been right about the thoroughness of the count's research, he would have the answer they needed. Then all that would remain for them to do would be to go to the place where Sarak was buried and recover his crown. Then they hopefully would return to Cimmura with Bhelliom and—

There was a light tap on his door. He rose and opened it.

It was Sephrenia. Her face was ashen gray, and there were tears streaming down her cheeks. "Please, come with me, Sparhawk," she said. "I cannot face them alone any more."

"Face whom?"

"Just come with me. I'm hoping that I'm wrong, but I'm afraid I'm not." She led him down the hall and opened the room she shared with Flute, and once again Sparhawk smelled the familiar graveyard reek. Flute sat on the bed, her little face grave, but her eyes unafraid. She was looking at a shadowy figure in black armor. Then the figure turned, and Sparhawk saw the scarred face. "Olven," he said in a stricken voice.

The ghost of Sir Olven did not reply but simply extended its hands with its sword lying across them.

Sephrenia was weeping openly as she stepped forward to receive the sword.

The ghost looked at Sparhawk and raised one hand in a kind of half salute.

And then it vanished.

■  CHAPTER TWELVE  ■

Their mood was very bleak the following morning as they saddled their horses in the predawn darkness.

"Was he a good friend?" Ulath asked, heaving Kalten's saddle up onto the back of the blond Pandion's horse.

"One of the best," Sparhawk answered. "He never said very much, but you always knew you could depend on him. I'm going to miss him."

"What are we going to do about those Zemochs following us?" Kalten asked.

"I don't think there's much we can do," Sparhawk replied. "We're a little under strength until you and Tynian and Bevier recover. As long as all they're doing is trailing along behind us, they're not much of a problem."

"I think I've told you before that I don't like having enemies behind me," Ulath said.

"I'd rather have them behind me where I can keep an eye on them instead of hiding in ambush somewhere ahead," Sparhawk said.

Kalten winced as he pulled his saddle cinch tight. "That's going to get aggravating," he noted, laying one hand gently against his side.

"You'll heal," Sparhawk told him. "You always do."

"The only problem is that it takes longer to heal every time. We're not getting any younger, Sparhawk. Is Bevier going to be all right to ride?"

"As long as we don't push him," Sparhawk replied. "Tynian's better, but we'll take it slowly for the first day or so. I'm going to put Sephrenia in the wagon. Every time she gets another of those swords, she gets a little weaker. She's carrying more than she's willing to let us know about."

Kurik led the rest of the horses out into the yard. He was wearing his customary black leather vest. "I suppose I should give Bevier his armor back," he said hopefully.

"Keep it for the time being," Sparhawk disagreed. "I don't want him to start feeling brave just yet. He's a little headstrong. Let's not encourage him until we're sure he's all right."

"This is very uncomfortable, Sparhawk," Kurik said.

"I explained the reasons to you the other day."

"I'm not talking about reasons. Bevier and I are close to the same size, but there are differences. I've got raw places all over me."

"It's probably only for a couple more days."

"I'll be a cripple by then."

Berit assisted Sephrenia out through the door of the inn. He helped her up into the wagon and then lifted Flute up beside her. The small Styric woman was wan-looking, and she cradled Olven's sword gently, almost as one would carry a baby.

"Are you going to be all right?" Sparhawk asked her.

"I just need some time to get used to it, that's all," she replied.

Talen led his horse out of the stable.

"Just tie him on behind the wagon," Sparhawk told the boy. "You'll be driving."

"Whatever you say, Sparhawk," Talen agreed.

"No arguments?" Sparhawk was a little surprised.

"Why should I argue? I can see the reason for it. Besides, that wagon seat's more comfortable than my saddle—much more comfortable, when you get right down to it."

Tynian and Bevier came out of the inn. Both wore mail shirts and walked a bit slowly.

"No armor?" Ulath asked Tynian lightly.

"It's heavy," Tynian replied. "I'm not sure I'm up to it just yet."

"Are you sure we didn't leave anything behind?" Sparhawk asked Kurik.

Kurik gave him a flat, unfriendly stare.

"Just asking," Sparhawk said mildly. "Don't get irritable this early in the morning." He looked at the others. "We're not going to push today," he told them. "I'll be satisfied with five leagues, if we can manage it."

"You're saddled with a group of cripples, Sparhawk," Tynian said. "Wouldn't it be better if you and Ulath went on ahead? The rest of us can catch up with you later."

"No," Sparhawk decided. "There are unfriendly people roaming about, and you and the others aren't in any condition to defend yourselves just yet." He smiled briefly at Sephrenia. "Besides," he added, "we're supposed to be ten. I wouldn't want to offend the Younger Gods."

They helped Kalten, Tynian, and Bevier to mount and then rode slowly out of the innyard into the still-dark and largely deserted streets of Paler. They proceeded at a walk to the north gate, and the gate guards hurriedly opened it for them.

"Bless you, my children," Kalten said grandly to them as he rode through.

"Did you have to do that?" Sparhawk asked him.

"It's cheaper than giving them money. Besides, who knows? My blessing might actually be worth something."

"I think he's going to get better," Kurik said.

"Not if he keeps that up, he won't," Sparhawk disagreed.

The sky to the east was growing lighter, and they moved at an easy pace along the road that ran northwesterly from Paler to Lake Venne. The land lying between the two lakes was rolling and given over largely to the growing of grain. Grand estates dotted the countryside, and here and there were villages of the long huts of the serfs. Serfdom had been abolished in western Eosia centuries before, but it still persisted here in Pelosia, since, as best as Sparhawk could tell, the Pelosian nobility lacked the administrative skills to make any other system work. They saw a few of those nobles, usually in bright satin doublets, supervising the work of the linen-shirted serfs from horseback. Despite everything Sparhawk had heard of the evils of serfdom, the workers in the fields seemed well fed and not particularly mistreated.

Berit was riding several hundred yards to the rear and he kept turning in his saddle to look back.

"He's going to wrench my armor completely askew if he keeps doing that," Kalten said critically.

"We can always stop by a smith and have it retailored for you," Sparhawk said. "Maybe we could have some of the seams let out at the same time, since you're so bent on stuffing yourself full of food every chance you get."

"You're in a foul humor this morning, Sparhawk."

"I've got a lot on my mind."

"Some people are just not suited for command," Kalten observed grandly to the others. "My ugly friend here seems to be one of them. He worries too much."

"Do you want to do this?" Sparhawk asked flatly.

"Me? Be serious, Sparhawk. I couldn't even herd geese, much less direct a body of knights."

"Then would you like to shut up and let me do it?"

Berit rode forward, his eyes narrowed and his hand slipping his ax up and down in the sling at the side of his saddle. "The Zemochs are back there, Sir Sparhawk," he said. "I keep catching glimpses of them."

"How far back?"

"About a half a mile. Most of them are hanging back, but they've got scouts out. They're keeping an eye on us."

"If we charged to the rear, they'd just scatter," Bevier advised. "And then they'd pick up our trail again."

"Probably," Sparhawk agreed glumly. "Well, I can't stop them. I don't have enough men. Let them trail along if it makes them happy. We'll get rid of them when we're all feeling a little better. Berit, drop back and keep an eye on them—and no heroics."

"I understand completely, Sir Sparhawk."

The day grew hot before noon, and Sparhawk began to sweat inside his armor.

"Am I being punished for something?" Kurik asked him, mopping his streaming face with a piece of cloth.

"You know I wouldn't do that."

"Then why am I locked up in this stove?"

"Sorry. It's necessary."

About midafternoon, when they were passing through a long, verdant valley, a dozen or so gaily dressed young men galloped from a nearby estate to bar their way. "Go no farther," one of them, a pale, pimply young fellow in a green velvet doublet and with a supercilious, self-important expression commanded, holding up one hand imperiously.

"I beg your pardon?" Sparhawk asked.

"I demand to know why you are trespassing on my father's lands." The young fellow looked around at his sniggering friends with a smugly self-congratulatory expression.

"We were led to believe that this is a public road," Sparhawk replied.

"Only at my father's sufferance." The pimply fellow puffed himself up, trying to look dangerous.

"He's showing off for his friends," Kurik muttered. "Let's just sweep them out of the way and ride on. Those rapiers they're carrying aren't really much of a threat."

"Let's try some diplomacy first," Sparhawk replied. "We really don't want a crowd of angry serfs on our heels."

"I'll do it. I've handled his sort before." Kurik rode forward deliberately, Bevier's armor gleaming in the afternoon sun and his white cape and surcoat resplendent. "Young man," he said in a stern voice, "you seem to be a bit unacquainted with the customary courtesies. Is it possible that you don't recognize us?"

"I've never seen you before."

"I wasn't talking about *who* we are. I was talking about *what*. It's understandable, I suppose. It's obvious that you're not widely travelled."

The young fellow's eyes bulged with outrage. "Not so. Not so," he objected in a squeaky voice. "I have been to the city of Venne at least twice."

"Ah," Kurik said. "And when you were there, did you perhaps hear about the Church?"

"We have our own chapel right here on the estate. I need no instruction in that foolishness." The young man sneered. It seemed to be his normal expression.

An older man in a black brocade doublet was riding furiously from the estate.

"It's always gratifying to speak with an educated man," Kurik was saying. "Have you ever by chance heard of the Knights of the Church?"

The young fellow looked a bit vague at that. The man in the black doublet was approaching rapidly from behind the group of young men. His face appeared white with fury.

"I'd strongly advise you to stand aside," Kurik continued smoothly. "What you're doing imperils your soul—not to mention your life."

"You can't threaten me—not on my father's own estate."

"Jaken!" the man in black roared, "have you lost your mind?"

"Father," the pimply young man faltered, "I was just questioning these trespassers."

"*Trespassers?*" the older man spluttered. "This is the king's highway, you jackass!"

"But—"

The man in the black doublet moved his horse in closer, rose in his stirrups, and knocked his son from the saddle with a solid blow of his fist. Then he turned to face Kurik. "My apologies, Sir Knight," he said. "My half-wit son didn't know to whom he was speaking. I revere the Church and honor her knights. I hope and pray that you were not offended."

"Not at all, my Lord," Kurik said easily. "Your son and I had very nearly resolved our differences."

The noble winced. "Thank God I arrived in time then. That idiot isn't much of a son, but his mother would have been distressed if you'd been obliged to cut off his head."

"I doubt that it would have gone that far, my Lord."

"Father!" the young man on the ground said in horrified shock. "You *hit* me!" There was blood streaming from his nose. "I'm going to tell Mother!"

"Good. I'm sure she'll be very impressed." The noble looked apologetically at Kurik. "Excuse me, Sir Knight. I think some long overdue discipline is in order." He glared at his son. "Return home, Jaken," he said coldly. "When you get there, pack up this covey of parasitic wastrels and send them away. I want them off the estate by sundown."

"But they're my *friends!*" his son wailed.

"Well, they're not mine. Get rid of them. You will also pack. Don't bother to take fine clothing, because you're going to a monastery. The brothers there are very strict, and they'll see to your education—which I seem to have neglected."

"Mother won't let you do that!" his son exclaimed, his face going very pale.

"She doesn't have anything to say about it. Your mother has never been more to me than a minor inconvenience."

"But—" The young brat's face seemed to disintegrate.

"You sicken me, Jaken. You're the worst excuse for a son a man has ever been cursed with. Pay close attention to the monks, Jaken. I have some nephews far more worthy than you. Your inheritance is not all that secure, and you could be a monk for the remainder of your life."

"You can't do that."

"Yes, actually, I can."

"Mother will punish you."

The noble's laugh was chilling. "Your mother has begun to tire me, Jaken," he said. "She's self-indulgent, shrewish, and more than a little stupid. She's turned you into something I'd rather not look at. Besides, she's not very attractive any more. I think I'll send her to a nunnery for the rest of her life. The prayer and fasting may bring her closer to heaven, and the amendment of her spirit is my duty as a loving husband, wouldn't you say?"

The sneer had slid off Jaken's face, and he began to shake violently as his world crashed down around his ears.

"Now, my son," the noble continued disdainfully, "will you do as I tell you, or shall I unleash this Knight of the Church to administer the chastisement you so richly deserve?"

Kurik took his cue from that and slowly drew Bevier's sword. It made a singularly unpleasant sound as it slid from its sheath.

The young man scrambled away on his hands and knees. "I have a dozen friends with me," he threatened shrilly.

Kurik looked the pampered boys up and down; then he spat derisively. "So?" he said, shifting his shield and flexing his sword arm. "Did you want to keep his head, my Lord?" he asked the noble politely, "as a keepsake naturally?"

"You wouldn't!" Jaken was very nearly in a state of collapse now.

Kurik moved his horse forward, his sword glinting ominously in the sunlight. "Try me," he said in a tone dreadful enough to make the very rocks shrink.

The young man's eyes bulged in horror, and he scrambled back into his saddle with his satin-dressed sycophants rushing along behind him.

"Was that more or less what you had in mind, my Lord?" Kurik asked the noble.

"It was perfect, Sir Knight. I've wanted to do that myself for years." Then he sighed. "Mine was an arranged marriage, Sir Knight," he said by way of explanation. "My wife's family had a noble title, but they were deeply in debt. My family had money and land, but our title was not impressive. Our parents felt that the arrangement was sound, but she and I scarcely speak to one another. I've avoided her whenever possible. I've solaced myself with other women, I'm ashamed to admit. There are many accommodating young ladies—if one has the price. My wife's solaced herself with that abomination you just saw. She has few other enthusiasms—aside from making my life as miserable as she possibly can. I've neglected my duties, I'm afraid."

"I have sons myself, my Lord," Kurik told him as they all rode on. "Most of them are good boys, but one has been a great disappointment to me."

Talen rolled his eyes heavenward, but didn't say anything.

"Do you travel far, Sir Knight?" the noble asked, obviously wanting to change the subject.

"We go toward Venne," Kurik replied.

"A journey of some distance. I have a summer house near the west end of my estate. Might I offer you its comfort? We should reach it by evening, and the servants there can see to your needs." He made a wry face. "I'd offer you the hospitality of the manor, but I'm afraid tonight may be a bit noisy there. My wife has a penetrating voice, and she's not going to take kindly to certain decisions I've made this afternoon."

"You're most kind, my Lord. We'll be happy to accept your hospitality."

"It's the least I can do in recompense for my son's behavior. I wish I could think of some appropriate form of discipline to salvage him."

"I've always gotten good results with a leather belt, my Lord," Kurik suggested.

The nobleman laughed wryly. "That might not be a bad idea, Sir Knight," he agreed.

They rode on through a lovely afternoon, and as the sun was just going down, they reached the "summer house," which appeared to be only slightly less opulent than a mansion. The nobleman gave instructions to the household servants and then remounted his horse. "I'd gladly stay, Sir Knight," he said to Kurik, "but I think I'd better get back home before my wife breaks every dish in the house. I'll find a comfortable cloister for her, and live out my life in peace."

"I quite understand, my Lord," Kurik replied. "Good luck."

"Godspeed, Sir Knight." And the noble turned and rode back the way they had come.

"Kurik," Bevier said gravely as they entered the marble-floored foyer of the house, "you did honor to my armor back there. I'd have had my sword through that young fellow after his second remark."

Kurik grinned at him. "It was much more fun this way, Sir Bevier."

The Pelosian noble's summer house was even more splendid on the inside than it had appeared from the exterior. Rare woods, exquisitely carved, panelled the walls. The floors and fireplaces were all of marble, and the furnishings were covered with the finest brocade. The serving staff was efficient and unobtrusive, and they saw to every need.

Sparhawk and his friends dined splendidly in a dining room only slightly smaller than a grand ballroom. "Now *this* is what I call living." Kalten sighed contentedly. "Sparhawk, why is it that *we* can't have a bit more luxury in our lives?"

"We're Knights of the Church," Sparhawk reminded him. "Poverty toughens us up."

"But do we have to have so much of it?"

"How are you feeling?" Sephrenia asked Bevier.

"Much better, thanks," the Arcian replied. "I haven't coughed up any blood since this morning. I think I'll be up to a canter tomorrow, Sparhawk. This leisurely stroll is costing us time."

"Let's go easy for one more day," Sparhawk said. "According to my map, the country beyond the city of Venne is a little rugged and very underpopulated. It's ideal for ambushes, and we're being followed. I want you and Kalten and Tynian fit to defend yourselves."

"Berit," Kurik said.

"Yes?"

"Would you do me a favor before we leave here?"

"Of course."

"First thing in the morning, take Talen out into the courtyard and search him—thoroughly. The noble who owns this place was very hospitable, and I don't want to offend him."

"What makes you think I'd steal anything?" Talen objected.

"What makes me think you wouldn't? It's just a precaution. There are a great number of small, valuable things in this house. Some of them might just accidentally find their way into your pockets."

The beds in the house were down-filled, and they were deep and comfortable. They rose at dawn and ate a splendid breakfast. Then they thanked the servants, mounted their waiting horses, and rode on out. The new-risen sun was golden, and larks whirled and sang overhead. Flute, sitting in the wagon, accompanied them on her pipes. Sephrenia seemed stronger, but, at Sparhawk's insistence, she still rode in the wagon.

It was shortly before noon when a group of perhaps fifty fierce-looking men came galloping over a nearby hill. They were booted and dressed in leather, and their heads were all shaved.

"Tribesmen from the eastern marches," Tynian, who had been in Pelosia before, warned. "Be very careful, Sparhawk. These are reckless men."

The tribesmen swooped down the hill with superb horsemanship. They had savage-looking sabers at their belts, carried short lances and wore round shields on their left arms. At a curt signal from their leader, most of them reined in so sharply that their horses' rumps skidded on the grass. With five cohorts, the leader, a lean man with narrow eyes and a scarred scalp, came forward. With ostentatious display, the advancing tribesmen moved their horses sideways, the proud stallions prancing in perfect unison. Then, plunging their lances into the earth, the warriors drew their flashing sabers with a grand flourish.

"No!" Tynian said sharply as Sparhawk and the others instinctively went for their swords. "This is a ceremony. Stand fast."

The shaved-headed men came forward at a stately walk, and then at some hidden signal, their horses all went down on their front knees in a kind of genuflection as the riders raised their sabers to their faces in salute.

"Lord!" Kalten breathed. "I've never seen a horse do that before!"

Faran's ears flicked, and Sparhawk could feel him twitching irritably.

"Hail, Knights of the Church," the leather-garbed leader intoned formally. "We salute you, and stand at your service."

"Can I handle this?" Tynian suggested to Sparhawk. "I've had some experience."

"Feel free, Tynian," Sparhawk agreed, eyeing the pack of savage men on the hill.

Tynian moved forward, holding his black horse in tightly so that its pace was measured and slow. "Gladly we greet the Peloi," the Deiran declaimed formally. "Glad also are we of this meeting, for brothers should always greet each other with respect."

"You know our ways, Sir Knight," the scar-headed man approved.

"I have been in times past on the eastern marches, Domi," Tynian acknowledged.

"What's 'Domi' mean?" Kalten whispered.

"An ancient Pelosian word," Ulath supplied. "It means 'chief'—sort of."

"Sort of?"

"It takes a long time to translate."

"Will you take salt with me, Sir Knight?" the warrior asked.

"Gladly, Domi," Tynian replied, stepping slowly down from his saddle. "And might we season it with well-roasted mutton?" he suggested.

"An excellent suggestion, Sir Knight."

"Get it," Sparhawk said to Talen. "It's in that green pack. And don't argue."

"I'd sooner bite out my tongue," Talen agreed nervously, digging into the pack.

"Warm day, isn't it?" the Domi said conversationally, sitting cross-legged on the lush turf.

"We were saying the same thing just a few minutes ago," Tynian agreed, also sitting.

"I am Kring," the scarred man introduced himself, "Domi of this band."

"I am Tynian," the Deiran replied, "an Alcione Knight."

"I surmised as much."

Talen went a bit hesitantly to where the two men sat, carrying a roast leg of lamb.

"Well-prepared meat," Kring proclaimed, unhooking a leather bag of salt from his belt. "The Knights of the Church eat well." He ripped the lamb roast in two with teeth and fingernails and handed half to Tynian. Then he held out his leather bag. "Salt, brother?" he offered.

Tynian dipped his fingers into the bag, took out a generous pinch, and sifted it over his lamb. Then he shook his fingers in the direction of the four winds.

"You are well versed in our ways, friend Tynian," the Domi approved, imitating the gesture. "And is this excellent young fellow perhaps your son?"

"Ah, no, Domi." Tynian sighed. "He's a good lad, but he's addicted to thievery."

"Ho-ho!" Kring laughed, fetching Talen a clap on the shoulder that sent the boy rolling. "Thievery is the second most honorable profession in the world—next to fighting. Are you any good, boy?"

Talen smiled thinly, and his eyes went narrow. "Would you care to try me, Domi?" he challenged, coming to his feet. "Protect what you can, and I'll steal the rest."

The warrior rolled back his head, roaring with laughter. Talen, Sparhawk noticed, was already close to him, his hands moving fast.

"All right, my young thief," the Domi chortled, holding his widespread hands out in front of him, "steal what you can."

"Thank you all the same, Domi," Talen said with a polite bow, "but I already have. I believe I've got just about everything of value you own."

Kring blinked and began to pat himself here and there, his eyes filled with consternation.

Kurik groaned.

"It may turn out all right after all," Sparhawk muttered to him.

"Two brooches," Talen catalogued, handing them over, "seven rings—the one on your left thumb is really tight, you know. A gold bracelet—have that checked. I think there's brass mixed with it. A ruby pendant—I hope you didn't pay too much for it. It's really an inferior stone, you know. Then there's this jewelled dagger, and the pommel-stone off your sword." Talen brushed his hands together professionally.

The Domi roared with laughter. "I'll buy this boy, friend Tynian," he declared. "I'll give you a herd of the finest horses for him and raise him as my own son. Such a thief I've never seen before."

"Ah—sorry, friend Kring," Tynian apologized, "but he's not mine to sell."

Kring sighed. "Could you even steal horses, boy?" he asked wistfully.

"A horse is a little hard to fit in your pocket, Domi," Talen replied. "I could probably work it out, though."

"A lad of genius," the warrior said reverently. "His father is a man of great fortune."

"I hadn't noticed that very much," Kurik muttered.

"Ah, young thief," Kring said almost regretfully, "I seem to be also missing a purse—a fairly heavy one."

"Oh, did I forget that?" Talen said, slapping his forehead. "It must have completely slipped my mind." He fished a bulging leather bag out from under his tunic and handed it over.

"Count it, friend Kring," Tynian warned.

"Since the boy and I are now friends, I will trust his integrity."

Talen sighed and fished a large number of silver coins out of various hiding places. "I wish people wouldn't do that," he said, handing the coins over. "It takes all the fun out of it."

"*Two* herds of horses?" the Domi offered.

"Sorry, my friend," Tynian said regretfully. "Let us take salt and talk of affairs."

The two sat eating their salted lamb as Talen wandered back to the wagon. "He should have taken the horses," he muttered to Sparhawk. "I could have slipped away just after dark."

"He'd have chained you to a tree," Sparhawk told him.

"I can wriggle my way out of any chain in less than a minute. Do you have any idea of how much horses like he's got are worth, Sparhawk?"

"Training this boy may take longer than we'd expected," Kalten noted.

"Will you require an escort, friend Tynian?" Kring was asking. "We are engaged in no more than a slight diversion, and we will gladly put it aside to assist our holy mother Church and her revered knights."

"Thank you, friend Kring," Tynian declined, "but our mission involves nothing we can't deal with."

"Truly. The prowess of the Knights of the Church is legendary."

"What is this diversion you mentioned, Domi?" Tynian asked curiously. "Seldom have I seen the Peloi this far west."

"We normally haunt the eastern marches," Kring admitted, ripping a large chunk of lamb off the bone with his teeth, "but from time to time over the past few generations, Zemochs have been trying to slip across the border into Pelosia. The king pays a gold half crown for their ears. It's an easy way to make money."

"Does the king demand both ears?"

"No, just the right ones. We still have to be careful with our sabers, though. You can lose the whole bounty with a misaimed stroke. Anyway, my friends and I flushed a fair-sized group of Zemochs near the border. We took a number of them, but the rest fled. They were coming this way last we saw them, and some were wounded. Blood leaves a good trail. We'll run them down and collect their ears—and the gold. It's just a question of time."

"I think I might be able to save you a bit of that, my friend," Tynian said with a broad smile. "From time to time in the last day or so, we've seen a fairly large party of Zemochs riding to our rear. It might just be that they're the ones you're seeking. In any case, though, an ear is an ear, and the king's gold spends just as sweetly, even if it chances to be mistakenly dispensed."

Kring laughed delightedly. "It does indeed, friend Tynian," he agreed. "And who knows, it could just be that there are *two* bags of gold available out here. How many are they, would you say?"

"We've seen forty or so. They're coming up the road from the south."

"They won't come much farther," Kring promised, grinning a wolflike grin. "This was indeed a fortunate meeting, Sir Tynian—at least for me and my comrades. But why didn't you and your companions turn around and collect the bounty?"

"We weren't really aware of the bounty, Domi," Tynian confessed, "and we're on Church business of some urgency." He made a wry face. "Besides, even if we did gain that bounty, our oaths would require that we hand it over to the Church. Some fat abbot somewhere would profit from our labors. I don't propose to sweat that much to enrich a man who's never done an honest day's work in his life. I'd far rather point a friend in the direction of honest gain."

Impulsively, Kring embraced him. "My brother," he said, "you are a true friend. It's an honor to have met you."

"The honor is mine, Domi," Tynian said gravely.

The Domi wiped his greasy fingers on his leather breeches. "Well, I suppose we should be on our way, friend Tynian," he said. "Slow riding earns no bounty." He paused. "Are you sure you don't want to sell that boy?"

"He's the son of a friend of mine," Tynian said. "I wouldn't mind getting rid of the boy, but the friendship's valuable to me."

"I understand perfectly, friend Tynian." Kring bowed. "Commend me to God next time you talk with Him." He vaulted into his saddle from a standing start, and his horse was running before he was even settled.

Ulath walked up to Tynian and gravely shook his hand. "You're fast on your feet," he observed. "That was absolutely brilliant."

"It was a fair trade," Tynian said modestly. "We get the Zemochs off our backs, and Kring gets the ears. No bargain between friends is fair unless both sides get something they want."

"Very, very true," Ulath agreed. "I've never heard of selling ears before, though. Usually it's heads."

"Ears are lighter," Tynian said professionally, "and they don't stare at you every time you open your saddlebags."

"Would you gentlemen *mind*?" Sephrenia said tartly. "We have children with us, after all."

"Sorry, little mother," Ulath apologized easily. "Just talking shop."

She stalked back to the wagon, muttering. Sparhawk was fairly certain that some of the Styric words she was saying under her breath were never used in polite society.

"Who were they?" Bevier asked, looking at the warriors who were rapidly disappearing toward the south.

"They're of the Peloi," Tynian replied, "nomadic horse herders. They were the first Elenes in this region. The Kingdom of Pelosia is named after them."

"Are they as fierce as they look?"

"Even fiercer. Their presence on the border was probably why Otha invaded Lamorkand instead of Pelosia. No one in his right mind attacks the Peloi."

They reached Lake Venne late the following day. It was a large, shallow body of water into which nearby peat bogs continually drained, making the water turbid and brown-stained. Flute seemed strangely agitated as they made camp some distance back from the marshy lake shore. As soon as Sephrenia's tent was erected, she darted inside and refused to come out.

"What's the matter with her?" Sparhawk asked Sephrenia, absently rubbing the ring finger on his left hand. It seemed to be throbbing for some reason.

"I really don't know," Sephrenia frowned. "It's almost as if she's afraid of something."

After they had eaten and Sephrenia had carried Flute's supper in to her, Sparhawk closely questioned each of his injured companions. They all claimed perfect health, a claim he was sure was spurious. "All right, then." He gave up finally. "We'll go back to doing it the old way. You gentlemen can have your armor back, and we'll try a canter tomorrow. No galloping; no running; and if we run into any trouble, try to hold back unless things get serious."

"He's just like an old mother hen, isn't he?" Kalten observed to Tynian.

"If he scratches up a worm, you get to eat it," Tynian replied.

"Thanks all the same, Tynian," Kalten declined, "but I've already had my supper."

Sparhawk went to bed.

It was about midnight, and the moon was very bright outside the tent. Sparhawk sat bolt upright in his blankets, jolted awake by a hideous, roaring bellow.

"Sparhawk!" Ulath said sharply from outside the tent. "Rouse the others! Fast!"

Sparhawk shook Kalten awake and pulled on his mail shirt. He grabbed up his sword and ducked out of the tent. He looked around quickly and saw that the others needed no rousing. They were already struggling into their mail and were taking up weapons. Ulath stood at the edge of camp, his round shield in place and his ax in his hand. He was looking off intently into the darkness.

Sparhawk joined him. "What is it?" he asked quietly. "What makes a noise like that?"

"Troll," Ulath replied shortly.

"Here? In Pelosia? Ulath, that's impossible. There aren't any Trolls in Pelosia."

"Why don't you go out there and explain that to *him*?"

"Are you absolutely sure it's a Troll?"

"I've heard that sound too many times to miss it. It's a Troll, all right, and he's absolutely enraged about something."

"Maybe we should build up the fire," Sparhawk suggested as the others joined them.

"It wouldn't do any good," Ulath said. "Trolls aren't afraid of fire."

"You know their language, don't you?"

Ulath grunted.

"Why don't you call to him and tell him that we mean him no harm?"

"Sparhawk," Ulath said with a pained look, "in this situation, it's the other way around. If he attacks, try to strike at his legs," he warned them all. "If you swing at his body, he'll jerk your weapons out of your hands and feed them to you. All right, I'll try to talk with him." He lifted his head and bellowed something in a horrid, guttural language.

Something out there in the darkness replied, snarling and spitting.

"What did it say?" Sparhawk asked.

"He's cursing. It may take him an hour or so to get finished. Trolls have a lot of swearwords in their language." Ulath frowned. "He doesn't really seem all that sure of himself," he said, sounding puzzled.

"Perhaps our numbers are making it cautious," Bevier suggested.

"They don't know what the word means," Ulath disagreed. "I've seen a lone Troll attack a walled city."

There was another snarling bellow from out in the darkness, this time a little closer.

"Now, what's *that* supposed to mean?" Ulath said in bafflement.

"What?" Sparhawk asked.

"He's demanding that we turn the thief over to him."

"Talen?"

"I don't know. How could Talen pick a Troll's pocket? They don't *have* pockets."

Then they heard the sound of Flute's pipes coming from Sephrenia's tent. Her melody was stern and vaguely threatening. After a moment, the beast out in the darkness howled—a sound partially of pain and partially of frustration. Then the howling faded off into the distance.

"Why don't we all go to Sephrenia's tent and kiss that little girl about the head and shoulders for a while?" Ulath suggested.

"What happened?" Kalten asked.

"Somehow she ran him off. I've never seen a Troll run from anything. I saw one try to attack an avalanche once. I think we'd better talk with Sephrenia. Something's going on here that I don't understand."

Sephrenia, however, was as puzzled as they. She was holding Flute in her arms, and the little girl was crying. "Please, gentlemen," the Styric woman said softly, "just leave her alone for now. She's very, very upset."

"I'll stand watch with you, Ulath," Tynian said as they came out of the tent. "That bellow froze my blood. I'll never get back to sleep now."

They reached the city of Venne two days later. Once the Troll had been frightened away, they neither saw nor heard any further sign of him. Venne was not a very attractive city. Because local taxes were based on the number of square feet on the ground floor of each house, the citizens had circumvented the law by building overhanging second stories. In most cases, the overhang was so extreme that the streets were like narrow, dark tunnels, even at noon. They put up at the cleanest inn they could find, and Sparhawk took Kurik and went in search of information.

For some reason, however, the word *Ghasek* made the citizens of Venne very nervous. The answers Sparhawk and Kurik received were vague and contradictory, and the citizens usually went away from them very fast.

"Over there," Kurik said shortly, pointing at a man staggering from the door of a tavern. "He's too drunk to run."

Sparhawk looked critically at the reeling man. "He could also be too drunk to talk," he added.

Kurik's methods, however, were brutally direct. He crossed the street, seized the drunkard by the scruff of the neck, dragged him to the end of the street, and shoved his head into the fountain that stood there. "Now, then," he said pleasantly, "I think we understand each other. I'm going to ask you some questions, and you're going to give me the answers—unless you can figure out a way to sprout gills."

The fellow was spluttering and coughing. Kurik pounded on his back until the paroxysm passed.

"All right," Kurik said, "the first question is, 'Where is Ghasek?'"

The drunken man's face went pasty white, and his eyes bulged in horror.

Kurik shoved his head under water again. "This is starting to make me very tired," he said conversationally to Sparhawk, looking across the bubbles coming up out of the fountain. He pulled the fellow out by the hair. "This isn't going to get any more enjoyable, friend," he warned. "I really think you ought to start to cooperate. Let's try again. Where is Ghasek?"

"N-north," the fellow choked, spewing water all over the street. He seemed to be almost sober now.

"We know that. Which road do we take?"

"Go out the north gate. A mile or so after you get out of town, the road branches. Take the left fork."

"You're doing fine. See, you're even staying sort of dry. How far is it to Ghasek?"

"A-about forty leagues." The man writhed in Kurik's iron grip.

"Last question," Kurik promised. "Why does everybody in Venne wet himself whenever he hears the name Ghasek?"

"I-it's a horrible place. Things happen there that are too hideous to describe."

"I've got a strong stomach," Kurik assured him. "Go ahead. Shock me."

"They drink blood up there—and bathe in it—and even feed on human flesh. It's the most awful place in the world. Even to mention its name brings down a curse on your head." The man shuddered and began to weep.

"There, there," Kurik said, releasing him and patting him gently on the shoulder. He gave the man a coin. "You seem to have gotten all wet, friend," he added. "Why don't you go back to the tavern and see if you can get dry?"

The fellow scurried off.

"Doesn't sound like too pleasant a place, does it?" Kurik said.

"No, not really," Sparhawk admitted, "but we're going there all the same."

Because the road they proposed to follow was reputed not to be very good, they arranged to leave the wagon with the innkeeper and rode out on horseback the next morning through shadowy streets illuminated by torches. Sparhawk had passed on the information Kurik had wrung out of the drunken man the day before, and they all looked around warily as they passed out through the north gate of Venne.

"It's probably just some local superstition," Kalten scoffed. "I've heard awful stories about places before, and they usually turned out to be about things that had happened generations before."

"It doesn't really make much sense," Sparhawk agreed. "That tanner back in Paler said that Count Ghasek's a scholar. That's not usually the sort of man who goes in for exotic entertainments. Let's stay alert anyway. We're a long way from home, and it might be a little hard to call in help."

"I'll hold back a bit," Berit volunteered. "I think we'd all feel better if we're sure those Zemochs aren't still trailing us."

"I think we can count on the Domi's efficiency," Tynian said.

"Still—" Berit said.

"Go ahead, Berit," Sparhawk agreed. "It's just as well not to take chances."

They rode at an easy canter; as the sun was rising, they reached the fork in the road. The left fork was rutted, narrow, and poorly maintained. The rain that had swept through the area for some days back had left it muddy and generally unpleasant, and thick brush lined both sides of it.

"It's going to be slow going," Ulath noted. "I've seen smoother roads, and it's not going to get better once we get up into those hills." He looked toward the low range of forested mountains lying just ahead.

"We'll do the best we can," Sparhawk said, "but you're right. Forty leagues is quite a distance, and a bad road isn't going to make it seem any shorter."

They started up the muddy road at a trot. As Ulath had predicted, it grew steadily worse. After about an hour, they entered the forest. The trees were evergreens, and they cast a somber shade, but the air was cool and damp, a welcome relief for the armored knights. They stopped briefly for a meal of bread and cheese at noon and then pressed on, climbing higher and higher into the mountains.

The region was ominously deserted, and even most of the birds seemed muted, the only exception being the sooty ravens, who seemed to croak from every tree. As evening began to settle over the gloomy wood, Sparhawk led the others some distance away from the road, and they made camp for the night.

The dismal forest had subdued even the irrepressible Kalten, and they were all very quiet as they ate their evening meal. After they had eaten, they went to their beds.

It was about midnight when Ulath woke Sparhawk to take his turn on watch.

"There seem to be a lot of wolves out there," the big Genidian said quietly. "It might not be a bad idea to put your back to a tree."

"I've never heard of a wolf attacking a man," Sparhawk replied, also speaking softly to avoid waking the others.

"They usually don't," Ulath agreed, "unless they're rabid."

"That's a cheerful thought."

"I'm glad you liked it. I'm going to bed. It's been a long day."

Sparhawk left the circle of firelight and stopped about fifty yards back in the forest to allow his eyes to adjust to the darkness. He heard the howling of wolves back off in the woods. He thought he had found the source of many of the stories that had been circulating about Ghasek. This gloomy forest alone would be sufficient to stir up the fears in superstitious people. Add to that the flocks of ravens—always a bird of ill omen—and the chill howling of packs of wolves, and it was easy to see how the stories had gotten started. Sparhawk carefully circled the camp, his eyes and ears alert.

Forty leagues. Given the worsening condition of the road, it would be unlikely that they could cover more than ten leagues a day. Sparhawk chafed at their slow pace, but there was nothing he could do about it. They had to go to Ghasek. The thought came to him that the count might very well not have found anyone who knew the whereabouts of King Sarak's grave, and that this tedious and time-consuming trek might all be for nothing. He quickly pushed that thought out of his mind.

Idly, still watching the surrounding woods, he began to wonder what his life would be like if they were successful in curing Ehlana. He had known her only as a child, but she was no longer a little girl. He had received a few hints about her adult personality, but nothing definite enough to make him feel that he really knew her. She would be a good Queen, of that he was certain, but exactly what kind of a woman was she?

He saw a movement out in the shadows and stopped, his hand going to his sword as he searched the darkness. Then he saw a pair of blazing green eyes that reflected back the light of their fire. It was a wolf. The animal stared at the flames for a long time, then turned to slink silently back into the forest.

Sparhawk realized that he had been holding his breath, and he let it out explosively. No one is ever really prepared for a meeting with a wolf, and even though he knew it was irrational, he nonetheless felt the instinctive chill.

The moon rose, casting its pale light over the dark forest. Sparhawk looked up and saw the clouds coming in. Gradually, they obscured the moon and inexorably continued to build up. "Oh, fine," he muttered. "That's all we need—more rain." He shook his head and walked on, his eyes probing the darkness around him.

Somewhat later, Tynian relieved him, and he went back to his tent.

"Sparhawk." It was Talen, and his shaking of Sparhawk's shoulder was light as he woke the big Pandion.

"Yes." Sparhawk sat up, recognizing the note of urgency in the boy's voice.

"There's something out there."

"I know. Wolves."

"This wasn't a wolf—unless they've learned to walk on their hind legs."

"What did you see?"

"It was back in the shadows under those trees. I couldn't see it very well, but it seemed to have a kind of robe over it, and the robe didn't fit very well."

"The Seeker?"

"How would I know? I only caught a glimpse of it. It came to the edge of the woods and then dropped back into the shadows. I probably wouldn't even have seen it except for the glow coming off its face."

"Green?"

Talen nodded.

Sparhawk started to swear.

"When you run out of words, let me know," Talen offered. "I'm a pretty good swearer."

"Did you warn Tynian?"

"Yes."

"What were you doing out of bed?"

Talen sighed. "Grow up, Sparhawk," he said in a tone far older than his years. "No thief ever sleeps more than two hours at a time without going out to look around."

"I didn't know that."

"You should have. It's a nervous life, but it's a lot of fun."

Sparhawk cupped his hand about the back of the young fellow's neck. "I'm going to make a normal boy out of you yet," he said.

"Why bother? I outgrew all that a long time ago. It might have been nice to run and play—if things had been different—but they weren't, and this is much more fun. Go back to sleep, Sparhawk. Tynian and I'll keep an eye on things. Oh, by the way, it's going to rain tomorrow."

But it was not raining the following morning, though murky clouds obscured the sky. About midafternoon, Sparhawk reined Faran in.

"What's the trouble?" Kurik asked him.

"There's a village down there in that little valley."

"What could they possibly be doing out here in these woods? You can't farm with all these trees in the way."

"We could ask them, I suppose. I want to talk with them anyway. They're closer to Ghasek than the people back in Venne were, and I'd like to get a little more up-to-date information. There's no point in riding into something blind if you don't have to. Kalten," he called.

"Now what?" Kalten demanded.

"Take the others and keep on going. Kurik and I are going down to that village to ask a few questions. We'll catch up with you."

"All right." Kalten's tone was abrupt and slightly surly.

"What's the matter?"

"These woods depress me."

"They're only trees, Kalten."

"I know, but do there have to be so many of them?"

"Keep your eyes open. That Seeker's out there someplace."

Kalten's eyes brightened. He drew his sword and tested its edge with his thumb.

"What have you got in mind?" Sparhawk asked him.

"This might just be the chance we've been waiting for to get that thing off our backs once and for all. Otha's bug is very skinny. One good stroke should cut it in two. I think I'll just hang back a little bit and set up an ambush of my own."

Sparhawk thought very quickly at that point. "Nice plan," he seemed to agree, "but somebody has to lead the others to safety."

"Tynian can do that."

"Maybe, but do you feel like trusting Sephrenia's well-being to somebody we've only known for six months and who's still recovering from an injury?"

Kalten called his friend a number of obscene names.

"Duty, my friend," Sparhawk said calmly. "Duty. Its stern call pulls us away from various entertainments. Just do as I asked you to do, Kalten. We'll take care of the Seeker later."

Kalten continued to swear. Then he wheeled his horse and rode off to join the others.

"You were right on the edge of a fight there," Kurik commented.

"I noticed that."

"Kalten's a good man in a fight, but he's a hothead sometimes."

Then the two of them turned their horses and rode on down the hill toward the village.

The houses were made of logs, and they had sod roofs. The villagers had made some effort to clear the trees surrounding their community, creating stump-dotted fields extending perhaps a hundred paces back from their houses.

"They've cleared the land," Kurik observed, "but about all I see are kitchen gardens. I still wonder what they're doing out here."

That question was answered as soon as they rode into the place. A number of villagers were laboriously sawing boards from logs lying atop crude trestles. Stacks of warped green lumber beside the houses explained the purpose of the village.

One of the men stopped sawing, mopping at his brow with a dirty rag. "There's no inn here," he said to Sparhawk in an unfriendly tone.

"We're not really looking for an inn, neighbor," Sparhawk said, "just some information. How much farther is it to the house of Count Ghasek?"

The villager's face went slightly pale. "Not far enough away to suit me, my Lord," he replied, eyeing the big man in black armor nervously.

"What's the trouble, friend?" Kurik asked him.

"No sensible man goes near Ghasek," the villager replied. "Most people don't even want to talk about it."

"We heard some of the same sort of thing back in Venne," Sparhawk said. "What's going on at the count's house, anyway?"

"I couldn't really say, my Lord," the man said evasively. "I've never been there. I've heard some stories, though."

"Oh?"

"People have been disappearing around there. They're never seen again, so nobody really knows for sure what happened to them. The count's serfs have been running away, though, and he's not reputed to be a hard master. Something evil is going on in his house, and all the people who live nearby are terrified."

"Do you think the count's responsible?"

"It's not very likely. The count's been away from home for the past year. He travels around a lot."

"We heard that about him." Sparhawk thought of something. "Tell me, neighbor, have you seen any Styrics lately?"

"Styrics? No, they don't come into this forest. People up here don't like them, and we make the fact well known."

"I see. How far did you say it is to the count's house?"

"I didn't say. It's about fifteen leagues, though."

"A fellow in Venne said that it was forty leagues from there to Ghasek," Kurik told him.

The villager snorted derisively. "City folk don't even know how far a league is. It can't be much over thirty from Venne to Ghasek."

"We happened to see somebody back in the woods last night," Kurik said in a mildly conversational tone. "He was wearing a black robe and had his hood up. Could that have been one of your neighbors?"

The sawyer's face went very, very pale. "Nobody around here wears that kind of clothes," he said shortly.

"Are you sure?"

"You heard me. I said nobody in this district dresses like that."

"It must have been some traveller then."

"That must be it." The villager's tone had become unfriendly again, and his eyes were a little wild.

"Thank you for your time, neighbor," Sparhawk said, turning Faran around to leave the village.

"He knows more than he's saying," Kurik observed as the two of them were passing the last houses.

"Right," Sparhawk agreed. "The Seeker doesn't own him, but he's very, very much afraid. Let's move right along. I want to catch up with the others before dark."

They overtook their friends just as the sky to the west took on the ruddy glow of sunset, and they made camp beside a silent mountain lake not far from the road.

"You think it's going to rain?" Kalten asked after they had eaten supper and were sitting around the fire.

"Don't say that," Talen said. "I only just got dry from all that rain in Lamorkand."

"It's always possible, of course," Kurik said in reply to Kalten's question. "It's the time of year for it, but I don't smell very much moisture in the air."

Berit came back from where they had picketed the horses. "Sir Sparhawk," he said quietly, "there's somebody coming."

Sparhawk came to his feet. "How many?"

"I only heard one horse. Whoever it is is coming down the road from the direction we're going." The novice paused. "He's pushing his horse very hard," he added.

"That's not too wise," Ulath grunted, "considering the dark and the condition of that road."

"Should we put out the fire?" Bevier asked.

"I think he's already seen it, Sir Bevier," Berit replied.

"Let's see if he decides to stop," Sparhawk said. "One man all by himself isn't much of a threat."

"Unless it's the Seeker," Kurik said, shaking out his chain mace. "All right, gentlemen," he said in his gruff, drill sergeant's voice, "spread out and get ready."

The knights automatically responded to that note of command. They all instinctively recognized the fact that Kurik probably knew more about close fighting than any man in the four orders. Sparhawk drew his sword, suddenly feeling an enormous pride in his friend.

The traveller reined in his horse on the road not too far from their camp. They could all hear the horse panting and gasping for breath. "May I approach?" the man out in the darkness pleaded. His voice was shrill and seemed to hover on the very brink of hysteria.

"Come on in, stranger," Kalten replied easily after a quick glance at Kurik.

The man who came riding out of the darkness was flamboyantly, even gaudily dressed. He wore a wide-brimmed, plumed hat, a red satin doublet, blue hose, and knee-length leather boots. He had a lute slung across his back; except for a small dagger at his waist, he carried no weapons. His horse lurched and staggered with exhaustion, and the rider himself appeared to be in much the same condition. "Thank God," the man said when he saw the armored knights standing around the fire. He swayed dangerously in his saddle and would have fallen had not Bevier jumped forward to catch him.

"The poor fellow seems to be just about played out," Kalten said. "I wonder what's chasing him."

"Wolves, maybe." Tynian shrugged. "I expect he'll tell us just as soon as he gets his breath."

"Get him some water, Talen," Sephrenia instructed.

"Yes, ma'am." The boy took a pail and went down to the lake.

"Just lie back for a few moments," Bevier told the stranger. "You're safe now."

"There's no time," the man gasped. "There's something of vital urgency I must tell you."

"What's your name, friend?" Kalten asked him.

"I am Arbele, a minstrel by profession," the stranger replied. "I write poetry and compose the songs I sing for the entertainment of lords and ladies. I have just come from the house of that monster, Count Ghasek."

"That doesn't sound too promising," Ulath muttered.

Talen brought the pail of water, and Arbele drank greedily.

"Take his horse down to the lake," Sparhawk told the boy. "Don't let him drink too much right at first."

"Right," Talen said.

"Why do you call the count a monster?" Sparhawk asked then.

"What else would you call a man who seals up a fair damsel in a tower?"

"Who is this fair damsel?" Bevier asked, his voice strangely intent.

"His own sister!" Arbele choked in a tone of outrage. "A lady incapable of wrongdoing."

"Did he happen to tell you why?" Tynian asked.

"He rambled out some nonsense, accusing her of foul misdeeds. I refused to listen to him."

"Are you sure about this?" Kalten's tone was skeptical. "Did you ever see the lady?"

"Well, no, not really, but the count's servants told me about her. They said that she's the greatest beauty in the district, and that the count sealed her in that tower when he returned from a journey. He drove me and all the servants from the castle, and now he proposes to keep his sister in that tower for the rest of her life."

"Monstrous!" Bevier exclaimed, his eyes afire with indignation.

Sephrenia had been watching the minstrel very closely. "Sparhawk," she said urgently, motioning him away from the fire. The two of them walked off, and Kurik followed them.

"What is it?" Sparhawk asked once they were out of earshot.

"Don't touch him," she replied, "and warn the others to avoid him as well."

"I don't quite follow."

"Something's wrong with him, Sparhawk," Kurik said. "His eyes aren't right, and he's talking a little too fast."

"He's infected with something," Sephrenia said.

"A disease?" Sparhawk shuddered back from the word. In a world where plagues were rampant, that word rang in human imagination like the clap of doom.

"Not in the sense you mean," she replied. "This is not a physical disease. Something has contaminated his mind— something evil."

"The Seeker?"

"I don't think so. The symptoms aren't the same. I've got a strong feeling that he might be contagious, so keep everybody away from him."

"He's talking," Kurik said, "and he doesn't have that wooden face. I think you're right, Sephrenia. I don't believe it's the Seeker. It's something else."

"He's very dangerous just now," she said.

"Not for long," Kurik said bleakly, reaching for his mace.

"Oh, Kurik," she said in a resigned tone of voice, "stop that. What would Aslade say if she found out you were assaulting helpless travellers?"

"We really don't have to tell her, Sephrenia."

"When will the day come when Elenes stop thinking with their weapons?" she said in exasperation. Then she said something in Styric that Sparhawk did not recognize.

"I beg your pardon?" he said.

"Never mind."

"There's a problem, though," Kurik said seriously. "If the minstrel's infectious, then Bevier's got it too. He touched him when he fell off his horse."

"I'll keep an eye on Bevier," she said. "Perhaps his armor protected him. I'll know better in a little while."

"And Talen?" Sparhawk asked. "Did he touch the minstrel when he brought him that pail of water?"

"I don't think so," she said.

"Could you cure Bevier if he's caught it?" Kurik asked.

"I don't even know what it is yet. All I know is that something has taken possession of that minstrel. Let's go back and try to keep the others away from him."

"I charge you, Knights of the Church," the minstrel was saying in strident tones, "ride forthwith to the house of the wicked count. Punish him for his cruelty, and free his beautiful sister from her undeserved punishment."

"Yes!" Bevier said fervently.

Sparhawk looked quickly at Sephrenia, and she gravely nodded to advise him that Bevier had been infected. "Stay with him, Bevier," he told the Arcian. "The rest of you, come with me."

They walked a short distance from the fire, and Sephrenia quietly explained.

"And now Bevier's got it too?" Kalten asked her.

"I'm afraid so. He's already beginning to behave irrationally."

"Talen," Sparhawk said seriously, "when you gave him that pail of water, did you touch him?"

"I don't think so," the boy replied.

"Are you feeling any urges to run around rescuing ladies in distress?" Kurik asked him.

"Me? Kurik, be serious."

"He's all right," Sephrenia said with a sound of relief in her voice.

"All right," Sparhawk said, "what do we do?"

"We ride to Ghasek as quickly as we can," she replied. "I have to find out what's causing the infection before I can cure it. We absolutely *have* to get into that castle—even if it involves force."

"We can handle that," Ulath said, "but what are we going to do about that minstrel? If he can infect others just by touching them, he's likely to come back at the head of an army."

"There's a simple way to deal with it," Kalten said, putting his hand on his sword hilt.

"No," Sephrenia said sharply. "I'll put him to sleep instead. A few days' rest might do him some good anyway." She looked sternly at Kalten. "Why is your first answer to any problem always a sword?"

"Overtrained, I guess." He shrugged.

Sephrenia began to speak the incantation, weaving the spell with her fingers and quietly releasing it.

"What about Bevier?" Tynian asked. "Wouldn't it be a good idea for him to go to sleep too?"

She shook her head. "He has to be able to ride. We can't leave him behind. Just don't get close enough to him to let him touch you. I've got problems enough already."

They walked back to the fire.

"The poor fellow's gone to sleep," Bevier reported. "What are we going to do about this?"

"Tomorrow morning, we're going to ride on to Ghasek," Sparhawk replied. "Oh, one thing, Bevier," he added. "I know you're outraged about this, but try to keep your emotions under control when we get there. Keep your hand away from your sword, and keep your tongue under control. Let's feel this situation out before we take any action."

"That's the course of prudence, I suppose," Bevier admitted grudgingly. "I'll feign illness when we get there. I'm not sure I could restrain my anger if I have to look this monstrous count in the face too many times."

"Good idea," Sparhawk agreed. "Put a blanket over our friend here, and then get to bed. Tomorrow's going to be a hard day."

After Bevier had gone to his tent, Sparhawk spoke quietly with his fellow knights. "Don't wake Bevier to stand watch tonight," he cautioned. "I don't want him getting any ideas about riding out on his own in the middle of the night."

They all nodded and went to their blankets.

It was still cloudy the following morning, a dense, gray overcast that filled the dismal wood with a kind of murky twilight. After they had finished breakfast, Kurik erected a sheet of canvas on poles over the sleeping minstrel. "Just in case it rains," he said.

"Is he all right?" Bevier asked.

"Just exhausted," Sephrenia replied evasively. "Let him sleep."

They mounted and rode back out to the rutted track. Sparhawk led them at first at a trot to warm up the horses, and then, after about a half hour, he pushed Faran into a gallop. "Keep your eyes on the road," he shouted to the others. "Let's not cripple any of the horses."

They rode hard through the murky wood, slowing briefly from time to time to rest their mounts. As the day progressed, they began to hear rumbles of thunder off to the west, and the impending storm increased their desire to reach the questionable safety of the house at Ghasek.

As they drew closer to the count's castle, they passed deserted villages that had fallen into ruin. The storm clouds roiled overhead, and the distant thunder marched steadily toward them.

Late in the afternoon, they rounded a curve and saw the large castle perched atop a crag on the far side of a desolate field where ruined houses stood huddled together as if fearful of the bleak structure glowering down at them. Sparhawk reined Faran in. "Let's not just go charging up there," he said to the others. "We don't want the people in the castle to misunderstand our intentions." He led them at a trot across the field. They passed the village and approached the base of the craggy hill.

There was a narrow track leading up the side of the crag, and they rode up it in single file.

"Gloomy-looking place," Ulath said, craning his neck to look up at the brooding structure atop the crag.

"It doesn't really help to generate much enthusiasm for this visit," Kalten agreed.

The track they followed led ultimately to a barred gate. Sparhawk reined in, leaned over in his saddle, and pounded on the gate with one steel-clad fist.

They waited, but nothing happened.

Sparhawk pounded again.

After some time, a small panel in the center of the gate slid open. "What is it?" a hollow voice demanded shortly.

"We are travellers," Sparhawk replied, "and we seek shelter from the storm which approaches."

"The house is closed to strangers."

"Open the gate," Sparhawk said flatly. "We are Knights of the Church, and failure to comply with our reasonable request for shelter is an offense against God."

The unseen man on the other side of the gate hesitated. "I must ask the count's permission," he said grudgingly in a deep, rumbling voice.

"Do so at once then."

"Not a very promising beginning, is it?" Kalten said.

"Gatekeepers sometimes take themselves too seriously," Tynian told him. "Keys and locks do strange things to some people's sense of proportion."

They waited while lightning streaked the purple sky to the west.

Then, after what seemed a very long time, they heard the rattling of a chain followed by the sound of a heavy iron bar sliding through massive rings. Grudgingly, the gate groaned open.

The man inside was huge. He wore bullhide armor, and his eyes were deep-sunk beneath heavy brows. His lower jaw protruded, and his face was bleak.

Sparhawk knew him. He had seen him once before.

## CHAPTER FOURTEEN

The corridor into which the surly gate guard led them was draped with cobwebs and dimly lighted by flickering torches set in iron rings at widely spaced intervals. Sparhawk quite deliberately lagged behind to fall in beside Sephrenia. "You recognized him too?" he whispered to her.

She nodded. "There's more going on here than we realized," she whispered back. "Be very careful, Sparhawk. This is dangerous."

"Right," he grunted.

At the far end of the cobwebbed hallway stood a large, heavy door. When their silent escort pulled it open, the rusty hinges squealed in protest. They came out at the head of a curved stairway that led down into a very large room. The room was vaulted, its walls were painted white, and the polished stone floor was as black as night. A fire burned fitfully in the arched fireplace, and the only other light came from a single candle on the table before the fire. Seated at the table was a pale-faced, gray-haired man dressed all in black. His face was melancholy and had the pallor of one who is seldom out in the sun. He looked somehow unhealthy, a victim of some obscure malaise. He was reading a large, leather-bound book by the light of his single candle.

"The people I spoke of, Master," the lantern-jawed man in the bullhide armor said deferentially in his deep, hollow voice.

"Very well, Occuda," the man at the table replied in a weary voice. "Prepare chambers for them. They will stay until the storm abates."

"It shall be as you say, Master." The big servant turned and went back up the stairs.

"Very few people travel into this part of the kingdom," the man in black informed them. "The region is desolate and unpopulated. I am Count Ghasek, and I offer you the meager shelter of my house until the weather clears. In time, you may wish that you had not found my gate."

"My name is Sparhawk," the big Pandion told him, and then he introduced the others.

Ghasek nodded politely to each. "Seat yourselves," he invited his guests. "Occuda will return shortly and prepare refreshments for you."

"You are very kind, my Lord of Ghasek," Sparhawk said, removing his helmet and gauntlets.

"You may not think so for long, Sir Sparhawk," Ghasek said ominously.

"That's the second time you've hinted at some kind of trouble within your walls, my Lord," Tynian said.

"And it may not be the last, Sir Tynian. The word 'trouble,' however, is far too mild, I'm afraid. To be quite honest with you, had you not been Knights of the Church, my gates would have remained closed to you. This is an unhappy house, and I do not willingly inflict its sorrows on strangers."

"We passed through Venne a few days ago, my Lord," Sparhawk said carefully. "All manner of rumors are going about concerning your castle."

"I'm not in the least surprised," the count replied, passing a trembling hand across his face.

"Are you unwell, my Lord?" Sephrenia asked him.

"Advancing age perhaps, and there's only one cure for that."

"We saw no other servants in your house, my Lord," Bevier said, obviously choosing his words carefully.

"Occuda and I are the only ones here now, Sir Bevier."

"We encountered a minstrel in the forest, Count Ghasek," Bevier told him almost accusingly. "He mentioned the fact that you have a sister."

"You must mean the fool called Arbele," the count replied. "Yes, I do in fact have a sister."

"Will the lady be joining us?" Bevier's tone was sharp.

"No," the count replied shortly. "My sister is indisposed."

"Lady Sephrenia here is highly skilled in the healing arts," Bevier pressed.

"My sister's malady is not susceptible to cure." The count said it with a note of finality.

"That's enough, Bevier," Sparhawk told the young Cyrinic in a tone of command.

Bevier flushed and rose from his chair to walk to the far end of the room.

"The young man seems distraught," the count observed.

"The minstrel Arbele told him some things about your house," Tynian said candidly. "Bevier's an Arcian, and they're an emotional people."

"I see," the melancholy nobleman replied. "I can imagine the kind of wild tales Arbele is telling. Fortunately, few will believe him."

"I'm afraid you're in error, my Lord," Sephrenia disagreed. "The tales Arbele tells are a symptom of a disorder that clouds his reason, and the disorder is infectious. For a time at least, everyone he encounters will accept what he says as absolute truth."

"My sister's arm grows longer, I see."

From somewhere far back in the house there came a hideous shriek, followed by peal upon peal of mindless laughter.

"Your sister?" Sephrenia asked gently.

Ghasek nodded, and Sparhawk could see the tears brimming in his eyes.

"And her malady is not physical?"

"No."

"Let us not pursue this further, gentlemen," Sephrenia said to the knights. "The subject is painful to the count."

"You're very kind, Madame," Ghasek said gratefully. He sighed, then said, "Tell me, Sir Knights, what brings you into this melancholy forest?"

"We came expressly to see you, my Lord," Sparhawk told him.

"Me?" The count looked surprised.

"We are on a quest, Count Ghasek. We seek the final resting place of King Sarak of Thalesia, who fell during the Zemoch invasion."

"The name is vaguely familiar to me."

"I thought it might be. A tanner in the town of Paler—a man named Berd—"

"Yes. I know him."

"Anyway, he told us of the chronicle you're compiling."

The count's eyes brightened, bringing life to his face for the first time since they had entered the room. "The labor of a lifetime, Sir Sparhawk."

"So I understand, my Lord. Berd told us that your research has been more or less exhaustive."

"Berd may be a bit overgenerous in that regard." The count smiled modestly. "I have, however, gathered *most* of the folklore in northern Pelosia and even in some parts of Deira. Otha's invasion was far more extensive than is generally known."

"Yes, so we discovered. With your permission, we'd like to examine your chronicle for clues that might lead us to the place where King Sarak is buried."

"Certainly, Sir Sparhawk, and I'll help you myself, but the hour grows late, and my chronicle is weighty." He smiled self-deprecatingly. "Once I begin, we could be up for most of the night. I lose all track of time once I immerse myself in those pages. Suppose we wait until morning before we begin."

"As you wish, my Lord."

Then Occuda entered, bringing a large pot of thick stew and a stack of plates. "I fed her, Master," he said quietly.

"Is there any change?" the count asked.

"No, Master. I'm afraid not."

The count sighed, and his face became melancholy again.

Occuda's skills in the kitchen appeared to be limited. The stew he provided was marginal at best, but the count was so immersed in his studies that he appeared to be indifferent to what was set before him.

After they had eaten, the count bade them good night, and Occuda led them up the stairs and down a long corridor toward the rooms he had prepared. As they approached the chambers, they heard the shrieks of the madwoman once again. Bevier suppressed a sob. "She's suffering," he said in an anguished voice.

"No, Sir Knight," Occuda disagreed. "She's completely insane, and people in her condition cannot comprehend their circumstances."

"I'd be interested to know how a servant came to be such an expert in diseases of the mind."

"That's enough, Bevier," Sparhawk said again.

"No, Sir Knight," Occuda said. "Your friend's question is pertinent." He turned toward Bevier. "In my youth, I was a monk," he said. "My order devoted itself to caring for the infirm. One of our abbeys had been converted into a hospice for the deranged, and that's where I served. I have had much experience with the insane. Believe me when I tell you that Lady Bellina is hopelessly mad."

Bevier looked a little less certain of himself, but then his face hardened again. "I don't believe you," he snapped.

"That's entirely up to you, Sir Knight," Occuda said. "This will be your chamber." He opened a door. "Sleep well."

Bevier went into the room and slammed the door behind him.

"You know that as soon as the house grows quiet, he'll go in search of the count's sister, don't you?" Sephrenia murmured.

"You're probably right," Sparhawk agreed. "Occuda, is there some way you can lock that door?"

The huge Pelosian nodded. "I can chain it shut, my Lord," he said.

"You'd better do it then. We don't want Bevier wandering around the halls in the middle of the night." Sparhawk thought a moment. "We'd better post a guard outside his door as well," he told the others. "He's got his Lochaber ax with him, and if he gets desperate enough, he might try to chop the door down."

"That could get a little tricky, Sparhawk," Kalten said dubiously. "We don't want to hurt him, but we don't want him coming at us with that gruesome ax of his either."

"If he tries to get out, we'll just have to overpower him," Sparhawk said.

Occuda showed the others to their rooms, and Sparhawk's was the last. "Will that be all, Sir Knight?" the servant asked politely as they entered.

"Stay a moment, Occuda," Sparhawk said.

"Yes, my Lord."

"I've seen you before, you know."

"Me, my Lord?"

"I was in Chyrellos some time ago, and Sephrenia and I were watching a house belonging to some Styrics. We saw you accompany a woman into that house. Was that Lady Bellina?"

Occuda sighed and nodded.

"It was what happened in that house that drove her mad, you know."

"I'd guessed as much. Can you tell me the whole story? I don't want to bother the count with painful questions, but we've got to rid Sir Bevier of his obsession."

"I understand, my Lord. My first loyalty is to the count, but perhaps you *should* know the details. At least that way you may be able to protect yourselves from that madwoman." Occuda sat down, his rugged face mournful. "The count is a scholarly man, Sir Knight, and he's frequently away from home for long periods, pursuing the stories he's been collecting for decades. His sister, Lady Bellina, is—or was—a plain, rather dumpy woman of middle years with very little prospect of ever catching a husband. This is a remote and isolated house, and Bellina suffered from loneliness and boredom. Last winter, she begged the count to permit her to visit friends in Chyrellos, and he gave her his consent, provided that I accompany her."

"I'd wondered how she got there," Sparhawk said, sitting on the edge of the bed.

"Anyway," Occuda continued, "Bellina's friends in Chyrellos are giddy, senseless ladies, and they filled her ears with stories about a Styric house where a woman's youth and beauty could be restored by magic. Bellina became inflamed with a wild desire to go to the house. Women do things for strange reasons sometimes."

"Did she in fact grow younger?"

"I wasn't permitted to accompany her into the room where the Styric magician was, so I can't say what happened in there, but when she came out, I scarcely recognized her. She had the body and face of a sixteen-year-old, but her eyes were dreadful. As I told your friend, I've worked with the insane before, so I recognize the signs. I bundled her up and brought her straight back to this house, hoping that I might be able to treat her here. The count was away on one of his journeys, so he had no way of knowing what began to happen after I got her home."

"And what was that?"

Occuda shuddered. "It was horrible, Sir Knight," he said in a sick voice. "Somehow, she was able to dominate the other servants completely. It was as if they were powerless to resist her commands."

"All except you?"

"I think the fact that I had been a monk may have protected me—either that or she didn't think I was worth the trouble."

"What exactly did she do?" Sparhawk asked him.

"Whatever it was that she encountered in that house in Chyrellos was totally evil, Sir Knight, and it possessed her utterly. She would send the servants who were her slaves out to surrounding villages by night, and they would abduct innocent serfs for her. I discovered later that she'd had a torture chamber set up in the cellar of this house. She gloried in blood and agonies." Occuda's face twisted with revulsion. "Sir Knight, she fed on human flesh and bathed her naked body in human blood. I saw her with my own eyes."

He paused and then continued. "It was no more than a week ago when the count returned to the castle. It was late one night when he arrived, and he sent me to the cellar for a bottle of wine, though he seldom drinks anything but water. When I was down there, I heard what sounded like a scream. I went to investigate, and opened the door to her secret chamber. I wish to God I never had!" He covered his face with his hands, and a racking sob escaped him. "Bellina was naked," he continued after he had regained his composure, "and she had a serf girl chained down on a table. Sir Knight, she was cutting the poor girl to pieces while the girl was still alive, and she was cramming quivering pieces of flesh into her own mouth!" Occuda made a retching sound, then clenched his teeth together.

Sparhawk never knew what impelled him to ask the question. "Was she alone in there?"

"No, my Lord. The servants who were her slaves were there as well, lapping the blood from those dank stones. And—" The lantern-jawed man hesitated.

"Go on."

"I cannot swear to this, my Lord. My head was reeling, but it seemed that at the back of the chamber there was a hooded figure all in black, and its presence chilled my soul."

"Can you give me any details about it?" Sparhawk asked.

"Tall, very thin, totally enshrouded in a black robe."

"And?" Sparhawk pressed, knowing with icy certainty what came next.

"The room was dark, my Lord," Occuda apologized, "except for the fires in which Bellina heated her torturing irons, but from that back corner I seemed to see a glow of green. Is that in any way significant?"

"It may be," Sparhawk replied bleakly. "Go on with the story."

"I ran to inform the count. At first he refused to believe me, but I forced him to go to the cellar with me. I thought at first he would kill her when he saw what she was doing. Would to God that he had! She started screeching when she saw him in the doorway and tried to attack him with the knife she'd been using on the serf girl, but I wrested it from her."

"Was that when he locked her in the tower?" Sparhawk was shaken by the horrible story.

"That was my idea, actually," Occuda said grimly. "At the hospice where I served, the violent ones were always confined. We dragged her to the tower, and I chained the door shut. She will remain there for the rest of her life if there's any way I can manage it."

"What happened to the other servants?"

"At first they made attempts to free her, and I had to kill several of them. Then, yesterday, the count heard a few of them telling a wild story to that silly fool of a minstrel. He instructed me to drive them all out of the castle. They milled around outside the gate for a while, and then they all ran off."

"Was there anything strange about them?"

"They all had absolutely blank faces," Occuda replied, "and the ones I killed died without making a sound."

"I was afraid of that. We've encountered that before."

"What happened to her in that house, Sir Knight? What drove her mad?"

"You've been trained as a monk, Occuda," Sparhawk said, "so you've probably had some theological instruction. Are you familiar with the name Azash?"

"The God of the Zemochs?"

"That's him. The Styrics in that house in Chyrellos were Zemochs, and it's

Azash who owns Lady Bellina's soul. Is there any way she could possibly have gotten out of that tower?"

"Absolutely impossible, my Lord."

"Somehow she managed to infect that minstrel, and he was able to pass it on to Bevier."

"She could not have gotten out of the tower, Sir Knight," Occuda said adamantly.

"I'll need to talk with Sephrenia," Sparhawk said. "Thank you for being so honest, Occuda."

"I told you all this in the hope that you could help the count." Occuda rose to his feet.

"We'll do what we can."

"Thank you. I'll go chain your friend's door shut." He started toward the door, then turned back. "Sir Knight," he said in a somber tone, "do you think I should kill her? Might that not be better?"

"It may come to that, Occuda," Sparhawk said frankly, "and if you do, you'll have to cut off her head. Otherwise, she'll just rise again."

"I can do that if I have to. I have an ax, and I'll do anything to spare the count more suffering."

Sparhawk put a comforting hand on the servant's shoulder. "You're a good and true man, Occuda," he said. "The count's lucky to have you in his service."

"Thank you, my Lord."

Sparhawk removed his armor and went down the corridor to Sephrenia's door.

"Yes?" she said in response to his knock.

"It's me, Sephrenia," he said.

"Come in, dear one," she said.

He entered her room. "I had a talk with Occuda," he said.

"Oh?"

"He told me what's been happening here. I'm not sure if you want to hear it."

"If I'm to cure Bevier, I'm afraid I'll have to."

"We were right," Sparhawk began. "The Pelosian woman we saw going into that Zemoch house in Chyrellos was the count's sister."

"I was sure of it. What else?"

Briefly, Sparhawk repeated what Occuda had told him, glossing over the more gory details.

"It's consistent," she said almost clinically. "That form of sacrifice is a part of the worship of Azash."

"There's more," Sparhawk told her. "When he entered the chamber in the cellar, Occuda saw a shadowy figure back in one of the corners. It was robed and hooded, and its face glowed green."

She drew in her breath sharply.

"Could Azash have more than one Seeker out there?" Sparhawk asked.

"With an Elder God, anything is possible."

"It couldn't be the same one," he said. "Nothing can be in two places at the same time."

"As I said, dear one, with an Elder God, anything is possible."

"Sephrenia," he said in a strained voice, "I hate to say it, but all this is beginning to frighten me just a little."

"And me as well, dear Sparhawk. Keep the spear of Aldreas close to you. The power of Bhelliom may protect you. Now go to bed. I need to think."

"Will you bless me before I sleep, little mother?" he asked, dropping to his knees. He suddenly felt like a small, helpless child. He gently kissed her palms.

"With all my heart, my dear one," she replied, enfolding his head in her arms and drawing him to her. "You are the best of them all, Sparhawk," she said to him, "and if you be but strong, not even the gates of Hell can prevail against you."

As he rose to his feet, Flute slid down off her bed and gravely came to him. He felt suddenly unable to move. The little girl took him by the wrists in a gentle grasp that he was powerless to resist. She turned his hands over and gently kissed each of his palms, and her kisses burned in his blood like holy fire. Shaken, Sparhawk left the room without a further word.

He slept fitfully, waking often and stirring uneasily in his bed. The night seemed interminable, and the rumble of thunder shook the very foundations of the castle. The rain the storm had brought with it clawed at the window of the room in which Sparhawk tried to sleep, and water ran in torrents from the slate roof to hammer the stones of the courtyard. It must have been well past midnight when he finally gave up. He threw off his blankets and sat moodily on the edge of the bed. What were they going to do about Bevier? He knew that the Arcian's faith was strong, but the Cyrinic Knight did not have Occuda's iron will. He was young and ingenuous, and he had the native passion of all Arcians. Bellina could use that to her advantage. Even if Sephrenia could rid Bevier of his obsessive compulsion, what guarantee would there be that Bellina could not reimpose it upon him at any time it pleased her? Although he shrank from the idea, Sparhawk was forced to admit that the course Occuda had suggested might be the only one available to them.

Then, quite suddenly, he was almost overcome by a sense of dread. Something overpoweringly evil was nearby. He rose from the bed, seeking his sword in the darkness. Then he went to the door and opened it.

The hallway outside his room was dimly lit by a single torch. Kurik sat dozing in the chair outside Bevier's room, but otherwise, the hallway was empty. Then Sephrenia's door opened, and she came hurrying out with Flute directly behind her. "Did you feel it, too?"

"Yes. Can you locate it?"

She pointed at Bevier's door. "It's in there."

"Kurik," Sparhawk said, touching his squire's shoulder.

Kurik's eyes came open immediately. "What's the trouble?" he asked.

"Something's in there with Bevier. Be careful." Sparhawk unhooked Occuda's chain, slipped the latch, and slowly pushed the door open.

The room was filled with an eerie light. Bevier lay tossing on his bed, and over him hovered the misty, glowing shape of a naked woman. Sephrenia drew in her breath sharply. "Succubus," she whispered. She immediately began an incantation, motioning sharply to Flute. The little girl lifted her pipes and began to play a melody so complex that Sparhawk could not even begin to follow it.

The glowing and indescribably beautiful woman at the bedside turned toward

the door, drawing its lips back to reveal its dripping fangs. It hissed at them spitefully and the hiss seemed overlaid by an insectlike stridulation, but the glowing figure seemed unable to move. The spell continued, and the succubus began to shriek,
clutching at its head. Flute's song grew more stern, and Sephrenia's incantation grew
louder. The succubus began to writhe, screaming imprecations so vile that Sparhawk flinched back from them. Then Sephrenia lifted one hand and spoke, surprisingly in Elene rather than Styric. "Return to the place from which you came!" she
commanded, "and venture forth no more this night!"

The succubus vanished with a disjointed howl of frustration, leaving behind it
the foul odor of decay and corruption.

## CHAPTER FIFTEEN

"How did she get out of that tower?" Sparhawk asked in a hushed voice.
"There's only one door, and Occuda's got it chained shut."

"She didn't get out," Sephrenia replied absently, her brow creased with a frown.
"I've only seen this happen once before," she added. Then she smiled a bit wryly.
"We're lucky I remembered the spell."

"You're not making any sense, Sephrenia," Kurik said. "She was right here."

"No, actually she wasn't. The succubus is not of the flesh. It's the spirit of the
one who sends it. Bellina's body is still confined in that tower, but her spirit roams
the halls of this melancholy house, infecting everything it touches."

"Bevier's lost then, isn't he?" Sparhawk asked bleakly.

"No. I've at least partially freed him of her influence. If we move quickly
enough, I can clear his mind entirely. Kurik, go find Occuda. I need to ask him
some questions."

"Right away," the squire replied, going out the door.

"Won't she come back tomorrow night and infect Bevier again?" Sparhawk
asked.

"I think there's a way to prevent that, but I've got to question Occuda to be
sure. Don't talk so much, Sparhawk. I need to think." She sat on the bed, rather absently laying her hand on Bevier's forehead. He stirred restlessly. "Oh, stop that,"
she snapped at the sleeping man. She muttered a few words in Styric, and the young
Arcian suddenly sank back into his pillow.

Sparhawk waited nervously as the small woman pondered the situation. Several
minutes later, Kurik returned with Occuda. Sephrenia rose to her feet. "Occuda,"
she began, but then seemed to change her mind. "No," she said, almost to herself.
"There's a faster way. Here's what I want you to do. I want you to think back to the
moment you opened that door in the cellar—only the moment when you opened
it. Don't dwell on what Bellina was doing."

"I don't quite understand, my Lady," Occuda said.

"You don't have to. Just do it. We don't have much time." She murmured briefly to herself and then reached up to touch his shaggy brow. She had to stand on her tiptoes. "Why are you people all so tall?" she complained. She kept her fingers lightly on Occuda's forehead for a moment and then let out an explosive breath. "Just as I thought," she said exultantly. "It *had* to be there. Occuda, where's the count right now?"

"I believe he's still in that central room, Lady. He usually reads for most of the night."

"Good." She looked at the bed and snapped her fingers. "Bevier, get up."

The Arcian rose stiffly, his eyes blank.

"Kurik," she said, "you and Occuda help him. Don't let him fall down. Flute, you go back to bed. I don't want you to see this."

The little girl nodded.

"Come along, gentlemen," Sephrenia said crisply. "We haven't much time left."

"Just exactly what are we doing?" Sparhawk asked as he followed her down the hall. For a small person she moved very fast.

"There isn't time to explain," she said. "We need the count's permission to go to the cellar—and his presence, I'm afraid."

"The cellar?" Sparhawk was baffled.

"Don't ask foolish questions, Sparhawk." She stopped and looked at him critically. "I told you to keep your hands on that spear," she scolded him. "Now go back to your room and get it."

He threw his hands helplessly in the air and turned around.

"Run, Sparhawk!" she shouted after him.

He caught up with them just as they entered the doorway that opened out onto the stairs leading down into the sunken room near the center of the castle. Count Ghasek still sat hunched over his book in the flickering light of his guttering candle. His fire had burned down to embers, and the wind from the storm outside howled fitfully in the chimney.

"You're going to ruin your eyes, my Lord," Sephrenia told him. "Put aside the book. We have things to do."

He stared at her in astonishment.

"I need to ask a favor of you, my Lord."

"A favor? Of course, Madame."

"Don't be too quick to agree, Count Ghasek—not until you know what I'm going to ask you. There's a room in the cellar of your house. I need to visit it with Sir Bevier here, and I'll need to have you accompany us. If we move quickly enough, I can cure Bevier and rid this house of its curse."

Ghasek stared at Sparhawk, his face totally baffled.

"I'd advise doing as she says, my Lord," Sparhawk told him. "You'll do it in the end anyway, and it's a lot less embarrassing if you just agree gracefully."

"Is she like this often?" the count asked, rising to his feet.

"Frequently."

"Time is passing, gentlemen," Sephrenia said, her foot tapping impatiently on the floor.

"Come with me, then," the count said, giving up. He led them up the stairs and into the cobwebby corridor. "The entrance to the cellar is this way." He pointed down a narrow side hall and then led the way again. He took a large iron key from his doublet and unlocked a narrow door. "We'll need light," he said.

Kurik took a torch down from its ring and handed it to him.

The count lifted the torch and started down a long flight of narrow stone stairs. Occuda and Kurik supported the somnolent Bevier to keep him from falling as they descended. At the foot of the stairs, the count turned to his left. "One of my ancestors considered himself to be quite a connoisseur of fine wines," he said, pointing at dusty casks and bottles lying on their sides on wooden racks back in the dimness as they passed. "I have little taste for wine myself, so I seldom come down here. It was only by chance that I happened to send Occuda down here one night, and he came upon that dreadful room."

"This is not going to be very pleasant for you, my Lord," Sephrenia warned him. "Perhaps you might want to wait outside the room."

"No, Madame," he said. "If you can endure it, I can as well. It's only a room now. What happened in it is in the past."

"It's the past which I intend to resurrect, my Lord."

He looked at her sharply.

"Sephrenia is an adept in the secrets," Sparhawk explained. "She can do many things."

"I have heard of such people," the count admitted, "but there are few Styrics in Pelosia, so I've never seen those arts performed."

"You may not wish to, my Lord," she warned him ominously. "It's necessary for Bevier to see the full extent of your sister's perversions for him to be cured of his obsession. Your presence as the owner of the house is necessary, but if you stand just outside the room, it will suffice."

"No, Madame, witnessing what happened here may stiffen my resolve. If my sister cannot be restrained by confinement, I may find it necessary to take sterner measures."

"Let's hope it doesn't come to that."

"This is the door to the room," the count said, producing another key. He unlocked the door and opened it wide. The sickening stench of blood and decaying flesh washed out over them.

By the flickering light of the torch, Sparhawk saw immediately why this chamber had inspired such horror. A rack stood in the center of the bloodstained floor, and cruel hooks jutted from the walls. He winced when he saw that many of the hooks had gobbets of blackened flesh clinging to them. On one wall hung the gruesome implements of the torturer's trade, knives, pincers, branding irons, and needle-sharp hooks. There were also thumbscrews and an iron boot, as well as assorted whips.

"This may take some time," Sephrenia said, "and we must complete the task before morning. Kurik, take the torch and hold it as high over your head as you can. Sparhawk, hold the spear in readiness. Something may try to interfere." She took Bevier's arm and led him toward the rack. "All right, Bevier," she said to him, "wake up."

Bevier blinked and looked around in confusion. "What is this place?" he said.

"You're here to watch, not to talk, Bevier," she told him crisply. She began to speak in Styric, her fingers moving rapidly in the air in front of her. Then she pointed at the torch to release the spell.

At first nothing seemed to happen, but then Sparhawk saw a faint movement near the brutal rack. The figure was dim and hazy at first, but then the torch flared up, and he could see it more clearly. It was the form of a woman, and he recognized her face. She was the Pelosian woman he had seen emerging from the Styric house in Chyrellos. Her face was also the face of the succubus that had hovered over Bevier's bed earlier this night. She was naked, and her face was exultant. In one hand she held a long, cruel knife, in the other, a hook. Gradually, another figure began to appear, strapped down on the rack. The second figure appeared to be that of a serf girl, judging from her clothing. Her face was contorted into an expression of mindless terror, and she struggled futilely with her bonds.

The woman with the knife approached the bound figure on the rack and with deliberate slowness began to cut her victim's clothing away. When the serf girl had been stripped, the count's sister methodically began on her flesh, muttering all the while in an alien Styric dialect. The serf girl was screaming, and the look of cruel exultation on Lady Bellina's face locked into a hideous grin. Sparhawk saw with revulsion that her teeth had been filed to points. He looked away, unable to watch any longer, and he saw Bevier's face. The Arcian watched in horrified disbelief as Bellina gorged herself on the girl's flesh.

When it was done, blood was running from the corners of Bellina's mouth, and her body was smeared with it.

Then the images changed. This time Bellina's victim was a male, and he writhed on one of the hooks protruding from the wall while Bellina slowly carved small chunks from his body and ate them with relish.

One after another, the procession of victims continued. Bevier was sobbing now and trying to cover his eyes with his hands.

"No!" Sephrenia said sharply, pulling his hands down. "You must see it all."

On and on the horror went as victim after victim came under Bellina's knife. The worst were all the children. Sparhawk could not bear that.

And then, after an eternity of blood and agony, it was over. Sephrenia looked intently into Bevier's face. "Do you know who I am, Sir Knight?" she asked him.

"Of course," he sobbed. "Please, Lady Sephrenia," he begged, "no more, I pray you."

"How about this man?" She pointed at Sparhawk.

"Sir Sparhawk of the Pandion Order, my brother knight."

"And him?"

"Kurik, Sparhawk's squire."

"And this gentleman?"

"Count Ghasek, the owner of this unhappy house."

"And him?" She pointed at Occuda.

"He's the count's servant, a good and honest man."

"Is it still your intention to release the count's sister?"

"Release her? Are you mad? That fiend belongs in the deepest pit in Hell."

"It's worked," Sephrenia said to Sparhawk. "We won't have to kill him now." There was a great relief in her voice.

Sparhawk cringed back from the implication in her matter-of-fact tone.

"Please, my Lady," Occuda said in a shaking voice, "can we go out of this horrible place now?"

"We're not finished yet. Now we come to the dangerous part. Kurik, take the torch to the back of the room. Go with him, Sparhawk, and be ready for anything."

Shoulder to shoulder the two slowly walked to the back of the chamber. And then in the flickering torchlight they saw the small stone idol set in a niche in the back wall. It was grotesquely misshapen and had a hideous face.

"What is it?" Sparhawk gasped.

"That is Azash," Sephrenia replied.

"Does he actually look like *that*?"

"Approximately. There are some things about him that are too horrible for any sculptor to capture."

The air in front of the idol seemed to waver, and a tall, skeletal figure in a hooded black robe suddenly appeared between the image of Azash and Sparhawk. The green glow coming out of the hood grew brighter and brighter.

"Don't look at its face!" Sephrenia warned them sharply. "Sparhawk, slide your left hand up the shaft of the spear until you're holding the blade."

He vaguely understood, and when his hand reached the blade socket, he felt an enormous surge of power.

The Seeker shrieked and flinched back from him, and the glow from its face flickered and began to fade. Grimly, step by step, Sparhawk advanced on the hooded creature, holding the spear blade out in front of him like a knife. The Seeker shrieked again and then vanished.

"Destroy the idol, Sparhawk," Sephrenia commanded.

Still holding the spear, he reached forward with one hand and took the idol from its niche. It seemed terribly heavy, and it was hot to the touch. He raised it overhead and dashed it to the floor where it shattered into hundreds of pieces.

From high up in the house came a shriek of unutterable despair.

"Done!" Sephrenia said. "Your sister is powerless now, Count Ghasek. The destruction of the image of her God has bereft her of all supernatural capabilities, and I think that, were you to look at her, you'd find that she once again appears as she did before she entered the Styric house in Chyrellos."

"I will never be able to thank you enough, Lady Sephrenia," he said with gratitude.

"Was that the same thing that's been following us?" Kurik asked.

"Its image," Sephrenia replied. "Azash summoned it when he realized that the idol was in danger."

"If it was only an image, then it wasn't really dangerous, was it?"

"Don't ever make that mistake, Kurik. The images Azash summons are sometimes even more dangerous than the real things." She looked around with distaste. "Let us leave this revolting place," she suggested. "Lock the door again, Count Ghasek—for the time being. Later on, it might be wise to wall up the entrance."

"I'll see to it," he promised.

They went back up the narrow stairs and returned to the vaulted room where they had found the count. The others had already gathered there.

"What was all that awful screaming?" Talen asked. The boy's face was pale.

"My sister, I'm afraid," Count Ghasek replied sadly.

Kalten looked warily at Bevier. "Is it safe to talk about her in front of him?" he quietly asked Sparhawk.

"He's all right now," Sparhawk answered, "and Lady Bellina has been stripped of her powers."

"That's a relief. I wasn't sleeping too well under the same roof with her." He looked at Sephrenia. "How did you manage it?" he asked. "Cure Bevier, I mean?"

"We found out how the lady was influencing others," she said. "There's a spell that temporarily counteracts that sort of thing. Then we went to a room in the cellar and completed the cure." She frowned. "There's still a problem, though," she said to the count. "That minstrel's still out there. He's infected, and the servants you sent away probably are as well. They can infect others, and they could return with a large number of people. I cannot remain here to cure them all. Our quest is far, far too important for such a delay."

"I will send for armed men," the count declared. "I have enough resources for that, and I will seal up the gates of this castle. If necessary, I will kill my sister to prevent her escape."

"You may not have to go that far, my Lord," Sparhawk told him, remembering something Sephrenia had said in the cellar. "Let's go have a look at this tower."

"You have a plan, Sir Sparhawk?"

"Let's not get our hopes up until I see the tower."

The count led them out into the courtyard. The storm had largely passed. The lightning was flickering on the eastern horizon now, and the pounding rain had diminished to intermittent tatters that raked the shiny stones of the yard. "It's that one, Sir Sparhawk," the count said, pointing at the southeast corner of the castle.

Sparhawk took a torch from beside the entryway, crossed the rainy courtyard, and began his examination of the tower. It was a squat, round structure perhaps twenty feet high and fifteen or so in diameter. A stone stairway wound halfway around the side of it to a solidly barred and chained door at the top. The windows were no more than narrow slits. There was a second door at the base of the tower, and it was unlocked. Sparhawk opened it and went inside. It appeared to be a storeroom. Boxes and bags were piled along the walls, and the room appeared dusty and unused. Unlike the tower, however, the room was not round but semicircular. Buttresses jutted out from the walls to hold up the stone floor of the chamber above. Sparhawk nodded with satisfaction and went back outside again. "What's behind that wall in this storeroom, my Lord?" he asked the count.

"There's a wooden staircase that runs up from the kitchen, Sir Sparhawk. In times when the tower had to be defended, the cooks could take food and drink to the men up there. Occuda uses it now to feed my sister."

"Do the servants you sent away know about the stairway?"

"Only the cooks knew, and they were among the ones Occuda killed."

"Better and better. Is there a door at the top of those stairs?"

"No. Just a narrow slot to push the food through."

"Good. The lady's misbehaved a bit, but I don't think any of us would want to starve her to death." He looked around at the others. "Gentlemen," he said to them, "we're going to learn a new trade."

"I don't quite follow you, Sparhawk," Tynian admitted.

"We're now going to be stonemasons. Kurik, do you know how to lay brick and stone?"

"Of course I do, Sparhawk," Kurik said disgustedly. "You should know that."

"Good. You'll be our foreman then. Gentlemen, what I'm going to suggest may shock you, but I don't think we have any choice." He looked at Sephrenia. "If Bellina ever gets out of that tower, she's probably going to go looking for Zemochs or the Seeker. Would they be able to restore her powers?"

"Yes, I'm sure they could."

"We can't allow that. I don't want that cellar ever to be used that way again."

"What are you proposing, Sir Sparhawk?" the count asked.

"We're going to wall up that door at the top of those stairs," Sparhawk replied. "Then we'll tear the stairway down and use the stones to wall in this door at the base of the tower as well. Then we'll conceal the door that leads from the kitchen to that stairway inside the tower. Occuda will still be able to feed her, but if the minstrel or those servants ever manage to get inside the castle, they'll never figure out how to get to that room up there. Lady Bellina will live out the rest of her life right where she is."

"That's a rather horrible thing to suggest, Sparhawk," Tynian said.

"Would you rather kill her?" Sparhawk asked bluntly.

Tynian's face blanched.

"That's it, then. We brick her up inside."

Bevier's smile was chill. "Perfect, Sparhawk," he said. Then he looked at the count. "Tell me, my Lord, which of the structures inside your walls can you spare?"

The count gave him a puzzled look.

"We're going to need building stone," Bevier explained. "Quite a bit of it, I think. I want the wall across that door up there good and thick."

# CHAPTER SIXTEEN

They removed their armor and put on the plain workmen's smocks that Occuda provided, and then they went to work. They knocked out a portion of the back wall of the stable, working under Kurik's direction. Occuda mixed a large tub of mortar, and they began to carry building stones up the curved stairway to the door at the top of the tower.

"Before you begin, gentlemen," Sephrenia said, "I'll need to see her."

"Are you sure of that?" Kalten asked her. "She might still be dangerous, you know."

"That's what I have to find out. I'm positive that she's powerless, but it's best to be certain, and I can't do that unless I see her."

"And I'd like to see her face one last time as well," Count Ghasek added. "I can't bear what she's become, but I did love her once."

They mounted the stairs, and Kurik pried the heavy chain away from the door with a steel bar. Then the count took yet another key and unlocked the door.

Bevier drew his sword.

"Is that really necessary?" Tynian asked him.

"It may be," Bevier replied bleakly.

"All right, my Lord," Sephrenia said to the count, "open the door."

The Lady Bellina stood just inside. Her wildly contorted face was pouchy and her neck wrinkled. Her tangled hair was streaked with gray, and her naked body sagged in unlovely folds. Her eyes were totally insane, and she pulled back her lips from her pointed teeth in a snarl of hate.

"Bellina," the count began sadly, but she hissed at him and lunged forward with her fingers extended like claws.

Sephrenia spoke a single word, pointing her finger, and Bellina reeled back as if she had been struck a heavy blow. She howled in frustration and tried to rush at them again, but suddenly stopped, clawing at the air in front of her as if at some wall that none of them could see.

"Close it again, my Lord," Sephrenia instructed sadly. "I've seen enough."

"So have I," the count replied in a choked voice and with tear-filled eyes as he closed the door. "She's hopelessly mad now, isn't she?"

"Completely. Of course she's been mad since she left that house in Chyrellos, but she's absolutely gone now. She's no longer a danger to anyone but herself." Sephrenia's voice was filled with pity. "There are no mirrors in that room, are there?"

"No. Would that pose some threat?"

"Not really, but at least she'll be spared the sight of herself. That would be too cruel." She paused thoughtfully. "There are some common weeds hereabouts, I've noticed. There's a way to extract their juices, and they have a calming effect. I'll talk with Occuda and give him instructions for putting them in her food. They won't cure her, but they'll make it less likely that she'll hurt herself. Lock the door, my Lord. I'll go back inside while you gentlemen do what needs to be done. Let me know when you're finished." Flute and Talen trailed after her as she walked back toward the castle.

"Hold it right there, young man," Kurik said to his son.

"Now what?" Talen said.

"You stay here."

"Kurik, I don't know anything about bricklaying."

"You don't have to know all that much to carry stones up those stairs."

"You're not serious!"

Kurik reached for his belt, and Talen hurried over to the pile of squared-off stones at the back of the stable.

"Good lad there," Ulath noted. "He grasps reality almost immediately."

Bevier insisted upon being in the forefront of their work. The young Cyrinic laid building stones almost in a frenzy.

"Keep them level," Kurik barked at him. "This is a permanent structure, so let's make a workmanlike job of it."

In spite of himself, Sparhawk laughed.

"Something amusing, my Lord?" Kurik asked him coldly.

"No. I just remembered something, that's all."

"You'll have to share it with us later. Don't just stand there, Sparhawk. Help Talen carry stones."

The embrasure into which the door was set was quite thick, since this tower was a part of the castle's fortifications. They built one wall flush against the door as the count's sister shrieked insanely inside and pounded wildly against the door that they were sealing. Then they began a second wall tightly against the first. It was midmorning when Sparhawk went into the castle to tell Sephrenia that they had finished.

"Good," she said. The two of them went back out into the courtyard. The rain had ceased now, and the sky had begun to clear. Sparhawk looked upon that as a good omen. He led Sephrenia to the stair that half encircled the tower.

"Very nice, gentlemen," Sephrenia called up to the others, who were putting the finishing touches on the wall they had constructed. "Now, come down from there. I have one last thing to do."

They trooped down, and the small woman went on up. She began to chant in Styric. When she released the spell, the fresh-built wall seemed to shimmer for a moment. Then the shimmering was gone. She came back down. "All right," she said, "you can knock down the stairs now."

"What did you do?" Kalten asked curiously.

She smiled. "Your work was much better than you might have thought, dear one," she told him. "The wall you built is totally impregnable now. That minstrel or the servants can pound on it with sledges until they're old and gray without damaging it in the slightest."

Kurik, who had gone back up the steps, leaned out and looked down at them. "The mortar's completely dry," he reported. "That usually takes days."

Sephrenia pointed at the door at the base of the tower. "Let me know when you finish this one. It's a bit damp and chilly out there. I think I'll go back inside where it's warm."

The count, who had been more saddened by the necessary entombment of his sister than he had readily admitted, accompanied her back inside while Kurik instructed his makeshift work crew on how to proceed.

It took them most of the rest of the day to knock down the stone stairway leading to the now-walled-in upper door and to seal off the lower one. Then Sephrenia came out, repeated the spell, and went back into the castle.

Sparhawk and the others adjourned to the kitchen, which was located in a wing of the castle abutting the tower.

Kurik considered the small door leading to the inside staircase.

"Well?" Sparhawk asked him.

"Don't rush me, Sparhawk."

"It's getting late, Kurik."

"Do you want to do this?"

Sparhawk closed his mouth and watched without saying a word as Talen slipped away. The boy looked tired, and Kurik was a hard taskmaster. Sparhawk was like that on occasion.

Kurik consulted with Occuda for a few moments, then looked at his mortar-spattered crew. "Time to learn a new trade, gentlemen," he said. "You're now going to become carpenters. We're going to build a china cabinet out from that door. The hinges will still work, and I can fashion a hidden latch. The door will be completely concealed." He thought a moment, cocking his head to listen to the muffled shrieks coming from above. "I think I'll need some quilts, Occuda," he said thoughtfully. "We'll nail them to the other side of the door to keep the noise from being too loud in here."

"Good idea," Occuda agreed. "With no other servants around, I'll be spending a fair amount of time in here, and that screaming might get on my nerves."

"That's not the only reason we're doing it, but that's all right. Very well, gentlemen, let's get to work." Kurik grinned. "I'll make useful people out of you all yet," he said.

When they were done, the china cabinet was a solid piece of work. Kurik rather liberally laid a dark stain over it, then stepped back and viewed the new woodwork critically. "Wax it a couple times after the stain dries," he said to Occuda, "and then scuff it up a bit. You'd probably better scratch it in a few places as well and blow dust into the corners. Then load it with crockery. Nobody will ever know that it hasn't been here for a century or more."

"That is a very good man you've got there, Sparhawk," Ulath noted. "Would you consider selling him?"

"His wife would kill me," Sparhawk replied. "Besides, we don't sell people in Elenia."

"We're not *in* Elenia."

"Why don't we go back to that main room?"

"Not just yet, Sir Knights," Kurik said firmly. "First you have to sweep the sawdust up from the floor and put the tools away."

Sparhawk sighed and went looking for a broom.

After they had cleaned up the kitchen, they washed the mortar and sawdust off themselves, changed back into tunics and hose, and returned to the large room with the vaulted ceiling, where they found the count and Sephrenia deep in conversation while Talen and Flute sat not far away. The boy appeared to be teaching the little girl how to play draughts.

"You look much neater now," Sephrenia told them approvingly. "You were all really very messy out there in the courtyard."

"You can't lay brick or stone without getting mud on you." Kurik shrugged.

"I seem to have picked up a blister," Kalten mourned, looking at the palm of his hand.

"It's the first honest work he's done since he was knighted," Kurik said to the count. "With a little training, he might not make a bad carpenter, but the rest of them have a long way to go, I'm afraid."

"How did you conceal the door in the kitchen?" the count asked him.

"We built a china cabinet against it, my Lord. Occuda's going to do a few things to it to make it look old and then fill it with dishes. We padded the back of it to muffle the sound of your sister's screaming."

"Is she still doing that?" The count sighed.

"It will not diminish as the years go by, my Lord," Sephrenia told him. "I'm afraid she'll scream until the day she dies. When she stops, you'll know that it's over."

"Occuda's fixing us something to eat," Sparhawk said to the count. "It's going to take him awhile, so this might not be a bad time to have a look at the chronicle you've compiled."

"Excellent idea, Sir Sparhawk," the count said, rising from his chair. "Will you excuse us, Madame?"

"Of course."

"Perhaps you might care to accompany us?"

She laughed. "Ah, no, my Lord. I'd be of no use in a library."

"Sephrenia doesn't read," Sparhawk explained. "It has something to do with her religion, I think."

"No," she disagreed. "It has to do with language, dear one. I don't want to get into the habit of thinking in Elene. It might interfere at some point when I need to think—and speak—very rapidly in Styric."

"Bevier, Ulath, why don't you come with the count and me?" Sparhawk suggested. "Between you, you might be able to fill in some details that will help him pinpoint the story we need."

They went back up the stairs and left the room. The three knights followed the count through the dusty hallways of the castle until they reached a door in the west wing. The count opened the door and led them into a dark room. He fumbled around on a large table for a moment, took up a candle, and went back into the hallway to light it from the torch burning outside.

The room was not large, and it was crammed with books. They stood on shelves stretching from floor to ceiling and were piled in the corners.

"You are well read, my Lord," Bevier said to him.

"It's what scholars do, Sir Bevier. The soil hereabouts is poor—except for growing trees—and the cultivation of trees is not a very stimulating activity for a civilized man." He looked around fondly. "These are my friends," he said. "I'll need their companionship now more than ever, I'm afraid. I won't be able to leave this house ever again. I'll have to stay here to guard my sister."

"The insane don't usually live for very long, my Lord," Ulath assured him. "Once they go mad, they begin to neglect themselves. I had a cousin who lost her mind one winter. She was gone by spring."

"It's a painful thing to hope for the death of a loved one, Sir Ulath, but God help me, I find that I do." The count put his hand on a foot-thick stack of unbound paper lying on his desk. "My life's work, gentlemen." He seated himself. "To business then. Exactly what are we looking for?"

"The grave of King Sarak of Thalesia," Ulath told him. "He didn't reach the battlefield down in Lamorkand, so we assume he fell in some skirmish up here in Pelosia or in Deira—unless his ship was lost at sea."

Sparhawk had never thought of that. The possibility that Bhelliom lay at the bottom of the Straits of Thalesia or the Sea of Pelos chilled him.

"Can you generalize a bit?" the count asked. "Which side of the lake was the king's destination? I've broken my chronicle down by districts to give it some organization."

"In all probability, King Sarak was bound for the east side," Bevier replied. "That's where the Thalesian army engaged the Zemochs."

"Are there any clues at all about where his ship landed?"

"Not any that I've ever heard," Ulath admitted. "I've made a few guesses, but they could be off by a hundred leagues or so. Sarak might have sailed to some seaport along the north coast, but Thalesian ships don't always do that. We're reputed to be pirates in some quarters, and Sarak might have wanted to avoid the tiresome questions and just driven his prow up onto some deserted beach."

"That makes it a little more difficult," Count Ghasek said. "If I knew where he'd landed, I'd know which districts he might have passed through. Does Thalesian tradition provide any description of the king?"

"Not in very much detail," Ulath replied, "only that he was about seven feet tall."

"That helps a bit. The common people probably wouldn't have known his name, but a man of that size would have been remembered." He began to leaf through his manuscript. "Could he possibly have landed on the north coast of Deira?" he asked.

"It's possible, but unlikely," Ulath said. "Relations between Deira and Thalesia were a bit strained in those days. Sarak probably wouldn't have put himself in a position to have been captured."

"Let's begin up around the port of Apalia then. The shortest route to the east side of Lake Randera would run south from there." He began to leaf through the pages in front of him. He frowned. "There doesn't seem to be anything useful here," he said. "How large was the king's party?"

"Not very sizeable," Ulath rumbled. "Sarak left Emsat in a hurry, and he only took a few retainers with him."

"All of the accounts I picked up in Apalia mention large bodies of Thalesian troops. Of course, it could be as you suggested, Sir Ulath. King Sarak might have landed on some lonely beach and bypassed Apalia entirely. Let's try the port of Nadera before we start combing beaches and isolated fishing villages." He consulted a map and then turned to a place about halfway through the manuscript and began to skim through it. "I think we've got something!" he exclaimed with a scholar's enthusiasm. "A peasant up near Nadera told me about a Thalesian ship that slipped past the city during the night early in the campaign and sailed several leagues up the river before she landed. A number of warriors disembarked, and one of them stood head and shoulders above the rest. Was there anything unusual about Sarak's crown?"

"It had a large blue jewel on top of it," Ulath said, his face intent.

"That was him, then," the count said exultantly. "The story makes particular mention of that jewel. They say that it was the size of a man's fist."

Sparhawk let out an explosive breath. "At least Sarak's ship didn't sink at sea," he said with relief.

The count took a length of string and stretched it diagonally across the map. Then he dipped his pen into his inkwell and made a number of notes. "All right, then," he said crisply. "Assuming King Sarak took the shortest course from Nadera to the battlefield, he'd have passed through the districts on this list. I've done research in all of them. We're getting closer, Sir Knights. We'll track down this king of yours yet." He began to leaf through rapidly. "No mention of him here," he muttered, half to himself, "but there weren't any engagements in that district." He read on, his lips pursed. "Here!" he said, his face breaking into a smile of triumph. "A group of Thalesians rode through a village twenty leagues to the north of Lake Venne. Their leader was a very large man wearing a crown. We're narrowing it down."

Sparhawk found that he was actually holding his breath. He had been on many missions and quests in his life, but this searching out a trail through paper had a strange excitement to it. He began to understand how a man could devote his life to scholarship with absolute contentment.

"And here it is!" the count said excitedly. "We've found him."

"Where?" Sparhawk demanded eagerly.

"I'll read you the entire passage," the count replied. "You understand, of course, that I've cast the account in more gentlemanly language that that of the man who told it to me." He smiled. "The language of peasants and serfs is colorful, but hardly suitable for a scholarly work." He squinted at the page. "Oh, yes. Now I remember. This fellow was a serf. His master told me that the fellow liked to tell stories. I found him breaking up clods with a mattock in a field near the east side of Lake Venne. This is what he told me:

" 'It was early in the campaign, and the Zemochs under Otha had penetrated the eastern border of Lamorkand and were devastating the countryside as they marched. The western Elenian kings were rushing to meet them with all the forces they could muster, and large bodies of troops were crossing into Lamorkand from the west, but they were primarily farther south than Lake Venne. The troops coming down from the north were mostly Thalesians. Even before the Thalesian army landed, however, an advance party of them rode south past Lake Venne.

" 'Otha, as we all know, had sent out skirmishers and patrols well in advance of his main force. It was one of those patrols that intercepted the party of Thalesians mentioned above at a place called Giant's Mound.' "

"Was the place named before or after the battle?" Ulath asked.

"It almost had to have been after," the count replied. "Pelosians don't erect burial mounds. That's a Thalesian custom, isn't it?"

"Right, and the word *giant* describes Sarak rather well, wouldn't you say?"

"Exactly my thought. There's more, though." The count continued to read. " 'The engagement between the Thalesians and the Zemochs was short and very savage. The Zemochs vastly outnumbered the small band of northern warriors and soon swarmed them under. Among the last to fall was the leader, a man of enormous proportions. One of his retainers, though sorely wounded, took something from his fallen leader's body and fled west toward the lake with it. There is no clear account of what it was that he took or what he did with it. The Zemochs pursued the retainer hotly, and he died of his wounds on the shore of the lake. However, a column of Alcione Knights, men who had been returned to their mother house in Deira to recuperate from wounds received in the campaign in Rendor, happened by on their way to Lake Randera and exterminated the Zemoch patrol to the last man. They buried the faithful retainer and rode on, by purest chance missing the site of the original engagement.

" 'As it happened, a sizeable force of Thalesians had been following the first party by no more than a day. When the local peasants informed them of what had transpired, they buried their countrymen and erected the mound over their graves. This second Thalesian force never reached Lake Randera, since they were ambushed two days later, and all were slain.' "

"And that explains why no one ever knew what had happened to Sarak," Ulath said. "There was no one left alive to tell anybody about it."

"This retainer," Bevier mused, "might it have been the king's crown he took?"

"It's possible," Ulath conceded. "More likely, though, it would have been his sword. Thalesians put great value on royal swords."

"It won't be hard to find out," Sparhawk said. "We'll go to Giant's Mound and Tynian can raise Sarak's ghost. He'll be able to tell us what happened to his sword—and his crown."

"Here's something odd," the count said. "I remember that I almost didn't write it down because it happened *after* the battle. The serfs have been seeing a monstrously deformed shape in the marshes around Lake Venne for centuries now."

"Some swamp creature?" Bevier suggested. "A bear perhaps?"

"I think that serfs would recognize a bear," the count said.

"Maybe a moose," Ulath said. "The first time I ever saw a moose, I couldn't believe anything could get that big, and a moose hasn't got the prettiest face in the world.".

"I remember that the serfs said that the thing walks on its hind legs."

"Could it possibly be a Troll?" Sparhawk asked. "That one who was roaring outside our camp down by the lake?"

"Did the serfs describe it as shaggy and very tall?" Ulath asked.

"It's shaggy, right enough, but they say it's squat, and its limbs are all twisted."

Ulath frowned. "That doesn't sound like any Troll I've ever heard about—except maybe—" His eyes suddenly went wide. "Ghwerig!" he shouted, snapping his fingers. "It *has* to be Ghwerig. That nails it down, Sparhawk. Ghwerig's looking for Bhelliom, and he knows right where to look."

"I think we'd better go back to Lake Venne," Sparhawk said, "and just as fast as we can. I don't want Ghwerig to find Bhelliom before I do. I definitely don't want to have to wrestle him for it."

## CHAPTER SEVENTEEN

"I am eternally in your debt, my friends," Ghasek said to them in the castle courtyard the next morning as they were preparing to leave.

"And we are in yours as well, my Lord," Sparhawk assured him. "Without your aid, we'd have had no chance of finding what we seek."

"Godspeed then, Sir Sparhawk," Ghasek said, shaking the big Pandion's hand warmly.

Sparhawk led the way out of the courtyard and back down the narrow track to the foot of the crag.

"I wonder what's going to happen to him," Talen said rather sadly as they rode along.

"He has no choice," Sephrenia said. "He has to stay there until his sister dies. She's no longer a danger, but she still has to be guarded and cared for."

"I'm afraid the rest of his life is going to be very lonely." Kalten sighed.

"He has his books and chronicles," Sparhawk disagreed. "That's all the company a scholar really needs."

Ulath was muttering under his breath.

"What's the trouble?" Tynian asked him.

"I should have known that the Troll at Lake Venne was there for some specific reason," Ulath replied. "I could have saved us some time if I'd investigated."

"Would you have recognized Ghwerig if you'd seen him?"

Ulath nodded. "He's dwarfed, and there aren't very many dwarfed Trolls about. She-Trolls usually eat deformed cubs as soon as they're born."

"That's a brutal practice."

"Trolls aren't famous for their gentle dispositions. They don't even get along with each other most of the time."

The sun was very bright that morning, and the birds sang in the bushes near the deserted village in the center of the field below Count Ghasek's castle. Talen turned aside to ride into the village.

"There won't be anything in there to steal," Kurik called after him.

"Just curious is all," Talen called back. "I'll catch up with you in a couple of minutes."

"Do you want me to go get him?" Berit asked.

"Let him look around," Sparhawk said. "He'll complain all day if we don't."

Then Talen came galloping out of the village. His face was deathly pale, and his eyes were wild. When he reached them, he tumbled from his horse and lay on the ground retching and unable to speak.

"We'd better go have a look," Sparhawk said to Kalten. "The rest of you wait here."

The two knights rode warily into the deserted village with their lances at the ready.

"He went this way," Kalten said quietly, pointing to the tracks of Talen's horse in the muddy street with the tip of his lance.

Sparhawk nodded, and they followed the tracks to a house that was somewhat larger than the others in the village. The two dismounted, drew their swords and entered.

The rooms inside were dusty and devoid of any furniture. "Nothing at all in here," Kalten said. "I wonder what frightened him so much."

Sparhawk opened the door to a room at the back of the house and looked inside. "You'd better go get Sephrenia," he said bleakly.

"What is it?"

"A child. It's not alive, and it's been dead for a long time."

"Are you sure?"

"Look for yourself."

Kalten looked into the room and made a gagging sound. "Are you sure you want her to see that?" he asked.

"We need to know what happened."

"I'll go get her then."

The two went back outside. Kalten remounted and rode out to where the others waited while Sparhawk stood near the door of the house. A few minutes later, the blond knight returned with Sephrenia.

"I told her to leave Flute with Kurik," Kalten said. "We wouldn't want her to see what's in there."

"No," Sparhawk replied somberly. "Little mother," he apologized to Sephrenia, "this will not be pleasant."

"Few things are," she said resolutely.

They took her inside the house to that back room.

She took one quick look and then turned aside. "Kalten," she said, "go dig a grave."

"I don't have a shovel," he objected.

"Then use your hands!" Her tone was intense, almost savage.

"Yes, Sephrenia." He seemed awed by her uncharacteristic vehemence. He left the house quickly.

"Oh, poor thing," Sephrenia mourned, hovering over the desiccated little body.

The body of the child was withered and dry. Its skin was gray, and its sunken eyes were open.

"Bellina again?" Sparhawk asked. His voice seemed loud, even to himself.

"No," she replied. "This is the work of the Seeker. This is how it feeds. Here," she pointed at dry puncture marks on the child's body, "and here, here, and here. This is where the Seeker fed. It draws out the body's fluids and leaves only a dry husk."

"Not anymore," Sparhawk said, his fist closing about the haft of Aldreas' spear. "The next time we meet, it dies."

"Can you afford to do that, dear one?"

"I can't afford not to. I'll avenge this child—against the Seeker or Azash or even against the gates of Hell itself."

"You're angry, Sparhawk."

"Yes. You could say that." It was stupid and served no purpose, but Sparhawk suddenly tore his sword from its scabbard and destroyed an unoffending wall with it. It didn't accomplish anything, but it made him feel a little better.

The others came silently down into the village and to the open grave Kalten had grubbed out of the earth with his bare hands. Sephrenia came out of the house with the dry body of the child in her arms. Flute came forward with a light linen cloth, and the two carefully wrapped the dead child in it. Then they deposited it in the rude grave.

"Bevier," Sephrenia said, "would you? This is an Elene child, and you are the most devout among these knights."

"I am unworthy." Bevier was weeping openly.

"Who *is* worthy, dear one?" she said. "Will you send this unknown child into the darkness alone?"

Bevier stared at her and then fell to his knees beside the grave and began to recite the ancient prayer for the dead of the Elene church.

Rather peculiarly, Flute came up beside the kneeling Arcian. Her fingers gently wove through his curly blue-black hair in a strangely comforting way. For some reason, Sparhawk began to feel that the strange little girl might be far, far older than any of them realized. Then she raised her pipes. The hymn was an ancient one, almost at the core of the Elene faith, but there was a minor Styric overtone to it. Briefly, in the sound of the little girl's song, Sparhawk began to perceive some unbelievable possibilities.

When the burial was complete, they mounted and rode on. They were all very quiet for the rest of that day, and they stopped for the night at the campsite beside the small lake where they had encountered the wandering minstrel. The man was gone.

"I was afraid of that," Sparhawk said. "It was too much to hope that he'd still be here."

"Maybe we'll catch up with him farther south," Kalten suggested. "That horse of his wasn't in very good shape."

"What can we do about him even if we do catch him?" Tynian said. "You weren't planning to kill him, were you?"

"Only as a last resort," Kalten replied. "Now that Sephrenia knows how Bellina influenced him, she could probably cure him."

"Your confidence is very nice, Kalten," she said, "but it might be misplaced."

"Will the spell she put on him ever wear off?" Bevier asked.

"To some degree. He'll grow less desperate as time goes on, but he'll never be entirely free of it. It might even make him write better poetry, though. The important thing is that he'll grow less and less infectious. Unless he meets a fair number of people in the next week or so, he won't be much of a danger to the count, and neither will those servants."

"That's something at least," the young Cyrinic said. He frowned slightly. "Since I was already infected, why did that creature come to me that night? Wasn't that just a waste of her time?" Bevier seemed still strongly shaken by the funeral service for the dead child.

"It was for reinforcement, Bevier," she told him. "You were agitated, but you wouldn't have gone so far as to attack your companions. She had to make sure you'd go to any lengths to free her from that tower."

As they were setting up their night's camp, something occurred to Sparhawk. He went over to where Sephrenia sat by the fire with her teacup in her hands. "Sephrenia," he said, "what's Azash up to? Why is he suddenly going out of his way to corrupt Elenes? He's never done that before, has he?"

"Do you remember what the ghost of King Aldreas said to you that night in the crypt?" she said. "That the time had come for Bhelliom to re-emerge?"

"Yes."

"Azash knows that too, and he's growing desperate. I'd guess that he's found that his Zemochs aren't reliable. They follow orders, but they're not very bright. They've been digging up that battlefield for centuries now and they just keep plowing over the same ground. We've found out more about Bhelliom's location in the past few weeks than they've found out in the past five hundred years."

"We were lucky."

"That's not entirely true, Sparhawk. I know that I tease you sometimes about Elene logic, but that was precisely what's gotten us so close to Bhelliom. A Zemoch is incapable of logic. That's Azash's weakness. A Zemoch doesn't think because he doesn't have to. Azash does all his thinking for him. That's why Azash so desperately needs Elene converts. He doesn't need their adoration; he needs their minds. He has Zemochs all over the western kingdoms gathering old stories—in the same way that we did. I think he believes that one of them will stumble over the right story and that then his Elene converts will be able to piece together the meaning of it."

"That's the long way around, isn't it?"

"Azash has time. He's not pressed by the same sense of urgency that we are."

Later that night, Sparhawk was standing watch some distance away from the fire, looking out over the small lake that glittered in the moonlight. Again, the howls of wolves echoed back in the dismal woods, but now for some reason the sound did not seem so ominous. The ghastly spirit that had haunted this forest was locked away forever, and the wolves were only wolves now and not harbingers of evil. The Seeker, of course, was an entirely different matter. Grimly Sparhawk promised himself that the next time they encountered it, he would bury the spear of Aldreas in the hideous creature.

"Sparhawk, where are you?" It was Talen. He spoke quietly and stood near the fire peering out into the darkness.

"Over here."

The boy came toward him, putting his feet down carefully to avoid hidden obstructions on the ground.

"What's the problem?" Sparhawk asked him.

"I couldn't sleep. I thought you might like some company."

"I appreciate that, Talen. Standing watch is a lonely business."

"I'm certainly glad to be away from that castle," Talen said. "I've never been so scared in my life."

"I was a little nervous myself," Sparhawk admitted.

"Do you know something? There were all sorts of very nice things in Ghasek's castle, and I didn't once think of stealing any of them. Isn't that odd?"

"Maybe you're growing up."

"I've known some very old thieves," Talen disagreed. Then he sighed disconsolately.

"Why so mournful, Talen?"

"I wouldn't tell just anyone this, Sparhawk, but it's not as much fun as it used to be. Now that I know I can take just about anything I want from almost anybody, the thrill has sort of gone out of it."

"Maybe you should look for another line of work."

"What else am I suited for?"

"I'll give it some thought and let you know what I come up with."

Talen laughed suddenly.

"What's so funny?" Sparhawk asked him.

"I might have just a little trouble getting references," the boy replied, still laughing. "My customers didn't usually know they were doing business with me."

Sparhawk grinned. "It could be a problem," he agreed. "We'll work something out."

The boy sighed again. "It's almost over, isn't it, Sparhawk? We know where that king's buried now. All we have left to do is go dig up his crown, and then we'll go back to Cimmura. You'll go to the palace, and I'll go back to the streets."

"I don't think so," Sparhawk said. "Maybe we can come up with an alternative to the streets."

"Maybe, but the minute it gets tedious, I'll just run away again. I'm going to miss all this, you know? There've been a few times when I was so scared I almost wet myself, but there have been good times, too. Those are the ones I'll remember."

"At least we gave you something." Sparhawk put his hand on the boy's shoulder. "Go back to bed, Talen. We'll be getting up early tomorrow."

"Whatever you say, Sparhawk."

They set out at dawn, riding carefully along the rutted road to avoid injury to the horses. They passed the woodcutters' village without stopping and pressed on.

"How far do you make it?" Kalten asked about midmorning.

"Three, maybe four more days—five more at the most," Sparhawk replied. "Once we get out of this forest, the roads improve and we'll make better time."

"Then all we have to do is find Giant's Mound."

"That shouldn't be much of a problem. From what Ghasek said, the local peasantry uses it as a landmark. We'll ask around."

"Then we get to start digging."

"It's not really the sort of thing you want to have somebody do for you."

"Do you remember what Sephrenia said at Alstrom's castle back in Lamorkand?" Kalten said seriously. "The business about Bhelliom's re-emergence ringing through the whole world?"

"Vaguely," Sparhawk replied.

"Then the minute we dig it up, Azash is going to know about it, and the road back to Cimmura could be lined on both sides with Zemochs. It could be a very nervous trip."

Ulath was riding directly behind them. "Not really," he disagreed. "Sparhawk's already got the rings. I can teach him a few words in the language of the Trolls. Once he's got Bhelliom in his hands, there's almost nothing he won't be able to do. He'll be able to bowl over whole regiments of Zemochs."

"Is it really that powerful?"

"Kalten, you have no idea. If even half the stories are true, Bhelliom can do almost anything. Sparhawk could probably stop the sun with it, if he wanted to."

Sparhawk looked back over his shoulder at Ulath. "Do you have to know Troll language to use Bhelliom?" he asked.

"I'm not really sure," Ulath replied, "but they say that it's infused with the power of the Troll-Gods. They might not respond to words spoken in Elene or Styric. The next time I talk with a Troll-God, I'll ask him."

They camped in the forest again that night. After supper, Sparhawk walked away from the fire to do some thinking. Bevier quietly joined him. "Will we stop in Venne when we reach it?" the Cyrinic asked.

"More than likely," Sparhawk replied. "I doubt that we'd be able to get much farther tomorrow."

"Good. I'll need to find a church."

"Oh?"

"I've been contaminated by evil. I need to pray for a while."

"It wasn't really your fault, Bevier. It could have happened to any one of us."

"But it was me, Sparhawk," Bevier sighed. "The witch probably sought me out because she knew that I'd be susceptible."

"Nonsense, Bevier. You're the most devout man I've ever met."

"No," Bevier disagreed sadly. "I know my own weaknesses. I am powerfully attracted to members of the fair sex."

"You're young, my friend. What you feel is only natural. It subsides in time— or so I'm told."

"Do you still feel those urges? I'd hoped that by the time I reached your age, they would no longer trouble me."

"It doesn't work exactly that way, Bevier. I've known some very old men whose heads could still be turned by a pretty face. It's part of being human, I suppose. If God didn't want us to feel that way, He wouldn't permit it. Patriarch Dolmant explained it to me once when I was having a problem with it. I'm not sure I entirely believed him, but it made me feel a little less guilty."

Bevier chuckled. "You, Sparhawk? This is a side of you I hadn't seen. I thought you were totally consumed with your sense of duty."

"Not entirely, Bevier. I still have a little time for other thoughts as well. I'm sorry you didn't get the chance to meet Lillias."

"Lillias?"

"A Rendorish woman. I lived with her while I was in exile."

"*Sparhawk!*" Bevier gasped.

"It was part of a necessary disguise."

"But surely you didn't—" Bevier left it hanging. Sparhawk was sure that the young man was blushing furiously, but the darkness concealed it.

"Oh, yes," he assured his friend. "Lillias would have left me otherwise. She's a woman of strong appetites. I needed her to help conceal my real identity, so I more or less had to try to keep her happy."

"I'm shocked at you, Sparhawk, truly shocked."

"The Pandions are a more pragmatic order than the Cyrinics, Bevier. We do what has to be done in order to get the job finished. Don't worry, my friend. Your soul hasn't been damaged—at least not very much."

"I still need to spend some time in a church."

"Why? God is everywhere, isn't he?"

"Of course."

"Talk with Him here, then."

"It wouldn't be quite the same."

"Whatever makes you feel right, I suppose."

They set out again at first light. The road now tended downward, for they were coming down out of the low range of forested hills. On occasion, when rounding a curve or cresting a hill, they could see Lake Venne sparkling in the spring sun off in the distance; by midafternoon, they reached the fork in the road. The main road was much better than had been the one leading down from Ghasek, and they reached the north gate of Venne just before the sunset filled the western sky with its fire.

Once again they rode through the narrow streets with the overhanging houses casting a premature darkness, and arrived back at the inn where they had previously stayed. The innkeeper, a jovial fat Pelosian, welcomed them and led them upstairs to the second floor where the sleeping rooms were located. "Well, my Lords," he said, "how was your sojourn in those accursed woods?"

"Quite successful, neighbor," Sparhawk replied, "and I think you can begin to pass the word around that Ghasek's no longer a place to be feared. We found out what was causing the problem and took care of it."

"Thanks be to God for the Knights of the Church!" the innkeeper cried enthusiastically. "The stories that have been going around have been very bad for business here in Venne. People have been choosing other routes because they didn't want to go into those woods."

"It's all taken care of now," Sparhawk assured him.

"Was it some kind of monster?"

"In a manner of speaking," Kalten replied.

"Did you kill it?"

"We entombed it." Kalten shrugged, starting to remove his armor.

"Good for you, my Lord."

"Oh, by the way," Sparhawk said, "we need to find a place called Giant's Mound. Do you by any chance happen to know where we should start looking?"

"I think it's on the east side of the lake," the innkeeper replied. "There are some villages down there. They're back a ways from the lake shore because of all those peat bogs." He laughed. "The villages won't be hard to find. The peasants down there burn peat in their stoves. It puts out quite a bit of smoke, so about all you have to do is follow your noses."

"What are you planning to offer for supper tonight?" Kalten asked eagerly.

"Is that all you ever think about?" Sparhawk said.

"It's been a long trip, Sparhawk. I need some real food. You gentlemen are good companions, but your cooking leaves a bit to be desired."

"I've had a haunch of beef turning on the spit since this morning, my Lord," the innkeeper said. "It should be well-done by now."

Kalten smiled beatifically.

True to his word, Bevier spent the night in a nearby church and rejoined them in the morning. Sparhawk chose not to question him concerning the state of his soul.

They rode out of Venne and took the road south along the lake. They made much better time than they had when they had made the trip to the city. On that occasion, Kalten, Bevier, and Tynian had been recovering from their encounter with the monstrous thing that had emerged from the burial mound at the north end of Lake Randera, but now they were wholly restored and able to ride at a gallop.

It was late afternoon when Kurik pulled up beside Sparhawk. "I just caught a trace of peat smoke in the air," he reported. "There's a village of some kind around here."

"Kalten," Sparhawk called.

"Yes?"

"There's a village nearby. Kurik and I are going to go have a look. Set up camp and build a good fire. It might be after dark before the two of us get back, and we'll need something to guide us in."

"I know what to do, Sparhawk."

"All right. Do it then." Sparhawk and his squire turned aside from the road and galloped across an open field toward a low band of trees a mile or so to the east.

The smell of burning peat grew stronger—a strangely homelike scent. Sparhawk leaned back in his saddle, feeling strangely at ease.

"Don't get too confident," Kurik warned. "The smoke does strange things to their heads. Peat burners are not always very reliable. In some ways, they're worse than Lamorks."

"Where did you get all this information, Kurik?"

"There are ways, Sparhawk. The Church and the nobility get their information in dispatches and reports. The commons go to the heart of things."

"I'll remember that. There's the village."

"You'd better let me do most of the talking when we get there," Kurik advised. "No matter how hard you try, you don't sound much like a commoner."

It was a low village. Shallow, wide houses built of gray fieldstone and roofed with thatch lined both sides of the single street. A thick-bodied peasant sat on a stool in an open-sided shed, milking a brown cow.

"Hello there, friend," Kurik called to him, slipping down from his horse.

The peasant turned and stared at him in slack-lipped stupidity.

"Do you happen to know about a place called Giant's Mound?" Kurik asked him.

The fellow continued to gape at him without answering.

Then a lean man with squinting eyes came out of a nearby house. "Won't do you no good to talk to him," he said. "He got kicked in the head by a horse when he was young, and he ha'n't been right since."

"Oh," Kurik said. "Sorry to hear about that. Maybe you could help us. We're looking for a place called Giant's Mound."

"You're not plannin' to go there at night, are you?"

"No, we thought we'd wait until daylight."

"That's a little better, but not much. It's haunted, you know."

"No, I didn't know that. Whereabouts is it?"

"You see that lane as runs off toward the southeast?" The lean man pointed.

Kurik nodded.

"Come sunup, follow that. It runs right past the mound—four, maybe five mile from here."

"Have you ever seen anybody poking around it? Maybe somebody digging?"

"Never heard tell of nothin' like that. People as has good sense don't poke around haunted places."

"We've heard that you've got a Troll in this area."

"What's a Troll?"

"Ugly brute all covered with hair. This one is pretty badly deformed."

"Oh, that thing. It's got a lair someplace out in the bogs. It only comes out at night. It wanders up an' down the lake shore. It makes awful noises for a while an' then pounds on the ground with its front paws as if it was real mad about somethin'. I seen it a couple times myself when I was cuttin' peat. I'd stay away from it if it was me. It seems like it's got a awful bad temper."

"Sounds like good advice to me. Ever see any Styrics hereabouts?"

"No. They don't come around here. People in this district don't hold with heathens much. You sure are full of questions, friend."

Kurik shrugged. "Best way to learn things is to ask questions," he said easily.

"Well, go ask somebody else. I got work to do." The fellow's expression had turned unfriendly. He scowled at the stupid fellow in the shed. "You done with the milkin' yet?" he demanded.

The slack-lipped idiot shook his head apprehensively.

"Well, get at it. You don't get no supper till yer done."

"Thanks for your time, friend," Kurik said, remounting.

The lean man grunted and went back into the house.

"Useful," Sparhawk said as they rode out of the village in the ruddy light of the setting sun. "At least there aren't any Zemochs around."

"I'm not so sure, Sparhawk," Kurik disagreed. "I don't think that fellow was the best source of information in the world. He doesn't seem to take too much interest in what's going on around him. Besides, Zemochs aren't the only ones we have to worry about. That Seeker thing could set just about anybody on us, and we've also got to keep an eye out for that Troll. If Sephrenia's right about that jewel's making its re-emergence known, the Troll would be one of the first ones to know, wouldn't he?"

"I don't know. We'll have to ask her."

"I think we'd better assume that he will. If we dig the crown up, we should more or less expect a visit from him."

"That's a cheery thought. At least we found out where the mound is located. Let's go see if we can find Kalten's camp before it gets dark."

Kalten had set up for the night in a copse of beech trees a mile or so back from the lake, and he had built a large fire at the edge of the grove. He was standing beside it when Sparhawk and Kurik rode in. "Well?" he asked.

"We got directions to the mound," Sparhawk replied, climbing down from his saddle. "It's not very far. Let's go talk with Tynian."

The heavily armored Alcione was standing by the fire, talking with Ulath.

Sparhawk related the information Kurik had obtained from the villager, then looked at Tynian. "How are you feeling?" he asked directly.

"I'm fine. Why? Am I looking unwell?"

"Not really. I was just wondering if you felt up to necromancy again. The last time took quite a bit out of you, as I recall."

"I'm up to it, Sparhawk," Tynian assured him, "provided you don't want me to raise whole regiments."

"No, just one. We need to talk with King Sarak before we dig him up. He'll probably know what happened to his crown, and I want to be sure he's not going to object to being taken back to Thalesia. I don't want an angry ghost trailing along behind us."

"Truly," Tynian agreed fervently.

They rose before dawn the next morning and waited impatiently for the first sign of daylight along the horizon to the east. When it came, they were ready and they set out across the still-dark fields.

"I think we should have waited for more light, Sparhawk," Kalten grumbled. "We're likely to run around in circles out here."

"We're going east, Kalten. That's where the sun comes up. All we have to do is ride toward the lightest part of the sky."

Kalten muttered something to himself.

"I didn't quite catch that," Sparhawk said.

"I wasn't talking to you."

"Oh. Sorry."

The pale predawn light gradually increased, and Sparhawk looked around to get his bearings. "That's the village over there," he said, pointing. "The lane we want to follow is on the far side of it."

"Let's not rush too much," Sephrenia cautioned, drawing her white robe about Flute. "I want the sun to be up when we reach the mound. The talk of haunting may be just a local superstition, but let's not take any chances."

Sparhawk curbed his impatience with some difficulty.

They rode through the silent village at a walk and entered the lane the surly villager had pointed out. Sparhawk nudged Faran into a trot. "It's not all that fast, Sephrenia," he said in response to her disapproving expression. "The sun will be well up by the time we get there."

The lane was lined on both sides by low fieldstone walls and, like all country lanes, it wandered. Farmers, by and large, took little interest in straight lines and usually followed the path of least resistance. Sparhawk's impatience grew greater with each passing mile.

"There it is," Ulath said finally, pointing ahead. "I've seen hundreds like it in Thalesia."

"Let's wait until the sun gets a little higher," Tynian said, squinting at the sunrise. "I don't want any shadows around when I do this. Where's the king likely to be buried?"

"In the center," Ulath replied, "with his feet pointed toward the west. His retainers will be in ranks on either side of him."

"It helps to know that."

"Let's ride around it," Sparhawk said. "I want to see if anybody's been digging, and I definitely want to make sure that nobody's around. This is the sort of thing we want lots of privacy for." They cantered around the mound. It was quite high, and it was perhaps a hundred feet long and twenty wide. Its sides were covered with grass, and it was smoothly symmetrical. There were no signs of any excavations.

"I'm going up on top," Kurik said when they returned to the road. "That's the highest point around here. If anybody's in the area, I should be able to see them from up there."

"You would actually walk on a grave?" Bevier's tone was shocked.

"We're all going to be walking on it in a little while, Bevier," Tynian said. "I'll need to be fairly close to where King Sarak's buried to raise his ghost."

Kurik clambered up the side of the mound and stood atop it, peering around. "I don't see anybody," he called down, "but there are some trees off to the south. It might not hurt to have a look before we get started."

Sparhawk ground his teeth together, but he had to admit to himself that his squire was probably right.

Kurik slid down the grassy side of the mound and remounted.

"Sephrenia," Sparhawk said, "why don't you stay here with the children?"

"No, Sparhawk," she refused. "If there are people hiding in those trees, we don't want them to know that we have any particular interest in this mound."

"Good point," he agreed. "Let's just ride on down to those trees as if we intended to keep going south."

They moved out, following the winding country lane across the fields.

"Sparhawk," Sephrenia said quietly as they approached the edge of the trees, "there are people in those woods, and they aren't friendly."

"How many?"

"A dozen at least."

"Hold back a little bit with Talen and Flute," he told her. "All right, gentlemen," he said to the others, "you know what to do."

But before they could enter the woods, a group of poorly armed peasants dashed out from under the trees. They had that vacant look that immediately identified them. Sparhawk lowered his lance and charged with his companions thundering along at either side of him.

The fight did not last for very long. The peasants were unskilled with their weapons and they were on foot. It was all over in a few minutes.

"Nicely done, Sssir Knightsss," a chillingly metallic voice said sardonically from the shadows back under the trees. Then the robed and hooded Seeker rode out into the morning sunlight. "But no matter," it continued. "I know where ye are now."

Sparhawk handed his lance to Kurik and drew Aldreas' spear out from under his saddle skirt. "And we know where you are as well, Seeker," he said in an ominously quiet voice.

"Do not be foolisssh, Sssir Sssparhawk," it hissed. "Thou art no match for me."

"Why don't we try it and find out?"

The hooded figure's hidden face began to glow green. Then the light flickered and faded. "Thou hassst the ringsss!" it hissed, seeming much less sure of itself now.

"I thought you already knew that."

Then Sephrenia joined them.

"It hasss been quite sssome time, Sssephrenia," the thing said in its hissing voice.

"Not nearly long enough to suit me," she replied coldly.

"I will ssspare thy life if thou wilt fall down and worsssship me."

"No, Azash. Never. I will remain faithful to my Goddess."

Sparhawk stared at her and then at the Seeker in astonishment.

"Thinkessst thou that Aphrael canssst protect thee if I decide that thy life ssservesss no further purpossse?"

"You've decided that before without much noticeable effect. I will still serve Aphrael."

"Asss thou sssseessst fit, Sssephrenia."

Sparhawk moved Faran forward at a walk, sliding his ringed hand up the shaft of the spear until it rested on the metal shank. Once again he felt that enormous surge of power.

"The game isss almossst played out, and itsss conclusssion isss foregone. We will meet once again, Sssephrenia, and for the lassst time." Then the hooded creature wheeled its horse and fled from Sparhawk's menacing approach.

PART THREE

# THE TROLL CAVE

THALESIA

R. Horset
Horset
Heid
Husdal
Ghwerig's cave
R. Ksema
R. Emsat
Yosut
Ksema
Emsat

Straits of Thalesia

Asabel
Amir
R. Asabel
Endahl

DEIRA

R. Acie
Gatas

Gulf
of Acie
Acie
Adera
Endde
Endde R.
Styric R.

DEIRAN
SEA

ELENIA
Cardos
Lenda
Cimmura
Cimmur R.
Vardenais
Ucera R.
Dieros
Ucera
ARCIUM
Coombe R.
Coombe

The Troll Cave

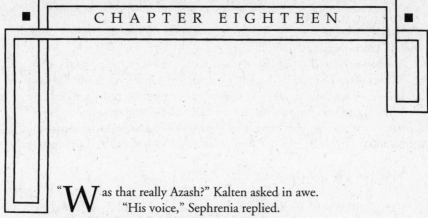

## CHAPTER EIGHTEEN

"Was that really Azash?" Kalten asked in awe.

"His voice," Sephrenia replied.

"Does he really talk like that? All that hissing?"

"Not really. The Seeker's mouth parts distort things."

"I gather that you've met him before," Tynian said, shifting the shoulder plates of his bulky armor.

"Once," she said shortly, "a very long time ago." Sparhawk got the distinct impression that she didn't really want to talk about it. "We may as well go back to the mound," she added. "Let's get what we came for and leave before the Seeker comes back with reinforcements."

They turned their horses and rode back along the winding lane. The sun had fully risen by now, but Sparhawk nonetheless felt cold. The encounter with the Elder God, even though by proxy, had chilled his blood and seemed to have even dulled the sun.

When they reached the mound, Tynian took his coil of rope and laboriously led the way up the steep side. Again he laid out the peculiar pattern on the ground.

"Are you sure you won't raise one of the king's retainers by mistake?" Kalten asked him.

Tynian shook his head. "I'll call Sarak by name." He began the incantation, and concluded it by clapping his hands sharply together.

At first nothing seemed to happen, and then the ghost of the long-dead King Sarak began to emerge from the mound. His chain-mail armor was archaic and showed huge rents in it from sword and ax. His shield had been battered, and his ancient sword was nicked and scarred. He was enormous, but he wore no crown. "Who art thou?" the ghost demanded in a hollow voice.

"I am Tynian, your Majesty, an Alcione Knight from Deira."

King Sarak stared sternly at him with hollow eyes. "This is unseemly, Sir Tynian. Return me at once to the place where I sleep, lest I grow wroth."

"Pray forgive me, your Majesty," Tynian apologized. "We would not have disturbed thy rest but for a matter of desperate urgency."

"Nothing hath sufficient urgency to concern the dead."

Sparhawk stepped forward. "My name is Sparhawk, your Majesty," he said.

"A Pandion, judging from thine armor."

"Yes, your Majesty. The Queen of Elenia is gravely ill, and only Bhelliom can heal her. We have come to entreat thee to permit us to use the jewel to restore her health. We will return it to thy grave when we have completed our task."

"Return it or keep it, Sir Sparhawk," the ghost said indifferently. "Thou shalt not find it in my grave, however."

Sparhawk felt as if he had been struck a sharp blow to the pit of the stomach.

"This Queen of Elenia, what malady hath she so grave that only Bhelliom can heal it?" There was only the faintest hint of curiosity in the ghost's voice.

"She was poisoned, your Majesty, by those who would seize her throne."

Sarak's expression, which had been blankly indifferent, suddenly became angry. "A treasonous act, Sir Sparhawk," he said harshly. "Knowest thou the perpetrators?"

"I do."

"And hast thou punished them?"

"Not as yet, your Majesty."

"They still have their heads? Have the Pandions become weaklings over the centuries?"

"We thought it best to return the Queen to health, your Majesty, so that *she* might have the pleasure of pronouncing their doom upon them."

Sarak seemed to consider that. "It is fitting," he approved finally. "Very well then, Sir Sparhawk, I will aid thee. Despair not that Bhelliom is not in the place where I lie, for I can direct thee to the place where it lies hidden. When I fell upon this field, my kinsman, the Earl of Heid, seized up my crown and fled with it to keep it out of the hands of our foes. Hard was he pressed and gravely wounded. He reached the shores of yon lake ere he died, and he hath sworn to me in the House of the Dead that with his dying breath, he cast the crown into the murky waters, and that our foes found it not. Seek ye, therefore, in that lake, for doubtless Bhelliom still lies there."

"Thank you, your Majesty," Sparhawk replied with profound gratitude.

Then Ulath pushed forward. "I am Ulath of Thalesia," he declared, "and I claim distant kinship with thee, my King. It is unseemly that thy final resting place be in foreign soil. As God gives me strength, I vow to thee that with thy permission I will return thy bones to our homeland and lay thee to rest in the royal sepulcher at Emsat."

Sarak regarded the braided Genidian with some approval. "Let it be so then, my kinsman, for in truth, my sleep hath been unquiet in this rude place."

"Sleep here but for a short while longer, my King, for as soon as our task is completed, I will return here and take thee home." There were tears in Ulath's ice-blue eyes. "Let him rest, Tynian," he said. "His final journey will be long."

Tynian nodded and let King Sarak sink back into the earth.

"That's it then, isn't it?" Kalten said eagerly. "We ride to Lake Venne and go swimming."

"It's easier than digging," Kurik told him. "All we have to worry about is the Seeker and that Troll." He frowned slightly. "Sir Ulath," he said, "if Ghwerig knows exactly where Bhelliom is, why hasn't he retrieved it in all these years?"

"The way I understand it, Ghwerig can't swim," Ulath replied. "His body's too twisted. We'll probably still have to fight him, though. As soon as we bring Bhelliom out of the lake, he'll attack us."

Sparhawk looked toward the west where the light from the newly risen sun sparkled on the waters of the lake. The tall, summer-green grass of the fields near the mound moved in long waves in the fitful morning breeze, and the fields were bounded near the lake by the grayish sedge and marsh grass that covered the peat bogs. "We'll worry about Ghwerig when we see him," he said. "Let's go have a closer look at this lake."

They all slid down the grassy side of the mound and climbed into their saddles. "Bhelliom shouldn't be too far out from shore," Ulath said as they rode toward the lake. "Crowns are made of gold, and gold's heavy. A dying man couldn't throw something like that very far." He scratched at his chin. "I've looked for things underwater before," he said. "You have to be very methodical about it. Just floundering around doesn't accomplish very much."

"When we get there, show us how it's done," Sparhawk replied.

"Right. Let's ride due west until we come to the lake. If the Earl of Heid was dying, he wouldn't have taken any side trips."

They rode on. Sparhawk's elation was overshadowed with some anxiety. There was no way to know how long it would be before the Seeker returned with a horde of numb-faced men at its back, and he knew that he and his friends could not wear armor while they probed the depths of the lake. They would be defenseless. Not only that, as soon as the spirit of Azash saw them in the lake, he would know exactly what they were doing, and for that matter, so would Ghwerig.

The light breeze was still blowing as they rode west, and puffy white clouds marched at a stately pace across the deep blue sky.

"There's a grove of cedar trees up ahead," Kurik said, pointing to a low, dark green patch of vegetation a quarter of a mile away. "We're going to need to build a raft when we get to the lake. Come along, Berit. Let's go start chopping." He led his string of packhorses toward the grove with the novice close behind him.

Sparhawk and his friends reached the lake about midmorning and stood looking out over the water rippling in the breeze. "That's going to make looking for something on the bottom very difficult," Kalten said, pointing toward the murky, peat-stained depths.

"Any notion of where the Earl of Heid might have come out on the lake shore?" Sparhawk asked Ulath.

"Count Ghasek's story said that some Alcione Knights came along and buried him," the Genidian replied. "They were in a hurry, so they probably wouldn't have moved his body very far from where he fell. Let's look around for a grave."

"After five hundred years?" Kalten said skeptically. "There won't be much to mark it, Ulath."

"I think you're wrong, Kalten," Tynian disagreed. "Deirans build cairns over graves when they bury somebody. The earth might flatten out over a grave, but rocks are a bit more permanent."

"All right," Sparhawk said, "let's spread out and start looking for a pile of rocks."

It was Talen who found the grave, a low mound of brown-stained stones partially covered by muddy silt that had accumulated over centuries of high water. Tynian marked it by sinking the butt of his pennon-tipped lance into the mud at the foot of the grave.

"Shall we get started?" Kalten asked.

"Let's wait for Kurik and Berit," Sparhawk said. "The lake bottom's a little too soupy for wading. We're going to need that raft."

It was perhaps a half hour later when the squire and the novice joined them. The packhorses were laboriously pulling a dozen cedar logs behind them.

It was shortly after noon when they finished lashing the logs together with ropes to form a crude raft. The knights had discarded their armor and worked in loincloths, sweating in the hot sun.

"You're getting sunburned," Kalten told the pale-skinned Ulath.

"I always do," Ulath replied. "Thalesians don't tan very well." He straightened as he finished tying the last knot in the rope that held one end of the raft together. "Well, let's launch it and see if it floats," he suggested.

They pushed the raft down the slippery mud beach into the water. Ulath looked at it critically. "I wouldn't want to make a sea voyage on that thing," he said, "but it's good enough for our purposes here. Berit, go over to that willow thicket and cut yourself a couple of saplings."

The novice nodded and returned a few minutes later with two long, springy wands.

Ulath went to the grave and picked up two stones somewhat larger than his fist. He hefted them a couple of times, one in each hand, then tossed one to Sparhawk. "What do you think?" he asked. "Does that feel to be about the same weight as a gold crown?"

"How would I know?" Sparhawk asked. "I've never worn a crown."

"Guess, Sparhawk. The day's wearing on, and the mosquitoes are going to come out before long."

"All right, that's probably about the weight of a crown, give or take a few pounds."

"That's what I thought. All right, Berit, take your saplings and pole the raft out into the lake. We're going to mark the area we want to search."

Berit looked a little puzzled, but did as he was told.

Ulath hefted one of his rocks. "That's far enough, Berit," he called. He gave the rock an underhand toss toward the shaky raft. "Mark that place!" he bellowed.

Berit wiped the water the rock had splashed on him from his face. "Yes, Sir Ulath," he said, poling the raft toward the widening circles on the surface of the lake. Then he took one of his willow saplings and sank one end of it down into the muddy bottom.

"Now pole the raft off to the left," Ulath shouted. "I'll throw the next rock a ways beyond you."

"Your left or mine, Sir Ulath?" Berit asked politely.

"Take your pick. I just don't want to brain you with this." Ulath was tossing his rock from one hand to the other and squinting out at the brown-stained waters of the lake.

Berit pushed the raft out of the way, and Ulath launched his rock with a mighty heave.

"Lord!" Kalten said. "No dying man could ever throw anything that far."

"That was the idea," Ulath said modestly. "That's the absolute outer limit of the area we search. Berit!" he bellowed in a shattering voice, "mark that spot and then go down. I need to know how deep we're going and what kind of bottom we've got to work with."

Berit hesitated after he marked the place where the second rock had struck the water. "Would you please ask Lady Sephrenia to turn her back?" he asked plaintively, his face suddenly bright red.

"If anyone laughs, he'll spend the rest of his life as a toad," Sephrenia threatened, resolutely turning her back on the lake and pulling the curious little girl Flute around at the same time.

Berit stripped and went over the edge of the raft like an otter. He re-emerged a minute later. Everyone on shore, Sparhawk noticed, had held his breath while the agile novice had been down. Berit exhaled explosively, spraying water. "It's about eight feet deep, Sir Ulath," he reported, clinging to the end of the raft, "but the bottom's muddy—two feet of it at least—mucky and not very nice. The water's dark brown. You can't see your hand in front of your face."

"I was afraid of that," Ulath muttered.

"How's the water?" Kalten called out to the young man in the lake.

"Very, very cold," Berit chattered.

"I was afraid of that, too," Kalten said glumly.

"Well, gentlemen," Ulath said, "time to get wet."

The rest of the afternoon was distinctly unpleasant. As Berit had announced, the water was cold and murky, and the soft bottom was thick with brown mud from the nearby peat bogs. "Don't try to dig around in that with your hands," Ulath instructed. "Probe with your feet."

They found nothing. By the time the sun went down, they were all exhausted and blue with the cold.

"We have a decision to make," Sparhawk said soberly after they had dried themselves and put on tunics and mail shirts. "How long is it going to be safe for us to stay here? The Seeker knows almost exactly where we are, and our scent will lead it right to us. As soon as it sees us in the lake, Azash will know where Bhelliom is. That's something we can't let him find out."

"You're right, Sparhawk," Sephrenia agreed. "It will take the Seeker awhile to gather its forces, and awhile longer to lead them back here, but I think we'll need to set a time limit on how long we stay in this place."

"But we're so close," Kalten objected.

"It's not going to do us any good to find Bhelliom just to turn it over to Azash," she pointed out. "If we ride off, we'll lead the Seeker away from this spot. We know where Bhelliom is now. We can always come back later when it's safe."

"Noon tomorrow?" Sparhawk asked her.

"I don't think we should stay any longer."

"That's it then," Sparhawk said. "At noon we'll pack up and go back to the city of Venne. I get the feeling that the Seeker won't take its men into a town. They'd be very conspicuous the way they shamble around."

"A boat," Ulath said, his face ruddy in the light of their fire.

"Where?" Kalten asked, peering out at the night-shrouded lake.

"No. What I mean is, why don't we ride to Venne and hire a boat? The Seeker will follow our trail to Venne, but it won't be able to sniff our tracks over water, will it? It'll camp outside Venne waiting for us to come out, but we'll be back here by then. We'll be free to search for Bhelliom until we find it."

"It's a good idea, Sparhawk," Kalten said.

"Is he right?" Sparhawk asked Sephrenia. "Will travelling by water throw the Seeker off our trail?"

"I believe it will," she replied.

"Good. We'll try it then."

They ate a meager supper and went to their beds.

They rose at sunrise the following morning, took a quick breakfast, and poled the raft back out to the markers that indicated where they had left off the previous day. They anchored the raft and once again went into the chill waters to probe at the muddy bottom with their feet.

It was almost noon when Berit surfaced not far from where Sparhawk was treading water and catching his breath. "I think I've found something," the novice said, gasping for air. Then he upended himself and swam down headfirst. After a painfully long minute, he came up again. It was not a crown he held in his hand, though, but a brown-stained human skull. He swam to the raft and laid the skull up on the logs. Sparhawk squinted up at the sun and swore. Then he followed Berit to the raft. He hauled himself up on the logs. "That's it," he called to Kalten, whose head had just popped up out of the water. "We can't stay here any longer. Gather up the others, and let's get back to shore."

When they reached the shore, the sunburned Ulath curiously examined the skull. "Seems awfully long and narrow for some reason," he said.

"That's because he was a Zemoch," Sephrenia told him.

"Did he drown?" Berit asked.

Ulath scraped some of the mud off the skull and then poked one finger into an aperture in the left temple. "Not with this hole in the side of his head, he didn't." He went down to the lake shore and sloshed the skull around in the water to rinse centuries of accumulated mud out of it. Then he brought it back and shook it. Something rattled inside. The big Thalesian laid it on the mounded-up stones of the grave of the Earl of Heid, took up a rock, and cracked the skull open as casually as a man might crack a walnut. Then he picked something up out of the fragments. "I thought so," he said. "Somebody put an arrow in his brainpan, probably from shore." He handed the rusty arrowhead to Tynian. "Do you recognize it?"

"It's Deiran forging," Tynian said after examining it.

Sparhawk thought back for a moment. "Ghasek's account said that Alcione Knights from Deira came along and wiped out the Zemochs who'd been pursuing the Earl of Heid. We can be fairly certain that the Zemochs saw the earl throw the crown into the lake. They'd have gone out after it, wouldn't they? And to the exact spot where it hit the water. Now we find this one with a Deiran arrow in his head. It's not too hard to reconstruct what happened. Berit, can you pinpoint the precise spot where you found the skull?"

"To within a few feet, Sir Sparhawk. I was taking bearings on things along the shore. It was straight out from that dead snag over there and about thirty feet out into the lake."

"That's it, then," Sparhawk said exultantly. "The Zemochs were diving after the crown, and the Alciones came along and raked them with arrows from shore. That skull was probably lying no more than a few yards from Bhelliom."

"We know where it is now," Sephrenia said. "We'll come back for it later."

"But—"

"We must leave immediately, Sparhawk, and it would be far too dangerous to have Bhelliom in our possession with the Seeker right behind us."

Grudgingly, Sparhawk had to admit that she was probably right. "All right, then," he said in a disappointed tone, "let's break down the camp and get out of here. We'll wear mail instead of armor so we won't be so conspicuous. Ulath, push that raft back out into the lake. We'll wipe out any traces that we've been here and ride on up to Venne."

It took them about a half an hour; then they moved out. They rode north along the lake, moving at a gallop. As usual, Berit rode to the rear, watching for signs of pursuit.

Sparhawk was melancholy. Somehow it seemed that for weeks he had been trying to run in soft sand. No matter how close he got to the one thing that would save his Queen, something always seemed to interfere, to force him away from the goal. He began to have darkly superstitious feelings. Sparhawk was an Elene and a Church Knight. He was at least nominally committed to the Elene faith and its rigid rejection of anything remotely related to what the Church called "heathenism." Sparhawk had been abroad in the world too long, however, and seen far too many things to accept the dictates of his Church at face value. He realized that in many ways he hung suspended between absolute faith and total skepticism. Something somewhere was desperately trying to keep him away from the Bhelliom, and he was fairly certain he knew who it was—but why would Azash bear such enmity toward the young Queen of Elenia? Sparhawk grimly began to think of armies and invasions. If Ehlana died, he vowed to himself that he would obliterate Zemoch and leave Azash weeping alone in the ruins without one single human to worship him.

They reached the city of Venne not long after noon the following day and returned through the gloomy streets to the now-familiar inn. "Why don't we just buy this place?" Kalten suggested as they dismounted in the courtyard. "I'm starting to feel as if I've lived here all my life."

"Go ahead and make the arrangements," Sparhawk told him. "Kurik, let's walk down to the lake shore and see if we can find a boat before the sun goes down."

The knight and his squire walked out of the innyard and down the cobbled street that led toward the lake. "This town doesn't get any prettier when you get to know it," Kurik observed.

"We're not here for the scenery," Sparhawk growled.

"What's the matter, Sparhawk?" Kurik asked. "You've been in a foul humor for the last week or more."

"Time, Kurik." Sparhawk sighed. "Time. Sometimes it's almost as if I can feel it dribbling through my fingers. We were within no more than a few feet of Bhelliom, and then we had to pack up and leave. My Queen is dying inch by inch, and things keep getting in my way. I'm starting to feel a very powerful urge to hurt some people."

"Don't look at me."

Sparhawk smiled faintly. "I think you're safe, my friend," he said, putting his hand affectionately on Kurik's shoulder. "If nothing else, I'd hate to make wagers on the outcome if you and I ever had a really serious disagreement."

"There's that, too," Kurik agreed. Then he pointed. "Over there," he said.

"Over there what?"

"That tavern. People with boats go in there."

"How do you know that?"

"I just saw one go in. Boats tend to leak, and the men who own them try to seal up the seams with tar. Anytime you see a man with tar on his tunic, you can be fairly sure that he has something to do with boats."

"You're an absolute sink of information sometimes, Kurik."

"I've been around in the world for quite a long time, Sparhawk. If a man keeps his eyes open, he can learn a great deal. When we go inside, let me do the talking. It'll be faster." Kurik's stride suddenly took on a peculiar roll, and he banged open the tavern door with unnecessary force. "Hello there, mates," he said in a raspy voice. "Have we chanced by luck on a place where men as works on the water be accustomed to gather?"

"You've found the right place, friend," the barman said.

"Praise be," Kurik said. "I hate to drink with landsmen. All they can talk about is the weather an' their crops, an' once you've said it's cloudy an' that the turnips is growin', you've exhausted the possibilities of conversation."

The men in the tavern laughed appreciatively.

"Forgive me if I seem to pry," the barman apologized, "but you seem to have the speech of a salt-water man."

"Indeed," Kurik said, "an' sore do I miss the smell of brine an' the gentle kiss of spray upon my cheek."

"You're a long way from any salt water, mate," one tar-smeared fellow sitting at a table in the corner said with an odd note of respect in his voice.

Kurik sighed deeply. "Missed me boat, mate," he said. "We made port in Apalia, sailin' down from Yosut up in Thalesia, an' I went out on the town an' got sore took by the grog. The cap'n was not one to wait for stragglers, so he upped an' sailed with the mornin' tide an' left me beached. As luck had it, I fell in with this man," he clapped Sparhawk familiarly on the shoulder, "an' he give me employment. Says he needs to hire a boat here in Venne an' he needed someone as knew the way of boats to make sure he doesn't wind up on the bottom of the lake."

"Well, now, mate," the tarry man in the corner said with narrowed eyes, "what would your employer be willing to pay for the hire of a boat?"

" 'Twould only be for a couple of days," Kurik said. He looked at Sparhawk. "What thinkee, Cap'n? Would a half crown strain your purse?"

"I could manage a half crown," Sparhawk replied, trying to conceal his amazement at Kurik's sudden alteration.

"Two days, you say?" the man in the corner said.

"Dependin' on the wind and weather, mate, but it's always that way on the water, isn't it?"

"Truly. It could just be that we can do some business here. I happen to own a fair-sized fishing boat, and the fishing hasn't been very good of late. I could hire out the boat to you and spend the two days mending my nets."

"Why don't we just nip on down to the water's edge an' have a look at your vessel?" Kurik suggested. "It might just could be that we could strike a bargain."

The tar-smeared fellow drained his tankard and rose to his feet. "Come along then," he said, moving toward the door.

"Kurik," Sparhawk said quietly in a pained tone, "don't spring surprises like that on me. My nerves aren't as good as they used to be."

"Variety keeps life interestin', Cap'n." Kurik grinned as they left the tavern in the wake of the fisherman.

The boat was perhaps thirty feet long, and it sat low in the water.

"She appears to have a leak or two, mate," Kurik noted, pointing at the foot or so of water standing in the hull.

"We were just patching her," the fisherman apologized. "I hit a submerged log and sprung a seam. The men as works for me wanted to get something to eat before they came back to finish up and bail her out." He patted the boat's rail affectionately. "She's a good old tub," he said modestly. "She responds to the helm well, an' she can take whatever kind of weather this lake can throw at her."

"An' you'll have her patched by mornin'?"

"Shouldn't be no trouble, mate."

"What thinkee, Cap'n?" Kurik asked Sparhawk.

"Looks all right to me," Sparhawk replied, "but I'm no expert. That's what I hired you for."

"All right then, we'll try her, mate," Kurik told the fisherman. "We'll come back down sunup an' settle up then." He spat on his hand, and he and the fisherman slapped their palms together. "Come along, Cap'n," Kurik told his lord. "Let's find us some grog an' supper an' then a bed. 'Twill be a long day tomorrow." And then with that rolling swagger, he led the way up from the lake front.

"Would you like to explain all that?" Sparhawk asked when they were some distance away from the boat owner.

"It's not too difficult, Sparhawk," Kurik said. "Men who sail on lakes always have a great deal of respect for salt-water sailors, and they'll go out of their way to be accommodating."

"So I noticed, but how did you ever learn to talk that way?"

"I went to sea once when I was about sixteen. I've told you that before."

"Not that I remember, no."

"I must have."

"Maybe it slipped my mind. What possessed you to go to sea?"

"Aslade." Kurik laughed. "She was about fourteen then and just blossoming out. She had that marrying sort of look in her eye. I wasn't ready yet, so I ran away to sea. Biggest mistake I ever made. I hired on as a deckhand on the leakiest bucket on the west coast of Eosia. I spent six months bailing water out of the bilges. When I got back to shore, I swore I'd never set foot on a ship again. Aslade was very happy to see me again, but then she's always been an emotional girl."

"Was that when you decided to marry her?"

"Shortly after that. When I got home, she took me up to her father's hayloft and did some fairly serious persuading. Aslade can be very, very persuasive when she sets her mind to it."

*"Kurik!"* Sparhawk was actually shocked.

"Grow up, Sparhawk. Aslade's a country girl, and most country girls have already started to swell when they get married. It's a relatively direct form of courtship, but it has its compensations."

"In a *hayloft*?"

Kurik smiled. "Sometimes you have to improvise, Sparhawk."

## CHAPTER NINETEEN

Sparhawk sat in the room he shared with Kalten, poring over his map while his friend snored on a nearby bed. Ulath's idea of a boat was a good one. Sephrenia's statement that it would indeed evade the Seeker's most dangerous means of tracking them down was reassuring. They could return to that lonely mud beach where the Earl of Heid slumbered and resume their interrupted search without looking over their shoulders for signs of a hooded figure sniffing at the ground behind them. The Zemoch skull Berit had found on the murky bottom had almost precisely pinpointed Bhelliom's location. With only a little luck, they would be able to find it within the space of a single afternoon. They'd have to return here to Venne for the horses, however, and that was the problem. If, as they had surmised, the Seeker's blank-minded cohorts likely would be lurking in the fields and woods around the town, they'd have to fight their way out. Under ordinary circumstances, fighting would not have concerned Sparhawk; it was what he had trained a lifetime to do. If he had Bhelliom in his possession, however, it would not only be his own life he would be risking, but Ehlana's as well, and that was unacceptable. Moreover, as soon as Azash sensed Bhelliom's re-emergence, the Seeker would hurl whole armies against them in a desperate attempt to seize the jewel.

The solution was simple, of course. All they had to do was to come up with a way to convey the horses to the west side of the lake. Then the Seeker could haunt the region around Venne until it grew old and died without causing Sparhawk and his friends any further inconvenience. The boat that he and Kurik had hired, though, would not be capable of carrying more than two horses at a time. The notion of making eight or nine separate trips halfway down the lake to deposit the horses on some lonely beach on the west side of the lake made Sparhawk almost want to scream with impatience. Hiring several boats was an alternative, though not a very good one. A single boat probably would not attract attention; a fleet of them, though, would. Perhaps they could find someone dependable enough to herd the horses down the west shore. The only problem with that was that Sparhawk was not sure whether the Seeker could identify the smell of the horses as well as that of the people who rode them. He scratched absently at the finger that bore his ring. The finger seemed to be tingling and throbbing for some reason.

There was a light tap at the door.

"I'm busy," he said irritably.

"Sparhawk." The voice was light and musical, and it had that peculiar lilt that identified the speaker as Styric. Sparhawk frowned. He didn't recognize the voice.

"Sparhawk, I need to talk with you."

He rose and went to the door. To his astonishment, it was Flute. She slipped into the room and closed the door behind her.

"So you *can* talk?" he asked, surprised.

"Of course I can."

"Why haven't you then?"

"It wasn't necessary before. You Elenes babble far too much." Although her voice was that of a little girl, her words and inflections were peculiarly adult. "Listen to me, Sparhawk. This is very important. We must all leave immediately."

"It's the middle of the night, Flute," he objected.

"How terribly observant of you," she said, looking toward the darkened window. "Now please be still and listen. *Ghwerig has retrieved Bhelliom!* We have to intercept him before he can get to the north coast and sneak aboard a ship bound for Thalesia. If he evades us, we'll have to follow him to his cave in the mountains of Thalesia, and that would take quite a while."

"According to Ulath, nobody even knows where the cave is."

"I know where it is. I've been there before."

"You *what*?"

"Sparhawk, you're wasting time. I have to get out of this city. There's too much distraction here. I can't feel what's happening. Put on your iron suit and let's go." Her tone was abrupt, even imperious. She looked at him, her large, dark eyes grave. "Is it possible that you're such a total lump that you can't feel Bhelliom moving through the world? Isn't that ring telling you anything?"

He started slightly and looked at the ruby ring on his left hand. It still seemed to be throbbing. The small child standing in front of him seemed to know far too much. "Does Sephrenia know about all this?"

"Of course. She's getting our things together."

"Let's go talk with her."

"You're beginning to irritate me, Sparhawk." Her dark eyes flashed, and the corners of her bowlike pink mouth turned down.

"I'm sorry, Flute, but I still have to talk with Sephrenia."

She rolled her eyes upward. "Elenes," she said in a tone so like Sephrenia's that Sparhawk almost laughed. He took her hand and led her from the room and down the hallway.

Sephrenia was busily stowing clothing, both hers and Flute's, in the canvas bag sitting on the bed in her room. "Come right in, Sparhawk," she said to him as he paused in the doorway. "I've been expecting you."

"What's going on, Sephrenia?" he asked in a baffled tone of voice.

"Didn't you tell him?" she asked Flute.

"Yes, but he doesn't seem to believe me. How can you tolerate these stubborn people?"

"They have a certain charm. Believe her, Sparhawk," she said gravely to him. "She knows what she's talking about. Bhelliom has emerged from the lake. I felt it myself, and now Ghwerig has it. We have to get out into open country so that Flute and I can sense which way he's going with it. Go rouse the others and have Berit saddle our horses."

"You're sure about this?"

"Yes. Hurry, Sparhawk, or Ghwerig will get away."

He turned quickly and went back out into the hall. This was all moving so rapidly that he did not have time to think. He went from room to room, waking the others and instructing them all to gather in Sephrenia's room. He sent Berit to the stable to saddle the horses and, last of all, he woke Kalten.

"What's the problem?" the blond Pandion asked, sitting up and rubbing sleepily at his eyes.

"Something's come up," Sparhawk replied. "We're leaving."

"In the middle of the night?"

"Yes. Get dressed, Kalten, and I'll pack our things."

"What's going on, Sparhawk?" Kalten swung his legs over the edge of the bed.

"Sephrenia will explain it. Hurry, Kalten."

Grumbling, Kalten began to dress while Sparhawk jammed their spare clothing into the pack they had brought up to their room. Then the two of them went back down the hall, and Sparhawk rapped on the door to Sephrenia's room.

"Oh, *do* come in, Sparhawk. This is no time to stand on ceremony."

"Who's that?" Kalten asked.

"Flute," Sparhawk replied, opening the door.

"Flute? She can talk?"

The others had already gathered in the room, and they were all looking at the little girl they had thought was mute with some astonishment.

"To save time," she said, "yes, I *can* talk, and no, I didn't want to before. Does that answer all the tiresome questions? Now listen very carefully. The Troll-Dwarf Ghwerig has managed to get his hands on Bhelliom again, and he's trying to take it to his cave up in the mountains of Thalesia. Unless we hurry, he'll get away from us."

"How did he get it out of the lake when he hasn't ever been able to do it before?" Bevier asked.

"He had help." She looked around at their faces and muttered a naughty word in Styric. "You'd better show them, Sephrenia. Otherwise they'll stand here all night asking foolish questions."

There was a large mirror—a sheet of polished brass, actually—on one wall of Sephrenia's room. "Would you all come over here, please?" Sephrenia said, going to the mirror.

They gathered around the mirror, and she began an incantation Sparhawk had not heard before. Then she gestured. The mirror became momentarily cloudy. When it cleared, they seemed to be looking down at the lake.

"There's the raft," Kalten said in astonishment, "and that's Sparhawk coming to the surface. I don't understand, Sephrenia."

"We're looking at things that happened just before noon yesterday," she told him.

"We already know what happened."

"We knew what *we* were doing," she corrected. "There were others there as well, however."

"I didn't see anybody."

"They didn't want you to see them. Just keep watching."

The perspective in the mirror seemed to change, moving away from the lake toward the sedge that grew thickly on the peat bog. A dark-robed shape was crouched down, hidden in the marsh grass.

"The Seeker!" Bevier exclaimed. "It was watching us!"

"It wasn't the only one," Sephrenia told him.

The perspective changed again, sliding several hundred yards north along the lake to a clump of scrubby trees. A shaggy, grotesquely deformed shape was hidden in the grove.

"And that's Ghwerig," Flute told them.

"That's a *dwarf*?" Kalten exclaimed. "It's as big as Ulath. How big is a normal one?"

"About twice as big as Ghwerig." Ulath shrugged. "Ogres are even bigger."

The mirror clouded again as Sephrenia spoke rapidly in Styric. "Nothing important went on for quite a while, so we're skipping that part," she explained.

The mirror cleared again. "There we go, riding away from the lake," Kalten said.

Then the Seeker rose from the marsh grass, and with it about ten wooden-faced men who appeared to be Pelosian serfs. Numbly, the serfs shambled down to the lake shore and waded into the water.

"We were afraid that might happen," Tynian said.

The mirror clouded again. "They continued the search all through yesterday, last night, and today," Sephrenia told them. "Then, just over an hour ago, one of them found Bhelliom. This part might be a little hard to see, because it was dark. I'll lighten the image as much as I can for you."

It was a bit hard to make out, but it seemed that one of the serfs emerged from the lake carrying a mud-caked object in his hand. "King Sarak's crown," Sephrenia identified the object.

The black-robed Seeker rushed along the lake shore, its scorpionlike claws extended and clicking eagerly, but Ghwerig reached the serf before Azash's creature could. With a mighty blow of his gnarled fist, he crushed in the side of the serf's head and seized the crown. Then he turned and ran before the Seeker could summon its followers out of the lake. Ghwerig's run was a peculiar loping gait involving both legs and one extraordinarily long arm. A man might be able to run faster, but not by very much.

The image faded.

"What happened next?" Kurik asked.

"Ghwerig stopped from time to time when one of the serfs began to overtake him," Sephrenia replied. "It looked as if he were deliberately slowing down. He killed them one by one."

"Where's Ghwerig now?" Tynian asked.

"We can't tell," Flute told him. "It's very hard to follow a Troll in the dark. That's why we have to get out into the open countryside. Sephrenia and I can feel Bhelliom, but only if we can get clear of all these townsmen."

Tynian considered it. "The Seeker's more or less out of the picture now," he said. "It's going to have to go out and gather more people before it can go after Ghwerig."

"That's a comforting thought," Kalten said. "I wouldn't want to have to take them both on at once."

"We'd better get started," Sparhawk told them. "Put on your armor, gentlemen," he suggested. "When we run across Ghwerig, we might need it."

They went back to their rooms to gather their belongings and to dress themselves in steel. Sparhawk clanked down the stairs to settle up with the fat innkeeper, who stood leaning against the doorway of the empty taproom, sleepy-eyed and yawning.

"We're going to be leaving now," Sparhawk said to him.

"It's still dark outside, Sir Knight."

"I know, but something came up."

"You've heard the news then, I gather."

"What news was that?" Sparhawk asked him cautiously.

"There's trouble down in Arcium. I haven't been able really to get the straight of it, but there's even been talk that it might be a war of some kind."

Sparhawk frowned. "That doesn't make much sense, neighbor. Arcium's not like Lamorkand. The Arcian nobles foreswore their blood feuds generations ago at the king's command."

"I can only repeat what I heard, Sir Knight. The word that I've picked up is that the kingdoms of western Eosia are all mobilizing. Earlier tonight some fellows came through Venne in quite a hurry—fellows who weren't very interested in going off to fight in a foreign war—and they say that there's a huge army gathering to the west of the lake conscripting every man they run across."

"The western kingdoms wouldn't mobilize because of a civil war in Arcium," Sparhawk told him. "That kind of thing is an internal matter."

"That's what puzzles me too," the innkeeper agreed, "but what puzzles me even more is that some of those timid fellows have said that a fair portion of that army is made up of Thalesians."

"They must have been wrong," Sparhawk said. "King Wargun drinks quite a bit, but he still wouldn't invade a friendly kingdom. If these men you mentioned were trying to avoid being conscripted, they probably wouldn't have stopped to examine the men who were chasing them, and one man in a mail shirt looks much like another."

"That's probably very true, Sir Knight."

Sparhawk paid for their night's lodging. "Thank you for the information, neighbor," he said to the innkeeper as the others began to come down the stairway. He turned and went out to the courtyard.

"What's going on, Sir Sparhawk?" Berit asked, handing Sparhawk Faran's reins.

"The Seeker was watching us while we were in the lake," Sparhawk replied. "One of its men found Bhelliom, but Ghwerig the Troll took it away from him. Now we have to go find Ghwerig."

"That might be a little difficult, Sir Sparhawk. There's fog rolling in off the lake."

"Hopefully, it'll burn off before Ghwerig gets this far north."

The others came out of the inn. "Let's all get mounted," Sparhawk said to them. "Which way do we go, Flute?"

"North for now," she replied as Kurik lifted her up to Sephrenia.

Berit blinked. "She knows how to talk!" he exclaimed.

"Please, Berit," she said to him, "don't repeat the obvious. Let's go, Sparhawk. I can't pinpoint Bhelliom's location until we get away from here."

They rode out of the innyard and into the foggy street. The fog was thick, hovering just this side of rainy drizzle, and it carried with it the acidic reek of the peat bogs that surrounded the lake.

"This isn't a good night for coming up against a Troll," Ulath said, falling in beside Sparhawk.

"I doubt very much that we'll run across Ghwerig tonight," Sparhawk said. "He's on foot, and it's a long way from here to where he found Bhelliom—that's assuming he's even coming this way."

"He almost has to, Sparhawk," the Genidian said. "He wants to get to Thalesia, and that means he's got to get to a seaport on the north coast."

"We'll know better which way he's moving once we get Sephrenia and Flute out of town."

"My guess would be Nadera," Ulath speculated. "It's a bigger seaport than Apalia, and there are more ships there. Ghwerig's going to have to sneak on board one. It's not likely that he could book passage. Most sea captains are superstitious about sailing with Trolls aboard."

"Would Ghwerig understand enough of our language to find out which ships are going to Thalesia by eavesdropping?"

Ulath nodded. "Most Trolls have a smattering of Elene and even Styric. They usually can't speak any language but their own, but they can understand a few words of ours."

They passed through the city gate and reached the fork in the road north of Venne shortly before daybreak. They looked dubiously at the rutted track that led up into the mountains toward Ghasek and ultimately to the seaport at Apalia. "I hope he doesn't decide to go that way," the white-cloaked Bevier said with a shudder. "I don't really want to go back to Ghasek."

"Is he moving at all?" Sparhawk asked Flute.

"Yes," she replied. "He's coming north along the lake shore."

"I don't quite understand this," Talen said to the little girl. "If you can sense where Bhelliom is, why didn't we just stay at the inn until he got closer with it?"

"Because there are too many people in Venne," Sephrenia told him. "We can't get a clear picture of Bhelliom's location in the middle of all that welter of thoughts and emotions."

"Oh," the boy said, "that makes sense—I guess."

"We could ride down the lake shore and meet him," Kalten suggested. "Save us all a lot of time."

"Not in the fog," Ulath said firmly. "I want to be able to see him coming. I don't want to get surprised by a Troll."

"He's going to have to pass through here," Tynian said, "or at least very close to here, if he's headed toward the north coast. He can't swim across the lake, and he can't go into Venne. Trolls are a little conspicuous, or so I'm told. When he gets closer, we can ambush him."

"It's got some possibilities, Sparhawk," Kalten said. "If we've got his probable line of travel pinpointed, we can catch him unawares up here. We can kill him and be halfway to Cimmura with Bhelliom before anyone is the wiser."

"Oh, Kalten," Sephrenia sighed.

"Killing is what we do, little mother," he told her. "You don't have to watch if you don't want to. One Troll more or less in the world isn't going to make all that much difference."

"There could be a problem, though," Tynian said to Flute. "The Seeker's going to be hot on Ghwerig's heels just as soon as it gathers up enough men, and it can probably sense Bhelliom in the same way you and Sephrenia can, can't it?"

"Yes," she admitted.

"Then you're forgetting that we may have to face it just as soon as we dispose of Ghwerig, aren't you?"

"And you're forgetting that we'll have Bhelliom at that point and that Sparhawk has the rings."

"Would Bhelliom eliminate the Seeker?"

"Quite easily."

"Let's pull back into those trees a ways," Sparhawk suggested. "I don't know how long it's going to take Ghwerig to get here, and I don't want him coming up on us while we're all standing in the middle of the road talking about the weather and other things."

They withdrew into the shadowy cover of a stand of trees and dismounted.

"Sephrenia," Bevier said in a puzzled tone of voice, "if Bhelliom can destroy the Seeker with magic, couldn't you use ordinary Styric magic to do the same thing?"

"Bevier," she replied patiently, "if I could do that, don't you think I'd have done it a long time ago?"

"Oh," he said, sounding a bit abashed, "I didn't think of that, I guess."

The sun came up blearily that morning. The pervading fog from the lake and the heavy mist out of the forest to the north half clouded the air at ground level, although the sky above was clear. They set out watches and checked over saddles and equipment. After that, most of them dozed in the muggy heat, frequently changing watch. A man on short sleep in sultry weather is not always very alert.

It was not long after noon when Talen woke Sparhawk. "Flute wants to talk to you," he said.

"I thought she'd be asleep."

"I don't think she ever really sleeps," the boy said. "You can't get near her without her eyes popping open."

"Someday maybe we'll ask her about that." Sparhawk threw off his blanket, rose to his feet, and splashed some water from a nearby spring on his face. Then he went to where Flute cuddled comfortably next to Sephrenia.

The little girl's huge eyes opened immediately. "Where have you been?" she asked.

"It took me a moment to get fully awake."

"Stay alert, Sparhawk," she said. "The Seeker's coming."

He swore and reached for his sword.

"Oh, don't do that," she said disgustedly. "It's still a mile or so away."

"How did it get this far north so fast?"

"It didn't stop to pick up any people the way we thought it would. It's alone, and it's killing its horse. The poor beast is dying right now."

"And Ghwerig's still a good ways away?"

"Yes, Bhelliom's still south of the city of Venne. I can get snatches of the Seeker's thought." She shuddered. "It's hideous, but it has much the same idea that we have. It's trying to get far enough ahead of Ghwerig to set up an ambush for him. It can pick up local people to do its work for it up here. I think we'll have to fight it."

"Without Bhelliom?"

"I'm afraid so, Sparhawk. It doesn't have any people to help it, and that might make it easier to deal with."

"Can we kill it with ordinary weapons?"

"I don't think so. There's something that might work, though. I've never tried it, but my older sister told me how to do it."

"I didn't think you had any family."

"Oh, Sparhawk!" She laughed. "My family is far, far larger than you could possibly imagine. Get the others. The Seeker will be coming up that road in just a few minutes. Confront it, and I'll bring Sephrenia. It will stop to think—which is to say that Azash will, since Azash is really its mind. But Azash is far too arrogant to avoid a chance to taunt Sephrenia, and that's when I'll strike at the Seeker."

"Are you going to kill it?"

"Of course not. We don't kill things, Sparhawk. We let nature do that. Now go. We don't have much time."

"I don't understand."

"You don't have to. Just go get the others."

They ranged out across the road at the fork, their lances set.

"Does she really know what she's talking about?" Tynian asked dubiously.

"I certainly hope so," Sparhawk murmured.

And then they heard the labored breathing of a horse very near to fatal exhaustion, the unsteady thudding of staggering hooves, and the savage whistle and crack of a whip. The Seeker, black-robed and hunched in its saddle, came around the bend, flogging unmercifully at its dying horse.

"Stay, hound of Hell!" Bevier cried out in a ringing voice, "for here ends your reckless advance!"

"We're going to have to talk to that boy someday," Ulath muttered to Sparhawk.

The Seeker, however, had reined in cautiously.

Then Sephrenia, with Flute at her side, stepped out of the trees. The small Styric woman's face was even paler than usual. Oddly enough, Sparhawk had never fully realized how tiny his teacher really was—scarcely taller than Flute herself. Her presence had always been so commanding that somehow in his mind she had seemed even taller that Ulath. "And is this the meeting thou hast promised, Azash?" she demanded contemptuously. "If so, then I am ready."

"Ssso, Sssephrenia," the hateful voice said, "we meet again and all unexssspectedly. Thisss may be thy lassst day of life."

"Or thine, Azash," she replied with calm courage.

"Thou canssst not dessstroy me." The laugh was hideous.

"Bhelliom can," she told the thing, "and we will deny Bhelliom unto thee and turn it to our own ends. Flee, Azash, if thou wouldst cling to thy life. Pull the rocks of this world over thine head and cower in fear before the wrath of the Younger Gods."

"Isn't she pushing this a little?" Talen said in a strangled voice.

"They're up to something," Sparhawk murmured. "Sephrenia and Flute are deliberately goading that thing into doing something rash."

"Not while I have breath!" Bevier declared fervently, couching his lance.

"Hold your ground, Bevier!" Kurik barked. "They know what they're doing! God knows, none of the rest of us do."

"And art thou ssstill continuing thine unwholesssome dalliancece with these Elene children, Sssephrenia?" the voice of Azash said. "If thine appetite isss ssso vassst, come thou unto me, and I ssshall give thee sssurfeit."

"That is no longer within thy power, Azash, or hast thou forgotten thy unmanning? Thou art an abomination in the sight of all the Gods, and that is why they cast thee out, emasculated thee, and confined thee in thy place of eternal torment and regret."

The thing on the exhausted horse hissed in fury, and Sephrenia nodded calmly to Flute. The little girl lifted her pipes to her lips and began to play. Her melody was rapid, a series of skittering, discordant notes, and the Seeker seemed to shrink back. "It ssshall avail thee not, Sssephrenia," Azash declared in a shrill voice. "There isss yet time."

"Thinkest thou so, mighty Azash?" she said in a taunting voice. "Then thine endless centuries of confinement have bereft thee of thy wits as well as thy manhood."

The Seeker's shriek was one of sheer rage.

"Impotent godling," Sephrenia continued her goading, "return to foul Zemoch and gnaw upon thy soul in vain regret for the delights now eternally denied thee."

Azash howled, and Flute's song grew even faster.

Something was happening to the Seeker. Its body seemed to be writhing under its black robe, and terrible, inarticulate noises came out from under its hood. With an awful jerking motion it clambered down from its dying horse. It half staggered forward, its scorpion claws extended.

Instinctively, the Church Knights moved to protect Sephrenia and the little girl.

"Stay back!" Sephrenia snapped. "It cannot stop what is happening now."

The Seeker fell squirming to the road, tearing off the black robe. Sparhawk suppressed a powerful urge to retch. The Seeker had an elongated body divided in the middle by a waist like that of a wasp, and it glistened with a puslike grayish slime. Its spindly limbs were jointed in many places, and it did not have what one could really call a face, but only two bulging eyes and a gaping maw surrounded by a series of sharp-pointed, fanglike appendages.

Azash shrieked something at Flute. Sparhawk recognized the inflection as Styric, but—and he was forever grateful for the fact—he recognized none of the words.

And then the Seeker began to split apart with an awful ripping sound. There was something inside of it, something that squirmed and wriggled, trying to break free. The rip in the Seeker's body grew wider, and that which was inside began to emerge. It was shiny black and wet. Translucent wings hung from its shoulders. It had two huge protruding eyes, delicate antennae, and no mouth. It shuddered and struggled, pulling itself free of the now-shrunken husk of the Seeker. Then, finally fully emerging, it crouched in the dirt of the road, rapidly fanning its insect wings to dry them. When the wings were dry and flushed with something that might even have been blood, they began to whir, moving so rapidly now that they seemed to blur, and the creature that had been so hideously born before their eyes rose into the air and flew off toward the east.

"Stop it!" Bevier shouted. "Don't let it get away!"

"It's harmless now," Flute told him calmly, lowering her pipes.

"What did you do?" he asked in awe.

"The spell simply speeded up its maturing," she replied. "My sister was right when she taught me that spell. It's an adult now, and all of its instincts are bent on breeding. Not even Azash can override its desperate search for a mate."

"What was the purpose of that little exchange of insults?" Kalten asked Sephrenia.

"Azash had to be so enraged that he would begin to lose his control of the Seeker so that Flute's spell would work," she explained. "That's why I threw certain unpleasant realities in his face."

"Wasn't that a little dangerous?"

"Very," she admitted.

"Will the adult find a mate?" Tynian asked Flute in an awed voice. "I'd hate to see the world crawling with Seekers."

"It will find no mate," she told him. "It is the only one of its kind on the surface of the earth. It no longer has a mouth, so it can no longer feed. It will fly around in its desperate search for a week or so."

"And then?"

"And then? And then it will die." She said it in a chillingly indifferent voice.

## CHAPTER TWENTY

They dragged the husk of the Seeker off the road and returned to the trees to await Ghwerig. "Where is he now?" Sparhawk asked Flute.

"Not far from the north end of the lake," she replied. "He's not moving right now. It's my guess that now that the fog has burned off, the serfs have gone to the fields. There are probably so many people about that he has to hide."

"That means that he's likely to come through here after nightfall, doesn't it?"

"It's probable, yes."

"I'm really not very excited about meeting a Troll in the dark."

"I can make light, Sparhawk—enough for our purposes, anyway."

"I'd appreciate it." He frowned. "If you could do that to the Seeker, why didn't you do it before?"

"There wasn't time. It always came on us by surprise. It takes awhile to prepare oneself for that particular spell. Do you really have to talk so much, Sparhawk? I'm trying to concentrate on Bhelliom."

"Sorry. I'll go talk with Ulath. I want to find out exactly how to go about attacking a Troll."

He found the big Genidian Knight dozing under a tree. "What's happening?" Ulath said, one of his blue eyes opening.

"Flute says that Ghwerig's probably hiding right now. He's not moving, at any rate. He's likely to come past here sometime tonight."

Ulath nodded. "Trolls like to move around in the dark," he said. "It's their customary hunting time."

"What's the best way to deal with him?"

"Lances might work—if we all charge him at the same time. One of us might be able to get in a lucky thrust."

"This is a little too serious to be trusting to luck."

"It's worth a try—for a start, anyway. We'll probably still have to fall back on swords and axes. We'll need to be very careful, though. You have to watch out for a Troll's arms. They're very long, and Trolls are much more agile than they look."

"You seem to know a great deal about them. Have you ever fought one?"

"A few times, yes. It's not really the sort of thing you want to make a habit of. Has Berit still got that bow of his?"

"I think so, yes."

"Good. That's usually the best way to start on a Troll—slow him down with a few arrows and then move in to finish up."

"Will he have any weapons?"

"Maybe a club. Trolls don't really have the knack of working in iron or steel."

"How did you ever learn their language?"

"We had a pet Troll in our chapterhouse at Heid. Found him when he was a cub, but Trolls are born knowing how to speak their language. He was an affectionate little rascal—at least at first. Turned mean on us later on, though. I learned the language from him while he was growing up."

"You say he turned mean?"

"It wasn't really his fault, Sparhawk. When a Troll grows up, he starts to get these urges, and we didn't have time to hunt down a female for him. And then his appetite started to get out of hand. He'd eat a couple of cows or a horse every week."

"What finally happened to him?"

"One of our brothers went out to feed him, and he attacked. The brothers couldn't have that, so we decided that we'd have to kill him. It took five of us, and most of us had to take to our beds for a week or so afterward."

"Ulath," Sparhawk said suspiciously, "are you pulling my leg?"

"Would I do that? Trolls aren't really too bad—as long as you've got plenty of armed men around you. An arrow in the belly usually makes them kind of cautious. It's the Ogres you've got to watch out for. They don't have enough brains to be cautious." He scratched at his cheek. "There was an Ogress once who developed an unreasoning passion for one of the brothers at Heid," he said. "She wasn't too bad looking—for an Ogress. She kept her fur fairly clean and her horns shiny. She even used to polish her fangs. They chew granite to do that, you know. Anyhow, as I was saying, she was wildly in love with this knight at Heid. She used to lurk in the woods and sing to him—most awful sound you ever heard. She could sing all the needles off a pine tree at a hundred paces. The knight finally couldn't stand it any more, and he entered a monastery. She just pined away after that."

"Ulath, I *know* you're pulling my leg now."

"Why, Sparhawk," Ulath protested mildly.

"Then the best way to get Ghwerig out of the way is to stand back and shoot him full of arrows?"

"For a start. We'll still have to get in close, though. Trolls have very tough hide and thick fur. Arrows don't usually penetrate very deep, and trying to do it in the dark is going to make it very tricky."

"Flute says she can make enough light for us."

"She's a very strange person, isn't she—even for a Styric?"

"That she is, my friend."

"How old do you think she really is?"

"I have no idea. Sephrenia won't even give me a clue. I do know that she's much, much older than she appears to be, and much wiser than any of us can guess."

"After the way she got that Seeker off our backs, I don't think it would hurt us to do as she says for a while."

"I'd agree to that," Sparhawk said.

"Sparhawk," the little girl called sharply, "come here."

"I just wish she wouldn't be so imperious all the time," Sparhawk muttered, turning around to answer the summons.

"Ghwerig's doing something I don't understand," she said when he rejoined her.

"What's that?"

"He's moving out onto the lake."

"He must have found a boat," Sparhawk said. "Ulath tells us that he can't swim. Which way's he going?"

She closed her eyes in concentration. "More or less to the northwest. He'll miss the city of Venne and come out on the west side of the lake. We're going to have to ride on down there if we're going to intercept him."

"I'll tell the others," Sparhawk said. "How fast is he moving?"

"Very slowly right now. I don't think he knows how to row a boat very well."

"That might give us a little time to get there before he does."

They broke their minimal encampment and rode south along the west side of Lake Venne as twilight settled over western Pelosia.

"Will you be able to pinpoint his approximate landing place by the sense you're picking up from Bhelliom?" Sparhawk asked Flute, who rode in Sephrenia's arms.

"To within a half mile or so," she replied. "It gets more precise as he gets closer to shore. There are currents and winds and that sort of thing, you understand."

"Is he still moving slowly?"

"Even more so. Ghwerig has certain difficulties with his shoulders and hips. It would make rowing very difficult for him."

"Can you make any kind of guess about when he'll make it to shore here on the west side of the lake?"

"In his present condition, not until well after daybreak tomorrow. At this point he's fishing. He needs food."

"With his hands?"

"Trolls are very, very fast with their hands. The lake surface confuses him. Most of the time, he's not even sure which way he's going. Trolls have a very poor sense of direction—except for north. They can feel the pull of the pole through the earth. On water, though, they're almost helpless."

"We've got him then."

"Don't plan the victory celebration until after you've won the fight, Sparhawk," she said tartly.

"You're a very disagreeable little girl, Flute. Do you know that?"

"But you do love me, don't you?" she said with disarming ingenuousness.

"What can you do?" he helplessly asked Sephrenia. "She's impossible."

"Answer her question, Sparhawk," his tutor suggested. "It's more important than you realize."

"Yes, God help me," he said to Flute, "I do. There are times when I want to spank you, but I *do* love you."

"That's all that's important." She sighed. Then she snuggled up in Sephrenia's protective robe and went promptly to sleep.

They patrolled a long stretch of the western shore of Lake Venne, peering out into the darkness that had settled over the lake. Gradually during the long night, Flute narrowed the area of their patrol, bringing them closer and closer together.

"How can you tell?" Kalten demanded of her a few hours past midnight.

"Would he understand?" Flute asked Sephrenia.

"Kalten? Probably not, but you can try to explain it, if you'd like." Sephrenia smiled. "We all need a bit of frustration in our lives from time to time."

"It feels different when Bhelliom's moving at a diagonal than when it's coming at you head-on," Flute tried.

"Oh," he said dubiously, "that makes sense, I suppose."

"See," Flute said triumphantly to Sephrenia, "I knew I could make him understand."

"Only one question," Kalten added. "What's a diagonal?"

"Oh dear," she said, pressing her face against Sephrenia in a gesture of despair.

"Well, what is it?" Kalten appealed to his fellow knights.

"Let's swing south a bit, Kalten, and keep an eye on the lake," Tynian said. "I'll explain it to you as we go along."

"You!" Sephrenia said to Ulath, who had a faint smile on his face. "Not a word."

"I didn't say anything."

Sparhawk turned Faran and rode slowly back toward the north, looking out at the dark waters.

The moon rose late that night, and it cast a long, glittering path across the surface of the lake. Sparhawk relaxed a bit then. Looking for a Troll in the dark had been a very tense business. It seemed somehow almost too easy now. All they had to do was wait for Ghwerig to reach the lake shore. After all the difficulties and setbacks that had dogged them since they had set out in search of Bhelliom, the idea of just being able to sit and wait for it to be delivered to them made Sparhawk a little nervous. He had an ominous suspicion that something was going to go wrong. If all the things that had happened in Lamorkand and here in Pelosia were any indication, something was bound to go wrong. Their quest had been dogged by near-disaster almost from the moment they had left the chapterhouse at Cimmura, and Sparhawk saw no reason to hope that this situation would be any different.

Once again, the sun rose in a rusty sky, a coppery disk hanging low over the brown-stained waters of the lake. Sparhawk rode wearily back through the grove of trees from which they kept watch to where Sephrenia and the children were waiting. "How far away is he now?" he asked Flute.

"He's about a mile out in the lake," she replied. "He's stopped again."

"Why does he keep stopping?" Sparhawk was growing increasingly irritated about these periodic halts in the Troll's progress across the lake.

"Would you like to hear a guess?" Talen asked.

"Go ahead."

"I stole a boat once because I had to get across the Cimmura River. The boat leaked. I had to stop every five minutes or so to bail out the water. Ghwerig's been stopping about every half hour. Maybe his boat doesn't leak as much as mine did."

Sparhawk stared at the boy for a moment, and then he suddenly burst out laughing. "Thanks, Talen," he said, feeling suddenly much better.

"No charge," the boy replied impudently. "You see, Sparhawk, the easiest answer is usually the right one."

"Then I've got a Troll out there in a leaky boat, and I've got to wait here on shore until he gets all the water out of it."

"That pretty well sums it up, yes."

Tynian rode in at a canter. "Sparhawk," he said quietly, "we've got some riders coming in from the west."

"How many?"

"Too many to count conveniently."

"Let's take a look." The two rode back through the trees to where Kalten, Ulath, and Bevier were sitting their horses, looking off to the west. "I've been watching them, Sparhawk," Ulath said. "I think they're Thalesians."

"What are Thalesians doing here in Pelosia?"

"Remember what that innkeeper told you back in Venne?" Kalten said, "about a war going on down in Arcium? Didn't he say that the western kingdoms are mobilizing?"

"I'd forgotten about that," Sparhawk admitted. "Well, it's none of our concern—at least not for the moment."

Kurik and Berit rode up. "I think we've seen him, Sparhawk," Kurik reported. "At least Berit has."

Sparhawk looked quickly at the novice.

"I climbed a tree, Sir Sparhawk," Berit explained. "There's a small boat some distance off shore. I couldn't make out too many details, but it looks as if it's just drifting, and there seems to be some splashing going on."

Sparhawk laughed wryly. "I guess Talen was right," he said.

"I don't quite follow, Sir Sparhawk."

"He said that Ghwerig probably stole a leaky boat, and that he has to stop every so often to bail out the water."

"You mean we've been waiting all night while Ghwerig scoops the water out of his boat?" Kalten asked.

"It looks that way," Sparhawk said.

"They're getting closer, Sparhawk," Tynian said, pointing to the west.

"And they're definitely Thalesians," Ulath added.

Sparhawk swore and went to the edge of the trees. The approaching men were formed up in a column; at the head of the column rode a large man in a mail shirt and a purple cape. Sparhawk recognized him. It was King Wargun of Thalesia, and he appeared to be roaring drunk. Beside him rode a pale, slender man in a highly decorated but somewhat delicate suit of armor.

"The one beside Wargun is King Soros of Pelosia," Tynian said quietly. "I don't think he poses much of a danger. He spends most of his time praying and fasting."

"We do have a problem, though, Sparhawk," Ulath said gravely. "Ghwerig's going to be coming ashore very shortly, and he's got the royal crown of Thalesia with him. Wargun would give his very soul to get that crown back. I hate to say it, but we'd better lead him away from here before Ghwerig reaches the lake shore."

Sparhawk began to swear in frustration. His suspicions of the previous night had turned out to be all too correct.

"We'll be all right, Sparhawk," Bevier assured him. "Flute can follow Bhelliom's trail. We'll get King Wargun some distance away and then take our leave of him. We can come back later and chase down the Troll."

"It doesn't look as if we have much choice," Sparhawk conceded. "Let's go get Sephrenia and the children and draw Wargun away from here."

They mounted quickly and rode back to where Sephrenia, Talen, and Flute waited. "We're going to have to leave," Sparhawk said tersely. "There are some Thalesians coming, and King Wargun's with them. Ulath says that if Wargun finds out what we're here for, he'll try to take the crown away from us as soon as we get our hands on it. Let's ride."

They left the trees on the margin of the lake at a gallop, headed north. As they had anticipated, the column of Thalesian troops moved in pursuit. "We need a couple of miles at least," Sparhawk shouted to the others. "We've got to give Ghwerig a chance to get away."

They reached the road that bore northeasterly back toward the city of Venne and galloped along, rather ostentatiously not looking back at the pursuing Thalesians.

"They're coming up fast," Talen, who could look back over his shoulder without seeming to, called to Sparhawk.

"I'd like to get them a little farther away from Ghwerig," Sparhawk said regretfully, "but I guess this is as far as we can go."

"Ghwerig's a Troll, Sparhawk," Ulath said. "He knows how to hide."

"All right," Sparhawk agreed. He made some show of looking back over his shoulder and then held up one hand in the signal for a halt. They reined in and turned their horses to face the oncoming Thalesians.

The Thalesians also halted, and one of their number came forward at a walk. "King Wargun of Thalesia would have words with you, Sir Knights," he said respectfully. "He will join us presently."

"Very well," Sparhawk said curtly.

"Wargun's drunk," Ulath muttered to his friend. "Try to be diplomatic, Sparhawk."

King Wargun and King Soros rode up and reined in their horses. "Ho-ho, Soros!" Wargun roared, swaying dangerously in his saddle. "We seem to have snared us a covey of Church Knights." He blinked and peered at the knights. "I know that one," he said. "Ulath, what are you doing here in Pelosia?"

"Church business, your Majesty," Ulath replied blandly.

"And that one with the broken nose is the Pandion Sparhawk," Wargun added to King Soros. "Why were you running so hard, Sparhawk?"

"Our mission is of a certain urgency, your Majesty," Sparhawk said.

"And what mission is that?"

"We're not at liberty to discuss it, your Majesty. Standard Church practice, you understand."

"Politics then," Wargun snorted. "I wish the Church would keep her nose out of politics."

"Will you ride along with us for a ways, your Majesty?" Bevier inquired politely.

"No, I think it's going to be the other way around, Sir Knight—and it's going to be more than just a ways." Wargun looked at them all. "Do you know what's been going on in Arcium?"

"We've heard a few garbled rumors, your Majesty," Tynian said, "but nothing very substantial."

"All right," Wargun said, "I'll give you some substance. The Rendors have invaded Arcium."

"That's impossible!" Sparhawk exclaimed.

"Go tell the people who used to live in Coombe about impossible. The Rendors sacked and burned the town. Now they're marching north toward the capital at Larium. King Dregos has invoked the mutual defense treaties. Soros here and I are gathering up every able-bodied man we can lay our hands on. We're going to ride south and stamp out the Rendorish infection once and for all."

"I wish we could accompany your Majesty," Sparhawk said, "but we have another commitment. Perhaps, once our task is finished, we may be able to join you."

"You already have, Sparhawk," Wargun said bluntly.

"We have another urgent commitment, your Majesty," Sparhawk repeated.

"The Church is eternal, Sparhawk, and she's very patient. Your other commitment will have to wait."

That did it. Sparhawk, whose temper was never really all that much under control, looked the monarch of Thalesia full in the face. Unlike the anger of other men, whose rage was dissipated in shouting and oaths, Sparhawk's grew more and more icy calm. "We are Church Knights, your Majesty," he said in a flat, unemotional voice. "We are not subject to earthly kings. Our responsibility is to God and to our mother, the Church. We will obey *her* commands, not yours."

"I have a thousand picked men at my back," Wargun blustered.

"And how many are you prepared to lose?" Sparhawk asked in his deadly quiet voice. He drew himself up in his saddle and slowly lowered his visor. "Let's save some time, Wargun of Thalesia," he said formally, removing his right gauntlet. "I find your attitude unseemly, even irreligious, and it offends me." With a negligent-appearing toss, he threw his gauntlet into the dust of the road in front of the Thalesian king.

"*That's* his idea of diplomacy?" Ulath murmured to Kalten in some dismay.

"That's about as close as he can usually get," Kalten said, loosening his sword in its sheath. "You may as well go ahead and draw your ax, Ulath. This promises to be an interesting morning. Sephrenia, take the children to the rear."

"Are you mad, Kalten?" Ulath exploded. "You want me to draw my ax on my own king?"

"Of course not," Kalten grinned, "only on his funeral cortege. If Wargun goes up against Sparhawk, he'll be drinking heavenly mead after the first pass."

"Then I'll have to fight Sparhawk," Ulath said regretfully.

"That's up to you, my friend," Kalten said with equal regret, "but I don't advise it. Even if you get past Sparhawk, you'll still have to face me, and I cheat a lot."

"I will not permit this!" a booming voice roared. The man who shouldered his horse through the surrounding Thalesians was huge, bigger even than Ulath. He wore a mail shirt, and an Ogre-horned helmet, and carried a massive ax. A wide black ribbon about his neck identified him as a churchman. "Pick up your gauntlet, Sir Sparhawk, and withdraw your challenge! This is the command of our mother, the Church!"

"Who's that?" Kalten asked Ulath.

"Bergsten, the Patriarch of Emsat," Ulath replied.

"A *patriarch*? Dressed like that?"

"Bergsten's not your average churchman."

"Your Grace," King Wargun faltered. "I—"

"Put up your sword, Wargun," Bergsten thundered, "or would you face *me* in single combat?"

"*I* wouldn't," Wargun said almost conversationally to Sparhawk. "Would *you*?"

Sparhawk looked appraisingly at the Patriarch of Emsat. "Not if I could help it," he admitted. "How *did* he get that big?"

"He was an only child," Wargun said. "He didn't have to fight with nine brothers and sisters for his supper every night. What's your feeling about a truce at this point, Sparhawk?"

"It sounds like the course of prudence to me, your Majesty. We really have something important to do, though."

"We'll talk about it later—when Bergsten's at prayers."

"This is the command of the Church!" the Patriarch of Emsat roared. "The Church Knights will join us in this holy mission. The Eshandist heresy is an offense against God. It will die on the rocky plains of Arcium. As God gives us strength, my children, let us proceed with this great work that we are about." He wheeled his horse to face south. "Don't forget your gauntlet, Sir Sparhawk," he said over his shoulder. "You might need it when we get to Arcium."

"Yes, your Grace," Sparhawk replied through clenched teeth.

# CHAPTER TWENTY-ONE

Promptly at noon, King Soros of Pelosia called a halt. He instructed his servants to erect his pavilion, and he and his private chaplain retired inside for noon prayers.

"Choirboy," King Wargun muttered under his breath. "Bergsten!" he bellowed.

"Right here, your Majesty," the militaristic patriarch said mildly from behind his king.

"Have you gotten over your siege of bad temper yet?"

"I wasn't really bad tempered, your Majesty. I was merely trying to save lives—yours included."

"What's that supposed to mean?"

"Had you been foolish enough to accept Sir Sparhawk's challenge, you'd be dining in Heaven tonight—or supping in Hell, depending on Divine Judgment."

"That's direct enough."

"Sir Sparhawk's reputation precedes him, your Majesty, and you would be no match for him. Now, what was it you had on your mind?"

"How far is Lamorkand from here?"

"The south end of the lake, my Lord—about two days."

"And the closest Lamork city?"

"That would be Agnak, your Majesty. It's just across the border and a bit to the east."

"All right. We'll go there then. I want to get Soros out of his own country and away from all these religious shrines. If he stops to pray one more time, I'm going to strangle him. We'll pick up the bulk of the army late today. They're already marching south. I'm going to send Soros on down to mobilize the Lamork barons. You go with him, and if he tries to pray more than once a day, you have my permission to brain him."

"That could have some interesting political ramifications, your Majesty," Bergsten noted.

"Lie about it," Wargun growled. "Say it was an accident."

"How can you brain somebody by accident?"

"Think something up. Now, listen to me, Bergsten. I need those Lamorks. Don't let Soros get side-tracked on some religious pilgrimage. Keep him moving. Quote sacred texts to him if you have to. Pick up every Lamork you can lay your hands on and then swing into Elenia. I'll meet you on the Arcian border. I've got to go to Acie in Deira. Obler's called a council of war." He looked around. "Sparhawk," he said disgustedly, "go someplace and pray. A Church Knight should be above eavesdropping."

"Yes, your Majesty," Sparhawk replied.

"That's a very ugly horse you've got there, you know?" Wargun said, looking critically at Faran.

"We're a matched set, your Majesty."

"I'd be careful, King Wargun," Kalten advised over his shoulder as he and Sparhawk started back to where their friends had dismounted. "He bites."

"Which one? Sparhawk or the horse?"

"Take your pick, your Majesty."

The two swung down from their horses and joined their friends. "What's Ghwerig doing?" Sparhawk asked Flute.

"He's still hiding," the little girl replied. "At least I think he is. Bhelliom's not moving. He's probably going to wait until dark before he starts out again."

Sparhawk grunted.

Kalten looked at Ulath. "What's the story behind Bergsten?" he asked. "I've never seen a churchman in armor before."

"He used to be a Genidian Knight," Ulath replied. "He'd be preceptor by now if he hadn't entered the priesthood."

Kalten nodded. "He *did* seem to be carrying that ax as if he knew how to use it. Isn't it a bit unusual for a member of one of the militant orders to take the cloth?"

"Not that unusual, Kalten," Bevier disagreed from nearby. "A fair number of the high churchmen in Arcium used to be Cyrinics. Someday I myself may leave our order so that I can serve God more personally."

"We're going to have to find some nice accommodating girl for that boy, Sparhawk," Ulath muttered. "Let's get him involved in some serious sin so that he gives up that notion. He's too good a man to waste by putting him in a cassock."

"How about Naween?" Talen, who was standing beside them, suggested.

"Who's Naween?" Ulath asked.

Talen shrugged. "The best whore in Cimmura. She's enthusiastic about her work. Sparhawk's met her."

"Really?" Ulath said, looking at Sparhawk with one raised eyebrow.

"It was on business," Sparhawk said shortly.

"Of course—but yours or hers?"

"Do you suppose we could drop this?" Sparhawk cleared his throat and then looked around to make sure that none of King Wargun's soldiers was within earshot. "We've got to get clear of this lot before Ghwerig gets too far ahead of us," he said.

"Tonight," Tynian suggested. "Rumor has it that King Wargun drinks himself to sleep every night. We should be able to slip away without too much problem."

"We surely cannot disobey the direct command of the Patriarch of Emsat," Bevier said in a shocked tone.

"Of course not, Bevier," Kalten said easily. "We'll just slip out and find some country vicar or the abbot of a monastery and get him to order us to go back to what we were doing."

"That's immoral!" Bevier gasped.

"I know." Kalten smirked. "Disgusting, isn't it?"

"But it *is* technically legitimate, Bevier," Tynian assured the young Cyrinic. "A bit devious, I'll admit, but still legitimate. We're oath-bound to follow the orders of consecrated members of the clergy. The order of a vicar or an abbot would super-sede the order of Patriarch Bergsten, wouldn't it?" Tynian's eyes were wide and inno-cent.

Bevier looked at him helplessly, and then he began to laugh.

"I think he's going to be all right, Sparhawk," Ulath said, "but let's keep your friend Naween in reserve—just in case."

"Who's Naween?" Bevier asked, puzzled.

"An acquaintance of mine," Sparhawk replied distantly. "Someday I may intro-duce you."

"I'd be honored," Bevier said sincerely.

Talen went off some distance and collapsed in helpless laughter.

They caught up with the mob of disconsolate-looking Pelosian conscripts late that afternoon. As Sparhawk had feared, the perimeter of their encampment was being patrolled by Wargun's heavily armed thugs.

The soldiers set up a pavilion for them just before sunset, and they went inside. Sparhawk removed his armor and put on a mail shirt instead. "The rest of you wait here," he said. "I want to take a look around before it gets dark." He put on his sword belt and stepped out of the tent.

There were two evil-looking Thalesians outside. "Where do you think you're going?" one of them demanded.

Sparhawk gave him a flat, unfriendly stare and waited.

"My Lord," the fellow grudgingly added.

"I want to check on my horses," Sparhawk said.

"We have farriers to do that, Sir Knight."

"We're not going to have an argument about this, are we, neighbor?"

"Ah—no, I don't think so, Sir Knight."

"Good. Where are the horses picketed?"

"I'll show you, Sir Sparhawk."

"There's no need of that. Just tell me."

"I have to accompany you anyway, Sir Knight. The king's orders."

"I see. Lead on then."

As they started out, Sparhawk heard a sudden boisterous voice. "Ho there, Sir Knight!" He looked around.

"I see they got you and your friends, too." It was Kring, the Domi of the marauding band of Peloi.

"Hello, my friend," Sparhawk greeted the shaved-headed tribesman. "Did you catch up with those Zemochs?"

Kring laughed. "I've got a whole sackful of ears," he said. "They tried to make a stand. Stupid people, the Zemochs. But then King Soros took up with this ragtag army, and we had to follow along in order to collect the bounty." He rubbed at his shaved head. "That's all right, though. We didn't have anything pressing to do back home anyway, now that the mares have all foaled. Tell me, do you still have that young thief with you?"

"Last time I looked he was still around. Of course, he might have stolen a few things and then bolted. He bolts very well when the occasion demands it."

"I'll wager he does, Sir Knight. I'll wager he does. How's my friend Tynian? I saw you all when you rode in, and I was just on my way to visit him."

"He's well."

"Good." The Domi looked seriously at Sparhawk then. "Perhaps you can give me some information about military etiquette, Sir Knight. I've never been a part of a formal army before. What are the general rules about pillage?"

"I don't think anybody would get too concerned," Sparhawk replied, "as long as you limit your plundering to the enemy dead. It's considered bad form to loot the bodies of our own soldiers."

"Stupid rule, that one," Kring sighed. "What does a dead man care about possessions? How about rape?"

"It's frowned on. We'll be in Arcium, and that's a friendly country. Arcians are sensitive about their womenfolk. Wargun's gathered up a fair number of camp followers if those urges are bothering you."

"Camp followers always act so bored. Give me a nice young virgin every time. You know, this campaign is turning out to be less and less enjoyable. How about arson? I love a good fire."

"I'd definitely advise against it. As I said, we'll be in Arcium, and all the towns and houses belong to the people who live there. I'm sure they'd object."

"Civilized warfare leaves a lot to be desired, doesn't it, Sir Knight?"

"What can I say, Domi?" Sparhawk apologized, spreading his hands helplessly.

"If you don't mind my saying so, it's the armor, I think. You people are so encased in steel that you lose sight of the main things—booty, women, horses. It's a failing, Sir Knight."

"It is a failing, Domi," Sparhawk conceded. "Centuries of tradition, you understand."

"There's nothing wrong with tradition—as long as it doesn't get in the way of important things."

"I'll bear that in mind, Domi. Our tent's right over there. Tynian will be glad to see you." Sparhawk followed the Thalesian sentry on through the camp to where the horses were picketed. He made some pretense of checking Faran's hooves, looking intently out into the twilight at the perimeter of the camp. As he had noted earlier, there were dozens of men riding around the outside. "Why so many patrols?" he asked the Thalesian.

"The Pelosian conscripts are unenthusiastic about this campaign, Sir Knight," the warrior replied. "We didn't go to all the trouble of gathering them up only to have them sneak off in the middle of the night."

"I see," Sparhawk said. "We can go back now."

"Yes, my Lord."

Wargun's patrols seriously complicated things, not to mention the presence of the two sentries outside their tent. Ghwerig was getting farther and farther away with Bhelliom, and it seemed that there was very little Sparhawk could do about it. He knew that by himself, using a mixture of stealth and main force, he could escape from the camp, but what would that accomplish? Without Flute, he'd have little chance of tracking down the fleeing Troll, and to take her along without the others to help guard her would be to place her in unacceptable danger. They were going to have to come up with some other idea.

The Thalesian warrior was leading him past the tent of some Pelosian conscripts when he saw a familiar face. "Occuda?" he said incredulously, "is that you?"

The lantern-jawed man in bullhide armor rose to his feet, his bleak face showing no particular pleasure at the meeting. "I'm afraid it is, my Lord," he said.

"What happened? What forced you to leave Count Ghasek?"

Occuda looked briefly at the men who shared the tent with him. "Might we discuss this privately, Sir Sparhawk?"

"Certainly, Occuda."

"Over there, my Lord."

"I'll be in plain sight," Sparhawk told his escort. Together Sparhawk and Occuda walked away from the tent and stopped near a grove of sapling fir trees that stood so closely together that they precluded the possibility of anyone's pitching a tent among them.

"The count has fallen ill, my Lord," Occuda said somberly.

"And you left him alone with that madwoman? I'm disappointed in you, Occuda."

"The circumstances have changed somewhat, my Lord."

"Oh?"

"The Lady Bellina is dead now."

"What happened to her?"

"I killed her." Occuda said it in a numb voice. "I could no longer bear her endless screaming. At first the herbs the Lady Sephrenia advised quieted Bellina somewhat, but after a short while, she seemed to shake off their effects. I tried to increase the dosage, but to no avail. Then one night, as I was pushing her supper through that slot in the tower wall, I saw her. She was raving and frothing at the mouth like a rabid dog. She was obviously in agony. That's when I made the decision to put her to rest."

"We all knew it might come to that," Sparhawk said gravely.

"Perhaps. I could not bring myself simply to slaughter her, however. The herbs no longer quieted her. The nightshade, however did. She stopped screaming shortly after I gave it to her." There were tears in Occuda's eyes. "I took my sledge and broke a hole in the tower wall. Then I did as you instructed with my ax. I've never done anything so difficult in my life. I wrapped her body in canvas and took her outside the castle. There I burned her. After what I had done, I could not face the count. I left him a note confessing my crime and then went to a woodcutter's village not far from the castle. I hired servants there to care for the count. Even after I told them there was no longer any danger at the castle, I had to pay them double wages to get them to agree. Then I came away from that place and joined this army. I hope the fighting starts soon. Everything in my life is over. All I want now is to die."

"You did what you had to, Occuda."

"Perhaps, but that does not absolve me of my guilt."

Sparhawk made a decision at that point. "Come with me," he said.

"Where are we going, my Lord?"

"To see the Patriarch of Emsat."

"I could not enter the presence of a high churchman with Lady Bellina's blood on my hands."

"Patriarch Bergsten is a Thalesian. I doubt that he's very squeamish. We need to see the Patriarch of Emsat," he told his Thalesian escort. "Take us to his tent."

"Yes, my Lord."

The sentry led them through camp to the pavilion of Patriarch Bergsten. Bergsten's brutish face looked particularly Thalesian by candlelight. He had heavy bone ridges across his brows, and his cheekbones and jaw were prominent. He was still wearing his mail shirt, although he had removed his Ogre-horned helmet and stood his ax in the corner.

"Your Grace," Sparhawk said with a bow, "my friend here has a problem of a spiritual nature. I wonder if you could help him?"

"That is my calling, Sir Sparhawk," the patriarch replied.

"Thank you, your Grace. Occuda here was at one time a monk. Then he entered the service of a count in northern Pelosia. The count's sister became involved with an evil cult, and she began to practice rites involving human sacrifice, which gave her certain powers."

Bergsten's eyes widened.

"At any rate," Sparhawk continued, "when the count's sister was finally stripped of those powers, she went mad, and her brother was forced to confine her. Occuda took care of her until he could no longer bear her agonies. Then, out of compassion, he poisoned her."

"That's a dreadful story, Sir Sparhawk," Bergsten said in his deep voice.

"It was a dreadful series of events," Sparhawk agreed. "Occuda feels overcome with guilt now, and he's convinced that his soul is lost. Can you absolve him so that he can face the rest of his life?"

The armored Patriarch Bergsten looked thoughtfully at Occuda's suffering face, his eyes at once shrewd and compassionate. He seemed to consider the matter for several moments, then he straightened, and his expression grew hard. "No, Sir Sparhawk, I can't," he said flatly.

Sparhawk was about to protest, but the patriarch raised one thick hand. He looked at the hulking Pelosian. "Occuda," he said sternly, "you were once a monk?"

"I was, your Grace."

"Good. This shall be your penance then. You will resume your monk's habit, Brother Occuda, and you will enter my service. When I have decided that you have paid for your sin, I will grant you absolution."

"Y-your Grace," Occuda sobbed, falling to his knees, "how can I ever thank you?"

Bergsten smiled bleakly. "You may change your mind in time, Brother Occuda. You will find that I'm a very hard master. You'll pay for your sin many times over before your soul is washed clean. Now, go gather your possessions. You'll be moving in here with me."

"Yes, your Grace." Occuda rose and left the tent.

"If you don't mind my saying so, your Grace," Sparhawk said, "you are a very devious man."

"No, not really, Sir Sparhawk." The huge churchman smiled. "It's just that I've had enough experience to know that the human spirit is a very complex thing. Your friend feels that he must suffer in order to expiate his sin, and if I were simply to absolve him, he would always doubt that he had been throughly cleansed. He feels that he has to suffer, so I'll make sure that he suffers—in moderation, of course. I'm not a monster, after all."

"Was what he did really a sin?"

"Of course not. He acted out of mercy. He'll make a very good monk, and after I think he's suffered long enough, I'll find a nice quiet monastery some place and make him the abbot. He'll be too busy to brood about things, and the Church will get a good, faithful abbot. This is not to mention all those years when I'll have his services at no cost."

"You're not really a very nice man, your Grace."

"I have never pretended to be, my son. That will be all, Sir Sparhawk. Go with my blessing." The patriarch winked slyly.

"Thank you, your Grace," Sparhawk said without cracking a smile.

He felt somehow very pleased with himself as he and the sentry walked back across the camp. He might not always be able to solve his own problems, but he certainly seemed able to solve those of others.

"Kring was telling us that the outside of the camp is being patrolled," Tynian said when Sparhawk re-entered the tent. "That's going to make it more difficult to get away, isn't it?"

"Much more," Sparhawk agreed.

"Oh," Tynian added. "Flute's been asking some questions about distances. Kurik looked in the packs, but he couldn't find your map."

"It's in my saddlebag."

"I should have thought of that, I suppose," Kurik said.

"What is it you want to know?" Sparhawk asked the little girl, opening his saddlebag for the map.

"How far is it from this Agnak place to Acie?"

Sparhawk spread his map out on the table in the center of the pavilion.

"It's a very pretty picture, but it doesn't answer my question," she said.

Sparhawk measured it off. "It's about three hundred leagues," he replied.

"That still doesn't answer my question, Sparhawk. I need to know how long it will take."

He computed it. "About twenty days."

She frowned. "Perhaps I can shorten that a bit," she said.

"What are we talking about here?" he asked her.

"Acie's on the coast, isn't it?"

"Yes."

"We're going to need a boat to get us to Thalesia. Ghwerig's taking Bhelliom to his cave up in the mountains there."

"There are enough of us to overpower the sentries," Kalten said, "and dealing with a patrol in the middle of the night's not all that hard. We're still not so far behind Ghwerig that we can't catch him."

"We have something to do in Acie," she told him. "At least I do—and it must be done before we go after Bhelliom. We know where Ghwerig's going, so he won't be hard to find. Ulath, go tell Wargun that we'll accompany him to Acie. Think up some plausible reason."

"Yes, lady," he said with the faintest hint of a smile.

"I wish you'd all stop doing that," she complained. "Oh, by the way, on your way to Wargun's tent, ask someone to bring us some supper."

"What would you like?"

"Goat would be nice, but anything will do as long as it's not pork."

They reached Agnak just before sunset the following day and set up their huge camp. The local citizenry immediately closed the city gates. King Wargun insisted that Sparhawk and the other Church Knights accompany him under a flag of truce to the north gate. "I am Wargun of Thalesia," he roared at the city walls. "I have King Soros of Pelosia with me—as well as these Knights of the Church. The Kingdom of Arcium has been invaded by the Rendors, and I call upon every able-bodied man with faith in God to join with us in our efforts to stamp out the Eshandist heresy. I'm not here to inconvenience you in any way, my friends, but if that gate isn't open by the time the sun goes down, I'll reduce your walls to rubble and drive you all into the wilderness where you can watch your city burn down to ashes."

"Do you think they heard him?" Kalten asked.

"They probably heard him in Chyrellos," Tynian replied. "Your king has a most penetrating voice, Sir Ulath."

"It's a long way from one mountain top to another in Thalesia." Ulath shrugged. "You have to talk very loud if you want to be heard."

King Wargun grinned crookedly at him. "Would anyone care to wager on whether or not that gate opens before the sun slips behind yon hill?" he asked.

"We are Church Knights, your Majesty," Bevier replied piously. "We take a vow of poverty, so we're not really in a position to gamble on sporting events."

King Wargun roared with laughter.

The city gate opened somewhat hesitantly.

"Somehow I knew they'd see it my way," Wargun said, leading the way into the city. "Where will I find your chief magistrate?" he asked one of the trembling gate guards.

"I-I believe he's in the council house, your Majesty," the guard stammered. "Probably hiding in the cellar."

"Be a good fellow and go fetch him for me."

"At once, your Majesty." The guard threw down his pike and ran off down the street.

"I like Lamorks," Wargun said expansively. "They're always so eager to be obliging."

The chief magistrate was a pudgy man. His face was pale, and he was sweating profusely as the gate guard bodily dragged him into Wargun's presence.

"I will require suitable quarters for King Soros, myself, and our entourage, your Excellency," Wargun informed him. "This won't inconvenience your citizens all that much, because they'll be up all night equipping themselves for an extended military campaign anyway."

"As your Majesty commands," the magistrate replied in a squeaky voice.

"You see what I mean about Lamorks?" Wargun said. "Soros will have smooth going down here. He'll sweep the whole kingdom clean in a week—if he doesn't stop to pray too often. Why don't we go someplace and get something to drink while his excellency here empties a dozen or so houses for us?"

After a consultation with King Soros and Patriarch Bergsten the following morning, Wargun took a troop of Thalesian cavalry and led them toward the west with Sparhawk riding at his side. It was a fine morning. The sunlight sparkled on the lake, and there was a light breeze blowing in from the west.

"I suppose you're still not going to tell me what you were doing in Pelosia?" Wargun said to Sparhawk. The Thalesian King seemed relatively sober this morning, so Sparhawk decided to risk his mood.

"You know about Queen Ehlana's illness, of course," he began.

"The whole world knows about it. That's why her bastard cousin is trying to seize power."

"There's a bit more to it than that, your Majesty. We've finally isolated the cause of the illness. Primate Annias needed access to her treasury, so he had her poisoned."

"He did *what?*"

Sparhawk nodded. "Annias is not overburdened with scruples and he'll do anything to reach the Archprelacy."

"The man's a scoundrel," Wargun growled.

"At any rate, we've discovered a possible cure for Ehlana. It involves the use of magic, and we need a certain talisman to make it work. We found out that the talisman is in Lake Venne."

"What is this talisman?" Wargun asked, his eyes narrowed.

"It's a kind of an ornament," Sparhawk replied evasively.

"Do you really put that much store in all that magic nonsense?"

"I've seen it work a few times, your Majesty. Anyhow, that's why we objected so much when you insisted that we join you. We weren't trying to be disrespectful. Ehlana's life is being sustained by a spell, but it's only good for just so long. If she dies, Lycheas will take the throne."

"Not if I can help it, he won't. I don't want any throne in Eosia occupied by a man who doesn't know his own father."

"The idea doesn't appeal to me either, but I think Lycheas does in fact know who his father is."

"Oh? Who is it? Do you know?"

"The Primate Annias."

Wargun's eyes went wide. "Are you sure of that?"

Sparhawk nodded. "I have it on the very best authority. The ghost of King Aldreas told me. His sister was a bit profligate."

Wargun made the sign to ward off evil, a peasant gesture that looked peculiar coming from a reigning monarch. "A ghost, you say? The word of a ghost won't stand up in any court, Sparhawk."

"I wasn't planning to take it to court, your Majesty," Sparhawk said grimly, resting his hand on his sword hilt. "As soon as I have the leisure, the principals will be standing before a higher judgment."

"Good man," Wargun approved. "I wouldn't have thought that a churchman would have succumbed to Arissa, though."

"Arissa can be very persuasive sometimes. Anyway, this campaign of yours is directed at another one of Annias' plots. I strongly suspect that the Rendorish invasion is being led by a man named Martel. Martel works for Annias, and he's been trying to stir up enough trouble to draw the Church Knights away from Chyrellos during the election. Our preceptors could probably keep Annias off the Archprelate's throne, so he had to get them out of his way."

"The man's a real snake, isn't he?"

"That's a pretty fair description."

"You've given me a lot to think about this morning, Sparhawk. I'll mull it over, and we'll talk some more about it later."

A sudden light sprang into Sparhawk's eyes.

"Don't get your hopes up too much, though. I still think I'm going to need you when I get to Arcium. Besides, the militant orders have already marched south. You're Vanion's right arm, and I think he'd miss you if you stayed away."

Time and distance seemed to drag on interminably as they rode west. They crossed into Pelosia again and rode across the unending plains in bright summer sunlight.

One night when they were still some distance from the border of Deira, Kalten was in a bad humor. "I thought you said you were going to speed this trip up," he said accusingly to Flute.

"I did," she replied.

"Really?" he said with heavy sarcasm. "We've been on the road for a week already, and we haven't even reached Deira yet."

"Actually, Kalten, we've only been on the road for two days. I have to make it *seem* longer so that Wargun doesn't get suspicious."

He looked at her disbelievingly.

"I've got another question for you, Flute," Tynian said. "Back at the lake, you were very eager to catch Ghwerig and take Bhelliom away from him. Then you suddenly changed your mind and said that we have to go to Acie. What happened?"

"I received word from my family," she told him. "They told me about this task I have to complete at Acie before we can go after Bhelliom." She made a wry face. "I probably would have thought of it myself."

"Let's get back to this other thing," Kalten said impatiently. "How did you squeeze time together the way you said you have?"

"There are ways," she said evasively.

"I wouldn't pursue it, Kalten," Sephrenia advised. "You wouldn't understand what she's been doing, so why worry about it? Besides, if you keep asking her questions, she might decide to answer you, and the answers would probably upset you very much."

## CHAPTER TWENTY-TWO

It seemed that it took them two more weeks to reach the foothills above Acie, the bleak, ugly capital of Deira, which perched on an eroded bluff overlooking the original harbor and the long, narrow Gulf of Acie. Flute advised them that evening, however, that no more than five days had passed since they had left the city of Agnak in Lamorkand. Most of them chose to take her at her word, but Sir Bevier, who was of a scholarly and resolutely Elenian frame of mind, questioned her about how this seeming miracle had come to pass. Her explanation was patient, although dreadfully obscure. Bevier finally excused himself and went outside the tent for a time to look at the stars and to re-establish his relations with things he had always considered immutable and eternal.

"Did you understand anything she said at all?" Tynian asked him when he returned, pale and sweating, to the tent.

"A little," Bevier replied, sitting down again. "Just around the edges." He looked at Flute with frightened eyes. "I think perhaps that Patriarch Ortzel was right. We should have no dealings with these Styric people. Nothing is sacred to them."

Flute crossed the tent on her grass-stained little feet and laid a consoling hand on his cheek. "Dear Bevier," she said sweetly, "so serious and so devout. We must get to Thalesia quickly—just as soon as I can finish what I have to do in Acie. We simply did not have the time to plod halfway across the continent at the usual pace. That's why I did it the other way."

"I understand the reasons," he said, "but—"

"I will never hurt you, you know, and I won't let anybody else hurt you either, but you must try not to be so rigid. It makes it so very hard to explain things to you. Does that help at all?"

"Not appreciably."

She raised up on her tiptoes and kissed him. "Now then," she said brightly, "everything's all right again, isn't it?"

He gave up. "Do as you will, Flute," he said to her with a gentle, almost shy smile. "I can't refute your arguments and your kisses at the same time."

"He's such a *nice* boy," she said delightedly to the others.

"We sort of feel the same way about him ourselves," Ulath said blandly, "and we have some plans for him."

"You, however," she said critically to the Genidian Knight, "are most definitely *not* a nice boy."

"I know," he admitted, unruffled, "and you have no idea how much that disappointed my mother—and a number of other ladies from time to time as well."

She gave him a dark look and stalked away, muttering to herself in Styric. Sparhawk recognized some of the words, and he wondered if she really knew what they meant.

As had become his custom, Wargun asked Sparhawk to ride beside him the following morning as they trekked down the long, rocky slope from the foothills of the Deiran mountains toward the coast. "I should really get out more often," the King of Thalesia confided. "After almost three weeks coming from Agnak, I should be nearly ready to fall out of my saddle, but I feel as if we've been on the road for only a few days."

"Perhaps it was the mountains," Sparhawk suggested carefully. "Mountain air is always invigorating."

"Maybe that's it," Wargun agreed.

"Have you given any more thought to the discussion we had awhile back, your Majesty?" Sparhawk asked cautiously.

"I've had a lot on my mind, Sparhawk. I appreciate your personal concern about Queen Ehlana, but, from a political standpoint, the important thing now is to crush this Rendorish invasion. Then the preceptors of the militant orders will be able to return to Chyrellos and block the Primate of Cimmura. If Annias fails to gain the Archprelacy, Lycheas the bastard won't have any chance of ascending the throne of Elenia. I realize that it's a hard choice, but politics is a hard game."

A little later, when Wargun was conferring with his troop commander, Sparhawk relayed the gist of their conversation to his companions.

"He's not any more reasonable when he's sober, is he?" Kalten said.

"From his own standpoint, he's right, though," Tynian observed. "The politics of the situation dictate that we do everything we can to get all the preceptors back to Chyrellos before Cluvonus dies. I doubt that he cares much one way or the other about Ehlana. There's one other possibility, though. We're in Deira now, and Obler's the king here. He's a very wise old man. If we explain the situation to him, he might overrule Wargun."

"I don't think I'd care to hang Ehlana's life on that slim a possibility," Sparhawk said. He turned to rejoin Wargun.

Despite Flute's assurances concerning the actual elapsed time their journey had consumed, Sparhawk was still impatient. The apparent slow pace nagged at him. While he could intellectually accept what she said, he could not come to grips with it emotionally. Twenty days is twenty days to one's senses, and Sparhawk's senses were strung wire-taut just now. He began to have dark thoughts. Things had been going wrong so consistently that seeming premonitions tugged at his mind. He began to think about the forthcoming encounter with Ghwerig with a great deal less certainty about the outcome.

About noon they reached Acie, the capital city of the Kingdom of Deira. The Deiran army was encamped around the city, and their camp was bustling with activity as they prepared for the march south.

Wargun had been drinking again, but he looked around with satisfaction. "Good," he said, "they're almost ready. Come along, Sparhawk, and bring your friends. Let's go talk to Obler."

As they rode through the narrow, cobbled streets of Acie, Talen pulled his horse in beside Sparhawk's. "I'm going to drop behind a ways," he said very quietly. "I want to look around. Getting away in the open countryside's very hard. This is a town, though, and there are always lots of places to hide in towns. King Wargun's not going to miss me. He hardly knows I'm along. If I can find us a good hiding place, maybe we can slip away to it and stay there until the army moves out. Then we can make a run for Thalesia."

"Just be very careful."

"Naturally."

A few streets farther on, Sephrenia reined in sharply and pulled her white palfrey off to the side of the street. She and Flute quickly dismounted and went to the entrance of a narrow alley to greet an aged Styric with a long, snowy beard who wore an intensely white robe. Some sort of ritual ceremony seemed to take place among the three of them, but Sparhawk could not quite make out the details. Sephrenia and Flute spoke earnestly to the old man at some length, and then he bowed in acknowledgment and went back on up the alley.

"What was that all about?" Wargun asked suspiciously when Sephrenia and the little girl rejoined them.

"He's an old friend, your Majesty," Sephrenia replied, "and the most revered and wise man in all of western Styricum."

"A king, you mean?"

"That's a word that has no meaning in Styricum, your Majesty," she told him.

"How can you have a government if you don't have a king?"

"There are other ways, your Majesty, and besides, Styrics have outgrown the need for government."

"That's absurd."

"Many things seem that way—at first. It may come to you Elenes in time."

"That's a very infuriating woman sometimes, Sparhawk," Wargun growled, pushing his horse back to the front of the column.

"Sparhawk," Flute said very lightly.

"Yes?"

"The task here in Acie is complete. We can leave for Thalesia at any time now."

"How do you propose to manage that?"

"I'll tell you later. Go keep Wargun company. He gets lonesome without you."

The palace was not a particularly imposing building. It looked to be more like a complex of administrative offices than something built for ostentation and display. "I don't know how Obler can live in this hovel," Wargun said disdainfully, swaying in his saddle. "You there," he bellowed at one of the guards posted at the main door, "go tell Obler that Wargun of Thalesia has arrived. We need to confer about a few things."

"At once, your Majesty." The guard saluted and went inside.

Wargun dismounted and unhooked the wineskin from the skirt of his saddle. He uncorked it and took a long drink. "I hope Obler's got some chilled ale," he said. "This wine's beginning to sour my stomach."

The guard returned. "King Obler will receive you, your Majesty," he said. "Please follow me."

"I know the way," Wargun replied. "I've been here before. Have somebody see to our horses." He blinked his bloodshot eyes at Sparhawk. "Come along then," he commanded. He did not appear to have missed Talen.

They trooped through the unadorned hallways of King Obler's palace and found the aged king of Deira sitting behind a large table littered with maps and papers.

"Sorry to be so late, Obler," Wargun said, untying his purple cloak and dropping it on the floor. "I made a swing through Pelosia to pick up Soros and a sort of an army." He sprawled out in a chair. "I've been sort of out of touch. What's been going on?"

"The Rendors have laid siege to Larium," the white-haired King of Deira replied. "The Alciones, Genidians, and Cyrinics are holding the city, and the Pandions are out in the countryside dealing with Rendorish raiding parties."

"That's more or less what I'd expected," Wargun grunted. "Can you send for some ale, Obler? My stomach's been bothering me for the past few days. You remember Sparhawk, don't you?"

"Of course. He's the man who saved Count Radun down in Arcium."

"And this one is Kalten. The big one there is Ulath. The one with the dark skin is Bevier, and I'm sure you know Tynian. The Styric woman is called Sephrenia—I'm not really sure about her real name. I'm sure neither one of us could even pronounce it. She teaches the Pandions magic, and that adorable child there is her little girl. The other two work for Sparhawk. I wouldn't aggravate either one of them." He looked around, his eyes bleary. "What happened to that boy you had with you?" he asked Sparhawk.

"Probably exploring," Sparhawk replied blandly. "Political discussions bore him."

"Sometimes they bore me as well," Wargun said. He looked back at King Obler. "Have the Elenes mobilized yet?"

"My agents have found no evidence of it."

Wargun started to swear. "I think I'll stop in Cimmura on my way south and hang that young bastard Lycheas."

"I'll lend you a rope, your Majesty," Kalten offered.

Wargun laughed. "What's happening in Chyrellos, Obler?"

"Cluvonus is in delirium," Obler replied. "He can't last much longer, I'm afraid. Most of the major churchmen are already there preparing for the election of his successor."

"The Primate of Cimmura, most likely," Wargun growled sourly. He took a tankard of ale from a servant. "That's all right, boy," he said. "Just leave the keg." His voice was slurred. "This is the way I see it, Obler. We'd better get to Larium as quickly as we can. We'll push the Rendors back into the sea so that the militant orders can go to Chyrellos and keep Annias from becoming Archprelate. If that happens, we may have to declare war."

"On the Church?" Obler sounded startled.

"Archprelates have been deposed before, Obler. Annias won't have any use for a miter if he doesn't have a head. Sparhawk has already volunteered to use his knife."

"You'll start a general civil war, Wargun. No one has directly confronted the Church for centuries."

"Then maybe it's about time. Anything else happening?"

"The Earl of Lenda and Preceptor Vanion of the Pandion order arrived no more than an hour ago," Obler said. "They wanted to get cleaned up. I sent for them just as soon as I'd heard that you'd arrived. They'll join us in a bit."

"Good. We'll be able to settle a lot of things here then. What's the date?"

King Obler told him.

"Your calendar must be wrong, Obler," Wargun said after counting days off on his fingers.

"What did you do with Soros?" Obler asked.

"I came close to killing him," Wargun growled. "I've never seen anybody pray so much when there was work to be done. I sent him into Lamorkand to pick up the barons down there. He's riding at the head of the army, but Bergsten's actually the one in charge. Bergsten would make a good Archprelate, if we could ever get him out of that armor." He laughed. "Can you imagine the reaction of the Hierocracy to an Archprelate in a mail shirt and a horned helmet, and with a battle-ax in his hands?"

"It might enliven the Church a bit, Wargun," Obler conceded with a faint smile.

"God knows she needs it," Wargun said. "She's been acting like a frigid old maid since Cluvonus fell ill."

"Would your Majesties excuse me?" Sparhawk asked deferentially. "I'd like to look in on Vanion. We haven't seen each other for a while, and there are things I need to report to him."

"More of this everlasting Church business?" Wargun asked.

"You know how it is, your Majesty."

"No, thank God, I don't. Go ahead, Knight of the Church. Talk with your father superior, but don't keep him too long. We've got important business here."

"Yes, your Majesty." Sparhawk bowed to the two kings and quietly left the room.

Vanion was trying to struggle into his armor when Sparhawk entered the room.

He stared at his subordinate in some astonishment. "What are you doing here, Sparhawk?" he demanded. "I though you were in Lamorkand."

"Just passing through, Vanion," Sparhawk replied. "Some things have changed. I'll give you the gist of it now, and we can fill you in on more detail after King Wargun goes to bed." He looked critically at his preceptor. "You're looking tired, my friend."

"Old age," Vanion said ruefully, "and all of those swords I made Sephrenia give me are getting heavier every day. You know that Olven died?"

"Yes. His ghost brought his sword to Sephrenia."

"I was afraid of that. I'll take it away from her."

Sparhawk tapped Vanion's breastplate with one knuckle. "You don't have to wear this, you know. Obler's fairly informal, and Wargun doesn't even know what the word formal means."

"Appearances, my friend," Vanion said, "and the honor of the Church. Sometimes it's boring, I'll admit, but—" He shrugged. "Help me into this contraption, Sparhawk. You can talk while you're tightening straps and buckling buckles."

"Yes, my Lord Vanion." Sparhawk began to assist his friend into the suit of armor, briefly summarizing the events that had taken place in Lamorkand and Pelosia.

"Why didn't you chase down the Troll?" Vanion asked him.

"Some things came up," Sparhawk said, fastening Vanion's black cape to his shoulder plates. "Wargun, for one thing. I even offered to fight him, but Patriarch Bergsten interfered."

"You challenged a *king*?" Vanion looked stunned.

"It seemed appropriate at the time, Vanion."

"Oh, my friend." Vanion sighed.

"We'd better get going," Sparhawk said. "There's a lot more to tell you, but Wargun's getting impatient." Sparhawk squinted at Vanion's armor. "Brace yourself," he said. "You're lopsided." Then he banged both of his fists down on Vanion's shoulder plates. "There," he said. "That's better."

"Thanks," Vanion said dryly, his knees buckling slightly.

"The honor of the order, my Lord. I don't want you to look as if you were dressed in cheap tin plates."

Vanion decided not to answer that.

The Earl of Lenda was in the room when Sparhawk and Vanion entered.

"There you are, Vanion," King Wargun said. "Now we can get started. What's happening down in Arcium?"

"The situation hasn't changed all that much, your Majesty. The Rendors are still besieging Larium, but the Genidians, Cyrinics, and Alciones are inside the walls along with most of the Arcian army."

"Is the city in any real danger?"

"Hardly. It's built like a mountain. You know the Arcian fondness for stonework. It could probably hold out for twenty years." Vanion looked over at Sparhawk. "I saw an old friend of yours down there," he said. "Martel appears to be in command of the Rendorish army."

"I'd sort of guessed that. I thought I'd nailed his feet to the floor down in Rendor, but apparently he managed to talk his way around Arasham."

"He really didn't have to," King Obler said. "Arasham died a month ago—under highly suspicious circumstances."

"It sounds as if Martel's had his hand in the poison jar again," Kalten said.

"Who's the new spiritual leader in Rendor then?" Sparhawk asked.

"A man named Ulesim," King Obler replied. "I gather he was one of Arasham's disciples."

Sparhawk laughed. "Arasham didn't even know he existed. I've met Ulesim. The man's an idiot. He won't last six months."

"Anyway," Vanion continued, "I have the Pandion order out in the countryside dealing with Rendorish foraging parties. Martel's going to start getting hungry before long. That's about all, your Majesty," he concluded.

"Nice and to the point. Thanks, Vanion. Lenda, what's going on in Cimmura?"

"Things are about the same, your Majesty—except that Annias has gone to Chyrellos."

"And he's probably perched on the foot of the Archprelate's bed like a vulture," Wargun surmised.

"I wouldn't be at all surprised, your Majesty," Lenda agreed. "He left Lycheas in charge. I have a number of people in the palace who work for me, and one of them managed to hear Annias giving Lycheas his final instructions. He ordered Lycheas to withhold the Elenian army from the campaign in Rendor. As soon as Cluvonus dies, the army—and the Church soldiers in Cimmura—are supposed to march on Chyrellos. Annias wants to flood the Holy City with his own men to help intimidate the uncommitted members of the Hierocracy."

"The Elenian army's mobilized then?"

"Fully, your Majesty. They have an encampment about ten leagues south of Cimmura."

"We'll probably have to fight them, your Majesty," Kalten said. "Annias dismissed most of the old generals and replaced them with men loyal to him."

Wargun started to swear.

"It may not be quite as serious as it sounds, your Majesty," the Earl of Lenda said. "I've made an extended study of the law. In times of religious crisis, the militant orders are empowered to take command of all forces in Western Eosia. Wouldn't you say that an invasion by the Eshandist heresy qualifies as a religious crisis?"

"By God, you're right, Lenda. Is that Elenian law?"

"No, your Majesty. Church law."

Wargun suddenly howled with laughter. "Oh, that's too rare!" he roared, pounding on the arm of his chair with one beefy fist. "Annias is trying to become the head of the Church, and we use Church law to spike his wheel. Lenda, you're a genius."

"I have my moments, your Majesty," Lenda replied modestly. "I'd imagine that Preceptor Vanion here can persuade the General Staff to join your forces—particularly in view of the fact that Church law empowers him to resort to extreme measures should any officer refuse to accept his authority in such situations."

"I'd imagine that a few beheadings might prove instructional to the General Staff," Ulath said. "If we shorten four or five generals, the rest will probably fall in line."

"Quickly," Tynian added with a grin.

"Keep your ax good and sharp then, Ulath," Wargun said.

"Yes, your Majesty."

"About the only problem remaining is what we're going to do about Lycheas," the Earl of Lenda said.

"I've already decided that," Wargun said. "As soon as we get to Cimmura, I'm going to hang him."

"Splendid notion," Lenda said smoothly, "but I think we might want to consider that just a bit. You *do* know that Annias is the Prince Regent's father, don't you?"

"So Sparhawk tells me, but I don't really care who his father is; I'm going to hang him anyway."

"I'm not really sure just how fond Annias is of his son, but he *did* go to some fairly extreme measures to put him on the Elenian throne. It might just be that the militant orders can use him to some advantage when they get to Chyrellos. An offer to put him to the torture might just persuade Annias to move his troops out of Chyrellos so that the election can proceed without their interference."

"You're taking all the fun out of this, Lenda," Wargun complained. He scowled. "You're probably right, though. All right, when we get to Cimmura, we'll throw him in the dungeon—along with all his toadies. Are you up to taking charge at the palace?"

"If your Majesty wishes," Lenda sighed. "But wouldn't Sparhawk or Vanion be a better choice?"

"Maybe, but I'm going to need them when I get to Arcium. What do you think, Obler?"

"I have absolute confidence in the Earl of Lenda," King Obler replied.

"I'll do my best, your Majesties," Lenda said, "but keep in mind the fact that I'm getting very old."

"You're not as old as I am, my friend," King Obler reminded him, "and nobody's offered to let *me* evade my responsibilities."

"All right, that's settled then," Wargun said. "Now, let's get down to cases. We'll march south to Cimmura, imprison Lycheas, and bully the Elenian General Staff into joining us with their army. We may as well pick up the Church soldiers as well. Then we join Soros and Bergsten on the Arcian border. We march south to Larium, encircle the Rendors, and exterminate the lot of them."

"Isn't that a bit extreme, your Majesty?" Lenda objected.

"No, as a matter of fact, it's not. I want it to be at least ten generations before the Eshandist heresy raises its head again." He grinned crookedly at Sparhawk. "If you serve well and faithfully, my friend, I'll even let you kill Martel."

"I'd appreciate that, your Majesty," Sparhawk replied politely.

"Oh, dear," Sephrenia sighed.

"It needs to be done, little lady," Wargun told her. "Obler, is your army ready to move?"

"They're only awaiting orders, Wargun."

"Good. If you don't have anything else planned, why don't we start for Elenia tomorrow?"

"We might as well." Old King Obler shrugged.

Wargun stood up and stretched, yawning broadly. "Let's all get some sleep then," he said. "We'll be starting early tomorrow."

Later, Sparhawk and his friends gathered in Vanion's room to tell the preceptor in much greater detail what had happened in Lamorkand and Pelosia.

When they had finished, Vanion looked curiously at Flute. "Just exactly what's your part in all this?" he asked her.

"I was sent to help," she replied with a shrug.

"By Styricum?"

"In a manner of speaking."

"And what is this task you have to perform here in Acie?"

"I've already done it, Vanion. Sephrenia and I had to talk with a certain Styric here. We saw him in the street on our way to the palace and took care of it."

"What did you have to say to him that was more important than getting the Bhelliom?"

"We had to prepare Styricum for what is about to happen."

"The invasion by the Rendors, you mean?"

"Oh, that's nothing, Vanion. This is much, much more serious."

Vanion looked at Sparhawk. "You're going to Thalesia then?"

Sparhawk nodded. "Even if I have to walk on water to get there."

"All right, I'll do what I can to help you get out of the city. There's one thing that concerns me, though. If you *all* leave, Wargun's going to notice that you're gone. Sparhawk and one or two others might be able to get away without alerting Wargun, but that's about all."

Flute stepped into the middle of the room and looked them over. "Sparhawk," she said, pointing, "and Kurik. Sephrenia and me—and Talen."

"That's absurd!" Bevier exploded. "Sparhawk's going to need knights with him if he's going to come up against Ghwerig."

"Sparhawk and Kurik can take care of it," she said complacently.

"Isn't it dangerous to take Flute along?" Vanion asked Sparhawk.

"Maybe so, but she's the only one who knows the way to Ghwerig's cave."

"Why Talen?" Kurik said to Flute.

"There's something he has to do in Emsat," she replied.

"I'm sorry, my friends," Sparhawk told the other knights, "but we're more or less committed to doing things her way."

"Are you going to leave now?" Vanion said.

"No, we have to wait for Talen."

"Good. Sephrenia, go get Olven's sword."

"But—"

"Just do it, Sephrenia. Please don't argue with me."

"Yes, dear one." She sighed.

After she had delivered Olven's sword to him, Vanion was so weak he could barely stand.

"You're going to kill yourself doing this, you know," she told him.

"Everybody dies from something. Now then, gentlemen," he said to the knights, "I have a troop of Pandions with me. Those of you who are staying behind should mingle yourselves in among them when we ride out. Lenda and Obler are both quite old. I'll suggest to Wargun that we put them in a carriage and that he ride along with them. That should keep him from being able to count noses. I'll try to keep him occupied." He looked at Sparhawk. "A day or two is probably all I'll be able to manage for you," he apologized.

"That should be enough," Sparhawk said. "Wargun's likely to think that I'm going back to Lake Venne. He'll send any pursuit in that direction."

"The only problem now is getting you out of the palace," Vanion said.

"I'll take care of that," Flute told him.

"How?"

"Maa-gic," she said, comically drawing the word out and wiggling her fingers at him.

He laughed. "How did we ever get along without you?"

She sniffed. "Badly, I'd imagine."

It was about an hour later when Talen slipped into the room.

"Any problems?" Kurik asked him.

"No." Talen shrugged. "I made a few contacts and found us a place to hide."

"Contacts?" Vanion asked him. "With whom?"

"A few thieves, some beggars, and a couple of murderers. They sent me to the man who controls the underside of Acie. He owes Platime a few favors, so when I mentioned Platime's name, he became very helpful."

"You live in a strange world, Talen," Vanion said.

"No stranger than the one you live in, my Lord," Talen said with an extravagant bow.

"That may be entirely true, Sparhawk," Vanion said. "We may all be thieves and brigands when you get right down to it. All right," he said to Talen, "where is this hiding place?"

"I'd rather not say," Talen replied evasively. "You're sort of an official person, and I gave my word."

"There's honor in your profession?"

"Oh yes, my Lord. It's not based on any knightly code, though. It's based on not getting your throat cut."

"You have a very wise son, Kurik," Kalten said.

"You had to go ahead and say it, didn't you, Kalten?" Kurik asked acidly.

"Are you ashamed of me, Father?" Talen asked in a small voice, his face downcast.

Kurik looked at him. "No, Talen," he said, "actually I'm not." He put his burly arm about the boy's shoulders. "This is my son, Talen," he said defiantly, "and if anybody wants to make an issue of it, I'll be more than happy to give him satisfaction, and we can throw out the nonsense about the nobility and the commons not being allowed to fight each other."

"Don't be absurd, Kurik," Tynian said with a broad grin. "Congratulations to you both."

The other knights gathered about the husky squire and his larcenous son, clapping them on the shoulders and adding their congratulations to Tynian's.

Talen looked around at them, his eyes suddenly very wide and filled with tears at his sudden acknowledgment. Then he fled to Sephrenia, fell to his knees, buried his face in her lap, and wept.

Flute smiled.

## CHAPTER TWENTY-THREE

It was that same peculiarly drowsy melody Flute had played on the docks at Vardenais and again outside the chapterhouse in Cimmura.

"What's she doing now?" Talen whispered to Sparhawk as they all crouched behind the balustrade of the wide porch at the front of King Obler's palace.

"She's putting Wargun's sentries to sleep," Sparhawk replied. There was no point in extended explanations. "They'll ignore us as we pass them." Sparhawk wore his mail shirt and his traveller's cloak.

"Are you sure about that?" Talen sounded dubious.

"I've seen it work a few times before."

Flute stood up and walked to the wide staircase leading down to the courtyard. Still holding her pipes in one hand, she motioned for them to follow with the other.

"Let's go," Sparhawk said, rising to his feet.

"Sparhawk," Talen warned, "you're right out in plain sight."

"It's all right, Talen. They won't pay any attention to us."

"You mean they can't see us?"

"They can see us," Sephrenia told the boy, "at least with their eyes, but our presence doesn't mean anything to them."

Sparhawk led them to the stairs, and they followed Flute on down into the yard.

One of the Thalesian soldiers was posted at the foot of the stairs, and he gave them no more than a glance as they passed, his eyes dull and uninterested.

"This is very hard on my nerves, you know," Talen whispered.

"You don't have to whisper, Talen," Sephrenia told him.

"They can't hear us either?"

"They can hear us all right, but our voices don't register on them."

"You wouldn't mind if I got ready to run anyhow, would you?"

"It's not really necessary."

"I'll do it all the same."

"Relax, Talen," Sephrenia said. "You're making it harder for Flute."

They went into the stables, saddled their horses, and led them out into the courtyard as Flute continued to play her pipes. Then they walked out through the gate past King Obler's indifferent sentries and King Wargun's patrol in the street outside the palace.

"Which way?" Kurik asked his son.

"That alley just down the street."

"Is this place very far?"

"About halfway across town. Meland doesn't like to get too close to the palace because the streets around here are patrolled."

"Meland?"

"Our host. He controls all the thieves and beggars here in Acie."

"Is he dependable?"

"Of course not, Kurik. He's a thief. He won't betray us though. I asked for thieves' sanctuary. He's obliged to take us in and hide us from anybody who might come looking for us. If he had refused, he'd have had to answer to Platime at the next meeting of the thieves' council in Chyrellos."

"There's a whole world out there that we don't know anything about," Kurik said to Sparhawk.

"I've noticed," Sparhawk replied.

The boy led them through the crooked streets of Acie to a shabby section not too far from the city gates. "Stay here," he said when they reached a seedy-looking tavern. He went inside and emerged a moment later with a ferret-like man. "He's going to take care of our horses."

"Watch out for this one, neighbor," Sparhawk warned the fellow as he handed him Faran's reins. "He's playful. Faran, behave yourself."

Faran flicked his ears irritably as Sparhawk carefully pulled the spear of Aldreas out from under his saddle skirt.

Talen led them into the tavern. It was lighted by smoky tallow candles and had long, scarred tables flanked by rickety-looking benches. There were a number of rough-looking men sitting at the tables. None of them paid any particular attention to Sparhawk and his friends, though their eyes were busy. Talen went to a stairway at the back. "It's up here," he said, pointing up the stairs.

The loft at the top of the stairs was very large, and it looked oddly familiar to Sparhawk. It was sparsely furnished and there were straw pallets on the floor along the walls. It seemed somehow very similar to Platime's cellar back in Cimmura.

Meland was a thin man with an evil-looking scar running down his left cheek. He was sitting at a table with a sheet of paper and an inkpot in front of him. There was a heap of jewelry near his left hand, and he seemed to be cataloguing the pieces.

"Meland," Talen said as they approached the table, "these are the friends I told you about."

"I thought you said there would be ten of you." Meland had a nasal, unpleasant voice.

"The plans have changed. This is Sparhawk. He's the one who's more or less in charge."

Meland grunted. "How long do you plan to be here?" he asked Sparhawk shortly.

"If I can find a ship, only until tomorrow morning."

"You shouldn't have any trouble finding a ship. There are ships from all over western Eosia down at the harbor, Thalesian, Arcian, Elenian, and even a few from Cammoria."

"Are the city gates open at night?"

"Not usually, but there's that army camped outside the walls. The soldiers are going in and out of town, so the gates are open." Meland looked critically at the knight. "If you're going down to the harbor, you'd better not wear that mail—or the sword. Talen says that you'd prefer not to be noticed. The people down there would remember someone dressed the way you are. There are some clothes hanging on those pegs over there. Find something that fits." Meland's tone was abrupt.

"What's the best way to get down to the harbor?"

"Go out the north gate. There's a wagon track that leads down to the water. It branches off the main road on the left about a half mile out of town."

"Thank you, neighbor," Sparhawk said.

Meland grunted and went back to his catalogue.

"Kurik and I are going to go down to the harbor to see about a ship," Sparhawk told Sephrenia. "You'd better stay here with the children."

"As you wish," she said.

Sparhawk found a somewhat shabby blue doublet hanging on one of the pegs that looked as if it might fit. He took off his mail shirt and sword and put it on. Then he pulled on his cloak again.

"Where are all of your people?" Talen was asking Meland.

"It's nighttime," Meland replied. "They're out working—or at least they'd better be."

"Oh, I hadn't thought of that, I guess."

Sparhawk and Kurik went back downstairs to the tavern.

"You want me to get our horses?" Kurik asked.

"No. Let's walk. People pay attention to mounted men."

"All right."

They went out through the city gate and on along the main road until they came to the wagon road Meland had mentioned. Then they walked on down to the harbor.

"Shabby-looking sort of place, isn't it?" Sparhawk noted, looking around at the settlement surrounding the harbor.

"Waterfronts usually are," Kurik said. "Let's ask a few questions." He accosted a passerby who appeared to be a seagoing man. "We be lookin' for a ship as is bound for Thalesia," he said, reverting to the sailor language he had used in Venne. "Tell me, mate, could y' maybe tell us if there be a tavern hereabouts where the ship captains gather?"

"Try the Bell and Anchor," the sailor replied. "It's that way a couple of streets—right near the water."

"Thanks, mate."

Sparhawk and Kurik walked down toward the long wharves jutting out into the dark, garbage-strewn waters of the Gulf of Acie. Kurik suddenly stopped. "Sparhawk," he said, "doesn't there seem to be something familiar about that ship out at the end of this wharf?"

"She does seem to have a familiar rake to her masts, doesn't she?" Sparhawk agreed. "Let's go have a closer look."

They walked a ways out on the wharf. "She's Cammorian," Kurik advised.

"How can you tell?"

"By the rigging and the slant of her masts."

"You don't think—" Then Sparhawk broke off, looking incredulously at the vessel's name painted on her bow. "Well, I'll be," he said. "That's Captain Sorgi's ship. What's he doing all the way up here?"

"Why don't we see if we can find him and ask him? If it's really Sorgi and not just somebody who bought his ship from him, this could solve our problem."

"Provided he plans to sail in the right direction. Let's go find the Bell and Anchor."

"Do you remember all the details of that story you told Sorgi?"

"Enough to get by, I think."

The Bell and Anchor was a tidy, sedate tavern, as befitted a place frequented by ship captains. The taverns visited by common sailors tended to be rowdier and usually showed evidence of hard use. Sparhawk and Kurik entered and stood in the doorway, looking around. "Over there," Kurik said, pointing at a husky man with silver-shot, curly hair drinking with a group of substantial-looking men at a table in the corner. "It's Sorgi, all right."

Sparhawk looked at the man who had conveyed them from Madel in Cammoria to Cippria in Rendor and nodded his agreement. "Let's drift on over there," he said. "It might be best if he saw us first." They went across the room, doing their best to appear to be only casually looking around.

"Why, strike me blind if it isn't Master Cluff!" Sorgi exclaimed. "What are you doing up here in Deira? I thought you were going to stay down in Rendor until all those cousins got tired of looking for you."

"Why, I believe it's Captain Sorgi," Sparhawk said in mock astonishment to Kurik.

"Join us, Master Cluff," Sorgi invited expansively. "Bring your man as well."

"You're very kind, Captain," Sparhawk murmured, taking a chair at the seamen's table.

"What happened to you, my friend?" Sorgi asked.

Sparhawk put on a mournful expression. "Somehow the cousins tracked me down," he said. "I was lucky enough to see one of them in a street in Cippria before he saw me, and I bolted. I've been on the run ever since."

Sorgi laughed. "Master Cluff here has a bit of a problem," he told his companions. "He made the mistake of paying court to an heiress before he got a look at her face. The lady turned out to be remarkably ugly, and he ran away from her screaming."

"Well, I didn't exactly scream, Captain," Sparhawk said. "I'll admit that my hair stood on end for a week or so, though."

"Anyway," Sorgi continued, grinning broadly, "as it turns out, the lady has a multitude of cousins, and they've been pursuing poor Master Cluff for months now. If they catch him, they're going to drag him back and force him to marry her."

"I think I'd rather kill myself first," Sparhawk said in a mournful tone of voice. "But what are you doing this far north, Captain? I thought you plied the Arcian Strait and the Inner Sea."

"I happened to be in the port of Zenga on the south coast of Cammoria," Sorgi explained, "and I ran across the opportunity to buy a cargo of satins and brocade. There's no market for that sort of merchandise in Rendor. They all wear those ugly black robes, you know. The best market for Cammorian fabrics is in Thalesia. You wouldn't think so, considering the climate, but Thalesian ladies are passionate for satins and brocades. I stand to make a tidy profit on the cargo."

Sparhawk felt a sudden surge of elation. "You're going to Thalesia then?" he said. "Might you have room for some passengers?"

"Do you want to go to Thalesia, Master Cluff?" Sorgi asked with some surprise.

"I want to go *anywhere*, Captain Sorgi," Sparhawk told him in a desperate-sounding voice. "I've got a group of those cousins no more than two days behind me. If I can get to Thalesia, maybe I can go up and hide in the mountains."

"I'd be careful, my friend," one of the other captains advised. "There are robbers up in the mountains of Thalesia—not to mention the Trolls."

"I can outrun robbers, and Trolls can't be any uglier than the lady in question," Sparhawk said, feigning a shudder. "What do you say, Captain Sorgi," he pleaded. "Will you help me out of my predicament again?"

"Same price?" Sorgi asked shrewdly.

"Anything," Sparhawk said in apparent desperation.

"Done then, Master Cluff. My ship is at the end of the third wharf down from here. We sail for Emsat with the morning tide."

"I'll be there, Captain Sorgi," Sparhawk promised. "Now, if you'll excuse us, my man and I have to go pack a few things." He rose to his feet and extended his hand to the seaman. "You've saved me again, Captain," he said with genuine gratitude. Then he and Kurik quietly left the tavern.

Kurik was frowning as they went back out into the street. "Do you get the feeling that somebody may be tampering with things?" he asked.

"How do you mean?"

"Isn't it peculiar that we just happened to run across Sorgi again—the one man we can usually count on to help us? And isn't it even more peculiar that he just happens to be going to Thalesia—the one place we really want to go?"

"I think your imagination's getting away with you, Kurik. You heard him. It's perfectly logical that he should be here."

"But at just the right time for us to run across him?"

That was a somewhat more troubling question. "We can ask Flute about it when we get back up to the city," he said.

"You think she might be responsible?"

"Not really, but she's the only one I know of who might have been able to arrange something like this—although I doubt if even *she* could have managed it."

There was, however no chance to speak with Flute when they returned to the loft above the seedy tavern, because a familiar figure sat across the table from Meland. Large and grossly bearded and wearing a nondescript cloak, Platime was busily haggling. "Sparhawk!" the huge man roared his greeting.

Sparhawk stared at him in some astonishment. "What are you doing in Acie, Platime?"

"Several things, actually," Platime said. "Meland and I always trade stolen jewelry. He sells what I steal in Cimmura, and I take what he steals around here back to Cimmura and sell it there. People tend to recognize their own jewelry, and it's not always safe to sell things in the same town where you stole them."

"This piece isn't worth what you're asking for it, Platime," Meland said flatly, holding up a jewel-studded bracelet.

"All right, make me an offer," Platime suggested.

"Another coincidence, Sparhawk?" Kurik asked suspiciously.

"We'll see," Sparhawk said.

"The Earl of Lenda's here in Acie, Sparhawk," Platime said seriously. "He's the closest thing to an honest man on the royal council, and he's attending some kind of conference at the palace. Something's afoot, and I want to know about it. I don't like surprises."

"I can tell you what's going on," Sparhawk told him.

"You can?" Platime looked a little surprised.

"If the price is right." Sparhawk grinned.

"Money?"

"No, a little more than that, I think. I sat in on the conference you mentioned. You know about the war in Arcium, of course?"

"Naturally."

"And what I tell you will go no further?"

Platime motioned Meland away from the table, then looked closely at Sparhawk and grinned. "Only in the way of business, my friend."

This was not a particularly reassuring reply. "You've professed some degree of patriotism in the past," Sparhawk said carefully.

"I have those feelings from time to time," Platime admitted grudgingly. "As long as they don't interfere with honest profit."

"All right, I need your cooperation."

"What have you got in mind?" Platime asked suspiciously.

"My friends and I are seeking to restore Queen Ehlana to her throne."

"You have been for quite some time, Sparhawk, but can that pale little girl really manage a kingdom?"

"I think she can, yes, and I'll be right behind her."

"That gives her a certain edge. What are you going to do about Lycheas the bastard?"

"King Wargun wants to hang him."

"I don't normally approve of hangings; but in the case of Lycheas, I'd make an exception. Do you think I could reach an accommodation with Ehlana?"

"I wouldn't wager any money on it."

Platime grinned. "It was worth a try," he said. "Just tell my Queen that I am her most faithful servant. She and I can work out the details later."

"You're a bad man, Platime."

"I never pretended to be anything else. All right, Sparhawk, what do you need? I'll go along with you—up to a point."

"I need information more than anything. You know Kalten?"

"Your friend? Of course."

"He's at the palace right now. Put on something that makes you look more or less respectable. Go there and ask for him. Make arrangements with him to pass on information. I gather that you have ways to pick up details about most of the things that are going on in the known world?"

"Would you like to know what's going on in the Tamul Empire right now?"

"Not really. I've got enough trouble here in Eosia at the moment. We'll deal with the Daresian continent when the time comes."

"You're ambitious, my friend."

"Not really. For the moment, I just want our Queen back on her throne."

"I'll settle for that," Platime said. "Anything to get rid of Lycheas and Annias."

"We're all working in the same direction then. Talk with Kalten. He can set up ways for you to get information to him, and he'll pass it on to people who can use it."

"You're turning me into a spy, Sparhawk," Platime said in a pained voice.

"It's at least as honorable a profession as thievery."

"I know. The only problem, though, is that I don't know how well it pays. Where are you going from here?"

"We have to go to Thalesia."

"Wargun's own kingdom? After you just ran away from him? Sparhawk, you're either braver or stupider than I thought you were."

"You know that we slipped out of the palace then?"

"Talen told me." Platime thought a moment. "You'll probably make port at Emsat, won't you?"

"That's what our captain says."

"Talen, come here," Platime called.

"What for?" the boy replied flatly.

"Haven't you broken him of that habit yet, Sparhawk?" Platime asked sourly.

"It was only for old times' sake, Platime." Talen grinned.

"Listen carefully," Platime said to the boy. "When you get to Emsat, look up a man named Stragen. He more or less runs things there—the same way I do in Cimmura and Meland does here in Acie. He'll be able to give you whatever help you'll need."

"All right," Talen said.

"You think of everything, don't you, Platime?" Sparhawk said.

"In my business, you sort of have to. People who don't tend to wind up dangling unpleasantly."

They reached the harbor shortly after sunrise the following morning and, after they had seen to the loading of the horses, they went on board.

"You seem to have picked up another retainer, Master Cluff," Captain Sorgi said to Sparhawk when he saw Talen.

"My man's youngest son," Sparhawk replied truthfully.

"Just as an indication of the friendship I bear you, Master Cluff, there won't be any extra charge for the boy. Speaking of that, why don't we settle up before we set sail?"

Sparhawk sighed and reached for his purse.

There was a good following wind as they sailed out of the Gulf of Acie and around the promontory that lay to the north. Then they entered the Straits of Thalesia and left the land behind. Sparhawk stood on deck talking with Sorgi. "How long do you think it's going to take to get to Emsat?" he asked the curly-haired seaman.

"We'll probably make port by noon tomorrow," Sorgi replied, "if the wind holds. We'll furl sail and rig sea-anchors tonight. I'm not as familiar with these waters as I am with the Inner Sea or the Arcian Strait, so I'd rather not take chances."

"I like prudence in the captain of a ship I'm sailing on," Sparhawk told him. "Oh, and speaking of prudence, do you imagine we might be able to find some secluded cove before we reach Emsat? Towns make me very nervous for some reason."

Sorgi laughed. "You see those cousins around every corner, don't you, Master Cluff? Is that why you're under arms?" Sorgi looked meaningfully at Sparhawk's mail shirt and sword.

"A man in my circumstances can't be too careful."

"We'll find you a cove, Master Cluff. The coast of Thalesia is one long secluded cove. We'll find you a quiet beach and put you ashore so you can sneak north to visit the Trolls without the inconvenience of having cousins dogging your heels."

"I appreciate that, Captain Sorgi."

"You up there!" Sorgi bellowed to one of the sailors aloft, "look lively! You're up there to work, not to daydream!"

Sparhawk walked a ways up the deck and leaned on the rail, idly watching the intensely blue rollers sparkling in the midday sun. Kurik's questions were still troubling him. Had the chance meetings with Sorgi and Platime indeed been coincidence? Why should they both have been in Acie at precisely the same time that Sparhawk and his friends had made good their escape from the palace? If Flute indeed could tamper with time, could she also reach out over tremendous distances to draw in people they needed at precisely the right moment? How powerful was she?

Almost as if his thought had summoned her, Flute came up the companionway and looked around. Sparhawk crossed the deck to meet her. "I have a question or two for you," he said.

"I thought you might have."

"Did you have anything to do with bringing both Platime and Sorgi to Acie?"

"Not personally, no."

"But you knew they'd be there?"

"It saves time when you deal with people who already know you, Sparhawk. I made some requests, and certain members of my family arranged the details."

"You keep mentioning your family. Just exactly—"

"What on earth is that?" she exclaimed, pointing off to starboard.

Sparhawk looked. A huge surging was just beneath the surface, and then a great flat tail burst up out of the water and crashed down, sending up a great cloud of spray. "A whale, I think," he said.

"Do fish really get that big?"

"I don't think they're actually fish—at least that's what I've heard."

"He's *singing*!" Flute said, clapping her hands in delight.

"I don't hear anything."

"You're not listening, Sparhawk." She ran forward and leaned out over the bow of the ship.

"Flute!" he shouted. "Be careful!" He rushed to the rail at the bow and took hold of her.

"Stop that," she said. She lifted her pipes to her lips, but a sudden lurch of the ship made her lose her grip on them, and they fell from her hands into the sea. "Oh, bother," she said. Then she made a face. "Oh, well, you'll find out soon enough any-way." Then she lifted her small face. The sound that came from her throat was the sound of those rude shepherd's pipes. Sparhawk was stunned. The pipes had been simply for show. What they had been hearing all along had been the sound of Flute's own voice. Her song soared out over the waves.

The whale rose again and rolled slightly over on one side, his vast eye curious. Flute sang to him, her voice trilling. The enormous creature swam closer, and one of the sailors aloft shouted with alarm, "There be whales here, Captain Sorgi!"

And then there were other whales rising from the deep as if in response to the little girl's song. The ship rocked and bobbed in their surging wake as they gathered about the bow, sending huge clouds of mist from great blowholes in the tops of their heads.

One sailor ran forward with a long boat hook, his eyes filled with panic.

"Oh, don't be silly," Flute told him. "They're only playing."

"Uh—Flute," Sparhawk said in an awed voice, "don't you think you should tell them to go home?" He realized even as he said it just how foolish it sounded. The whales *were* home.

"But I *like* them," she protested. "They're beautiful."

"Yes, I know, but whales don't make very good pets. As soon as we get to Thale-sia, I'll buy you a kitten instead. Please, Flute, say good-bye to your whales and make them go away. They're slowing us down."

"Oh." Her face was disappointed. "All right, I guess." She lifted her voice again with a peculiar trilling sound of regret. The whales moved off and then sounded, their vast flukes crashing against the surface of the sea, tearing it to frothy tatters.

Sparhawk glanced around. The sailors were gaping openmouthed at the little girl. Explanations at this point would be extremely difficult. "Why don't we go back to our cabin and have some lunch?" he suggested.

"All right," she agreed. Then she lifted her arms to him. "You can carry me, if you'd like."

It was the quickest way to get her out from under the awed stares of Sorgi's crew, so he picked her up and carried her to the companionway.

"I really wish you wouldn't wear this," she said, picking at his mail shirt with one small fingernail. "It smells absolutely awful, you know."

"In my business, it's sort of necessary. Protection, you understand."

"There are other ways to protect yourself, Sparhawk, and they're not nearly so offensive."

When they reached the cabin, they found Sephrenia sitting, pale-faced and shaken, with a ceremonial sword in her lap. Kurik, who looked a little wild about the eyes, hovered over her. "It was Sir Gared, Sparhawk," he said quietly. "He walked right straight through the door as if it wasn't even there and gave his sword to Sephrenia."

Sparhawk felt a sharp wrench of pain. Gared had been a friend. Then he straightened and sighed. If all went well, this would be the last sword Sephrenia would be forced to bear. "Flute," he said, "can you help her to sleep?"

The little girl nodded, her face grave.

Sparhawk lifted Sephrenia in his arms. She seemed to have almost no weight. He carried her to her bunk and gently laid her down. Flute came to the bunk and began to sing. It was a lullaby such as one would sing to a small child. Sephrenia sighed and closed her eyes.

"She'll need to rest," Sparhawk told Flute. "It's going to be a long ride to Ghwerig's cave. Keep her asleep until we reach the coast of Thalesia."

"Of course, dear one."

They reached the Thalesian coast about noon of the following day, and Captain Sorgi hove to in a small cove just to the west of the port city of Emsat.

"You have no idea how much I appreciate your help, Captain," Sparhawk said to Sorgi as he and the others were preparing to disembark.

"My pleasure, Master Cluff," Sorgi told him. "We bachelors need to stick together in these affairs."

Sparhawk grinned at him.

The little group led their horses down a long gangway and out onto the beach. They mounted as the sailors were carefully maneuvering the ship out of the cove.

"Do you want to go with me into Emsat?" Talen asked. "I have to go talk with Stragen."

"I'd probably better not," Sparhawk said. "Wargun might have had time to get a messenger to Emsat by now, and I'm fairly easy to describe."

"I'll go with him," Kurik volunteered. "We're going to need supplies anyway."

"All right. Let's go back into the woods a ways and set up for the night first, though."

They made camp in a small glade in the forest, and Kurik and Talen rode out about midafternoon.

Sephrenia was wan, and her face was drawn-looking as she sat by the fire cradling Sir Gared's sword.

"This is not going to be easy for you, I'm afraid," Sparhawk said regretfully. "We're going to have to ride fast if we want to reach Ghwerig's cave before he seals it up. Is there any way you could give me Gared's sword?"

She shook her head. "No, dear one. You weren't present in the throne room. Only one of us who was there when we cast the spell can keep Gared's sword."

"I was afraid that might be the case. I guess I'd better see about some supper."

It was about midnight when Kurik and Talen returned.

"Any problems?" Sparhawk asked.

"Nothing worth mentioning." Talen shrugged. "Platime's name opens all kinds of doors. Stragen told us that the countryside north of Emsat is infested with robbers, though. He's going to provide us with an armed escort and spare horses—the horses were my father's idea."

"We can move faster if we change horses every hour or so," Kurik explained. "Stragen's also going to send supplies along with the men who'll be riding with us."

"You see how nice it is to have friends, Sparhawk?" Talen asked impudently.

Sparhawk ignored that. "Are Stragen's men going to come here?" he asked.

"No," Talen replied. "Before sunrise we'll meet them a mile or so up the road that runs north out of Emsat." He looked around. "What's for supper? I'm starving."

## CHAPTER TWENTY-FOUR

They rode out at first light, circled through the forest lying to the north of Emsat, and stopped not far from the north road. "I hope this Stragen keeps his word," Kurik muttered to Talen. "I've never been in Thalesia before, and I don't like the notion of riding into hostile country without knowing what's going on."

"We can trust Stragen, Father," Talen replied confidently. "Thalesian thieves have this peculiar sense of honor. It's the Cammorians you have to watch out for. They'd cheat themselves if they could figure out a way to make a profit out of it."

"Sir Knight," a soft voice said from back in the trees.

Sparhawk immediately went for his sword.

"There's no need of that, my Lord," the voice said. "Stragen sent us. There are robbers out there in the foothills, and he told us to get you safely past them."

"Come out of the shadows then, neighbor," Sparhawk said.

"Neighbor." The man laughed. "I like that. You have a very wide neighborhood, neighbor."

"Most of the world lately," Sparhawk admitted.

"Welcome to Thalesia then, neighbor." The man who rode out of the shadows had pale, flaxen hair. He was clean-shaven and roughly dressed and he carried a brutal-looking pike and had an ax slung to his saddle. "Stragen says you want to go north. We're to accompany you as far as Heid."

"Will that work out?" Sparhawk asked Flute.

"Perfectly," she replied. "We'll be leaving the road a mile or so beyond there."

"You take orders from a child?" the flaxen-haired man asked.

"She knows the way to the place where we're going." Sparhawk shrugged. "Never argue with your guide."

"That's probably true, Sir Sparhawk. My name is Tel—if it makes any difference. I've got a dozen men and spare horses—along with the supplies your man Kurik requested." He rubbed one hand over his face. "This sort of baffles me, Sir Knight," he admitted. "I've never seen Stragen so eager to accommodate a stranger."

"Have you ever heard of Platime?" Talen asked him.

Tel looked at the boy sharply. "The chief down in Cimmura?" he asked.

"That's the one," Talen said. "Stragen owes Platime some favors, and I work for Platime."

"Oh, that explains it, I guess," Tel admitted. "The day's wearing on, Sir Knight," he said to Sparhawk. "Why don't we go to Husdal?"

"Why don't we?" Sparhawk agreed.

Tel's men were all dressed in utilitarian Thalesian peasant garb, and they all carried weapons as if they knew how to use them. They were uniformly blond and had the bleak faces of men with little concern for the politer amenities of life.

When the sun came up, they increased their pace. Sparhawk knew that having Tel and his cutthroats along might slow them considerably, but he was grateful for the additional safety they provided for Sephrenia and Flute. He had been more than a little concerned about their vulnerability in the event of an ambush in the mountains.

They passed briefly through farm country, and neat farmsteads stood here and there along the road. An attack was unlikely in such well-populated country. The danger would come when they reached the mountains. They rode hard that day and covered considerable distance. They camped some distance from the road and left again early the following morning.

"I'm starting to feel a little saddle-weary," Kurik admitted as they set out at first light.

"I thought you'd be used to it by now," Sparhawk said.

"Sparhawk, we've been riding almost constantly for the last six months. I think I'm starting to wear out my saddle with my backside."

"I'll buy you a new one."

"So I can have all the entertainment of breaking it in? No thanks."

The country became more rolling, and they could clearly see the dark green mountains to the north now. "If I can make a suggestion, Sparhawk," Tel said, "why don't we make camp before we get up into the hills? There are robbers up there, and a night attack could cause us some inconvenience. I doubt that they'd come down onto this plain, though."

Sparhawk had to admit that Tel was probably right, even though he chafed at the delay. The safety of Sephrenia and Flute was of far more importance than any arbitrary time limits.

They stopped for the night before the sun set and took shelter in a shallow dell. Tel's men were very good at concealment, Sparhawk noticed.

The next morning they waited for daylight before setting out. "All right," Tel said as they rode along at a trot. "I know some of the fellows who hide up here in the mountains, and they've got some favorite places for their ambushes. I'll let you know when we start to get close to those places. The best way to get through them is to ride at a gallop. It takes people hiding in ambush by surprise, and they usually need a minute or two to get on their horses. We can be well past them before they can give chase."

"How many of them are there likely to be?" Sparhawk asked him.

"About twenty or thirty altogether. They'll split up, though. They've got more than one place, and they'll probably want to cover them all."

"Your plan isn't bad, Tel," Sparhawk said, "but I think I've got a better one. We ride through the ambush at a gallop the way you suggested until they start to come after us. Then we turn on them. There's no point in letting them join forces with others farther up on the trail."

"You're a bloodthirsty one, aren't you, Sparhawk?"

"I've got a friend from up here in Thalesia who keeps telling me that you should never leave live enemies behind you."

"He may have a point there."

"How did you learn so much about those fellows up here?"

"I used to be one of them, but I got tired of sleeping out of doors in bad weather. That's when I went to Emsat and started working for Stragen."

"How far is it from here to Husdal?"

"About fifty more leagues. We can make it by the end of the week if we hurry along."

"Good. Let's go then."

They rode up into the mountain at a trot, keeping a wary eye on the trees and bushes at the side of the road.

"Just ahead," Tel said quietly. "That's one of their places. The road goes through a gap there."

"Then let's ride," Sparhawk said. He led the way at the gap. They heard a startled shout from the top of the bluff on the left side of the road. A single man stood up there.

"He's there alone," Tel shouted, looking back over his shoulder. "He watches the road for travellers and then lights a fire to signal on up ahead."

"Not this time he won't," one of Tel's men growled, unslinging a longbow from across his back. He stopped his horse and smoothly shot an arrow at the lookout atop the bluff. The lookout doubled over when the arrow took him in the stomach and toppled off the bluff to lie motionless in the dusty road.

"Good shot," Kurik said.

"Not too bad," the archer said modestly.

"Do you think anyone heard him yell?" Sparhawk asked Tel.

"That depends on how close they are. They probably won't know what it meant, but a few of them might ride down here to investigate."

"Let them," the man with the bow said grimly.

"We'd better go a little slowly along here," Tel advised. "It wouldn't do to go around a corner and come face to face with them."

"You're very good at this, Tel," Sparhawk said.

"Practice, Sparhawk, and I know the ground. I lived up here for more than five years. That's why Stragen sent me instead of somebody else. You'd better let me have a look around that bend in the road just ahead." He slipped down off his horse and took his pike. He ran ahead at a crouch; just before he reached the bend, he eased his way into the bushes and disappeared. A moment later he reappeared and made a few obscure gestures.

"Three of them," the man with the bow translated in a muted voice. "They're coming at a trot." He set an arrow to his bowstring and raised the bow.

Sparhawk drew his sword. "Guard Sephrenia," he told Kurik.

The first man around the bend toppled out of his saddle with an arrow in his throat. Sparhawk shook his reins and Faran charged.

The two other men were staring at their fallen companion in blank amazement. Sparhawk cut one of them out of the saddle, and the other turned to flee. Tel, however, stepped out of the bushes and drove his pike at an angle up into the man's body. The man gave a gurgling groan and fell from his horse.

"Get the horses!" Tel barked to his men. "Don't let them get back to where the other brigands are hiding!"

His men galloped after the fleeing horses and brought them back a few minutes later.

"A nice piece of work," Tel said, pulling his pike free of the body lying in the road. "No yelling, and none of them got away." He rolled the body over with his foot. "I know this one," he said. "Those other two must be new. The life expectancy of a highway robber isn't really very good, so Dorga has to find new recruits every so often."

"Dorga?" Sparhawk asked, dismounting.

"He's the chief of this band. I never really cared for him very much. He's a little too self-important."

"Let's drag these into the bushes," Sparhawk said. "I'd rather not have the little girl see them."

"All right."

After the bodies had been concealed, Sparhawk stepped back around the bend and signalled Sephrenia and Kurik to come on ahead.

They rode on carefully.

"This may be much easier than I'd thought," Tel said. "I think they're splitting up into very small groups so they can watch more of the road. We should go into the woods a ways on the left side of the road just ahead. There's a rockslide coming down on the right side, and Dorga usually has a few archers there. Once we get past them, I'll send a few men around behind them to deal with them."

"Is that really necessary?" Sephrenia asked.

"I'm just following Sir Sparhawk's advice, lady," Tel said. "Don't leave live enemies behind you—particularly not ones armed with bows. I don't really need an arrow in my back, and neither do you."

They rode into the woods before they reached the rockslide and continued at a very careful walk. One of Tel's men crept out to the edge of the trees and rejoined them a few minutes later. "Two of them," he reported quietly. "They're about fifty paces up the slide."

"Take a couple of men," Tel instructed. "There's cover about two hundred paces up ahead. You'll be able to get across the road there. Work your way up along the edge of the slide and get behind them. Try not to let them make any noise."

The stubble-faced blond cutthroat grinned, signalled to two of his companions, and rode on ahead.

"I'd forgotten how much fun this is," Tel said. "At least in good weather. It's miserable in the winter, though."

They had ridden perhaps half a mile past the slide when the three ruffians caught up with them.

"Any problems?" Tel asked.

"They were half-asleep." One of the men chuckled. "They're all the way asleep now."

"Good." Tel looked around. "We can gallop for a ways now, Sparhawk. The roadsides are too open for ambushes for the next few miles."

They galloped until almost noon, when they reached the crest of the ridge where Tel signalled for a halt. "The next part might be tricky," he told Sparhawk. "The road runs down a ravine, and there's no way for us to work our way around it from this end. The place is one of Dorga's favorites, so he's likely to have quite a few men there. I'd say that the best thing for us to do is to go through it at a dead run. An archer has a little trouble shooting downhill at moving targets—at least I always did."

"How far is it until we come out of the ravine?"

"About a mile."

"And we'll be in plain sight all the way?"

"More or less, yes."

"We don't have much choice, though, do we?"

"Not unless you want to wait until dark, and that would make the rest of the road to Husdal twice as dangerous."

"All right," Sparhawk decided. "You know the country, so you lead the way." He unhooked his shield from his saddlehorn and strapped it on his arm. "Sephrenia, you ride right beside me. I can cover you and Flute with the shield. Lead on, Tel."

Their plunging run down the ravine took the concealed brigands by surprise. Sparhawk heard a few startled shouts from the top of the ravine, and a single arrow fell far behind them.

"Spread out!" Tel shouted. "Don't ride all clustered together!"

They plunged on. More arrows came whizzing down into the ravine, dropping among them now. One arrow shattered on the shield that Sparhawk was holding protectively over Sephrenia and Flute. He heard a muffled cry and glanced back. One of Tel's men was swaying in his saddle, his eyes filled with pain. Then he slumped over and fell heavily to the ground.

"Keep going!" Tel ordered. "We're almost clear now!"

The road ahead came out of the ravine, passed through a stretch of trees, and then curved along the side of a cliff that dropped steeply down into a gorge.

A few more arrows arced down from the top of the ravine, but they were falling far behind now.

They galloped through the stretch of trees and on out along the side of the cliff. "Keep going!" Tel commanded again. "Let them think we're going to run all the way through here."

They galloped on along the face of the cliff. Then the wide ledge upon which the road was built bent sharply inward to the point where the cliff face ended and the road ran steeply down into the forest again. Tel reined in his panting horse. "This looks like a good place," he said. "The road narrows a little ways back there, so they'll only be able to come at us a couple at a time."

"You really think they'll try to follow us?" Kurik asked.

"I know Dorga. He may not know exactly who we are, but he definitely doesn't want us to get to the authorities in Husdal. Dorga's very nervous about the notion of having large groups of the sheriff's men sweeping though these mountains. They have a very stout gallows in Husdal."

"Is that forest down there safe?" Sparhawk asked, pointing down the road.

Tel nodded. "The brush is too thick to make ambushes feasible. That ravine was the last stretch that's really dangerous on this side of the mountains."

"Sephrenia," Sparhawk said, "ride on down there. Kurik, you go with her."

Kurik's face showed that he was about to protest, but he said nothing. He led Sephrenia and the children on down the road toward the safety of the forest.

"They'll come fast," Tel said. "We went past them at a dead run, and they'll be trying to catch up." He looked at the ruffian with a longbow. "How fast can you shoot that thing?" he asked.

"I can have three arrows in the air at the same time." The fellow shrugged.

"Try for four. It doesn't matter if you hit the horses. They'll fall off the edge of the cliff and take their riders with them. Get as many as you can, and then the rest of us will charge. Does that sound all right, Sparhawk?"

"It's workable," Sparhawk agreed. He shifted the shield on his left arm and then drew his sword.

Then they heard the clatter of horses' hooves coming fast along the rocky ledge on the other side of the sharp curve. Tel's archer climbed down from his horse and hung his quiver of arrows on a stunted tree at the roadside where they would be close at hand. "These are going to cost you a quarter crown apiece, Tel," he said calmly, drawing an arrow from the quiver and setting it to his bowstring. "Good arrows are expensive."

"Take your bill to Stragen," Tel suggested.

"Stragen pays very slowly. I'd rather collect from you and let you argue with him."

"All right." Tel's tone was slightly sulky.

"Here they come," one of the other cutthroats said without any particular excitement.

The first two brigands to come around the curve probably didn't even see them. Tel's laconic archer was at least as good as he had claimed to be. The two men fell from their saddles, one at the side of the road and the other vanishing into the gorge. Their horses ran on a few yards and then pulled up when they saw Tel's mounted men blocking the road.

The archer missed one of the next pair that came around the sharp curve. "He ducked," he said. "Let's see him try to get out of the way of this one." He pulled his bow and shot again, and his arrow took the fellow in the forehead. The man tumbled over backward and lay in the road kicking.

Then the brigands came around the curve in a cluster. The archer loosed several arrows into their midst. "You'd better go now, Tel," he said. "They're coming on a little too fast."

"Let's ride!" Tel shouted, settling his pike under his arm in a manner curiously reminiscent of that used by armored knights. Tel's men had a peculiar assortment of weapons, but they handled them in a professional manner.

Because Faran was by far the strongest and fastest horse they had, Sparhawk outdistanced the others in the fifty-pace intervening stretch of road. He crashed into the center of the startled group of men, swinging his sword to the right and left in broad overhand strokes. The men he was attacking wore no mail to protect them, and so Sparhawk's blade bit deep into them. A couple of them feebly tried to hold rusty swords up to ward off his ruthless blows, but Sparhawk was a trained swordsman who could alter his point of aim even in midswing, and the two fell howling into the road, clutching at the stumps of missing right hands.

A red-bearded man had been riding at the back of the ambushers. He turned to flee, but Tel plunged past Sparhawk, his blond hair flying, his pike lowered, and the two disappeared around the curve.

Tel's men followed along behind Sparhawk, cleaning up with brutal efficiency.

Sparhawk trotted Faran around the curve. Tel, it appeared, had picked the red-bearded man out of the saddle with his pike, and the fellow lay writhing on the road with the pike protruding from his back. Tel dismounted and squatted beside the mortally wounded man. "It didn't turn out so well, did it, Dorga?" he said in an almost friendly tone. "I told you a long time ago that waylaying travellers was a risky business." Then he pulled the pike out of his former chieftain's back and calmly kicked him off the edge of the cliff. Dorga's despairing shriek faded down into the gorge.

"Well," Tel said to Sparhawk, "I guess that takes care of all this. Let's go on down. It's still some distance to Husdal."

Tel's men were disposing of the bodies of the dead and wounded ambushers by casually throwing them into the gorge.

"It's safe now," Tel told them. "Some of you stay here and round up those people's horses. We ought to be able to get a good price for them. The rest of you, come with us. Coming, Sparhawk?" He led the way on down the road.

The days seemed to drag on as they moved through the unpopulated mountains of central Thalesia. At one point, Sparhawk reined Faran back to ride beside Sephrenia and Flute. "To me it seems as if we've been out here on this road for five days at least," he said to the little girl. "How long has it really been?"

She smiled and raised two fingers.

"You're playing with time again, aren't you?" he accused.

"Of course," she said. "You didn't buy me that kitten the way you promised you would, so I have to play with something."

He gave up at that point. Nothing in the world was more immutable than the rising and setting of the sun, but Flute seemed able to alter those events at will. Sparhawk had seen Bevier's consternation when she had patiently explained the inexplicable to him. He decided that he did not wish to experience that personally.

It seemed to be several days later—though Sparhawk would not have taken an oath to that effect—when, at sunset, the flaxen-haired Tel pulled his horse in beside Faran. "That smoke down there is coming from the chimneys at Husdal," he said. "My men and I'll be turning back here. I believe there's still a price on my head in Husdal. It's all a misunderstanding, of course, but explanations are tiresome—particularly when you're standing on a ladder with a noose around your neck."

"Flute," Sparhawk said back over his shoulder, "has Talen done what he came here to do?"

"Yes."

"I sort of thought so. Tel, would you do me a favor and take the boy back to Stragen? We'll pick him up on our way back. Tie him very tightly and loop a rope about his ankles and under his horse's belly. Jump him from behind and be careful, he's got a knife in his belt."

"There's a reason, I suppose," Tel said.

Sparhawk nodded. "Where we're going is very dangerous. The boy's father and I would rather not expose him to that."

"And the little girl?"

"She can take care of herself—probably better than any of the rest of us."

"You know something, Sparhawk," Tel said skeptically, "when I was a boy, I always wanted to become a Church Knight. Now I'm glad I didn't. You people don't make any sense at all."

"It's probably all the praying," Sparhawk told him. "It tends to make a man a little vague."

"Good luck, Sparhawk," Tel said shortly. Then he and two of his men roughly jerked Talen from his saddle, disarmed him, and tied him on the back of his horse. The names Talen called Sparhawk as he and his captors rode off to the south were wide-ranging and, for the most part, very unflattering.

"She doesn't really understand all those words, does she?" Sparhawk asked Sephrenia, looking meaningfully at Flute.

"Will you stop talking as if I weren't here?" the little girl snapped. "Yes, as a matter of fact, I do know what the words mean, but Elene is such a puny language to swear in. Styric is more satisfying, but if you really want to curse, try Troll."

"You speak Troll?" He was surprised.

"Of course. Doesn't everyone? There's no point in going into Husdal. It's a depressing place—all mud and rotting logs and mildewed thatching. Circle it to the west, and we'll find the valley we want to follow."

They bypassed Husdal and moved up into steeper mountains. Flute watched intently and finally pointed one finger. "There," she said. "We turn left here."

They stopped at the entrance to the valley and peered with some dismay at the track to which she had directed them. It was a path more than a road, and it seemed to wander quite a bit.

"It doesn't look too promising," Sparhawk said dubiously, "and it doesn't look as if anybody's been on it for years."

"People don't use it," Flute told him. "it's a game trail—sort of."

"What kind of game?"

"Look there." She pointed.

It was a boulder with one flat side, and an image had been crudely chiselled into it. The image looked very old and weathered, and it was hideous.

"What's that?" Sparhawk asked.

"It's a warning," she replied calmly. "That's a picture of a Troll."

"You're taking us into Troll country?" he asked in alarm.

"Sparhawk, Ghwerig's a Troll. Where else do you think he'd live?"

"Isn't there any other way to get to his cave?"

"No, there isn't. I can frighten off any Trolls we happen to run across, and the Ogres don't come out in the daytime, so they shouldn't be any problem."

"Ogres, too?"

"Of course. They always live in the same country with Trolls. Everybody knows that."

"I didn't."

"Well, now you do. We're wasting time, Sparhawk."

"We'll have to go in single file," the knight told Kurik and Sephrenia. "Stay as close behind me as you can. Let's not get spread out." He started up the trail at a trot with the spear of Aldreas in his hand.

The valley to which Flute had led them was narrow and gloomy. The steep walls were covered with tall fir trees so dark as to look nearly black, and the sides of the valley were so high that the sun seldom shone into this murky place. A mountain river rushed down the center of the narrow gap, roaring and foaming. "This is worse than the road to Ghasek," Kurik shouted over the noise of the river.

"Tell him to be still," Flute told Sparhawk. "Trolls have very sharp ears."

Sparhawk turned in his saddle and laid a finger across his lips. Kurik nodded.

There seemed to be an inordinate number of dead white snags dotting the dark forest that rose steeply on either side. Sparhawk leaned forward and put his lips close to Flute's ear. "What's killing the trees?" he asked.

"Ogres come out at night and gnaw on the bark," she said. "Eventually the tree dies."

"I thought Ogres were meat eaters."

"Ogres eat anything. Can't you go any faster?"

"Not through here I can't. This is a very bad trail. Does it get any better on up ahead?"

"After we go up out of this valley, we'll come to a flat place in the mountains."

"A plateau?"

"Whatever you want to call it. There are a few hills, but we can go around those. It's all covered with grass."

"We'll be able to make better time there. Does the plateau stretch all the way to Ghwerig's cave?"

"Not quite. After we cross that, we'll have to go up into the rocks."

"Who brought you all the way up here? You said you'd been here before."

"I came alone. Somebody who knew the way told me how to get to the cave."

"Why would you want to?"

"I had something to do there. Do we really have to talk so much? I'm trying to listen for Trolls."

"Sorry."

"Hush, Sparhawk." She put her finger to his lips.

It was a day later when they reached the plateau. As Flute had told them, it was a vast, rolling grassland with snow-covered peaks lining the horizon on all sides.

"How long is it going to take us to get across this?" Sparhawk asked.

"I'm not sure," Flute replied. "The last time I was here I was on foot. The horses should be able to go much faster."

"You were up here alone and on foot with Trolls and Ogres about?" he asked incredulously.

"I didn't see any of those. There was a young bear that followed me for a few days, though. I think he was only curious, but I got tired of having him behind me, so I made him go away."

Sparhawk decided not to ask her any more questions. The answers were far too disturbing.

The high grassland seemed interminable. They rode for hours, but the skyline did not appear to change. The sun sank low above the snowy peaks, and they made their camp in a small clump of stunted pines.

"It's big country up here," Kurik said, looking around. He pulled his cloak closer about him. "Cold too, once the sun goes down. Now I can see why most Thalesians wear fur."

They hobbled the horses to keep them from straying and built up the fire.

"There's no real danger here in this meadow," Flute assured them. "Trolls and Ogres like to stay in the forest. The hunting's easier for them when they can hide behind trees."

The next morning dawned cloudy, and a chilly wind swept down from the mountain peaks, bending the tall grass in long waves. They rode hard that day, and by evening they had reached the foot of the peaks that towered white above them.

"We can't make any fire tonight," Flute said. "Ghwerig may be watching."

"Are we that close?" Sparhawk asked.

"You see that ravine just ahead?"

"Yes."

"Ghwerig's cave is at the upper end of it."

"Why didn't we just go on up there, then?"

"That wouldn't have been a good idea. You can't sneak up on a Troll at night. We'll wait until the sun's well up tomorrow before we start out. Trolls usually doze in the daytime. They don't actually ever really sleep, but they're a little less alert when the sun's out."

"You seem to know a great deal about them."

"It's not too hard to find things out—if you know the right people to ask. Make Sephrenia some tea and some hot soup. Tomorrow's likely to be very difficult for her, and she'll need all her strength."

"It's a little hard to make hot soup without a fire."

"Oh, Sparhawk, I know that. I'm small, but I'm not stupid. Heap up a pile of rocks in front of the tent. I'll take care of the rest."

Grumbling to himself, he did as she directed.

"Get back from it," she said. "I don't want to burn you."

"Burn? How?"

She began to sing softly, and then she made a brief gesture with one small hand. Sparhawk immediately felt the heat radiating out from his pile of rocks.

"That's a useful spell," he said admiringly.

"Start cooking, Sparhawk. I can't keep the rocks hot all night."

It was very strange, Sparhawk thought as he set Sephrenia's teakettle up against one of the heated rocks. Somehow in the past weeks, he had almost begun to stop thinking of Flute as a child. Her tone and manner were adult, and she ordered him around like a lackey. Even more surprising was the fact that he automatically obeyed her. Sephrenia was right, he decided. This little girl was in all probability one of the most powerful magicians in all of Styricum. A disturbing question came to him. Just how old *was* Flute anyway? Could Styric magicians control or modify their ages? He knew that neither Sephrenia nor Flute would answer those questions, so he busied himself with cooking and tried not to think about it.

They awoke at dawn, but Flute insisted that they wait until midmorning before they attempted to ascend the ravine. She also instructed them to leave the horses at the camp, since the sound of their hoofs on the rocks might alert the sharp-eared Troll lurking inside the cave.

The ravine was narrow with sheer sides, and it was filled with dense shadows. The four of them moved slowly up its rocky floor, placing their feet carefully to avoid dislodging any loose stones. They spoke but rarely and then only in whispers. Sparhawk carried the ancient spear. For some reason it seemed right.

The climb grew steeper, and they were forced to clamber over rounded boulders now in order to continue their ascent. As they neared the top, Flute motioned them to a halt and crept on ahead a few yards. Then she came back. "He's inside," she whispered, "and he's already started his enchantments."

"Is the cave mouth blocked?" Sparhawk whispered back.

"In a manner of speaking. When we get up there, you won't be able to see it. He's created an illusion to make it look as if the mouth of the cave is just a part of the cliff face. The illusion is solid enough so that we won't be able just to walk through it. You'll need to use the spear to break through." She whispered for a moment to Sephrenia, and the small woman nodded. "All right, then," Flute said, taking a deep breath, "let's go."

They climbed up the last few yards and entered a bleak, unwholesome-looking basin choked with brambles and dead white snags. On one side of the basin there was a steep overhanging cliff that did not appear to have any openings in it.

"There it is," Flute whispered.

"Are you sure this is the right place?" Kurik murmured. "It looks like solid rock."

"This is the place," she replied. "Ghwerig's hiding the entrance." She led the way along a scarcely defined path to the face of the cliff. "It's right here," she said softly, laying one small hand on the rock. "Now, this is what we're going to do. Sephrenia and I are going to cast a spell. When we release it, it's going to pour into you, Sparhawk. You'll feel very strange for a moment, and then you'll feel the power starting to build up inside you. At the right moment, I'll tell you what to do." She began to sing very softly, and Sephrenia spoke in Styric almost under her breath. Then, in unison, they both gestured at Sparhawk.

His eyes went suddenly dim, and he almost fell. He felt very weak, and the spear he held in this left hand seemed almost too heavy to bear. Then, just as quickly, it seemed to have no weight at all. He felt his shoulders surging with the force of the spell.

"Now," Flute said to him. "Point the spear at the face of the cliff."

He lifted his arm and did as she had told him.

"Walk forward until the spear touches the wall."

He took two steps and felt the spear point touch the unyielding rock.

"Release the power—*through* the spear."

He concentrated, gathering the power within him. The ring on his left hand seemed to throb. Then he sent the power along the shaft of the spear into the broad blade.

The seemingly solid rock in front of him wavered; then it was gone, revealing an irregularly shaped opening.

"And there it is," Flute said in a triumphant whisper, "Ghwerig's cave. Now let's go find him."

# CHAPTER TWENTY-FIVE

The cave had the musty smell of long-damp earth and rock, and there was the sound of water endlessly dripping somewhere off in the darkness. "Where's he most likely to be?" Sparhawk whispered to Flute.

"We'll start in his treasure chamber," she replied. "He likes to look at his hoard. It's down there." She pointed at the opening of a passageway.

"It's completely dark back in there," he said dubiously.

"I'll take care of that," Sephrenia told him.

"But quietly," Flute cautioned. "We don't know exactly where Ghwerig is, and he can hear and feel magic." She looked closely at Sephrenia. "Are you all right?" she asked.

"It's not as bad as it was," Sephrenia replied, shifting Sir Gared's sword to her right hand.

"Good. I'm not going to be able to do anything in here. Ghwerig would recognize my voice. You're going to have to do almost everything."

"I can manage," Sephrenia said, but her voice sounded weary. She held up the sword. "As long as I have to carry this anyway, I may as well use it." She muttered briefly and made a small motion with her left hand. The tip of sword began to glow, a tiny incandescent spark. "It's not much of a light," she said critically, "but it's going to have to do. If I made it any brighter, Ghwerig would see it." She raised the sword and led the way into the mouth of the gallery. The glowing tip of the sword looked almost like a firefly in the oppressive darkness, but it cast just enough faint light to make it possible for them to find their way and avoid obstructions on the rough floor of the passageway they were following.

The passage curved steadily downward and to the right. After they had gone a few hundred paces, Sparhawk realized that it was not a natural gallery, but had been carved out of the rock, and it moved in a steady spiral down and down. "How did Ghwerig make this?" he whispered to Flute.

"He used Bhelliom. The old passage is much longer, and it's very steep. Ghwerig's so badly deformed that it used to take him days to climb up out of the cave."

They moved on, walking as quietly as they could. At one point the gallery passed through a large cavern where limestone icicles hung from the ceiling, dripping continually. Then the passage continued on into the rock. Occasionally, their faint light disturbed a colony of bats hanging from the ceiling, and the creatures chittered shrilly as they flapped frantically away in huge, dark clouds.

"I *hate* bats," Kurik said with an oath.

"They won't hurt you," Flute whispered. "A bat will never run into you, not even in total darkness."

"Are their eyes that good?"

"No, but their ears are."

"Do you know *everything*?" Kurik's whisper sounded a little grumpy.

"Not yet," she said quietly, "but I'm working on that. Do you have anything to eat? I'm a little hungry for some reason."

"Some dried beef," Kurik replied, reaching inside the tunic that covered his black leather vest. "It's very salty, though."

"There's plenty of water in this cave." She took the chunk of leather-hard beef he offered and bit into it. "It *is* a little salty, isn't it?" she admitted, swallowing hard.

They moved on. Then they saw a light coming from somewhere ahead, faint at first but growing steadily stronger as they moved on down the spiral gallery. "His treasure cave is just ahead," Flute whispered. "Let me have a look." She crept on ahead and then returned. "He's there," she said, her face breaking into a smile.

"Is he making that light?" Kurik whispered.

"No. It comes down from the surface. There's a stream that drops down into the cavern. It catches the sunlight at certain times of the day." She was speaking in a normal tone now. "The sound of the waterfall will muffle our voices. We still have to be careful, though. His eyes will catch any movement." She spoke briefly to Sephrenia, and the small Styric woman nodded. She reached up and extinguished the spark at the tip of the sword between two fingers. Then she began to weave an incantation.

"What's she doing?" Sparhawk asked Flute.

"Ghwerig's talking to himself," she replied, "and it might just be that he'll say something useful to us. He's speaking in the language of the Trolls, so Sephrenia's making it possible for us to understand him."

"You mean that she's going to make him speak in Elene?"

"No. The spell isn't directed at him." She smiled that impish little smile of hers. "You're learning many things, Sparhawk. Now you'll understand the language of the Trolls—for a time at least."

Sephrenia released the spell, and quite suddenly Sparhawk could hear much more than he had during their long descent through the spiralling gallery. The rushing sound of the waterfall dropping into the cavern ahead became almost a roar, and Ghwerig's rasping mutter came clearly over it.

"We'll wait here for a time," Flute told them. "Ghwerig's an outcast, so he talks to himself most of the time, and he says whatever is crossing his mind. We can find out a great deal by eavesdropping. Oh, by the way, he has Sarak's crown, and Bhelliom's still attached to it."

Sparhawk felt a sudden rush of excitement. The thing he had sought for so long was no more than a few hundred paces away. "What's he doing?" he asked Flute.

"He's sitting at the edge of the chasm that the waterfall has carved out of the rock. All his treasures are piled up around him. He's cleaning the peat stains off of Bhelliom with his tongue. That's why we can't understand him at the moment. Let's move a little closer, but stay back from the mouth of the gallery."

They crept on down toward the light and stopped a few yards from the opening. The reflected light from the waterfall shimmered and seemed to waver liquidly. It was peculiarly like a rainbow.

"Stealers! Thieves!" The voice was harsh, far harsher than any Elenian or Styric throat could have produced. "Dirty. She all dirty." There was more of the slobbering sound as the Troll-Dwarf licked at his treasure. "Stealers all dead now," Ghwerig chortled hideously. "All dead. Ghwerig not dead, and his rose come home at last."

"He sounds as if he's mad," Kurik muttered.

"He always has been," Flute told him. "His mind's as twisted as his body."

"Talk to Ghwerig, blue rose!" the unseen monstrosity commanded. Then he howled out a hideous oath directed at the Styric Goddess Aphrael. "Bring back rings! Bring back rings! Bhelliom not talk to Ghwerig if Ghwerig not got rings!" There was a blubbering sound, and Sparhawk realized with revulsion that the beast was crying. "Lonely," the Troll sobbed. "Ghwerig so lonely!"

Sparhawk felt a wrench of almost unbearable pity for the misshapen dwarf.

"Don't do that," Flute said sharply. "It will weaken you when you face him. You're our only hope now, Sparhawk, and your heart must be like stone."

Then Ghwerig spoke for a time in terms so vile that there were no counterparts in the Elenian language.

"He's invoking the Troll-Gods," Flute explained quietly. She cocked her head. "Listen," she said sharply. "The Troll-Gods are answering him."

The muted roar of the waterfall seemed to change tone, becoming deeper, more resonant.

"We'll have to kill him very soon," the little girl said in a chillingly matter-of-fact tone. "He still has some fragments of the original sapphire left in his workshop. The Troll-Gods instructed him to make new rings. Then they'll infuse them with the force to unlock the power of Bhelliom. He'll be able to destroy us at that point."

Then Ghwerig chuckled hideously. "Ghwerig beat you, Azash. Azash a God, but Ghwerig beat him. Azash not ever see Bhelliom now."

"Can Azash possibly hear him?" Sparhawk asked.

"Probably," Sephrenia said calmly. "Azash knows the sound of his own name. He listens when somebody says something to him."

"Man-things swim in lake to find Bhelliom," Ghwerig rambled on. "Bug-thing belong Azash watch from weeds and see them. Man-things go away. Bug-thing bring man-things with no minds. Man-things swim in water. Many drown. One man-thing find Bhelliom. Ghwerig kill man-thing and take blue rose. Azash want Bhelliom? Azash come seek Ghwerig. Azash cook in Troll-God fire. Ghwerig never eat God-meat before. Ghwerig wonder how God-meat taste."

Deep within the earth there was a rumbling sound, and the floor of the cave seemed to shudder.

"Azash definitely heard him," Sephrenia said. "You almost have to admire that twisted creature out there. No one has ever thrown that kind of insult into the face of one of the Elder Gods."

"Azash mad at Ghwerig?" the Troll was saying. "Or maybe-so Azash shake from fear. Ghwerig have Bhelliom now. Soon make rings. Ghwerig not need Troll-Gods then. Cook Azash in Bhelliom fire. Cook slow so juice not burn away. Ghwerig eat Azash. Who is pray to Azash when Azash deep in Ghwerig's belly?"

The rumble this time was accompanied by sharp cracking sounds as rocks deep in the earth shattered.

"He's sticking his neck out, wouldn't you say?" Kurik said in a strained voice. "Azash isn't the sort you want to play with."

"The Troll-Gods are protecting Ghwerig," Sephrenia replied. "Not even Azash would risk a confrontation with them."

"Stealers! All stealers!" the Troll howled. "Aphrael steal rings! Adian-of-Thalesia steal Bhelliom! Now Azash and Sparhawk-from-Elenia try to steal her from Ghwerig again! Talk to Ghwerig, blue rose! Ghwerig lonely!"

"How did he find out about me?" Sparhawk was startled by the breadth of the Troll-Dwarf's knowledge.

"The Troll-Gods are old and very wise," Sephrenia replied. "There's very little that happens in the world that they don't know, and they'll pass it on to those who serve them—for a price."

"What sort of price would satisfy a God?"

"Pray that you never have to know, dear one," she said with a shudder.

"Take Ghwerig ten years to carve one petal here, blue rose. Ghwerig love blue rose. Why she not talk to Ghwerig?" He mumbled inaudibly for a time. "Rings. Ghwerig make rings so Bhelliom speak again. Burn Azash in Bhelliom fire. Burn Sparhawk in Bhelliom fire. Burn Aphrael in Bhelliom fire. All burn. All burn. Then Ghwerig eat."

"I think it's time for us to get to it," Sparhawk said grimly. "I definitely don't want him getting into his workshop." He reached for his sword.

"Use the spear," Flute told him. "He can grab your sword out of your hand, but the spear has enough power to hold him off. Please, my noble father, try to stay alive. I need you."

"I'm doing my very best," he told her.

"Father?" Kurik asked in a tone of surprise.

"It's a Styric form of address," Sephrenia said rather quickly, throwing a look at Flute. "It has to do with respect—and love."

At that point Sparhawk did something he had seldom done before. He set his palms together in front of his chest and bowed to this strange Styric child.

Flute clasped her hands together in delight, then hurled herself into his arms and kissed him soundly with her rosebud little mouth. "Father," she said. For some reason, Sparhawk felt profoundly embarrassed. Flute's kiss was not that of a little girl.

"How hard is a Troll's head?" Kurik asked Flute gruffly, obviously as disturbed as Sparhawk by the little girl's open display of affection that seemed far beyond her years. He was shaking out his brutal chain mace.

"Very, very hard," she told him.

"We've heard that he's deformed," Kurik continued. "How good are his legs?"

"Weak. It's all he can do to stand."

"All right then, Sparhawk," Kurik said in a professional tone. "I'll edge around to the side of him and whip him across the knees, hips, and ankles with this." He swung his mace whistling through the air. "If I can put him down, shove the spear into his guts and then I'll try to brain him."

"*Must* you be so graphic, Kurik?" Sephrenia protested in a sick voice.

"This is business, little mother," Sparhawk told her. "We have to know exactly what we're going to do, so don't interfere. All right, Kurik, let's go." Quite deliberately he walked to the mouth of the gallery and stepped out into the cavern, making no attempt to conceal himself.

The cavern was a place of wonder. Its roof was lost in purple shadow, and the seething waterfall plunged in glowing, golden mist into an unimaginably deep chasm from which the hollow roar of falling water echoed up in endless babble. The walls, stretching out as far as the eye could reach, glittered with flecks and veins of gold, and gems more precious than the ransom of kings sparkled in the shifting, rainbow-hued light.

The misshapen Troll-Dwarf, shaggy and grotesque, squatted at the edge of the chasm. Piled around him were lumps and chunks of pure gold and heaps of gems of every hue. In his right hand Ghwerig held the stained gold crown of King Sarak, and surmounting that crown was Bhelliom, the sapphire rose. The jewel seemed to glow as it caught and reflected the light that came tumbling down with the falling water. Sparhawk looked for the first time at the most precious object on earth, and for a moment a kind of wonder almost overcame him. Then he stepped forward, the ancient battle spear held low in his left hand. He wasn't sure if Sephrenia's spell would make it possible for the grotesque Troll to understand him, but he felt a peculiar moral compunction to speak. Simply to destroy this deformed monstrosity without a word was not in Sparhawk's nature. "I have come for Bhelliom," he said. "I am not Adian, King of Thalesia, so I will not try to trick you. I will take what I want from you by main force. Defend yourself if you can." It was as close as Sparhawk could come to a formal challenge under the circumstances.

Ghwerig came to his feet, his twisted body hideous, and his flat lips peeled back from his yellow fangs in a snarl of hatred. "You not take Ghwerig's Bhelliom from him, Sparhawk-from-Elenia. Ghwerig kill first. Here you die, and Ghwerig eat—not even pale Elene God save Sparhawk now."

"That hasn't been decided yet," Sparhawk replied coolly. "I need the use of Bhelliom for a time, and then I will destroy it to keep it out of the hands of Azash. Surrender it up to me or die."

Ghwerig's laughter was hideous. "Ghwerig die? Ghwerig immortal, Sparhawk-from-Elenia. Man-thing cannot kill."

"That also hasn't been decided yet." Quite deliberately, Sparhawk took the spear in both hands and advanced on the Troll-Dwarf. Kurik, his spiked chain mace hanging from his right fist, came out of the mouth of the gallery and edged around his lord to come at the Troll from the side.

"Two?" Ghwerig said. "Sparhawk should have brought a hundred." He bent and lifted a huge stone club bound with iron out of a pile of gems. "You not take Ghwerig's Bhelliom from him, Sparhawk-from-Elenia. Ghwerig kill first. Here you die, and Ghwerig eat. Not even Aphrael save Sparhawk now. Little man-things doomed. Ghwerig feast this night. Roasted man-things have much juice." He smacked his lips grossly. He straightened, his rough-furred shoulders bulking ominously. The term "dwarf" as applied to a Troll, Sparhawk saw, was grossly deceptive. Ghwerig, despite his deformity, was at least as tall as he, and the Troll's arms, twisted like old stumps, hung down below his knees. His face was furred rather than bearded, and his green eyes seemed to glow malevolently. He shambled forward, his vast club swinging in his right hand. In his left he still clutched Sarak's crown with Bhelliom glowing at its apex.

Kurik stepped in and swung his whistling chain mace at the monster's knees, but Ghwerig almost disdainfully blocked the blow with his club. "Flee, weak man-thing," he said, his voice grating horribly. "All flesh is food for me." He swung his horrid club at that point, and the reach of his abnormally long arms made him doubly dangerous. Kurik jumped back as the ironbound stone cudgel whistled past his face.

Sparhawk lunged in, driving the spear at the Troll's chest, but again Ghwerig deflected the stroke. "Too slow, Sparhawk-from-Elenia." He laughed.

Then Kurik's mace caught him high on the left hip. Ghwerig fell back, but, with catlike speed, smashed his club into a pile of glittering gems, spraying them out like missiles. Kurik winced and put his free hand to his face to wipe the blood from a gash in his forehead out of his eyes.

Sparhawk jabbed again with his spear, lightly slicing the off-balance Troll across the chest. Ghwerig roared with rage and pain, then stumbled forward with vast swings of his club. Sparhawk jumped back, coolly watching for an opening. He saw that the Troll was totally without fear. No injury short of one that was mortal would make the thing retreat. Ghwerig was actually foaming at the mouth now, and his green eyes glowed with madness. He spat out hideous curses and lurched forward again, swinging his horrid club.

"Keep him away from the edge!" Sparhawk shouted to Kurik. "If he goes over, we may never find the crown!" Then he quite clearly realized that he had found the key. Somehow they had to make the deformed Troll drop the crown. It was obvious by now that not even the two of them could prevail against this shaggy creature with its long arms and its eyes ablaze with insane rage. Only a distraction would give them the opportunity to leap in and deliver a mortal wound. He shook his right hand to get Kurik's attention, then reached over and clapped the hand on his left elbow. Kurik's eyes looked puzzled for a moment, but then they narrowed, and he nodded. He circled around to Ghwerig's left, his mace at the ready.

Sparhawk tightened his grip on the spear with both hands again and feinted with it. Ghwerig swung his club at the extended weapon, and Sparhawk jerked it back.

"Ghwerig's rings!" the Troll shouted in triumph. "Sparhawk-from-Elenia brings the rings back to Ghwerig. Ghwerig feel their presence!" With a hideous roar he leaped forward, his club tearing at the air.

Kurik struck, his spiked chain mace tearing a huge chunk of flesh from the Troll's massive left arm. Ghwerig, however, paid little heed to the injury, but continued his rush, his club whistling as he bore down on Sparhawk. His left hand was still tightly locked on the crown.

Sparhawk gave ground grudgingly. He had to keep the Troll away from the brink of the chasm for as long as he held the crown.

Kurik swung his mace again, but Ghwerig shied away, and the blow missed the shaggy elbow. It appeared that the first stroke had caused the Troll more pain than had been evident. Sparhawk took advantage of that momentary flinch and stabbed quickly, opening a gash in Ghwerig's right shoulder. Ghwerig howled, more in rage than in pain, and immediately swung the club again.

Then, from behind him, Sparhawk heard the sound of Flute's voice rising clear and bell-like above the muted roar of the waterfall. Ghwerig's eyes went wide, and his brutish mouth gaped. "You!" he shrieked. "Now Ghwerig pay you back, girl-child! Girl-child's song ends here!"

Flute continued to sing, and Sparhawk risked a quick glance over his shoulder. The little girl stood in the mouth of the gallery with Sephrenia hovering behind her. Sparhawk sensed that the song was not in fact a spell but rather was intended to distract the dwarf so that either he or Kurik could catch the monster off guard. Ghwerig hobbled forward again, swinging his club to force Sparhawk out of his path. The Troll's eyes were fixed on Flute, and his breath hissed between his tightly clenched fangs. Kurik crashed his mace into the monster's back, but Ghwerig gave no indication that he even felt the stroke as he bore down on the Styric child. Then Sparhawk saw his opportunity. As the Troll passed him, the wide swings of the stone club left the hairy flank open. He struck with all his strength, driving the broad blade of the ancient spear into Ghwerig's body just beneath the ribs. The Troll-Dwarf howled as the razor-sharp blade penetrated his leathery hide. He tried to swing his club, but Sparhawk jumped back, jerking the spear free. Then Kurik whipped his chain mace at the deformed side of Ghwerig's right knee, and Spar-hawk heard the sickening sound of breaking bone. Ghwerig toppled, losing his grip on his club. Sparhawk reversed his grip on the spear and drove it down into the Troll's belly.

Ghwerig screamed, clutching at the spear with his right hand as Sparhawk wrenched it back and forth, slicing the sharp blade through the Troll's entrails. The crown, however, still remained tightly clenched in that twisted left hand. Only death, Sparhawk saw, would release that iron grip.

The Troll rolled away from the spear, gashing himself open even more horribly as he did so. Kurik smashed him in the face with the mace, crushing out one of his eyes. With a hideous howl, the monster rolled toward the brink of the chasm, scattering his hoarded jewels in the process. Then, with a scream of triumph, he toppled over the edge with Sarak's crown still in his grip!

Filled with chagrin, Sparhawk rushed to the brink of the abyss and stared down in dismay. Far below he could see the deformed body plunging down and down into unimaginable darkness. Then he heard the light patter of bare feet on the stony floor of the cavern, and Flute sped past him, her glossy black hair flying. To his horror, the little girl did not hesitate nor falter, but ran directly off the edge and plunged down after the falling Troll. "Oh, my God!" he choked, reaching vainly out toward her even as Kurik, his face aghast, came up beside him.

And then Sephrenia was there, Sir Gared's sword still in her hand.

"Do something, Sephrenia," Kurik pleaded.

"There's no need, Kurik," she replied calmly. "Nothing can happen to her."

"But—"

"Hush, Kurik. I'm trying to listen."

The light from the glowing waterfall seemed to dim somewhat as if far overhead a cloud had passed over the sun. The roar of the falling water seemed mocking now, and Sparhawk realized that tears were streaming down his cheeks.

Then, in the deep darkness of that unimaginable abyss, he saw what appeared to be a spark of light. It grew steadily brighter, rising, or so it seemed, from that ghastly chasm. And as it rose, he could see it more clearly. It appeared to be a brilliant shaft of pure white light topped by a spark of intense blue.

Bhelliom rose from the depths, resting on the palm of Flute's incandescent little hand. Sparhawk gaped in astonishment as he realized that he could see through her, and that what had risen glowing from the darkness below was as insubstantial as mist. Flute's tiny face was calm and imperturbable as she held the sapphire rose over her head with one hand. She reached out with the other to Sephrenia. To Sparhawk's horror, his beloved tutor stepped off the ledge.

But she did not fall.

As if walking on solid earth, she calmly strolled out across the bottomless gulf of air to take Bhelliom from Flute's hand. Then she turned and spoke in a strangely archaic form. "Wrench open thy spear, Sir Sparhawk, and put the ring of thy Queen upon thy right hand, lest Bhelliom destroy thee when I deliver it up to thee." Beside her, Flute lifted her face in exultant song, a song that rang with the voices of multitudes.

Sephrenia reached out a hand to touch that insubstantial little face in a gesture of infinite love. Then she walked back across the emptiness with Bhelliom held lightly between her two palms. "Here endeth thy quest, Sir Sparhawk," she said gravely. "Reach forth thy hands to receive Bhelliom from me and from my Child-Goddess Aphrael."

And quite suddenly, everything became clear. Sparhawk fell to his knees with Kurik beside him, and the knight accepted the sapphire rose from Sephrenia's hands. She knelt between the two of them in adoration as they gazed at the glowing face of the one they had called Flute.

The eternal Child-Goddess Aphrael smiled at them, her voice still raised in choral song that filled all the cave with shimmering echoes. The light that filled her misty form grew brighter and brighter, and she speared upward faster than any arrow.

Then she vanished.

# THE SAPPHIRE
# ROSE

*Author's note: My wife has advised me that she would like to write the dedication for this book. Since she's responsible for much of the work, her suggestion seems only fair.*

*You reached up and pulled the fire*
*down from the sky.*

*Love,*
*Me.*

# PROLOGUE

*Otha and Azash—Excerpted from* A Cursory History of Zemoch. *Compiled by the History Department of the University of Borrata.*

Following the invasion of the Elenic-speaking peoples from the steppes of central Daresia lying to the east, the Elenes gradually migrated westward to displace the thinly scattered Styrics who inhabited the Eosian continent. The tribes that settled in Zemoch were late-comers, and they were far less advanced than their cousins to the west. Their economy and social organization were simplistic, and their towns rude by comparison with the cities that were springing up in the emerging western kingdoms. The climate of Zemoch, moreover, was at best inhospitable, and life there existed at the subsistence level. The Church found little to attract her attention to so poor and unpleasant a region; and as a result, the rough chapels of Zemoch became largely unpastored and their simple congregations untended. Thus the Zemochs were obliged to take their religious impulses elsewhere. Since there were few Elene priests in the region to enforce the Church ban on consorting with the heathen Styrics, fraternization became common. As the simple Elene peasantry perceived that their Styric neighbors were able to reap significant benefits from the use of the arcane arts, it is perhaps only natural that apostasy became rampant. Whole Elenic villages in Zemoch were converted to Styric pantheism. Temples were openly erected in honor of this or that topical God, and the darker Styric cults flourished. Intermarriage between Elene and Styric became common, and by the end of the first millennium, Zemoch could no longer have been considered in any light to be a true Elenic nation. The centuries and the close contact with the Styrics had even so far corrupted the Elenic language in Zemoch that it was scarcely intelligible to western Elenes.

It was in the eleventh century that a youthful goatherd in the mountain village of Ganda in central Zemoch had a strange and ultimately earth-shaking experience. While searching in the hills for a straying goat, the lad, Otha by name, came across a hidden, vine-covered shrine that had been erected in antiquity by one of the numerous Styric cults. The shrine had been raised to a weathered idol that was at once grotesquely distorted and oddly compelling. As Otha rested from the rigors of his climb, he heard a hollow voice address him in the Styric tongue. "Who art thou, boy?" the voice inquired.

"My name is Otha," the lad replied haltingly, trying to remember his Styric.

"And hast thou come to this place to pay obeisance to me, to fall down and worship me?"

"No," Otha answered with uncharacteristic truthfulness. "What I'm really doing is trying to find one of my goats."

There was a long pause. Then the hollow, chilling voice continued. "And what must I give thee to wring from thee thine obeisance and thy worship? None of thy kind hath attended my shrine for five thousand years, and I hunger for worship—and for souls."

Otha was certain at this point that the voice was that of one of his fellow herders playing a prank on him and he determined to turn the joke around. "Oh," he said in an offhand manner, "I'd like to be the king of the world, to live forever, to have a thousand ripe young girls willing to do whatever I wanted them to do, and a mountain of gold—and, oh yes, I want my goat back."

"And wilt thou give me thy soul in exchange for these things?"

Otha considered it. He had been scarcely aware of the fact that he had a soul, and so its loss would hardly inconvenience him. He reasoned, moreover, that if this were not, in fact, some juvenile goatherd prank, and if the offer were serious, failure to deliver even one of his impossible demands would invalidate the contract. "Oh, all right," he agreed with an indifferent shrug. "But first I'd like to see my goat—just as an indication of good faith."

"Turn thee around then, Otha," the voice commanded, "and behold that which was lost."

Otha turned, and sure enough, there stood the missing goat, idly chewing on a bush and looking curiously at him. Quickly he tethered her to the bush.

At heart, Otha was a moderately vicious lad. He enjoyed inflicting pain on helpless creatures. He was given to cruel practical jokes, to petty theft, and, whenever it was safe, to a form of the seduction of lonely shepherdesses that had only directness to commend it. He was avaricious and slovenly, and he had a grossly overestimated opinion of his own cleverness.

His mind worked very fast as he tied his goat to the bush. If this obscure Styric divinity could deliver a lost goat upon demand, what else might he be capable of? Otha decided that this might very well be the opportunity of a lifetime. "All right," he said, feigning simplemindedness, "one prayer—for right now—in exchange for the goat. We can talk about souls and empires and wealth and immortality and women later. Show yourself. I'm not going to bow down to empty air. What's your name, by the way? I'll need to know that in order to frame a proper prayer."

"I am Azash, most powerful of the Elder Gods, and if thou wilt be my servant and lead others to worship me, I will grant thee far more than thou hast asked. I will exalt thee and give thee wealth beyond thine imagining. The fairest of maidens shall be thine. Thou shalt have life unending, and, moreover, power over the spirit world such as no man hath ever had. All I ask in return, Otha, is thy soul and the souls of those others thou wilt bring to me. My need and my loneliness are great, and my rewards unto thee shall be equally great. Look upon my face now, and tremble before me."

There was a shimmering in the air surrounding the crude idol, and Otha saw the reality of Azash hovering about the roughly carved image. He shrank in horror before the awful presence that had so suddenly appeared before him, and fell to the ground, abasing himself before it. This was going much too far. At heart, Otha was a coward, however, and he was afraid that the most rational response to the materialized Azash—instant flight—might provoke the hideous God into doing nasty things to him, and Otha was extremely solicitous of his own skin.

"Pray, Otha," the idol gloated. "Mine ears hunger for thine adoration."

"Oh, mighty—uh—Azash, wasn't it? God of Gods and Lord of the World, hear my prayer and receive my humble worship. I am as the dust before thee, and thou towerest above me like the mountain. I worship thee and praise thee and thank thee from the depths of my heart for the return of this miserable goat—which I will beat senseless for straying just as soon as I get her home." Trembling, Otha hoped that the prayer might satisfy Azash—or at least distract him enough to provide an opportunity for escape.

"Thy prayer is adequate, Otha," the idol acknowledged. "Barely. In time thou wilt become more proficient in thine adoration. Go now thy way, and I will savor this rude prayer of thine. Return again on the morrow, and I will disclose my mind further unto thee."

As he trudged home with his goat, Otha vowed never to return, but that night he tossed on his rude pallet in the filthy hut where he lived, and his mind was afire with visions of wealth and subservient young women upon whom he could vent his lust. "Let's see where this goes," he muttered to himself as the dawn marked the end of the troubled night. "If I have to, I can always run away later."

And that began the discipleship of a simple Zemoch goatherd to the Elder God, Azash, a God whose name Otha's Styric neighbors would not even utter, so great was their fear of him. In the centuries that followed, Otha realized how profound was his enslavement. Azash patiently led him through simple worship into the practice of perverted rites and beyond into the realms of spiritual abomination. The formerly ingenuous and only moderately disgusting goatherd became morose and somber as the dreaded idol fed gluttonously upon his mind and soul. Though he lived a half dozen lifetimes and more, his limbs withered, while his paunch and head grew bloated and hairless and pallid white as a result of his abhorrence of the sun. He grew vastly wealthy, but took no pleasure in his wealth. He had eager concubines by the score, but he was indifferent to their charms. A thousand wraiths and imps and creatures of ultimate darkness responded to his slightest whim, but he could not even summon sufficient interest to command them. His only joy became the contemplation of pain and death as his minions cruelly wrenched and tore the lives of the weak and helpless from their quivering bodies for his entertainment. In that respect, Otha had not changed.

During the early years of the third millennium, after the sluglike Otha had passed his nine hundredth year, he commanded his infernal underlings to carry the rude shrine of Azash to the city of Zemoch in the northeast highlands. An enormous semblance of the hideous God was constructed to enclose the shrine, and a vast temple erected about it. Beside that temple, and connected to it by a labyrinthine series of passageways, stood his own palace, gilt with fine, hammered gold and inlaid with pearl and onyx and chalcedony and with its columns surmounted with intricately carved capitals of ruby and emerald. There he indifferently proclaimed himself Emperor of all Zemoch, a proclamation seconded by the thunderous but somehow mocking voice of Azash booming hollowly from the temple and cheered by multitudes of howling fiends.

There began then a ghastly reign of terror in Zemoch. All opposing cults were ruthlessly extirpated. Sacrifices of the newborn and virgins numbered in the thousands, and Elene and Styric alike were converted by the sword to the worship of Azash. It took perhaps a century for Otha and his henchmen to eradicate totally all traces of decency from his enslaved subjects. Blood lust and rampant cruelty became common, and the rites performed before the altars and shrines erected to Azash became increasingly degenerate and obscene.

In the twenty-fifth century, Otha deemed that all was in readiness to pursue the ultimate goal of his perverted God, and he massed his human armies and their dark allies upon the western borders of Zemoch. After a brief pause, while he and Azash gathered their strength, Otha struck, sending his forces down onto the plains of Pelosia, Lamorkand, and Cammoria. The horror of that invasion cannot be fully described. Simple atrocity was not sufficient to slake the savagery of the Zemoch horde, and the gross cruelties of the inhumans who accompanied the invading army are too hideous to be mentioned. Mountains of human heads were erected, captives were roasted alive and then eaten, and the roads and highways were lined with occupied crosses, gibbets, and stakes. The skies grew black with flocks of vultures and ravens, and the air reeked with the stench of burned and rotting flesh.

Otha's armies moved with confidence toward the battlefield, fully believing that their hellish allies could easily overcome any resistance, but they had reckoned without the power of the Knights of the Church. The great battle was joined on the plains of Lamorkand just to the south of Lake Randera. The purely physical struggle was titanic enough, but the supernatural battle on that plain was even more stupendous. Every conceivable form of spirit joined in the fray. Waves of total darkness and sheets of multicolored light swept the field. Fire and lightning rained from the sky. Whole battalions were swallowed up by the earth or burned to ashes in sudden flame. The shattering crash of thunder rolled perpetually from horizon to horizon, and the ground itself was torn by earthquake and the eruption of searing liquid rock that poured down slopes to engulf advancing legions. For days the armies were locked in dreadful battle upon that bloody field before, step by step, the Zemochs were pushed back. The horrors that Otha hurled into the fray were overmatched one by one by the concerted power of the Church Knights, and for the first time the Zemochs tasted defeat. Their slow, grudging retreat became more rapid, eventually turning into a rout as the demoralized horde broke and ran toward the dubious safety of the border.

The victory of the Elenes was complete, but not without dreadful cost. Fully half of the militant knights lay slain upon the battlefield, and the armies of the Elene kings numbered their dead by the scores of thousands. The victory was theirs, but they were too exhausted and too few to pursue the fleeing Zemochs past the border.

The bloated Otha, his withered limbs no longer even able to bear his weight, was bourne on a litter through the labyrinth at Zemoch to the temple, there to face the wrath of Azash. He groveled before the idol of his God, blubbering and begging for mercy.

And at long last Azash spoke. "One last time, Otha," the God said in a horribly quiet voice. "Once only will I relent. I *will* possess Bhelliom, and thou wilt obtain it for me and deliver it up to me here, for if thou dost not do this thing, my generosity unto thee shall vanish. If gifts do not encourage thee to bend to my will, perhaps torment will. Go, Otha. Find Bhelliom for me and return with it here that I may be unchained and my maleness restored. Shouldst thou fail me, surely wilt thou die, and thy dying shall consume a million million years."

Otha fled, and thus, even in the ruins and tatters of his defeat, was born his last assault upon the Elene kingdoms of the west, an assault that was to bring the world to the brink of universal disaster.

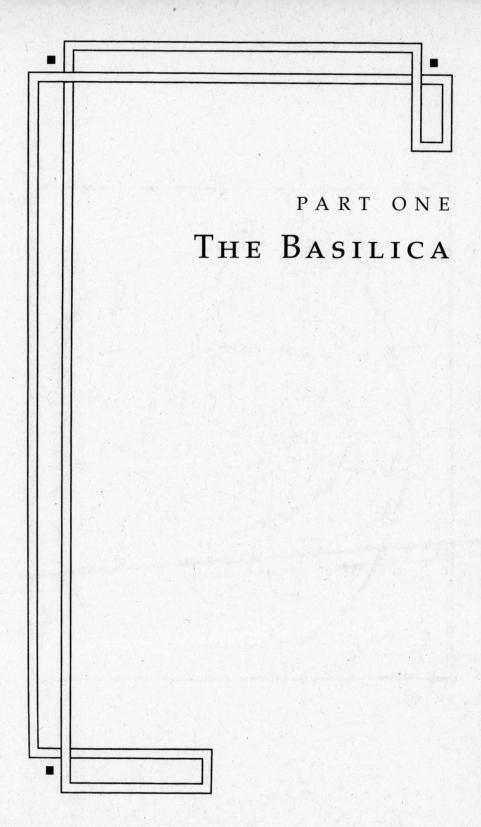

PART ONE

# THE BASILICA

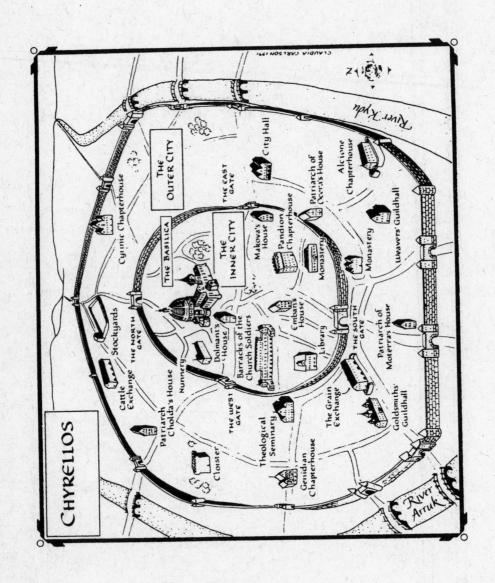

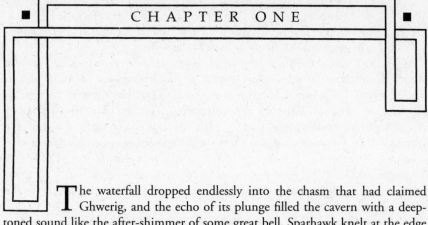

The waterfall dropped endlessly into the chasm that had claimed Ghwerig, and the echo of its plunge filled the cavern with a deep-toned sound like the after-shimmer of some great bell. Sparhawk knelt at the edge of the abyss with the Bhelliom held tightly in his fist. Thought had been erased, and he could only kneel at the brink of the chasm, his eyes dazzled by the light of the sun-touched column of water falling into the depths from the surface above and his ears full of its sound.

The cave smelled damp. The mistlike spray from the waterfall bedewed the rocks, and the wet stones shimmered in the shifting light of the torrent to mingle with the last fading glimmerings of Aphrael's incandescent ascension.

Sparhawk slowly lowered his eyes to look at the jewel he held in his fist. Though it appeared delicate, even fragile, he sensed that the sapphire rose was all but indestructible. From deep within its azure heart there came a kind of pulsating glow, deep blue at the tips of the petals and darkening down at the gem's center to a lambent midnight. Its power made his hand ache, and something deep in his mind shrieked warnings at him as he gazed into its depths. He shuddered and tore his eyes from its seductive glow.

The hard-bitten Pandion Knight looked around, irrationally trying to cling to the fading bits of light lingering in the stones of the Troll-Dwarf's cave as if the Child-Goddess Aphrael could somehow protect him from the jewel he had labored so long to gain and that he now strangely feared. There was more to it than that, though. At some level below thought Sparhawk wanted to hold that faint light forever, to keep the spirit if not the person of the tiny, whimsical divinity in his heart.

Sephrenia sighed and slowly rose to her feet. Her face was weary and at the same time exalted. She had struggled hard to reach this damp cave in the mountains of Thalesia, but she had been rewarded with that joyful moment of epiphany when she had looked full into the face of her Goddess. "We must leave this place now, dear ones," she said sadly.

"Can't we stay a few minutes longer?" Kurik asked her with an uncharacteristic longing in his voice. Of all the men in the world, Kurik was the most prosaic—most of the time.

"It's better that we don't. If we stay too long, we'll start finding excuses to stay even longer. In time, we may not want to leave at all." The small, white-robed Styric looked at Bhelliom with revulsion. "Please get it out of sight, Sparhawk, and command it to be still. Its presence contaminates us all." She shifted the sword that the ghost of Sir Gared had delivered to her aboard Captain Sorgi's ship. She muttered in Styric for a moment and then released the spell that ignited the tip of the sword with a brilliant glow to light their way back to the surface.

Sparhawk tucked the flower-gem inside his tunic and bent to pick up the spear of King Aldreas. His chain-mail shirt smelled very foul to him just now, and his skin cringed away from its touch. He wished that he could rid himself of it.

Kurik stooped and lifted the iron-bound stone club the hideously malformed Troll-Dwarf had wielded against them before his fatal plunge into the chasm. He hefted the brutal weapon a couple of times and then indifferently tossed it into the abyss after its owner.

Sephrenia lifted the glowing sword over her head, and the three of them crossed the gem-littered floor of Ghwerig's treasure cave toward the entrance of the spiralling gallery that led to the surface.

"Do you think we'll ever see her again?" Kurik asked wistfully as they entered the gallery.

"Aphrael? It's hard to say. She's always been a little unpredictable." Sephrenia's voice was subdued.

They climbed in silence for a time, following the spiral of the gallery steadily to the left. Sparhawk felt a strange emptiness as they climbed. They had been four when they had descended; now they were only three. The Child-Goddess, however, had not been left behind, for they all carried her in their hearts. There was something else bothering him, though. "Is there any way we can seal up this cave once we get outside?" he asked his tutor.

Sephrenia looked at him, her eyes intent. "We can if you wish, dear one, but why do you want to?"

"It's a little hard to put into words."

"We've got what we came for, Sparhawk. Why should you care if some swineherd stumbles across the cave now?"

"I'm not entirely sure." He frowned, trying to pinpoint it. "If some Thalesian peasant comes in here, he'll eventually find Ghwerig's treasure hoard, won't he?"

"If he looks long enough, yes."

"And after that it won't be long before the cave's swarming with other Thalesians."

"Why should that bother you? Do you want Ghwerig's treasure for yourself?"

"Hardly. Martel's the greedy one, not me."

"Then why are you so concerned? What does it matter if the Thalesians start wandering around in here?"

"This is a very special place, Sephrenia."

"In what way?"

"It's holy," he replied shortly. Her probing had begun to irritate him. "A Goddess revealed herself to us here. I don't want the cave profaned by a crowd of drunken, greedy treasure hunters. I'd feel the same way if someone profaned an Elene Church."

"Dear Sparhawk," she said, impulsively embracing him. "Did it really cost you all that much to admit Aphrael's divinity?"

"Your Goddess was very convincing, Sephrenia," he replied wryly. "She'd have shaken the certainty of the Hierocracy of the Elene Church itself. Can we do it? Seal the cave, I mean?"

She started to say something, then stopped, frowning. "Wait here," she told them. She leaned Sir Gared's sword point up against the wall of the gallery and walked back down the passage for a ways and then stopped again at the very edge of the light from the glowing sword tip, where she stood deep in thought. After a time, she returned.

"I'm going to ask you to do something dangerous, Sparhawk," she said gravely. "I think you'll be safe though. The memory of Aphrael is still strong in your mind, and that should protect you."

"What do you want me to do?"

"We're going to use Bhelliom to seal the cave. There are other ways we could do it, but we have to be sure that the jewel will accept your authority. I *think* it will, but let's make certain. You're going to have to be strong, Sparhawk. Bhelliom won't want to do what you ask, so you'll have to compel it."

"I've dealt with stubborn things before." He shrugged.

"Don't make light of this, Sparhawk. It's something far more elemental than anything *I've* ever done. Let's move on."

They continued upward along the spiralling passageway with the muted roar of the waterfall in Ghwerig's treasure cave growing fainter and fainter. Then, just as they moved beyond the range of hearing, the sound seemed to change, fragmenting its one endless note into many, becoming a complex chord rather than a single tone—some trick perhaps of the shifting echoes in the cave. With the change of that sound, Sparhawk's mood also changed. Before, there had been a kind of weary satisfaction at having finally achieved a long-sought goal, coupled with the sense of awe at the revelation of the Child-Goddess. Now, however, the dark, musty cave seemed somehow ominous, threatening. Sparhawk felt something he had not felt since early childhood. He was suddenly afraid of the dark. Things seemed to lurk in the shadows beyond the circle of light from the glowing sword tip, faceless things filled with a cruel malevolence. He nervously looked back over his shoulder. Far back, beyond the light, something seemed to move. It was brief, no more than a flicker of a deeper, more intense darkness. He discovered that when he tried to look directly at it, he could no longer see it, but when he glanced off to one side, it was there—vague, unformed, and hovering on the very edge of his vision. It filled him with an unnamed dread. "Foolishness," he muttered, and moved on, eager to reach the light above them.

It was midafternoon when they reached the surface, and the sun seemed very bright after the dark cave. Sparhawk drew in a deep breath and reached inside his tunic.

"Not yet, Sparhawk," Sephrenia advised. "We want to collapse the ceiling of the cave, but we don't want to bring that overhanging cliff down on our heads at the same time. We'll go back down to where the horses are and do it from there."

"You'll have to teach me the spell," he said as the three of them crossed the bramble-choked basin in front of the cave mouth.

"There isn't any spell. You have the jewel and the rings. All you have to do is give the command. I'll show you how when we get down."

They clambered down the rocky ravine to the grassy plateau and their previous night's encampment. It was nearly sunset when they reached the pair of tents and the picketed horses. Faran laid his ears back and bared his teeth as Sparhawk approached him.

"What's your problem?" Sparhawk asked his evil-tempered war horse.

"He senses Bhelliom," Sephrenia explained. "He doesn't like it. Stay away from him for a while." She looked critically up the gap from which they had just emerged. "It's safe enough here," she decided. "Take out Bhelliom and hold it in both hands so that the rings are touching it."

"Do I have to face the cave?"

"No. Bhelliom will know what you're telling it to do. Now, remember the inside of the cave—the look of it, the feel, and even the smell. Then imagine the roof collapsing. The rocks will tumble down and bounce and roll and pile up on top of each other. There'll be a lot of noise. A great cloud of dust and a strong wind will come rushing out of the cave mouth. The ridgeline above the cave will sag as the roof of the cavern collapses, and there'll probably be avalanches. Don't let any of that distract you. Keep the images firmly in your mind."

"It's a bit more complicated than an ordinary spell, isn't it?"

"Yes. This is not, strictly speaking, a spell, though. You'll be unleashing elemental magic. Concentrate, Sparhawk. The more detailed you make the image, the more powerfully Bhelliom will respond. When you've got it firmly in your mind, tell the jewel to make it happen."

"Do I have to speak to it in Ghwerig's language?"

"I'm not sure. Try Elenic first. If that doesn't work, we'll fall back on Troll."

Sparhawk remembered the mouth of the cave, the antechamber just inside, and the long, spiralling gallery leading down to Ghwerig's treasure cave. "Should I bring down the roof on that waterfall as well?" he asked.

"I don't think so. That river might come to the surface again somewhere downstream. If you dam it up, someone might notice that it's not running any more and start investigating. Besides, that particular cavern is very special, isn't it?"

"Yes, it is."

"Let's enclose it, then, and protect it forever."

Sparhawk pictured the ceiling of the cave collapsing with a huge, grinding roar and a billowing cloud of rock dust. "What do I say?" he asked.

"Call it 'Blue-Rose.' That's what Ghwerig called it. It might recognize the name."

"Blue-Rose," Sparhawk said in a tone of command, "make the cave fall in."

The sapphire rose went very dark, and angry red flashes appeared deep in its center.

"It's fighting you," Sephrenia said. "This is the part I warned you about. The cave is the place where it was born, and it doesn't want to destroy it. Force it, Sparhawk."

"Do it, Blue-Rose!" Sparhawk barked, bending every ounce of his will on the jewel in his hands. Then he felt a surge of incredible power, and the sapphire seemed to throb in his hands. He felt a sudden wild exaltation as he unloosed the might of the stone. It was far beyond mere satisfaction; it verged almost on physical ecstasy.

There was a low, sullen rumbling from deep in the ground, and the earth shuddered. Rocks deep beneath them began to pop and crack as the earthquake shattered layer upon layer of subterranean rock. Far up the ravine, the rock face looming over the mouth of Ghwerig's cave began to topple outward, then dropped straight down into the weedy basin as its base crumbled out from under it. The sound of the collapsing cliff was very loud even at this distance, and a vast cloud of dust boiled up from the rubble and then drifted off to the northeast as the prevailing wind that raked these mountains swept it away. Then, even as it had in the cave, something flickered at the edge of Sparhawk's vision—something dark and filled with malevolent curiosity.

"How do you feel?" Sephrenia asked, her eyes intent.

"A little strange," he admitted. "Very strong for some reason."

"Keep your mind away from that. Concentrate on Aphrael instead. Don't even think about Bhelliom until that feeling wears off. Get it out of sight again. Don't look at it."

Sparhawk tucked the sapphire back inside his tunic.

Kurik looked up the ravine toward the huge pile of rubble filling the basin that had lain before the mouth of Ghwerig's cave. "That all seems so final," he said regretfully.

"It is," Sephrenia told him. "The cavern's safe now. Let's keep our minds on other things, gentlemen. Don't dwell on what we've just done, or we might be tempted to undo it."

Kurik squared his heavy shoulders and looked around. "I'll get a fire going," he said. He walked back toward the mouth of the ravine to gather firewood while Sparhawk rummaged through the packs for cooking utensils and something suitable for supper. After they had eaten, they sat around the fire, their faces subdued.

"What was it like, Sparhawk?" Kurik asked. "Using Bhelliom, I mean?" He glanced at Sephrenia. "Is it all right to talk about it now?"

"We'll see. Go ahead, Sparhawk. Tell him."

"It was like nothing else I've ever experienced," the big knight replied. "I suddenly felt as if I were a hundred feet tall and that there was nothing in the world I couldn't do. I even caught myself looking around for something else to use it for—a mountain to tear down, maybe."

"Sparhawk! Stop!" Sephrenia told him sharply. "Bhelliom's tampering with your thoughts. It's trying to lure you into using it. Each time you do, its hold on you grows stronger. Think about something else."

"Like Aphrael?" Kurik suggested. "Or is she dangerous, too?"

Sephrenia smiled. "Oh yes, very dangerous. She'll capture your soul even faster than Bhelliom will."

"Your warning's a little late, Sephrenia. I think she already has. I miss her, you know."

"You needn't. She's still with us."

He looked around. "Where?"

"In spirit, Kurik."

"That's not exactly the same."

"Let's do something about Bhelliom right now," she said thoughtfully. "Its grip is even more powerful than I'd imagined." She rose and went to the small pack that contained her personal belongings. She rummaged around in it and took out a canvas pouch, a large needle, and a hank of red yarn. She took up the pouch and began to stitch a crimson design on it, a peculiarly asymmetrical design. Her face was intent in the ruddy firelight, and her lips moved constantly as she worked.

"It doesn't match, little mother," Sparhawk pointed out. "That side's different from the other."

"It's supposed to be. Please don't talk to me just now, Sparhawk. I'm trying to concentrate." She continued her sewing for a time, then pinned her needle into her sleeve and held the pouch out to the fire. She spoke intently in Styric, and the fire rose and fell, dancing rhythmically to her words. Then the flame suddenly billowed out as if trying to fill the pouch. "Now, Sparhawk," she said, holding the pouch open. "Put Bhelliom in here. Be very firm. It's probably going to try to fight you again."

He was puzzled, but he reached inside his tunic, took the stone, and tried to put it into the pouch. A screech of protest seemed to fill his ears, and the jewel actually grew hot in his hand. He felt as if he were trying to push the thing through solid rock, and his mind reeled, shrieking to him that what he was trying to do was impossible. He set his teeth together and shoved harder. With an almost audible wail, the sapphire rose slipped into the pouch, and Sephrenia pulled the drawstring tight. She tied the ends into an intricate knot, then took her needle and wove red yarn through that knot. "There," she said, biting off the yarn, "that should help."

"What did you do?" Kurik asked her.

"It's a form of a prayer. Aphrael can't diminish Bhelliom's power, but she can confine it so that it can't influence us or reach out to others. It's not perfect, but it's the best we can do on short notice. We'll do something a little more permanent later on. Put it away, Sparhawk. Try to keep your chain mail between the pouch and your skin. I think that may help. Aphrael once told me that Bhelliom can't bear the touch of steel."

"Aren't you being a little overcautious, Sephrenia?" Sparhawk asked her.

"I don't know, Sparhawk. I've never dealt with anything like Bhelliom before and I can't even begin to imagine the limits of its power. I know enough, though, to know that it can corrupt anything—even the Elene God or the Younger Gods of Styricum."

"All except Aphrael," Kurik corrected.

She shook her head. "Even Aphrael was tempted by Bhelliom when she was carrying it up out of that abyss to bring it to us."

"Why didn't she just keep it for herself then?"

"Love. My Goddess loves us all, and she gave up Bhelliom willingly out of that love. Bhelliom can't begin to understand love. In the end, that may be our only defense against it."

Sparhawk's sleep was troubled that night, and he tossed restlessly on his blankets. Kurik was on watch near the edge of the circle of firelight, and so Sparhawk was left to wrestle with his nightmares alone. He seemed to see the sapphire rose hanging in mid-air before his eyes, its deep blue glow seductive. Out of the center of that glow there came a sound—a song that pulled at his very being. Hovering around him, so close almost as to touch his shoulders, were shadows—more than one, certainly, but less than ten, or so it seemed. The shadows were *not* seductive. They seemed to be filled with a hatred born from some towering frustration. Beyond the glowing Bhelliom stood the obscenely grotesque mud idol of Azash, the idol he had smashed at Ghasek, the idol that had claimed Bellina's soul. The idol's face was moving, twisting hideously into expressions of the most elemental passions—lust and greed and hatred and a towering contempt that seemed born of its certainty of its own absolute power.

Sparhawk struggled in his dream, dragged first this way and then that. Bhelliom pulled at him; Azash pulled at him; and the hateful shadows pulled as well. The power of each was irresistible, and his mind and body seemed almost torn apart by those titanic conflicting forces.

He tried to scream. And then he awoke. He sat up and realized that he was sweating profusely. He swore. He was exhausted, but a sleep filled with nightmares was no cure for that bone-deep weariness. Grimly he lay back down, hoping for an oblivion without dreams.

It began again, however. Once again he wrestled in his sleep with Bhelliom and with Azash and with the hateful shadows lurking behind him.

"Sparhawk," a small, familiar voice said in his ear, "don't let them frighten you. They can't hurt you, you know. All they can do is try to frighten you."

"Why are they doing it?"

"Because they're afraid of you."

"That doesn't make sense, Aphrael. I'm only a man."

Her laughter was like the peal of a small, silver bell. "You're so innocent sometimes, father. You're not like any other man who's ever lived. In a rather peculiar way, you're more powerful than the Gods themselves. Go to sleep now. I won't let them hurt you."

He felt a soft kiss on his cheek, and a pair of small arms seemed to embrace his head with a peculiarly maternal tenderness. The terrible images of his nightmare wavered. And then they vanished.

It must have been hours later when Kurik entered the tent and shook him into wakefulness. "What time is it?" Sparhawk asked his squire.

"About midnight," Kurik replied. "Take your cloak. It's chilly out there."

Sparhawk arose, put on his mail shirt and tunic, and then buckled his sword belt around his waist. Then he tucked the pouch under the tunic. He picked up his traveller's cloak. "Sleep well," he told his friend, and left the tent.

The stars were very bright, and a crescent moon had just risen above the jagged line of peaks to the east. Sparhawk walked away from the embers of their fire to allow his eyes to adjust to the darkness. He stood with his breath steaming slightly in the chill mountain air.

The dream still troubled him, though it was fading now. About the only sharp memory he really had of it was the lingering feel of the soft touch of Aphrael's lips on his cheek. He firmly closed the door of the chamber where he stored his nightmares and thought of other things.

Without the little Goddess and her ability to tamper with time, it was probably going to take them a week to reach the coast, and they were going to have to find a ship to carry them to the Deiran side of the Straits of Thalesia. By now King Wargun had undoubtedly alerted every nation in the Elene kingdoms to their escape. They'd have to move carefully to avoid capture, but they nonetheless needed to go into Emsat. They had to retrieve Talen for one thing, and ships are hard to come by on deserted shores.

The night air in these mountains was chill even in summer, and Sparhawk pulled his cloak tighter about his shoulders. His mood was somber, troubled. The events of this day were the kind that led to long thoughts. Sparhawk's religious convictions were not really all that profound. His commitment had always been to the Pandion Order rather than to the Elene faith. The Church Knights were largely engaged in making the world safe for other, gentler, Elenes to perform those ceremonies the clergy felt were pleasing to God. Sparhawk seldom concerned himself with God. Today, however, he had gone through some rather profoundly spiritual events. Ruefully he admitted to himself that a man with a pragmatic turn of mind is never really prepared for religious experiences of the kind that had been thrust upon him today. Then, almost as if his hand were acting of its own volition, it strayed toward the neck of his tunic. Sparhawk resolutely drew his sword, stabbed its point into the turf, and wrapped both hands firmly about its hilt. He pushed his mind away from religion and the supernatural.

It was almost over now. The time his queen would be compelled to remain confined in the crystal that sustained her life could be measured in days rather than weeks or months. Sparhawk and his friends had trekked all over the Eosian continent to discover the one thing that would cure her, and now that cure lay in the canvas pouch under his tunic. Nothing could stop him now that he had Bhelliom. He could destroy whole armies with the sapphire rose if need be. He sternly pulled his mind back from that thought.

His broken face grew bleak. Once his queen was safe, he was going to do some more or less permanent things to Martel, the Primate Annias, and anyone who had aided them in their treason. He began mentally to draw up a list of people who had things to answer for. It was a pleasant way to pass the nighttime hours, and it kept his mind occupied and out of mischief.

At dusk six days later, they crested a hill and looked down at the smoky torches and candlelit windows of the capital of Thalesia. "You'd better wait here," Kurik said to Sparhawk and Sephrenia. "Wargun's probably spread descriptions of you through every city in Eosia by now. I'll go into town and locate Talen. We'll see what we can find in the way of a ship."

"Will you be all right?" Sephrenia asked. "Wargun could have sent out your description as well, you know."

"King Wargun's a nobleman," Kurik growled. "Nobles pay very little attention to servants."

"You're not a servant," Sparhawk objected.

"That's how I'm defined, Sparhawk, and that's how Wargun saw me—when he was sober enough to see anything. I'll waylay some traveller and steal his clothes.

That should get me by in Emsat. Give me some money in case I have to bribe some people."

"Elenes," Sephrenia sighed, as Sparhawk led her back some distance from the road and Kurik rode at a walk on down toward the city. "How did I ever get involved with such unscrupulous people?"

The dusk faded slowly, and the tall, resinous fir trees around them turned into looming shadows. Sparhawk tethered Faran, their pack horse, and Ch'iel, Sephrenia's white palfrey. Then he spread his cloak on a mossy bank for her to sit on.

"What's troubling you, Sparhawk?" she asked him.

"Tired, maybe." He tried to shrug it off. "And there's always a kind of letdown after you've finished something."

"There's more to it than that though, isn't there?"

He nodded. "I wasn't really prepared for what happened in that cave. It all seemed very immediate and personal, somehow."

She nodded. "I'm not trying to be offensive, Sparhawk, but the Elene religion has become institutionalized, and it's very hard to love an institution. The Gods of Styricum have a much more personal relationship with their devotees."

"I think I prefer being an Elene. It's easier. Personal relationships with Gods are very upsetting."

"But don't you love Aphrael—just a little?"

"Of course I do. I was a lot more comfortable with her when she was just Flute, but I still love her." He made a face. "You're leading me in the direction of heresy, little mother," he accused.

"Not really. For the time being, all Aphrael wants is your love. She hasn't asked you for your worship—yet."

"It's that 'yet' that concerns me. Isn't this a rather peculiar time and place for a theological discussion, though?"

Just then there was the sound of horses on the road, and the unseen riders reined in not far from where Sparhawk and Sephrenia were concealed. Sparhawk rose quickly, his hand going to his sword hilt.

"They have to be around here somewhere," a rough voice declared. "That was his man who just rode into the city."

"I don't know about you two," another voice said, "but I'm not really all that eager to find him, myself."

"There are three of us," the first voice declared pugnaciously.

"Do you think that would really make any difference to him? He's a Church Knight. He could probably cut all three of us down without even working up a sweat. We're not going to be able to spend the money if we're all dead."

"He's got a point there," a third voice agreed. "I think the best idea is just to locate him for now. Once we know where he is and which way he's going, we'll be able to set up an ambush for him. Church Knight or not, an arrow in his back ought to make him docile. Let's keep looking. The woman's riding a white horse. That should make it easier to locate them."

The unseen horses moved on, and Sparhawk slid his half-drawn sword back into its scabbard.

"Are they Wargun's men?" Sephrenia whispered to Sparhawk.

"I wouldn't think so," Sparhawk murmured. "Wargun's a little erratic, but he's not the sort who sends out paid assassins. He wants to yell at me and maybe throw me in his dungeon for a while. I don't think he's angry enough to want to murder me—at least I hope not."

"Someone else, then?"

"Probably." Sparhawk frowned. "I don't seem to recall having offended anyone in Thalesia lately, though."

"Annais has a long arm, dear one," she reminded him.

"That might be it, little mother. Let's lie low and keep our ears open until Kurik comes back."

After about an hour they heard the slow plodding of another horse coming up the rutted road from Emsat. The horse stopped at the top of the hill. "Sparhawk?" The quiet voice was vaguely familiar.

Sparhawk quickly put his hand to his sword hilt, and he and Sephrenia exchanged a quick glance.

"I know you're in there somewhere, Sparhawk. It's me, Tel, so don't get excited. Your man said you wanted to go into Emsat. Stragen sent me to fetch you."

"We're over here," Sparhawk replied. "Wait. We'll be right out." He and Sephrenia led their horses to the road to meet the flaxen-haired brigand who had escorted them to the town of Heid on their journey to Ghwerig's cave. "Can you get us into the city?" Sparhawk asked.

"Nothing easier." Tel shrugged.

"How do we get past the guards at the gate?"

"We just ride on through. The gate guards work for Stragen. It makes things a lot simpler. Shall we go?"

Emsat was a northern city, and the steep-pitched roofs of the houses bespoke the heavy snows of winter. The streets were narrow and crooked, and there were only a few people abroad. Sparhawk, however, looked about warily, remembering the three cutthroats on the road outside of town.

"Be kind of careful with Stragen, Sparhawk," Tel cautioned as they rode into a seedy district near the waterfront. "He's the bastard son of an earl and he's a little touchy about his origins. He likes to have us address him as 'Milord.' It's foolish, but he's a good leader, so we play his games." He pointed down a garbage-littered street. "We go this way."

"How's Talen getting along?"

"He's settled in now, but he was seriously put out with you when he first got here. He called you some names I'd never even heard before."

"I can imagine." Sparhawk decided to confide in the brigand. He knew Tel and he was at least partially sure he could trust him. "Some people rode by the place where we were hiding before you came," he said. "They were looking for us. Were those some of your men?"

"No," Tel replied. "I came alone."

"I sort of thought you might have. These fellows were talking about shooting me full of arrows. Would Stragen be involved in that sort of thing in any way?"

"Out of the question, Sparhawk," Tel said quite firmly. "You and your friends have thieves' sanctuary. Stragen would never violate that. I'll talk to Stragen about it. He'll see to it that these itinerant bowmen stay out of your hair." Tel laughed a chilling little laugh. "He'll probably be more upset with them because they've gone into business for themselves than because they threaten you, though. Nobody cuts a throat or steals a penny in Emsat without Stragen's permission. He's very keen about that." The blond brigand led them to a boarded-up warehouse at the far end of the street. They rode around to the back, dismounted, and were admitted by a pair of burly cutthroats standing guard at the door.

The interior of the warehouse belied the shabby exterior. It appeared only slightly less opulent than a palace. There were crimson drapes covering the boarded-up windows, deep blue carpets on the creaky floors, and tapestries concealing the rough plank walls. A semicircular staircase of polished wood curved up to a second floor, and a crystal chandelier threw soft, glowing candlelight over the entryway.

"Excuse me for a minute," Tel said. He went into a side chamber and emerged a bit later wearing a cream-colored doublet and blue hose. He also had a slim rapier at his side.

"Elegant," Sparhawk observed.

"Another one of Stragen's foolish ideas," Tel snorted. "I'm a working man, not a clothes rack. Let's go up, and I'll introduce you to Milord."

The upper floor was, if anything, even more extravagantly furnished than the one below. It was expensively floored with intricate parquet, and the walls were panelled with highly polished wood. Broad corridors led off toward the back of the house, and chandeliers and standing candelabra filled the spacious hall with golden light. It appeared that some kind of ball was in progress. A quartet of indifferently talented musicians sawed at their instruments in one corner, and gaily dressed thieves and whores circled the floor in the mincing steps of the latest dance. Although their clothing was elegant, the men were unshaven, and the women had tangled hair and smudged faces. The contrast gave the entire scene an almost nightmarish quality, heightened by voices and laughter that were coarse and raucous.

The focus of the entire room was a thin man with elaborate curls cascading over his ruffed collar. He was dressed in white satin, and the chair upon which he sat near the far end of the room was not quite a throne—but very nearly. His expression was sardonic, and his deep-sunk eyes had about them a look of obscure pain.

Tel stopped at the head of the staircase and talked for a moment with an ancient cutpurse holding a long staff and wearing elegant scarlet livery. The white-haired knave turned, rapped the butt of his staff on the floor, and spoke in a booming voice. "Milord," he declaimed, "the Marquis Tel begs leave to present Sir Sparhawk, Knight of the Church and champion of the Queen of Elenia."

The thin man rose and clapped his hands together sharply. The musicians broke off their sawing. "We have important guests, dear friends," he said to the dancers. His voice was very deep and quite consciously well modulated. "Let us pay our proper respects to the invincible Sir Sparhawk, who, with the might of his hands, defends our Holy Mother Church. I pray you, Sir Sparhawk, approach that we may greet you and make you welcome."

"A pretty speech," Sephrenia murmured.

"It should be," Tel muttered back sourly. "He probably spent the last hour composing it." The flaxen-haired brigand led them through the throng of dancers, who all bowed or curtsied jerkily to them as they passed.

When they reached the man in white satin, Tel bowed. "Milord," he said, "I have the honor to present Sir Sparhawk the Pandion. Sir Sparhawk, Milord Stragen."

"The thief," Stragen added sardonically. Then he bowed elegantly. "You honor my inadequate house, Sir Knight," he said.

Sparhawk bowed in reply. "It is I who am honored, Milord." He rigorously avoided smiling at the airs of this apparently puffed-up popinjay.

"And so we meet at last, Sir Knight," Stragen said. "Your young friend Talen has given us a glowing account of your exploits."

"Talen sometimes tends to exaggerate things, Milord."

"And the lady is . . . ?"

"Sephrenia, my tutor in the secrets."

"Dear sister," Stragen said in flawless Styric, "will you permit me to greet you?"

If Sephrenia was startled by this strange man's knowledge of her language, she gave no indication of it. She extended her hands, and Stragen kissed her palms. "It is surprising, Milord, to meet a civilized man in the midst of a world filled with all these Elene savages," she said.

He laughed. "Isn't it amusing, Sparhawk, to discover that even our unblemished Styrics have their little prejudices?" The blond pseudo aristocrat looked around the hall. "But we're interrupting the grand ball. My associates do so enjoy these frivolities. Let's withdraw so that their joy may be unconfined." He raised his resonant voice slightly, speaking to the throng of elegant criminals. "Dear friends," he said to them, "pray excuse us. We will go apart for our discussions. We would not for all the world interrupt your enjoyment of this evening." He paused, then looked rather pointedly at one ravishing dark-haired girl. "I trust that you'll recall our discussion following the last ball, Countess," he said firmly. "Although I stand in awe of your ferocious business instincts, the culmination of certain negotiations should take place in private rather than in the center of the dance floor. It was very entertaining—even educational—but it did somewhat disrupt the dance."

"It's just a different way of dancing, Stragen," she replied in a coarse, nasal voice that sounded much like the squeal of a pig.

"Ah, yes, Countess, but *vertical* dancing is in vogue just now. The horizontal form hasn't yet caught on in the more fashionable circles, and we *do* want to be stylish, don't we?" He turned to Tel. "Your services this evening have been stupendous, my dear Marquis," he said to the blond man. "I doubt that I shall ever be able to adequately repay you." He languidly lifted a perfumed handkerchief to his nostrils.

"That I have been able to serve is payment enough, Milord," Tel replied with a low bow.

"Very good, Tel," Stragen approved. "I may yet bestow an earldom upon you." He turned and led Sparhawk and Sephrenia from the ballroom. Once they were in the corridor outside, his manner changed abruptly. The veneer of bored gentility dropped away, and his eyes became alert, hard. They were the eyes of a very dangerous man. "Does our little charade puzzle you, Sparhawk?" he asked. "Maybe you feel that those in our profession should be housed in places like Platime's cellar in Cimmura or Meland's loft in Acie?"

"It's more commonplace, Milord," Sparhawk replied cautiously.

"We can drop the 'Milord,' Sparhawk. It's an affectation—at least partially. All of this has a more serious purpose than satisfying some obscure personal quirk of mine, though. The gentry has access to far more wealth than the commons, so I train my associates to prey upon the rich and idle rather than the poor and industrious. It's more profitable in the long run. This current group has a long way to go, though, I'm afraid. Tel's coming along rather well, but I despair of ever making a lady of the countess. She has the soul of a whore, and that voice—" He shuddered. "Anyway, I train my people to assume spurious titles and to mouth little civilities to each other in preparation for more serious business. We're all still thieves, whores, and cutthroats, of course, but we deal with a better class of customers."

They entered a large, well-lighted room to find Kurik and Talen sitting together on a large divan. "Did you have a pleasant journey, my Lord?" Talen asked Sparhawk in a voice that had just a slight edge of resentment to it. The boy was dressed in a formal doublet and hose, and for the first time since Sparhawk had met him, his hair was combed. He rose and bowed gracefully to Sephrenia. "Little mother," he greeted her.

"I see you've been tampering with our wayward boy, Stragen," she observed.

"His Grace had a few rough edges when he first came to us, dear lady," the elegant ruffian told her. "I took the liberty of polishing him a bit."

"His Grace?" Sparhawk asked curiously.

"I have certain advantages, Sparhawk." Stragen laughed. "When nature—or blind chance—bestows a title, she has no way to consider the character of the recipient and to match the eminence to the man. I, on the other hand, can observe the true nature of the person involved and can select the proper adornment of rank. I saw at once that young Talen here is an extraordinary youth, so I bestowed a duchy upon him. Give me three more months, and I could present him at a court." He sat down in a large, comfortable chair. "Please, friends, find places to sit, and then you can tell me how I can be of further service to you."

Sparhawk held a chair for Sephrenia and then took a seat not far from their host. "What we really need at the moment, neighbor, is a ship to carry us to the north coast of Deira."

"That's what I wanted to discuss with you, Sparhawk. Our excellent young thief here tells me that your ultimate goal is Cimmura, and he also tells me that there may be some unpleasantness awaiting you in the northern kingdoms. Our tipsy monarch is a man much in need of friends, and he bitterly resents defections. As I understand it, he's presently displeased with you. All manner of unflattering descriptions are being circulated in western Eosia. Wouldn't it be faster—and safer— to sail directly to Cardos and go on to Cimmura from there?"

Sparhawk considered that. "I was thinking of landing on some lonely beach in Deira and going south through the mountains."

"That's a tedious way to travel, Sparhawk, and a very dangerous one for a man on the run. There are lonely beaches on every coast, and I'm sure we can find a suitable one for you near Cardos."

"We?"

"I think I'll go along. I like you, Sparhawk, even though we've only just met. Besides, I need to talk some business with Platime anyway." He rose to his feet then. "I'll have a ship waiting in the harbor by dawn. Now I'll leave you. I'm sure you're tired and hungry after your journey, and I'd better return to the ball before our overenthusiastic countess sets up shop in the middle of the ballroom floor again." He bowed to Sephrenia. "I bid you good night, dear sister," he said to her in Styric. "Sleep well." He nodded to Sparhawk and quietly left the room.

Kurik rose, went to the door, and listened. "I don't think that man's entirely sane, Sparhawk," he said in a low voice.

"Oh, he's sane enough," Talen disagreed. "He's got some strange ideas, but some of them might even work." The boy came over to Sparhawk. "All right," he said, "let me see it."

"See what?"

"The Bhelliom. I risked my life more than once to help steal it, and then I got disinvited to go along at the last minute. I think I'm at least entitled to take a look at it."

"Is it safe?" Sparhawk asked Sephrenia.

"I don't really know, Sparhawk. The rings will control it, though—at least partially. Just a brief look, Talen. It's very dangerous."

"A jewel is a jewel." Talen shrugged. "They're all dangerous. Anything one man wants, another is likely to try to steal, and that's the sort of thing that leads to killing. Give me gold every time. It all looks the same and you can spend it anyplace. Jewels are hard to convert into money, and people usually spend all their time trying to protect them—and that's really inconvenient. Let's see it, Sparhawk."

Sparhawk took out the pouch and picked open the knot. Then he shook the glowing blue rose into the palm of his right hand. Once again a brief flicker darkened the edge of his vision, and a chill passed over him. For some reason the flicker of the shadow brought the memory of the nightmare sharply back, and he could almost feel the hovering presence of those obscurely menacing shapes that had haunted his sleep that night a week ago.

"God!" Talen exclaimed. "That's incredible." He stared at the jewel for a moment, then he shuddered. "Put it away, Sparhawk. I don't want to look at it anymore."

Sparhawk slipped Bhelliom back into its pouch.

"It really ought to be bloodred, though," Talen said moodily. "Look at all the people who've died over it." He looked at Sephrenia. "Was Flute really a Goddess?"

"Kurik told you about that, I see. Yes, she was—and is—one of the Younger Gods of Styricum."

"I liked her," the boy admitted, "when she wasn't teasing me. But if she's a God—or Goddess—she could be any age she wanted to be, couldn't she?"

"Of course."

"Why a child, then?"

"People are more truthful with children."

"I've never particularly noticed that."

"Aphrael's more loveable than you are, Talen." She smiled. "And that may be the real reason behind her choice of form. She needs love—all Gods do, even Azash. People tend to pick little girls up and kiss them. Aphrael enjoys being kissed."

"Nobody ever kissed *me* all that much."

"That may come in time, Talen—if you behave yourself."

## CHAPTER TWO

The weather on the Thalesian peninsula, like that in every northern kingdom, was never really settled, and it was drizzling rain the following morning as bank after bank of thick, dirty clouds rolled into the Straits of Thalesia off the Deiran Sea.

"A splendid day for a voyage," Stragen observed dryly as he and Sparhawk looked through a partially boarded-up window at the rain-wet streets below. "I hate rain. I wonder if I could find any career opportunities in Rendor."

"I don't recommend it," Sparhawk told him, remembering a sun-blasted street in Jiroch.

"Our horses are already on board the ship," Stragen said. "We can leave as soon as Sephrenia and the others are ready." He paused. "Is that roan horse of yours always so restive in the morning?" he asked curiously. "My men report that he bit three of them on the way to the docks."

"I should have warned them. Faran's not the best-tempered horse in the world."

"Why do you keep him?"

"Because he's the most dependable mount I've ever owned. I'll put up with a few of his crotchets in exchange for that. Besides, I like him."

Stragen looked at Sparhawk's chain-mail shirt. "You really don't have to wear that, you know."

"Habit." Sparhawk shrugged. "And there are a fair number of unfriendly people looking for me at the moment."

"It smells awful, you know."

"You get used to it."

"You seem moody this morning, Sparhawk. Is something wrong?"

"I've been on the road for a long time, and I've run into some things I wasn't really prepared to accept. I'm trying to sort them out in my mind."

"Maybe someday when we get to know each other better, you can tell me about it." Stragen seemed to think of something. "Oh, incidentally, Tel mentioned those three ruffians who were looking for you last night. They aren't looking anymore."

"Thank you."

"It was a sort of internal matter, really. They violated one of the primary rules when they didn't check with me before they went looking for you. I can't really afford to have people setting that kind of precedent. We couldn't get much out of them, I'm afraid. They were acting on the orders of someone outside of Thalesia, though—we were able to get that much from the one who was still breathing. Why don't we go see if Sephrenia's ready?"

There was an elegant coach awaiting them outside the rear door of the warehouse about fifteen minutes later. They entered it, and the driver maneuvered his matched team around in the narrow alley and out into the street.

When they reached the harbor, the coach rolled out onto a wharf and stopped beside a ship that appeared to be one of the kind normally used for coastal trade. Her half-furled sails were patched and her heavy railings showed signs of having been broken and repaired many times. Her sides were tarred, and she bore no name on her bow.

"She's a pirate, isn't she?" Kurik asked Stragen as they stepped down from the coach.

"Yes, as a matter of fact, she is," Stragen replied. "I own a fair number of vessels in that business, but how did you recognize her?"

"She's built for speed, Milord," Kurik said. "She's too narrow in the beam for cargo capacity, and the reinforcing around her masts says that she was built to carry a lot of sail. She was designed to run other ships down."

"Or to run away from them, Kurik. Pirates live nervous lives. There are all sorts of people in the world who yearn to hang pirates just on general principles." Stragen looked around at the drizzly harbor. "Let's go on board," he suggested. "There's not much point in standing out here in the rain discussing the finer points of life at sea."

They went up the gangway, and Stragen led them to their cabins below decks. The sailors slipped their hawsers, and the ship moved out of the rainy harbor at a stately pace. Once they were past the headland and in deep water, however, the crew crowded on more sail, and the questionable vessel heeled over and raced across the Straits of Thalesia toward the Deiran coast.

Sparhawk went up on deck about noon and found Stragen leaning on the rail near the bow looking moodily out over the gray, rain-dappled sea. He wore a heavy brown cloak, and his hat brim dripped water down his back.

"I thought you didn't like rain," Sparhawk said.

"It's humid down in that cabin," the brigand replied. "I needed some air. I'm glad you came up, though, Sparhawk. Pirates aren't very interesting conversationalists."

They stood for a time listening to the creaking of rigging and ship's timbers and to the melancholy sound of rain hissing into the sea.

"How is it that Kurik knows so much about ships?" Stragen asked finally.

"He went to sea for a while when he was young."

"That explains it, I guess. I don't suppose you'd care to talk about what you were doing in Thalesia?"

"Not really. Church business, you understand."

Stragen smiled. "Ah, yes. Our taciturn Holy Mother Church," he said. "Sometimes I think she keeps secrets just for the fun of it."

"We sort of have to take it on faith that she knows what she's doing."

"*You* have to, Sparhawk, because you're a Church Knight. I haven't taken any of those vows, so I'm perfectly free to view her with a certain skepticism. I did give some thought to entering the priesthood when I was younger, though."

"You might have done very well. The priesthood and the army are always interested in the talented younger sons of noblemen."

"I rather like that." Stragen smiled. " 'Younger son' has a much nicer sound to it than 'bastard,' doesn't it? It doesn't really matter to me, though. I don't need rank or legitimacy to make my way in the world. The Church and I wouldn't have gotten along too well, I'm afraid. I don't have the humility she seems to require, and a congregation reeking of unwashed armpits would have driven me to renounce my vows fairly early on." He looked back out at the rainy sea. "When you get right down to it, life didn't leave me too many options. I'm not humble enough for the Church, I'm not obedient enough for the army, and I don't have the bourgeois temperament necessary for trade. I did dabble for a time at court, though, since the government always needs good administrators, legitimate or not, but after I'd beaten out the dull-witted son of a duke for a position we both wanted, he became abusive. I challenged him, of course, and he was foolish enough to show up for our appointment wearing chain mail and carrying a broadsword. No offense intended, Sparhawk, but chain mail has a few too many small holes in it to be a good defense against a well-sharpened rapier. My opponent discovered that fairly early on in the discussion. After I'd run him through a few times, he sort of lost interest in the whole business. I left him for dead—which proved to be a pretty good guess—and quietly removed myself from government service. The dullard I'd just skewered turned out to be distantly related to King Wargun, and our drunken monarch has very little in the way of a sense of humor."

"I've noticed."

"How did you manage to get on the wrong side of him?"

Sparhawk shrugged. "He wanted me to participate in that war going on down in Arcium, but I had pressing business in Thalesia. How's that war going, by the way? I've been a little out of touch."

"About all we've had in the way of information are rumors. Some say that the Rendors have been exterminated; others say that Wargun has, and that the Rendors are marching north burning everything that's the least bit flammable. Whichever rumor you choose to believe depends on your view of the world, I suppose." Stragen looked sharply aft.

"Something wrong?" Sparhawk asked him.

"That ship back there." Stragen pointed. "She *looks* like a merchantman, but she's moving a little too fast."

"Another pirate?"

"I don't recognize her—and believe me, I'd recognize her if she were in my line of business." He peered aft, his fact tight. Then he relaxed. "She's veering off now." He laughed briefly. "Sorry if I seem a little overly suspicious, Sparhawk, but unsuspicious pirates usually end up decorating some wharf-side gallows. Where were we?"

Stragen was asking a few too many questions. It was probably a good time to divert him. "You were about to tell me about how you left Wargun's court and set up one of your own," Sparhawk suggested.

"It took a little while," Stragen admitted, "but I'm rather uniquely suited for a life of crime. I haven't been the least bit squeamish since the day I killed my father and my two half brothers."

Sparhawk was a bit surprised at that.

"Killing my father might have been a mistake," Stragen admitted. "He wasn't really a bad sort, and he *did* pay for my education, but I took offense at the way he treated my mother. She was an amiable young woman from a well-placed family who'd been put in my father's household as the companion of his ailing wife. The usual sort of thing happened, and I was the result. After my disgrace at court, my father decided to distance himself from me, so he sent my mother home to her family. She died not long afterward. I suppose I could justify my patricide by claiming that she died of a broken heart, but as a matter of fact, she choked to death on a fishbone. Anyway, I paid a short visit to my father's house, and his title is now vacant. My two half brothers were stupid enough to join in, and now all three of them share the same tomb. I rather imagine that my father regretted all the money he'd spent on my fencing lessons. The expression on his face while he was dying seemed to indicate that he was regretting *something*." The blond man shrugged. "I was younger then. I'd probably do it differently now. There's not much profit involved in randomly rendering relatives down to dog meat, is there?"

"That depends on how you define profit."

Stragen gave him a quick grin. "Anyway, I realized almost as soon as I took to the streets that there's not that much difference between a baron and a cutpurse or a duchess and a whore. I tried to explain that to my predecessor, but the fool wouldn't listen to me. He drew his sword on me, and I removed him from office. Then I began training the thieves and whores of Emsat. I've adorned them with imaginary titles, purloined finery, and a thin crust of good manners to give them a semblance of gentility. Then I turned them loose on the aristocracy. Business is very, very good, and I'm able to repay my former class for a thousand slights and insults." He paused. "Have you had about enough of this malcontented diatribe yet, Sparhawk? I must say that your courtesy and forbearance are virtually superhuman. I'm tired of being rained on anyway. Why don't we go below? I've got a dozen flagons of Arcian red in my cabin. We can both get a little tipsy and engage in some civilized conversation."

Sparhawk considered this complex man as he followed him below. Stragen's motives were clear, of course. His resentment and that towering hunger for revenge were completely understandable. What was unusual was his total lack of self-pity. Sparhawk found that he liked the man. He didn't trust him, of course—that would have been foolish—but he liked him nonetheless.

"So do I," Talen agreed that evening in their cabin when Sparhawk briefly recounted Stragen's story and confessed his liking for the man. "That's probably natural, though. Stragen and I have a lot in common."

"Are you going to throw that in my teeth again?" Kurik asked him.

"I'm not lobbing stones in your direction, Father," Talen said. "Things like that happen, and I'm a lot less sensitive about it than Stragen is." He grinned then. "I was able to use our similar backgrounds to some advantage while I was in Emsat, though. I think he took a liking to me, and he made me some very interesting offers. He wants me to come to work for him."

"You've got a promising future ahead of you, Talen," Kurik said sourly. "You could inherit either Platime's position or Stragen's—assuming you don't get yourself caught and hanged first."

"I'm starting to think on a larger scale," Talen said grandly. "Stragen and I did some speculating about it while I was in Emsat. The thieves' council is very close to being a government right now. About all it really needs to qualify is some single leader—a king, maybe, or even an emperor. Wouldn't it make you proud to be the father of the Emperor of the Thieves, Kurik?"

"Not particularly."

"What do you think, Sparhawk?" the boy asked, his eyes filled with mischief. "Should I go into politics?"

"I believe we can find something more suitable for you to do, Talen."

"Maybe, but would it be as profitable—or as much fun?"


They reached the Elenian coast a league or so to the north of Cardos a week later and disembarked about midday on a lonely beach bordered on its upper end with dark fir trees.

"The Cardos road?" Kurik asked Sparhawk as they saddled Faran and Kurik's gelding.

"Might I make a suggestion?" Stragen asked from nearby.

"Certainly."

"King Wargun's a maudlin man when he's drunk—which is most of the time. Your defection probably has him blubbering in his beer every night. He offered a sizeable reward for your capture in Thalesia and Deira, and he's probably circulated the same offer here. Your face is well known in Elenia, and it's about seventy leagues from here to Cimmura—a good week of hard travel at least. Do you really want to spend that much time on a well-travelled road under those circumstances? Particularly in view of the fact that *somebody* wants to shoot you full of arrows rather than just turn you over to Wargun?"

"Perhaps not. Can you think of an alternative?"

"Yes, as a matter of fact, I can. It may take us a day or so longer, but Platime once showed me a different route. It's a bit rough, but very few people know about it."

Sparhawk looked at the thin blond man with a certain amount of suspicion. "Can I trust you, Stragen?" he asked bluntly.

Stragen shook his head in resignation. "Talen," he said, "haven't you ever explained thieves' sanctuary to him?"

"I've tried, but sometimes Sparhawk has difficulty with moral concepts. It goes like this, Sparhawk. If Stragen lets anything happen to us while we're under his protection, he'll have to answer to Platime."

"That's more or less why I came along, actually," Stragen admitted. "As long as I'm with you, you're still under my protection. I like you, Sparhawk, and having a

Church Knight to intercede with God for me in case I happen to be accidentally hanged couldn't hurt." His sardonic expression returned then. "Not only that, watching out for all of you might expiate some of my grosser sins."

"Do you really have that many sins, Stragen?" Sephrenia asked him gently.

"More than I can remember, dear sister," he replied in Styric, "and many of them are too foul to be described in your presence."

Sparhawk looked quickly at Talen, and the boy nodded gravely. "Sorry, Stragen," he apologized. "I misjudged you."

"Perfectly all right, old boy." Stragen grinned. "And perfectly understandable. There are days when I don't even trust myself."

"Where's this other road to Cimmura?"

Stragen looked around. "Why, do you know, I actually believe it starts just up there at the head of this beach. Isn't that an amazing coincidence?"

"That was your ship we sailed on?"

"I'm a part owner, yes."

"And you suggested to the captain that this beach might be a good place to drop us off?"

"I *do* seem to recall such a conversation, yes."

"An amazing coincidence, all right," Sparhawk said dryly.

Stragen stopped, looking out to sea. "Odd," he said, pointing at a passing ship. "There's that same merchantman we saw up in the straits. She's sailing very light, otherwise she couldn't have made such good time." He shrugged. "Oh, well. Let's go to Cimmura, shall we?"

The "alternative route" they followed was little more than a forest trail that wound up across the range of mountains that lay between the coast and the broad tract of farmland drained by the Cimmura River. Once the track came down out of the mountains, it merged imperceptibly with a series of sunken country lanes meandering through the fields.

Early one morning when they were midway across that farmland, a shabby-looking fellow on a spavined mule cautiously approached their camp. "I need to talk with a man named Stragen," he called from just out of bowshot.

"Come ahead," Stragen called back to him.

The man did not bother to dismount. "I'm from Platime," he identified himself to the Thalesian. "He told me to warn you. There were some fellows looking for you on the road from Cardos to Cimmura."

"*Were?*"

"They couldn't really identify themselves after we encountered them, and they aren't looking for anything anymore."

"Ah."

"They were asking questions before we intercepted them, though. They described you and your companions to a number of peasants. I don't think they wanted to catch up with you just to talk about the weather, Milord."

"Were they Elenians?" Stragen asked intently.

"A few of them were. The rest seemed to be Thalesian sailors. Someone's after you and your friends, Stragen, and I think they've got killing on their minds. If I were you, I'd get to Cimmura and Platime's cellar just as quickly as I could."

"My thanks, friend," Stragen said.

The ruffian shrugged. "I'm getting paid for this. Thanks don't fatten my purse at all." He turned his mule and rode off.

"I *knew* I should have turned and sunk that ship," Stragen noted. "I must be getting soft. We'd better move right along, Sparhawk. We're awfully exposed out here."

Three days later, they reached Cimmura and reined in on the north rim of the valley to look down at the city, smoky and mist-plagued. "A distinctly unattractive place, Sparhawk," Stragen said critically.

"It's not much," Sparhawk conceded, "but we like to call it home."

"I'll be leaving you here," Stragen said. "You have things to attend to, and so do I. Might I suggest that we all forget we ever met each other? You're involved in politics and I in theft. I'll leave it to God to decide which occupation is the more dishonest. Good luck, Sparhawk, and keep your eyes open." He half bowed to Sephrenia from his saddle, turned his horse, and rode down to the grimy city below.

"I could almost grow to like that man," Sephrenia said. "Where to, Sparhawk?"

"The chapterhouse," the big Pandion decided. "We've been away for quite some time, and I'd like to know how things stand before I go to the palace." He squinted up at the noonday sun, bleary and wan-looking in the pervading haze that hung over Cimmura. "Let's stay out of sight until we find out who's controlling the city."

They kept to the trees and rode on around Cimmura on the north side. Kurik slipped down from his gelding at one point and crept to the edge of the bushes to have a look. His expression was grave when he returned. "There are church soldiers manning the battlements," he reported.

Sparhawk swore. "Are you sure?"

"The men up there are wearing red."

"Let's move on anyway. We've got to get inside the chapterhouse."

The dozen or so ostensible workmen were still laying cobblestones outside the fortress of the Pandion Knights.

"They've been at that for almost a year now," Kurik muttered, "and they still haven't finished. Do we wait for dark?"

"I don't think that would do much good. They'll still be watching, and I don't want it generally known that we're back in Cimmura."

"Sephrenia," Talen said, "can you make a column of smoke come up from just inside the city walls near the gate?"

"Yes," she replied.

"Good. We'll make those bricklayers go away then." The boy quickly explained his plan.

"That isn't really too bad, Sparhawk," Kurik said rather proudly. "What do you think?"

"It's worth a try. Let's do it and see what happens."

The red uniform Sephrenia created for Kurik did not look all that authentic, but the smudges and smoke stains she added covered most of the discrepancies. The important things were the gold-embroidered epaulets that identified him as an officer. The burly squire then led his horse through the bushes to a spot near the city gate.

Then Sephrenia began to murmur in Styric, gesturing with her fingers as she did so.

The column of smoke that rose from inside the walls was very convincing: thick, oily black, and boiling dreadfully.

"Hold my horse," Talen said to Sparhawk, slipping down from his saddle. He ran out to the edge of the bushes and began to shriek "Fire!" at the top of his lungs.

The so-called workmen gaped at him stupidly for a moment, then turned to stare in consternation at the city.

"You always have to yell 'fire,' " Talen explained when he returned. "It gets people to thinking in the right direction."

Then Kurik galloped up to the spies outside the gate of the chapterhouse. "You men," he barked, "there's a house on fire on Goat Lane. Get in there and help put the fire out before the whole city starts to burn."

"But sir," one of the workmen objected, "we were ordered to stay here and keep an eye on the Pandions."

"Do you have anything you value inside the city walls?" Kurik asked him bluntly. "If that fire gets away from us, you can stand here and keep an eye on it while it burns. Now move, all of you! I'm going up to that fortress to see if I can persuade the Pandions to lend a hand."

The workmen looked at him, then dropped their tools and ran toward the illusory conflagration as Kurik rode on toward the drawbridge of the chapterhouse.

"Slick," Sparhawk complimented Talen.

"Thieves do it all the time." The boy shrugged. "We have to use real fire, though. People run outside to gawk at fires. That provides an excellent opportunity to look around inside their houses for things of value." He looked toward the city gate. "Our friends seem to be out of sight. Why don't we ride on before they come back?"

Two Pandion Knights in black armor rode gravely out to meet them as they reached the drawbridge. "Is that a fire in the city, Sparhawk?" one of them asked in some alarm.

"Not really," Sparhawk replied. "Sephrenia's entertaining the church soldiers."

The other knight grinned at Sephrenia. Then he straightened. "Who are thou who entreateth entry into the house of the soldiers of God?" he began the ritual.

"We don't have time for that, brother," Sparhawk told him. "We'll go through it twice next time. Who's in charge now?"

"Lord Vanion."

That was surprising. Preceptor Vanion had been much involved in the campaign in Arcium when last Sparhawk had heard of him. "Do you have any idea where I might locate him?"

"He's in his tower, Sparhawk," the second knight advised.

Sparhawk grunted. "How many knights are here right now, brother?"

"About a hundred."

"Good. I may need them." Sparhawk nudged Faran with his heels. The big roan turned his head to look at his master with some surprise. "We're busy, Faran," Sparhawk explained to his horse. "We'll go through the ritual some other time."

Faran's expression was disapproving as he started across the drawbridge.

"Sir Sparhawk!" a ringing voice came from the stable door. It was the novice Berit, a rangy, rawboned young man whose face was split with a broad grin.

"Shout a little louder, Berit," Kurik said reprovingly. "Maybe they'll be able to hear you in Chyrellos."

"Sorry, Kurik," Berit apologized, looking abashed.

"Get some other novices to look after our horses and come with us," Sparhawk told the young man. "We have things to do, and we have to talk with Vanion."

"Yes, Sir Sparhawk." Berit ran back into the stable.

"He's such a nice boy." Sephrenia smiled.

"He might work out," Kurik said grudgingly.

"*Sparhawk?*" a hooded Pandion said with some surprise as they entered the arched door leading into the chapterhouse. The knight pushed back his hood. It was Sir Perraine, the Pandion who had posed as a cattle buyer in Dabour. Perraine spoke with a slight accent.

"What are you doing back in Cimmura, Perraine?" Sparhawk asked, clasping his brother knight's hand. "We all thought you'd taken root in Dabour."

Perraine seemed to recover from his surprise. "Ah," he began, "once Arasham died, there wasn't much reason for me to remain in Dabour. But what are you doing here? We'd heard that King Wargun was pursuing you all over western Eosia."

"Pursuing isn't catching, Perraine." Sparhawk grinned. "We can talk later. Right now my friends and I have to go talk with Vanion."

"Of course." Perraine bowed slightly to Sephrenia and walked out into the courtyard.

They went up the stairs to the south tower where Vanion's study was located. The Preceptor of the Pandion Order wore a white Styric robe, and his face had aged even more in the short time since Sparhawk had last seen him. The others were also there, Ulath, Tynian, Bevier, and Kalten. Their presence seemed somehow to make the room shrink. These were very large men, not only in sheer physical size, but also in terms of their towering reputations. The room seemed somehow full of bulky shoulders. As was customary among Church Knights when inside their chapterhouses, they all wore monks' robes over their mail shirts.

"Finally!" Kalten said, letting out an explosive breath. "Sparhawk, why didn't you get word to us to let us know how you were?"

"Messengers are a little hard to find in Troll country, Kalten."

"Any luck?" Ulath asked eagerly. Ulath was a huge, blond-braided Thalesian, and Bhelliom had a special meaning for him.

Sparhawk looked quickly at Sephrenia, silently asking permission.

"All right," she said, "but only for a minute."

Sparhawk reached down inside his tunic and drew out the canvas pouch in which he carried Bhelliom. He pulled open the drawstring, lifted out the most precious object in the world, and placed it on the table Vanion used for a writing desk. Even as he did so, there came again that faint flicker of darkness somewhere off in a dim corner. The hound of darkness his nightmare had conjured up in the mountains of Thalesia followed him still, and the shadow seemed larger and darker now, as if each re-emergence of Bhelliom somehow increased its size and its brooding menace.

"Do not look too deeply into those petals, gentlemen," Sephrenia warned. "Bhelliom can capture your souls if you look at it too long."

"God!" Kalten breathed. "Look at that thing!"

Each glowing petal of the sapphire rose was so perfect that one could almost see dew clinging to it. From deep within the jewel emanated a blue light and an almost overpowering command to look upon it and observe its perfection.

"Oh, God," Bevier prayed fervently, "defend us from the seduction of this stone." Bevier was a Cyrinic Knight and an Arcian. Sometimes Sparhawk felt that he was excessively pious. This, however, was not one of those times. If even half of what he had already sensed was true, Sparhawk knew that Bevier's fear of Bhelliom was well placed.

Ulath, the huge Thalesian, was muttering in Troll. "Not kill, Bhelliom-Blue-Rose," he said. "Church Knights not enemies to Bhelliom. Church Knights protect Bhelliom from Azash. Help make what is wrong right again, Blue-Rose. I am Ulath-from-Thalesia. If Bhelliom have anger, send anger against Ulath."

Sparhawk straightened. "No," he said firmly in the hideous Troll-tongue. "I am Sparhawk-from-Elenia. I am he who kill Ghwerig-Troll-Dwarf. I am he who brings Bhelliom-Blue-Rose to this place to heal my queen. If Bhelliom-Blue-Rose do this and still have anger, send anger against Sparhawk-from-Elenia and not against Ulath-from-Thalesia."

"You fool!" Ulath exploded. "Have you got any idea of what that thing can do to you?"

"Wouldn't it do the same sort of things to you?"

"Gentlemen, please," Sephrenia said wearily. "Stop this nonsense at once." She looked at the glowing rose on the table. "Listen to me, Bhelliom-Blue-Rose," she said firmly, not even bothering to speak in the language of the Trolls. "Sparhawk-from-Elenia has the rings. Bhelliom-Blue-Rose must acknowledge his authority and obey him."

The jewel darkened briefly, and then the deep blue light returned.

"Good," she said. "I will guide Bhelliom-Blue-Rose in what must be done, and Sparhawk-from-Elenia will command it. Blue-Rose must obey."

The jewel flickered, and then the light returned.

"Put it away now, Sparhawk."

Sparhawk put the rose back into its pouch and slipped it back under his tunic.

"Where's Flute?" Berit asked, looking around.

"*That,* my young friend, is a very, very long story," Sparhawk told him.

"Not dead?" Sir Tynian asked in a shocked tone. "Surely not dead."

"No," Sparhawk told him. "That would be impossible. Flute is immortal."

"No human is immortal, Sparhawk," Bevier protested in a shocked voice.

"Exactly," Sparhawk replied. "Flute's *not* human. She's the Styric Child-Goddess Aphrael."

"Heresy!" Bevier gasped.

"You wouldn't think so if you'd been in Ghwerig's cave, Sir Bevier," Kurik told him. "I saw her rise from a bottomless abyss with my own eyes."

"A spell, perhaps?" But Bevier did not seem quite so sure of himself now.

"No, Bevier," Sephrenia said. "No spell could have accomplished what she did in that cave. She was—and is—Aphrael."

"Before we get involved in a theological dispute here, I need some information," Sparhawk said. "How did you all get away from Wargun, and what's happening in the city?"

"Wargun wasn't really a problem," Vanion told him. "We came through Cimmura on our way south, and things went more or less the way we'd planned them at Acie. We threw Lycheas into the dungeon, put the Earl of Lenda in charge, and persuaded the army and the church soldiers here in Cimmura to march south with us."

"How did you manage that?" Sparhawk asked with some surprise.

"Vanion's a very good persuader." Kalten grinned. "Most of the generals were loyal to Primate Annias, but when they tried to object, Vanion invoked that Church law the Earl of Lenda mentioned back at Acie and took command of the army. The generals still objected until he marched them all down to the courtyard. After Ulath beheaded a few of them, most of the rest decided to change sides."

"Oh, *Vanion,*" Sephrenia said in a tone of profound disappointment.

"I was a bit pressed for time, little mother," he apologized. "Wargun was in a hurry to get started. He wanted to butcher the entire Elenian officer corps, but I talked him out of that. Anyway, we joined with King Soros of Pelosia at the border and marched down into Arcium. The Rendors turned tail and ran when they saw us coming. Wargun intends to chase them down, but I think that's just for his personal entertainment. The other preceptors and I managed to convince him that our presence in Chyrellos during the election of the new archprelate was vital, so he let each of us take a hundred knights."

"That was generous of him," Sparhawk said sardonically. "Where are the knights from the other orders?"

"They're camped outside Demos. Dolmant doesn't want us to move into Chryellos until the situation there solidifies."

"If Lenda's in charge at the palace, why are there church soldiers on the walls of the city?"

"Annias found out what we'd done here, of course. There are members of the Hierocracy who are loyal to him, and they all have their own troops. He borrowed some of those men and sent them here. They freed Lycheas and imprisoned the Earl of Lenda. They control the city at the moment."

"We ought to do something about that."

Vanion nodded. "We were on our way to Demos with the other orders when we chanced to find out what was happening here. The other orders went on to Demos to be in position to move on Chyrellos, and we came here to Cimmura. We only arrived late last night. The knights were all eager to go into the city as soon as we got here, but we've been campaigning hard, and they're all tired. I want them to be a little better rested before we correct things inside the walls."

"Are we likely to have any problems?"

"I doubt it. Those church soldiers aren't Annias' men. They're on loan from the other patriarchs, and their loyalties are a little vague. I think a show of force is probably about all it's going to take to make them capitulate."

"Are the remaining six knights who were involved in the spell in the throne room among your hundred?" Sephrenia asked him.

"Yes," Vanion replied a little wanly. "We're all here." He looked at the Pandion sword she was carrying. "Do you want to give me that?" he asked.

"No," she said firmly. "You're carrying enough already. It isn't going to be much longer, anyway."

"You're going to reverse the spell?" Tynian asked. "Before you use Bhelliom to cure the queen, I mean?"

"We have to," she told him. "Bhelliom has to touch her skin in order to cure her."

Kalten went to the window. "It's late afternoon now," he said. "If we're going to do this today, we'd better get started."

"Let's wait until morning," Vanion decided. "If the soldiers try to resist, it might take awhile to subdue them, and I don't want any of those people slipping away in the dark to warn Annias until we've had time to get reinforcements here."

"How many soldiers are at the palace?" Sparhawk asked.

"My spies report a couple hundred," Vanion replied, "hardly enough to cause us any problems."

"We're going to have to come up with a way to seal the city for a few days if we don't want to see a relief column wearing red tunics coming up the river," Ulath said.

"I can take care of that," Talen told him. "I'll slip into town just before dark and go talk to Platime. He'll seal the gates for us."

"Can he be trusted?" Vanion asked.

"Platime? Of course not, but I think he'll do that much for us. He hates Annias."

"That's it, then," Kalten said gaily. "We can move out at dawn and have everything tidied up by lunch time."

"Don't bother to set a place at the table for the bastard Lycheas," Ulath said bleakly, testing the edge of his ax with his thumb. "I don't think he's going to have much of an appetite."

## CHAPTER THREE

Kurik woke Sparhawk early the following morning and helped him into his formal black armor. Then, carrying his sword belt and plumed helmet, Sparhawk went to Vanion's study to await the dawn and the arrival of the others. This was the day. He had striven toward this day for half a year and more. Today he would look full into the eyes of his queen, salute her, and swear his oath of fealty.

A terrible impatience welled up in him. He wanted to get on with it, and he swore at the sluggard sun for its leisurely rising. "And then, Annias," he almost purred, "you and Martel are going to become no more than footnotes to history."

"Did you get hit on the head when you had that fight with Ghwerig?" It was Kalten, who was also wearing his formal black armor and who entered with his helmet under his arm.

"Not really," Sparhawk replied. "Why?"

"You're talking to yourself. Most people don't do that, you know."

"You're wrong, Kalten. Almost everybody does it. Most of the time, though, it involves rewriting past conversations—or planning ones yet to come."

"Which were you doing just now?"

"Neither. I was sort of warning Annias and Martel what to expect."

"They couldn't hear you, you know."

"Maybe not, but giving them some kind of warning is the knightly thing to do. At least *I'll* know I said it—even if they don't."

"I don't think I'll bother with that when I go after Adus." Kalten grinned. "Do you have any idea of how long it would take to pound a thought into Adus? Oh, who gets to kill Krager, by the way?"

"Let's give him to somebody who does something nice for us."

"Sounds fair." Kalten paused, and his face grew serious. "Is it going to work, Sparhawk? Will Bhelliom *really* cure Ehlana, or have we just been fooling ourselves?"

"I think it's going to work. We have to believe that it will. Bhelliom's very, very powerful."

"Have you ever used it at all?"

"Once. I collapsed a ridgeline in the mountains of Thalesia with it."

"Why?"

"It needed to be done. Don't think about Bhelliom, Kalten. It's very dangerous to do that."

Kalten looked skeptical. "Are you going to let Ulath shorten Lycheas a bit when we get to the palace? Ulath really enjoys doing that to people—or I could hang the bastard, if you'd prefer."

"I don't know," Sparhawk said. "Maybe we should wait and let Ehlana make the decision."

"Why bother her with it? She's probably going to be a little weak after all this, and as her champion, you really ought to try to spare her any exertion." Kalten squinted at Sparhawk. "Don't take this wrong," he said, "but Ehlana *is* a woman, after all, and women are notoriously tenderhearted. If we leave it up to her, she may not let us kill him at all. I'd rather have him safely dead before she wakes up. We'll apologize to her of course, but it's very hard to unkill somebody, no matter how sorry you are."

"You're a barbarian, Kalten."

"Me? Oh, by the way, Vanion's got our brothers putting on their armor. We should all be ready by the time the sun's up and the people in the city open the gates." Kalten frowned. "That might present a problem, though. There'll be church soldiers at the gates, and they may try to slam them shut in our faces when they see us coming."

"That's what battering-rams are for." Sparhawk shrugged.

"The queen might get a little cross with you if she finds out that you've been knocking down the gates of her capital city."

"We'll make the church soldiers repair them."

"It's honest work right enough, and that's something church soldiers know very little about. I'd suggest you take a hard look at that stretch of cobblestones outside our gates before you make any final decisions, though. Church soldiers aren't very handy with tools." The big blond man sank into a chair, his armor creaking. "It's taken us a long time, Sparhawk, but it's almost over now, isn't it?"

"Very nearly," Sparhawk agreed, "and once Ehlana's well again, we can go looking for Martel."

Kalten's eyes brightened. "And Annias," he added. "I think we should hang him from the arch of the main gate of Chyrellos."

"He's a Church primate, Kalten," Sparhawk said in a pained voice. "You can't do that to him."

"We can apologize to him later."

"How exactly do you propose to do that?"

"I'll work something out," Kalten replied in an offhand manner. "Maybe we could call it a mistake or something."

The sun had risen by the time they gathered in the courtyard. Vanion, looking pale and drawn, struggled down the stairs with a large case. "The swords," he explained tersely to Sparhawk. "Sephrenia says we'll need them when we get to the throne room."

"Can't somebody else carry them for you?" Kalten asked him.

"No. They're my burden. As soon as Sephrenia comes down, we'll get started."

The small Styric woman seemed very calm, even remote, when she emerged from the chapterhouse with Sir Gared's sword in her hands and with Talen close behind her.

"Are you all right?" Sparhawk asked her.

"I've been preparing myself for the ritual in the throne room," she replied.

"There might be some fighting," Kurik said. "Is it really a good idea for us to bring Talen along with us?"

"I can protect him," she said, "and his presence is necessary. There are reasons, but I don't think you'd understand them."

"Let's mount up and go," Vanion said.

There was a great deal of clinking as the hundred black-armored Pandion Knights climbed into their saddles. Sparhawk took his customary place at Vanion's side with Kalten, Bevier, Tynian, and Ulath close behind them and the column of Pandions strung out to the rear. They crossed the drawbridge at a trot and bore down on the startled group of church soldiers outside the gate. At a curt signal from Vanion, a score of Pandions swung out from the column and encircled the so-called workmen. "Hold them here until the rest of us take the city gates," Vanion instructed. "Then bring them into the city and rejoin us."

"Yes, my Lord," Sir Perraine replied.

"All right, gentlemen," Vanion said then, "I think a gallop is in order at this point. Let's not give the soldiers in the city too much time to prepare for our arrival."

They thundered across the rather short distance between the chapterhouse and the east gate of Cimmura. Despite Kalten's concern about the possibility of the gates being closed to them, the soldiers there were too surprised to react in time.

"Sir Knights!" an officer protested shrilly. "You can't enter the city without the Prince Regent's authorization!"

"With your permission, Lord Vanion?" Tynian asked politely.

"Of course, Sir Tynian," Vanion consented. "We have pressing matters to attend to, and we don't really have time for idle chitchat here."

Tynian moved his horse forward. The knight from Deira was deceptively moonfaced. He had the sort of countenance one would normally associate with good humor and a generally happy approach to life. His armor, however, concealed a massively developed upper torso and powerful arms and shoulders. He drew his sword. "My friend," he said pleasantly to the officer, "would you be so good as to step aside so that we may proceed? I'm sure none of us wants any unpleasantness here." His tone was civil, almost conversational.

Many of the church soldiers, long accustomed to having things their own way in Cimmura, were not really prepared to have anyone question their authority. It was the officer's misfortune to be one of those soldiers. "I must forbid your entry into the city without specific authorization from the Prince Regent," he declared stubbornly.

"That's your final word, then?" Tynian asked in a regretful tone.

"It is."

"It's your decision, friend," Tynian said. Then he raised up in his stirrups and swung a vast overhand blow with his sword.

Since the officer could not believe that anyone would actually defy him, he made no move to protect himself. His expression was one of amazement as Tynian's heavy, broad-bladed sword struck the angle between his neck and shoulder and sheared diagonally down into his body. Blood fountained up from the dreadful wound, and the suddenly limp body hung from Tynian's sword, held there by the crushed-in edges of the great rent in the officer's steel breastplate. Tynian leaned back in his saddle, removed his foot from his stirrup, and kicked the body off his sword blade. "I *did* ask him to move out of our way, Lord Vanion," he explained. "Since he chose not to, what just happened is entirely his responsibility, wouldn't you say?"

"It was indeed, Sir Tynian," Vanion agreed. "I see no blame accruing to you in this matter. You were the very soul of courtesy."

"Let's proceed, then," Ulath said. He slipped his war ax from its sling at the side of his saddle. "All right," he said to the wide-eyed church soldiers, "who's next?"

The soldiers fled.

The knights who had been guarding the workmen came up at a trot, herding their prisoners ahead of them. Vanion left ten of them to hold the gates, and the column moved on into the city. The citizens of Cimmura were fully aware of the situation at the palace and, when they saw a column of bleak-faced Pandion Knights in their ominous black armor riding through the cobbled streets, they knew immediately that a confrontation was imminent. Doors slammed up and down the street, and shutters were hastily closed from the inside.

The knights rode on through now-deserted streets.

There was a sudden spiteful buzz from behind them, and a heavy clang. Sparhawk half wheeled Faran.

"You really ought to watch your back, Sparhawk," Kalten told him. "That was a crossbow bolt, and it would have taken you right between the shoulder blades. You owe me what it's going to cost me to have my shield re-enamelled."

"I owe you more than that, Kalten," Sparhawk said gratefully.

"Strange," Tynian said. "The crossbow's a Lamork weapon. Not many church soldiers carry them."

"Maybe it was something personal," Ulath grunted. "Have you offended any Lamorks lately, Sparhawk?"

"Not that I know of."

"There won't be much point in extended conversation when we get to the palace," Vanion said. "I'll order the soldiers to throw down their arms when we arrive."

"Do you think they'll do it?" Kalten asked.

Vanion grinned mirthlessly. "Probably not—at least not without several object lessons. When we get there, Sparhawk, I want you to take your friends here and secure the door to the palace. I don't think we'll want to chase church soldiers up and down the halls."

"Right," Sparhawk agreed.

The church soldiers, warned by the men who had fled from the city gates, had formed up in the palace courtyard, and the largely ornamental palace gates were closed.

"Bring up the ram," Vanion called.

A dozen Pandions rode forward with a heavy log carried in rope slings attached to their saddles. It took them perhaps five minutes to batter down the gates, and then the Church Knights streamed into the courtyard.

"Throw down your weapons!" Vanion shouted to the confused soldiers in the yard.

Sparhawk led his friends around the perimeter of the courtyard to the large doors that gave entry into the palace. There they dismounted and climbed the stairs to confront the dozen soldiers on guard in front of the door. The officer in charge drew his sword. "No one may enter!" he barked.

"Get out of my way, neighbor," Sparhawk said in his deadly quiet voice.

"I don't take orders from—" the officer began. Then his eyes glazed as there was a sudden sound like that a melon might make when dropped on a stone floor as Kurik deftly brained him with his spiked chain mace. The officer dropped, twitching.

"That's something new," Sir Tynian said to Sir Ulath. "I never saw a man with brains coming out of his ears before."

"Kurik's very good with that mace," Ulath agreed.

"Any questions?" Sparhawk asked the other soldiers ominously.

They stared at him.

"I believe you were told to drop your weapons," Kalten told them.

They hurriedly shed their arms.

"We're relieving you here, neighbors," Sparhawk informed them. "You may join your friends out there in the yard."

They quickly went down the stairs.

The mounted Pandions were slowly advancing on the church soldiers standing in the courtyard. There was some sporadic resistance from the more fanatic of the soldiers, and the Pandion Knights provided a sizeable number of those "object lessons" their preceptor had mentioned. The center of the courtyard soon flowed with blood, and it was littered with unattached heads, arms, and a few legs. More and more of the soldiers saw the direction the fight was going, threw away their weapons, and raised their hands in surrender. There was one stubborn pocket of resistance, but the knights pushed the struggling soldiers up against one wall and slaughtered them.

Vanion looked around the yard. "Herd the survivors into the stables," he ordered, "and post a few guards." Then he dismounted and walked back to the shattered gate. "It's all over, little mother," he called to Sephrenia, who had waited outside with Talen and Berit. "It's safe to come in now."

Sephrenia rode her white palfrey into the courtyard, shielding her eyes with one hand. Talen, however, looked around with bright, vicious eyes.

"Let's get rid of this," Ulath said to Kurik, bending to pick up the shoulders of the dead officer. The two of them carried the body off to one side, and Tynian thoughtfully scraped the puddle of brains off the top step with one foot.

"Do you people always chop your enemies to pieces like this?" Talen asked Sparhawk as he dismounted and went over to help Sephrenia down from her horse.

Sparhawk shrugged. "Vanion wanted the soldiers to see what would happen to them if they offered any more resistance. Dismemberment is usually quite convincing."

"*Must* you?" Sephrenia shuddered.

"You'd better let us go in first, little mother," Sparhawk said as Vanion joined them with twenty knights. "There may be soldiers hiding in there."

As it turned out, there were a few, but Vanion's knights efficiently flushed them from their hiding places and took them to the main door and gave them pointed instructions to join their comrades in the stables.

The doors to the council chamber were unguarded, and Sparhawk opened the door and held it for Vanion.

Lycheas was cowering, slack-lipped and trembling, behind the council table with a fat man in red, and Baron Harparin was desperately yanking on one of the bellpulls. "You can't come in here!" Harparin said shrilly to Vanion in his high-pitched, effeminate voice. "I command you to leave at once on the authority of King Lycheas."

Vanion looked at him coldly. Sparhawk knew that Vanion bore a towering contempt for the disgusting pederast. "This man irritates me," he said in a flat voice, pointing at Harparin. "Will someone please do something about him?"

Ulath strode around the table, his war ax in his hands.

"You wouldn't dare!" Harparin squealed, cringing back and still yanking futilely at the bellpull. "I'm a member of the royal council. You wouldn't dare do anything to me."

Ulath did, in fact, dare. Harparin's head bounced once and then rolled across the carpet to come to rest near the window. His mouth was agape, and his eyes were still bulging in horror. "Was that more or less what you had in mind, Lord Vanion?" the big Thalesian asked politely.

"Approximately, yes. Thank you, Sir Ulath."

"How about these other two?" Ulath pointed his ax at Lycheas and the fat man.

"Ah—not just yet, Sir Ulath." The Pandion preceptor approached the council table carrying the case containing the swords of the knights who had fallen. "Now, Lycheas, where is the Earl of Lenda?" he demanded.

Lycheas gaped at him.

"Sir Ulath," Vanion said in a tone like ice.

Ulath grimly lifted his blood-stained ax.

"No!" Lycheas screamed. "Lenda's confined down in the cellars. We didn't hurt him at all, Lord Vanion. I swear to you that he's—"

"Take Lycheas and this other one down to the dungeon," Vanion ordered a pair of his knights. "Release the Earl of Lenda and replace him in the cell with these. Then bring Lenda here."

"If I may, my Lord?" Sparhawk asked.

"Of course."

"Lycheas the bastard," Sparhawk said formally, "as Queen's Champion, it is my distinct pleasure to place you under arrest on the charge of high treason. The penalty is rather well known. We'll attend to that just as soon as it's convenient. Thinking about it might give you something to occupy the long, tedious hours of your confinement."

"I could save you a great deal of time and expense, Sparhawk," Ulath offered helpfully, hefting his ax again.

Sparhawk pretended to consider it. "No," he said regretfully. "Lycheas has run roughshod over the people of Cimmura. I think they're entitled to the spectacle of a nice, messy public execution."

Lycheas was actually blubbering in terror as Sir Perraine and another knight dragged him past the wide-eyed head of Baron Harparin and out of the room.

"You're a hard and ruthless man, Sparhawk," Bevier noted.

"I know." Sparhawk looked at Vanion. "We'll have to wait for Lenda," he said. "He's got the key to the throne room. I don't want Ehlana to wake up and find that we've chopped her door down."

Vanion nodded. "I need him for something anyway," he said. He put the sword case on the council table and sat down in one of the chairs. "Oh, by the way," he said, "cover Harparin up before Sephrenia gets here. Things like that distress her." It was yet another clue, Sparhawk thought, that Vanion's concern for Sephrenia went far beyond what was customary.

Ulath went to the window, jerked down one of the drapes, and turned back, pausing only to kick Harparin's head back over beside the pederast's body, then he covered the remains with the drape.

"A whole generation of little boys will sleep more securely now that Harparin's no longer with us," Kalten observed lightly, "and they'll probably mention Ulath in their prayers every night."

"I'll take all the blessings I can get." Ulath shrugged.

Sephrenia entered with Talen and Berit in tow. She looked around. "I'm pleasantly surprised," she noted. "I was more or less expecting additional carnage." Then her eyes narrowed. She pointed at the draped body lying by the wall. "What's that?" she demanded.

"The late Baron Harparin," Kalten told her. "He left us rather suddenly."

"Did you do that, Sparhawk?" she accused.

"Me?"

"I know you all too well, Sparhawk."

"Actually, Sephrenia, it was me," Ulath drawled. "I'm very sorry if it bothers you, but then, I'm Thalesian. We're widely reputed to be barbarians." He shrugged. "One is more or less obliged to uphold the reputation of his homeland, wouldn't you say?"

She refused to answer that. She looked around at the faces of the other Pandions in the room. "Good," she said. "We're all here. Open that case, Vanion."

Vanion opened the sword case.

"Sir Knights," Sephrenia addressed the Pandions in the room as she laid Sir Gared's sword on the table beside the case. "Some months ago, twelve of you joined with me in casting the enchantment that has sustained the life of Queen Ehlana. Six of your brave companions have gone into the House of the Dead since then. Their swords, however, must be present when we undo the enchantment that we may cure the queen. Thus, each of you who was there must carry the sword of one of your fallen brothers as well as your own. I will work the spell that will make it possible for you to take up those swords. We will then proceed to the throne room, where the swords of the fallen will be taken from you."

Vanion looked startled. "Taken? By whom?"

"Their original owners."

"You're going to summon ghosts into the throne room?" he asked in astonishment.

"They will come unsummoned. Their oaths insure that. As before, you'll encircle the throne with your swords extended. I'll undo the spell, and the crystal will disappear. The rest is up to Sparhawk—and Bhelliom."

"What exactly am I supposed to do?" Sparhawk asked her.

"I'll tell you at the proper time," she replied. "I don't want you to do anything prematurely."

Sir Perraine escorted the aged Earl of Lenda into the council chamber.

"How was the dungeon, my Lord of Lenda?" Vanion asked lightly.

"Damp, Lord Vanion," Lenda replied. "Also dark and very smelly. You know how dungeons are."

"No." Vanion laughed. "Not really. It's an experience I'd prefer to forgo." He looked at the old courtier's lined face. "Are you all right, Lenda?" he asked. "You look very tired."

"Old men always look very tired, Vanion." Lenda smiled gently. "And I'm older than most." He straightened his thin old shoulders. "Being thrown into the dungeon from time to time is an occupational hazard for those in public service. You get used to it. I've been in worse."

"I'm sure Lycheas and that fat fellow will enjoy the dungeon, my Lord," Kalten said lightly.

"I doubt that, Sir Kalten."

"We've made them aware of the fact that the end of their confinement will mark their entrance into another world. I'm sure they'll prefer the dungeon. Rats aren't all *that* bad."

"I didn't notice Baron Harparin," Lenda said. "Did he escape?"

"Only in a manner of speaking, my Lord," Kalten replied. "He was being offensive. You know how Harparin was. Sir Ulath gave him a lesson in courtesy—with his ax."

"This day is topfilled with joyful surprises, then." Lenda chortled.

"My Lord of Lenda," Vanion said rather formally, "we're going to the throne room now to restore the queen. I'd like to have you witness that restoration so that you can confirm her identity in case any doubts arise later. The commons are superstitious, and there are those who might want to circulate rumors to the effect that Ehlana is not who she appears to be."

"Very well, my Lord Vanion," Lenda agreed, "but how do you plan to restore her?"

"You'll see." Sephrenia smiled. She held out her hands over the swords and spoke at some length in Styric. The swords glowed briefly as she released the spell, and the knights who had been present during the encasement of the Queen of Elenia stepped to the table. She talked to them briefly in low tones, and then each of them took up one of the swords. "Very well," she said, "let us proceed to the throne room."

"This is all very mysterious," Lenda said to Sparhawk as they walked down the corridor toward the throne room.

"Have you ever seen real magic performed, my Lord?" Sparhawk asked him.

"I don't believe in magic, Sparhawk."

"That may change shortly, Lenda." Sparhawk smiled.

The old courtier produced the key from an inside pocket and unlocked the door to the throne room. Then they all followed Sephrenia inside. The room was dark. During Lenda's confinement, the candles had been allowed to go out. Sparhawk, nonetheless, could still hear the measured drumbeat of his queen's heart echoing in the darkness. Kurik stepped back outside and brought in a torch. "Fresh candles?" he asked Sephrenia.

"Definitely," she replied. "Let's not awaken Ehlana to a dark room."

Kurik and Berit replaced the burned-out candle stubs with fresh tapers. Then Berit looked curiously at the young queen he had served so faithfully without ever having seen her. His eyes grew suddenly wide as he stared at her, and he seemed to catch his breath. His look was one of totally appropriate veneration, but there was, Sparhawk thought, perhaps a bit more to it than simple respect. Berit was about the same age as Ehlana, and she *was* very beautiful, after all.

"That's much better," Sephrenia said, looking around at the candlelit throne room. "Sparhawk, come with me." She led him to the dais upon which the throne stood.

Ehlana sat as she had for all these months. She wore the crown of Elenia on her pale, blonde head and she was enfolded in her state robes. Her eyes were closed, and her face serene.

"Just a few more moments, my Queen," Sparhawk murmured. Strangely, his eyes were filled with tears, and his heart was in his throat.

"Remove your gauntlets, Sparhawk," Sephrenia told him. "You'll want the rings to touch Bhelliom when you use it."

He took off his mailed gauntlets, then reached inside his surcoat, removed the canvas pouch, and untied the drawstring.

"All right, gentlemen," Sephrenia said then to the surviving knights, "take your places."

Vanion and the other five Pandions spaced themselves out around the throne, each of them holding his own sword and that of one of his fallen brothers.

Sephrenia stood beside Sparhawk and began to form the incantation in Styric, her fingers weaving an accompaniment. The candles dimmed and flared almost in time to the sonorous spell. At some time during her incantation, the room became gradually filled with that familiar smell of death. Sparhawk tore his eyes from Ehlana's face to risk a quick look around the circle of knights. Where there had been six before, there were now twelve. The filmy shapes of those who had fallen one by one in the preceding months had returned unbidden to take their swords one last time.

"Now, Sir Knights," Sephrenia instructed the living and the dead alike, "point your swords at the throne." And she began to speak a different incantation. The tip of each sword began to glow, and those incandescent points of light grew brighter and brighter until they surrounded the throne with a ring of pure light. Sephrenia raised her arm, spoke a single word, then brought the arm sharply down. The crystal encasement surrounding the throne wavered like water, and then it was gone.

Ehlana's head sagged forward, and her body began to tremble violently. Her breathing was suddenly labored, and the heartbeat that still echoed through the room faltered. Sparhawk leaped up onto the dais to go to her aid.

"Not yet!" Sephrenia told him sharply.

"But—"

"Do as I say!"

He stood helplessly over his stricken queen for a minute that seemed to last for an hour. Then Sephrenia stepped forward and lifted Ehlana's chin with both her hands. The queen's gray eyes were wide and vacant, and her face was twisted grotesquely.

"Now, Sparhawk," Sephrenia said, "take Bhelliom in your hands and touch it to her heart. Be sure the rings are touching the stone. At the same time, command it to heal her."

He seized the sapphire rose in both hands, then he gently touched the flower-gem to Ehlana's breast. "Heal my queen, Bhelliom-Blue-Rose!" he commanded in a loud voice.

The enormous surge of power coming from the jewel between his hands sent

Sparhawk to his knees. The candles flickered and dimmed as if some dark shadow had passed over the room. Was it something fleeing? Or was it perhaps that shadow of dread that followed him and haunted all his dreams? Ehlana stiffened, and her slender body was slammed against the back of her throne. A hoarse gasp came from her throat. Then her wide-eyed stare was suddenly rational, and she gazed at Sparhawk in astonishment.

"It is done!" Sephrenia said in a trembling voice, and then she slumped weakly down on the dais.

Ehlana drew in a deep, shuddering breath. "My Knight!" she cried out feebly, extending her arms to the black-armored Pandion kneeling before her. Though her voice was weak, it nonetheless was full and rich, a woman's voice now and not the childish one Sparhawk remembered. "Oh, my Sparhawk, you have come back to me at last." She laid her trembling arms about his armored shoulders, inserted her face beneath his raised visor, and kissed him lingeringly.

"Enough of that for now, children," Sephrenia told them. "Sparhawk, carry her to her chambers."

Sparhawk was very disturbed. Ehlana's kiss had been anything but childlike. He tucked Bhelliom away, removed his helmet, and tossed it to Kalten. Then he gently picked up his queen. She put her pale arms about his shoulders and her cheek to his. "Oh, I have found thee," she breathed, "and I love thee, and I will not let thee go."

Sparhawk recognized the passage she was quoting, and it seemed wildly inappropriate. He grew even more troubled. There was obviously a serious mistake here someplace.

## CHAPTER FOUR

Ehlana was going to be a problem, Sparhawk decided as he removed his armor not long after he had presented himself to his queen the following morning. Though she had never been far from his thoughts during his exile, he found that he had to make a number of difficult adjustments. When he had left, their relative positions had been clearly defined. He was the adult; she was the child. That had changed now, and they were both treading the unfamiliar ground of the monarch-and-subject relationship. He had been told by Kurik and others that the girl he had raised almost from babyhood had shown remarkable mettle during the few months before Annias had poisoned her. Hearing about it was one thing; experiencing it was another. This is not to say that Ehlana was harsh or peremptory with him, for she was not. She felt, he thought—and hoped—a genuine affection for him, and she did not give him direct commands so much as give the impression that she *expected* him to accede to her wishes. They were functioning in a gray area, and there were all sorts of opportunities for serious missteps on either side.

THE BASILICA · 583

Several recent incidents were perfect examples of that sort of thing. In the first place, her request that he sleep in a chamber adjoining hers was, he felt, highly inappropriate, even slightly scandalous. When he had tried to point that out, however, she had laughed at his fears. His armor, he reasoned, had provided some small defense against wagging tongues. Times were troubled, after all, and the Queen of Elenia needed protection. As her champion, Sparhawk had the obligation—the right even—to stand guard over her. When he had presented himself to her that morning once again in full armor, however, she had wrinkled her nose and suggested that he change clothes immediately. He knew that would be a serious mistake. The queen's champion in armor was one thing, and no one with a reasonable regard for his own health would be likely to make an issue of Sparhawk's proximity to the royal person. If he were dressed in doublet and hose, though, that would be quite another thing. The servants were bound to talk, and the gossip of palace servants had a way of spreading throughout the city.

Now Sparhawk looked dubiously into the mirror. His doublet was silver-trimmed black velvet, and his hose were gray. The clothing bore some faint resemblance to a uniform, and the black half boots he had chosen had a more military appearance than the pointed shoes currently in fashion at court. He rejected the slender rapier out of hand and belted on his heavy broadsword instead. The effect was slightly ludicrous, but the presence of the heavier weapon quite clearly stated that Sparhawk was in the queen's apartments on business.

"That's absolutely absurd, Sparhawk," Ehlana laughed when he returned to the sitting room where she lay prettily propped up by pillows on a divan, a blue satin coverlet across her knees.

"My Queen?" he said coolly.

"The broadsword, Sparhawk. It's completely out of place with those clothes. Please take it off at once and wear the rapier I ordered provided for you."

"If my appearance offends you, your Majesty, I'll withdraw. The sword, however, stays where it is. I can't protect you with a knitting needle."

Her gray eyes flashed. "You—" she began hotly.

"*My* decision, Ehlana," he cut across her objections. "Your safety is my responsibility, and the steps I take to insure it are not open to discussion."

They exchanged a long, hard stare. This would not be the last time their wills would clash, Sparhawk was sure.

Ehlana's eyes softened. "So stern and unbending, my Champion," she said.

"Where your Majesty's safety is concerned, yes." He said it flatly. It was probably best to get that clearly understood right at the outset.

"But why are we arguing, my knight?" She smiled whimsically, fluttering her eyelashes at him.

"Don't do that, Ehlana," he told her, automatically assuming the tutorial manner he had used when she was a little girl. "You're the queen, not some coy chambermaid trying to get her own way. Don't ask or try to be charming. Command."

"Would you take off the sword if I commanded you to, Sparhawk?"

"No, but the usual rules don't apply to me."

"Who decided that?"

"I did. We can send for the Earl of Lenda if you'd like. He's well versed in the law, and he can give us his opinion on the matter."

"But if he decides against you, you'll ignore him, won't you?"

"Yes."

"That's not fair, Sparhawk."

"I'm not trying to be fair, my Queen."

"Sparhawk, when we're alone like this, do you suppose we could dispense with the 'your Majestys' and 'my Queens'? I do have a name, after all, and you weren't afraid to use it when I was a child."

"As you wish." He shrugged.

"Say it, Sparhawk. Say 'Ehlana.' It's not a hard name, and I'm sure you won't choke on it."

He smiled. "All right, Ehlana," he gave up. After her defeat on the issue of the sword, she needed a victory of some kind to restore her dignity.

"You're so much more handsome when you smile, my Champion. You should try it more often." She leaned back on her pillows, her face thoughtful. Her pale blonde hair had been carefully combed that morning, and she wore a few modest but quite expensive pieces of jewelry. Her cheeks were prettily rosy, which was in quite some contrast to her very fair skin. "What did you do in Rendor after the idiot Aldreas sent you into exile?"

"That's hardly the proper way to speak of your father, Ehlana."

"He wasn't much of a father, Sparhawk, and his intellect wasn't exactly what you'd call towering. The efforts he expended entertaining his sister must have softened his brains."

"Ehlana!"

"Don't be such a prude, Sparhawk. The whole palace knew about it—the whole city, probably."

Sparhawk decided that it was time to find a husband for his queen. "How did you find out so much about Princess Arissa?" he asked her. "She was sent to that cloister near Demos before you were born."

"Gossip lingers, Sparhawk, and Arissa was hardly what you'd call discreet."

Sparhawk cast about for a way to change the subject. Although Ehlana *seemed* to be aware of the basic implications of what she was saying, he could not bring himself to give credence to the notion that she could be so worldly. Some part of his mind stubbornly clung to the notion that beneath her evident maturity, she was still the same innocent child he had left ten years before. "Hold out your left hand," he told her. "I have something for you."

The tone of their relationship was still indistinct. They both felt that keenly, and it made them uncomfortable. Sparhawk swung back and forth between a stiffly correct formality and an abrupt, almost military manner of command. Ehlana seemed to fluctuate, too, at one moment the coltish, knobby-kneed girl he had trained and molded, and in the next a full-fledged queen. At a somewhat deeper level, they were both extremely aware of the changes a short decade had brought to Ehlana. The process known as "filling out" had done some very significant things to the Queen of Elenia. Since Sparhawk had not been present to grow gradually accustomed to them, they were thrust upon his awareness in full flower. He tried as best he could to avoid looking at her without giving offense. For her part, Ehlana seemed quite self-conscious about her recently acquired attributes. She seemed to waver between a desire to show them off—even to flaunt them—and an embarrassed wish to conceal them behind anything that lay at hand. It was a difficult time for them both.

At this point something should be clarified in Sparhawk's defense. Ehlana's almost overpowering femininity, coupled with her queenly manner and disconcerting candor, had distracted him, and the rings looked so much alike that he should be forgiven for taking his own off by mistake. He slipped it on her finger without giving any thought to the implications.

Despite the similarity of the two rings, there were a few minuscule differences, and women are notoriously adept at recognizing such tiny variations. Ehlana gave the ruby ring he had just placed on her finger what appeared to be no more than a cursory glance, then with a squeal of delight she threw her arms about his neck, nearly pulling him off balance in the process, and glued her lips to his.

It is unfortunate, perhaps, that Vanion and the Earl of Lenda chose that moment to enter the room. The old earl coughed politely, and Sparhawk, flushing to the roots of his hair, gently but firmly disengaged the queen's arms from about his neck.

The Earl of Lenda was smiling knowingly, and one of Vanion's eyebrows was curiously raised. "Sorry to interrupt, my Queen," Lenda said diplomatically, "but since your recovery appears to be progressing so well, Lord Vanion and I thought it might be a suitable time to bring you up to date on certain matters of state."

"Of course, Lenda," she replied, brushing aside the implied question of just exactly what she and Sparhawk had been doing when the pair had entered the room.

"There are some friends outside, your Majesty," Vanion said. "They will be able to brief you on some events in greater detail than the earl and I would be able to."

"Then show them in, by all means."

Sparhawk stepped to a sideboard and poured himself a glass of water; his mouth was very dry for some reason.

Vanion went outside for a moment and returned with Sparhawk's friends. "I believe you know Sephrenia, Kurik, and Sir Kalten, your Majesty," he said. He then introduced the others, judiciously omitting references to Talen's professional activities.

"I'm so pleased to meet you all," Ehlana said graciously. "Now, before we begin, I have an announcement to make. Sir Sparhawk here has just proposed marriage to me. Wasn't that nice of him?"

Sparhawk had the glass to his lips at that point and he went into an extended fit of choking.

"Why, whatever is the matter, dear?" Ehlana asked innocently.

He pointed at his throat, making strangling noises.

When Sparhawk had somewhat regained his breath and a few shreds of his composure, the Earl of Lenda looked at his queen. "I gather then that your Majesty has accepted your champion's proposal?"

"Of course I have. That's what I was doing when you came in."

"Oh," the old man said. "I see." Lenda was a consummate politician and he was able to make statements like that without cracking a smile.

"Congratulations, my Lord," Kurik said gruffly, seizing Sparhawk's hand in a grip of iron and shaking it vigorously.

Kalten was staring at Ehlana. *"Sparhawk?"* he demanded incredulously.

"Isn't it odd how your closest friends never fully understand your greatness, my dear?" she said to Sparhawk. "Sir Kalten," she said then, "your boyhood friend is the paramount knight in the world. Any woman would be honored to have him as her husband." She smiled smugly. "I'm the one who *got* him, however. All right, friends, please be seated and tell me what's been happening to my kingdom while I've been ill. I trust you'll be brief. My betrothed and I have many plans to make."

Vanion had remained standing. He looked around at the others. "If I leave out anything important, don't hesitate to step in and correct me," he said. He looked up at the ceiling. "Where to begin?" he mused.

"You might start by telling me what it was that made me so ill, Lord Vanion," Ehlana suggested.

"You were poisoned, your Majesty."

*"What?"*

"A very rare poison from Rendor—the same one that killed your father."

"Who was responsible?"

"In your father's case, it was his sister. In yours, it was the Primate Annias. You knew that he's had his eyes on the throne of the archprelate in Chyrellos, didn't you?"

"Of course. I was doing what I could to stand in his way. If he reaches that throne, I think I'll convert to Eshandism—or maybe even become Styric. Would your God accept me, Sephrenia?"

"Goddess, your Majesty," Sephrenia corrected. "I serve a Goddess."

"What an extraordinarily practical notion. Would I have to cut off my hair and sacrifice a few Elene children to her?"

"Don't be absurd, Ehlana."

"I'm only teasing, Sephrenia." Ehlana laughed. "But isn't that what the Elene commons say about Styrics? How did you find out about the poisonings, Lord Vanion?"

Vanion quickly described Sparhawk's meeting with the ghost of King Aldreas and the recovery of the ring that now—mistakenly—decorated the champion's hand. He then moved on, covering the de facto rulership of Annias and the elevation of the queen's cousin to the Prince Regency.

"Lycheas?" she exclaimed at that point. "Ridiculous. He can't even dress himself." She frowned. "If I was poisoned and it was the same poison that killed my father, how is it that I'm still alive?"

"We used magic to sustain you, Queen Ehlana," Sephrenia told her.

Vanion then spoke of Sparhawk's return from Rendor and their growing conviction that Annias had poisoned her primarily to gain access to her treasury in order to finance his campaign for the archprelacy.

Sparhawk took up the story at that point and told the young lady who had so recently netted him of the trip of the group of Church Knights and their companions to Chyrellos, then to Borrata, and finally down into Rendor.

"Who is Flute?" Ehlana interrupted him at one point.

"A Styric foundling," he replied. "At least we *thought* she was. She seemed to be about six years old, but she turned out to be much, much older than that." He continued his account, describing the trek across Rendor and the meeting with the physician in Dabour who had finally told them that only magic could save the stricken queen. He then went on to tell her of the meeting with Martel.

"I never liked him," she declared, making a face.

"He's working for Annias now," Sparhawk told her, "and he was in Rendor at the same time we were. There was a crazy old religious fanatic down there—Arasham—and he was the spiritual leader of the kingdom. Martel was trying to persuade him to invade the western Elene kingdoms as a diversion to give Annias a free hand during the election of the new archprelate. Sephrenia and I went to Arasham's tent, and Martel was there."

"Did you kill him?" Ehlana asked fiercely.

Sparhawk blinked. This was a side of her he had never seen. "The time wasn't exactly right, my Queen," he apologized. "I came up with a subterfuge instead and persuaded Arasham not to invade until he received word from me. Martel was furious, but he couldn't do anything about it. He and I had a nice chat later, and he told me that he was the one who had found the poison and passed it on to Annias."

"Would that stand up in a court of law, my Lord?" Ehlana asked the Earl of Lenda.

"It would depend on the judge, your Majesty," he replied.

"We have nothing to worry about on that score, Lenda," she said grimly, "because *I'm* going to be the judge—also the jury."

"Most irregular, your Majesty," he murmured.

"So was what they did to my father and me. Go on with the story, Sparhawk."

"We returned here to Cimmura and went to the chapterhouse. That's where I received the summons to go to the royal crypt under the cathedral to meet with your father's ghost. He told me a number of things—first that it was your aunt who had poisoned him and that it was Annias who'd poisoned you. He also told me that Lycheas was the result of certain intimacies between Annias and Arissa."

"Thank God!" Ehlana exclaimed. "I was half-afraid that he was my father's bastard. It's bad enough to have to admit that he's my cousin, but a brother? Unthinkable."

"Your father's ghost also told me that the only thing that could save your life was the Bhelliom."

"What's the Bhelliom?"

Sparhawk reached inside his doublet and pulled out the canvas pouch. He opened it and drew out the sapphire rose. "This is Bhelliom, your Majesty," he told her. Once again he felt more than saw the annoying flicker of darkness at the very edge of his vision. He shook off the feeling as he held out the jewel.

"How exquisite!" she cried, reaching out for it.

*"No!"* Sephrenia said sharply. "Don't touch it, Ehlana! It could destroy you!"

Ehlana shrank back, her eyes wide. "But Sparhawk's touching it," she objected.

"It knows him. It may know you as well, but let's not take any chances. We've all spent too much time and effort on you to waste it at this point."

Sparhawk tucked the jewel back into its pouch and put it away.

"There's something else you should know, Ehlana," Sephrenia continued. "Bhelliom is the most powerful and precious object in the world, and Azash wants it desperately. That's what was behind Otha's invasion of the west five hundred years ago. Otha has Zemochs—and others—here in the west trying to find the jewel. We must deny it to him at any cost."

"Should we destroy it now?" Sparhawk asked her bleakly. The question cost him a great deal of effort to say for some reason.

"Destroy it?" Ehlana cried. "But it's so beautiful!"

"It's also evil," Sephrenia told her. She paused. "Perhaps evil isn't the right term, though. It has no concept of the difference between good and evil. No, Sparhawk, let's keep it for a while longer until we're certain Ehlana is past any danger of a relapse. Go on with the story. Try to be brief. Your queen is still very weak."

"I'll cut this short then," he said. He told his queen of their search of the battlefield at Lake Randera and of how they were finally able to locate Count Ghasek. The queen listened intently, almost seeming to hold her breath as he recounted the events at Lake Venne. He quickly sketched in King Wargun's interference—though he did not use that exact word—and finally described the dreadful encounter in Ghwerig's cave and the revelation of Flute's real identity. "And that's where things stand right now, my Queen," he concluded. "King Wargun's battling the Rendors down in Arcium; Annias is in Chyrellos awaiting the death of Archprelate Cluvonus; and you're back on your throne where you belong."

"And also newly betrothed," she reminded him. She was obviously not going to let him forget that. She thought for a moment. "And what have you done with Lycheas?" she asked intently.

"He's back in the dungeon where he belongs, your Majesty."

"And Harparin and that other one?"

"The fat one's in the dungeon with Lycheas. Harparin left us rather suddenly."

"You let him escape?"

Kalten shook his head. "No, your Majesty. He started screaming and trying to order us out of the council chamber. Vanion got bored with all the noise and had Ulath chop off his head."

"How very appropriate. I want to see Lycheas."

"Shouldn't you rest?" Sparhawk asked her.

"Not until I have a few words with my cousin."

"I'll fetch him," Ulath said. He turned and left the room.

"My Lord of Lenda," Ehlana said then, "will you head up my royal council?"

"As your Majesty wishes," Lenda said with a low bow.

"And Lord Vanion, would you also serve—when your other duties permit?"

"I'd be honored, your Majesty."

"As my consort and champion, Sparhawk will also have a seat at the council table—and I think Sephrenia as well."

"I am Styric, Ehlana," Sephrenia pointed out. "Would it be wise to put a Styric on your council, given the feelings of the Elene commons about our race?"

"I'm going to put an end to that nonsense once and for all," Ehlana said firmly. "Sparhawk, can you think of anyone else who might be useful on the council?"

He thought about it, and suddenly an idea came to him. "I know a man who isn't of noble birth, your Majesty, but he's very clever and he understands a great deal about a side of Cimmura you probably don't even know exists."

"Who is this man?"

"His name's Platime."

Talen burst out laughing. "Have you lost your mind, Sparhawk?" he said. "You're going to let Platime into the same building with the treasury and the crown jewels?"

Ehlana looked a bit puzzled. "Is there some problem with this man?" she asked.

"Platime's the biggest thief in Cimmura," Talen told her. "I know that for a fact because I used to work for him. He controls every thief and beggar in the city—also the swindlers, cutthroats, and whores."

"Watch your language, young man!" Kurik barked.

"I've heard the term before, Kurik," Ehlana said calmly. "I know what it means. Tell me, Sparhawk, what's your reasoning behind this suggestion?"

"As I said, Platime's very clever—in some ways almost brilliant, and, though it's a little odd, he's a patriot. He has a vast understanding of the society of Cimmura, and he has ways of finding information that I can't even guess at. There's nothing that happens in Cimmura—or in most of the rest of the world, for that matter— that he doesn't know about."

"I'll interview him," Ehlana promised.

Then Ulath and Sir Perraine dragged Lycheas into the room. Lycheas gaped at his cousin, his mouth open and his eyes bulging in astonishment. "How—" he began, then broke off, biting his lip.

"You didn't expect to see me alive, Lycheas?" she asked in a deadly tone.

"I believe it's customary to kneel in the presence of your queen, Lycheas," Ulath growled, kicking the bastard's feet out from under him. Lycheas crashed to the floor and grovelled there.

The Earl of Lenda cleared his throat. "Your Majesty," he said, "during the time of your illness, Prince Lycheas insisted that he be addressed as 'your Majesty.' I'll have to consult the statutes, but I believe that constitutes high treason."

"That's what I arrested him for, at least," Sparhawk added.

"That's good enough for me," Ulath said, raising his ax. "Say the word, Queen of Elenia, and we'll have his head on a pole at the palace gate in a matter of minutes."

Lycheas gaped at them in horror and then began to cry, pleading for his life while his cousin pretended to think it over. At least Sparhawk *hoped* that she was pretending. "Not here, Sir Ulath," she said a bit regretfully. "The carpeting, you understand."

"King Wargun wanted to hang him," Kalten said. He looked up. "You've got a nice high ceiling in here, your Majesty, and good stout beams. It won't take me but a moment to fetch a rope. We can have him dancing in the air in no time, and hanging's not nearly as messy as beheading."

Ehlana looked at Sparhawk. "What do you think, dear? Should we hang my cousin?"

Sparhawk was profoundly shocked at the cold-blooded way she said it.

"Ah—he has a great deal of information that could be useful to us, my Queen," he said.

"That might be true," she said. "Tell me, Lycheas, have you anything you'd like to share with us while I think this over?"

"I'll say anything you want, Ehlana," he blubbered.

Ulath cuffed him across the back of the head. "Your Majesty," he prompted.

"What?"

"You call the queen 'your Majesty,' " Ulath said, cuffing him again.

"Y-your Majesty," Lycheas stammered.

"There's something else, too, my Queen," Sparhawk continued. "Lycheas is Annias' son, you recall."

"How did you find out about that?" Lycheas exclaimed.

Ulath cuffed him again. "He wasn't talking to you. Speak when you're spoken to."

"As I was saying," Sparhawk went on, "Lycheas is Annias' son, and he might be a useful bargaining chip in Chyrellos when we go there to try to keep Annias off the archprelate's throne."

"Oh," Ehlana said petulantly, "all right—I guess—but as soon as you're done with him, turn him over to Sir Ulath and Sir Kalten. I'm sure they'll find a way to decide which one of them gets to send him on his way."

"Draw straws?" Kalten asked Ulath.

"Or we could roll the dice," Ulath countered.

"My Lord Lenda," Ehlana said then, "why don't you and Lord Vanion take this wretch someplace and question him. I'm getting sick of the sight of him. Take Sir Kalten, Sir Perraine, and Sir Ulath with you. Their presence might encourage him to be more forthcoming."

"Yes, your Majesty," Lenda said, concealing a smile.

After Lycheas had been dragged from the room, Sephrenia looked the young queen full in the face. "You weren't seriously considering that, were you, Ehlana?" she asked.

"Oh, of course not—well, not *too* seriously, anyway. I just want Lycheas to sweat a bit. I think I owe him that." She sighed wearily. "I think I'd like to rest now," she said. "Sparhawk, do be a dear and carry me in to bed."

"That's hardly proper, Ehlana," he said stiffly.

"Oh, bother proper. You may as well get used to thinking of me and beds at the same time anyway."

"*Ehlana!*"

She laughed and held out her arms to him.

As Sparhawk bent and lifted his queen in his arms, he happened to catch a glimpse of Berit's face. The young novice was giving him a look of undisguised hatred. There was going to be a problem here, Sparhawk saw. He decided to have a long talk with Berit just as soon as the opportunity presented itself.

He carried Ehlana into the other room and tucked her into a very large bed. "You've changed a great deal, my Queen," he said gravely. "You're not the same person I left ten years ago." It was time to get that out into the open so that they could both stop tiptoeing around it.

"You've noticed," she said archly.

"That's part of it right there," he told her, reverting to his professorial tone. "You're still only eighteen years old, Ehlana. It's not becoming for you to assume the worldly airs of a woman of thirty-five. I strongly recommend a more innocent public pose."

She squirmed around in the bed until she was lying on her stomach with her head at the foot. She rested her chin in her hands, wide-eyed and ingenuous, her lashes fluttering and with one foot coyly kicking at her pillow. "Like this?" she asked.

"Stop that."

"I'm just trying to please you, my betrothed. Was there anything else about me you'd like to change?"

"You've grown hard, child."

"Now it's your turn to stop something," she said firmly. "Don't call me 'child' any more, Sparhawk. I stopped being a child the day Aldreas sent you to Rendor. I could be a child as long as you were here to protect me, but once you were gone, I couldn't afford that any more." She sat up cross-legged on the bed. "My father's court was a very unfriendly place for me, Sparhawk," she told him gravely. "I was dressed up and displayed at court functions where I could watch Annias smirking. Any friends I had were immediately sent away—or killed—so I was forced to entertain myself by eavesdropping on the empty-headed gossip of the chambermaids. As a group, chambermaids tend to be quite wanton. I drew up a chart once—you taught me to be methodical, you'll remember. You wouldn't believe what goes on below stairs. My chart indicated that one aggressive little minx had very nearly outstripped Arissa herself in her conquests. Her availability was almost legendary. If I sometimes seem 'worldly'—wasn't that your term?—you can blame it on the tutors who took up my education when you left. After a few years—since any friendship I displayed for the lords and ladies of the court was an immediate cause for their exile or worse—I came to rely on the servants. Servants expect you to give them orders, so I gave orders. It's a habit now. It worked out rather well for me, though. Nothing happens in the palace that the servants don't know about, and before long they were telling me everything. I was able to use that information to protect myself from my enemies, and everybody at court except Lenda was my enemy. It wasn't much of a childhood, Sparhawk, but it prepared me far better than empty hours spent rolling hoops or wasting affection on rag dolls or puppies. If I seem hard, it's because I grew up in hostile territory. It may take you some years to soften those sharp edges, but I'm sure I'll enjoy your efforts in that direction." She smiled winsomely, but there was still a kind of pained defensiveness in her gray eyes.

"My poor Ehlana," he said, his heart in his throat.

"Hardly poor, dear Sparhawk. I have you now, and that makes me the richest woman in the world."

"We've got a problem, Ehlana," he said seriously.

"I don't see any problems. Not now."

"I think you misunderstood when I gave you my ring by mistake." He regretted that instantly. Her eyes opened as wide as they might have had he slapped her in the face. "Please don't take what I just said wrong," he rushed on. "I'm just too old for you, that's all."

"I don't care how old you are," she said defiantly. "You're mine, Sparhawk, and I'll *never* let you go." Her voice was so filled with steel that he almost shrank from her.

"I was sort of obliged to point it out," he back-stepped. He *had* to ease her past that dreadful moment of injury. "Duty, you understand."

She stuck her tongue out at that. "All right, now that you've made your genuflection in duty's direction, we won't ever mention it again. When do you think we should have the wedding—before or after you and Vanion go to Chyrellos and kill Annias? I'm rather in favor of getting right on with it, personally. I've heard all sorts of things about what goes on between a husband and wife when they're alone, and I'm really very, very curious."

Sparhawk turned bright red at that.

# CHAPTER FIVE

"Is she asleep?" Vanion asked when Sparhawk emerged from Ehlana's bedroom.

Sparhawk nodded. "Did Lycheas tell you anything useful?" he asked.

"A number of things—mostly verification of things we've already guessed," Vanion replied. The preceptor's face was troubled, and the strain of bearing the swords of the fallen knights still showed on him, although he looked more vigorous now. "My Lord of Lenda," he said, "is the queen's apartment here secure? I'd rather not have some of the things Lycheas told us become general knowledge."

"The rooms are quite secure, my Lord," Lenda assured him, "and the presence of your knights in the corridors will probably discourage anyone who's afflicted with a burning curiosity."

Kalten and Ulath entered, and they both had vicious grins on their faces. "Lycheas is having a very bad day." Kalten smirked. "Ulath and I were recalling a number of lurid executions we'd seen in the past while we were escorting him back to his cell. He found the notion of being burned at the stake particularly distressing."

"And he almost fainted when we raised the possibility of racking him to death." Ulath chuckled. "Oh, by the way, we stopped by the palace gate on our way back here. The church soldiers we captured are repairing it." The towering Genidian

Knight set his ax in the corner. "Some of your Pandions have been out in the streets, Lord Vanion. It seems that quite a number of the citizens of Cimmura have dropped out of sight."

Vanion gave him a puzzled look.

"They seem a bit nervous for some reason," Kalten explained. "Annias has been in control of the city for quite a while now, and some people, nobles and commons alike, always have their eyes open for the main chance. They went out of their way to accommodate the good primate. Their neighbors know who they are, though, and there have been a few . . . incidents, I understand. When there's a sudden change of power, many people want to demonstrate their loyalty to the new regime in some visible way. There appear to have been several spontaneous hangings and a fair number of houses are on fire. Ulath and I suggested to the knights that they put a stop to that, at least. Fires do tend to spread, you know."

"I just love politics, don't you?" Tynian grinned.

"Mob rule should always be suppressed," the Earl of Lenda said critically. "The mob is the enemy of *any* government."

"By the way," Kalten said curiously to Sparhawk, "did you *really* propose to the queen?"

"It's a misunderstanding."

"I was fairly sure it was. You've never struck me as the marrying kind. She's going to hold you to it anyway, though, isn't she?"

"I'm working on that."

"I wish you all the luck in the world, but quite frankly, I don't hold out much hope for you. I saw some of the looks she used to throw your way when she was a little girl. You're in for an interesting time, I think." Kalten was grinning.

"It's such a comfort to have friends."

"It's time you settled down anyway, Sparhawk. You're getting to be too old to be running around the world picking fights with people."

"You're as old as I am, Kalten."

"I know, but that's different."

"Have you and Ulath decided who gets to dispose of Lycheas yet?" Tynian asked.

"We're still discussing it." Kalten gave the big Thalesian a suspicious look. "Ulath's been trying to foist off a set of dice on me."

"Foist?" Ulath protested mildly.

"I saw one of those dice, my friend, and it had four sixes on it."

"That's a lot of sixes," Tynian noted.

"It is indeed." Kalten sighed. "To be honest with you, though, I don't really think Ehlana's going to let us kill Lycheas. He's such a pathetic lump that I don't think she'll have the heart. Oh, well," he added, "there's always Annias."

"And Martel," Sparhawk reminded him.

"Oh, yes. There's *always* Martel."

"Which way did he go after Wargun chased him away from Larium?" Sparhawk asked. "I always like to keep track of Martel. I wouldn't want him to get himself into any trouble."

"The last time we saw him, he was going east," Tynian said, shifting the shoulder plates of his heavy Deiran armor.

"East?"

Tynian nodded. "We thought he'd go south to Umanthum, but we found out later that he'd moved his fleet to Sarinium after the burning of Coombe—probably because Wargun has ships patrolling the Straits of Arcium. He's most likely back in Rendor by now."

Sparhawk grunted. He unhooked his sword belt, laid it on the table, and sat down. "What did Lycheas tell you?" he asked Vanion.

"Quite a bit. It's fairly obvious that he didn't know everything Annias was doing, but surprisingly, he's managed to pick up a great deal of information. He's brighter than he looks."

"He'd almost have to be," Kurik said. "Talen," he said to his son, "don't do that."

"I was just looking, Father," the boy protested.

"Don't. You might be tempted."

"Lycheas told us that his mother and Annias have been lovers for years now," Vanion told them, "and it was Annias who suggested to Arissa that she attempt to seduce her brother. He'd come up with a rather obscure bit of Church doctrine that appeared to permit a marriage between them."

"The Church would never permit such an obscenity," Sir Bevier declared flatly.

"The Church has done many things in her history that don't conform to contemporary morality, Bevier," Vanion said. "At one time, she was very weak in Cammoria, and there had been a tradition of incestuous marriages in the royal house of that kingdom. The Church made allowances in order to continue her work there. Anyway, Annias reasoned that Aldreas was a weak king and Arissa would be the real ruler of Elenia if she married him. Then, since Annias more or less controlled Arissa, he'd be the one making the decisions. At first that seemed to be enough for him, but then his ambition began to run away with him. He started eyeing the archprelate's throne in Chyrellos. That was about twenty years ago, I gather."

"How did Lycheas find out about it?" Sparhawk asked him.

"He used to visit his mother in that cloister at Demos," Vanion replied. "Arissa's reminiscences were rather wide-ranging, I understand, and she was quite candid with her son."

"That's revolting," Bevier said in a sick voice.

"Princess Arissa has a peculiar kind of morality," Kalten told the young Arcian.

"At any rate," Vanion said, "Sparhawk's father stepped in at that point. I knew him very well, and *his* morality was much more conventional. He was greatly offended by what Aldreas and Arissa were doing. Aldreas was afraid of him, so when he suggested a marriage to a Deiran princess instead, Aldreas rather reluctantly agreed. The rest is fairly well known. Arissa went into an absolute fury and ran off to that brothel down by the riverside—sorry about that, Sephrenia."

"I've heard about it before, Vanion," she replied. "Styrics are not nearly as unworldly as you Elenes sometimes believe."

"Anyway, Arissa stayed in the brothel for several weeks, and when she was finally apprehended, Aldreas had no choice but to confine her in that cloister."

"That raises a question," Tynian said. "Considering the amount of time she spent in that brothel and the number of customers she had, how can anyone be sure *who* Lycheas' father was?"

"I was just coming to that," Vanion replied. "She assured Lycheas during one of his visits that she was pregnant to Annias *before* she went to the brothel. Aldreas married the Deiran princess, and she died giving birth to Queen Ehlana. Lycheas was about six months old at the time, and Annias was doing his best to get Aldreas to legitimize him and make him his heir. That was too much even for Aldreas, and he flatly refused. It was about at that time that Sparhawk's father died, and Sparhawk here took his hereditary position as King's Champion. Annias began to grow alarmed at Ehlana's progress after Sparhawk took charge of her education. By the time she was eight, he decided that he had to get her champion away from her before he could make her so strong that Annias wouldn't be able to control her. That's when he persuaded Aldreas to send Sparhawk into exile in Rendor, and then he sent Martel to Cippria to kill him to make sure he'd never come back and complete Ehlana's education."

"But he was too late, wasn't he?" Sparhawk smiled. "Ehlana was already too strong for him."

"How did you manage that, Sparhawk?" Kalten asked. "You've never really been what you'd call a very inspiring teacher."

"Love, Kalten," Sephrenia said quite softly. "Ehlana's loved Sparhawk since she was very young, and she tried to do things the way he'd have wanted her to do them."

Tynian laughed. "You did it to yourself then, Sparhawk," he said.

"Did what?"

"You made a woman of steel, and now she's going to force you to marry her—and she's strong enough to get away with it."

"Tynian," Sparhawk said acidly, "you talk too much." The big Pandion was suddenly irritated—all the more so because he privately had to admit that Tynian was probably right.

"The point here, though, is that none of this is really very new or surprising," Kurik noted. "It's certainly not enough to keep Lycheas' head on his shoulders."

"That came a little later," Vanion told him. "Ehlana frightened him so much when she seemed on the verge of having him summarily executed that he was babbling at first. Anyway, after Annias had forced Aldreas to send Sparhawk into exile, the king began to change. He actually started to develop some backbone. It's a little hard sometimes to know why people do things."

"Not really, Vanion," Sephrenia disagreed. "Aldreas was under the thumb of the primate, but in his heart he knew that what he was doing was wrong. Perhaps he felt that his champion might have been able to rescue his soul, but once Sparhawk was gone, Aldreas began to realize that he was totally alone. If his soul was going to be saved, he was going to have to do it himself."

"She might be very close to right, you know," Bevier marvelled. "Perhaps I should make some study of the ethics of Styricum. A synthesis of Elene and Styric ethical thought might be very interesting."

"Heresy," Ulath observed flatly.

"I beg your pardon?"

"We're not supposed to consider the possibility that other ethics have any validity, Bevier. It's a little shortsighted, I'll admit, but our Church is like that sometimes."

Bevier rose to his feet, his face flushed. "I will not listen to insults directed at our Holy Mother," he declared.

"Oh, sit down, Bevier," Tynian told him. "Ulath's only teasing you. Our Genidian brothers are much more deeply versed in theology than we give them credit for."

"It's the climate," Ulath explained. "There's not a great deal to do in Thalesia in the winter—unless you like to watch it snow. We have a lot of time for meditation and study."

"For whatever reason, Aldreas began to refuse some of Annias' more outrageous demands for money," Vanion continued his account, "and Annias started to get desperate. That's when he and Arissa decided to murder the king. Martel provided the poison, and Annias made arrangements to slip Arissa out of that cloister. He probably could have poisoned Aldreas himself, but Arissa begged him to let her do it because she wanted to kill her brother herself."

"Are you really sure you want to marry into that family, Sparhawk?" Ulath asked.

"Do I have any choice at this point?"

"You could always run away. I'm sure you could find work in the Tamul Empire on the Daresian continent."

"Ulath," Sephrenia said, "hush."

"Yes, ma'am," he said.

"Go ahead, Vanion," she instructed.

"Yes, ma'am." He duplicated Ulath's intonation perfectly. "After Arissa had killed Aldreas, Ehlana ascended the throne. She turned out to be Sparhawk's true pupil. She absolutely denied Annias access to her treasury and she was on the verge of packing him off to a monastery. That's when he poisoned her."

"Excuse me, Lord Vanion," Tynian interrupted. "My Lord of Lenda, attempted regicide is a capital offense, isn't it?"

"Throughout the civilized world, Sir Tynian."

"I thought that might be the case. Kalten, why don't you put in an order for a bale of rope? And Ulath, you'd better send to Thalesia for a couple of spare axes."

"What's this?" Kalten asked.

"We have evidence now that Lycheas, Annias, and Arissa have all committed high treason—along with a fair number of other confederates."

"We knew that before," Kalten said.

"Yes." Tynian smiled. "But now we can prove it. We have a witness."

"I was sort of hoping to take care of suitable rewards myself," Sparhawk objected.

"It's always better to do such things legally, Sparhawk," Lenda told him. "It avoids arguments later on, you understand."

"I wasn't really planning to leave anyone around to argue with me, my Lord."

"I think you'd better shorten his chain a bit, Lord Vanion," Lenda suggested with a sly smile. "His fangs seem to be getting longer."

"I noticed that," Vanion agreed. Then he went on. "Annias was a little confounded when Sephrenia's spell kept Ehlana from dying the way her father had, but he went ahead and set Lycheas up as prince regent anyway, reasoning that an incapacitated queen was the same as a dead one. He took personal charge of the Elenian treasury and started buying patriarchs right and left. That's when his campaign to gain the archprelacy gained momentum and became more obvious. It was at about that point in Lycheas' story that my Lord of Lenda here suggested to him quite firmly that he hadn't yet said anything momentous enough to keep his neck off Ulath's chopping block."

"Or out of my noose," Kalten added grimly.

Vanion smiled. "Lenda's suggestion had the desired effect on Lycheas," he said. "The prince regent became a gold mine of information at that point. He said that he can't actually prove it, but he's picked up some strong hints that Annias has been in contact with Otha, and that he's seeking his aid. The primate has always pretended to be violently prejudiced against Styrics, but that may have been a pose to conceal his real feelings."

"Probably not," Sephrenia disagreed. "There's a world of difference between western Styrics and Zemochs. The annihilation of western Styricum would have been one of Otha's first demands in exchange for any assistance."

"That's probably true," Vanion conceded.

"Did Lycheas have anything at all solid to base his suspicions upon?" Tynian asked.

"Not much," Ulath told him. "He saw a few meetings taking place, is about all. It's not quite enough to justify a declaration of war just yet."

"War?" Bevier exclaimed.

"Naturally." Ulath shrugged. "If Otha's been involving himself in the internal affairs of the western Elene kingdoms, that's cause enough to go east and do war upon him."

"I've always liked that expression," Kalten said. " 'Do war.' It sounds so permanent—and so messy."

"We don't need justification if you really want to go destroy Zemoch, Ulath," Tynian said.

"We don't?"

"Nobody ever got around to drawing up a peace treaty after the Zemoch invasion five hundred years ago. Technically, we're still at war with Otha—aren't we, my Lord of Lenda?"

"Probably, but resuming hostilities after a five-hundred-year truce might be a little hard to justify."

"We've just been resting up, my Lord." Tynian shrugged. "I don't know about these other gentlemen, but *I* feel fairly well rested now."

"Oh, dear," Sephrenia sighed.

"The important thing here," Vanion went on, "is that on several occasions Lycheas saw one particular Styric closeted with Annias. Once he was able to overhear a part of what they were saying. The Styric had a Zemoch accent—or so Lycheas believes."

"That's Lycheas, all right," Kurik observed. "He's got the face of a sneak and an eavesdropper."

"I'll agree to that," Vanion said. "Our excellent Prince Regent couldn't hear the whole conversation, but he told us that the Styric was telling Annias that Otha had to get his hands on a particular jewel or the Zemoch God would withdraw his support. I think we can all make some fairly educated guesses about which jewel he was talking about."

Kalten's face grew mournful. "You're going to be a spoilsport about this, aren't you, Sparhawk," he lamented.

"That one escapes me."

"You're going to tell the queen about this, I suppose, and then she'll decide that the information's important enough to keep Lycheas' head on his neck or his feet on the floor."

"I'm sort of obliged to keep her advised, Kalten."

"I don't suppose we could persuade you to wait awhile, could we?"

"Wait? How long?"

"Only until after the bastard's funeral."

Sparhawk grinned at his friend. "No, I'm afraid not, Kalten," he said. "I'd really like to oblige you, but I've got my own skin to consider. It might make my queen cross with me if I start hiding things from her."

"That's about all Lycheas really knows," Vanion told them. "Now, we need to make a decision. Cluvonus is almost dead, and as soon as he dies, we'll have to join the other orders at Demos for the ride to Chyrellos. That's going to leave the queen totally unprotected here. We don't know when Dolmant's going to send us the command to march, and we don't know how long it's going to take the Elenian army to get back from Arcium. What are we going to do about the queen?"

"Take her with us." Ulath shrugged.

"I think you might get quite an argument there," Sparhawk said. "She's only recently been restored to her throne, and she's the sort who takes her responsibilities very seriously. She'll definitely get her back up if you suggest that she abandon her capital at this point."

"Get her drunk," Kalten said.

"Do *what*?"

"You don't want just to rap her on the head, do you? Get her tipsy, wrap her in a blanket, and tie her across a saddle."

"Have you lost your mind? This is the *queen*, Kalten, not one of your blowzy barmaids."

"You can apologize later. The important thing is to get her to safety."

"It may not come to any of that," Vanion said. "Cluvonus might hang on for a while yet. He's been on the brink of death for months now, but he's still alive. He might even outlive Annias."

"That shouldn't be too hard for him," Ulath said bleakly. "Annias doesn't have much in the way of a life expectancy just now."

"If I could persuade you gentlemen to curb your blood lust for a moment," the Earl of Lenda interposed, "I think the important thing right now is to get someone to King Wargun down in Arcium and to persuade him to release the Elenian army—and enough Pandion Knights to keep the general staff in line when they get here. I'll compose a letter to him advising in the strongest terms that we need the Elenian army back here in Cimmura just as quickly as they can get here."

"You'd better ask him to release the militant orders as well, my Lord," Vanion suggested. "I think we're going to need them in Chyrellos."

"You might also send a letter to King Obler," Tynian added, "and to Patriarch Bergsten. Between them, they can probably prevail on Wargun. The King of Thalesia drinks too much, and he enjoys a good war, but he's still a thoroughly political animal. He'll see the necessity of protecting Cimmura and taking control of Chyrellos immediately—if someone explains it to him."

Lenda nodded his agreement.

"All this still doesn't solve our problem, gentlemen," Bevier said. "Our messenger to Wargun could very well be no more than a day's ride away when word reaches us that the archprelate has died. That puts us right back in the same situation. Sparhawk will have to persuade a reluctant queen to abandon her capital with no visible danger in view."

"Blow in her ear," Ulath said.

"What was that?" Sparhawk asked.

"It usually works," Ulath said, "at least it does in Thalesia. I blew in a girl's ear in Emsat once, and she followed me around for days."

"That's disgusting!" Sephrenia said angrily.

"Oh, I don't know," Ulath said mildly. "*She* seemed to enjoy it."

"Did you pat her on top of the head, too, and scratch her chin—the way you'd have done if she'd been a puppy?"

"I never thought of that," Ulath admitted. "Do you think it might have worked?"

She began to swear at him in Styric.

"We're getting a little far afield here," Vanion said. "We can't compel the queen to leave Cimmura, and there's no way to be absolutely certain that a force large enough to hold the walls can reach the city before we're called away."

"I think the force is already here, Lord Vanion," Talen disagreed. The boy was dressed in the elegant doublet and hose Stragen had provided for him in Emsat, and he looked not unlike a youthful nobleman.

"Don't interrupt, Talen," Kurik said. "This is serious business. We don't have time for childish jokes."

"Let him speak, Kurik," the Earl of Lenda said intently. "Good ideas can sometimes come from the most unusual places. Exactly what is this force you spoke of, young man?"

"The people," Talen replied simply.

"That's absurd, Talen," Kurik said. "They aren't trained."

"How much training do you really need in order to pour boiling pitch down on the heads of a besieging army?" Talen shrugged.

"It's a very interesting notion, young man," Lenda said, "There *was*, in fact, an outpouring of popular support for Queen Ehlana after her coronation. The people of Cimmura—and of the surrounding towns and villages—might very well come to her aid. The problem, though, is that they don't have any leaders. A mob of people milling around in the street without anyone to direct them wouldn't be much of a defense."

"There *are* leaders about, my Lord."

"Who?" Vanion asked the boy.

"Platime for one," Talen offered, "and if Stragen's still here, he'd probably be fairly good at it as well."

"This Platime's a sort of a scoundrel, isn't he?" Bevier asked dubiously.

"Sir Bevier," Lenda said, "I've served on the royal council of Elenia for many years, and I can assure you that not only the capital, but the entire kingdom has been in the hands of scoundrels for decades now."

"But—" Bevier started to protest.

"Is it the fact that Platime and Stragen are *official* scoundrels that upsets you, Sir Bevier?" Talen asked lightly.

"What do you think, Sparhawk?" Lenda asked. "Do you think this Platime fellow could really direct some kind of military operation?"

Sparhawk thought it over. "He probably could," he said, "particularly if Stragen's still here to help him."

"Stragen?"

"He holds a position similar to Platime's among the thieves in Emsat. Stragen's a strange one, but he's extremely intelligent, and he's had an excellent education."

"They can call in old debts as well," Talen said. "Platime can draw men from Vardenias, Demos, the towns of Lenda and Cardos—not to mention the men he can get from the robber bands operating out in the countryside."

"It's not really as if they were going to have to hold the city for an extended period of time," Tynian mused, "only until the Elenian army gets here, and a great deal of what they'll be doing is going to be pure intimidation. It's unlikely that Primate Annias will be able to spare more than a thousand church soldiers from Chyrellos to cause problems here, and if the tops of the city walls are lined with a superior force, those soldiers will be very reluctant to attack. You know, Sparhawk, I think the boy's come up with a remarkably good plan."

"I'm overcome by your confidence, Sir Tynian," Talen said with an extravagant bow.

"There are veterans here in Cimmura as well," Kurik added, "former army men who can help direct the workers and peasants in the defense of the city."

"It's all terribly unnatural, of course," the Earl of Lenda said sardonically. "The whole purpose of government has always been to keep the commons under control and out of politics entirely. The only purpose the common people really have for existing is to do the work and pay the taxes. We may be doing something here that we'll all live to regret."

"Do we really have any choice, Lenda?" Vanion asked him.

"No, Vanion, I don't think we have."

"Let's get started with it then. My Lord of Lenda, I believe you have some correspondence to catch up with, and Talen, why don't you go see this Platime fellow?"

"May I take Berit with me, my Lord Vanion?" the boy asked, looking at the young novice.

"I suppose so, but why?"

"I'm sort of the official envoy from one government to another. I should have an escort of some kind to make me look more important. That sort of thing impresses Platime."

"One government to another?" Kalten asked. "Do you actually think of Platime as a head of state?"

"Well, isn't he?"

As Sparhawk's friends were filing out, Sparhawk briefly touched Sephrenia's sleeve. "I need to talk with you," he said quietly.

"Of course."

He went to the door and closed it. "I probably should have told you about this before, little mother," he said, "but it all seemed so innocuous at the beginning . . ." He shrugged.

"Sparhawk," she told him, "you know better than that. You must tell me everything. I'll decide what's innocuous and what isn't."

"All right. I think I'm being followed."

Her eyes narrowed.

"I had a nightmare right after we took Bhelliom away from Ghwerig. Azash was mixed up in it and so was Bhelliom. There was something else as well, though—something I can't put a name to."

"Can you describe it?"

"Sephrenia, I can't even see it. It seems to be some sort of shadow—something dark that's right on the very edge of my vision—like a flicker of movement to one side and slightly behind me. I get the feeling that it doesn't like me very much."

"Does it only come to you when you're dreaming?"

"No. I see it now and then when I'm awake, too. It seems to appear whenever I take Bhelliom out of its pouch. There are other times as well, but I can almost count on seeing it any time I open the pouch."

"Do that now, dear one," she instructed. "Let's find out if I can see it, too."

Sparhawk reached inside his doublet, took out the pouch, and opened it. He removed the sapphire rose and held it in his hand. The flicker of darkness was immediately there. "Can you see it?" he asked.

Sephrenia looked carefully around the room. "No," she admitted. "Can you feel anything coming from the shadow?"

"I can tell that it isn't fond of me." He put Bhelliom back into the pouch. "Any ideas?"

"It might be something connected with Bhelliom itself," she suggested a bit dubiously. "To be perfectly honest with you, though, I don't really know that much about Bhelliom. Aphrael doesn't like to talk about it. I think the Gods are afraid of it. I know a little bit about how to use it, but that's about all."

"I don't know if there's any connection," Sparhawk mused, "but somebody's definitely interested in doing me in. There were those men on the road outside

Emsat, that ship that Stragen thought might be following us, and those outlaws who were looking for us on the Cardos road."

"Not to mention the fact that somebody tried to shoot you in the back with a crossbow when we were on our way to the palace," she added.

"Could it be another Seeker, perhaps?" he suggested.

"Something like that, maybe. Once the Seeker takes control of somebody, the man becomes a mindless tool. These attempts on your life seem to be a bit more rational."

"Could Azash have some creature who could manage that?"

"Who knows what kinds of creatures Azash can raise? I know of a dozen or so different varieties, but there are probably scores of others."

"Would you be offended if I tried logic?"

"Oh, I *suppose* you can—if you feel you must." She smiled at him.

"All right. First off, we know that Azash has wanted me dead for a long time now."

"All right."

"It's probably even more important to him now, though, because I've got Bhelliom, and I know how to use it."

"You're stating the obvious, Sparhawk."

"I know. Logic's like that sometimes. But these attempts to kill me *usually* come sometime not long after I've taken out the Bhelliom and caught a glimpse of that shadow."

"Some kind of connection, you think?"

"Isn't it possible?"

"Almost anything's possible, Sparhawk."

"All right, then. If the shadow's something like the Damork or the Seeker, it's probably coming from Azash. That 'probably' makes the logic a little shaky, but it's something to sort of consider, wouldn't you say?"

"Under the circumstances I'd almost have to agree."

"What do we do about it, then? It's an interim hypothesis, and it ignores the possibility of pure coincidence, but shouldn't we take some steps just in case there *is* some connection?"

"I don't think we can afford not to, Sparhawk. I think the first thing you should do is to keep Bhelliom inside that pouch. Don't take it out unless you absolutely have to."

"That makes sense."

"And if you *do* have to take it out, be on your guard for an attempt on your life."

"I sort of do that automatically anyway—all the time. I'm in a nervous kind of profession."

"*And,* I think we'd better keep this to ourselves. If that shadow comes from Azash, it can turn our friends against us. Any one of them could turn on you at any time at all. If we tell them what we suspect, the shadow—or whatever it is—will probably know what's in their thoughts. Let's not warn Azash that we know what he's doing."

Sparhawk steeled himself to say it, and when he did, it was with a vast reluctance. "Wouldn't it solve everything if we were just to destroy Bhelliom right here and now?" he asked her.

She shook her head. "No, dear one," she said. "We may still need it."

"It's a simple answer, though."

"Not really, Sparhawk." Her smile was bleak. "We don't know for sure what kind of force the destruction of Bhelliom might release. We might lose something fairly important."

"Such as?"

"The city of Cimmura—or the entire Eosian continent, for all I know."

## CHAPTER SIX

It was nearly dusk when Sparhawk quietly opened the door to his queen's bedroom and looked in on her. Her face was framed by that wealth of pale blonde hair fanning out on the pillow and catching the golden light of the single candle on the stand at the side of her bed. Her eyes were closed, and her face softly composed. He had discovered in the past day or so that an adolescence spent in the corrupt court dominated by the Primate Annias had marked her face with a kind of defensive wariness and a flinty determination. When she slept, however, her expression had the same soft, luminous gentleness that had caught at his heart when she was a child. Privately, and now without reservation, he admitted that he loved this pale girl-child, although he was still adjusting his conception of her in that regard. Ehlana was much a woman now and no longer a child. With an obscure kind of twinge, Sparhawk admitted to himself that he really was wrong for her. There was a temptation to take advantage of her girlish infatuation, but he knew that to do so would not only be morally wrong, but could also cause her much suffering later in her life. He determined that under no circumstances would he inflict the infirmities of his old age upon the woman he loved.

"I know you're there, Sparhawk." Her eyes did not open, and a soft smile touched her lips. "I always used to love that when I was a child, you know. Sometimes, particularly when you started lecturing me on theology, I'd doze off—or pretend to. You'd talk on for a while, and then you'd just sit there, watching me. It always made me feel so warm and secure and totally safe. Those moments were probably the happiest in my life. And just think, after we're married, you'll watch me go to sleep in your arms every night, and I'll know that nothing in the world can ever hurt me, because you'll always be there watching over me." She opened her calm gray eyes. "Come here and kiss me, Sparhawk," she told him, extending her arms.

"It's not proper, Ehlana. You're not fully dressed, and you're in bed."

"We're betrothed, Sparhawk. We have a certain leeway in such matters. Besides, I'm the queen. *I'll* decide what's proper and what's not."

Sparhawk gave up and kissed her. As he had noted before, Ehlana was most definitely no longer a child. "I'm too old for you, Ehlana," he reminded her gently once again. He wanted to keep that firmly in front of both of them. "You do know that I'm right, don't you?"

"Nonsense." She had not yet removed her arms from about his neck. "I forbid you to get old. There, does that take care of it?"

"You're being absurd. You might as well order the tide to stop."

"I haven't tried that yet, Sparhawk, and until I do, we won't really know that it wouldn't work, will we?"

"I give up," he laughed.

"Oh, good. I just *adore* winning. Was there something important you wanted to tell me, or did you just stop by to ogle me?"

"Do you *mind*?"

"Being ogled? Of course not. Ogle to your heart's content, beloved. Would you like to see more?"

*"Ehlana!"*

Her laughter was a silvery cascade.

"All right, let's get down to more serious matters."

"I *was* being serious, Sparhawk—*very* serious."

"The Pandion Knights, myself included, are going to have to leave Cimmura before long, I'm afraid. The revered Cluvonus is failing fast, and as soon as he dies, Annias is going to make a try for the archprelate's throne. He's flooded the streets of Chyrellos with troops loyal to him, and unless the militant orders are there to stop him, he'll gain that throne."

Her face took on that flinty expression again. "Why don't you take that gigantic Thalesian, Sir Ulath, run on down to Chyrellos, and chop Annias' head off? Then come right back. Don't give me time to get lonely."

"Interesting notion, Ehlana. I'm glad you didn't suggest it in front of Ulath, though. He'd be on his way to the stables to saddle the horses by now. The point I was trying to make is that when we leave, you're going to be left defenseless here. Would you consider coming along with us?"

She thought about it. "I'd love to, Sparhawk," she said, "but I don't really see how I can just now. I've been incapacitated for quite some time, and I've got to stay here in Cimmura to repair the damage Annias caused while I was asleep. I have responsibilities, love."

"We were fairly sure you'd feel that way about it, so we've come up with an alternative plan to insure your safety."

"You're going to use magic and seal me up in the palace?" Her eyes were impish as she teased him.

"We hadn't considered that," he conceded. "It probably wouldn't work, though. As soon as Annias found out what we'd done, he'd likely send soldiers here to try to retake the city. His underlings would be able to run the kingdom from outside the palace walls, and you wouldn't be able to do much to stop them. What we *are* going to do is put together a kind of an army to protect you—and the city— until your own army has time to come back from Arcium."

"The term 'a kind of an army' sounds a little tentative, Sparhawk. Where are you going to get that many men?"

"Off the streets, and from the farms and villages."

"Oh, that's just fine, Sparhawk. Wonderful." Her tone was sarcastic. "I'm to be defended by ditchdiggers and plowboys?"

"Also by thieves and cutthroats, my Queen."

"You're actually serious about this, aren't you?"

"Very much so. Don't close your mind just yet, though. Wait until you hear the details—and there are a pair of scoundrels on their way here to meet you. Don't make any decisions until after you've talked with them."

"I think you're completely mad, Sparhawk. I still love you, but your mind seems to be slipping. You can't make an army out of hod carriers and clodhoppers."

"Really? Where do you suppose the common soldiers in your army come from, Ehlana? Aren't they recruited from the streets and farms?"

She frowned. "I hadn't thought of that, I suppose," she conceded, "but without generals, I'm not going to have much of an army, you know."

"That's what the two men I just mentioned are coming here to discuss with you, your Majesty."

"Why is it that 'your Majesty' always sounds so cold and distant when you say it, Sparhawk?"

"Don't change the subject. You'll agree to withhold judgment, then?"

"If you say so, but I'm still a little dubious about this. I wish *you* could stay here."

"So do I, but . . ." He spread his hands helplessly.

"When will there ever be time for just us?"

"It won't be much longer, Ehlana, but we *have* to beat Annias. You understand that, don't you?"

She sighed. "I suppose so."

Talen and Berit returned not long afterward with Platime and Stragen. Sparhawk met them in the sitting room while Ehlana attended to those minute details that are always involved in making a woman "presentable."

Stragen was at his elegant best, but the waddling, black-bearded Platime, chief of beggars, thieves, cutthroats, and whores, looked distinctly out of place. "Ho, Sparhawk!" the fat man bellowed. He had forgone his food-spotted orange doublet in favor of one in blue velvet that didn't fit him very well.

"Platime," Sparhawk replied gravely. "You're looking quite natty this evening."

"Do you like it?" Platime plucked at the front of his doublet with a pleased expression. He turned a full circle, and Sparhawk noted several knife holes in the back of the thief's finery. "I've had my eye on it for several months now. I finally persuaded the former owner to part with it."

"Milord." Sparhawk bowed to Stragen.

"Sir Knight," Stragen responded, also bowing.

"All right, what's this all about, Sparhawk?" Platime demanded. "Talen was babbling some nonsense about forming up a home guard of some kind."

"Home guard. That's a good term," Sparhawk approved. "The Earl of Lenda will be along in a few moments, and then I'm sure her Majesty will make her entrance from that room over there—where she's probably listening at the door right now."

From the queen's bedchamber came the stamp of an angry foot.

"How's business been?" Sparhawk asked the gross leader of the underside for Cimmura.

"Quite good, actually." The fat man beamed. "Those foreign church soldiers the primate sent to prop up the bastard Lycheas were very innocent. We robbed them blind."

"Good. I always like to see friends get on in the world."

The door opened, and the ancient Earl of Lenda shuffled into the room. "Sorry to be late, Sparhawk," he apologized. "I'm not very good at running anymore."

"Quite all right, my Lord of Lenda," Sparhawk replied. "Gentlemen," he said to the two thieves, "I have the honor to present the Earl of Lenda, head of her Majesty's council of advisors. My Lord, these are the two men who will lead your home guard. This is Platime, and this, Milord Stragen from Emsat."

They all bowed—at least Platime *tried* to bow. "Milord?" Lenda asked Stragen curiously.

"An affectation, my Lord of Lenda," Stragen smiled ironically. "It's a carryover from a misspent youth."

"Stragen's one of the best," Platime put in. "He's got some strange ideas, but he does very well—better even than me some weeks."

"You're too kind, Platime," Stragen murmured with a bow.

Sparhawk crossed the room to the door to the queen's bedchamber. "We're all assembled, my Queen," he said through the panel.

There was a pause, and then Ehlana, wearing a pale blue satin gown and a discreet diamond tiara, entered. She stopped, looking around with a queenly bearing. "Your Majesty," Sparhawk said formally, "may I present Platime and Stragen, your generals?"

"Gentlemen," she said with a brief inclination of her head.

Platime tried to bow again, badly, but Stragen more than made up for it.

"Pretty little thing, isn't she?" Platime observed to his blond companion. Stragen winced.

Ehlana looked a bit startled. To cover the moment, she looked around the room. "But where are our other friends?" she asked.

"They've returned to the chapterhouse, my Queen," Sparhawk informed her. "They have preparations to make. Sephrenia promised to come back later, though." He extended his arm and escorted her to a rather ornate chair by the window. She sat and carefully arranged the folds of her gown.

"May I?" Stragen said to Sparhawk.

Sparhawk looked puzzled.

Stragen went to the window, nodding to Ehlana as he passed, and drew the heavy drapes. She stared at him. "It's most imprudent to sit with one's back to an open window in a world where there are crossbows, your Majesty," he explained with another bow. "You have many enemies, you know."

"The palace is totally secure, Milord Stragen," Lenda objected.

"Do you want to tell him?" Stragen wearily asked Platime.

"My Lord of Lenda," the fat man said politely, "I could get thirty men inside the palace grounds in about ten minutes. Knights are all very well on a battlefield, I suppose, but it's hard to look up when you're wearing a helmet. In my youth, I studied the art of burglary. A good burglar is as much at home on a rooftop as he is on a street." He sighed. "Those were the days," he reminisced. "There's nothing like a nice neat burglary to set the pulse to racing."

"But it might be a bit difficult for a man weighing twenty-one stone," Stragen added. "Even a slate roof can only hold so much weight."

"I'm not really all *that* fat, Stragen."

"Of course not."

Ehlana looked genuinely alarmed. "What are you doing to me, Sparhawk?" she asked.

"Protecting you, my Queen," he replied. "Annias wants you dead. He's already proved that. As soon as he finds out about your recovery, he'll try again. The men he sends to kill you won't be gentlemen. They won't leave their cards with the footman at the door when they come to call. Between them, Platime and Milord Stragen know just about everything there is to know about slipping into places unobserved, and they'll be able to take the proper steps."

"We can guarantee your Majesty that no one will get past us alive," Stragen assured her in his beautiful deep voice. "We'll try not to inconvenience you overly, but there'll be certain restrictions on your freedom of movement, I'm afraid."

"Such as not sitting near an open window?"

"Precisely. We'll draw up a list of suggestions and pass them on to you through the Earl of Lenda. Platime and I are men of business, and your Majesty might find our presence distressing. We'll remain in the background as much as possible."

"Your delicacy is exquisite, Milord," she told him, "but I'm not all that much distressed by the presence of honest men."

"Honest?" Platime laughed coarsely. "I think we've just been insulted, Stragen."

"Better an honest cutthroat than a dishonest courtier," Ehlana said. "Do you really do that? Cut throats, I mean?"

"I've slit a few in my time, your Majesty," he admitted with a shrug. "It's a quiet way to find out what a man has in his purse, and I've always been curious about that sort of thing. Speaking of that, you might as well tell her, Talen."

"What's this?" Sparhawk asked.

"There's a small fee involved, Sparhawk," Talen said.

"Oh?"

"Stragen volunteered his services free of charge," the boy explained.

"Just for the experience, Sparhawk," the blond northerner said. "King Wargun's court is a bit crude. The court of Elenia is reputed to be exquisitely courteous and totally depraved. A studious man always seizes these opportunities to expand his education. Platime, on the other hand, is not quite so studious. He wants something a little more tangible."

"Such as?" Sparhawk bluntly asked the fat man.

"I'm beginning to give some thought to retirement, Sparhawk—some quiet country estate where I can entertain myself in the company of a bevy of immoral young women—begging your Majesty's pardon. Anyway, a man can't really enjoy his declining years if there are a number of hanging offenses lurking in his background. I'll protect the queen with my life if she can find it in her heart to grant me a full pardon for my past indiscretions."

"Just what sort of indiscretions are we talking about here, Master Platime?" Ehlana asked suspiciously.

"Oh, nothing really worth mentioning, your Majesty," he replied deprecatingly. "There were a few incidental murders, assorted thefts, robberies, extortions, burglaries, arson, smuggling, highway robbery, cattle rustling, pillaging a couple of monasteries, operating unlicensed brothels—that sort of thing."

"You *have* been busy, haven't you, Platime?" Stragen said admiringly.

"It's a way to pass the time. I think we'd better just make it a general pardon, your Majesty. I'm bound to forget a few offenses here and there."

"Is there any crime you *haven't* committed, Master Platime?" she asked sternly.

"Barratry, I think, your Majesty. Of course I'm not sure what it means, so I can't be entirely positive."

"It's when a ship captain wrecks his ship in order to steal the cargo," Stragen supplied.

"No, I've never done that. Also, I've never had carnal knowledge of an animal, I've never practiced witchcraft, and I've never committed treason."

"Those are the more really serious ones, I suppose," Ehlana said with a perfectly straight face. "I *do* so worry about the morals of foolish young sheep."

Platime roared with sudden laughter. "I do, myself, your Majesty. I've spent whole nights tossing and turning about it."

"What kept you untainted by treason, Master Platime?" the Earl of Lenda asked curiously.

"Lack of opportunity, probably, my Lord," Platime admitted, "although I rather doubt I'd have gone into that sort of thing anyway. Unstable governments make the general populace nervous and wary. They start protecting their valuables, and that makes life very hard for thieves. Well, your Majesty, do we have a bargain?"

"A general pardon in exchange for your services? For so long as I require them?" she countered.

"What's that last bit supposed to mean?" he demanded suspiciously.

"Oh, nothing at all, Master Platime," she said innocently. "I don't want you to get bored and abandon me just when I need you the most. I'd be desolate without your company. Well?"

"Done, by God!" he roared. He spat in his hand and held it out to her.

She looked at Sparhawk, her face confused.

"It's a custom, your Majesty," he explained. "You also spit in your hand, and then you and Platime smack your palms together. It seals the bargain."

She cringed slightly, then did as he instructed. "Done," she said uncertainly.

"And there we are," Platime said boisterously. "You're now the same as my very own little sister, Ehlana, and if anybody offends you, or threatens you, I'll gut him for you, and then you can pour hot coals into his gaping belly with your own two little hands."

"You're so very kind," she said weakly.

"You've been had, Platime." Talen howled with laughter.

"What are you talking about?" Platime's face darkened.

"You've just volunteered for a lifetime of government service, you know."

"That's absurd."

"I know, but you did it all the same. You agreed to serve the queen for as long as she wants you to, and you didn't even raise the question of pay. She can keep you here in the palace until the day you die."

Platime's face went absolutely white. "You wouldn't do that to me, would you, Ehlana?" he pleaded in a choked voice.

She reached up and patted his bearded cheek. "We'll see, Platime," she said. "We'll see."

Stragen was doubled over with silent laughter. "What's this homeguard business, Sparhawk?" he asked when he had recovered.

"We're going to mobilize the common people to defend the city," Sparhawk said. "As soon as Kurik gets here, we'll work out the details. He suggested that we round up army veterans and press them into service as sergeants and corporals. Platime's men can serve as junior officers, and you and Platime, under the direction of the Earl of Lenda, will act as our generals until the regular Elenian army returns to relieve you."

Stragen thought it over. "It's a workable plan," he approved. "It doesn't take nearly as much training to defend a city as it does to attack one." He looked at his large, crestfallen friend. "If it's all right, your Majesty," he said to Ehlana, "I'll take your protector here someplace and pour some ale into him. He looks a trifle distraught for some reason."

"As you wish, Milord." She smiled. "Can you think of any crimes *you* might have committed in my kingdom you'd like to have me pardon—on the same terms?"

"Ah, no, your Majesty," he replied. "The thieves' code forbids my poaching in Platime's private preserve. If it weren't for that, I'd rush out and murder somebody—just for the sake of spending the rest of my life in your divine company." His eyes were wicked.

"You're a very bad man, Milord Stragen."

"Yes, your Majesty," he agreed, bowing. "Come along, Platime. It won't seem nearly so bad once you get used to it."

"That was very, very slick, your Majesty," Talen said after they had left. "Nobody's *ever* swindled Platime that way before."

"Did you really like it?" She sounded pleased.

"It was brilliant, my Queen. Now I can see why Annias poisoned you. You're a very dangerous woman."

She beamed at Sparhawk. "Aren't you proud of me, dear?"

"I think your kingdom's safe, Ehlana. I just hope the other monarchs are on their guard, that's all."

"Would you excuse me for a moment?" she asked, looking at her still-moist palm. "I'd like to go wash my hands."

It was not long afterward when Vanion gravely led the others into the Queen's sitting room. The preceptor bowed perfunctorily to Ehlana. "Have you talked with Platime yet?" he asked Sparhawk.

"It's all arranged," Sparhawk assured him.

"Good. We're going to have to ride to Demos tomorrow morning. Dolmant sent word that Archprelate Cluvonus is on his deathbed. He won't last out the week."

Sparhawk sighed. "We knew it was coming," he said. "Thank God we had time to take care of things here before it happened. Platime and Stragen are somewhere in the palace, Kurik—drinking, probably. You'd better get together with them and work out some kind of organizational plans."

"Right," the squire said.

"A moment, Master Kurik," the Earl of Lenda said. "How are you feeling, your Majesty?" he asked Ehlana.

"I'm fine, my Lord."

"Do you think you're strong enough to make a public appearance?"

"Of course, Lenda. I'm perfectly all right."

"Good. Once our generals and Master Kurik have gathered up our home guard, I think a few short speeches from you might go a long way toward firing them up—appeals to their patriotism, denunciations of the church soldiers, a few veiled references to the perfidy of the Primate Annias, that sort of thing."

"Of course, Lenda," she agreed. "I like to make speeches anyway."

"You'll have to stay here until you've got things all set up," Sparhawk said to Kurik. "You can join us in Chyrellos when Cimmura's secure."

Kurik nodded and quietly left.

"That's a very good man, Sparhawk," Ehlana said.

"Yes."

Sephrenia had been looking critically at the rosy-cheeked queen. "Ehlana," she said.

"Yes?"

"You really shouldn't pinch your cheeks like that to make them pink, you know. You'll bruise your skin. You're very fair, and your skin is delicate."

Ehlana blushed. Then she laughed ruefully. "It *is* a bit vain, isn't it?"

"You're a queen, Ehlana," the Styric woman told her, "not a milkmaid. Fair skin is more regal."

"Why do I always feel like a child when I'm talking with her?" Ehlana asked no one in particular.

"We all do, your Majesty," Vanion assured her.

"What's happening in Chyrellos right now?" Sparhawk asked his friend. "Did Dolmant give you any details?"

"Annias controls the streets," Vanion replied. "He hasn't done anything overt yet, but his soldiers are letting themselves be seen. Dolmant thinks he'll try to call for the election before Cluvonus is even cold. Dolmant has friends, and they're going to try to stall things until we get there, but there's only so much they'll be able to do. Speed is vital now. When we rejoin the other orders, there'll be four hundred of us. We'll be outnumbered, but our presence should be felt. There's something else, too. Otha's crossed the border into Lamorkand. He's not advancing yet, but he's issuing ultimatums. He's demanding the return of Bhelliom."

"Return? He never had it."

"Typical diplomatic flimflammery, Sparhawk," the Earl of Lenda explained. "The weaker your position, the bigger the lie you tell." The old man pursed his lips thoughtfully. "We know—or at least we can presume—that there's an alliance between Otha and Annias, right?"

"Yes," Vanion agreed.

"Annias knows—or should—that our tactic to counter him will be to play for time. Otha's move at this point gives the election a certain urgency. Annias will argue that the Church must be united to face the threat. Otha's presence on the border will terrify the more timid members of the Hierocracy, and they'll rush to confirm Annias. Then both he and Otha will get what they want. It's very clever, actually."

"Did Otha go so far as to mention Bhelliom by name?" Sparhawk asked.

Vanion shook his head. "He's accused you of stealing one of the national treasures of Zemoch, that's all. He left it rather deliberately vague. Too many people know about the significance of Bhelliom. He can't really come right out and mention it by name."

"It's fitting together more and more tightly," Lenda said. "Annias will declare that only *he* knows a way to make Otha withdraw. He'll stampede the Hierocracy into electing him. Then he'll wrest Bhelliom from Sparhawk and deliver it to Otha as a part of their bargain."

"It's going to take quite a bit of 'wresting,' " Kalten said bleakly. "The militant orders will all fall into line behind Sparhawk."

"That's probably what Annias hopes you'll do," Lenda told him. "Then he'll have every justification for disbanding the militant orders. Most of the Church Knights will obey the archprelate's command to disband. The rest of you will be outlaws, and Annias will let the commons know that you're keeping the one thing that will stave off Otha. As I said, it's very clever."

"Sparhawk," Ehlana said in a ringing voice, "when you get to Chyrellos, I want Annias apprehended on the charge of high treason. I want him delivered to me in chains. Bring Arissa and Lycheas as well."

"Lycheas is already here, my Queen."

"I know that. Take him with you to Demos and imprison him with his mother. I want him to have plenty of time to describe the present circumstances to Arissa."

"It's a useful idea, your Majesty," Vanion said delicately, "but we'll hardly have enough force in Chyrellos to take Annias into custody right at first."

"I know that, Lord Vanion, but if the arrest warrant and the specification of charges is delivered to Patriarch Dolmant, it may help him in delaying the election. He can always call for a Church investigation of the charges, and those things take time."

Lenda rose and bowed to Sparhawk. "My boy," he said, "no matter what else you may have done or may yet do, your finest work sits upon that throne. I'm proud of you, Sparhawk."

"I think we'd better start moving," Vanion said. "We've got a lot of preparations to make."

"I'll have copies of the warrant for the primate's arrest in your hands by the third hour after midnight, Lord Vanion," Lenda promised, "along with a number of others. We have a splendid opportunity here to clean up the kingdom. Let's not waste it."

"Berit," Sparhawk said. "My armor's in that room over there. Take it back to the chapterhouse—if you would, please. I think I'm going to need it."

"Of course, Sir Sparhawk." Berit's eyes, however, were still flat and unfriendly.

"Stay a moment, Sparhawk," Ehlana said as they all started toward the door. He dropped behind the others and waited until the door closed.

"Yes, my Queen," he said.

"You must be so very, very careful, my beloved," she said with her heart in her eyes. "I'd die if I lost you now." Mutely, she held out her arms to him.

He crossed to where she sat and embraced her. Her kiss was fierce. "Go quickly, Sparhawk," she said in a voice near to tears. "I don't want you to see me crying."

# CHAPTER SEVEN

They left for Demos shortly after sunrise the following morning, riding at a jingling trot with a forest of pennon-tipped lances strung out behind them as the hundred Pandions rode resolutely eastward.

"It's a good day to be on the road," Vanion said, looking around at the sun-drenched fields. "I just wish . . . oh, well."

"How are you feeling now, Vanion?" Sparhawk asked his old friend.

"Much better," the preceptor replied. "I'll be honest with you, Sparhawk. Those swords were very, *very* heavy. They gave me some fairly strong hints of what it's going to be like to grow old."

"You'll live forever, my friend." Sparhawk smiled.

"I certainly *hope* not, not if it means feeling the way I felt when I was carrying those swords."

They rode on in silence for a while.

"This is a long chance, Vanion," Sparhawk said somberly. "We're going to be badly outnumbered in Chyrellos, and if Otha starts across Lamorkand, it's going to be a close race between him and Wargun. Whichever one gets to Chyrellos first will win."

"I think we're getting very close to one of those articles of faith, Sparhawk.

We're going to have to trust God in this. I'm sure he doesn't want Annias to be arch-prelate, and I'm *very* sure he doesn't want Otha in the streets of Chyrellos."

"Let's hope not."

Berit and Talen were riding not far behind. Over the months, a certain friendship had grown up between the novice and the young thief, a friendship based in part upon the fact that they were both a bit uncomfortable in the presence of their elders.

"Exactly what's this election business all about, Berit?" Talen asked. "What I'm getting at is, how does it work exactly? I'm a little shaky on that sort of thing."

Berit straightened in his saddle. "All right, Talen," he said, "when the old arch-prelate dies, the patriarchs of the Hierocracy gather in the Basilica. Most of the other high churchmen are there as well, and the kings of Eosia are usually also present. Each of the kings makes a short speech at the beginning, but no one else is permitted to speak during the Hierocracy's deliberations—only the patriarchs, and they're the only ones who have votes."

"You mean that the preceptors can't even vote?"

"The preceptors *are* patriarchs, young man," Perraine said from just behind them.

"I didn't know that. I wondered why everybody sort of stepped aside for the Church Knights. How is it that Annias is running the Church in Cimmura then? Where's the patriarch?"

"Patriarch Udale is ninety-three years old, Talen," Berit explained. "He's still alive, but we're not sure he even knows his own name. He's being cared for in the Pandion motherhouse at Demos."

"That makes it difficult for Annias, doesn't it? As a primate, he can't talk—or vote, and there's no way he can poison this Udale if he's in the motherhouse—not without being fairly obvious."

"That's why he needs money. He has to buy people to do his talking—and his voting—for him."

"Wait a minute. Annias is only a primate, isn't he?"

"That's right."

Talen frowned. "If he's only a primate and the others are patriarchs, how does he think he stands a chance at election?"

"A churchman doesn't have to be a patriarch to ascend the throne of the Church. On several occasions, some simple village priest has become the arch-prelate."

"It's all very complicated, isn't it? Wouldn't it just be simpler for us to move in with the army and put the man we want on the throne?"

"That's been tried in the past. It never really worked out. I don't think God approves."

"He'll approve a lot less if Annias wins, won't he?"

"There could be something to what you say, Talen."

Tynian rode forward, and there was a grin on his broad face. "Kalten and Ulath are amusing themselves by terrorizing Lycheas," he said. "Ulath's been lopping off saplings with his ax, and Kalten's coiled a noose. He's been pointing out overhanging tree limbs to Lycheas. Lycheas keeps fainting. We had to chain his hands to his saddlebow to keep him from falling out of his saddle."

"Kalten and Ulath are simple fellows," Sparhawk observed. "It doesn't take much to keep them amused. Lycheas will have a great deal to tell his mother when we get to Demos."

About midday, they turned southeast to ride across country. The weather held fair. They made good time and reached Demos late the following day. Just before the column swung south toward the encampment of the knights of the other three orders, Sparhawk, Kalten, and Ulath took Lycheas around the northern edge of town to the cloister in which Princess Arissa was confined. The cloister had yellow sandstone walls, and it stood in a wooded glen where birds sang from the limbs in the late afternoon sunshine.

Sparhawk and his friends dismounted at the gate and rather roughly jerked the chained Lycheas from his saddle.

"We'll need to speak with your mother superior," Sparhawk told the gentle little nun who opened the gate for them. "Is Princess Arissa still spending most of her time in that garden near the south wall?"

"Yes, my Lord."

"Please ask the mother superior to join us there. We're delivering Arissa's son to her." He took Lycheas by the scruff of the neck and dragged him across the courtyard toward the walled garden where Arissa spent her long hours of confinement. Sparhawk was coldly angry for a number of reasons.

"Mother!" Lycheas cried when he saw her. He broke free from Sparhawk and stumbled toward her, his imploring hands hampered by his chains.

Princess Arissa came to her feet, her face outraged. The circles under her eyes had lessened, and her look of sullen discontent had faded, to be replaced by one of smug anticipation. "What's the meaning of this?" she demanded, embracing her cowering son.

"They threw me in the dungeon, Mother," Lycheas blubbered, "and they've been threatening me."

"How *dare* you treat the Prince Regent so, Sparhawk?" she burst out.

"The situation has greatly changed, Princess," Sparhawk informed her coolly. "Your son isn't prince regent any more."

"No one has the authority to depose him. You'll pay for this with your life, Sparhawk."

"I sort of doubt that, Arissa," Kalten disagreed with a broad grin. "I'm sure you'll be delighted to hear that your niece has recovered from her illness."

"Ehlana? That's impossible!"

"As a matter of fact, it isn't. I know that as a true daughter of the Church, you'll join with us all in praising God for his miraculous intervention. The royal council almost swooned with delight. The Baron Harparin was so pleased that he completely lost his head."

"But no one ever recovers from—" She bit her lip.

"From the effects of darestim?" Sparhawk completed her sentence for her.

"How did you—"

"It wasn't really all that hard, Arissa. It's all falling apart on you, Princess. The queen was most displeased with you and your son—and the Primate Annias as well, of course. She's commanded us to take the three of you into custody. You can consider yourself under arrest at this point."

"On what charge?" she exclaimed.

"High treason, wasn't it, Kalten?"

"I think those were the words the queen used, yes. I'm sure it's all a misunderstanding, your Highness." The blond man smirked at Queen Ehlana's aunt. "You, your son, and the good primate should have no trouble explaining things at your trial."

"Trial?" Her face blanched.

"I think that's the normal procedure, Princess. Ordinarily, we'd have just hanged your son and then you as well, but you both have a certain eminence in the kingdom, so certain necessary formalities are in order."

"That's absurd!" Arissa cried. "I'm a princess. I can't be charged with such a crime."

"You might try to explain that to Ehlana," Kalten replied. "I'm sure she'll listen carefully to your arguments—before she passes sentence."

"You'll also be charged with the murder of your brother, Arissa," Sparhawk added. "Princess or not, that alone would be enough to hang you. But we're a bit pressed for time. I'm sure your son will be able to explain it all to you in greater detail."

An aged nun entered the garden, her expression disapproving at the presence of men within her walls.

"Ah, Mother Superior," Sparhawk greeted her with a bow. "By order of the crown, I'm to confine these two criminals until they can be brought to trial. Do you by chance have penitents' cells within your walls?"

"I'm sorry, Sir Knight," the mother superior said very firmly, "but the rules of our order forbid confining penitents against their will."

"That's all right, Mother." Ulath smiled. "We'll take care of it. We'd sooner die than offend the ladies of the Church. I can assure you that the princess and her son will be unwilling to leave their cells—both of them being so engulfed in repentance, you understand. Let's see, I'll need a couple of lengths of chain, some stout bolts, a hammer, and an anvil. I'll close up those cells with no trouble whatsoever, and you and your good sisters won't need to concern yourselves with politics." He paused and looked at Sparhawk. "Or did you want me to chain them to the walls?"

Sparhawk actually considered it. "No," he decided finally, "probably not. They're still members of the royal family, and certain courtesies are involved."

"I have no choice but to accede to your demands, Sir Knights," the mother superior said. She paused. "There are rumors abroad that the queen has recovered," she said. "Can that possibly be true?"

"Yes, Mother Superior," Sparhawk told her. "The queen is well, and the government of Elenia is once again in her hands."

"Praise God!" the old nun exclaimed. "And will you soon be removing our unwanted guests from within our walls?"

"Soon, Mother. Very soon."

"We shall cleanse the chambers the princess has contaminated then—and offer prayers for her soul, of course."

"Of course."

"How very, very touching," Arissa said sardonically, appearing to have slightly recovered. "If this grows any more cloying, I think I'll vomit."

"You're starting to irritate me, Arissa," Sparhawk said coldly. "I don't recommend it. If I weren't under the queen's orders, I'd strike off your head here and now. I'd advise you to make your peace with God, because I'm quite sure you'll be meeting him face to face before long." He looked at her with extreme distaste. "Get her out of my sight," he told Kalten and Ulath.

About fifteen minutes later, Kalten and Ulath came back from within the cloister.

"All secure?" Sparhawk asked them.

"It'd take a blacksmith an hour to open those cell doors," Kalten replied. "Shall we go then?"

They had gone no more than a half mile when Ulath suddenly shouted, "Look out, Sparhawk!" and roughly shoved the big Pandion from his saddle.

The crossbow bolt whizzed through the empty air where Sparhawk had been an instant before and buried itself to the vanes in a tree at the roadside.

Kalten's sword came whistling from its sheath, and he spurred his horse in the direction from which the bolt had come.

"Are you all right?" Ulath asked, dismounting to help Sparhawk to his feet.

"A little bruised is all. You push very firmly, my friend."

"I'm sorry, Sparhawk. I got excited."

"Perfectly all right, Ulath. Push as hard as you like when these things happen. How did you see the bolt coming?"

"Pure luck. I happened to be looking that way, and I saw the bushes move."

Kalten was swearing when he rode back. "He got away," he reported.

"I'm getting *very* tired of that fellow," Sparhawk said, pulling himself back into the saddle.

"You think it might be the same one who took a shot at you back in Cimmura?" Kalten asked him.

"This isn't Lamorkand, Kalten. There isn't a crossbow standing in the corner of every kitchen in the kingdom." He thought about it for a moment. "Let's not make an issue of this when we see Vanion again," he suggested. "I can sort of take care of myself, and he's got enough on his mind already."

"I think it's a mistake, Sparhawk," Kalten said dubiously, "but it's your skin, so we'll do it your way."

The knights of the four orders were waiting in a well-concealed encampment a league or so to the south of Demos. Sparhawk and his friends were directed to the pavilion where their friends were conversing with Preceptor Abriel of the Cyrinic Knights, Preceptor Komier of the Genidians, and Preceptor Darellon of the Alciones. "How did Princess Arissa take the news?" Vanion asked.

"She was moderately discontented about it all." Kalten smirked. "She wanted to make a speech, but since about all she really wanted to say was 'You can't do this,' we cut her off."

"You did *what?*" Vanion exclaimed.

"Oh, not that way, my Lord Vanion," Kalten apologized. "Poor choice of words there, perhaps."

"Say what you mean, Kalten," Vanion told him. "This is no time for misunderstandings."

"I wouldn't actually behead the princess, Lord Vanion."

"*I* would," Ulath muttered.

"May we see the Bhelliom?" Komier asked Sparhawk.

Sparhawk looked at Sephrenia, and she nodded, although a bit dubiously.

Sparhawk reached inside his surcoat and removed the canvas pouch. He untied the drawstring, then shook the sapphire rose out into his hand. It had been several days since he felt even the faintest twinge of that shadowy, unnamed dread, but it returned once again as soon as his eyes touched the petals of the jewel, and once again that shapeless shadow, even darker and larger now, flickered just beyond his field of vision.

"Dear God," Preceptor Abriel gasped.

"That's it, all right," the Thalesian Komier grunted. "Get it out of sight, Sparhawk."

"But—" Preceptor Darellon protested.

"Did you want to keep your soul, Darellon?" Komier asked bluntly. "If you do, don't look at that thing for more than a few seconds."

"Put it away, Sparhawk," Sephrenia said.

"Have we had any news about what Otha's doing?" Kalten asked as Sparhawk dropped Bhelliom back into its pouch.

"He appears to be holding firm at the border," Abriel replied. "Vanion told us about the confession of the bastard Lycheas. It's very likely that Annias has asked Otha to stand on the border making menacing noises. Then the Primate of Cimmura can claim that he knows a way to stop the Zemochs. That should sway a few votes his way."

"Do we think that Otha knows Sparhawk's got Bhelliom?" Ulath asked.

"Azash does," Sephrenia said, "and that means Otha does as well. Whether the news reached Annias yet is anybody's guess."

"What's happening in Chyrellos?" Sparhawk asked Vanion.

"The latest word we have is that Archprelate Cluvonus is still hanging on by a thread. There's no way we can hide the fact that we're coming, so we're just going to bull our way on through to Chyrellos. There's been a change of plans now that Otha's made his move. We want to reach Chyrellos *before* Cluvonus dies. It's obvious that Annias is going to try to force the election as soon as he can now. He can't really start giving orders until after that. Once Cluvonus dies, though, the patriarchs Annias controls can start calling for votes. Probably the first thing they'll vote on is sealing the city. That won't be a matter of substance, so Annias probably has the votes to get it passed."

"Can Dolmant make any kind of estimate about how the vote stands just now?" Sparhawk asked.

"It's close, Sir Sparhawk," Preceptor Abriel told him. Abriel was the leader of the Cyrinic Knights in Arcium. He was a solidly built man in his sixties with silvery hair and an ascetic expression. "A fair number of patriarchs aren't in Chyrellos."

"A tribute to the efficiency of Annias' assassins," the Thalesian Komier said dryly.

"Most probably," Abriel agreed. "At any rate, there are one hundred and thirty-two patriarchs in Chyrellos right now."

"Out of how many?" Kalten asked.

"One hundred and sixty-eight."

"Why such an odd number?" Talen asked curiously.

"It was arranged that way, young man," Abriel explained. "The number was selected so that it would take one hundred votes to elect a new archprelate."

"One hundred and sixty-seven would have been closer," Talen said after a moment.

"To what?" Kalten asked.

"The hundred votes. You see, one hundred votes is sixty percent of—" Talen looked at Kalten's uncomprehending expression. "Ah—never mind, Kalten," he said. "I'll explain later."

"Can you come up with those numbers in your head, boy?" Komier asked with some surprise. "We've wasted a bale of paper grinding out computations, then."

"It's a trick, my Lord," Talen said modestly. "In my business you sometimes have to deal with numbers very rapidly. Could I ask how many votes Annias has right now?"

"Sixty-five," Ariel replied, "either firm or strongly leaning toward him."

"And we have?"

"Fifty-eight."

"Nobody wins, then. He needs thirty-five more votes, and we need forty-two."

"It's not quite that simple, I'm afraid." Abriel sighed. "The procedure set down by the Church fathers says that it takes one hundred votes—or a like proportion of those present and voting—to elect a new archprelate, or to decide all matters of substance."

"And *that's* what used up that bale of paper," Komier said sourly.

"All right," Talen said after a moment's thought. "Annias only needs eighty votes then, but he's still fifteen short." He frowned. "Wait a minute," he said. "Your numbers don't add up. You've only accounted for one hundred and twenty-three votes, and you said there were one hundred and thirty-two patriarchs in Chyrellos."

"Nine of the patriarchs have still not decided," Abriel told him. "Dolmant suspects that they're just holding out for bigger bribes. There are votes from time to time on nonsubstantive matters. In those cases, it only takes a simple majority to win. Sometimes the nine will vote with Annias and sometimes they won't. They're demonstrating their power to him. They'll vote to their own advantage, I'm afraid."

"Even if they all vote with Annias every time, they still won't make any difference," Talen said. "No matter how you stretch nine votes, you can't turn them into fifteen."

"But he doesn't need fifteen," Preceptor Darellon said wearily. "Because of all the assassinations and all the church soldiers in the streets of Chyrellos, seventeen of the patriarchs opposed to Annias have gone into hiding somewhere in the Holy City. They aren't present and voting, and that changes the numbers."

"This is beginning to make my head ache," Kalten said to Ulath.

Talen was shaking his head. "I think we're in trouble, my Lords," he said. "Without those seventeen to raise the total, the number to win is sixty-nine. Annias only needs four more votes."

"And as soon as he can come up with enough money to satisfy four of those nine holdouts, he'll win," Sir Bevier said. "The boy's right, my Lords. We're in trouble."

"We have to change the numbers, then," Sparhawk said.

"How do you change numbers?" Kalten asked. "A number is a number. You can't change it."

"You can if you add to it. What we have to do when we get to Chyrellos is find those seventeen patriarchs who are hiding and get them safely back to the Basilica to vote. That would bring the number Annias needs to win back up to eighty, and he can't reach that number."

"But neither can we," Tynian pointed out. "Even if we brought them back, we'd still only have fifty-eight votes."

"Sixty-two actually, Sir Tynian," Berit corrected respectfully. "The preceptors of the four orders are also patriarchs, and I don't think any of them would vote for Annias, would you, my Lords?"

"That changes the number again," Talen said. "Add the seventeen and the four, and the total is one hundred and thirty-six. That raises the number needed to win to eighty-two—eighty-one and a fraction, actually."

"An unreachable number for either side," Komier said in a gloomy voice. "There's still no way we can win."

"We don't have to win the vote to come out on top, Komier," Vanion said. "We're not trying to elect anybody. All we're trying to do is keep Annias *off* the throne. We can win with a stalemate." Sparhawk's friend rose to his feet and began to pace up and down in the pavilion. "As soon as we reach Chyrellos, we'll have Dolmant send a message to Wargun down in Arcium declaring that there's a religious crisis in the Holy City. That will put Wargun under *our* orders. We'll include a command signed by the four of us that he's to suspend his operations in Arcium and ride for Chyrellos with all possible speed. If Otha starts to move, we're going to need him there anyway."

"How are we going to get enough votes for such a declaration?" Preceptor Darellon asked.

"I wasn't planning to put it to a vote, my friend." Vanion smiled thinly. "Dolmant's reputation will convince Patriarch Bergsten that the declaration is official, and Bergsten can order Wargun to march on Chyrellos. We can apologize for the misunderstanding later. By then, though, Wargun will be in Chyrellos with the combined armies of the west."

"Less the Elenian army," Sparhawk insisted. "My queen is sitting in Cimmura with only a pair of thieves to protect her."

"I'm not trying to offend you, Sir Sparhawk," Darellon said, "but that's hardly crucial at this point."

"I'm not so sure, Darellon," Vanion disagreed. "Annias desperately needs money right now. He has to have access to the Elenian treasury—not only to bribe the remaining nine, but also to keep the votes he already has. It wouldn't take too many defections to put the throne completely out of his reach. Protecting Ehlana—and her treasury—is even more vital now than it was before."

"Perhaps you're right, Vanion," Darellon conceded. "I hadn't thought of that, I guess."

"All right, then," Vanion continued his analysis, "when Wargun reaches Chyrellos with his forces, the balance of power in the Holy City shifts. Annias' grip on his adherents is fairly tenuous as it is, and I'd guess that in many cases it's based rather strongly on the fact that his soldiers control the streets. As soon as that changes, I think a goodly part of his support will begin to dissolve. As I see it, gentlemen, our job is to reach Chyrellos before Cluvonus dies, get that message off to Wargun, and then start rounding up the patriarchs who are in hiding so that we can get them back into the Basilica to participate in the voting." He looked at Talen. "How many do we need—what's the absolute minimum we need to keep Annias from winning?"

"If he can somehow get those nine, he'll have seventy-four votes, my Lord. If we can find six of the ones in hiding, the total number voting will be one hundred and twenty-five. Sixty percent of that is seventy-five. He loses at that point."

"Very good, Talen," Vanion said. "That's it, then, gentlemen. We go to Chyrellos, take the city apart, and find six patriarchs who are willing to vote against Annias. We nominate somebody—anybody—to stand for election and we keep taking votes until Wargun arrives."

"It's still not the same as winning, Vanion," Komier grumbled.

"It's the next best thing," Vanion replied.

Sparhawk's sleep was restless that night. The darkness seemed filled with vague cries and moans and a sense of unnamed terror. Finally he rose from his bed, threw on a monk's robe, and went looking for Sephrenia.

As he had half expected, he found her sitting in the doorway of her tent with her teacup in her hands. "Don't you ever sleep?" he asked, with some irritation.

"Your dreams are keeping me awake, dear one."

"You know what I'm dreaming?" He was astounded.

"Not the details, but I know something's upsetting you."

"I saw the shadow again when I showed Bhelliom to Vanion and the other preceptors."

"Is that what's disturbing you?"

"In part. Someone took a shot at me with a crossbow when Ulath, Kalten, and I were coming here from the cloister where Arissa's confined."

"But that was *before* you took Bhelliom out of the pouch. Maybe the incidents aren't linked after all."

"Maybe the shadow saves them up—or maybe it can see them coming in the future. It might be that the shadow doesn't need to have me touch Bhelliom in order to send somebody to kill me."

"Does Elene logic usually involve so many maybes?"

"No, it doesn't, and that bothers me a little bit. It doesn't bother me enough to make me discard the hypothesis, though. Azash has been sending things to kill me for quite some time now, little mother, and they've all had some sort of supernatural quality about them. This shadow that I keep catching a glimpse of obviously isn't natural, or you'd have been able to see it, too."

"That's true, I suppose."

"Then I'd be sort of foolish to drop my guard just because I can't *prove* that Azash sent the shadow, wouldn't I?"

"Probably, yes."

"Even though I can't actually prove it, I *know* that there's some kind of connection between Bhelliom and that flicker in the corner of my eye. I don't know what the connection is just yet, and maybe that's why some random incidents seem to be clouding the issue. To be on the safe side, though, I'm going to assume the worst—that the shadow belongs to Azash and it's following Bhelliom and it's sending humans to kill me."

"That makes sense."

"I'm glad you approve."

"You'd already made up your mind about this, Sparhawk," she said to him, "so why did you come looking for me?"

"I needed to have you listen while I talked my way through it."

"I see."

"Besides, I like your company."

She smiled fondly at him. "You're such a good boy, Sparhawk. Now, why don't we talk about why you're keeping this last attempt on your life from Vanion?"

He sighed. "You *don't* approve of that, I see."

"No, as a matter of fact, I don't."

"I don't want him putting me in the middle of the column with armored knights holding their shields over me. I *have* to be able to see what's coming at me, Sephrenia. I'll start trying to claw my way out of my skin if I can't."

"Oh, dear," she sighed.

Faran was in a foul humor. A day and a half of nearly continual hard riding had made his disposition definitely take a turn for the worse. Some fifteen leagues from Chyrellos, the preceptors halted the column and ordered the knights to dismount and walk their horses for a time. Faran tried to bite Sparhawk three times as the big knight was climbing out of his saddle. The bites were more an indication of disapproval than any serious attempt to injure or maim; Faran had discovered early in life that biting his master when Sparhawk was wearing full armor only led to aching teeth. When the big roan half whirled and kicked Sparhawk solidly on the hip, however, Sparhawk felt it was time to take steps. With Kalten's help, he rose to his feet, pushed back his visor, and pulled himself hand over hand up the reins to glare directly into the ugly war horse's face. "Stop it!" he snapped.

Faran glared back at him with hate-filled eyes.

Sparhawk moved his hand very quickly and grasped the roan's left ear in his gauntleted fist. Grimly he began to twist.

Faran ground his teeth together, and tears actually appeared in his eyes. "Do we understand each other?" Sparhawk grated.

Faran kicked him in the knee with one forehoof.

"It's up to you, Faran," Sparhawk told him. "You're going to look ridiculous without that ear, though." He twisted harder until the horse grudgingly squealed in pain.

"Always nice talking with you, Faran," Sparhawk said, releasing the ear. Then he stroked the sweat-soaked neck. "You big old fool," he said gently. "Are you all right?"

Faran flicked his ears—his right one, anyway—with an ostentatious display of indifference.

"It's really necessary, Faran," Sparhawk explained. "I'm not riding you this hard for fun. It won't be much farther. Can I trust you now?"

Faran sighed and pawed at the ground with one forehoof.

"Good," Sparhawk said. "Let's walk for a ways."

"This is truly uncanny," Preceptor Abriel said to Vanion. "I've never seen horse and man so totally linked before."

"It's part of Sparhawk's advantage, my friend," Vanion said. "He's bad enough by himself, but when you put him on that horse, he turns into a natural disaster."

They walked for a mile or so, then remounted and rode on through the afternoon sunlight toward the Holy City.

It was nearly midnight when they crossed the wide bridge over the River Arruk and approached one of the west gates of Chyrellos. The gate, of course, was guarded by church soldiers. "I cannot grant you entry until sunrise, my Lords," the captain in charge of the guard detachment said firmly. "By order of the Hierocracy, no one under arms may enter Chyrellos during the hours of darkness."

Preceptor Komier reached for his ax.

"A moment, my friend," Preceptor Abriel cautioned mildly. "I believe there's a way to resolve this difficulty without unpleasantness. Captain," he addressed the red-tunicked soldier.

"Yes, my Lord?" The captain's voice was insultingly smug.

"This order you mentioned, does it apply to members of the Hierocracy itself?"

"My Lord?" The captain seemed confused.

"It's a simple question, Captain. A yes or a no will suffice. Does the order apply to the patriarchs of the Church?"

"No one may hinder a Church patriarch, my Lord," the captain floundered a bit.

"Your Grace," Abriel corrected.

The captain blinked stupidly.

"The correct form of address when speaking to a patriarch is 'your Grace,' Captain. By Church law, my three companions and I are, in fact, patriarchs of the Church. Form up your men, Captain. We will inspect them."

The captain hesitated.

"I speak for the Church, Lieutenant," Abriel said. "Will you defy her?"

"Uh—I'm a captain, your Grace," the man mumbled.

"You *were* a captain, Lieutenant, but not any more. Now, would you like to be a sergeant again? If not, you'll do as I say immediately."

"At once, your Grace," the shaken man replied. "You there!" he shouted. "All of you! Fall in and prepare for inspection!"

The appearance of the detachment at the gate was, in Preceptor—ah, should one say instead *Patriarch*?—Darellon's words, disgraceful. Reprimands were freely distributed in blistering terms, and then the column entered the Holy City without any further hindrance. There was no laughter—nor even any smiles—until the armored men were well out of earshot of the gates. The discipline of the Knights of the Church is the wonder of the known world.

Despite the lateness of the hour, the streets of Chyrellos were heavily patrolled by church soldiers. Sparhawk knew these kinds of men, and he knew that their loyalty was for sale. They served only for the pay in most cases. Because of their numbers here in the Holy City, they had become accustomed to behaving with a certain arrogant rudeness. The appearance of four hundred armored Church Knights in the streets at the ominous hour of midnight engendered what Sparhawk felt to be a becoming humility, however—at least among the common troops. It took the officers a bit longer to grasp the truth. It always does, somehow. One obnoxious young fellow tried to block their path, demanding to examine their documents. He seemed quite puffed up with his own importance and failed to look behind him. He was thus unaware of the fact that his troops had discreetly gone someplace else. He continued to deliver his peremptory commands in a shrill voice, demanding this and insisting on that until Sparhawk loosened Faran's reins and rode him down at a brisk walk. Faran made a special point of grinding steel-shod hooves into a number of sensitive places on the officer's body.

"Feel better now?" Sparhawk asked his horse.

Faran nickered wickedly.

"Kalten," Vanion said, "let's get started. Break the column up into groups of ten. Fan out through the city and let it be generally known that the Knights of the Church offer their protection to any patriarch desiring to go to the Basilica to participate in the voting."

"Yes, my Lord Vanion," Kalten said. "I'll go wake up the Holy City. I'm sure everybody is breathlessly waiting to hear the news I bring."

"Do you think there's any hope that someday he'll grow up?" Sparhawk said.

"I rather hope not," Vanion said gently. "No matter how old the rest of us get, we'll always have an eternal boy in our midst. That's sort of comforting, really."

The preceptors, followed by Sparhawk, his friends, and a twenty-man detachment under the command of Sir Perraine, proceeded along the broad avenue.

Dolmant's modest house was guarded by a platoon of soldiers, and Sparhawk recognized their officer as one loyal to the Patriarch of Demos. "Thank God!" the young man exclaimed as the knights reined in just outside Dolmant's gate.

"We were in the area and thought we'd stop by to pay a courtesy call," Vanion said with a dry smile. "His Grace has been well, I trust?"

"He'll be much better now that you and your friends are here, my Lord. It's been a bit tense here in Chyrellos."

"I can imagine. Is his Grace still awake?"

The officer nodded. "He's meeting with Emban, Patriarch of Ucera. Perhaps you know him, my Lord?"

"Heavy-set fellow—sort of jolly?"

"That's him, my Lord. I'll tell his Grace you've arrived."

Dolmant, Patriarch of Demos, was as lean and severe as always, but his ascetic face actually broke into a broad smile when the Church Knights trooped into his study. "You made good time, gentlemen," he told them. "You all know Emban, of course." He indicated his stout fellow patriarch.

Emban was definitely more than "heavy-set." "Your study's starting to resemble a foundry, Dolmant." He chuckled, looking around at the armored knights. "I haven't seen so much steel in one place in years."

"Comforting, though," Dolmant said.

"Oh, my, yes."

"How do things stand in Cimmura, Vanion?" Dolmant asked intently.

"I'm happy to report that Queen Ehlana has recovered and now has her government firmly in her own hands," Vanion replied.

"Thank God!" Emban exclaimed. "I think Annias just went into bankruptcy."

"You managed to find the Bhelliom, then?" Dolmant asked Sparhawk.

Sparhawk nodded. "Would you like to see it, your Grace?" he asked.

"I don't believe so, Sparhawk. I'm not supposed to admit its power, but I've heard some stories. Folklorish superstition no doubt—but let's not take any chances."

Sparhawk heaved an inward sigh of relief. He did not much fancy another encounter with that flickering shadow or the prospect of walking around for several days with the uneasy feeling that someone might be aiming a crossbow at him.

"It's peculiar that the news of the queen's recovery hasn't reached Annias yet," Dolmant observed. "At least he's shown no signs of chagrin so far."

"I'd be very surprised if he's heard of it yet, your Grace," Komier rumbled. "Vanion sealed the city to keep the Cimmurans at home. As I understand it, people who try to leave are turned back quite firmly."

"You didn't leave your Pandions there, did you, Vanion?"

"No, your Grace. We found assistance elsewhere. How's the archprelate?"

"Dying," Emban replied. "Of course, he's been dying for several years, but he's a little more serious about it this time."

"Is Otha making any more moves, your Grace?" Darellon asked.

Dolmant shook his head. "He's still encamped just inside the border of Lamorkand. He's making all kinds of threats and demanding that the mysterious Zemoch treasure be returned to him."

"It's not so mysterious, Dolmant," Sephrenia told him. "He wants Bhelliom, and he knows Sparhawk has it."

"Someone's bound to suggest that Sparhawk turn it over to him in order to prevent an invasion," Emban observed.

"That will never happen, your Grace," she said firmly. "We'll destroy it first."

"Have any of the patriarchs who were in hiding returned as yet?" Preceptor Abriel asked.

"Not a one," Emban snorted. "They're probably down the deepest ratholes they can find. Two of them had fatal accidents a couple of days ago, and the rest went to ground."

"We have knights scouring the city looking for them," Preceptor Darellon reported. "Even the most timid of rabbits might regain some degree of courage if they're protected by Church Knights."

"Darellon," Dolmant said reproachfully.

"Sorry, your Grace," Darellon said perfunctorily.

"Will that change the numbers?" Komier asked Talen. "The two that died, I mean?"

"No, my Lord," Talen said. "We weren't counting them anyway."

Dolmant looked puzzled.

"The lad has a gift for figures," Komier explained. "He can compute things in his head faster than I can with a pencil."

"Sometimes you amaze me, Talen," Dolmant said. "Could I perhaps interest you in a career in the Church?"

"Counting the contributions of the faithful, your Grace?" Talen asked eagerly.

"Ah—no, I don't think so, Talen."

"Have the votes changed at all, your Grace?" Abriel asked.

Dolmant shook his head. "Annias still has a simple majority. He can bull through anything that isn't a matter of substance. His toadies are calling for votes on just about anything that comes up. He wants to keep a running count, for one thing, and the voting keeps us all locked in the audience chamber."

"The numbers are about to change, your Grace," Komier said. "My friends and I have decided to participate this time."

"Now *that's* unusual," Patriarch Emban said. "The preceptors of the militant orders haven't participated in a vote of the Hierocracy for two hundred years."

"We're still welcome, aren't we, your Grace?"

"As far as I'm concerned you are, your Grace. Annias might not like it too much, though."

"How very unfortunate for him. What does that do to the numbers, Talen?"

"It just went up from sixty-nine votes to seventy-one and a fraction, my Lord Komier. That's the sixty percent Annias needs to win."

"And a simple majority?"

"He's still got that. He only needs sixty-one."

"I don't think any of the neutral patriarchs will go over to him on a matter of substance until he meets their price," Dolmant said. "They'll probably abstain, and then Annias needs—" He frowned, thinking hard.

"Sixty-six votes, your Grace," Talen supplied. "He's one vote short."

"Delightful boy," Dolmant murmured. "Our best course then is to make every vote a vote of substance—even a vote to light more candles."

"How do we do that?" Komier asked. "I'm a little rusty on the procedure."

Dolmant smiled faintly. "One of us rises to his feet and says 'substance.'"

"Won't we just be voted down?"

Emban chuckled. "Oh, no, my dear Komier," he said. "A vote on whether a question is a matter of substance or not is itself a matter of substance. I think we've got him, Dolmant. That one vote he doesn't have will keep him off the archprelate's throne."

"Unless he can get his hands on some money," Dolmant said, "or unless more patriarchs happen to die. How many of us does he have to kill in order to win, Talen?"

"All of you might help him a bit." Talen grinned.

"Mind your manners," Berit barked.

"Sorry," Talen apologized, "I should have added 'your Grace,' I suppose. Annias needs to reduce the total number voting by at least two in order to have the sixty percent he needs, your Grace."

"We'll have to assign knights to protect the loyal patriarchs, then," Abriel said, "and that's going to reduce the number out in the city trying to locate the missing members. It's starting to hinge on taking control of the streets. We need Wargun very badly."

Emban looked at him, puzzled.

"It's something we came up with at Demos, your Grace," Abriel explained. "Annias is intimidating patriarchs because Chyrellos is awash with church soldiers. If a patriarch—either you or Patriarch Dolmant—declares a religious crisis and orders Wargun to suspend operations down in Arcium and to bring his armies here to Chyrellos, the whole picture changes. The intimidation starts going the other way at that point."

"Abriel," Dolmant said in a pained voice, "we do not elect an archprelate by intimidation."

"We live in the real world, your Grace," Abriel replied. "Annias was the one who chose the rules of this game, so we're obliged to play his way—unless you happen to have another set of dice."

"Besides," Talen added, "it would give us at least one more vote."

"Oh?" Dolmant said.

"Patriarch Bergsten's with Wargun's army. We could probably persuade him to vote right, couldn't we?"

"Why don't we put our heads together and compose a letter to the King of Thalesia, Dolmant?" Emban grinned.

"I was just about to suggest that myself, Emban. And perhaps we should forget to tell anyone else about it. Conflicting orders from some other patriarch would just confuse Wargun, and he's confused enough as it is."

## CHAPTER EIGHT

Sparhawk was tired, but he slept poorly. His mind seemed filled with numbers. Sixty-nine changed into seventy-one, then eighty, then back, and the nine and seventeen—no, fifteen—hovered ominously in the background. He started to lose track of what the numbers meant, and they became just numbers that arrayed themselves threateningly before him, armored and with weapons in their hands. And, as it almost always did when he slept now, the shadowy thing haunted his dreams. It did not do anything, but merely watched—and waited.

Sparhawk did not really have the temperament for politics. Too many things reduced themselves in his mind to battlefield imagery, and superior strength and training and individual bravery counted for much on a battlefield. In politics, however, the feeblest were equal to the strongest. A palsied hand shakingly raised to vote had a power equal to that of a mailed fist. His instincts told him that the solution to the problem rested in his scabbard, but the killing of the Primate of Cimmura would tear the west apart at a time when Otha stood armed and poised on the eastern marches.

He finally gave up and slipped quietly from his bed to avoid waking the sleeping Kalten. He put on his soft monk's robe and padded through the night-dark halls to Dolmant's study.

Sephrenia was there, sitting before a small fire that crackled on the hearth, her teacup in her hands and her eyes a mystery. "You're troubled, aren't you, dear one?" she said to him quietly.

"Aren't you?" He sighed and sank into a chair, extending his long legs out in front of him. "We're not suited for this, little mother," he said moodily, "neither one of us. I'm not arranged in such a way that I can palpitate with delight over the change of a number, and I'm not positive that you even understand what numbers mean. Since Styrics don't read, can any of you actually understand any number larger than the sum of your fingers and toes?"

"Are you trying to be insulting, Sparhawk?"

"No, little mother, I could never do that—not to you. I'm sorry. I'm a bit sour this morning. I'm fighting the kind of war I don't understand. Why don't we frame some sort of prayer and ask Aphrael to change the minds of certain members of the Hierocracy? That would be nice and simple and probably head off a great deal of bloodshed."

"Aphrael wouldn't do that, Sparhawk."

"I was afraid you might say that. That leaves us the unpleasant alternative of playing somebody else's game, then, doesn't it? I wouldn't mind so much—if I understood the rules a little better. Frankly, I'd much prefer swords and oceans of blood." He paused. "Go ahead and say it, Sephrenia."

"Say what?"

"Sigh and roll your eyes heavenward and say 'Elenes' in your most despairing tone."

Her eyes went hard. "That was uncalled for, Sparhawk."

"I was only teasing you." He smiled. "We can do that with those we love without giving offense, can't we?"

Patriarch Dolmant entered quietly, his face troubled. "Is no one sleeping tonight?" he asked.

"We have a big day ahead of us tomorrow, your Grace," Sparhawk replied. "Is that why you're up as well?"

Dolmant shook his head. "One of my servants fell ill," he explained, "a cook. I don't know why the other servants sent for me. I'm no physician."

"I think it's called trust, your Grace." Sephrenia smiled. "You're supposed to have certain special contacts with the Elene God. How is the poor fellow—the cook, I mean?"

"It appears to be quite serious. I sent for a physician. He isn't much of a cook, but I'd rather he didn't die. But now, tell me—what really happened in Cimmura, Sparhawk?"

Sparhawk quickly sketched in the events that had occurred in the throne room and the substance of the confession of Lycheas.

"Otha?" Dolmant exclaimed. "Annias actually went *that* far?"

"We can't really prove it, your Grace," Sparhawk told him. "It might be useful at some point to let the information drop in Annias' presence, however. It might throw him off balance a bit. Anyway, at Ehlana's command, we've confined Lycheas and Arissa in that cloister near Demos, and I'm carrying a sizeable number of warrants for the arrest of assorted people on charges of high treason. Annias' name figures quite prominently in one of those warrants." He paused. "There's a thought," he said. "We could march the knights to the Basilica, arrest Annias, and take him back to Cimmura in chains. Ehlana was talking very seriously of hangings and beheadings when we left."

"You can't take Annias out of the Basilica, Sparhawk," Dolmant said. "It's a church, and a church is sanctuary for all civil crimes."

"Pity," Sparhawk murmured. "Who's in charge of Annias' toadies in the Basilica?"

"Makova, Patriarch of Coombe. He's been more or less running things for the past year. Makova's an ass, totally venal, but he's an expert on Church law and he knows a hundred technicalities and loopholes."

"Is Annias attending the meetings?"

"Most of the time, yes. He likes to keep a running count of the votes. He's spending his spare time making offers to the neutral patriarchs. Those nine men are very shrewd. They never come right out and openly accept his offers. They answer with their votes. Would you like to watch us play, little mother?" Dolmant said it with a faint irony.

"Thank you all the same, Dolmant," she declined, "but there are a goodly number of Elenes who are firmly convinced that if a Styric ever enters the Basilica, the dome will fall in on itself. I don't enjoy being spat on all that much, so I think I'll stay here, if I may."

"When have the meetings usually been commencing?" Sparhawk asked the patriarch.

"It varies," Dolmant replied. "Makova holds the chair—that was a simple majority vote. He's been playing with his authority. He calls the meetings on a whim, and the messengers delivering those calls somehow always seem to lose their way when they come looking for those of us opposed to Annias. I think Makova started out by trying to slip through a substantive vote while the rest of us were still in bed."

"What if he calls a vote in the middle of the night, Dolmant?" Sephrenia asked.

"He can't," Dolmant explained. "Sometime in antiquity, some patriarch with nothing better to do codified the rules dealing with meetings of the Hierocracy. History tells us that he was a tiresome old windbag with an obsession about meaningless detail. He was the one responsible for the absurd rule about the one hundred votes—or sixty percent—on substantive matters. He also—probably out of pure whim—set down the rule that the Hierocracy could only deliberate during the hours of daylight. Many of his rules are stupid frivolities, but he talked for six straight weeks, and finally his brothers voted to accept his rules just to shut him up." Dolmant touched his cheek reflectively. "When this is all over, I may just nominate the silly ass for sainthood. Those petty, ridiculous rules of his may be all that's keeping Annias off the throne right now. At any rate, we've made a practice of all being in place at dawn, just to be safe. It's a rather petty form of retaliation, actually. Makova's not customarily an early riser, but he's been greeting the sun with the rest of us for the past several weeks. If he's not there, we can vote in a new chairman and proceed without him. All sorts of inconvenient votes could take place."

"Couldn't he just have those votes repealed?" she asked.

Dolmant actually smirked. "A vote to repeal is a matter of substance, Sephrenia, and he doesn't have the votes."

There was a respectful knock on the door, and Dolmant answered it. A servant spoke with him for a moment.

"That cook just died," Dolmant said to Sparhawk and Sephrenia, sounding a bit shocked. "Wait here a moment. The physician wants to talk with me."

"Strange," Sparhawk murmured.

"People *do* die of natural causes, Sparhawk," Sephrenia told him.

"Not in *my* profession—at least not very often."

"Maybe he was old."

Dolmant returned, his face very pale. "He was poisoned!" he exclaimed.

"What?" Sparhawk demanded.

"That cook of mine was poisoned, and the physician says that the poison was in the porridge the man was preparing for breakfast. That porridge could have killed everyone in the house."

"Perhaps you'd like to reconsider your position on the notion of arresting Annias, your Grace," Sparhawk said grimly.

"Surely you don't believe—" Dolmant broke off, his eyes suddenly very wide.

"He's already had a hand in the poisoning of Aldreas and Ehlana, your Grace," Sparhawk said. "I doubt that he'd choke very much over a few patriarchs and a score or so Church Knights."

"The man's a monster!" Then Dolmant started to swear, using oaths more common to a barracks than a theological seminary.

"You'd better tell Emban to circulate word of this to the patriarchs loyal to us, Dolmant," Sephrenia advised. "It appears that Annias may have come up with a cheaper way to win an election."

"I'd better start rousing the others," Sparhawk said, rising to his feet. "I want to tell them about this, and it takes awhile to get into full armor."

It was still dark when they set out for the Basilica accompanied by fifteen ar-

mored knights from each of the four orders. Sixty Church Knights, it had been decided, was a force with which few would care to interfere.

The sky to the east was beginning to show that first pale stain of daylight when
they reached the great domed church that was at the very center of the Holy City—
its thought and spirit as well as its geography. The entrance into the city of the column of Pandions, Cyrinics, Genidians, and Alciones the previous night had not
gone unnoticed, and the torchlit bronze portal leading into the vast court before the
Basilica was guarded by a hundred and a half red-tunicked church soldiers under
the command of that same captain who, at Makova's orders, had attempted to prevent the departure of Sparhawk and his companions from the Pandion chapterhouse on their journey to Borrata. "Halt!" he commanded in an imperious, even
insulting tone.

"Would you attempt to deny entrance to patriarchs of the Church, Captain?"
Preceptor Abriel asked in a level tone, "knowing that you thereby imperil your
soul?"

"His neck, too," Ulath muttered to Tynian.

"Patriarch Dolmant and Patriarch Emban may freely enter, my Lord," the captain said. "No true son of the Church could refuse them entry."

"But what of these other patriarchs, Captain?" Dolmant asked him.

"I see no other patriarchs, your Grace." The captain's tone hovered on insult.

"You're not looking, Captain," Emban told him. "By Church law, the preceptors of the militant orders are also patriarchs. Stand aside and let us pass."

"I have heard of no such Church law."

"Are you calling me a liar, Captain?" Emban's normally good-humored face
had gone iron-hard.

"Why—certainly not, your Grace. May I consult with my superiors on this
matter?"

"You may not. Stand aside."

The captain started to sweat. "I thank your Grace for correcting my error," he
floundered. "I was not aware that the preceptors also enjoyed ecclesiastical rank. All
patriarchs may freely enter. The rest, I'm afraid, must wait outside."

"He'd *better* be afraid if he's going to try to enforce that," Ulath grated.

"Captain," Preceptor Komier said, "all patriarchs are entitled to a certain administrative staff, aren't they?"

"Certainly, my Lord—uh, your Grace."

"These knights are *our* staff. Secretaries and the like, you understand. If you
deny *them* entrance, I'll expect to see a long file of the black-robed underlings of the
*other* patriarchs filing out of the Basilica in about five minutes."

"I can't do *that,* your Grace," the captain said stubbornly.

"Ulath," Komier barked.

"If I may, your Grace," Bevier interposed. Bevier, Sparhawk noted, was holding his Lochaber ax loosely in his right hand. "The captain and I have met before.
Perhaps I can reason with him." The young Cyrinic Knight moved his horse forward. "Though our relations have never been cordial, Captain," he said, "I beseech
you not to so risk your soul by defying our Holy Mother, the Church. With this in
mind, will you freely stand aside as the Church has commanded you to do?"

"I will not, Sir Knight."

Bevier sighed regretfully. Then, with an almost negligent swing of his dreadful ax, he sent the captain's head flying. Bevier, Sparhawk had noted, did that on occasion. Just as soon as he was certain that he was on firm theological ground, the young Arcian habitually took sometimes shockingly direct action. Even now, his face was serene and untroubled as he watched the captain's headless body standing stock still for several seconds, and then he sighed as the body collapsed.

The church soldiers gasped and cried out in horror and alarm as they recoiled and reached for their weapons.

"That tears it," Tynian said. "Here we go." He reached for his sword.

"Dear friends," Bevier addressed the soldiers in a gentle but commanding voice, "you have just witnessed a truly regrettable incident. A soldier of the Church has wilfully defied our Mother's lawful command. Let us join together now to offer up a fervent prayer that All-Merciful God shall see fit to forgive his dreadful sin. Kneel, dear friends, and pray." Bevier shook the blood off his ax, spattering a number of soldiers in the process.

First a few, then more, and finally all of the soldiers sank to their knees.

"Oh, God!" Bevier led them in prayer, "we beseech thee to receive the soul of our dear brother, but recently departed, and grant him absolution for his grievous sin." He looked around. "Continue to pray, dear friends," he instructed the kneeling soldiers. "Pray not only for your former captain, but for yourselves as well, lest sin, ever devious and cunning, creep into *your* hearts even as it crept into his. Defend your purity and humility with vigor, dear friends, lest you share your captain's fate." Then the Cyrinic Knight, all in burnished steel and pristine white surcoat and cape, moved his horse forward at a walk, threading his way through the ranks of the kneeling soldiers, bestowing blessings with one hand and holding his lochaber ax in the other.

"I *told* you he was a good boy," Ulath said to Tynian as the party followed the beatifically smiling Bevier.

"I never doubted it for a moment, my friend," Tynian replied.

"Lord Abriel," Patriarch Dolmant said as he guided his horse past the kneeling soldiers, many of whom were actually weeping, "have you questioned Sir Bevier of late on the actual substance of his beliefs? I may be wrong, but I seem to detect certain deviations from the true teachings of our Holy Mother."

"I shall catechize him most penetratingly on the matter, your Grace—just as soon as I have the opportunity."

"There's no great rush, my Lord," Dolmant said benignly. "I don't feel that his soul is in any immediate danger. That is a truly *ugly* weapon he carries, however."

"Yes, your Grace," Abriel agreed. "It truly is."

Word of the sudden demise of the offensive captain at the gate spread rather quickly. There was no interference from church soldiers at the massive doors of the Basilica—indeed, there seemed to be no church soldiers around at all. The heavily armed knights dismounted, formed up into a military column, and followed their preceptors and the two patriarchs into the vast nave. There was a noisy clatter as the party knelt briefly before the altar. Then they rose and marched off down a candlelit corridor toward the administrative offices and the archprelate's audience chamber.

632 • THE SAPPHIRE ROSE

The men standing guard at the door to the chamber were not church soldiers, but rather were members of the archprelate's personal guard. Their loyalties were to the office itself, and they were totally incorruptible. They were also, however, sticklers for the letter of Church law, in which they were probably more well versed than many of the patriarchs sitting in the chamber. They immediately recognized the ecclesiastical eminence of the preceptors of the four orders. Coming up with a reason why the rest of the entourage should be admitted took a bit longer, however. It was Patriarch Emban—fat, sly, and with a nearly encyclopedic knowledge of Church law and custom—who pointed out the fact that any churchman with proper credentials and at the invitation of a patriarch must be freely admitted. Once the guards had agreed to that, Emban gently pointed out that the Church Knights were de facto churchmen as members of technically cloistered orders. The guards mulled that over, conceded Emban's point, and ceremoniously opened the huge doors. Sparhawk noticed a number of poorly concealed smiles as he and his friends filed inside. The guards by definition were incorruptible and totally neutral. This did not, however, preclude their having private opinions.

The audience chamber was as large as any secular throne room. The throne itself—massive, ornate, constructed of solid gold, and standing on a raised dais backed by purple drapes—was at one end of the hall, and on either side, rising in tier upon tier, stood the high-backed benches. The first four tiers were crimson-cushioned, indicating that those seats were reserved for the patriarchs. Above those seats and separated from them by velvet ropes of deepest purple were the plain wooden seats of the galleries for the spectators. A lectern stood before the throne, and Patriarch Makova of Coombe in Arcium stood at the lectern, droning out a speech filled with ecclesiastic bombast. Makova, lean-faced, pock-marked, and obviously sleepy, turned irritably as the huge doors opened and the knights followed the patriarchs of Demos and Ucera into the vast chamber.

"What's the meaning of this?" Makova demanded in an outraged tone.

"Nothing out of the ordinary, Makova," Emban replied. "Dolmant and I are merely escorting some of our brother patriarchs in to join our deliberations."

"I see no patriarchs," Makova snapped.

"Don't be tiresome, Makova. All the world knows that preceptors of the militant orders hold rank equal to ours and are, therefore, members of the Hierocracy."

Makova glanced quickly at a weedy-looking monk sitting off to one side at a table piled high with massive books and ancient scrolls. "Will the assemblage hear the words of the law clerk on this matter?" he asked.

There was a rumble of assent, though the looks of consternation on the faces of at least some of the patriarchs clearly showed that they already knew the answer. The weedy monk consulted several large tomes, then rose, cleared his throat, and spoke in a rusty-sounding voice. "His Grace, the Patriarch of Usara, has correctly cited the law," he said. "The preceptors of the militant orders are indeed members of the Hierocracy, and the names of the current holders of those offices have been duly entered in the rolls of this body. The preceptors have not chosen to participate in deliberations for some two centuries past, but they have the rank nonetheless."

"Authority not exercised no longer exists," Makova snapped.

"I'm afraid that's not entirely true, your Grace," the monk apologized. "There are many historical precedents for resuming participation. At one time, the patriarchs of the kingdom of Arcium refused to participate in the deliberations of the Hierocracy for eight hundred years as a result of a dispute over proper vestments, and—"

"All right. All right," Makova said angrily, "but these armored assassins have no right to be here." He glared at the knights.

"Wrong again, Makova," Emban said smugly. "By definition, the Church Knights are members of religious orders. Their vows are no less binding and legitimate than ours. They are, thus, churchmen and may act as observers—provided that they are invited by a sitting patriarch." He turned. "Sir Knights," he said, "would you be so good as to accept my personal invitation to witness our proceedings?"

Makova looked quickly at the scholarly monk, and the weedy fellow nodded.

"What it boils down to, Makova," Emban said in an unctuous tone tinged with malice, "is that the Knights of the Church have as much right to be present as the serpent Annias, who sits in unearned splendor in the north gallery—chewing his lower lip in dismay, I note."

"You go too far, Emban!"

"I don't really think so, old boy. Shall we take a vote on something, Makova, and find out how much your support has been eroded?" Emban looked around. "But we're interrupting the proceedings. I pray you, my brother patriarchs and dear guests, let us take our seats so that the Hierocracy may continue its empty deliberations."

"Empty?" Makova gasped.

"Totally empty, old boy. Until Cluvonus dies, nothing we decide here has any meaning whatsoever. We're simply amusing ourselves—and earning our pay, of course."

"That's a very offensive little man," Tynian murmured to Ulath.

"Good, though." The huge Genidian Knight grinned.

Sparhawk knew exactly where he was going. "You," he muttered to Talen, who had probably been admitted by mistake, "come with me."

"Where are we going?"

"To irritate an old friend." Sparhawk grinned mirthlessly. He led the boy up the stairs to an upper gallery where the emaciated Primate of Cimmura sat with a writing desk in front of him and a fair number of black-robed sycophants on either side. Sparhawk and Talen went to places on the bench directly behind Annias. Sparhawk saw that Ulath, Berit, and Tynian were following, and he waved them off warningly even as Dolmant and Emban escorted the armored preceptors to places on the lower, cushioned tiers.

Sparhawk knew that Annias sometimes blurted things out when he was surprised and he wanted to find out if his enemy had in any way been involved in the attempted mass poisoning at Dolmant's house that morning. "Why, can that *possibly* be the Primate of Cimmura?" he said in feigned surprise. "What on *earth* are you doing so far away from home, Annias?"

Annias turned to glare at him. "What are you up to, Sparhawk?" he demanded.

"Observing, that's all," Sparhawk replied, removing his helmet and depositing his gauntlets in it. He unbuckled his shield and removed his sword belt. He leaned them against the back of Annias' seat. "Will those be in your way, neighbor?" he asked mildly. "It's a bit hard to sit down comfortably when you're so encumbered with the tools of your trade, you know." He sat. "How have you been, Annias? I haven't seen you for months now." He paused. "You're looking a bit gaunt and pasty-faced, old boy. You really ought to get more fresh air and exercise."

"Be still, Sparhawk," Annias snapped. "I'm trying to listen."

"Oh, of course. We can have a nice long talk later—catch up on each other's accomplishments and the like." There was nothing out of the ordinary in Annias' reaction, and Sparhawk became a little less certain of the man's guilt.

"If it pleases you, my brothers," Dolmant was saying, "a number of events have recently occurred, and I feel obligated to report them to the Hierocracy. Though our primary tasks are ageless, we nonetheless function in the world and must keep abreast of current events."

Makova looked questioningly up toward Annias. The primate took up a quill and a scrap of paper. Sparhawk rested his arms on the back of his enemy's seat and looked over the man's shoulder as he scribbled the terse instruction, "Let him talk."

"Tiresome, isn't it, Annias," Sparhawk said in a pleasant tone. "It would be so much more convenient if you could do your own talking, wouldn't it?"

"I told you to shut up, Sparhawk," Annias grated, handing his note to a young monk to carry to Makova.

"My, aren't *we* testy this morning," Sparhawk observed. "Didn't you sleep well last night, Annias?"

Annias turned to glare at his tormentor. "Who's that?" he demanded, pointing at Talen.

"My page," Sparhawk replied. "It's one of the encumbrances of knightly rank. He sort of fills in while my squire is otherwise occupied."

Makova had glanced at the note. "We always welcome the words of the learned Primate of Demos," he declaimed loftily, "but please be brief, your Grace. We have important business to attend to here." He stepped away from the lectern.

"Of course, Makova," Dolmant replied, stepping to the vacated place. "Briefly, then," he began, "as a result of the full recovery of Queen Ehlana, the political situation in the kingdom of Elenia has radically changed, and—"

Cries of astonishment echoed through the hall, and there was a confused babble of voices. Sparhawk, still leaning on the back of Annias' seat, was pleased to see the primate's face grow totally white as he half started to his feet. "Impossible!" the churchman gasped.

"Amazing, isn't it, Annias?" Sparhawk said, "and so totally unexpected. I'm sure you'll be happy to know that the queen sends you her *very* best wishes."

"Explain yourself, Dolmant!" Makova half shouted.

"I was only trying to be brief—as you requested, Makova. No more than a week ago, Queen Ehlana recovered from her mysterious ailment. Many look upon that as miraculous. Upon her recovery, certain facts came to light, and the former Prince Regent—and his mother, I understand—are currently under arrest on the charge of high treason."

Annias fell back in his seat in a near faint.

"The revered and respected Earl of Lenda now heads the royal council, and warrants for a number of co-conspirators in the foul plot against the queen have been issued over his seal. The Queen's Champion is presently searching out these miscreants and will doubtless bring them all before the bar of justice—either human or divine."

"The Baron Harparin was next in line to head the Elenian Royal Council," Makova protested.

"The Baron Harparin is presently standing before the bar of the Highest Justice, Makova," Dolmant said in a deadly tone. "He faces the Ultimate Judge. There is, I fear, scant hope for his acquittal—though we may pray that it be otherwise."

"What happened to him?" Makova gasped.

"I'm told that he was accidentally beheaded during the changeover of administrations in Cimmura. Regrettable, perhaps, but that sort of thing happens now and then."

"Harparin?" Annias gasped in dismay.

"He made the mistake of offending Preceptor Vanion," Sparhawk murmured in his ear, "and you know how short-tempered Vanion can be at times. He was very sorry afterward, of course, but by then Harparin was lying in two separate places. He absolutely *destroyed* the carpeting in the council chamber—all that blood, you know."

"Who else are you chasing, Sparhawk?" Annias demanded.

"I don't have the list with me at the moment, Annias, but there *are* a number of prominent names on it—names I'm sure you'd recognize."

There was a stir at the door, and two frightened-looking patriarchs crept into the hall and then scurried to places on the red-cushioned benches. Kalten stood grinning at the door for a moment, then left again.

"Well?" Sparhawk whispered to Talen.

"Those two bring the total up to one hundred nineteen," Talen whispered back. "We've got forty-five, and Annias still has sixty-five. He needs seventy-two now instead of seventy-one. We're getting closer, Sparhawk."

It took the secretary of the Primate of Cimmura some while longer to complete *his* computations. Annias scribbled a one-word note to Makova. Sparhawk, watching over the primate's shoulder, read the single word "vote."

The issue Makova put to the vote was a pure absurdity. Everyone knew that. The only question the vote was designed to answer was upon which side the nine neutral patriarchs clustered in a now-frightened group near the door would come down. After the tally, Makova announced the results in a tone of dismay. The nine had voted in a block *against* the Primate of Cimmura.

The huge door opened again, and three black-robed monks entered. Their cowls were raised, and their pace was ritualistically slow. When they reached the dais, one of their number removed a folded black cover from beneath his robe, and the three solemnly spread it over the throne to announce that the Archprelate Cluvonus had finally died.

"How long will the city be in mourning?" Tynian asked Dolmant that afternoon when they had gathered once again in the patriarch's study.

"A week," Dolmant replied. "The funeral takes place then."

"And nothing happens during that period?" the blue-cloaked Alcione Knight asked. "No sessions of the Hierocracy or anything?"

Dolmant shook his head. "No. We're supposed to spend the period in prayer and meditation."

"It's a breathing space," Vanion said, "and it should give Wargun time to get here." He frowned. "We still have a problem, though. Annias doesn't have any more money, and that means that his hold on his majority grows shakier every day. He's probably growing desperate by now, and desperate men do rash things."

"He's right," Komier agreed. "I expect Annias will take to the streets at this point. He'll hold his own votes by terror and try to reduce the number voting by eliminating patriarchs loyal to us until he gets the number down to the point where he has a substantive majority. I think it's time to fort up, gentlemen. We'd better get our friends all together behind some good stout walls where we can protect them."

"I'll certainly agree," Abriel concurred. "Our position is vulnerable right now."

"Which of your chapterhouses is closest to the Basilica?" Patriarch Emban asked them. "Our friends are going to have to file back and forth through the streets to participate in deliberations. Let's not expose them to any more danger than we have to."

"Our house is closest," Vanion told him, "and it has its own well. After what happened this morning, I don't want to give Annias access to our drinking water."

"Supplies?" Darellon asked.

"We keep enough on hand to withstand a six-month siege," Vanion replied. "Soldiers' rations, I'm afraid, your Grace," he apologized to the corpulent Emban.

Emban sighed. "Oh, well," he said, "I've been meaning to lose some weight anyway."

"It's a good plan," the white-cloaked Preceptor Abriel said, "but it does have a drawback. If we're all in one chapterhouse, the church soldiers can surround us. We'll be penned up inside with no way to get to the Basilica at all."

"Then we'll fight our way through," Komier said, cramming his ogre-horned helmet on his head irritably.

Abriel shook his head. "People get killed in fights, Komier. The vote is very close. We can't afford to lose a single patriarch at this point."

"We can't win either way," Tynian said.

"I'm not so sure," Kalten disagreed.

"Can you see a way out of it?"

"I think so." Kalten looked at Dolmant. "I'll need permission for this, your Grace," he said.

"I'm listening. What's your plan?"

"If Annias decides to resort to naked force, that means that any semblance of civil order goes out the window, doesn't it?"

"More or less, yes."

"Then if he's not going to pay any attention to the rules, why should we? If we want to cut down on the number of church soldiers surrounding the Pandion chapterhouse, all we have to do is give them something more important to do."

"Set fire to the city again?" Talen suggested.

"That might be a little extreme," Kalten said. "We can keep the notion in reserve, though. Right now, however, the votes Annias has got are the most important things in his life. If we start peeling them off one by one, he'll do just about anything to protect what he's got left, won't he?"

"I will *not* allow you to start butchering patriarchs, Kalten," Dolmant said in a shocked voice.

"We don't have to kill anybody, your Grace. All we have to do is imprison a few. Annias is fairly intelligent. He'll get the point after a while."

"You'll need *some* kind of charge, Sir Kalten," Abriel said. "You can't just imprison patriarchs of the Church for no reason at all—regardless of the circumstances."

"Oh, we have charges, my Lord Abriel—all sorts of charges—but 'crimes against the crown of Elenia' has the nicest ring to it, wouldn't you say?"

"I hate it when he tries to be clever," Sparhawk muttered to Tynian.

"You'll love this one, Sparhawk," Kalten said. He threw back his black cloak with an expression of insufferable smugness. "How many of those arrest warrants Lenda signed for you back in Cimmura have you still got in your pocket?"

"Eight or ten, why?"

"Are there any of those people whose company you'd absolutely die without for the next several weeks?"

"I could probably live without most of them." Sparhawk thought he saw which way his friend was going.

"All we have to do is substitute a few names then," Kalten said. "The documents are official, so it's going to *look* legal—sort of. After we've picked up four or five of his bought-and-paid-for patriarchs and dragged them off to the Alcione chapterhouse—which just *happens* to be way over on the far side of town—won't Annias do everything in his power to get them back? I'd sort of expect the number of soldiers gathered around the Pandion chapterhouse to diminish drastically at that point."

"Amazing," Ulath said. "Kalten actually came up with a workable idea."

"About the only thing I can see wrong with it is the business of substituting names," Vanion said. "You can't just scratch out one name and replace it with another—not on an official document."

"I didn't say anything about scratching out names, my Lord," Kalten said modestly. "Once, when we were novices, you gave Sparhawk and me leave to go home for a few days. You scribbled a note to get us out through the gate. We just happened to keep the note. The scribes in the scriptorium have something that totally washes out ink. They use it when they make mistakes. The date on that note of yours kept mysteriously changing. You might almost call it miraculous, mightn't you?" He shrugged. "But then, God's always been sort of fond of me."

"Would it work?" Komier bluntly asked Sparhawk.

"It did when we were novices, my Lord," Sparhawk assured him.

"You actually *knighted* these two, Vanion?" Abriel asked.

"It was a slow week."

The grins in the room were broad now.

"Totally reprehensible, Kalten," Dolmant said. "I'd have to absolutely forbid it—if I thought that you were in any way serious about it. You were just speculating, weren't you, my son?"

"Oh, absolutely, your Grace."

"I was sure that was the case." Dolmant smiled benignly, even piously, and then he winked.

"Oh, dear," Sephrenia sighed. "Isn't there *one* honest Elene in the world? You, too, Dolmant?"

"I didn't agree to anything, little mother," he protested with exaggerated innocence. "We were only speculating, weren't we, Sir Kalten?"

"Certainly, your Grace. Pure speculation. Neither of us would ever *seriously* consider something so reprehensible."

"My feelings exactly," Dolmant said. "There, Sephrenia, does that set your mind at rest?"

"You were a much nicer boy when you were a Pandion novice, Dolmant," she reproved him.

There was a stunned silence as they all stared at the Patriarch of Demos.

"Oops," Sephrenia said mildly, her eyes dancing and a faint smile hovering at the corners of her mouth. "I suppose I really shouldn't have said that, should I have, Dolmant?"

"Did you really have to do that, little mother?" he asked her in a pained tone.

"Yes, dear one, I believe I did. You've started to become just a little too impressed with your own cleverness. It's my responsibility as your teacher—and your friend—to curb that whenever possible."

Dolmant tapped one finger on the table in front of him. "I trust we'll all be discreet about this, gentlemen?"

"Wild horses couldn't drag it out of us, Dolmant." Emban grinned. "As far as I'm concerned, I never even heard it—and that'll probably hold true until the next time I need a favor from you."

"Were you any good, your Grace?" Kalten asked respectfully. "As a Pandion, I mean?"

"He was the best, Kalten," Sephrenia said rather proudly. "He was even a match for Sparhawk's father. We were all saddened when the Church found other duties for him. We lost a very good Pandion when he took holy orders."

Dolmant was still looking around at his friends, his expression suspicious. "I thought I'd buried it completely," he sighed. "I never thought you'd betray me, Sephrenia."

"It's not exactly as if it were shameful, your Grace," Vanion said.

"It might prove to be politically inconvenient," Dolmant said. "At least *you* were able to control your tongue, brother."

"Not to worry, Dolmant," Emban said expansively. "I'll keep an eye on your friends here, and as soon as I suspect that one of them is starting to have difficulty controlling his tongue, I'll order him to that monastery at Zemba down in Cammoria where the brothers all take vows of silence."

"All right then," Vanion said, "let's get started, gentlemen. We have a number of friendly patriarchs to round up, and Kalten, I want you to go start practicing forgery. The names you'll be substituting on those arrest warrants will have to be in the handwriting of the Earl of Lenda." He paused thoughtfully, looking at his blond subordinate. "You'd better take Sparhawk with you," he added.

"I can manage, my Lord."

Vanion shook his head. "No, Kalten," he disagreed, "I don't think so. I've seen your attempts at spelling before."

"Bad?" Darellon asked him.

"Terrible, my friend. Once he wrote down a six-letter word, and he didn't manage to get a single letter right."

"Some words are difficult to spell, Vanion."

"His own *name*?"

"But you can't do this!" the Patriarch of Cardos protested shrilly as Sparhawk and Kalten dragged him from his house a few days later. "You can't arrest a patriarch of the Church for anything while the Hierocracy's in session."

"But the Hierocracy's not in session just now, your Grace," Sparhawk pointed out. "They're in recess during the period of official mourning."

"I still cannot be tried by a civil court. I demand that you present these specious charges before an ecclesiastical court."

"Take him outside," Sparhawk curtly instructed the black-armored Sir Perraine.

The Patriarch of Cardos was dragged from the room.

"Why the delay?" Kalten asked.

"Two things. Our prisoner didn't really seem all that surprised at the charges, did he?"

"Now that you mention it, no."

"I think maybe Lenda missed a few names when he was drawing up that list."

"That's always possible. What was the other thing?"

"Let's send a message to Annias. He knows that we can't touch him as long as he stays inside the Basilica, doesn't he?"

"Yes."

"All right, then, let's imprison him there and curtail his freedom of movement—for its irritation value if nothing else. We still owe him for that poisoned cook."

"How do you plan to do that?"

"Watch—and follow my lead."

"Don't I always?"

They went out to the courtyard of the patriarch's luxurious house, a house built, Sparhawk was sure, on the backs of the Elenian taxpayers. "My colleague and I have considered your request for an ecclesiastical hearing, your Grace," the big Pandion said to the prisoner. "We find that your argument has merit." He began to leaf through his sheaf of warrants.

"You'll deliver me to the Basilica for a hearing, then?" the patriarch asked.

"Hmm?" Sparhawk said absently, still reading.

"I said, are you going to take me to the Basilica and present these absurd charges there?"

"Ah, I don't think so, your Grace. That would really be inconvenient." Sparhawk pulled out the warrant for the arrest of the Primate of Cimmura and showed it to Kalten.

"That's the one, all right," Kalten said. "That's the fellow we want."

Sparhawk rolled up the warrant and tapped it against his cheek. "Here's what we're going to do, your Grace," he said. "We're going to take you to the Alcione chapterhouse and confine you there. These charges originated in the kingdom of Elenia, and any ecclesiastical proceedings would have to be conducted by the head of the Church in that kingdom. Since Primate Annias is acting for the Patriarch of Cimmura during his Grace's incapacity, that makes him the man who would head up this hearing. Strange how things work out, isn't it? Since Primate Annias is the one in authority in this matter, we'll freely turn you over to him. All he has to do is to come out of the Basilica, go to the Alcione chapterhouse, and order us to turn you over to him." He glanced at a red-tunicked officer being guarded by the bleak-looking Sir Perraine. "The captain of your guard here will serve as an excellent messenger. Why don't you have a word with him and explain the situation? Then we'll send him to the Basilica to tell Annias about it. Have him ask the good primate to come and visit us. We'll be overjoyed to see him on neutral ground, won't we, Kalten?"

"Oh, absolutely," Kalten replied fervently.

The Patriarch of Cardos gave them a suspicious look, then quickly conferred with the captain of his guard detachment. He kept glancing at the rolled-up warrant in Sparhawk's hand as he spoke.

"Do you think he got the point?" Kalten murmured.

"I certainly hope so. I did everything but hit him over the head with it."

The Patriarch of Cardos returned, his face stiff with anger.

"Oh, one other thing, Captain," Sparhawk said to the church soldier, who was preparing to leave. "Would you be so good as to convey a personal message to the Primate of Cimmura for us? Tell him that Sir Sparhawk of the Pandion Order invites him to come out from under the dome of the Basilica to play in the streets—where certain petty little restrictions won't interfere with our fun."

Kurik arrived that evening. He was travel-stained and looked weary. Berit escorted him into Dolmant's study, and he sank into a chair. "I'd have been here a bit sooner," he apologized, "but I stopped off in Demos to see Aslade and the boys. She gets very cross when I ride through town and don't stop."

"How is Aslade?" Patriarch Dolmant asked.

"Fatter." Kurik smiled. "And I think she's getting a little silly as the years creep up on her. She was feeling nostalgic, so she took me up into the hayloft." His jaw set slightly. "Later I had a long talk with the boys about letting thistles grow in the hayfield."

"Do you have any idea of what he's talking about, Sparhawk?" Dolmant asked in perplexity.

"Yes, your Grace."

"But you're not going to explain it to me, are you?"

"No, your Grace, I don't think so. How's Ehlana?" he asked his squire.

"Difficult," Kurik grunted. "Unprincipled. Abrasive. Willful. Overbearing. Demanding. Sneaky. Unforgiving. Just your average, run-of-the-mill young queen. I like her, though. She reminds me of Flute for some reason."

"I wasn't asking for a description, Kurik," Sparhawk said. "I was inquiring as to her health."

"She seems fine to me. If there was anything wrong with her, she wouldn't be able to run that fast."

"Run?"

"She seems to feel that she missed a great deal while she was asleep, so she's trying to catch up. She's had her nose in every corner of the palace by now. Lenda's seriously contemplating suicide, I think, and the chambermaids are all in a state of despair. You can't hide a speck of dust from her. She may not have the best kingdom in the world when she's finished, but she's certainly going to have the neatest." Kurik reached inside his leather vest. "Here," he said, pulling out a very thick packet of folded parchment. "She wrote you a letter. Give yourself time to read it, my Lord. It took her two days to write it."

"How's the home guard idea working out?" Kalten asked.

"Quite well, actually. Just before I left, a battalion of church soldiers arrived outside the city. The battalion commander made the mistake of standing too near the gate when he demanded admittance. A couple of citizens dumped something on him."

"Burning pitch?" Tynian surmised.

"No, Sir Tynian." Kurik grinned. "The two fellows make their living draining and cleaning cesspools. The officer received the fruit of their day's labor—about a hogshead full. The colonel—or whatever he was under all of that—lost his head and ordered an assault on the gate. That's when the rocks and burning pitch came into play. The soldiers set up camp not too far from the east wall to think things over, and late that night a score or so of Platime's cutthroats climbed down ropes from the parapet and visited their camp. The soldiers didn't have too many officers left the following morning. They milled around out there for a while, and then they went away. I think your queen's quite safe, Sparhawk. As a group, soldiers aren't very imaginative, and unconventional tactics tend to confuse them. Platime and Stragen are having the time of their lives, and the common people are beginning to take a certain pride in their city. They're even sweeping the streets on the off chance that Ehlana might ride by on one of her morning inspections."

"Those idiots aren't letting her out of the palace, are they?" Sparhawk exclaimed angrily.

"Who's going to stop her? She's safe, Sparhawk. Platime put the biggest woman I've ever seen to guarding her. The woman's almost as big as Ulath, and she carries more weapons than a platoon."

"That would be Mirtai, the giantess," Talen said. "Queen Ehlana's perfectly safe, Sparhawk. Mirtai's an army all by herself."

"A woman?" Kalten asked incredulously.

"I wouldn't recommend calling her that to her face, Kalten," the boy said seriously. "She thinks of herself as a warrior, and nobody in his right mind argues with her. She wears men's clothes most of the time, probably because she doesn't want to be pestered by fellows who like their women large. She's got knives attached to her in some of the most unexpected places. She's even got a pair built into the soles of her shoes. Not much of those two knives sticks out past her toes, but it's enough. You *really* wouldn't want her to kick you in certain tender places."

"Where did Platime ever come across a woman like that?" Kalten asked him.

"He bought her." Talen shrugged. "She was about fifteen at the time and hadn't reached her full growth. She didn't speak a word of Elene, I've been told. He tried to put her to work in a brothel, but after she'd crippled or killed a dozen or so potential customers, he changed his mind."

"Everybody speaks Elene," Kalten objected.

"Not in the Tamul Empire, I understand. Mirtai's a Tamul. That's why she has such a strange name. I'm afraid of her, and I don't say that about many people."

"It's not only the giantess, Sparhawk," Kurik continued. "The common people know their neighbors, and they know everybody who has unreliable political opinions. The people are fanatically loyal to the queen now, and every one of them makes it his personal business to keep an eye on his neighbors. Platime's rounded up just about everybody in town who's the least bit suspect."

"Annias has a lot of underlings in Cimmura," Sparhawk fretted.

"He *used* to, my Lord," Kurik corrected. "There were a number of messy object lessons, and if there's anyone left in Cimmura who doesn't love the queen, he's being very careful to keep that fact to himself. Can I have something to eat? I'm famished."

The funeral of Archprelate Cluvonus was suitably stupendous. Bells tolled for days, and the air inside the Basilica was tainted with incense and with chants and hymns solemnly delivered in archaic Elene, a language very few present could still comprehend. All clerics wore sober black in most situations, but such solemn occasions as this brought forth a rainbow of brightly colored vestments. The patriarchs all wore crimson, and the primates were robed in the colors of their kingdoms of origin. Each of the nineteen cloistered orders of monks and nuns had its own special color, and each color had its own special significance. The nave of the Basilica was a riot of often-conflicting colors, more closely resembling the site of a Cammorian country fair than a place where a solemn funeral was being conducted. Obscure little rituals and superstitious holdovers from antiquity were religiously performed, although no one had the faintest notion of their significance. A sizeable number of priests and monks, whose sole duties in life were to perform those rituals and antiquated ceremonies, appeared briefly in public for the only times in their lives. One aged monk, whose sole purpose in life was to carry a black velvet cushion upon which rested a dented and very tarnished saltcellar thrice around the archprelate's bier, became so excited that his heart fluttered and stopped, and a replacement for him had to be appointed on the spot. The replacement, a pimply-faced young novice of indifferent merit and questionable piety, wept with gratitude as he realized that his position in life was completely secure now, and that he would only be required actually to do any work once every generation or so.

The interminable funeral droned on and on, punctuated by prayers and hymns. At specified points, the congregation stood; at others, they knelt; and at still others they sat back down again. It was all very solemn, and not very much of it made any real sense.

The Primate Annias sat as near as he dared to the velvet rope separating the patriarchs from the spectators on the north side of the vast nave, and he was surrounded by flunkies and sycophants. Since Sparhawk could not get close to him, the big Pandion settled instead for sitting in the south gallery directly opposite, where, surrounded by his friends, he could look directly into the gray-faced churchman's eyes. The gathering of the patriarchs opposed to Annias inside the walls of the Pandion chapterhouse had proceeded according to plan, and the apprehension and imprisonment of six patriarchs loyal to the primate—or at least to his money—had also gone off without a hitch. Annias, his frustration clearly showing on his face, busied himself by scribbling notes to the Patriarch of Coombe, which were delivered by various members of a squad of youthful pages. For each note Annias dispatched to Makova, Sparhawk dispatched one to Dolmant. Sparhawk had a certain advantage in this. Annias actually had to write the notes. Sparhawk simply sent folded scraps of blank paper. It was a ploy to which Dolmant had rather surprisingly agreed.

Kalten slipped into a seat on the other side of Tynian, scribbled a note of his own, and passed it down to Sparhawk.

Good luk. Fyve moor of are missing patriarks showd up at the bak gait of the chapterhowse a half our ago. They herd we were protekting our frends, and they maid a run for it. Forchunate, wot?

Sparhawk winced slightly. Kalten's grasp of the spelling of the Elene language was probably even looser than Vanion had feared. He showed the note to Talen. "How does this affect things?" he whispered.

Talen squinted. "The number voting only changes by one," he whispered back. "We locked away six of Annias' votes and got back five more of ours. We've got fifty-two now, he's got fifty-nine, and there are still the nine neutrals. That's a total of one hundred and twenty votes. It still takes seventy-two to win, but not even the nine votes would help him now. They'd only give him sixty-eight, which makes him four votes short."

"Give me the note," Sparhawk said. He scribbled the numbers under Kalten's message and then added the two sentences, "I'd suggest that we suspend all negotiations with the neutrals at this point. We don't need them now." He handed the note to Talen. "Take this to Dolmant," he instructed, "and it's perfectly all right to grin just a bit while you're on your way down to him."

"A vicious grin, Sparhawk? A smirk, maybe?"

"Do your best." Sparhawk took another piece of paper, wrote the information on it, and passed it among his armored friends.

The Primate Annias was suddenly confronted by a group of Church Knights beaming at him from across the nave of the Basilica. His face darkened, and he began to gnaw nervously on one fingernail.

At long last the funeral ceremony wound to its conclusion. The throng in the nave rose to its feet to file along behind the body of Cluvonus to its resting place in the crypt beneath the floor of the Basilica. Sparhawk took Talen and dropped back to have a word with Kalten. "Where did you learn how to spell?" he asked.

"Spelling is the sort of thing with which no gentleman ought to concern himself, Sparhawk," Kalten replied loftily. He looked around carefully to be sure he wouldn't be heard. "Where *is* Wargun?" he whispered.

"I haven't any idea," Sparhawk whispered back. "Maybe they had to sober him up. Wargun's sense of direction isn't too good when he's been drinking."

"We'd better come up with an alternative plan, Sparhawk. The Hierocracy's going back into session just as soon as Cluvonus gets laid away."

"We've got enough votes to hold Annias off."

"It's only going to take about two ballots to prove that to him, my friend. He'll start getting rash at that point, and we're badly outnumbered here." Kalten looked at the heavy wooden beams lining the stairway down into the crypt. "Maybe I should set fire to the Basilica," he said.

*"Are you out of your mind?"*

"It would delay things, Sparhawk, and we need a delay very badly right about now."

"I don't think we have to go *that* far. Let's keep those five patriarchs under wraps for right now. Talen, without those five votes, where do we stand?"

"One hundred and fifteen voting, Sparhawk. That means sixty-nine to win."

"That makes him one vote short again—even if he can buy the neutrals. He'll probably hold off on any kind of confrontation if he thinks he's that close. Kalten, take Perraine and go back to the chapterhouse and get those five patriarchs. Put them in bits and pieces of armor to disguise them and then form up fifty or so knights to bring them here. Take them into an antechamber. We'll let Dolmant decide when he needs them."

"Right." Kalten grinned wickedly. "We've beaten Annias, though, haven't we, Sparhawk?"

"It looks that way, but let's not start celebrating until there's someone else sitting on that throne. Now get moving."

There were speeches when the still crimson-robed Hierocracy resumed its deliberations. The speeches were for the most part eulogies delivered by patriarchs too unimportant to have participated in the formal services in the nave. The Patriarch Ortzel of Kadach, brother of the Baron Alstrom in Lamorkand, was particularly tedious. The session broke up early and resumed again the following morning. The patriarchs who were opposed to Annias had gathered the previous evening and had selected Ortzel to be their standard-bearer. Sparhawk still had grave reservations about Ortzel, but he kept them to himself.

Dolmant held the five patriarchs who had so recently returned to his ranks in reserve. Disguised in mismatched armor, they sat with a platoon of Church Knights in a squad room not far from the audience chamber.

After the Hierocracy had come to order, Patriarch Makova rose to his feet and placed the name of Primate Annias in nomination for the archprelacy. His nominating speech went on for almost an hour, but the applause greeting it was not particularly fulsome. Then Dolmant rose and nominated Ortzel. Dolmant's speech was more to the point, but it was followed by more enthusiastic applause.

"Do they vote now?" Talen whispered to Sparhawk.

"I don't know," Sparhawk admitted. "That's up to Makova. He's holding the chair at the moment."

"I'd *really* like to see a vote, Sparhawk," Talen said urgently.

"Aren't you sure of your numbers?" Sparhawk said it with a certain apprehension.

"Of course I am, but numbers are only numbers. A lot of things can happen when you get people involved in something. Take that, for example." Talen pointed at a page hurriedly carrying a note from the nine uncommitted patriarchs to Dolmant. "What are they up to now?"

"They probably want to know why Dolmant suddenly stopped offering them money," Sparhawk replied. "Their votes are worthless at this point, although they probably don't fully understand that as yet."

"What do you think they'll do now?"

"Who knows?" Sparhawk shrugged. "And who cares?"

Makova, standing at the lectern, glanced over a sheaf of notes. Then he looked up and cleared his throat. "Before we move on to our initial vote, my brothers," he began, "a matter of great urgency has just come to my attention. As some of you may be aware, the Zemochs are massing on the eastern border of Lamorkand with obviously warlike intent. I believe that we may expect with some certainty that Otha will invade the west—possibly within the next few days. It is, therefore, vital that the deliberations of this body be concluded with all possible haste. Our new archprelate will be faced almost immediately upon his elevation with the direst crisis to face our Church and her faithful sons in the past five centuries."

"What's he doing?" Sir Bevier whispered to Sparhawk. "Everybody in Chyrellos knows that Otha's already in eastern Lamorkand."

"He's stalling," Sparhawk said, frowning, "but he doesn't have any reason to stall."

"What's Annias up to?" Tynian asked, glaring across the audience chamber at the Primate of Cimmura, who sat smiling smugly.

"He's waiting for something to happen," Sparhawk replied.

"What?"

"I don't have any idea, but Makova's going to keep talking until it does."

Then Berit slipped into the audience chamber, his face pale and his eyes wild. He half stumbled up the stairs and pushed his way along the bench to where Sparhawk sat. "Sir Sparhawk!" he burst out.

"Keep your voice down, Berit!" Sparhawk hissed. "Sit down and pull yourself together!"

Berit sat and drew in a deep breath.

"All right," Sparhawk said. "Speak quietly and tell us what's happening."

"There are two armies approaching Chyrellos, my Lord," the novice said tersely.

"*Two?*" Ulath said in some surprise. Then he spread his hands. "Maybe Wargun split his forces for some reason."

"It's not King Wargun's army, Sir Ulath," Berit said. "As soon as we saw them coming, some Church Knights rode out to find out just who was approaching the city. The ones coming down from the north seem to be Lamorks."

"Lamorks?" Tynian asked, puzzled. "What are *they* doing here? They should be on the border facing Otha."

"I don't think these particular Lamorks are interested in Otha, my Lord," Berit told him. "Some of the knights who rode out were Pandions, and they identified the leaders of the Lamork army as Adus and Krager."

"*What?*" Kalten exclaimed.

"Keep it quiet, Kalten!" Sparhawk grated. "And the other army, Berit?" he asked, although he already knew the answer.

"Mostly Rendors, my Lord, but there are a fair number of Cammorians as well."

"And their leader?"

"Martel, my Lord."

PART TWO

# THE ARCHPRELATE

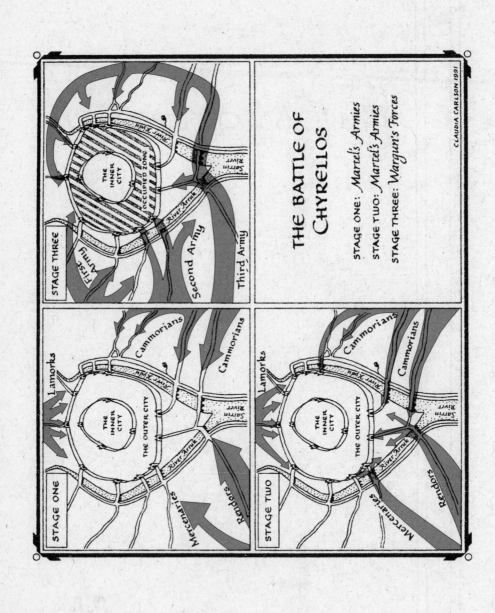

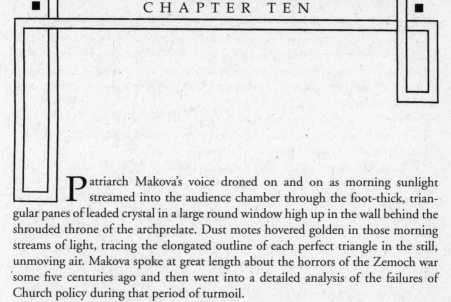

# CHAPTER TEN

Patriarch Makova's voice droned on and on as morning sunlight streamed into the audience chamber through the foot-thick, triangular panes of leaded crystal in a large round window high up in the wall behind the shrouded throne of the archprelate. Dust motes hovered golden in those morning streams of light, tracing the elongated outline of each perfect triangle in the still, unmoving air. Makova spoke at great length about the horrors of the Zemoch war some five centuries ago and then went into a detailed analysis of the failures of Church policy during that period of turmoil.

Sparhawk scribbled a brief note to Dolmant, Emban, and the preceptors to advise them of the armies approaching the Holy City.

"Will the church soldiers defend Chyrellos?" Bevier whispered.

"I think the best we can hope for is some token resistance," Sparhawk replied.

"What's *keeping* Wargun?" Kalten demanded of Ulath.

"I can't even begin to guess."

"Might this not be a good time to make our apologies and leave quietly?" Tynian suggested. "Makova's not really telling us anything we don't already know."

"Let's see what Dolmant says first," Sparhawk replied. "I don't want to give Annias any clues about what we might do at this point. We know why he was stalling now, but let's see what he does next. It's going to take Martel awhile to deploy his forces anyway, so we've got time yet."

"Not very much," Tynian muttered.

"The usual course of action in such circumstances is to demolish the bridges," Bevier advised. "That would delay the approaching armies."

Sparhawk shook his head. "There are ten different bridges across those two rivers, Bevier, and we only have four hundred knights. I don't think we dare risk those men just for the sake of a few hours' delay."

"Not to mention the fact that the Lamorks coming from the north won't have any bridges to cross at all," Tynian added.

The door to the ornate audience chamber opened, and an excited monk hurried to the lectern, his sandals slapping on the polished marble floor and the breath of his passing setting the illuminated dust motes hanging in the sunny triangles to swirling and dancing. The monk bowed deeply and handed Makova a folded sheet of paper.

Makova quickly read the message, and a thin smile of triumph crossed his pock-marked face. "I have just received some important information, my brothers," he announced. "Two sizeable bodies of pilgrims are approaching Chyrellos. While I

know that many of us are otherworldly and abstracted from current events, it's no
secret that certain tensions exist in Eosia at this time. Mightn't it be wise of us to adjourn so that we may use such resources as are available to us to gather more information about these men so that we might better assess the situation?" He looked
around. "Without objection, it is so ordered. The Hierocracy stands in recess until
tomorrow morning."

"Pilgrims," Ulath snorted contemptuously as he rose to his feet.

Sparhawk, however, sat staring hard across the chamber at the Primate of Cimmura, who looked back at him with a faint smile on his face.

Vanion had risen with the other patriarchs and looked quickly up at Sparhawk.
He made a curt motion with one hand and moved toward the door.

"Let's get out of here," Sparhawk muttered to his friends over the sound of the
excited conversation in the chamber. The black-robed patriarchs were filing slowly
toward the door, their progress impeded by knots of their brothers who had stopped
to discuss the matter. Sparhawk led his armored friends out to the stairway and then
down to the marble floor of the audience chamber. The big Pandion resisted his impatient impulse to shove assorted clergymen out of his way as he descended.

He encountered Annias near the door. "Ah, there you are, Sparhawk," the thin,
gray-faced Primate of Cimmura said with a faintly malicious smile. "Do you plan to
visit the city wall to witness the approach of the throngs of the faithful?"

Sparhawk kept a very tight rein on his temper at that point. "Interesting notion, neighbor," he drawled in a tone hovering on insult, "but I thought I might go
have a bite of lunch instead. Would you care to join me, Annias? Sephrenia's roasting a goat, I think. Roast goat thickens the blood, I'm told, and you've been looking just a bit watery of late, if you don't mind my saying so."

"So kind of you to invite me, Sparhawk, but I have a pressing engagement elsewhere. Church business, you understand."

"Of course. Oh, by the way, Annias, when you speak with Martel, give him my
regards. Tell him how eager I am to continue the conversation we began back in
Dabour."

"I'll be certain to tell him, Sir Knight. Now, if you'll excuse me." There was a
faint look of annoyance on the primate's face as he turned and went out through the
wide doorway.

"What was that all about?" Tynian asked.

"You have to know Sparhawk a little better," Kalten told him. "He'd have died
before he gave Annias any satisfaction right there. He didn't even blink the time I
broke his nose. He just gave me a friendly smile and then kicked me in the stomach."

"Did *you* blink?"

"No, as a matter of fact, I was too busy trying to get my breath back. What are
we doing, Sparhawk?"

"Vanion wants to talk with us."

The preceptors of the militant orders were talking together tensely just to one
side of the huge door. Patriarch Emban of Ucera was with them. "I think our major
concern at the moment is the condition of the city gates," Preceptor Abriel was saying. Abriel's burnished armor and his gleaming white surcoat and cloak gave him a

deceptively saintlike appearance, but there was not much of saintliness in his face just now.

"Do you think we can count on the church soldiers at all?" the blue-cloaked Preceptor Darellon asked. Darellon was a slender man and seemed not quite robust enough to carry his heavy Deiran armor. "They could demolish the bridges at least."

"I wouldn't advise it," Emban said bluntly. "They take their orders from Annias, and Annias isn't likely to put any impediments in the way of this Martel person. Sparhawk, exactly what are we facing out there?"

"You tell him, Berit," Sparhawk told the rawboned young novice. "You're the one who actually saw them."

"Yes, my Lord," Berit agreed. "We have Lamorks coming down from the north, your Grace," he told Emban, "and Cammorians and Rendors coming up from the south. Neither army is actually massive, but in combination they're serious enough to threaten the Holy City."

"This army to the south," Emban said, "how are they deployed?"

"The Cammorians are in the van, your Grace, and covering the flanks. The Rendors are in the center and bringing up the rear."

"Are they wearing those traditional black Rendorish robes?" Emban pressed, his eyes intent.

"It's rather difficult to say, your Grace," Berit replied. "They're beyond the rivers, and there's a great deal of dust out there. They seemed to be dressed differently from the Cammorians, though. That's about all I can really say."

"I see. Vanion, is this young man any good?"

"Very good, your Grace," Sparhawk answered for his preceptor. "We have high expectations for him."

"Good. Can I borrow him? And I think I'll want your squire Kurik as well. I need something, and I want them to go get it for me."

"Of course, your Grace," Sparhawk agreed. "Go with him, Berit. Kurik's at the chapterhouse. You can pick him up there."

Emban waddled away with Berit close behind him.

"We'd better split up, my Lords," Preceptor Komier suggested. "Let's go have a look at those gates. Ulath, you're with me."

"Yes, my Lord."

"Sparhawk," Vanion said, "you come with me. Kalten, I want you to stay close to Patriarch Dolmant. Annias might try to take advantage of the confusion, and Dolmant's the one he has to worry about the most. Do your very best to keep his Grace inside the Basilica. It's a little safer in here." Vanion put on his plumed black helmet and turned with a swirl of his inky cloak.

"Which way, my Lord?" Sparhawk asked when they emerged from the Basilica and started down the marble steps to the broad court below.

"We'll go to the south gate," Vanion said grimly. "I want to have a look at Martel."

"Right," Sparhawk agreed. "I'd be the last in the world to say 'I told you so,' Vanion, but I did, you know. I wanted to kill Martel right from the start."

"Don't push it, Sparhawk," Vanion snapped tersely as he hauled himself up into his saddle. His face became grimly set. "The situation's changed, though. You have my permission now."

"It's a little late," Sparhawk muttered as he mounted Faran.

"What was that?"

"Nothing, my Lord."

The south gate of the city of Chyrellos had not been closed for over two centuries, and its condition was painfully obvious. Many of its timbers showed signs of dry rot, and the massive chains that operated it were thick with rust. Vanion took one look and shuddered. "Totally indefensible," he growled. "I could kick that thing down all by myself. Let's go up on top of the wall, Sparhawk. I want to see these armies."

The top of the city wall was crowded with citizens, artisans, merchants, and common laborers. There was an almost holiday air in the colorfully dressed throng as it milled about atop the wall, gaping at the approaching army.

"Watch who you're shoving," one workman said belligerently to Sparhawk. "We got our right to look, same as you." He smelled strongly of cheap ale.

"Go someplace else and look, neighbor." Sparhawk told him.

"You can't order me around. I got my rights."

"You want to look, is that it?"

"That's what I'm here for."

Sparhawk seized him by the front of his canvas smock, lifted him out over the edge of the wall, and dropped him. The wall was about fifteen feet high at that point, and the breath wooshed out of the drunken laborer as he hit the ground. "The approaching army's out that way, neighbor," Sparhawk said pleasantly, leaning out over the edge and pointing southward. "Why don't you stroll on out there and have a closer look—just to exercise your rights?"

"You can be very abrasive when you set your mind to it, Sparhawk," Vanion chided his friend.

"I didn't like his attitude," Sparhawk grunted. "Neighbors," he said then to those crowded around them, "would anyone else like to assert his rights?" He glanced over the wall. The drunken laborer was scrambling toward the questionable safety of the city, limping and wailing incoherently.

A place on the top of the wall immediately opened for the two Pandions.

Vanion looked out at the approaching force of Cammorians and Rendors. "That's sort of what I'd hoped," he said to Sparhawk. "The bulk of Martel's forces is still marching up from the rear, and they're piling up behind the bridges." He pointed at the vast dust cloud rising for several miles to the south. "He won't be able to get those men here until almost dark. I doubt that his deployment will be complete before noon tomorrow. That gives us a little bit of time at least. Let's go back down."

Sparhawk turned to follow his preceptor, but then stopped and turned back. An ornate carriage with the emblem of the Church prominently embossed on its sides had just emerged from the south gate. The monk who was driving it had a suspiciously familiar set to his shoulders. Just before the carriage turned west, a bearded man wearing the cassock of a patriarch peered briefly out of the carriage window.

The carriage was no more than thirty yards away, so Sparhawk could easily identify the supposed clergyman inside.

It was Kurik.

Sparhawk started to swear.

"What's the matter?" Vanion asked him.

"I'm going to have a long talk with Patriarch Emban," Sparhawk grated. "That's Kurik and Berit in that carriage."

"Are you sure?"

"I'd recognize Kurik a hundred yards away on a dark night. Emban had no right to endanger them like that."

"It's too late to do anything about it now. Come along, Sparhawk. I want to go talk with Martel."

"Martel?"

"Maybe we can surprise an answer or two out of him. Do you think he's arrogant enough to honor a flag of truce—just to demonstrate his advantage at this point?"

Sparhawk nodded slowly. "Probably. Martel's ego's a vast open sore. He'd go through the motions of being honorable even if it involved walking through fire."

"That's more or less the way I see him, too. Let's go find out if we're right, but don't get so caught up in exchanging insults with him that you forget to keep your eyes open, Sparhawk. What we really want to do is get a closer look at his army. I need to know if it's just some rabble he's scraped together from country fairs and roadside taverns or something more serious."

A commandeered bed sheet—although Vanion *did* offer to pay the frightened innkeeper for it even as Sparhawk was stripping it from the bed of an upstairs room—provided them with a flag of truce. It popped and flapped quite satisfyingly from Sparhawk's lance as the two black-armored knights thundered out through the south gate toward the approaching army. They rode to a hilltop and stopped there. Sparhawk turned Faran slightly so that the stiff breeze caught their improvised flag and blew it out for all to see. Though they were some distance from the van of Martel's army, Sparhawk could hear distant shouts and commands. The army gradually undulated to a stop, and not long after, Martel, accompanied by one of his soldiers, rode out from the midst of their troops. Martel also carried a lance, and a white cape that looked suspiciously like that of a Cyrinic Knight flapped from it. Sparhawk squinted at him. "I wonder," he mused. "Bhelliom brought Ehlana back from the brink of death. I wonder if I could persuade it to do the same for Martel."

"Why would you want to?"

"So I could kill him again, my Lord. I could make killing Martel over and over again my life's work with just a little encouragement."

Vanion gave him a very hard look, but he didn't say anything.

Martel wore a very expensive suit of armor, its cuirass and shoulder plates embossed with gold and silver and with the steel itself highly burnished. It appeared to be of Deiran forging, and it was much more elegant than the functional armor of the Church Knights. When he was within a few yards of Sparhawk and Vanion, he thrust the butt of his lance into the ground and removed his ornate, white-plumed helmet. His white hair flowed out behind him in the stiff breeze. "My Lord," he said with exaggerated courtesy, inclining his head toward Vanion.

Vanion's face was icy. He did not speak to the knight he had expelled from the Pandion Order, but motioned Sparhawk forward instead.

"Ah," Martel said in a tone that might even have been one of genuine regret, "I expected better of you, Vanion. Oh, well, I'll talk with Sparhawk instead. Feel free to listen in, if you like."

Sparhawk also drove the butt of his lance into the turf and he, also, removed his helmet as he nudged Faran forward.

"You're looking well, old boy," Martel said.

"You look about the same—except for the fancy armor."

"I recently had occasion to do some thinking," Martel replied. "I've gathered up a great deal of money in the last several years, but it occurred to me that I wasn't enjoying it very much. I decided to buy some new toys."

"That's a new horse, too, isn't it?" Sparhawk looked at Martel's bulky black mount.

"Do you like him? I could get you one from the same stable, if you'd like."

"I'll stick with Faran."

"Did you ever civilize that ugly brute?"

"I sort of like him the way he is. What are your intentions here, Martel?"

"Isn't it obvious, old boy? I'm going to seize the Holy City. If I were speaking for public approval, I could put a better face on it and use the word 'liberate,' I suppose, but since we're such old friends, I suppose I can afford to be frank. To put it in plain terms, Sparhawk, I'm going to march into the Holy City, and, as the saying goes, bend it to my will."

"You mean you're going to *try*, Martel."

"Who's going to stop me?"

"Your own good sense, I hope. You're a bit deranged, but you've never been stupid."

Martel gave him a mocking half bow.

"Where did you come up with all the troops on such short notice?"

"Short notice?" Martel laughed. "You don't pay much attention to things, do you, Sparhawk? You spent too much time in Jiroch, I'm afraid. All that sun." He shuddered. "By the way, have you heard from the lovely Lillias lately?" He threw that in quickly, obviously showing off his knowledge of Sparhawk's activities for the past several years in the hope of discomfitting his former brother.

"She was well—last I heard." Sparhawk gave no hint that he was at all surprised.

"I may just take her when this is all over. She's a significant sort of woman, I noticed. It might amuse me to dally with your former mistress."

"Get lots of rest, Martel. I don't really think you've got enough stamina for Lillias. You still haven't answered my question, though."

"Thought you could answer it for yourself, old boy, now that I've nudged your memory a bit. I gathered the Lamorks while I was up there fomenting discord between Baron Alstrom and Count Gerrich. The Cammorian mercenaries are always available. All I had to do was pass the word, and they came running. The Rendors weren't that difficult, once I'd disposed of Arasham. Incidentally, he kept croaking the word 'Ramshorn' while he was dying. Could that possibly have been that secret word you cooked up? Very pedestrian, Sparhawk. Most unimaginative. The new spiritual leader of Rendor is a much easier man to manage."

"I've met him," Sparhawk said shortly. "I wish you joy in his companionship."

"Oh, Ulesim's not so bad—as long as you stay upwind of him. Anyway, I landed in Arcium, sacked and burned Coombe, and marched on Larium. I must say that Wargun took his own sweet time getting there, though. When he arrived, I rode away and then led him around in circles down in Arcium. It was a way to amuse myself while I was awaiting word of the passing of the revered Cluvonus. Did you give him a nice funeral, by the way?"

"Fairly standard."

"I'm sorry I missed it."

"There's something else you should be sorry about, Martel. Annias isn't going to be able to pay you. Ehlana's recovered and cut him off from her treasury again."

"Yes, I'd heard about that—from Princess Arissa and her son. I freed them from that cloister as a favor to the Primate of Cimmura. There was a slight misunderstanding while I was releasing them, though, and all the nuns in that cloister died quite suddenly. Regrettable, perhaps, but you religious types really shouldn't become involved in politics, you know. My soldiers also set fire to the cloister as we were riding away. I'll convey your best wishes to Arissa when I rejoin my troops. She's been staying in my pavilion since we left Demos. The horrors of her confinement quite unnerved her, and I've been sort of offering what comfort I could."

"That's one more you owe me, Martel," Sparhawk grated.

"One more what?"

"Those nuns are another reason for me to kill you."

"Feel free to try at any time, old boy. How on earth did you manage to cure Ehlana, though? I was assured down in Rendor that there was no possible cure."

"Your informants were wrong. We found out what the cure was in Dabour. Actually, that's why Sephrenia and I were really there. You might call spoiling your plans there in Arasham's tent sort of a bonus."

"I was really put out with you about that, you know."

"How are you going to pay your troops?"

"Sparhawk," Martel said wearily, "I'm about to capture the richest city in the world. Have you any idea of how much loot's available inside the walls of Chyrellos? My troops joined me eagerly—for no pay at all—just for the chance to browse around in there."

"I hope they're ready for a protracted siege, then."

"It's not going to take me all that long to get inside, Sparhawk. Annias will open the gates for me."

"Annias doesn't have enough votes in the Hierocracy to do that."

"I rather imagine that my presence here will alter the vote somewhat."

"Would you like to settle this right here and now? Just you and me?" Sparhawk offered.

"Why should I do that when I've already got the advantage, old boy?"

"All right. Try to get into Chyrellos then, and maybe we can find one of those alleys you're so fond of."

"I yearn for the day, dear brother." Martel smiled. "Well, Vanion, has your tame ape here wheedled enough answers out of me to suit you yet, or should I go on?"

"Let's go back," Vanion said abruptly to Sparhawk.

"Always a pleasure talking with you, Lord Vanion," Martel called mockingly after them.

"Do you really think Bhelliom might possibly bring him back from the grave?" Vanion asked Sparhawk as they rode back toward the city. "I wouldn't mind killing him a time or two myself."

"We can ask Sephrenia, I suppose."

They gathered once again in the red-draped study of Sir Nashan, the portly Pandion who was in charge of the chapterhouse here. The chapterhouse, unlike those of the other orders, was just inside the walls of the ancient inner city, the original Chyrellos. Each of the preceptors gave a report on one of the gates of the city. None of the reports was particularly encouraging. Abriel, as senior preceptor, rose to his feet. "What do we think, gentlemen?" he said. "Is there any possible way we can hold the entire city?"

"Absolutely out of the question, Abriel," Komier said bluntly. "Those gates wouldn't keep out a herd of sheep, and even counting the church soldiers, we don't have enough men to hold off the kind of force gathering out there."

"You're raising a very unpleasant notion, Komier," Darellon said.

"I know, but I don't see very many options, do you?"

"Not really."

"I'm sorry, my Lords," Sir Nashan said deferentially, "but I don't quite follow what you've got in mind."

"We'll have to pull back to the walls of the inner city, Nashan," Vanion told him.

"And abandon the rest?" Nashan exclaimed. "My Lords, we're talking about the largest—and richest—city in the world!"

"We have no choice, Sir Nashan," Abriel explained. "The walls of the inner city were built in antiquity. They're much higher and stronger than the largely ornamental walls that encircle the rest of Chyrellos. We can defend the inner city—for a time, at least—but we have no chance of holding the whole city."

"We're going to have to make some hard and unpleasant choices here," Preceptor Darellon said. "If we pull back to the inner walls, we're going to have to close the gates to the general population. We won't have sufficient supplies in the old city to sustain that many people."

"We won't be able to do a thing until we can take command of the church soldiers, though," Vanion said. "Four hundred of us couldn't possibly hold out against Martel's army."

"I might be able to help you there," Patriarch Emban said. Emban was sprawled in a large chair, his fat hands on his paunch. "It's going to depend on just how arrogant Makova's feeling in the morning, however." Emban had been evasive when Sparhawk had demanded some sort of explanation about what he had sent Kurik and Berit to do.

"We're going to have a certain tactical advantage," Komier said thoughtfully. "Martel's troops are mercenaries. As soon as they get inside the outer city, they're going to stop for some constructive looting. That's going to give us more time."

Emban chuckled. "It's also going to distract a sizeable portion of the Hierocracy." He grinned. "Many of my fellow patriarchs have lavish houses out beyond the inner walls. They'll view the sacking of the outer city with a certain anguish, I'd imagine. That *might* just reduce their enthusiasm for the candidacy of the Primate of Cimmura. *My* house, however, is here inside the old walls. I'll be able to think quite clearly—and so will you, won't you, Dolmant?"

"You're a bad man, Emban," Dolmant told him.

"But God appreciates my efforts, Dolmant, no matter how sneaky or underhanded. All of us live but to serve—each in his own special way." He paused, frowning slightly. "Ortzel's our candidate. I'd have probably chosen someone else, but there's a tide of conservatism in the Church just now, and Ortzel's so conservative that he doesn't even believe in fire. We may have to work on him just a bit, Dolmant. He's not exactly what you'd call loveable."

"That's *our* problem, Emban—yours and mine," Dolmant pointed out. "I think we should concern ourselves with military matters at the moment."

"I suspect that our next step will have to be charting out routes for withdrawal," Abriel said. "If the Patriarch of Ucera here is successful in transferring command of the church soldiers over to us, we'll have to move them back inside the inner walls rapidly before the general population realizes what we're doing. Otherwise, we'll have mobs of refugees in here with us."

"This is brutal, my Lords," Sephrenia chided them. "You're abandoning innocent people to the mercy of a horde of savages. Martel's men won't be satisfied with just looting. There are certain to be atrocities out there."

Dolmant sighed. "War is never civilized, little mother," he told her. "One other thing. From now on, you *will* accompany us to the Basilica every day. I want you where we can protect you."

"As you wish, dear one," she replied.

Talen's face was mournful. "I don't suppose you could see your way clear to sort of let me slip outside the inner walls before you close the gates, could you?" he asked Sparhawk.

"No," Sparhawk replied, "but why would you want to be out there?"

"To look after my share of the loot, naturally. This is a once-in-a-lifetime opportunity."

"You would surely not join in the looting of houses, would you, Talen?" Bevier asked in a shocked tone.

"Of course not, Sir Bevier. I'd let Martel's soldiers do that. It's when they're back out in the street with their arms full of the things that they've stolen that the thieves of Chyrellos will move in and pick them over. Martel's going to lose a lot of men in the next few days, I'd imagine. I can almost guarantee that an epidemic of

stab wounds is going to break out in his ranks before this is all over. There are beggars out there who'll never have to beg again." The boy sighed again. "You're rob-
bing my childhood of all its fun, Sparhawk," he accused.

"There is absolutely no danger whatsoever, my brothers," Makova scoffed the
following morning when the Hierocracy reconvened. "The commander of my own
personal guard, Captain Gorta—" He paused a moment to give the preceptors of
the militant orders a hard stare. The sudden demise of the previous captain of his
troops obviously still rankled. "Captain Erden, that is—went out at great personal
risk to question these approaching pilgrims most closely, and he assures me that
they are no more than that—pilgrims, faithful sons of the Church—and that they
are making this pilgrimage to the Holy City in order to join their voices with others in thanksgiving when the new archprelate is elevated to the holy throne."

"Now, that's really amazing, Makova," Patriarch Emban drawled. "As it so happens, I sent observers of my own out of the city, and they had an entirely different
kind of report. How do you imagine we can reconcile these differences?"

Makova's smile was brief, even frosty. "The Patriarch of Ucera is well known for
his jocularity," he said. "He is indeed a droll and jolly fellow, and his merry japes frequently relax our tensions at stressful moments, but is this really the time for hilar-
ity, my dear Emban?"

"Do you see me smiling, Makova?" Emban's tone had quite nearly the bite of a
dagger thrust to the kidneys. He rose, grunting. "What *my* people report, dear
brothers, is that this horde of so-called pilgrims at our gates is anything but
friendly."

"Nonsense," Makova snapped.

"Perhaps," Emban said, "but I've taken the liberty of having one of these 'pilgrims' brought here to the Basilica so that we may examine him more closely. He
may not choose to speak very much, but much can be gleaned from observing a
man's demeanor, his bearing, his origins—even his clothing." Emban clapped his
hands sharply together before Makova could object or exert his authority.

The door to the chamber opened, and Kurik and Berit entered. They each held
an ankle of the black-robed man they were bringing in to be interviewed, and they
dragged the inert body across the marble floor, leaving a long crimson smear of
blood on the white stone behind them.

"What are you *doing*?" Makova half shrieked.

"Merely presenting evidence, Makova. No rational decision can be made without a thorough examination of the evidence, can it?" Emban pointed at a spot not
too far in front of the lectern. "Put the witness there, my friends," he instructed
Kurik and Berit.

"I *forbid* this!" Makova howled.

"Forbid away, old boy." Emban shrugged. "But it's too late now. Everybody in
the chamber has already seen this man, and we all know what he is, don't we?"
Emban waddled over to the corpse lying spread-eagled on the marble floor. "We can
all tell by this man's features what his nation of origin was, and his black clothing
confirms it. My brothers, what we have here was obviously a Rendor."

"Patriarch Emban of Ucera," Makova said desperately, "I arrest you on the charge of murder."

"Don't be an ass, Makova," Emban said. "You can't arrest me while the Hierocracy's in session. Besides, we're inside the Basilica, and I claim sanctuary." He looked at Kurik. "Did you really have to kill him?" he asked.

"Yes, your Grace," the burly squire replied. "The situation made it necessary—but we said a brief prayer over him afterward, though."

"Most exemplary, my son," Emban said. "I will therefore grant you and your young companion here full absolution for your part in sending this miserable heretic to face the infinite mercy of God." The fat man looked around the chamber. "Now," he said, "to return to our interrogation of this 'pilgrim.' We have here a Rendor—armed with a sword, you'll note. Since the only Rendors currently on this part of the Eosian continent are Eshandists, we must conclude that this 'pilgrim' was one as well. Given their views, would we expect Eshandist heretics to come to the Holy City to celebrate the elevation of a new archprelate? Has our dear brother Makova somehow miraculously converted the heretics of the south to the worship of the true God and rejoined them with the body of our Holy Mother Church? I pause for the reply of the esteemed Patriarch of Coombe." He stood looking expectantly at Makova.

"I'm certainly glad he's on *our* side," Ulath murmured to Tynian.

"Truly."

"Ah," Emban said as Makova looked at him helplessly. "It was too much to hope for, I suppose. We must all apologize to God for our failure to seize this opportunity to heal the wound in the body of our Holy Mother. Our regret, however, and our bitter tears of disappointment must not dim our eyes to the harshness of reality. The 'pilgrims' at our gates are not what they seem. Our dear brother Makova has been cruelly deceived, I'm afraid. What stands at the gates of Chyrellos is not a multitude of the faithful, but a ravening army of our most hated foes bent on destroying and desecrating the very center of the true faith. Our own personal fate, my brothers, is of no moment, but I should advise you all to make your peace with God. The horrors the Eshandist heretics inflict upon members of the higher clergy are too well known to require repeating. I myself am totally resigned to facing the flames." He paused, then grinned. He clapped both hands to his huge paunch. "I'll make a jolly fire, though."

A titter of nervous laughter rippled through the chamber.

"Our own fates, my brothers, are not important," Emban continued. "What matters here is the fate of the Holy City and the fate of the Church. We face a cruel but simple decision. Do we surrender our Mother to the heretics, or do we fight?"

"Fight!" one patriarch shouted, springing to his feet. "Fight!"

The cry was quickly taken up. Soon the entire Hierocracy was on its feet, roaring out the word "Fight!"

Emban clasped his hands behind his back somewhat theatrically and bowed his head. When he lifted his face, tears were actually streaming down his cheeks. He turned slowly, giving everyone in the audience chamber ample opportunity to see those tears. "Alas, my brothers," he said in a broken voice. "Our vows forbid us to lay aside our cassocks and vestments and to take up the sword. We stand helpless in this dreadful crisis. We are doomed, my brothers, and our Holy Mother Church is doomed with us. Alas that I have lived so long that I must witness this terrible day. Where can we turn, brothers? Who will come to our aid? Who has the power to protect us in this darkest hour? What manner of men are there in all the world who can defend us in this dreadful, fatal conflict?"

There was a breathless pause.

"The Church Knights!" a feeble old voice wheezed from one of the red-cushioned benches. "We must turn to the Knights of the Church! Not even the powers of Hell can prevail against them!"

"The Church Knights!" the Hierocracy roared as in one voice. "The Church Knights!"

## CHAPTER ELEVEN

The excited tumult in the large chamber continued for some time as Patriarch Emban of Ucera stood gravely in the center of the long marble floor, just *happening* to have placed himself in the precise center of that elongated circle of light streaming down through the round window behind the vacant throne. As the babble of voices began to die out, Emban raised one pudgy hand. "Indeed, my brothers," he continued, his voice carrying just that right note of gravity, "the invincible Knights of the Church could easily defend Chyrellos, but the knights are committed at this time to the defense of Arcium. The preceptors are here, of course, taking their rightful places among us, but each of them has but a token force here, certainly not enough to fight off the armies of darkness encircling us. We cannot whisk the full might of the militant orders from the rocky plains of Arcium to the Holy City in the twinkling of an eye; and even if we could, how could we convince the commanders of the army in that sorely beset kingdom that our need is greater than theirs and thus persuade them to release the knights to come to our aid?"

Patriarch Ortzel of Kadach rose to his feet, his severe face framed by his pale, graying hair. "If I may speak, Emban," he said. The Patriarch of Kadach was the compromise candidate of the factions opposed to Annias, and he spoke with a certain authority.

"Of course," Emban said. "I eagerly await the wisdom of my esteemed brother from Lamorkand."

"The paramount duty of the Church is to survive so that she may continue her work," Ortzel said in his harsh voice. "All other considerations must be secondary to that. Will we all concede that point?"

There was a murmur of agreement.

"There are times when sacrifices must be made," Ortzel continued. "If a man's leg be caught between the rocks at the bottom of a tidal pool and the rising waters be lapping at his chin, must not the man regretfully sacrifice the limb in order to save his life? Thus it is with us. In sorrow must we sacrifice the whole of Arcium if need be to save our life—which is our Holy Mother Church. What we are faced with here, my brothers, is a crisis. In times past, the Hierocracy has been extremely reluctant to impose the stern and stringent requirements of this most extreme of measures, but the situation facing us is doubtless the severest trial facing our Holy Mother since the Zemoch invasion five centuries ago. God is watching us, my brothers, and will surely judge us and our fitness to continue our stewardship of his beloved Church. I, therefore, as the laws that govern us require, demand that an immediate vote be taken. The question upon which we will vote can be stated most simply. 'Does the current situation in Chyrellos constitute a Crisis of the Faith?' Yes or no?"

Makova's eyes were wide with shock. "Surely," he burst out, "surely the situation is not *that* critical! We have not even tried negotiation with the armies at our gates as yet, and—"

"The patriarch is not in order," Ortzel said abruptly. "The question of Crisis of the Faith is not open to discussion."

"Point of law!" Makova shouted.

Ortzel looked intimidatingly at the weedy monk who served as law clerk. "Speak the law," he commanded.

The monk was trembling violently and he began to paw desperately through his books.

"What's happening here?" Talen asked in confusion. "I don't understand."

"Crisis of the Faith is almost never invoked," Bevier told him, "probably because the kings of western Eosia object so violently. In a Crisis of the Faith, the Church assumes control of everything—governments, armies, resources, money—everything."

"But wouldn't a Crisis of the Faith require a substantive vote?" Kalten asked, "or even unanimity?"

"I don't think so," Bevier said. "Let's see what the law clerk has to say."

"Isn't it sort of redundant at this point anyway?" Tynian asked. "We've already sent for Wargun and told him that there's a Church crisis."

"Somebody probably neglected to tell Ortzel," Ulath replied. "He's a stickler for legalities, and there's no real point in disturbing his sensibilities, is there?"

The weedy monk, his face absolutely white, rose and cleared his throat. His voice was squeaky with fright as he began. "The Patriarch of Kadach has correctly cited the law," he declared. "The question of Crisis of the Faith must be put to an immediate secret vote."

"*Secret?*" Makova exclaimed.

"Such is the law, your Grace, and the vote is to be decided by a simple majority."

"But—"

"I must remind the Patriarch of Coombe that further discussion is not in order." Ortzel's voice cracked like a whip. "I call for the vote." He looked around.

"You," he snapped at the clergyman sitting not far from the goggle-eyed Annias, "fetch the instruments of the vote. They are, as I recall, in the chest at the right hand of the archprelate's throne."

The clergyman hesitated, looking fearfully at Annias.

*"Move, man!"* Ortzel roared.

The priest jumped to his feet and ran to the shrouded throne.

"Somebody's going to have to explain this to me a little better," Talen said in a baffled tone.

"Later, Talen," Sephrenia told him softly. Sephrenia, wearing a heavy black robe that looked slightly ecclesiastical and concealed her race and sex, sat among the Church Knights, almost totally concealed by their armored bulk. "Let's watch the exquisite dance being performed before us."

"Sephrenia," Sparhawk chided her.

"Sorry," she apologized. "I'm not poking fun at your Church, Sparhawk, just at all this involuted maneuvering."

The instruments of the vote consisted of a fairly large black box, quite dusty and totally unadorned, and two plain leather bags securely held shut with stamped leaden seals.

"Patriarch of Coombe," Ortzel said quite concisely. "You hold the chair at the moment. It is your duty to break the seals and cause the ballots to be distributed."

Makova glanced quickly at the law clerk, and the little monk nodded. Then Makova took up the two bags, pried open the leaden seals, and took an object from each. They were perhaps the size of a common penny. One was white and the other black. "We will vote with these," he declared to his fellow patriarchs, holding the counters up. "Is it agreed that the black means no and the white yes?"

There was a rumble of agreement.

"Distribute the counters, then," Makova instructed a pair of youthful pages. "Each member of the Hierocracy shall receive one white counter and one black." He cleared his throat. "As God gives you wisdom, my brothers, vote your consciences in this matter." Some trace of color had returned to Makova's face.

"He's been counting votes," Kalten said. "He's got fifty-nine, and he *thinks* we've only got forty-seven. He doesn't know about the five patriarchs hiding in that closet. I'd imagine those five votes will come as quite a surprise to him. He'll still win, though."

"You're forgetting the neutrals, Kalten," Bevier reminded him.

"They'll just abstain, won't they? They're still looking for bribes. They're not going to offend either side."

"They can't abstain, Kalten," Bevier told him, "not on *this* vote. Church law says that they have to come down on one side or the other of this question."

"Where did you learn so much about this, Bevier?"

"I told you that I'd studied military history."

"What's military history got to do with this?"

"The Church declared a Crisis of the Faith during the Zemoch invasion. I looked into it as part of my study."

"Oh."

As the two pages were distributing the counters, Dolmant rose and walked to the huge doors. He spoke briefly to the members of the archprelate's guard standing outside and returned to his seat. It was when the two boys distributing the counters were nearly at the end of the fourth row of the crimson-cushioned benches that the door opened, and the five nervous patriarchs who had been in hiding filed in.

"What's the meaning of this?" Makova was goggle-eyed.

"The Patriarch of Coombe is not in order," Ortzel reminded him. Ortzel seemed to enjoy saying that to Makova. "My brothers," he began to address the five, "we are presently voting on—"

"It is *my* responsibility to instruct our brothers," Makova said vehemently.

"The Patriarch of Coombe is in error," Ortzel said in a clipped voice. "It was *I* who put the question before the Hierocracy, and, therefore, the responsibility is *mine.*" He quickly explained the vote to his five fellow patriarchs. He stressed the gravity of the situation to them, something Makova surely would not have done.

Makova regained his composure.

"He's counting votes again," Kalten murmured. "He's still got more than we have. It all hangs on the neutrals now."

The black box was placed on a table in front of Makova's lectern, and the patriarchs filed by, each depositing one of his counters in the slot on the top of the box. Some were quite obvious about which counter they were depositing. Others were not.

"I'll take care of the tallying," Makova declared.

"No," Ortzel said flatly, "at least not alone. It was *I* who placed the question before the Hierocracy, and *I* will assist you."

"I'm beginning to like Ortzel more and more," Tynian said to Ulath.

"Yes," Ulath agreed. "Maybe we misjudged him."

Makova's face grew more gray as he and Ortzel began to tally up the votes. There was a hushed, almost breathless silence as the tallying continued.

"And done," Ortzel said curtly. "Announce the totals, Makova."

Makova threw a quick, apologetic glance at Annias. "The vote stands at sixty-four yes and fifty-six no," he muttered almost inaudibly.

"Say it again, Makova," Ortzel prompted. "Some of our brothers have failing hearing."

Makova gave him a look filled with hatred and repeated the totals in a louder voice.

"We got the neutrals!" Talen exulted, "*and* we stole three of Annias' votes as well."

"Well, then," Emban said mildly, "I'm glad that's been settled. We have much to consider, my brothers, and very little time. Am I correct in assuming that it is the will of the Hierocracy that we send immediately for the Church Knights—*and* the armies of western Eosia as well—to come to our defense with all possible haste?"

"Will you leave the kingdom of Arcium totally defenseless, Emban?" Makova demanded.

"Just what's threatening Arcium at the moment, Makova? All the Eshandists are camped outside *our* gates. Do you want another vote?"

"Substance," Makova said flatly, insisting on a sixty-percent majority on the question.

"Point of law," Emban replied. His fat face had an almost saintly expression. He looked at the law clerk. "What is the law on matters of substance under these circumstances?" he asked.

"Saving only the election of an archprelate, a substantive vote is not required in times of Crisis of the Faith, your Grace," the monk replied.

"I rather thought that might be the case." Emban smiled. "Well, Makova, do we vote or not?"

"I'll withdraw the question of substance," Makova conceded grudgingly, "but exactly how do you propose to get a messenger out of a besieged city?"

Ortzel rose again. "As my brothers may be aware, I am a Lamork," he said. "We are well accustomed to sieges in Lamorkand. Last night I sent twenty of my own men in disguise to the outskirts of the city and beyond. They are awaiting only that signal that even now rises as a plume of red smoke from the dome of this very Basilica. I would surmise that they are already riding hard for Arcium—at least they'd better be, if they know what's good for them."

"I'm going to *like* him." Kalten grinned.

"You dared to do this without the consent of the Hierocracy as a whole, Ortzel?" Makova gasped.

"Was there ever any doubt concerning the outcome of the voting, Makova?"

"I begin to catch a strong smell of collusion here," Sephrenia said lightly.

"My brothers," Emban continued, "the crisis we presently face is clearly a military one, and for the most part, we are not military men. How may we avoid the errors, the confusion, the delays that untrained and unworldly churchmen must inevitably cause as they flounder through unfamiliar complexities? The leadership of the Patriarch of Coombe has been exemplary, and I'm sure we join together in expressing our heartfelt gratitude to him, but, regrettably, the Patriarch of Coombe is no more well versed in military science than I, and I'll confess it freely, my brothers, I can't tell one end of a sword from the other." He smiled broadly. "Quite obviously, *my* training has been with eating implements rather than with those of war. I'd be happy to accept any challenge in that area, however. My opponent and I could happily duel to the death on a well-roasted ox."

The Hierocracy laughed at that. The tension was somewhat relaxed by the laughter.

"We need a military man, my brothers," Emban continued. "We need a general now instead of a chairman. We have four such generals in our very midst. These, of course, are the preceptors of the four orders."

There was an excited stir, but Emban held up one hand. *"But,"* he continued, "do we dare distract one of these towering military geniuses from the vital task of defending Chyrellos? I think not. Where then should we look?" He paused. "I must now break a solemn promise I made to one of my brothers," he confessed. "I pray that both he and God will be able to find it in their hearts to forgive me. We do, in fact, have a man with military training in our midst, dear brothers. He had modestly concealed this fact, but a modesty that deprives us of his talent in this time of crisis is no virtue." His broad round face took on an expression of genuine regret. "Forgive me, Dolmant," he said, "but I have no choice in this matter. My duty to the Church comes even before my duty to a friend."

Dolmant's eyes were frosty.

Emban sighed. "I expect that when we conclude this meeting, my dear brother from Demos will thrash me thoroughly, but I'm well padded, and the bruises won't be all that visible—I hope. In his youth, the Patriarch of Demos was an acolyte in the Pandion Order, and—"

There was a sudden amazed babble in the chamber.

Emban raised his voice. "Preceptor Vanion of that order, who was himself a novice at the selfsame time, assures me that our saintly brother from Demos was a consummate warrior and might very well have risen to the rank of preceptor himself had not our Holy Mother found other uses for his vast talents." He paused again. "Praise God, my brothers, that we were never faced with *that* decision. Choosing between Vanion and Dolmant would likely have been a task beyond our combined wisdom." He continued for a time, heaping praise upon Dolmant. Then he looked around. "What is our decision, my brothers? Shall we beseech our brother of Demos to guide us in this time of our gravest peril?"

Makova stared at him. His mouth opened a couple of times as if he were on the verge of speaking, but each time he clamped it tightly shut.

Sparhawk put his hands on the bench in front of him, leaned forward, and spoke quietly to the elderly monk sitting in front of him. "Has Patriarch Makova been suddenly struck dumb, neighbor?" he asked. "I'd have thought he'd be climbing the walls by now."

"In a very real sense the Patriarch of Coombe *has* been struck dumb, Sir Knight," the monk replied. "There's a long-standing custom—even a rule—in the Hierocracy that a patriarch may not speak to his own candidacy for any post—no matter how remote that candidacy may be. It's considered immodest."

"Sensible custom, that one," Sparhawk said.

"I feel much the same way, Sir Knight." The monk smiled. "Makova tends to put me to sleep for some reason."

Sparhawk grinned at him. "Me, too," he said. "I suppose we should both pray for greater patience—one of these days."

Makova looked around desperately, but none of his friends saw fit to speak—either because of a lack of anything flattering to say about him, or because they could see which way a vote would go. "Vote," he said somewhat sullenly.

"Good idea, Makova." Emban smiled. "Let's move right along. Time's fleeing even as we speak."

The vote this time was sixty-five for Dolmant's assuming the chair and fifty-five against. Another of the supporters of the Primate of Cimmura had defected.

"My brother from Demos," Emban said to Dolmant when the tally had been completed and announced, "would you be so kind as to assume the chair?"

Dolmant came forward while Makova angrily gathered up his papers and stalked away from the lectern.

"You honor me beyond my ability to express my gratitude, my brothers," Dolmant said. "For the moment, let me merely say thank you so that we may more quickly deal with the crisis at hand. Our most immediate need is for a greater force under the command of the Knights of the Church. How may we address that need?"

Emban had not even bothered to sit down. "The force of which our revered chairman speaks is at hand, my brothers," he said to the assemblage. "Each of us has a detachment of church soldiers at his disposal. In view of the current crisis, I propose that we immediately turn control of those troops over to the militant orders."

"Will you strip us of our only protection, Emban?" Makova protested.

"The protection of the Holy City is far more important, Makova," Emban told him. "Will history say of us that we were so cowardly that we refused our aid to our Holy Mother in her time of need out of timidity and a craven concern for our own skins? Pray God that no such poltroon contaminates us by his presence in our midst. What says the Hierocracy? Shall he make this insignificant sacrifice for the sake of the Church?"

The rumble of assent this time was slightly pained in some quarters.

"Will any patriarch call for a vote on the matter?" Dolmant asked with cool correctness. He looked around at the now-silent tiers. "Then let the recorder set down the fact that the suggestion of the Patriarch of Ucera was accepted by general acclamation. The scribes will then draw up suitable documents which each member of the Hierocracy will sign, transferring command of his personal detachment of church soldiers over to the militant orders for the defense of the city." He paused. "Will someone please ask the commander of the archprelate's personal guard to present himself before the Hierocracy?"

A priest scurried to the door, and shortly thereafter, a brawny officer with red hair, a polished breastplate, and armed with an embossed shield and antiquated short sword entered. His expression clearly showed that he was aware of the army at the city gates.

"One question, Colonel," Dolmant said to him. "My brothers have asked me to chair their deliberations. In the absence of an archprelate, do I speak in his stead?"

The colonel considered it for a moment. "You do, your Grace," he admitted, looking somewhat pleased.

"That's unheard of," Makova protested, obviously a bit chagrined that he had not taken advantage of this obscure rule during his *own* tenure as chairman.

"So is this situation, Makova," Dolmant told him. "A Crisis of the Faith has only been declared five times in the history of the Church, and in each of the four preceding crises, a vigorous archprelate occupied the throne that so sadly stands empty before us. When faced with unique circumstances, we must improvise. This is what we're going to do, Colonel. The patriarchs are each going to sign documents turning command of their individual detachments of soldiers over to the Church Knights. To save time and unnecessary arguments, as soon as those documents are signed, you and your men will escort each patriarch to the barracks of his sundry forces, where the patriarch may confirm his written command in person." He turned then to look at the preceptors. "Lord Abriel," he said, "will you and your fellow preceptors dispatch knights to take command of the soldiers just as soon as they are released and to assemble them in a place of your choosing? Our deployment must be quick and unfaltering."

Abriel stood. "We will, your Grace," he declared, "and gladly."

"Thank you, my Lord Abriel," Dolmant said. He looked back at the ranks of the Hierocracy, rising tier upon tier above him. "We have done what we can, my brothers," he said to them. "It seems most appropriate now that we proceed immediately to turn our soldiers over to the Knights of the Church, and then perhaps we might each devote ourselves to seeking counsel from God. Perhaps he, in his infinite wisdom, will suggest further steps we might take to defend his beloved Church. Therefore, without objection, the Hierocracy stands in recess until such time as this crisis has passed."

"Brilliant," Bevier exclaimed. "In one series of master strokes, they've wrested control of the Hierocracy from Annias, stripped him of all his soldiers, and forestalled the taking of any votes while we're not here to stop them."

"It's kind of a shame that they broke off so quickly," Talen said. "The way things stand right now, we only need one more vote to elect our *own* archprelate."

Sparhawk was elated as he and his companions joined the crush at the door to the audience chamber. Although Martel was still a grave threat to the Holy City, they had succeeded in wresting control of the Hierocracy from Annias and his underlings, and the weakness of the Primate of Cimmura's grasp on his votes was clearly demonstrated by the defection of four of his bought and paid-for patriarchs. As he started to move slowly from the chamber, he felt again that now-familiar sense of overpowering dread. He half turned. This time, he even partially saw it. The shadow was back behind the archprelate's throne, seeming to undulate softly in the dimness. Sparhawk's hand went to the front of his surcoat to make sure that Bhelliom was still where it belonged. The jewel was secure, and he knew that the drawstring on the pouch was tightly tied. It appeared that his reasoning had been slightly faulty. The shadow *could* make an appearance independently of the Bhelliom. It was even here inside the most consecrated building of the Elene faith. He had thought that here of all places he would be free of it, but it was not so. Troubled, he continued with his friends from the room that now seemed dark and chill.

The attempt on Sparhawk's life came almost immediately after he saw the shadow. A cowled monk, one of the many in the crowd at the door, spun suddenly and drove a small dagger directly at the big Pandion's unvisored face. It was only Sparhawk's trained reflexes that saved him. Without thinking, he blocked the dagger stroke with his armored forearm and then seized the monk. With a despairing cry, the monk drove his little dagger into his own side. He stiffened abruptly, and Sparhawk felt a violent shudder pass through the body of the man he was holding. Then the monk's face went blank, and he sagged limply.

"Kalten!" Sparhawk whispered to his friend. "Give me a hand! Keep him on his feet."

Kalten stepped swiftly to the other side of the monk's body and took his arm.

"Is our brother unwell?" another monk asked them as they half carried the body out through the door.

"Fainted," Kalten replied in an offhand manner. "Some people can't stand crowds. My friend and I will take him into some side chamber and let him get his breath."

"Slick," Sparhawk muttered a quick compliment.

"You see, Sparhawk, I *can* think on my feet." Kalten jerked his head toward the door of a nearby antechamber. "Let's take him in there and have a look at him."

They dragged the body into the chamber and closed the door behind them. Kalten pulled the dagger from the monk's side. "Not much of a weapon," he said disdainfully.

"It was enough," Sparhawk growled. "One little nick with it stiffened him up like a plank."

"Poison?" Kalten guessed.

"Probably—unless the sight of his own blood overpowered him. Let's have a look." Sparhawk bent and tore open the monk's robe.

The "monk" was a Rendor.

"Isn't *that* interesting?" Kalten said. "It looks as if that crossbowman who's been trying to kill you has started hiring outside help."

"Maybe this *is* the crossbowman."

"No way, Sparhawk. The crossbowman's been hiding in the general population. Anybody with half a brain would recognize a Rendor. He couldn't have just mingled with the crowd."

"You're probably right. Give me the dagger. I think I'd better show it to Sephrenia."

"Martel really doesn't want to meet you, does he?"

"What makes you think Martel's behind this?"

"What makes you think he isn't? What about this?" Kalten pointed at the body on the floor.

"Leave it. The caretakers here in the Basilica will run across it eventually and dispose of it for us."


Many of the church soldiers submitted their resignations when they discovered that they were being placed under the command of the Church Knights—the officers did, at any rate. Resignation is not an option available to common soldiers. These resignations, however, were not accepted, but the Knights were not totally insensitive to the feelings of the various colonels, captains, and lieutenants who felt strong moral compunctions about commanding their forces under such circumstances. They graciously divested such officers of their rank and enrolled them as common soldiers. They then marched the red-tunicked troops to the great square in front of the Basilica for deployment on the walls and at the gates of the inner city.

"Did you have any trouble?" Ulath asked Tynian as the two of them, each leading a sizeable detachment of soldiers, met at an intersection.

"A few resignations was about all." Tynian shrugged. "I have a whole new group of officers in this batch."

"So do I," Ulath replied. "A lot of old sergeants are in charge now."

"I ran across Bevier awhile back," Tynian said as the two rode toward the main gate of the inner city. "He doesn't seem to be having the same problem for some reason."

"The reason should be fairly obvious, Tynian." Ulath grinned. "Word of what he did to that captain who tried to keep us out of the Basilica has gotten around." Ulath pulled off his ogre-horned helmet and scratched his head. "I think it was the praying afterward that chilled everybody's blood the most. It's one thing to lop off a man's head in the heat of a discussion, but praying for his soul afterward has a very unsettling effect on most people for some reason."

"That's probably it," Tynian agreed. He looked back at the soldiers straggling disconsolately toward the site of what was very likely to be actual fighting. Church soldiers for the most part did not enlist in order to fight, and they viewed the impending unpleasantness with a vast lack of enthusiasm. "Gentlemen, gentlemen," Tynian chided them, "this won't do at all. You must try to *look* like soldiers at least. Please straighten up those ranks and try to march in step. We *do* have some reputation to maintain, after all." He paused a moment. "How about a song, gentlemen?" he suggested. "The people are always encouraged when soldiers sing as they march into battle. It's a demonstration of bravery, after all, and it shows a manly contempt for death and dismemberment."

The song that rose from the ranks was feeble, and Tynian insisted that the soldiers start over—several times—until the full-throated bawling of the column satisfied his need for a display of martial enthusiasm.

"You're a cruel sort of fellow, Tynian," Ulath noted.

"I know," Tynian agreed.


Sephrenia's reaction to the news of the failed attack by the disguised Rendor was almost one of indifference. "You're sure you saw the shadow behind the archprelate's throne just before the attack?" she asked Sparhawk.

He nodded.

"Our hypothesis still seems quite valid then." She said it almost with satisfaction. She looked at the small, poison-smeared dagger lying on the table between them. "Hardly the sort of thing you'd want to use against an armored man," she observed.

"A scratch would have done the trick, little mother."

"How could he have scratched you when you were wrapped in steel?"

"He tried to stab me in the face, Sephrenia."

"Keep your visor closed then."

"Won't that look a little ridiculous?"

"Which do you prefer? Ridiculous or dead? Did any of our friends see the attempt?"

"Kalten did—or at least he knew that it happened."

She frowned. "That's too bad. I know you were hoping that we could sort of keep this between ourselves—at least until we know what's going on."

"Kalten knows that someone's been trying to kill me—they all do, for that matter. They all think it's just Martel and that he's up to his usual tricks."

"Let's sort of leave it at that then, shall we?"

"There have been some desertions, my Lord," Kalten reported to Vanion as the group gathered on the steps of the Basilica. "There was no way we could keep word of what we were doing from reaching some of those outlying barracks."

"It was to be expected," Vanion said. "Did anybody happen to look over the outer wall to see what Martel's doing?"

"Berit's been keeping an eye on things, my Lord," Kalten replied. "That boy's going to make an awfully good Pandion. We ought to try to keep him alive if we can. Anyway, he reports that Martel's almost completed his deployment. He could probably give the order to march on the city right now. I'm surprised that he hasn't, really. I'm sure some of Annias' toadies have reached him by now to report what happened in the Basilica this morning. Every moment he delays just gives us more time to get ready for him."

"Greed, Kalten," Sparhawk told his friend. "Martel's very greedy, and he can't believe that his greed's not universal. He thinks we'll try to defend the whole of Chyrellos, and he wants to give us time to get spread so thin that he'll be able to walk over us. He'd never be able to bring himself to believe that we'd abandon the outer city and concentrate on defending the inner walls."

"I suspect that many of my brother patriarchs feel much the same way," Emban said. "The voting might have been much tighter if those of them with palaces in the outer city had been aware of the fact that we're going to abandon their houses to Martel."

Komier and Ulath came up the marble steps to join them. "We're going to have to pull down some houses just outside the walls," Komier said. "Those are Lamorks to the north of the city, and Lamorks use crossbows. We don't want any rooftops out there for them to shoot at us from." The Genidian Preceptor paused. "I'm not very experienced at sieges," he admitted. "What kind of engines is this Martel likely to bring against us?"

"Battering-rams," Abriel told him, "catapults, assault towers."

"What's an assault tower?"

"It's a sort of high structure. They roll it up until it's flush against the wall. Then the soldiers come spilling out right in the middle of us. It's a way to cut down on the sort of casualties they'll take with scaling ladders."

"Roll?" Komier asked.

"The towers are on wheels."

Komier grunted. "We'll leave the rubble from the houses we pull down lying in the streets, then. Wheels don't run too well across piles of building blocks."

Berit came galloping into the broad square and along the quickly opened path through the ranks of the church soldiers massed in front of the Basilica. He leaped from his saddle and ran up the stairs. "My Lords," he said a little breathlessly. "Martel's men are beginning to assemble their siege engines."

"Will someone explain that to me?" Komier asked.

"The engines are transported in pieces, Komier," Abriel told him. "When you get to the place where you're going to fight, you have to put them together."

"How long's that likely to take? You Arcians are the experts on castles and sieges."

"Quite a few hours, Komier. The mangonels will take longer. He'll have to construct those here."

"What's a mangonel?"

"It's a sort of oversized catapult. It's too big to transport—even if you break it down. They use whole trees when they build them."

"How big a rock can it throw?"

"A half ton or so."

"The walls won't take too many of those."

"That's sort of the idea, I think. He'll be using the standard catapults at first, though. The mangonels will probably take at least a week to build."

"The catapults and battering-rams and towers should keep us occupied until then, I suppose," Komier said sourly. "I *hate* sieges." Then he shrugged. "We'd better get at it." He looked disdainfully at the church soldiers. "Let's set these enthusiastic volunteers to work tearing down houses and cluttering up the streets."

At some point not long after dark, some of Martel's scouts discovered that the outer walls of Chyrellos were undefended. A few of them, the stupider ones, reported back. For the most part, however, these scouts proved to be the vanguard of the looters. An hour or so before midnight, Berit woke Sparhawk and Kalten to report that there were troops in the outer city. Then he turned to leave again.

"Where are you going?" Sparhawk asked bluntly.

"Back out there, Sir Sparhawk."

"No you're not. You stay inside the inner walls now. I don't want you getting yourself killed."

"Somebody has to keep an eye on things, Sir Sparhawk," Berit objected.

"There's a cupola on top of the dome of the Basilica," Sparhawk told him. "Go get Kurik, and then the two of you go up there to watch."

"All right, Sir Sparhawk." Berit's tone was slightly sullen.

"Berit," Kalten said as he pulled on his mail shirt.

"Yes, Sir Kalten?"

"You don't have to like it, you know. You just have to do it."

Sparhawk and the others went through the ancient narrow streets of the inner city and mounted the wall. The streets of the outer city were filled with bobbing torches as the mercenaries under Martel's command ran from house to house, stealing what they could. The occasional screams of women clearly said that looting was not the only thing on the minds of the attacking force. A crowd of panicky and wailing citizens stood outside the now-closed gates of the inner city, pleading to be admitted, but the gates remained steadfastly closed to them.

A somewhat delicate patriarch with sagging pouches under his eyes came running up the stairs to the top of the wall. "What are you *doing*?" he almost shrieked at Dolmant. "Why aren't these soldiers out there defending the city?"

"It's a military decision, Cholda," Dolmant replied calmly. "We don't have enough men to defend the whole of Chyrellos. We've had to pull back inside the walls of the old city."

"*Are you mad?* My house is out there!"

"I'm sorry, Cholda," Dolmant told him, "but there's nothing I can do."

"But I *voted* for you!"

"I appreciate that."

"My house! My things! My treasures!" Patriarch Cholda of Mirishum stood wringing his hands. "My beautiful house! All my furnishings! My gold!"

"Go take refuge in the Basilica, Cholda," Dolmant told him coldly. "Pray that your sacrifice may find favor in the eyes of God."

The Patriarch of Mirishum turned and stumbled back down the stairs, weeping bitterly.

"I think you lost a vote there, Dolmant," Emban said.

"The voting's all over, Emban, and I'm sure I could live without that particular vote anyway."

"I'm not so sure, Dolmant," Emban disagreed. "There's still one ballot yet to come. It's fairly important, and we might just need Cholda before it's over."

"They've started," Tynian said sadly.

"What have?" Kalten asked him.

"The fires," Tynian replied, pointing out across the city as a sudden pillar of golden orange flame and black smoke shot up through the roof of a house. "Soldiers always seem to get careless with their torches when they're looting at night."

"Isn't there something we can do?" Bevier asked urgently.

"Not a thing, I'm afraid," Tynian said, "except maybe pray for rain."

"It's the wrong season for it," Ulath said.

"I know." Tynian sighed.

# CHAPTER TWELVE

The looting of the outer city continued into the night. The fires spread quickly, since no one was available to check them, and the city was soon enveloped in a thick pall of smoke. From the top of the wall, Sparhawk and his friends could see wild-eyed mercenaries running through the streets, each carrying an improvised sack over his shoulder. The crowd of citizens gathered before the gates of the inner city to plead for admittance melted away as Martel's mercenaries began to appear.

There were murders, of course—some of them in plain sight—and there were other atrocities as well. One unshaven Cammorian dragged a young woman from a house by the hair and disappeared with her up an alley. Her screams quite clearly told the watchers what was happening to her.

A red-tunicked young church soldier standing beside Sparhawk atop the city wall began to weep openly. Then, as the somewhat shamefaced Cammorian emerged from the alley, the soldier raised his bow, aimed, and released—all in one motion. The Cammorian doubled over, clutching at the arrow buried to the feathers in his belly.

"Good man," Sparhawk said shortly to the young fellow.

"That could have been my sister, Sir Knight," the soldier said, wiping at his tears.

Neither of them was really prepared for what happened next. The woman, dishevelled and weeping, emerged from the alley and saw her attacker writhing in the rubble-littered street. She lurched to where he lay and kicked him solidly in the face several times. Then, seeing that he was unable to defend himself, she snatched his dagger from his belt. It were best, perhaps, not to describe what she did to him next. His screams, however, echoed in the streets for quite some time. When at last he fell silent, she discarded the bloody knife, opened the sack he had been carrying, and looked inside. Then she wiped her eyes on her sleeve, tied the sack shut, and dragged it back to her house.

The soldier who had shot the Cammorian started to retch violently.

"Nobody's very civilized in those circumstances, neighbor," Sparhawk told him, laying a comforting hand on his shoulder, "and the lady *did* have a certain justification for what she just did."

"That must have hurt," the soldier said in a shaking voice.

"I think that's what she had in mind, neighbor. Go get a drink of water and wash your face. Try not to think about it."

"Thank you, Sir Knight," the young fellow said, swallowing hard.

"Perhaps not *all* church soldiers are so bad," Sparhawk muttered to himself, revising a long-held opinion.

As the sun went down, they gathered in Sir Nashan's red-draped study in the Pandion chapterhouse, what Sir Tynian and Sir Ulath had come to call—not entirely in jest—"the high command": the preceptors, the three patriarchs, and Sparhawk and his friends. Kurik, Berit, and Talen, however, were not present.

Sir Nashan hovered diffidently near the door. Nashan was an able administrator, but he was just a bit uncomfortable in the presence of so much authority. "If there's nothing further you need, my Lords," he said, "I'll leave you to your deliberations now."

"Stay, Nashan," Vanion told him. The preceptor smiled. "We certainly don't want to dispossess you, and your knowledge of the city may prove very useful."

"Thank you, Lord Vanion," the stout knight said, slipping into a chair.

"I think we've stolen a march on your friend Martel, Vanion," Preceptor Abriel said.

"Have you looked over the wall lately, Abriel?" Vanion asked dryly.

"As a matter of fact, I have," Abriel said, "and that's exactly what I'm talking about. As Sir Sparhawk told us yesterday, this Martel couldn't believe that we'd abandon the outer city without a fight, so he didn't take it into account when he made his plans. He made no attempt to keep his scouts out of the city, and those scouts were just the forerunners of the main body of looters. As soon as his scouts found that the city was unprotected, they rushed in to loot the houses and most of the rest of the army followed. Martel's completely lost control of his forces now, and he won't regain it until the outer city is picked clean. Not only that, as soon as his soldiers have as much as they can carry, they'll begin to desert."

"I cannot encourage theft," Patriarch Ortzel said rigidly, "but under the circumstances . . ." A faint, almost sly smile touched his thin lips.

"Wealth needs to be redistributed from time to time, Ortzel," Emban pontificated. "People with too much money have too much time to think up assorted sins to commit. Perhaps this is God's way of restoring the filthy rich to a condition of wholesome poverty."

"I wonder if you'd feel the same way if your *own* house were being looted."

"That might influence my opinion, all right," Emban conceded.

"God's ways are mysterious," Bevier said devoutly. "We had no choice but to abandon the outer city, and that may be the one thing that will save us."

"I don't think we can count on enough desertions from Martel's ranks to grow complacent, gentlemen," Vanion said. "The rampage of his troops will gain us some time, I'll grant you." He looked around at the other preceptors. "A week, perhaps?" he asked.

"At the very most," Komier said. "There are a lot of men out there, and they're very busy. It's not going to take them all that long to strip the city."

"And that's when the killing's going to start," Kalten said. "As you said, Lord Komier, there are a lot of men out there, and I'm fairly sure that not all of them got into the city. The ones who are still outside are just as greedy as the ones who got here first. It's going to be chaotic for a while, I think, and it's going to take Martel quite a bit longer to regain control."

"He's probably right," Komier grunted. "Either way, we've got some time. There are four gates into the inner city here, and most of them aren't much better than the ones in the outer wall. One gate's easier to defend than four, so why don't we fix it that way?"

"Are you going to make the gates disappear by magic, Komier?" Emban asked. "I know the Church Knights are trained to do many unusual things, but this *is* the Holy City, after all. Would God really approve of that sort of thing on his own doorstep?"

"I never even thought of magic," Komier admitted. "Actually, I wasn't going to use anything like that. It's very hard to batter down a gate if there are two or three collapsed houses piled up behind it, isn't it?"

"Almost impossible," Abriel agreed.

Emban grinned broadly. "Isn't Makova's house fairly close to the east gate of the inner city?" he asked.

"Now that you mention it, your Grace, I do believe it is," Sir Nashan replied.

"A fairly substantial house?" Komier said.

"It certainly should be," Emban said, "considering what he paid for it."

"What the Elenian taxpayers paid for it, your Grace," Sparhawk corrected.

"Ah, yes. I'd almost forgotten that. Would the Elenian taxpayers be willing to contribute that very expensive house to the defense of the Church?"

"They'd be delighted, your Grace."

"We'll certainly look the house of the Patriarch of Coombe over very carefully when we're selecting the ones to tear down," Komier promised.

"The only question now is the whereabouts of King Wargun," Dolmant said.

"Martel's blunder has bought us some time, but it won't keep him out of the inner city forever. Could your messengers have gone astray, Ortzel?"

"They're good, solid men," Ortzel said, "and an army the size of Wargun's shouldn't be hard to find. Besides, the messengers you and Emban sent earlier should have reached him quite some time ago, shouldn't they?"

"Not to mention the ones the Earl of Lenda sent from Cimmura," Sparhawk added.

"The absence of the King of Thalesia is a mystery," Emban said, "and it's becoming increasingly inconvenient."

The door opened, and Berit entered. "Excuse me, my Lords," he apologized, "but you wanted to be informed if anything unusual was happening out in the city."

"What have you seen, Berit?" Vanion asked him.

"I was up in that little house on top of the dome of the Basilica, my Lord—"

"Cupola," Vanion corrected.

"I can never remember that word," Berit confessed. "Anyway, you can see the whole city from up there. The ordinary people are fleeing from Chyrellos. They're streaming out through all of the gates in the outer wall."

"Martel doesn't want them underfoot," Kalten said.

"*And* he wants the women out of town," Sparhawk added bleakly.

"I didn't quite understand that, Sparhawk," Bevier said.

"I'll explain it to you later," Sparhawk told him, glancing at Sephrenia.

There was a knock on the door, and a Pandion Knight entered. He was holding Talen by the arm, and the boy from the streets of Cimmura had a disgusted expression on his face and a fair-sized sack in one hand. "You wanted to see this young fellow, Sir Sparhawk?" the Pandion asked.

"Yes," Sparhawk replied. "Thank you, Sir Knight." He looked rather sternly at Talen. "Where have you been?" he asked directly.

Talen's expression grew evasive. "Ah—here and there, my Lord," he replied.

"You *know* that's not going to work, Talen," Sparhawk said wearily. "I'll get the answer out of you eventually anyway, so why bother trying to hide it?"

"To keep in practice, I suppose." Talen shrugged. "You'll twist my arm until I tell you, won't you, Sparhawk?"

"Let's hope it doesn't come to that."

"All right." Talen sighed. "There are thieves in the streets of the inner city, and there are a lot of interesting things going on out beyond the walls. I managed to find a way to slip out there. I've been selling that information."

"How's business?" Patriarch Emban asked him. Emban's eyes were bright.

"Not too bad, actually," Talen said professionally. "Most of the thieves here inside the walls don't have too much to bargain with. You don't make much profit sitting on the things you've stolen, but I'm easy to do business with. I just charge them a percentage of what they're able to steal from the soldiers outside the walls."

"Open the sack, Talen," Sparhawk ordered him.

"I'm really shocked at you, Sparhawk," Talen said. "These are holy men in this room. Is it really proper to expose them to—well, you know."

"Open the sack, Talen."

The boy sighed, laid the sack on Sir Nashan's desk, and opened it. There were a number of largely decorative items inside—metal goblets, small statues, thick chains, assorted eating utensils, and a rather intricately engraved tray about the size of a dinner plate. All of the items appeared to be made of solid gold.

"You got all *this* just for selling information?" Tynian asked incredulously.

"Information's the most valuable thing in the world, Sir Tynian," Talen replied loftily, "and I'm not doing anything immoral or illegal. My conscience is perfectly clear. Not only that, I'm making my contribution to the defense of the city."

"I don't quite follow that reasoning," Sir Nashan said.

"The soldiers out there aren't willingly giving up what they've stolen, Sir Knight." Talen smirked. "The thieves know they'll feel that way, so they don't bother to make requests. Martel's lost a fair number of his troops since the sun went down."

"Most reprehensible, young man," Ortzel said reprovingly.

"My hands are completely clean, your Grace," Talen replied innocently. "I haven't personally stabbed a single soldier in the back. What the villains from the street do out there isn't *my* responsibility, is it?" The boy's eyes shone with innocence.

"Give it up, Ortzel." Emban chuckled. "None of us are worldly enough to argue with this young fellow." He paused. "Dolmant," he said, "tithing is a well-established practice, isn't it?"

"Of course," the Patriarch of Demos said.

"I was sure it was. Given the unusual circumstances here, I'd say that the young fellow should contribute a quarter of his profits to the Church, wouldn't you?"

"It sounds about right to me," Dolmant agreed.

"A *quarter*?" Talen exclaimed. "That's highway robbery!"

"Actually, we aren't on a highway, my son." Emban smiled. "Would you like to settle up after each of your excursions? Or should we wait until you've gathered all your profits and we can take care of it all at once?"

"After you've settled up with the Patriarch Emban, Talen," Vanion said, "I have a burning curiosity about this secret way you've found to get in and out of the city."

"It's not really much of a secret, Lord Vanion," Talen said deprecatingly. "About all it really consists of are the names of a squad of enterprising church soldiers who have the night watch in one of the towers on the wall. They've got a nice long rope with knots tied in it to make climbing up and down easy. They're willing to rent out the rope, and I'm willing to rent out their names and the location of the tower they're guarding. Everybody's making a nice profit."

"Including the Church," Patriarch Emban reminded him.

"I was sort of hoping you'd forgotten about that, your Grace."

"Hope is a cardinal virtue, my son," Emban said piously, "even when it's misplaced."

Kurik came in carrying a Lamork crossbow. "I think we may be in luck, my Lords," he said. "I happened to look into the armory of the archprelate's personal guard in the Basilica. They've got racks and racks of these down there, and barrels of bolts."

"An eminently suitable weapon," Ortzel approved. Ortzel *was* a Lamork, after all.

"They're slower than a longbow, your Grace," Kurik pointed out, "but they *do* have an extraordinary range. I think they'll be very effective in breaking up charges against the inner city before they can pick up much momentum."

"Do you know how to use this weapon, Kurik?" Vanion asked him.

"Yes, Lord Vanion."

"Start training some church soldiers, then."

"Yes, my Lord."

"A number of things are turning our way, my friends," Vanion said. "We have a defensible position, a parity of weapons, and a certain delay working for us."

"I'd still be happier if Wargun were here," Komier said.

"So would I," Vanion agreed, "but we'll just have to make do with what we've got until he gets here, I'm afraid."

"There's something else we need to concern ourselves with, gentlemen," Emban said gravely. "Assuming that all goes well, the Hierocracy's going to go back into session just as soon as Martel's been driven off. Abandoning the outer city is going to alienate a sizeable number of patriarchs. If you let a man's house be looted and burned, he's not going to be very fond of you or want to vote for you. We've got to find some way to prove the connection between Annias and Martel. If we don't, we're doing all this just for the exercise. I can talk as fast as the next man, but I can't perform miracles. I need something to work with."

It was about midnight when Sparhawk climbed the stairs to the wall of the old city not far from the south gate, the most defensible of the four and the one it had been decided to leave unblocked. Chyrellos was burning in earnest now. A looter entering a house to find it already empty feels a certain angry frustration, and he usually vents his feelings by setting fire to the place. Such behavior is totally predictable and, in a certain sense, quite natural. The looters, their faces more desperate now as the number of unpillaged houses diminished, ran from building to building waving torches and weapons. Kurik, always practical, had stationed the church soldiers he was training with crossbows on the walls, and the looters provided those men with moving targets upon which to practice. There were not too many hits, but the soldiers appeared to be improving.

Then, from a narrow street at the edge of the zone of collapsed houses just beyond practical crossbow range, a sizeable number of well-armed men on horseback emerged. The man in the lead bestrode a glossy black horse, and he wore embossed Deiran armor. He removed his helmet. It was Martel, and close behind him were the brutish Adus and the weasel-like Krager.

Kurik joined Sparhawk and his blond friend. "I can have the soldiers shoot at them, if you'd like," the squire said to Sparhawk. "Somebody might get lucky."

Sparhawk scratched his chin. "No, I don't think so, Kurik," he said.

"You're passing up an awfully good opportunity, Sparhawk," Kalten said. "If Martel catches a stray crossbow bolt in the eye, that whole army out there will fall apart."

"Not just yet," Sparhawk said. "Let's see if I can irritate him just a bit first. Mar-

tel sometimes blurts things out when he's irritated. Let's see if I can jolt something
out of him."

"That's a fair distance for shouting," Kalten said.

"I don't have to shout." Sparhawk smiled.

"I wish you wouldn't do that," Kalten complained. "It always makes me feel so
inadequate."

"You should have paid attention to your lessons when you were a novice."
Sparhawk focused his attention on the white-haired man and wove the intricate
Styric spell. "It sort of went to pieces on you, didn't it, Martel?" he asked in a con-
versational tone.

"Is that you, Sparhawk?" Martel's voice was just as conversational as he, too,
utilized the spell they had both learned as novices. "So awfully good to hear your
voice again, old boy. I didn't quite follow your comment, though. Things seem to
be going fairly well from where *I* sit."

"Why don't you see how many of your soldiers you can interest in an assault on
these walls about now? Take as long as you want, old boy, I'm not going anyplace."

"It was really very clever to desert the city, Sparhawk. I wasn't expecting that."

"We sort of liked it. It must be causing you a great deal of anguish every time
you think about all the loot that's getting away from you, though."

"Who said it's getting away? I made a few speeches to my men. Most of my
army's still under control—out there in the meadows on the other sides of those
rivers. I pointed out to them that it's much easier to let the enterprising types do all
the work of looting. Then, when they come out, we take the loot away from them
and put it all into a common pile. Everybody will share equally."

"Even you?"

"Oh, good God! No, Sparhawk." Martel laughed. "I'm the general. I take my
share first."

"The lion's share?"

"I *am* the lion, after all. We'll all grow very, very wealthy once we break into the
treasure vaults below the Basilica."

"That's going a little far even for *you*, Martel."

"Business is business, Sparhawk. You and Vanion stripped me of my honor, so
now all I can do is solace myself with money—and satisfaction, of course. I think
I'll have your head mounted when this is all over, my friend."

"It's right here, Martel. All you have to do is come and claim it. It's going to
take your soldiers a long time to loot the city, and you don't really have much time
to waste."

"It won't take them all *that* long, Sparhawk. They're moving along at a very
good clip, you know. A man who thinks he's working for himself is always more industrious."

"That's only the first wave of looters. They're the ones who are concentrating
on gold. The next wave will go looking for silver. Then the third wave will start tearing houses apart looking for the hiding places where people keep valuables. I'd guess
that it's going to be a month or so before they've stolen everything in Chyrellos—
down to the last brass candlestick. You don't really have a month, old boy—not with
Wargun wandering around out there with half the manpower in Eosia behind him."

"Ah yes, Wargun, the drunken King of Thalesia. I'd almost forgotten him. What *do* you suppose happened to him? It's so unlike him to be this tardy."

Sparhawk broke the spell. "Have your soldiers drop some arrows on him, Kurik," he said bleakly.

"What's the trouble, Sparhawk?" Kalten asked.

"Martel's found some way to keep Wargun away from Chyrellos. We'd better go advise the preceptors. I'm afraid we're all alone here."

# CHAPTER THIRTEEN

"He didn't say it exactly, Vanion," Sparhawk reported. "You know how he is, but there was that sort of implied smirk in his voice that he knows is so irritating. We both know Martel well enough to know what he meant."

"What exactly did he say again, Sir Sparhawk?" Dolmant asked.

"We were talking about Wargun, your Grace, and he said, 'What *do* you suppose has happened to him? It's so unlike him to be this tardy.' " Sparhawk did his best to imitate Martel's intonation.

"It does have a knowing sort of ring to it, doesn't it?" Dolmant agreed. "I don't know Martel as well as the two of you do, but that has the sound of a man who's terribly pleased with himself."

"Sparhawk's right," Sephrenia told them. "Martel's worked out some way to keep Wargun away. The question is how."

"How isn't important, little mother," Vanion said. The four of them were sitting together in a small room adjacent to Sir Nashan's study. "What's important now is keeping this information away from the soldiers. The Church Knights are trained to accept desperate circumstances. The soldiers aren't. About all they're clinging to at the moment is the expectation of seeing Wargun's armies coming across the meadows lying to the west of the River Arruk. The inner city's not really surrounded yet, and the looters aren't paying any attention to other people. We could have desertions by the score if word of this gets out. Advise the Church Knights quietly—and in confidence. I'll tell the other preceptors."

"And I'll tell Emban and Ortzel," Dolmant promised.

The week seemed to drag, although there were many, many things that had to be done. Houses were pulled down and their rubble used to block the three gates that Komier had decided were only marginally defensible. Kurik continued to train selected church soldiers in the use of their crossbows. Berit gathered a group of young monks, and they traded off keeping watch from the cupola atop the Basilica dome. Emban scurried about inside the Basilica itself, trying to maintain his hold on votes, although that grew more and more difficult. None of the defenders had the temerity to refuse the patriarchs of the Church the right to ascend the walls to look out at the city, and the view from those walls was not very encouraging. A fair number of patriarchs, several of them in the very forefront of the fight to keep the Primate of Cimmura off the throne, lamented bitterly as the fires approached the quarters of the city in which their houses lay, and not a few told Emban to his face that he could forget about any future support. Emban grew drawn-looking and he began to complain of pains in his stomach as he watched his support melting before his eyes.

Annias did nothing. He simply waited.

And Chyrellos continued to burn.

Sparhawk stood atop the wall early one evening looking out over the burning city. His mood was somber. He heard a slight clinking behind him and turned quickly.

It was Sir Bevier. "Not too promising, is it?" the young Arcian said, also looking out at Chyrellos.

"Not really," Sparhawk agreed. He looked directly at his young friend. "How long do you think these walls will stand up to a mangonel, Bevier?"

"Not very long, I'm afraid. The walls were built in antiquity. They weren't meant to stand up to modern siege engines. Perhaps Martel won't bother to construct them. They take a long time to build, and the workers have to know exactly what they're doing. A poorly constructed mangonel will kill more of its crew than it will the enemy. There's a great deal of stress involved when you load one."

"We can hope, I suppose. I think these walls will stand up to ordinary catapults, but if he starts lobbing half-ton boulders at us . . ." Sparhawk shrugged.

"Sparhawk." It was Talen. The boy came quickly up the stairs from below. "Sephrenia wants to see you at the chapterhouse. She says it's urgent."

"Go ahead, Sparhawk," Bevier said. "I'll keep watch here."

Sparhawk nodded and went down the stairs to the narrow street below.

Sephrenia met him in the lower hall. Her face was even more pale than usual.

"What is it?" Sparhawk asked her.

"It's Perraine, dear one," she replied in a hushed voice. "He's dying."

"*Dying?* There haven't been any attacks yet. What happened to him?"

"He's killed himself, Sparhawk."

"*Perraine?*"

"He's taken poison of some kind, and he refuses to tell me what it is."

"Is there any way—"

She shook her head. "He wants to talk with you, Sparhawk. You'd better hurry. I don't think there's much time."

Sir Perraine lay on the narrow cot in a cell-like room. His face was deathly pale, and he was sweating profusely. "You certainly took your time, Sparhawk," he said in a weak-sounding voice.

"What's this all about, Perraine?"

"It's something appropriate. Let's not waste any time with this. There are some things you need to know before I leave."

"We can talk about that after Sephrenia gives you the antidote."

"There isn't going to be any antidote. Just be still and listen to me." Perraine sighed deeply. "I've betrayed you, Sparhawk."

"You aren't capable of that, Perraine."

"Anyone's capable of it, my friend. All he needs is some kind of reason. I had one, believe me. Hear me out. I don't have much time left." He closed his eyes for a moment. "You've noticed that someone's been trying to kill you lately, haven't you?"

"Yes, but what's—"

"It was me, Sparhawk—or people I'd hired."

*"You?"*

"Thank God I failed."

"Why, Perraine? Have I insulted you somehow?"

"Don't be foolish, Sparhawk. I was acting on orders from Martel."

"Why would you take orders from Martel?"

"Because he was holding something over my head. He was threatening someone who was more precious to me than my life itself."

Sparhawk was stunned. He started to speak, but Perraine held up one hand. "Don't talk, Sparhawk," he said. "Listen. There isn't much time. Martel came to me in Dabour just after Arasham died. I went for my sword, of course, but he just laughed at me. He told me to put up the sword if I cared anything at all about Ydra."

"Ydra?"

"She's from northern Pelosia. Her father's barony adjoins the one belonging to my father. Ydra and I have loved each other since we were children. I'd die for her without giving it a second thought. Martel knew that somehow, and he reasoned that if I were willing to die for her, I'd also be willing to kill. He told me that he'd given her soul to Azash. I didn't believe him. I didn't think he could really do that."

Sparhawk remembered Count Ghasek's sister, Bellina. "It can be done, Perraine," he said bleakly.

"That's what I found out. Martel and I travelled to Pelosia, and he showed Ydra to me when she was performing some obscene rite before an image of Azash." Tears stood openly in Perraine's eyes. "It was horrible, Sparhawk, horrible." He choked back a sob. "Martel told me that if I didn't do exactly as he told me, her corruption would increase until her soul was totally lost. I wasn't sure if he could really do what he said he would, but I couldn't take that chance."

"He could do it all right," Sparhawk assured him. "I've seen it."

"I was going to kill her," Perraine went on, his voice growing weaker, "but I just couldn't bring myself to do it. Martel watched me struggle with myself, and he just laughed at me. If you ever get the opportunity, I hope you kill him."

"You have my word on that, Perraine."

Perraine sighed again, and his face grew even more pale. "An excellent poison, this one," he noted. "Anyway, Martel had his fist around my heart. He told me to go to Arcium and to join Vanion and the other Pandions there. At the first opportunity, I was to make my way back to the chapterhouse in Cimmura. Somehow he knew that you were going to Thalesia and that you'd most likely be returning through Emsat. He gave me money and instructed me to start hiring murderers. I had to do everything he told me to do . . . Most of the time it was my assassins who made the attempts on you, but once, when we were coming through Demos on our way here, I actually shot a crossbow at you myself. I could try to pretend that I missed on purpose, but that would be a lie. I was really trying to kill you, Sparhawk."

"And the poison at Dolmant's house?"

"Yes. I was getting desperate. You have uncommonly good luck, my friend. I tried everything I could think of, and I just couldn't kill you."

"And the Rendor who tried to stick a poisoned knife in me in the Basilica?"

Perraine looked a bit startled. "I had nothing to do with that, Sparhawk. I swear. We've both been in Rendor, and we both know how undependable they are. Someone else must have sent him—maybe even Martel himself."

"What made you change your mind, Perraine?" Sparhawk asked sadly.

"Martel's lost his hold on me. Ydra's dead."

"I'm sorry."

"I'm not. Somehow she realized what was happening. She went to the chapel in her father's house and prayed all night. Then, just as the sun was coming up, she drove a dagger into her heart. She'd sent one of her footmen here with a letter explaining everything that had happened. He arrived just before Martel's army encircled the city. She's free now, and her soul is safe."

"Why did you take poison then?"

"I'm going to follow her, Sparhawk. Martel's stolen my honor, but he can never steal my love." Perraine stiffened on his narrow cot, and he twisted in agony for a moment. "Yes," he gasped, "an excellent poison. I'd recommend it by name, but I don't altogether trust our little mother here. Given half a chance, I think she could resurrect a stone." He smiled at their teacher. "Can you find it in your heart to forgive me, Sparhawk?"

"There's nothing to forgive, Perraine," Sparhawk said in a thick voice, taking his friend's hand.

Perraine sighed. "I'm sure they'll strike my name from the Pandion rolls, and I'll be remembered with contempt."

"Not if I can help it, they won't," Sparhawk told him. "I'll protect your honor, my friend." He gripped Perraine's hand tightly in an unspoken pledge.

Sephrenia reached across the bed and took the dying man's other hand.

"It's almost over," Perraine said in a faint whisper. "I wish—" And then he fell silent.

Sephrenia's wail of grief was almost like that of a hurt child. She pulled Perraine's limp body to her.

"There's no time for that!" Sparhawk told her sharply. "Will you be all right here for a while? I have to go get Kurik."

She stared at him in astonishment.

"We have to dress Perraine in his armor," he explained. "Then Kurik and I can take him to one of those streets just inside the wall. We'll shoot a crossbow bolt into his chest and lay him in the street. They'll find him later, and everyone will believe that one of Martel's mercenaries shot him off the wall."

"But, Sparhawk, why?"

"Perraine was my friend, and I promised to protect his honor."

"But he tried to kill you, dear one."

"No, little mother, *Martel* tried to kill me. He forced Perraine to help him. The guilt's all Martel's, and one of these days before very long, I'm going to make him answer for it." He paused. "You might start thinking about that hypothesis of ours," he added. "This seems to poke quite a large hole in it." Then he remembered the Rendor with the poisoned knife. "Either that or there's more than just one assassin out there to worry about," he added.

The first probing attacks came after five days of looting. They were tentative, designed primarily to identify strong points—and weak ones. The defenders had certain advantages here. Martel had received his training from Vanion, and Vanion could, therefore, predict almost exactly what the white-haired former Pandion would do, and, moreover, he could marshal his forces so as to dissemble and deceive. The probing attacks grew stronger. They came sometimes at dawn, sometimes late in the day, and sometimes in the middle of the night when darkness shrouded the smoky city. The Church Knights were always on the alert. They never removed their armor, and they slept in snatches whenever and wherever they could.

It was when the outer city lay almost entirely in ruins that Martel moved his siege engines into place to begin the steady pounding of the inner city. Large rocks rained from the sky, crushing soldiers and citizens alike. Large baskets were mounted on some of Martel's catapults, and bushels of crossbow bolts were launched high into the air to drop indiscriminately into the ancient city. Then came the fire. Balls of burning pitch and naphtha came sailing over the walls to ignite the roofs and to fill the streets with great splashes of searing fire. There were as yet no half-ton boulders, however.

The defenders endured. There was nothing else they could do.

Lord Abriel began to construct engines of his own to respond, but aside from the rubble of destroyed houses, there was very little at hand to throw at Martel in reply.

They endured, and each stone, each fireball, each shower of arrows dropping from the sky in a deadly rain only increased their hatred of the besiegers.

The first serious assault came not long after midnight eight days after the looting had begun. A disorganized horde of Rendorish fanatics came shrieking out of the dark, smoky streets to the southwest bent on attacking a somewhat shaky bartizan on the corner of the old wall in that quarter. The defenders rushed to that point. Sheets of arrows and crossbow bolts swept through the black-robed ranks of the Rendors, felling them in windrows like new-mown wheat. The shrieks took on that note of agony that has risen from every battlefield since the beginning of time. On and on, however, came the Rendors, men so wildly gripped by religious frenzy that they paid no heed to their dreadful casualties, some of them even ignoring mortal wounds as they dragged themselves toward the walls.

"The pitch!" Sparhawk shouted to the soldiers who were feverishly shooting arrows and bolts down into the seething mass of the attackers below. Cauldrons of boiling pitch were dragged to the edge of the walls even as the scaling ladders came angling up from below to clatter against the weather-worn battlements. The Rendors, shrieking war cries and religious slogans, came scrambling up the rude ladders only to fall howling and writhing from those ladders as great waves of scalding pitch engulfed them, burning, searing.

"Torches!" Sparhawk commanded.

Half a hundred flaming torches sailed out over the walls to ignite the pools of liquid pitch and naphtha below. A great sheet of flame shot up to bathe the walls and to burn those Rendors still clinging to their ladders as ants sizzle, shrivel, and fall from a log cast into a fire. Burning men ran from the crowd below, shrieking, stumbling blindly, and trailing streams of dripping flame like comets as they ran.

Still the Rendors came, and still the scaling ladders ponderously rose from their ranks, pushed from the rear by hundreds of hands to swing up and up, then to hesitate, standing vertically, and then to fall slowly against the wall. Fanatics, wild-eyed and some actually foaming at the mouth, were desperately climbing even before the ladders fell into place. From the top of the walls, the defenders pushed the ladders away with long poles, and the ladders reversed their rise, teetered back out to stand momentarily motionless, and then toppled backward, carrying the men near their tops to their deaths below. Hundreds of Rendors crowded near the base of the walls to avoid the arrows from above, and they dashed out to scramble up the ladders toward the tops of the walls.

"Lead!" Sparhawk commanded then. The lead had been Bevier's idea. Each sarcophagus in the crypt beneath the Basilica had been surmounted by a leaden effigy of its inhabitant. The sarcophagi were now unadorned, and the effigies had been melted down. Bubbling cauldrons stood at intervals along the tops of the walls, and at Sparhawk's command, they were pushed forward and overturned to pour down in great silvery sheets on the Rendors clustered at the base of the wall. The shrieks this time did not last for long, and no man ran blazing from the attack after he had been entombed in liquid lead.

Some few, then more, did reach the tops of the walls. The church soldiers met them with a bravery born of desperation, and they held the fanatics long enough to permit the Knights to come to their aid. Sparhawk strode forward at the head of the phalanx of black-armored Pandions. He swung his heavy broadsword steadily, rhythmically. The broadsword is not a weapon with much finesse, and the big Pandion Knight did not so much fight his way through the shrieking Rendors as he did chop open a wide path. His sword was an instrument of dismemberment, and hands and whole arms flew spinning from his strokes to rain down on the faces of attackers still on the scaling ladders. Heads went sailing out to fall either on the outside of the wall or on the inside, depending on the direction of Sparhawk's swing. The Knights following him and disposing of the wounded were soon wading in blood. One Rendor, quite skinny and waving a rusty saber, stood howling before the man in black armor bearing down on him. Sparhawk altered his swing slightly and sheared the man almost in two at the waist. The Rendor was hurled against the battlements by the force of the blow, and the remaining shred of flesh ripped as the upper torso toppled outward. The man's lower half caught up on one of the battlements, the legs threshing wildly. The Rendor's upper torso did not quite reach the ground below, but hung head downward from a long rope of purple bowel that steamed in the cool night air. The torso swung slowly back and forth, jerking slightly downward as its intestines gradually unravelled.

"Sparhawk!" Kalten shouted as Sparhawk's arm began to grow weary. "Get your breath! I'll take over here!"

And so it went until the top of the wall was once again secure and all the scaling ladders had been shoved away. The Rendors milled around below, still falling victim to arrows and to large rocks thrown down on them from the walls.

And then they broke and fled.

Kalten came back, panting and wiping his sword. "Good fight," he said, grinning.

"Tolerable," Sparhawk agreed laconically. "Rendors aren't very good fighters, though."

"Those are the best kind to face." Kalten laughed. He pulled back one foot to kick the bottom half of the skinny Rendor off the wall.

"Leave him where he is," Sparhawk said shortly. "Let's give the next wave of attackers something to look at while they're crossing the field to get here. You might as well tell the people cleaning up down on the inside of the wall to save any loose heads they come across as well. We'll set them on stakes along the battlements."

"Object lessons again?"

"Why not? A man who's attacking a defended wall is entitled to know what's likely to happen to him, wouldn't you say?"

Bevier came hurrying down the bloody parapet. "Ulath's been hurt!" he shouted to them from several yards away. He turned to lead them back to their injured friend, and the church soldiers melted out of his way. Perhaps unconsciously, Bevier was still brandishing his Lochaber ax.

Ulath lay on his back. His eyes were rolled back in his head, and blood was running out of his ears.

"What happened?" Sparhawk demanded of Tynian.

"A Rendor ran up behind him and hit him on the head with an ax."

Sparhawk's heart sank.

Tynian gently removed Ulath's horned helmet and gingerly probed through the Genidian Knight's blond hair. "I don't think his head's broken," he reported.

"Maybe the Rendor didn't swing hard enough," Kalten surmised.

"I saw the blow. The Rendor swung as hard as he could. That blow should have split Ulath's head like a melon." Tynian frowned, tapping on the bulging knot of horn that joined the two curling points jutting from each side of their friend's conical helmet. Then he examined the helmet closely. "Not a scratch," he marveled. He took out his dagger and scraped at the horn, but was unable even to mar its shiny surface. Then, finally overcome by curiosity, he picked up Ulath's fallen war ax and hacked at the horn several times without even chipping it. "That's amazing," he said. "That's the hardest stuff I've ever come across."

"That's probably why Ulath's still got his brains inside his head," Kalten said. "He doesn't look too good, though. Let's carry him to Sephrenia."

"You three go on ahead," Sparhawk told them regretfully. "I've got to go talk with Vanion."

The four preceptors stood together some distance away where they had been observing the attack.

"Sir Ulath's been hurt, my Lord," Sparhawk reported to Komier.

"Is it bad?" Vanion asked quickly.

"There's no such thing as a good injury, Vanion," Komier said. "What happened, Sparhawk?"

"A Rendor hit him in the head with an ax, my Lord."

"In the head, you say? He'll be all right then." He reached up and rapped his knuckles on his own ogre-horned helmet. "That's why we wear these."

"He didn't look very good," Sparhawk said gravely. "Tynian, Kalten, and Bevier are taking him to Sephrenia."

"He'll be all right," Komier insisted.

Sparhawk pushed Ulath's injury to the back of his mind. "I think I've put my finger on some of Martel's strategy, my Lords. He saddled himself with those Rendors for a specific reason. Rendors aren't really very good at modern warfare. They don't wear any kind of protective armor—not even helmets—and they're pitifully incapable of any form of swordsmanship. We swept them off the top of that wall the way you'd mow a hayfield. All they really have is a raging fanaticism, and they'll attack in the face of insurmountable odds. Martel's going to keep throwing them at us to wear us down and to reduce our numbers. Then, after he's weakened and exhausted us, he'll throw in his Cammorian and Lamork mercenaries. We've got to work out some way to keep those Rendors off the walls. I'm going to go talk with Kurik. Maybe he can come up with a few ideas."

Kurik, as a matter of fact, could. His years of experience, and the reminiscences of grizzled old veterans he had met from time to time, provided him with a large number of very nasty ideas. There were objects he called caltrops, fairly simple, four-pronged steel things that could be made in such a way that no matter how far they were thrown, they would always land with one sharp-pointed steel prong pointing upward. Rendors did not wear boots, but only soft leather sandals. A generous smearing of poison on the pointed prongs made the caltrops lethal as opposed to merely inconvenient. Ten-foot-long beams with sharpened stakes attached to them to protrude like the spines of a hedgehog and once again doctored with poison provided fairly insurmountable barriers when rolled down long beams to lie in profusion out in front of the walls. Long log pendulums swinging from the battlements parallel to the walls would sweep scaling ladders away like cobwebs. "None of these will actually hold off really serious attacks, Sparhawk," Kurik said, "but they'll slow people down to the point where crossbowmen and regular archers can pick them off. Not very many attackers will reach the walls."

"That's sort of what we had in mind," Sparhawk said. "Let's commandeer the citizenry and put them to work on these ideas. All that the people of Chyrellos are doing right now is sitting around eating. Let's give them a chance to earn their keep."

The construction of Kurik's obstacles took several days, and there were several more Rendorish attacks in the interim. Then Preceptor Abriel's catapults scattered the caltrops in profusion in front of the walls, and the hedgehogs rolled down long beams to lie in tangles and clusters some twenty yards or so out from the walls. After that, very few Rendors reached the walls, and the ones who did were not encumbered by scaling ladders. They would normally mill around shouting slogans and hacking at the walls with their swords until the bowmen on top of the walls had the leisure to kill them. After a few of those abortive attacks, Martel pulled back for a day or so to reconsider his strategy. It was still summer, however, and the hordes of dead Rendors lying outside the walls began to bloat in the sun. The smell of rotting flesh made the inner city distinctly unpleasant.

One evening, Sparhawk and his companions took advantage of the lull to return to the chapterhouse for much-needed baths and a hot meal. Before they did anything else, however, they stopped by to visit Sir Ulath. The big Genidian Knight lay in his bed. His eyes were still unfocused, and he had a confused look on his face. "I'm getting tired of just lying around, brothers," he said in a slurred voice, "and it's hot in here. Why don't we go out and hunt down a Troll? Slogging through the snow should cool off our blood a little."

"He thinks he's in the Genidian motherhouse at Heid," Sephrenia told the knights quietly. "He keeps wanting to go Troll hunting. He thinks I'm a serving wench, and he's been making all sorts of improper suggestions to me."

Bevier gasped.

"And then sometimes he cries," she added.

"Ulath?" Tynian said in some amazement.

"It may be a subterfuge, though. The first time he did it, I tried to comfort him, and it turned into a sort of wrestling match. He's very strong, considering his condition."

"Will he be all right?" Kalten asked. "I mean, will he regain his senses?"

"It's very hard to say, Kalten. That blow bruised his brain, I think, and you never know how something like that's going to turn out. I think you'd better leave, dear ones. Don't excite him."

Ulath began to make a long, rambling speech in the language of the Trolls, and Sparhawk was surprised to discover that he still understood the language. The spell Sephrenia had cast in Ghwerig's cave seemed to still have some of its potency left.

After he had bathed and shaved, Sparhawk put on a monk's robe and joined the others in the nearly deserted refectory where their meal was laid on a long table.

"What's Martel going to do next?" Preceptor Komier was asking Abriel.

"He'll probably fall back on fairly standard siege tactics," Abriel replied. "Most likely he'll settle down and let his siege engines pound us for a while. Those fanatics were just about his only chance for a quick victory. This may drag out for quite some time."

They all sat quietly, listening to the monotonous crash of large rocks falling into the city around them.

Then Talen burst into the room. His face was smudged and his clothes were dirty. "I just saw Martel, my Lords!" he said excitedly.

"We've all seen him, Talen," Kalten said, sprawling deeper into his chair. "He rides up outside the walls now and then to have a look around."

"He wasn't outside the walls, Kalten," Talen said. "He was in the cellar under the Basilica."

"What are you saying, boy?" Dolmant demanded.

Talen drew in a deep breath. "I—uh—well, I wasn't entirely honest with you gentlemen when I told you how I was getting the thieves of Chyrellos out of the inner city," he confessed. He held up one hand. "I *did* arrange for a meeting between the thieves and those church soldiers on the wall with their rope. That part was completely true. About the only thing I *didn't* tell you was that I found another way as well. I just didn't want to bore you with a lot of extra details. Anyway, not long after we got here, I happened to be down in the lowest cellar under the Basilica, and I found a passageway. I don't know what it was used for originally, but it leads off to the north. It's perfectly round, and the stones of the walls and floor are very smooth. I followed it, and it took me out into the city."

"Does it show any signs of being used as a passageway at all?" Patriarch Emban asked.

"Not when I went through it the first time, no, your Grace. The cobwebs were as thick as ropes."

"Oh, that thing," Sir Nashan said. "I've heard about it, but I never got around to investigating it. The old torture chambers are down in that cellar. It's the sort of place most people want to avoid."

"The passageway, Nashan," Vanion said to him. "What's it for?"

"It's an old aqueduct, my Lord. It was part of the original construction of the Basilica. It runs north to the River Kydu to carry water to the inner city. Everybody tells me that it collapsed centuries ago."

"Not all of it, Sir Knight," Talen told him. "It runs far enough out into the main city to be useful. To make it short, I was looking around and I found this—what was it you called that passage?"

"An aqueduct," Nashan supplied.

"That's a peculiar word. Anyway, I found it, and I followed it, and it came out in the cellar of a warehouse several streets on out in the city. It doesn't go any farther than that, though, but it doesn't really have to. There's a door leading out from the cellar into an alley. That's the information I was selling to the thieves of Chyrellos. Anyway, I was down in that cellar this afternoon, and I saw Martel come sneaking out of that passageway. I hid and he went on by. He was alone, so I followed him, and he went into a kind of storeroom. Annias was waiting for him there. I couldn't hear what they were saying, but they had their heads very close together like men doing some very serious plotting. They talked together for a while, and then they left the storeroom. Martel told Annias to wait for the usual signal and then to meet him again down there. He said, 'I'll want you someplace safe when the fighting starts.' Then Annias said that he was still worried about the possibility of Wargun showing up, but Martel laughed and said, 'Don't worry about Wargun, my friend. He's blithely ignorant of everything that's happening here.' Then they left. I waited awhile and came right here."

"How did Martel find out about the aqueduct?" Kalten asked him.

"Some of his men probably chased one of the thieves and found it." Talen shrugged. "Everybody gets civic-spirited when it comes to chasing thieves. I've been chased by absolute strangers sometimes."

"That explains Wargun's absence," Komier said bleakly. "All our messengers have probably been ambushed."

"And Ehlana's still sitting in Cimmura with only Stragen and Platime to defend her," Sparhawk said in a worried tone. "I think I'll go down to that cellar and wait for Martel. He'll come along eventually and I can waylay him."

"Absolutely not!" Emban said sharply.

"Your Grace," Sparhawk objected, "I think you're overlooking the fact that if Martel dies, this siege dies with him."

"And I think *you're* overlooking the fact that our real goal here is to defeat Annias in the election. I need a report of a conversation between Annias and Martel to swing the votes I need to beat the Primate of Cimmura. Our situation here is getting very tenuous, gentlemen. Every time those fires out there sweep into a new quarter, we lose a few more votes."

"Wouldn't Talen's report of a meeting between Annias and Martel make the Hierocracy suspicious, your Grace?" Kalten asked.

"Most of the Hierocracy never heard of Martel, Sir Kalten," Emban replied, "and this boy's not the most reliable of witnesses. *Somebody* in Chyrellos is bound to know that he's a thief. We have to have a totally incorruptible and reliable witness. One whose neutrality and objectivity can never be questioned."

"The commander of the archprelate's personal guard, perhaps?" Ortzel suggested.

"The very man," Emban agreed, snapping his fingers. "If we can get him down into the cellar where he can hear Martel and Annias talking, it might give me something to place before the Hierocracy."

"Aren't you overlooking the fact that when Martel comes through that aqueduct, he's going to have a small army with him, your Grace?" Vanion asked. "He said something about wanting to get Annias to safety before the fighting starts. That sounds to me as if he plans to lead a surprise attack into the Basilica itself. Your witness won't find a very attentive audience if all the patriarchs are running for their lives."

"Don't trouble me with these details, Vanion," Emban said airily. "Just post some men down there."

"Gladly, but where do I get the men?"

"Take some of those fellows off the walls. They're not doing anything useful anyway."

Vanion's face turned very red, and a thick vein started to throb in his forehead.

"You'd better let me tell him, Vanion," Komier suggested. "We don't want you to come down with the apoplexy." He turned casually to the fat little patriarch. "Your Grace," he said mildly, "when you're planning a surprise attack, you usually want to divert your enemy's attention. Doesn't that sort of make sense?"

"Well—" Emban said a bit dubiously.

"At least that's the way *I'd* do it, and Martel's had a great deal of training. I sort of suspect that what's going to happen is that Martel's going to wait until he gets those mangoes built—"

"Mangonels," Preceptor Abriel corrected.

"Whatever." Komier shrugged. "Then he's going to start bashing down our walls. *Then* he's going to attack the walls with every man he can muster. Believe me, your Grace, the men on the walls—or what's left of the walls—are going to be very,

very busy. *That's* when Martel's going to come into the cellar, and we're *not* going to have any men to spare to meet him."

"Why do you have to be so blasted clever, Komier?" Emban snapped.

"What do we do then?" Dolmant asked them.

"We don't have any choice, your Grace," Vanion replied. "We're going to have to collapse that aqueduct so that Martel can't get through."

"But if you do that, we won't have any report of the meeting between Annias and Martel!" Emban protested shrilly.

"Try to look at the whole picture, Emban," Dolmant said patiently. "Do we really want Martel voting when we elect a new archprelate?"

## CHAPTER FOURTEEN

"They're ceremonial troops, your Grace," Vanion objected. "This isn't a parade or a formal changing of the guard." The four of them, Vanion, Dolmant, Sparhawk, and Sephrenia, were gathered in Sir Nashan's study.

"I've seen them training in the courtyard outside their barracks, Vanion," Dolmant said patiently. "I still remember enough of my own training to recognize professionals when I see them."

"How many of them are there, your Grace?" Sparhawk asked.

"Three hundred," the patriarch replied. "As the archprelate's personal guard, they're wholly committed to the defense of the Basilica." Dolmant leaned back in his chair, tapping his fingertips together. "I don't see that we have much choice, Vanion," he said. His lean, ascetic face seemed almost to glow in the candlelight. "Emban was right, you know. All our scrambling for votes has gone out the window now. My brothers in the Hierocracy are very attached to their houses." He made a sour face. "It's one of the few forms of vanity left for members of the higher clergy. We all wear plain cassocks, so we can't show off our clothing; we don't marry, so we can't show off our wives; we're committed to peace, so we can't demonstrate our prowess on the battlefield. All that's left for us are our palaces. We lost at least twenty votes when we pulled back to the walls of the inner city and abandoned the palaces of my brothers to Martel's looters. We absolutely *must* have some evidence of the collusion between Annias and Martel. If we can do that, we turn it around. The burning of the palaces becomes Annias' fault instead of ours." He looked at Sephrenia then. "I'm going to have to ask you to do something, little mother," he said.

"Of course, Dolmant." She smiled at him fondly.

"I can't even ask you officially," he said with a rueful smile, "because it has to do with things I'm not supposed to believe in any more."

"Ask me as a former Pandion, dear one," she suggested. "That way we can both ignore the fact that you've fallen in with evil companions."

"Thank you," he said dryly. "Is there some way you can collapse that aqueduct without actually being in the cellar?"

"I can take care of that, your Grace," Sparhawk offered. "I can use Bhelliom."

"No, actually you can't," Sephrenia reminded him. "You don't have both rings." She looked back at Dolmant. "I can do what you ask," she told him, "but Sparhawk will have to be in the cellar. I can channel the spell through him."

"Better and better, actually," Dolmant said. "Vanion, see what you think of this. You and I talk with Colonel Delada, the commander of the archprelate's guard. We put his guardsmen in the cellar under the command of somebody reliable."

"Kurik?" Sparhawk suggested.

"The very man," Dolmant approved. "I suspect that I'd still obey automatically if Kurik barked an order at me." Dolmant paused. "Why didn't you ever knight him, Vanion?"

"Because of his class prejudices, Dolmant." Vanion laughed. "Kurik believes that knights are frivolous, empty-headed men. Sometimes I almost think he's right."

"All right then," Dolmant continued. "We put Kurik and the guardsmen in the cellar to wait for Martel—well out of sight, of course. What's likely to be the first sign that Martel's main assault on our walls is starting?"

"Boulders dropping out of the sky, I'd say, wouldn't you, Sparhawk? That'll be the sign that his mangonels are in place. He won't start his attack until he's sure that they're working properly."

"And that would be the most probable time for him to start through the aqueduct, wouldn't it?"

Vanion nodded. "There'd be too much chance of them being discovered if they crept into the cellar any sooner."

"This is fitting together even more tightly." Dolmant seemed pleased with himself on that score. "We have Sparhawk and Colonel Delada wait on the walls for the first boulders. When they start crashing down, the two of them go down to the cellar to eavesdrop on the conversation between Martel and Annias. If the archprelate's guard can't hold the entrance to the aqueduct, Sephrenia will collapse the tunnel. We block the secret attack, get the evidence against Annias, and we may very well capture Annias and Martel themselves. What do you think, Vanion?"

"It's an excellent plan, your Grace," Vanion said with a straight face. Sparhawk also saw a number of gaps. The years seemed to have clouded Dolmant's strategic sense in a few areas. "I can only see one drawback," Vanion added.

"Oh?"

"Once those engines batter down the walls, we're likely to have hordes of mercenaries here in the inner city with us."

"That would be a bit inconvenient, wouldn't it?" Dolmant conceded with a slight frown. "Let's go talk with Colonel Delada anyway. I'm sure something will turn up."

Vanion sighed and followed the Patriarch of Demos from the room.

"Was he always like that?" Sparhawk asked Sephrenia.

"Who?"

"Dolmant. I think he's pushing optimism about as far as it can be pushed."

"It's your Elene theology, dear one." She smiled. "Dolmant's professionally committed to the notion of providence. Styrics look upon that as the worst form of fatalism. What's troubling you, dear one?"

"A perfectly good logical construction has fallen apart on me, Sephrenia. Now that we know about Perraine, I don't have any way at all to connect that shadow with Azash."

"Why are you so obsessed with hard evidence, Sparhawk?"

"I beg your pardon?"

"Just because you can't logically prove a connection, you're ready to discard the whole idea. Your reasoning was fairly tenuous to begin with anyway. About all you were really doing was trying to distort things to make your logic fit your feelings— a sort of a justification for a leap of faith. You felt—you believed—that the shadow came from Azash. That's good enough for me. I'm more comfortable with the notion of trusting your feelings than your logic anyway."

"Be nice," he chided.

She smiled. "I think it's time to discard logic and start relying on those leaps of faith, Sparhawk. Sir Perraine's confession erases any connection between that shadow you keep seeing and the attempts on your life, doesn't it?"

"I'm afraid so," he admitted, "and to make matters even worse, I haven't even *seen* the shadow lately."

"Just because you haven't seen it doesn't mean it's not still there. Tell me exactly what you felt each time you saw it."

"There was a chill," he replied, "and an overpowering sense that whatever it was hated me. I've been hated before, Sephrenia, but not like that. It was inhuman."

"All right, we can rely on that then. It's something supernatural. Anything else?"

"I was afraid of it." He admitted it flatly.

"You? I didn't think you knew what the word meant."

"I know, all right."

She thought about it, her tiny, perfect face creased with thought. "Your original theory was really quite shaky, Sparhawk," she told him. "Would it *really* make much sense for Azash to have some brigand kill you and then have to chase down the brigand in order to retrieve Bhelliom from him?"

"It's a little cumbersome and roundabout, I suppose."

"Exactly. Let's look at the possibility of pure coincidence."

"I'm not supposed to do that, little mother. Providence, you understand."

"Stop that."

"Yes, ma'am."

"Suppose that Martel subverted Perraine on his own—without consulting with Annias—that's assuming that it's Annias who's the one dealing with Otha and not Martel."

"I don't really think Martel would go so far as to have personal dealings with Otha."

"I wouldn't be too sure, Sparhawk. But let's assume that killing you was Martel's idea and not Otha's—or some involuted scheme Azash came up with. *That* would cover the hole in your logic. The shadow could still be related to Azash and have absolutely no connection whatsoever with the attempts on your life."

"What's it doing then?"

"Watching, most likely. Azash wants to know where you are, and he *definitely* wants to know where Bhelliom is. That might explain why you almost always see that shadow when you remove the jewel from the pouch."

"This is starting to make my head ache, little mother. But if everything goes the way Dolmant's planned it, we'll have both Martel and Annias in custody before long. We ought to be able to get a few answers out of them—enough to clear up my headache, anyway."

Colonel Delada, commander of the archprelate's personal guard, was a stocky, solidly built man with short-cut reddish hair and a lined face. Despite his largely ceremonial position, he carried himself like a warrior. He wore the burnished breastplate, round embossed shield, and traditional short sword of his unit. His knee-length cape was crimson, and his visorless helmet had a horsehair crest. "Are they really that big, Sir Sparhawk?" he asked as the two of them looked out at the smoking ruins from the flat roof of a house abutting the inner-city wall.

"I really don't know, Colonel Delada," Sparhawk replied. "I've never seen one either. Bevier has, though, and he tells me that they're at least as big as a fair-sized house."

"And they can really throw rocks the size of oxen?"

"That's what they tell me."

"What's the world coming to?"

"They call it progress, my friend," Sparhawk said wryly.

"The world would be a better place if we hanged all the scientists and engineers, Sir Sparhawk."

"And the lawyers, too."

"Oh yes, definitely the lawyers. *Everybody* wants to hang all the lawyers." Delada's eyes narrowed. "Why are all of you being so secretive around me, Sparhawk?" he demanded irritably. In Delada's case all the clichés about red-haired people seemed to apply.

"We have to protect your strict neutrality, Delada. You're going to see something—and we hope hear something—that's very important. Later on, you're going to be called on to give testimony about it. There are going to be people who'll try very hard to throw doubts on your testimony."

"They'd better not," the colonel said hotly.

Sparhawk smiled. "Anyway, if you don't know anything at all in advance about what you're going to see and hear, nobody will be able to raise any question at all about your impartiality."

"I'm not stupid, Sparhawk, and I *have* got eyes. This has to do with the election, hasn't it?"

"Just about everything in Chyrellos has to do with the election right now, Delada—except maybe that siege out there."

"And I wouldn't wager any significant amounts of money that the siege isn't in-volved too."

"That's one of those areas we aren't supposed to talk about, Colonel."

"Aha!" Delada said triumphantly. "Just as I thought!"

Sparhawk looked out over the wall. The important thing was to be able to prove beyond doubt the collusion between Martel and Annias. Sparhawk was a bit apprehensive about that. If the conversation between the Primate of Cimmura and the renegade Pandion did *not* reveal Martel's identity, all Delada would be able to report to the Hierocracy would be a highly suspicious conversation between Annias and an unnamed stranger. Emban, Dolmant, and Ortzel, however, had been adamant. Delada was absolutely *not* to be supplied with any information that could contaminate his testimony. Sparhawk was particularly disappointed in Patriarch Emban on that score. The fat churchman was devious and deceitful on every other count. Why should he suddenly become ethical on this one crucial point?

"It's starting, Sparhawk," Kalten called from the torchlit wall. "The Rendors are coming out to clear away our obstructions."

The rooftop was slightly higher than the wall, and Sparhawk could clearly see over the fortification. The Rendors came rushing out, howling as before. Heedless of the poison smeared on the stakes of the hedgehogs, they rolled the obstructions out of the way. Many, caught up in a frenzied religious ecstasy, even went so far as to throw themselves needlessly on the poisoned stakes. Broad avenues were soon cleared away, and the assault towers began to trundle out of the still-smoking city, moving slowly toward the walls. The assault towers, Sparhawk saw, were con-structed of thick planks covered by green cowhides that had been dipped in water so many times that rivulets actually ran from them. No crossbow bolt or javelin would be able to penetrate the planks, and burning pitch and naphtha would not be able to set fire to the dripping hides. One by one, Martel was countering all their defenses.

"Do you actually anticipate fighting in the Basilica, Sir Sparhawk?" Delada asked.

"We can hope not, Colonel," Sparhawk replied. "It's best to be ready, though. I really appreciate your deploying those guardsmen of yours down in that cellar—particularly since I can't tell you why we need them there. We'd have had to pull men off the walls otherwise."

"I have to assume you know what you're doing, Sparhawk," the colonel said ruefully. "Putting the whole detachment under the command of your squire sort of upset my second in command, though."

"It was a tactical decision, colonel. That cellar's full of echoes. Your men won't be able to understand shouted commands. Kurik and I have been together for a long time, and we've worked out ways to deal with situations like that one."

Delada looked out at the assault towers lumbering across the open space in front of the walls. "Big, aren't they?" he said. "How many men can you crowd into one of those things?"

"That depends on how fond of the men you are," Sparhawk told him, moving his shield in front of his body to ward off the arrows that had already begun to drop onto the roof, "several hundred at least."

"I'm not familiar with siege tactics," Delada admitted. "What happens now?"

"They roll up to the walls and try to charge the defenders. The defenders try to push the towers over. It's very confusing and very noisy and a lot of people get hurt."

"When do those mangonels come into play?"

"Probably when several of the towers are firmly in place against the walls."

"Won't they be dropping boulders on their own men?"

"The men in the towers aren't very important. A lot of them are Rendors—like the ones out there who got killed clearing away the obstructions. The man who's in charge of that army isn't exactly what you'd call a humanitarian."

"Do you know him?"

"Oh, yes, very well."

"And you want to kill him, don't you?" Delada asked shrewdly.

"The thought's crossed my mind a few times."

One of the towers was now quite close to the wall, and the defenders, trying to dodge the hail of arrows and crossbow bolts, threw grappling hooks on long ropes over the roof of the lumbering structure. Then they began to pull on the ropes. The tower swayed, rocked back and forth, and finally toppled with a resounding crash. The men inside began to scream, some in pain and some in terror. They knew what came next. The fall of the tower had broken the planks, and the tower lay open like a shattered egg. The cauldrons of pitch and naphtha poured down upon the wreckage and the struggling men, and the torches set the boiling liquid on fire.

Delada swallowed hard as the despairing screams of the burning men came shockingly up from the base of the wall. "Does that happen very often?" he asked in a sick voice.

"We *hope* so," Sparhawk said bleakly. "Every one of them we kill outside the walls is one less who gets inside." Sparhawk wove a quick spell and spoke to Sephrenia, who was waiting inside the chapterhouse. "We're just about ready to engage out here, little mother," he reported. "Any hints of Martel yet?"

"Nothing, dear one." Her voice seemed almost to whisper in his ear. "Be very careful, Sparhawk. Aphrael will be very cross with you if you allow yourself to be killed."

"Tell her she's welcome to lend a hand, if she'd like."

"Sparhawk!" The tone was half-shocked and half-amused.

"To whom were you speaking, Sir Sparhawk?" Delada's voice was baffled, and he was looking around to see if anyone was near them.

"You're relatively devout, aren't you, Colonel?" Sparhawk asked him.

"I'm a son of the Church, Sparhawk."

"It might upset you if I told you, then. The militant orders have permission to go beyond what's allowed to ordinary members of the Elene faith. Why don't we just let it go at that."

Despite the best efforts of the defenders, several towers reached the wall, and the drawbridges at their tops swung down onto the battlements. One of the towers touched the wall just beside the gate, and Sparhawk's friends were ready for it. Tynian led their charge as they dashed across the drawbridge and into the tower itself. Sparhawk held his breath as his friends struggled inside the tower out of his sight. The sounds from within bespoke the ferocity of the fight. There was the crash of arms, and screams and groans. Then Tynian and Kalten came back out, ran across the thick-planked drawbridge, and seized a large bubbling cauldron of boiling pitch and naphtha in their steel-clad arms. They lurched back across the drawbridge with it and disappeared inside again. The screams from within suddenly intensified as they dumped the pitch down into the faces of the men on ladders inside the tower.

The knights emerged from the tower. When Kalten reached the wall, he took up a torch and flipped it into the structure with a negligent-appearing toss. The tower acted much like a chimney. Black smoke billowed from the gaping doorway the drawbridge had covered, and then dark orange flame boiled out through the roof. The screaming inside the tower increased, and then it died out.

The counterattacks of the knights along the walls were sufficient to ward off the first wave of attackers, but the defense of the battlements had cost many lives. The sheets of arrows and the heavier bolts from the crossbows had raked the tops of the walls in a virtual storm, and many of the church soldiers and not a few of the knights had fallen prey to them.

"They'll come again?" Delada asked somberly.

"Of course," Sparhawk said shortly. "The siege engines will pound the walls for a time now, and then more towers will come across that open area."

"How long can we hold out?"

"Four—maybe five of those attacks. Then the mangonels will start to break down the walls. The fighting will start inside the city at that point."

"We can't possibly win, can we, Sparhawk?"

"Probably not."

"Chyrellos is doomed, then?"

"Chyrellos was doomed the moment those two armies appeared, Delada. The strategy behind the attack on the city was very thorough—you might almost say brilliant."

"That's a peculiar attitude under these circumstances, Sparhawk."

"It's called professionalism. One's supposed to admire the genius of one's opponent. It's a pose, of course, but it helps to build a certain abstraction. Last stands are very gloomy, and you need something to keep your spirits up."

Then Berit clambered up through the trapdoor on the roof upon which Sparhawk and Delada stood. The novice's eyes were wide, seemingly slightly unfocused, and his head was jerking. "Sir Sparhawk!" he exclaimed, his voice unnecessarily loud.

"Yes, Berit?"

"What did you say?'

Sparhawk looked at him more closely. "What's the matter, Berit?" he asked.

"I'm sorry, Sir Sparhawk. I can't hear you. They rang the bells in the Basilica when the attack started. All the bells are up in the cupola on top of the dome. You never heard so much noise." Berit reached up and thumped the heel of his hand against the side of his head.

Sparhawk took him by the shoulders and looked directly into his face. "What's happening?" he bellowed, exaggeratedly mouthing the words.

"Oh, I'm sorry, Sir Sparhawk. The bells sort of rattled me. There are thousands of torches coming across the meadows on the other side of the River Arruk. I thought you ought to know."

"Reinforcements?" Delada said hopefully.

"I'm sure they are," Sparhawk replied, "but for which army?"

There was a heavy, booming crash behind them, and a fair-sized house collapsed in on itself as a huge boulder caved in its roof.

"God!" Delada exclaimed. "That boulder was enormous! These walls will never withstand that kind of pounding."

"No," Sparhawk agreed. "It's time for us to go to the cellar, Colonel."

"They started throwing those big rocks earlier than you thought, Sparhawk," the colonel noted. "That's sort of a good sign, wouldn't you say?"

"I'm afraid I don't quite follow that."

"Wouldn't that suggest that the army to the west is a relief column for us?"

"The troops outside our walls are mercenaries, Colonel. They *could* be in a hurry to get through our walls so that they won't have to share the loot with their friends out there on the other side of the river."


The lowest cellars of the Basilica were constructed of gigantic stones that had been laboriously chiseled and then carefully laid in long, low barrel vaults supported here and there by massive buttresses. The weight of the entire structure towering above rested entirely upon those mighty arches. It was dim and cool and quite damp in these cellars lying even below the crypt where the bones of long-dead churchmen moldered in dark silence.

"Kurik!" Sparhawk hissed to his squire as he and Delada passed the barred gate of an area set off from the rest of the cellar where Sparhawk's squire and Delada's guardsmen waited.

Kurik came to the bars on quiet feet.

"The mangonels have started," Sparhawk told him, "and there's a big army coming in from the west."

"You're just full of good news, aren't you, my Lord?" Kurik paused. "This isn't really a very nice place in here, Sparhawk. There are chains and manacles hanging from the walls, and there's a place toward the back that would have warmed Bellina's heart."

Sparhawk looked briefly at Delada.

Delada coughed. "It's no longer used," he said shortly. "There was a time when the Church would go to any lengths to stamp out heresy. Interrogations were conducted down here and confessions obtained. It wasn't one of the brighter chapters in the history of our Holy Mother."

"Some stories about that have leaked out." Sparhawk nodded. "Wait here with the guardsmen, Kurik. The colonel and I have to go get into place before either of our visitors arrive. When I whistle for the attack, don't wait around, because I'll really need you at that point."

"Have I ever let you down, Sparhawk?"

"No, as a matter of fact, you haven't. Sorry I even mentioned it." He led the colonel deeper into the labyrinthine cellar. "We're going to go into a fairly large room, Colonel," he explained. "There are all sorts of nooks and crannies along the walls. The young fellow who found the place brought me down here and showed it to me. He tells me that the two men we're interested in are likely to meet there. You'll be able to identify at least one of them. Hopefully, their conversation will identify the other. Pay very close attention to what they say, please. As soon as the conversation's over, I want you to go directly back to your quarters and lock your door. Don't open it for anybody but me, Lord Vanion, or Patriarch Emban. If it makes you feel better, for a brief period of time, you'll be the most important man in Chyrellos, and we'll set whole armies to protecting you."

"This is all very mysterious, Sparhawk."

"It has to be for right now, my friend. I hope that when you hear the conversation, you'll understand why. Here's the door." Sparhawk carefully pushed the rotting door open, and the two of them entered a large, dark chamber festooned with cobwebs. A rough table and two chairs sat near the door, and the thick stub of a single candle sat on a cracked saucer in the center of the table. Sparhawk led the way to the rear of the chamber and back into a deep alcove. "Take off your helmet," he whispered, "and wrap your cloak around your breastplate. We don't want any chance of reflection to warn anybody that we're here."

Delada nodded.

"I'm going to blow out our candle now," Sparhawk told him, "and we'll have to be absolutely quiet. If we need to talk, we'll have to whisper very softly into each other's ears." He blew out the candle, bent and laid it on the floor.

They waited. Somewhere far off in the darkness, water was dripping slowly. No matter how tight any drain may seem, there is always seepage, and water, like smoke, will always find the place it is seeking.

It might have been five minutes—or an hour—or even a century, when a muffled clinking came from the very far end of the vast cellar. "Soldiers," Sparhawk breathed to Delada. "Let's hope the man leading them doesn't bring them all inside this place."

"Indeed," Delada breathed back.

Then a dark-robed and hooded man slipped through the doorway, shielding a single candle with one hand. He lighted the candle on the table, blew out his own, and threw back his hood.

"I should have known," Delada whispered to Sparhawk. "It's the Primate of Cimmura."

"It is indeed, my friend. It is indeed."

The soldiers came nearer. They were making some effort to muffle the clinking of their equipment, but soldiers as a group have never been much good at stealth. "This is far enough," a familiar voice commanded. "Draw back a ways. I'll call if I need you."

There was a pause, and then Martel entered. He was carrying his helmet, and his white hair shone in the light of the single guttering candle on the table in front of the primate. "Well, Annias," he drawled, "we made a good try, but the game's played out."

"What are you talking about, Martel?" Annias snapped. "Everything's going our way."

"It changed direction on us about an hour ago."

"Stop trying to be cryptic, Martel. Tell me what's happening."

"There's an army marching in from the west, Annias."

"That other wave of Cammorian mercenaries you told me about?"

"I rather suspect that those mercenaries have been ground into dog meat by now, Annias." Martel unbuckled his sword belt. "Hate to break it to you this way, old boy, but that's Wargun's army marching in from the west. They stretch out as far as the eye can reach."

Sparhawk's heart leaped with exultation.

"Wargun?" Annias cried. "You said you'd taken care of keeping him away from Chyrellos."

"Thought I had, old boy, but somehow someone got through to him."

"His army's even bigger than yours?"

Martel sank wearily into his chair. "God, I'm tired," he confessed. "I haven't slept for two days. You were saying?"

"Has Wargun got more men than you have?"

"Lord, yes. He could chew me up in the space of a few hours. I really don't think we ought to wait for him. All *I* have to worry about is how long it's going to take Sparhawk to kill me. In spite of that face of his, Sparhawk's a gentle person. I'm sure he'd make quick work of me. I'm really disappointed in Perraine. I thought he might be able to do something permanent about my former brother. Oh, well. Ydra pays the penalty for his failure, I suppose. As I was saying, Sparhawk should be able to do for me in well under a minute. He's a much better swordsman than I am. *You,* however, have much more to be concerned about. Lycheas tells me that Ehlana wants your head on a plate. I once caught a glimpse of her face in Cimmura just after her father died and before you poisoned her. Sparhawk's gentle, but Ehlana's made of stone, and she hates you, Annias. She might very well decide to take your head off all by herself. She's a slender girl, and it might take her half a day to hack through your neck."

"But we're so *close,*" Annias protested in anguished frustration. "The archprelate's throne is almost within my grasp."

"You'd better ungrasp it then. It might be very heavy to carry when you're running for your life. Arissa and Lycheas are in my pavilion packing a few things already, but you're not going to have that kind of time, I'm afraid. You'll be leaving from here—with me. Get one thing very clear, Annias. I won't wait for you—not ever. If you start to fall behind, I'll leave you."

"There are things I *have* to have, Martel."

"I'm sure there are. I can think of a few right offhand myself—your head for one—and Lycheas says that the blond ape who runs with Sparhawk has developed an unwholesome passion for hanging people. I know Kalten well enough to realize how clumsy he is. He's almost certain to botch the job, and being the guest of honor at a botched hanging isn't my idea of a pleasant way to pass an afternoon."

"How many men did you bring here into this cellar?" Annias' voice was fearful.

"About a hundred is all."

"Are you mad? We're right in the middle of an encampment of Church Knights!"

"Your cowardice is starting to show, Annias." Martel's voice was thick with contempt. "That aqueduct isn't very wide. Would you really want to have to clamber over the top of a thousand well-armed mercenaries when the time comes to start running?"

"Run? Where can we run to? Where can we possibly go?"

"Where else? We go to Zemoch. Otha will protect us."

Colonel Delada drew in his breath with a sharp hiss.

"Be still, man," Sparhawk muttered.

Martel rose to his feet and began to pace up and down, his face ruddy in the candlelight. "Try to follow me on this, Annias," he said. "You gave Ehlana darestim, and darestim's *always* fatal. There's no cure, and ordinary magic could not have reversed the effects. I know that because I was trained in magic by Sephrenia myself."

"That Styric witch!" Annias said from between clenched teeth.

Martel seized him by the front of his robe and half lifted him from his chair. "Be very careful what you say, Annias," Martel said from between his teeth. "Don't insult my little mother, or you'll wish that it was Sparhawk who caught you. As I said, he's basically a gentle sort of person. I'm not. I can do things to you Sparhawk would never dream of."

"Surely you don't still have any feeling for her."

"That's *my* business, Annias. All right, then. If only magic could have cured the queen and ordinary magic wouldn't have worked, what does that leave us?"

"Bhelliom?" Annias guessed, rubbing his hand over the wrinkles Martel's fist had gathered up in the front of his robe.

"Precisely. Sparhawk's somehow managed to get his hands on it. He used it to cure Ehlana, and more than likely he's still got it with him. It's not the sort of thing you leave lying around. I'll send the Rendors out to knock down the bridges over the Arruk. That should delay Wargun for a while and give you and me more time to run. We'd better go north for a ways and get out of the main battle zone before we turn east toward Zemoch." He grinned mirthlessly. "Wargun's always wanted to exterminate the Rendors anyway. If I send them out to destroy the bridges, he'll get his chance, and God knows *I* won't miss them all that much. I'll order the rest of my troops to make a stand against Wargun on the east bank of the river. They'll engage him in a splendid battle—which might even last for a couple of hours before he butchers the lot of them. That's about all the time you and I and our friends are going to have to get clear of this place. We can count on Sparhawk to be right behind us, and we can be absolutely sure that he'll have Bhelliom with him."

"How do we know that? You're guessing, Martel."

"Do you mean to say that you've been around Sparhawk for all these years and haven't gotten to know him yet? I'm not trying to be insulting, old boy, but you're an absolute idiot, do you know that? Otha's massed in eastern Lamorkand, and he'll be marching into western Eosia within a matter of days. He'll slaughter everything in sight—men, women, children, cattle, dogs, wild animals, even fish. Preventing that is the primary duty of the Church Knights, and Sparhawk's what they had in mind when they founded the four orders. He's all duty and honor and implacable resolve. I'd give my soul to be a man like Sparhawk. He's got the one thing in his possession that will absolutely stop Otha cold. Do you really think there's anything in the world that would prevent him from bringing Bhelliom with him? Use your head, Annias."

"What good's it going to do us to run if we know that Sparhawk's right behind us with Bhelliom in his hands? He'll obliterate Otha and us along with him."

"Not very likely. Sparhawk's moderately stupendous, but he's not a God. Azash, however, is, and Azash has wanted Bhelliom since before the beginning of time. Sparhawk will chase us, and Azash will be waiting for him. Azash will destroy him in order to take Bhelliom from him. Then Otha will invade. Since we'll have done such a tremendous service for him, he'll reward us—lavishly. He'll put you on the archprelate's throne and give *me* the crown of any Elenian kingdom I choose— perhaps even all of them. Otha's lost his hunger for power in the last thousand years or so. I'll even set Lycheas up as regent—or even king—of Elenia, if you want— although I can't for the life of me think of any reason you'd want that. Your son's a snivelling cretin, and the sight of him turns my stomach. Why don't you have him strangled, and then you and Arissa can try again? If you both concentrate, you might even be able to produce a real human being instead of a dung-beetle."

Sparhawk felt a sudden chill. He looked around. Though he could not see it, he knew that the shadowy watcher that had followed him from Ghwerig's cave was somewhere here in the room. Could it possibly be that merely the mention of Bhelliom's name was enough to summon it?

"But how do we know that Sparhawk will be able to follow us?" Annias was asking. "He doesn't know about our arrangement with Otha, so he won't have the faintest idea of where we're going."

"You *are* naive, aren't you, Annias?" Martel laughed. "Sephrenia can listen in on a conversation from at least five miles away, and she can arrange to have everyone in the room with her hear it as well. Not only that, there are hundreds of places in this cellar that are within earshot of this room. Believe me, Annias, one way or another, Sparhawk's listening to us at this very moment." He paused. "Aren't you, Sparhawk?" he added.

## CHAPTER FIFTEEN

Martel's question hung in the musty dimness. "Stay here," Sparhawk whispered bleakly to Delada. He reached for his sword.

"Not very likely," the colonel replied, his tone just as grim. He also drew his sword.

It was really neither the time nor the place for arguments. "All right, but be careful. I'll take Martel. You grab Annias."

The two of them stepped out of their place of concealment and walked toward the single candle guttering on the table.

"Why, if it isn't my dear brother Sparhawk," Martel drawled. "So awfully good to see you again, old boy."

"Look quickly, Martel. You aren't going to be seeing much of anything for very long."

"I'd love to oblige you, Sparhawk, but I'm afraid we'll have to postpone it again. Pressing business, you understand." Martel took Annias by the shoulder and pushed him toward the door. "Move!" he snapped. The two of them went quickly out as Sparhawk and Delada rushed forward, swords in hand.

"Stop!" Sparhawk snapped to his companion.

"They're getting away, Sparhawk!" Delada objected.

"They already have." Sparhawk said it with a hot disappointment souring his mouth. "Martel's got a hundred men out there in those corridors. We need you alive, Colonel." Sparhawk whistled shrilly even as he heard the rush of many feet in the corridor outside. "We'll have to defend the door until Kurik and the guardsmen get here."

The two of them went quickly to the rotting door and took their places, one on either side of it. At the last moment, Sparhawk stepped out into plain view a few feet back from the arched opening in the massive stone wall. His position gave his sword full play, but the soldiers rushing through the entrance were hampered in their swings by the rocks of the sides and top of the archway.

Martel's mercenaries discovered very quickly what a bad idea it was to rush up on Sparhawk when he was angry, and Sparhawk was very angry at that point. The bodies piled up in the doorway as he savagely vented his rage on the scruffy-looking soldiers.

Then Kurik was there with Delada's guardsmen, and Martel's men fell back, defending the passageway leading toward the opening of the aqueduct into which Martel and Annias had already fled. "Are you all right?" the squire asked quickly, looking in through the doorway.

"Yes," Sparhawk replied. Then he reached out and caught Delada's arm as the colonel started to push past him.

"Let me go, Sparhawk," Delada said from between tight lips.

"No, Colonel. Do you remember what I told you awhile ago about your being the most important man in Chyrellos for a while?"

"Yes." Delada's tone was sullen.

"That particular eminence started just a few minutes ago, and I'm *not* going to let you get yourself killed just because you're feeling pugnacious at the moment. I'll take you to your quarters now and post a guard outside your door."

Delada rammed his sword back into its sheath. "You're right, of course," he said. "It's just that—"

"I know, Delada. I feel the same way myself."

After he had seen to the colonel's safety, Sparhawk returned to the cellar. The guardsmen under Kurik's command were in the process of mopping up and flushing out any mercenaries who were trying to hide. Kurik came back through the torchlit darkness. "I'm afraid Martel and Annias got completely away, Sparhawk," he reported.

"He was ready for us, Kurik," Sparhawk said glumly. "Somehow he knew we'd either be down here or that Sephrenia could work a spell so that we could hear him. He was saying a lot of things for my benefit."

"Oh?"

"The army coming in from the west is Wargun's."

"It's about time he got here." Kurik suddenly grinned.

"Martel also announced which way he's going. He *wants* us to follow him."

"I'll be overjoyed to oblige him. Did we get what *we* want, though?"

Sparhawk nodded. "When Delada's done with his report, Annias won't get a single vote."

"That's something anyway."

"Put some captain in charge of these guardsmen, and let's go find Vanion."

The preceptors of the four orders were standing atop the walls near the gates looking with some puzzlement out at the now-retreating mercenaries. "They just broke off the attack for no reason," Vanion said as Sparhawk and Kurik joined them.

"They had a reason, right enough," Sparhawk replied. "That's Wargun over there across the river."

"Thank God!" Vanion exclaimed. "Word must have reached him after all. How did things go in the cellar?"

"Colonel Delada heard a *very* interesting conversation. Martel and Annias got away, though. They're going to make a run for Zemoch to seek Otha's protection. Martel's going to send his Rendors out to destroy the bridges to give the rest of his mercenaries time to deploy. He doesn't have much hopes that they'll be able to do much more than inconvenience Wargun. All he's really hoping for is enough delay to give him time to get away."

"I think we'd better go talk with Dolmant," Preceptor Darellon said. "The situation has changed a bit. Why don't you round up your friends, Sir Sparhawk, and we'll go back to the chapterhouse."

"Pass the word, Kurik," Sparhawk told his squire. "Let all our friends know that King Wargun's come to our rescue."

Kurik nodded.

The patriarchs were enormously relieved to hear of King Wargun's approach and even more relieved to hear that Annias had incriminated himself. "The colonel can even testify about the arrangement Annias and Martel have with Otha," Sparhawk told them. "The only unfortunate part of the whole business was that Annias and Martel escaped."

"How long will it take for word of this turn of events to reach Otha?" Patriarch Emban asked.

"I think we'll almost have to assume that Otha will know about the change in the situation here almost as soon as it happens, your Grace," Preceptor Abriel told him.

Emban nodded with a look of distaste. "More of that magic business, I suppose."

"It's going to take Wargun quite some time to regroup and start to march into Lamorkand to meet the Zemochs, isn't it?" Dolmant said.

"A week or ten days, your Grace," Vanion agreed, "and even that's cutting it a little fine. Advance elements from both armies will be able to move out more rapidly, but neither main force will be able to start in less than a week."

"How far can an army move in a day?" Emban asked.

"Ten miles maximum, your Grace," Vanion replied.

"That's absurd, Vanion. Even *I* can walk ten miles in four hours, and I don't move very fast."

"That's when you're walking alone, your Grace." Vanion smiled. "A man out for a stroll doesn't have to worry about keeping the rear of a column from straggling, and when the time comes to sleep for the night, he can roll himself in his cloak under a bush. It takes quite a bit longer to set up an encampment for an army."

Emban grunted, laboriously hauled himself to his feet and waddled to the map of Eosia hanging on the wall of Sir Nashan's study. He measured off some distances. "They'll meet about here then," he said, stabbing one finger at a spot on the map, "on that plain to the north of Lake Cammoria. Ortzel, what's the country like around there?"

"Relatively flat," the Lamork Patriarch replied. "It's mostly farmland with a few patches of woods here and there."

"Emban," Dolmant said gently, "why don't we let King Wargun work out the strategy? We have our own business to attend to, you know."

Emban laughed a bit sheepishly. "I guess I'm a born busybody," he said. "I can't stand to let anything go by without sticking my nose into it." He clasped his hands reflectively behind his back. "We'll have everything under control here in Chyrellos just as soon as Wargun gets here. I think it's safe to say that Colonel Delada's testimony will eliminate the candidacy of the Primate of Cimmura once and for all, so why don't we clear away this election business right away—before the Hierocracy has time to gather its collective breath. Patriarchs are political animals, and as soon as they've had the time to collect their wits, they're going to start to see all sorts of opportunities in the present situation. We don't really need a number of unanticipated candidacies clouding things over right now. Let's keep it simple if we can. Not only that, we alienated a fair number of patriarchs when we decided to let the outer city burn. Let's catch the Hierocracy while it's still overwhelmed with thanksgiving and gratitude and fill that empty chair in the Basilica before they start brooding about lost houses and the like. We've got the upper hand for the moment. Let's use it before our support starts to crumble."

"That's all you ever really think about, isn't it, Emban?" Dolmant said.

"Somebody has to, my friend."

"We'd better get Wargun into the city first, though," Vanion told them. "Is there anything we can do to help him?"

"We can move out of the inner city just as soon as Martel's generals start turning around to face his army," Komier suggested. "We can hit them from behind and sting them enough to force them to chase us back inside the walls. Then they'll have to divert enough troops to keep us penned up in here. That should reduce the force facing Wargun a little bit."

"What I'd *really* like to do is figure out some way to defend those bridges across the Arruk," Abriel said. "Replacing them is what's going to cost Wargun time—and lives."

"I don't see that there's very much we can do about that," Darellon said. "We don't have enough men to keep the Rendors away from the riverbank."

"We *have* got enough to disrupt things inside the city though," Komier asserted. "Why don't we go back to the wall and size things up a bit? I need something to do to take the taste of that siege out of my mouth anyway."

There was fog as dawn approached, for the summer was drawing to a close and the two rivers that joined at Chyrellos fumed gray, wispy tendrils of mist from their dark surfaces in the cool of the night, and the tendrils joined together to form first a haze that softened the orange torchlight, then a mist that enshrouded distant houses, and finally that thick, clinging fog as common in cities that are built along rivers.

There was enthusiasm in the ranks for the action. There were tactical reasons for the plan, of course, but tactics are for generals, and the common soldiery was more interested in revenge. They had endured the pounding of siege engines; they had beaten off fanatics climbing scaling ladders; and they had faced the assault towers. Until now they had been forced to bear whatever the besiegers had hurled at them. This was their chance to even some scores, to chastise their chastisers, and they marched forth from the inner city with looks of grim anticipation on their faces.

Many of Martel's mercenaries had joined him with enthusiasm when there had been the prospect of loot and rapine and easy assaults on meagerly defended walls. Their enthusiasm waned, however, at the notion of meeting a vastly superior force in open country. They became peace-loving men at that point and crept through the foggy streets in search of places where their newly found pacifist sentiments would not be offended. The sortie in force from the inner city came as a great surprise and an even greater disappointment to men bent merely upon leading simple lives untainted by strife.

The fog, of course, helped enormously. The defenders of the inner city had only to fall upon men who were not wearing the armor of Church Knights or the red tunics of church soldiers. The torches these sudden pacifists carried made them easy targets for Kurik's now-proficient crossbowmen.

Since men on horseback make too much noise, the Church Knights moved through the streets on foot. After a time, Sparhawk joined Vanion. "All we're doing here is picking off deserters," he advised his preceptor.

"Not entirely, Sparhawk," Vanion disagreed. "The church soldiers have been under siege, and that sort of thing wears down men's spirits. Let's give our questionable allies the chance for a little revenge before we turn them back over to the patriarchs."

Sparhawk nodded his agreement and then he, Kalten, and Kurik moved out to take the lead.

A shadowy figure carrying an ax appeared at a torchlit intersection. The outline showed that whoever it was wore neither armor nor the tunic of a church soldier. Kurik raised his crossbow and took aim. At the last instant, he jerked his weapon upward, and the bolt whizzed up toward the predawn sky. Kurik started to swear sulphurously.

"What's the matter," Kalten hissed.

"That's Berit," Kurik said from between clenched teeth. "He always rolls his shoulders that way when he walks."

"Sir Sparhawk?" the novice called into the darkness, "are you down there?"

"Yes."

"Thank God. I think I've walked down every burned-out alley in Chyrellos looking for you."

Kurik banged one fist against a wall.

"Talk to him about it later," Sparhawk said. "All right, Berit," he called, "you've found me. What's important enough for you to go around risking your skin to try to share it?"

Berit came down the street to join them. "The Rendors appear to be gathering near the west gate, Sir Sparhawk. There are thousands of them."

"What are they doing?"

"I think they're praying. They're having some kind of ceremony at any rate. There's a skinny, bearded fellow standing on a pile of rubble haranguing them."

"Could you hear any of what he was saying?"

"Not very much, Sir Sparhawk, but he did say one word fairly often, and all the rest bellowed out the word each time he said it."

"What was the word?" Kurik demanded.

" 'Ramshorn,' I think it was, Kurik."

"That's got a familiar ring to it, Sparhawk," Kurik said.

Sparhawk nodded. "It appears that Martel brought Ulesim along to keep the Rendors in line."

Berit gave him a puzzled look. "Who's Ulesim, Sir Sparhawk?"

"The current spiritual leader of the Rendors. There's a twisted piece of a sheep's horn that's a kind of badge of office." He thought of something. "The Rendors are just sitting around listening to sermons?" he asked the novice.

"If that's what you want to call all that babbling, yes."

"Why don't we go back and talk with Vanion?" Sparhawk suggested. "This might be very useful."

The preceptors and Sparhawk's friends were not far behind. "I think we've just had a bit of luck, my Lords," Sparhawk reported. "Berit's been out wandering around in the streets. He says that the Rendors are all gathered near the west gate and that their leader's whipping them into a frenzy."

"You actually let a novice go out there alone, Sir Sparhawk?" Abriel asked disapprovingly.

"Kurik's going to talk to him about that later, my Lord."

"What was this leader's name again?" Vanion asked thoughtfully.

"Ulesim, my Lord. I've met him. He's a total idiot."

"What would the Rendors do if something happened to him?"

"They'd disintegrate, my Lord. Martel said that he was going to order them to tear down the bridges. Apparently they haven't started yet. Rendors need a lot of encouragement and some rather careful directions before they start on anything. Anyway, they look upon their religious leader as a semidivinity. They won't do anything without his express command."

"That might just be the way to save your bridges, Abriel," Vanion said. "If something happens to this Ulesim, the Rendors may just forget what they're supposed to do. Why don't we gather up our forces and go pay them a call?"

"Bad idea," Kurik said shortly. "Sorry, Lord Vanion, but it really is. If we march on the Rendors in force, they'll fight to the death to defend their holy man. All we'll do is get a lot of men needlessly killed."

"Do you have an alternative?"

Kurik patted his crossbow. "Yes, my Lord," he said confidently. "Berit says that Ulesim's making a speech to his people. A man who's talking to a crowd usually stands up on something. If I can get to within two hundred paces of him . . ." Kurik left it hanging.

"Sparhawk," Vanion decided, "take your friends and protect Kurik. Try to slip through the city until you can get him and that crossbow close enough to this Ulesim to remove him. If those Rendorish fanatics fly all to pieces and don't destroy the bridges, Wargun will be able to cross the river before the other mercenaries are ready for him. Mercenaries are the most practical soldiers in the world. They're not very enthusiastic about hopeless battles."

"You think they'll capitulate?" Darellon asked.

"It's worth a try," Vanion said. "A peaceful solution of some kind here could save us a lot of men on both sides, and I think we're going to need every man we can lay our hands on—even the Rendors—when we come up against Otha."

Abriel suddenly laughed. "I wonder how God's going to feel about having his Church defended by Eshandist heretics?"

"God's tolerant." Komier grinned. "He might even forgive them—a little."

The four knights, Berit, and Kurik crept through the streets of Chyrellos toward the west gate. A faint breeze had come up, and the fog was rapidly dissipating. They reached a large burned-out area near the west gate to find thousands of tightly packed and heavily armed Rendors gathered in the thinning mist about a heaped-up pile of rubble. Atop the rubble stood a familiar figure.

"That's him, all right," Sparhawk whispered to his companions as they took refuge in the gutted remains of a house. "There he stands in all his glory—Ulesim, most-favored-disciple-of-holy-Arasham."

"What was that?" Kalten asked.

"That's what he called himself down in Rendor. It was a self-bestowed title. I guess he wanted to spare Arasham the effort of selecting somebody."

Ulesim was in a state bordering on hysteria, and his speech had little in the way of coherence to recommend it. He held one bony arm aloft, and he was tightly clutching something. After about every fifteen words, he would shake the object in his hand vigorously and bellow, *"Ramshorn!"* His followers then would roar back, *"Ramshorn!"*

"What do you think, Kurik?" Sparhawk whispered as they all looked over a half-collapsed wall.

"I think he's crazy."

"Of course he's crazy, but is he in range?"

Kurik squinted across the top of the crowd at the ranting fanatic. "It's a goodly way," he said dubiously.

"Give it a try anyway," Kalten said. "If your bolt falls short—or even goes over—somebody of Rendorish persuasion's bound to catch it for you."

Kurik laid his crossbow across the top of the broken wall to steady it and took careful aim.

"God has revealed it to me!" Ulesim was shrieking to his followers. "We must destroy the bridges that are the work of the Evil One! The forces of darkness beyond the river will assault you, but Ramshorn will protect you! The power of the Blessed Eshand has joined with that of Holy Arasham to fill the talisman with unearthly might! Ramshorn will give you victory!"

Kurik squeezed the lever of his crossbow slowly. The thick bow made a deep-toned *twang* as it sped the bolt toward its mark.

"You are invincible!" Ulesim was shrieking. "You are—"

Whatever else it was that they were was never revealed. The vanes of a crossbow bolt were suddenly protruding from Ulesim's forehead just above his eyebrows. He stiffened, his eyes wide and his mouth suddenly gaping. Then he crumpled into a heap atop the rubble.

"Good shot," Tynian congratulated Kurik.

"Actually, I was trying to hit him in the belly," Kurik confessed.

"That's all right, Kurik." The Deiran laughed. "It was more spectacular this way anyhow."

A vast groan of shock and dismay ran through the crowd of Rendors.

Then the word "crossbow" raced through the crowd. A number of unfortunates had obtained such weapons from the Lamorks in one way or another. They were torn to pieces on the spot by their frenzied compatriots. A fair number of the black-robed men from the south ran off through the streets, howling and tearing at their garments. Others slumped to the ground, weeping in despair. Still others stood staring in stunned disbelief at the place where Ulesim had only recently stood haranguing them. There was also, Sparhawk noticed, a fair amount of on-the-spot politics going on. There were those in the crowd who felt that they had a claim on the recently vacated position, and they began to take steps to insure their elevation to eminence, reasoning that power rests more securely in the hands of sole survivors. Adherents of this or that candidate joined in, and the huge crowd was soon embroiled in what could only be called a general riot.

"Political discussion is quite spirited among the Rendors, isn't it?" Tynian observed mildly.

"I noticed that," Sparhawk agreed. "Let's go tell the preceptors about Ulesim's accident."

Since the Rendors were now militantly indifferent to bridges, sheep's horns, or the impending battle, the commanders of Martel's army saw that they had no chance whatsoever against the human sea on the far side of the river. Mercenaries are the most realistic of all soldiers, and soon a sizeable detachment of officers rode across one of the bridges under a flag of truce. They returned just before daybreak. The mercenary commanders conferred for a few moments, and then they formed up and, pushing the rioting Rendors ahead of them, marched out of Chyrellos and laid down their arms in surrender.

Sparhawk and the others gathered atop the wall of the outer city right beside the open west gate as the kings of western Eosia rode quite formally across the bridge to enter the Holy City. King Wargun, flanked by the mail-shirted Patriarch Bergsten, King Dregos of Arcium, King Soros of Pelosia, and the ancient King Obler of Deira, rode at the head of the column. Directly behind them came an ornate open carriage. Four people sat in the carriage. They were all robed and hooded, but the sheer bulk of one of them sent a chill through Sparhawk. Surely they wouldn't have— And then, apparently at some command from the slightest of them, the four pushed back their hoods. The fat one was Platime. Stragen was the second. The third was a woman whom Sparhawk did not recognize, and the fourth, slender and blonde and looking altogether lovely, was Ehlana, Queen of Elenia.

# CHAPTER SIXTEEN

Wargun's entry into Chyrellos was hardly triumphant. The commoners of the Holy City had not been in a position to stay abreast of current affairs, and one army looks very much like another to ordinary people. For the most part, they stayed under cover as the kings of Eosia passed on their way to the Basilica.

Sparhawk had little chance to speak with his queen when they all arrived at the Basilica. He had things to say to her, of course, but they were not the sort of things he wanted to say in public. King Wargun gave his generals a few abrupt commands, and then they followed the Patriarch of Demos inside for one of the get-togethers that normally mark such occasions.

"I'll have to admit that this Martel of yours is very clever," the King of Thalesia conceded a bit later, leaning back in a chair with an ale tankard in his hand. They had gathered in a large, ornate meeting room in the Basilica. The room had a long, polished table, a marble floor, and thick burgundy drapes at the windows. The kings were present, as were the preceptors of the four orders, patriarchs Dolmant, Emban, Ortzel, and Bergsten, and Sparhawk and the others, including Ulath, who still exhibited moments of vagueness but appeared to be on the mend. Sparhawk's face was stony as he looked across the table at his bride-to-be. He had many things he wanted to say to Ehlana, and a few he was saving up for Platime and Stragen as well. He was controlling his temper with some difficulty.

"After the burning of Coombe," Wargun went on, "Martel took a weakly defended castle perched on top of a crag. He strengthened the defenses, left a sizeable garrison there, and then moved on to lay siege to Larium. When we came up behind him, he fled east. Then he swung south, and finally he went west again toward

Coombe. I spent weeks chasing him. It *seemed* that he'd led his whole army into that castle, and I settled down to starve him out. What I *didn't* know was that he'd been detaching whole regiments from his army to hide in the countryside as he marched, and so he reached that castle with no more than a very small force. He sent that force inside the walls and closed the gates, and then he rode away, leaving *me* to besiege an impregnable castle, and leaving *him* free to regather his forces and march on Chyrellos."

"We sent a great many messages to you, your Majesty," Patriarch Dolmant said.

"I'm sure you did, your Grace," Wargun said sourly, "but only one of them reached me. Martel cluttered most of Arcium with small bands of ambushers. I expect that most of your messengers are lying in ditches down there in God's own rock garden. Sorry, Dregos," he apologized to the Arcian king.

"That's all right, Wargun," King Dregos forgave him. "God had a reason for putting so much rock in Arcium. Paving roads and building walls and castles gives my people something to do other than starting wars with each other."

"If there were ambushers out, how did *anybody* manage to reach you, your Majesty?" Dolmant asked.

"That was the strange part of it, Dolmant," Wargun replied, scratching at his tousled head. "I never really *did* get the straight of it. The fellow who got through is from Lamorkand, and it appears that he just rode openly all the way across Arcium and no one paid any attention to him. Either he's the luckiest man alive, or God loves him more than most—and he doesn't look all that loveable to me."

"Is he nearby, your Majesty?" Sephrenia asked the King of Thalesia, her eyes strangely intent.

"I think so, little lady." Wargun belched. "He said something about wanting to make a report to the Patriarch of Kadach. He's probably out there in the hall somewhere."

"Do you suppose we might ask him a few questions?"

"Is it really important, Sephrenia?" Dolmant asked her.

"Yes, your Grace," she replied, "I think it might be. There's something I'd like to verify."

"You," Wargun said sharply to one of the soldiers standing at the door, "see if you can find that seedy-looking Lamork who's been trailing after us. Tell him to come in here."

"At once, your Majesty."

"Naturally 'at once.' I gave an order, didn't I? *All* my orders are obeyed at once." King Wargun was already on his fourth tankard of ale, and his grip on civility was beginning to slip. "Anyway," he went on, "the fellow arrived at that castle I was besieging no more than two weeks ago. After I read his message, I gathered up the army and we all came here."

The Lamork who was escorted into the room was, as Wargun had said, a bit on the seedy-looking side. He was obviously neither a warrior nor a churchman. He had thin, lank, dun-colored hair and a big nose.

"Ah, Eck," Patriarch Ortzel said, recognizing one of his servants. "I should have guessed that you'd have been the one to make it through. My friends, this is one of my servants—Eck by name—a very sneaky fellow, I've found. He's most useful when stealth is required."

"I don't think stealth had much to do with it this time, your Grace," Eck admitted. He had a nasal sort of voice that seemed to go with his face. "As soon as we saw your signal, we all rode off to the west as fast as our horses could run. We started to run into ambushes before we even reached the Arcian border, though. That's when we decided to split up. We thought that one of us at least might get through. Personally, I didn't have much hope of that. There seemed to be a man with a long-bow behind every tree. Anyway, I hid out in a ruined castle near Darra to think things over. I couldn't see any way to get your message through at all. I didn't know where King Wargun was, and I didn't dare ask any travellers for fear that they were some of the men who'd been killing my friends."

"Perilous situation," Darellon said.

"I thought so myself, my lord," Eck agreed. "I hid in that ruin for two days, and then one morning, I heard the strangest sound. It seemed to be music of some kind. I thought it might be a shepherd, but it turned out to be a little girl with a few goats. She was making the music on those pipes that herders carry. The little girl seemed to be about six or so, and I knew as soon as I saw her that she was Styric. Everyone knows that it's bad luck to have anything at all to do with Styrics, so I stayed hidden in the ruins. I certainly didn't want her to give me away to any of the people who were looking for me. She came right up to me as if she knew exactly where I was, though, and she told me to follow her." He paused, his face troubled. "Now, I'm a grown man, your Grace, and I don't take orders from children—and particularly not from Styric ones—but there was something very strange about this little girl. When she told me to do something, I went right ahead and started to do it before I even stopped to think about it. Isn't that odd? To make it short, she led me out of those ruins. The men who were looking for me were all around, but they just acted as if they couldn't even see us. The little girl led me all the way across Arcium. Now, that's a long, long ways, but for some reason it only took us three days—four actually when you count the day when we stopped so that one of her nanny goats could give birth to a pair of kids—cute little beasts they were, too. The little girl even insisted that I carry them on my horse when we moved on. Well, sir, we reached the castle where King Wargun's army was laying siege to some Rendors inside, and that's when the little girl left me. It's the oddest thing. I don't like Styrics, but I actually cried when she went away. She gave me a little kiss before she left, and I can still feel it on my cheek. I've thought about it a lot since then, and I've decided that maybe Styrics aren't so bad after all."

"Thank you," Sephrenia murmured.

"Well, sir," Eck went on, "I went to the army and told them that I had a message for King Wargun from the Hierocracy. The soldiers took me to his Majesty, and I gave him the document. After he read it through, he gathered up his army, and we made a forced march to get here. That's about all there was, my Lords."

Kurik was smiling gently. "Well, well," he said to Sephrenia, "it looks as if Flute's still around—and in more than just spirit—doesn't it?"

"So it would seem," she agreed, also smiling.

"Document?" Patriarch Emban said to Patriarch Ortzel.

"I took the liberty of speaking for the Hierocracy," Ortzel confessed. "I gave each of my messengers a copy for King Wargun. I thought it might be all right, under the circumstances."

"It's quite all right with *me*," Emban said. "Makova might not have liked it very much, though."

"I'll apologize to him someday—if I happen to think about it. I wasn't really sure whether any of the other messages had reached King Wargun, so I more or less briefed him on everything that's been happening."

It had taken a few moments for what they were saying to seep through King Wargun's awareness. "Are you saying that I moved my army on the orders of one single patriarch—who isn't even a Thalesian?" he roared.

"No, Wargun," the huge Patriarch Bergsten said firmly. "I fully approve of the actions of the Patriarch of Kadach, so you moved your army on *my* orders. Would you like to argue with *me* about it?"

"Oh," Wargun said contritely, "that's different then." Patriarch Bergsten was not really the sort one argued with. Wargun moved on quickly. "I read over the document a couple of times and decided that a side trip to Cimmura might be in order. I sent Dregos and Obler with the main body of the army on ahead and took the Elenian army back up there so that they could defend their capital city. When we got there, we found the place defended by the common citizens, if you can imagine that, and when I demanded entry, they wouldn't open the gates for me until that fat one over there gave his approval. To be honest with you, I couldn't really see where Cimmura was in all that much danger. Those shopkeepers and common workmen were handling themselves in a very professional manner up on those walls, I'll tell the world. Anyway, I went to the palace to meet with the Earl of Lenda and this pretty young lady who wears the crown. That's when I saw that rascal over there." He pointed at Stragen. "He'd hemstitched a fourth cousin of mine with that rapier of his up in Emsat, and I'd put a price on his head—more out of family feeling than for any particular affection for the cousin, since the man made me sick just to look at him. He had a habit of picking his nose in public, and I find that disgusting. He won't do it any more, though. Stragen skewered him thoroughly. Anyway, I was going to have this rogue hanged, but Ehlana there talked me out of it." He took a long drink. "Actually—" He belched, "—she threatened to declare war on me if I didn't drop the idea. She's a very feisty young lady, I discovered." He suddenly grinned at Sparhawk. "I understand that congratulations are in order, my friend, but I don't know that I'd take off my armor until you get to know her better."

"We know each other very well, Wargun," Ehlana said primly. "Sparhawk virtually raised me from a baby, so if I sometimes have a few rough edges, you have him to thank for it."

"I probably should have suspected something like that." Wargun laughed to the others. "When I told Ehlana about what was happening here in Chyrellos, she insisted on bringing her army along to help with the fighting. I absolutely forbade it, and all she did was reach out, tweak my whiskers, and say, 'That's all right, Wargun. I'll race you to Chyrellos then.' Now, I don't let *anyone* pull my whiskers, so I was going to spank her right there on the spot, queen or no queen, but then that enormous woman over there stepped in." He looked at the woman Sparhawk surmised was Mirtai, the Tamul giantess, and shuddered. "I couldn't believe that she could move that fast. She had a knife to my throat before I could even blink. I tried to explain to Ehlana that I had more than enough men to capture Chyrellos, but she said something about having an investment to protect. I never really got the straight of that. Anyway, we all marched out of Cimmura and joined with Dregos and Obler and came on down here to the Holy City. Now, could somebody explain to me what's really been happening here?"

"The usual Church politics," Patriarch Emban told him dryly. "You know how much our Mother adores intrigue. We were fighting a delaying action in the meetings of Hierocracy, manipulating votes, kidnapping patriarchs—that sort of thing. We were barely able to keep the Primate of Cimmura off the throne, and then Martel showed up and laid siege to the Holy City. We pulled back inside the walls of the inner city for one of those tedious last stands. Things were starting to get serious by the time you arrived last night."

"Has Annias been seized as yet?" King Obler asked.

"I'm afraid not, your Majesty," Dolmant replied. "Martel managed to spirit him out of the city just before dawn."

"That's truly unfortunate." Obler sighed. "He could still come back and make a serious bid for the archprelacy then, couldn't he?"

"We'd be overjoyed to see him, your Majesty," Dolmant said with a mirthless smile. "I'm sure you've heard of the connection between Annias and Martel and the suspicions we have about some sort of arrangements between them and Otha. As luck had it, we were able to take the commander of the archprelate's personal guard to a place where he could overhear Annias and Martel talking. The colonel's completely neutral, and everybody knows it. Once he reports what he heard to the Hierocracy, Annias will be expelled from the Church—at the very least." He paused. "Now, then," he went on, "the Zemochs are massed in eastern Lamorkand as a part of the arrangement between Otha and Annias. As soon as Otha finds out that their plans have gone awry here in Chyrellos, he'll start to march west. I'd suggest that we do something about that."

"Have we any idea of which way Annias went?" Ehlana asked, her eyes glittering.

"He and Martel took Princess Arissa and your cousin Lycheas, and they're all running to Otha for protection, my Queen," Sparhawk told her.

"Is there any way you could intercept them?" she demanded fiercely.

"We can try, your Majesty." He shrugged. "I wouldn't hold out much hope, though."

"I *want* him, Sparhawk," she said fiercely.

"I'm very sorry, your Majesty," Patriarch Dolmant interposed, "but Annias has committed crimes against the Church. *We* get him first."

"So that you can lock him away in some monastery to pray and sing hymns the rest of his life?" she asked with disdain. "I have much more interesting plans for him, your Grace. Believe me, if I get my hands on him first, I will *not* surrender him to the Church—at least not until I've finished with him. After that, you can have what's left."

"That will do, Ehlana," Dolmant told her sharply. "You're right on the verge of open disobedience to the Church. Don't make the mistake of pushing this too far. In point of fact, though, it's not a monastery that's awaiting Annias. The nature of the crimes he's committed against the Church merits burning at the stake."

Their eyes locked, and Sparhawk groaned inwardly.

Then Ehlana laughed, a bit shamefaced. "Forgive me, your Grace," she apologized to Dolmant. "I spoke in haste. Burning, did you say?"

"At the very least, Ehlana," he replied.

"I will, of course, defer to our Holy Mother. I would sooner die than appear undutiful."

"The Church appreciates your obedience, my daughter," Dolmant said blandly.

Ehlana clasped her hands piously and gave him a wholly spurious little smile of contrition.

Dolmant laughed in spite of himself. "You're a naughty girl, Ehlana," he chided.

"Yes, your Grace," she admitted. "I suppose I am at that."

"This is a very dangerous woman, my friends," Wargun told his fellow monarchs. "I think we should all make a special point of not getting in her way. All right, what's next?"

Emban slid lower in his chair and sat tapping his fat fingertips together. "We'd more or less decided that we should settle the question of the archprelacy once and for all, your Majesty. That was before you even entered the city. It's going to take some time for you to prepare your forces to march toward central Lamorkand, isn't it?" he asked.

"At least a week," Wargun replied glumly, "possibly two. I've got units strung out halfway back to Arcium—mostly stragglers and supply wagons. It's going to take a while to get them organized, and troops really get jammed up when they have to cross bridges."

"We can give you ten days at most," Dolmant told him. "Do your staging and organizing as you march."

"It's not done that way, your Grace," Wargun objected.

"It will be this time, your Majesty. Soldiers on a march spend more time sitting around waiting than they do walking. Let's put that time to good use."

"You'll also want to keep your soldiers out of Chyrellos," Patriarch Ortzel added. "Most of the citizens have fled, so the city's deserted. If your men become distracted with looking through unoccupied houses, they'll be a little difficult to round up when the time comes to march."

"Dolmant," Emban said, "you're holding the chair in the Hierocracy. I think we should go into session first thing tomorrow morning. Let's keep our brothers away from the outer city today—for their own safety, of course, since there still might be a few of Martel's mercenaries hiding in the ruins. Primarily, though, we don't want them to get a chance to examine the damage to their houses too closely before we go into formal session. We've seriously alienated a fair number of patriarchs, and even with Annias discredited, we don't want some spur-of-the-moment coalition confusing the issues here. I think we should hold some sort of service in the nave before we go into session. Probably something solemn and having to do with thanksgiving. Ortzel, would you officiate? You're going to be our candidate, so let's give everybody the chance to get used to looking at you. And, Ortzel, try to smile now and then. Honestly, your face won't break."

"Am I so very, very stern, Emban?" Ortzel replied with a faint half smile.

"Perfect," Emban said. "Practice that exact smile in a mirror. Remember that you're going to be a kindly, loving father—at least that's what we want them to think. What you do after you get to the throne is between you and God. All right, then. The services will remind our brothers that they're churchmen first and property owners second. We'll march directly to the audience chamber from the nave. I'll talk to the choirmaster and have a lot of singing echoing through the Basilica—something exalted to put our brothers in the proper mood. Dolmant will call us to order, and we'll begin with an update—let everybody know the details of what's been happening. That's for the benefit of the patriarchs who've been hiding in cellars since the siege began. It's perfectly proper to call in witnesses under those circumstances. I'll select them to make sure they're eloquent. We want a lot of lurid descriptions of rape, arson, and pillage to stir up a certain disapproval of the behavior of the recent visitors to our city. Our parade of witnesses will culminate with Colonel Delada, and he'll report the conversation between Annias and Martel. Let them mull that over for a little bit. I'll talk to some of our brothers and have them prepare speeches full of outraged indignation and denunciations of the Primate of Cimmura. Then Dolmant will appoint a committee to investigate the matter. We don't want the Hierocracy to get sidetracked." The fat little patriarch thought it over. "Let's adjourn for a noon meal at that point. Give them a couple of hours to work themselves up about the perfidy of Annias. Then, when we go back into session, Bergsten will make a speech about the need for all considered speed. Don't give the appearance of rushing things, Bergsten, but remind them that we're in a Crisis of the Faith. Then urge that we proceed directly with the voting. Wear your armor and carry that ax. Let's set the tone of being on a wartime footing. Then we'll have the traditional speeches by the kings of Eosia. Make them stirring, your Majesties. Lots of references to cruel war and Otha and the foul designs of Azash. We want to frighten our brothers enough so that they'll vote their consciences instead of politicking in back hallways and trying to make deals with each other. Keep your eyes on me, Dolmant. I'll nose out any patriarchs with the uncontrollable urge toward political chicanery and identify them to you. As chairman, you can recognize whomever you choose. And under *no* circumstances whatsoever accept a move to adjourn. Don't let anybody break the momentum. Go immediately into the nominations at that point. Let's get into the voting before our brothers have time to start thinking up mischief. Speed the vote right along. We want Ortzel on that throne before the sun goes down. And Ortzel, you keep your mouth shut during the deliberations. Some of your opinions are controversial. Don't air them in public—at least not tomorrow."

"I feel like an infant," King Dregos said wryly to King Obler. "I thought I knew a *little* bit about politics, but I've never seen the art practiced so ruthlessly before."

"You're in the big city now, your Majesty." Emban grinned at him. "And *this* is the way we play here."

King Soros of Pelosia, a man of extreme piety and an almost childlike reverence, had nearly fainted a number of times during Patriarch Emban's cold-blooded scheme to manipulate the Hierocracy. He finally bolted, muttering something about wanting to pray for guidance.

"Keep an eye on Soros tomorrow, your Grace," Wargun advised Emban. "He's a religious hysteric. When he makes his speech, he might just decide to expose us. Soros spends all his time talking to God, and sometimes that unsettles a man's wits. Is there any possible way we can skip over him during the speeches?"

"Not legitimately," Emban said.

"We'll talk with him, Wargun," King Obler said. "Maybe we can persuade him to be too ill to attend tomorrow's session."

"I'll make him sick, all right," Wargun muttered.

Emban rose to his feet. "We all have things to attend to, ladies and gentlemen," he said, "so as they say, let's get cracking."

Sparhawk stood up. "The Elenian embassy was damaged during the siege, my Queen," he said to Ehlana in a neutral tone. "May I offer you the somewhat Spartan comfort of the Pandion chapterhouse instead?"

"You're cross with me, aren't you, Sparhawk?" she asked him.

"It might be more appropriate if we discussed that in private, my Queen."

"Ah," she sighed. "Well, let's go ahead and go to your chapterhouse so you can scold me for a while. Then we can move right on into the kissing and making up. That's the part *I'm* really interested in. At least you won't be able to spank me—not with Mirtai standing guard over me. Have you ever met Mirtai, by the way?"

"No, my Queen." Sparhawk looked at the silent Tamul woman who stood behind Ehlana's chair. Mirtai's skin had a peculiarly exotic bronze tinge to it, and her braided hair was a glossy black. In a woman of normal size, her features would have been considered beautiful, and her dark eyes, slightly upturned at the corners, ravishing. Mirtai, however, was not of normal size. She towered a good hand's breadth above Sparhawk. She wore a white satin blouse with full sleeves and a garment that was more like a knee-length kilt than a skirt, belted at her waist. She wore black leather boots and had a sword at her side. Her shoulders were broad and her hips lithely slender. Despite her size, she seemed perfectly proportioned. There was, however, something ominous about her expressionless gaze. She did not look at Sparhawk the way a woman would normally look at a man. She was an unsettling sort of person.

Sparhawk, stiffly correct, offered his steel-clad arm to his queen and escorted her out through the nave and to the marble steps outside the Basilica. There was a ringing tap on his armored back as they stepped out onto the broad landing at the top of the stairs. He looked around. Mirtai had rapped on his armor with one knuckle. She took a folded cloak from off her arm, shook it out, and held it for Ehlana.

"Oh, it's not really *that* cool, Mirtai," Ehlana objected.

Mirtai's face went flinty, and she shook the cloak once commandingly.

Ehlana sighed and permitted the giantess to settle the cloak about her shoulders. Sparhawk was looking directly at the bronze woman's face, so there could be no question about what happened next. Without changing expression, Mirtai gave him a slow wink. For some reason, that made him feel a great deal better. He and Mirtai were going to get along very well, he decided.

Since Vanion was busy, Sparhawk escorted Ehlana, Sephrenia, Stragen, Platime, and Mirtai to Sir Nashan's study for their discussions. He had spent the morning preparing and sharpening a number of scathing remarks that verged just on the edge of being treasonous.

Ehlana, however, had studied politics since childhood, and she knew that one needs to be quick—even abrupt—when one's position is none too strong. "You're unhappy with us," she began before Sparhawk even had the door closed. "You feel that I have no business being here and that my friends here are at fault for allowing me to place myself in danger. Is that more or less it, Sparhawk?"

"Approximately, yes." *His* tone was frosty.

"Let's simplify things then," she went on quickly. "Platime, Stragen, and Mirtai *did*, in fact, protest most violently, but I'm the queen, so I overruled them. Do we agree that I have that authority?" *Her* tone had an edge to it, a note of challenge.

"She really did, Sparhawk," Platime said in a conciliatory tone. "Stragen and I yelled at her for an hour about it, and then she threatened to have us thrown into the dungeon. She even threatened to revoke my pardon."

"Her Majesty is a very effective bully, Sparhawk," Stragen concurred. "Don't ever trust her when she smiles at you. That's when she's the most dangerous, and when the time comes, she uses her authority like a bludgeon. We even went so far as to try to lock her in her apartment, but she just had Mirtai kick the door down."

Sparhawk was startled. "That's a very thick door," he said.

"It *used* to be. Mirtai kicked it twice, and it split right down the middle."

Sparhawk looked at the bronze woman with some surprise.

"It wasn't difficult," she said. Her voice was soft and musical, and it was touched with just the faintest tinge of an exotic accent. "Doors inside of houses dry out, and they split quite easily if you kick them just right. Ehlana can use the pieces for firewood when winter comes." She spoke with quiet dignity.

"Mirtai is very protective of me, Sparhawk," Ehlana said. "I feel completely secure when she's around, and she's teaching me to speak the language of the Tamuls."

"Elene is a coarse and ugly language," Mirtai observed.

"I've noticed that." Sephrenia smiled.

"I'm teaching Ehlana the Tamul tongue so that I will not be ashamed to have my owner clucking at me like a chicken."

"I'm *not* your owner any longer, Mirtai," Ehlana insisted. "I gave you your freedom right after I bought you."

Sephrenia's eyes were outraged. *"Owner!"* she exclaimed.

"It's a custom of Mirtai's people, little sister," Stragen explained. "She's an Atan. They're a warrior race, and it's generally believed that they need guidance. The Tamuls feel that they aren't emotionally equipped to handle freedom. It seems to cause too many casualties."

"Ehlana was ignorant even to make the suggestion," Mirtai said calmly.

*"Mirtai!"* Ehlana exclaimed.

"Dozens of your people have insulted me since you became my owner,

Ehlana," the Tamul woman said sternly. "They would all be dead now if I were free. That old one—Lenda—even let his shadow touch me once. I know that you're fond of him, so I'd have regretted killing him." She sighed philosophically. "Freedom is very dangerous for one of my kind. I prefer not to be burdened with it."

"We can talk about it some other time, Mirtai," Ehlana said. "Right now we have to pacify my champion." She looked Sparhawk full in the face. "You have no reason to be angry with Platime, Stragen, or Mirtai, my beloved," she told him. "They did everything they could to keep me in Cimmura. Your quarrel is with me and with me alone. Why don't we excuse them so that we can scream at each other privately?"

"I'll go along with them," Sephrenia said. "I'm sure you'll both be able to speak more freely if you're alone." She followed the two thieves and the bronze giantess from the room. She paused at the door. "One last thing, children," she added. "Scream all you want, but no hitting—and I don't want either of you to come out of here until you've resolved this." She went out and closed the door behind her.

"Well?" Ehlana said.

"You're stubborn," Sparhawk said flatly.

"It's called being strong-willed, Sparhawk. That's considered to be a virtue in kings and queens."

"What on earth possessed you to come to a city under siege?"

"You forget something, Sparhawk," she said. "I'm not really a woman."

He looked her slowly up and down until she blushed furiously—he owed her that, he felt. "Oh?" He knew he was going to lose this fight anyway.

"Stop that," she said. "I'm the queen—a reigning monarch. That means that I sometimes have to do things that an ordinary woman wouldn't be allowed to do. I'm already at a disadvantage because I'm a woman. If I hide behind my own skirts, none of the other kings will take me seriously, and if they don't take *me* seriously, they won't take Elenia seriously either. I *had* to come here, Sparhawk. You understand that, don't you?"

He sighed. "I don't like it, Ehlana, but I can't argue with your reasoning."

"Besides," she added softly, "I was lonesome for you."

"You win." He laughed.

"Oh, good," she exclaimed, clapping her hands together delightedly. "I just *adore* winning. Now, why don't we move right on into the kissing and making up?"

They did that for a while. "I've missed you, my stern-faced champion." She sighed. Then she banged her knuckles on his cuirass. "I didn't miss *this,* though," she added. She gave him an odd look. "Why did you have such a strange expression on your face when that Ick fellow—"

"Eck," he corrected.

"Sorry—when he was talking about the little girl who guided him through Arcium to King Wargun?"

"Because the little girl was Aphrael."

"A Goddess? She actually appears before ordinary people? Are you absolutely sure?"

He nodded. "Absolutely," he told her. "She made him more or less invisible, and she compressed a ten-day journey into three. She did the same things for us on a number of occasions."

"How remarkable." She stood, idly drumming her fingertips on his armor.

"Please don't do that, Ehlana," he said. "It makes me feel like a bell with legs."

"Sorry. Sparhawk, are we *really* sure we want Patriarch Ortzel on the archprelate's throne? Isn't he awfully cold and stern?"

"Ortzel's rigid, right enough, and his archprelacy's going to cause the militant orders some difficulty. He's violently opposed to our using magic, for one thing."

"What earthly good is a Church Knight if he can't use magic?"

"We *do* have other resources as well, Ehlana. Ortzel wouldn't have been my first choice, I'll admit, but he holds strictly to the teachings of the Church. No one like Annias will ever get into a position of any kind of authority if Ortzel's in charge. He's rigid, but he follows Church doctrine to the letter."

"Couldn't we find somebody else—somebody we like a little more?"

"We don't select archprelates because we're fond of them, Ehlana," he chided. "The Hierocracy tries to select the man who'll be best for the Church."

"Well, of *course* it does, Sparhawk. Everybody knows that." She turned sharply. "There it is again," she said with exasperation.

"There what is?" he asked her.

"You wouldn't be able to see it, love," she told him. "Nobody can see it but me. At first I thought that everyone around me was going blind. It's a sort of shadow or something. I can't really see it—not clearly, anyway—but it sort of hovers around behind my back where I can only catch very brief glimpses of it. It always makes me very cold for some reason."

Chilled, Sparhawk half turned, being careful to make it look casual. The shadow hovered at the edge of his vision, looming larger and darker, and its malevolence was more pronounced. Why should it have been following Ehlana, though? She had not even touched the Bhelliom. "It should go away in time," he said carefully, not wanting to alarm her. "Don't forget that Annias gave you a very rare and powerful poison. There are bound to be some lingering aftereffects."

"I suppose that's it."

Then he understood. It was her ring, of course. Sparhawk silently berated himself for not having thought of that possibility earlier. Whatever it was that was behind the shadow would certainly want to keep an eye on both rings.

"I thought we were making up," Ehlana said.

"We are."

"Why aren't you kissing me, then?"

He was attending to that when Kalten came in.

"Didn't you ever learn how to knock?" Sparhawk asked him sourly.

"Sorry," Kalten said. "I thought Vanion was in here. I'll see if I can find him someplace else. Oh, by the way, here's something to brighten your day a little more, though—if it really needs it. Tynian and I were out with Wargun's soldiers flushing deserters out of the houses. We found an old friend hiding in the cellar of a wine shop."

"Oh?"

"For some reason, Martel left Krager behind. We'll all get together with him for a nice chat—just as soon as he sobers up, and after you two have finished whatever it is you're doing here." He paused. "Would you like to have me lock the door for you?" he asked. "Or maybe stand guard outside?"

"Get out of here, Kalten." It wasn't Sparhawk who gave the command, however.

## CHAPTER SEVENTEEN

Krager was not in very good shape when Kalten and Tynian half carried him into Sir Nashan's study early that evening. His thin hair was dishevelled, he was unshaven, and his nearsighted eyes were bloodshot. His hands were shaking violently, and his expression was one of misery, a misery that had nothing to do with his capture. The two knights dragged Martel's underling to a plain chair in the center of the room and sat him in it. Krager buried his face in his shaking hands.

"I don't think we're going to get much out of him when he's in this condition," King Wargun growled. "I've been through that sort of thing myself, and I know. Give him some wine. He'll be more or less coherent when his hands stop shaking."

Kalten looked at Sir Nashan, and the plump Pandion pointed at an ornate cabinet in the corner. "It's only for medicinal purposes, Lord Vanion," Nashan explained quickly.

"Of course," Vanion said.

Kalten opened the cabinet and took out a crystal decanter of Arcian red wine. He poured a large gobletful and handed it to Krager. The suffering man spilled half of it, but he did manage to get the rest down. Kalten poured him another. And then another. Krager's hands began to grow more steady. He looked around, blinking. "I see that I've fallen into the hands of mine enemies," he said in a voice made rusty by years of hard drinking. "Ah, well." He shrugged. "Fortunes of war, I suppose."

"Your situation here is not enviable," Lord Abriel told him ominously.

Ulath took out a whetstone and began sharpening his ax. It made a very unpleasant sound.

"Please," Krager said wearily, "I'm not feeling well. Spare me the melodramatic threats. I'm a survivor, gentlemen. I fully understand the situation here. I'll cooperate with you in exchange for my life."

"Isn't that just a bit contemptible?" Bevier sneered.

"Of course it is, Sir Knight," Krager drawled, "but I'm a contemptible sort of person—or hadn't you noticed? Actually, I deliberately placed myself in a position so that you could capture me. Martel's plan was very good—as far as it went—but when it started to fall apart, I decided that I didn't really want to share his fortunes when they were on the decline. Let's save time, gentlemen. We all know that I'm too valuable to kill. I know too much. I'll tell you everything I know in exchange for my life, my freedom, and ten thousand gold crowns."

"What about your loyalties?" Patriarch Ortzel asked sternly.

"Loyalty, your Grace?" Krager laughed. "To Martel? Don't be absurd. I worked for Martel because he paid me well. We both knew that. But now you're in a position to offer me something of much greater value. Do we have a bargain?"

"Some time on the rack might lower your asking price a bit," Wargun told him.

"I'm not a robust man, King Wargun," Krager pointed out, "and my health's never been what you'd call very good. Do you really want to gamble on my expiring under the ministrations of your torturers?"

"Let it lie," Dolmant said. "Give him what he wants."

"Your Grace is a wise and gracious man." Krager laughed suddenly. "Awfully sorry about the pun there, Patriarch Dolmant. It was accidental, I assure you."

"There's one restriction, however," Dolmant went on. "Under the circumstances, we could hardly set you free until such time as your former master is apprehended. By your own admission, you're not very dependable. Besides, we'll need a little confirmation of what you tell us."

"Perfectly understandable, your Grace," Krager agreed. "But no dungeons. My lungs aren't very strong, and I really should avoid damp places."

"A monastery, then?" Dolmant countered.

"Totally acceptable, your Grace—on the condition that Sparhawk is not permitted to come within ten miles of the place. Sparhawk's irrational sometimes, and he's wanted to kill me for years now—haven't you, Sparhawk?"

"Oh, yes," Sparhawk admitted freely. "I'll tell you what, Krager. I'll pledge myself to keep my hands off you until after Martel is dead."

"Fair enough, Sparhawk," Krager replied, "if you'll also vow to give me a week's head start before you come after me. Do we have a bargain, gentlemen?"

"Tynian," Preceptor Darellon said, "take him out into the hallway while we discuss this."

Krager rose shakily to his feet. "Come along then, Sir Knight," he said to Tynian. "You, too, Kalten, and don't forget to bring the wine."

"Well?" King Wargun asked after the closely guarded prisoner had left the room.

"Krager himself is unimportant, your Majesty," Vanion said, "but he's absolutely right about the importance of the information he has. I'd advise accepting his terms."

"I hate to give him all that gold, though," Wargun growled moodily.

"In Krager's case, it's not really a gift," Sephrenia said quietly. "If you give Krager that much money, he'll drink himself to death within six months."

"That doesn't sound like much of a punishment to me."

"Have you ever seen a man die of the aftereffects of drink, Wargun?" she asked.

"I can't say that I have."

"You might stop by an asylum sometime and watch the process. You may find it very educational."

"Are we agreed, then?" Dolmant asked, looking around. "We give this sewer rat what he asks and confine him to the monastery until such time as we know that he can't report anything significant to Martel?"

"All right," Wargun gave in grudgingly. "Bring him back in and let's get on with this."

Sparhawk went to the door and opened it. A scarred man with a shaved head was speaking urgently with Tynian.

"Kring?" Sparhawk asked with some surprise, recognizing the Domi of the band of marauding horsemen from the eastern marches of Pelosia. "Is that you?"

"Well, Sparhawk," Kring said. "It's good to see you again. I was just bringing friend Tynian here some news. Did you know that the Zemochs are massed in eastern Lamorkand?"

"We'd heard about it, yes. We were more or less planning to take steps."

"Good. I've been off with the army of the king of the Thalesians, and one of my men from back home caught up with me here. When you ride out to take those steps you were talking about, don't concentrate too much on Lamorkand. The Zemochs are marauding into eastern Pelosia as well. My tribesmen have been gathering ears by the bale. I thought the Knights of the Church ought to know about that."

"We're in your debt, Domi," Sparhawk said. "Why don't you show friend Tynian here where you're camped? We're a bit involved with the kings of Eosia at the moment, but just as soon as we can break free, we'll pay you a call."

"I'll make preparations, then, Sir Knight," Kring promised. "We'll take salt together and talk of affairs."

"Indeed we will, my friend," Sparhawk promised.

Tynian followed Kring back down the corridor, and Sparhawk and Kalten took Krager back into Nashan's study.

"Very well, Krager," Patriarch Dolmant said quite firmly. "We'll agree to your terms—provided that you'll agree to confinement in a monastery until it's safe to release you."

"Of course, your Grace," Krager agreed quickly. "I need some rest anyway. Martel's had me running back and forth across the continent for over a year now. What would you like to hear first?"

"How did this connection between Otha and the Primate of Cimmura begin?"

Krager leaned back in his chair, crossing his legs and swirling his wine glass thoughtfully. "As I understand it, it all started shortly after the old Patriarch of Cimmura fell ill and Annias took over his responsibilities in the cathedral there. Up until then, the primate's goal appeared to have been largely political. He wanted to marry his doxy off to her brother so that he'd be able to run the kingdom of Elenia. After he got a taste of the kind of power the Church could put into a man's hands, however, his horizons began to expand. Annias is a realist, and he's fully aware of the fact that he's not universally loved."

"That may be the understatement of the century," Komier muttered.

"You've noticed that, my Lord," Krager said dryly. "Even Martel despises him, and I can't for the life of me understand how Arissa can bring herself to crawl into the same bed with him. Anyway, Annias knew that he was going to need help in reaching the archprelate's throne. Martel got wind of what he had in mind, and he disguised himself and slipped into Cimmura to talk with him. I'm not sure exactly how, but at some time in the past, Martel had made contact with Otha. He wouldn't ever really talk about it, but I sort of gather that it was in some way connected with his being expelled from the Pandion Order."

Sparhawk and Vanion exchanged a look. "It was," Vanion said. "Go on."

"Annias rejected the notion at first, but Martel can be very convincing when he wants to be, and finally the primate agreed at least to open negotiations. They found a disreputable Styric who was outcast from his band, and they had a long talk with him. He agreed to act as their emissary to Otha, and in due time, a bargain was struck."

"And what was this bargain?" King Dregos of Arcium asked.

"I'll get to that in a bit, your Majesty," Krager promised. "If I jump around in this, I might forget details." He paused and looked around. "I hope you're all taking note of how cooperative I'm being here. Otha sent some of his people to Elenia to provide assistance to Annias. A great deal of that assistance was in the form of gold. Otha's got tons of it."

"What!" Ehlana exclaimed. "I thought Annias had poisoned my father and me primarily to get his hands on the Elenian treasury in order to finance his drive for the archprelacy."

"I'm not trying to be offensive, your Majesty," Krager said, "but the Elenian treasury couldn't have begun to cover the kind of expenses Annias was incurring. His control of it, however, concealed the *real* source of his funding. Embezzlement is one thing, but consorting with Otha is quite something else. You and your father were actually poisoned for no other reason than to hide the fact that Annias had an unlimited supply of Otha's gold. Things went on more or less according to plan. Otha provided money and some occasional Styric magic to help Annias obtain his interim goals. Everything was going along fairly well until Sparhawk came back from Rendor. You're a very disruptive sort of fellow, Sparhawk."

"Thank you," Sparhawk replied.

"I'm sure you know most of the rest of the details, my Lords," Krager continued. "Ultimately, we all wound up here in Chyrellos, and the rest, as they say, is history. Now, getting back to your question, King Dregos. Otha bargains very hard, and he asked a great price from Annias for his aid."

"What did Annias have to give him?" Patriarch Bergsten, the huge Thalesian churchman, asked.

"His soul, your Grace," Krager replied with a shudder. "Otha insisted that Annias convert to the worship of Azash before he'd provide any magic or any money. Martel witnessed the ceremony, and he told me about it. That was one of my duties, incidentally. Martel gets lonesome from time to time, and he needs somebody to talk to. Martel's not particularly squeamish, but even *he* was sickened by the rites that celebrated Annias' conversion."

"Did Martel convert, too?" Sparhawk asked intently.

"I sort of doubt it, Sparhawk. Martel doesn't really have *any* religious convictions. He believes in politics, power, and money, not Gods."

"Which one of them is really in charge?" Sephrenia asked. "Which one is the leader and which the follower?"

"Annias *thinks* he's the one who's giving the orders, but frankly, I rather doubt it. All of his contacts with Otha are through Martel, but Martel makes contacts of his own that Annias doesn't know about. I can't swear to it, but I think there's a separate arrangement between Martel and Otha. It's the sort of thing Martel would do."

"There's something more behind all of this, isn't there?" Patriarch Emban asked shrewdly. "Otha—and Azash—weren't really very likely to expend all that money and energy just for the sake of the badly tarnished soul of the Primate of Cimmura, were they?"

"Of course not, your Grace," Krager agreed. "The plan, of course, was to attempt to get what they wanted by following the plan Annias and Martel had already laid out. If the Primate of Cimmura had managed to bribe his way into the archprelacy, he'd have been able to achieve everything they all wanted without resorting to war, and wars are sometimes chancy."

"And what are the things they wanted?" King Obler asked.

"Annias is obsessed with becoming archprelate. Martel's willing to let him have that. It's not going to mean anything anyway, if this all goes according to plan. What Martel wants is power, wealth, and legitimacy. Otha wants domination of the entire Eosian continent, and, of course, Azash wants the Bhelliom—and the souls of everyone in the whole world. Annias will live forever—or very close to it—and he was going to spend the next several centuries using his power as archprelate to bring the Elenes gradually over to the worship of Azash."

"That's monstrous!" Ortzel exclaimed.

"Moderately so, yes, your Grace," Krager agreed. "Martel will get an imperial crown with only slightly less power than Otha's. He'll rule all of western Eosia. Then you'll have the four of them—Otha and Martel as emperors, Annias as high priest of the Church, and Azash as God. Then they'll be able to turn their attention to the Rendors and to the Tamul Empire in Daresia."

"How did they propose to get Bhelliom for Azash?" Sparhawk asked bleakly.

"Subterfuge, deceit, outright purchase, or main force, if necessary. Listen to me, Sparhawk." Krager's face was suddenly deadly serious. "Martel's led you to believe that he'll go north a ways and then turn toward eastern Lamorkand to join with Otha. He's going to Otha, all right, but Otha's *not* in Lamorkand. His generals are much better at fighting wars than he is. He's still in his capital in the city of Zemoch itself. *That's* where Martel and Annias are going, and they want you to follow them." He paused. "I was told to tell you that, of course," he admitted. "Martel wants you to follow him to Zemoch and to bring Bhelliom with you. They're all afraid of you for some reason, and I don't think it's just because you've managed to find Bhelliom. Martel doesn't want to face you directly, and that's not really like him. They want you to go to Zemoch so that *Azash* can deal with you." Krager's face twisted in sudden anguish and horror. "Don't go, Sparhawk," he pleaded. "For God's sake, don't go! If Azash takes Bhelliom away from you, the world is doomed."

· · ·

The vast nave of the Basilica was filled to overflowing very early the following morning. The citizens of Chyrellos had begun timidly returning to what was left of their homes almost as soon as King Wargun's army had rounded up the last of Martel's mercenaries. The people of the Holy City were probably no more pious than other Elenes, but Patriarch Emban made a gesture of pure humanitarianism. He let word be spread through the city that the Church storehouses would be opened to the populace immediately after the thanksgiving services were concluded. Since there was no food to be had anywhere else in Chyrellos, the citizens responded. Emban reasoned that a congregation numbering in the thousands would impress upon his fellow patriarchs the gravity of the situation and encourage them to take their duties seriously. Besides, Emban *did* feel a certain compassion for the truly hungry. His own bulk made him peculiarly sensitive to the pangs of hunger.

Patriarch Ortzel celebrated the rites of thanksgiving. Sparhawk noticed that the lean, harsh churchman spoke in an altogether different tone when addressing a congregation. His voice was almost gentle, and he sometimes verged on actual compassion.

"Six times," Talen whispered to Sparhawk as the Patriarch of Kadach led the throng in the final prayer.

"What?"

"He smiled six times during his sermon. I counted. A smile doesn't look all that natural on his face, though. What did we decide to do about what Krager told us yesterday? I fell asleep."

"We noticed that. We're going to have Krager repeat what he told us to the entire Hierocracy right after Colonel Delada reports the conversation between Martel and Annias."

"Will they believe him?"

"I think so. Delada's the unimpeachable witness. Krager's merely providing confirmation and filling in details. Once they've been forced to accept Delada's testimony, they won't have much difficulty choking down what Krager has to say."

"Clever," Talen said admiringly. "Do you know something, Sparhawk? I've almost decided to give up the idea of becoming the emperor of thieves. I think I'll enter the Church instead."

"God defend the faith," Sparhawk prayed.

"I'm sure He will, my son." Talen smiled benignly.

As the celebration concluded and the choir broke into exalted song, pages moved through the ranks of the patriarchs delivering the announcement that the Hierocracy would resume deliberations immediately. Six more of the missing ecclesiasts had been discovered in various places in the outer city, and two emerged from hiding places within the Basilica itself. The rest were still unaccounted for. As the patriarchs of the Church solemnly filed out of the nave and into the corridor leading toward the audience chamber, Emban, who had stayed behind to speak with a number of people, scurried past Sparhawk and Talen, puffing and sweating. "Almost forgot something," he said as he passed them. "Dolmant's got to order the Church storehouses opened. Otherwise, we're liable to have a riot on our hands."

"Would I have to get as fat as he is if I want to run things in the Church?" Talen whispered. "Fat men don't run very well when things go wrong, and something's bound to go wrong for Emban eventually."

Colonel Delada stood near the door to the audience chamber. His breastplate and helmet gleamed, and his crimson cloak was immaculate. Sparhawk stepped out of the line of Church Knights and clergymen entering the chamber and spoke briefly to him. "Nervous?" he asked.

"Not really, Sir Sparhawk. I'll admit that I'm not looking forward to this, though. Do you think they'll ask me any questions?"

"They might. Don't let them rattle you. Just take your time and report exactly what you heard in that cellar. Your reputation will be speaking with you, so nobody can doubt your word."

"I just hope I don't start a riot in there," Delada said wryly.

"Don't worry about that. The riot's going to start when they hear the witness who's going to come *after* you."

"What's he going to say, Sparhawk?"

"I'm not at liberty to tell you—at least not until after you've delivered your report. I'm not permitted to do anything at all to tamper with your neutrality at this point. Good luck in there."

The patriarchs of the Church were gathered in little clusters in the chamber talking in subdued tones. Emban's carefully staged thanksgiving service had lent a solemn tone to the morning, and no one really wanted to break it. Sparhawk and Talen mounted to the gallery where they customarily sat with their friends. Bevier was hovering protectively over Sephrenia, his face showing his concern. Sephrenia sat serenely in her gleaming white robe. "There's no reasoning with her," Bevier said as Sparhawk joined them. "We managed to slip Platime, Stragen, and even the Tamul woman in here disguised as clergymen, but Sephrenia absolutely insisted upon wearing her Styric robe. I've tried time and again to explain to her that no one is permitted to witness the deliberations of the Hierocracy but the kings and members of the clergy, but she won't listen to me."

"I *am* a member of the clergy, dear Bevier," she told him simply. "I'm a priestess of Aphrael—the high priestess, actually. Let's just say that I'm here to observe as a sort of tentative gesture in the direction of ecumenism."

"I wouldn't mention that until after the election's over, little mother," Stragen advised. "You'll start a theological debate that might just go on for several centuries, and we're a little pressed for time just now."

"I sort of miss our friend from across the way," Kalten said, pointing at the place in the gallery where Annias had customarily sat. "I'd give a great deal to watch his face crumble as this morning's proceedings unfold."

Dolmant had entered and, after a brief conference with Emban, Ortzel, and Bergsten, he took his place at the lectern. His presence there brought order to the room. "My brothers and my dear friends," he began, "we have seen momentous events since last we gathered here. I've taken the liberty of asking a number of witnesses to testify so that we may all be fully familiar with the situation here before we begin our deliberations. First, however, I must speak to the present condition of the citizens of Chyrellos. The besieging army has stripped the city of food, and the people are in desperate need. I ask the permission of the Hierocracy to open the Church storehouses so that we may alleviate their suffering. As representatives of the Church, charity is one of our primary duties." He looked around. "Do I hear any objections?" he asked.

There was total silence.

"Then it is so ordered. Let us then without further delay welcome the reigning monarchs of western Eosia as our most honored observers."

The people in the chamber rose to their feet respectfully.

There was a brazen trumpet fanfare from the front of the chamber, and a large bronze door swung ponderously open to admit the royalty of the continent. All were garbed in their state robes and wore their crowns. Sparhawk scarcely glanced at Wargun and the other kings, but fixed his eyes on the perfect face of his betrothed. Ehlana was radiant. Sparhawk sensed that during the ten years of his exile in Rendor, very few people had paid much attention to his queen, and that it was only at court functions and ceremonies that she had been granted any significance whatsoever. Thus, she enjoyed ceremonial occasions more than is common among the various members of other royal families. She moved with the other monarchs at a stately pace, her hands resting lightly on the arm of her distant kinsman, the ancient King Obler of Deira, toward the thrones sitting in a semicircle extending from the sides of the dais and the golden throne of the archprelate. As chance had it—or perhaps not entirely chance—the circle of prismed light from the large round window behind the thrones fell full upon the throne of Elenia, and Ehlana took her place surrounded by a blazing halo of golden sunshine. That seemed altogether appropriate to Sparhawk.

After the monarchs had seated themselves, the others in the chamber resumed their places. Dolmant greeted the monarchs each in turn and even made passing reference to the absent King of Lamorkand, who, with Otha camped just inside his border, had other things on his mind. Then the Patriarch of Demos moved smoothly into the business of providing a quick summary of recent events, a summary that seemed to many to be directed to people who had spent the past several weeks on the moon. Emban's witnesses dwelt fulsomely upon the destruction of the outer city and the atrocities committed by Martel's mercenaries. Everyone knew of these horrors, of course, but describing them in lurid detail aroused a certain mood of outrage and a thirst for revenge that Emban had felt might be helpful in moving the Hierocracy in the direction of militancy and impressing upon them the need for expeditious action. Probably the most important fact to be revealed by this half dozen or so witnesses was the name of the man who had commanded the attacking army. Martel's name figured prominently in the accounts of three of the witnesses, and, before he called Colonel Delada, Dolmant provided a brief history of the renegade Pandion, describing him as primarily a mercenary but omitting any reference to his connection to the Primate of Cimmura. He then called for the testimony of the commander of the archprelate's personal guard, noting in passing the legendary neutrality of these dedicated men.

Delada's memory proved to be remarkable. He glossed over the source of his knowledge of the location of the meeting, ascribing it to the "excellent military intelligence activities of the Church Knights." He described the cellar and the long-forgotten aqueduct that had provided such dangerous access to the Basilica itself.

He then repeated the conversation between Martel and Annias almost verbatim. The fact that he delivered his account in a completely unemotional tone lent a great deal of weight to his report. Despite his personal feelings in the matter, Delada hewed strictly to his code of neutrality. His report was punctuated frequently by cries of shock and stunned amazement from the Hierocracy and the assembled spectators.

Patriarch Makova, his pock-marked face pale and his speech faltering, rose to question the colonel. "Is it at all possible that the voices you heard in the dark cellar were *not,* in fact, the voices of the two men who were supposedly speaking—that this was some elaborate subterfuge designed to discredit the Primate of Cimmura?"

"No, your Grace," Delada replied firmly. "That is not in any way possible. The one man was most definitely the Primate Annias, and he addressed the other man as Martel."

Makova began to perspire. He tried another tack. "Who was it that escorted you to that cellar, Colonel?"

"Sir Sparhawk of the Pandion Order, your Grace."

"Well, now," Makova said triumphantly, smirking around at the other members of the Hierocracy, "there we have it, then. Sir Sparhawk has long held a personal enmity for Primate Annias. He has quite obviously swayed this witness."

Delada came to his feet, his face a fiery red. "Are you calling me a liar?" he demanded, his hand reaching for his sword hilt.

Makova recoiled, his eyes suddenly very wide.

"Sir Sparhawk told me absolutely nothing in advance, Patriarch Makova," Delada said from between clenched teeth. "He wouldn't even tell me who either of the men in that cellar were. I identified Annias all on my own and Martel from Annias' own mouth. And I'll tell you something else as well. Sparhawk is the champion of the Queen of Elenia. If *I* held that position, the head of the Primate of Cimmura would be decorating a pole in front of the Basilica right now."

"How *dare* you?" Makova gasped.

"The man you're so eager to put on the archprelate's throne poisoned Sparhawk's queen and he's running to Zemoch right now to beg Otha to protect him from Sparhawk's anger. You'd better find somebody else to vote for, your Grace, because even if the Hierocracy makes the mistake of electing Annias of Cimmura to the archprelacy, he'll never live to assume that throne, since if Sparhawk doesn't kill him—*I will!*" Delada's eyes were ablaze and his sword was half-drawn.

Makova shrank back.

"Ah—" Dolmant said mildly. "Would you like a moment to compose yourself, Colonel?" he suggested.

"I *am* composed, your Grace," Delada retorted, ramming his sword back into its scabbard. "I'm not nearly as angry now as I was a few hours ago. I haven't once questioned the honor of the Patriarch of Coombe."

"Spirited, isn't he?" Tynian whispered to Ulath.

"Red-haired people are like that sometimes," Ulath replied sagely.

"Did you want to ask the colonel any more questions, Makova?" Emban inquired with an innocent expression.

Makova stalked back to his seat, refusing to answer.

"Wise decision," Emban murmured just loud enough to be heard.

A nervous laugh ran through the Hierocracy.

It was not so much the information that Annias had been behind the attack on the city that so shocked and outraged the Hierocracy—they were all ranking churchmen, and they fully understood the lengths to which ambition could drive a man. Although Annias' methods were extreme and totally reprehensible, the Hierocracy could understand his motives and perhaps even secretly admire a man willing to go to such lengths to achieve his goal. It was his alliance with Otha, however, that went completely beyond the pale. Many of the patriarchs who had quite willingly sold their votes to Annias squirmed uncomfortably as they began to realize the full extent of the depravity of the man with whom they had allied themselves.

Lastly, Dolmant called Krager, and the Patriarch of Demos made no attempt whatsoever to conceal Krager's character and fundamental unreliability.

Krager had been tidied up a bit, he was wearing chains on his wrists and ankles as an indication of his status, and he turned out to be a brilliant witness. He made no effort to offer excuses for himself, but was bluntly, even brutally, honest about his many flaws. He even went so far as to provide the details of the arrangement that was protecting his head. The implication that he had very solid reasons for absolute truthfulness was not lost on the Hierocracy. Faces blanched. Many patriarchs prayed audibly. There were cries of outrage and horror as Krager in a matter-of-fact tone described in detail the monstrous conspiracy that had come so very close to success. He did *not*, however, make any reference to Bhelliom. That omission had been decided upon fairly early on in the planning. "It might have all worked, too," Krager concluded in a tone of regret. "If only we'd had one more day before the armies of the western kingdoms arrived in Chyrellos, the Primate of Cimmura would be sitting on that very throne. His first act would have been to order the militant orders disbanded, and his second to order the Elene monarchs to return to their own kingdoms and demobilize their armies. Then Otha would have marched in without any resistance, and within generations, we'd all be bowing to Azash. It was such a very good plan." Krager sighed. "And it would have made me one of the richest men in the world." He sighed again. "Ah, well," he concluded.

Patriarch Emban had been sprawled in his seat, carefully assessing the mood of the Hierocracy. He hauled himself to his feet. "Do we have any questions for this witness?" he asked, looking pointedly at Makova.

Makova would not answer him. Makova would not even look at him.

"Perhaps, my brothers," Emban continued, "this might be the proper time to adjourn for lunch." He smiled rather broadly and clapped his hands to his paunch. "That suggestion coming from me didn't really surprise anyone very much, did it?" he asked them.

They laughed, and that seemed to relax the tension. "This morning has given us many things to consider, my brothers," the little fat man continued seriously, "and unfortunately we'll have little time to consider them. With Otha camped in eastern Lamorkand, we don't have much time for extended contemplation."

Dolmant adjourned the Hierocracy then and declared that they would reconvene within the hour.

At Ehlana's request, Sparhawk and Mirtai joined her in a small chamber in the

Basilica for a light lunch. The young queen seemed a bit distracted and scarcely touched her food but sat instead scribbling rapidly on a scrap of paper.

"Ehlana," Mirtai said sharply. "Eat. You'll waste away if you don't eat."

"Please, Mirtai," the queen said, "I'm trying to compose a speech. I have to address the Hierocracy this afternoon."

"You don't have to say all that much, Ehlana," Sparhawk told her. "Just tell them how honored you are to be allowed to witness their deliberations, say a few unflattering things about Annias, and invoke the blessings of God on the proceedings."

"This is the first time they've ever been addressed by a queen, Sparhawk," she said tartly.

"There have been queens before."

"Yes, but none of them sat on a throne during an election. I looked it up. This is going to be an historic first, and I don't want to make a fool of myself."

"You don't want to faint, either," Mirtai said, pointedly pushing the queen's plate back in front of her. Mirtai, Sparhawk noticed, had the soul of a bully.

There was a light rap at the door, and Talen entered, grinning impishly. He bowed to Ehlana. "I just came by to tell you that King Soros won't be addressing the Hierocracy this afternoon," he told Sparhawk, "so you won't have to worry about being exposed as a scoundrel."

"Oh?"

"His Majesty must have taken a chill, and it settled in his throat. He can't speak above a whisper."

Ehlana frowned. "How strange. It hasn't really been that cold lately. I don't want to wish the King of Pelosia any bad luck, but isn't this a lucky sort of thing to have happen just now?"

"Luck had very little to do with it, your Majesty." Talen grinned. "Sephrenia almost dislocated her jaw and very nearly braided her fingers putting the spell together. Excuse me. I'm supposed to go tell Dolmant and Emban. Then I have to report it to Wargun so that he doesn't bash in Soros' head to keep him quiet."

After they had finished with their lunch, Sparhawk escorted the two ladies back to the audience chamber. "Sparhawk," Ehlana said just before they entered, "do you like Dolmant, the Patriarch of Demos?"

"Very much," he replied. "He's one of my oldest friends—and that's not just because he used to be a Pandion."

She smiled. "I like him, too." She said it as if something had just been settled.

Dolmant reconvened the Hierocracy and then asked each of the kings to address the assembled patriarchs. As Sparhawk had suggested to Ehlana earlier, each monarch rose, thanked the Hierocracy for being permitted to be present, made a few references to Annias, Otha, and Azash, and then invoked the blessing of God upon the deliberations.

"And now, brothers and friends," Dolmant said, "we have a rare occasion here today. For the first time in history, a queen will address us." He smiled ever so faintly. "I would not for the world offend the mighty kings of western Eosia, but I must in all candor say that Ehlana, Queen of Elenia, is far lovelier than they are, and I think we may be surprised to discover that she's as wise as she is beautiful."

Ehlana blushed charmingly. For the remainder of his life, Sparhawk was never able to discover how she could blush at will. She even tried to explain it to him a few times, but it was quite beyond his understanding.

The Queen of Elenia rose and stood with her face downcast for a moment as if in some confusion at Dolmant's prettily turned compliment. "I thank you, your Grace," she said in a clear, ringing voice as she raised her head. All traces of the blush were now gone, and Ehlana had a very determined expression on her face.

Sparhawk's heart gave a sudden suspicious lurch. "Get hold of something solid, gentlemen," he warned his friends. "I know that look. I think she has a few surprises in store for us here."

"I, too, must express my gratitude to the Hierocracy for allowing me to be present," Ehlana began, "and I will add my prayers to those of my brother monarchs, asking God to grant these nobles of the Church wisdom in their deliberations. Since I am the first woman ever to address the Hierocracy in such circumstances, however, might I ask the indulgence of the assembled patriarchs that I might address a few additional remarks to them? If my words seem frivolous, I'm sure the learned patriarchs will forgive me. I am but a woman and not very old. And we all know that young women are sometimes silly when they become excited." She paused.

"Excited, did I say?" she continued, her voice like a silver trumpet. "Nay, gentlemen, say instead that I am enraged! This monster, this cold, bloodless beast, this—this Annias murdered my beloved father. He struck down the wisest and gentlest monarch in all Eosia!"

*"Aldreas?"* Kalten whispered in disbelief.

"And then," Ehlana continued in that ringing voice, "not content with breaking my heart, this ravening savage sought my life as well! Our Church is tainted now, gentlemen, besmirched because this villain ever professed holy orders. I would come here as a suppliant, a petitioner, to demand justice, but I will wring my *own* justice from the body of the man who murdered my father. I am but a weak woman, but I have a champion, gentlemen, a man who at my command will search out and find this monstrous Annias even though the beast seeks to hide himself in the very bowels of Hell itself. Annias *will* face me. I swear this to you all, and generations yet unborn shall tremble at the memory of his fate. Our Holy Mother Church need not concern herself with dispensing justice to this wretch. The Church is gentle, compassionate, but *I,* gentlemen, am not." So much for his queen's apparent submission to the dictates of the Church, Sparhawk thought.

Ehlana had paused again, her young face lifted in vengeful resolve. "But what of this prize?" she asked, turning to look pointedly at the shrouded throne. "Upon whom will you bestow this chair for which Annias was willing to drown the world in blood? To whom shall this piece of ornate furniture descend? For mistake me not, friends, that's all it is, a piece of furniture, heavy, ungainly, and, I'm sure, not very comfortable. Whom will you sentence to bear the awful burdens of care and responsibility that go with this chair, and that he will be forced to carry in this darkest hour of our Holy Mother's life? He must be wise, of course, that goes without saying, but all of the patriarchs of the Church are wise. He must also be courageous, but are you not all as brave as lions? He must be shrewd, and make no mistake, there is a vast difference between wisdom and shrewdness. He must be clever, for he faces the master of deceit—not Annias, though Annias is deceitful enough; not Otha, sunk in his own foul debauchery; but Azash himself. Which of you will match strength and cunning and will with that spawn of Hell?"

"What is she *doing*?" Bevier whispered in a stunned voice.

"Isn't it obvious, Sir Knight?" Stragen murmured urbanely. "She's selecting a new archprelate."

"That's absurd!" Bevier gasped. "The Hierocracy chooses the archprelate!"

"Right now, Sir Bevier, they'd elect *you* if she pointed that small pink finger at you. Look at them. She has the entire Hierocracy in the palm of her hand."

"You have warriors among you, reverend patriarchs," Ehlana was saying, "men of steel and valor, but could an armored archprelate match the guile of Azash? You have theologians among you, my Lords of the Church, men of such towering intellect that they can perceive the mind and intent of God Himself, but would such a man, attuned to the voice of Divine Truth, be prepared to counter the Master of Lies? There are those versed in Church law and those who are masters of Church politics. There are those who are strong, and those who are brave. There are those who are gentle, and those who are compassionate. If we could but choose the entire Hierocracy itself to lead us, we would be invincible, and the gates of Hell could not prevail against us!" Ehlana swayed, raising one trembling hand to her brow. "Forgive me, gentlemen," she said in a weak voice. "The effects of the poison with which the serpent Annias sought to steal away my life do linger yet."

Sparhawk half started to his feet.

"Oh, *do* sit down, Sparhawk," Stragen told him. "You'll spoil her performance if you go clanking down there right now. Believe me, she's perfectly fine."

"Our Holy Mother needs a champion, my Lords of the Church," Ehlana continued in a weary voice, "a man who is the distillation and essence of the Hierocracy itself, and I think that in your hearts you all know who that man is. May God give you the wisdom, the enlightenment, to turn to the one who even now is in your very midst, shrouded with true humility, but who extends his gentle hand to guide you, perhaps not even knowing that he does so, for this self-effacing patriarch perhaps does not even know himself that he speaks with the Voice of God. Seek him in your hearts, my Lords of the Church, and lay this burden upon *him*, for only he can be our champion!" She swayed again, and her knees began to buckle. Then she wilted like a flower. King Wargun, his face awed and his eyes full of tears, leaped to his feet and caught her even as she fell.

"The perfect touch," Stragen said admiringly. He grinned. "Poor, poor Sparhawk," he said. "You haven't got a chance, you know."

"Stragen, *will* you shut up?"

"What was that really all about?" Kalten asked in a baffled tone.

"She just appointed an archprelate, Sir Kalten," Stragen told him.

"Who? She didn't mention a single name."

"Isn't it clear to you yet? She very carefully eliminated all the other contenders. There's only one possibility left. The other patriarchs all know who he is, and they'll elect him—just as soon as one of them dares to mention his name. I'd tell you myself, but I don't want to spoil it for you."

King Wargun had lifted the apparently unconscious Ehlana in his arms and was carrying her toward the bronze door at one side of the chamber.

"Go to her," Sephrenia said to Mirtai. "Try to keep her calm. She's very exhilarated right now—and *don't* let King Wargun come back in here. He might blurt something out and ruin everything."

Mirtai nodded and rushed down to the floor.

The chamber was alive with excited conversation. Ehlana's fire and passion had ignited them all. Patriarch Emban sat with his eyes wide in stunned amazement. Then he grinned broadly, and then he covered his mouth with one hand and began to laugh.

"—obviously possessed by the Divine Hand of God Himself," one nearby monk was saying excitedly to another. "But a *woman*? Why would God speak to us in the voice of a woman?"

"His ways are mysterious," the other monk said in an awed voice, "and unfathomable to man."

It was with some difficulty that Patriarch Dolmant restored order. "My brothers and friends," he said. "We must, of course, forgive the Queen of Elenia for her emotional outburst. I have known her since childhood, and I assure you that she is normally a completely self-possessed young woman. It is doubtless as she herself suggested. The last traces of the poison still linger and make her sometimes irrational."

"Oh, this is *too* rare." Stragen laughed to Sephrenia. "*He* doesn't even know."

"Stragen," she said crisply, "hush."

"Yes, little mother."

Patriarch Bergsten, mail-shirted and dreadful in his ogre-horned helmet, rose and rapped the butt of his war ax on the marble floor. "Permission to speak?" He didn't actually ask.

"Of course, Bergsten," Dolmant said.

"We are not here to discuss the vaporish indisposition of the Queen of Elenia," the massive Patriarch of Emsat declared. "We are here to select an archprelate. I suggest that we move on with it. To that end, I place in nomination the name of Dolmant, Patriarch of Demos. Who will join his voice with mine in this nomination?"

"No!" Dolmant exclaimed in stunned dismay.

"The Patriarch of Demos is not in order," Ortzel declared, rising to his feet. "By custom and by law, as one who has been nominated, he may not speak further until this question has been decided. With the consent of my brothers, I would ask the esteemed Patriarch of Ucera to assume the chair." He looked around. There appeared to be no dissent.

Emban, still grinning openly, waddled to the lectern and rather cavalierly dismissed Dolmant with a wave of one chubby hand. "Has the Patriarch of Kadach concluded his remarks?" he asked.

"No," Ortzel said, "I have not." Ortzel's face was still stern and bleak. Then, with no sign of the pain it must have caused him, he spoke firmly. "I join my voice with that of my brother of Emsat. Patriarch Dolmant is the only possible choice for the archprelacy."

Then Makova rose. His face was dead white, and his jaws were clenched. "God will punish you for this outrage!" he almost spat at his fellow patriarchs. "I will have no part in this absurdity!" He spun on his heel and stormed from the chamber.

"At least he's honest," Talen observed.

"Honest?" Berit exclaimed. "Makova?"

"Of course, revered teacher." The boy grinned. "Once somebody buys Makova, he stays bought—no matter how things turn out."

Patriarch after patriarch rose to approve Dolmant's nomination. Emban's face grew sly as the last patriarch, a feeble old man from Cammoria, was helped to his feet to murmur the name "Dolmant" in a creaky voice.

"Well, Dolmant," Emban said in mock surprise, "it seems that only you and I are left. Is there someone you'd like to nominate, my friend?"

"I beg of you, my brothers," Dolmant pleaded, "don't do this." He was openly weeping.

"The Patriarch of Demos is not in order," Ortzel said gently. "He must place a name in nomination or stand mute."

"Sorry, Dolmant." Emban grinned. "But you heard what he said. Oh, incidentally, I'll join my voice with those of the others in nominating you. Are you *sure* you wouldn't like to nominate somebody?" He waited. "Very well, then. I make it one hundred and twenty-six nominations for the Patriarch of Demos, one bolted, and one abstention. Isn't that amazing? Shall we vote, my brothers, or shall we save some time and just declare Patriarch Dolmant the archprelate by acclamation? I pause for your reply."

It began with a single deep voice coming from somewhere down front. "Dolmant!" the voice boomed. "Dolmant!"

It was soon picked up. "Dolmant!" they roared, "Dolmant!" It went on for quite some time.

Then Emban raised his hand for silence. "Awfully sorry to be the one to tell you, old boy," he drawled to Dolmant, "but you don't seem to be a patriarch any more. Why don't you and a couple of our brothers retire to the vestry for a few moments so they can help you try on your new robes?"

## CHAPTER EIGHTEEN

The audience chamber was still filled with excited conversation, some of it in shouts. Patriarchs with looks of exaltation on their faces milled about on the marble floor, and Sparhawk heard the phrase "inspired by God" repeated over and over in awed tones as he pushed his way through the crowd. Churchmen are traditionally very conservative, and they found that any hint that a mere woman might have actually guided the Hierocracy in its decision was unthinkable. The notion of divine inspiration was a convenient way out. Obviously, it had not been Ehlana who had spoken, but God Himself. At the moment, Sparhawk was not concerned about theology. What he *was* concerned about was the condition of his queen. Stragen's explanation was plausible, of course, but Stragen had been talking about Sparhawk's queen—and his betrothed. Sparhawk wanted to see for himself that she was well.

She appeared to be not only well but in glowing health as he opened the door through which King Wargun had carried her. She even looked a bit ridiculous as she stood half bent over with her ear pressed to the spot where the closed door had only recently been.

"You could hear much better from your seat out there in the chamber, my Queen," Sparhawk said with some asperity.

"Oh, be still, Sparhawk," she said tartly, "and come in and shut the door."

Sparhawk stepped through the doorway.

King Wargun stood with his back against the wall and his eyes a bit wild. Mirtai stood in front of him, poised. "Get this she-dragon away from me, Sparhawk," Wargun begged.

"Have you decided not to make an issue of my queen's theatrics, your Majesty?" Sparhawk asked him politely.

"Admit that she made a fool of me? Don't be absurd, Sparhawk. I wasn't going to run out there and declare that I'd been a jackass in public. All I wanted to do was to tell everyone that your queen was all right, but I didn't even make it as far as the door when this huge woman came in here. She *threatened* me, Sparhawk! *Me,* of all people. Do you see that chair there?"

Sparhawk looked. The chair was upholstered, and large wads of horsehair were protruding out of a long gash in its back.

"It was merely a suggestion, Sparhawk," Mirtai said mildly. "I wanted Wargun to understand what might happen if he made any wrong decisions. It's all right now. Wargun and I are almost friends." Mirtai, Sparhawk had noticed, never used titles.

"It's very improper to draw a knife on a king, Mirtai," Sparhawk told her reprovingly.

"She didn't," Wargun said. "She did that with her knee." He shuddered.

Sparhawk looked at the Tamul woman, puzzled.

Mirtai pulled aside her monk's robe, reached down, and modestly lifted her kilt a few inches. As Talen had told him, she had curved knives strapped to her lower thighs so that the blades rode along the inside of her calves for about four inches. The knives appeared to be very sharp. He also noted in passing that both her knees were dimpled. "It's a practical arrangement for a woman," she explained. "Men sometimes become playful at inconvenient times. The knives persuade them to go play with someone else."

"Isn't that illegal?" Wargun asked.

"Would you like to try to arrest her, your Majesty?"

"*Will* you all stop that chattering?" Ehlana said sharply to them. "You sound like a flock of magpies. This is what we're going to do. In a few moments, things will start to quiet down out there. Then Wargun will escort me back inside, and Mirtai and Sparhawk will follow. I'll lean on Wargun's arm and look properly weak and trembly. After all, I've either just fainted or had a divine visitation—depending on which of the rumors I hear buzzing around out there you care to believe. We all want to be in our places before the archprelate is escorted to his throne."

"How are you going to explain that speech to them, Ehlana?" Wargun demanded.

"I'm not," she replied. "I'll have absolutely no memory of it whatsoever. They'll believe whatever they want to believe, and no one will dare to call me a liar, because either Sparhawk or Mirtai will challenge them if they do." She smiled then. "Was the man I chose more or less the one you had in mind, dear?" she asked Sparhawk.

"Yes, I think he is."

"You may thank me properly then—when we're alone. Very well, then, let's go back inside."

They all looked suitably grave as they reentered the chamber. Ehlana leaned heavily on Wargun, her face looking wan and exhausted. There was a sudden, awed silence as the two monarchs resumed their places.

Patriarch Emban waddled forward, his face looking concerned. "Is she all right?" he asked.

"She seems a bit better," Sparhawk told him. It was not *exactly* a lie. "She tells us that she has no memory of anything she said when she was addressing the Hierocracy. It might be better if we didn't press her on that point in her present condition, your Grace."

Emban gave Ehlana a shrewd look. "I understand perfectly, Sparhawk. I'll make a few suitable remarks to the Hierocracy." He smiled at Ehlana. "I'm so glad to see that you're feeling better, your Majesty," he said.

"Thank you, your Grace," she replied in a trembling little voice.

Emban returned to the lectern as Sparhawk and Mirtai went back up into the gallery to rejoin their friends. "My brothers," he said. "I'm sure you'll all be happy to know that Queen Ehlana is recovering. She's asked me to apologize for anything she may have said during her remarks. The queen's health is still not good, I'm afraid, and she journeyed here to Chyrellos at great personal risk, so firm was her resolve to be present for our deliberations."

They murmured their admiration for such devotion.

"It were best, I think," Emban continued, "if we were not to question her Majesty too closely concerning the content of her remarks. It appears that she has no memory of her speech. This can be quite easily explained by her weakened condition. There is perhaps another explanation as well, but I think wisdom and consideration for her Majesty dictate to us that we not pursue it." Of such stuff legends are made.

And then there was a brassy fanfare of trumpets, and the door to the left side of the throne swung open. Dolmant, flanked by Ortzel and Bergsten, entered. The new archprelate wore a plain white cassock, and his face was calm now. Sparhawk was struck by an odd notion. There were marked similarities between Dolmant's white cassock and Sephrenia's white robe. The thought led him to the brink of a speculation that might just have been mildly heretical.

The two patriarchs, the one from Lamorkand and the other from Thalesia, escorted Dolmant to the throne, which had been unshrouded during their absence, and the archprelate took his seat.

"And will Sarathi address us?" Emban said, stepping from behind the lectern and genuflecting.

"Sarathi?" Talen whispered to Berit.

"It's a very old name," Berit explained quietly. "When the Church was finally unified almost three thousand years ago, the very first archprelate was named Sarathi. His name is remembered—and honored—by addressing the archprelate this way."

Dolmant sat gravely on his gold throne. "I have not sought this eminence, my brothers," he told them, "and I would be far happier had you not seen fit to thrust it upon me. We can only hope—all of us—that this is truly God's will." He raised his face slightly. "Now, we have much that needs to be done. I will call upon many of you to aid me, and, as is always the case, there will be changes here in the Basilica. I pray you, my brothers, do not be chagrined or downcast when Church offices are being reassigned, for it has ever been thus when a new archprelate comes to this throne. Our Holy Mother faces her gravest challenge in half a millennium. My first act, therefore, must be to confirm the state of Crisis of the Faith, and I decree that this state shall continue until we have met the challenge and prevailed. And now, my brothers and dear friends, let us pray, and then shall we depart and go to our sundry duties."

"Nice and short," Ulath approved. "Sarathi's getting off to a good start."

"Was the queen *really* in hysterics when she made that speech?" Kalten curiously asked Sparhawk.

"Of course she wasn't," Sparhawk snorted. "She knew exactly what she was doing every second."

"I sort of thought she might have been. I think your marriage is going to be filled with surprises, Sparhawk, but that's all right. The unexpected always keeps a man on his toes."

As they were leaving the Basilica, Sparhawk fell back to have a word with Sephrenia. He found her a few feet back down a side passage deep in conversation with a man wearing a monk's robe. When the man turned, however, Sparhawk saw that he was not an Elene, but rather was a silvery-bearded Styric. The man bowed to the approaching knight. "I will leave you now, dear sister," he said to Sephrenia in Styric. His voice, deep and rich, belied his evident age.

"No, Zalasta, stay," she said, laying one hand on his arm.

"I would not offend the Knights of the Church by my presence in their holy place, sister."

"Sparhawk takes a bit more offending than the usual Church Knight, my dear friend." She smiled.

"This is the legendary Sir Sparhawk?" the Styric said with some surprise. "I am honored, Sir Knight." He spoke in heavily accented Elene.

"Sparhawk," Sephrenia said, "this is my oldest and dearest friend, Zalasta. We were children together in the same village."

"I am honored, *sioanda*," Sparhawk said in Styric, also bowing. *Sioanda* was a Styric word meaning "friend of my friend."

"Age has dimmed my eyes it seems," Zalasta noted. "Now that I look more closely at his face, I can indeed see that this is Sir Sparhawk. The light of his purpose shines all around him."

"Zalasta has offered us his aid, Sparhawk," Sephrenia said then. "He is very wise and deeply schooled in the secrets."

"We would be honored, learned one," Sparhawk said.

Zalasta smiled. "I would be of small use on your quest, Sir Sparhawk," he said in a slightly self-deprecating way. "Were you to encase me in steel, I'm sure I would wither like a flower."

Sparhawk tapped his breastplate. "It's an Elene affectation, learned one," he said, "like pointed hats or brocade doublets. We can only hope that someday steel wardrobes will go out of fashion."

"I had always thought Elenes to be a humorless race," the Styric noted, "but you are droll, Sir Sparhawk. I would be of little use to you in your trek, but at some future time I may be able to assist you in some other matter of a certain importance."

"Trek?" Sparhawk asked.

"I know not where you and my sister will go, Sir Knight, but I perceive many leagues hovering about you both. I have come to advise you both to steel your hearts and to be ever watchful. A danger avoided is sometimes preferable to a danger overcome." Zalasta looked around. "And my presence here is one of those avoidable dangers, I think. You are cosmopolitan, Sir Sparhawk, but I think that perhaps some of your comrades may be less sophisticated." He bowed to Sparhawk, kissed Sephrenia's palms, and then glided silently back up the shadowy side passage.

"I haven't seen him in more than a century," Sephrenia said. "He's changed— just a little."

"Most of us would change in that long a period, little mother." Sparhawk smiled. "Except you, of course."

"You're such a nice boy, Sparhawk." She sighed. "It all seems so long ago. Zalasta was always so serious when he was a child. Even then he was wise beyond belief. His grasp of the secrets is profound."

"What's this trek he was talking about?"

"Do you mean to say you can't feel it? You can't feel the distance stretching in front of you?"

"Not noticeably, no."

"Elenes." She sighed. "Sometimes I'm surprised that you can even feel the seasons turn."

He ignored that. "Where are we going?"

"I don't know. Not even Zalasta can perceive that. The future lying before us is dark, Sparhawk. I should have known that it would be, but I didn't think my way completely through it, I guess. We *are* going someplace, though. Why aren't you with Ehlana?"

"The kings are all being solicitous. I can't get near her." He paused. "Sephrenia, she can see it, too—the shadow, I mean. I think it's probably because she's wearing one of the rings."

"That would stand to reason. Bhelliom's useless without the rings."

"Does it put her in any kind of danger?"

"Of course it does, Sparhawk, but Ehlana's been in danger since the day she was born."

"Isn't that just a little fatalistic?"

"Perhaps. I just wish *I* could see this shadow of yours. I might be able to identify it a little more precisely."

"I can borrow Ehlana's ring and give them both to you," he offered. "Then *you* can take Bhelliom out of the pouch. I can almost guarantee that you'll see the shadow at that point."

"Don't even suggest that, Sparhawk." She shuddered. "I wouldn't be much good to you if I were suddenly to vanish—permanently."

"Sephrenia," he said a bit critically, "was I some sort of an experiment? You keep warning everybody not to touch Bhelliom, but you didn't even turn a hair when you were telling me to chase it down and take it away from Ghwerig. Wasn't *I* in a certain amount of danger, too? Did you just wait to see if I'd explode when I put my hands on it?"

"Don't be silly, Sparhawk. Everyone *knows* that you were destined to wield Bhelliom."

"*I* didn't."

"Let's not pursue this, dear one. We have enough problems already. Just accept the fact that you and Bhelliom are linked. I think that shadow should be our concern right now. What is it, and what is it doing?"

"It seems to be following Bhelliom—and the rings. Can we discount the things Perraine was trying to do? Wasn't that Martel's idea—one that he came up with on his own?"

"I don't know that we'd be safe to assume that. Martel was controlling Perraine, but something else may have been controlling Martel—without his even knowing it."

"I see that this is going to be another of the kind of discussions that give me headaches."

"Just take precautions, dear one," she told him. "Don't relax your guard. Let's see if we can catch up with Ehlana. She'll be upset if you're not attentive."

They were all somewhat subdued when they gathered together that evening. This time, however, they did not gather in the Pandion chapterhouse but rather in a large overdecorated chamber attached to the archprelate's personal apartments. The room was normally the site of the meetings of the highest councils of the Church, and they had assembled there at Sarathi's personal request. Tynian, Sparhawk noticed, was conspicuously absent. The walls of the room were panelled, and it was adorned with blue drapes and carpeting. A very large religious fresco decorated the ceiling. Talen looked up and sniffed disdainfully. "I could do a better job than that with my left hand," he declared.

"There's a thought," Kurik said. "I think I'll ask Dolmant if he'd like to have the ceiling of the nave here in the Basilica decorated."

"Kurik," Talen said with some shock, "that ceiling's bigger than a cow pasture. It'd take forty years to paint enough pictures to cover it."

"You're young." Kurik shrugged. "Steady work might keep you out of trouble."

The door opened, and Dolmant entered. They all rose from their seats and genuflected.

"Please," Dolmant said wearily, "spare me. People have been doing that ever since the overly clever Queen of Elenia jammed me into a seat I didn't really want."

"Why, Sarathi," she protested, "what a thing to say."

"We have things to discuss, my friends," Dolmant said, "and decisions to make." He took his seat at the head of the large conference table in the center of the room. "Please sit down, and let's get to work."

"When would you like to have us schedule your coronation, Sarathi?" Patriarch Emban asked.

"That can wait. Let's push Otha off our doorstep first. I don't think I'd care to have him attend. How do we proceed?"

King Wargun looked around. "I'll throw out some ideas and see how the rest respond," he said. "The way I see it, we've got two options. We can march east until we run into the Zemochs and then fight them in open fields, or we can move out until we find suitable terrain and stop and wait for them. The first option would keep Otha farther away from Chyrellos, and the second would give us time to erect field fortifications. Both approaches have their advantages, and they both have their drawbacks as well." He looked around again. "What do you think?" he asked.

"I think we need to know what kind of a force we're facing," King Dregos said.

"There are a lot of people in Zemoch," old King Obler said.

"That's God's own truth." Wargun scowled. "They breed like rabbits."

"We can expect to be outnumbered then," Obler continued. "If I remember my military strategy correctly, that would almost compel us to take up defensive positions. We'll have to erode Otha's forces before we can go on the offensive."

"Another siege," Komier groaned. "I *hate* sieges."

"We don't always get what we want, Komier," Abriel told him. "There's a third option, however, King Wargun. There are many fortified keeps and castles in Lamorkand. We can move out, occupy those strongholds in force, and hold them. Otha won't be able to bypass them, because if he does, the troops inside will be able to come out and decimate his reserves and destroy his supply trains."

"Lord Abriel," Wargun said, "that strategy will spread us out all over central Lamorkand."

"I'll admit that it has drawbacks," Abriel conceded, "but the last time Otha invaded, we met him head-on at Lake Randera. We virtually depopulated the continent in the process, and it took centuries for Eosia to recover. I'm not sure we want to repeat that."

"We won, didn't we?" Wargun said bluntly.

"Do we really want to win that way again?"

"There may be another alternative," Sparhawk said quietly.

"I'd certainly be glad to hear it," Preceptor Darellon said. "I'm not too happy with any of the options I've heard so far."

"Sephrenia," Sparhawk said, "just how powerful *is* the Bhelliom really?"

"I've told you that it's the most powerful object in the world, dear one."

"Now there's a thought," Wargun said. "Sparhawk could use Bhelliom to obliterate whole chunks of Otha's army. Incidentally, Sparhawk, you *are* going to return Bhelliom to the royal house of Thalesia when you're finished with it, aren't you?"

"We might discuss that, your Majesty," Sparhawk said. "It wouldn't really do you all that much good, though. It won't do anything at all without the rings, and I don't feel much like surrendering *mine* yet. You can ask my queen how she feels about hers, if you wish."

"My ring stays where it is," Ehlana said flatly.

Sparhawk had been mulling over his earlier conversation with Sephrenia. He was growing increasingly certain that the impending confrontation was *not* going to be settled by vast armies clashing in central Lamorkand in the way that the one five hundred years earlier had been. He had no way to justify his certainty, since he had not reached it by logic but rather by some intuitive leap that was more Styric in nature than Elene. He somehow knew that it would be a mistake for him to immerse himself in an army. Not only would that delay him in something he must do, but it would also be dangerous. If the subversion of Sir Perraine had *not* been an independent act on Martel's part, then he would be exposing himself and his friends to thousands of potential enemies, all completely unidentifiable and all armed to the teeth. Once again he absolutely had to get clear of an Elene army. His idea grew more out of that necessity than out of any real conviction that it would work. "Is there enough power in Bhelliom to destroy Azash?" he asked Sephrenia. He already knew the answer, of course, but he wanted her to confirm it for the others.

"What are you saying, Sparhawk?" she asked in a tone of profound shock. "You're talking about destroying a God. The whole world trembles at such a suggestion."

"I'm not raising the question to start a theological debate," he said. "Would Bhelliom be able to do it?"

"I don't know. No one's ever had the temerity even to suggest it before."

"Where is Azash most vulnerable?" he asked.

"Only in his confinement. The Younger Gods of Styricum chained him within that clay idol Otha found centuries ago. That's one of the reasons he's been seeking Bhelliom so desperately. Only the sapphire rose can free him."

"And if the idol were to be destroyed?"

"Azash would be destroyed with it."

"And what would happen if I went to the city of Zemoch, discovered that I couldn't destroy Azash with Bhelliom, and smashed the jewel instead?"

"The city would be obliterated," she said in a troubled tone, "along with any mountain ranges in the vicinity."

"I can't really lose then, can I? Either way, Azash ceases to exist. And, if what Krager told us is true, Otha's at Zemoch as well, along with Martel, Annias, and various others. I could get them all. Once Azash and Otha are gone, the Zemoch invasion would disintegrate, wouldn't it?"

"You're talking about throwing your life away, Sparhawk," Vanion said.

"Better one life than millions."

"I absolutely forbid it!" Ehlana shouted.

"Forgive me, my Queen," Sparhawk told her, "but you ordered me to deal with Annias and the others. You can't really rescind that command—at least not to me, you can't."

There was a polite rap on the door, and Tynian entered with the Domi, Kring. "Sorry to be late," the Deiran Knight apologized. "The Domi and I have been busy with some maps. For some reason, the Zemochs have sent forces north from their main encampment on the Lamork border. There's an infestation of them in eastern Pelosia."

Kring's eyes brightened when he saw King Soros. "Ah, there you are, my King," he said. "I've been looking all over for you. I've got all sorts of Zemoch ears I'd like to sell you."

King Soros whispered something. He still appeared to have a sore throat for some reason.

"It's starting to fit together," Sparhawk told the council. "Krager told us that Martel was taking Annias to the city of Zemoch to seek refuge with Otha." He leaned back in his chair. "I think the final solution to the problem we've been having for the last five centuries lies in the city of Zemoch and not on the plains of Lamorkand. *Azash* is our enemy, not Martel or Annias or Otha and his Zemochs, and we've got the means to destroy Azash once and for all in our hands right now. Wouldn't we be foolish not to use it? I could wear the petals off Bhelliom destroying Zemoch infantry units with it, and we'd all grow old and gray on some fluid battlefield to the north of Lake Cammoria. Wouldn't it be better to go right to the heart of the problem—to Azash himself? Let's have done with this so that it doesn't keep cropping up every half eon or so."

"It's strategically unsound, Sparhawk," Vanion said flatly.

"Excuse me, my friend, but what's so strategically sound about a stalemate on a flat battlefield? It took more than a century to recover from the last battle between the Zemochs and the west. This way we at least have a chance to end it once and for all. If it appears not to be working, I'll destroy Bhelliom. Then Azash won't have any reason to come west again. He'll go pester the Tamuls or something instead."

"You'd never get through, Sparhawk," Preceptor Abriel said. "You heard what this Peloi said. There are Zemochs in eastern Pelosia as well as the ones down in eastern Lamorkand. Do you propose to wade through them all by yourself?"

"I think they'll stand aside for me, my Lord. Martel's going north—at least that's what he said. He may go as far north as Paler, or he may not. It doesn't really matter, because I'm going to follow him no matter *where* he goes. He *wants* me to follow him. He made that fairly clear down in that cellar, and he was very careful to make sure that I heard him because he wants to deliver me to Azash. I think I can trust him not to put anything in my way. I know it sounds a little peculiar, but I think we can actually trust Martel this time. If he really has to, he'll take his sword and clear a path for me." He smiled bleakly. "My brother's tender concern for my welfare touches my heart." He looked at Sephrenia. "You said that even suggesting the destruction of a God is unthinkable, didn't you? What would be the general reaction to the idea of destroying Bhelliom?"

"That's even more unthinkable, Sparhawk."

"Then the notion that I might be considering it won't even occur to them, will it?"

She shook her head mutely, her eyes strangely frightened as she looked at him.

"That's our advantage then, my Lords," Sparhawk declared. "I can do the one thing that no one can bring himself to believe that I'll do. I can destroy the Bhelliom—or threaten to. Somehow I have the feeling that people—and Gods—are going to start getting out of my way if I do that."

Preceptor Abriel was still stubbornly shaking his head. "You'll be trying to bull your way through primitive Zemochs in eastern Pelosia and along the border, Sparhawk. Not even Otha has control over those savages."

"Permission to speak, Sarathi?" Kring asked in a profoundly respectful tone.

"Of course, my son." Dolmant looked a bit puzzled. He had no idea who this fierce man was.

"I can get you through eastern Pelosia and well into Zemoch, friend Sparhawk," Kring said. "If the Zemochs are all spread out, my horsemen can ride right through them. We'll leave a swath of bodies five miles wide from Paler to the Zemoch border—all minus their right ears, of course." Kring's broad grin was wolfish. He looked around in a self-congratulatory way. Then he saw Mirtai, who sat demurely beside Ehlana. His eyes went wide, and he first went pale and then bright red. Then he sighed lustily.

"I wouldn't, if I were you," Sparhawk warned him.

"What?"

"I'll explain later."

"I hate to admit it," Bevier said, "but this plan's looking better and better. We really shouldn't have much trouble at all getting to Otha's capital."

"*We?*" Kalten asked.

"We *were* going to go along, weren't we, Kalten?"

"Has it got any chance at all of working, little mother?" Vanion asked.

"No, Lord Vanion, it hasn't!" Ehlana interrupted him. "Sparhawk *can't* go to Zemoch and use Bhelliom to kill Azash because he doesn't have both rings. I've got one of them, and he'll have to kill me to get it away from me."

That was something Sparhawk had not considered. "My Queen—" he began.

"I have *not* given you leave to speak, Sir Sparhawk!" she told him. "You will *not* pursue this vain and foolhardy scheme! You will *not* throw your life away! Your life is *mine*, Sparhawk! Mine! You do *not* have our permission to take it from us!"

"That's plain enough," Wargun said, "and it takes us right back to where we started from."

"Perhaps not," Dolmant said quietly. He rose to his feet. "Queen Ehlana," he said sternly, "will you submit to the will of our Holy Mother, the Church?"

She looked at him defiantly.

"*Will* you?"

"I am a true daughter of the Church," she said sullenly.

"I'm delighted to hear it, my child. It is the command of the Church that you surrender this trinket into her hands for some brief time that she may use it in furtherance of her work."

"That's not fair, Dolmant," she accused.

"Will you defy the Church, Ehlana?"

"I—I *can't*!" she wailed.

"Then give me the ring." He held out his hand.

Ehlana burst into tears. She clutched his arms and buried her face in his robe.

"Give me the ring, Ehlana," he repeated.

She looked up at him, dashing the tears from her eyes with one defiant hand.

"Only on one condition, Sarathi," she countered.

"Will you try to bargain with our Holy Mother?"

"No, Sarathi, I am merely obeying one of her earlier commands. She instructs us to marry so that we may increase the congregation of the faithful. I will surrender the ring to you on the day you join me with Sir Sparhawk in marriage. I've worked too hard to get him to let him escape me now. Will our Holy Mother consent to this?"

"It seems fair to me," Dolmant said, smiling benignly at Sparhawk, who was gaping at the two of them as he was traded off like a side of beef.

Ehlana had a very good memory. As Platime had instructed her, she spat in her hand. "Done, then!" she said.

Dolmant had been around for a long time, so he recognized the gesture. He also spat on his palm. "Done!" he said, and the two of them smacked their palms together, sealing Sparhawk's fate.

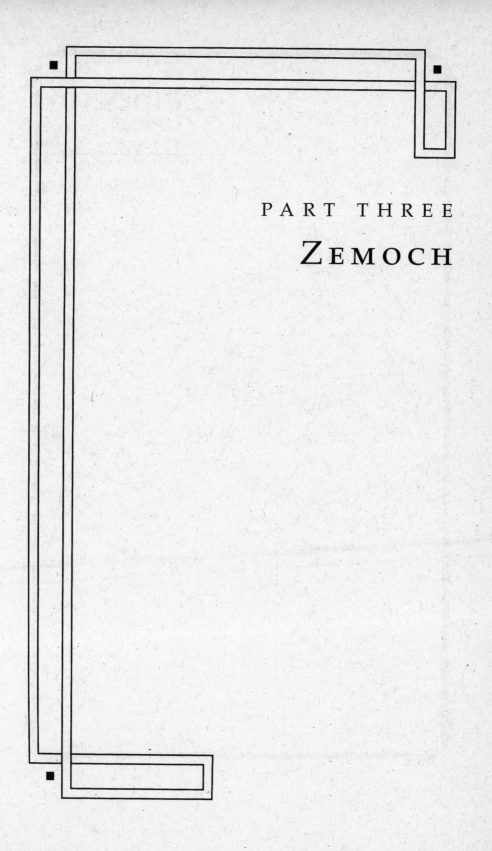

PART THREE

# ZEMOCH

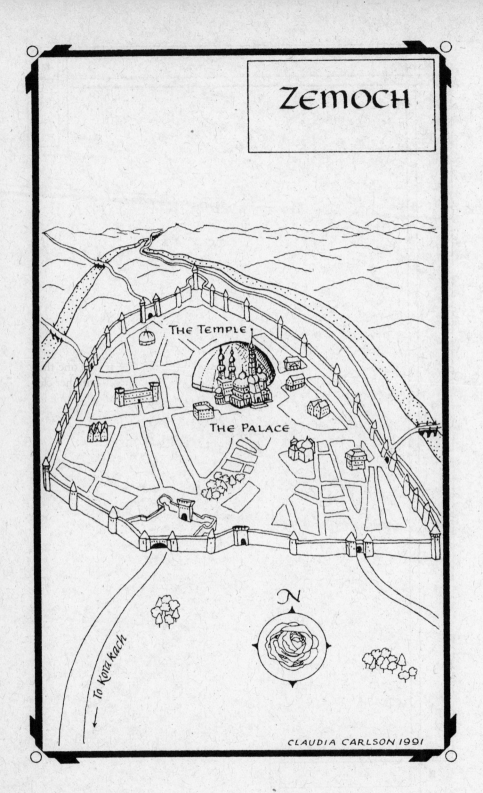

ZEMOCH

The Temple

The Palace

To Kotukach

N

CLAUDIA CARLSON 1991

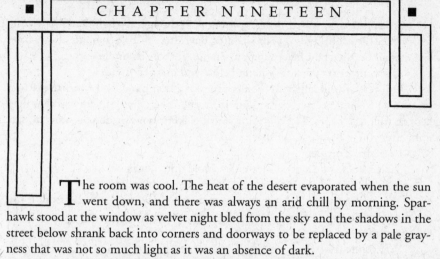

The room was cool. The heat of the desert evaporated when the sun went down, and there was always an arid chill by morning. Sparhawk stood at the window as velvet night bled from the sky and the shadows in the street below shrank back into corners and doorways to be replaced by a pale grayness that was not so much light as it was an absence of dark.

Then the first of them emerged from a shadowy alley with a clay vessel balanced on her shoulder. She was robed and hooded in black, and a black veil covered the lower half of her face. She moved through the pale light with a grace so exquisite that it made Sparhawk's heart ache. Then there were others. One by one they emerged from doorways and alleys to join the silent procession, each with her clay vessel upon her shoulder, and each following a ritual so old that it had become instinctive. However it was that the men began their day, the women inevitably started theirs by going to the well.

Lillias stirred. "Mahkra," she said in a voice slurred with sleep, "come back to bed."

He could hear the bells in the distance even over the incessant bawling of the half-wild cows in the yards around him. The religion of this kingdom discouraged bells, so Sparhawk knew that the sound came from a place where members of his own faith were gathered. There was no other place to go, so he stumbled on toward the sound of the bells. The hilt of his sword was slippery with blood, and the weapon seemed very heavy now. He wanted to be free of its weight, and it would be so easy to let it slip from his fingers to lie lost in the dung-smelling darkness. A true knight, however, surrendered his sword only to death, and Sparhawk grimly clamped his fist about the sword hilt and lurched on, following the bells. He was cold, and the blood flowing from his wounds seemed very warm, even comforting. He staggered on through the chill night with the blood flowing from one side, warming him.

"Sparhawk." It was Kurik's voice, and the hand shaking his shoulder was firm. "Sparhawk, wake up. You're having a nightmare again."

Sparhawk opened his eyes. He was sweating profusely.

"The same one?" Kurik asked.

Sparhawk nodded.

"Maybe you'll be able to put it to rest when you finally kill Martel."

Sparhawk sat up in bed.

Kurik's face was creased with a broad grin. "I thought it might have been a different one," he said. "This *is* your wedding day, after all. Bridegrooms always have bad dreams on the night before their weddings. It's sort of an old custom."

"Was your sleep uneasy the night before you married Aslade?"

"Oh, yes." Kurik laughed. "Something was chasing me, and I had to get to a seacoast so I could get on board a ship to escape. The only problem was that they kept moving the ocean. Do you want your breakfast now, or do you want to wait until after you've bathed and I shave you?"

"I can shave myself."

"That wouldn't be a good idea today. Hold out your hand."

Sparhawk extended his right hand. It was visibly trembling.

"You *definitely* shouldn't try to shave yourself today, my Lord. Let's call it my wedding present to the queen. I won't let you go to her bed on her wedding night with your face in tatters."

"What time is it?"

"A half hour or so before dawn. Get up, Sparhawk. You've got a full day ahead of you. Oh, by the way, Ehlana sent you a present. It came last night after you fell asleep."

"You should have got me up."

"Why? You can't wear it in bed."

"What is it?"

"Your crown, my Lord."

"My *what*?"

"Crown. It's a sort of a hat. It won't keep off much in the way of weather, though."

"What's she thinking about?"

"Propriety, my Lord. You're the Prince Consort—or you will be by tonight. It's not a bad crown—as crowns go. Gold, jewels, that sort of thing."

"Where did she get it?"

"She had it made for you right after you left Cimmura to come here. She brought it along with her—sort of the way a fisherman always has a coil of line and a hook somewhere in his pocket. I gather that your bride didn't want to be unprepared in case an opportunity arose. She wants me to carry it on a velvet cushion during the ceremony tonight. As soon as the two of you are married, she's going to put it on your head."

"Foolishness." Sparhawk snorted, swinging his legs out of bed.

"Perhaps, but you'll learn in time that women look at the world differently from the way we do. It's one of the things that makes life interesting. Now, what's it to be? Your breakfast or your bath?"

They met that morning in the chapterhouse, since things in the Basilica were in turmoil. The changes Dolmant was making were sweeping, and the clergy was scrambling about like ants rooted from a ripped-open anthill. The huge Patriarch Bergsten, still in his mail shirt and wearing his ogre-horned helmet, was grinning as he entered Sir Nashan's study and stood his war ax in the corner.

"Where's Emban?" King Wargun asked him. "And Ortzel?"

"They're busy dismissing people. Sarathi's giving the Basilica a thorough house cleaning. Emban's drawn up a list of the politically unreliable, and the populations of a number of monasteries are expanding sharply."

"Makova?" Tynian asked.

"He was among the first to leave."

"Who's first secretary?" King Dregos asked.

"Who else? Emban, of course, and Ortzel's the new head of the college of theologians. It's probably what he's best suited for anyway."

"And you?" Wargun asked him.

"Sarathi's given me a rather specialized position," Bergsten replied. "We haven't come up with a name for it as yet." He looked rather sternly at the preceptors of the Church Knights. "There's been some rather long-standing dissention among the militant orders," he told them. "Sarathi's asked me to put a stop to it." His shaggy brows lowered ominously. "I trust we understand each other, gentlemen."

The preceptors looked at each other a bit nervously.

"Now," Bergsten continued, "have we made any decisions here yet?"

"We're still arguing about that, your Grace," Vanion answered. Vanion's face was gray this morning for some reason, and he looked definitely unwell. Sparhawk sometimes forgot that Vanion was quite a bit older than he looked. "Sparhawk's still bent on suicide, and we haven't been able to come up with any convincing alternatives. The rest of the Church Knights are going to move out tomorrow to occupy various fortresses and castles in Lamorkand, and the army will follow once they've been organized."

Bergsten nodded. "Exactly what are you going to do, Sparhawk?"

"I thought I'd go destroy Azash, kill Martel, Otha, and Annias, and then come home, your Grace."

"Very funny," Bergsten said dryly. "Details, man. Give me details. I have to make a report to Sarathi, and he loves details."

"Yes, your Grace. We've all more or less agreed that we don't have much chance of catching up with Martel and his party before they get across into Zemoch. He's got a three-day start on us—counting today. Martel isn't very considerate of horses, and he has a lot of incentive to stay ahead of us."

"Are you going to follow him, or just ride straight on to the Zemoch border?"

Sparhawk leaned back in his chair. "We're a little tenuous on that, your Grace," he said thoughtfully. "I'd like to catch Martel, certainly, but I'm not going to let that sidetrack me. My main goal is to get to the city of Zemoch before a general war breaks out in central Lamorkand. I had a talk with Krager, and he says that Martel plans to go north and then to try to cross over into Zemoch from somewhere up in Pelosia. I more or less want to do the same thing, so I'll follow him—but only up to a point. I'm not going to waste time chasing Martel all over northern Pelosia. If he starts wandering around up there, I'll break off the chase and go straight on to Zemoch. I've been playing Martel's game ever since I came back from Rendor. I don't think I want to play any more."

"What are you going to do about all the Zemochs in eastern Pelosia?"

"That's where I come in, your Grace," Kring told him. "There's a pass that leads into the interior. The Zemochs don't seem to know about it for some reason. My horsemen and I have been using it for years—anytime ears get scarce along the border." He stopped abruptly and looked with some consternation at King Soros. The King of Pelosia, however, was busy praying and appeared not to have heard the Domi's inadvertent revelation.

"That's about all there is to it, your Grace," Sparhawk concluded. "Nobody really knows for sure what's going on in Zemoch, so we'll have to improvise once we get there."

"How many of you are there?" Bergsten asked.

"The usual group. Five knights, Kurik, Berit, and Sephrenia."

"What about me?" Talen objected.

"*You* are going back to Cimmura, young man," Sephrenia told him. "Ehlana can keep an eye on you. You'll stay at the palace until we come back."

"That's not fair!"

"Life is filled with injustice, Talen. Sparhawk and your father have plans for you, and they don't propose to let you get yourself killed before they have a chance to put them in motion."

"Can I appeal to the Church for sanctuary, your Grace?" Talen asked Bergsten quickly.

"No, I don't think so," the armored patriarch replied.

"You have no idea how disappointed I am in our Holy Mother, your Grace," Talen sulked. "Just for that, I don't think I'll join the Church after all."

"Praise God," Bergsten murmured.

"Amen," Abriel sighed.

"May I be excused?" Talen asked in a huffy tone.

"No." It was Berit, who sat by the door with his arms crossed and one leg thrust out to block the doorway.

Talen sat back down, looking injured.

The remainder of the discussion dealt with the deployment of troops at the various fortresses and castles in central Lamorkand. Sparhawk and his friends were not going to be involved in that, so the bridegroom's attention wandered. He did not actually think of anything very coherently, but sat instead staring wide-eyed at the floor.

The meeting broke up about noon, and they began to file out. There were many preparations to make, and they all had things to do.

"Friend Sparhawk," Kring said as they left Nashan's study, "might I have a word with you?"

"Of course, Domi."

"It's sort of personal."

Sparhawk nodded and led the scarred chief of the Peloi to a small chapel nearby. They both perfunctorily genuflected to the altar and then sat on a polished bench near the front of the chapel. "What is it, Kring?" Sparhawk asked.

"I'm a plain man, friend Sparhawk," Kring began, "so I'll speak to the point. I'm mightily taken with that tall, beautiful woman who guards the Queen of Elenia."

"I thought I detected something like that."

"Do you think I might have any chance with her at all?" Kring's heart was in his eyes.

"I'm not really sure, my friend," Sparhawk told him. "I scarcely know Mirtai."

"Is that her name? I never really had the chance to find out. Mirtai—it's got a nice sound to it, doesn't it? Everything about her is perfect. I have to ask this. Is she married?"

"I don't think so."

"Good. It's always awkward to pay court to a woman if you have to kill her husband first. It seems to get things off to a bad start for some reason."

"I think you should know that Mirtai's not an Elene, Kring. She's a Tamul, and her culture—and religion—are not the same as ours. Are your intentions honorable?"

"Of course. I think too much of her to insult her."

"That's the first step anyway. If you approached her on any other footing, she'd probably kill you."

"*Kill?*" Kring blinked in astonishment.

"She's a warrior, Kring. She's not like any other woman you've ever encountered."

"Women can't be warriors."

"Not Elene women, no. But as I said, Mirtai's an Atan Tamul. They don't look at the world the same way we do. As I understand it, she's already killed ten men."

"Ten?" Kring gasped incredulously, swallowing hard. "That's going to be a problem, Sparhawk." Kring squared his shoulders. "No matter, though. Perhaps after I marry her, I can train her to behave more properly."

"I wouldn't make any wagers on that, my friend. If there's going to be any training, I think *you're* the one who'll be on the receiving end of it. I'd really advise you to drop the whole idea, Kring. I like you, and I'd hate to see you get yourself killed."

"I'm going to have to think about this, Sparhawk," Kring said in a disturbed tone of voice. "This is a very unnatural situation we have here."

"Yes."

"Nonetheless, could I ask you to serve as my *oma?*"

"I don't understand the word."

"It means friend. The one who goes to the woman—and to her father and brothers. You start by telling her how much I'm attracted to her and then tell her what a good man I am—the usual thing, you understand—what a great leader I am, how many horses I own, how many ears I've taken, and what a great warrior I am."

"That last should impress her."

"It's just the simple truth, Sparhawk. I *am* the best, after all. I'll have all the time while we're riding to Zemoch to think it over. You might mention it to her before we leave, though—just to give *her* something to think about. Oh, I almost forgot. You can tell her that I'm a poet, too. That always impresses women."

"I'll do my best, Domi," Sparhawk promised.

Mirtai's reaction was none too promising when Sparhawk broached the subject to her later that afternoon. "That little bald one with the bandy legs?" she said incredulously. "The one with all the scars on his face?" Then she collapsed in a chair, laughing uncontrollably.

"Well," Sparhawk murmured philosophically as he left her, "I tried."

It was going to be an unconventional sort of wedding. There were no Elenian noblewomen in Chyrellos to attend Ehlana, for one thing. The only two ladies who were really close to her were Sephrenia and Mirtai. She insisted on their presence, and that raised some eyebrows. Even the worldly Dolmant choked on it. "You *can't* bring two heathens into the nave of the Basilica during a religious ceremony, Ehlana."

"It's my wedding, Dolmant. I can do anything I want to. I *will* have Sephrenia and Mirtai as attendants."

"I forbid it."

"Fine." Her eyes grew flinty. "No attendants, no wedding—and if there isn't a wedding, my ring stays right where it is."

"That is an impossible young woman, Sparhawk," the archprelate fumed as he stormed out of the room where Ehlana was making her preparations.

"We prefer the term 'spirited,' Sarathi," Sparhawk said mildly. Sparhawk was dressed in black velvet trimmed with silver. Ehlana had summarily rejected the idea of his being married in his armor. "I don't want a blacksmith in our bedchamber to help you get undressed, love," she had told him. "If you need help, I'll provide it—but I don't want to break all my fingernails in the process."

There were noblemen by the score in the armies of western Eosia, and legions of clergy in the Basilica, and so that evening the vast, candlelit nave was almost as packed as it had been on the day of the funeral of the revered Cluvonus. The choir sang joyful anthems as the wedding guests filed in, and incense by the bale perfumed the air.

Sparhawk waited nervously in the vestry with those who were to attend him. His friends were all there, of course—Kalten, Tynian, Bevier, Ulath, and the Domi, as well as Kurik, Berit, and the preceptors of the four orders. Ehlana's attendants, appropriately, were, in addition to Sephrenia and Mirtai, the kings of western Eosia and, oddly enough, Platime, Stragen, and Talen. The queen had given no reason for these selections. It was altogether possible that there *were* no reasons.

"Don't do that, Sparhawk," Kurik told his lord.

"Do what?"

"Don't keep pulling at the neck of your doublet like that. You'll rip it."

"The tailor cut it too tight. It feels like a noose."

Kurik did not answer that. He did, however, give Sparhawk an amused look.

The door opened, and Emban thrust his sweating face into the room. He was grinning broadly. "Are we just about ready?" he asked.

"Let's get on with it," Sparhawk said abruptly.

"Our bridegroom grows impatient, I see," Emban said. "Ah, to be young again. The choir's going to sing the traditional wedding hymn," he told them. "I'm sure that some of you are familiar with it. When they get to the final chord, I'll open the door, and then you gentlemen can escort our sacrificial lamb here to the altar. Please don't let him run away. That always disrupts the ceremony so much." He chuckled wickedly and closed the door again.

"That's a very nasty little man," Sparhawk grated.

"Oh, I don't know," Kalten said. "*I* sort of like him."

The wedding hymn was one of the oldest pieces of sacred music in the Elene faith. It was a song filled with joy. Brides traditionally paid very close attention to it. Grooms, on the other hand, usually scarcely heard it.

As the last notes died away, Patriarch Emban opened the door with a flourish, and Sparhawk's friends formed up around him to escort him into the nave. It would be perhaps inappropriate here to dwell upon the similarities of such a procession to the gathering of bailiffs escorting a condemned prisoner to the scaffold.

They proceeded directly across the front of the nave to the altar where Archprelate Dolmant, robed all in white trimmed with gold, awaited them. "Ah, my son," Dolmant said to Sparhawk with a faint smile, "so good of you to join us."

Sparhawk did not trust himself to answer that. He *did*, however, reflect rather bitterly on the fact that all his friends viewed the occasion as one filled with an enormous potential for humor.

Then, after a suitable pause, during which all the wedding guests rose to their feet, fell silent, and craned their necks to gaze toward the back of the nave, the choir broke into the processional hymn, and the bridal party emerged from either side of the vestibule. First, one from either side, came Sephrenia and Mirtai. The disparity of the size of the two women was not immediately noted by the onlookers. What *was* noted and what raised a shocked gasp from the crowd was the obvious fact that both were clearly heathens. Sephrenia's white robe was almost defiantly Styric. A garland of flowers encircled her brow, and her face was calm. Mirtai's gown was of a style unknown in Elenia. It was of a deep, royal blue and seemed to be unseamed. It was fastened at each shoulder with a jeweled clip, and a long gold chain caught it below the bust, crossed the Tamul woman's back, encircled her waist, and then hugged her hips to the intricate knot low in the front with the tasseled ends nearly reaching the floor. Her golden arms were bare to the shoulders, flawlessly smooth, yet solidly muscled. She wore golden sandals, and her now-unbraided and glossy black hair flowed smoothly down her back, reaching to mid-thigh. A simple silver band encircled her head. About her wrists she wore not bracelets but rather burnished steel cuffs embossed with gold. As a concession to Elene sensibilities, she was not visibly armed.

The Domi Kring sighed lustily as she entered and, with Sephrenia at her side, paced slowly down the aisle toward the altar.

Again there was the customary pause, and then the bride, her left hand resting lightly on the arm of old King Obler, emerged from the vestibule to stop so that all present might view her—not so much as a woman, but as a work of art. Her gown was of white satin, but brides are almost always gowned in white satin. This particular gown was lined with gold lamé, and the long sleeves were turned back to reveal that contrast. The sleeves themselves were cut long at the backs of the arms, reaching quite nearly to the floor. Ehlana wore a wide belt of beaten mesh gold inlaid with precious gems about her waist. A fabulous golden cape descended to the floor behind her to add its weight to her gleaming satin train. Her pale blonde hair was surmounted by a crown—not the traditional royal crown of Elenia, but rather a lacework of gold mesh highlighted with small, brightly colored gems interspersed with pearls. The crown held her veil in place, a veil that reached to her bodice in the front and overlaid her shoulders in the back and was so delicate and fine as to be scarcely more than mist. She carried a single white flower, and her pale young face was radiant.

"Where did they get the gowns on such short notice?" Berit whispered to Kurik.

"Sephrenia wriggled her fingers, I'd imagine."

Dolmant gave the two of them a stern look, and they stopped whispering.

After the Queen of Elenia there came the crowned kings, Wargun, Dregos, and Soros, and the Crown Prince of Lamorkand, who was standing in for his absent father, followed by the ambassador of Cammoria, who was the representative of that kingdom. The Kingdom of Rendor was unrepresented, and no one had even thought to invite Otha of Zemoch.

The procession began to move slowly down the aisle toward the altar and the waiting bridegroom. Platime and Stragen brought up the rear, one of them on each side of Talen, who bore the white velvet cushion upon which rested that pair of ruby rings. It should be noted in passing that both Stragen and Platime were keeping a very close eye on the youthful thief.

Sparhawk considered his bride as, with glowing face, she approached. In those last few moments while he was still able to think coherently, he realized something at last that he had never fully admitted to himself. Ehlana had been a chore when she had been placed in his care years ago—not only a chore, but a humiliation as well. It is to his credit that he had felt no personal resentment toward her, for he had realized that she had been as much a victim of her father's caprice as he was himself. The first year and more had been trying. The girl-child who now so radiantly approached him had been timorous, and at first had spoken only to Rollo, a small, somewhat bedraggled stuffed toy animal that in those days was her constant and probably only companion. In time, however, she had grown accustomed to Sparhawk's battered face and stern demeanor, and a somewhat tenuous friendship had been cemented on the day when an arrogant courtier had offered Princess Ehlana an impertinence and had been firmly rebuked by her knight-protector. It was undoubtedly the first time anyone had ever shed blood for her—the courtier's nose had bled profusely—and an entire new world had opened for the small, pale princess. From that moment, she had confided everything to her knight—even things he might have preferred she had not. She had no secrets from him, and he had come to know her as he had never known anyone else in the world. And that, of course, had ruined him for any other woman. The slight, as yet unformed princess had so intricately intertwined her very being with his that there was no possible way they could ever truly be separated, and that, finally, was why they were here in this place at this time. If there had been only his own pain to consider, Sparhawk might have held firm in his rejection of the idea. He could not, however, endure *her* pain, and so—

The hymn concluded. Old King Obler delivered his kinswoman to her knight, and the bride and groom turned to face Archprelate Dolmant. "I'm going to preach to you for a while," Dolmant told them quietly. "It's a sort of convention, and people expect me to do it. You don't really have to listen, but try not to yawn in my face if you can avoid it."

"We wouldn't dream of it, Sarathi," Ehlana assured him.

Dolmant spoke of the state of marriage—at some length. He then assured the bridal couple that once the ceremony had been completed, it would be perfectly all right for them to follow their natural inclinations—that it would not only be all right, but was, in fact, encouraged. He strongly suggested that they be faithful to each other and reminded them that any issue of their union must be raised in the Elenian faith. Then he came to the "wilt thous," asking them in turn if they consented to be wed, bestowed all their worldly goods upon each other, and promised to love, honor, obey, cherish, and so forth. Then, since things were going so well, he moved right along into the exchanging of the rings, neither of which Talen had even managed to steal.

It was at that point that Sparhawk heard a soft, familiar sound that seemed to echo down from the dome itself. It was the faint trilling of pipes, a joyful sound filled with abiding love. Sparhawk glanced at Sephrenia. Her glowing smile said everything. For a moment he irrationally wondered what protocols had been involved when Aphrael had applied to the Elene God for permission to be present, and, it appeared, to add her blessing to His.

"What *is* that music?" Ehlana whispered, her lips not moving.

"I'll explain later," Sparhawk murmured.

The song of Aphrael's pipes seemed to go unnoticed by the throng in the candlelit nave. Dolmant's eyes, however, widened slightly, and his face went a bit pale. He regained his composure and finally declared that Sparhawk and Ehlana were permanently, irrevocably, unalterably, and definitively man and wife. He then invoked the blessings of God upon them in a nice little concluding prayer and finally gave Sparhawk permission to kiss his bride.

Sparhawk tenderly lifted Ehlana's veil and touched his lips to hers. No one actually kisses someone else very well in public, but the couple managed without looking too awkward about the whole business.

The wedding ceremony was followed immediately by Sparhawk's coronation as Prince Consort. He knelt to have the crown Kurik had carried into the nave on a purple velvet cushion placed upon his head by the young woman who had just promised—among other things—to obey him, but who now assumed the authority of his queen. Ehlana made a nice speech in a ringing voice with which she could probably have commanded rocks to move with some fair expectation of being obeyed. She said a number of things about him in her speech, mostly flattering, and concluded by firmly settling the crown on his head. Then, since he was on his knees anyway and his upturned face was convenient, she kissed him again. He noticed that she got much, much better at it with practice. "You're *mine* now, Sparhawk," she murmured with her lips still touching his. Then, though he was far from decrepit, she helped him to his feet. Mirtai and Kalten came forward with ermine-trimmed robes to place on the shoulders of the royal pair, and then the two of them turned to receive the cheers of the throng within the nave.

▪   ▪   ▪

There was a wedding supper following the ceremony. Sparhawk never remembered what was served at that supper nor even if he ate any of it. All he remembered was that it seemed to go on for centuries. Then at last he and his bride were escorted to the door of a lavish chamber high up in the east wing of one of the buildings that comprised the church complex. He and Ehlana entered, and he closed and locked the door behind them.

There were furnishings in the room—chairs, tables, divans, and the like—but all Sparhawk really saw was the stark reality of the bed. It was a high bed on a raised dais, and it had a substantial post at each corner.

"Finally," Ehlana said with relief. "I thought all of that was going to go on forever."

"Yes," Sparhawk agreed.

"Sparhawk," she said then, and her tone was not the tone of a queen, "do you *really* love me? I know I forced you into this—first back in Cimmura and then here. Did you marry me because you really love me, or did you just defer to me because I'm the queen?" Her voice was trembling, and her eyes were very vulnerable.

"You're asking silly questions, Ehlana," he told her gently. "I'll admit that you startled me at first—probably because I had no idea that you felt this way. I'm not much of a catch, Ehlana, but I do love you. I've never loved anyone else, and never will. My heart's a little battered, but it's entirely yours." Then he kissed her, and she seemed to melt against him.

The kiss lasted for quite some time, and after a few moments he felt one small hand slide caressingly up the back of his neck to remove his crown. He drew his face back and looked into her lustrous gray eyes. Then he gently removed *her* crown and let her veil slide to the floor. Gravely, each unfastened the other's ermine-trimmed robe and let it fall.

The window was open, and the night breeze billowed the gauzy curtains and carried with it the nighttime sounds of Chyrellos far below. Sparhawk and Ehlana did not feel the breeze, and the only sound they heard was the beating of each other's hearts.


The candles no longer burned, but the room was not dark. The moon had risen, a full moon that filled the night with a pale, silvery luminescence. The moonlight seemed caught in the filmy net of the curtains blowing softly at the window, and the glow of those curtains provided a subtler, more perfect light than that of any candle.

It was very late—or to be more precise, very early. Sparhawk had dozed off briefly, but his pale, moon-drenched wife shook him awake. "None of that," she told him. "We only have this one night, and you're not going to waste it by sleeping."

"Sorry," he apologized. "I've had a busy day."

"Also a busy night," she added with an arch little smile. "Did you know that you snore like a thunderstorm?"

"It's the broken nose, I think."

"That may cause problems in time, love. I'm a light sleeper." Ehlana nestled down in his arms and sighed contentedly. "Oh, this is very nice," she said. "We should have gotten married years ago."

"I think your father might have objected—and if he hadn't, Rollo certainly would have. Whatever happened to Rollo, by the way?"

"His stuffings all came out after my father sent you into exile. I washed him and then folded him up and put him on the top shelf in my closet. I'll have him restuffed after our first baby is born. Poor Rollo. He saw some hard use after you were sent away. I cried all over him extensively. He was a very soggy little animal for several months."

"Did you really miss me all that much?"

"Miss you? I thought I'd die. I wanted to die, actually."

His arms tightened around her.

"Well, now," she said, "why don't we talk about that?"

He laughed. "Do you absolutely have to say everything that pops into your head?"

"When we're alone, yes. I have no secrets from you, my husband." She remembered something. "You said you were going to tell me about that music we heard during the ceremony."

"That was Aphrael. I'll have to check with Sephrenia, but I rather strongly suspect that we've been married in more than one religion."

"Good. That gives me another hold on you."

"You don't really need any more, you know. You've had me in thrall since you were about six years old."

"That's nice," she said, snuggling even closer to him. "God knows I was trying." She paused. "I must say, though, that I'm getting just a bit put out with your impertinent little Styric Goddess. She always seems to be around. For all we know, she's hovering unseen in some corner right now." She stopped suddenly and sat up in bed. "Do you suppose she might be?" she asked with some consternation.

"I wouldn't be surprised." He was deliberately teasing her.

"*Sparhawk!*" The pale light of the moon made it impossible to be sure, but Sparhawk strongly suspected that his wife was blushing furiously.

"Don't concern yourself, love." He laughed. "Aphrael's exquisitely courteous. She'd never think of intruding."

"But we can never really be sure, can we? I'm not sure I like her. I get the feeling that she's very much attracted to you, and I don't much care for the notion of immortal competition."

"Don't be absurd. She's a child."

"I was only about five years old the first time I saw you, Sparhawk, and I decided to marry you the minute you walked into the room." She slid from the bed, crossed to the glowing window, and parted the gauzy curtains. The pale moonlight made her look very much like an alabaster statue.

"Shouldn't you put on a robe?" he suggested. "You're exposing yourself to public scrutiny, you know."

"Everybody in Chyrellos has been asleep for hours now. Besides, we're six floors above the street. I want to look at the moon. The moon and I are very close, and I want her to know how happy I am."

"Pagan." He smiled.

"I suppose I am, at that," she admitted, "but all women feel a peculiar attachment to the moon. She touches us in ways a man could never understand."

Sparhawk crawled out of bed and joined her at the window. The moon was very pale and very bright, but the fact that its pale light washed out all color concealed to some degree the ruin Martel's siege had inflicted on the Holy City, although the smell of smoke was still very strong in the night air. The stars glittered in the sky. There was nothing really unusual about that, but they seemed especially brilliant on this night of all nights.

Ehlana pulled his arms about her and sighed. "I wonder if Mirtai's sleeping outside my door," she said. "She does that, you know. Wasn't she ravishing tonight?"

"Oh, yes. I didn't get the chance to tell you this, but Kring's completely overwhelmed by her. I've never seen a man so bowled over by love."

"At least he's open and honest about it. I have to drag affectionate words out of you."

"You know that I love you, Ehlana. I always have."

"That's not precisely true. When I was still carrying Rollo around, you were only mildly fond of me."

"It was more than that."

"Oh, really? I saw the pained looks you used to give me when I was being childish and silly, my noble Prince Consort." She frowned. "That's a very cumbersome title. When I get back to Cimmura, I think I'll have a talk with Lenda. It seems to me there's an empty duchy somewhere—or if there isn't, I'll vacate one. I'm going to dispossess a few of Annias' henchmen anyway. How would you like to be a duke, your Grace?"

"Thanks all the same, your Majesty, but I think I can forgo the encumbrance of additional titles."

"But I *want* to give you titles."

"I'm sort of taken with 'husband,' personally."

"Any man can be a husband."

"But I'm the only one who's yours."

"Oh, that's very nice. Practice a bit, Sparhawk, and you might even turn into a perfect gentleman."

"Most of the perfect gentlemen I know are courtiers. They're not generally held in high regard."

She shivered.

"You're cold," he accused. "I *told* you to put on a robe."

"Why do I need a robe when I have this nice warm husband handy?"

He bent, picked her up in his arms, and carried her back to the bed.

"I've dreamed of this," she said as he gently put her on the bed, joined her, and drew the covers over them. "You know something, Sparhawk?" She snuggled down against him again. "I used to worry about this night. I thought I'd be all nervous and shy, but I'm not at all—and do you know why?"

"No, I don't think so."

"I think it's because we've really been married since the first moment I laid my eyes on you. All we were really doing was waiting for me to grow up so that we could formalize things." She kissed him lingeringly. "What time do you think it is?"

"A couple of hours until daylight."

"Good. That gives us lots more time. You *are* going to be careful in Zemoch, aren't you?"

"I'm going to do my very best."

"Please don't do heroic things just to impress me, Sparhawk. I'm already impressed."

"I'll be careful," he promised.

"Speaking of that—do you want my ring now?"

"Why don't you give it to me in public? Let Sarathi see us keep our part of the bargain."

"Was I really too terrible to him?"

"You startled him a bit. Sarathi's not used to dealing with women like you. I think you unnerve him, my love."

"Do I unnerve you, too, Sparhawk?"

"Not really. I raised you, after all. I'm used to your little quirks."

"You're really lucky, you know. Very few men have the opportunity to rear their own wives. That may give you something to think about on your way to Zemoch." Her voice quavered then, and a sudden sob escaped her. "I *swore* I wouldn't do this," she wailed. "I don't want you to remember me as being all weepy."

"It's all right, Ehlana. I sort of feel the same way myself."

"Why does the night have to run so fast? Could this Aphrael of yours stop the sun from coming up if we asked her to? Or maybe you could do it with the Bhelliom."

"I don't think anything in the world has the power to do that, Ehlana."

"What good are they all then?" She began to cry, and he took her into his arms and held her until the storm of her weeping had passed. Then he gently kissed her. One kiss became several, and the rest of the night passed without any further weeping.

## CHAPTER TWENTY

"But why does it have to be in public?" Sparhawk demanded, clanking around the room to settle his armor into place.

"It's expected, dear," Ehlana replied calmly. "You're a member of the royal family now, and you're obliged to appear in public on occasion. You get used to it after a while." Ehlana, wearing a fur-trimmed blue velvet robe, sat at her dressing table.

"It's no worse than a tournament, my Lord," Kurik told him. "That's in public, too. Now will you stop pacing around so I can get your sword belt on straight?" Kurik, Sephrenia, and Mirtai had arrived at the bridal chamber with the sun, Kurik carrying Sparhawk's armor, Sephrenia carrying flowers for the queen, and Mirtai carrying breakfast. Emban came with them, and *he* carried the news that the formal farewell would take place on the steps of the Basilica.

"We haven't given the people or Wargun's troops much in the way of detail, Sparhawk," the fat little churchman cautioned, "so you probably shouldn't get too specific if you start making speeches. We'll give you a rousing send-off and hint at the fact that you're going to save the world all by yourself. We're used to lying, so we'll even be able to sound convincing. It's all very silly, of course, but we'd appreciate your cooperation. The morale of the citizens and particularly of Wargun's troops is very important just now." His round face took on a slightly disappointed cast. "I suggested that we have you do something spectacular in the way of magic to top things off, but Sarathi put his foot down."

"Your tendency toward theatrics sometimes gets out of hand, Emban," Sephrenia told him. The small Styric woman was toying with Ehlana's hair, experimenting with comb and brush.

"I'm a man of the people, Sephrenia," Emban replied. "My father was a tavern keeper, and I know how to please a crowd. The people love a good show, and that's what I wanted to give them."

Sephrenia had lifted Ehlana's hair into a mass atop the queen's head. "What do you think, Mirtai?" she asked.

"I liked it the way it was before," the giantess replied.

"She's married now. The way she wore her hair before was the way a young girl would wear it. We have to do something with it to indicate that she's a married woman."

"Brand her." Mirtai shrugged. "That's what my people do."

"Do *what?*" Ehlana exclaimed.

"Among my people, a woman is branded with her husband's mark when she marries—usually on the shoulder."

"To indicate that she's his property?" the queen asked scornfully. "What sort of mark does the *husband* wear?"

"He wears his wife's mark. Marriages are not undertaken lightly among my people."

"I can see why," Kurik said with a certain awe.

"Eat your breakfast before it gets cold, Ehlana," Mirtai commanded.

"I don't really care all that much for fried liver, Mirtai."

"It's not for you. My people lay some importance on the wedding night. Many brides became pregnant on that night—or so they say. That might be the result of practicing before the ceremony, though."

"*Mirtai!*" Ehlana gasped, flushing.

"You mean you didn't? I'm disappointed in you."

"I didn't think of it," Ehlana confessed. "Why didn't you say something, Sparhawk?"

Emban for some reason was blushing furiously. "Why don't I just run along?" he said. "I have a million things to take care of." And he bolted from the room.

"Was it something I said?" Mirtai asked innocently.

"Emban's a churchman, dear," Sephrenia told her, trying to stifle a laugh. "Churchmen prefer not to know too much about such things."

"Foolishness. Eat, Ehlana."

The gathering on the steps of the Basilica was not *quite* a ceremony, but rather one of those informally formal affairs customarily put on for public entertainment. Dolmant was there to lend solemnity to the affair. The kings, crowned and robed, were present to give an official tone, and the preceptors of the militant orders to add a martial note. Dolmant began things with a prayer. That was followed by brief remarks from the kings and then by slightly longer ones from the preceptors. Sparhawk and his companions then knelt to receive the archprelate's blessing, and the whole affair was concluded by the farewell between Ehlana and her Prince Consort. The Queen of Elenia, speaking once again in that oratorical tone, commanded her champion to go forth and conquer. She concluded by removing her ring and bestowing it upon him as a mark of her special favor. He responded by replacing it upon her hand with a ring surmounted with a heart-shaped diamond. Talen had been a bit evasive about how the ring had come into his possession when he had pressed it upon Sparhawk just prior to the gathering on the steps.

"And now, my Champion," Ehlana concluded, perhaps a bit dramatically, "go forth with your brave companions, and know that our hopes, our prayers, and all our faith ride with you. Take up the sword, my husband and Champion, and defend me and our faith and our beloved homes against the vile hordes of heathen Zemoch!" And then she embraced him and bestowed a single brief kiss upon his lips.

"Nice speech, love," he murmured his congratulations.

"Emban wrote it," she confessed. "He's got the soul of a meddler. Try to get a word to me now and then, my husband, and in the name of God, be careful."

He gently kissed her forehead, and then he and his friends strode purposefully to the foot of the marble stairs and their waiting horses as the bells of the Basilica rang out their own farewell. The preceptors of the militant orders, who were to ride out with them a ways, followed. Kring and his mounted Peloi were already waiting in the street. Before they set out, Kring rode forward to where Mirtai stood, and his horse performed that ritual genuflection to her. Neither of them spoke, but Mirtai *did* look slightly impressed.

"All right, Faran," Sparhawk said as he swung up into the saddle, "it's all right for you to indulge yourself just a bit."

The big, ugly roan's ears pricked forward eagerly, and he began to prance outrageously as the warlike party moved off in the direction of the east gate.

Once they had passed the gate, Vanion left Sephrenia's side and drew his horse in beside Faran. "Stay alert, my friend," he advised. "Have you got Bhelliom where you can get your hands on it in a hurry if you have to?"

"It's inside my surcoat," Sparhawk said. He looked closely at his friend. "Don't take this wrong," he said, "but you're looking decidedly seedy this morning."

"I'm tired more than anything, Sparhawk. Wargun kept us running pretty hard down there in Arcium. Take care of yourself, my friend. I want to go talk with Sephrenia before we separate."

Sparhawk sighed as Vanion rode back along the column to rejoin the small, beautiful woman who had tutored generations of Pandions in the secrets of Styricum. Sephrenia and Vanion would never say anything overtly, even to each other, but Sparhawk knew how things stood between them, and he also knew how totally impossible their situation was.

Kalten pulled in beside him. "Well, how did the wedding night go?" he asked, his eyes very bright.

Sparhawk gave him a long, flat look.

"You don't want to talk about it, I gather."

"It's sort of private."

"We've been friends since boyhood, Sparhawk. We've never had any secrets from each other."

"We have now. It's about seventy leagues to Kadach, isn't it?"

"That's fairly close. If we push, we should be able to make it in five days. Did Martel sound at all concerned when he was talking with Annias down in that cellar? What I'm getting at is, do you think he'll be worried enough about our following him to hurry right along?"

"He definitely wanted to leave Chyrellos."

"He's probably pushing his horses hard then, wouldn't you say?"

"That's a safe bet."

"His horses will tire if he runs them hard, so we still might have a chance to catch up with him after a few days. I don't know how you feel about *him*, but *I'd* certainly like to catch Adus."

"It's something to think about, all right. How's the country between Kadach and Moterra?"

"Flat. Mostly farmland. Castles here and there. Farm villages. It's a great deal like eastern Elenia." Kalten laughed. "Have you taken a look at Berit this morning? He's having a little trouble adjusting to his armor. It doesn't fit him all that well." Berit, the rawboned young novice, had been promoted to a rank seldom used by the militant orders. He was now an apprentice knight rather than a novice. This legally enabled him to wear his own armor, but he did not as yet rate a "sir."

"He'll get used to it," Sparhawk said. "When we stop for the night, take him aside and show him how to pad the raw spots. We don't want him to start bleeding out of the joints of his armor. Be discreet about it, though. If I remember rightly, a young fellow's very proud and a little touchy when he first puts his armor on. That sort of passes after the first few blisters break."

It was when they reached a hilltop several miles from Chyrellos that the preceptors turned back. The advice and the cautions had all been given, and so there was little to do but clasp hands and to wish each other well. Sparhawk and his friends rather soberly watched as their leaders rode back to the Holy City.

"Well," Tynian said, "now that we're alone—"

"Let's talk for a few moments first," Sparhawk said. He raised his voice. "Domi," he called, "would you join us for a moment, please?"

Kring rode up the hill, an inquiring look on his face.

"Now then," Sparhawk began, "Martel seems to think that Azash will want us to get through without any difficulty, but Martel might be wrong. Azash has many servants, and he may very well loose them on us. He wants Bhelliom, not any satis-faction he might get from a personal confrontation. Kring, I think you'd better put out scouts. Let's not be taken by surprise."

"I will, friend Sparhawk," the Domi promised.

"If we *should* happen to encounter any of the servants of Azash, I want all of you to fall back and let me deal with them. I've got Bhelliom, and that should be all the advantage I'll need. Kalten raised the point that we might just overtake Martel. If we do, try to take Martel and Annias alive. The Church wants them to stand trial. I doubt that Arissa or Lycheas will offer much resistance, so take them as well."

"And Adus?" Kalten asked eagerly.

"Adus can barely talk, so he wouldn't be of much value in any trial. You can have him—as a personal gift from me."

They had gone perhaps another mile when they found Stragen sitting under a tree. "I thought perhaps you'd gotten lost," the slender thief drawled, rising to his feet.

"Do I sense a volunteer here?" Tynian suggested.

"Hardly, old boy," Stragen said. "I've never had occasion to visit Zemoch, and I think I want to keep it that way. Actually, I'm here as the queen's messenger, and her personal envoy. I'll ride along with you as far as the Zemoch border, if I may, and then I'll return to Cimmura to give her my report."

"Aren't you spending a great deal of time away from your own business?" Kurik asked him.

"My business in Emsat sort of runs itself. Tel's looking out for my interests there. I need a vacation anyway." He patted at his doublet in various places. "Oh, yes, here it is." He drew out a folded sheet of parchment. "A letter for you from your bride, Sparhawk," he said, handing it over. "It's the first of several I'm supposed to give you when the occasion dictates."

Sparhawk moved Faran away from the others and broke the seal on Ehlana's note.

Beloved,

You've been gone for only a few hours, and I already miss you desper-ately. Stragen is carrying other messages for you—messages that I hope will inspire you when things aren't going well. They will also convey to you my unbending love and faith in you. I love you, my Sparhawk.

Ehlana.

"How did you get ahead of us?" Kalten was asking when Sparhawk rejoined them.

"You're wearing armor, Sir Kalten," Stragen replied, "and I'm not. You'd be amazed at how fast a horse can run when he's not burdened with all that excess iron."

"Well?" Ulath asked Sparhawk, "do we send him back to Chyrellos?"

Sparhawk shook his head. "He's acting under orders from the queen. There's an implicit command to me involved in that as well. He comes along."

"Remind me never to become a royal champion," the Genidian Knight said. "It seems to involve all sorts of politics and complications."

The weather turned cloudy as they rode northeasterly along the Kadach road, although it did not rain as it had the last time they had been here. The southeastern border country of Lamorkand was more Pelosian in character than it was Lamork, and there were few castles atop the surrounding hilltops. Because of its proximity to Chyrellos, however, the landscape was dotted with monasteries and cloisters, and the sound of bells echoed mournfully across the fields.

"The clouds are moving in the wrong direction," Kurik said as they were saddling their horses on the second morning out from Chyrellos. "An east wind in mid-autumn is very bad news. I'm afraid we're in for a hard winter, and that's not going to be pleasant for the troops campaigning on the plains of central Lamorkand."

They mounted and rode on toward the northeast. About midmorning, Kring and Stragen rode forward to join Sparhawk at the head of the column. "Friend Stragen here has been telling me some things about that Tamul woman, Mirtai," Kring said. "Did you ever get the chance to talk to her about me?"

"I sort of broke the ice on the subject," Sparhawk said.

"I was afraid of that. Some of the things Stragen told me are giving me some second thoughts about the whole notion."

"Oh?"

"Did you know that she has knives strapped to her knees and elbows?"

"Yes."

"I understand that they stick out whenever she bends one of her arms or legs."

"I think that's the idea, yes."

"Stragen tells me that once when she was young, three ruffians set upon her. She bent an elbow and slashed one across the throat, drove her knee into the second one's crotch, knocked the third down with her fist and knifed him in the heart. I'm not entirely sure that I want a woman like that for a wife. What did she say? When you told her about me, I mean?"

"She laughed, I'm afraid."

"*Laughed?*" Kring sounded shocked.

"I sort of gather that you're not exactly to her taste."

"Laughed? At *me?*"

"I think your decision's wise, though, friend Kring," Sparhawk said. "I don't think you two would get along very well."

Kring's eyes, however, were bulging. "*Laughed* at me, did she?" he said indignantly. "Well, we'll just *see* about that!" And he whirled his horse and rode back to join his men.

"That might have worked out if you hadn't told him about the laughing," Stragen observed. "Now he'll go out of his way to pursue her. I sort of like him, and I hate to think of what Mirtai's likely to do to him if he gets too persistent."

"Maybe we can talk him out of it," Sparhawk said.

"I wouldn't really count on it."

"What are you actually doing here, Stragen?" Sparhawk asked the blond man. "In the southern kingdoms, I mean?"

Stragen looked off toward a nearby monastery, his eyes distant. "Do you want the real truth, Sparhawk? Or would you like to give me a moment or two to fabricate a story for you?"

"Why don't we start out with the truth? If I don't like that, then you can make something up."

Stragen flashed him a quick grin. "All right," he agreed. "Up in Thalesia, I'm a counterfeit aristocrat. Down here, I'm the real thing—or very close to it. I associate with kings and queens, the nobility and the higher clergy on a more or less equal footing." He raised one hand. "I'm not deluding myself, my friend, so don't become concerned about my sanity. I know what I am—a bastard thief—and I know that my proximity to the gentry down here is only temporary and that it's based entirely on my usefulness. I'm tolerated, not really accepted. My ego, however, is sizeable."

"I noticed that," Sparhawk said with a gentle smile.

"Be nice, Sparhawk. Anyway, I'll accept this temporary and superficial equality—if only for the chance of some civilized conversation. Whores and thieves aren't really very stimulating companions, you understand, and about all they can really offer in the way of conversation is shop talk. Have you ever heard a group of whores sitting around talking shop?"

"I can't say that I have."

Stragen shuddered. "Absolutely awful. You learn things about men—and women—that you really don't want to know."

"This won't last. You know that, don't you, Stragen? The time will come when things will return to normal, and people will start closing their doors to you again."

"You're probably right, but it's fun to pretend for a little while. And when it's all over, I'll have that much more reason to despise you stinking aristocrats." Stragen paused. "I do sort of like *you*, though, Sparhawk—for the time being, at least."

As they rode northeasterly, they began to encounter groups of armed men. The Lamorks were never very far from full mobilization anyway, and they were able to respond to their king's call to arms quickly. In a melancholy repetition of the events of some five centuries earlier, men from all the kingdoms of western Eosia streamed toward a battlefield in Lamorkand. Sparhawk and Ulath passed the time conversing in Troll. Sparhawk was not certain when he might have occasion to talk to a troll, but since he had learned the language—even if by magic—it seemed a shame to let it slip away.

They reached Kadach at the end of a gloomy day when the sunset was staining the clouds to the west with an orange glow much like that of a distant forest fire. The wind from the east was stiff, and it carried with it the first faint chill of the oncoming winter. Kadach was a walled town, stiff and gray and rigidly unlovely. In what was to become a custom, Kring bade them good night and led his men on through the city and out the east gate to set up camp in the fields beyond. The Peloi were uncomfortable when confined in cities with such urban frivolities as walls, rooms, and roofs. Sparhawk and the rest of his friends found a comfortable inn near the center of town, bathed, changed clothes, and gathered in the common room for a supper of boiled ham and assorted vegetables. Sephrenia, as usual, declined the ham.

"I've never understood why people would want to boil a perfectly good ham," Sir Bevier noted with some distaste.

"Lamorks oversalt their hams when they cure them," Kalten explained. "You have to boil a Lamork ham for quite a while before it's edible. They're a strange people. They try to make everything an act of courage—even eating."

"Shall we go for a walk, Sparhawk?" Kurik suggested to his Lord after they had eaten.

"I think I've had just about enough exercise for one day."

"You *did* want to know which way Martel went, didn't you?"

"That's true, isn't it? All right, Kurik. Let's go nose around a bit."

When they reached the street, Sparhawk looked around. "This is likely to take us half the night," he said.

"Hardly," Kurik disagreed. "We'll go to the east gate first, and if we don't find anything out there, we'll try the north one."

"We just start asking people in the street?"

Kurik sighed. "Use your head, Sparhawk. When people are on a journey, they usually start out first thing in the morning—about the same time that other people are going to work. A lot of workmen drink their breakfasts, and so the taverns are usually open. When a tavern keeper's waiting for the first customer of the day, he watches the street fairly closely. Believe me, Sparhawk, if Martel left Kadach in the last three days, at least half a dozen tavern keepers saw him."

"You're an extraordinarily clever fellow, Kurik."

"Somebody in this party has to be, my Lord. As a group, knights don't spend a great deal of their time thinking."

"Your class prejudices are showing, Kurik."

"We all have our little flaws, I guess."

The streets of Kadach were very nearly deserted, and the few citizens abroad hurried along with their cloaks whipping around their ankles in the stiff wind. The torches set in the walls at intersections flared and streamed as the wind tore at them, casting wavering shadows that danced on the cobblestones of the streets.

The keeper of the first tavern they tried appeared to be his own best customer, and he had absolutely no idea of what time of day he normally opened his doors for business—or even what time of day it was now. The second tavern keeper was an unfriendly sort who spoke only in grunts. The third, however, proved to be a garrulous old fellow with a great fondness for conversation. "Well, now," he said, scratching at his head. "Lessee iff'n I kin call it t' mind. The last three days, y' say?"

"About that, yes," Kurik told him. "Our friend said he'd meet us here, but we got delayed, and it looks as if he went on without us."

"Kin ye describe him agin?"

"Fairly large man. He might have been wearing armor, but I couldn't swear to that. If his head was uncovered you'd have noticed him. He's got white hair."

"Can't seem t' recollect nobody like that. Might could be he went out one t'other gates."

"That's possible, I suppose, but we're fairly sure he was going east. Maybe he left town before you opened for business."

"Now that's hardly likely. I opens 'at door there when the watch opens the gate.

Some of the fellers as works here in town lives on farms out yonder, an' I usually gets some fairly brisk trade of a mornin'. Would yer friend a-bin travellin' alone?"

"No," Kurik replied. "He had a churchman with him and a lady of aristocratic background. There'd also have been a slack-jawed young fellow who looks about as stupid as a stump, and a big, burly man with a face like a gorilla."

"Oh, 'at bunch. You shoulda tole me 'bout ape-face right off. They rode thoo here 'bout daylight yestiddy mornin'. 'At 'ere gorilla ye was talkin' about, he clumb down off'n his horse an' he come in here bellerin' fer ale. He don't talk none too good, does he?"

"It usually takes him about half a day to think up an answer when somebody says hello to him."

The tavern keeper cackled shrilly. " 'At's him, all right. He don't smell none too sweet neither, does he?"

Kurik grinned at him and spun a coin across the counter to him. "Oh, I don't know," he said. "He isn't *too* much worse than an open cesspool. Thank you for the information, my friend."

"Y' think ye'll be able t' ketch up with 'em?"

"Oh, we'll catch them all right," Kurik replied fervently, "sooner or later. Were there any others with them?"

"No. Jist 'em five. 'Ceptin' fer the gorilla, they all had ther cloaks pulled up 'round ther heads. 'At's probably how come I couldn't see the one with the white hair. They was movin' along at a purty good clip, though, so's iff'n ye wants t' ketch 'em, yer gonna have t' push yer horses some."

"We can do that, my friend. Thanks again." And Kurik and Sparhawk went back out into the street. "Was that more or less what you needed to know, my Lord?" Kurik asked.

"That old fellow was a gold mine, Kurik. We've gained a bit of time on Martel, we know that he doesn't have any troops with him, and we know that he's going toward Moterra."

"We know something else, too, Sparhawk."

"Oh? What's that?"

"Adus still needs a bath."

Sparhawk laughed. "Adus always needs a bath. We'll probably have to pour about a hogshead of water on him before we bury him. Otherwise the ground might just spit him back out again. Let's go on back to the inn."

When Sparhawk and Kurik reentered the low-beamed common room of the inn, however, they found that their party had expanded slightly. Talen sat all innocent-eyed at the table with a number of hard stares focused on him.

"I'm a royal messenger," the boy said quickly as Sparhawk and Kurik approached the table, "so don't start reaching for your belts, either of you."

"You're a royal *what*?" Sparhawk asked him.

"I'm carrying a message to you from the queen, Sparhawk."

"Let's see the message."

"I committed it to memory. We really wouldn't want messages like that falling into unfriendly hands, would we?"

"All right. Let's hear it then."

"It's sort of private, Sparhawk."

"That's all right. We're among friends."

"I can't see why you're behaving this way. I'm just obeying the queen's command, that's all."

"The message, Talen."

"Well, she's getting ready to leave for Cimmura."

"That's nice." Sparhawk's tone was flat.

"And she's very worried about you."

"I'm touched."

"She's feeling well, though." The additions Talen was tacking on were growing more and more lame.

"That's good to know."

"She—uh—she says that she loves you."

"And?"

"Well—that's all, really."

"It's a strangely garbled message, Talen. I think maybe you've left something out. Why don't you go over it again?"

"Well—uh—she was talking to Mirtai and Platime—and me, of course—and she said that she wished there was some way she could get word to you to let you know what she was doing and exactly how she felt."

"She said this to you?"

"Well, I was in the room when she said it."

"Then we can't really say that she ordered you to come here, can we?"

"Not in so many words, I suppose, but aren't we supposed to sort of anticipate her wishes? She *is* the queen, after all."

"May I?" Sephrenia asked.

"Of course," Sparhawk replied. "I've already found out what *I* want to know."

"Maybe," she said, "maybe not." She turned to the boy. "Talen?"

"Yes, Sephrenia?"

"That's the weakest, most clumsy, and obviously false story I've ever heard from you. It doesn't even make any sense, particularly in view of the fact that she's already sent Stragen to do more or less the same thing. Is that really the best you could come up with?"

He even managed to look embarrassed. "It's not a lie," he said. "The queen said exactly what I told you she did."

"I'm sure she did, but what was it that moved you to come galloping after us to repeat some idle comments?"

He looked a little confused.

"Oh, dear," Sephrenia sighed. She began to scold Aphrael in Styric at some length.

"I think I missed something there." Kalten sounded baffled.

"I'll explain in a moment, Kalten," Sephrenia said. "Talen, you have an enormous gift for spontaneous prevarication. What happened to it? Why didn't you just cook up a lie that was at least a little bit plausible?"

He squirmed a bit. "It just wouldn't have seemed right," he said sullenly.

"You felt that you shouldn't really lie to your friends, is that it?"

"Something like that, I guess."

"Praise God!" Bevier said in stunned fervor.

"Don't be too quick to start offering up prayers of thanksgiving, Bevier," she told him. "Talen's apparent conversion isn't entirely what it seems to be. Aphrael's involved in it, and she's a terrible liar. Her convictions keep getting in the way."

"Flute?" Kurik said. "Again? Why would she send Talen here to join us?"

"Who knows?" Sephrenia laughed. "Maybe she likes him. Maybe it's part of her obsession with symmetry. Maybe it's something else—something she wants him to do."

"Then it wasn't really my fault, was it?" Talen said quickly.

"Probably not." She smiled at him.

"That makes me feel better," he said. "I knew you wouldn't like it if I came after you, and I almost choked on all that truth. You should have spanked her when you had the chance, Sparhawk."

"Do you have any idea at all of what they're talking about?" Stragen asked Tynian.

"Oh, yes," Tynian replied. "I'll explain it to you someday. You won't believe me, but I'll explain it anyway."

"Did you find out anything about Martel?" Kalten asked Sparhawk.

"He rode out through the east gate early yesterday morning."

"We've gained a day on him then. Did he have any troops with him?"

"Only Adus," Kurik replied.

"I think it's time for you to tell them everything, Sparhawk," Sephrenia said gravely.

"You're probably right," he agreed. He drew in a deep breath. "I'm afraid I haven't been entirely honest with you, my friends," he admitted.

"What's new and different about that?" Kalten asked.

Sparhawk ignored him. "I've been followed ever since I left Ghwerig's cave up in Thalesia."

"That crossbowman?" Ulath suggested.

"He might have been involved, but we can't really be sure. The crossbowman— and the people he had working for him—was probably something Martel came up with. I can't be sure if it's still a problem or not. The one who was responsible is dead now."

"Who was it?" Tynian asked intently.

"That's not particularly important." Sparhawk had decided some time ago to keep Perraine's involvement an absolute secret. "Martel has ways to force people to do what he tells them to do. That's one of the reasons we had to get away from the main body of the army. We wouldn't have been very effective if we'd had to spend most of our time trying to guard our backs from the attacks of people we could supposedly trust."

"Who was following you if it wasn't the crossbowman?" Ulath persisted.

Sparhawk told them about the shadowy form that had haunted him for months now.

"And you think it's Azash?" Tynian asked him.

"It sort of fits together, wouldn't you say?"

"How would Azash have known where Ghwerig's cave was?" Sir Bevier asked. "If that shadow's been following you since you left the cave, Azash would almost have to have known, wouldn't he?"

"Ghwerig was saying some fairly insulting things to Azash before Sparhawk killed him," Sephrenia told them. "There was a certain amount of evidence that Azash could hear him."

"What sort of insults?" Ulath asked curiously.

"Ghwerig was threatening to cook Azash and eat him," Kurik said shortly.

"That's a little daring—even for a Troll," Stragen noted.

"I'm not so sure," Ulath disagreed. "I think Ghwerig was totally safe in that cave of his—at least safe from Azash. He didn't have too much to protect him from Sparhawk as it turned out, though."

"Would one of you like to clarify that a bit?" Tynian asked him. "You Thalesians are the experts on Trolls."

"I'm not sure how much light we can throw on it," Stragen said. "We know a *little* bit more about Trolls than other Elenes, but not very much." He laughed. "When our ancestors first came to Thalesia, they couldn't tell Trolls from Ogres or bears. The Styrics told us most of what we know. It seems that when the Styrics first came to Thalesia, there were a few confrontations between the Younger Styric Gods and the Troll-Gods. The Troll-Gods realized fairly early on that they were badly overmatched, and they went into hiding. The legends say that Ghwerig and Bhelliom and the rings were sort of involved in hiding them. It's generally believed that they're somewhere in Ghwerig's cave and that Bhelliom's somehow protecting them from the Styric Gods." He looked at Ulath. "Wasn't that sort of what you were getting at?" he asked.

Ulath nodded. "When you combine Bhelliom and the Troll-Gods, you're talking about enough power to make even Azash step around it a little carefully. That's probably why Ghwerig could make the kind of threats he did."

"How many Troll-Gods are there?" Kalten asked.

"Five, aren't there, Ulath?" Stragen said.

Ulath nodded. "The God of eat," he supplied, "the God of kill, the God of—"

He broke off and gave Sephrenia a slightly embarrassed look. "Uh—let's just call it the God of fertility," he continued lamely. "Then there's the God of ice—all kinds of weather, I suppose—and the God of fire. Trolls have a fairly simple view of the world."

"Then Azash *would* have known about it when Sparhawk came out of the cave with Bhelliom and the rings," Tynian said, "and he probably would have followed."

"With unfriendly intentions," Talen added.

"He's done it before." Kurik shrugged. "He sent the Damork to chase Sparhawk all over Rendor and the Seeker to try to run us down in Lamorkand. At least he's predictable."

Bevier was frowning. "I think we're overlooking something here," he said.

"Such as?" Kalten asked.

"I can't quite put my finger on it," Bevier admitted, "but I get the feeling that it's fairly important."


They left Kadach at dawn the following morning and rode eastward toward the city of Moterra under skies that continued gray and cloudy. The murky sky, coupled with their conversation of the previous evening, made them all gloomy and downcast, and they rode mostly in silence. About noon, Sephrenia suggested a halt. "Gentlemen," she said quite firmly, "this isn't a funeral procession, you know."

"You could be wrong there, little mother," Kalten said to her. "I didn't find much to lift my spirits in last night's discussion."

"I think we'd all better start looking for cheerful things to think about," she told them. "We're riding into some fairly serious danger. Let's not make it worse by piling gloom and depression on top of it. People who *think* they're going to lose usually do."

"There's a lot of truth there," Ulath agreed. "One of my brother knights at Heid is absolutely convinced that every set of dice in the world hates him. I've never seen him win—not even once."

"If he's been playing with *your* dice, I can see why," Kalten accused.

"I'm hurt," Ulath said plaintively.

"Enough to throw those dice away?"

"Well, no, not quite *that* much. We really ought to come up with something cheerful to talk about, though."

"We could find some wayside tavern and get drunk, I suppose," Kalten said hopefully.

"No," Ulath shook his head. "I've found that ale just makes a bad mood worse. After four or five hours of drinking, we'd probably all be crying into our tankards."

"We could sing hymns," Bevier suggested brightly.

Kalten and Tynian exchanged a long look, and then they both sighed.

"Did I ever tell you about the time when I was down in Cammoria and this lady of high station became enamored of me?" Tynian began.

"Not that I recall," Kalten replied rather quickly.

"Well, as I remember it . . ." Tynian began, and then told them a long, amusing, and just slightly off-color account of what was probably an entirely fictitious amorous adventure. Ulath followed by telling them the story of the unfortunate Genidian Knight who had aroused a passion in the heart of an Ogress. His description of the singing of the love-stricken female reduced them all to helpless laughter. The stories, richly embellished with detail and humor, lightened their mood, and they all felt much better by sunset, when they halted for the day.

Even with frequent changes of horses, it took them twelve days to reach Moterra, an unlovely town lying on a flat, marshy plain extending out from the west fork of the River Geras. They reached the city about midday. Sparhawk and Kurik once again sought out information while the rest of the party rested their horses in preparation for the ride northward toward Paler. Since they still had a number of hours of daylight left, they saw no reason to spend the night in Moterra.

"Well?" Kalten asked Sparhawk as the big Pandion and his squire rejoined the group.

"Martel went north," Sparhawk answered.

"We're still right behind him then," Tynian said. "Did we pick up any more time?"

"No," Kurik replied. "He's still two days ahead of us."

"Well—" Tynian shrugged. "—since we're going that way anyhow—"

"How far is it to Paler?" Stragen asked.

"A hundred and fifty leagues," Kalten told him. "Fifteen days at least."

"We're moving on in the season," Kurik said. "We're bound to run into snow in the mountains of Zemoch."

"That's a cheery thought," Kalten said.

"It's always good to know what to expect."

The sky continued gloomy, though the air was cool and dry. About midway through their journey, they began to encounter the extensive diggings that had turned the ancient battlefield at Lake Randera into a wasteland. They saw a few of the treasure hunters, but passed them without incident.

Perhaps something had changed it, or perhaps it was because he was out of doors instead of in some candlelit room, but *this* time when Sparhawk caught that faint glimmer of darkness and menacing shadow at the very corner of his vision, something was actually there. It was late in the afternoon of a depressing day that they had spent riding through a landscape denuded of all vegetation and littered with great mounds of raw, dug-over earth. When Sparhawk caught that familiar flicker and its accompanying chill, he half turned in his saddle and looked squarely at the shadow that had haunted him for so long. He reined Faran in. "Sephrenia," he said quite calmly.

"Yes?"

"You wanted to see it. I think that if you turn around rather slowly, you'll be able to look as much as you want. It's just beyond that large pond of muddy water."

She turned to look.

"Can you see it?" he asked her.

"Quite clearly, dear one."

"Gentlemen," Sparhawk said to the others then, "our shadowy friend seems to have come out of hiding. It's about a hundred and fifty yards behind us."

They turned to look.

"It's almost like a cloud of some kind, isn't it?" Kalten noted.

"I've never seen a cloud like *that* before." Talen shuddered. "Dark, isn't it?"

"Why do you suppose it decided not to hide anymore?" Ulath murmured.

They all turned, looking to Sephrenia for some kind of explanation.

"Don't ask *me,* gentlemen," she said helplessly. "Something has changed, though."

"Well, at least we know that Sparhawk hasn't just been seeing things for all this time," Kalten said. "What do we do about it?"

"What *can* we do about it?" Ulath asked him. "You don't have much luck fighting with clouds and shadows with axes or swords."

"So? What do you suggest, then?"

"Ignore it." Ulath shrugged. "It's the king's highway, so it's not breaking any laws if it wants to follow along, I guess."

The next morning, however, the cloud was nowhere to be seen.

It was late in the autumn when they once again rode into the familiar city of Paler. As had become their custom, the Domi and his men camped outside the city walls, and Sparhawk and the others rode on to the same inn where they had stayed before.

"It's good to see you again, Sir Knight," the innkeeper greeted Sparhawk as the black-armored Pandion came back down the stairs.

"It's good to be back," Sparhawk replied, not really meaning it. "How far is it to the east gate from here?" he asked. It was time to go start asking questions about Martel again.

"About three streets over, my Lord," the innkeeper replied.

"It's closer than I thought." Then something occurred to Sparhawk. "I was just about to go out to ask around about a friend of mine who passed through Paler two days ago," he said. "You might be able to save me some time, neighbor."

"I'll do what I can, Sir Knight."

"He has white hair, and there's a fairly attractive lady with him, as well as a few others. It is possible that he stopped here in your inn?"

"Why, yes, my Lord. As a matter of fact, he did. They were asking questions about the road to Vileta—although I can't for the life of me think why anyone in his right mind would want to go into Zemoch at this particular time."

"He has something he wants to take care of there, and he's always been a rash and foolhardy man. Was I right? Was it two days ago when he stopped?"

"Exactly two days, my Lord. He's riding hard, judging from the condition of his horses."

"Do you happen to remember which room was his?"

"It's the one the lady with your party's staying in, my Lord."

"Thank you, neighbor," Sparhawk told him. "We certainly wouldn't want our friend to get away from us."

"Your friend was nice enough, but I certainly didn't care much for that big one who's with him. Does he improve at all once you get to know him?"

"Not noticeably, no. Thanks again, friend." Sparhawk went back upstairs and rapped on Sephrenia's door.

"Come in, Sparhawk," she replied.

"I wish you wouldn't do that," he said as he entered.

"Do what?"

"Call me by name before you've even seen me. Couldn't you at least pretend that you don't know who's knocking at your door?"

She laughed.

"Martel went through here two days ago, Sephrenia. He stayed in this very room. Could that in any way be useful to us?"

She thought about it a moment. "It may just be, Sparhawk. What did you have in mind?"

"I'd sort of like to find out what his plans are. He knows we're right on his heels, and he's likely to try to delay us. I'd like to get a few specifics on any traps he may be laying for us. Can you arrange to let me see him? Or hear him at least?"

She shook her head. "He's too far away."

"Well, so much for that idea."

"Perhaps not." She thought for a moment. "I think that perhaps it's time for you to get to know Bhelliom a little better, Sparhawk."

"Would you like to clarify that?"

"There's some sort of connection between Bhelliom and the Troll-Gods and the rings. Let's investigate that."

"Why involve the Troll-Gods at all, Sephrenia? If there's a way to use Bhelliom, why not just do that, and leave the Troll-Gods out of it altogether?"

"I'm not sure if Bhelliom would understand us, Sparhawk; and if it did, I'm not sure that *we'd* understand what it was doing to obey us."

"It collapsed that cave, didn't it?"

"That was very simple. This is a little more complicated. The Troll-Gods would be much easier to talk with, I think, and I want to find out just how closely Bhelliom's linked to them if I can—*and* just how much you can control them by using Bhelliom."

"You want to experiment, in other words."

"You might put it that way, I suppose, but it might be safer to experiment now, when there's nothing crucial at stake, than later, when our lives might hinge on the outcome. Lock the door, Sparhawk. Let's not expose the others to this just yet."

He crossed to the door and slid the iron bolt into place.

"You're not going to have time to think when you talk with the Troll-Gods, dear one, so get everything set in your mind before you start. You're going to issue commands and nothing else. Don't ask them questions, and don't seek out explanations. Just tell them to do things and don't worry about how they manage to obey. We want to see and hear the man who was in this room two sleeps ago. Just tell them to put his image—" She looked around the room, then pointed at the hearth. "—in that fire there. Tell Bhelliom that you *will* talk with one of the Troll-Gods— probably Khwaj, the Troll-God of fire. He's the most logical one to deal with flame and smoke." Sephrenia obviously knew a great deal more about the Troll-Gods than she had told them.

"Khwaj," Sparhawk repeated. Then he had a sudden idea. "What's the name of the Troll-God of eat?" he asked her.

"Ghnomb," she replied. "Why?"

"It's something I'm still working on. If I can put it together, I might try it and see if it works."

"Don't extemporize, Sparhawk. You know how I feel about surprises. Take off your gauntlets, and remove Bhelliom from the pouch. Don't let it out of your grasp, and be sure that the rings are touching it at all times. Do you still remember the Troll language?"

"Yes. Ulath and I have been practicing."

"Good. You can speak to Bhelliom in Elene, but you'll have to speak to Khwaj in his own tongue. Tell me what you did today—in Troll."

The words were halting at first, but after a few moments he became more fluent. The changeover from the Elene language to Troll involved a profound shift in his thinking. In their language itself lay some of the character of the Trolls. It was not a pleasant character, and it involved concepts entirely alien to the Elene mind—except at the deepest, most primitive level.

"All right," she told him, "come to the fire, and let's begin. Be like iron, Sparhawk. Don't hesitate or explain anything. Just give commands."

He nodded and removed his gauntlets. The two blood-red rings, one on each of his hands, glowed in the firelight. He reached inside his surcoat and took out the pouch. Then he and his tutor stood before the hearth and looked into the crackling flames. "Open the pouch," Sephrenia instructed.

He worked the knots free.

"Now, take Bhelliom out. Order it to bring Khwaj to you. Then tell Khwaj what you want. You don't have to be too explicit. Khwaj will understand your thoughts. Pray that you never understand his."

He drew in a deep breath and set the pouch down on the hearth. "Here goes," he said. He pulled the pouch open and took the Bhelliom out. The sapphire rose was icy cold as he touched it. He lifted it, trying to keep his sense of awe at the sight of it far away from his mind. "Blue-Rose!" he snapped, holding the jewel in both hands. "Bring the voice of Khwaj to me!"

He felt a strange shift in the jewel, and a single spot of bright red appeared deep within the azure petals. The Bhelliom suddenly grew hot in his hands.

"Khwaj!" Sparhawk barked in the language of Trolls, "I am Sparhawk-from-Elenia. I have the rings. Khwaj must do as I command."

Bhelliom shuddered in his hand.

"I seek Martel-from-Elenia," Sparhawk continued. "Martel-from-Elenia stayed in this place two sleeps ago. Khwaj *will* show Sparhawk-from-Elenia what he wishes to see in the fire. Khwaj *will* make it so Sparhawk-from-Elenia can hear what he wishes to hear. Khwaj *will* obey! *Now!*"

Faintly, as from very far away in some hollow place filled with echoes, there came a howl of rage, a howl overlaid with a crackling sound as of some huge fire. The flames dancing along the tops of the oak logs in the fireplace lowered until they were little more than a sickly glimmering. Then they rose, bright yellow and filling the entire opening with a sheet of nearly incandescent fire. Then they froze, no longer a flickering or a dancing but simply a flat, unwavering sheet of motionless yellow. The heat from the fireplace stopped at once as if a pane of thick glass had been set in front of it.

Sparhawk found himself looking into a tent. Martel, drawn and weary-looking, sat at a rough table across from Annias, who looked even worse.

"*Why* can't you find out where they are?" the Primate of Cimmura was demanding.

"I don't know, Annias," Martel grated. "I've called up every creature Otha gave me, and none of them has found anything."

"Oh, mighty Pandion," Annias sneered. "Maybe you should have stayed in your order longer to give Sephrenia time to teach you more than parlor tricks for the amusement of children."

"You're getting very close to the point of outliving your usefulness to me, Annias," Martel said ominously. "Otha and I can put *any* churchman on the archprelate's throne and achieve what we want. You're not really indispensable, you know." And that answered the question of just *who* was taking orders from *whom* once and for all.

The tent flap opened, and the apelike Adus slouched in. His armor was a mismatched accumulation of bits and pieces of rust-splotched steel drawn from a half dozen different cultures. Adus, Sparhawk noticed again, had no forehead. His hairline began at his shaggy eyebrows. "It died," he reported in a voice that was half snarl.

"I should make you walk, you idiot," Martel told him.

"It was a weak horse." Adus shrugged.

"It was perfectly fine until you spurred it to death. Go steal another one."

Adus grinned. "A farm horse?"

"Any kind of horse you can find. Don't take all night killing the farmer, though—or amusing yourself with his women. And don't burn the farmstead down. Let's not light up the sky and announce our location."

Adus laughed—at least it *sounded* like a laugh. Then he left the tent.

"How can you stand that brute?" Annias shuddered.

"Adus? He's not so bad. Think of him as a walking battle-ax. I use him for killing people; I don't sleep with him. Speaking of that, have you and Arissa resolved your differences yet?"

"That harlot!" Annias said with a certain contempt.

"You knew what she was when you took up with her, Annias," Martel told him. "I thought her depravity was part of what attracted you to her." Martel leaned back. "It must be Bhelliom," he mused.

"What must?"

"It's probably the Bhelliom that's keeping my creatures from locating Sparhawk."

"Wouldn't Azash himself be able to find out?"

"I don't give orders to Azash, Annias. If he wants me to know something, he tells me. It could just be that Bhelliom's more powerful than he is. When we get to his temple, you can ask him, if you're really curious about it. The question might offend him, but it's entirely up to you."

"How far have we come today?"

"No more than seven leagues. Our pace slowed noticeably after Adus ripped out his horse's guts with his spurs."

"How far to the Zemoch border?"

Martel unrolled a map and consulted it. "I make it about fifty more leagues—five days or so. Sparhawk can't be more than three days behind us, so we'll have to keep up the pace."

"I'm exhausted, Martel. I can't keep on going like this."

"Every time you start brooding about how tired you are, just imagine how it would feel to have Sparhawk's sword sliding through your guts—or how exquisitely painful it's going to be when Ehlana beheads you with a pair of sewing scissors—or a bread knife."

"Sometimes I wish I'd never met you, Martel."

"The feeling's entirely mutual, old boy. Once we cross the border into Zemoch, we should be able to slow Sparhawk down a bit. A few ambushes along the way ought to make him a bit more cautious."

"We were ordered not to kill him," Annias objected.

"Don't be an idiot. As long as he has Bhelliom, no human could possibly kill him. We were ordered not to kill *him*—even if we could—but Azash didn't say anything about the others. The loss of a few of his companions might upset our invincible enemy. He doesn't look very much like it, but Sparhawk's a sentimentalist at heart. You'd better go get some sleep. We'll start out again just as soon as Adus gets back."

"In the dark?" Annias sounded incredulous.

"What's the matter, Annias? Are you afraid of the dark? Think about swords in the belly or the sound of a bread knife sawing on your neck bone. That should make you brave."

"Khwaj!" Sparhawk said sharply. "Enough! Go away now!"

The fire returned to normal.

"Blue-Rose!" Sparhawk said then. "Bring the voice of Ghnomb to me!"

"What are you *doing*?" Sephrenia exclaimed, but Bhelliom had already started to respond. The pinpoint of light within the glowing blue petals was a sickly mixture of green and yellow, and Sparhawk suddenly had a foul taste in his mouth, a taste much like the smell of half-decayed meat.

"Ghnomb!" Sparhawk said in that harsh voice. "I am Sparhawk-from-Elenia, and I have the rings. Ghnomb must do as I command. I hunt. Ghnomb will help me hunt. I am two sleeps behind the man-thing that is my prey. Ghnomb will make it so that my hunters and I can catch the man-thing we seek. Sparhawk-from-Elenia will tell Ghnomb when, and Ghnomb will aid our hunt. Ghnomb *will* obey!"

Again there was that hollow, echoing howl of rage, a howl filled this time with a slobbering gnawing sound and a horrid, wet smacking of lips.

"Ghnomb! Go away now!" Sparhawk commanded. "Ghnomb *will* come again at Sparhawk-from-Elenia's command!"

The greenish-yellow spot vanished, and Sparhawk thrust the Bhelliom back into the pouch.

"Are you *mad*?" Sephrenia exclaimed.

"No, I don't think so. I want to be so close behind Martel that he won't have time to set up any ambushes." He frowned. "It's beginning to look as if the attempts to kill me really *were* Martel's own idea," he said. "He seems to have different orders now. That clarifies things a bit, but now I have to start worrying about how to protect you and the others." He made a face. "There's always *something*, isn't there?"

## CHAPTER TWENTY-TWO

"Sparhawk." It was Kurik, and he was shaking his Lord into wakefulness. "It's about an hour before dawn. You wanted me to wake you."

"Don't you ever sleep?" Sparhawk sat up in his bed, yawning. Then he swung his legs out of bed and put his feet on the floor.

"I slept fine." Kurik looked critically at his friend. "You're not eating enough," he accused. "Your bones are sticking out. Get dressed. I'll go wake the others, and then I'll come back and help you into your armor."

Sparhawk rose and pulled on his quilted and rust-splotched undergarments.

"Very chic," Stragen observed sardonically from the doorway. "Is there some obscure part of the knightly code that prohibits laundering those garments?"

"They take a week to dry."

"Are they really necessary?"

"Have you ever worn armor, Stragen?"

"God forbid."

"Try it sometime. The padding keeps the armor from grinding off your skin in unusual places."

"Ah, the things we endure in order to be stylish."

"Are you really planning to turn back at the Zemoch border?"

"The queen's orders, old boy. Besides, I'd just be in your way. I'm profoundly unsuited to confront a God. Frankly, I think you're insane—no offense intended, of course."

"Are you going back to Emsat from Cimmura?"

"If your wife gives me permission to leave. I really should get back—if only to check over the books. Tel's fairly dependable, but he *is* a thief, after all."

"And then?"

"Who knows?" Stragen shrugged. "I'm at loose ends in the world, Sparhawk. I have a unique sort of freedom. I don't have to do anything I don't want to do. Oh, I almost forgot. I didn't really come by this morning to discuss the ins and outs of liberty with you." He reached inside his doublet. "A letter for you, my Lord," he said with a mocking bow. "From your wife, I believe."

"How many of these do you have?" Sparhawk asked, taking the folded sheet. Stragen had delivered one of Ehlana's brief, impassioned notes to her husband in Kadach and yet another in Moterra.

"That's a state secret, my friend."

"Do you have some sort of agenda? Or are you distributing them when the spirit moves you?"

"A little of each, old boy. There *is* an agenda, of course, but I'm to use my own judgment in these matters. If I see that you're becoming downcast or moody, I'm supposed to brighten your day. I'll leave you to your reading now." He stepped back out into the hallway and moved off down the corridor toward the stairs leading to the lower floor of the inn.

Sparhawk broke the seal and opened Ehlana's letter.

Beloved,

If all has gone well, you're in Paler by now—this is terribly awkward, you know. I'm trying to look into the future, and my eyes aren't strong enough for that. I'm talking to you from weeks and weeks in the past, and I haven't the faintest idea of what's been happening to you. I dare not tell you of my anguish or my desolation at this unnatural separation, for should I unburden my heart to you, I would weaken your resolve, and that could endanger you. I love you, my Sparhawk, and I am torn between wishing that I were a man so that I could share your danger and, if need be, lay down my life for you, and glorying in the fact that I am a woman and can lose myself in your embrace.

From there Sparhawk's young queen launched into detailed reminiscence of their wedding night that was far too personal and private to bear repeating.

"How was the queen's letter?" Stragen asked as they were saddling their horses in the courtyard while the emerging dawn laid a dirty stain across the cloudy eastern horizon.

"Literate," Sparhawk replied laconically.

"That's an unusual characterization."

"Sometimes we lose sight of the real person lying behind the state robes, Stragen. Ehlana's a queen, right enough, but she's also an eighteen-year-old girl who seems to have read too many of the wrong books."

"I'd hardly have expected such a clinical description from a new bridegroom."

"I have a lot on my mind just now." Sparhawk pulled the cinch of his saddle tighter. Faran grunted, filled his belly with air, and deliberately stepped on his master's foot. Almost absently, the Pandion kneed his mount in the stomach. "Keep your eyes open today, Stragen," he advised. "Some peculiar things are likely to happen."

"Such as what?"

"I'm not really sure. If everything goes well, we'll cover a great deal more ground today than usual. Stay with the Domi and his Peloi. They're an emotional people, and out-of-the-ordinary things sometimes upset them. Just keep assuring them that everything's under control."

"Is it?"

"I haven't got the foggiest idea, old boy. I'm trying very hard to be optimistic about it, however." Stragen, he felt, sort of had that coming.

The dawn came slowly that morning, since the cloud cover rolling in from the east had thickened during the night. At the top of the long slope leading up from the northern end of the lead-gray sheet of Lake Randera, Kring and his Peloi joined them. "It's good to be back in Pelosia again, friend Sparhawk," Kring said, a good-humored grin on his scarred face, "even in this cluttered and overplowed part of the kingdom."

"How many days to the Zemoch border, Domi?" Tynian asked.

"Five or six, friend Tynian," the Domi replied.

"We'll start out in just a few moments," Sparhawk told his friends. "There's something Sephrenia and I have to do." He motioned to his tutor, and they rode some distance away from the group sitting their horses on the grassy hilltop. "Well?" he said to her.

"Must you really do this, dear one?" she pleaded.

"I think so, yes. It's the only way I can think of to protect you and the others from ambushes when we reach the Zemoch border." He reached inside his surcoat, removed the pouch, and took off his gauntlets. Once again the Bhelliom felt very cold in his hands, a chill almost like the touch of ice. "Blue-Rose!" he commanded, "bring the voice of Ghnomb to me!"

The jewel sullenly warmed in his hands. Then the greenish-yellow spot appeared within its depths, accompanied by the rotten-meat taste in Sparhawk's mouth. "Ghnomb!" he said, "I am Sparhawk-from-Elenia, and I have the rings. I hunt now. Ghnomb *will* aid my hunting as I commanded. Ghnomb *will* do it! *Now!*"

He waited tensely, but nothing happened. He sighed. "Ghnomb!" he said. "Go away now!" He put the sapphire rose back into its pouch, knotted the strings, and thrust the pouch back inside his surcoat. "Well," he said ruefully, "so much for that. You said he'd let me know if he couldn't help. He just let me know, all right. It's a little awkward to find out about it at this stage of the proceedings, though."

"Don't give up just yet, Sparhawk," Sephrenia told him.

"Nothing happened, little mother."

"Don't be too sure."

"Well, let's go on back. It seems we're going to have to do this the hard way."

The party rode out at a brisk trot, moving down the far side of the hill with the pale disk of the new-risen sun hanging behind the clouds on the eastern horizon. The farmland lying to the east of Paler was in the last stages of the harvest, and serfs were already in the fields, small figures in dun or blue looking like immobile toys far back from the road.

"Serfdom doesn't seem to encourage much enthusiasm for work," Kurik observed critically. "Those people out there don't seem to be moving at all."

"If I were a serf, I don't think I'd be very interested in exerting myself either," Kalten said.

They rode on at a canter, crossed a wide valley, and climbed a low chain of hills. The clouds were a bit thinner here to the east, and the sun, just above the horizon, was more distinct. Kring sent out his patrols, and they rode on.

Something was wrong, but Sparhawk could not exactly put his finger on what it was. The air was very still, and the sound of the horses' hooves seemed quite loud and unnaturally crisp in the soft dirt of the road. Sparhawk looked around and saw that his friends' expressions seemed uneasy.

They were halfway across the next valley when Kurik reined in with a sudden oath. "*That* does it," he said.

"What's the matter?" Sparhawk asked him.

"How long would you say we've been on the road?"

"An hour or so. Why?"

"Look at the sun, Sparhawk."

Sparhawk looked at the eastern horizon where the almost obscured disk of the sun hung just over a gently rounded line of hills. "It seems to be where it always is, Kurik," he said. "Nobody's moved it."

"That's just the point, Sparhawk. It's *not* moving. It hasn't moved an inch since we started. It came up, and then it stopped."

They all stared toward the east.

"It's fairly common, Kurik," Tynian said. "We've been riding up and down hills. That always seems to put the sun in a different position. Where it seems to be depends on how high up—or down—the hill you are."

"I thought so myself, Sir Tynian—at first—but I'll swear to you that the sun hasn't moved since we left that hilltop to the east of Paler."

"Be serious, Kurik," Kalten scoffed. "The sun *has* to move."

"Not *this* morning, apparently. What's going on here?"

"Sir Sparhawk!" Berit's voice was shrill, hovering just on the edge of hysteria. "Look!"

Sparhawk turned his head in the direction the apprentice knight was pointing a shaking hand.

It was a bird—a completely ordinary-looking bird, a lark of some kind, Sparhawk judged. Nothing at all was unusual about it—if one were to overlook the fact that it hung absolutely motionless in mid-air, looking for all the world as if it had been stuck there with a pin.

They all looked around, their eyes a little wild. Then Sephrenia began to laugh.

"I don't really see anything funny about this, Sephrenia," Kurik told her.

"Everything's fine, gentlemen," she told them.

"*Fine?*" Tynian said. "What's happened to the sun and that idiotic bird?"

"Sparhawk stopped the sun—and the bird."

"*Stopped the sun!*" Bevier exclaimed. "That's impossible!"

"Apparently not. Sparhawk talked with one of the Troll-Gods last night," she told them. "He said that we were hunting and that our prey was far ahead of us. He asked the Troll-God Ghnomb to help us catch up, and Ghnomb seems to be doing just that."

"I don't follow you," Kalten said. "What's the sun got to do with hunting?"

"It's not all that complicated, Kalten," she said calmly. "Ghnomb stopped time, that's all."

"*That's all?* How do you stop time?"

"I have no idea." She frowned. "Maybe 'stopping time' isn't quite accurate. What's really happening is that we're moving outside of time. We're in that winking of an eye between one second and the next."

"What's keeping that bird up in the air, Lady Sephrenia?" Berit demanded.

"His last wingbeat, probably. The rest of the world is moving along quite normally. People out there aren't even aware of the fact that we're passing through. When the Gods do the things we ask them to do, they don't always do them in the way we expect. When Sparhawk told Ghnomb that he wanted to catch up to Martel, he was thinking about time more than the miles, so Ghnomb is moving us through time, not distance. He'll control time for as long as it takes us. Covering the distance is up to us."

Then Stragen came forward at a gallop. "Sparhawk!" he cried. "What in God's name did you do?"

Sparhawk briefly explained. "Just go back and calm the Peloi. Tell them that it's an enchantment. Explain that the world is frozen. Nothing will move until we get to where we want to go."

"Is that the truth?"

"More or less, yes."

"Do you actually think they'll believe me?"

"Invite them to come up with their own explanations if they don't like mine."

"You *can* unfreeze things later, can't you?"

"Of course—at least I hope so."

"Ah—Sephrenia?" Talen said tentatively. "All the rest of the world is stopped dead, right?"

"Well, that's the way it appears to *us*. Nobody else perceives it that way, though."

"Other people can't even see us then, right?"

"They won't even know we're here."

A slow, almost reverent smile came to the boy's lips. "Well, now," he said. "Well, well, well."

Stragen's eyes also became very bright. "Well now indeed, your Grace," he agreed.

"Never mind, you two," Sephrenia said sharply.

"Stragen," Sparhawk added as an afterthought, "tell Kring that there's no real need to hurry. We might as well conserve the horses. Nobody out there is going to go anywhere or do anything until we get to where we want to go anyway."

It was eerie to canter through that perpetual murky sunrise. It was neither cold nor warm nor damp nor dry. The world around them was silent, and unmoving birds dotted the air. Serfs stood like statues in the fields, and once they passed a tall white birch tree that had been brushed by a passing breeze just before the Troll-God Ghnomb had frozen time. A cloud of motionless golden leaves hung in the air to the leeward side of the tree.

"What time do you think it is?" Kalten asked after they had ridden for several leagues.

Ulath squinted at the sky. "I make it about sunrise," he replied.

"Oh, very, very funny, Ulath," Kalten said sarcastically. "I don't know about the rest of you, but I'm starting to get a little hungry."

"You were born hungry," Sparhawk told him.

They ate trail rations and moved on again. There was no real need to hurry, but the sense of urgency they had all felt since they had left Chyrellos nagged at them, and they were soon cantering. To have proceeded at a leisurely walk would have seemed unnatural.

An hour or so later—though it was really impossible to tell—Kring came up from the rear. "I think there's something behind us, friend Sparhawk," he said. Kring's tone had a respectful awe about it. It's not every day that one can talk with a man who stops the sun.

Sparhawk looked at him sharply. "Are you sure?" he asked.

"Not really," Kring admitted. "It's a feeling more than anything. There's a very dark cloud low to the ground off to the south. It's a goodly way off, so it's hard to tell for sure, but it seems to be pacing us."

Sparhawk looked toward the south. It was that same cloud again, larger, blacker, and more ominous. The shadow could follow him even *here*, it appeared. "Have you seen it move at all?" he asked Kring.

"No, but we've come quite some distance since we stopped to eat, and it's still just over my right shoulder where it was when we set out."

"Keep an eye on it," Sparhawk said tersely. "See if you can catch it actually moving."

"Right," the Domi agreed, wheeling his horse.

They set up camp for the "night" after they had covered approximately the distance they would have gone in a normal day. The horses were confused, and Faran kept watching Sparhawk with a hard-eyed look of suspicion.

"It's not *my* fault, Faran," Sparhawk said as he unsaddled the big roan.

"How can you lie to that poor beast like that, Sparhawk?" Kalten said from nearby. "Have you no shame? It *is* your fault."

Sparhawk slept poorly. The unchanging light was always there. He slept for as long as he could, and then rose. The others were also stirring.

"Good morning, Sparhawk," Sephrenia said ironically. Her expression was a bit put out.

"What's the matter?"

"I miss my morning tea. I tried to heat some rocks in order to boil water, but it didn't work. Nothing works, Sparhawk—no spells, no magic, nothing. We're totally defenseless in this never-never land you and Ghnomb have created, you know."

"What can attack us, little mother?" he asked gravely. "We're outside of time. We're someplace where nothing can reach us."

It was about "noon" when they discovered just how wrong that particular assessment had been.

"It's moving, Sparhawk!" Talen shouted as they approached an immobile village. "That cloud! It's moving!"

The cloud that Kring had noticed the day before was definitely moving now. It was inky black. It rolled across the ground toward the small cluster of thatch-roofed serfs' huts huddled in a shallow dale, and a low rumble of sullen thunder, the first sound they had heard since Ghnomb had locked them in time, accompanied its inexorable march. Behind it, the trees and grasses were all dead and decaying, as if that momentary touch of darkness had blighted them in an instant. The cloud engulfed the village, and when it had passed, the village was gone as if it had never existed.

As the cloud drew nearer, Sparhawk heard a rhythmic sound, a kind of thudding as of dozens of bare heels striking the earth, and accompanying that a brutish grunting as might come from a throng of beasts uttering low, guttural barks in evenly spaced unison.

"Sparhawk!" Sephrenia cried urgently. "Use the Bhelliom! Break up that cloud! Call Khwaj!"

Sparhawk fumbled with the pouch, then threw his gauntlets to the ground and tore open the canvas sack with his bare hands. He lifted out the sapphire rose in both hands. "Blue-Rose!" he half shouted. "Bring Khwaj!" The Bhelliom grew hot in his hands, and that single spark of red appeared in its petals.

"Khwaj!" Sparhawk half shouted. "I am Sparhawk-from-Elenia! Khwaj *will* burn away the dark that comes! Khwaj *will* make it so Sparhawk-from-Elenia can see what is inside the cloud! Do it, Khwaj! *Now!*"

Again there was that howl of frustration and rage as the Troll-God was compelled against his will to obey. Then, immediately in front of the rolling black cloud there rose a long, high sheet of roaring flame. Brighter and brighter the flame grew, and Sparhawk could feel the waves of intense heat blasting back at them from the wall of fire. The cloud advanced inexorably, seeming to ignore the wall.

"Blue-Rose!" Sparhawk snarled in the Troll tongue. "Help Khwaj! Blue-Rose *will* send its power and the power of all the Troll-Gods to help Khwaj! Do it! *Now!*"

The answering blast of power nearly knocked Sparhawk from his saddle, and Faran reeled back, flattening his ears and baring his teeth.

Then the cloud stopped. Great rents and tears appeared in it, only to be almost instantly repaired. The flame undulated, rising, then falling into sickly glimmerings, then flaring anew as the two forces contended with each other. At last the darkness of the cloud began to fade, even as night fades from the sky with the approach of dawn. The flames grew higher, more intensely bright. The cloud sickened yet more. It grew wispy and tattered.

"We're winning!" Kalten exclaimed.

"We?" Kurik said, picking up Sparhawk's gauntlets.

Then, as if it had been ripped away by a gale, the cloud streamed away. Sparhawk and his friends saw what had made the grunting sound. They were immense and humanlike, which is to say that they had arms and legs and heads. They were dressed in furs and carried weapons crafted of stone—axes and spears for the most part. Their humanity ended there. They had receding brows and protruding, muzzlelike mouths, and they were not so much hairy as they were furred. Although the cloud had dissipated, they continued their advance, a kind of shuffling trot. Their feet struck the ground in unison, and they barked that guttural grunt with each thudding step. They momentarily paused at regular intervals, and from somewhere in their midst there arose a high-pitched wail, a kind of shrill ululation. Then the rhythmic barking and stamping trot would begin again. They wore helmets of a sort, the skullcaps of unimaginable beasts decorated with horns, and their faces were smeared with colored mud in intricate designs.

"Are they Trolls?" Kalten's voice was shrill.

"Not like any Trolls I've ever seen," Ulath replied, reaching for his ax.

"All right, my children!" the Domi shouted to his men. "Let us clear the beasts from our path!" He drew his saber, held it aloft, and shouted a great war cry.

The Peloi charged.

"Kring!" Sparhawk yelled. "Wait!"

But it was too late. Once unleashed, the savage tribesmen from the eastern marches of Pelosia could not again be reined in.

Sparhawk swore. He stuffed the Bhelliom inside his surcoat. "Berit!" he commanded, "take Sephrenia and Talen to the rear! The rest of you, let's go lend a hand!"

It was not an organized fight in any sense of the word that civilized men would understand. After the first charge of Kring's tribesmen, everything disintegrated into a general mêlée of random savagery. The Church Knights discovered almost immediately that the grotesque creatures they faced did not seem to feel pain. It was impossible to determine if this was a natural characteristic of their species or if whatever had unleashed them had provided them with some additional defense. Beneath their shaggy fur lay a hide of unnatural toughness. This is not to say that swords bounced off them, but more often than not they did not cut cleanly. The best strokes opened only minimal wounds.

The Peloi, however, appeared to be having greater success with their sabers. The quick thrust of a sharp-pointed weapon was more effective than the massive overhand blow of heavy broadswords, and once their leathery hides had been penetrated, the savage brutes howled with pain. Stragen, his eyes alight, rode through the shaggy mass, the point of his slender rapier dancing, avoiding the clumsy strokes of stone axes, slipping the brutal thrusts of flint-tipped spears, and then sinking effortlessly, almost delicately, deep into fur-covered bodies. "Sparhawk!" he shouted. "Their hearts are lower down in their bodies! Thrust at the belly, not the chest!"

It grew easier then. The Church Knights altered their tactics, thrusting with the points of their swords rather than chopping with the broad blades. Bevier regretfully hung his lochaber from his saddle horn and drew his sword. Kurik discarded his mace and drew his short blade. Ulath, however, stubbornly clung to his ax. His only concession to the exigencies of the situation was to use both hands to swing the weapon. His prodigious strength was sufficient to overcome such natural defenses as horn-tough hide and inch-thick skulls.

The tide of the struggle turned then. The huge, uncomprehending beasts were unable to adjust to a changing situation, and more and more of them fell to the thrusting swords. One last, small cluster continued to fight even after the majority of their pack mates had been slain, but the lightninglike dashes of Kring's warriors whittled them away. The last one left standing was bleeding from a dozen saber thrusts. He raised his brutish face and shrieked that high-pitched ululation. The sound cut off abruptly as Ulath rode in, stood up in his stirrups to raise his ax high overhead, and then split the wailing brute's head from crown to chin.

Sparhawk wheeled, his bloody sword in his fist, but all the creatures had fallen. He looked around more closely. Their victory had been costly. A dozen of Kring's men had been felled—not merely felled, but torn apart as well—and fully as many lay groaning on the bloody ground.

Kring sat cross-legged on the turf, cradling the head of one of his dying men. His face was filled with sorrow.

"I'm sorry, Domi," Sparhawk said. "Find out how many of your men are injured. We'll work out some way to have them cared for. How close would you say we are to the lands of your people?"

"A day and a half of hard riding, friend Sparhawk," Kring replied, sadly closing the vacant eyes of the warrior who had just died, "a bit less than twenty leagues."

Sparhawk rode toward the rear where Berit sat his horse with his ax in his hands guarding Talen and Sephrenia.

"Is it over?" Sephrenia asked, her eyes averted.

"Yes," Sparhawk replied, dismounting. "What were they, little mother? They looked like Trolls, but Ulath didn't think they really were."

"They were dawn-men, Sparhawk. It's a very old and very difficult spell. The Gods—and a few of the most powerful magicians of Styricum—can reach back into time and bring things, creatures and men, forward. The dawn-men haven't walked this earth for countless thousands of years. That's what we all were once—Elenes, Styrics, even Trolls."

"Are you saying that humans and Trolls are related?" he asked her incredulously.

"Distantly. We've all changed over the eons. Trolls went one way, and we went another."

"Ghnomb's frozen instant doesn't appear to be as safe as we thought it was."

"No. Definitely not."

"I think it's time to set the sun in motion again. We don't seem to be able to hide from whatever's chasing us by slipping through the cracks in time, and Styric magic doesn't work here. We'll be safer in ordinary time."

"I think you're right, Sparhawk."

Sparhawk took Bhelliom from its pouch once more and commanded Ghnomb to break the spell.

Kring's Peloi fashioned litters in which to carry their dead and wounded, and the party moved on, relieved to some degree that the birds actually flew now and that the sun was moving once again.

The next morning a roving Peloi patrol found them, and Kring rode forth to confer with his friends. His face was bleak when he returned. "The Zemochs are setting fire to the grass," he said angrily. "I won't be able to help you much longer, friend Sparhawk. We have to protect our pastures, and that means we'll have to spread out all over our lands."

Bevier looked at him speculatively. "Wouldn't it be easier if the Zemochs all gathered in one place, Domi?" he asked.

"It would indeed, friend Bevier, but why would they do that?"

"To capture something of value, friend Kring."

Kring looked interested. "Such as what?"

"Gold." Bevier shrugged. "And women, and your herds."

Kring looked shocked.

"It would be a trap, of course," Bevier continued. "You gather all your herds and your treasures and your womenfolk in one place with only a few of your Peloi to guard them. Then take the rest of your warriors and ride off, making sure that Zemoch scouts can see you leave. Then, once it gets dark, you slip back and take up positions nearby, keeping well out of sight. The Zemochs will all come running to steal your herds and treasures and women. Then you can fall on them all at once. That way you spare yourself the trouble of hunting them down one by one. Besides, it would give your women a glorious opportunity to witness your bravery. I'm told that women melt with love when they have the chance to watch their menfolk destroy a hated enemy." Bevier's grin was sly.

Kring's eyes narrowed as he thought it over. "I like it!" he burst out after a moment. "God strike me blind if I don't! We'll do it!" And he rode off to tell his people.

"Bevier," Tynian said, "sometimes you amaze me."

"It's a fairly standard strategy for light cavalry, Tynian," the young Cyrinic said modestly. "I came across it in my study of military history. Lamork barons used that ploy a number of times before they started building castles."

"I know, but you actually suggested using women for bait. I think you're just a little more worldly than you appear, my friend."

Bevier blushed.

They followed after Kring at a somewhat slower pace, hindered by the wounded and the sorrowful line of horses carrying the dead. Kalten had a distant look on his face, and he seemed to be counting something up on his fingers.

"What's the trouble?" Sparhawk asked him.

"I'm trying to figure up just how much time we gained on Martel."

"Not quite a day and a half," Talen said promptly. "A day and a third, actually. We're about six or seven hours behind him now. We average about a league an hour."

"Twenty miles then," Kalten said. "You know, Sparhawk, if we rode all night tonight, we could be right inside his camp when the sun rises tomorrow."

"We're not going to ride at night, Kalten. There's something very unfriendly out there, and I'd rather not have it surprise us in the dark."

They made camp at sunset, and after they had eaten, Sparhawk and the others gathered in a large pavilion to consider their options.

"We more or less know what we're going to do," Sparhawk began. "Getting to the border shouldn't be any problem. Kring's going to lead his men away from his womenfolk anyway, so we'll have most of the Peloi warriors with us for at least part of the way. That's going to keep the Zemoch conventional forces at a distance, so we'll be safe from them until we reach the border. It's after we cross that line that we'll run into trouble, and the key to that is Martel. We're still going to have to push him to the point that he won't have time to gather up Zemochs to stand in our way."

"Make up your mind, Sparhawk," Kalten said. "First you say we're not going to ride at night, and then you say you're going to push Martel."

"We don't have to be actually on top of him to push him, Kalten. As long as he *thinks* we're close, he'll start running. I think I'll have a little talk with him while I've still got some daylight." He looked around. "I'll need about a dozen candles," he said. "Berit, would you mind?"

"Of course not, Sir Sparhawk."

"Set them up on this table—close together and all in a row." Sparhawk reached inside his surcoat and took out the Bhelliom again. He put it down on the table and laid a cloth over it to hide its seduction. When the lighted candles were in place, he uncovered the jewel and laid his ringed hands on it. "Blue-Rose," he commanded, "bring Khwaj to me!"

The stone grew hot under his hands again, and the glowing red spot appeared deep within its petals. "Khwaj!" Sparhawk said sharply. "You know me. I will see the place where my enemy will sleep tonight. Make it appear in the fire, Khwaj! Now!"

The howl of anger was no longer a howl, but had diminished to a sullen whine. The candle flames lengthened, and their edges joined to form a solid sheet of bright yellow fire. The image appeared in the fire.

It was a small encampment, three tents only, and it lay in a grassy basin with a small lake at its center. A grove of dark cedar trees stood across the lake from the camp, and a single campfire flickered in the lowering dusk at the center of that half circle of tents on the lake shore. Sparhawk carefully fixed the details in his mind. "Take us closer to the fire, Khwaj!" he barked. "Make it so that we can hear what is being said."

The image changed as the apparent viewpoint drew nearer. Martel and the others sat around the fire, their faces gaunt with exhaustion. Sparhawk motioned to his friends, and they all leaned forward to listen.

"Where are they, Martel?" Arissa was asking acidly. "Where are these brave Zemochs you counted on to protect us? Gathering wildflowers?"

"They're diverting the Peloi, Princess," Martel replied. "Do you really want those savages to catch up with us? Don't worry, Arissa. If your appetites are growing uncontrollable, I'll lend you Adus. He doesn't smell very nice, but that's no great drawback where you're concerned, is it?"

Her eyes blazed with sudden hatred, but Martel ignored her. "The Zemochs will hold off the Peloi," he said to Annias, "and unless Sparhawk's been riding horses to death—which he'd never do—he's still three days behind us. We don't really need any Zemochs until we cross the border. That's when I'll want to find some of them to start laying traps for my dear brother and his friends."

"Khwaj!" Sparhawk said shortly, "make it so that they can hear me! Now!"

The candle flames flickered, then steadied again.

"Awfully nice camp you have there, Martel," Sparhawk said in an offhand manner. "Are there any fish in the lake?"

"Sparhawk!" Martel gasped. "How can you reach this far?"

"Far, old boy? It's not really all that far at all. I'm almost on top of you. If it'd been me, though, I'd have made camp in that cedar grove across the lake. There are whole races of people who want to kill you, brother mine, and it's hardly safe to make camp right out in the open the way you have."

Martel sprang to his feet. "Get the horses!" he shouted to Adus.

"Leaving so soon, Martel?" Sparhawk asked mildly. "What a shame. I was so looking forward to meeting you face-to-face again. Ah, well, no matter. I'll see you first thing in the morning. I think we can both stand to wait that long." Sparhawk's grin was vicious as he watched the five of them saddling their horses. Their movements were panicky, and their eyes darted about wildly. They clambered onto their mounts and bolted off toward the east at a dead run, flogging their horses unmercifully.

"Come back, Martel," Sparhawk called after them. "You forgot your tents."

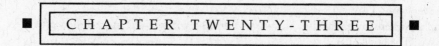

# CHAPTER TWENTY-THREE

The land of the Peloi was a vast, unfenced grassland that had never known the touch of the plow. The winds of late autumn swept that eternal grassland under a lowering sky, sighing a mournful dirge for summer. They rode eastward toward a high, rocky pinnacle out in the center of the plain with their cloaks drawn tightly around them to ward off the arid chill, and with their mood made somber by the unending gloom.

They reached the rock pinnacle late that afternoon and found the land around it bustling with activity. Kring, who had gone on ahead to gather the Peloi, rode up to meet them, a rough bandage encircling his head.

"What happened to you, friend Kring?" Tynian asked him.

"There was some small dissatisfaction with Sir Bevier's plan, I'm afraid," Kring replied ruefully. "One of the dissidents slipped up behind me."

"I would never have thought Peloi warriors would attack from the rear."

"Of course they wouldn't, but my attacker wasn't a man. A Peloi woman of high rank sneaked around behind me and banged me on the head with a cooking pot."

"I hope you had her suitably punished."

"I couldn't really do that, friend Tynian. She's my own sister. Our mother would never have forgiven me if I'd had the little brat flogged. None of the women like Bevier's idea at all, but my sister was the only one who dared to reprimand me about it."

"Are your womenfolk concerned about their own safety?" Bevier asked him.

"Of course not. They're as brave as lionesses. What *does* concern them is the fact that one of them will be placed in charge of this women's camp. Peloi women are very sensitive about status. All the menfolk thought your plan was a splendid idea, but the women—" He spread his hands helplessly. "What man can ever understand a woman?" He squared his shoulders then and got down to business. "I've put my subchiefs to work on organizing the camp here. We'll leave a minimal force, and all the rest of us will make some show of riding toward the Zemoch border as if we planned to invade. From time to time at night we'll detach forces to sneak back here and take up positions in the surrounding hills to wait for the Zemochs. You'll all ride along and slip away when we get near the border."

"A very sound plan, friend Kring," Tynian approved.

"I sort of thought so myself." Kring grinned. "Come along, my friends. I'll take you to the tents of my clan. We're roasting a span of oxen for supper. We'll take salt together and talk of affairs." He seemed to think of something. "Friend Stragen," he said, "you know the Tamul woman Mirtai better than our other friends do. Is she at all gifted in the art of cooking?"

"I've never eaten anything she prepared, Domi," Stragen admitted. "She once told us of a journey she made on foot when she was a girl, though. As I understand it, she subsisted primarily on wolf."

"*Wolf?* How do you cook a wolf?"

"I don't think she did. She was in a hurry, I guess, so she just ate the wolf as she went."

Kring swallowed very hard. "She ate him raw?" he asked in wonder. "How did she manage to catch one?"

Stragen shrugged. "Chased him down, more than likely," he replied. "Then she tore off some of the choicer parts and ate him as she ran."

"The poor wolf!" Kring exclaimed. Then he looked suspiciously at the Thalesian thief. "Are you making this up, Stragen?" he demanded.

"Me?" Stragen's ice-blue eyes were as innocent as those of a child.

They rode out at dawn the next morning, and Kring came back to ride beside Sparhawk. "Stragen was only trying to fool me last night, wasn't he, Sparhawk?" he asked with a worried look.

"Probably," Sparhawk replied. "Thalesians are a strange people, and they have a peculiar sense of humor."

"She *could* probably do it, though," Kring said in admiration. "Chase down a wolf and eat him raw, I mean."

"I suppose she could if she wanted to," Sparhawk admitted. "I see that you're still thinking of her."

"I think of very little else, Sparhawk. I've tried to push her from my mind, but it's of no use." He sighed. "My people will never accept her, I'm afraid. It might be all right if my rank were not such as it is, but if I marry her, she'll be Doma among the Peloi—the Domi's mate, and chief among the women. The other women would gnaw their livers in jealousy and would speak against her to their husbands. Then the men would speak against her in our councils, and I'd have to kill many of the friends I've had since boyhood. Her presence among us would tear my people asunder." He sighed again. "Perhaps I can arrange to get myself killed during the impending war. That way I can avoid making the choice between love and duty." He straightened in his saddle. "Enough of such womanly talk," he said. "After my people and I have annihilated the main force of the Zemochs, we'll harry the border country on both sides of the line. The Zemochs will have little time to concern themselves with you and your friends. Zemochs are easy to divert. We'll destroy their shrines and temples. That drives them insane for some reason."

"You've thought this through rather carefully, haven't you, Kring?"

"It's always good to know where you're going, Sparhawk. When we march eastward, we'll stay on the road that leads northeasterly toward the Zemoch town of Vileta. Listen carefully, my friend. You're going to need directions if you want to find that pass I mentioned earlier." He then spoke at some length to tell Sparhawk which way to go, stressing landmarks and distances as he went along.

"That's about it, friend Sparhawk," he concluded. "I wish I could do more. Are you sure you wouldn't like to have me bring a few thousand horsemen and come along with you?"

"I wouldn't mind the company, Kring," Sparhawk replied, "but that large a force would draw resistance, and that would delay us. We have friends on the plains of Lamorkand who are counting on us to reach the temple of Azash before the Zemochs overwhelm them."

"I understand completely, friend Sparhawk."

They rode east for two days, and then Kring told Sparhawk that he should turn south in the morning. "I'd advise leaving about two hours before daylight, friend Sparhawk," he said. "If some Zemoch scout sees you and your friends ride out of the encampment in the daylight, he might get curious and follow you. The country to the south is fairly flat, so riding in the dark won't be all that dangerous. Good luck, my friend. There's a very great deal riding on your shoulders. We'll pray for you—when we're not busy killing Zemochs." The moon was rising above scattered clouds when Sparhawk came out of their pavilion for a breath of fresh air. Stragen followed him. "Nice night," the slender blond man said in his resonant voice.

"A bit chilly, though," Sparhawk replied.

"Who'd want to live in a land of endless summer? I probably won't see you when you ride out, Sparhawk. I'm not what you'd call an early riser." Stragen reached inside his doublet and drew out a packet of paper somewhat thicker than the previous ones. "This is the last of them," he said, handing over the packet. "I've completed the task your queen laid upon me."

"You did well, Stragen—I guess."

"Give me a little more credit than *that*, Sparhawk. I did exactly as Ehlana commanded."

"You could have saved yourself a long ride if you'd just given me all the letters at once, you know."

"I didn't mind the ride all that much. I rather like you and your companions, you know—not enough to emulate your overwhelming nobility, of course, but I *do* like you."

"I like you, too, Stragen—not enough to trust you, of course, but well enough, I suppose."

"Thank you, Sir Knight," Stragen said with a mocking bow.

"Don't mention it, Milord." Sparhawk grinned.

"Be careful in Zemoch, my friend," Stragen said seriously. "I'm very fond of your iron-willed young queen, and I'd rather you didn't break her heart by doing something stupid. Also, if Talen tells you something, pay attention to him. I know he's just a boy—and a thief to boot—but he has very good instincts and a rather astounding mind. It's altogether possible that he's the most intelligent person either of us will ever meet. Besides, he's lucky. Don't lose, Sparhawk. I don't much fancy bowing down to Azash." He made a face. "Enough of that. I've got a maudlin streak in me sometimes. Let's go back inside and crack open a flagon or two for old times' sake—unless you want to read your mail."

"I think I'll save it. I may get downhearted somewhere in Zemoch, and I'll need something to lift my spirits at that point."

The clouds had once again obscured the moon as they gathered early the next morning. Sparhawk sketched in their route, laying some stress on the landmarks Kring had mentioned. Then they mounted and rode out of the camp.

The darkness was so dense as to be virtually impenetrable. "We could be riding around in circles out here, you know," Kalten complained, his voice slightly sullen. Kalten had sat up late with the Peloi the previous evening, and his eyes had been bloodshot and his hands palsied when Sparhawk had awakened him.

"Just keep riding, Kalten," Sephrenia told him.

"Of course," he said sarcastically, "but which way?"

"Southeast."

"Fine, but which way is southeast?"

"That way." She pointed off into the darkness.

"How do you know?"

She spoke rapidly to him in Styric for a moment, "There," she said. "That should explain everything to you."

"Little mother, I didn't understand one single word you said."

"That's not my fault, dear one."

The dawn came slowly that morning, since the cloud banks lying to the east were particularly dense. As they rode south, they began to see the outlines of ragged peaks lying leagues off to the east—peaks that could only be in Zemoch.

It was late in the morning when Kurik reined in. "There's that red peak you mentioned, Sparhawk," he said, pointing.

"It looks as if it's bleeding, doesn't it?" Kalten observed. "Or is that just my eyes?"

"A little of each perhaps, Kalten," Sephrenia said. "You shouldn't have drunk so much ale last night."

"You should have told me about that last night, little mother," he said mournfully.

"Very well then, gentlemen," she said, "it's time for you to change clothing, I think. Your armor might be a bit ostentatious in Zemoch. Put on your mail shirts if you must, but I have Styric smocks for each of you. After you've changed, I'll do something about your faces."

"I'm more or less used to mine," Ulath told her.

"*You* may be, Ulath, but it might startle the Zemochs."

The five knights and Berit removed their formal armor—the knights with a certain relief, and Berit with obvious reluctance. Then they pulled on their only slightly less uncomfortable chain mail and lastly the Styric smocks.

Sephrenia looked at them critically. "Leave your sword belts on over the smocks for now," she said. "I doubt that the Zemochs have any really set customs about how they wear their weapons. If we find out differently later, we can make adjustments. Now, stand still, all of you." She went from man to man, touching their faces and repeating the same Styric incantation for each of them.

"It didn't seem to have worked, Lady Sephrenia," Bevier said, looking around at his companions. "They all still look the same to me."

"I'm not trying to disguise them from *you*, Bevier." She smiled. She went to her saddlebag and took out a small hand mirror. "*This* is how the Zemochs will see you." She handed him the mirror.

Bevier took one look and then made the sign to ward off evil. "Dear God!" he gasped, "I look hideous!" He handed the mirror quickly to Sparhawk, and Sparhawk examined his strangely altered face carefully. His hair was still horsetail black, but his weathered skin had become pale, a racial characteristic of all Styrics. His brows and cheekbones had become prominent, almost roughhewn. Sephrenia, he noted with a certain disappointment, had left his nose as it was. As much as he told himself that he really didn't mind the broken nose all that much, he nonetheless found that he had been curious to find out just how he might appear with a straight one for a change.

"I've made you resemble a pure Styric strain," she told them. "It's common enough in Zemoch, and I'm more comfortable with it. The sight of a mixed Elene and Styric nauseates me, for some reason."

Then she extended her right arm, spoke at some length in Styric, and then gestured. A dark spiral band that looked much like a tattoo encircled her forearm and wrist and culminated in an amazingly lifelike representation of a snake's head on her palm.

"There's a reason for that, I suppose," Tynian said, looking curiously at the marking.

"Of course. Shall we go then?"

The border between Pelosia and Zemoch was ill-defined, seeming to lie along a meandering line marked by the end of the tall grass. The soil to the east of that line was thin and rocky, and the vegetation stunted. The dark edge of a coniferous forest lay a mile or so up the steep slope. When they had covered perhaps half that distance, a dozen riders in dirty white smocks emerged from the trees and approached them.

"I'll handle this," Sephrenia said. "Just don't say anything, any of you, and try to look menacing."

The approaching Zemochs reined in. Some of them had those unfinished-looking Styric features; some could easily pass for Elenes, and some appeared to be an unwholesome mixture of the two.

"All glory to the dread God of the Zemochs," their leader intoned in bastardized Styric. The tongue he spoke was a mixture of that tongue and Elene, combining the worst features of both languages.

"You did not say his name, Kedjek," Sephrenia said coldly.

"How did she know the fellow's name?" Kalten whispered to Sparhawk. Kalten obviously understood more Styric than he could pronounce.

" 'Kedjek' isn't a name," Sparhawk replied. "It's an insult."

The Zemoch's face went even more pale, and his black eyes narrowed with hate. "Women and slaves do not speak so to members of the imperial guard!" he snapped.

"Imperial guard," Sephrenia sneered. "Neither you nor any of your men would make a wart on any part of an imperial guardsman. Say the name of our God so that I may know that you are of the true faith. Say it, Kedjek, lest ye die."

"Azash," the now-uncertain man muttered.

"His name is fouled by the tongue that speaks it," she told him, "but Azash sometimes enjoys defilement."

The Zemoch straightened. "I am commanded to gather the people," he declared. "The day is at hand when Blessed Otha will stretch forth his fist to crush and enslave the unbelievers of the west."

"Obey then. Continue with your work. Be diligent, for Azash rewards lack of zeal with agonies."

"I need no woman to instruct me," he said coldly. "Prepare to take your servants to the place of war."

"Your authority does not extend to me." She raised her right hand, her palm toward him. The markings about her forearm and wrist seemed to writhe and surge, and the image of the snake's head hissed, its forked tongue flickering. "You have my permission to greet me," she told him.

The Zemoch recoiled, his eyes wide with horror. Since the ritual Styric greeting involved the kissing of the palms, Sephrenia's "permission" was an open invitation to suicide. "Forgive me, High Priestess," he begged in a shaking voice.

"I don't think so," she said flatly. She looked at the other Zemochs, who were goggle-eyed with fright. "This piece of offal has offended me," she told them. "Do what is customary."

The Zemochs leaped from their saddles, pulled their struggling leader from his horse, and beheaded him on the spot. Sephrenia, who normally would have viewed such savagery with revulsion, looked on with no change of expression. "Adequate," she said flatly. "Display what remains of him in the usual fashion and go on with your task."

"Ah—uh—Dread Priestess," one of them faltered, "we have no leader now."

"You have spoken. Therefore you will lead. If you do well, you will be rewarded. If you do not do well, the punishment will be on your head. Now take this carrion out of my path." She touched Ch'iel's flanks with her heels, and the slender white mare moved forward, delicately avoiding the puddles of blood on the ground.

"Leadership among the Zemochs appears to have certain hazards," Ulath observed to Tynian.

"Truly," Tynian agreed.

"Did you really have to do that to him, Lady Sephrenia?" Bevier asked in a choked voice.

"Yes. A Zemoch who offends the priesthood is always punished, and in Zemoch, there is only one punishment."

"How did you make the picture of the snake move?" Talen asked her, his eyes a little frightened.

"I didn't," she replied. "It only *seemed* to move."

"Then it wouldn't really have bitten him, would it?"

"He'd have *thought* it had, and the results would have been the same. How far did Kring tell you to go into this forest, Sparhawk?"

"About a day's ride," he told her. "We turn south at the eastern edge of the woods—just before we get to the mountains."

"Let's ride on, then."

They were all a bit awed by the apparent change in Sephrenia. The soulless arrogance she had displayed during the encounter with the Zemochs had been so radically different from her normal behavior that she even frightened *them* to some degree. They rode on through the shadowy forest in subdued silence, casting frequent looks in her direction. Finally, she reined in her palfrey. "*Will* you all stop that?" she said tartly. "I haven't grown another head, you know. I'm posing as a Zemoch priestess, and I'm behaving in exactly the way a priestess of Azash would. When you imitate a monster, you sometimes have to do monstrous things. Now, let's ride on. Tell us a story, Tynian. Take our minds off the recent unpleasantness."

"Yes, little mother," the broad-faced Deiran agreed. Sparhawk had noticed that they had all, unconsciously perhaps, taken to addressing her in that form.

They camped in the forest that night and continued the following morning under still-cloudy skies. They were climbing steadily through the forest, and as they progressed, the air grew colder. It was about midday when they reached the eastern edge of the wood and turned south, staying perhaps a hundred yards back under the trees to take advantage of the concealment they offered.

As Kring had advised Sparhawk they would, they reached an extensive grove of blighted trees late in the day. The stark white band of dead trees spilled down from the mountainside like a leprous waterfall, foul smelling, fungus-ridden, and about a league wide. "This place looks—and smells—like the outskirts of Hell," Tynian said in a somber tone.

"Maybe it's because of the cloudy weather," Kalten told him.

"I don't think sunshine would help this place very much," Ulath disagreed.

"What could have laid waste so vast a region?" Bevier asked with a shudder.

"The earth itself is diseased," Sephrenia told him. "Let's not linger too long in this accursed wood, dear ones. A man is not a tree, but the noxious miasma of this forest cannot be healthy."

"We're losing daylight, Sephrenia," Kurik said.

"That won't be a problem. There'll be light enough for us to press on after it grows dark."

"What was it that diseased the earth, Lady Sephrenia?" Berit asked, looking around at the white trees thrusting upward from the contaminated soil like imploring skeletal hands.

"There's no way to know, Berit, but the reek of this place is the reek of death.

Horrors beyond imagining may lie under the ground. Let's put this place behind us."

The sky darkened with the approach of evening, but as night fell, the dead trees around them began to give off a sickly, greenish glow.

"Are you doing this, Sephrenia?" Kalten asked, "making the light, I mean?"

"No," she replied. "The light isn't the result of magic."

Kurik laughed a bit ruefully. "I should have remembered that," he said.

"Remembered what?" Talen asked him.

"Rotten logs and the like glow in the dark sometimes."

"I didn't know that."

"You've spent too much time in cities, Talen."

"You have to go where your customers are." The boy shrugged. "You don't make much profit swindling frogs."

They rode on through the first hours of night in that faint greenish glow, covering their noses and mouths with their cloaks. Not long before midnight they reached a steep, forested ridge. They rode on for some distance and then set up camp for the remainder of the night in a shallow, wooded basin where the night air seemed unusually sweet and pure after the endless hours in the fetid stink of the dead forest.

The prospect they viewed the following morning as they crested the ridge was not a great deal more encouraging. What they had faced the previous day had been dead white. What lay in store for them today was just as dead, but it was black.

"What on earth is that?" Talen gasped, staring out over the bubbling expanse of sticky-looking black muck.

"The tar bogs Kring mentioned," Sparhawk replied.

"Can we go around them?"

"No. The tar seeps out of the face of a cliff, and the bogs run on for leagues out into the foothills."

The tar bogs appeared to be vast puddles of shiny black, glistening wet, bubbling and stretching to a rocky spur perhaps five miles to the south. Near the far side there rose a plume of bluish flame quite nearly as tall as the spire rising above the cathedral of Cimmura.

"How can we hope to cross that?" Bevier exclaimed.

"Carefully, I'd imagine," Ulath replied. "I've crossed a few quicksand bogs up in Thalesia. You spend a lot of time probing in front of you with a stick—a long one, preferably."

"The Peloi have the trail marked," Sparhawk assured them. "They've poked sticks into solid ground."

"Which side of the sticks are we supposed to stay on?" Kalten asked.

"Kring didn't say." Sparhawk shrugged. "I imagine we'll find out before we go very far, though."

They rode down the ridge and moved at a careful walk out into the sticky black quagmire. The air hanging above the bogs was thick with the penetrating odor of naphtha, and Sparhawk began to feel somewhat lightheaded after a short distance.

They plodded on, their pace slowed by the need for caution. Great viscous bubbles rose up from the depths of the naphtha sinks around them to pop with odd belching sounds. When they neared the southern end of the bog, they passed the burning pillar, a column of blue flame that roared endlessly as it shot up from the earth. Once they had passed that blazing shaft, the ground began to rise and they were soon out of the bogs. Perhaps it had been the heat from the burning grasses spurting from the earth that made the contrast so noticeable, but when they left the bogs behind, the air seemed much, much colder.

"We've got weather coming," Kurik warned. "Rain at first most likely, but I think there might be snow behind it."

"No trip through the mountains is complete without snow," Ulath observed.

"What are we supposed to look for now?" Tynian asked Sparhawk.

"That," Sparhawk replied, pointing at a high cliff with broad yellow bands running diagonally across its face. "Kring gives very good directions." He peered on ahead and saw a tree with a patch of bark slashed away. "Good," he said. "The trail to the pass is marked. Let's ride on before the rain starts."

The pass was in fact an ancient stream bed. The climate of Eosia had changed over the eons, and as Zemoch had grown more and more arid, the stream that had patiently carved the narrow ravine had dried up at its source leaving a steep gully running back up into the towering cliff.

As Kurik had predicted, the rain began in the late afternoon. It was a steady drizzle that dampened everything.

"Sir Sparhawk," Berit called from the rear. "I think you should take a look at this."

Sparhawk reined in and rode back. "What is it, Berit?"

Berit pointed toward the west where the sunset was no more than a lighter shade of gray in the rainy sky. In the center of that lighter spot hovered an amorphous cloud of inky black. "It's moving the wrong way, Sir Sparhawk," Berit said. "All the other clouds are moving west. That one's coming east, right toward us. It looks sort of like the cloud these dawn-men were hiding in, doesn't it? The one that's been following us?"

Sparhawk's heart sank. "It does indeed, Berit. Sephrenia!" he called.

She rode back to join them.

"It's there again," Sparhawk told her, pointing.

"So I see. You didn't expect it just to go away, did you, Sparhawk?"

"I was hoping. Can we do anything?"

"No."

He squared his shoulders. "We keep going then," he said.

The steep ravine wound up through the rock, and they followed it slowly as evening began to descend. Then they rounded a sharp bend in the ancient course and saw a rockslide, which was not a slide strictly speaking, but rather a collapsed wall—a place where the south face of the gap had broken free and fallen into the ravine apparently to block it entirely.

"That's fairly intimidating," Bevier observed. "I hope Kring gave you good directions, Sparhawk."

"We're supposed to bear to the left here," Sparhawk told them. "We'll find a clump of limbs and logs and brush on the downhill side of the rockfall right up against the north wall of the ravine. When we pull those out of the way, we'll find a passageway leading under the slide. The Peloi use it when they ride back into Zemoch looking for ears."

Kalten wiped his face. "Let's go look," he said.

The pile of broken-off trees and tangled brush looked quite natural in the rapidly fading light, and it appeared to be no more than one of those random accumulations of driftwood and debris that wash down every ravine during the spring runoff. Talen dismounted, climbed up a steeply slanted log, and peered into a dark gap in the tangle. "Hello," he shouted into the opening. The sound of his voice returned as a hollow echo.

"Let us know if someone answers," Tynian called to him.

"This is it, Sparhawk," the boy said. "There's a large open space behind this pile."

"We may as well get to work then," Ulath suggested. He looked up at the rainy, darkening sky. "We might want to give some thought to spending the night in there," he added. "It's out of the weather, and it's getting dark anyway."

They fashioned yokes from pieces of driftwood and used the pack horses to pull aside the pile of logs and brush. The mouth of the passageway was triangular, since the outward side leaned against the north face of the ravine. The passage was narrow and smelled musty.

"It's dry," Ulath noted, "and it's out of sight. We could go back in there a ways and build a fire. If we don't dry our clothes off, these mail shirts are going to be solid rust by morning."

"Let's cover this opening first, though," Kurik said. He didn't sound too hopeful about the notion of trying to hide behind a brush pile from the shadowy cloud that had followed them since Thalesia, however.

After they had covered the opening, they took torches from one of the packs, lighted them, and followed the narrow passageway a hundred yards or so to a place where it widened out.

"Good enough?" Kurik asked.

"At least it's dry," Kalten said. He kicked at the sandy floor of the passage, turning up a chunk of bleached wood buried there. "We might even be able to find enough wood for a fire."

They set up their camp in the somewhat confined space, and they soon had a small fire going.

Talen came back from the passageway on ahead. "It goes on for another few hundred yards," he reported. "The upper end's blocked with brush the same way the lower one was. Kring's very careful to keep this passage hidden."

"What's the weather like on up ahead?" Kurik asked.

"There's some snow mixed with the rain now, Father."

"It looks as if I was right then. Oh, well, we've all been snowed on before, I guess."

"Whose turn is it to do the cooking?" Kalten asked.

"Yours," Ulath told him.

"It can't be mine again already."

"Sorry, but it is."

Grumbling, Kalten went to the packs and began to rummage around.

The meal consisted of Peloi trail rations, smoked mutton, dark bread, and a thick soup made from dried peas. It was nourishing, but the flavor was hardly spectacular. After they had finished eating, Kalten began to clean up. He was gathering their plates when he suddenly stopped. "Ulath?" he said suspiciously.

"Yes, Kalten?"

"In all the time we've been travelling together, I haven't seen you cook more than once or twice."

"No, you probably haven't."

"When does your turn come?"

"It doesn't. My job is to keep track of whose turn it is. You wouldn't really expect me to do that and cook, too, would you? Fair is fair, after all."

"Who appointed you?"

"I volunteered. Church Knights are supposed to do that when unpleasant tasks come up. That's one of the reasons people respect us so much."

They sat around after that, staring moodily into the fire. "It's days like today that make me wonder why I took up knighting for a career," Tynian said. "I had a chance to go into law when I was younger. I thought it would be boring, so I chose this instead. I wonder why."

There was a general murmur of agreement.

"Gentlemen," Sephrenia said, "push this kind of thinking from your minds. I've told you before that if we grow melancholy or fall into despair, we'll be falling right into the hands of our enemies. One dark cloud hanging over our heads is enough. Let's not add clouds of our own making. When the light falters, the darkness wins."

"If you're trying to cheer us up, you're going at it in a strange way, Sephrenia," Talen told her.

She smiled faintly. "Perhaps that *was* a bit dramatic, wasn't it? The point, my dear ones, is that we all have to be very alert. We must be wary of depression, dejection, and above all, melancholy. Melancholy's a form of madness, you know."

"What are we supposed to do?" Kalten asked her.

"It's really quite simple, Kalten," Ulath said. "You watch Tynian very closely. As soon as he begins behaving like a butterfly, tell Sparhawk about it. I'll watch *you* for signs of froggishness. Just as soon as you start trying to catch flies with your tongue, I'll know that you're starting to lose your grip on things."

# CHAPTER TWENTY-FOUR

There were snowflakes the size of half crowns mixed with the drizzle that swirled down into the narrow pass. Sooty ravens hunched on tree limbs, their feathers wet and their eyes angry. It was the kind of morning that cried out for stout walls, a sturdy roof, and a cheery fire, but those amenities were not available, so Sparhawk and Kurik wormed their way deeper into the juniper thicket and waited.

"Are you sure?" Sparhawk whispered to his squire.

Kurik nodded. "It was definitely smoke, Sparhawk," he replied in a low voice, "and somebody was doing a very bad job of frying bacon."

"There isn't much we can do but wait," Sparhawk said sourly. "I don't want to blunder into anybody." He tried to shift his position, but he was wedged in between the trunks of two scrubby trees.

"What's the matter?" Kurik whispered.

"There's water dripping off a limb just over me. It's running down the back of my neck."

Kurik gave him a long, speculative look. "How are you feeling, my Lord?" he asked.

"Wet. Thanks for asking, though."

"You know what I mean. I'm supposed to keep an eye on you. You're the key to this whole business. It doesn't really matter if the rest of us start feeling sorry for ourselves, but if *you* start having doubts and fears, we're *all* in trouble."

"Sephrenia's like a mother hen sometimes."

"She loves you, Sparhawk. It's only natural for her to be concerned."

"I'm a big boy now, Kurik. I'm even married."

"Why, I do believe you're right. How strange that I missed that."

"Very funny."

They waited, straining their ears, but all they could hear was the sound of water dripping from tree limbs.

"Sparhawk," Kurik said finally.

"Yes?"

"If something happens to me, you'll look after Aslade, won't you? And the boys?"

"Nothing's going to happen to you, Kurik."

"Probably not, but I need to know anyway."

"You've got a pension coming—quite a sizeable one, actually. I may have to sell off some acreage to cover it. Aslade will be well taken care of."

"That's assuming *you* survive this trip as well," Kurik said wryly.

"You don't have to worry about that, my friend. It's in my will. Vanion will see to it—or Ehlana."

"You think of everything, don't you, Sparhawk?"

"I'm in a dangerous line of work. I'm sort of obliged to make provisions—just in case of accidents." Sparhawk grinned at his friend. "Is this particular subject designed to cheer me up in some obscure way?" he asked.

"I just wanted to know, that's all," Kurik said. "It's good to have your mind at rest about such things. Aslade should be able to set the boys up in trades of their own then."

"Your boys already have a trade, Kurik."

"Farming? Sometimes that's a little dubious."

"I wasn't talking about farming. I've talked with Vanion about them. Your oldest boy's probably going to be entering his novitiate when this business is all over."

"That's ridiculous, Sparhawk."

"Not really. The Pandion Order always needs good men, and if they're at all like their father, your sons are some of the best. We'd have had *you* knighted years ago, but you wouldn't even let me talk about it. You're a stubborn man, Kurik."

"Sparhawk, you—" Kurik broke off. "Somebody's coming!" he hissed.

"This is pure idiocy," a voice from the other side of the thicket said in the crude mixture of Elene and Styric that identified the speaker as a Zemoch.

"What did he say?" Kurik whispered. "I can't follow that gibberish."

"I'll tell you later."

"Why don't you go back and tell Surkhel that he's an idiot, Houna?" the other voice suggested. "I'm sure he'll be very interested in your opinion."

"Surkhel *is* an idiot, Timak. He's from Korakach. They're all either insane or feeble-minded there."

"Our orders come from Otha, not from Surkhel, Houna," Timak said. "Surkhel's just doing what he's told to do."

"Otha," Houna snorted. "I don't believe there *is* an Otha. The priesthood just made him up. Who's ever seen him?"

"You're lucky I'm your friend, Houna. You could get yourself fed to the vultures for that kind of talk. Stop complaining so much. This isn't so bad. All we have to do is ride around looking for people in a countryside where there aren't any people. They've all been rounded up and sent off to Lamorkand already."

"I'm tired of all the rain, that's all."

"Be glad it's only raining water, Houna. When our friends encounter the Church Knights on the plains of Lamorkand, they'll probably run into cloudbursts of fire—or lightning—or poisonous snakes."

"The Church Knights can't be *that* bad," Houna scoffed. "We've got Azash to protect us."

"Some protection," Timak sneered. "Azash boils Zemoch babies down for soup stock."

"That's superstitious nonsense, Timak."

"Have you ever known anybody who went to his temple and came back?"

A shrill whistle came from some distance off.

"That's Surkhel," Timak said. "It's time to move on, I guess. I wonder if he knows how irritating that whistling is?"

"He *has* to whistle, Timak. He hasn't learned how to talk yet. Let's go."

"What did they say?" Kurik whispered. "Who are they?"

"They seem to be part of a patrol of some kind," Sparhawk replied.

"Looking for us? Did Martel manage to send people out in spite of everything?"

"I don't think so. From what those two said, they're out to round up everybody who hasn't gone off to war. Let's gather up the others and move on."

"What were they saying?" Kalten asked as they set out again.

"They were complaining," Sparhawk said. "They sounded like soldiers the whole world over. I think if we push aside all these horror stories, we'll find that Zemochs aren't really all that much different from common people anywhere else."

"They worship Azash," Bevier said stubbornly. "That makes them monsters by definition."

"They *fear* Azash, Bevier," Sparhawk corrected. "There's a difference between fear and worship. I don't really think we need to embark on a war of total annihilation here in Zemoch. We need to clean out the fanatics and the elite troops—along with Azash and Otha, of course. After that, I think we can leave the common people alone to pick out their own theology, whether it's Elene or Styric."

"They're a degenerate race, Sparhawk," Bevier insisted stubbornly. "The intermarriage of Styric and Elene is an abomination in the eyes of God."

Sparhawk sighed. Bevier was an archconservative, and nothing would be gained by arguing with him. "We can sort all that out after the war, I think," he said. "It's safe enough to ride on now. Let's keep our eyes open, but I don't think we'll have to try to sneak through the countryside."

They remounted and rode on up out of the pass onto a hilly plateau dotted here and there with groves of trees. The rain continued to fall, and the large, wet snowflakes mingled with it grew thicker as they continued eastward. They camped that night in a grove of spruce trees, and their fire, fed by damp twigs and branches, was small and sickly. They awoke the following morning to find the plateau covered with wet, slushy snow to a depth of perhaps three inches.

"It's time for a decision, Sparhawk," Kurik said, looking out at the still-falling snow.

"Oh?"

"We can keep trying to follow this trail—which isn't very well marked to begin with and will probably disappear altogether in about an hour—or we can strike out to the north. We could be on the Vileta road by noon."

"You have a certain preference, I gather?"

"You could say that, yes. I don't fancy wandering around in strange country trying to find a trail that might not even lead to where we want to go."

"All right, then, Kurik," Sparhawk said. "Since you're so keen on this, we'll do it your way. All I was really concerned about was getting through the border country where Martel was planning to leave ambushes in our path anyway."

"We'll lose half a day," Ulath pointed out.

"We'll lose a lot more if we get turned around in these mountains," Sparhawk replied. "We don't have any specific appointment with Azash. He'll welcome us any time we get there."

They rode north through the slushy snow, with the thickly falling flakes and the mist that accompanied them obscuring nearby hills. The wet snow plastered itself against them in sodden blankets, and their discomfort added to their gloom. Neither Ulath nor Tynian could lighten the mood with their few tentative efforts at humor, and after a while they rode in silence, each sunk in moody melancholy.

As Kurik had predicted, they reached the Vileta road about midday and turned east again. There was no evidence that the road had been travelled since the snow had begun to fall. Evening was undefined on that snow-clogged day, a gradual darkening of the pervading gloom. They took shelter for the night in an ancient, decrepit barn, and as they always did in hostile country, they took turns standing watch.

They bypassed Vileta late the following day. There was nothing in the town they wanted anyway, and there was no point in taking chances.

"Deserted," Kurik said shortly as they rode past the town.

"How do you know that?" Kalten asked him.

"No smoke. The weather's chilly, and it's still snowing. They'd have fires going."

"Oh."

"I wonder if they forgot anything when they left," Talen said, his eyes bright.

"Never mind," Kurik told him flatly.

The snow abated somewhat the following day, and their mood noticeably brightened; but when they awoke the morning after that, it was snowing again, and their spirits plummeted once more.

"Why are we doing this, Sparhawk?" Kalten asked morosely toward the end of the day. "Why does it have to be us?"

"Because we're Church Knights."

"There are other Church Knights, you know. Haven't we done enough already?"

"Do you want to go back? I didn't ask you—any of you—to come along, you know."

Kalten shook his head. "No, of course not. I don't know what came over me. Forget I said anything."

Sparhawk, however, did not. That evening he drew Sephrenia to one side. "I think we have a problem," he said to her.

"Are you starting to have unusual feelings?" she asked quickly. "Something that may be coming from somewhere outside of yourself?"

"I didn't exactly follow that."

"I think we've all noticed it a few times before. We've all been having these sudden bouts of doubt and depression." She smiled slightly. "That's not really in the character of Church Knights, you know. Most of the time you're optimistic to the point of insanity. These doubts and gloom are being imposed on us from the outside. Is that the sort of thing you're feeling? Is that the problem?"

"It's not me," he assured her. "I'm feeling a little low, but I think that's just the weather. It's the others I'm talking about. Kalten came up to me today, and he was asking me why *we* had to be the ones to do this. Kalten would never ask that kind of question. You usually have to hold him back, but now I think he just wants to pack it all up and go home. If my friends are all feeling this way, why don't I feel it, too?"

She looked out into the still-falling snow. Once again he was struck by just how agelessly beautiful she was. "I think he's afraid of you," she said after a while.

"Kalten? That's nonsense."

"That's not the one I meant. It's Azash who's afraid of you, Sparhawk."

"That's absurd."

"I know, but I think it's true all the same. Somehow you have more control over Bhelliom than anyone else has ever had. Not even Ghwerig had such absolute power over the stone. That's what Azash is *really* afraid of. That's why he won't risk confronting you directly, and that's why he's trying to dishearten your friends. He's attacking Kalten and Bevier and the others because he's afraid to attack you."

"You, too?" he asked her. "Are you in despair, too?"

"Of course not."

"Why of course?"

"It would take too long to explain. I'll take care of this, Sparhawk. Go to bed."

They awoke the following morning to a familiar sound. It was clear and pure, and though the song of the pipes was in a minor key, it seemed filled with an ageless joy. A slow smile came to Sparhawk's lips, and he shook Kalten awake. "We've got company," he said.

Kalten sat up quickly, reaching for his sword, and then he heard the sound of the pipes. "Well, now!" He grinned. "It's about time. I'll be glad to see her again."

They emerged from the tent and looked around. It was still snowing, and the stubborn mist hung back among the trees. Sephrenia and Kurik sat by the small fire in front of her tent.

"Where is she?" Kalten asked, looking out into the settling snow.

"She's here," Sephrenia said calmly, sipping her tea.

"I can't see her."

"You don't have to, Kalten. All you really need to know is that she's here."

"It's not the same, Sephrenia." His voice was just slightly disappointed.

"She finally went and did it, didn't she?" Kurik laughed.

"Did what?" Sephrenia asked him.

"She poached a group of Church Knights right out from under the nose of the Elene God."

"Don't be silly. She wouldn't do that."

"Oh, really? Take a look at Kalten there. That's the closest thing to adoration I've ever seen on his face. If I put together something that looked like an altar right now, he'd probably genuflect."

"That's nonsense," Kalten said, looking slightly embarrassed. "I just like her, that's all. She makes me feel good when she's around."

"Of course," Kurik said skeptically.

"I don't know that we should pursue this line of thought when Bevier joins us," Sephrenia cautioned. "Let's not confuse him."

The others also emerged from their tents smiling broadly. Ulath was actually laughing.

Their mood had lightened enormously, and the bleak morning seemed almost sunny. Even their horses seemed alert, almost frisky. Sparhawk and Berit went to where they were picketed to feed them their morning rations of grain. Faran normally greeted the morning with a flat look of dislike, but on this particular day the big, ugly roan seemed calm, even serene. He was looking intently at a large, spreading beech tree. Sparhawk glanced at the tree and then froze. The tree was half-concealed by mist, but he seemed to see quite clearly the familiar figure of the little girl who had just banished their despair with her joyful song. She appeared to be exactly the same as she had been the first time he had seen her. She sat upon a limb, holding her shepherd's pipes to her lips. The headband of plaited grass encircled her glossy black hair, she still wore the short, belted linen smock, and her grass-stained little feet were crossed at the ankles. Her large, dark eyes looked directly at him, and there was the hint of a dimple on each of her cheeks.

"Berit," Sparhawk said quietly, "look."

The young apprentice turned, and then he suddenly stopped. "Hello, Flute," he greeted her, sounding strangely unsurprised.

Aphrael blew him a little trill of recognition and continued her song. Then the mist swirled about the tree, and when it cleared, she was no longer there. Her melody, however, continued.

"She looks well, doesn't she?" Berit said.

"How could she look otherwise?" Sparhawk laughed.

The days seemed to race by after that. What had been tedious plodding through gloom and snow now took on an almost holiday air. They laughed and joked and even ignored the weather, though it did not noticeably improve. It continued to snow each night and on into the morning, but at about noon each day, the snow gradually turned to rain, and the rain melted down each night's accumulation so that, although they rode through continual slush, the drifts did not pile up sufficiently to impede their progress. Intermittently as they rode, the sound of Aphrael's pipes hauntingly drifted out of the mist, urging them on.

It was several days later when they came over a hill to look down at the lead-gray expanse of the Gulf of Merjuk stretching before them, half-shrouded by mist and the chill drizzle. Huddled on the near shore was a sizeable cluster of low buildings.

"That would be Albak," Kalten said. He wiped at his face and peered down at the town intently. "I don't see any smoke," he noted. "No, wait. There's one live chimney—right near the center of town."

"We may as well go down there," Kurik said. "We're going to have to steal a boat."

They rode down the hill and entered Albak. The streets were unpaved and clogged with slushy snow. The snow had not been churned into soupy muck, a clear indication that the town was uninhabited. The single column of smoke, thin and sickly-looking, rose from the chimney of a low, shedlike building facing what appeared to be a town square. Ulath sniffed at the air. "A tavern, judging from the smell," he said.

They dismounted and went inside. The room was long and low, with smoke-stained beams and moldy straw on the floor. It was cold and damp and smelled foul. There were no windows, and the only light came from a small fire flickering on a hearth at the far end. A hunchbacked man dressed in rags was kicking a bench to pieces to feed the fire. "Who's there?" he cried out as they entered.

"Travellers," Sephrenia replied in Styric, her tone strangely alien. "We're looking for a place to spend the night."

"Don't look here," the hunchback growled. "This is *my* place." He threw several pieces of the bench into the fireplace, pulled a greasy blanket about his shoulders, and sat back down, pulling an open beer keg closer to him and then extending his hands toward the feeble flames.

"We'll gladly go somewhere else," she said to him. "We need a little information, though."

"Go ask somebody else." He squinted at her. His eyes were oddly disconnected, looking off in different directions, and he looked to one side of her in that peculiar way of the nearly blind.

Sephrenia crossed the straw-littered floor and faced the uncivil hunchback. "You seem to be the only one here," she told him.

"I am," he said sullenly. "All the rest went off to die in Lamorkand. I'll die here. That way I don't have to walk so far. Now get out of here."

She extended her arm and then turned it over in front of his stubbled face. The image of the serpent's head rose from her palm, its tongue flickering. The half-blind hunchback puckered his face, turning his head this way and that in an effort to see what she was holding. Then he cried out in fright, half rose, and stumbled back over his stool, spilling his beer keg.

"You have my permission to offer your greeting," Sephrenia said in an implacable tone.

"I didn't know who you were, Priestess," he gibbered. "Forgive me, please."

"We'll see. Is there no one else in the town?"

"None, Priestess—only me. I'm too crippled to travel, and I can hardly see. They left me behind."

"We seek another group of travellers—four men and a woman. One of the men has white hair. Another looks like an animal. Have you seen them?"

"Please don't kill me."

"Then speak."

"Some people passed through here yesterday. They may have been the ones you're looking for. I can't say for sure because they didn't come close enough to the fire for me to see their faces. I could hear them talking, though. They said they were going to Aka and from there to the capital. They stole Tassalk's boat." The hunchback sat up on the floor, clasped his arms about him, and began to rock back and forth rhythmically, moaning to himself.

"He's crazy," Tynian said quietly to Sparhawk.

"Yes," Sparhawk agreed sadly.

"All gone," the hunchback crooned. "All gone off to die for Azash. Kill the Elenes, then die. Azash loves death. All die. All die. All die for Azash."

"We're going to take a boat," Sephrenia cut through his ravings.

"Take. Take. Nobody will come back. All die, and Azash will eat them."

Sephrenia turned her back on him and returned to where the others stood. "We'll leave here now," she said in a steely tone.

"What's going to happen to him?" Talen asked her, his voice subdued. "He's all by himself here and nearly blind."

"He'll die," she replied in an abrupt tone of voice.

"All alone?" Talen's voice was half-sick.

"Everybody dies alone, Talen." She resolutely led them from the stinking tavern.

Once she was outside, however, she broke down and wept.

Sparhawk went to his saddlebags and took out his map. He studied it with a frown. "Why would Martel go to Aka?" he muttered to Tynian. "It's leagues out of his way."

"There's a road from Aka to Zemoch," Tynian said, pointing at the map. "We've been pushing him hard, and his horses are probably nearly exhausted."

"Maybe that's it," Sparhawk agreed. "And Martel's never been very fond of going across country."

"Will we follow the same route?"

"I don't think so. He doesn't know much about boats, so he'll wallow around out there in the gulf for several days. Kurik's a sailor, though, so he can take us straight across. We should be able to make it from the east shore to the capital in about three days. We can still get there before he does. Kurik," he called, "let's go find a boat."

Sparhawk was leaning against the rail of the large, tar-smeared scow Kurik had selected. The surface winds had swung briefly around to the west, and their ship sped across the choppy waters of the gulf toward the east. Sparhawk reached inside his tunic and took out Ehlana's letter.

Beloved,

If all has gone well, you're very close to the Zemoch border by now— and I *must* believe that all has gone well or else I shall go mad. You and your companions *will* succeed, dearest Sparhawk. I know that as surely as if God Himself had told it to me. Our lives are strangely controlled, my love. We were destined to love each other—and to marry. We had no real choice in this, I think—though I would certainly have chosen no other. Our meeting each other and our marriage were all a part of some grander design—even as was the gathering of your companions. Who in all the world could be more perfectly suited to aid you than the great men who ride with you? Kalten and Kurik, Tynian and Ulath, Bevier and dear Berit, so young and so very brave, all of them have joined with you in love and common purpose. You surely cannot fail, my beloved, not with such men at your side. Hasten, my Champion and husband. Take your invincible companions to the lair of our ancient foe and confront him there. Let Azash tremble, for the Knight Sparhawk comes with Bhelliom in his fist, and not all the powers of Hell can prevail against him. Hasten, my beloved, and know that you are armed not merely with Bhelliom, but with my love as well.

I love you,
Ehlana.

Sparhawk read through the letter several times. His bride, he saw, had a very strong tendency toward oratory. Even her letters had the tone of a public address. Stirring though the message was, he might have preferred something a bit less polished, something more genuine. Although he knew that the emotions she expressed came from her heart, her fondness for the well-turned phrase somehow intruded itself between them. "Oh well," he sighed. "She'll probably relax as we get to know each other better."

Then Berit came up on deck, and Sparhawk remembered something. He read through the letter again and made a quick decision. "Berit," he called, "do you suppose I could have a word with you?"

"Of course, Sir Sparhawk."

"I thought you might like to see this." Sparhawk handed him the letter.

Berit looked at it. "But this is personal, Sir Sparhawk," he objected.

"It concerns you, I think. It may help you to deal with a problem you've been having lately."

Berit read through the letter, and a strange expression came over his face.

"Does that help at all?" Sparhawk asked him.

Berit flushed. "Y-you knew?" he stammered.

Sparhawk smiled a bit wryly. "I know it may be hard for you to believe, my friend, but I was young once myself. What's happened to you has probably happened to every young man who's ever lived. In my case, it was when I first went to court. She was a young noblewoman, and I was absolutely certain that the sun rose and set in her eyes. I still think of her on occasion—rather fondly, actually. She's older now, of course, but her eyes still make me weak when she looks at me."

"But you're married, Sir Sparhawk."

"That's fairly recent, and it has nothing whatsoever to do with what I felt for that young noblewoman. You'll waste a lot of dreams on Ehlana, I expect. We all do that in these cases, but maybe it makes better men of us."

"Surely you won't tell the queen." Berit seemed shocked.

"Probably not, no. It doesn't really concern her, so why should I worry her about it? The point I'm trying to make here, Berit, is that what you're feeling is a part of growing up. Everybody goes through the same thing—if he's lucky."

"You don't hate me then, Sir Sparhawk?"

"Hate you? God no, Berit. I'd be disappointed in you if you *didn't* feel this way about *some* young, pretty girl."

Berit sighed. "Thank you, Sir Sparhawk," he said.

"Berit, before very long, you're going to be a full-fledged Pandion Knight, and then we'll be brothers. Do you suppose we could drop that 'sir'? Just 'Sparhawk' will do. I more or less recognize the name."

"If you wish, Sparhawk," Berit said. He offered his friend the letter.

"Why don't you keep it for me? I've got a lot of clutter in my saddlebags, and I wouldn't want to lose it."

Then the two of them, their shoulders almost touching, went aft to see if Kurik needed any help with the ship.

They rigged a sea anchor that evening, and when they awoke the following morning, they found that the rain and snow had passed, though the sky was still lead gray.

"That cloud's there again, Sparhawk," Berit reported, coming forward from the stern. "It's a good long ways behind us, but it's definitely there."

Sparhawk looked aft. Now that he could actually see it, it did not seem quite so menacing. When it had been that vague shadow hovering always at the very edge of his vision, it had filled him with an unnamed dread. Now he had to be very careful not to think of it as little more than some minor annoyance. It *was* still dangerous, after all. A faint smile touched his lips. It appeared that even a God could blunder, could push something past the point of effectiveness.

"Why don't you just dissolve that thing with the Bhelliom, Sparhawk?" Kalten asked irritably.

"Because it would just form up again. Why waste the effort?"

"You aren't going to do anything about it then?"

"Of course I am."

"What?"

"I'm going to ignore it."

About midmorning they landed on a snowy beach, waded the horses ashore, and set the boat adrift. Then they mounted and rode inland.

The eastern side of the gulf was far more arid than the mountains to the west had been, and the rocky hills were covered with a layer of fine black sand, thinly dusted in sheltered spots with skiffs of powdery snow. The wind was bitingly cold, and it lifted clouds of dust and snow to engulf them as they pushed on. They rode through what seemed a perpetual twilight, their mouths and noses covered with scarves.

"Slow going," Ulath observed laconically, carefully wiping dust from his eyes. "Martel's decision to go by way of Aka might have been wise."

"I'm sure it's just as cold and dusty on the road from Aka to Zemoch," Sparhawk said. He smiled faintly. "Martel's a fastidious sort. He absolutely abhors getting dirty. The notion of a couple of pounds of fine black sand mixed with snow sifting down the back of his neck sort of appeals to me for some reason."

"That's very petty, Sparhawk," Sephrenia chided.

"I know," he replied. "I'm like that sometimes."

They took shelter that night in a cave, and when they emerged the following morning they found that the sky had cleared, although the wind had picked up and was stirring up clouds of the perpetual dust.

Berit was the sort of young man who took his responsibilities very seriously. He had taken it upon himself to scout around at first light and he was just returning as the rest of them gathered at the cave mouth. They could clearly see his look of revulsion as he came nearer. "There are some people out there, Sparhawk," he said as he dismounted.

"Soldiers?"

"No. They have old people and women and children with them. They have a few weapons, but they don't seem to know how to handle them."

"What are they doing?" Kalten asked.

Berit coughed nervously and looked around. "I'd really rather not say, Sir Kalten, and I don't think we want Lady Sephrenia to see them. They've set up a sort of an altar with a clay idol on it, and they're doing things people shouldn't do in public. I think they're just a group of degenerate peasants."

"We'd better tell Sephrenia," Sparhawk decided.

"I couldn't do that, Sparhawk," Berit said, blushing. "I *couldn't* describe what they're doing in front of her."

"Generalize, Berit. You don't have to be too specific."

Sephrenia, however, proved to be curious. "Exactly what are they doing, Berit?"

"I *knew* she was going to ask," Berit muttered reproachfully to Sparhawk. "They're—uh—they're sacrificing animals, Lady Sephrenia, and they aren't wearing any clothes—even in this cold. They're smearing blood from the sacrifices on their bodies, and they're—uh—"

"Yes," she said. "I'm familiar with the rite. Describe the people. Do they look Styric? Or are they more Elene?"

"Many of them are fair-haired, Lady Sephrenia."

"Ah," she said, "that's who they are, then. They don't pose any particular danger. The idol is another matter, though. We can't leave it behind us. We have to smash it."

"For the same reason we had to break the one in the cellar at Ghasek?" Kalten asked.

"Exactly." She made a little face. "I shouldn't really say this, but the Younger Gods blundered when they confined Azash to that clay idol in the shrine near Ghanda. The idea was sound enough, but they overlooked something. The idol can be duplicated by men, and if certain rites are performed, the Spirit of Azash can enter the duplicates."

"What do we do?" Bevier asked.

"We go smash the idol before the rite's completed."

The unclad Zemochs in the canyon were none too clean, and their hair was tangled and matted. Sparhawk had never truly realized before just how much of human ugliness is concealed by clothing. The naked worshippers appeared to be peasants and herdsmen, and they squealed with fright as the mail-shirted knights burst upon them. The fact that the attackers were disguised as Zemochs added to their confusion. They ran this way and that, bawling in terror.

Four of their number wore crude ecclesiastical robes, and they stood before the altar where they had just finished sacrificing a goat. Three of them gaped in stunned disbelief at the knights, but the fourth, a scraggly-bearded fellow with a narrow head, was weaving his fingers and speaking desperately in Styric. He released a series of apparitions that were so ineptly formed as to be laughable.

The knights rode directly through the apparitions and the milling crowd.

"Defend our God!" the priest shrieked, his lips flecked with foam. His parishioners, however, chose not to do that.

The mud idol on the crude altar seemed to be moving slightly, even as a distant hill seems to dance and waver in the shimmering heat of a summer afternoon. Wave upon wave of sheer malevolence emanated from it, and the air was suddenly deathly cold. Sparhawk suddenly felt his strength draining away, and Faran faltered. Then the ground before the altar seemed to bulge. Something was stirring beneath the earth, something so dreadful that Sparhawk turned his eyes away in sick revulsion. The ground heaved, and Sparhawk felt cold fear grip his heart. The light began to fade from his eyes.

"No!" Sephrenia's voice rang out. "Stand firm! It cannot hurt you!" She began to speak rapidly in Styric, then quickly held out her hand. What appeared there glowed brightly and seemed at first no larger than an apple, but as it rose into the air, it expanded and grew brighter and brighter until it was almost as if she had conjured up a small sun to hang in the air before the idol, and that sun brought with it a summerlike warmth that burned away the deathly chill. The ground ceased its restless heaving, and the idol froze, once again becoming motionless.

Kurik spurred his trembling gelding forward and swung his heavy chain mace once. The grotesque idol shattered beneath the blow, and its shards flew out in all directions.

The naked Zemochs wailed in absolute despair.

## CHAPTER TWENTY-FIVE

"Round them up, Sparhawk," Sephrenia said, looking with a shudder at the naked Zemochs, "and please make them put their clothes back on." She looked at the altar. "Talen," she said, "gather up the fragments of the idol. We won't want to leave them here."

The boy didn't even argue with her.

The "rounding up" did not take very long. Naked, unarmed people do not customarily resist when mailed men with sharp steel in their hands start giving orders. The priest with the narrow head continued to shriek at them, however, although he was very careful not to give them any other reason to chastise him. "Apostates!" he howled. "Defilers! I call upon Azash to—" His words trailed off into a kind of croak as Sephrenia extended her arm and the serpent head reared from her palm, its tongue flickering. He stared at the swaying image of the reptile, his eyes bulging. Then he collapsed and grovelled in the dirt before her.

Sephrenia looked around sternly, and the other Zemochs also sank to the ground with a horrified moan. "Perverted ones!" she snarled at them in the corrupt Zemoch dialect. "Your rite has been forbidden for centuries. Why have you chosen to disobey mighty Azash?"

"Our priests beguiled us, Dread Priestess," one shaggy-haired fellow gibbered. "They told us that the prohibition of our rite was a Styric blasphemy. They said that it was the Styrics in our midst who were leading us away from the true God." He seemed blind to the fact that Sephrenia herself was Styric. "We are Elene," he said proudly, "and we know that we are the chosen ones."

Sephrenia gave the Church Knights a look that conveyed volumes. Then she looked at the ragtag band of unwashed "Elenes" grovelling before her. She seemed about to speak once, her breath drawn in to deliver a shattering denunciation. Instead, however, she let out the breath, and when she spoke, her voice was clinically detached. "You have strayed," she told them, "and that makes you unfit to join your countrymen in their holy war. You will return to your homes now. Go back to Merjuk and beyond, and venture no more to this place. Do not go near the temple of Azash, lest he destroy you."

"Should we hang our priests?" the shaggy fellow asked her hopefully, "or burn them perhaps?"

"No. Our God seeks worshippers, not corpses. Henceforth you will devote yourselves to the rites of purification and of reconciliation and the rites of the seasons only. You are as children, and as children shall you worship. Now go!" She straightened her arm, and the serpent head emerging from her palm reared up, swelling, growing, and becoming not so much a serpent as a dragon. The dragon roared, and sooty flames shot from its mouth.

The Zemochs fled.

"You should have let them hang that one fellow at least," Kalten said.

"No," she replied. "I just set them on the path of a different religion, and that religion forbids killing."

"They're Elenes, Lady Sephrenia," Bevier objected. "You should have instructed them to follow the Elene faith."

"With all its prejudices and inconsistencies, Bevier?" she asked. "No, I don't think so. I pointed them in a gentler way. Talen, have you finished yet?"

"I've got all the pieces I could find, Sephrenia."

"Bring them along." She turned her white palfrey then and led them away from the rude altar.

They returned to the cave, gathered up their belongings, and set out again.

"Where did they come from?" Sparhawk asked Sephrenia as they rode along in the biting cold.

"Northeastern Zemoch," she replied, "from the steppes north of Merjuk. They're primitive Elenes who haven't had the benefits of contact with civilized people the way the rest of you have."

"Styrics, you mean?"

"Naturally. What other civilized people are there?"

"Be nice," he chided her.

She smiled. "The inclusion of orgies in the worship of Azash was a part of Otha's original strategy. It brought in the Elenes. Otha's an Elene himself, and he knows how strong those appetites are in your race. We Styrics have more exotic perversions. Azash really prefers those, but the primitives in the back country still hold to the old ways. They're relatively harmless."

Talen drew in beside them. "What do you want me to do with the pieces of that idol?" he asked.

"Throw them away," she replied, "one piece every mile or so. Scatter them thoroughly. The rite had already begun, and we don't want someone to gather up the pieces and put them back together again. The cloud's trouble enough. We don't want Azash himself behind us as well."

"Amen," the boy said fervently. He rode off to one side, stood up in his stirrups, and hurled a fragment of mud some distance away.

"We're safe then, aren't we?" Sparhawk said, "now that the idol's smashed, I mean, and as soon as Talen finishes scattering it?"

"Hardly, dear one. That cloud's still there."

"But the cloud's never really hurt us, Sephrenia. It tried to make us melancholy and afraid, but that's about all—and Flute took care of that for us. If that's the best it can really do, it's not much of a threat."

"Don't let yourself grow overconfident, Sparhawk," she warned. "The cloud—or shadow, whichever it is—is probably a creature of Azash, and that could make it at least as dangerous as the Damork or the Seeker."

The countryside did not improve as they rode eastward, nor did the weather. It was bitterly cold, and the billowing clouds of black dust erased the sky. What little vegetation they saw was stunted and sickly. They were following something that sort of looked like a trail, though its drunken meanderings suggested wild cattle rather than men. The water holes were infrequent and the water in them was ice that had to be melted down to water the horses.

"Cursed dust!" Ulath suddenly bellowed at the sky, throwing aside the cloth that covered his mouth and nose.

"Steady," Tynian said to him.

"What's the use of all this?" Ulath demanded, spitting out dust. "We can't even tell which way we're going!" He pulled the cloth back across his face and rode on, muttering to himself.

The horses continued to plod on, their hooves kicking up little puffs of frozen dust.

The melancholy that had beset them in the mountains lying to the west of the Gulf of Merjuk was obviously returning, and Sparhawk rode on cautiously, watching with chagrin as the mood of his companions rapidly deteriorated even as he kept a wary eye on nearby ravines and rocky outcrops.

Bevier and Tynian were deep in a somber conversation. "It is a sin," Bevier was saying stubbornly. "To even suggest it is a heresy and a blasphemy. The fathers of the Church have reasoned it out, and reason, coming as it does *from* God, is *of* God. Thus God himself tells us that He and He alone is divine."

"But—" Tynian began to object.

"Hear me out, my friend," Bevier said to him. "Since God tells us that there are no other divinities, for us to believe otherwise is blackest sin. We are embarked upon a quest founded in childish superstition. The Zemochs are a danger, certainly, but they are a *worldly* danger, even as the Eshandists. They have no supernatural allies. We are throwing our lives away searching for a mythical foe who exists only in the diseased imaginations of our heathen enemies. I will reason with Sparhawk about this presently, and I have no doubt that he can be persuaded to abandon this vain quest."

"That might be best," Tynian agreed, albeit somewhat dubiously. The two of them seemed totally unaware that Sparhawk was clearly riding within earshot.

"You've got to talk with him, Kurik," Kalten was saying to Sparhawk's squire. "We haven't got a chance in the world."

"*You* tell him," Kurik growled. "I'm a servant. It's not my place to tell my Lord that he's a suicidal madman."

"I honestly believe we should slip up behind him and tie him up. I'm not just trying to save my own life, you understand. I'm trying to save his, too."

"I feel the same way, Kalten."

"They're coming!" Berit screamed, pointing at a nearby cloud of swirling dust. "Arm yourselves!"

The warlike shouts of Sparhawk's friends were shrill, tinged with panic, and their charge had an air of desperation about it. They crashed into the dust cloud, swinging their swords and axes at the unfeeling air.

"Help them, Sparhawk!" Talen cried, his voice shrill.

"Help them with what?"

"The monsters! They'll all be killed!"

"I rather doubt that, Talen," Sparhawk replied coolly, watching his friends flailing at the dust cloud with their weapons. "They're more than a match for what they're facing."

Talen glared at him for a moment, then rode several yards away, swearing to himself.

"I take it that you don't see anything in the dust either," Sephrenia said calmly.

"That's all it is, little mother, just dust."

"Let's deal with that right now." She spoke briefly in Styric, then gestured.

The thickly billowing dust cloud seemed to shudder and flinch in upon itself for a moment, and then it gave a long, audible sigh as it slithered to the ground.

"Where did they go?" Ulath roared, looking around and brandishing his ax.

The others looked equally baffled, and the looks they directed at Sparhawk were darkly suspicious.

They avoided him after that and rode with dark scowls, whispering to each other and frequently casting covert looks at him, looks filled with hostility. They made their night's encampment on the leeward side of a steep bluff where pale, sand-scoured rocks protruded from an unwholesome, diseased-looking bank of leprous clay. Sparhawk cooked their meal, and his friends chose not to linger with him at the fire after the meal as was customary. He shook his head in disgust and went to his blankets.


"Awaken, Sir Knight, an' it please thee." The voice was soft and gentle, and it seemed filled with love. Sparhawk opened his eyes. He found himself in a gaily colored pavilion, and beyond the open tent flap was a broad green meadow, all aswirl with wildflowers. There were trees, ancient and vast, their branches heavy with fragrant blossoms, and beyond the trees lay a sparkling sea of deep, deep blue, bejewelled with the gleams of reflected sunlight. The sky was as no other sky had ever been. It was a rainbow that covered the entire dome of the heavens, blessing all the world beneath.

The speaker who had awakened him stood nudging him with her nose and pawing impatiently at the carpeted floor of the pavilion with one forehoof. She was small for a deer, and her coat was of such dazzling whiteness as to be almost incandescent. Her eyes were large and meltingly brown, and they reflected a docility, a trust, and a sweet nature that tugged at the heart. Her manner, however, was insistent. She most definitely wanted him to get up.

"Have I slept overlong?" he asked, a bit concerned that he might have offended her.

"Thou wert a-weary, Sir Knight," she replied, automatically, it seemed, coming to his defense even against self-criticism. "Dress thyself with some care," the gentle hind instructed, "for I am bidden to bring thee into the presence of my mistress, who doth rule this realm and whom all her subjects adore."

Sparhawk fondly stroked her snowy neck, and her great eyes melted with love. He rose and looked to his armor. It was as it should have been, jet black and embossed with silver. He was pleased to note as he drew it on that it had no more weight than gossamer silk. It was not steel, however. Though his great sword was imposing, it was, he knew, no more than ornamental in this fairy kingdom begirt by a jewelled sea and lying in happy contentment beneath its multicolored sky. Here were no dangers, no hate, no discord, and all was abiding peace and love.

"We must hasten," the white deer told him. "Our boat doth await us on yon strand where wavelets play in wanton abandon in the ever-changing light of our enchanted sky." She led him with precise and delicate steps into the flower-kissed meadow, a meadow so sweet smelling as to make the senses swoon.

They passed a white tigress lolling indolently upon her back in the warm morning sunlight as her cubs, large-footed and awkward, wrestled in the grass nearby in mock ferocity. The white deer paused briefly to nuzzle at the face of the tigress, and she was rewarded by a broad, affectionate swipe of a huge pink tongue that bedampened one side of her snowy face from chin to ear tip.

The flower-tipped grasses bowed before the warm breeze as Sparhawk followed the white deer across the meadow to the blue-tinged shade beneath the ancient trees. Beyond the trees, an alabaster gravel strand sloped gently down to an azure sea, and there awaited them a craft more bird than ship. Slender was her prow, and graceful as the neck of a swan. Two wings of snowy sail rose above her oaken deck, and she tugged at her moorings as if eager to be off.

Sparhawk considered the white doe, bent, and, placing one arm beneath her breast and the other behind her haunch, he lifted her quite easily. She made no effort to struggle, but a momentary alarm showed in her huge eyes.

"Calm thyself," he told her. "I do but bear thee unto our waiting ship that thou wilt encounter no sudden chill from the waters that do stand between us and our craft."

"Thou art kind, gentle knight," she said, trustingly resting her chin upon his shoulder as, with purposeful strides, he waded out into the playful wavelets.

Once they had boarded, their eager craft leaped forward, bravely breasting the waves, and their destination soon emerged before them. It was a small, verdant eyot crowned with a sacred grove ancient beyond imagining, and Sparhawk could clearly see the gleaming marble columns of a temple beneath those spreading limbs.

Other craft, no less graceful than his own and heedless of the vagaries of the wanton breeze, also made their way across that sapphire sea toward the eyot that beckoned to them. And as they stepped out upon a golden strand, Sir Sparhawk recognized the dearly loved faces of his companions. Sir Kalten, steadfast and true; Sir Ulath, bull-strong and lion-brave, Sir—

Sparhawk half woke, shaking his head to clear the cobwebs of cloying image and extravagant expression from his mind.

Somewhere a tiny foot stamped in exasperation. "That *really* makes me cross, Sparhawk!" a familiar voice scolded him. "Now go back to sleep at once!"

Slowly the valiant knights climbed the gentle slope leading to the eyot's grove-crested top, recounting to each other their morning's adventures. Sir Kalten was guided by a white badger, Sir Tynian by a white lion, Sir Ulath by a great white bear, and Sir Bevier by a snowy dove. The young knight-to-be, Berit, was led by a white lamb, Kurik by a faithful white hound, and Talen by a mink in ermine coat.

Sephrenia, clad in white and with her brow encircled by a garland of flowers, awaited them on the marble steps of the temple, and, seated quite calmly on the branch of an oak that predated every other living thing, was the queen of this fairy realm, the Child-Goddess Aphrael. She wore a gown instead of that rude smock, and her head was crowned with light. The playful subterfuge of the pipes was no longer necessary, and she raised her voice in a clear, pure song of greeting. Then she rose and walked down through the empty air as calmly as she might have descended a stair, and when she reached the cool, lush grass of the sacred grove, she danced, whirling and laughing among them, bestowing kisses by the score with her bowlike little mouth. Her tiny feet but lightly crushed the soft grass, but Sparhawk immediately saw the source of those greenish stains that had always perplexed him. She even kissed those snowy creatures that had guided the heroes into her exalted presence. The flowery descriptions came into Sparhawk's mind despite his best efforts to keep them out, and he groaned inwardly. Aphrael imperiously motioned for him to kneel, encircled his neck with her small arms, and kissed him several times. "If you don't stop making fun of me, Sparhawk," she murmured for his ears alone, "I'll strip you of your armor and turn you out to graze with the sheep."

"Forgive mine error, Divine One." He grinned at her.

She laughed and kissed him again. Sephrenia had once mentioned the fact that Aphrael enjoyed kisses. That did not appear to have changed very much.

They breakfasted on fruits unknown to man, then lounged at their ease on the soft grass as birds carolled to them from the limbs of the sacred grove. Then Aphrael rose to her feet and, after circling through the group once more for kisses, she spoke to them quite gravely. "Though I have been desolate to have been absent from your midst for the past lonely months," she began, "I have not summoned ye here solely for this joyful reunion, glad though it makes my heart. Ye have gathered at my request and with my dear sister's aid—" She gave Sephrenia a smile of radiant love "—so that I may impart unto ye certain truths. Forgive me that I must touch these truths but lightly, for they are the truths of the Gods, and are far beyond your grasp, I do fear; for much as I melt with love for each of ye, I must tell ye, not unkindly, that even as I have appeared as a child to ye, so ye now appear to me. Thus I will not assault the outer bounds of your understanding with matters beyond your reach." She looked around at their uncomprehending expressions. "What *is* the matter with you all?" she said in exasperation.

Sparhawk rose to his feet, crooked a finger at the little Goddess, and led her off to one side.

"What?" she demanded crossly.

"Are you in the mood for some advice?" he asked her.

"I'll listen." Her tone made no promises.

"You're stupefying them with eloquence, Aphrael. Kalten looks like a poleaxed ox at the moment. We're plain men, little Goddess. You'll have to speak to us plainly if you want us to understand."

She pouted. "I worked for weeks on that speech, Sparhawk."

"It's a lovely speech, Aphrael. When you tell the other Gods about this—and I'm sure you will—recite it to them as if you had delivered it to us verbatim. They'll swoon with delight, I'm sure. For the sake of brevity—this night won't last forever, you know—*and* for the sake of clarity, give us the abbreviated version. You might consider suspending the 'thees' and 'thous' as well. They make you sound as if you're preaching a sermon, and sermons tend to put people to sleep."

She pouted slightly. "Oh, very well, Sparhawk," she said, "but you're taking all the fun out of this for me."

"Can you ever forgive me?"

She stuck her tongue out at him and led him back to rejoin the others.

"This grouchy old bear suggests that I get to the point," Aphrael said, giving Sparhawk a sly, sidelong glance. "He's nice enough as a knight, I suppose, but he's a bit lacking in poetry. Very well, then, I've asked you to come here so that I can tell you a few things about Bhelliom—why it's so powerful, and so very dangerous." She paused, knitting her ravenlike brows. "Bhelliom isn't substance," she continued. "It's spirit, and it predates the stars. There are many such spirits, and each of them has many attributes. One of their more important attributes is color. You see, what happens is—" She looked around at them. "Maybe we can save that for some other day," she decided. "Anyway, these spirits were cast across the sky so that—" She broke off again. "This is *very* difficult, Sephrenia," she said in a plaintive little voice. "*Why* must these Elenes be so dense?"

"Because their God chooses not to explain things to them, Aphrael," Sephrenia told her.

"He's such an old stick," Aphrael said. "He makes rules for no reason at all. That's all He ever does—makes rules. He's so tiresome sometimes."

"Why don't you go on with your story, Aphrael?"

"Very well." The Child-Goddess looked at the knights. "The spirits have colors, and they have a purpose," she told them. "I think you'll have to settle for that at the moment. One of the things they do is to make worlds. Bhelliom—which isn't its real name—made the blue ones. Seen from afar, this world is blue, because of its oceans. Other worlds are red, or green, or yellow, or any of countless other colors. These spirits make worlds by attracting the dust that blows forever through the emptiness, and the dust congeals around them like churned butter. But when Bhelliom made *this* world, it made a mistake. There was too much red dust. Bhelliom's essence is blue, and it can't bear red, but when you gather red dust together, you have—"

"Iron!" Tynian exclaimed.

"And you said they wouldn't understand," Aphrael said reproachfully to Sparhawk. She rushed to Tynian and kissed him several times. "Very well, then," she said happily. "Tynian is exactly right. Bhelliom cannot bear iron because iron is red. To protect itself, it hardened its essence of blue into the sapphire—which Ghwerig later carved into the shape of a rose. The iron—the red—congealed around it, and Bhelliom was trapped within the earth."

They stared at her, still only vaguely comprehending.

"Just make it short," Sparhawk advised.

"I *am.*"

"It's your story, Aphrael." He shrugged.

"Bhelliom's been congealed even more because the Troll-Gods are trapped in-side it," she continued.

"They're *what?*" Sparhawk gasped.

"Everybody knows *that,* Sparhawk. Where do you think Ghwerig hid them from us when we were looking for them?"

He uneasily remembered that Bhelliom and its unwilling inhabitants lay no more than a few inches from his heart.

"The point of all this is that Sparhawk has threatened to destroy Bhelliom, and because he's an Elene Knight, he'll probably use his sword—or an ax—or the spear of Aldreas, or something like that—something made of steel, which is to say iron. If he strikes Bhelliom with something made of steel, he *will* destroy it, and Bhelliom and the Troll-Gods are doing everything in their power to keep him from ever com-ing near enough to Azash for him to be tempted to raise his sword against it. First they tried to attack *his* mind, and when that didn't work, they began to attack *yours.* It won't be long, dear ones, before one of you tries to kill him."

"Never!" Kalten half shouted.

"If they continue to twist you, it *will* happen, Kalten."

"We'll fall on our swords first," Bevier declared.

"Why on earth would you want to do that?" she asked him. "All you have to do is confine the jewel in something made of steel. That canvas pouch is marked with the Styric symbols for iron, but Bhelliom and the Troll-Gods are growing desperate, and symbols aren't enough now. You'll have to use the real thing."

Sparhawk made a sour face, suddenly feeling just a little foolish. "I've been thinking all along that the shadow—and now that cloud—had come from Azash," he confessed.

Aphrael stared at him. "You *what?*" she exclaimed.

"It seemed sort of logical," he said lamely. "Azash has been trying to kill me since this all started."

"Why would Azash chase you around with clouds and shadows when he has much more substantial things at his command? Is that the very best all that logic could come up with?"

"I knew it!" Bevier exclaimed. "I *knew* we were overlooking something when you first told us about that shadow, Sparhawk! It didn't really *have* to be Azash after all."

Sparhawk suddenly felt very foolish.

"Why is it that I've got so much power over Bhelliom?" he asked her.

"Because of the rings."

"Ghwerig had the rings before I did."

"But they were clear stones then. Now they're red with the blood of your fam-ily and the blood of Ehlana's."

"Just the color is enough to make it obey me?"

Aphrael stared at him and then at Sephrenia. "Do you mean they don't *know* why their blood is red?" she asked incredulously. "What have you been *doing,* sister?"

"It's a difficult concept for them, Aphrael."

The little Goddess stamped away, flinging her arms in the air and muttering Styric words she should not have known existed.

"Sparhawk," Sephrenia said calmly, "your blood is red because it has iron in it."

"It *has*?" He was stunned. "How's that possible?"

"Just believe what I say, Sparhawk. It's those blood-stained rings that gives you so much power over the jewel."

"What an amazing thing," he said.

Aphrael returned then. "Once Bhelliom is confined in steel, you'll have no further interference from the Troll-Gods," she told them. "The rest of you will stop plotting to kill Sparhawk, and you'll all be as one again."

"Couldn't you have just told us what to do without all these explanations?" Kurik asked her. "These are Church Knights, Flute. They're used to following orders they don't understand. They almost have to be."

"I suppose I could have," she admitted, laying one small hand caressingly on his bearded cheek, "but I missed you—all of you—and I wanted you to see the place where I live."

"Showing off?" he teased her.

"Well—" She blushed slightly. "Is that so very, very improper?"

"It's a lovely island, Flute, and we're proud that you chose to show it to us."

She threw her arms about his neck and smothered him with kisses. Her face, Sparhawk noticed however, was wet with tears as she kissed the gruff squire.

"You must return now," she told them, "for the night is nearly over. First, however—"

The kissing went on for quite some time. When the dark-haired little Goddess came to Talen, she brushed her lips lightly against his and then started toward Tynian. She stopped, a speculative look on her face, and then returned to the young thief and did a more complete job on him. When she moved on, she was smiling mysteriously.

"And hath our gentle mistress resolved thy turmoil, Sir Knight?" the snowy hind asked as the swanlike boat returned the two of them to the alabaster strand where the gaily colored pavilion awaited them.

"I will know that with more certainty when mine eyes again open on the mundane world from which she summoned me, gentle creature," he replied. He found that he could not help himself. The flowery speech came to his lips unbidden. He sighed ruefully.

The note of the pipes was slightly discordant, a scolding sort of note.

"An' it please thee, dear Aphrael," he surrendered.

"That's much better, Sparhawk." The voice was no more than a whisper in his ears.

The small white deer led him back to the pavilion, and he lay down again, a strange, bemused drowsiness coming over him.

"Remember me," the hind said softly, nuzzling at his cheek.

"I will," he promised, "and gladly, for thy sweet presence doth ease my troubled soul and bids me rest."

And then again he slept.

He awoke in an ugly world of black sand and chill, blowing dust reeking of things long dead. His hair was clogged with the dust, and it abraded his skin beneath his clothing. What had really awakened him, however, was a small, *tink*ing sound, the sound of someone firmly tapping on ringing steel with a small hammer.

Despite the turmoil of the previous day, he felt enormously refreshed and at peace with the world.

The ringing sound of the hammer stopped, and Kurik crossed their dusty campsite with something in his hands. He held it out to Sparhawk. "What do you think?" he asked. "Will this lock it in?" What he was holding in his calloused hands was a chain-mail pouch. "It's about the best I can do for right now, my Lord. I don't have too much steel to work with."

Sparhawk took the pouch and looked at his squire. "You, too?" he asked. "You had a dream, too?"

Kurik nodded. "I talked with Sephrenia about it," he said. "We all had the same dream—it wasn't exactly a dream, though. She tried to explain it to me, but she lost me." He paused. "I'm sorry, Sparhawk. I doubted you. Everything seemed so futile and hopeless."

"That was the Troll-Gods, Kurik. Let's get Bhelliom into the steel pouch so that it doesn't happen to you again." He took up the canvas pouch and began to untie the strings.

"Wouldn't it be easier just to leave it inside the canvas sack?" Kurik asked.

"It might make it easier to put it into the steel one, but the time's coming when I might have to take it out in a hurry. I don't want any knots getting in my way when Azash is breathing down the back of my neck."

"Sound thinking, my Lord."

Sparhawk lifted the sapphire rose in both hands and held it directly in front of his face. "Blue-Rose," he said to it in Troll, "I am Sparhawk-from-Elenia. Do you know me?"

The Rose flickered sullenly.

"Do you acknowledge my authority?"

The Rose grew dark, and he could feel its hatred.

He inched his right thumb up along his palm and turned the ring on his finger around. Then he held the ring against the flower-gem—not the band this time but the blood-stained stone itself. He pressed his hand firmly against the sapphire rose.

Bhelliom shrieked, and he could feel it writhing in his hand like a live snake. He relaxed the pressure slightly. "I'm glad we understand each other," he said. "Hold open the pouch, Kurik."

There was no resistance. The jewel seemed almost eager to enter its imprisonment.

"Neat," Kurik said admiringly as Sparhawk wrapped a strand of soft iron wire around the top of the steel-link pouch.

"I thought it might be worth a try." Sparhawk grinned. "Are the others up yet?"

Kurik nodded. "They're standing in line over by the fire. You might give some thought to issuing a general amnesty, Sparhawk. Otherwise, they'll fill up half the morning with apologies. Be particularly careful about Bevier. He's been praying since before daylight. It's likely to take him a long time to tell you just how guilty he feels."

"He's a good boy, Kurik."

"Of course he is. That's part of the problem."

"Cynic."

Kurik grinned at him.

As the two of them crossed the camp, Kurik looked up at the sky. "The wind's died," he observed, "and the dust seems to be settling. Do you suppose—?" He left it tentative.

"Probably," Sparhawk said. "It sort of fits together, doesn't it? Well, here goes." He cleared his throat as he approached his shamefaced friends. "Interesting night, wasn't it?" he asked them conversationally. "I was really getting attached to that little white deer. She had a cold, wet nose, though."

They laughed, sounding a bit strained.

"All right," he said then. "Now we know where all the gloom was coming from, and there's not really much point in plowing over it again and again, is there? It was nobody's fault, so why don't we forget about it? We've got more important things to think about right now." He held up the steel-link pouch. "Here's our blue friend," he told them. "I hope it's comfortable in its little iron sack, but comfortable or not, that's where it's going to stay—at least until we need it. Whose turn is it to cook breakfast?"

"Yours," Ulath told him.

"I cooked supper last night."

"What's that got to do with it?"

"That's hardly fair, Ulath."

"I just keep track of these things, Sparhawk. If you're interested in justice, go talk with the Gods."

The rest of them laughed, and everything was all right again.

While Sparhawk was preparing breakfast, Sephrenia joined him at the fire. "I owe you an apology, dear one," she confessed.

"Oh?"

"I didn't even suspect that the Troll-Gods might have been the source of that shadow."

"I'd hardly call that your fault, Sephrenia. I was so convinced that it was Azash that I wasn't willing to admit any other possibility."

"I'm supposed to know better, Sparhawk. I'm not supposed to rely on logic."

"I think it might have been Perraine that led us in the wrong direction, little mother," he said gravely. "Those attacks of his came at Martel's direction, and Martel was simply following an earlier strategy laid down by Azash. Since it was just a continuation of what had been going on before, we had no reason to suspect that something new had entered the game. Even after we found out that Perraine had nothing to do with the shadow, the old idea still stuck. Don't blame yourself,

Sephrenia, because I certainly don't blame you. What surprises me is that Aphrael didn't see that we were making a mistake and warn us about it."

Sephrenia smiled a bit ruefully. "I'm afraid it was because she couldn't believe that we didn't understand. She has no real conception of just how limited we are, Sparhawk."

"Shouldn't you tell her?"

"I'd sooner die."

Kurik's speculation may or may not have been correct, but whether that constant wind that had choked them with dust for the past few days had been of natural origin or whether Bhelliom had roused it, it was gone now, and the air was clear and cold. The sky was bright, brittle blue, and the sun, cold and hard, hung above the eastern horizon. That, coupled with the vision of the preceding night, lifted their spirits enough to make it even possible for them to ignore the black cloud hovering on the horizon behind them.

"Sparhawk," Tynian said, pulling his horse in beside Faran, "I think I've finally figured it out."

"Figured what out?"

"I think I know how Ulath decides whose turn it is to cook."

"Oh? I'd like to hear that."

"He just waits until somebody asks, that's all. As soon as somebody asks whose turn it is, Ulath appoints *him* to do the cooking."

Sparhawk thought back. "You could be right, you know," he agreed, "but what if nobody asks?"

"Then Ulath has to do the cooking himself. It happened once as I recall."

Sparhawk thought it over. "Why don't you tell the others?" he suggested. "I think Ulath has a lot of turns coming, don't you?"

"He does indeed, my friend." Tynian laughed.

It was about midafternoon when they reached a steep ridge of sharply fractured black rock. There was a sort of a trail winding toward its top. When they were about halfway up, Talen called to Sparhawk from the rear. "Why don't we stop here?" he suggested. "I'll sneak on ahead and take a look."

"It's too dangerous," Sparhawk turned him down flatly.

"Grow up, Sparhawk. That's what I do. I'm a professional sneak. Nobody's going to see me. I can guarantee that." The boy paused. "Besides," he added, "if there's any kind of trouble, you're going to need grown men wearing steel to help you. I wouldn't be of much use in a fight, so I'm the only one you can really spare." He made a face. "I can't believe I just said that. I want you all to promise to keep Aphrael away from me. I think she's an unhealthy influence."

"Forget it," Sparhawk rejected the idea.

"No chance, Sparhawk," the boy said impudently, rolling out of his saddle and hitting the ground running. "None of you can catch me."

"He's long overdue for a good thrashing," Kurik growled as they watched the nimble boy scamper up the side of the ridge.

"He's right, though," Kalten said. "He's the only one we can really afford to lose. Somewhere along the way he's picked up a fairly wide streak of nobility. You should be proud of him, Kurik."

"Pride wouldn't do me much good when it came time to try to explain to his mother why I let him get himself killed."

Above them, Talen had disappeared almost as if the ground had opened and swallowed him. He emerged several minutes later from a fissure near the top of the ridge and ran back down the trail to rejoin them. "There's a city out there," he reported. "It would almost have to be Zemoch, wouldn't it?"

Sparhawk took his map out of his saddlebag. "How big is the city?"

"About the size of Cimmura."

"It has to be Zemoch, then. What does it look like?"

"I think it was sort of what they had in mind when they invented the word 'ominous.'"

"Was there any smoke?" Kurik asked him.

"Only coming from the chimneys of a couple of large buildings in the center of the city. They seemed to be sort of connected. One of them has all kinds of spires, and the other one's got a big black dome."

"The rest of the city must be deserted," Kurik said. "Have you ever been in Zemoch before, Sephrenia?"

"Once."

"What's the place with all the spires?"

"Otha's palace."

"And the one with the black dome?" Kurik did not really have to ask. They all knew the answer.

"The building with the black dome is the Temple of Azash. He's there—waiting for us."

# CHAPTER TWENTY-SIX

Subterfuge had never really been an option, Sparhawk concluded as he and his companions put aside their minimal disguises to don their armor. Deceiving unsophisticated peasants and third-rate militiamen out in the countryside was one thing, but attempting to pass unchallenged through a deserted city patrolled by elite troops would have been futile. Ultimately they would be obliged to resort to force of arms, and under the circumstances, that meant full armor. Chain mail was adequate for impromptu social get-togethers in rural surroundings, he thought wryly, but city life required greater formality. Country attire simply would not do.

"All right, what's the plan?" Kalten asked as the knights helped each other into their armor.

"I haven't exactly put one together yet," Sparhawk admitted. "To be perfectly honest with you, I didn't really think we'd get this far. I thought the best we could hope for was to get close enough to Otha's city to include it in the general destruction when I smashed the Bhelliom. As soon as we get settled into harness, we'll talk with Sephrenia."

High, thin clouds had begun to drift in from the east during the afternoon, and as the day moved on toward sunset, those clouds began to thicken. The desiccated chill began to lessen, and it was replaced by a peculiar sultriness. There were occasional rumblings of thunder far beyond the eastern horizon when, as the sun was dying amid bloody clouds, the knights gathered around Sephrenia.

"Our glorious leader here seems to have neglected a few strategic incidentals," Kalten announced to sort of start things off.

"Be nice," Sparhawk murmured to him.

"I am, Sparhawk. I haven't used the word 'idiot' even once. The question that makes us all burn with curiosity is, what do we do now?"

"Just offhand I'd say we could rule out a siege," Ulath observed.

"Frontal assaults are always fun," Tynian said.

"Do you mind?" Sparhawk said to them acidly. "This is sort of how I see it, Sephrenia. We've got what appears to be a deserted city out there, but there are sure to be patrols of Otha's elite guards. We might possibly be able to avoid them, but it wouldn't be a good idea to pin too many hopes on that. I just wish I knew a little bit more about the city itself."

"*And* about how good Otha's elite guards are," Tynian added.

"They're adequate soldiers," Bevier supplied.

"Would they be a match for Church Knights?" Tynian asked.

"No, but then who is?" Bevier said it with no trace of immodesty. "They're probably about on a par with the soldiers in King Wargun's army."

"You've been here before, Sephrenia," Sparhawk said. "Just exactly where are the palace and the temple located?"

"They're the same building, actually," she replied, "and they're in the exact center of the city."

"Then it wouldn't really matter which gate we used, would it?"

She shook her head.

"Isn't it rather odd for a palace and a temple to be under the same roof?" Kurik asked.

"Zemochs are odd people," she told him. "Actually there *is* some degree of separation, but you have to go *through* the palace to reach the temple. The temple itself doesn't have any outside entrances."

"Then all we have to do is ride to the palace and knock on the door," Kalten said.

"No," Kurik disagreed firmly. "We *walk* to the palace, and we'll talk about knocking when we get there."

"Walk?" Kalten sounded injured.

"Horses make too much noise on paved streets, and they're a little hard to hide when you need to take cover."

"Walking any distance in full armor isn't much fun, Kurik."

"You wanted to be a knight. As I remember it, you and Sparhawk even volunteered."

"Could you sort of whistle up that invisibility spell Sparhawk told us about?" Kalten asked Sephrenia. "The one Flute used to play on her pipes?"

She shook her head.

"Why not?"

She hummed a short musical phrase. "Do you recognize that melody?" she asked him.

He frowned. "I can't say that I do."

"That was the traditional Pandion hymn. I'm sure you're familiar with it. Does that answer your question?"

"Oh. Music isn't one of your strong points, I see."

"What would happen if you tried it and hit the wrong notes?" Talen asked curiously.

She shuddered. "Please don't ask."

"We skulk, then," Kalten said. "So let's get to skulking."

"Just as soon as it gets dark," Sparhawk said.

It was a mile or more across a flat, dusty plain to the grim walls of Zemoch, and the armored knights were all sweating profusely by the time they reached the west gate.

"Muggy," Kalten said quietly, wiping his streaming face. "Isn't there anything normal about Zemoch? It shouldn't be this sticky at this time of year."

"There's definitely some unusual weather coming in," Kurik agreed. The distant rumble of thunder and the pale flickers of lightning illuminating the cloud banks lying to the east confirmed their observations.

"Maybe we could appeal to Otha for shelter from the storm," Tynian said. "What are the Zemoch views on hospitality?"

"Undependable," Sephrenia replied.

"We'll want to be as quiet as we can once we're in the city," Sparhawk cautioned.

Sephrenia lifted her head and looked off to the east, her pale face scarcely visible in the sultry darkness. "Let's wait a bit," she suggested. "That storm's moving this way. Thunder would cover a great deal of incidental clanking."

They waited, leaning against the basalt walls of the city as the crack and tearing roar of the thunder marched inexorably toward them.

"That should cover any noise we make," Sparhawk said after about ten minutes. "Let's get inside before the rain comes."

The gate itself was made of crudely squared-off logs bound with iron, and it stood slightly ajar. Sparhawk and his companions drew their weapons and slipped through one by one.

There was a strange smell to the city, an odor that seemed to have no counterpart in any place Sparhawk had ever visited. It was an odor neither fair nor foul, but one that was more than anything peculiarly alien. There were no torches to provide illumination, of course, and they were forced to rely upon the intermittent flickers of lightning staining the purple cloud banks rolling in from the east. The streets revealed by those flashes were narrow, and their paving stones had been worn smooth by centuries of shuffling feet. The houses were tall and narrow, and their windows were small and for the most part barred. The perpetual dust storms that scoured the city had rubbed the stones of the houses quite smooth. The same gritty dust had gathered in corners and along the doorsills of the houses to give the city, which could not have been deserted for much more than a few months, the air of a ruin abandoned for eons.

Talen slipped up behind Sparhawk and rapped on his armor.

"Don't do that, Talen."

"It got your attention, didn't it? I've got an idea. Are you going to argue with me about it?"

"I don't think so. What was it you wanted to argue about?"

"I have certain talents that are rather unique in this group, you know."

"I doubt that you'll find very many purses to slit open, Talen. I don't see all that many people about."

"Ha," Talen said flatly. "Ha. Ha. Ha. Now that you're past that, are you ready to listen?"

"I'm sorry. Go ahead."

"None of the rest of you could really sneak through a graveyard without waking up half the occupants, right?"

"I wouldn't go quite *that* far."

"I would. I'll go on ahead—not too far, but just far enough. I'll be able to come back and tell you about anybody coming—or hiding in ambush."

Sparhawk didn't wait this time. He made a grab for the boy, but Talen slipped out of his reach quite easily. "Don't do that, Sparhawk. You just make yourself look foolish." He ran off a few feet, then stopped and slid his hand down into one boot. From its place of concealment he drew a long needle-pointed dirk. Then he vanished up the dark, narrow street.

Sparhawk swore.

"What's the matter?" Kurik asked from not far behind him.

"Talen just ran off."

"He did *what?*"

"He says he's going to scout on ahead. I tried to stop him, but I couldn't catch him."

From somewhere off in the maze of twisting streets there came a deep, mindless kind of howling.

"What's that?" Bevier asked, taking a tighter grip on his long-handled lochaber ax.

"The wind maybe?" Tynian replied without much conviction.

"The wind isn't blowing."

"I know, but I think I prefer to believe that's what's causing the noise anyway. I don't like the alternatives."

They moved on, staying close to the sides of the houses and freezing involuntarily in their tracks with each flash of lightning and crack of thunder.

Talen came back, running on silent feet. "There's a patrol coming," he said, staying just back out of reach. "Would you believe they're carrying torches? They're not trying to find anybody; they're trying to make sure they don't."

"How many?" Ulath asked.

"A dozen or so."

"Hardly enough to worry about, then."

"Why not just cut over to the next street through this alley? Then you won't even have to look at them, much less worry." The boy darted into an alleyway and disappeared again.

"The next time we choose a leader, I think I'll vote for him," Ulath murmured.

They moved on through the narrow, twisting streets. With Talen probing ahead of them, they were easily able to avoid the sporadic Zemoch patrols. As they worked their way nearer to the center of the city, however, they reached a quarter where the houses were more imposing and the streets were wider. The next time Talen came back, a momentary flash of ghostly lightning revealed a disgusted expression on his face. "There's another patrol just ahead," he reported. "The only trouble is that they're not patrolling. It looks as if they broke into a wine shop. They're sitting in the middle of the street drinking."

Ulath shrugged. "We'll just slip around them through the alleys again."

"We can't," Talen said. "There aren't any alleys leading off this street. I haven't found any way to get around them, and we have to use this street. As nearly as I can tell, it's the only one in the district that leads to the palace. This town doesn't make any sense at all. None of the streets go where they're supposed to."

"How many of these revellers do we have to contend with?" Bevier asked him.

"Five or six."

"And they have torches?"

Talen nodded. "They're just around this next turn in the street."

"With the torches flaring right in their eyes, they won't be able to see in the dark very well." Bevier flexed his arm, swinging his ax suggestively.

"What do you think?" Kalten asked Sparhawk.

"We might as well," Sparhawk said. "It doesn't sound as if they'll volunteer to get out of our way."

It was more in the nature of simple murder than a fight. The carouse of the Zemoch patrol had advanced to the point where they were aggressively inattentive. The Church Knights simply walked up to them and cut them down. One of them cried out briefly, but his surprised shout was lost in a tearing crash of thunder.

Without a word the knights dragged the inert bodies to nearby doorways and concealed them. Then they gathered protectively around Sephrenia and continued along that wide, lightning-illuminated street toward the sea of smoky torches that appeared to be encircling Otha's palace.

Once again they heard that howling sound, a sound devoid of any semblance of humanity. Talen returned, making no effort to evade them this time. "The palace isn't far ahead," he said, speaking quietly despite the now almost continuous thunder. "There are guards out front. They're wearing armor of some kind. It's got all kinds of steel points sticking out of it. They look like hedgehogs."

"How many?" Kalten asked.

"More than I had time to count. Do you hear that wailing noise?"

"I've been trying not to."

"I think you'd better get used to it. The guards are the ones making it."

Otha's palace was larger than the Basilica in Chyrellos, but it had no architectural grace. Otha had begun his life as a goatherd, and the principle that seemed to guide his sense of taste could best be summed up in the single word "large." So far as Otha was concerned, bigger was better. His palace had been constructed of fractured, rusty-black basalt rock. Because of its flat sides, basalt is easy for masons to work, but it offers little in the way of beauty. It lends itself to massive construction and not much else.

The palace reared like a mountain in the center of Zemoch. There were towers, of course. Palaces always have towers, but the rough black spires clawing at the air above the main building had no grace, no balance, and in most cases no evident purpose. Many of them had been started centuries before and then never finished. They jutted into the air, half-completed and surrounded by the rotting remains of crude scaffolding. The palace did not exude so much a sense of evil as it did of madness, of a kind of frenzied but purposeless effort.

Beyond the palace Sparhawk could see the swelling dome of the temple of Azash, a perfect rusty-black hemisphere constructed of huge, rigidly symmetrical hexagonal blocks of basalt that gave it the appearance of the nest of some enormous insect or a vast, scabbed-over wound.

The area surrounding the palace and the adjoining temple was a kind of paved dead zone where there were no buildings or trees or monuments. It was simply a flat place extending out perhaps two hundred yards from the walls. It was lighted on this darkest of nights by thousands of torches thrust at random into the cracks between the flagstones to form what almost appeared to be a knee-high field of tossing fire.

The broad avenue that the knights were following appeared to continue directly across the fiery plaza to the main portal of the house of Otha, where it entered with undiminished breadth through the widest and highest pair of arched doors Sparhawk had ever seen. Those doors stood ominously open.

The guards stood in the space between the walls and that broad grainfield of torches. They were armored, but their armor was more fantastic than any Sparhawk had ever seen. Their helmets had been wrought into the shape of skulls, and they were surmounted by branching steel antlers. The various joints—shoulder and elbow, hip and knee—were decorated with long spikes and flaring protrusions. Their forearms were studded with hooks, and the weapons they grasped were not so much weapons of death but of pain, with saw-tooth edges and razorlike barbs. Their shields were large and hideously painted.

Sir Tynian was Deiran, and Deirans from time immemorial have been the world's experts on armor. "Now that's the most idiotic display of pure childishness I've ever seen in my life," he said contemptuously to the others during a momentary lull in the thunder.

"Oh?" Kalten said.

"Their armor's almost useless. Good armor is supposed to protect the man wearing it but give him a certain freedom of movement. There's not much point in turning yourself into a turtle."

"It looks sort of intimidating, though."

"That's all it really is—something worn for its appearance. All those spikes and hooks are useless, and worse yet they'll just guide an opponent's weapon to vulnerable points. What were their armorers thinking of?"

"It's a legacy from the last war," Sephrenia explained. "The Zemochs were overwhelmed by the appearance of the Church Knights. They didn't understand the actual purpose of armor—only its frightening appearance, so their armorers concentrated on appearance rather than utility. Zemochs don't wear armor to protect themselves; they wear it to frighten their opponents."

"I'm not the least bit frightened, little mother," Tynian said gaily. "This is going to be almost too easy."

Then at some signal only Otha's hideously garbed warriors could perceive, they all broke into that mindless wailing, a kind of gibbering howl devoid of any meaning.

"Is that supposed to be some kind of war cry?" Berit asked nervously.

"It's about the best they can manage," Sephrenia told him. "Zemoch culture is basically Styric, and Styrics don't know anything about war. Elenes shout when they go to war. Those guards are just trying to imitate the sound."

"Why don't you take out the Bhelliom and erase them, Sparhawk?" Talen suggested.

"No!" Sephrenia said sharply. "The Troll-Gods are confined now. Let's not turn them loose again until we're in the presence of Azash. There's not too much point in unleashing Bhelliom on common soldiers and risking what we came here to do."

"She has a point," Tynian conceded.

"They aren't moving," Ulath said, looking at the guards. "I'm sure they can see us, but they aren't making any effort to form up and protect that doorway. If we can smash through to the door, go inside, and close it behind us, we won't have to worry about them anymore."

"Now that may just be the most inept plan I've ever heard," Kalten scoffed.

"Can you think of a better one?"

"No, as a matter of fact, I can't."

"Well, then?"

The knights formed up in their customary wedge formation and strode rapidly toward the gaping portal of Otha's palace. As they approached through that fiery field, an oddly familiar reek came momentarily to Sparhawk's nostrils.

As quickly as it had begun, the meaningless howling broke off, and the guards in their skull-faced armor stood motionless. They did not brandish their weapons or even attempt to gather more force before the portal. They simply stood.

Again there came that penetrating reek, but it was quickly swept away by a sudden wind. The lightning redoubled its fury and began to blast great chunks from nearby buildings with deafening crashes. The air about them seemed suddenly tinglingly alive.

"Down!" Kurik barked sharply. "Everybody get down on the ground!"

They did not understand, but they all immediately obeyed, diving for the ground with a great clattering of their armor.

The reason for Kurik's alarmed shout became immediately apparent. Two of the grotesquely armored guards to the left of the massive doors were suddenly engulfed in a brilliant ball of bluish fire and were quite literally blasted to pieces. Their fellows did not move or even turn to look as scorched bits and pieces of armor showered upon them.

"It's the armor!" Kurik shouted over the crashing thunder. "Steel attracts lightning! Stay down!"

The lightning continued to blast down into the metal-clad ranks of the skull-faced guardsmen, and the smell of burning flesh and hair gusted back across the broad plaza as the sudden wind swirled and rebounded from the high basalt walls of the palace.

"They're not even moving!" Kalten exclaimed. "Nobody's *that* disciplined."

Then as the storm continued its ponderous march, the sudden flurry of lightning moved on to shatter deserted houses instead of steel-clad men.

"Is it all right now?" Sparhawk demanded of his squire.

"I don't know for certain," Kurik told him. "If you start to feel any kind of tingling, get down immediately."

They rose warily to their feet. "Was that Azash?" Tynian asked Sephrenia.

"I don't think so. If Azash had thrown the lightning, I don't think he'd have missed us. It might have been Otha, though. Until we get to the temple, we're more likely to encounter Otha's work than anything conjured up by Azash."

"Otha? Is he really that skilled?"

"Skilled probably isn't the right word," she replied. "Otha has great power, but he's clumsy. He's too lazy to practice."

They continued their menacing advance, but the men awaiting them in that grotesque armor still made no move either to attack or even reinforce those of their number barring the door.

When Sparhawk reached the first of the guards, he raised his sword, and the previously motionless man howled at him and clumsily raised a broad-bladed ax embellished with useless spikes and barbs. Sparhawk slapped the ax aside and struck with his sword. The dreadful-looking armor was even less useful than Tynian had suggested. It was scarcely thicker than paper, and Sparhawk's sword stroke slashed down into the guard's body as if it had met no resistance whatsoever. Even had he struck at a totally unprotected man, his sword should not have cut so deeply into the body.

Then the man he had just slaughtered collapsed, and his gashed armor gaped open. Sparhawk recoiled in sudden revulsion. The body inside the armor had not been the body of a living man. It appeared to be no more than blackened, slimy bones with a few shreds of rotting flesh clinging to them. A dreadful stink suddenly boiled out of the armor.

"They aren't alive!" Ulath roared. "There's nothing in the armor but bones and rotting guts!"

Sickened, gagging with nausea, the knights fought on, hacking their way through their already dead enemies.

"Stop!" Sephrenia cried sharply.

"But—" Kalten started to object.

"Take one step backward—all of you!"

They grudgingly stepped back a pace, and the outrageously armored cadavers menacing them returned to immobility. Once again at that unseen and unheard signal they gave vent to that emotionless howl.

"What's going on?" Ulath demanded. "Why aren't they attacking?"

"Because they're dead, Ulath," Sephrenia said.

Ulath pointed at a crumpled form with his ax. "Dead or not, this one still tried to stick his spear into me."

"That's because you came to within reach of his weapon. Look at them. They're standing all around us, and they aren't making any move to assist their companions. Get me a torch, Talen."

The boy wrested a torch from between two flagstones and handed it to her. She raised it and peered at the paving beneath their feet. "That's frightening," she said with a shudder.

"We will protect you, Lady Sephrenia," Bevier assured her. "You have nothing to fear."

"There's nothing for any of us to fear, dear Bevier. What's truly frightening is the fact that Otha probably has more power at his command than any living human, but he's so stupid that he doesn't even know how to use it. We've spent centuries fearing an absolute imbecile."

"Raising the dead *is* fairly impressive, Sephrenia," Sparhawk suggested.

"Any Styric child can galvanize a corpse, but Otha doesn't even know what to do with them once he raises them. Each one of his dead guardians is standing on a flagstone, and that flagstone is all it's protecting."

"Are you sure?"

"Test it and see for yourself."

Sparhawk raised his shield and advanced on one of the stinking guards. As soon as his foot touched the flagstone, the skull-faced thing swung jerkily at him with a jagged-bladed ax. He easily deflected the stroke and stepped back. The guard returned to its former position and stood motionless as a statue.

The vast circle of guards ringing the palace and the temple howled their empty howl again.

Then, to Sparhawk's horror, Sephrenia gathered her white robe about her and quite calmly began to thread her way through the ranks of the stinking dead. She stopped and glanced back at them. "Oh *do* come along now. Let's get inside before the rain starts. Just don't step on any of their flagstones, that's all."

It was eerie to step around those savagely threatening figures with their foul reek and their skull-like faces in the ghastly light of the dancing lightning, but no more dangerous in fact than avoiding nettles on a forest trail.

When they had passed the last of the dead sentries, Talen stopped and squinted along a diagonal rank of those guardians. "Revered teacher," he said quietly to Berit.

"Yes, Talen?"

"Why don't you push this one over?" Talen pointed at the back of one of the armored figures. "Sort of off to the side?"

"Why?"

Talen grinned a wicked kind of grin. "Just give it a shove, Berit. You'll see."

Berit looked a bit puzzled, but he reached out with his ax and gave the rigid corpse a good shove. The armored figure fell, crashing into another. The second corpse promptly beheaded the first, staggering back as it did so, and it was immediately chopped down by a third.

The chaos spread rapidly, and a sizeable number of the intimidating dead were dismembered by their fellows in a mindless display of unthinking savagery.

"That's a *very* good boy you have there, Kurik," Ulath said.

"We have some hopes for him," Kurik said modestly.

They turned toward the portal and then stopped. Hanging in mid-air in the very center of the dark doorway was a misty face engraved upon the emptiness with sickly green flame. The face was grotesquely misshapen, a thing of towering, implacable evil—and it was familiar. Sparhawk had seen it before.

"*Azash!*" Sephrenia hissed. "Stay back, all of you!"

They stared at the ghastly apparition.

"Is that really him?" Tynian asked in an awed voice.

"An image of him," Sephrenia replied. "It's more of Otha's work."

"Is it dangerous?" Kalten asked her.

"To step into the doorway means death, and worse than death."

"Are there any other ways to get in?" Kalten asked her, eyeing the glowing apparition fearfully.

"I'm sure there are, but I doubt if we'd ever be able to find them."

Sparhawk sighed. He had decided a long time ago that he would do this when the time came. He regretted the argument it was going to cause more than the act itself. He detached Bhelliom's steel-mesh pouch from his belt. "All right," he said to his friends, "you'd better get started. I can't give you any guarantees about how much time I'll be able to give you, but I'll hold off for as long as I can."

"What are you talking about?" Kalten asked suspiciously.

"This is as close to Azash as we're going to get, I'm afraid. We all know what has to be done, and it's only going to take one of us to do it. If any of you ever makes it back to Cimmura, tell Ehlana that I wished that this had turned out differently. Sephrenia, is this close enough? Will Azash be destroyed?"

Her eyes were full of tears, but she nodded.

"Let's not get sentimental about this," Sparhawk said brusquely. "We don't have the time. I'm honored to have known you—all of you. Now get out of here. That's an order." He had to get them moving before they began making foolishly noble decisions. "Go!" he roared at them. "And watch how you step around those guards!"

They were moving now. Military men always respond to commands—if the commands are shouted. They were moving, and that was all that was important. The whole gesture was probably futile anyway. If what Sephrenia had said was true, they would need at least a day to get beyond the area that would be totally destroyed when he smashed the Bhelliom, and there was little hope that he could remain undiscovered for that long. He had to at least try to give them that one slim chance, though. Perhaps no one would come out of the palace, and none of the patrols roving the streets would chance to see him. It was nice to think so, anyway.

He did not want to watch them go. It would be better that way. There were things to be done anyway, things far more important than standing forlornly like a child who has misbehaved and is being left behind while the rest of the family goes off to the fair. He looked first to the right and then to the left. If Sephrenia had been right and if this was the only way into Otha's palace, it would be better to go off some distance from the gaping portal and its glowing apparition. That way, all he would need to concern himself about would be those patrols. Anyone—or any-thing— emerging from the palace wouldn't immediately see him. Left, or right? He shrugged. What difference did it make? Perhaps it might be better to slip around the outer perimeter of the palace and to wait against the wall of the temple itself. He'd be closer to Azash that way, and the Elder God would be closer to the center of that absolute obliteration. He half turned and saw them. They were standing beyond the ranks of the threatening dead. Their faces were resolute.

"What are you doing?" he called to them. "I told you to get out of here."

"We decided to wait for you," Kalten called back.

Sparhawk took a threatening step toward them.

"Don't be foolish, Sparhawk," Kurik said. "You can't afford to risk trying to sidestep your way through those dead men. If you make a single misstep, one of them will brain you from behind—and then Azash will get Bhelliom. Did we really come all this way just for that?"

## CHAPTER TWENTY-SEVEN

S parhawk swore. Why couldn't they just do as they had been told? Then he sighed. He should have known they wouldn't obey. There was no help for it now, and no point in berating them about it.

He pulled off his gauntlet to take his water bottle from his belt, and his ring flashed blood-red in the torchlight. He worked the stopper out of the bottle and drank. The ring flashed in his eyes again. He lowered the bottle, looking thought-fully at the ring. "Sephrenia," he said almost absently. "I need you."

She was at his side in a few moments.

"The Seeker was Azash, wasn't it?"

"That's an oversimplification, Sparhawk."

"You know what I mean. When we were at King Sarak's grave in Pelosia, Azash spoke to you through the Seeker, but he ran away when I started after him with Al-dreas' spear."

"Yes."

"And I used the spear to chase away that thing that came out of the mound in Lamorkand, and I killed Ghwerig with it."

"Yes."

"But it wasn't really the spear, was it? It isn't really all that much of a weapon, after all. It was the rings, wasn't it?"

"I don't see where you're going with this, Sparhawk."

"Neither do I exactly." He pulled off his other gauntlet and held his hands out, looking at the rings. "They have a certain amount of power themselves, don't they? I think maybe I've been getting a little overwhelmed by the fact that they're the keys to Bhelliom. Bhelliom's got so much power that I've been overlooking things that can be done with just the rings alone. Aldreas' spear didn't really have anything to do with it—which is a good thing, actually, since it's standing in a corner in Ehlana's apartment back in Cimmura. Any weapon would have served just as well, wouldn't it?"

"As long as the rings were touching it, yes. Please, Sparhawk, just get to the point. Your Elene logic is tedious."

"It helps me to think. I could clear that image out of the doorway with Bhelliom, but that would turn the Troll-Gods loose, and they'd be trying to stab me in the back every time I turned around. But the Troll-Gods have no connection with the rings. I can use the rings without waking Ghnomb and his friends. What would happen if I took my sword in both hands and touched it to that face hanging in the doorway?"

She stared at him.

"We aren't really talking about Azash here. We're dealing with Otha. I may not be the greatest magician in the world, but I really don't have to be as long as I have the rings. I think they may just be more than a match for Otha, wouldn't you say?"

"I can't tell you, Sparhawk." Her tone was subdued. "I don't know."

"Why don't we try it and find out?" He turned and looked back across the ranks of the reeking dead. "All right," he called to his friends, "come back here. We've got something to do."

They slipped warily past the armored cadavers and gathered around Sparhawk and his tutor. "I'm going to try something that might not work," he told them, "and if it doesn't, you're going to have to deal with Bhelliom." He took the steel-mesh pouch from his belt. "If what I try fails, spill Bhelliom out on the flagstones and smash it with a sword or an ax." He gave the pouch to Kurik, handed Kalten his shield, and drew his sword. He gripped its hilt in both hands and strode back to the vast doorway with the glowing apparition hanging in its center. He lifted his sword. "Wish me luck," he said. Anything else would have smacked of bombast.

He straightened his arms, levelling his sword at the image etched in green fire before him. He steeled himself and deliberately stepped forward to bring his sword point into contact with the burning enchantment.

The results were satisfyingly spectacular. The touch of the sword point exploded the burning image, showering Sparhawk with a waterfall of multicolored sparks, and the detonation probably shattered every window for miles in any direction. Sparhawk and all of his friends were hurled to the ground, and the armored corpses still standing guard before the palace were felled like new-mown wheat. Sparhawk shook his head to clear away the ringing in his ears and struggled to get back on his feet again as he stared at the portal. One of the vast doors had been split down the middle, and the other hung precariously from a single hinge. The apparition was gone, and in its place hung a few tatters of wispy smoke. From deep inside the palace there came a prolonged, batlike screech of agony.

"Is everybody all right?" Sparhawk shouted, looking at his friends.

They were struggling to their feet, their eyes slightly unfocused.

"Noisy," was all Ulath said.

"Who's making all that noise inside?" Kalten asked.

"Otha, I'd imagine," Sparhawk replied. "Having one of your spells shattered gives you quite a turn." He retrieved his gauntlets and the steel-mesh pouch:

"Talen!" Kurik shouted. "No!"

But the boy had already walked directly into the open doorway. "There doesn't seem to be anything here, Father," he reported, walking farther inside and then back out again. "Since I didn't vanish in a puff of smoke, I think we can say that it's safe."

Kurik started to move toward the boy, his hands outstretched hungrily. Then he thought better of it and stopped, muttering curses.

"Let's go inside," Sephrenia said, "I'm sure every patrol in the city heard that blast. We can hope that they thought it was only thunder, but some of them are bound to come to investigate."

Sparhawk picked up the pouch and tucked it back under his belt. "We'll want to get out of sight once we're inside. Which way should we go?"

"Bear to the left once we're through the doorway. The passages on that side lead to the kitchens and the storerooms."

"All right then. Let's go."


That alien smell Sparhawk had noticed when they had first entered the city was stronger here in the dark corridors of the palace. The knights moved cautiously, listening to the echoes of the shouts of the elite guards. The palace was in turmoil, and even in a place as vast as this there were bound to be encounters. In most cases, Sparhawk and his friends evaded these by simply stepping into the dark chambers that lined the corridors. Sometimes, however, that was not possible, but the Knights of the Church were far more skilled at close combat than the Zemochs, and what noise the encounters produced was lost in the shouting that echoed through the corridors. They pressed on, their weapons at the ready.

It was nearly an hour later when they entered a large pastry kitchen where the banked fires provided a certain amount of light. They stopped there and closed and barred the doors.

"I'm all turned around," Kalten confessed, stealing a small cake. "Which way do we go?"

"Through that door, I think," Sephrenia replied. "The kitchens all open into a corridor that leads to the throne room."

"Otha eats in his throne room?" Bevier asked in some surprise.

"Otha doesn't move around very much," she answered. "He can't walk any more."

"What happened to him to cripple him?"

"His appetite. Otha eats almost constantly, and he's never been fond of exercise. His legs are too weak to carry him any more."

"How many doors into the throne room?" Ulath asked her.

She thought a moment, remembering. "Four, I think. The one from the kitchens here, another coming in from the main palace, and the one leading to Otha's private quarters."

"And the last?"

"The last entrance doesn't have a door. It's the opening that leads into the maze."

"Our first move should be to block those, then. We'll want some privacy when we talk with Otha."

"And anybody else who happens to be there," Kalten added. "I wonder if Martel's managed to get here yet." He took another cake.

"There's one way to find out," Tynian said.

"In a moment," Sparhawk said. "What's this maze you mentioned, Sephrenia?"

"It's the route to the temple. There was a time when people were fascinated by labyrinths. It's very complicated and very dangerous."

"Is that the only way to get to the temple?"

She nodded.

"The worshippers walk *through* the throne room to get to the temple?"

"Ordinary worshippers don't go into the temple, Sparhawk—only priests and sacrifices."

"We should probably rush the throne room, then. We'll bar the doors, deal with whatever guards may be in there, and then take Otha prisoner. If we put a knife to his throat, I don't think any of his soldiers will interfere with us."

"Otha's a magician, Sparhawk," Tynian reminded him. "Taking him prisoner might not be as easy as it sounds."

"Otha's no particular danger at the moment," Sephrenia disagreed. "We've all had spells come apart on us before. It takes awhile to recover from that."

"Are we ready, then?" Sparhawk asked tensely.

They nodded, and he led them through the doorway.

The corridor leading from the kitchens to Otha's throne room was narrow and not very long. Its far end was illuminated by ruddy torchlight. As they neared that light, Talen slipped on ahead, his soft-shod feet making no sound on the flagstone floor. He returned in a few moments. "They're all there," he whispered in a voice tight with excitement. "Annias, Martel, and the rest. It looks as if they just got here. They're still wearing travellers' cloaks."

"How many guards in the room?" Kurik asked him.

"Not too many. Twenty or so at the most."

"The rest of them are probably out in the halls looking for us."

"Can you describe the room?" Tynian asked. "And the places where the guards are standing?"

Talen nodded. "This corridor opens out not far from the throne itself. You'll be able to pick Otha out of the rest almost immediately. He looks a lot like a garden slug. Martel and the others are gathered around him. There are two guards at each of the doors—except for the archway right behind the throne. Nobody's guarding that one. The rest of the guards are scattered along the walls. They're wearing mail and swords, and each one of them is holding a long spear. There are a dozen or so burly fellows in loincloths squatting near the throne. They don't have any weapons."

"Otha's bearers," Sephrenia explained.

"You were right," Talen told her. "There are four doors—this one just ahead of us, another over on the far side of the room, the archway, and a bigger one down at the end of the room."

"The door that leads out into the rest of the palace," Sephrenia said.

"*That's* the important one, then," Sparhawk decided. "There's nobody in these kitchens but a few cooks, I'd imagine, and not very many people in Otha's bedroom, but there'll be soldiers on the other side of that main door. How far is it from this door to that one?"

"About two hundred feet," the boy said.

"Who feels like running?" Sparhawk looked around at his friends.

"What do you say, Tynian?" Ulath asked. "How fast can you cover two hundred feet?"

"As fast as *you* can, my friend."

"We'll take care of it, Sparhawk," Ulath said.

"Don't forget that you promised to let me have Adus," Kalten reminded his friend.

"I'll try to save him for you."

They moved purposefully ahead toward the torchlit doorway. They paused just back from it, then they rushed through. Ulath and Tynian sprinted toward the main door. There were cries of shock and alarm as the knights burst into the throne room. Otha's soldiers shouted conflicting orders to each other, but one officer overrode them all with the hoarse bellow, "Protect the emperor!"

The mailed guards lining the walls deserted their comrades at the doors and rushed to form a protective ring around the throne with their spears. Kalten and Bevier had almost negligently cut down the two guards at the entrance to the corridor leading back into the kitchens, and then Ulath and Tynian reached the main door where the two guards were desperately trying to open it to cry for help. Both men fell in the first flurry of strokes, and then Ulath set his massive back against the door and braced himself while Tynian pawed behind the nearby draperies looking for the bar to lock the door.

Berit dashed through the doorway beside Sparhawk, leaped over the still weakly moving guards on the floor, and ran toward the door on the opposite side of the room with his ax raised. Even though he was encumbered by his armor, he ran like a deer across the polished floor of the throne room and fell upon the two men guarding the door that led back to Otha's bedchamber. He brushed aside their spears and disposed of them with two powerful ax blows.

Sparhawk heard the solid metallic clank behind him as Kalten slammed the heavy iron bar into place.

There was a pounding on the outside of the door Ulath was holding closed, and then Tynian found the iron bar and slid it into place. Berit barred his door as well.

"Very workmanlike," Kurik approved. "We still can't get to Otha, though."

Sparhawk looked at the ring of spears around the throne and then at Otha himself. As Talen had said, the man who had terrified the west for the past five centuries looked much like a common slug. He was pallid white and totally hairless. His face was grossly bloated and so shiny with sweat as to look almost as if it were covered with slime. His paunch was enormous, and it protruded so far in front of him that it gave his arms the appearance of being stunted. He was incredibly dirty, and priceless rings decorated his greasy hands. He half lay on his throne as if something had hurled him back. His eyes were glazed, and his limbs and body were twitching convulsively. He had obviously still not recovered from the shock of the breaking of his spell.

Sparhawk drew in a deep breath to steady himself, looking around as he did so. The room itself was decorated with the ransom of kings. The walls were covered with hammered gold, and the columns were sheathed in mother-of-pearl. The floor was of polished black onyx and the draperies flanking each door were of blood-red velvet. Torches protruded from the walls at intervals, and very large iron braziers stood one on each side of Otha's throne.

And then at last, Sparhawk looked at Martel.

"Ah, Sparhawk," the white-haired man drawled urbanely, "so good of you to drop by. We've been expecting you."

The words seemed almost casual, but there was the faintest hint of an edge to Martel's voice. He had *not* expected them to arrive so soon, and he had certainly not expected their sudden rush. He stood with Annias, Arissa, and Lycheas within the safety of the ring of spears while Adus encouraged the spearmen with kicks and curses.

"We were in the neighborhood anyway." Sparhawk shrugged. "How've you been, old boy? You look a bit travel-worn. Was it a difficult journey?"

"Nothing unbearable." Martel inclined his head toward Sephrenia. "Little mother," he said, sounding once again oddly regretful.

Sephrenia sighed, but said nothing.

"I see we're all here," Sparhawk continued. "I do so enjoy these little get-togethers, don't you? They give us the chance to reminisce." He looked at Annias, whose subordinate position to Martel was now clearly evident. "You should have stayed in Chyrellos, your Grace," he said. "You missed all the excitement of the election. Would you believe that the Hierocracy actually put Dolmant on the arch-prelate's throne?"

A look of sudden anguish crossed the face of the Primate of Cimmura. "Dolmant?" he choked in a stricken voice. In later years Sparhawk was to conclude that his revenge upon the primate had been totally complete in that instant. The pain his simple statement had caused his enemy was beyond his ability to comprehend it. The life of the Primate of Cimmura crumbled and turned to ashes in that single moment.

"Astonishing, isn't it?" Sparhawk continued relentlessly. "Absolutely the last man anyone would have expected. Many in Chyrellos feel that the hand of God was involved. My wife, the Queen of Elenia—you remember her, don't you? . . . blonde girl, rather pretty, the one you poisoned—made a speech to the patriarchs just as they were beginning their deliberations. It was *she* who suggested him. She was amazingly eloquent, but it's generally believed that her speech was inspired by God Himself—particularly in view of the fact that Dolmant was elected unanimously."

"That's impossible!" Annias gasped. "You're lying, Sparhawk!"

"You can verify it for yourself, Annias. When I take you back to Chyrellos, I'm sure you'll have plenty of time to examine the records of the meeting. There's quite a dispute in the works about who's going to have the pleasure of putting you on trial and executing you. It may drag on for years. Somehow you've managed to offend just about everybody west of the Zemoch border. They all want to kill you for some reason."

"You're being just a bit childish, Sparhawk," Martel sneered.

"Of course I am. We all do that sometimes. It's really a shame the sunset was so uninspiring this evening, Martel, since it was the last one you're ever going to see."

"That's true of one of us at any rate."

"Sephrenia." It was a rumbling, deep-toned gurgle more than a voice.

"Yes, Otha?" she replied calmly.

"Bid thy witless little Goddess farewell," the sluglike man on the throne rumbled in antique Elene. His little eyes were focused now, though his hands still trembled. "Thine unnatural kinship with the Younger Gods draws to its close. Azash awaits thee."

"I rather doubt that, Otha, for I bring the unknown one with me. I found him long before he was born, and I have brought him here with Bhelliom in his fist. Azash fears him, Otha, and you would be wise to fear him, too."

Otha sank lower on his throne, his head seeming to retract turtlelike into the folds of his fat neck. His hand moved with surprising speed, and a beam of greenish light shot from it, a light levelled at the small Styric woman. Sparhawk, however, had been waiting for that. He had been holding his shield in both bare hands in a negligent-appearing posture. The blood-red stones of the rings were quite firmly pressed against the shield's steel rim. With practiced speed he thrust the shield in front of his tutor. The beam of green light struck the shield and reflected back from its polished surface. One of the armored guards was suddenly obliterated in a soundless blast that sprayed the throne room with white-hot fragments of his chain mail.

Sparhawk drew his sword. "Have we just about finished with all this nonsense, Martel?" he asked bleakly.

"Wish I could oblige, old boy," Martel replied, "but Azash is waiting for us. You know how that goes."

The hammering on the heavy door Tynian and Ulath were guarding grew louder.

"Is that someone knocking?" Martel said mildly. "Be a good fellow, Sparhawk, and see who it is. All that banging sets my teeth on edge."

Sparhawk started forward.

"Take the emperor to safety!" Annias barked to the barely clad brutes squatting near the throne. With practiced haste, the men inserted stout steel poles into recesses in the jewelled seat, set their shoulders under the poles, and lifted the vast weight of their master from the pedestallike base of the throne. Then they wheeled with the litter and trotted ponderously toward the arched opening behind the throne.

"Adus!" Martel commanded, "keep them off me!" Then he, too, turned and herded Annias and his family along in Otha's wake as the brutish Adus pushed forward, flogging at Otha's spear-armed guards with the flat of his sword and bellowing unintelligible orders.

The hammering at the locked doors became a booming sound as the soldiers outside improvised battering-rams.

"Sparhawk!" Tynian shouted. "Those doors won't hold for long!"

"Leave them!" Sparhawk shouted back. "Help us here! Otha and Martel are getting away!"

The soldiers Adus commanded had spread out to face Sparhawk, Kurik, and Bevier not so much to engage them as to prevent their entering the arched doorway that led back into the labyrinth. Although he was in most respects profoundly, even frighteningly stupid, Adus was a gifted warrior, and a fight of this nature, involving as it did a simple situation and a manageable number of men, put him in his natural element. He directed Otha's guardsmen with grunts, kicks, and blows, deploying them in pairs and trios to block individual opponents with their spears. The concept implicit in Martel's command was well within Adus' limited grasp. His purpose was to delay the knights long enough to enable Martel to escape, and perhaps no one was better suited for that than Adus.

As Kalten, Ulath, Tynian, and Berit joined the fight, Adus gave ground. He had the advantage of numbers, but his Zemoch soldiers were no match for the steel-clad knights. He was, however, able to pull the bulk of his force back into the mouth of the maze where their spears could serve as an effective barrier.

And all the while the rhythmic booming of the battering-rams continued.

"We've got to get into that maze!" Tynian shouted. "When those doors give way, we're going to be surrounded!"

It was Sir Bevier who took action. The young Cyrinic Knight was bravery personified, and on many occasions he had demonstrated a total disregard for his own personal safety. He strode forward, swinging his brutal, hook-pointed lochaber ax. He swung not at the soldiers, but at their spears, and a spear without a point is nothing more than a pole. Within moments he had effectively disarmed Adus' Zemochs—and had received a deep wound in his side, just above the hip. He fell back weakly, with blood streaming from the rent in his armor.

"See to him!" Sparhawk barked to Berit, and lunged forward to engage the Zemochs. Without their spears, the Zemochs were forced to fall back on their swords, and the advantage shifted to the Church Knights at that point. The armored men chopped the Zemochs out of their path.

Adus assessed the situation quickly and stepped back into the doorway.

"Adus!" Kalten bellowed, kicking a Zemoch out of his way.

"Kalten!" Adus roared. The brute took a step forward, his piglike eyes hungry. Then he snarled and disembowelled one of his own soldiers to give vent to his frustration and disappeared back into the maze.

Sparhawk whirled about. "How is he?" he demanded of Sephrenia, who knelt over the wounded Bevier.

"It's serious, Sparhawk."

"Can you stop the bleeding?"

"Not entirely, no."

Bevier lay pale and sweating, with the breastplate of his armor unbuckled and lying open like a clamshell. "Go on, Sparhawk," he said. "I'll hold this doorway for as long as I can."

"Don't be stupid," Sparhawk snapped. "Pad the wound as best you can, Sephrenia. Then buckle his armor back up. Berit, bring him along. Carry him if you have to."

There was a splintering sound behind them in the throne room as the booming continued.

"The doors are giving way, Sparhawk," Kalten reported.

Sparhawk looked down the long arched corridor leading into the maze. Torches were set in iron rings at widely spaced intervals. A sudden hope flared up in him. "Ulath," he said, "you and Tynian bring up the rear. Shout if any of those soldiers breaking down the doors come up behind us."

"I'll just hold you back, Sparhawk," Bevier said weakly.

"No, you won't," Sparhawk replied. "We're not going to run through this maze. We don't know what's in here, so we're not going to take any chances. All right, gentlemen, let's move out."

They started down the long, straight corridor that led into the labyrinth, passing two or three unlighted entrances on either side as they went.

"Shouldn't we check those?" Kalten asked.

"It's probably not necessary," Kurik said. "Some of Adus' men were wounded, and there are blood spatters on the floor. We know that Adus at least went this way."

"That's no guarantee that *Martel* did," Kalten said. "Maybe he told Adus to lead us off in the wrong direction."

"It's possible," Sparhawk conceded, "but this corridor is lighted, and none of the others are."

"I'd hardly call it a maze if the way through it is marked with torches, Sparhawk," Kurik pointed out.

"Maybe not, but as long as the torches and the blood trail go the same way, we'll chance it."

The echoing corridor made a sharp turn to the left at its far end. The vaulted walls and ceiling curving upward and inward gave the twisting passages that oppressive sense of being too low, and Sparhawk found himself instinctively ducking his head.

"They've broken through the doors in the throne room, Sparhawk," Ulath called from the rear. "There are some torches bobbing around back in the entryway."

"That more or less settles it," Sparhawk said. "We don't have time to start exploring side passages. Let's go on."

The lighted corridor began to twist and turn at that point, and the spots of blood on the floor suggested that they were still on the same trail Adus had followed.

The corridor turned to the right.

"How are you bearing up?" Sparhawk asked Bevier, who was leaning heavily on Berit's shoulder.

"Fine, Sparhawk. As soon as I get my breath, I'll be able to make it without help."

The corridor turned to the left again, then to the left again after only a few yards.

"We're going back the same way we came, Sparhawk," Kurik declared.

"I know. Do we have any choice, though?"

"Not that I can think of, no."

"Ulath," Sparhawk called, "are the men behind us gaining at all?"

"Not that I can see."

"Maybe they don't know the way through the maze either," Kalten suggested. "I don't think anyone would visit Azash just for fun."

The rush came out of a side corridor. Five spear-armed Zemoch soldiers dashed out of the dark entryway and bore down on Sparhawk, Kalten, and Kurik. Their spears gave them some advantage—but not enough. After three of their number had been felled to lie writhing and bleeding on the flagstone floor, the other two fled back the way they had come.

Kurik seized a torch from one of the iron rings in the wall and led Sparhawk and Kalten into the dark, twisting corridor. After several minutes they saw the soldiers they were pursuing. The two men were fearfully edging their way through a stretch of the passage, each one of them hugging a wall.

"Now we've got them," Kalten exulted, starting forward.

"Kalten!" Kurik's voice cracked. "Stop!"

"What's wrong?"

"They're staying too close to the walls."

"So?"

"What's wrong with the middle of the passageway?"

Kalten stared at the two frightened men clinging to the walls, his eyes narrowing. "Let's find out," he said. He pried up a small flagstone with his sword point and hurled it at one of the soldiers, missing his mark by several feet.

"Let me do it," Kurik told him. "You can't throw anything with your armor binding up your shoulders the way it does." He pried loose another stone. His aim was much more true. The rock he had thrown bounced off the soldier's helmet with a loud clang. The man cried out as he reeled back, trying desperately to grab some kind of handhold on the stone wall. He failed, however, and stepped onto the floor in the center of the corridor.

The floor promptly fell open under him, and he dropped from sight with a despairing shriek. His companion, straining to see, also made a misstep and fell from the narrow ledge along the wall to follow his friend into the pit.

"Clever," Kurik said. He advanced to the brink of the gaping pit and raised his torch. "The bottom's studded with sharpened stakes," he observed, looking down at the two men impaled below. "Let's go back and tell the others. I think we'd better start watching where we put our feet."

They returned to that torchlit main corridor as Ulath and Tynian joined them from the rear. Kurik tersely described the trap that had claimed the two Zemochs. He looked thoughtfully at the soldiers who had fallen here in the corridor and picked up one of their spears. "These weren't Adus' men."

"How do you know that?" Kalten asked him.

"Sir Bevier broke the spears of the ones who were with Adus. That means there are other soldiers here in the labyrinth—probably in small groups the same as this one. I'd guess that they're here to lead us into traps in the side corridors."

"That's very obliging of them," Ulath said.

"I don't follow your reasoning, Sir Ulath."

"There are traps in the maze, but we have soldiers around to spring them for us. All we have to do is catch them."

"One of those silver linings people talk about?" Tynian asked.

"You could say that, yes. The Zemochs we catch might not look at it that way, though."

"Are those soldiers behind us coming up very fast?" Kurik asked him.

"Not very."

Kurik went back to the side corridor, holding his torch aloft. He was smiling grimly when he came back. "There are torch rings in the side passages the same as there are in this one," he told them. "Why don't we move a few torches as we go along? We've been following the torches, and those soldiers have been following us. If the torches start leading them off into the side passages where the traps are, wouldn't they sort of slow down a bit?"

"I don't know about *them*," Ulath said, "but I know *I* would."

---

## CHAPTER TWENTY-EIGHT

Zemoch soldiers periodically charged out of side corridors, their faces bearing the hopeless expressions of men who considered themselves already dead. The ultimatum "surrender or die," however, opened an option to them the existence of which they had not even been aware. Most of them leaped at the chance to seize it. Their effusive gratitude waned, however, when they found that they were expected to take the lead.

The traps designed to surprise the unwary were ingenious. In those passages where the floor did not drop open, the ceiling collapsed. The bottoms of most of the pits in the floor were studded with sharpened stakes, although several pits housed assorted reptiles—all venomous and all bad-tempered. Once, when the designer of the labyrinth had evidently grown bored with pits and falling ceilings, the walls smashed forcefully together.

"There's something wrong here," Kurik said, even as yet another despairing shriek echoed through the maze from behind them where the soldiers who had burst into the throne room were exploring side corridors.

"Things seem to be going rather well to me," Kalten said.

"These soldiers live here, Kalten," the squire said, "and they don't seem to be any more familiar with this labyrinth than we are. We've just run out of prisoners again. I think it's time to consider a few things. Let's not make any blunders."

They gathered in the center of the corridor. "This doesn't make any sense, you know," Kurik told them.

"Coming to Zemoch?" Kalten said. "I could have told you that back in Chyrellos."

Kurik ignored that. "We've been following a trail of blood spots on the floor, and that trail is still stretching on out in front of us—right down the middle of a torchlit corridor." He scraped one foot at a large blood spot on the floor. "If someone were really bleeding this hard, he would have been dead a long time ago."

Talen bent, touched one finger to a glistening red spot on the floor, and then touched the finger to his tongue. He spat. "It isn't blood," he said.

"What is it?" Kalten asked.

"I don't know, but it isn't blood."

"We've been bamboozled, then," Ulath said sourly. "I was beginning to wonder about that. What's worse, we're trapped in here. We can't even turn around and follow the torches back because we've been busily moving torches for the past half hour or more."

"This is what's known in logic as 'defining the problem,' " Bevier said with a weak smile. "I think the next step is called 'finding a solution.' "

"I'm no expert at it," Kalten admitted, "but I don't think we're going to be able to logic our way out of this."

"Why not use the rings?" Berit suggested. "Couldn't Sparhawk just blow a hole right straight through the maze?"

"The passages are mostly barrel vaults, Berit," Kurik said. "If we start blowing holes in the walls, we'll have the ceiling down on our heads."

"What a shame," Kalten sighed. "So many good ideas have to be discarded simply because they won't work."

"Are we absolutely bent on solving the riddle of the maze?" Talen asked them. "I mean, does finding the solution have some sort of religious significance?"

"None that I know of," Tynian replied.

"Why stay inside the maze, then?" the boy asked innocently.

"Because we're trapped here," Sparhawk told him, trying to control his irritation.

"That's not exactly true, Sparhawk. We've never been really trapped. Kurik might be right about the danger involved in knocking down the walls, but he didn't say a thing about the ceiling."

They stared at him. Then they all began to laugh a bit foolishly.

"We don't know what's up there, of course," Ulath noted.

"We don't know what's around the next corner either, Sir Knight. And we'll never know what's above the ceiling until we have a look, will we?"

"It could just be open sky," Kurik said.

"Is that any worse than what we have down here, Father? Once we get outside, Sparhawk might be able to use the rings to break through the outer wall of the temple. Otha may find mazes entertaining, but I think I've more or less gotten enough amusement out of this one. One of the first rules Platime ever taught me was that if you don't like the game, don't play."

Sparhawk looked questioningly at Sephrenia.

She was also smiling ruefully. "I didn't even think of it myself," she admitted. "Can we do it?"

"I don't see any reason why not—as long as we stand back a ways so that we don't get crushed by falling rubble. Let's have a look at this ceiling."

They raised their torches to look up at the barrel-vaulted ceiling. "Is that construction going to cause any kind of problem?" Sparhawk asked Kurik.

"Not really. The stones are laid in interlocking courses, so they'll hold—eventually. There's going to be a lot of rubble, though."

"That's all right, Kurik," Talen said gaily. "The rubble will give us something to climb up on."

"It's going to take a great deal of force to knock loose any of those stone blocks, though," Kurik said. "The weight of the whole corridor is holding the vault together."

"What would happen if a few of those blocks just weren't there any more?" Sephrenia asked him.

Kurik went to one of the upward-curving walls and probed at a crack between two stone blocks with his knife. "They used mortar," he said. "It's fairly rotten, though. If you can dissolve a half dozen of those blocks up there, a fairly sizeable piece of the ceiling will fall in."

"But the whole corridor won't collapse?"

He shook his head. "No. After a few yards of it tumble in, the structure will be sound again."

"Can you really dissolve rocks?" Tynian asked Sephrenia curiously.

She smiled. "No, dear one. But I *can* change them into sand—which amounts to the same thing, doesn't it?" She intently studied the ceiling for several moments. "Ulath," she said then, "you're the tallest. Lift me up. I have to touch the stones."

Ulath blushed a bright red, and they all knew why. Sephrenia was not the sort of person one put his hands on.

"Oh, don't be such a goose, Ulath," she told him. "Lift me up."

Ulath looked around menacingly. "We aren't going to talk about this, are we?" he said to his friends. Then he bent and lifted her easily.

She clambered upward, looking not unlike someone climbing a tree. When she was high enough, she reached up and put the palms of her hands on several of the stones, pausing briefly with each one. Her touch seemed almost caressing. "That should do it," she said. "You can put me down again, Sir Knight."

Ulath lowered her to the floor, and they retreated back down the corridor. "Be ready to run," she cautioned them. "This is a little inexact." She began to move her hands in front of her, speaking rapidly in Styric as she did so. Then she held out both hands, palms up, to release the spell.

Fine sand began to sift down from the ceiling, slithering out of the cracks between the roughly squared-off building blocks. At first it was only a trickle, but it steadily increased.

"Looks almost like water leaking out, doesn't it?" Kalten observed as the sand flow increased.

The walls began to creak, and there were popping noises as the mortar between the stones started to crack.

"We can go back a bit farther," Sephrenia said, looking apprehensively at all the rock around them. "The spell's working. We don't have to stand here to supervise it." Sephrenia was a very complex little woman. She was sometimes timid about very ordinary things and at other times indifferent to horrendous ones. They walked farther on back up the corridor as the building blocks near the place where the sand was now pouring down out of the ceiling creaked and groaned and grated together, settling in a fraction of an inch at a time to replace the sand.

When it came, it came all at once. A large section of the overhead vault collapsed with the grinding clatter of falling rock and a large cloud of eons-old dust that billowed down the corridor toward them, setting them all to coughing. As the dust gradually settled, they saw a large, jagged hole in the ceiling.

"Let's go have a look," Talen said. "I'm curious to find out what's up there."

"Could we wait just a bit longer?" Sephrenia asked fearfully. "I'd really like to be sure that it's safe."

They struggled up the pile of rubble from the fallen ceiling and boosted each other up through the hole. The area above the ceiling was a vast, domed emptiness, dusty and stale-smelling. The light from the torches they had brought with them from the corridor below seemed sickly and did not reach out as far as the walls—if walls to this dim place indeed existed. The floor resembled to a remarkable degree a field laced with the upward-bulging burrows of a colony of extraordinarily industrious moles, and they saw a number of structural peculiarities they had not perceived when down in the maze.

"Sliding walls," Kurik said, pointing. "They can change the maze any time they want to by closing off some passages and opening others. That's why those Zemoch soldiers didn't know where they were going."

"There's a light," Ulath told them, "way over there to the left. It seems to be coming up from down below."

"The temple maybe?" Kalten suggested.

"Or the throne room again. Let's go have a look."

They threaded their way along the tops of the vaults for some distance and then came to a straight path that stretched in one direction toward the light Ulath had seen and off into the darkness in the other.

"No dust," Ulath said, pointing at the stones of the path. "This is used fairly often."

The going was much faster on the straight pathway, and they soon reached the source of the flickering light. It was a flight of stone stairs leading down into a torch-lit room—a room with four walls and no doors.

"That's ridiculous," Kalten snorted.

"Not really," Kurik disagreed, raising his torch to peer over the side of the path.

"That front wall slides on those tracks." He pointed at a pair of metal tracks below that emerged from the room on the outside. He leaned forward to look more closely. "There's no machinery out here, so there has to be a latch of some kind in that room. Sparhawk, let's go down and see if we can find it."

The two of them went down the stairs into the room. "What are we looking for?" Sparhawk asked his friend.

"How should I know? Something that looks ordinary but isn't."

"That's not very specific, Kurik."

"Just start pushing on rocks, Sparhawk. If you find one that can be depressed, it's probably the latch."

They went along the walls pushing on rocks. After a few minutes, Kurik stopped, a slightly foolish look on his face. "You can stop, Sparhawk," he said. "I found the latches."

"Where?"

"There are torches on the side walls and on the back, right?"

"Yes. So what?"

"But there aren't any torches on the front wall—the one right in front of the foot of the stairs."

"So?"

"There *are* a couple of torch rings, though." Kurik went to the front wall and pulled on one of the rusty iron rings. There was a solid-sounding clank. "Pull the other one, Sparhawk," he suggested. "Let's open this door and see what's behind it."

"Sometimes you're so clever you make me sick, Kurik," Sparhawk said sourly. Then he grinned. "Let's get the others down here first," he said. "I'd rather not open that door and find half the Zemoch army behind it with only the two of us here to hold them off." He went to the stairs and beckoned to his waiting friends, touching one finger to his lips as he did so to signal the need for silence.

They came down quietly to avoid clinking.

"Kurik found the latches," Sparhawk whispered. "We don't know what's on the other side of the door, so we'd better be ready."

Kurik motioned to them. "The wall isn't too heavy," he said quietly, "and the track it slides on seems to be well greased. Berit and I should be able to move it. The rest of you should be ready for anything on the other side."

Talen moved quickly to the corner on the left side and put his face close to the two intersecting walls. "I'll be able to look through here just as soon as you get it open an inch or so," he told his father. "If I shout, slam it shut again."

Kurik nodded. "Are we ready?" he asked.

They all nodded, their weapons in their hands and their muscles tense.

Kurik and Berit pulled out on the torch rings and inched the wall aside slightly. "Anything yet?" Kurik hissed to his son.

"Nobody's there," Talen replied. "It's a short corridor with just one torch. It seems to go back about twenty paces and then it turns to the left. There's quite a bit of light coming from beyond that turn."

"All right, Berit," Kurik said, "let's open it all the way."

The two of them slid the wall the rest of the way open.

"Now *that* is very, very clever," Bevier said admiringly. "The labyrinth down here doesn't go anywhere at all. The *real* route to the temple is up above it."

"Let's find out where we are—in the temple or back at the throne room," Sparhawk said. "And let's be as quiet as we can."

Talen looked as if he were about to say something.

"Forget it," Kurik told him. "It's too dangerous. You just stay behind the rest of us with Sephrenia."

They moved out into the short corridor where the single torch near the far end provided a dim, flickering light.

"I don't hear anything," Kalten whispered to Sparhawk.

"People waiting in ambush don't usually make noise, Kalten."

They paused just before the corridor turned sharply to the left. Ulath edged to the corner, pulled off his helmet, and took a quick look, his head darting out and back once. "Empty," he said shortly. "It seems to turn right about ten or fifteen paces farther on."

They moved on around the corner and crept along the short passage. Again they stopped at the corner, and Ulath popped his head out again. "It's a kind of an alcove," he whispered. "There's an archway that opens out into a wider corridor. There's a lot of light out there."

"Did you see anybody?" Kurik asked him.

"Not a soul."

"That should be the main corridor out there," Bevier murmured. "The stairs that lead up out of the maze to the real route to the temple should be fairly close to the end of the labyrinth—either at the throne room or at the temple."

They rounded the corner into the alcove, and Ulath again took a quick look. "It's a main corridor, all right," he reported, "and there's a turn a hundred paces off to the left."

"Let's go up to that corner," Sparhawk decided. "If Bevier's right, the hallway beyond the corner should lead out of the maze. Sephrenia, you stay in here with Talen, Bevier, and Berit. Kurik, you guard the door. The rest of us will go have a look." He leaned close to his squire and whispered, "If things start to go wrong, get Sephrenia and the others back to the room at the foot of the stairs. Slide the wall shut and lock it."

Kurik nodded. "Be careful out there, Sparhawk," he said quietly.

"You, too, my friend."

The four knights stepped out into the broad, vaulted corridor and crept along toward the torchlit corner ahead. Kalten followed the rest of them, turning often to keep watch to the rear. At the corner, Ulath briefly poked out his head. Then he stepped back. "We might have known," he whispered disgustedly. "It's the throne room. We're right back where we started from."

"Is there anybody in there?" Tynian asked.

"Probably, but why bother them? Let's just go on back to that staircase, slide the wall shut again, and leave the people in the throne room to take care of their own entertainment."

It was as they were turning around that it happened. Adus, followed by a score of Zemoch soldiers, burst from a side passage not too far from the entrance to the alcove, and he was bellowing at the top of his lungs. Cries of alarm echoed into the corridor from the throne room itself.

"Tynian! Ulath!" Sparhawk snapped, "hold off the ones in the throne room! Let's go, Kalten!" Then he and his blond friend dashed back toward the opening where Kurik stood guard.

Adus was far too limited to be anything but predictable. He savagely drove his soldiers on ahead of him and slouched forward, a brutal war ax in his hand and an insane look in his piglike eyes.

It was too far. Sparhawk saw that immediately. Adus was much closer to the arched entrance to the alcove than he and Kalten were, and there were already soldiers between him and his friend and the archway. He chopped a Zemoch out of his way. "Kurik!" he shouted. "Fall back!"

But it was too late. Kurik had already engaged the apelike Adus. His chain mace whistled through the air, crunching into his opponent's armored shoulders and chest, but Adus was in the grip of a killing frenzy, and he ignored those dreadful blows. Again and again he smashed at Kurik's shield with his war ax.

Kurik was undoubtedly one of the most skilled men in the world when close fighting was involved, but Adus appeared totally mad. He hacked and kicked and bulled his way at Kurik, pushing and flailing with his battle ax. Kurik was forced to retreat, giving ground grudgingly step by step.

Then Adus threw his shield aside, took his ax handle in both hands, and began to swing a rapid series of blows at Kurik's head. Forced finally into one last defense, Kurik grasped his shield with both hands and raised it to protect his head from those massive blows. Roaring in triumph, Adus swung—not at Kurik's head, but at his body. The brutal ax bit deep into the side of his chest, and blood gushed from his mouth and from the dreadful wound in his chest. "Sparhawk!" he cried weakly, falling back against the side of the arch.

Adus raised his ax again.

*"Adus!"* Kalten roared, killing another Zemoch.

Adus checked the ax blow he had aimed at Kurik's unprotected head and half turned. *"Kalten!"* he bellowed back his challenge. He contemptuously kicked Sparhawk's friend out of his way and shambled toward the blond Pandion, his piggish eyes burning insanely beneath his shaggy brows.

Sparhawk and Kalten abandoned any semblance of swordsmanship and simply cut down anything in their paths, relying more on strength and fury than on skill.

Adus, totally insane now, also chopped his way through his own soldiers to reach them.

Kurik stumbled out into the corridor, clutching at his bleeding chest and trying to shake out his chain mace, but his legs faltered. He stumbled and fell. With enormous effort, he rose to his elbows and began to drag himself after the savage who had struck him down. Then his eyes went blank, and he fell onto his face.

"Kurik!" Sparhawk howled. The light seemed to fade from his eyes, and there was a deafening ringing in his ears. His sword suddenly appeared to have no weight. He cut down whatever appeared before him. At one point, he found himself chopping at the stones of the wall. It was the sparks somehow that returned him to his senses. Kurik would take him to task for damaging his sword edge.

Somehow Talen had reached his father's side. He knelt, struggling to turn Kurik over. And then he wailed, a cry of unspeakable loss. "He's dead, Sparhawk! My father's dead!"

The wrench of that cry nearly drove Sparhawk to his knees. He shook his head like some dumb animal. He hadn't heard that cry. He *could* not have heard it. He absently killed another Zemoch. Dimly, he heard the sound of fighting behind him and he knew that Tynian and Ulath were engaging the soldiers from the throne room.

Then Talen rose, sobbing and reaching down into his boot. His long, needle-pointed dirk came out gleaming in his fist, and he advanced on Adus from the rear, his soft-shod feet making no sound. Tears streamed down the boy's face, but his teeth were clenched with hate.

Sparhawk ran his sword through another Zemoch, even as Kalten sent another head rolling down the corridor.

Adus brained one of his own soldiers, roaring like an enraged bull.

The roar suddenly broke off. Adus gaped, his eyes bulging. His mismatched armor did not fit very well, and the back of his cuirass did not reach all the way to his hips. It was there, in that area covered only by chain mail, that Talen had stabbed him. Chain mail will ward off the blow of sword or ax, but it is no defense against a thrust. Talen's dirk drove smoothly into the half-witted brute's back just under the lower rim of the cuirass, seeking and finding Adus' kidney. Talen jerked his dirk free and stabbed again, on the other side this time.

Adus squealed like a stuck pig in a slaughterhouse. He stumbled forward, one hand clutching at the small of his back, his face suddenly dead white with pain and shock.

Talen drove his dirk into the back of the animal's knee.

Adus stumbled a few more steps, dropping his ax and grabbing at his back with both hands. Then he fell writhing to the floor.

Sparhawk and Kalten cut down the remaining Zemoch soldiers, but Talen had already snatched up a fallen sword and, standing astride Adus' body, was chopping at the brute's helmeted head. Then he reversed the sword and tried desperately to stab down through the breastplate into Adus' writhing body, but he did not have enough strength to make his weapon penetrate. "Help me!" he cried. "Somebody help me!"

Sparhawk stepped to the weeping boy's side, his own eyes also streaming tears. He dropped his sword and reached out to take the hilt of the one that Talen was try-ing to drive into Adus. Then he took hold of the sword's crosspiece with his other hand. "You do it like this, Talen," he said almost clinically, as if he were merely giv-ing instructions on the practice field.

Then, standing one on either side of the whimpering Adus, the boy and the man took hold of the sword, their hands touching on the hilt.

"We don't have to hurry, Sparhawk," Talen grated from between clenched teeth.

"No," Sparhawk agreed. "Not really, if you don't want to."

Adus shrieked as they slowly pushed the sword into him. The shriek broke off as a great fountain of blood gushed from his mouth. "Please!" he gurgled.

Sparhawk and Talen grimly twisted the sword.

Adus shrieked again, banging his head on the floor and beating a rapid tattoo on the flagstones with his heels. He arched his quivering body, belched forth another gusher of blood, and collapsed in an inert heap.

Talen, weeping, sprawled across the body, clawing at the dead man's staring eyes. Then Sparhawk bent, gently picked the boy up, and carried him back to where Kurik lay.

## CHAPTER TWENTY-NINE

There was still fighting in the torchlit corridor, the clash of steel on steel, cries, shouts, and groans. Sparhawk knew that he must go to the aid of his friends, but the enormity of what had just happened left him stunned, unable to move. Talen knelt beside Kurik's lifeless body, weeping and pounding his fist on the flagstone floor.

"I have to go," the big Pandion told the boy.

Talen did not answer.

"Berit," Sparhawk called, "come here."

The young apprentice came cautiously out of the alcove, his ax in his hands.

"Help Talen," Sparhawk said. "Take Kurik back inside."

Berit was staring in disbelief at Kurik.

"Move, boy!" Sparhawk said sharply, "and take care of Sephrenia."

"Sparhawk!" Kalten shouted. "There are more of them coming!"

"On the way!" Sparhawk looked at Talen. "I have to go," he told the boy again.

"Go ahead," Talen replied. Then he looked up, his tear-streaked face savage. "Kill them all, Sparhawk," he said fiercely. "Kill them all."

Sparhawk nodded. That would help Talen a bit, he thought as he returned to retrieve his sword. Anger was a good remedy for grief. He picked up his sword and turned, feeling his own rage burning in his throat. He almost pitied the Zemoch soldiers as he went to rejoin Kalten. "Fall back," he told his friend in a coldly level tone. "Get your breath."

"Is there any hope?" Kalten asked, parrying a Zemoch spear thrust.

"No."

"I'm sorry, Sparhawk."

It was a small group of soldiers, no doubt one of the detachments that had been trying to lure the knights into side passages. Sparhawk went toward them purposefully. It was good to be fighting. Fighting demanded every bit of a man's attention and pushed everything else from his mind. Sparhawk moved deftly against the half-dozen Zemochs. There was a certain obscure justice working now. Kurik had taught him every move, every technical nuance he was bringing to bear, and those skills were supplemented by a towering rage over his friend's death. In a very real sense,

Kurik had made Sparhawk invincible. Even Kalten seemed shocked at his friend's sheer savagery. It was the work of no more than a few moments to kill five of the soldiers facing him. The last turned to flee, but Sparhawk passed his sword quickly to his shield hand, bent, and picked up a Zemoch spear. "Take this with you," he called after the fleeing man. Then he made a long, practiced cast. The spear took the soldier squarely between the shoulder blades.

"Good throw," Kalten said.

"Let's go help Tynian and Ulath." Sparhawk still felt a powerful need to kill people. He led his friend back toward the turn in the corridor where the Alcione Knight and his Genidian comrade were holding back the soldiers who had rushed into the maze from the throne room in response to Adus' bellowed command.

"I'll take care of this," Sparhawk said flatly.

"Kurik?" Ulath asked.

Sparhawk shook his head and began killing Zemochs again. He waded on, leaving the maimed behind him for his companions to dispatch.

"Sparhawk!" Ulath shouted. "Stop! They're running!"

"Hurry!" Sparhawk yelled back. "We can still catch them!"

"Let them go!"

"No!"

"You're keeping Martel waiting, Sparhawk," Kalten said sharply. Kalten sometimes made a show of being stupid, but Sparhawk saw immediately just how smoothly his blond friend had brought him up short. Killing relatively innocent soldiers was no more than an idle pastime when compared to dealing once and for all with the white-haired renegade.

He stopped. "All right," he panted, nearly exhausted from his exertions, "let's go back. We've got to get past that sliding wall before the soldiers come back anyway."

"Are you feeling any better?" Tynian asked as they started back toward the alcove.

"Not really," Sparhawk said.

They passed Adus' body. "Go on ahead," Kalten told them. "I'll be right along."

Berit and Bevier awaited them at the entrance to the alcove.

"Did you chase them off?" Bevier asked.

"Sparhawk did," Ulath grunted. "He was very convincing."

"Aren't they likely to gather reinforcements and come back?"

"Not unless their officers have very large whips, they won't."

Sephrenia had arranged Kurik's body in a posture of repose. His cloak covered the dreadful wound that had spilled out his life. His eyes were closed and his face calm. Once again Sparhawk felt an unbearable grief. "Is there any way—?" he began, even though he already knew the answer.

Sephrenia shook her head. "No, dear one," she replied. "I'm sorry." She sat beside the body, holding the weeping Talen in her arms.

Sparhawk sighed. "We're going to have to leave," he told them. "We have to get back to those stairs before anybody decides to follow us." He looked back over his shoulder. Kalten was hurrying to join them, and he was carrying something wrapped in a Zemoch cloak.

"I'll do this," Ulath said. He bent and picked Kurik up as if the powerful squire were no more than a child, and they retraced their steps to the foot of the stairs leading up into the dusty darkness above.

"Slide that wall back in place," Sparhawk said, "and see if you can find some way to wedge it shut."

"We can do that from up above," Ulath said. "We'll block the track it slides on."

Sparhawk grunted as he made some decisions. "Bevier," he said regretfully, "we're going to have to leave you here, I'm afraid. You're badly wounded, and I've already lost enough friends today."

Bevier started to object, but then changed his mind.

"Talen," Sparhawk went on, "you stay here with Bevier and your father." He smiled a sad smile. "We want to *kill* Azash; we don't want to steal him."

Talen nodded.

"And Berit—"

"Please, Sparhawk," the young man said, his eyes filled with tears. "*Please* don't make me stay behind. Sir Bevier and Talen are safe here, and I might be able to help when we get to the temple."

Sparhawk glanced at Sephrenia. She nodded. "All right," he said. He wanted to warn Berit to be careful, but that would have demeaned the apprentice, so he let it pass.

"Give me your war ax and shield, Berit," Bevier said, his voice weak. "Take these instead." He handed Berit his lochaber and his burnished shield.

"I won't dishonor them, Sir Bevier," Berit swore.

Kalten had stepped toward the rear of the chamber. "There's a space back here under the stairs, Bevier. It might be a good idea for you and Kurik and Talen to wait for us under there. If the soldiers manage to break through the wall, the three of you won't be in plain sight."

Bevier nodded as Ulath took up Kurik's body to conceal it behind the stairs.

"There's not much left to say, Bevier," Sparhawk told the Cyrinic Knight, taking his hand. "We'll try to come back as soon as we can."

"I'll pray for you, Sparhawk," Bevier said, "for all of you."

Sparhawk nodded, then knelt briefly at Kurik's side and took his squire's hand. "Sleep well, my friend," he murmured. Then he rose and started up the stairs without looking back.

The stairs at the far end of that broad, straight pathway that stretched across the mole-tunnel mounds of the labyrinth below were very wide and sheathed with marble. There was no sliding wall to conceal a chamber at the foot of those stairs, and no maze led away from the temple. No maze was needed.

"Wait here," Sparhawk whispered to his friends, "and put out those torches." He crept forward, pulled off his helmet, and lay down at the top of the stairs.

"Ulath," he murmured, "hold my ankles. I want to see what we're getting into." With the huge Thalesian keeping him from tumbling in a steely clatter down the stairs, Sparhawk inched his way headfirst down the stairs until he could see out into the room beyond.

The Temple of Azash was a place of nightmare. It was, as the dome that roofed it implied, circular, and it was fully a half a mile across. The curving, inwardly sloping walls were of polished black onyx, as was the floor. It was much like looking into the very heart of night. The temple was not lighted by torches but by huge bonfires flaring and roaring in enormous iron basins set on girderlike legs. The vast chamber was encircled by tier upon tier of polished black terraces stepping down and down to a black floor far beneath.

At evenly spaced intervals along the top terrace were twenty-foot marble statues of things that were for the most part not human. Then Sparhawk saw a Styric form among them and somewhat farther along an Elenian one. He realized that the statues were representations of the servants of Azash, and that humanity played a very small and insignificant part in that assemblage. The other servants dwelt in places at once very far away and at the same time very, very close.

Directly opposite the entrance through which he peered was the towering idol. Man's efforts to visualize and to represent his Gods are never wholly satisfactory. A lion-headed God is not really the image of a human body with the head of a lion tacked on for the sake of contrast. Mankind perceives the face as the seat of the soul; the body is largely irrelevant. The icon of a God is not meant to be representational, and the face of the icon is intended to suggest the spirit of the God rather than to be an accurate re-creation of his real features. The face of the idol rearing high above the polished black temple contained the sum of human depravity. Lust was there, certainly, and greed, and gluttony; but there were other attributes in that face as well, attributes for which there were no names in any human tongue. Azash, to judge from his face, craved—required—things beyond human comprehension. There was a haggard, unsatisfied look about that face. It was the face of a being with overpowering desires that were not—could not be—satisfied. The lips were twisted, the eyes brooding and cruel.

Sparhawk wrenched his eyes from that face. To look too long at it was to lose one's soul.

The body was not fully formed. It was as if the sculptor had been so overwhelmed by that face and all that it implied that he no more than sketched in the remainder of the figure. There was a spiderlike profusion of arms that extended in clusters of tentacles from vast shoulders. The body leaned back somewhat with its hips thrust forward obscenely, but what would have been the focus of that suggestive pose was not there. Instead there was a smooth, unwrinkled surface, shiny and looking very much like a burn scar. Sparhawk remembered the words Sephrenia had cast into the God's teeth during her confrontation with the Seeker at the north end of Lake Venne. Impotent, she had called him, and emasculate. He preferred not to speculate on the means the Younger Gods may have used to mutilate their older relative. There was a pale greenish nimbus emanating from the idol, a glow much like that that had come from the face of the Seeker.

There was a ceremony of some sort taking place on the circular black floor far below in the sickly green glow coming from the altar. Sparhawk's mind recoiled from the notion of calling that ceremony a religious rite. The celebrants cavorted naked before the idol. Sparhawk was not some unworldly, cloistered monk. He was acquainted with the world, but the levels of perversion being demonstrated in that rite turned his stomach. The orgy that had so engrossed the primitive Elene Zemochs back in the mountains had been childlike, almost pure, by comparison. *These* celebrants appeared to be attempting to duplicate the perversions of nonhumans, and their fixed stares and galvanic movements clearly showed that they would continue the ceremony until they died from sheer excess. The lower tiers of that huge, stair-stepped basin were packed with green-robed figures who raised a groaning discordant chant, an empty sound devoid of any thought or emotion.

Then a slight movement caught Sparhawk's eye, and he looked quickly toward his right. A group of people were gathered on the top terrace a hundred yards or more away beneath the leprous white statue of something that must have been dredged from the depths of madness. One of the figures had white hair.

Sparhawk twisted around and signalled to Ulath to pull him back up again.

"Well?" Kalten asked him.

"It's all one big room," Sparhawk murmured. "The idol is over on the far side, and there are wide terraces leading down to a floor in the middle."

"What's the noise?" Tynian asked.

"They're holding some sort of rite. I think that chant's a part of it."

"I'm not concerned about their religion," Ulath rumbled. "Are there any soldiers?"

Sparhawk shook his head.

"That's helpful. Anything else?"

"Yes. I need some magic, Sephrenia. Martel and the others are gathered on the top terrace. They're about a hundred paces off to the right. We need to know what they're saying. Are we close enough for your spell to work?"

She nodded. "Let's move back away from the stairs," she suggested. "The spell makes a certain amount of light, and we don't want anyone to know that we're here just yet."

They retreated back along the dusty pathway, and Sephrenia took Sir Bevier's polished shield from Berit. "This should do it," she said. She quickly cast the spell and released it. The knights gathered around the suddenly glowing shield, peering at the hazy figures appearing on its mirrorlike surface. The voices coming from the image were tinny-sounding, but they were intelligible.

"Thine assurances to me that my gold would buy thee that throne from which thou couldst further our purposes were hollow, Annias," Otha was saying in that gurgling rumble.

"It was Sparhawk again, your Majesty." Annias tried to excuse himself in an almost grovelling tone. "He disrupted things—as we had feared he would."

"Sparhawk!" Otha spat out a foul oath and slammed his fist down on the arm of his thronelike litter. "The man's existence doth canker my soul. His very name doth cause me pain. Thou wert to keep him away from Chyrellos, Martel. Why didst thou fail me and my God?"

"I didn't really fail, your Majesty," Martel replied calmly, "and neither did Annias for that matter. Putting his Grace on the archprelate's throne was only a means to an end, and we've achieved that end. Bhelliom is under this very roof. The scheme to elevate Annias so that he could force the Elenes to surrender the jewel to us was filled with uncertainties. This has been much faster and much more direct. Results are what Azash wants, your Majesty, not the success or failure of any of the interim steps."

Otha grunted. "Perhaps," he conceded, "but Bhelliom hath not been passively delivered into the possession of our God. It doth still lie in the hands of this Sparhawk. Ye have put armies in his path and he doth easily o'erwhelm them. Our Master hath sent servants more horrible than death itself to slay him, and he lives yet."

"Sparhawk's only a man, after all," Lycheas said in his whining voice. "His luck can't last forever."

Otha threw a look at Lycheas that quite plainly spoke of death. Arissa put her arm protectively around her son's shoulders and looked as if she were about to come to his defense, but Annias shook his head warningly.

"Thou hast defiled thyself by acknowledging this bastard of thine, Annias," Otha declared in a tone of towering contempt. He paused, looking at them. "Can none of ye *understand?*" he suddenly roared. "This Sparhawk is Anakha, the unknown. The destinies of all men are clearly visible—all men save Anakha. Anakha moves outside of destiny. Even the Gods fear him. He and Bhelliom are linked in some way beyond the comprehension of the men or the Gods of this world, and the Goddess Aphrael serves them. We do not know their purpose. All that doth save us from them lies in the fact that Bhelliom's submission to Sparhawk is reluctant. Should it ever yield to him willingly, he will be a God."

"But he's not a God yet, your Majesty." Martel smiled. "He's trapped in that maze, and he'll never leave his companions behind to assault us alone. Sparhawk's predictable. That's why Azash accepted Annias and me. We know Sparhawk, and we know what he'll do."

"And didst thou *know* that he would succeed as he hath?" Otha sneered. "Didst thou *know* that his coming here would threaten our very existence—and the existence of our God?"

Martel looked at the obscenely cavorting figures on the floor below. "How long will that continue?" he asked. "We need some guidance from Azash at this point, and we can't get his attention while that's going on."

"The rite is nearly complete," Otha told him. "The celebrants are beyond exhaustion. They will die soon."

"Good. Then we'll be able to speak with our master. He's *also* in danger."

"Martel!" Otha said sharply, his voice filled with alarm. "Sparhawk hath broken out of the maze! He hath reached the pathway to the temple!"

"Summon men to stop him!" Martel barked.

"I have, but they are far behind him. He will reach us before they can hinder him."

"We must rouse Azash!" Annias cried in a shrill voice.

"To interrupt this rite is death," Otha declared.

Martel straightened and took his ornate helmet out from under his arm. "Then it's up to me, I guess," he said bleakly.

Sparhawk raised his head. From far off in the direction of the palace he could hear the sound of battering-rams pounding on a stone wall. "That's enough," he said to Sephrenia. "We have to move. Otha's called soldiers to break down that wall that leads to the stairs near the palace."

"I hope Bevier and Talen are out of sight," Kalten said.

"They are," Sparhawk told him. "Bevier knows what he's doing. We're going to have to go down into the temple. This attic—or whatever you want to call it—is too open. If we try to fight here, we'll have soldiers coming at us from all sides." He looked at Sephrenia. "Is there some way we can block those stairs behind us?" he asked her.

Her eyes narrowed. "I *think* so," she replied.

"You sound a bit dubious."

"No, not really. I can block the stairway easily enough, but I can't be sure whether Otha knows the counterspell."

"He won't know that you've blocked it until his soldiers arrive and can't come down the stairs, will he?" Tynian asked her.

"No. Actually he won't. Very good, Tynian."

"Do we just run around that top terrace and confront the idol?" Kalten asked.

"We can't," Sephrenia told him. "Otha's a magician, you remember. He'd be hurling spells at our backs every step of the way. We'll have to confront him directly."

"And Martel as well," Sparhawk added. "Now then, Otha doesn't dare to interrupt Azash while that rite's going on. We can take advantage of that. All we'll have to worry about is Otha himself. Can we deal with him, Sephrenia?"

She nodded. "Otha's not brave," she replied. "If we threaten him, he'll use his power to shield himself from us. He'll count on the soldiers coming from the palace to deal with us."

"We'll try it," Sparhawk said. "Are we all ready then?"

They nodded.

"Just be careful," he told them, "and I don't want any interference when I go after Martel. All right, let's go."

They went to the head of the stairs, paused a moment, then drew in a collective deep breath and marched down with drawn weapons.

"Ah, there you are, old boy," Sparhawk drawled to Martel, deliberately imitating the white-haired renegade's nonchalance, "I've been looking all over for you."

"I was right here, Sparhawk," Martel replied, drawing his sword.

"So I see. I must have gotten turned around somehow. I hope I didn't keep you waiting."

"Not at all."

"Splendid. I hate being tardy." He looked them over. "Good. I see that we're all here." He looked a bit more closely at the Primate of Cimmura. "Really, Annias, you should try to get more sun. You're as white as a sheet."

"Oh, before you two get started, Martel," Kalten said, "I brought you a present—a little memento of our visit. I'm sure you'll cherish it always." He bent slightly and gave the cloak he was carrying a little flip, holding one edge firmly in his gauntleted fist. The cloak unfurled on the onyx floor. Adus' head rolled out and bounced across to stop at Martel's feet, where it lay staring up at him.

"How very kind of you, Sir Kalten," Martel said from between clenched teeth. Seemingly indifferent, he kicked the head off to one side. "I'm sure that obtaining this gift for me cost you a great deal."

Sparhawk's fist tightened about his sword hilt, and his brain seethed with hatred. "It cost me Kurik, Martel," he said in a flat voice, "and now it's time to settle accounts."

Martel's eyes widened briefly. "Kurik?" he said in a stunned voice. "I didn't expect that. I'm truly sorry, Sparhawk. I liked him. If you ever get back to Demos, give Aslade my sincerest apologies."

"I don't think so, Martel. I won't insult Aslade by mentioning your name to her. Shall we get on with this?" Sparhawk began to move forward, his shield braced and his sword point moving slowly back and forth like the head of a snake. Kalten and the others grounded their weapons and stood watching grimly.

"A gentleman to the end, I see," Martel said, putting on his helmet and moving away from Otha's litter to give himself fighting room. "Your good manners and your sense of fair play will be the death of you yet, Sparhawk. You had the advantage. You should have used it."

"I'm not going to need it, Martel. You still have a moment or two for repentance. I'd advise you to use the time well."

Martel smiled thinly. "I don't think so, Sparhawk," he said. "I made my choice. I won't demean myself by changing it now." He clapped down his visor.

They struck simultaneously, their swords ringing on each other's shields. They had trained together under Kurik's instruction as boys, so there was no possibility of some trick or feint giving either of them an opening. They were so evenly matched that there was no way to predict the outcome of this duel that had been a decade and more in the preparation.

Their first strokes were tentative as they carefully felt each other out, looking for alterations in technique or changes in their relative strength. To the untrained onlooker their hammering at each other might have seemed frenzied and without thought, but that was not the case. Neither of them was so enraged as to overextend himself and leave himself open. Great dents appeared in their shields, and showers of sparks cascaded down over them each time their sword edges clashed against each other. Back and forth they struggled, moving slowly away from the spot where Otha's jewelled litter sat and where Annias, Arissa, and Lycheas stood watching, wide-eyed and breathless. That, too, was a part of Sparhawk's strategy. He needed to draw Martel away from Otha so that Kalten and the others could menace the bloated emperor. To gain that end, he retreated a few paces now and then when it was not actually necessary, drawing Martel step by step away from his friends.

"You must be getting old, Sparhawk," Martel panted, hammering at his former brother's shield.

"No more than you are, Martel." Sparhawk delivered a massive blow that staggered his opponent.

Kalten, Ulath, and Tynian, followed by Berit, who swung Sir Bevier's hideous lochaber, fanned out to advance on Otha and Annias. Sluglike Otha waved one arm, and a shimmering barrier appeared around his litter and Martel's companions.

Sparhawk felt the faintest of tingles along the back of his neck, and he knew that Sephrenia was weaving the spell that would block the stairs. He rushed at Martel, swinging his sword as rapidly as he could to so distract the white-haired man that he would not feel that faint familiar sensation that always accompanied the release of a friend's spell. Sephrenia had trained Martel, and he would know her touch.

The fight raged on. Sparhawk was panting and sweating now, and his sword arm arched with weariness. He stepped back, lowering his sword slightly in the traditional wordless suggestion that they pause for long enough to get their breath. That suggestion was never considered a sign of weakness.

Martel also lowered his sword in agreement. "Almost like old times, Sparhawk," he panted, pushing open his visor.

"Close," Sparhawk agreed. "You've picked up some new tricks, I see." He also opened his visor.

"I spent too much time in Lamorkand. Lamork swordsmanship is clumsy, though. Your technique seems to be a little Rendorish."

"Ten years of exile there." Sparhawk shrugged, breathing deeply as he tried to regain his wind.

"Vanion would skin the both of us if he saw us flailing at each other this way."

"He probably would. Vanion's a perfectionist."

"That's God's own truth."

They stood panting and staring intently into each other's eyes, watching for that minuscule narrowing that would preface a surprise blow. Sparhawk could feel the ache slowly draining from his right shoulder. "Are you ready?" he asked finally.

"Any time you are."

They clanged their visors shut again and resumed the fight.

Martel launched a complicated and extended series of sword strokes. The series was familiar, since it was one of the oldest, and its conclusion was inevitable. Sparhawk moved his shield and his sword in the prescribed defense, but he had known as soon as Martel swung the first stroke that he was going to receive a near-stunning blow to the head. Kurik, however, had devised a modification to the Pandion helmet not long after Martel's expulsion from the order, and when the renegade swung his heavy blow at Sparhawk's head, Sparhawk ducked his chin slightly to take the stroke full on the crest of his helmet—a crest that was now heavily reinforced. His ears rang nonetheless, and his knees buckled slightly. He was, however, able to parry the follow-up stroke that might well have disabled him.

Martel's reactions seemed somehow slower than Sparhawk remembered them as having been. His own blows, he conceded, probably no longer had the crisp snap of youth. They were both older, and an extended duel with a man of equal strength and skill ages one rapidly.

Then he suddenly understood, and the action came simultaneously with understanding. He unleashed a series of overhand strokes at Martel's head, and the renegade was forced to protect himself with both sword and shield. Then Sparhawk followed that flurry to the head with the traditional body thrust. Martel knew it was coming, of course, but he simply could not move his shield rapidly enough to protect himself. The point of Sparhawk's sword crunched into his armor low on the right side of his chest and drove deeply into his body. Martel stiffened, then coughed a great spray of blood out through the slots of his visor. He tried weakly to keep his shield and sword up, but his hands were trembling violently. His legs began to shake. His sword fell from his hand, and his shield dropped to his side. He coughed again, a wet, tearing sound. Blood poured from his visor once more, and he slowly collapsed in a heap, facedown. "Finish it, Sparhawk," he gasped.

Sparhawk pushed him over onto his back with one foot. He raised his sword, then lowered it again. He knelt beside the dying man. "There's no need," he said quietly, opening Martel's visor.

"How did you manage that?" Martel asked.

"It's that new armor of yours. It's too heavy. You got tired and started to slow down."

"There's a certain justice there," Martel said, trying to breathe shallowly so that the blood rapidly filling his lungs would not choke him again. "Killed by my own vanity."

"That's probably what kills us all—eventually."

"It was a good fight, though."

"Yes. It was."

"And we finally found out which of us is the best. Perhaps it's the time for truth. I never had any real doubts, you know."

"I did."

Sparhawk knelt quietly, listening to Martel's breathing growing shallower and shallower. "Lakus died, you know," he said quietly, "and Olven."

"Lakus and Olven? I didn't know that. Was I in any way responsible?"

"No. It was something else."

"That's some small comfort anyway. Could you call Sephrenia for me, Sparhawk? I'd like to say good-bye to her."

Sparhawk raised his arm and motioned to the woman who had trained them both.

Her eyes were full of tears as she knelt across Martel's body from Sparhawk. "Yes, dear one?" she said to the dying man.

"You always said I'd come to a bad end, little mother," Martel said wryly, his voice no more than a whisper now, "but you were wrong. This isn't so bad at all. It's almost like a formal deathbed. I get to depart in the presence of the only two people I've ever really loved. Will you bless me, little mother?"

She put her hands to his face and spoke gently in Styric. Then, weeping, she bent and kissed his pallid forehead.

When she raised her face again, he was dead.

## CHAPTER THIRTY

S parhawk rose to his feet and helped Sephrenia to stand.
"Are you all right, dear one?" she whispered.

"I'm well enough." Sparhawk stared hard at Otha.

"Congratulations, Sir Knight," Otha rumbled ironically, his sweaty head gleaming in the light of the fires, "and I thank thee. Long have I pondered the problem of Martel. He sought, methinks, to rise above himself, and his usefulness to me ended when thou and thy companions brought Bhelliom to me. I am well rid of him."

"Call it a farewell gift, Otha."

"Oh? Art thou leaving?"

"No, but you are."

Otha laughed. It was a revolting sound.

"He's afraid, Sparhawk," Sephrenia whispered. "He's not sure that you can't break through his shield."

"Can I?"

"I'm not sure either. He's very vulnerable now, though, because Azash is totally distracted by that rite."

"That's a place to start then." Sparhawk drew in a deep breath and started toward the bloated Emperor of Zemoch.

Otha flinched back and made a quick signal to the half-naked brutes around him. The bearers picked up the litter upon which he grossly sprawled and started toward the terraces leading down toward the onyx floor where the naked celebrants, twitching and blank-faced with exhaustion, continued their obscene rite. Annias, Arissa, and Lycheas went with him, their eyes fearful as they stayed as close to his litter as possible to remain within the questionable safety of the glowing nimbus of his protective shield. When the litter reached the onyx floor, Otha shouted to the green-robed priests, and they rushed forward, their faces alight with mindless devotion as they drew weapons from beneath their vestments.

From behind them, Sparhawk heard a sudden cry of frustrated chagrin. The soldiers rushing to the aid of their emperor had just encountered Sephrenia's barrier. "Will it hold?" he asked her.

"It will unless one of those soldiers is stronger than I am."

"Not too likely. That leaves only the priests, then." He looked at his friends. "All right, gentlemen," he said to them. "Let's form up around Sephrenia and clear a path through here."

The priests of Azash wore no armor, and the way they handled their weapons showed little evidence of skill. They were Styric for the most part, and the sudden appearance of hostile Church Knights in the holy center of their religion had startled them and filled them with dismay. Sparhawk remembered something Sephrenia had once said. Styrics, she had told him, do not react well when they are surprised. The unexpected tends to confound them. He could feel a faint prickling sensation as he and his armored friends started down the stair-stepped terraces, a prickling that told him that some few of the priests at least were attempting to put some form of spell together. He roared an Elene war cry, a harsh bellow filled with a lust for blood and violence. The prickling evaporated. "Lots of noise, gentlemen!" he shouted to his friends. "Keep them off balance so they can't use magic!"

The Church Knights rushed down the black terraces bellowing war cries and brandishing their weapons. The priests recoiled, and then the knights were on them.

Berit pushed past Sparhawk, his eyes alight with enthusiasm and Sir Bevier's lochaber at the ready. "Save your strength, Sparhawk," he said gruffly, trying to make his voice deeper, more roughly masculine. He stepped purposefully in front of the startled Sparhawk and strode into the green-robed ranks facing them, swinging the lochaber like a scythe.

Sparhawk reached out to pull him back, but Sephrenia laid her hand on his wrist. "No, Sparhawk," she said. "This is important to him, and he's in no particular danger."

Otha had reached the polished altar in front of the idol and was staring at the carnage below in open-mouthed fright. Then he drew himself up. "Approach, then, Sparhawk!" he blustered. "My God grows impatient!"

"I doubt that, Otha," Sparhawk called back. "Azash wants Bhelliom, but he doesn't want *me* to deliver it to him, because he doesn't know what I'm going to do with it."

"Very good, Sparhawk," Sephrenia murmured. "Use your advantage. Azash will sense Otha's uncertainty, and He'll feel the same way."

The temple echoed with the noise of blows, shrieks, and groans as Sparhawk's friends systematically slaughtered the green-robed priests. They chopped their way through the tightly packed ranks until they reached the foot of the first terrace below the altar.

In spite of everything, Sparhawk felt tightly exultant. He had not expected to make it this far, and his unexpected survival filled him with a sense of euphoric invincibility. "Well, Otha," he said, looking up those stair-stepped terraces at the bloated emperor, "why don't you awaken Azash? Let's find out if the Elder Gods know how to die as well as men do."

Otha gaped at him, then scrambled from his litter and crumpled to the floor as his puny legs refused to support him. "Kneel!" he half screamed at Annias. "Kneel and pray to our God for deliverance!" The notion that his soldiers could not enter the temple obviously frightened Otha considerably.

"Kalten," Sparhawk called to his friend, "finish up with the priests, and then make sure that those soldiers don't break through and rush us from behind."

"That's not necessary, Sparhawk," Sephrenia said.

"I know, but it should keep them back out of harm's way." He drew in a deep breath. "Here we go, then." He shook off his gauntlets, tucked his sword blade under his arm, and took the steel-mesh pouch from his belt. He unwrapped the wire that bound the pouch shut and shook Bhelliom out into his hand. The jewel seemed very hot, and light, wavering like heat lightning on a summer's night, seethed among its petals. "Blue-Rose!" he said sharply. "You must do as I command!"

Otha, half-kneeling, half-squatting, was babbling a prayer to his God—a prayer made almost unintelligible by his fright. Annias, Lycheas, and Arissa also knelt, and they stared up at the hideous face of the idol looming above them. Their eyes were filled with horror as they more closely beheld the reality of that God they had so willing chosen to follow.

"Come, Azash!" Otha pleaded. "Awaken! Hear the prayer of thy servants!"

The idol's deep-sunk eyes had been closed, but now they slowly opened, and that greenish fire blazed from them. Sparhawk felt wave upon wave of malevolence blazing at him from those baleful eyes, and he stood, stunned into near-insensibility by the titanic presence of a God.

The idol was moving! A kind of undulation rippled down its body and the tentacle arms sinuously reached forth—reaching toward the glowing stone in Sparhawk's hand, yearning toward the one thing in all the world that offered restoration and freedom.

"No!" Sparhawk's voice was a harsh rasp. He raised his sword above the Bhelliom. "I'll destroy it!" he threatened. "And you along with it!"

The idol seemed to recoil, and its eyes were suddenly filled with amazed shock. "Why hast thou brought this ignorant savage into my presence, Sephrenia?" The voice was hollow, and it echoed throughout the temple and in Sparhawk's mind as well. Sparhawk knew that the mind of Azash could obliterate him in the space between two heartbeats, but for some reason Azash seemed afraid to bring his power to bear upon the rash man who stood menacing the sapphire rose with drawn sword.

"I do but obey my destiny, Azash," Sephrenia replied calmly. "I was born to bring Sparhawk to this place to face thee."

"But what of the destiny of this Sparhawk? Dost thou know what *he* is destined to do?" There was a kind of desperation in the voice of Azash.

"No man or God knoweth that, Azash," she reminded him. "Sparhawk is Anakha, and all the Gods have known and feared that one day Anakha would come and would move through this world committed to ends that none may perceive. I am the servant of his destiny, whatever it may be, and I have brought him here that he may bring those ends to fruition."

The idol seemed to tense itself, and then an irresistible command lashed out, overpowering and insistent, and the command was *not* directed at Sparhawk.

Sephrenia gasped and seemed almost to wilt like a flower before the first blast of winter. Sparhawk could actually feel her resolve fading. She wavered as the force of the mind of Azash peeled away her defenses.

He tensed his arm and raised his sword higher. If Sephrenia were to fall, they were lost, and he could not know if there would be time to deliver the last fatal stroke after her collapse. He drew the image of Ehlana's face in his mind and gripped his sword hilt even more tightly.

The sound was not audible to anyone else. He knew that. It was in his mind only; only he could hear it. It was the insistent, commanding sound of shepherd's pipes, and there was a very strong overtone of irritation to it.

*"Aphrael!"* he called out in sudden relief.

A small firefly spark appeared in front of his face. "Well, *finally!*" Flute's voice snapped angrily. "What took you so *long*, Sparhawk? Don't you know that you have to *call* me?"

"No. I didn't know that. Help Sephrenia."

There was no touch, no movement, no sound, but Sephrenia straightened, brushing at her brow with lightly touching fingers as the idol's eyes burned and fixed themselves on the firefly spark.

"My daughter," the voice of Azash said. "Wilt thou cast thy lot with these mortals?"

"I am no daughter of thine, Azash." Flute's voice was crisp. "I willed *myself* into existence, as did my brothers and sisters when thou and thy kindred did tear at the fabric of reality with thy childish contention. I am thy daughter only through thy fault. Hadst thou and thy kindred turned ye aside from that reckless course that would have destroyed all, there would have been no need for me and mine."

"I *will* have Bhelliom!" The hollow voice was the thunder and the earthquake, tearing at the very foundations of the earth.

"Thou shalt *not*!" Flute's voice was flatly contradictory. "It was to deny thee and thy kind possession of Bhelliom that I and my kind came into existence. Bhelliom is not of this place, and it must not be held here in bondage to thee or to me or to the Troll-Gods or any other Gods of this world."

*"I will have it!"* The voice of Azash rose to a scream.

"No. Anakha will destroy it first, and in its destruction shalt thou perish."

The idol seemed to flinch. "How *darest* thou!" it gasped. "How darest thou even *speak* such horror? In the death of one of us lieth the seeds of the deaths of us all."

"So be it then." Aphrael's tone was indifferent. Then her light little voice took on a cruel note. "Direct thy fury at *me*, Azash, and not at my children, for it was *I* who used the power of the rings to emasculate thee and to confine thee forever in that idol of mud."

"It was *thou*?" The terrible voice seemed stunned.

"It was *I*. Thy power is so abated by thine emasculation that thou canst not escape thy confinement. Thou wilt *not* have Bhelliom, impotent Godling, and thus shalt thou be forever imprisoned. Thou shalt remain unmanned and confined until the farthest star burns down to ashes." She paused, and when she spoke again it was in the tone of one slowly twisting a knife buried in the body of another. "It was thine absurd and transparent proposal that all the Gods of Styricum unite to seize Bhelliom from the TrollGods—'for the good of all'—that gave me the opportunity to mutilate and confine thee, Azash. Thou hast none to blame but thyself for what hath befallen thee. And now Anakha hath brought Bhelliom and the rings—and even the Troll-Gods locked within the jewel—here to confront thee. I call upon thee to submit to the power of the sapphire rose—or to perish."

There was a howl of inhuman frustration, but the idol made no move.

Otha, however, his eyes filled with panic, began to mutter a desperate spell. Then he hurled it forth, and the hideous statues encircling the interior of the vast temple began to shimmer, changing from marble-white to greens and blues and bloody reds, and the babble of their inhuman voices filled the dome. Sephrenia spoke two words in Styric, her voice calm. She gestured, and the statues froze again, congealing back into pallid marble.

Otha howled, then began to speak again, so frustrated and enraged that he did not even speak in Styric, but in his native Elene.

"Listen to me, Sparhawk." Flute's musical voice was very soft.

"But Otha—"

"He's only babbling. My sister can deal with him. Pay attention. The time will come very soon when you'll have to act. I'll tell you when. Climb these stairs to the idol and keep your sword poised over Bhelliom. If Azash or Otha or anything else tries to keep you from reaching the idol, smash the Bhelliom. If all goes well and you reach the idol, touch Bhelliom to that place that looks burned and scarred."

"Will that destroy Azash?"

"Of course not. The idol that's sitting there is only an encasement. The *real* idol is inside that big one. Bhelliom will shatter the big idol, and you'll be able to see Azash himself. The real idol is quite small, and it's made of dried mud. As soon as you can see it, drop your sword and hold Bhelliom in both hands. Then use these exact words, 'Blue-Rose, I am Sparhawk-from-Elenia. By the power of these rings I command Blue-Rose to return this image to the earth from which it came.' Then touch Bhelliom to the idol."

"What happens then?"

"I'm not sure."

"*Aphrael!*" Sparhawk said it in a tone of startled protest.

"Bhelliom's destiny is even more obscure than yours, and I can't tell from one minute to the next what *you're* going to do."

"Will it destroy Azash?"

"Oh, yes—and quite possibly the rest of the world as well. Bhelliom wants to be free of this world, and this might just be the chance it's been waiting for."

Sparhawk swallowed very hard.

"It's a gamble," she conceded in an offhand way, "but we never know which way the dice are going to turn up until we roll them, do we?"

The temple suddenly went totally dark as Sephrenia and Otha continued their struggle, and for a breathless moment it seemed as if that darkness might be eternal, so intense was it.

Then the light gradually returned. The fires in those great iron braziers renewed themselves, and gradually the flames rose again.

As the light returned, Sparhawk found that he was looking at Annias. The Primate of Cimmura's emaciated face was a ghastly white, and all thought had vanished from his eyes. Blinded by his obsessive ambition, Annias had never looked fully at the horror to which he had pledged his soul in his pursuit of the archprelate's throne. Now at last he obviously perceived it, and now, just as obviously, it was too late. He stared at Sparhawk, his eyes pleading mutely for something—anything— that would save him from the pit that had opened before his feet.

Lycheas was blubbering, gibbering in terror, and Arissa held him in her arms, clinging to him actually, and her face was no less filled with horror than that of Annias.

The temple filled with noise and light, shattering sound and boiling smoke as Otha and Sephrenia continued to grapple.

"It's time, Sparhawk." Flute's voice was very calm.

Sparhawk braced himself and started forward, his sword held threateningly over the sapphire rose, which seemed almost to cringe beneath that heavy steel blade.

"Sparhawk," the little voice was almost wistful, "I love you."

The next sound he heard was not one of love, however. It was a snarling howl in the language of the Trolls. It was more than one voice, and it came from Bhelliom itself. Sparhawk reeled as the hatred of the Troll-Gods lashed at him. The pain was unendurable. He burned and froze at the same time, and his bones heaved and surged within his flesh. "Blue-Rose!" he gasped, faltering, almost falling. "Command the Troll-Gods to be silent. Blue-Rose will do it—*now!*"

The agony continued, and the Trollish howling intensified.

"Then die, Blue-Rose!" Sparhawk raised his sword.

The howling broke off abruptly, and the pain stopped.

Sparhawk crossed the first onyx terrace and stepped up onto the next.

"Do not do this, Sparhawk." The voice was in his mind. "Aphrael is a spiteful child. She leads thee to thy doom."

"I was wondering how long it was going to be, Azash," Sparhawk said in a shaking voice as he crossed the second terrace. "Why did you not speak to me before?"

The voice that had spoken in his mind was silent.

"Were you afraid, Azash?" he asked. "Were you afraid that something you said might change that destiny that you cannot see?" He stepped up onto the third terrace.

"Do not do this, Sparhawk." The voice was pleading now. "I can give thee the world."

"No, thank you."

"I can give thee immortality."

"I'm not interested. Men are used to the idea of dying. It's only the Gods who find the thought so frightening." He crossed the third terrace.

"I will destroy thy comrades if thou dost persist."

"All men die sooner or later." Sparhawk tried to sound convincingly indifferent. He stepped up onto the fourth terrace. He felt as if he were suddenly trying to wade through solid rock. Azash did not dare attack him directly, since that might trigger the fatal stroke that would destroy them all. Then Sparhawk saw his one absolute advantage. Not only could the Gods not see his destiny; they could not see his thoughts either. Azash could not know when the decision to strike would come. Azash could not feel him make that decision and so he could not stop the sword stroke. He decided to play on that advantage. Still locked in place, he sighed. "Oh, well, if that's the way you want it." He raised his sword again.

"*No!*" The cry came not only from Azash but from the snarling Troll-Gods as well.

Sparhawk crossed the fourth terrace. He was sweating profusely. He could hide his thoughts from the Gods, but not from himself. "Now, Blue-Rose," he said quietly to Bhelliom as he stepped up onto the fifth terrace, "I am going to do this. You and Khwaj and Ghnomb and the others will aid me, or you will perish. A God must die here—one God or many. If you aid me, it will only be the one. If you do not, it will be the many."

*"Sparhawk!"* Aphrael's voice was shocked.

"Don't interfere."

There was a momentary hesitation. "Can I help?" she whispered in a little-girl voice.

He thought only for an instant. "All right, but this isn't the time for games—and don't startle me. My arm's set like a coiled spring."

The firefly spark began to expand, softening from intensity to a glow, and Aphrael emerged from that glow, her shepherd's pipes held to her lips. As always her little feet were grass-stained. Her face was somber as she lowered the pipes. "Go ahead and smash it, Sparhawk," she said sadly. "They'll never listen to you." She sighed. "I grow weary of unending life anyway. Smash the stone and have done with it."

The Bhelliom went absolutely dark, and Sparhawk felt it shudder violently in his hand. Then its blue glow returned, soft and submissive.

"They'll help now, Sparhawk," Aphrael told him.

"You lied to them," he accused.

"No, I lied to *you*. I wasn't talking to them."

He could not help but laugh.

He crossed the fifth terrace. The idol was much closer now, and it loomed large in his sight. He could also see Otha, sweating and straining as he and Sephrenia engaged in that duel that Sparhawk knew, could he but see it, was far more titanic than the one he had fought with Martel. He could see more clearly now the stark terror in the face of Annias and the near-collapse of Arissa and her son.

Sparhawk could sense the gigantic presence of the Troll-Gods. They seemed so overpoweringly real that he could almost see their gigantic, hideous forms hovering protectively just behind him. He stepped up onto the sixth terrace. Three more to go. Idly he wondered if the number nine had some significance in the twisted minds of the worshippers of Azash. The God of the Zemochs threw everything to the winds at that point. He saw death inexorably climbing the stairs toward him, and he began to unleash everything in his power in a desperate effort to ward off the black-armored messenger carrying his glowing blue death to him.

Fire burst from beneath Sparhawk's feet, but before he even felt its heat, it was quenched in ice. A monstrous form lunged at him, springing from nothingness, but an even more intense fire than that that the ice had just vanquished consumed it. The Troll-Gods, unwilling certainly, but left without a choice by Sparhawk's adamantine ultimatum, were aiding him now, beating aside the defenses of Azash to clear his path.

Azash began to shriek as Sparhawk stepped up onto the seventh terrace. A rush now was feasible, but Sparhawk decided against it. He did not want to be panting and shaking from exertion when the climactic moment arrived. He continued his steady, inexorable pace, crossing the seventh terrace as Azash unleashed horrors beyond imagining at him, horrors instantly quenched by the Troll-Gods or even by Bhelliom itself. He drew in a deep breath and stepped up onto the eighth terrace.

Then he was surrounded by gold—coins and ingots and lumps the size of a man's head. A cascade of bright jewels spilled out of nothing to run down over the gold like a river of blue and green and red, a rainbow-hued waterfall of wealth beyond imagining. Then the wealth began to diminish, great chunks of it vanishing to the gross sounds of eating. "Thank you, Ghnomb," Sparhawk murmured to the Troll-God of feeding.

A houri of heart-stopping loveliness beckoned to Sparhawk seductively, but was immediately assaulted by a lustful Troll. Sparhawk did not know the name of the Troll-God of mating, so he did not know whom to thank. He pushed on to step up onto the ninth and last terrace.

"Thou *canst* not!" Azash shrieked. Sparhawk did not reply as he marched grimly toward the idol with Bhelliom still in one fist and his menacing sword in the other. Lightning flashed around him, but each bolt was absorbed by the growing sapphire aura with which Bhelliom protected him.

Otha had abandoned his fruitless duel with Sephrenia and crawled, sobbing in fright, toward the right side of the altar. Annias had collapsed on the left side of that same narrow onyx slab, and Arissa and Lycheas, clinging to each other, wailed.

Sparhawk reached the narrow altar. "Wish me luck," he whispered to the Child-Goddess.

"Of course, father," she replied.

Azash shrank back as Bhelliom's glow intensified, and the idol's burning eyes bulged with terror. Sparhawk saw that an immortal suddenly faced with the possibility of his own death is peculiarly defenseless. The idea alone erased all other thought, and Azash could only react at the simplest, most childish level. He lashed out, blindly hurling elemental fire at the black-armored Pandion threatening his very existence. The shock was enormous as that incandescent green flame struck the equally brilliant blue flame of Bhelliom. The blue wavered, then solidified. The green shrank back, then pushed again at Sparhawk.

And there they locked, Bhelliom and Azash, each exerting irresistible force to protect its very existence. Neither of them would—or could—relent. Sparhawk had the unpleasant conviction that he might very well stand in this one place for all eternity with the jewel half extended as Azash and Bhelliom remained locked in their struggle.

It came from behind him, spinning and whirring through the air with a sound almost like bird wings. It passed over his head and clanged against the idol's stone chest, exploding forth a great shower of sparks. It was Bevier's hook-pointed lochaber ax. Berit, unthinking perhaps, had thrown the lochaber at the idol—a foolish gesture of puny defiance.

But it worked.

The idol flinched involuntarily from something that could not possibly hurt it, and its force, its fire, momentarily vanished. Sparhawk lunged forward with Bhelliom clutched in his left hand, thrusting it like a spear point at the burn scar low on the idol's belly. His hand went numb in the violent shock of contact.

The sound was deafening. Sparhawk was sure that it shook the entire world.

He bent his head and locked his muscles, pushing Bhelliom harder and harder against the shiny scar of Azash's emasculation. The God shrieked in agony. *"Ye have failed me!"* he howled, and writhing tentacle arms whipped out from either side of the idol's body to seize Otha—and Annias.

"Oh, my God!" the Primate of Cimmura shrieked, not to Azash, but to the God of his childhood. "Save me! Protect me! Forgive—" His voice rose to an inarticulate screech as the tentacle tightened about him.

There was no finesse in the punishment inflicted upon the Emperor of Zemoch and the Primate of Cimmura. Maddened by pain and fear and a hunger to lash out at those he considered responsible, Azash reacted like an infuriated child. Other arms lashed out to seize the shrieking pair, and then, with cruel slowness, the undulating arms began to turn in opposite directions in that motion used by a washerwoman to wring out a dripping rag. Blood and worse spurted out from between the God's eellike fingers as he inexorably wrung the lives of Otha and Annias from their writhing bodies.

Sickened, Sparhawk closed his eyes—but he could not close his ears. The shrieking grew worse, rising to strangled squeals at the very upper edge of hearing.

Then they fell silent, and there were two sodden thumps as Azash discarded what was left of his servants.

Arissa was retching violently over the unrecognizable remains of her lover and the father of her only child as the vast idol shuddered and cracked, raining chunks of carved rock as it disintegrated. Writhing arms solidified as they broke free and fell to smash into fragments on the floor. The grotesque face slid in pieces from the front of the head. A large piece of rock struck Sparhawk's armored shoulder, and the impact quite nearly jarred Bhelliom from his hands. With a great cracking noise, the idol broke at the waist, and the vast upper trunk toppled backward to smash into a million pieces on the polished black floor. A stump only remained, a kind of crumbling stone pedestal upon which sat that crude mud idol that Otha had first seen almost two thousand years before.

*"Thou canst not!"* The voice was the squeal of a small animal, a rabbit maybe, or perhaps a rat. *"I am a God! Thou art nothing! Thou art an insect! Thou art as dirt!"*

"Perhaps," Sparhawk said, actually feeling pity for the pathetic little mud figurine. He dropped his sword and clasped Bhelliom firmly in both hands. "Blue-Rose!" he said sharply. "I am Sparhawk-from-Elenia! By the power of these rings I command Blue-Rose to return this image to the earth from which it came!" He thrust both hands and the sapphire rose forward. "Thou hast hungered for Bhelliom, Azash," he said. "Have it, then. Have it and all that it brings thee." Then the Bhelliom touched the misshapen little idol. "Blue-Rose will obey! *Now!*" He clenched himself as he said it, expecting instant obliteration.

The entire temple shuddered, and Sparhawk felt a sudden oppressive sense of heaviness bearing down on him as if the air itself had the weight of tons. The flames of the huge fires sickened, lowering into fitful flickers as if some great weight pressed them down, smothering them.

And then the vast dome of the temple exploded upward and outward, hurling the hexagonal blocks of basalt miles away. With a sound that was beyond sound, the fires belched upward, becoming enormous pillars of intensely brilliant flame, columns that shot up through the gaping hole that had been the dome to illuminate the pregnant bellies of the clouds that had spawned the thunderstorm. Higher and higher those incandescent columns roared, searing the cloud mass above. And still they reared higher, wreathed with lightning as they burned the clouds away and ascended still into the darkness above, reaching toward the glittering stars.

Sparhawk, implacable and unrelenting, held the sapphire rose against the body of Azash, the skin of his wrist crawling as the God's tiny, impotent tentacles clutched at it as a mortally stricken warrior might clutch at the arm of a foe slowly twisting a sword blade in his vitals. The voice of Azash, Elder God of Styricum, was a tiny squeal, a puny wail such as any small creature might make as it died. Then a change came over the little idol. Whatever had made it adhere together was gone, and with a slithering kind of sigh it came apart and settled into a heap of dust.

The great columns of flame slowly subsided, and the air that flooded into the ruined temple from the outside once again had the chill of winter.

Sparhawk felt no sense of triumph as he straightened. He looked at the sapphire rose glowing in his hand. He could feel its terror, and he could dimly hear the whimpering of the Troll-Gods locked in its azure heart.

Flute had somehow stumbled back down the terraces and wept in Sephrenia's arms.

"It's over, Blue-Rose," Sparhawk said wearily to the Bhelliom. "Rest now." He slipped the jewel back into the pouch and absently twisted the wire to hold it shut.

There was the sound of running then, of frantic flight. Princess Arissa and her son fled down the onyx terraces toward the shiny floor below. So great was their fright that neither appeared to be even aware of the other as they stumbled down and down. Lycheas was younger than his mother, and his flight was swifter. He left her behind, leaping, falling, and scrambling back to his feet again as he bolted.

Ulath, his face like stone, was waiting for him at the bottom—with his ax.

Lycheas shrieked once, and then his head flew out in a long, curving arc and landed on the onyx floor with a sickening sound such as a dropped melon might make.

"Lycheas!" Arissa shrieked in horror as her son's headless body fell limply at Ulath's feet. She stood frozen, gaping at the huge, blond-braided Thalesian who had begun to mount the onyx terraces toward her, his bloody ax half-raised. Ulath was not one to leave a job half-finished.

Arissa fumbled at the sash about her waist, pulled out a small glass vial, and struggled to pull the stopper free.

Ulath did not slow his pace.

The vial was open now, and Arissa lifted her face and drank its contents. Her body instantly stiffened, and she gave a hoarse cry. Then she fell twitching to the floor of the terrace, her face black and her tongue protruding from her mouth.

"Ulath!" Sephrenia said to the still-advancing Thalesian. "No. It isn't necessary."

"Poison?" he asked her.

She nodded.

"I hate poison," he said, stripping the blood off the edge of his ax with his thumb and forefinger. He flung the blood away and then ran a practiced thumb along the edge. "It's going to take a week to polish out all these nicks," he said mournfully, turning and starting back down again, leaving the Princess Arissa sprawled on the terrace above him.

Sparhawk retrieved his sword and descended. He felt very, very tired now. He wearily picked up his gauntlets and crossed the littered floor to Berit, who stood staring at him in awe. "That was a nice throw," he said to the young man, putting his hand on Berit's armored shoulder. "Thank you, brother."

Berit's smile was like the sun coming up.

"Oh, by the way," Sparhawk added, "you'd probably better go find Bevier's ax. He's very fond of it."

Berit grinned. "Right away, Sparhawk."

Sparhawk looked around at the corpse-littered temple, then up through the shattered dome at the stars twinkling overhead in the cold winter sky. "Kurik," he said without thinking, "what time do you make it?" Then he broke off as a wave of unbearable grief overwhelmed him. He steeled himself. "Is everybody all right?" he asked his friends, looking around. Then he grunted, not really trusting himself to speak. He drew in a deep breath. "Let's get out of here," he said gruffly.

They crossed the polished floor and went up the wide terraces to the top. Somehow in the vast upheaval of the encounter at the altar, all the statues encircling the wall had been shattered. Kalten stepped on ahead and looked up the marble stairs. "The soldiers seem to have run off," he reported.

Sephrenia countered the spell that had blocked the stairs and they started up.

"Sephrenia." The voice was hardly more than a croak.

"She's still alive," Ulath said almost accusingly.

"That happens once in a while," Sephrenia said. "Sometimes the poison takes a little longer."

"Sephrenia, help me. Please help me."

The small Styric woman turned and looked back across the temple at Princess Arissa, who had weakly raised her head to plead for her life.

Sephrenia's tone was as cold as death itself. "No, Princess," she replied. "I don't think so." Then she turned again and went on up the stairs with Sparhawk and the rest of them close behind her.

# CHAPTER THIRTY-ONE

The wind had changed at some time during the night, and it now blew steadily out of the west, bringing snow with it. The violent thunderstorm that had engulfed the city the previous night had unroofed many houses and exploded others. The streets were littered with debris and with a thin covering of wet snow. Berit had retrieved their horses, and Sparhawk and his friends rode slowly. There was no longer any need for haste. The cart Kalten had found in a side street trundled along behind them with Talen at the reins and Bevier resting in the back with Kurik's covered body. Kurik, Sephrenia assured them as they set out, would remain untouched by the corruption that is the final destiny of all men. "I owe Aslade that much at least," she murmured, nestling her cheek against Flute's glossy black hair. Sparhawk was a bit surprised to find that in spite of everything, he still thought of the Child-Goddess as Flute. She did not look all that much like a Goddess at the moment. She clung to Sephrenia, her face tear-streaked, and each time she opened her eyes, they were filled with horror and despair.

The Zemoch soldiers and the few remaining priests of Azash had fled the deserted city, and the slushy streets echoed with a kind of mournful emptiness. Something quite peculiar was happening to Otha's capital. The nearly total destruction of the temple had been completely understandable, of course. The only slightly less severe damage to the adjoining palace was probably to be expected. It was what was happening to the rest of the city that was inexplicable. The inhabitants had not really left the city that long ago, but their houses were collapsing—not all at once as might have been expected, given the explosive nature of what had taken place in the temple, but singly or in groups of two or three. It was somehow as if the decay that overcomes any abandoned city were taking place in the space of hours instead of centuries. The houses sagged, creaked mournfully, and then slowly fell in on themselves. The city walls crumbled, and even the paving stones of the streets heaved up and then settled back, broken and scattered.

Their desperate plan had succeeded, but the cost had been beyond what any of them had been prepared to pay. There was no sense of triumph in their success, none of that exultation warriors normally feel in a victory. It was not merely the sorrowful burden of the cart that dampened their mood, however, but something deeper.

Bevier was pale from loss of blood, but his face was profoundly troubled. "I still don't understand," he confessed.

"Sparhawk is Anakha," Sephrenia replied. "It's a Styric word that means 'without destiny.' All men are subject to destiny, to fate—all men except Sparhawk. Somehow he moves outside destiny. We've known that he would come, but we didn't know when—or even who he would be. He's like no other man who's ever lived. He makes his *own* destiny, and his existence terrifies the Gods."

They left the slowly collapsing city of Zemoch behind in the thickly swirling snow slanting in from the west, although they could hear the grinding rumble of falling buildings for quite some time as they rode southward along the road leading to the city of Korakach, some eighty leagues to the south. About midafternoon, as the snow was beginning to let up, they took shelter for the night in a deserted village. They were all very tired, and the thought of riding even one more mile was deeply repugnant to them. Ulath prepared their supper without even any attempt to resort to his usual subterfuge, and they sought their beds even before the light had begun to fade.

·   ·   ·

Sparhawk awoke suddenly, startled to find that he was in the saddle. They were riding along the brink of a windswept cliff with an angry sea ripping itself to tattered froth on the rocks far below. The sky overhead was threatening, and the wind coming in off the sea had a biting chill. Sephrenia rode in the lead, and she held Flute enfolded in her arms. The others trailed along behind Sparhawk, their cloaks drawn tightly around them and wooden expressions of stoic endurance on their faces. They all seemed to be there, Kalten and Kurik, Tynian and Ulath, Berit and Talen and Bevier. Their horses plodded up the winding, weather-worn trail that followed the edge of the long, ascending cliff toward a jutting promontory that thrust a crooked, stony finger out into the sea. At the outermost tip of the rocky promontory stood a gnarled and twisted tree, its streaming branches flailing in the wind.

When she reached the tree, Sephrenia reined in her horse, and Kurik walked forward to lift Flute down. The squire's face was set, and he did not speak to Sparhawk as he passed. It seemed to Sparhawk that something was wrong—terribly wrong—but he could not exactly put his finger on it.

"Very well, then," the little girl said to them. "We're here to finish this, and we don't have all that much time."

"Exactly what do you mean by 'finish this'?" Bevier asked her.

"My family has agreed that we must put Bhelliom beyond the reach of men or Gods. No one must ever be able to find it or use it again. The others have given me one hour—and all of their power—to accomplish this. You may see some things that are impossible—you might have even noticed them already. Don't concern yourselves about them, and don't pester me with questions. We don't have that much time. We were ten when we set out, and we're the same ten now. It has to be that way."

"We're going to throw it into the sea then?" Kalten asked her.

She nodded.

"Hasn't that been tried before?" Ulath asked her. "The Earl of Heid threw King Sarak's crown into Lake Venne, as I recall, and Bhelliom still reemerged."

"The sea is much deeper than Lake Venne," she told him. "The water out there is much deeper than it is anywhere else in the world, and no one knows where this particular shoreline is."

"We do," Ulath disagreed.

"Oh? Where is it? On which particular coast of which particular continent?" She pointed upward at the dense cloud racing overhead. "And where's the sun? Which way is east and which is west? All you can really say for sure is that you're on a seacoast somewhere. You can tell anyone you like, and then every man who will ever live can start wading in the sea tomorrow, and they'll never find Bhelliom, because they'll never know exactly where to look."

"Then you want me to throw it into the sea?" Sparhawk asked her as he dismounted.

"Not quite yet, Sparhawk," she replied. "There's something we have to do first. Would you get that sack I asked you to keep for me, Kurik?"

Kurik nodded, went back to his gelding, and opened one of his saddlebags. Once again Sparhawk had that strong sense that something was wrong.

Kurik came back carrying a small canvas sack. He opened it and took out a small steel box with a hinged lid and a stout hasp. He held it out to the little girl. She shook her head and held her hands behind her. "I don't want to touch it," she said. "I just want to look at it to make sure it's right." She bent forward and examined the box closely. When Kurik opened the lid, Sparhawk saw that the interior of the box was lined with gold. "My brothers did well," she approved. "It's perfect."

"Steel *will* rust in time, you know," Tynian told her.

"No, dear one," Sephrenia told him. "That particular box will never rust."

"What about the Troll-Gods, Sephrenia," Bevier asked. "They've shown us that they can reach out to the minds of men. Won't they be able to call someone and direct him to the place where the box lies hidden? I don't think they'll be happy lying at the bottom of the sea for all eternity."

"The Troll-Gods can't reach out to men without the aid of Bhelliom," she explained, "and Bhelliom's powerless as long as it's locked in steel. It lay helpless in that iron deposit in Thalesia from the time this world was made until the day Ghwerig freed it. This may not be entirely foolproof, but it's the best we can do, I think."

"Set the box down on the ground, Kurik," Flute instructed, "and open it. Sparhawk, take Bhelliom out of the pouch and tell it to sleep."

"Forever?"

"I sort of doubt that. This world won't last that long, and once it's gone, Bhelliom will be free to continue its journey."

Sparhawk took the pouch from his belt and untwisted the wire that held it closed. Then he upended the pouch and the sapphire rose fell out into his hand. He felt it shudder with a kind of relief as it was freed from its steel confinement. "Blue-Rose," he said calmly, "I am Sparhawk-from-Elenia. Do you know me?"

It glowed a deep, hard blue, neither hostile nor particularly friendly. The muted snarls he seemed to hear deep in his mind, however, told him that the Troll-Gods did not share that neutrality.

"The time has come for you to sleep, Blue-Rose," Sparhawk said to the jewel. "There will be no pain, and when you awaken, you will be free."

The jewel shuddered again, and its crystal glitter softened, almost as if in gratitude.

"Sleep now, Blue-Rose," he said gently, holding the priceless thing in both hands. Then he placed it in the box and firmly closed the lid.

Wordlessly, Kurik handed him a small, cunningly wrought lock. Sparhawk nodded and snapped the lock shut on the hasp, noting as he did that the lock had no keyhole. He looked questioningly at the Child-Goddess.

"Throw it into the sea," she said, watching him intently.

A vast reluctance came over him. He knew that Bhelliom, confined as it was, could not be influencing him. The reluctance was his own. For a time, for a few short months, he had possessed something even more eternal than the stars, and he had somehow shared that just by touching it. It was this that made Bhelliom so infinitely precious. Its beauty, its perfection, had never really had anything to do with it, though he yearned for just one last glimpse of it, one last touch of that soft blue glow on his hands. He knew that once he had cast it away, something very important would be gone from his life and that he would pass the remainder of his days with a vague sense of loss that might diminish with the passing of years, but would never wholly be gone.

He steeled himself, willing the pain of loss to come so that he might teach himself to endure it. Then he leaned back and threw the small steel object as far as he could out over the angry sea.

The hurtling steel box arched out over the crashing waves far below, and as it flew it began to glow, neither red nor blue nor any other color, but rather sheer incandescent white. Far it went, farther than any man could have thrown it, and then, like a shooting star, it fell in a long, graceful curve into the endlessly rolling sea.

"That's it then?" Kalten asked. "That's all we have to do?"

Flute nodded, her eyes filled with tears. "You can all go back now," she told them. She sat down beneath the tree and sadly took her pipes out from under her tunic.

"Aren't you coming with us?" Talen asked her.

"No," she sighed. "I'll stay here for a while." Then she lifted her pipes and began to play a sad song of regret and loss.

They had only ridden a short distance with the sound of the pipes sadly following them when Sparhawk turned to look back. The tree was still there, of course, but Flute was gone. "She's left us again," he told Sephrenia.

"Yes, dear one," she sighed.

The wind picked up as they rode down from the promontory, and driven spray began to sting their faces. Sparhawk tried to pull the hood of his cloak forward to shield his face, but it was no use. No matter how hard he tried, the driving spray lashed at his cheeks and nose.

His face was still wet when he suddenly awoke and sat up. He mopped the salt brine away and reached inside his tunic.

Bhelliom was not there.

He knew that he would have to talk with Sephrenia, but there was something he wanted to find out first. He rose and went out of the house where they had set up their camp the previous day. Two doors down the street was the stable where they had put the cart in which Kurik lay. Sparhawk gently turned back the blanket and touched his friend's cold face.

Kurik's face was wet, and when Sparhawk touched his fingertip to his tongue, he could taste the salt brine of the sea. He sat for a long time, his mind reeling back from the immensity of what the Child-Goddess had so casually dismissed as mere "impossibilities." The combined might of the Younger Gods of Styricum, it appeared, could accomplish *anything*. He decided at last not to even attempt a definition of what had happened. Dream or reality or something in between—what difference did it make? Bhelliom was safe now, and that was all that mattered.

They rode south to Korakach and on to Gana Dorit, where they turned west toward Kadum on the Lamork border. Once they reached the lowlands, they began to encounter Zemoch soldiers fleeing to the east. There were no wounded with the soldiers, so there did not appear to have been a battle.

There was no sense of accomplishment or even of victory as they rode. The snow turned to rain as they came down out of the highlands, and the mournful dripping of the sky seemed to match their mood. There were no stories or cheerful banter as they rode westward. They were all very tired, and all they really wanted to do was to go home.

King Wargun was at Kadum with a huge army. He was not moving, but sat firmly in place, waiting for the weather to break and for the ground to dry out. Sparhawk and the others were led to his headquarters, which, as might have been expected, were in a tavern.

"Now there's a real surprise," the half-drunk monarch of Thalesia said to the Patriarch Bergsten as Sparhawk and his friends entered. "I never thought I'd see *them* again. Ho, Sparhawk! Come over by the fire. Have something to drink and tell us what you've been up to."

Sparhawk removed his helmet and crossed the rush-covered tavern floor. "We went to the city of Zemoch, your Majesty," he reported briefly. "As long as we were there anyway, we killed Otha and Azash. Then we started back."

Wargun blinked. "That's right to the point." He laughed. He looked around blearily. "You there!" he bellowed at one of the guards at the door. "Go find Lord Vanion. Tell him that his men have arrived. Did you find someplace to lock up your prisoners, Sparhawk?"

"We didn't take any prisoners, your Majesty."

"Now *that's* the way to make war. Sarathi's going to be cross with you, though. He really wanted Annias to stand trial."

"We'd have brought him, Wargun," Ulath told his king, "but he wasn't very presentable."

"Which one of you killed him?"

"Actually it was Azash, your Majesty," Tynian explained. "The Zemoch God was very disappointed in Otha and Annias, so he did what seemed appropriate."

"How about Martel—and Princess Arissa—and the bastard Lycheas?"

"Sparhawk killed Martel," Kalten told him. "Ulath chopped Lycheas' head off, and Arissa took poison."

"Did she die?"

"We assume so. She was doing a fairly good job of it when we left her."

Then Vanion came in and went immediately to Sephrenia. Their secret, which wasn't really a secret anyway, since everyone with eyes knew how they felt about each other, went out the window as they embraced each other with a kind of fierceness uncharacteristic of either of them. Vanion kissed the cheek of the small woman he had loved for decades. "I thought I'd lost you," he said in a voice thick with emotion.

"You know that I'll never leave you, dear one," she said.

Sparhawk smiled faintly. That "dear one" that she addressed to them all had rather neatly concealed the real "dear ones" she directed to Vanion. There was a significant difference in the way she said it, he noticed.

Their recounting of what had taken place since they had left Zemoch was fairly complete. It was subdued, however, and it omitted a significant number of theological issues.

Then Wargun began a rambling and somewhat drink-slurred account of what had happened in Lamorkand and eastern Pelosia during the lengthy interval. The armies of the west, it appeared, had followed the strategy that had been worked out in Chyrellos before the campaign had begun, and the strategy seemed to have worked quite well.

"And then," the tipsy monarch concluded, "just when we were ready to get down to some serious fighting, the cowards all turned tail and ran. Why won't *anyone* stand and fight me?" Wargun's tone was plaintive. "Now I'm going to have to chase them all over the mountains of Zemoch to catch them."

"Why bother?" Sephrenia asked him.

"Why bother?" he exclaimed. "To keep them from ever attacking us again, that's why." Wargun was swaying in his seat and he clumsily dipped another tankard of ale from the keg at his side.

"Why waste the lives of your men?" she asked. "Azash is dead. Otha is dead. The Zemochs will never come again."

Wargun glared at her. Then he pounded his fist on the table. "I want to exterminate somebody!" he roared. "You wouldn't let me wipe out the Rendors! You called me to Chyrellos before I could finish up! But I'll be a cross-eyed Troll if I'll let you steal the Zemochs from me as well!" Then his eyes glazed, and he slid slowly under the table and began to snore.

"Your king has an amazing singleness of purpose, my friend," Tynian said to Ulath.

"Wargun's a simple man." Ulath shrugged. "There isn't room in his head for more than one idea at a time."

"I'll go with you to Chyrellos, Sparhawk," Vanion said. "I might be able to help you persuade Dolmant to pull Wargun up short." That, of course, was not Vanion's real reason for accompanying them, but Sparhawk chose not to question his friend any more closely.

They left Kadum early the following morning. The knights had removed their armor and travelled in mail shirts, tunics, and heavy cloaks. That did not appreciably increase their speed, but it did make them more comfortable. The rain went on day after day, a dreary, foggy drizzle that seemed to wash out all signs of color. They travelled through the sullen tag end of winter, almost never really warm and certainly never wholly dry. They passed through Moterra and rode on to Kadach, where they crossed the river and moved at a canter south toward Chyrellos. Finally, on a rainy afternoon they reached the top of a hill and looked down at the war-ravaged Holy City.

"I think our first step is to find Dolmant," Vanion decided. "It's going to take awhile for a messenger to get back to Kadum to stop Wargun, and a break in the weather could start to dry out the fields in Zemoch." Vanion began to cough, a tearing kind of cough.

"Aren't you feeling well?" Sparhawk asked him.

"I think I've picked up a cold, that's all."

They did not enter Chyrellos as heroes. There were no parades, no fanfares, no cheering throngs throwing flowers. In point of fact, nobody even seemed to recognize them, and the only thing that was thrown was garbage from the windows of the upper floors of the houses they passed. Very little had been done in the way of repairs or reconstruction since Martel's armies had been driven out, and the citizens of Chyrellos existed in squalor among the ruins.

They entered the Basilica still muddy and travel-worn and went directly up to the administrative offices on the second floor. "We have urgent news for the archprelate," Vanion said to the black-robed churchman who sat at an ornate desk shuffling papers and trying to look important.

"I'm afraid that's absolutely out of the question," the churchman said, looking disdainfully at Vanion's muddy clothing. "Sarathi's meeting with a deputation of Cammorian Primates at the moment. It's a very important conference, and it mustn't be interrupted by some unimportant military dispatch. Why don't you come back tomorrow?"

Vanion's nostrils went white, and he thrust back his cloak to free his sword-arm. Before things had the chance to turn ugly, however, Emban came along the hall. "Vanion?" he exclaimed, "and *Sparhawk*? When did you get back?"

"We only just arrived, your Grace," Vanion replied. "There seems to be some question about our credentials here."

"Not as far as I'm concerned. You'd better come inside."

"But, your Grace," the churchman objected, "Sarathi's meeting with the Cammorian Patriarchs, and there are other deputations who have been waiting and are far more—" He broke off as Emban slowly turned on him.

"Who is this man?" Emban seemed to direct the question at the ceiling. Then he looked at the man behind the desk. "Pack your things," he instructed. "You'll be leaving Chyrellos first thing in the morning. Take plenty of warm clothing. The monastery at Husdal is in northern Thalesia, and it's very cold there at this time of year."

The Cammorian Primates were summarily dismissed, and Emban ushered Sparhawk and the others into the room where Dolmant and Ortzel waited.

"Why didn't you send word?" Dolmant demanded.

"We thought Wargun was going to take care of that, Sarathi," Vanion told him.

"You trusted Wargun with a message *that* important? All right, what happened?"

Sparhawk, with occasional help from the others, recounted the story of the trip to Zemoch and told them what had happened there.

"Kurik?" Dolmant said in a stricken voice at one point in the narrative.

Sparhawk nodded.

Dolmant sighed and bowed his head in sorrow. "I imagine that one of you did something about that," he said, his voice almost savage.

"His son did, Sarathi," Sparhawk replied.

Dolmant was aware of Talen's irregular parentage. He looked at the boy with some surprise. "How did you manage to kill a warrior in full armor, Talen?" he asked.

"I stabbed him in the back, Sarathi," Talen replied in a flat tone of voice, "right in the kidneys. Sparhawk had to help me drive the sword into him, though. I couldn't get through his armor with it all by myself."

"And what will happen to you now, my boy?" Dolmant sadly asked him.

"We're going to give him a few more years, Sarathi," Vanion said, "and then we're going to enroll him as a novice in the Pandion Order—along with Kurik's other sons. Sparhawk made Kurik a promise."

"Isn't anybody going to ask *me* about this?" Talen demanded in an outraged tone.

"No," Vanion told him, "as a matter of fact, we're not."

"A knight?" Talen protested. "*Me?* Have you people all taken leave of your senses?"

"It's not so bad, Talen." Berit grinned. "Once you get used to it."

Sparhawk continued with the story. A number of things had happened in Zemoch that Ortzel was theologically unprepared to accept, and as the story wound down, his eyes became glazed, and he sat in stupefied shock.

"And that's more or less what happened, Sarathi," Sparhawk concluded. "It's going to take me awhile to get it all sorted out in my mind—the rest of my life, more than likely—and even then there are still going to be a lot of things I won't understand."

Dolmant leaned thoughtfully back in his chair. "I think that Bhelliom—and the rings—should be in Church custody," he said.

"I'm sorry, Sarathi," Sparhawk told him, "but that's impossible."

"You said *what?*"

"We don't have the Bhelliom anymore."

"What did you do with it?"

"We threw it into the sea, Sarathi," Bevier replied.

Dolmant stared at him in dismay.

Patriarch Ortzel came to his feet with a look of outrage on his face. "Without the permission of the Church?" he almost screamed. "You did not even seek counsel from God?"

"We were acting on the instructions of another God, your Grace," Sparhawk told him. "A Goddess, actually," he corrected.

"*Heresy!*" Ortzel gasped.

"I don't really think so, your Grace," Sparhawk disagreed. "Aphrael was the one who brought Bhelliom to me. She carried it up out of the chasm in Ghwerig's cave. After I'd done what we needed to do with it, it was only proper for me to return it to her. She didn't want it, though. She told me to throw it into the sea, so I did. We *are* instructed to be courteous, after all."

"That does not apply in a situation such as this!" Ortzel stormed. "The Bhelliom's too important to be treated as some mere trinket! Go back and find it at once and hand it over to the Church!"

"I think he's right, Sparhawk," Dolmant said gravely. "You're going to have to go retrieve it."

Sparhawk shrugged. "As you wish, Sarathi," he said. "We'll start just as soon as you tell us which ocean to look in."

"Surely you—" Dolmant looked at them helplessly.

"We have absolutely no idea, Sarathi," Ulath assured him. "Aphrael took us to a cliff somewhere on some coast, and we threw Bhelliom into the sea. It could have been any coast and any ocean. It may not even be on this world, for all I know. Do they have oceans on the moon? Bhelliom's gone for good, I'm afraid."

The churchmen stared at him in open dismay.

"I don't think your Elene God really wants Bhelliom, anyway, Dolmant," Sephrenia told the archprelate. "I think your God—like all the others—is very relieved to know that it's lost for good. I think it frightens all of them. I know that it frightened Aphrael." She paused. "Have you noticed how long and dreary this winter's been?" she asked then. "And how low your spirits are?"

"It's been a troubled time, Sephrenia," Dolmant reminded her.

"Granted, but I didn't notice you dancing for joy when you heard that Azash and Otha are gone. Not even *that* could lift your spirits. Styrics believed that winter's a state of mind in the Gods. Something happened at Zemoch that's never happened before. We found out once and for all that the Gods can die, too. I seriously doubt that any of us will feel spring in our souls until our Gods are able to come to grips with that. They're distracted and frightened now—and not really very interested in us—or our problems. They've left us to fend for ourselves for a while, I'm afraid. Our magic doesn't even seem to work any more for some reason. We're all alone now, Dolmant, and we'll have to endure this interminable winter until the Gods return."

Dolmant leaned back in his chair again. "You trouble me, little mother," he said. He passed one hand wearily across his eyes. "I'll be honest with you, though. I've felt this winter despair myself for the last month and a half. I awoke in the middle of the night once weeping uncontrollably. I haven't smiled since, or felt any lightness of spirit. I thought it was only me, but perhaps not." He paused. "And that brings us face-to-face with our duty as representatives of the Church. We absolutely *must* find something to distract the minds of the faithful from this universal despair—something to give them purpose, if not joy. What could possibly do that?"

"The conversion of the Zemochs, Sarathi," Bevier replied simply. "They've followed an evil God for eons. Now they're Godless. What better task for the Church?"

"Bevier," Emban said with a pained look, "are you by any chance striving for sainthood?" He looked at Dolmant. "It's really a very good idea, though, Sarathi. It would keep the faithful busy. There's no question about that."

"You'd better stop Wargun then, your Grace," Ulath advised. "He's poised in Kadum. As soon as the ground gets dry enough to hold a horse, he's going to march into Zemoch and kill anything that moves."

"I'll take care of that," Emban promised, "even if I have to ride to Kadum myself and arm wrestle him into submission."

"Azash is—was—a Styric God," Dolmant said, "and Elene priests have never had much success trying to convert Styrics. Sephrenia, could you possibly help us? I'll even find some way to give you authority and official status."

"No, Dolmant," she said firmly.

"Why is everybody saying no to me today?" he asked plaintively. "What's the problem, little mother?"

"I won't assist you in converting Styrics to a heathen religion, Dolmant."

"*Heathen?*" Ortzel choked.

"It's a word that's used to describe someone who isn't of the true faith, your Grace."

"But the Elene faith *is* the true faith."

"Not to me, it isn't. I find your religion repugnant. It's cruel, rigid, unforgiving, and smugly self-righteous. It's totally without humanity, and I reject it. I'll have no part of this ecumenicism of yours, Dolmant. If I should aid you in converting the Zemochs, you'll turn next to western Styricum, and *that* is where you and I will fight." She smiled then, a gentle, surprising smile that shone through the pervading gloom. "As soon as she's feeling better, I think I'll have a little talk with Aphrael. She may just take an interest in the Zemochs herself." The smile she directed at Dolmant at that point was almost radiant. "That would put us on opposite sides of the fence, wouldn't it, Sarathi?" she suggested. "I wish you all the best, though, old dear, but as they say, may the better man—or woman—win."

The weather altered only slightly as they rode westward. The rain had ceased for the most part, but the sky remained cloudy, and the blustery wind still had the chill of winter in it. Their destination was Demos. They were taking Kurik home. Sparhawk was not really looking forward to telling Aslade that he had finally managed to get her husband killed. The gloom that had fallen over the earth following the death of Azash was heightened by the funereal nature of their journey. The armorers at the Pandion chapterhouse in Chyrellos had hammered the dents out of the armor of Sparhawk and his friends, and had even buffed off most of the rust. They rode now with a somewhat ornate black carriage that bore Kurik's body.

They made camp in a grove not far back from the road some five leagues from Demos, and Sparhawk and the other knights saw to their armor. They had decided by unspoken agreement that they would wear their formal garb the next day. When he was satisfied that his equipment was ready for tomorrow, Sparhawk started across the camp toward the black carriage that stood some distance from the fire. Talen rose from his place to join him. "Sparhawk," he said as they walked.

"Yes?"

"You're not really serious about this notion, are you?"

"Which notion was that?"

"Putting me in training to become a Pandion."

"Yes, as a matter of fact I am. I made some promises to your father."

"I'll run away."

"Then I'll catch you—or send Berit to do it."

"That's not fair."

"You didn't really expect life to throw honest dice, did you?"

"Sparhawk, I don't want to go to knight school."

"We don't always get what we want, Talen. This is something your father wanted, and I'm not going to disappoint him."

"What about me? What about what *I* want?"

"You're young. You'll adjust to it. After a while, you might even find that you like it."

"Where are we going right now?" Talen's tone was sulky.

"I'm going to visit your father."

"Oh. I'll go back to the fire then. I'd rather remember him the way he was."

The carriage creaked as Sparhawk climbed up into it and sat down beside his squire's silent body. He did not say anything for quite some time. His grief had run itself out now and had been replaced with only a profound regret. "We've come a long way together, haven't we, my old friend?" he said finally. "Now you're going home to rest, and I have to go on alone." He smiled faintly in the darkness. "That was really very inconsiderate of you, Kurik. I was looking forward to growing old with you—older, that is."

He sat quietly for a time. "I've taken care of your sons," he added. "You'll be very proud of them—even of Talen, although he may take awhile to come around to the idea of respectability."

He paused again. "I'll break the news to Aslade as gently as I can," he promised. Then he laid his hand on Kurik's. "Good-bye, my friend," he said.

The part he had dreaded the most, telling Aslade, turned out not to be necessary, since Aslade already knew. She wore a black country dress when she met them at the gate of the farm on which she and her husband had labored for so many years. Her four sons, as tall as young trees, stood with her, also in their best clothes. Their somber faces told Sparhawk that his carefully prepared speech was unnecessary. "See to your father," Aslade told her sons.

They nodded and went to the black carriage.

"How did you find out?" Sparhawk asked her after she had embraced him.

"That little girl told us," she replied simply. "The one you brought with you when you were on your way to Chyrellos that time. She just appeared at the door one evening and told us. Then she went away."

"You believed her?"

Aslade nodded. "I knew that I must. She's not at all like other children."

"No, she isn't. I'm very, very sorry, Aslade. When Kurik started getting older, I should have made him stay home."

"No, Sparhawk. That would have broken his heart. You're going to have to help me with something right now, though."

"Anything at all, Aslade."

"I need to talk with Talen."

Sparhawk was not sure where this was leading. He motioned to the young thief, and Talen joined them.

"Talen," Aslade said.

"Yes?"

"We're very proud of you, you know."

"Me?"

"You avenged your father's death. Your brothers and I share that with you."

He stared at her. "Are you trying to say that you knew? About Kurik and me, I mean?"

"Of course I knew. I've known for a long time. This is what you're going to do—and if you don't, Sparhawk here will thrash you. You're going to Cimmura, and you're going to bring your mother back here."

"*What?*"

"You heard me. I've met your mother a few times. I went to Cimmura to have a look at her just before you were born. I wanted to talk with her so that we could decide which of us would be best for your father. She's a nice girl—a little skinny, perhaps, but I can fatten her up once I get her here. She and I get along quite well, and we're all going to live here until you and your brothers enter your novitiates. After that, she and I can keep each other company."

"You want *me* to live on a farm?" he asked incredulously.

"Your father would have wanted that, and I'm sure your mother wants it, and so do I. You're too good a boy to disappoint all three of us."

"But—"

"Please don't argue with me, Talen. It's all settled. Now, let's go inside. I've cooked a dinner for us, and I don't want it to get cold."

They buried Kurik beneath a tall elm tree on a hill overlooking his farm about noon the following day. The sky had been ominous all morning, but the sun broke through as Kurik's sons carried their father up the hill. Sparhawk was not as good as his squire had been at judging the weather, but the sudden appearance of a patch of blue sky and bright sunlight hovering just over the farm and touching no other part of the city of Demos made him more than a little suspicious.

The funeral was very simple and very moving. The local priest, an elderly, almost doddering man, had known Kurik since boyhood, and he spoke not so much of sorrow as of love. When it was over, Kurik's eldest son, Khalad, joined Sparhawk as they all walked back down the hill. "I'm honored that you thought I might be worthy to become a Pandion, Sir Sparhawk," he said, "but I'm afraid I'll have to decline."

Sparhawk looked sharply at the husky, plain-faced young man whose black beard was only beginning to sprout.

"It's nothing personal, Sir Sparhawk," Khalad assured him. "It's just that my father had other plans for me. In a few weeks—after you've had the chance to get settled in—I'll be joining you in Cimmura."

"You will?" Sparhawk was slightly taken aback by the lad's matter-of-fact manner.

"Of course, Sir Sparhawk. I'll be taking up my father's duties. It's a family tradition. My grandfather served yours—and your father, and my father served your father and you, so I'll be taking up where he left off."

"That's not really necessary, Khalad. Don't you want to be a Pandion Knight?"

"What I want isn't important, Sir Sparhawk. I have other duties."

· · ·

They left the farmstead the next morning, and Kalten rode forward to join Sparhawk. "Nice funeral," he noted, "if you happen to like funerals. I'd rather keep my friends around me, personally."

"Do you want to help me with a problem?" Sparhawk asked him.

"I thought we'd already killed everybody who needs it."

"Can you be serious?"

"That's a lot to ask, Sparhawk, but I'll try. What's this problem?"

"Khalad insists on being my squire."

"So? It's the sort of thing country boys do—follow their fathers' trades."

"I want him to become a Pandion Knight."

"I still don't see any problem. Go ahead and get him knighted then."

"He can't be a squire and a knight both, Kalten."

"Why not? Take *you,* for example. You're a Pandion Knight, a member of the royal council, Queen's Champion, *and* the Prince Consort. Khalad's got broad shoulders. He can handle both jobs."

The more Sparhawk thought about that, the more he liked it. "Kalten—" He laughed. "—what would I ever do without you?"

"Flounder, most likely. You complicate things too much, Sparhawk. You really ought to try to keep them simple."

"Thanks."

"No charge."


It was raining. A soft, silvery drizzle sifted down out of the late-afternoon sky and wreathed around the blocky watchtowers of the city of Cimmura. A lone rider approached the city. He was wrapped in a dark, heavy traveller's cloak and rode a tall, shaggy roan horse with a long nose and flat, vicious eyes. "We always seem to come back to Cimmura in the rain, don't we, Faran," the rider said to his horse.

Faran flicked his ears.

Sparhawk had left his friends behind that morning and had ridden on ahead. They all knew why, and they had not argued with him about it.

"We can send word on ahead to the palace, if you'd like, Prince Sparhawk," one of the guards at the east gate offered. Ehlana, it appeared, had made some issue of his new title. Sparhawk wished that she had not. It was going to take some getting used to.

"Thanks all the same, neighbor," Sparhawk told the guard, "but I'd sort of like to surprise my wife. She's young enough still to enjoy surprises."

The guard grinned at him.

"Get back inside the guardhouse, neighbor," Sparhawk advised. "You'll catch cold out here in the weather."

He rode on into Cimmura. The rain was keeping almost everyone inside, and Faran's steel-shod hooves echoed on the cobblestones of the nearly empty streets.

Sparhawk dismounted in the palace courtyard and handed Faran's reins to a groom. "Be a little careful of the horse, neighbor," he cautioned the stableman. "He's bad-tempered. Give him some hay and grain and rub him down, if you would, please. He's had a hard trip."

"I'll see to it, Prince Sparhawk." There it was again. Sparhawk decided to have a word with his wife about it.

"Faran," he said to his horse, "behave yourself."

The big roan gave him a flat, unfriendly look.

"It was a good ride," Sparhawk said, laying one hand on Faran's powerfully muscled neck. "Get some rest." Then he turned and went up the stairs into the palace. "Where's the queen?" he asked one of the soldiers at the door.

"In the council chamber, I believe, my Lord."

"Thank you." Sparhawk started down a long, candlelit corridor toward the council chamber.

The Tamul giantess Mirtai was emerging from the council chamber when he reached the door. "What took you so long?" she asked, showing no particular sign of surprise.

"Some things came up." He shrugged. "Is she in there?"

Mirtai nodded. "She's with Lenda and the thieves. They're talking about repairing streets." She paused. "Don't greet her *too* enthusiastically, Sparhawk," she cautioned. "She's with child."

Sparhawk gave her a stunned look.

"Wasn't that sort of what you two had in mind on your wedding night?" She paused again. "Whatever happened to that bandy-legged man who shaves his head?"

"Kring? The Domi?"

"What does 'Domi' mean?"

"Chief—sort of. He's the leader of his people. He's still alive and well as far as I know. The last time I saw him, he was working on a plan to lure the Zemochs into a trap so that he could slaughter them."

Her eyes suddenly glowed warmly.

"Why do you ask?" he wanted to know.

"No reason. Just curious."

"Oh. I see."

They went into the council chamber, and Sparhawk unfastened the neck of his dripping cloak. As chance had it, the Queen of Elenia had her back to the door when he entered. She and the Earl of Lenda, Platime, and Stragen were bent over the large map spread out on the council table. "I've been through that quarter of the city," she was saying insistently, "and I don't really think there's any help for it. The streets are so bad that patching just won't do. It's all going to have to be repaved." Her rich, vibrant voice touched Sparhawk's heart, even when she was discussing so mundane a matter. He smiled and laid his wet cloak across a chair near the door.

"Of course we can't start until spring, your Majesty," Lenda pointed out, "and even then we're going to be fearfully short of workers until the army returns from Lamorkand, and—" The old man broke off, staring at Sparhawk in astonishment.

The Prince Consort touched one finger to his lips as he approached the table to join them. "I hate to disagree with your Majesty," he said in a clinical tone, "but I think you should give more consideration to the condition of the highways rather than the streets here in Cimmura. Bad streets inconvenience the burgers, but if the farmers can't get their crops to market, it's more than just an inconvenience."

"I *know* that, Sparhawk," she said, still staring at the map, "but—" She raised her flawless young face, her gray eyes stunned. "Sparhawk?" Her voice was hardly more than a whisper.

"I really think your Majesty should concentrate on the highways," he continued seriously. "The one between here and Demos is in really shocking—" That was about as far as he got with that particular subject.

"Gently," Mirtai cautioned him as Ehlana hurled herself into his arms. "Remember what I told you outside."

"When did you get back?" Ehlana demanded.

"Just now. The others are a ways behind. I rode on ahead—for several reasons." She smiled and kissed him again.

"Well, gentlemen," Lenda said to Platime and Stragen, "I think perhaps we can continue this discussion later." He smiled. "Somehow I don't really think we'll be able to command her Majesty's full attention this evening."

"Would you all mind too terribly much?" Ehlana asked them in a little-girl sort of voice.

"Of course not, baby sister," Platime boomed. He grinned at Sparhawk. "It's good to have you back, my friend. Maybe you can distract Ehlana enough so that she won't be poking her nose into the details of certain public works projects I have an interest in."

"We won, I gather," Stragen said.

"Sort of," Sparhawk replied, remembering Kurik. "Otha and Azash won't be bothering us any more at least."

"That's the important thing," the blond thief said. "You can fill us in on the details later." He looked at Ehlana's radiant face. "*Much* later, I'd imagine," he added.

"Stragen," Ehlana said firmly.

"Yes, your Majesty?"

"Out." She pointed imperiously at the door.

"Yes, ma'am."

Sparhawk and his bride adjourned to the royal apartments shortly after that, accompanied only by Mirtai. Sparhawk was not really sure just how long the Tamul giantess intended to remain in attendance. He didn't want to offend her, but—

Mirtai, however, was very businesslike. She gave a number of crisp commands to the queen's personal servants—commands having to do with hot baths, suppers, privacy, and the like, and then, after everything in the royal apartment was to her satisfaction, she went to the door, drawing a large key from under her sword belt. "Will that be all for tonight, Ehlana?" she asked.

"Yes, Mirtai," the queen replied, "and thank you so very much."

Mirtai shrugged. "It's what I'm supposed to do. Don't forget what I told you, Sparhawk." She tapped the key firmly against the door. "I'll let you out in the morning," she said. Then she went out and closed the door behind her. The sound of the key turning in the lock was very loud.

"She's such a bully." Ehlana laughed a bit helplessly. "She absolutely ignores me when I give her any orders."

"She's good for you, love." Sparhawk smiled. "She helps you to keep your perspective."

"Go bathe, Sparhawk," Ehlana commanded. "You smell all rusty. Then you can tell me about everything that happened. Oh, by the way, I'll have my ring back now, if you don't mind."

He held out his hands. "Which one is it?" he asked her. "I can't for the life of me tell them apart."

"It's this one, of course." She pointed at the ring on his left hand.

"How do you know?" he asked, removing the ring and slipping it on her finger.

"Anyone can see that, Sparhawk."

"If you say so." He shrugged.

Sparhawk was really not accustomed to bathing in the presence of young ladies, but Ehlana seemed unwilling to let him out of her sight. Thus he began the story even as he bathed and continued it while they ate. There were things that Ehlana did not grasp and others she misunderstood, but she was able to accept most of what had taken place. She cried when he told her that Kurik had died, and her expression grew fierce when he described the fates of Annias and her aunt and cousin. There were a number of things he glossed over and others he did not mention at all. He found the evasive remark "You almost had to have been there" very useful a number of times. He made a rather special point of avoiding any mention of the nearly universal depression that seemed to have fallen over the world since the destruction of Azash. It did not seem to be a proper subject to be mentioned to a young woman in the initial months of her first pregnancy.

And then as they lay together in the close and friendly darkness, Ehlana told him of the events that had taken place here in the west during his absence.

Perhaps it was because they were in bed where such things normally happen, but for some reason the subject of dreams came up. "It was so very strange, Sparhawk," Ehlana said as she nestled down in the bed beside him. "The entire sky was covered with a rainbow, and we were on an island, the most beautiful place I've ever seen. There were trees—very old—and a kind of marble temple with graceful white columns, and I was waiting there for you and our friends. And then you came, each of you led by a beautiful white animal. Sephrenia was waiting with me, and she looked very young, hardly more than a girl, and there was a child who played some shepherd's pipes and danced. She was almost like a little empress, and everybody obeyed her orders." She giggled. "She even called you a grouchy old bear. Then she started to talk about Bhelliom. It was all very deep, and I only could understand a little of it."

None of them had grasped it all, Sparhawk remembered, and the dream had been more widespread than he had imagined. But why had Aphrael included Ehlana?

"That was sort of the end of that dream," she continued, "and you know all about the next one."

"Oh?"

"You just described it to me," she told him, "right down to the last detail. For some reason, I dreamed every single thing that happened in the Temple of Azash in Zemoch. My blood kept running cold while you were telling me about it."

"I wouldn't worry all that much about it," he told her, trying to keep his voice casual. "We're very close together, you know, and it's not really too strange that you'd know what I was thinking about."

"Are you serious?"

"Of course. It happens all the time. Ask any married woman, and she'll tell you that she always knows what's on her husband's mind."

"Well," she said dubiously, "maybe." She snuggled closer to him. "You're not being very attentive tonight, love," she accused. "Is it because I'm getting fat and ugly?"

"Of course not. You're in what's called a 'delicate condition.' Mirtai kept warning me to be careful. She'll carve out my liver if she thinks I've hurt you."

"Mirtai isn't here, Sparhawk."

"But she's still the only one with a key to that door."

"Oh, no, she isn't, Sparhawk," his queen said smugly, reaching under her pillow. "The door locks from either side, and it won't open unless it's been unlocked from both sides." She handed him a large key.

"A very cooperative door." He smiled. "Why don't I just slip on out to the other room and lock it from this side?"

"Why don't you do that? And don't get lost on your way back to bed. Mirtai told you to be careful, so you ought to practice that for a while."

Later—quite a bit later, actually—Sparhawk slipped out of bed and went to the window to look out at the rain-swept night. It was over now. He would no longer rise before the sun to watch the veiled woman of Jiroch going to the well in the steely gray light of dawn, nor would he ride strange roads in distant lands with the sapphire rose nestled near his heart. He had returned at last, older certainly and sadder and infinitely less certain of things he had always before accepted without question. He had come home at last, his wars over, he hoped, and his travels complete. They called him Anakha, the man who makes his own destiny, and he grimly resolved that his entire destiny lay here in this unlovely city with the pale, beautiful young woman who slept only a few feet away.

It was good to have that settled once and for all, and it was with some sense of accomplishment that he turned back to the bed and to his wife.

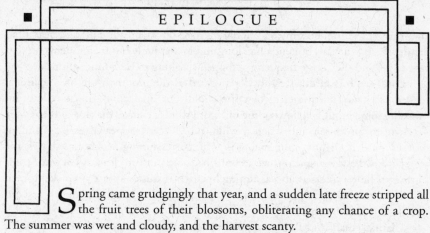

# EPILOGUE

S pring came grudgingly that year, and a sudden late freeze stripped all the fruit trees of their blossoms, obliterating any chance of a crop. The summer was wet and cloudy, and the harvest scanty.

The armies of western Eosia returned home from Lamorkand to immerse themselves in unrewarding toil in stubborn fields where only thistles grew in abundance. Civil war erupted in Lamorkand, but there was nothing unusual about that; there was a serf rebellion in Pelosia, and the number of beggars near the churches and at the gates of the cities of the west increased dramatically.

Sephrenia received the news of Ehlana's pregnancy with astonishment. The undeniable fact of that pregnancy seemed to baffle her, and that bafflement made her short-tempered, even waspish. In the usual course of time Ehlana gave birth to her first child, a daughter, whom she and Sparhawk named Danae. Sephrenia gave the infant an extended examination, and it seemed somehow to Sparhawk that his tutor was almost offended by the fact that Princess Danae was totally normal and disgustingly healthy.

Mirtai calmly rearranged the queen's schedule to add the task of nursing to Ehlana's other royal duties. It should be noted in passing perhaps that Ehlana's ladies-in-waiting all jealously hated Mirtai, even though the giantess had never physically assaulted or even spoken sharply to a single one of them.

The Church soon lost sight of her grand design in the east, turning instead to the south to seize an opportunity that presented itself there. Martel's enlistment of the most fervent Eshandists and his subsequent defeat at Chyrellos had decimated the ranks of that sect, leaving Rendor ripe for reassimilation into the congregation of the faithful. Although Dolmant sent his priests into Rendor in a spirit of love and reconciliation, that spirit lasted in most of his missionaries for only so long as the dome of the Basilica remained in view. The missions to Rendor were vengeful and punitive, and the Rendors responded in a fairly predictable fashion. After a number of the more strident and abrasive missionaries had been murdered, larger and larger detachments of Church Knights were sent into that southern kingdom to protect the unwelcome clergy and their meager congregations of converts. Eshandist sentiments began to reemerge, and there were once again rumors of caches of weapons out in the desert.

Civilized man believes that his cities are the crown of his culture and seems incapable of grasping the fact that the foundation of any kingdom is the land upon which it rests. When a nation's agriculture falters, its economy begins to collapse, and governments starved for revenue inevitably fall back on the most regressive of all forms of taxation, heaping additional burdens on an already suffering peasantry. Sparhawk and the Earl of Lenda had long and increasingly bitter arguments on that very issue, and they quite frequently stopped speaking to each other entirely.

Lord Vanion's health steadily deteriorated as the months wore on. Sephrenia tended his many infirmities as best she could, but finally on a blustery autumn morning some months following the birth of Princess Danae, the two of them were nowhere to be found, and when a white-robed Styric appeared at the Pandion motherhouse at Demos, announcing that he was assuming Sephrenia's duties, the worst of Sparhawk's suspicions were confirmed. Despite his pleadings of prior commitments, he was pressed into assuming his friend's duties as interim preceptor, an appointment Dolmant wished to make permanent, although Sparhawk resisted that notion strenuously.

Ulath, Tynian, and Bevier stopped by the palace from time to time for visits, and their reports of what was happening in their homelands were no more cheerful than the news Sparhawk was receiving from the outlying districts of Elenia. Platime gravely reported that his far-flung informants had advised him that near famine, epidemics, and civil unrest were well-nigh universal. "Hard times, Sparhawk," the fat thief said with a philosophic shrug. "No matter what we do to try to hold them off, hard times come along now and then."

Sparhawk enrolled Kurik's four elder sons as Pandion novices, overriding Khalad's objections. Since Talen was still a bit young for military training, he was ordered to serve as a page in the palace where Sparhawk could keep an eye on him. Stragen, unpredictable as always, came often to Cimmura. Mirtai guarded Ehlana, bullied her when it was necessary, and laughingly avoided the repeated marriage proposals of Kring, who seemed to be able to find all manner of excuses to ride across the continent from eastern Pelosia to Cimmura.

The years ground on, and conditions did not improve. That first year of excessive rain was followed by three years of drought. Food was continually in short supply, and the governments of Eosia were starved for revenue. Ehlana's pale, beautiful face grew careworn, although Sparhawk did what he could to transfer as many burdens as possible from her shoulders to his own.

It was on a clear, chilly afternoon in late winter when something quite profound happened to the Prince Consort. He had spent the morning in a violent argument with the Earl of Lenda about a proposed new tax, and Lenda had become shrill, even abusive, accusing Sparhawk of systematically dismantling the government in his excessive concern for the well-being of the pampered, lazy peasantry. Sparhawk won the argument in the end, although he took no particular pleasure in that, since each victory drove the wedge between him and his old friend that much deeper.

He sat near the fire in the royal apartment in a kind of moody discontent, half watching the activities of his four-year-old daughter, the Princess Danae. His wife, accompanied by Mirtai and Talen, was off on some errand in the city, and so Sparhawk and the tiny princess were alone.

Danae was a grave, serious child with glossy black hair, large eyes as dark as night, and a mouth like a pink rosebud. Despite her serious demeanor, she was affectionate, frequently showering her parents with spontaneous kisses. At the moment, she was near the fireplace doing important things involving a ball.

It was the fireplace that brought everything to a head and changed Sparhawk's life forever. Danae miscalculated slightly, and her ball rolled directly into the grate. Without giving it any apparent thought, she quickly went to the fireplace, and before her father could stop her or even cry out, she reached into the flames and retrieved her toy. Sparhawk leaped to his feet with a strangled cry and rushed to her. He snatched her up and closely examined her hand.

"What is it, Father?" she asked him quite calmly. Princess Danae was a precocious child. She had begun to speak early, and her speech by now was very nearly adult.

"Your hand! You burned it! You know better than to stick your hand into a fire."

"It's not burned," she protested, holding it up and wiggling her fingers. "See?"

"Don't go near the fire again," he commanded.

"No, Father." She wriggled to be let down and then crossed the floor with her ball to continue her game in a safe corner.

Troubled, Sparhawk returned to his chair. One *can* thrust one's hand into a fire and snatch it back out again without being burned, but it had not seemed that Danae had moved her hand that quickly. Sparhawk began to look more closely at his child. He had been very busy for the past several months, so he had not really looked at her but had simply accepted the fact that she was there. Danae was at an age when certain changes occur quite rapidly, and those changes, it seemed, had taken place right under Sparhawk's inattentive gaze. As he looked at her now, however, a sudden chill gripped his heart. Unbelievingly, he saw something for the first time. He and his wife were Elenes.

Their daughter was not.

He stared for a long time at his Styric daughter, then seized on the only possible explanation. *"Aphrael?"* he said in a stunned voice. Danae only looked a little bit like Flute, but Sparhawk could see no other possibility.

"Yes, Sparhawk?" Her voice betrayed no surprise.

"What have you done with my daughter?" he shouted, half rising to his feet in agitation.

"Don't be absurd, Sparhawk," she said quite calmly. "I *am* your daughter."

"That's impossible. How—?"

"You know I am, Father. You were there when I was born. Did you think I was some kind of changeling? Some starling planted in your nest to supplant your own chick? That's a foolish Elene superstition, you know. We don't ever do that."

He began to gain some control over his emotions. "Do you plan to explain this?" he asked in as level a tone as he could manage, "or am I supposed to guess?"

"Be nice, Father. You wanted children, didn't you?"

"Well—"

"And Mother's a queen. She has to give birth to a successor, doesn't she?"

"Of course, but—"

"She wouldn't have, you know."

"*What?*"

"The poison Annias gave her made her barren. You have no idea how difficult it was for me to overcome that. Why do you think Sephrenia was so upset when she discovered that Mother was pregnant? She knew about the effects of the poison, of course, and she was *very* put out with me for interfering—probably more because Mother's an Elene than for any other reason. Sephrenia's very narrow-minded sometimes. Oh, *do* sit down, Sparhawk. You look ridiculous all stooped over like that. Either sit or stand. Don't hover in between."

Sparhawk sank back into his chair, his mind reeling. "But *why?*" he demanded.

"Because I love you and Mother. She was destined to be childless, so I had to change her destiny just a bit."

"And did you change mine as well?"

"How could I possibly do that? You're Anakha, remember? Nobody knows what your destiny is. You've always been a problem for us. Many felt that we shouldn't let you be born at all. I had to argue for centuries to persuade the others that we really needed you." She looked down at herself. "I'm going to have to pay attention to growing up, I suppose. I was Styric before, and Styrics can take these things in stride. You Elenes are more excitable, and people might begin to talk if I were to remain a child for several centuries. I guess I'll have to do it the right way this time."

"*This* time?"

"Of course. I've been born dozens of times." She rolled her eyes. "It helps to keep me young." Her small face grew very serious. "Something terrible happened in the Temple of Azash, Father, and I needed to hide from it for a while. Mother's womb was the perfect place to hide. It was so safe and secure there."

"Then you *knew* what was going to happen in Zemoch," he accused.

"I knew that *something* was going to happen, so I just covered all the possibilities." She pursed her pink little mouth thoughtfully. "This might be very interesting," she said. "I've never been a grown woman before—and certainly never a queen. I wish my sister were here. I'd like to talk with her about it."

"Your sister?"

"Sephrenia." She said it almost absently. "She was the eldest daughter of my last parents. It's very nice having an older sister, you know. She's always been so very, very wise, and she always forgives me when I do something foolish."

A thousand things suddenly clicked into place in Sparhawk's mind, things that had never really been explained before. "How old *is* Sephrenia?" he asked.

She sighed. "You *know* I'm not going to answer that, Sparhawk. Besides, I'm not really sure. The years don't mean as much to us as they do to you. In a general way, though, Sephrenia's hundreds of years old, maybe even a thousand—whatever that means."

"Where is she now?"

"She and Vanion are off together. You knew how they felt about each other, didn't you?"

"Yes."

"Astonishing. You *can* use your eyes after all."

"What are they doing?"

"They're looking after things for me. I'm too busy to attend to business this time, and somebody has to mind the shop. Sephrenia can answer prayers as well as I can, and I don't have all that many worshippers."

"Do you absolutely *have* to make all of this sound so commonplace?" His tone was plaintive.

"But it *is,* Father. It's your Elene God who takes Himself so seriously. I've never once seen Him laugh. *My* worshippers are much more sensible. They love me, so they're tolerant of my mistakes." She laughed suddenly, climbed up into his lap, and kissed him. "You're the best father I've ever had, Sparhawk. I can actually talk with you about these things without making your eyes pop out of their sockets." She rested her head against his chest. "What's really been going on, Father? I know that things aren't going well, but Mirtai keeps putting me down for naps when people come to make reports to you, so I can't get very many details."

"It hasn't been a good time for the world, Aphrael," he said gravely. "The weather's been very bad, and there have been famine and pestilence. Nothing seems to be going the way it should. If I were at all superstitious, I'd say that the whole world's been going through a long spell of very bad luck."

"That's my family's fault, Sparhawk," she admitted. "We started feeling very sorry for ourselves after what happened to Azash, so we haven't been attending to business. I think that maybe it's time for *all* of us to grow up. I'll talk with the others and let you know what we decide."

"I'd appreciate that." Sparhawk could not actually believe this conversation was taking place.

"We have a bit of a problem, though," she told him.

"Only one?"

"Stop that. I'm serious. What are we going to tell Mother?"

"Oh, my God!" he said, his eyes suddenly going very wide. "I hadn't thought of that."

"We'll have to decide right now, you know, and I don't like to make up my mind in a hurry. She'd have a great deal of trouble believing this, wouldn't she? Particularly if it meant that she'd have to accept the fact that she's really barren and that I'm here as a result of my own choice instead of her personal appetites and fertility. Will it break her heart if we tell her who I really am?"

He thought about it. He knew his wife better than anyone else in the world possibly could. He remembered with an icy chill that momentary look of anguish that had filled her gray eyes when he had suggested that his gift of the ring had been a mistake. "No," he said finally, "we can't tell her."

"I didn't think so either, but I wanted to be sure."

Something occurred to Sparhawk. "Why did you include her in that dream, the one about the island? And why did she dream about what happened in the temple? It was almost as if she'd been there."

"She *was* there, Father. She had to be. I was hardly in a position to leave her behind and go places by myself, was I? Let me down, please."

He unwrapped his arms from about her, and she went to the window. "Come here, Sparhawk," she said after a moment.

He joined her at the window. "What is it?" he asked her.

"Mother's coming back. She's down in the courtyard with Mirtai and Talen."

Sparhawk looked out the window. "Yes," he agreed.

"I'm going to be a queen someday, aren't I?"

"Unless you decide to throw it all over and go herd goats someplace, yes."

She let that pass. "I'll need a champion then, won't I?"

"I suppose so. I could do it if you like."

"When you're eighty years old? You're very imposing right now, Father, but I suspect you'll begin to get a little decrepit when you get older."

"Don't rub it in."

"Sorry. And I'll need a Prince Consort as well, won't I?"

"It's customary. Why are we talking about this now, though?"

"I want your advice, Father, and your consent."

"Isn't this a little premature? You're only four years old, you know."

"A girl can't start thinking about these things too early." She pointed down toward the courtyard. "I think that one right down there will do very nicely, don't you?" She sounded almost as if she were choosing a new ribbon for her hair.

"*Talen?*"

"Why not? I like him. He's going to be a knight—*Sir* Talen, if you can believe that. He's funny and really much nicer than he seems—besides, I can beat him at draughts, and we can't spend *all* our time in bed, the way you and Mother do."

"*Danae!*"

"What?" She looked up at him. "Why are you blushing, Father?"

"Never mind. You just watch what you say, young lady, or I *will* tell your mother who you really are."

"Fine," she said serenely, "and then I'll tell her about Lillias. How would you like that?"

They looked at each other, and then they laughed.


It was about a week later. Sparhawk was hunched over a desk in the room he used as an office glaring at the Earl of Lenda's latest proposal, an absurd idea that would quite nearly double the government payroll. He scribbled an angry note at the bottom. "Why not just make everyone in the whole kingdom a government employee, Lenda? Then we can all starve together."

The door opened, and his daughter entered, carrying a rather disreputable-looking stuffed toy animal by one leg.

"I'm busy, Danae," he said shortly.

She closed the door firmly. "You're a grouch, Sparhawk," she said crisply.

He looked around quickly, went to the door to the adjoining room, and carefully closed it. "Sorry, Aphrael," he apologized. "I'm a little out of sorts."

"I noticed that. Everybody in the palace has noticed that." She held out her toy. "Would you like to kick Rollo across the room? He won't mind, and it might make you feel better."

He laughed, feeling just a little silly. "That *is* Rollo, isn't it? Your mother used to carry him in exactly the same way—before his stuffings fell out."

"She had him restuffed and gave him to me," Aphrael said. "I guess I'm sup-

posed to carry him around, though I can't for the life of me think why. I'd really much rather have a baby goat."

"This is something important, I take it?"

"Yes. I had a long talk with the others."

His mind shied away from the implications contained in that simple statement. "What did they say?"

"They weren't really very nice, Father. They're all blaming *me* for what happened in Zemoch. They wouldn't even listen to me when I tried to tell them that it was all *your* fault."

"*My* fault? Thanks."

"They're not going to help at all," she continued, "so it's going to be up to you and me, I'm afraid."

"We're going to go fix the world? All by ourselves?"

"It's not really all *that* difficult, Father. I've made some arrangements. Our friends will begin arriving very soon. Act as if you're surprised to see them, and then don't let them leave."

"Are they going to help us?"

"They're going to help *me*, Father. I'll need them around me when I do this. I'm going to need a great deal of love to make it work. Hello, Mother." She said it without even turning toward the door.

"Danae," Ehlana chided her daughter, "you know you're not supposed to disturb your father when he's working."

"Rollo wanted to see him, Mother," Danae lied glibly. "I told him that we weren't supposed to bother Father when he's busy, but you know how Rollo is." She said it so seriously that it almost sounded plausible. Then she lifted the disreputable-looking toy animal and shook her finger in his face. "Bad, bad Rollo," she scolded.

Ehlana laughed and rushed to her daughter. "Isn't she adorable?" she said happily to Sparhawk as she knelt to embrace the little girl.

"Oh, yes." He smiled. "She's that, all right. She's even better at that than you were." He made a rueful face. "I think it's my destiny to be wrapped around the fingers of a pair of very devious little girls."

The Princess Danae and her mother put their cheeks together and gave him an almost identical look of artfully contrived innocence.

Their friends began to arrive the next day, and each of them had a perfectly legitimate reason for being in Cimmura. For the most part, those reasons involved the bringing of bad news. Ulath had come south from Emsat to report that the years of hard drinking had finally begun to take their toll on King Wargun's liver. "He's the color of an apricot," the big Thalesian told them. Tynian told them that the ancient King Obler appeared to be slipping into his dotage, and Bevier advised that word coming out of Rendor hinted at the strong possibility of another Eshandist uprising. In marked contrast, Stragen reported that *his* business had taken a marked turn for the better, and that particular news was probably even worse than all the rest.

Despite all the bad news, the old friends took advantage of what appeared to be a chance meeting to stage something in the nature of a reunion.

It was good to have them all around him again, Sparhawk decided one morning as he slipped out of bed quietly to avoid awakening his sleeping wife, but sitting up talking with them for half the night and then rising early to attend to his other duties were leaving him more than a little short of sleep.

"Close the door, Father," Danae said quietly as he came out of the bedroom. She sat curled up in a large chair near the fire. She was wearing her nightdress, and her bare feet had those telltale grass stains on them.

Sparhawk nodded, closed the door, and joined her by the fire.

"They're all here now, Sparhawk," Danae told him, "so let's get started with this."

"Exactly what are we going to do?" he asked her.

"*You're* going to suggest a ride in the country."

"I'll need a reason for that, Danae. The weather's not really suitable for pleasure trips."

"Any sort of reason will do, Father. Think something up and suggest it. They'll all think it's a wonderful idea—I can guarantee that. Take them toward Demos. Sephrenia, Vanion, and I will join you a little way out of town."

"Would you like to clarify that a bit? You're already here."

"I'll be there, too, Sparhawk."

"You're going to be in two places at the same time?"

"It's not really all *that* difficult, Sparhawk. We do it all the time."

"Maybe, but that's not really a good way to keep your identity a secret, you know."

"No one will guess. I'll look like Flute to them."

"There's not really all that much difference between you and Flute, you know."

"Not to you, perhaps, but the others see me a little differently." She rose from her chair. "Take care of it, Sparhawk," she told him with an airy wave of her hand. Then she went toward the door, negligently dragging Rollo behind her.

"I give up," Sparhawk muttered.

"I heard that, Father," she said without even turning.

When they all gathered for breakfast later that morning, it was Kalten who provided the opening Sparhawk needed. "I wish there were some way we could all get out of Cimmura for a few days," the blond Pandion said critically. He looked at Ehlana. "I'm not trying to be offensive, your Majesty, but the palace isn't really a very good place to have a reunion. Every time things get off to a good start, some courtier comes in with something that absolutely *has* to have Sparhawk's immediate attention."

"He's got a point there," Ulath agreed. "A good reunion's a lot like a good tavern brawl. It's not nearly as much fun if it's interrupted every time it gets going."

Sparhawk suddenly remembered something. "Were you serious the other day, love?" he asked his wife.

"I'm always serious, Sparhawk. Which day were we talking about?"

"The day when you were talking about bestowing a duchy on me?"

"I've been trying to do that for four years now. I don't know why I bother anymore. You always find some reason to decline them."

"I shouldn't really do that, I suppose—at least not until I've had a chance to look them over."

"Where are you going with this, Sparhawk?" she asked.

"We need a place for uninterrupted celebration, Ehlana."

"Brawling," Ulath corrected.

Sparhawk grinned at him. "Anyway," he continued, "I really should go have a look at this duchy. It's off toward Demos, as I recall. We might want to have a rather close look at the manor house."

"We?" she asked him.

"A little advice never hurts a man when he's trying to make a decision. I think we *all* ought to go take a look at this duchy. What do the rest of you think?"

"The strength of a good leader lies in his ability to make the obvious appear innovative," Stragen drawled.

"We really ought to get out more often anyway, dear," Sparhawk told his wife. "We can take a little holiday, and all we'll really have to worry about is whether or not Lenda puts two dozen of his relatives on the public payroll while we're gone."

"I wish you all the enjoyment in the world, my friends," Platime said, "but I'm a kindly sort of fellow, and it distresses me to see a full-grown horse break down and cry every time I go to mount him. I'll stay here and keep an eye on Lenda."

"You can ride in the carriage," Mirtai told him.

"Which carriage was that, Mirtai?" Ehlana asked her.

"The one you're going to ride in to keep the weather off you."

"I don't need a carriage."

Mirtai's eyes flashed. "Ehlana!" she snapped. "Don't argue!"

"But—"

"Hush, Ehlana!"

"Yes, Mirtai," the queen sighed submissively.

They approached the outing with an almost holiday air. Even Faran felt it, and as *his* contribution to the festivities, he managed to step on both of Sparhawk's feet at the same time while his master was trying to mount.

The weather seemed to be almost in abeyance as they set out. The sky was overcast rather than cloudy, and the biting chill that had characterized the winter moderated, becoming, if not warm, at least bearable. There was not even a hint of a breeze, and Sparhawk was uneasily reminded of the endless now of that moment the Troll-God Ghnomb had frozen for them on the road leading eastward from Paler.

They left Cimmura behind and followed the road leading toward the cities of Lenda and Demos. Sparhawk had been spared the unsettling possibility of actually seeing his daughter in two places at the same time by Mirtai's decision that the weather was not suitable for the little princess to be making journeys and that she should remain in the palace in the care of her nurse. Sparhawk foresaw a titanic clash of wills looming in the future. The time was bound to come when Mirtai and Danae would run into each other head-on. He was rather looking forward to it, actually.

It was not far from the place on the road where they had encountered the Seeker that they found Sephrenia and Vanion seated by a small fire with Flute characteristically seated on the limb of a nearby oak. Vanion, looking younger and more fit than he had in years, rose to greet his friends. As Sparhawk had more or less expected, Vanion wore a white Styric robe and no sword. "You've been well, I trust," the big Pandion asked as he dismounted.

"Tolerable, Sparhawk. And you?"

"No complaints, my Lord."

And then they abandoned that particular pose and embraced each other roughly as the others all gathered around them.

"Who's been chosen to replace me as preceptor?" Vanion asked.

"We've been urging the Hierocracy to appoint Kalten, my Lord," Sparhawk told him blandly.

"You *what?*" Vanion's face was filled with chagrin.

"Sparhawk," Ehlana reproached her husband, "that's cruel."

"He's just trying to be funny, Vanion," Kalten said sourly. "Sometimes his humor's as twisted as his nose. Actually *he's* the one who's in charge."

"Thank God!" Vanion said fervently.

"Dolmant's been trying to persuade him to accept a permanent appointment, but our friend here keeps begging off—some nonsense about having too many jobs already."

"If you people spread me any thinner, you'll be able to see daylight through me," Sparhawk complained.

Ehlana had been looking with a certain awe at Flute, who, as she usually did, sat on the tree limb with her grass-stained feet crossed at the ankles and her pipes to her lips. "She looks exactly the way she did in that dream," she murmured to Sparhawk.

"She never changes," Sparhawk replied. "Well, not *too* much, anyway."

"Are we permitted to talk to her?" The young queen's eyes were actually a little frightened.

"Why are you standing over there whispering, Ehlana?" Flute asked.

"How do I address her?" the queen nervously asked her husband.

He shrugged. "We call her Flute. Her other name's a little formal."

"Help me down, Ulath," the little girl commanded.

"Yes, Flute," the big Thalesian replied automatically. He went to the tree and lifted the small divinity down and set her feet on the winter-browned grass.

Flute took outrageous advantage of the fact that as Danae she already knew Stragen, Platime, Kring, and Mirtai in addition to her mother. She spoke with them all quite familiarly, which noticeably added to their sense of awe. Mirtai in particular seemed quite shaken. "Well, Ehlana," the little girl said finally, "are we just going to stand here and stare at each other? Aren't you even going to thank me for the splendid husband I provided you?"

"You're cheating, Aphrael," Sephrenia scolded her.

"I know, dear sister, but it's so much fun."

Ehlana laughed helplessly and held out her arms. Flute crowed with delight and ran to her.

Flute and Sephrenia joined Ehlana, Mirtai, and Platime in the carriage. Just before they set out, however, the little Goddess thrust her head out the window. "Talen," she called sweetly.

"What?" Talen's tone was wary. Sparhawk rather suspected that Talen might just have had one of those chilling premonitions that beset young men and deer in almost the same way when they sense that they are being hunted.

"Why don't you join us here in the carriage?" Aphrael suggested in honeyed tones.

Talen looked a bit apprehensively at Sparhawk.

"Go ahead," Sparhawk told him. Talen was his friend, certainly—but Danae *was* his daughter, after all.

They rode on then. After several miles, Sparhawk began to have a vague sense of unease. Although he had been travelling the road between Demos and Cimmura since he had been a young man, it suddenly began to look strange to him. There were hills in places where there should not have been hills, and they passed a large, prosperous-looking farmstead Sparhawk had never seen before. He began to check his map.

"What's the matter?" Kalten asked him.

"Is there any way we could have made a wrong turn? I've been travelling this road back and forth for over twenty years now, and suddenly the usual landmarks aren't there any more."

"Oh, that's fine, Sparhawk," Kalten said sarcastically. He turned and looked back over his shoulder at the others. "Our glorious leader here has managed to get us lost," he announced. "We blindly followed him halfway across the world, and now he manages to lose his way not five leagues from home. I don't know about the rest of you, but I'm beginning to experience a severe erosion of confidence."

"Do *you* want to do this?" Sparhawk asked him flatly.

"And lose this opportunity to sit back and carp and criticize? Don't be silly."

They were obviously not going to reach any recognizable destination before dark, and they had not come prepared for camping out in the open. Sparhawk began to grow alarmed.

Flute thrust her head out of one of the windows of the carriage. "What's the matter, Sparhawk?" she asked.

"We're going to have to find some place to stay the night," he told her, "and we haven't passed any kind of house for the last ten miles."

"Just keep going, Sparhawk," she instructed.

"It's going to start getting dark before long, Flute."

"Then we'd better hurry, hadn't we?" She disappeared back inside the carriage.

They reached a hilltop just at dusk and looked out over a valley that absolutely *could not* have been where it was. The land below was grassy and gently rolling, dotted here and there with copses of white-trunked birch trees. About halfway down the hill was a low, sprawling, thatch-roofed house with golden candlelight streaming from its windows.

"Maybe they'll put us up for the night," Stragen suggested.

"Hurry right along now, gentlemen," Flute instructed from the carriage. "Supper's waiting, and we don't want it to get cold."

"She enjoys doing that to people, doesn't she?" Stragen said.

"Oh, yes," Sparhawk agreed, "probably more than anything else she gets to do."

Had it been somewhat smaller, the house might have been called a cottage. The rooms, however, were large, and there were many of them. The furnishings were rustic but well made, there were candles everywhere, and each scrupulously cleaned fireplace had a cheery fire dancing on the grate. There was a long table in the central room and it was set with what could only be called a banquet. There was not a single soul in the house, however.

"Do you like it?" Flute asked them with an anxious expression.

"It's lovely," Ehlana exclaimed, impulsively embracing the little girl.

"I'm awfully sorry," Flute apologized, "but I just couldn't bring myself to offer you ham. I know you Elenes all love it, but—" She shuddered.

"I think we can make do with what's here, Flute," Kalten said, surveying the table with his eyes alight, "don't you, Platime?"

The fat thief was looking almost reverently at all the food. "Oh, my goodness, yes, Kalten," he agreed enthusiastically. "This'll be just fine."

They all ate more than was really good for them and sat, afterward, sighing with that most pleasant of discomforts.

Berit came around the table and leaned over Sparhawk's shoulder. "She's doing it again, Sparhawk," the young knight murmured.

"Doing what?"

"The fires have been burning ever since we got here, and they still don't need any more wood, and the candles aren't even melting down."

"It's her house, I suppose," Sparhawk shrugged.

"I know, but—" Berit looked uncomfortable. "It's unnatural," he said finally.

"Berit," Sparhawk pointed out with a gentle smile, "we just rode through an impossible landscape to reach a house that isn't really here to eat a banquet that nobody prepared, and you're going to worry about a few little things like perpetually burning candles and fireplaces that don't need wood?"

Berit laughed and went back to his chair.

The Child-Goddess took her duties as hostess very seriously. She even seemed anxious as she escorted them to their rooms and carefully explained a number of things that did not really need to be explained.

"She's such a dear little thing, isn't she?" Ehlana said to Sparhawk when they were alone. "She seems so desperately concerned about the comfort and well-being of her guests."

"Styrics are a bit more casual about these things," Sparhawk explained. "Flute's not really used to Elenes, and we make her nervous." He smiled. "She's trying very, very hard to make a good impression."

"But she's a Goddess."

"She still gets nervous."

"Is it my imagination, or is she a great deal like our own Danae?"

"All little girls are similar, I suppose," he replied carefully, "just like all little boys."

"Perhaps," Ehlana conceded, "but she even seems to *smell* like Danae, and they both seem to be very fond of kisses." She paused, and then her face brightened. "We really should introduce them to each other, Sparhawk. They'd love each other, and they'd be wonderful playmates."

Sparhawk nearly choked on *that* idea.


The rhythm of the hoofbeats was familiar, and it was that more than anything that awakened Sparhawk early the next morning. He muttered an oath and swung his legs out of the bed.

"What is it, dear?" Ehlana asked in a sleepy voice.

"Faran got loose," he said in an irritated tone. "He managed to pull his picket line free somehow."

"He won't run away, will he?"

"And miss all the entertainment staying just out of my reach all morning will give him? Of course not." Sparhawk pulled on a robe and went to the window. It was only then that he heard the sound of Flute's pipes.

The sky over this mysterious valley was overcast, as it had been all winter. Dirty-looking clouds, chill and unpromising, stretched from horizon to horizon, hurried along by a blustery wind.

There was a broad meadow not far from the house, and Faran was cantering easily in a wide circular course around the meadow. He wore no saddle or bridle, and there was something almost joyful in his stride. Flute lay face up on his back with her pipes to her lips. Her head was nestled comfortably on his surging front shoulders, her knees were crossed, and she was beating time on the big roan's rump with one little foot. The scene was so familiar that all Sparhawk could do was stare.

"Ehlana," he said finally. "I think you might want to see this."

She came to the window. "What on *earth* is she doing?" she exclaimed. "Go stop her, Sparhawk. She'll fall off and get hurt."

"No, actually she won't. She and Faran have played together like this before. He won't let her fall off—even if she could."

"What are they doing?"

"I have no idea," he admitted, although that was not entirely true. "I think it's significant, though," he added. He leaned out the window and looked first to the left and then to the right. The others were all at the windows, their faces filled with surprise as they watched their little hostess.

The blustery wind faltered, then died as Flute continued her lilting tune, and the winter-brown grass in the dooryard ceased its dead rattling.

The joyous trilling song of the Child-Goddess rose into the sky as Faran continued tirelessly to circle the meadow, and as she played, the dirty-looking murk overhead opened and rolled back almost as a bolster is turned back on a bed, and a deep blue sky dotted with fluffy, sunrise-touched clouds appeared.

Sparhawk and the others stared up in wonder at that suddenly revealed sky, and, as children sometimes will, they saw pink dragons and rosy griffins caught somehow in the wonder of the clouds that streamed and coalesced, piling higher and higher only to come apart again as all the spirits of air and earth and sky joined to welcome that spring that the world had feared might never come.

The Child-Goddess Aphrael rose to her feet and stood on the big roan's surging back. Her glossy black hair streamed out behind her, and the sound of her pipes soared up to meet the sunrise. Then, even as she played, she began to dance, whirling and swaying, her grass-strained little feet flickering as she danced and joyously lifted her song.

Earth and sky and Faran's broad back were all one to Aphrael as she danced, and she whirled as easily on insubstantial air as upon the now-verdant turf or that surging roan back.

Awestruck, they watched from the house that wasn't really there, and their somber melancholy dropped away. Their hearts grew full as the Child-Goddess played for them that joyous, forever-new song of redemption and renewal, for now at last the dread winter had passed, and spring had once again returned.